# ROBERT LUDLUM
# The Second Bourne Trilogy

D1344399

Robert Ludlum
The Second Bourne Trilogy

# The Bourne Legacy
# The Bourne Betrayal
# The Bourne Sanction

Eric Van Lustbader

First published in Great Britain in 2009 by Orion Books,
an imprint of The Orion Publishing Group Ltd
Orion House, 5 Upper Saint Martin's Lane
London  WC2H 9EA

An Hachette UK Company

3  5  7  9  10  8  6  4  2

A CIP catalogue record for this book is
available from the British Library.

ISBN: 978 1 4091 1430 7

Printed in Great Britain by Clays Ltd, St Ives plc

The Orion Publishing Group's policy is to use papers
that are natural, renewable and recyclable products and
made from wood grown in sustainable forests. The logging
and manufacturing processes are expected to conform to
the environmental regulations of the country of origin.

# Contents

# The Bourne Legacy

In Memory of Bob

# Prologue

Khalid Murat, leader of the Chechen rebels, sat still as a stone in the center vehicle of the convoy making its way through the bombed-out streets of Grozny. The BTR-60BP armored personnel carriers were standard Russian military issue and, as such, the convoy was indistinguishable from all the others rumbling through the city on patrol. Murat's heavily armed men were crammed into the other two vehicles – one in front and one behind his own. They were heading toward Hospital Number Nine, one of six or seven different hideouts Murat used to keep three steps ahead of the Russian forces searching for him.

Murat was darkly bearded, close to fifty, with a bear's broad stance and the fire-lit eyes of the true zealot. He had learned early on that the iron fist was the only way to rule. He had been present when Jokhar Dudayev had imposed Islamic Shariah law to no avail. He had seen the carnage wreaked when it had all begun, when the Chechnya-based warlords, foreign associates of Osama bin Laden, invaded Daghestan and executed a string of bombings in Moscow and Volgodonsk that killed some two hundred people. When the blame for the foreigners' actions was falsely put on Chechen terrorists, the Russians began their devastating bombing of Grozny, reducing much of the city to rubble.

The sky over the Chechen capital was blurred, made indistinct by a constant flux of ash and cinder, a shimmering incandescence so lurid it seemed almost radioactive. Oil-fueled fires burned everywhere across the rubble-strewn landscape.

Khalid Murat stared out the tinted windows as the convoy passed a burned-out skeleton of a building, massive, hulking, the roofless interior filled with flickering flames. He grunted, turned to Hasan Arsenov, his second in command, and said, 'Once Grozny was the beloved home to lovers strolling down the wide tree-lined boulevards, mothers pushing prams across the leafy squares. The great circus was nightly filled to overflowing with joyous, laughing faces, and architects the world over made their pilgrimage to tour the magnificent buildings that once made Grozny one of the most beautiful cities on earth.'

He shook his head sadly, slapped the other's knee in a comradely gesture. 'Allah, Hasan!' he cried. 'Look how the Russians have crushed everything that was good and fine!'

Hasan Arsenov nodded. He was a brisk, energetic man fully ten years Murat's junior. A former biathlon champion, he had the wide shoulders and narrow hips of a natural athlete. When Murat had taken over as rebel leader, he was at his side. Now he pointed out to Murat the charred husk of a building on the convoy's right. 'Before the wars,' he said with grave intent, 'when Grozny was still a major oil-

5

refining center, my father worked there at the Oil Institute. Now instead of profits from our wells, we get flash fires that pollute our air and our water.'

The two rebels were chastened into silence by the parade of bombed-out buildings they passed, the streets empty save for scavengers, both human and animal. After several minutes, they turned to each other, the pain of their people's suffering in their eyes. Murat opened his mouth to speak but froze at the unmistakable sound of bullets pinging against their vehicle. It took him but an instant to realize that the vehicle was being hit by small-arms fire too weak to penetrate their vehicle's sturdy armor plate. Arsenov, ever vigilant, reached for the radio.

'I'm going to order the guards in the lead and tail vehicles to return fire.'

Murat shook his head. 'No, Hasan. Think. We're camouflaged in Russian military uniforms, riding in Russian personnel carriers. Whoever is firing on us is more likely an ally than a foe. We need to make sure before there's innocent blood on our hands.'

He took the radio from Arsenov, ordered the convoy to a halt.

'Lieutenant Gochiyayev,' he said into the radio, 'organize your men into a recon. I want to find out who's shooting at us, but I don't want them killed.'

In the lead vehicle, Lieutenant Gochiyayev gathered his men and ordered them to fan out behind the cover of the armored convoy. He followed them onto the rubble-strewn street, hunching his shoulders against the bitter cold. Using precise hand signals, he directed his men to converge from the left and right onto the place from which the small-arms fire had come.

His men were well trained; they moved swiftly and silently from rock to wall to pile of twisted metal beams, scrunched down, presenting as small a target as possible. However, no more shots were heard. They made their final run at once, a pincer move, designed to trap the enemy and crush them in a blistering cross-fire.

In the center vehicle, Hasan Arsenov kept his eye on the place where Gochiyayev had converged the troops and waited for the sounds of gunfire that never came. Instead, the head and shoulders of Lieutenant Gochiyayev appeared in the distance. Facing the center vehicle, he waved his arm back and forth in an arc, signaling that the area had been secured. At this sign, Khalid Murat moved past Arsenov, stepped out of the personnel carrier and without hesitation walked through the frozen rubble toward his men.

'Khalid Murat!' Arsenov called in alarm, running after his leader.

Clearly unperturbed, Murat walked toward a low crumbling stone wall, the place where the gunfire had emanated. He caught a glimpse of the piles of garbage; on one was a waxy white-skinned corpse that had some time ago been stripped of its clothes. Even at a distance the stench of putrefaction was like being hit with a poleax. Arsenov caught up with him and drew his sidearm.

When Murat reached the wall, his men were on either side, their arms at the ready. The wind gusted fitfully, howling and whining through the ruins. The dull metallic sky had darkened further and it began to snow. A light dusting quickly coated Murat's boots, created a web in the wiry jumble of his beard.

'Lieutenant Gochiyayev, you've found the attackers?'

'I have, sir.'

'Allah has guided me in all things; he guides me in this. Let me see them.'

'There's only one,' Gochiyayev replied.

'One?' Arsenov cried. 'Who? Did he know we're Chechen?'

'You're Chechen?' a small voice said. A pallid face emerged from behind the wall, a boy not more than ten years old. He wore a filthy wool hat, threadbare sweater over a few thin plaid shirts, patched trousers and a pair of cracked rubber boots far too big for his feet, which had probably been taken off a dead man. Though only a child, he had the eyes of an adult; they watched everything with a combination of wariness and mistrust. He stood protecting the skeleton of an unexploded Russian rocket he had scavenged for bread money, likely all that stood between his family and starvation. He held a gun in his left hand; his right arm ended at the wrist. Murat immediately looked away but Arsenov continued to stare.

'A land mine,' the boy said with a heartbreaking matter-of-factness. 'Laid by the Russian scum.'

'Allah be praised! What a little soldier!' Murat exclaimed, directing his dazzling, disarming smile at the boy. It was this smile that had drawn his people to him like filings to a magnet. 'Come, come.' He beckoned, then held his empty palms up. 'As you can see, we're Chechen, like you.'

'If you're like me,' the boy said, 'why do you ride in Russian armored cars?'

'What better way to hide from the Russian wolf, eh?' Murat squinted, laughed to see that the boy held a Gyurza. 'You carry a Russian Special Forces gun. Such bravery must be rewarded, yes?'

Murat knelt next to the boy and asked his name. When the boy told him, he said, 'Aznor, do you know who I am? I am Khalid Murat and I, too, wish to be free of the Russian yoke. Together we can do this, yes?'

'I never meant to shoot at fellow Chechens,' Aznor said. With his mutilated arm, he pointed to the convoy. 'I thought this was a *zachistka*.' He meant the monstrous clean-up operations perpetrated by Russian soldiers who searched for suspected rebels. More than twelve thousand Chechens had been killed during the *zachistkas*; two thousand had simply disappeared, countless others injured, tortured, maimed and raped. 'The Russians murdered my father, my uncles. If you were Russians I would've killed you all.' A spasm of rage and frustration played across his face.

'I believe you would've,' Murat said solemnly. He dug in his pocket for some bills. The boy had to tuck the gun into his waistband in order to take them in his remaining hand. Leaning toward the boy, Murat said in a collusive whisper, 'Now listen to me – I'll tell you where to buy more ammunition for your Gyurza so you'll be prepared when the next *zachistka* comes.'

'Thank you.' Aznor's face cracked open in a smile

Khalid Murat whispered a few words, then stepped back and ruffled the boy's hair. 'Allah be with you, little soldier, in everything you do.'

The Chechen leader and his second in command watched the small boy as he clambered back over the rubble, pieces of an unexploded Russian rocket tucked under one arm. Then they returned to their vehicle. With a grunt of disgust, Hasan slammed shut the armor-plated door on the world outside, Aznor's world. 'Doesn't it bother you that you're sending a child to his death?'

Murat glanced at him. The snow had melted to trembling droplets on his beard, making him seem in Arsenov's eyes more like a liturgical imam than a military commander. 'I've given this *child* – who must feed and clothe and, most important, *protect* the rest of his family as if he were an adult – I have given him hope, a specific objective. In short, I've provided him with *a reason to live*.'

Bitterness had turned Arsenov's face hard and pale; his eyes had a baleful look. 'Russian bullets will tear him to ribbons.'

'Is that what you truly think, Hasan? That Aznor is stupid or, worse, careless?'

'He's but one child.'

'When the seed is planted, the shoots will rise out of even the most inhospitable ground. It's always been this way, Hasan. The belief and courage of one inevitably grows and spreads, and soon that one is ten, twenty, a hundred, a thousand!'

'And all the while our people are being murdered, raped, beaten, starved and penned like cattle. It's not enough, Khalid. Not nearly enough!'

'The impatience of youth hasn't yet left you, Hasan.' He gripped the other's shoulder. 'Well, I shouldn't be surprised, yes?'

Arsenov, catching the look of pity in Murat's eyes, clenched his jaw and turned his face away. Curls of snow made visible wind devils along the street, whirling like Chechen dervishes in ecstatic trance. Murat took this as a sign of the import of what he had just done, of what he was about to say. 'Have faith,' he said in hushed, sacramental tones, 'in Allah and in that courageous boy.'

Ten minutes later, the convoy stopped in front of Hospital Number Nine. Arsenov looked at his wristwatch. 'Almost time,' he said. The two of them were riding in the same vehicle, against standard security precautions, owing to the extreme importance of the call they were about to receive.

Murat leaned over, pressed a button, and the soundproof barrier rose into place, cutting them off from the driver and four bodyguards sitting forward. Well-trained, they stared straight ahead through the bullet-proof windshield.

'Tell me, Khalid, as the moment of truth is upon us, what reservations you have.'

Murat raised his bristling eyebrows in a display of incomprehension that Arsenov thought rather transparent. 'Reservations?'

'Don't you want what's rightfully ours, Khalid, what Allah decrees we should have?'

'The blood runs high in you, my friend. I know this only too well. We've fought side by side many times – we've killed together and we owe each other our very lives, yes? Now, listen to me. I bleed for our people. Their pain fills me with a rage I can barely contain. You know this better, perhaps, than anyone. But history warns that one should beware what one wants the most. The consequences of what's being proposed – '

'What we've been planning for!'

'Yes, planning for,' Khalid Murat said. 'But the consequences must be considered.'

'Caution,' Arsenov said bitterly. 'Always caution.'

'My friend.' Khalid Murat smiled as he gripped the other's shoulder. 'I don't want to be misled. The reckless foe is easiest to destroy. You must learn to make patience a virtue.'

'Patience!' Arsenov spat. 'You didn't tell the boy back there to be patient. You gave him money, told him where to buy ammunition. You set him against the Russians. Each day we delay is another day that boy and thousands like him risk being killed. It's the very future of Chechnya that will be decided by our choice here.'

Murat pressed his thumbs into his eyes, rubbing with a circular motion. 'There are other ways, Hasan. There are *always* other ways. Perhaps we should consider – '

'There's no *time*. The announcement has been made, the date set. The Shaykh is right.'

'The Shaykh, yes.' Khalid Murat shook his head. 'Always the Shaykh.'

At that moment, the car phone rang. Khalid Murat glanced at his trusted companion and calmly clicked on the speakerphone. 'Yes, Shaykh,' he said in a deferential tone of voice. 'Hasan and I are both here. We await your instructions.'

High above the street where the convoy was idling, a figure crouched on a flat rooftop, elbows atop the low parapet. Lying along the parapet was a Finnish Sako TRG-41 bolt-action sniper rifle, one of many he had modified himself. Its aluminum and polyurethane stock made it as light as it was deadly accurate. He was dressed in the camouflage uniform of the Russian military, which did not look out of place with the Asian caste of his smooth features. Over the uniform, he wore a lightweight Kevlar harness from which hung a metal loop. In his right palm, he cradled a small matte-black box, no larger than the size of a pack of cigarettes. It was a wireless device in which were set two buttons. There was a stillness about him, a kind of aura that intimidated people. It was as if he understood silence, could gather it to him, manipulate it, unleash it as a weapon.

In his black eyes grew the world entire, and the street, the buildings upon which he now gazed were nothing more than a stage set. He counted the Chechen soldiers as they emerged from the guard vehicles. There were eighteen: the drivers still behind the wheels and in the center vehicle at least four guards as well as the principals.

As the rebels entered the main entrance of the hospital on their way to secure the site, he depressed the top button of the wireless remote and C4 charges went off, collapsing the hospital entrance. The percussion shook the street, set the heavy vehicles to rocking on their oversized shocks. The rebels caught directly in the blast were either blown to bits or crushed beneath the weight of falling rubble, but he knew that at least some of the rebels could have been far enough inside the hospital lobby to have survived, a possibility he had factored into his plan.

With the sound of the first explosion still ringing and the dust not yet settled, the figure looked down at the wireless device in his hand and depressed the lower button. The street in front and back of the convoy erupted in a deafening blast, collapsing the shell-pocked macadam.

Now, even as the men below struggled to come to grips with the carnage he had visited upon them, the assassin took up the Sako, moving with a methodical, unhurried precision. The rifle was loaded with special non-fragmentation bullets of the smallest caliber the rifle could accommodate. Through its IR-enabled scope, he saw three rebels who had managed to escape the blasts with only minor injuries. They were running toward the middle vehicle, screaming at the occupants to get out before it was destroyed by another blast. He watched as they yanked open the right-hand doors, allowed Hasan Arsenov and one guard to emerge. That left the driver and three remaining bodyguards inside the car with Khalid Murat. As Arsenov turned away, the figure sighted on his head. Through the scope, he noted the expression of command plastered on Arsenov's face. Then he moved the barrel in a smooth, practiced motion, this time sighting on the Chechen's thigh. The figure squeezed off a shot and Arsenov grabbed his left leg, shouting as he went down. One of the guards ran to Arsenov, dragged him to cover. The two remaining guards, swiftly determining where the shot had come from, ran across the street, entering the building on whose roof the figure crouched.

As three more rebels appeared, racing out a side entrance to the hospital, the assassin dropped the Sako. He watched now as the vehicle containing Khalid Murat slammed into reverse. Behind and below him, he could hear the rebels pounding up the stairs leading to his rooftop perch. Still unhurried, he fitted titanium and corundum spikes to his boots. Then he took up a composite crossbow and shot a line into a light pole just behind the middle vehicle, tying off the line to make sure it was taut. Shouting voices reached him. The rebels had gained the floor directly below him.

The front of the vehicle was now facing him as the driver tried to maneuver it around the huge chunks of concrete, granite and macadam that had erupted in the explosion. The assassin could see the soft glint of the two panes of glass that comprised the windshield. That was the one problem the Russians had yet to overcome: Bullet-proofing the glass made the panes so heavy it required two of them for the windshield. The personnel carrier's one vulnerable spot was the strip of metal between the two panes.

He took the sturdy metal loop attached to his harness and snapped himself to the taut line. Behind him, he heard the rebels burst through the door, emerging onto the roof a hundred feet away. Spotting the assassin, they swung around to fire on him as they ran toward him, setting off an unnoticed trip wire. Immediately, they were engulfed in a fiery detonation from the last remaining packet of C4 the assassin had planted the night before.

Never turning around to acknowledge the carnage behind him, the assassin tested the line and then launched himself from the rooftop. He slid down the line, lifting his legs so that the spikes were aimed at the windshield divider. Everything now depended on the speed and the angle with which he would strike the divider between the bullet-proof panes of the windshield. If he was off by just a fraction, the divider would hold and he had a good chance of breaking his leg.

The force of the impact ran up his legs, jolting his spine as the titanium and corundum spikes on his boots crumpled the divider like a tin can, the panes of glass caving in without its support. He crashed through the windshield and into the interior of the vehicle, carrying with him much of the windshield. A chunk of it struck the driver in the neck, half-severing his head. The assassin twisted to his left. The bodyguard in the front seat was covered in the driver's blood. He was reaching for his gun when the assassin took his head between his powerful hands and broke his neck before he had a chance to squeeze off a round.

The other two bodyguards in the jumpseat just behind the driver fired wildly at the assassin, who pushed the bodyguard with the broken neck so that his body absorbed the bullets. From behind this makeshift protection, he used the bodyguard's gun, fired precisely, one shot through the forehead of each man.

That left only Khalid Murat. The Chechen leader, his face a mask of hatred, had kicked open the door and was shouting for his men. The assassin lunged at Murat, shaking the huge man as if he were a water rat; Murat's jaws snapped at him, almost taking off an ear. Calmly, methodically, almost joyously he seized Murat around the throat and, staring into his eyes, jabbed his thumb into the cricoid cartilage of the Chechen leader's lower larynx. Blood immediately filled Murat's throat, choking him, draining him of strength. His arms flailed, his hands beating against the assassin's face and head. To no avail. Murat was drowning in his own blood. His lungs filled and his breathing became ragged, thick. He vomited blood and his eyes rolled up in their sockets.

Dropping the now-limp body, the assassin climbed back into the front seat, hurling the driver's corpse out of the door. He slammed the vehicle into gear and stepped on the gas before what remained of the rebels could react. The vehicle leaped forward like a racehorse from the gate, hurtled over rubble and tarmac, then vanished into thin air as it plummeted into the hole the explosives had made in the street.

Underground, the assassin upshifted, racing through the tight space of a storm drain that had been widened by the Russians, who had intended to use them for clandestine assaults on rebel strongholds. Sparks flew as the metal fenders now and again scraped against the curving concrete walls. But for all that, he was safe. His plan had concluded as it had begun: with perfect clockwork precision.

After midnight the noxious clouds rolled away, at last revealing the moon. The detritus-laden atmosphere gave it a reddish glow, its lambent light intermittently disturbed by the still burning fires.

Two men stood in the center of a steel bridge. Below them, the charred remains of an unending war were reflected in the surface of the sluggish water.

'It's done,' the first one said. 'Khalid Murat has been killed in a manner that will cause maximum impact.'

'I would expect nothing less, Khan,' the second man said. 'You owe your impeccable reputation in no small part to the commissions I've given you.' He was taller than the assassin by a good four inches, square-shouldered, long-legged. The only thing that marred his appearance was the strange glassy utterly hairless skin on the left side of his face and neck. He possessed the charisma of a born leader, a man not to be trifled with. Clearly, he was at home in the great halls of power, in public forums or in thuggish back alleys.

Khan was still basking in the look in Murat's eyes as he died. The look was different in every man. Khan had learned there was no common thread, for each man's life was unique, and though all sinned, the corrosion those sins caused differed from one to the next, like the structure of a snowflake, never to be repeated. In Murat, what had it been? Not fear. Astonishment, yes, rage, surely, but something more, deeper – sorrow at leaving a life's work undone. The dissection of the last look was always incomplete, Khan thought. He longed to know whether there was betrayal there, as well. Had Murat known who had ordered his assassination?

He looked at Stepan Spalko, who was holding out an envelope, heavy with money.

'Your fee,' Spalko said. 'Plus a bonus.'

'Bonus?' The topic of money refocused Khan's attention fully on the immediate. 'There was no mention of a bonus.'

Spalko shrugged. The ruddy moonlight made his cheek and neck shine like a bloody mass. 'Khalid Murat was your twenty-fifth commission with me. Call it an anniversary present, if you wish.'

'You're most generous, Mr. Spalko.' Khan stowed the envelope away without looking inside. To have done otherwise would have been very bad manners.

'I've asked you to call me Stepan. I refer to you as Khan.'

'That's different.'

'How so?'

Khan stood very still, and the silence flowed toward him. It gathered in him, making him seem taller, broader.

'I'm not required to explain myself to you, Mr. Spalko.'

'Come, come,' Spalko said with a conciliatory gesture. 'We're far from strangers. We share secrets of the most intimate nature.'

The silence built. Somewhere on the outskirts of Grozny an explosion lit up the night, and the sound of small-arms fire came to them like strings of children's firecrackers.

At length, Khan spoke. 'In the jungle I learned two mortal lessons. The first was to trust absolutely only myself. The second was to observe the most minute proprieties of civilization, because knowing your place in the world is the only thing standing between you and the anarchy of the jungle.'

Spalko regarded him for a long time. The fitful glow from the firefight was in Khan's eyes, lending him a savage aspect. Spalko imagined him alone in the jungle, prey to privations, the quarry of greed and wanton bloodlust. The jungle of Southeast Asia was a world unto itself. A barbarous, pestilential area with its own peculiar laws. That Khan had not only survived there, but flourished, was, in Spalko's mind at least, the essential mystery surrounding him.

'I'd like to think we're more than businessman and client.'

Khan shook his head. 'Death has a particular odor. I smell it on you.'

'And I on you.' A slow smile crept across Spalko's face. 'So you agree, there is something special between us.'

'We're men of secrets,' Khan said, 'aren't we?'

'A worship of death; a shared understanding of its power.' Spalko nodded his assent. 'I have what you requested.' He held out a black file folder.

Khan looked into Spalko's eyes for a moment. His discerning nature had caught a certain air of condescension that he found inexcusable. As he had long ago learned to do, he smiled at the offense, hiding his outrage behind the impenetrable mask of his face. Another lesson he had learned in the jungle: Acting in the moment, in hot blood, often led to an irreversible mistake; waiting in patience for the hot blood to cool was where all successful vengeance was bred. Taking the folder, he busied himself with opening the dossier. Inside, he found a single sheet of onionskin with three brief close-typed paragraphs and a photo of a handsome male face. Beneath the picture was a name: David Webb. 'This is all of it?'

'Culled from many sources. All the information on him anyone has.' Spalko spoke so smoothly Khan was certain he had rehearsed the reply.

'But this is the man.'

Spalko nodded.

'There can be no doubt.'

'None whatsoever.'

Judging by the widening glow, the firefight had intensified. Mortars could be heard, bringing their rain of fire. Overhead, the moon seemed to glow a deeper red.

Khan's eyes narrowed and his right hand curled slowly into a tight fist of hate. 'I could never find a trace of him. I'd suspected he was dead.'

'In a way,' Spalko said, 'he is.'

He watched Khan walk across the bridge. He took out a cigarette and lit up, drawing the smoke into his lungs, letting it go reluctantly. When Khan had disappeared into the shadows, Spalko pulled out a cell phone, dialed an overseas number. A voice answered, and Spalko said, 'He has the dossier. Is everything in place?'

'Yes, sir.'

'Good. At midnight your local time you'll begin the operation.'

# Book 1

# 1

David Webb, professor of linguistics at Georgetown University, was buried beneath a stack of ungraded term papers. He was striding down the musty back corridors of gargantuan Healy Hall, heading for the office of Theodore Barton, his department head, and he was late, hence this shortcut he had long ago discovered using narrow, ill-lighted passageways few students knew about or cared to use.

There was a benign ebb and flow to his life bound by the strictures of the university. His year was defined by the terms of the Georgetown semesters. The deep winter that began them gave grudging way to a tentative spring and ended in the heat and humidity of the second semester's finals week. There was a part of him that fought against serenity, the part that thought of his former life in the clandestine service of the U.S. government, the part that kept him friends with his former handler, Alexander Conklin.

He was about to round a corner when he heard harsh voices raised and mocking laughter and saw ominous-seeming shadows playing along the wall.

'Muthfucka, we gonna make your gook tongue come out the back of your head!'

Bourne dropped the stack of papers he had been carrying and sprinted around the corner. As he did so, he saw three young black men in coats down to their ankles arrayed in a menacing semicircle around an Asian, trapping him against a corridor wall. They had a way of standing, their knees slightly bent, their upper limbs loose and swinging slightly that made their entire bodies seem like blunt and ugly aspects of weapons, cocked and ready. With a start, he recognized their prey was Rongsey Siv, a favorite student of his.

'Muthafucka,' snarled one, wiry, with a strung-out, reckless look on his defiant face, 'we come in here, gather up the goods to trade for the bling-bling.'

'Can't ever have enough bling-bling,' said another with an eagle tattoo on his cheek. He rolled a huge gold square-cut ring, one of many on the fingers of his right hand, back and forth. 'Or don't you know the bling-bling, gook?'

'Yah, gook,' the strung-out one said, goggle-eyed. 'You don't look like you know *shit.*'

'He wants to stop us,' the one with the tattooed cheek said, leaning in toward Rongsey. 'Yah, gook, whatcha gonna do, *kung-fuckin-fu* us to death?'

They laughed raucously, making stylized kicking gestures toward Rongsey, who shrank back even farther against the wall as they closed in.

The third black man, thick-muscled, heavyset, drew a baseball bat from underneath the voluminous folds of his long coat. 'That right. Put your hands up, gook. We gonna break your knuckles good.' He slapped the bat against his cupped palm.

'You want it all at once or one at a time?'

'Yo,' the strung-out one cried, 'he don't get to choose.' He pulled out his own baseball bat and advanced menacingly on Rongsey.

As the strung-out kid brandished his bat, Webb came at them. So silent was his approach, so intent were they on the damage they were about to inflict that they did not become aware of him until he was upon them.

He grabbed the strung-out kid's bat in his left hand as it was coming down toward Rongsey's head. Tattoo-cheek, on Webb's right, cursed mightily, swung his balled fist, knuckles bristling with sharp-edged rings, aiming for Webb's ribs.

In that instant, from the veiled and shadowed place inside Webb's head, the Bourne persona took firm control. Webb deflected the blow from tattoo-cheek with his biceps, stepped forward and slammed his elbow into tattoo-cheek's sternum. He went down, clawing at his chest.

The third thug, bigger than the other two, cursed and, dropping his bat, pulled a switchblade. He lunged at Webb, who stepped into the attack, delivering a short, sharp blow to the inside of the assailant's wrist. The switchblade fell to the corridor floor, skittering away. Webb hooked his left foot behind the other's ankle and lifted up. The big thug fell on his back, turned over and scrambled away.

Bourne yanked the baseball bat out of the strung-out thug's grip. 'Muthafuckin' Five-O,' the thug muttered. His pupils were dilated, unfocused by the effects of whatever drugs he'd taken. He pulled a gun – a cheap Saturday-night special – and aimed it at Webb.

With deadly accuracy, Webb flung the bat, striking the strung-out thug between the eyes. He staggered back, crying out, and his gun went flying.

Alerted by the noise of the struggle, a pair of campus security guards appeared, rounding the corner at a run. They brushed past Webb, pounding after the thugs, who fled without a backward glance, the two helping the strung-out one. They burst through the rear door to the building, out into the bright sunshine of the afternoon, with the guards hot on their heels.

Despite the guards' intervention, Webb felt Bourne's desire to pursue the thugs run hot in his body. How quickly it had risen from its psychic sleep, how easily it had gained control of him. Was it because he wanted it to? Webb took a deep breath, gained a semblance of control and turned to face Rongsey Siv.

'Professor Webb!' Rongsey tried to clear his throat. 'I don't know – ' He seemed abruptly overcome. His large black eyes were wide behind the lenses of his glasses. His expression was, as usual, impassive, but in those eyes Webb could see all the fear in the world.

'It's okay now.' Webb put his arm across Rongsey's shoulders. As always, his fondness for the Cambodian refugee was showing through his professorial reserve. He couldn't help it. Rongsey had overcome great adversity – losing almost all his family in the war. Rongsey and Webb had been in the same Southeast Asian jungles, and try as he might, Webb could not fully remove himself from the tangle of that hot, humid world. Like a recurring fever, it never really left you. He felt a shiver of recognition, like a dream one has while awake.

'*Loak soksapbaee chea tay?*' How are you? he asked in Khmer.

'I'm fine, Professor,' Rongsey replied in the same language. 'But I don't . . . I mean, how did you . . . ?'

'Why don't we go outside?' Webb suggested. He was now quite late for Barton's meeting, but he couldn't care less. He picked up the switchblade and the gun. As he checked the gun's mechanism, the firing pin broke. He threw the useless gun in a trash bin but pocketed the switchblade.

Around the corner, Rongsey helped him with the spill of term papers. They then walked in silence through the corridors, which became increasingly crowded as they neared the front of the building. Webb recognized the special nature of this silence, the dense weight of time returning to normal after an incident of shared violence. It was a wartime thing, a consequence of the jungle; odd and unsettling that it should happen on this teeming metropolitan campus.

Emerging from the corridor, they joined the swarm of students crowding through the front doors to Healy Hall. Just inside, in the center of the floor, gleamed the hallowed Georgetown University seal. A great majority of the students were walking around it because a school legend held that if you walked on the seal you'd never graduate. Rongsey was one of those who gave the seal a wide berth, but Webb strode right across it with no qualms whatsoever.

Outside, they stood in the buttery spring sunlight, facing the trees and the Old Quadrangle, breathing the air with its hint of budding flowers. At their backs rose the looming presence of Healy Hall with its imposing Georgian red-brick facade, nineteenth-century dormer windows, slate roof and central two-hundred-foot clock spire.

The Cambodian turned to Webb. 'Professor, thank you. If you hadn't come . . .'

'Rongsey,' Webb said gently, 'do you want to talk about it?'

The student's eyes were dark, unreadable. 'What's there to say?'

'I suppose that would depend on you.'

Rongsey shrugged. 'I'll be fine, Professor Webb. Really. This isn't the first time I've been called names.'

Webb stood looking at Rongsey for a moment, and he was swept by sudden emotion that caused his eyes to sting. He wanted to take the boy in his arms, hold him close, promise him that nothing else bad would ever happen to him. But he knew that Rongsey's Buddhist training would not allow him to accept the gesture. Who could say what was going on beneath that fortresslike exterior. Webb had seen many others like Rongsey, forced by the exigencies of war and cultural hatred to bear witness to death, the collapse of a civilization, the kinds of tragedies most Americans could not understand. He felt a powerful kinship with Rongsey, an emotional bond that was tinged with a terrible sadness, recognition of the wound inside him that could never truly be healed.

All this emotion stood between them, silently acknowledged perhaps but never articulated. With a small, almost sad smile, Rongsey formally thanked Webb again and they said their good-byes.

Webb stood alone amid the students and faculty hurrying by, and yet he knew that he wasn't truly alone. Despite his best efforts, the aggressive personality of Jason Bourne had once again asserted itself. He breathed slowly and deeply, concentrating hard, using the mental techniques his psychiatrist friend, Mo Panov, had taught him for pushing the Bourne identity down. He concentrated first on his surrounding, on the blue and gold colors of the spring afternoon, on the gray stone and red brick of the buildings around the quad, of the movement of the students, the smiling faces of the girls, the laughter of the boys, the earnest talk of the professors. He absorbed each element in its entirety, grounding himself in time and place. Then, and only then, did he turn his thoughts inward.

Years ago he had been working for the foreign service in Phnom Penh. He'd been married then, not to Marie, his current wife, but to a Thai woman named Dao. They had two children, Joshua and Alyssa, and lived in a house on the bank of the river. America was at war with North Vietnam, but the war had spilled over into Cambodia. One afternoon, while he was at work and his family had been swimming in the river, a plane had strafed them, killing them.

Webb had almost gone mad with grief. Finally, fleeing his house and Phnom Penh, he'd arrived in Saigon, a man with no past and no future. It had been Alex Conklin who had taken a heartsick, half-mad David Webb off the streets of Saigon and forged him into a first-rate clandestine operative. In Saigon, Webb had learned to kill, had turned his own self-hatred outward, inflicting his rage on others. When a member of Conklin's group – an evil-tempered drifter named Jason Bourne – had been discovered to be a spy, it was Webb who had executed him. Webb had come to loathe the Bourne identity, but the truth was that it had often been his life-line. Jason Bourne had saved Webb's life more times than he could remember. An amusing thought if it hadn't been so literal.

Years later, when they had both returned to Washington, Conklin had given him a long-term assignment. He had become what amounted to a sleeper agent, taking the name of Jason Bourne, a man long dead, forgotten by everyone. For three years Webb *was* Bourne, turned himself into an international assassin of great repute in order to hunt down an elusive terrorist.

But in Marseilles, his mission had gone terribly wrong. He'd been shot, cast into the dark waters of the Mediterranean, thought dead. Instead, he had been pulled from the water by members of a fishing boat, nursed back to health by a drunkard doctor in the port they'd set him down in. The only problem was that in the shock of almost dying he'd lost his memory. What had come slowly back were the Bourne memories. It was only much later, with the help of Marie, his wife-to-be, that he had come to realize the truth, that he was David Webb. But by that time the Jason Bourne personality was too well ingrained, too powerful, too cunning to die.

In the aftermath, he'd become two people: David Webb, linguistics professor with a new wife and, eventually, two children, and Jason Bourne, the agent trained by Alex Conklin to be a formidable spy. Occasionally, in some crisis, Conklin called on Bourne's expertise and Webb reluctantly rose to duty. But the truth was that Webb often had little control over his Bourne personality. What had just happened with Rongsey and the three street thugs was evidence enough. Bourne had a way of asserting himself that was beyond Webb's control, despite all the work he and Panov had done.

Khan, having watched David Webb and the Cambodian student talking from across the quad, ducked into a building diagonally across from Healy Hall, mounted the stairs to the third floor. Khan was dressed much like all the other students. He looked younger than his twenty-seven years and no one gave him a second look. He was wearing khakis and a jeans jacket, over which was slung an outsize backpack. His sneakers made no sound as he went down the hallway, past the doors to classrooms. In his mind's eye was a clear picture of the view across the quad. He was again calculating angles, taking into account the mature trees that might obscure his view of his intended target.

He paused in front of the sixth door, heard a professor's voice from inside. The talk about ethics brought an ironic smile to his face. In his experience – and it was great and varied – ethics was as dead and useless as Latin. He went on to the next classroom, which he had already determined was empty, and went in.

Quickly now, he shut and locked the door behind him, crossed to the line of windows overlooking the quad, opened one and got to work. From his backpack, he removed a 7.62-mm SVD Dragunov sniper rifle with a collapsible stock. He fitted the optical sight onto it, leaned it on the sill. Peering through the sight, he found David Webb, by this time standing alone across the quad in front of Healy Hall. There were trees just to his left. Every once in a while, a passing student would obscure him. Khan took a deep breath, let it out slowly. He sighted on Webb's head.

Webb shook his head, shaking off the effect his memories of the past had on him, and refocusing on his immediate surroundings. The leaves rustled in a gathering breeze, their tips gilded with sunlight. Close by, a girl, her books clutched to her chest, laughed at the punchline of a joke. A waft of pop music came from an open window somewhere. Webb, still thinking of all the things he wanted to say to Rongsey, was about to turn up the front steps of Healy Hall when a soft *phutt!* sounded in his ear. Reacting instinctively, he stepped into the dappled shadows beneath the trees.

*You're under attack!* shouted Bourne's all-too-familiar voice, reemerging in his mind. *Move now!* And Webb's body reacted, scrambling as another bullet, its initial percussion muffled by a silencer, splintered the tree bark beside his cheek.

*A crack marksman.* Bourne's thoughts began to flood through Webb's brain in response to the organism finding itself under attack.

The ordinary world was in Webb's eyes, but the extraordinary world that ran parallel to it, Jason Bourne's world – secret, rarefied, privileged, deadly – flared like napalm in his mind. In the space of a heartbeat, he had been torn from David Webb's everyday life, set apart from everyone and everything Webb held dear. Even the chance meeting with Rongsey seemed now to belong to another lifetime. From behind, out of the sniper's sight, he gripped the tree, the pad of his forefinger feeling for the mark the bullet had made. He looked up. It was Jason Bourne who traced the trajectory of the bullet back to a third-floor window in a building diagonally across the quad.

All around him, Georgetown students walked, strolled, talked, argued and debated. They had seen nothing, of course, and if by chance they had heard anything at all, the sounds meant nothing to them and were quickly forgotten. Webb left his protection behind the tree, moving quickly into a knot of students. He mingled with them, hurrying, but as much as possible keeping to their pace. They were his best protection now, blocking Webb from the sniper's line of sight.

It seemed as if he was only semiconscious, a sleepwalker who nevertheless saw and sensed everything with a heightened awareness. A component of this awareness was a contempt for those civilians who inhabited the ordinary world, David Webb included.

After the second shot, Khan had drawn back, confused. This was not a state he knew well. His mind raced, assessing what had just happened. Instead of panicking, running like a frightened sheep back into Healy Hall as Khan had anticipated, Webb had calmly moved into the cover of the trees, impeding Khan's view. That had been improbable enough – and totally out of character for the man briefly described in Spalko's dossier – but then Webb had used the gash the second bullet had made in the tree to gauge its trajectory. Now, using the students as cover, he was heading toward this very building. Improbably, he was attacking instead of fleeing.

Slightly unnerved by this unexpected turn of events, Khan hurriedly broke down the rifle, stowed it away. Webb had gained the steps to the building. He'd be here within minutes.

Bourne detached himself from the pedestrian flow, raced into the building. Once inside, he leaped up the stairway to the third floor. He turned left. Seventh door on the left: a classroom. The corridor was filled with the buzz of students from all over the world – Africans, Asians, Latin Americans, Europeans. Each face, no matter how briefly glimpsed, registered on the screen of Jason Bourne's memory.

The low chatter of the students, their fitful bursts of laughter, belied the danger lurking in the immediate environment. As he approached the classroom door, he opened the switchblade he had confiscated earlier, curled his fist around it so that the blade protruded like a spike from between his second and third fingers. In one smooth motion, he pushed open the door, curled into a ball and tumbled inside, landing behind the heavy oak desk, some eight feet from the doorway. His knife hand was up; he was ready for anything.

He rose cautiously. An empty classroom leered at him, filled only with chalk dust and mottled patches of sunlight. He stood looking around for a moment, his nostrils dilated, as if he could drink in the scent of the sniper, make his image appear out of thin air. He crossed to the windows. One was open, the fourth from the left. He stood at it, staring out at the spot beneath the tree where moments ago he had been standing, talking with Rongsey. This is where the sniper had stood. Bourne could imagine him resting the rifle barrel on the sill, fitting one eye to the powerful scope, sighting across the quad. The play of light and shadow, the crossing students, a sudden burst of laughter or cross words. His finger on the trigger, squeezing in an even pull. *Phutt! Phutt!* One shot, two.

Bourne studied the windowsill. Glancing around, he went to the metal tray that ran below the wall of blackboards, scooped out a measure of chalk dust. Returning to the window, he gently blew the chalk dust from his fingers onto the slate surface of the sill. Not a single print appeared. It had been wiped clean. He knelt, cast his gaze along the wall beneath the window, the floor at his feet. He found nothing – no telltale cigarette butt, no stray hairs, no spent shells. The meticulous assassin had vanished just as expertly as he had appeared. His heart was pounding, his mind racing. Who would try to kill him? Surely, it was no one from his current life. The worst that could be said about it was his argument last week with Bob Drake, the head of the ethics department, whose penchant for droning on about his chosen field was both legendary and annoying. No, this threat was coming from Jason Bourne's world. Doubtless, there were many candidates from his past, but how many of them would be able to trace Jason Bourne back to David Webb? This was the real question that worried him. Though part of him wanted to go home, talk this through with Marie, he knew that the one person with sufficient knowledge of Bourne's shadow existence to be able to help was Alex Conklin, the man who like a conjurer had created Bourne out of thin air.

He crossed to the phone on the wall, lifted the receiver and punched in his faculty access code. When he reached an outside line, he dialed Alex Conklin's private number. Conklin, now semiretired from the CIA, would be at home. Bourne got a busy signal.

Either he could wait here for Alex to get off the phone – which, knowing Alex, could be a half hour or more – or he could drive to his house. The open window seemed to mock him. It knew more than he did about what had taken place here.

He left the classroom, heading back down the stairs. Without thinking, he scanned those around him, looking to match up anyone he had passed on his way to the room.

Hurrying across the campus, he soon reached the car park. He was about to get into his car when he thought better of it. Making a quick but thorough inspection of the car's exterior and its engine, he determined that it had not been tampered with. Satisfied, he slid behind the wheel, turned on the ignition and drove out of the campus.

Alex Conklin lived on a rural estate in Manassas, Virginia. Once Webb reached the outskirts of Georgetown, the sky took on a deeper radiance; an eerie kind of stillness had taken root, as if the passing countryside was holding its breath.

As with the Bourne personality, Webb both loved and loathed Conklin. He was father, confessor, coconspirator, exploiter. Alex Conklin was the keeper of the keys to Bourne's past. It was imperative he talk to Conklin now because Alex was the only one who would know how someone stalking Jason Bourne could find David Webb on campus at Georgetown University.

He'd left the city behind him, and by the time he'd reached the Virginia countryside, the brightest part of the day had slipped away. Thick banks of clouds obscured the sun, and gusts of wind swept through the verdant Virginia hillsides. He pressed down on the accelerator and the car leaped forward, its big engine purring.

As he followed the banked curves of the highway, it suddenly occurred to him that he hadn't seen Mo Panov in over a month. Mo, an Agency psychologist recommended by Conklin, was trying to repair Webb's fractured psyche, to suppress the Bourne identity for good and help Webb recover his lost memories. Through Mo's techniques, Webb had found chunks of memory he had assumed lost floating back up to his conscious mind. But the work was arduous, exhausting, and it wasn't unusual for him to halt the sessions during ends of terms when his life became unbearably hectic.

He turned off the main highway and headed northwest on a two-lane blacktop road. Why had Panov come into his mind at just this moment? Bourne had learned to trust his senses and his intuition. Mo popping up out of the blue was a kind of signpost. What meaning did Panov have for him now? Memory, yes, but what else? Bourne thought back. The last time they had been together, he and Panov had been talking about silence. Mo had told him that silence was a useful tool in memory work. The mind, needing to be busy, did not like silence. If you could induce a complete enough silence in your conscious mind, it was possible that a memory lost to you would appear to fill the space. *Okay,* Bourne thought, *but why think about silence just at this moment?*

It wasn't until he had turned into Conklin's long, gracefully curving drive that he made the connection. The sniper had used a silencer, the main purpose of which was to keep the shooter from being noticed. But a silencer had its drawbacks. In a long-range weapon, like the one the sniper had been using, it would significantly impair the accuracy of the shot. He should have been aiming at Bourne's torso – a higher-percentage shot because of body mass – but instead, he'd fired at Bourne's head. That wasn't logical, if you assumed the sniper was trying to kill Bourne. But if he was only attempting to frighten, to give warning – that was another matter. This unknown sniper had an ego, then, but he was not a showboat; he had left no token of his prowess behind. And yet he had a specific agenda – that much was clear.

Bourne passed the looming misshapen hulk of the old barn, the other smaller outbuildings – utility facilities, storage sheds and the like. Then the main house was in sight. It stood within stands of tall pines, clumps of birch and blue cedars, old wood that had been here for close to sixty years, predating the stone house by a decade. The estate had belonged to a now-deceased army general who had been deeply involved in clandestine and rather unsavory activities. As a result, the manor house – the entire estate, actually – was honeycombed with underground tunnels, entrances and egresses. Bourne imagined it amused Conklin to live in a place filled with so many secrets.

As he pulled up, he saw not only Conklin's BMW 7-series but Mo Panov's Jaguar parked side by side. As he walked across the bluestone gravel, his heart felt suddenly lighter. The two best friends he had in the world – both in their own ways the keepers of his past – were inside. Together, they would solve this mystery as they had all the others before. He climbed onto the front portico, rang the bell. There was no answer. Pressing his ear to the polished teak door, he could hear voices from within. He tried the handle, found the door unlocked.

An alarm went off inside his head and, for a moment, he stood behind the half-open door, listening to everything inside the house. No matter that he was out here in the countryside where crime was practically unheard of – old habits never died. Conklin's overactive sense of security would dictate locking the front door whether or not he was home. Opening the switchblade, he entered, all too aware that an attacker – one of a termination team sent to kill him – could be lurking inside.

The chandeliered foyer gave out onto a wide sweep of polished wood stairs leading up to an open gallery that ran the width of the foyer. To the right was the formal living room, to the left the denlike media room with its wet bar and deep, masculine leather sofas. Just beyond there was a smaller, more intimate room that Alex had made into his study.

Bourne followed the sound of the voice into the media room. On the large-screen TV a telegenic CNN commentator was standing outside the front of the Oskjuhlid Hotel. A superimposed graphic indicated that he was on location in Reykjavík, Iceland. '. . . the tenuous nature of the upcoming terrorism summit is on everyone's mind here.'

No one was in the room, but there were two old-fashioned glasses on the cock-tail table. Bourne picked one up, sniffed. Speyside single-malt, aged in sherry casks. The complex aroma of Conklin's favorite Scotch disoriented him, brought back a memory, a vision of Paris. It was autumn, fiery horse-chestnut leaves tumbling down the Champs-Elysées. He was looking out the window from an office. He struggled with this vision, which was so strong he seemed to be pulled out of him-self, to actually be in Paris, but, he reminded himself grimly, he was in Manassas, Virginia, at Alex Conklin's house, and all was not well. He struggled, trying to maintain his vigilance, his focus, but the memory, triggered by the scent of the sin-gle-malt, was overpowering, and he so yearned to *know*, to fill in the gaping holes in his memory. And so he found himself in the Paris office. Whose? Not Conklin's – Alex had never had an office in Paris. That smell, someone in the office with him. He turned, saw for the briefest instant the flash of a half-remembered face.

He tore himself away. Even though it was maddening to have a life you remembered only in fitful bursts, with all that had happened and things here feel-ing just slightly off-kilter, he couldn't afford to get sidetracked. What had Mo said about these triggers? They could come from a sight, a sound, a smell, even the touch of something, that once the memory was triggered he could tease it out by repeating the stimulus that had provoked it in the first place. But not now. He needed to find Alex and Mo.

He looked down, saw a small notepad on the table and picked it up. It seemed blank; the top leaf had been ripped off. But when he turned it slightly, he could see faint indentations. Someone – presumably Conklin – had written 'NX 20.' He pocketed the pad.

'So, the countdown has begun. In five days' time, the world will know whether a new day, a new world order will emerge, whether the law-abiding peoples of the world will be able to live in peace and harmony.' The anchor continued to drone on, segueing into a commercial.

Bourne switched off the TV with the remote and silence descended. It was possible that Conklin and Mo were out walking, a favorite way for Panov to let off steam while in conversation, and he, no doubt, would want the old man to get his exercise. But there was the anomaly of the unlocked door.

Bourne retraced his steps, re-entering the foyer and going up the stairs two at a time. Both guest bedrooms were empty, devoid of any sign of recent habitation, as were their en suite bathrooms. Down the hall, he went into Conklin's master suite, a Spartan space befitting an old soldier. The bed was small and hard, not much more than a pallet. It was unmade, clear that Alex had slept there last night. But as befitted a master of secrets, there was very little in the way of his past on display. Bourne picked up a silver-framed snapshot of a woman with long wavy hair, light eyes and a gently mocking smile. He recognized the regal stone lions of the fountain at Saint-Sulpice in the background. Paris. Bourne put the photo down, checked the bath. Nothing there of interest.

Back downstairs, two chimes sounded the hour on the clock in Conklin's study.

It was an antique ship's clock, its note bell-like, musical. But for Bourne the sound had unaccountably taken on an ominous cast. It seemed to him as if the tolling of the bell was rushing through the house like a black wave, and his heart beat fast.

He went down the hallway, past the kitchen into whose doorway he momentarily poked his head. A teakettle was on the stove, but the stainless-steel counters were spotlessly clean. Inside the refrigerator, the ice machine ground out cubes. And then he saw it – Conklin's walking stick, polished ash with the turned silver knob at its top. Alex had a bum leg, the result of a particularly violent encounter overseas; he would never have gone out on the grounds without the stick.

The study was around to the left, a comfortable wood-paneled room in a corner of the house that looked out onto a tree-shaded lawn, a flagstone terrace in the middle of which was sunk a lap-pool and, beyond, the beginning of the pine and hardwood forest that ran for most of the property. With a mounting sense of urgency, Bourne headed for the study. The moment he entered, he froze.

He was never so aware of the dichotomy inside himself, for part of him had become detached, an objective observer. This purely analytic section of his brain noted that Alex Conklin and Mo Panov lay on the richly dyed Persian carpet. Blood had flowed out of their head wounds, soaked into the carpet, in some places overflowing it, pooling on the polished wood floor. Fresh blood, still glistening. Conklin was staring up at the ceiling, his eyes filmed over. His face was flushed and angry, as if all the bile he had been holding deep inside had been forced to the surface. Mo's head was turned as if he had been trying to look behind him when he was felled. An unmistakable expression of fear was etched on his face. In the last instant, he had seen his death coming.

*Alex! Mo! Jesus! Jesus!* All at once, the emotional dam burst and Bourne was on his knees, his mind reeling with shock and horror. His entire world was shaken to its core. Alex and Mo dead – even with the grisly evidence before him it was hard to believe. Never to speak to them again, never to have access to their expertise. A jumble of images paraded before him, remembrances of Alex and Mo, times they had spent together, tense times filled with danger and sudden death, and then, in the aftermath, the ease and comfort of an intimacy that could only come from shared peril. Two lives taken by force, leaving behind nothing but anger and fear. With a stunning finality, the door onto his past slammed shut. Both Bourne and Webb were mourning. Bourne struggled to gather himself, swept aside Webb's hysterical emotionalism, willed himself not to weep. Mourning was an indulgence he could not afford. He had to think.

Bourne got busy absorbing the murder scene, fixing details in his mind, trying to work out what had happened. He moved closer, careful not to step in the blood or to otherwise disturb the scene. Alex and Mo had been shot to death, apparently with the gun lying on the carpet between them. They had received one shot each. This was a professional hit, not an intruder break-in. Bourne's eye caught the glint of the cell phone gripped in Alex's hand. It appeared as if he had been speaking to someone when he was shot. Had it been when Bourne was trying to get through to him earlier? Quite possibly. By the look of the blood, the lividity of the bodies, the lack of rigor mortis in the fingers, it was clear the murders had happened within the hour.

A faint sound in the distance began to intrude on his thoughts. Sirens! Bourne left the study and raced to the front-facing window. A fleet of Virginia State Police cruisers was careening down the driveway, lights flashing. Bourne was caught in a house with the bodies of two murdered men, and no plausible alibi. He had been set up. All at once, he felt the prongs of a clever trap closing around him.

# 2

The pieces came together in his mind. The expert shots fired at him on campus had not been meant to kill him but to herd him, to force him to come to Conklin. But Conklin and Mo had already been killed. Someone was still here, watching and waiting to call the police as soon as Bourne had shown up. The man who'd shot at him on campus?

Without a second thought, Bourne grabbed Alex's cell phone, ran into the kitchen, opened a narrow door onto a steep flight of stairs down into the basement and peered down into pitch blackness. He could hear the crackling of the police radios, the crunch of gravel, the pounding on the front door. Querulous voices raised.

Bourne went to the kitchen drawers, scrabbled around until he found Conklin's flashlight, then went through the basement door; for a moment he was in utter darkness. The concentrated beam of light illuminated the steps as he descended quickly, silently. He could smell the scents of concrete, old wood, lacquer and oil from the furnace. He found the hatch underneath the stairs, pulled it out. Once, on a cold and snowy winter's afternoon, Conklin had shown him the underground entrance the general had used to get to the private heliport near the stables. Bourne could hear the boards creaking above his head. The cops were inside the house. Possibly they had already found the bodies. Three cars, two dead men. It would not be long before they traced the license tags to his car.

Ducking down, he entered the low passageway, fitted the hatch back into place. Too late he thought of the old-fashioned glass he had picked up. *When the forensics people dust, they'll find my prints. Those, along with my car parked in the driveway . . .*

No good thinking about that now, he had to move! Bent over, he made his way along the cramped passageway. Within ten feet it opened up so that he was able to walk normally. There was a new dampness in the air; from somewhere close at hand he could hear the slow drip of water seeping. He determined that he had gone beyond the foundation of the house. Bourne quickened his pace and, not three minutes later, came upon another set of stairs. These were of metal, military in nature. He mounted them and, at the top, pushed up with his shoulder. Another hatch opened. Fresh air, the hushed and tranquil light at the end of the day, the droning of insects washed over him. He was at the edge of the general's heliport.

The tarmac was littered with twigs and bits of dead branches. At some point, a family of raccoons had made their way into the small ramshackle shingle-roofed shed at the edge of the tarmac. The place bore the unmistakable air of abandonment. The heliport was not, however, his objective. He turned his back on it and plunged into the thick pine forest.

His goal was to make a long sweeping curve away from the house, the entire estate, eventually ending up on the highway far enough away from any cordon the police threw around the estate. However, his immediate objective was the stream that ran more or less diagonally through the property. It would not be long, he knew, before the police brought in dogs. He could do very little about leaving his scent on dry land, but in the moving water even the dogs would lose his trail.

Snaking through the thorny snarl of underbrush, he crested a small ridge, stood between two cedars, listening intently. It was vital to catalog all the normal sounds of this specific environment so that he would instantly be alerted to the sound of an intruder. He was keenly aware that an enemy was in all likelihood somewhere close by. The murderer of his friends, of the moorings of his old life. The desire to stalk that enemy was weighed against the necessity of escaping from the police. As much as he wanted to track down the killer, Bourne knew it was crucial for him to be outside the radius of the police cordon before it was fully set up.

The moment Khan had entered the dense pine and hardwood forest on Alexander Conklin's estate he felt as if he had come home. The deep green vault closed over his head, plunging him into a premature twilight. Overhead, he could see sunlight filtering through the topmost branches, but here all was murk and gloom, the better for him to stalk his prey. He had followed Webb from the university campus to Conklin's house. During the course of his career, he had heard of Alexander Conklin, knew him for the legendary spymaster he had been. What puzzled him was why David Webb should come here? Why would he even know Conklin? And how was it that so many police had shown up at the estate mere minutes after Webb himself?

In the distance, he could hear baying, and he knew the police must have let loose their tracking dogs. Up ahead, he saw Webb moving through the forest as if he knew it well. Another question without an obvious answer. Khan picked up his pace, wondering where Webb was headed. Then he heard the sound of a stream and he knew precisely what his quarry had on his mind.

Khan hurried on, reaching the stream before Webb. He knew his prey would head downstream, away from the direction in which the hounds were headed. That was when he saw the huge willow and a grin captured his face. A sturdy tree with a network of spreading branches was just what he needed.

The ruddy sunlight of early evening threaded itself like needles of fire through the trees, and Bourne's eye was caught by the splotches of crimson that fired the edge of the leaves.

On the far side of the ridge, the land fell away rather steeply, and the way became more rocky. He could pick out the soft burbling sound of the nearby stream, and he headed for it as quickly as he could. The winter's snowpack had combined with the early spring rains to leave the stream swollen. Without hesitation, he stepped into the chill water, wading downstream. The longer he stayed in the water the better, as the dogs would lose all scent of him and become confused, and the farther away he emerged, the harder it would be for them to pick up his scent again.

Safe for the moment, he began thinking of his wife, Marie. He needed to contact her. Going home was out of the question now; doing so would put them in immediate jeopardy. But he had to contact Marie, warn her. The Agency was sure to come looking for him at home, and not finding him there, they were certain to detain Marie, interrogate her, assuming she would know his whereabouts. And there was the even more chilling possibility that whoever had set him up would now try to get to him through his family. In a sudden sweat of anxiety, he pulled out Conklin's cell phone, dialed Marie's cell phone, input a text message. It was one word only: *Diamond*. This was the code word he and Marie had previously agreed upon, to be used only in dire emergencies. It was a directive for her to take the kids and leave immediately for their safe house. They were to stay there, incommunicado, secure, until Bourne gave Marie the 'all clear' signal. Alex's phone rang and Bourne saw Marie's text: *Repeat please*. This was not the prescribed response. Then he realized why she was confused. He had contacted her on Alex's cell phone, not his. He repeated the message: *DIAMOND*, this time typing it in all capital letters. He waited, breathless, and then Marie's response came: *HOURGLASS*. Bourne exhaled in relief. Marie had acknowledged; he knew the message was real. Even now, she would be gathering up the kids, bundling them into the station wagon, driving off, leaving everything behind.

Still, he was left with a feeling of anxiety. He would feel a whole lot better once he heard her voice, once he could explain to her what had happened, that he was fine. But he wasn't fine. The man she knew – David Webb – had already been subsumed again by Bourne. Marie hated and feared Jason Bourne. And why shouldn't she? It was possible that one day Bourne would be all that was left of the personality in David Webb's body. And whose doing would that be? Alexander Conklin's.

It seemed astonishing and altogether improbable to him that he could both love and loathe this man. How mysterious the human mind that it could simultaneously contain such extreme contradictory emotions, that it could rationalize away those evil qualities it knew were there in order to feel affection for someone. But, Bourne knew, the need to love and be loved was a human imperative.

He continued this train of thought as he followed the stream, which, for all its bright sparkle, was exceptionally clear. Small fish darted this way and that, terrified by his advance. Once or twice he glimpsed a trout in a silvery flash, bony mouth slightly open as if seeking something. He had come to a bend in which a large willow, its roots greedy for moisture, overhung the streambed. Alert to any noise, any sign that his pursuers were drawing near, Bourne detected nothing but the rushing of the stream itself.

The attack came from above. He heard nothing, but he felt the shift in the light, then a weight pressing down on him in the instant before he was driven into the water. He felt the crushing pressure of the body on his midsection and lungs. As he struggled to breathe, his attacker slammed his head on the slick rocks of the streambed. A fist drove into his kidney and all the breath went out of him.

Instead of tensing against the attack, Bourne willed his body to go completely limp. At the same time, instead of striking out, he drew his elbows into his side and, at the moment when his body was at its most slack, he reared up onto them, twisting his torso. As he hurled himself around, he struck out and up with the edge of his hand. He gasped air into his lungs as the weight came off. Water streamed across his face, blurring his vision, so that he could see only the outline of his assailant. He struck out at him but connected with nothing but air.

His assailant vanished as quickly as he had appeared.

Khan, gasping and retching as he scrambled down the streambed, tried to force air past the spasming muscles and bruised cartilage of his throat. Stunned and enraged, he gained the underbrush and was soon lost within the tangle of the forest. Trying to force himself to breathe normally, he gently massaged the tender area Webb had struck. That had not been a lucky blow but a calculated, expert counterattack. Khan was confused, a tinge of fear creeping through him. Webb was a dangerous man – far more than any academic had any right to be. He had been shot at before; he could trace a bullet's trajectory, could track through wilderness, fight hand-to-hand. And at the first sign of trouble he had come to Alexander Conklin. Who was this man? Khan asked himself. One thing was certain, he would not underestimate Webb again. He would track him, regain the psychological advantage. Before the inevitable end, he wanted Webb to be afraid of him.

Martin Lindros, Deputy Director of the CIA, arrived at the Manassas estate of the late Alexander Conklin at precisely six minutes past six. He was met by the ranking Virginia State Police detective, a harried, balding man named Harris who was trying to mediate the territorial dispute that had sprung up between the state police, the county sheriff's office and the FBI, all of whom had begun vying for jurisdiction as soon as the identities of the deceased had been discovered. When Lindros emerged from his car, he counted a dozen vehicles, three times that number of people. What was needed was a sense of order and purpose.

As he shook hands with Harris, he looked him straight in the eye and said, 'Detective Harris, the FBI is out. You and I will be working this double homicide ourselves.'

'Yessir,' Harris said crisply. He was tall and, perhaps in compensation, had developed a slight stoop, which along with his large watery eyes and lugubrious face made him seem as if he had run out of energy long ago. 'Thanks. I've got some – '

'Don't thank me, Detective, I guarantee you this is going to be one bitch of a case.' He dispatched his assistant to deal with the FBI and the sheriff's personnel. 'Any sign of David Webb?' He'd gotten word from the FBI when he'd been patched through to them that Webb's car had been found parked in Conklin's driveway. Not Webb, really. Jason Bourne. Which was why the Director of Central Intelligence had dispatched him to take over the investigation personally.

'Not yet,' Harris said. 'But we have the dogs out.'

'Good. Have you established a cordon perimeter?'

'I tried to send my men out, but then the FBI . . .' Harris shook his head. 'I told them time was of the essence.'

Lindros glanced at his watch. 'Half-mile perimeter. Use some of your men to work another cordon at a radius of a quarter-mile. They might pick up something useful. Call in more personnel if you have to.'

While Harris was talking on his walkie-talkie, Lindros eyed him appraisingly. 'What's your first name?' he asked when the detective was through giving orders.

The detective gave him an abashed look. 'Harry.'

'Harry Harris. You're kidding, right?'

'No, sir. I'm afraid not.'

'What were your parents thinking?'

'I don't think they were, sir.'

'Okay, Harry. Let's take a look at what we have here.' Lindros was in his late thirties, a smart sandy-haired Ivy Leaguer who had been recruited to the Agency out of Georgetown. Lindros' father had been a strong-willed man who spoke his mind and had his own way of doing things. He instilled this quirky independence in young Martin, along with the sense of duty to his country, and Lindros believed it was these qualities that had caught the attention of the DCI.

Harris brought him into the study but not before Lindros had marked the two old-fashioned glasses on the cocktail table in the media room. 'Anyone touch these, Harry?'

'Not to my knowledge, sir.'

'Call me Martin. We're going to get to know each other fast.' He looked up and smiled, to further put the other at ease. The manner in which he had thrown around the Agency's weight was deliberate. In cutting out the other law enforcement agencies, he had drawn Harris into his orbit. He had a feeling he was going to need a compliant detective. 'Have your forensics people dust both glasses for prints, will you?'

'Right away.'

'And now let's have a word with the coroner.'

High atop the road that snaked along the ridge bordering the estate, a heavyset man stood peering at Bourne through a pair of powerful night-vision glasses. He had a wide melon face distinctly Slavic in character. The fingertips of his left hand were yellow; he smoked constantly, compulsively. Behind him, his large black SUV was parked in a scenic turnout. To anyone passing, he would look like a tourist. Tracking backward, he found Khan creeping through the woods on Bourne's trail. Keeping one eye on Khan's progress, he flipped open his tri-band cell phone, punched in an overseas number.

Stepan Spalko answered at once.

'The trap has been sprung,' the heavyset Slav said. 'The target is on the run. So far he has eluded both the police and Khan.'

'Goddammit!' Spalko said. 'What is Khan up to?'

'Do you want me to find out?' the man asked in his cold, casual manner.

'Keep as far away from him as possible. In fact,' Spalko said, 'get out of there now.'

Staggering to the stream bank, Bourne sat down, slicked his hair back from his face. His body ached and his lungs felt as if they were on fire. Explosions went off behind his eyes, returning him to the jungles of Tam Quan, the missions David Webb had undertaken at Alex Conklin's behest, missions sanctioned by Saigon Command yet disavowed by them, insane missions so difficult, so deadly that no American military personnel could ever be associated with them.

Bathed in the failing light of a spring evening, Bourne knew that he had been thrust into the same kind of situation now. He was in a red zone – an area controlled by the enemy. The trouble was, he had no idea who the enemy was or what he intended. Was Bourne even now being herded as he apparently had been when he had been fired upon at Georgetown University, or had his enemy moved on to a new phase of his plan?

Far off, he heard the baying of dogs, and then, startlingly close at hand, the crisp, clear sound of a twig snapping. Had it been made by an animal or the enemy? His immediate objective had been altered. He still had to avoid the net of the police cordon but now, at the same time, he had to find a way to turn the tables on his attacker. The trouble was he had to find his assailant before he attacked Bourne again. If it was the same person as before, then he was not only a crack shot but also an expert at jungle warfare. In a way, knowing this much about his adversary heartened Bourne. He was getting to know his opponent. Now to avoid being killed before he could get to know him well enough to surprise him . . .

The sun had slipped below the horizon, leaving the sky the color of a banked fire. A cool wind caused Bourne to shiver in his wet clothes. He rose and began to move, both to get the stiffness out of his muscles and to warm himself. The forest was cloaked in indigo, and yet he felt as exposed as if he were in a treeless expanse beneath a cloudless sky.

He knew what he would do if he were in Tam Quan: He'd find shelter, a place to regroup and consider options. But finding shelter in a red zone was tricky; he might be putting his head in a trap. He moved through the forest slowly and deliberately, his eyes scanning tree trunk after tree trunk until he found what he was looking for. Virginia creeper. It was too early in the year for flowers, but the shiny five-lobed leaves were unmistakable. Using the switchblade, he carefully peeled off long lengths of the sturdy vine.

Moments after he was finished, his ears pricked up. Following a faint sound, he soon came to a small clearing. There. He saw a deer, a mid-sized buck. Its head was up, its black nostrils scenting the air. Had it smelled him? No. It was trying to find –

The deer took off, and Bourne with him. He ran lightly and silently through the forest paralleling the deer's path. Once, the wind shifted and he had to alter his course in order to remain downwind of the animal. They had covered perhaps a quarter of a mile when the deer slowed. The ground had risen, become harder, more compact. They were quite some distance from the stream and on the extreme edge of the estate. The deer leaped easily over the stone wall marking the northwestern corner of the property. Bourne clambered over the wall in time to see that the deer had led him to a salt lick. Salt licks meant rocks and rocks meant caves. He recalled Conklin telling him that the northwestern edge of the property abutted a series of caves honeycombed with chimneys, natural vertical holes the Indians had once used to vent their cooking fires. Such a cave was just what he was hoping for – a haven to temporarily hide in that, by virtue of its two egresses, would not become a trap.

*Now I have him*, Khan thought. Webb had made a huge mistake – he'd entered the wrong cave, one of the few without a second exit. Khan crept out from his hiding place, crossing the small clearing in silence and in stealth, entering the black mouth of the cave.

Creeping forward, he could sense Webb in the darkness up ahead. Khan knew by the smell that this one was shallow. It did not have the damp, sharp scent of built-up organic matter of a cave that went deep into the bedrock.

Up ahead, Webb had switched on the flashlight. In a moment he would see that there was no chimney, no other way out. The time to attack was now! Khan launched himself at his adversary, struck him flush in the face.

Bourne went down, the flashlight hitting the rock, the light bouncing crazily. At the same time, he could feel the rush of air as the balled fist flew toward him. He allowed it to strike him and, as the arm was extended to the fullest, chopped down hard on the exposed and vulnerable biceps.

Lunging forward, he jammed his shoulder into the sternum of the other body. A knee came up, connected with the inside of Bourne's thigh, and a line of nerve pain flashed through him. He seized a handful of clothes, jerked the body against the rock face. The body bounced back, rammed into him, bowling him off his feet. They rolled together, grappling at each other. He could hear the other's breathing, an incongruously intimate sound, like listening to a child's breath beside you.

Locked in an elemental struggle, Bourne was close enough to smell a complex melange rising off the other like steam from a sunlit swamp that made the jungle of Tam Quan rear up once more in his mind. In that instant, he felt a bar against his throat. He was being hauled backward.

'I won't kill you,' a voice said in his ear. 'At least not yet.'

He jabbed backward with an elbow, was rewarded with a knee to his already aching kidney. He doubled over but was hauled painfully erect by the bar against his windpipe.

'I could kill you now, but I won't,' the voice said. 'Not until there is enough light so that I can look into your eyes while you die.'

'Did you have to kill two innocent decent men just to get to me?' Bourne said.

'What are you talking about?'

'The two people you shot to death back at the house.'

'I didn't kill them; I never kill innocents.' There was a chuckle. 'On the other hand, I don't know that I could call anyone associated with Alexander Conklin an innocent.'

'But you herded me here,' Bourne said. 'You shot at me so I'd run to Conklin, so you could – '

'You're talking nonsense,' the voice said. 'I merely followed you here.'

'Then how did you know where to send the cops?' Bourne said.

'Why would I even call them?' the voice whispered harshly.

Startling though this information was, Bourne was only half-listening. He had relaxed a little during this conversation, leaning backward. This left the smallest bit of slack between the bar and his windpipe. Bourne now turned on the balls of his feet, dropping one shoulder as he did so, so that the other was obliged to focus his attention on keeping the bar in place. In that instant, Bourne used the heel of his hand to deliver a quick strike just below the ear. The body fell hard; the bar rang hollowly as it struck the rock floor.

Bourne took several deep breaths to clear his head, but he was still woozy from loss of oxygen. He took up the flashlight, illuminated the spot where the body had fallen, but it wasn't there. A sound, barely a whisper, came to him and he raised the beam. A figure sprang into the light against the mouth of the cave. As the light struck him, he turned, and Bourne got a glimpse of his face before he vanished into the trees.

Bourne ran after him. In a moment he heard the distinct snap and whoosh! He heard movement up ahead, and he pushed through the undergrowth to where he had set his trap. He had woven the Virginia creeper into a net and tied it to a green sapling he had bent almost double. It had caught his assailant. The hunter had become the prey. Bourne pushed forward to the base of the trees, prepared himself to face his attacker and cut the creeper netting down. But the net was empty.

Empty! He gathered it up, saw the rent his quarry had cut into its upper section. He had been quick, clever and prepared; he would be even more difficult to take by surprise again.

Bourne looked up, playing the cone of the flashlight beam in an arc across the maze of tree limbs. Despite himself, he experienced a fleeting twinge of admiration for his expert and resourceful adversary. Snapping off the flashlight, he was plunged into night. A whippoorwill cried out and then, in the lengthening silence, an owl's hoot echoed mournfully through the pine-clad hills.

He leaned his head back and took a deep breath. Against the screen of his mind's eye the flat planes, the dark eyes of the face was limned, and in a moment he was certain that it matched up with one of the students he had seen on his way to the university classroom the sniper had used.

At last, his enemy had a face as well as a voice.

'I could kill you now, but I won't. Not until there is enough light so that I can look into your eyes while you die.'

# 3

Humanistas, Ltd., an international human-rights organization known the world over for its worldwide humanitarian and relief work, was headquartered on the deep green western slope of Gellért Hill in Budapest. From this magnificent vantage point, Stepan Spalko, peering through the huge angled plate-glass windows, imagined the Danube and the entire city genuflecting at his feet.

He had come around from behind his huge desk to sit on an upholstered chair facing the very dark-skinned Kenyan president. Flanking the door were the Kenyan's bodyguards, hands tucked at the smalls of their backs, the blank look endemic to all such government personnel etched on their faces. Above them, molded in bas-relief on the wall, was the green cross held in the palm of a hand that was Humanistas' well-marketed logo. The president's name was Jomo and he was a Kikuyu, the largest ethnic tribe of Kenya, and a direct descendant of Jomo Kenyatta, the Republic's first president. Like his famous forebear, he was a *Mzee*, Swahili for a respected elder. Between them was an ornate silver service dating back to the 1700s. Fine black tea had been poured, biscuits and exquisitely turned-out small sandwiches artfully arranged on a chased oval tray. The two men were talking in low, even tones.

'One doesn't know where to begin to thank you for the generosity you and your organization have shown us,' Jomo said. He was sitting up very straight, his ramrod back pulled a little away from the comfort of the chair's plush back. Time and circumstance had combined to rob his face of much of the vitality it had held in his youth. There was, beneath the high gloss of his skin, a grayish pallor. His features had been compressed, ossified into stone by hardship and perseverance in the face of overwhelming odds. In short, he had the aspect of a warrior too long at siege. His legs were together, bent at the knee at a precise ninety-degree angle. He held in his lap a long, polished box of deep-grained bubinga wood. Almost shyly, he presented the box to Spalko. 'With the heartfelt blessings of the Kenyan people, sir.'

'Thank you, Mr. President. You are too kind,' Spalko said graciously.

'The kindness is surely yours, sir.' Jomo watched with keen interest as Spalko opened the box. Inside was a flat-bladed knife and a stone, more or less oval in shape, with a flattish bottom and top.

'My God, this isn't a *githathi* stone, is it?'

'It is, indeed, sir,' Jomo said with obvious delight. 'It is from my birth village, from the *kiama* to which I still belong.'

Spalko knew Jomo was referring to the council of elders. The *githathi* was of great value to tribal members. When a dispute arose within the council that could not otherwise be settled, an oath was taken on this stone. Spalko gripped the knife's handle, which was carved from carnelian. It, too, had a ritualistic purpose. In cases of life or death disputes, the blade of this knife was first heated, then laid onto the tongues of the disputants. The extent of the tongues' subsequent blistering determined their guilt or innocence.

'I wonder, though, Mr. President,' Spalko said with the hint of an impish tone, 'whether the *githathi* comes from your *kiama* or your *njama*?'

Jomo laughed, a rumble deep in his throat that made his small ears quiver. It was so rare he had cause to laugh these days. He could not remember the last time. 'So you have heard of our secret councils, have you, sir? I would say your knowledge of our customs and lore is formidable, indeed.'

'The history of Kenya is long and bloody, Mr. President. I am a firm believer that it is in history we learn all our most important lessons.'

Jomo nodded. 'I concur, sir. And I feel compelled to reiterate that I cannot imagine what state the Republic would be in without your doctors and their vaccines.'

'There is no vaccine against AIDS.' Spalko's voice was gentle but firm. 'Modern medicine can curtail the suffering and deaths from the disease with drug cocktails, but as for its spread, only the stringent application of contraceptives or abstinence will be effective.'

'Of course, of course.' Jomo wiped his lips fastidiously. He detested coming hat in hand to this man who had already so generously extended his help to all Kenyans, but what choice did he have? The AIDS epidemic was decimating the Republic. His people were suffering, dying. 'What we need, sir, is more of the drugs. You have done much to alleviate the level of suffering in my country. But there are thousands yet to receive your help.'

'Mr. President.' Spalko leaned forward, and with him, Jomo as well. His head was now in the sunlight streaming in through the high windows, lending him an almost preternatural glow. The light also threw into prominence the shiny poreless skin on the left side of his face. This accentuation of his disfigurement served to provide a slight shock to Jomo, jolting him out of his predetermined pattern. 'Humanistas, Ltd. is prepared to return to Kenya with twice the number of doctors, double the amount of drugs. But you – the government – must do your part.'

It was at this point that Jomo realized that Spalko was asking of him something quite apart from promoting safe-sex lectures and distributing condoms. Abruptly, he turned, dismissing his two bodyguards from the room. When the door had closed behind them, he said, 'An unfortunate necessity in these dangerous times, sir, but even so one sometimes wearies of never being alone.'

Spalko smiled. His knowledge of Kenyan history and tribal customs made it impossible for him to take the president lightly, as others might. Jomo's need might be great, but one never wanted to take advantage of him. The Kikuyu were prideful people, an attribute made all the more important since it was more or less the only thing of value they possessed.

Spalko leaned over, opened a humidor, offered a Cuban Cohiba to Jomo, took one himself. They rose, lighting their cigars, walked across the carpet to stand at the window, looking out at the tranquil Danube sparkling in the sunlight.

'A most beautiful setting,' Spalko said conversationally.

'Indeed,' Jomo affirmed.

'And so serene.' Spalko let go a blue cloud of aromatic smoke. 'Difficult to come to terms with the amount of suffering in other parts of the world.' He turned then to Jomo. 'Mr. President, I would consider it a great personal favor if you would grant me seven days' unlimited access to Kenyan airspace.'

'Unlimited?'

'Coming and going, landings and such. No customs, immigration, inspections, nothing to slow us down.'

Jomo made a show of considering. He puffed some on his Cohiba, but Spalko could tell that he was not enjoying himself. 'I can grant you only three,' Jomo said at length. 'Longer than that will cause tongues to wag.'

'That will have to do, Mr. President.' Three days was all Spalko had wanted. He could have insisted on the seven days, but that would have stripped Jomo of his pride. A stupid and possibly costly mistake, considering what was to happen. In any event, he was in the business of promoting goodwill, not resentment. He held out his hand and Jomo slipped his dry, heavily calloused hand into his. Spalko liked that hand; it was a hand of a manual laborer, someone who was not afraid to get dirty.

After Jomo and his entourage had left, it was time to give an orientation tour to Ethan Hearn, the new employee. Spalko could have delegated the orientation to any one of a number of assistants, but he prided himself on personally making sure all his new employees were settled. Hearn was a bright young spark who had previously worked at the Eurocenter Bio-I Clinic on the other side of the city. He was a highly successful fund-raiser and was well connected among the rich and elite of Europe. Spalko found him to be articulate, personable and empathetic – in short, a born humanitarian, just the sort he needed to maintain the stellar reputation of Humanistas, Ltd. Besides which, he genuinely liked Hearn. He reminded him of himself when he was young, before the incident that had burned off half the skin of his face.

He took Hearn through the seven floors of offices, comprising laboratories, departments devoted to compiling the statistics the development people used in fund-raising, the lifeblood of organizations such as Humanistas, Ltd., as well as accounting, procurement, human resources, travel, the maintenance of the company's fleets of private jets, transport planes, ships and helicopters. The last stop was the development department, where Hearn's new office awaited him. At the moment, the office stood empty save for a desk, swivel chair, computer and phone console.

'The rest of your furniture,' Spalko told him, 'will be arriving in a few days.'

'No problem, sir. A computer and phones are all I really need.'

'A warning,' Spalko added. 'We keep long hours here, and there will be times you'll be expected to work through the night. But we're not inhuman. The sofa we provide folds out into a bed.'

Hearn smiled. 'Not to worry, Mr. Spalko. I'm quite used to those hours.'

'Call me Stepan.' Spalko gripped the younger man's hand. 'Everyone else does.'

The Director of Central Intelligence was soldering the arm on a painted tin soldier – a British redcoat from the Revolutionary War – when the call came. At first he considered ignoring it, perversely letting the phone ring even though he knew who would be on the other end of the line. Perhaps, he thought, this was because he did not want to hear what the Deputy Director would have to say. Lindros believed the DCI had dispatched him to the crime scene because of the importance of the dead men to the Agency. This was true, as far as it went. The real reason, however, was that the DCI couldn't bear to go himself. The thought of seeing Alex Conklin's dead face was too much for him.

He was sitting on a stool in his basement workshop, a tiny, enclosed, perfectly ordered environment of stacked drawers, aligned cubbyholes, a world unto itself, a place his wife – and his children when they had lived at home – were forbidden to enter.

His wife, Madeleine, poked her head through the open door to the cellar. 'Kurt, the phone,' she said needlessly.

He took an arm out of the wooden bin of soldier parts, studied it. He was a large-headed man, but a mane of white hair combed back from his wide, domed forehead lent him the aspect of a wise man, if not a prophet. His cool blue eyes were still as calculating as ever, but the lines at the corners of his mouth had deepened, pulling them down into something of a perpetual pout.

'Kurt, do you hear me?'

'I am not deaf.' The fingers at the end of the arm were slightly cupped as if the hand was preparing to reach out for something unnameable and unknown.

'Well, are you going to answer it?' Madeleine called down.

'Whether I answer it or not is none of your goddamn business!' he shouted with vehemence. 'Will you go to bed now.' A moment later he heard the satisfying whisper of the basement door closing. Why couldn't she leave him alone at a time like this? he fumed. Thirty years married, you'd think she'd know better.

He returned to his work, fitting the arm with the cupped hand to the shoulder of the torso, red to red, deciding on the final position. This was how the DCI dealt with situations over which he had no control. He played god with his miniature soldiers, buying them, cutting them to pieces, then, later, reconstructing them, molding them into the positions that suited him. Here, in the world he himself had created, he controlled everyone and everything.

The phone continued to ring in its mechanical, monotonous fashion and the DCI gritted his teeth, as if the sound was abrasive. What marvelous deeds had been accomplished in the days when he and Alex had been young! The mission inside Russia when they had almost landed in the Lubyanka, running the Berlin Wall, extracting secrets from the Staasi, vetting the defector from the KGB in the Vienna safe house, discovering that he was a double. The killing of Bernd, their longtime contact, the compassion with which they had told his wife that they would take care of Bernd's son Dieter, take him back to America, put him through college. They had done precisely that and had been rewarded for their generosity. Dieter had never returned to his mother. Instead, he had joined the Agency, had for many years been the director of the Science & Technology Directorate until the fatal motorcycle accident.

Where had that life gone? Laid to rest in Bernd's grave, and Dieter's – now Alex's. How had it been reduced so quickly to flashpoints in his memory? Time and responsibilities had crippled him, no question. He was an old man now, in some respects with more power, yes, but the daring deeds of yesterday, the elan with which he and Alex had bestrode the secret world, changing the fate of nations, had burned to ash, never to return.

The DCI's fist hammered the tin soldier into a cripple. Then and only then did he pick up the phone.

'Yes, Martin.'

There was a weariness in his voice Lindros picked up on immediately. 'Are you all right, sir?'

'No, I fucking well am not all right!' This was what the DCI had wanted. Another opportunity to vent his anger and frustration. 'How could I be all right given the circumstances?'

'I'm sorry, sir.'

'No, you're not,' the DCI said waspishly. 'You couldn't be. You have no idea.' He stared at the soldier he had crushed, his mind hounded by past glories. 'What is it you want?'

'You asked for an update, sir.'

'Did I?' The DCI rested his head in his hand. 'Yes, I suppose I did. What have you found?'

'The third car in Conklin's driveway belongs to David Webb.'

The DCI's keen ear responded to a tone in Lindros' voice. 'But?'

'But there's no sign of Webb.'

'Of course there isn't.'

'He was definitely there, though. We gave the dogs a sniff at the interior of his car. They found his scent on the property and followed it into the woods but lost it at a stream.'

The DCI closed his eyes. Alexander Conklin and Morris Panov shot to death, Jason Bourne MIA and on the loose five days before the terrorism summit, the most important international meeting of the century. He shuddered. He abhorred loose ends, but not nearly as much as Roberta Alonzo-Ortiz, the National Security Advisor, and these days she was running the show. 'Ballistics? Forensics?'

'Tomorrow morning,' Lindros said. 'That was as much as I could push them.'

'As far as the FBI and other law-enforcement agencies – '

'I've already neutralized them. We have a clear field.'

The DCI sighed. He appreciated the DDCI's initiative, but he despised being interrupted. 'Get back to work,' he said gruffly, and cradled the receiver.

For a long time afterward, he stared into the wooden bin, listening to the house breathing. It sounded like an old man. Boards creaked, familiar as an old friend's voice. Madeleine must be making herself a cup of hot chocolate, her traditional sleep aid. He heard the neighbor's corgi bark, and for some reason he could not fathom, it seemed a mournful sound, full of sorrow and failed hope. At length, he reached into the bin, picked out a torso in Civil War gray, a new tin soldier to create.

# 4

'Must've been some accident, by the look of you,' Jack Kerry said.

'Not really, just a flat,' Bourne replied easily. 'But I didn't have a spare, and then I tripped on something – a tree root, I think. I took quite a tumble into the stream.' He made a deprecating gesture. 'I'm not exactly well coordinated.'

'Join the crew,' Kerry said. He was a large, rawboned man with a double chin and too much fat around his middle. He had picked Bourne up a mile back. 'One time my wife asked me to run the dishwasher, I filled it up with Tide. Jesus, you should've seen the mess!' He laughed good-naturedly.

The night was pitch-dark, no moon or stars. A soft drizzle had begun and Kerry put on the windshield wipers. Bourne shivered a little in his damp clothes. He knew he had to focus, but every time he closed his eyes he saw images of Alex and Mo; he saw blood seeping, bits of skull and brain. His fingers curled, hands tightening into fists.

'So what is it you do, Mr. Little?'

Bourne had given his name as Dan Little when Kerry introduced himself. Kerry, it appeared, was an old-style gentleman who put great store in the niceties of convention.

'I'm an accountant.'

'I design nuclear waste facilities, myself. Travel far and wide, yessir.' Kerry gave him a sideways glance, light spinning off his glasses. 'Hell, you don't look like an accountant, you don't mind me saying.'

Bourne forced himself to laugh. 'Everyone says that. I played football in college.'

'Haven't let yourself go to seed like many ex-athletes,' Kerry observed. He patted his rotund abdomen. 'Not like me. Except I never was an athlete. I tried once. Never knew which way to run. Got screamed at by the coach. And then I got tackled good.' He shook his head. 'That was enough for me. I'm a lover, not a fighter.' He glanced at Bourne again. 'You got a family, Mr. Little?'

Bourne hesitated a moment. 'A wife and two children.'

'Happy, are ya?'

A wedge of black trees hurried by, a telephone pole leaning into the wind, a shack abandoned, draped with thorny creeper, returned to the wild. Bourne closed his eyes. 'Very happy.'

Kerry manhandled the car around a sweeping curve. One thing you could say about him – he was an excellent driver. 'Me, I'm divorced. That was a bad one. My wife left me with my three-year-old in tow. That was ten years ago.' He frowned. 'Or is it eleven? Anyway, I haven't seen or heard from either her or the boy since.'

Bourne's eyes snapped open. 'You haven't been in touch with your son?'

'It's not that I haven't tried.' There was a querulous note to Kerry's voice as he turned defensive. 'For a while, I called every week, sent him letters, money, you know, for things he might like, a bike and such. Never heard a word back.'

'Why didn't you go to see him?'

Kerry shrugged. 'I finally got the message – he didn't want to see me.'

'That was your wife's message,' Bourne said. 'Your son's only a child. He doesn't know what he wants. How can he? He hardly knows you.'

Kerry grunted. 'Easy for you to say, Mr. Little. You've got a warm hearth, a happy family to go home to every night.'

'It's precisely because I have children that I know how precious they are,' Bourne said. 'If it was my son, I'd fight tooth and nail to know him and to get him back into my life.'

They were coming to a more populated area now, and Bourne saw a motel, a strip of closed stores. In the distance, he could see a red flash, then another. There was a roadblock up ahead and, by the look of it, a major one. He counted eight cars in all, in two ranks of four each, turned at forty-five degrees to the highway in order to afford their occupants the greatest protection while allowing the cars to quickly close ranks if need be. Bourne knew he couldn't allow himself to get any-where near the roadblock, not, at least, sitting in plain view. He would have to find some other way to get through it.

All at once, the neon sign of an all-night convenience store loomed out of the darkness.

'I think this is as far as I'll go.'

'You sure, Mr. Little? It's still pretty desolate out here.'

'Don't worry about me. I'll just have my wife come and pick me up. We don't live far from here.'

'Then I should take you all the way home.'

'I'll be fine here. Really.'

Kerry pulled over and slowed to a stop just past the convenience store. Bourne got out.

'Thanks for the lift.'

'Any time.' Kerry smiled. 'And, Mr. Little, thanks for the advice. I'll think on what you said.'

Bourne watched Kerry drive off, then he turned and walked into the conve-nience store. The ultra-bright fluorescent lights made his eyes burn. The attendant, a pimply-faced young man with long hair and bloodshot eyes, was smoking a ciga-rette and reading a paperback book. He looked up briefly as Bourne entered, nodded disinterestedly and went back to his reading. Somewhere a radio was on; someone was singing 'Yesterday's Gone,' in a world-weary, melancholy voice. She might have been singing it for Bourne.

One look at the shelves reminded him that he hadn't eaten since lunch. He grabbed a plastic jar of peanut butter, a box of crackers, some beef jerky, orange juice and water. Protein and vitamins were what he needed. He also purchased a T-shirt, a long-sleeved striped shirt, razor and shaving cream, other items he knew from long experience he would need.

Bourne approached the counter, and the attendant put down the dog-eared book he had been reading. *Dhalgren* by Samuel R. Delany. Bourne remembered reading it just after he returned from Nam, a book as hallucinatory as the war. Fragments of his life came hurtling back – the blood, the death, the rage, the reckless killing, all to blot out the excruciating, never-ending pain of what had happened in the river just outside his house in Phnom Penh. *'You've got a warm hearth, a happy family to go home to every night,'* Kerry had said. If only he knew.

'Anything else?' the pimply-faced young man said.

Bourne blinked, returning to the present. 'Do you have an electrical charger for a cell phone?'

'Sorry, bud, all out.'

Bourne paid for his purchases in cash, took possession of the brown paper bag and left. Ten minutes later he walked onto the motel grounds. There were few cars. A tractor-trailer was parked at one end of the motel, a refrigerated truck, by the look of the compressor squatting on its top. Inside the office a spindly man with the gray face of an undertaker shuffled out from behind a desk in the rear, where he'd been watching an ancient portable black-and-white TV. Bourne checked in using another assumed name, paying for the room in cash. He was left with precisely sixty-seven dollars.

'Goddamn strange night,' the spindly man rasped.

'How so?'

The spindly man's eyes lit up. 'Don't tell me ya didn't hear about the murders?'

Bourne shook his head.

'Not twenty miles away.' The spindly man leaned over the counter. His breath smelled unpleasantly from coffee and bile. 'Two men – *government people* – nobody sayin' nothin' else about 'em, an' y'know what *that* means around here: hush-hush, deep-throat, cloak-an'-dagger, who the *hell* knows what they was up to? You turn on CNN when you get to the room, we got cable an' everything.' He handed Bourne the key. 'Putcha in a room at the other end from Guy – he's the trucker, might have seen his semi when you came in. Guy makes a reg'lar run from Florida to D.C.; he'll be leavin' at five, don't wantcha disturbed, now do we?'

The room was a drab brown, timeworn. Even the smell of an industrial-strength cleaner could not entirely blot out the odor of decay. Bourne turned on the TV, switching channels. He took out the peanut butter and crackers, began to eat.

'There is no doubt that this bold, visionary initiative of the president's has a chance to build bridges toward a more peaceful future,' the CNN newsreader was saying. Behind her, a graphic banner in screaming red across the top of the screen proclaimed THE TERRORISM SUMMIT with all the subtlety of a London tabloid. 'The summit includes, besides the president himself, the president of Russia and the leaders of the major Arab nations. Over the course of the coming week, we'll be checking in with Wolf Blitzer with the president's party and Christiane Amanpour with the Russian and Arab leaders for in-depth commentaries. Clearly, the summit has the makings of the news story of the year. Now, for an up-to-the-minute report from Reykjavík, Iceland . . .'

The scene switched to the front of the Oskjuhlid Hotel, where the terrorism summit would take place in five days' time. An overearnest CNN reporter began to conduct an interview with the head of American security, Jamie Hull. Bourne stared at Hull's square-jawed face, his short brush-cut hair, ginger-colored mustache, cold blue eyes, and an alarm went off in his head. Hull was Agency, high up in its Counterterrorist Center. He and Conklin had butted heads more than once. Hull was a clever political animal; he had his nose up the ass of everyone who counted. But he went by the book even when situations dictated he take a more flexible approach. Conklin must have been apoplectic at his being named head of the American security at the summit.

While Bourne was considering this, a news update took over the crawl on the screen. It concerned the deaths of Alexander Conklin and Dr. Morris Panov, both, according to the crawl, high-level government officials. All at once, the scene shifted and a banner reading BREAKING NEWS flashed on, followed by another, MANASSAS MURDERS, which was superimposed above a government photo of David Webb that took up almost the entire screen. The newsreader began her update on the brutal murders of Alex Conklin and Dr. Morris Panov. 'Each was shot once in the head,' the newsreader said with all the grim delight of her ilk, 'indicating the work of a professional killer. The government's prime suspect is this man, David Webb. Webb may be using an alias, Jason Bourne. According to highly placed government sources, Webb, or Bourne, is delusional and is considered dangerous. If you see this man, do not approach. Call the number listed on your screen . . .'

Bourne switched off the sound. Christ, the shit had really hit the fan now. No wonder that roadblock up ahead had looked so well organized – it was Agency, not the local cops.

He had better get to work. Brushing crumbs off his lap, he pulled out Conklin's cell phone. It was time to find out who Alex had been talking to when he had been shot. He accessed the auto-redial key, listened to the ring on the other end. A prerecorded message came on. This wasn't a personal number; it was a business. Lincoln Fine Tailors. The thought that Conklin was talking to his tailor when he was shot to death was depressing, indeed. It was no way for a master spy to go out.

He accessed the last incoming call, which was from the previous evening. It was from the DCI. *Dead end,* Bourne thought. He rose. As he padded to the bathroom, he stripped off his clothes. For a long time he stood under the hot shower spray, his mind deliberately blank as he sluiced the dirt and sweat off his skin. It was good to feel warm again and clean. Now if only he had a fresh set of clothes. All at once his head came up. He wiped water out of his eyes, his heart beating fast, his mind fully engaged again. Conklin's clothes were made by Old World Tailors off M Street; Alex had been going there for years. He even had dinner with the owner, a Russian immigrant, once or twice a year.

In something of a frenzy Bourne dried himself off, took up Conklin's phone again and dialed information. After he had gotten Lincoln Fine Tailors' address in Alexandria, he sat on the bed, staring at nothing. He was wondering just what it was Lincoln Fine Tailors did besides cut fabric and sew hems.

Hasan Arsenov appreciated Budapest in ways Khalid Murat could never have. He said as much to Zina Hasiyev as they passed through Immigration.

'Poor Murat,' she said. 'A brave soul, a courageous fighter for independence, but his thinking was strictly nineteenth century.' Zina, Arsenov's trusted lieutenant as well as his lover, was small, wiry, as athletic as Arsenov himself. Her hair was long, black as night, swirling around her head like a corona. Her wide mouth and dark, lustrous eyes also contributed to her wild, gypsylike appearance, but her mind could be as detached and calculating as a litigator's, and she was stone-cold fearless.

Arsenov grunted in pain as he ducked into the back of the waiting limousine. The assassin's shot had been perfect, striking muscle only, the bullet exiting his thigh as cleanly as it had entered. The wound hurt like hell, but the pain was worth it, Arsenov thought as he settled in beside his lieutenant. No suspicion had fallen on him; even Zina had no idea he had colluded in Murat's assassination. But what choice had he had? Murat had been growing increasingly nervous regarding the consequences of the Shaykh's plan. He hadn't had Arsenov's vision, his monumental sense of social justice. He would have been content merely to win back Chechnya from the Russians, while the rest of the world turned its back in scorn.

Whereas, when the Shaykh had unfurled his bold and daring stratagem, it was, for Arsenov, the moment of revelation. He could vividly see the future the Shaykh was holding out to them like a ripe fruit. Gripped by the flash of supernal illumination, he had looked at Khalid Murat for confirmation, had seen instead the bitter truth. Khalid could not see past the borders of his homeland, could not understand that regaining the homeland was, in a way, secondary. Arsenov realized that the Chechens needed to gain power not only to throw off the yoke of the Russian infidel but to establish their place in the Islamic world, to gain the respect of the other Muslim nations. The Chechens were Sunnis who had embraced the teachings of the Sufi mystics, personified by the *zikr*, the remembrance of God, the common ritual involving chanted prayer and rhythmic dance that achieved a shared trancelike state during which the eye of God appeared to the assembled. Sunni, being as monolithic as other religions, abhorred, feared and therefore reviled those who deviated even slightly from its strict central doctrine. Mysticism, divine or otherwise, was anathema. *Nineteenth-century thinking, in every sense of the phrase*, Arsenov thought bitterly.

Since the day of the assassination, the long-dreamed-of moment when he had become the new leader of the Chechen freedom fighters, Arsenov had lived in a feverish almost-hallucinatory state. He slept heavily but not restfully, for his slumber was filled with nightmares in which he was trying to find something or someone through mazes of rubble and was defeated. As a consequence, he was edgy and short with his subordinates; he tolerated no excuses whatsoever. Only Zina had the power to calm him; her alchemical touch allowed him to return from the strange limbo into which he had somehow receded.

The twinge of his wound brought him back to the present. He stared out the window at the ancient streets, watched with an envy that bordered on agony as people went about their business without hindrance, without the slightest trace of fear. He hated them, each and every one who in the course of their free and easy lives gave not one thought to the desperate struggle he and his people had been engaged in since the 1700s.

'What is it, my love?' A frown of concern crossed Zina's face.

'My legs ache. I grow weary of sitting, that's all.'

'I know you. The tragedy of Murat's murder hasn't left you, despite our vengeance. Thirty-five Russian soldiers went to their graves in retaliation for the murder of Khalid Murat.'

'Not just Murat,' Arsenov said. 'Our men. We lost seventeen men to Russian treachery.'

'You've rooted out the traitor, shot him yourself in front of the sublieutenants.'

'To show them what awaits all traitors to the cause. The judgment was swift, the punishment hard. This is our fate, Zina. There aren't enough tears to shed for our people. Look at us. Lost and dispersed, hiding in the Caucasus, more than one hundred fifty thousand Chechens living as refugees.'

Zina did not stop Hasan as he enumerated once again this agonizing history because these stories needed to be repeated as often as possible. They were the history books of the Chechens.

Arsenov's fists went white, his nails drawing crescents of blood from beneath the skin of his palms. 'Ah, to have a weapon more deadly than an AK-47, more powerful than a packet of C4!'

'Soon, soon, my love,' Zina crooned softly in her deep, musical voice. 'The Shaykh has proved to be our greatest friend. Look how much aid his organization has provided our people in just the last year; look how much coverage his press people have gotten us in international magazines and newspapers.'

'And still the Russian yoke is around our necks,' Arsenov growled. 'Still we die by the hundreds.'

'The Shaykh has promised us a weapon that will change all that.'

'He's promised us the world.' Arsenov wiped grit out of his eye. 'The time for promises is over. Let us now see the proof of his covenant.'

The limousine the Shaykh had sent for the Chechens turned off the motorway at Kalmankrt Boulevard, which took them over the Arpad Bridge, the Danube with its heavy barges and brightly painted pleasure craft a dazzle below them. Zina glanced down. To one side were the breathtaking domed and needle-spired Gothic stone edifices of the Houses of Parliament; on the other was thickly forested Margaret Island, within which was the luxe Danubius Grand Hotel, where crisp white sheets and a thick down comforter were awaiting them. Zina, hard as armor plate during the day, reveled in her nights in Budapest, never more so than in the luxury of the huge hotel bed. She saw in this feast of pleasure no betrayal of her ascetic existence but rather a brief respite from hardship and degradation, a reward like a wafer of Belgian chocolate slipped beneath the tongue, there in secret to melt in a cloud of ecstasy.

The limo nosed into the car park in the basement level of the Humanistas, Ltd. building. As they got out of the car, Zina took the large rectangular package from the driver. Uniformed guards checked the pair's passports against photos in the data bank of their computer terminal, gave them laminated ID tags and ushered them into a rather grand bronze-and-glass elevator.

Spalko received them in his office. By this time the sun was high in the sky, beating the river to a sheet of molten brass. He embraced them both, asked after the comfort of their flight, the ease of their trip in from Ferihegy Airport and the status of Arsenov's bullet wound. When the amenities had been dispensed with, they went into an adjacent room, paneled in honey-toned pecan wood, where a table had been set with crisp white linen and sparkling dinnerware. Spalko had had a meal prepared, Western food. Steak, lobster, three different vegetables – all the Chechens' favorites. And not a potato anywhere in evidence. Potatoes were often all Arsenov and Zina had to eat for days on end. Zina put the package on an empty chair, and they sat at the table.

'Shaykh,' Arsenov said, 'as always, we're overwhelmed by the largesse of your hospitality.'

Spalko inclined his head. He was pleased with the name he had given himself in their world, which meant the Saint, friend of God. It struck the right note of reverence and awe, an exalted shepherd to his flock.

He rose now and opened a bottle of powerful Polish vodka, which he poured into three glasses. He lifted his and they followed suit. 'In memory of Khalid Murat, a great leader, a powerful warrior, a grim adversary,' he intoned solemnly in the Chechen fashion. 'May Allah grant him the glory he has earned in blood and courage. May the tales of his prowess as a leader and as a man be told and retold among all the faithful.' They downed the fiery liquor in one quick gulp.

Arsenov stood, refilled the glasses. He raised his glass, and the others followed suit. 'To the Shaykh, friend of the Chechens, who will lead us to our rightful place in the new order of the world.' They drank down the vodka.

Zina made to rise, doubtless to make her own toast, but Arsenov stayed her with a hand on her arm. The restraining gesture did not fail to catch Spalko's attention. What interested him most was Zina's response. He could see past her veiled expression to her seething core. There were many injustices in the world, he knew, on every scale imaginable. It seemed to him peculiar and not a little perverse that human beings could be outraged by injustice on a grand scale, all the while missing the small wrongs that were daily visited on individuals. Zina fought side by side with the men; why, then, should she not have an opportunity to raise her voice in a toast of her own choosing? Rage seethed within her; Spalko liked that – he knew how to use another person's anger.

'My compatriots, my friends.' His eyes were sparking with conviction. 'To the meeting of sorrowful past, desperate present and glorious future. We stand on the brink of tomorrow!'

They began to eat, speaking of general and inconsequential matters just as if they were at a rather informal dinner party. And yet an air of anticipation, of incipient change, had crept into the room. They kept their eyes on their plates or on one another, as if now so close to it, they were reluctant to look at the gathering storm that was pressing in upon them. At length, they were finished.

'It's time,' the Shaykh said. Arsenov and Zina rose to stand before him.

Arsenov bowed his head. 'One who dies for the love of the material world dies a hypocrite. One who dies for the love of the hereafter dies an ascetic. But one who dies for the love of the Truth dies a Sufi.'

He turned to Zina, who opened the package they had brought with them from Grozny. Inside were three cloaks. She handed one to Arsenov, who put it on. She donned hers. The third Arsenov held in his hands as he faced the Shaykh.

'The *kherqeh* is the garment of honor of the dervish,' Arsenov intoned. 'It symbolizes the divine nature and attributes.'

Zina said, 'The cloak is sewn with the needle of devotion and the thread of the selfless remembrance of God.'

The Shaykh bowed his head and said, '*La illaha ill Allah.*' There is no God but God, who is One.

Arsenov and Zina repeated, '*La illaha ill Allah.*' Then the Chechen rebel leader placed the *kherqeh* around the Shaykh's shoulders. 'It is enough for most men to have lived according to the Shariah, the law of Islam, in surrender to the divine will, to die in grace and to enter into Paradise,' he said. 'But there are those of us who yearn for the divine here and now and whose love for God compels us to seek the path of inwardness. We are Sufi.'

Spalko felt the weight of the dervish cloak and said, 'O thou soul which are at peace, return unto thy Lord, with gladness that is thine in Him and His in thee. Enter thou among My slaves. Enter thou My Paradise.'

Arsenov, moved by this quotation from the Qur'an, took Zina's hand, and together they knelt before the Shaykh. In a call-and-response three centuries old, they recited a solemn oath of obedience. Spalko produced a knife, handed it to them. Both in turn cut themselves and, in a stemmed glass, offered up to him their blood. In this manner, they became *murids*, disciples of the Shaykh, bound to him in both word and deed.

Then, even though it was painful for Arsenov with his wounded thigh, they sat cross-legged, facing one another, and in the manner of the Naqshibandi Sufis, they performed the *zikr*, the ecstatic union with God. They placed their right hands on their left thighs, left hands atop right wrists. Arsenov began to move his head and neck to the right in the arc of a semicircle, and Zina and Spalko followed in perfect time to Arsenov's soft, almost sensual chanting: 'Save me, my Lord, from the evil eye of envy and jealousy, which falleth upon Thy bountiful Gifts.' They made the same movement to the left. 'Save me, my Lord, from falling into the hands of the playful children of earth, lest they might use me in their games; they might play with me and then break me in the end, as children destroy their toys.' Back and forth, back and forth. 'Save me, my Lord, from all manner of injury that cometh from the bitterness of my adversaries and from the ignorance of my loving friends.'

The chanted prayers and the movement became one, merging into an ecstatic whole in the presence of God . . .

Much later, Spalko led them down a back corridor to a small stainless-steel elevator, which took them down below the basement into the very bedrock in which the building was set.

They entered a vaulted, high-ceilinged room, crisscrossed by iron struts. The low hiss of the climate control was the only sound they heard. A number of crates had been stacked along one wall. It was to these that Spalko led them. He handed a crowbar to Arsenov, watched with a good measure of satisfaction as the terrorist leader cracked open the nearest crate, stared down at the gleaming sets of AK-47 assault rifles. Zina took one up, inspected it with care and precision. She nodded to Arsenov, who opened another crate, which held a dozen shoulder-held rocket-launchers.

'This is the most advanced ordnance in the Russian arsenal,' Spalko said.

'But what price?' Arsenov said.

Spalko spread his hands. 'What price would be appropriate if this weaponry helped you gain your freedom?'

'How do you put a price on freedom?' Arsenov said with a frown.

'The answer is you cannot. Hasan, freedom has no known price tag. It is bought with the blood and the indomitable hearts of people like yourselves.' He moved his eyes to Zina's face. 'These are yours – all of them – to use as you see fit to secure your borders, make those around you take notice.' At last, Zina looked up at him, through long lashes. Their eyes locked, sparked, though their expressions remained impassive.

As if responding to Spalko's scrutiny, Zina said, 'Even this weaponry won't gain us entry to the Reykjavík Summit.'

Spalko nodded, the corners of his mouth turning up slightly. 'True enough. The international security is far too comprehensive. An armed assault would result in nothing but our own deaths. However, I have a plan that will not only gain us access to the Oskjuhlid Hotel but will allow us to kill every person inside without exposing ourselves. Within hours of the event, everything you have dreamed of for centuries will be yours.'

'Khalid Murat was *afraid* of the future, *afraid* of what we, as Chechens, can accomplish.' The fever of righteousness colored Arsenov's face. 'We have been too long ignored by the world. Russia beats us into the ground while their comrades in arms, the Americans, stand by and do nothing to save us. Billions of American dollars flow into the Middle East but to Chechnya not a ruble!'

Spalko had assumed the self-satisfied air of a professor who sees his prize pupil perform well. His eyes glittered balefully. 'That will all change. Five days from now all the world will be at your feet. Power will be yours, as well as the respect of those who have spit on you, abandoned you. Russia, the Islamic world and all of the West, *especially* the United States!'

'We're speaking here of changing the entire world order, Zina,' Arsenov fairly shouted.

'But *how?*' Zina asked. 'How is this *possible?*'

'Meet me in Nairobi in three days' time,' Spalko replied, 'and you'll see for yourself.'

*The water, dark, deep, alive with an unnameable horror, closes over his head. He is sinking. No matter how hard he struggles, how desperately he strikes out for the surface, he feels himself spiraling down, as if weighted with lead. Then he looks down, sees a thick rope, slimy with weed, tied around his left ankle. He cannot see what is at the end of the rope because it disappears into the blackness below him. But whatever it is must be heavy, must be dragging him down, because the rope is taut. Desperately, he reaches down, his bloated fingers scrabbling to free himself, and the Buddha drifts free, spinning slowly, falling away from him into the unfathomable darkness . . .*

Khan awoke with a start, as always, racked by a horrible sense of loss. He lay amid the humid tangle of sheets. For a time, the recurring nightmare still pulsed evilly in his mind. Reaching down, he touched his left ankle as if to reassure himself that the rope was not tied to him. Then, gingerly, almost reverently, he moved his fingers up the taut, slick muscles of his abdomen and chest until he touched the small carved stone Buddha that hung around his neck by a thin gold chain. He never took it off, even when he slept. Of course it was there. It was always there. It was a talisman, even though he had tried to convince himself that he didn't believe in talismans.

With a small sound of disgust, he rose, then padded into the bathroom, splashed cold water over his head. He turned on the light, blinking for a moment. Thrusting his head close to the mirror, he inspected his reflection, looking at himself as if for the first time. He grunted, relieved himself, then, turning on a table lamp, sat on the edge of the bed, read again the sparse dossier Spalko had given him. Nothing in it gave the slightest hint that David Webb possessed the abilities Khan had seen. He touched the black-and-blue mark on his throat, thought of the net Webb had fashioned out of vines and cleverly set. He tore up the single sheet of the dossier. It was useless, less than useless, since it had led him to underestimate his target. And there were other implications, just as immediate. Spalko had given him information that was either incomplete or incorrect.

He suspected that Spalko knew precisely who and what David Webb was. Khan needed to know if Spalko had set some gambit in motion that involved Webb. He had his own plans for David Webb and he was quite determined that no one – not even Stepan Spalko – got in the way.

With a sigh, he turned off the light and lay back down, but his mind was unprepared for sleep. He found his entire body abuzz with speculation. Up until making the deal for his last assignment with Spalko, he had had no idea David Webb even existed, much less was still alive. He doubted he would have taken the assignment had not Spalko dangled Webb in front of his face. He must have known that Khan would find the prospect of finding Webb irresistible. For some time now, working for Spalko had made Khan uncomfortable. Increasingly, Spalko seemed to believe that he owned Khan, and Spalko, Khan was sure, was a megalomaniac.

In the jungles of Cambodia, where he had been forced to make his way as a child and teenager, he had had more than a little experience with megalomaniacs. The hot, humid weather, the constant chaos of war, the uncertainty of daily life all combined to drive people to the edge of madness. In that malevolent environment, the weak died, the strong survived; everyone was in some elemental fashion changed.

As he lay in bed, Khan fingered the scars on his body. It was a form of ritual, a superstition, perhaps, a method of keeping him safe from harm – not from the violence one adult perpetrates on another, but from the creeping, nameless terror a child feels in the dead of night. Children, waking from such nightmares, run to their parents, crawl into the warmth and comfort of their bed and are soon fast asleep. But Khan had no parents, no one to comfort him. On the contrary, he had been constantly obliged to free himself from the clutches of addle-brained adults who thought of him only as a source of money or sex. Slavery was what he had known for many years, from both the Caucasians and the Asians he had had the misfortune to stumble across. He belonged to neither world and they knew it. He was a half-breed and, as such, reviled, cursed at, beaten, abused, laid low in every manner a human being can be degraded.

And still he had persevered. His goal, from day to day, had devolved simply to surviving. But he had learned from bitter experience that escape was not enough, that those who had enslaved him would come after him, punish him severely. Twice, he had almost died. That was when he understood that more was required of him if he was to survive. He would have to kill or, eventually, he would be killed.

*

It was just before five when the Agency assault team stole into the motel from their position at the highway roadblock. They had been alerted to the presence of Jason Bourne by the night manager, who had awakened from a Xanax-induced doze to see Bourne's face staring at him from the TV screen. He had pinched himself to make sure he wasn't dreaming, had taken a shot of cheap rye, and made his call.

The team leader had called for the motel's security lights to be switched off so the team could make their approach in darkness. As they began to move into position, however, the refrigerated truck at the opposite end of the motel started up and switched on its headlights, catching some of the team in its powerful beams. The team leader waved frantically to the hapless driver, then ran to his side of the truck, told him to haul ass out of there. The driver, goggle-eyed at the sight of the team, did as he was requested, turning out his lights until he was clear of the parking lot and rolling down the highway.

The team leader signed to his men and they headed directly toward Bourne's room. At his silent command two broke off, headed around the back. The leader gave them twenty seconds to position themselves before he gave the order for them to don gas masks. Two of his men knelt, fired canisters of tear gas through the front window of the room. The leader's extended arm came down and his men rushed the room, slamming open the door. Gas whooshed out as they scuttled in, machine guns at the ready. The TV was on, the sound muted. CNN was showing the face of their quarry. The remains of a hasty meal were strewn on the stained, worn carpet and the bed was stripped. The room was abandoned.

Inside the refrigerated truck hastening away from the motel, Bourne, wrapped in the bedding, lay amid wooden cases containing plastic baskets of strawberries stacked up almost to the ceiling. He had managed to get himself into a position above floor level, the crates on either side holding him in place. When he had entered the rear of the truck, he had locked the door behind him. All such refrigeration trucks had a safety mechanism that could open and lock the rear door from the inside to ensure no one inadvertently got trapped. Switching on his flashlight for a moment, he had made out the center aisle, wide enough for a man to pass through. On the upper right-hand wall was the exhaust grille for the refrigeration compressor.

All at once, he tensed. The truck was slowing now as it approached the road-block, then it stopped completely. The flashpoint of extreme danger had arrived.

There was utter silence for perhaps five minutes, then, abruptly, the harsh sound of the rear door being opened. Voices came to him. 'You pick up any hitchhikers?' a cop said.

'Uh-uh,' Guy, the truck driver, answered.

'Here, look at this photo. Seen this fella on the side of the road maybe?'

'No, sir. Never seen the man. What'd he do?'

'What you got in there?' Another cop's voice.

'Fresh strawberries,' Guy said. 'Listen, Officers, have a heart. It ain't good for them to have the door open like this. What rots comes outta my pay.'

Someone grunted. A powerful flashlight beam played along the center aisle, swept across the floor just beneath the spot where Bourne lay suspended amid the strawberries.

'Okay,' the first cop said, 'close it up, buddy.'

The flashlight beam snapped off and the door slammed shut.

Bourne waited until the truck was in gear, rolling at speed down the highway to D.C., before extricating himself. His mind was buzzing. The cops must have shown Guy the same photo of David Webb that was being broadcast on CNN.

Within a half hour, the smooth highway driving had given way to the constant stop and start of urban streets with traffic lights. It was time to exit. Bourne went to the door, pushed on the safety lever. It wouldn't move. He tried again, this time with more force. Cursing under his breath, he snapped on the flashlight he'd taken from Conklin's house. In the bright circle of the beam, he saw that the mechanism had jammed. He was locked in.

# 5

The Director of Central Intelligence was in a dawn conference with Roberta Alonzo-Ortiz, the National Security Advisor. They met in the president's Situation Room, a circular space in the bowels of the White House. Many floors above them were the wood-paneled, beautifully dentiled rooms most people associated with this storied, historical building, but down here the full muscle and might of the Pentagon oligarchs held sway. Like the great temples of the ancient civilizations, the Sit Room had been built to last for centuries. Carved out of the old subbasement, its proportions were intimidating, as befitted such a monument to invincibility.

Alonzo-Ortiz, the DCI and their respective staffs – as well as select members of the Secret Service – were going over, for the hundredth time, the security plans for the terrorism summit in Reykjavík. Detailed schematics for the Oskjuhlid Hotel were up on a projection screen, along with notes on security issues regarding entrances, exits, elevators, roof, windows and the like. A direct video hook-up to the hotel had been established, so that Jamie Hull, the DCI's emissary-in-place, could participate in the briefing.

'No margin for error will be tolerated,' Alonzo-Ortiz said. She was a formidable-looking woman with jet-black hair and bright, keen eyes. 'Every aspect of this summit must go off like clockwork,' she continued. 'Any breach of security no matter how minuscule will have disastrous effects. It would destroy what coin the president has spent eighteen months building up with the principal Islamic states. I don't have to tell any of you that beneath the facade of cooperation lurks an innate distrust of Western values, the Judeo-Christian ethic and all that stands for. Any hint that the president has deceived them will have the most dire and immediate consequences.' She looked slowly around the table. It was one of her special gifts that when addressing a group she made each and every member believe that she was speaking only to him. 'Make no mistake, gentlemen. We are talking about nothing less than a global war here, a massed *jihad* such as we have never before seen and, quite possibly, cannot imagine.'

She was about to turn the briefing over to Jamie Hull when a young, slim man entered the room, went silently over to the DCI, handed him a sealed envelope.

'My apologies, Dr. Alonzo-Ortiz,' he said as he slit open the envelope. He read the contents impassively, though his heart rate had doubled. The National Security Advisor did not like her briefings interrupted. Aware that she was glaring at him, he pushed back his chair and rose.

Alonzo-Ortiz directed at him a smile so compressed her lips fairly disappeared. 'I trust you have sufficient cause to leave us so abruptly.'

'I do, indeed, Dr. Alonzo-Ortiz.' The DCI, though an old hand and, therefore, a wielder of his own power, knew better than to butt heads with the one person the president relied on most. He remained on his best behavior even though he deeply resented Roberta Alonzo-Ortiz both because she had usurped his traditional role with the president and because she was a woman. For these reasons, he employed what little power was at his command – the withholding of what she wanted most to know: the nature of the emergency dire enough to take him away.

The National Security Advisor's smile tightened further. 'In that event, I would appreciate a full briefing of the crisis, whatever it may be, as soon as is practicable.'

'Absolutely,' the DCI said, beating a hasty retreat. As the thick door to the Sit Room swung shut behind him, he added, dryly, 'Your Highness,' eliciting a gust of laughter from the field agent his office had employed as a messenger.

It took the DCI less than fifteen minutes to return to HQ where a meeting of Agency directorate heads was awaiting his arrival. The subject: the murders of Alexander Conklin and Dr. Morris Panov. The prime suspect: Jason Bourne. These were whey-faced men in impeccably tailored conservative suits, rep ties, polished brogues. Not for them striped shirts, colored collars, the passing fads of fashion. Used to striding the corridors of power inside the Beltway, they were as immutable as their clothes. They were conservative thinkers from conservative colleges, scions from the correct families who, early on, had been directed by their fathers to the offices, and thence the confidences, of the right people – leaders with vision and energy who knew how to get the job done. The nexus in which they now sat was a tightly held secret world, but the tentacles that fanned out from it stretched far and wide.

As soon as the DCI entered the conference room, the lights were dimmed. On a screen appeared the forensic photos of the bodies *in situ*.

'For the love of God, take those down!' the DCI shouted. 'They're an obscenity. We shouldn't be viewing these men like that.'

Martin Lindros, the DDCI, pressed a button and the screen went blank. 'To bring everyone up to date, yesterday we confirmed that it was David Webb's car in Conklin's driveway.' He paused as the Old Man cleared his throat.

'Let's call a spade a spade.' The DCI leaned forward, fists upon the gleaming table. 'The world at large may know this . . . this man as David Webb but here he is known as Jason Bourne. We will use that name.'

'Yessir,' Lindros said, determined not to run afoul of the DCI's exceedingly black mood. He barely needed to consult his notes, so fresh and vivid in his mind were the findings. 'W – Bourne was last seen on the Georgetown campus approximately an hour before the murders. A witness observed him hurrying toward his car. We can assume he drove directly to Alex Conklin's house. Bourne was definitely in the house at or around the time of the murders. His fingerprints are on a glass of half-finished Scotch found in the media room.'

'What about the gun?' the DCI asked. 'Is it the murder weapon?'

Lindros nodded. 'Absolutely confirmed by ballistics.'

'And it's Bourne's, you're certain, Martin?'

Lindros consulted a photocopied sheet, spun it across the table to the DCI. 'Registration confirms that the murder weapon belongs to David Webb. *Our* David Webb.'

'Sonuvabitch!' The DCI's hands were trembling. 'Are the bastard's fingerprints on it?'

'The gun was wiped clean,' Lindros said, consulting another sheet. 'No fingerprints at all.'

'The mark of a professional.' The DCI looked abruptly weary. It wasn't easy to lose an old friend.

'Yessir. Absolutely.'

'And Bourne?' the DCI growled. It appeared painful for him even to utter the name.

'Early this morning we received a tip that Bourne was holed up in a Virginia motel near one of the roadblocks,' Lindros said. 'The area was immediately cordoned off, an assault team sent into the motel. If Bourne was in fact there, he'd already fled, slipped through the cordon. He's vanished into thin air.'

'Goddammit!' Color had risen to the DCI's cheeks.

Lindros' assistant came silently in, handed him a sheet of paper. He scanned it for a moment, then looked up. 'Earlier, I sent a team to Webb's home, in the event he turned up there or contacted his wife. The team found the house locked up and empty. There's no sign of Bourne's wife or two children. Subsequent investigation revealed that she appeared at their school and pulled them out of class with no explanation.'

'That seals it!' The DCI seemed almost apoplectic. 'In every area he's a step ahead of us because he had these murders planned out beforehand!' During the short, swift drive to Langley, he'd allowed his emotions to get the better of him. Between Alex's murder and Alonzo-Ortiz's maneuvering, he had entered the Agency briefing in a rage. Now, presented with the forensic evidence, he was more than ready to convict.

'It's clear that Jason Bourne has gone rogue.' The Old Man, still standing, fairly shook now. 'Alexander Conklin was an old and trusted friend. I cannot remember or list the number of times he put his reputation – his very *life* – on the line for this organization, for his country. He was a true patriot in every sense of the word, a man of whom we were all justly proud.'

Lindros, for his own part, was considering the number of times he could remember and list when the Old Man had ranted at Conklin's cowboy tactics, his rogue missions, his secret agendas. It was all well and good to eulogize the dead, but, he thought, in this business it was downright foolish to ignore the dangerous tendencies of agents past and present. That, of course, included Jason Bourne. He was a sort of sleeper agent, the worst kind really – one not fully under his own control. In the past, he had been activated by circumstance, not by his own choosing. Lindros knew very little about Jason Bourne, an oversight he was determined to rectify the moment this briefing was adjourned.

'If Alexander Conklin had one weakness, one blind spot, it was Jason Bourne,' the DCI went on. 'Years before he met and married his current wife, Marie, he lost the whole of his first family – his Thai wife and two kids – in an attack in Phnom Penh. The man was half-mad with grief and remorse when Alex picked him up off the street in Saigon and trained him. Years later, even after Alex enlisted the aid of Morris Panov, there were problems controlling the asset – despite Dr. Panov's regular reports to the contrary. Somehow, he too fell under the influence of Jason Bourne.

'I warned Alex over and over, I begged him to bring Bourne in to be evaluated by our team of forensic psychiatrists, but he refused. Alex, God rest his soul, could be a stubborn man; he believed in Bourne.'

The DCI's face was slick with sweat, his eyes wide as he glanced around the room. 'And what is the result of that belief? Both men have been gunned down like dogs by the very asset they sought to control. The simple truth is that Bourne is uncontrollable. And he is deadly, a poisonous viper.' The DCI slammed his fist down on the conference table. 'I will not have these heinous, cold-blooded murders go unpunished. I'm authorizing a worldwide sanction drawn up, ordering Jason Bourne's immediate termination.'

Bourne shivered, by now chilled through and through. He glanced up, played his beam over the refrigeration vent. Heading back down the center aisle, he clambered up the right-hand stack of crates, crawled his way across the top of the stacks until he came to the grate. Flipping open the switchblade, he used the spine of the blade to unscrew the grille. The soft light of dawn flowed into the interior. There appeared to be just enough room for him to squeeze through. He hoped.

He rolled his shoulders in toward his chest, squeezing himself into the aperture, and began to wriggle from side to side. All went well for the first several inches or so, and then his forward progress abruptly stopped. He tried to move but couldn't. He was stuck. He exhaled all the air out of his lungs, allowed his upper body to go slack. He pushed with his feet and legs. A crate slid and tumbled, but he had inched forward. He lowered his legs until his feet found purchase on the crates below. Locking the heels of his shoes against the upper bar, he pushed again and again he moved. By slowly and carefully repeating this maneuver he was at last able to get his head and shoulders through. He blinked up into the candy pink sky, where fluffy clouds rose up, shifting shapes as he rolled by beneath them. Reaching up, he grabbed the corner of the roof, levered himself all the way out of the semi and onto its roof.

At the next stoplight he jumped down, tucking his lead shoulder in, rolling to cushion his fall. He rose, gained the sidewalk, dusted himself off. The street was deserted. He offered the unsuspecting Guy a brief salute as the semi drove off in a blue haze of diesel fumes.

He was on the outskirts of D.C., in the poor northeast district. Light was coming into the sky, the long shadows of dawn retreating before the sun. The hum of traffic could be heard in the distance, as well as the wail of a police siren. He breathed deeply. Beneath the urban stink, there was for him something fresh in the air, the exhilaration of freedom after the long night's struggle to remain hidden, to remain free.

He walked until he saw the fluttering of faded red, white and blue pennants. The used-car lot was shut down for the night. He walked onto the deserted lot, chose a car at random and switched its plates with the car next to it. He jimmied the lock, opened the driver's side door and hot-wired the ignition. A moment later, he was driving out of the lot and down the street.

He parked in front of a diner whose chrome-plated facade was a relic of the fifties. A gigantic cup of coffee sat atop the roof, its neon lights long ago burned out. Inside, it was steamy. The smell of coffee grounds and hot oil was ingrained into every surface. To his left was a long Formica counter and a row of vinyl-topped chromium stools; to his right, against the bank of sun-streaked windows, were a line of booths, each one with one of those individual jukeboxes that held the cards of all the songs that could be played for a quarter.

Bourne's white skin was silently remarked upon by the dark faces that turned as the door shut behind him with a little tinkle of a bell. No one returned his smile. Some appeared indifferent to him, but others of a different nature seemed to interpret his presence as an evil omen of things to come.

Aware of the hostile glares, he slid into a lumpy booth. A waitress with a frizz of orange hair and a face like Eartha Kitt dropped a fly-blown menu in front of him, filled his cup with steaming coffee. Bright, overly made-up eyes in a care-worn face regarded him for a time with curiosity and something more – compassion, perhaps. 'Don't you mind the stares, sugah,' she breathed. 'They're scared of you.'

He ate an indifferent breakfast: eggs, bacon and home fries, washed down with the astringent coffee. But he needed the protein and the caffeine laid to rest his exhaustion, at least temporarily.

The waitress refilled his cup and he sipped, marking time until Lincoln Fine Tailors opened. But he was not idle. He dug out the notepad he had picked off the table in Alex's media room, once again looked at the imprint left on the top sheet. NX 20. It had the ring of something experimental, something ominous, but really it could be anything, including a new-model computer.

Glancing up, he observed the denizens of the neighborhood drifting in and out, discussing Welfare checks, drug scores, police beatings, the sudden deaths of family members, the illness of friends in jail. This was their life, more alien to him than life in Asia or Micronesia. The atmosphere inside the diner was darkened by their rage and sorrow.

Once, a police cruiser slid slowly by like a shark skirting a reef. All motion in the diner ceased, as if this significant moment was a frame in a photographer's lens. He turned his head away and looked at the waitress. She was watching the taillights of the cruiser disappear down the block. An audible sigh of relief swept the diner. Bourne experienced his own sense of relief. It seemed that, after all, he was in the company of fellow travelers in shadow.

His thoughts turned to the man who was stalking him. His face had an Asian cast, and yet not wholly so. Was there something familiar about it – the bold line of the nose, which was not Asian at all, or the shape of the full lips, which was very much so? Was he someone from Bourne's past, from Vietnam? But, no, that was impossible. Judging by his appearance, he was in his late twenties at most, meaning he couldn't have been more than five or six when Bourne had been there. Who was he, then, and what did he want? The questions continued to haunt Bourne. Abruptly, he set down his half-empty cup. The coffee was beginning to burn a hole in his stomach.

Not long after, he returned to the stolen car, switched on the radio, spun the dial until he came to a news announcer talking about the terrorism summit, followed by a brief rundown first of the national news, then the local items. First on the list were the murders of Alex Conklin and Mo Panov but, strangely, no new information was forthcoming.

'More news upcoming,' the announcer said, 'but first this important message . . .'

'. . . *this important message.*' At that moment, the office in Paris with its view down the Champs-Elysées to the Arc de Triomphe came roaring back to him, the memory sweeping away the diner and those who surrounded him. There was a chocolate-colored chair at his side from which he had just risen. In his right hand a glass of cut-crystal half full of the amber liquid. A voice, deep and rich, full of melody, was speaking, something about the time it would take to get everything Bourne needed. 'Not to worry, my friend,' the voice said, the English blurred by the heavy cast of its French accent, 'I'm meant to give you this important message.'

In the theater of his mind, he turned, straining to see the face of the man who had spoken, but all he saw was a blank wall. The memory had evaporated like the scent of the Scotch, leaving Bourne back staring bleakly out the grimy windows of the broken-down diner.

A spasm of fury drove Khan to pick up his cell phone and call Spalko. It took some time, and a bit of doing on his part, but at length he was put through.

'To what do I owe this honor, Khan?' Spalko said in his ear. Listening hard, Khan heard the slight slur in his voice and determined that he had been drinking. His knowledge of the habits of his sometime employer went deeper than Spalko himself might have realized, if he'd wanted to consider it at all. He knew, for instance, that Spalko liked drink, cigarettes and women, though not necessarily in that order. His capacity for all three was immense. He thought now that if Spalko was even half as drunk as he suspected, he would have an advantage. Where Spalko was concerned, that was rare.

'The dossier you gave me appears incorrect, or at the very least incomplete.'

'And what leads you to that sorry conclusion?' The voice had instantaneously hardened, like water into ice. Too late Khan knew the language he had used had been too aggressive. Spalko might be a great thinker – a visionary even, as he doubtless considered himself – but in the bedrock of his being he operated on instinct. So he had risen from his semi-stupor to fight aggression with more of the same. He was possessed of a furious temper quite at odds with his carefully cultivated public image. But then so much of him thrived beneath the saccharine surface of his day-to-day life.

'Webb's behavior has been curious,' Khan said softly.

'Oh? In what way?' Spalko's voice had returned to its slurring, lazy diction.

'He hasn't been acting like a college professor.'

'I'm wondering why it matters. Haven't you killed him?'

'Not yet.' Khan, sitting in his parked car, watched through the window glass as a bus pulled into a stop across the street. The door opened with a sigh and people emerged: an old man, two teenage boys, a mother and her toddler son.

'Well, that's a change of plan, isn't it?'

'You knew I meant to toy with him first.'

'Certainly, but the question is for how long?'

There was a verbal chess match of sorts in progress, as delicate as it was fevered, and Khan could only guess at its nature. What was it about Webb? Why had Spalko decided to use him as a pawn for the double murder of the government men, Conklin and Panov? Why, for that matter, had Spalko ordered them killed? Khan had no doubt this is what had happened.

'Until I'm ready. Until he understands who's coming for him.'

Khan's eyes followed the mother as she put her child down on the sidewalk. The boy tottered a little as he walked and she laughed. His head tilted as he looked up at her and he laughed, too, mimicking her pleasure. She took his small hand in hers.

'You're not having second thoughts, are you?'

Khan thought he detected a slight tautness, a tremor of intent, and all at once he wondered whether Spalko was drunk at all. Khan considered asking him why it mattered to him whether or not he killed David Webb but, after some consideration, rejected the idea, fearing it might reveal his own concerns. 'No, no second thoughts,' Khan said.

'Because we're the same under the skin, you and I. Our nostrils dilate at the scent of death.'

Lost in thought and unsure how to respond, Khan closed his cell phone. He put his hand up to the window, watched between his fingers as the woman walked her son down the street. She took tiny steps, trying as best she could to match her gait to his wobbly one.

Spalko was lying to him, Khan knew that much. Just as he had been lying to Spalko. For a moment, his eyes lost their focus and he was back in the jungles of Cambodia. He had been with the Vietnamese gunrunner for over a year, tied up in a shack like a mad dog, half-starved and beaten. The third time he had attempted to escape he had learned his lesson, beating the unconscious gunrunner's head to a pulp with the spade-shaped head of a shovel he used to dig latrine pits. He had spent ten days living off what he could before he had been taken in by an American missionary by the name of Richard Wick. He had been given food, clothing, a hot bath and a clean bed. In exchange, he responded to the missionary's English lessons. As soon as he was able to read, he was given a Bible, which he was required to memorize. In this way, he began to understand that in Wick's view he was on the road to not salvation but to civilization. Once or twice, he tried to explain to Wick the nature of Buddhism, but he was very young and the concepts he'd been taught at an early age didn't seem so well formed when they emerged from his mouth. Not that Wick would've been interested in any case. He held no truck with any religion that didn't believe in God, didn't believe in Jesus the Savior.

Khan's eyes snapped back into focus. The mother was leading her toddler past the chrome facade of the diner with the huge coffee cup on its roof. Just beyond and across the street, Khan could see the man he knew as David Webb through the reflection-streaked glass of a car window. He had to give Webb credit; he had led Khan on a tortured path from the edge of the Conklin estate. Khan had seen the figure on the ridge road, observing them. By the time he had scrambled up there after escaping from Webb's clever trap, he had been too late to accost the man, but with his IR field glasses, he had been able to follow Webb's progress onto the highway. He had been ready to follow when Webb had been picked up. He watched Webb now, knowing what Spalko already knew: that Webb was a very dangerous man. A man like that surely had no concern about being the only Caucasian in the diner. He looked lonely, although Khan could not be sure, loneliness being entirely alien to him.

His gaze turned again to the mother and child. Their laughter drifted back to him, insubstantial as a dream.

\*

Bourne arrived at Lincoln Fine Tailors in Alexandria at five minutes past nine. The shop looked like all the other independently owned businesses in Old Town; that is to say, it had a vaguely Colonial facade. He crossed the red-brick sidewalk, pushed open the door, and went inside. The public area of the shop was divided in half by a waist-high barrier made up of a counter on the left and cutting tables on the right. The sewing machines were midway back behind the counter, manned by three Latinas who did not even glance up when he entered. A thin man in shirt-sleeves and open striped vest stood behind the counter frowning down at something. He had a high, domed forehead, a fringe of light brown hair, a face with sagging cheeks and muddy eyes. His glasses were pushed up onto the crown of his scalp. He had a habit of pinching his hawklike nose. He paid no attention to the door opening but looked up as Bourne approached the counter.

'Yes?' he said with an expectant air. 'How can I help you?'

'You're Leonard Fine? I saw your name on the window outside.'

'That's me,' Fine said.

'Alex sent me.'

The tailor blinked. 'Who?'

'Alex Conklin,' Bourne repeated. 'My name is Jason Bourne.' He looked around. No one was paying them the slightest attention. The sound of the sewing machines made the air sparkle and hum.

Very deliberately, Fine pulled his glasses down onto the narrow bridge of his nose. He peered at Bourne with a decided intensity.

'I'm a friend of his,' Bourne said, feeling the need to prompt the fellow.

'There are no articles of clothing here for a Mr. Conklin.'

'I don't think he left any,' Bourne said.

Fine pinched his nose, as if he were in pain. 'A friend, you say?'

'For many years.'

Without another word, Fine reached over, opened a door in the counter for Bourne to step through. 'Perhaps we should discuss this in my office.' He led Bourne through a door, down a dusty corridor reeking of sizing and spray starch.

The office wasn't much, a small cubicle with scuffed and pitted linoleum on the floor, bare pipes running from floor to ceiling, a battered green metal desk with a swivel chair, two stacks of cheap metal filing cabinets, piles of cardboard boxes. The smell of mold and mildew rose like steam from the contents of the office. Behind the chair was a small square window, so grimed it was impossible to see the alley beyond.

Fine went behind the desk, pulled out a drawer. 'Drink?'

'It's a little early,' Bourne said, 'don't you think?'

'Yeah,' Fine muttered. 'Now that you mention it.' He removed a gun from a drawer and aimed it at Bourne's stomach. 'The bullet won't kill you right away, but while you're bleeding to death, you'll wish it had.'

'There's no reason to get excited,' Bourne said easily.

'But there's *every* reason.' the tailor said. His eyes were set close together, making him appear somewhat cross-eyed. 'Conklin's dead and I heard you did it.'

'I didn't,' Bourne said.

'That's what you all say. Deny, deny, deny. It's the government's way, isn't it?' A crafty smile crossed the other's face. 'Sit down, Mr. Webb – or Bourne – whatever you're calling yourself today.'

Bourne looked up. 'You're Agency.'

'Not at all. I'm an independent operator. Unless Alex told them, I doubt if any-one inside the Agency knows I even exist.' The tailor's smile grew wider. 'That's why Alex came to me in the first place.'

Bourne nodded. 'I'd like to know about that.'

'Oh, I have no doubt.' Fine reached for the phone on his desk. 'On the other hand, when your own people get hold of you, you'll be too busy answering their questions to care about anything else.'

'Don't do that,' Bourne said sharply.

Fine halted with the receiver in midair. 'Give me a reason.'

'I didn't kill Alex. I'm trying to find out who did.'

'But you did kill him. According to the bulletin I read, you were at his house at the time he was shot to death. Did you see anyone else there?'

'No, but Alex and Mo Panov were dead when I arrived.'

'Bullshit. Why did you kill him, I wonder.' Fine's eyes narrowed. 'I imagine it was because of Dr. Schiffer.'

'I never heard of Dr. Schiffer.'

The tailor emitted a harsh laugh. 'More bullshit. And I suppose you never heard of DARPA.'

'Of course I have,' Bourne said. 'It stands for Defense Advanced Research Projects Agency. Is that where Dr. Schiffer works?'

With a sound of disgust, Fine said, 'I've had enough of this.' When he momen-tarily took his eyes off Bourne to dial a number, Bourne lunged at him.

The DCI was in his capacious corner office, on the phone with Jamie Hull. Brilliant sunlight spilled in the window, firing the jewel tones of the carpet. Not that the magnificent play of colors had any effect on the DCI. He was still in one of his black moods. Bleakly, he looked at the photos of himself with presi-dents in the Oval Office, foreign leaders in Paris, Bonn and Dakar, entertainers in L.A. and Vegas, evangelical preachers in Atlanta and Salt Lake City, even, absurdly, the Dalai Lama in his perpetual smile and saffron robes, on a visit to New York City. These pictures not only failed to rouse him from his gloom but made him feel the years of his life, as if they were layers of chain-mail weighing him down.

'It's a fucking nightmare, sir,' Hull was saying from far-off Reykjavík. 'First off, setting up security in conjunction with the Russians and Arabs is like chasing your tail. I mean, half the time I don't know what the hell they're saying and the other half I don't trust the interpreters – ours or theirs – are telling me exactly what they're saying.'

'You should have taken foreign language courses in grad school, Jamie. Just get on with it. I'll send you other interpreters, if you like.'

'Really? And where would be we getting them? We've excised all the Arabists, haven't we?'

The DCI sighed. That was a problem, of course. Almost all the Arab-speaking intelligence officers they'd had on their payroll had been deemed sympathetic to the Islamic cause, always shouting down the hawks, trying to explain how peace-loving most Islamics really were. Tell that to the Israelis. 'We've got a whole crop of new ones due here day after tomorrow from the Center for the Study of Intelligence. I'll have a couple sourced out to you ASAP.'

'That's not all, sir.'

The DCI scowled, vexed that he heard no hint of gratitude in the other's voice. 'What now?' he snapped. What if he removed all the photos? he wondered. Would that improve the lugubrious atmosphere in here?

'Not to complain, sir, but I'm trying my damnedest to establish proper security measures in a foreign country with no particular allegiance to the United States. We don't give them aid, so they aren't beholden to us. I invoke the president's name and what do I get? Blank stares. That makes my job triply difficult. I'm a member of the most powerful nation on the planet. I know more about security than everyone in Iceland put together. Where's the respect I'm supposed to – '

The intercom buzzed, and with a certain amount of satisfaction, the Old Man put Hull on hold. 'What is it?' he barked into the intercom.

'Sorry to bother you, sir,' the duty officer said, 'but a call's just come in on Mr. Conklin's emergency line.'

'What? Alex is dead. Are you sure?'

'Absolutely, sir. That line has not been reassigned yet.'

'All right. Continue.'

'I heard the sound of a brief scuffle and someone said a name – Bourne, I think.'

The DCI sat ramrod straight, his black mood dissolving as quickly as it had come on. 'Bourne. That's the name you heard, son?'

'It sure sounded like it. And the same voice said something like "kill you."'

'Where did the call come from?' the Old Man demanded.

'It was cut off, but I did a reverse trace. The number belongs to a shop in Alexandria. Lincoln Fine Tailors.'

'Good man!' The DCI was standing now. The hand that held the phone was trembling slightly. 'Dispatch two teams of agents immediately. Tell them Bourne has surfaced! Tell them to terminate him on sight.'

Bourne, having wrested the gun away from Leonard Fine without a shot being fired, now shoved him so hard against the smudgy wall that a calendar was dislodged from its nail, fell to the floor. The phone was in Bourne's hand; he had just severed the connection. He listened for any commotion out front, any hint that the women had heard the sounds of the brief but violent struggle.

'They're on their way,' Fine said. 'It's over for you.'

'I don't think so.' Bourne was thinking furiously. 'The call went to the main switchboard. No one would know what to do with it.'

Fine shook his head, a smirk on his face. 'The call bypassed the normal Agency switchboard; it rang directly through to the DCI's duty officer. Conklin insisted I memorize the number, to be used only in event of an emergency.'

Bourne shook Fine until his teeth rattled. 'You idiot! What have you done?'

'Paid my final debt to Alex Conklin.'

'But I told you. I didn't kill him.' And then something occurred to Bourne, one last desperate try to win Fine over to his side, to get him to open up about what Conklin had been up to, a clue to why he might have been killed. 'I'll prove to you Alex sent me.'

'More bullshit,' Fine said. 'It's too late – '

'I know about NX 20.'

Fine stood immobile. There was a slackness to his face; his eyes were open wide in shock. 'No,' he said. 'No, no, no!'

'He told me,' Bourne said. 'Alex told me. That's why he sent me, you see.'

'Alex could never have been coerced to tell about NX 20. Never!' The shock was fading from Fine's face, to be replaced by a slow dawning of the grievous error he had made.

Bourne nodded. 'I'm a friend. Alex and I go all the way back to Vietnam. This is what I have been trying to tell you.'

'God in heaven, I was on the phone with him when . . . when it happened.' Fine put a hand to his forehead. 'I heard the shot!'

Bourne grabbed the tailor by his vest. 'Leonard, get hold of yourself. We don't have time for a replay.'

Fine stared into Bourne's face. He had responded, as people most often do, to his given name. 'Yes.' He nodded, licked his lips. He was a man coming out of a dream. 'Yes, I understand.'

'The Agency will be here within minutes. I need to be gone by then.'

'Yes, yes. Of course.' Fine shook his head in sorrow. 'Now let go of me. Please.' Freed from Bourne's grip, he knelt beneath the back window, pulled out the radiator grille, behind which was a modern safe built into the plaster and lathe wall. He spun the dial, unlocked it, swung the heavy door open, pulled out a small manila envelope. Closing the safe, he replaced the grille and rose, handing the envelope to Bourne.

'This arrived for Alex late the other night. He called me yesterday morning to check on it. He said he was coming to pick it up.'

'Who sent it?'

At that moment, they heard voices raised in sharp command emanating from the shop out front.

'They're here,' Bourne said.

'Oh God!' Fine's features were pinched, bloodless.

'You must have another way out.'

The tailor nodded. He gave Bourne quick instructions. 'Go on now,' he said urgently. 'I'll keep them occupied.'

'Wipe your face,' Bourne said, and when Fine took the sheen of sweat off his face, he nodded.

While the tailor hurried into the shop to confront the agents, Bourne ran silently down the filthy corridor. He hoped Fine would be able to hold up under their questioning; otherwise he'd be finished. The bathroom was larger than he would have expected. To the left was an old porcelain sink beneath which were a stack of old paint cans, the tops rusted shut. A toilet was set against the rear wall, a shower to the left. Following Fine's instructions, he stepped into the shower, located the panel in the tile wall, opened it. He stepped through, replacing the tile panel.

Raising his hand, he pulled the old-fashioned light cord. He found himself in a narrow passage that looked to be in the adjacent building. The place stank; black plastic garbage bags had been stuffed between the rough wooden studs, possibly in lieu of insulation. Here and there, rats had scratched their way through the plastic, had gorged themselves on the rotting contents, left the rest spilling out onto the floor.

By the meager illumination provided by the bare bulb he saw a painted metal door that opened out onto the alley behind the stores. As he made his way toward it, the door burst open and two Agency suits sprinted through, guns drawn, their eyes intent on him.

# 6

The first two shots flew over Bourne's head as he ducked into a crouch. Coming out of it, he kicked hard at a plastic bag of garbage, sending it flying toward the two agents. It struck one and came apart at the seam. Refuse flew everywhere, sending the agents backward, coughing, their eyes streaming, arms over their faces.

Bourne struck upward, shattering the light bulb, plunging the narrow space into darkness. He turned and, flicking on his flashlight, saw the blank wall at the other end of the passageway. But there was a doorway to the outside, how . . . ?

Then he saw it and immediately extinguished the narrow beam of light. He could hear the agents shouting to each other, regaining their equilibrium. He went quickly to the far end of the passageway and knelt, feeling for the metal ring he had seen in a dull glint lying flush with the floor. He hooked his forefinger through it, pulled up, and the trap door to the cellar opened. A waft of stale, damp air came to him.

Without a moment's hesitation, he levered himself through the opening. His shoes struck the rung of a ladder and he went down, closing the trap door behind him. He smelled the roach spray first, then, switching on his flashlight, saw the gritty cement floor littered with their withered bodies like leaves on the ground. Rooting around in the splay of boxes, cartons and crates, he found a crowbar. Racing up the ladder, he slid the thick metal bar through the grips on the hatch. It was not a good fit; the crowbar remained loose, but it was the best he could hope for. All he needed, he thought, as he crunched across the roach-littered concrete floor, was enough time to get to the sidewalk delivery access common in all commercial buildings.

Above his head, he could hear the hammering as the two agents tried to open the hatch. It would not take long, he knew, for the crowbar to slip free under such vibration. But he had found the double metal panels to the street, had climbed the short flight of concrete steps that led upward. Behind him, the hatch burst open. He switched off his flashlight as the agents dropped to the basement floor.

Bourne was trapped now, and he knew it. Any attempt to lift the metal panels would bring in enough daylight for them to shoot him before he was halfway to the sidewalk. He turned, crept down the stairs. He could hear them moving around, looking for the light switch. They were speaking to each other in brief, staccato undertones, marking them as seasoned professionals. He crept along the jumbled piles of supplies. He, too, was looking for something specific.

When the lights snapped on, the two agents were spread apart, one on either side of the basement.

'What a shithole,' one of them said.

'Never mind that,' the other cautioned. 'Where the fuck's Bourne?'

With their bland, impassive faces there was not much to distinguish them. They wore Agency-issue suits and Agency-issue expressions with equal assurance. But Bourne had had much experience with the people the Agency swept into its nets. He knew how they thought and, therefore, how they would act. Though not physically together, they moved in concert. They would not give much thought to where he might hide. Rather they had mathematically divided the basement into quadrants they would search as methodically as machines. He could not now avoid them, but he could surprise them.

Once he appeared, they would move very fast. He was counting on this and so positioned himself accordingly. He had wedged himself into a crate, his eyes smarting from the fumes of the caustic industrial cleansers with which he shared the cramped space. His hand scrabbled around in the darkness. Feeling something curved against the back of his hand, he picked it up. It was a can, heavy enough for his purpose.

He could hear his heart beating, a rat scratching at the wall against which the crate rested; all else was silent as the agents continued their painstakingly thorough search. Bourne waited, patient, coiled. His lookout, the rat, had ceased its scratching. At least one of the agents was near.

It was deathly quiet now. Then, all at once, the quick catch of a breath came to him, the rustle of fabric nearly directly above his head, and he uncoiled, popping the lid off. The agent, gun in hand, reared back. His partner, across the basement, whirled. With his left hand, Bourne grabbed a handful of the nearest agent's shirt, jerked him forward. Instinctively, the agent pulled back, resisting, and Bourne lunged forward, using the agent's own momentum to slam his spine and head against the brick wall. He could hear the rat squeak even as the agent's eyes rolled up and he slid down, unconscious.

The second agent had taken two steps toward Bourne, thought better of engaging him hand-to-hand and aimed the Glock at his chest. Bourne threw the can into the agent's face. As he recoiled, Bourne closed the gap between them, drove the edge of his hand into the side of the agent's neck, felling him.

An instant later, Bourne was up the concrete stairs, opening the metal panels into fresh air and blue sky. Dropping the panels back into place, he calmly walked down the sidewalk until he reached Rosemont Avenue. There, he lost himself in the crowd.

A half-mile away, after assuring himself that he had not been followed, Bourne went into a restaurant. As he was seated at a table, he scanned every face in the room, searching for anomalies – feigned nonchalance, covert scrutiny. He ordered a BLT and a cup of coffee, then got up and headed toward the rear of the restaurant. Determining the men's room was empty, he locked himself in a cubicle, sat down on the toilet and opened the envelope meant for Conklin that Fine had given him.

Inside, he found a first-class airline ticket in Conklin's name to Budapest, Hungary, and a room key for the Danubius Grand Hotel. He sat looking at the items for a moment, wondering why Conklin had been on his way to Budapest and whether the trip had anything to do with his murder.

He took out Alex's cell phone, dialed a local number. Now that he had a direction, he felt better. Deron picked up after the third ring.

'Peace, Love and Understanding.'

Bourne laughed. 'It's Jason.' He never knew how Deron was going to answer the phone. Deron was quite literally an artist at his trade. It just happened that his trade was forgery. He made his living painting copies of Old Master oils that hung on mansion walls. They were so exacting, so expert that every so often one was sold at auction or ended up in a museum collection. On the side, just for the fun of it, he forged other things.

'I've been following the news on you and it has a distinctly ominous tone,' Deron said, in his slight British accent.

'Tell me something I don't know.' At the sound of the men's room door opening, Bourne paused. He stood up, put his shoes on either side of the toilet, peered over the top of the stall. A man with gray hair, a beard and a slight limp had bellied up to the urinal. He wore a dark suede bomber jacket, black slacks, nothing special. And yet, all at once Bourne felt trapped. He had to curb his desire to get out immediately.

'Damn, is the man on your ass?' It was always interesting to hear argot coming out of that cultured mouth.

'He was, up until I lost him.' Bourne left the bathroom and went back into the restaurant, scanning every table as he went. By this time his sandwich had come, but his coffee was cold. He flagged down the waitress, asked for it to be replaced. When she had walked away, he said softly into the phone, 'Listen, Deron, I need the usual – passport and contact lenses in my prescription, and I need them yesterday.'

'Nationality?'

'Let's keep it American.'

'I get the idea. The man won't expect that.'

'Something like that. I want the name on the passport to be Alexander Conklin.'

Deron gave a low whistle. 'It's your call, Jason. Give me two hours.'

'Do I have a choice?'

Deron's odd little giggle exploded down the line. 'You can go away hungry. I have all your photos. Which one d'you want?'

When Bourne told him, he said, 'Are you sure? You've got your hair shaved down to the nub. Doesn't look like you at all now.'

'It will when I get through with my makeover,' Bourne replied. 'I've been put on the Agency hit list.'

'Number one with a bullet, I shouldn't think. Where should we meet?'

Bourne told him.

'Good enough. Yo, listen, Jason.' Deron's tone was abruptly more somber. 'That must have been tough. I mean, you saw them, didn't you?'

Bourne stared at his plate. Why had he ordered this sandwich? The tomato had a raw and bloody look. 'I saw them, yes.' What if he could somehow roll back time, make Alex and Mo reappear? That would be quite a trick. But the past stayed the past, receding further from memory with every day.

'It's not like *Butch Cassidy*.'

Bourne did not say a word.

Deron sighed. 'I knew Alex and Mo, too.'

'Of course you did. I introduced you,' Bourne said, as he closed the phone.

He sat at the table for a while, thinking. Something was bothering him. An alarm bell had gone off in his head as he had exited the men's room, but he had been distracted by his conversation with Deron and so he had not taken full note of it. What was it? Slowly, carefully, he scanned the room again. Then he had it. He did not see the man with the beard and slight limp. Perhaps he had finished his meal and had been on his way out. On the other hand, his presence in the men's room had made Bourne distinctly uneasy. There was something about him . . .

He threw some money onto the table and went to the front of the restaurant. The two windows that looked out onto the street were separated by a wide mahogany pillar. Bourne stood behind it, using it as a screen while he checked the street. Pedestrians were first – anyone walking at an unnaturally slow pace, anyone loitering, reading a newspaper, standing too long in front of the shop window directly across the street, possibly scanning it for the reflection of the restaurant's entrance. He saw nothing suspicious. He marked three people sitting inside parked cars – one woman, two men. He could not see their faces. And then, of course, there were the cars parked on the restaurant side of the street.

Without a second thought, he went out onto the street. It was late morning and the crowd was denser now. That suited his current needs. He spent the next twenty minutes surveilling his immediate environment, checking doorways, storefronts, passing pedestrians and vehicles, windows and rooftops. When he'd satisfied himself that the field contained no Agency suits, he crossed the street, went into a liquor store. He asked for a bottle of the Speyside sherry-cask single-malt that had been Conklin's drink. While the proprietor went to fetch it, he looked out the window. No one in any of the cars parked on the restaurant side of the street. As he watched, one of the men he had noted got out of his car, went into a pharmacy. He had neither a beard nor a limp.

He had nearly two hours before he had to meet Deron, and he wanted to use the time productively. The memory of the Paris office, the voice, the half-remembered face that had been pushed aside by the exigencies of current circumstance, had now returned. According to Mo Panov's methodology, he needed to inhale the Scotch again in order to pull out more of the memory. In this way, he hoped to try to find out who the man in Paris was and why the particular memory of him had surfaced now. Had it been simply the scent of the single-malt, or was it something in his current predicament that had provoked it?

Bourne paid for the Scotch with a credit card, feeling he was safe enough using it in a liquor store. A moment later, he exited the store with his package. He passed the car with the woman inside. A small child was sitting next to her in the passenger's seat. Since the Agency would never allow a child to be used on an active field surveillance, that left the second man as a possibility. Bourne turned, walking away from the car in which the man sat. He did not look behind him, did not try to use any covert methods of spying or the standard procedures for shaking a tail. He did keep track of all the cars immediately in front and behind him, however.

Within ten minutes, he had reached a park. He sat down on a wrought-iron bench, watched the pigeons rise and fall, wheeling against the blue sky overhead. The other benches were perhaps half-full. An old man came into the park; he held a brown bag as crumpled as his face from which he extracted handfuls of bread crumbs. The pigeons, it seemed, had been expecting him, for they swooped down, swirling around him, cooing and clucking in delight as they gorged themselves.

Bourne opened the bottle of single-malt, sniffed its elegant and complex aroma. Immediately, Alex's face flashed before him, and the slow creep of blood over the floor. Gently, almost reverently, he set this image aside. He took a small sip of the Scotch, holding it on his palate, allowing the fumes to rise up into his nose, to bring him back to the shard of memory he was finding so elusive. In his mind's eye, he saw again the view out onto the Champs-Elysées. He was holding the cut-crystal glass in his hand, and as he took another sip of the Scotch, he willed himself to bring the glass to his lips. He heard the strong, operatic voice, willed himself to turn back into the Paris office where he had been standing an unknown time ago.

Now, for the first time, he could see the plush appointments of the room, the painting by Raoul Dufy of an elegant horse and rider in the Bois de Boulogne, the dark green walls with their deep luster, the high cream ceiling etched in the clear, piercing light of Paris. *Go on*, he urged himself. *Go on* . . . A patterned carpet, two high-backed upholstered chairs, a heavy polished walnut desk in the Regency style of Louis XIV, behind which stood, smiling, a tall, handsome man with worldly eyes, a long Gallic nose and prematurely white hair. Jacques Robbinet, French Minister of Culture.

That was it! How Bourne knew him, why they had become friends and, in a sense, compatriots, was still a mystery, but at least now he knew that he had an ally he could contact and count on. Elated, Bourne put the Scotch bottle underneath the bench, a gift for the first vagrant who noticed it. He looked around without seeming to. The old man had gone and so had most of the pigeons; just a few of the largest ones, chests puffed out to protect their territory, were strutting around, scrounging the last of the crumbs. A young couple were kissing on a nearby bench; three kids with a boombox passed through, made lewd noises at the snuggled couple. His senses were on high alert – something was wrong, out of place, but he could not figure out what it was.

He was keenly aware that the deadline to meet Deron was fast approaching, but instinct warned him not to move until he had identified the anomaly. He looked again at all the people in the park. No bearded man, certainly none with a limp. And yet . . . Diagonally across from him was a man sitting forward, elbows on knees, hands together. He was watching a young boy whose father had just handed him an ice cream cone. What interested Bourne was that he was dressed in a dark suede bomber jacket and black slacks. His hair was black, not gray, he had no beard, and by the normal way his legs were bent, Bourne was certain that he didn't have a limp.

Bourne, himself a chameleon, an expert in disguise, knew that one of the best methods of keeping hidden was to change your gait, especially if one was trying to hide from a professional. An amateur might notice superficial aspects such as hair color and clothes, but to a trained agent the way you moved and walked was as individual as a fingerprint. He tried to bring up the image of the man in the restaurant men's room. Had he been wearing a wig and fake beard? Bourne couldn't be sure. What he was certain of, though, was that the man had been wearing a dark suede bomber jacket and black slacks. From this position he couldn't see the man's face, but it was clear that he was far younger than the man in the men's room had appeared.

There was something else about him, but what was it? He studied the side of the man's face for several moments before he had it. A flash image of the man who'd jumped him in the woods of Conklin's estate came to him. It was the shape of the ear, the deep brownish color, the configuration of the whorls.

Good God, he thought, abruptly disoriented, this was the man who'd shot at him, who'd almost succeeded in killing him in the Manassas cave! How had he trailed Bourne all the way from there when Bourne had given the slip to every Agency and state trooper in the area? He felt a momentary chill run through him. What kind of man could do that?

He knew there was only one way to find out. Experience told him that when you are up against a formidable foe the only way to get a true measure of him is to do the last thing he would expect. Still, for a moment, he hesitated. He'd never been up against an antagonist like this. He understood that he had crossed over into unknown territory.

Knowing this, he rose and slowly and deliberately crossed the park and sat down beside the man, whose face he now saw had a distinctly Asian cast to it. To his credit, the man did not start or give any overt indication of surprise. He continued to watch the little boy. As the ice cream started to melt, his father showed him how to turn the cone to lick up the drippings.

'Who are you?' Bourne said. 'Why do you want to kill me?'

The man beside him looked straight ahead, gave no sign at all that he had heard what Bourne had said. 'Such a beatific scene of domestic bliss.' There was an acid edge to his voice. 'I wonder if the child knows that at a moment's notice his father could abandon him.'

Bourne had an odd reaction to hearing the other's voice in this setting. It was as if he had moved out of the shadows to fully inhabit the world of those around them.

'No matter how much you want to kill me,' Bourne said, 'you can't touch me here in this public place.'

'The boy is, what, six, I would say. Far too young to understand the nature of life, far too young to fathom why his father would leave.'

Bourne shook his head. The conversation was not proceeding as he had intended. 'What makes you think that? Why would the father abandon his son?'

'An interesting question from a man with two children. Jamie and Alison, isn't it?'

Bourne started as if the other had plunged a knife into his side. Fear and anger swirled inside him but it was the anger that he allowed to rise to the surface. 'I won't even ask how you know so much about me, but I will tell you this, in threatening my family you've made a fatal mistake.'

'Oh, there's no need to think that. I have no designs on your children,' Khan said evenly. 'I was merely wondering how Jamie will feel when you never come back.'

'I'll never abandon my son. I'll do whatever it takes to come safely back to him.'

'It seems odd to me that you're so passionate about your current family when you failed Dao, Joshua and Alyssa.'

Now the fear was gaining ground inside Bourne. His heart was pounding painfully, and there was a sharp pain in his chest. 'What are you talking about? Where did you get the idea that I failed them?'

'You abandoned them to their fate, didn't you?'

Bourne felt as if he was losing his grip on reality. 'How dare you! They died! They were pulled away from me, and I've never forgotten them!'

The hint of a smile curled the edges of the other's lips, as if he had scored a victory in dragging Bourne across the invisible barrier. 'Not even when you married Marie? Not even when Jamie and Alison were born?' His tone was tightly wound now, as if he was struggling to keep something deep inside him held in check. 'You tried to replicate Joshua and Alyssa. You even used the same first letters in their names.'

Bourne felt as if he'd been beaten senseless. There was an inchoate roaring in his ears. 'Who are you?' he repeated in a strangled voice.

'I'm known as Khan. But who are *you*, David Webb? A professor of linguistics might possibly be at home in the wilderness, but he surely doesn't know hand-to-hand combat; he doesn't know how to fashion a Viet Cong cage-net; he doesn't know how to hijack a car. Above all, he doesn't know how to successfully conceal himself from the CIA.'

'It seems, then, that we're a mystery to one another.'

That same maddening enigmatic smile played around Khan's mouth. Bourne felt a prickling of the short hairs at the nape of his neck, the sense that something in his shattered memory was trying to surface.

'Keep telling yourself that. The fact is, I *could* kill you now, even in this public place,' Khan said with a great deal of venom. The smile had vanished as quickly as a cloud changes its shape, and there was a small tremor in the smooth bronze column of his neck, as if some fury, long held in check, had briefly escaped to the surface. 'I *should* kill you now. But such extreme action would expose me to the pair of CIA agents who have entered the park from the north entrance.'

Without moving his head, Bourne directed his gaze in the indicated direction. Khan was quite right. Two Agency suits were scanning the faces of those in the immediate vicinity.

'I believe that it's time we left.' Khan rose, looked down at Bourne for a moment. 'This is a simple situation. Either come with me or be taken.'

Bourne got up and, walking side by side with Khan, went out of the park. Khan was between Bourne and the agents, and he took a route that would keep him in that position. Again, Bourne was impressed with the young man's expertise as well as his thinking in extreme situations.

'Why are you doing this?' Bourne asked. He had not been immune to the other's significant flare of temper, an incandescence as enigmatic to Bourne as it was alarming. Khan didn't answer.

They entered the stream of pedestrians and were soon lost within the flow. Khan had witnessed the four agents heading into Lincoln Fine Tailors, and he had quickly memorized their faces. It hadn't been difficult; in the jungle where he had raised himself, the instant identification of an individual often meant the difference between life and death. In any event, unlike Webb, he knew where all four were and he was on the lookout for the other two now, because at this crucial juncture when he was leading his target to a place of his choosing, he did not want any intrusion.

Sure enough, up ahead in the crowd, he spotted them. They were in standard formation, one on either side of the street, heading directly toward them. He turned to Webb to alert him, only to find that he was alone in the throng. Webb had vanished into thin air.

# 7

Deep within the bowels of Humanistas, Ltd. was a sophisticated listening station that monitored the clandestine signals traffic from all the various major intelligence networks. No human ear heard the raw data because no human ear would be able to make sense of it. Since the signals were encrypted, the intercepted traffic was run through a series of sophisticated software programs made up of heuristic algorithms – that is to say, they had the ability to learn. There was a program for each intelligence network because each agency had selected a different encryption algorithm.

Humanistas' battery of programmers were more successful at breaking some codes than others, but the bottom line was that Spalko more or less knew what was going on all over the world. The American CIA code was one of the ones that had been broken, so within hours of the DCI ordering the termination of Jason Bourne, Stepan Spalko was reading about it.

'Excellent,' he said. 'Now everything is going according to plan.' He set down the decryption, then pulled up a map of Nairobi on a monitor screen. He kept moving around the city until he found the area on the outskirts where President Jomo wanted the Humanistas medical team sent in to minister to the quarantined known AIDS patients.

At that moment his cell phone rang. He listened to the voice on the other end of the line. He checked his watch, said, finally, 'There should be enough time. You've done well.' Then he took the elevator upstairs to Ethan Hearn's office. On the way up, he made a single call, achieving in minutes what many others in Budapest had tried in vain for weeks to get – an orchestra seat for that night's opera.

Humanistas, Ltd.'s newest young development officer was hard at work on his computer, but he stood up as soon as Spalko walked in. He looked as clean and neat as Spalko imagined he had when he had walked in to work this morning.

'No need to be formal around here, Ethan,' Spalko said with an easy smile. 'This isn't the army, you know.'

'Yes, sir. Thank you.' Hearn stretched his back. 'I've been at it since seven this morning.'

'How goes the fund-raising?'

'I have two dinners and a lunch with solid prospects set up for early next week. I've e-mailed you a copy of the pitch letters I want to give to them.'

'Good, good.' Spalko glanced around the room as if to make certain no one else was in hearing distance. 'Tell me, do you own a tux?'

'Absolutely, sir. I couldn't do my job otherwise.'

'Excellent. Go home and change into it.'

'Sir?' The young man's brows had knitted together in surprise.

'You're going to the opera.'

'Tonight? At such short notice? How did you manage to get tickets?'

Spalko laughed. 'You know, I like you, Ethan. I'm willing to bet you're the last honest man on earth.'

'Sir, I have no doubt that would be you.'

Spalko laughed again at the bewildered expression that had come over the young man. 'That was a joke, Ethan. Now, come on. There's no time to lose.'

'But my work.' Hearn gestured at the computer screen.

'In a way, tonight *will* be work. There'll be a man at the opera I want to recruit as a benefactor.' Spalko's demeanor was so relaxed, so nonchalant that Hearn never suspected a thing. 'This man – his name is László Molnar – '

'I've never heard of him.'

'You wouldn't.' Spalko's voice lowered, became conspiratorial. 'Though he is quite wealthy, he is paranoid about anyone knowing. He's not on any donor list, that I can assure you, and if you make any allusion to his wealth, you might as well forget ever talking to him again.'

'I understand completely, sir,' Hearn said.

'He is a connoisseur of sorts, though nowadays it seems to me the word has lost much of its meaning.'

'Yes, sir.' Hearn nodded. 'I think I know what you mean.'

Spalko was quite certain the young man had no idea what he meant, and a vague undertone of regret crept into his thoughts. He had once been as naive as Hearn, a hundred years ago, or so it now seemed. 'In any event, Molnar loves opera. He has had a subscription for years.'

'I know exactly how to proceed with difficult prospects like László Molnar.' Hearn deftly pulled on his suit jacket. 'You can count on me.'

Spalko grinned. 'Somehow I knew I could. Now, once you've hooked him, I want you to take him to Underground. Do you know the bar, Ethan?'

'Of course, sir. But it will be quite late. After midnight, surely.'

Spalko put his forefinger beside his nose. 'Another secret. Molnar is something of a night owl. He'll resist, however. It seems he enjoys being persuaded. You must persevere, Ethan, do you understand?'

'Perfectly.'

Spalko handed him a slip of paper with Molnar's seat number. 'Then go on. Have a good time.' He gave him a small shove. 'And good luck.'

The imposing Romanesque facade of Magyar Állami Operaház, the Hungarian State Opera House, was ablaze with light. Inside, the magnificent, ornate gilt-and-red interior, three stories high, glittered with what seemed like ten thousand spearpoints of light from the elaborate cut-crystal chandelier that descended from the muraled domed ceiling like a giant bell.

Tonight, the company was presenting Zoltán Kodály's *Háry János*, a traditional favorite that had been in its repertory since 1926. Ethan Hearn hurried into the vast marble lobby, echoing with the voices of Budapest society assembled for the evening's festivities. His tuxedo was of a fine worsted fabric and was well cut, but it was hardly a name brand. In his line of work, what he wore and how he wore it was extremely important. He tended toward elegant, muted clothes, never anything flashy or too expensive. Humility was the name of the game when one was asking for donations.

He did not want to be late, but he slowed himself down, reluctant to miss a moment of that peculiar electric time just before the curtain rose that made his heart thump.

Having assiduously boned up on the hobbies of Hungarian society, he fancied himself something of an opera buff. He liked *Háry János* both because of its music, which was derived from Hungarian folk music, and because of the tall tale the veteran soldier János spins of his rescue of the emperor's daughter, his promotion to general, his virtual single-handed defeat of Napoleon and his eventual winning of the heart of the emperor's daughter. It was a sweet fable, drenched in the bloody history of Hungary.

In the end, it was fortuitous that he had arrived late, because by consulting the slip of paper Spalko had given him, he was able to identify László Molnar, who, along with most others, was already seated. From what Hearn could determine at first sight, he was a middle-aged man of medium height, heavy around the gut, and, with a slicked-back mass of black hair, a head not unlike a mushroom. A forest of bristles sprouted from his ears and the backs of his blunt-fingered hands. He was ignoring the woman on his left, who, in any case, was speaking, rather too loudly, to her companion. The seat to Molnar's right was vacant. It appeared that he had come to the opera on his own. All the better, Hearn thought, as he took his seat near the rear of the orchestra. A moment later the lights dimmed, the orchestra struck up the prelude and the curtain slid smoothly up.

Later, during the intermission, Hearn took a cup of hot chocolate and mingled with the soigné crowd. This was how humans had evolved. As opposed to the animal world, the female was definitely the more colorful of the species. The women were sheathed in long dresses of shantung silk, Venetian moiré, Moroccan satin that just months ago had been displayed on the couturier runways of Paris, Milan and New York. The men, clad in designer tuxedos, appeared content to circle their mates, who gaggled in clusters, fetching them champagne or hot chocolate when needed but, for the most part, looking thoroughly bored.

Hearn had enjoyed the first half of the opera and was looking forward to the conclusion. He had not, however, forgotten his assignment. In fact, during the performance he had spent some time coming up with an approach. He never liked to lock himself into a plan; rather he used his first visual assessment of the prospect to figure out an approach. To the discerning eye, so much could be determined by visual cues. Did the prospect care about his appearance? Did he like food, or was he indifferent to it? Did he drink or smoke? Was he cultured or uncouth? All these factors and many more went into the mix.

So it was that by the time Hearn made his approach, he was confident he could strike up a conversation with László Molnar.

'Pardon me,' Hearn said in his most deprecating tone of voice. 'I'm a lover of opera. I was wondering if you were, too.'

Molnar had turned. He wore an Armani tuxedo that emphasized his broad shoulders while cleverly hiding the bulk of his gut. His ears were very large and, this close up, even hairier than they had seemed at first glance. 'I am a student of the opera,' he said slowly and, to Hearn's attuned senses, warily. Hearn smiled his most charming smile and engaged Molnar's dark eyes with his own. 'To be frank,' Molnar continued, apparently mollified, 'I'm consumed by it.'

This fit in perfectly with what Spalko had told him, Hearn thought. 'I have a subscription,' he said in his effortless fashion. 'I've had one for some years, and I couldn't help noticing that you have one also.' He laughed softly. 'I don't get to meet too many people with a love of opera. My wife prefers jazz.'

'Mine loved the opera.'

'You're divorced?'

'A widower.'

'Oh, I'm so sorry.'

'It happened some time ago,' Molnar said, warming a little now that he'd given up this intimate bit of knowledge. 'I miss her so terribly that I've never sold her seat.'

Hearn held out a hand. 'Ethan Hearn.'

After the slightest hesitation, László Molnar gripped it with his hairy-backed paw. 'László Molnar. I'm pleased to make your acquaintance.'

Hearn gave a courtly little bow. 'Would you care to join me in a hot chocolate, Mr. Molnar?'

This offer appeared to please the other, and he nodded. 'I'd be delighted.' As they walked together through the milling crowd, they exchanged lists of their favorite operas and opera composers. Since Hearn had asked Molnar to go first, he made certain they had many in common. Molnar was again pleased. As Spalko had noted, there was something open and honest about Hearn that even the most jaundiced eye could not help but appreciate. He possessed the knack of being natural even in the most artificial situations. It was this sincerity of spirit that caught Molnar, dissolving his defenses.

'Are you enjoying the performance?' he inquired as they sipped their hot chocolate.

'Very much,' Hearn said. 'But *Háry János* is so full of emotion I confess I'd enjoy it all the more if I could see the expressions on the principals' faces. Sad to say, when I bought the subscription I couldn't afford anything closer, and now it's quite impossible to obtain a better seat.'

For a moment, Molnar said nothing, and Hearn feared that he was going to let the opening pass. Then he said, as if he had just thought of it, 'Would you care to sit in my wife's seat?'

'Once more,' Hasan Arsenov said. 'We need to go over again the sequence of events that will gain us our freedom.'

'But I know them as well as I know your face,' Zina protested.

'Well enough to negotiate the route to our final destination blindfolded?'

'Don't be ridiculous,' Zina scoffed.

'In Icelandic, Zina. We speak now only in Icelandic.'

In their hotel room, the schematics for the Oskjuhlid Hotel in Reykjavík were spread out across the large desk. In the inviting glow of lamplight, every layer of the hotel was laid bare, from the foundation, to the security, sewage and heating and air-conditioning systems, to the floor plans themselves. On each oversized

bluesheet were neatly written a series of notes, directional arrows, markouts indicating the layers of security that had been added by each of the participating
nations for the terrorism summit. Spalko's intel was impeccably detailed.

'From the time we breach the hotel's defenses,' Arsenov said, 'we'll have very little
time to accomplish our goal. The worst part is we won't know *how* little time until
we get there and make a dry run. That makes it even more imperative that there be
no hesitation, no mistake – not one wrong turn!' In his ardor, his dark eyes were
blazing. Taking up a sash of hers, he led her to one end of the room. He wrapped it
around her head, tying it tightly enough so that he knew she couldn't see.

'We've just entered the hotel.' He let go of her. 'Now I want you to walk out the
route for me. I'll be timing you. Now go!'

For two-thirds of the circuitous journey, she did well, but then, at the junction
of what would be two branching corridors, she went left instead of right.

'You're finished,' he said harshly as he whipped off the blindfold. 'Even if you
corrected your mistake, you wouldn't make the target on time. Security – be it
American, Russian or Arab – would catch up to you and shoot you dead.'

Zina was trembling, furious with herself and with him.

'I know that face, Zina. Put your anger away,' Hasan said. 'Emotion breaks concentration, and concentration is what you need now. When you can make the path
blindfolded without making a mistake, we will be finished for this evening.'

An hour later, her mission accomplished, Zina said, 'Come to bed, my love.'

Arsenov, dressed now only in a simple muslin robe, dyed black, belted at the
waist, shook his head. He was standing by the huge window, looking out at the diamond night-sparkle of Budapest reflected in the dark water of the Danube.

Zina sprawled naked on the down comforter, laughed softly, deep in her throat.
'Hasan, feel.' She moved her palm, her long, splayed fingers over the sheets. 'Pure
Egyptian cotton, so luxurious.'

He wheeled on her, a frown of disapproval darkening his face. 'That's just it,
Zina.' He pointed to the half-empty bottle on the night table. 'Napoleon brandy,
soft sheets, a down comforter. These luxuries are not for us.'

Zina's eyes opened wide, her heavy lips forming a moue. 'And why not?'

'Has the lesson I've just taught you gone in one ear only to fly out the other?
Because we are *warriors*, because we have renounced all worldly possessions.'

'Have you renounced your weapons, Hasan?'

He shook his head, his eyes hard and cold. 'Our weapons have a purpose.'

'These soft things also have a purpose, Hasan. They make me happy.'

He made a guttural sound in the back of his throat, curt and dismissive.

'I don't want to possess these things, Hasan,' Zina said huskily, 'just use them
for a night or two.' She held out a hand to him. 'Can't you relax your iron-bound
rules for even that short a time? We've both worked hard today; we deserve a
little relaxation.'

'Speak for yourself. I won't be seduced by luxuries,' he said shortly. 'It disgusts
me that you have been.'

'I don't believe I disgust you.' She had seen something in his eyes, a sort of
self-denial that she naturally enough misinterpreted as the rock of his strict
ascetic nature.

'All right, then,' she said. 'I'll break the brandy bottle, sow the bed with glass, if only you'll come join me.'

'I've told you,' he warned darkly. 'Do not joke of these matters, Zina.'

She sat up, on her knees moved toward him, her breasts, sheened in golden lamplight, swaying provocatively. 'I'm perfectly serious. If it's your wish to lie in a bed of pain while we make love, who am I to argue?'

He stood looking at her for a long time. It did not occur to him that she might be mocking him still. 'Don't you understand?' He took a step toward her. 'Our path is set. We are bound to the *Tariqat*, the spiritual path to Allah.'

'Don't distract me, Hasan. I'm still thinking of weapons.' She grabbed a handful of muslin and pulled him toward her. Her other hand reached out, gently caressed the fabric of the bandage that wrapped the area of his thigh where he'd been shot. Then it moved higher.

Their lovemaking was as fierce as any hand-to-hand combat. It arose as much out of wanting to hurt the other as it did from physical need. In their jackhammer thrashing, moaning and release, it was doubtful that love played any role. For his part, Arsenov longed to be ground into the bed of glass shards that Zina had joked about, so that when her nails gripped him, he resisted her, obliging her to hold on tighter, to score his skin. He was rough enough to bait her, so that she bared her teeth, used them on the powerful muscles of his shoulders, his chest, his arms. It was only with the rising tide of pain threatening to overpower the pleasure that the strange hallucinatory sensation in which he was lost receded somewhat.

Punishment was required for what he had done to Khalid Murat, his compatriot, his friend. Never mind that he had done what was needed in order for his people to survive and flourish. How many times had he told himself that Khalid Murat had been sacrificed on the altar of Chechnya's future? And yet, like a sinner, an outcast, he was hounded by doubt and fear, in need of cruel punishment. Though truly, he thought now in the little death that comes in sexual release, was it not always thus with prophets? Was not this torture further proof that the road he had embarked upon was the righteous one?

Beside him, Zina lay in his arms. She might have been miles away, though in a manner of speaking her mind was also filled with thoughts of prophets. Or, more accurately, one prophet. This latter-day prophet had dominated her mind ever since she had drawn Hasan to the bed. She hated that Hasan could not let himself take pleasure in the luxuries around him, and so, when he grasped her, it was not him she was thinking of, when he entered her, in her mind it was not him at all, but Stepan Spalko to whom she crooned. And when, nearing her end, she bit her lip it was not out of passion, as Hasan believed, but out of a fear that she would shout Spalko's name. She so much wanted to, if only to hurt Hasan in a manner that would cut him to the quick, for she had no doubt of his love for her. This love she found dumb and unknowing, an infantile thing like a baby reaching for its mother's breast. What he craved from her was warmth and shelter, the quick thrust back into the womb. It was a love that made her skin crawl.

But what *she* craved . . .

Her thoughts froze in their tracks as he moved against her, sighing. She had supposed that he was asleep, but he was not, or else something had roused him. Now, attendant on his desires, she had no time for her own thoughts. She smelled his manly scent, rising like a pre-dawn mist, and his breathing quickened just a little.

'I was thinking,' he whispered, 'about what it means to be a prophet, whether one day I will be called that among our people.'

Zina said nothing, knowing that he wished her to be silent now, to listen only, as he reassured himself of his chosen path. This was Arsenov's weakness, the one unknown to anyone else, the one he showed only to her. She wondered if Khalid Murat had been clever enough to have suspected this weakness. She was almost certain Stepan Spalko was.

'The Qur'an tells us that each of our prophets is the incarnation of a divine attribute,' Arsenov said. 'Moses is the manifestation of the transcendent aspect of reality, because of his ability to speak with God without an intermediary. In the Qur'an, the Lord said to Moses, 'Fear not, you are transcendent.' Jesus is the manifestation of prophethood. As an infant, he cried, 'God gave me the book and placed me as a prophet.'

'But Mohammad is the spiritual incarnation and manifestation of all of God's names. Mohammad himself said, "What God first created was my light. I was a prophet while Adam was still between water and earth."'

Zina waited the space of several heartbeats to be certain that he had finished pontificating. Then, with a hand placed on his slowly rising and falling chest, she asked as she knew he wanted her to ask, 'And what is *your* divine attribute, my prophet?'

Arsenov turned his head on the pillow so that he could see her fully. The lamplight behind her cast most of her face in shadow, just a fiery line along her cheek and jawbone was limned in a long painterly stroke, and he was caught out in a thought he most often kept hidden, even from himself. He did not know what he would do without her strength and vitality. For him, her womb represented immortality, the sacred place from which his sons would issue, his line continuing through all eternity. But he knew this dream could not happen without Spalko's help. 'Ah, Zina, if you only knew what the Shaykh will do for us, what he will help us become.'

She rested her cheek against her folded arm. 'Tell me.'

But he shook his head, a small smile playing at the corners of his mouth. 'That would be a mistake.'

'Why?'

'Because you must see for yourself without any foreknowledge the devastation caused by the weapon.'

Now, peering into Arsenov's eyes, she experienced a chill deep in the core of her, where she rarely dared to look. Possibly she felt an intimation of the terrible power that would be unleashed in Nairobi in three days' time. But with the clairvoyance sometimes granted lovers, she understood that what interested Hasan most was the fear this form of death – whatever it would turn out to be – would engender. It was fear he meant to wield, that was clear enough. Fear to use as a righteous sword to regain all that had been lost to the Chechens over centuries of abuse, displacement and bloodshed.

From an early age, Zina had been on intimate terms with fear. Her father, weak and dying of the disease of despair that ran like a plague through Chechnya, who had once provided for his family as all Chechen men must but could not now even show his face on the street for fear of being picked up by the Russians. Her mother, once a beautiful young woman, in her last years a sunken-chested crone with thinning hair, bad eyesight and faulty memory.

After she came home from the long day's scavenging, she was obliged to walk three kilometers to the nearest public water pump, stand in the queue for an hour or two, only to walk back, lug the full bucket up the five flights to their filthy room.

That water! Sometimes, even now, Zina would awake, gagging, with its foul turpentine taste in her mouth.

One night her mother sat down and did not get up. She was twenty-eight but looked more than twice that age. From the constantly burning oil fires, her lungs were full of tar. When Zina's younger brother had complained of thirst, the old woman had looked at Zina and said, 'I can't get up. Even for our water. I can't go on . . .'

Zina rolled and, twisting her torso, turned off the lamp. The moon, previously unseen, filled the casement of the window. At the point where her upper torso dipped down to her narrow waist, a small pool of its cool light fell upon the bed, illuminating the tip of her breast, below which, under the deep curve, lay Hasan's hand. Outside that pool there was only darkness.

For a long time she lay with her eyes open, listening to Hasan's regular breathing, waiting for sleep to claim her. Who knew the meaning of fear better than Chechens? she wondered. In Hasan's face was written the lamentable history of their people. Never mind death, never mind ruin, there was only one outcome that he could see: vindication for Chechnya. And with a heart made heavy by despair, Zina knew that the attention of the world needed to be snapped into focus. These days, there was only one way to do that. She knew Hasan was right: Death had to come in a manner heretofore unthinkable, but what price they might all pay she could not begin to imagine.

# 8

Jacques Robbinet liked to spend mornings with his wife, drinking café au lait, reading the papers and talking with her about the economy, their children and the state of their friends' lives. They never spoke about his work.

He made it a strict rule never to come into the office before noon. Once there, he spent an hour or so scanning documents, interdepartmental memos and the like, writing e-mail responses when necessary. His phone was answered by his assistant, who logged calls and brought him messages deemed urgent by her. In this, as in all things she did for Robbinet, she was exemplary. She had been trained by him and her instincts were unerring.

Best of all, she was utterly discreet. This meant that Robbinet could tell her where he was lunching each day with his mistress – be it a quiet bistro or the mistress's apartment in the fourth arrondissement. This was crucial, since Robbinet took long lunches, even by French standards. He rarely returned to the office before four, but he was often at his desk until well past midnight, in signals with his counterparts in America. Robbinet's official title might be Minister of Culture, but in fact he was a spy at such a high level that he reported directly to the French president.

On this particular evening, however, he was out to dinner, the afternoon having proved so tiresomely hectic he'd had to postpone his daily tryst until late in the evening. There was a flap that concerned him greatly. A worldwide sanction had been routed to him by his American friends, and as he read it, his blood had run cold, for the target for termination was Jason Bourne.

Some years ago Robbinet had met Bourne at, of all places, a spa. Robbinet had booked a weekend at the spa just outside Paris so that he could be with his then-mistress, a tiny thing with enormous appetites. She had been a ballet dancer; Robbinet still recalled with great fondness the marvelous suppleness of her body. In any event, they had met in the steam room and they had gotten to talking. Eventually, in a most unsettling manner, he was to discover that Bourne had been there looking for a certain double agent. Having ferreted her out, he had killed her while Robbinet was getting a treatment – green mud, if memory served. Good thing, too, since the double agent was posing as Robbinet's therapist in order to assassinate him. Is there any place where one is more vulnerable than on a therapist's table? Robbinet wondered. What could he do after that, except take Bourne out to a lavish dinner. That night, over foie gras, veal kidneys in mustard-spiked *jus* and *tarte Tatin*, all washed down with three magnificent bottles of the finest ruby Bordeaux, having uncovered each other's secrets, they became fast friends.

It was through Bourne that Robbinet had met Alexander Conklin and had become Conklin's conduit to the operations of the Quai d'Orsay and Interpol.

In the end, Robbinet's trust in his assistant was Jason Bourne's good fortune, for it was over café and thoroughly decadent *millefeuille* at Chez Georges with Delphine that he received the call from her. He loved the restaurant for both its food and its location. Because it was across the street from the Bourse – the French equivalent of the New York Stock Exchange – it was frequented by brokers and businessmen, people far more discreet than the gossiping politicians with whom Robbinet was, from time to time, obliged to rub elbows.

'There's someone on the line,' his assistant said in his ear. Thankfully, she monitored his after-hours calls from home. 'He says it's urgent he speak with you.'

Robbinet smiled at Delphine. His mistress was an elegant, mature beauty whose looks were diametrically opposed to those of his wife of thirty years. They had been having a most delightful conversation about Aristide Maillot, whose voluptuous nudes graced the Tuilleries, and Jules Massenet, whose opera *Manon* they both thought overrated. Really, he could not understand the American male obsession with girls scarcely out of their teens. The thought of taking as a mistress someone his daughter's age seemed frightful to him, not to mention pointless. What on earth would there be to talk about over café and *millefeuille*? 'Has he given you his name?' he said into the phone.

'Yes. Jason Bourne.'

Robbinet's pulse started to pound. 'Put him through,' he said immediately. Then, because it was inexcusable to speak on the phone for any length of time in front of one's mistress, he excused himself, went outside into the fine mist of the Parisian evening and waited for the sound of his old friend's voice.

'My dear Jason. How long has it been?'

Bourne's spirits rose the moment he heard Jacques Robbinet's voice booming through his cell phone. At last the voice of someone inside who wasn't – he hoped! – trying to kill him. He was barreling down the Capital Beltway in another car he had stolen on his way to meet Deron.

'To tell you the truth, I don't know.'

'It's been years, can you believe it?' Robbinet said. 'But, really, I must tell you that I've kept track of you through Alex.'

Bourne, who'd felt some initial trepidation, now began to relax. 'Jacques, you've heard about Alex.'

'Yes, *mon ami*. The American DCI has sent out a worldwide sanction on you. But I don't believe a word of it. You couldn't possibly have murdered Alex. Do you know who did?'

'I'm trying to find out. All I know for certain at the moment is that someone named Khan may be involved.'

The silence at the other end of the line went on so long that Bourne was forced to say, 'Jacques? Are you there?'

'Yes, *mon ami*. You startled me, that's all.' Robbinet took a deep breath. 'This Khan, he is known to us. He's a professional assassin of the first rank. We ourselves know that he's been responsible for over a dozen high-level hits worldwide.'

'Whom does he target?'

'Mainly politicians – the president of Mali, for instance – but also from time to time prominent business leaders. As far as we've been able to determine, he's neither political nor an ideologue. He takes the commissions strictly for money. He believes in nothing but that.'

'The most dangerous kind of assassin.'

'Of that there can be no doubt, *mon ami*,' Robbinet said. 'Do you suspect him of murdering Alex?'

'It's possible,' Bourne said. 'I encountered him at Alex's estate just after I found the bodies. It might have been he who called the police because they showed up while I was still in the house.'

'A classic setup,' Robbinet concurred.

Bourne was silent for a moment, his mind filled with Khan, who could have shot him dead on campus or, later, from his vantage point in the willow. The fact that he didn't told Bourne a great deal. This apparently wasn't a normal commission for Khan; his stalking was personal, a vendetta of some sort that must have had its origins in the jungles of Southeast Asia. The most logical assumption was that Bourne had killed Khan's father. Now the son was out for revenge. Why else would he be obsessed with Bourne's family? Why else would he ask about Bourne abandoning Jamie? This theory fit the circumstances perfectly.

'What else can you tell me about Khan?' Bourne said now.

'Very little,' Robbinet replied, 'other than his age, which is twenty-seven.'

'He looks younger than that,' Bourne mused. 'Also, he's part Asian.'

'Rumor is he's half-Cambodian, but you know how reliable rumors can be.'

'And the other half?'

'Your guess is as good as mine. He's a loner, no known vices, residence unknown. He burst on the scene six years ago, killing the prime minister of Sierra Leone. Before that, it's as if he didn't exist.'

Bourne checked his rear-view mirror. 'So he made his first official kill when he was twenty-one.'

'Some coming-out party, eh?' Robbinet said dryly. 'Listen, Jason, about this man Khan, I can't overemphasize how dangerous he is. If he's involved in any way, you must use extreme caution.'

'You sound frightened, Jacques.'

'I am, *mon ami*. Where Khan is concerned, there's no shame in it. You should be, too. A healthy dose of fear makes one cautious, and believe me, now is a time for caution.'

'I'll keep that in mind,' Bourne said. He maneuvered through traffic, looking for the right exit. 'Alex was working on something, and I think he was killed because of it. You don't know anything about what he was involved with, do you?'

'I saw Alex here in Paris perhaps six months ago. We had dinner. My impression was that he was terribly preoccupied. But you know Alex, always secretive as the tomb.' Robbinet sighed. 'His death is a terrible loss for all of us.'

Bourne turned off the Beltway at the Route 123 exit, drove to Tysons Corner. 'Does 'NX 20' mean anything to you?'

'That's all you have? NX 20?'

He drove to the Tysons Corner center parking terrace C. 'More or less. Look up a name: Dr. Felix Schiffer.' He spelled it out. 'He works for DARPA.'

'Ah, now you have given me something useful. Let me see what I can do.'

Bourne gave him his cell phone number as he exited the car. 'Listen, Jacques, I'm on my way to Budapest but I'm just about out of cash.'

'No problem,' Robbinet said. 'Shall we use our same arrangement?'

Bourne had no idea what that was. He had no choice but to agree.

'*Bon*. How much?'

He went up the escalator, past Aviary Court. 'A hundred thousand should do it. I'll be staying at the Danubius Grand Hotel under Alex's name. Mark the packet "Hold for Arrival."'

'*Mais oui*, Jason. It will be done just as you wish. Is there any other assistance I can provide?'

'Not at the moment.' Bourne saw Deron up ahead, standing outside a store called Dry Ice. 'Thanks for everything, Jacques.'

'Remember caution, *mon ami*,' Robbinet said before signing off. 'With Khan in the field, anything can happen.'

Deron had spotted Bourne and began walking at a slower pace so Bourne could catch up to him. He was a slight man with skin the color of cocoa, a chiseled, high-cheekboned face and eyes that flashed his keen intelligence. With his lightweight coat, smartly tailored suit and gleaming leather attaché case, he looked every inch the businessman. He smiled as they walked side by side through the mall.

'It's good to see you, Jason.'

'Too bad the circumstances are so dire.'

Deron laughed. 'Hell, when disaster strikes is the *only* time I see you!'

While they spoke, Bourne was gauging sight lines, assessing escape routes, checking faces.

Deron unlocked his briefcase, handed Bourne a slim packet. 'Passport and contacts.'

'Thanks.' Bourne put the packet away. 'I'll get payment to you within the week.'

'Whenever.' Deron waved a long-fingered artist's hand. 'Your credit is good with me.' He handed Bourne another item. 'Dire situations require extreme measures.'

Bourne held the gun in his hand. 'What is this made of? It's so light.'

'Ceramic and plastic. Something I've been working on for a couple of months now,' Deron said with no little pride. 'Not useful for distance but spot-on at close range.'

'Plus, it won't be picked up at the airport,' Bourne said.

Deron nodded. 'Ammo, as well.' He handed Bourne a small cardboard box. 'Plastic-tipped ceramic, makes up for the small caliber. Another plus, look here, see these vents on the barrel – they dissipate the noise of percussion. The firing makes almost no sound.'

Bourne frowned. 'Doesn't that cut down on the stopping power?'

Deron laughed. 'Old school ballistics, m'man. Believe me, you take someone down with this, they stay down.'

'Deron, you're a man of unusual talents.'

'Hey, I gotta be me.' The forger sighed deeply. 'Copying the Old Masters has its charm, I suppose. You cannot believe how much I've learned studying their techniques. On the other hand, the world you opened up to me – a world no one else here in this entire mall but us knows exists – now that is what I call excitement.' A wind had come up, a damp harbinger of change, and he raised the collar of his coat against it. 'I admit I once harbored a secret desire to market some of my more unusual products to people like you.' He shook his head. 'But no more. What I do now on the side, I do for fun.'

Bourne saw a man in a trench coat stop in front of a store window to light up a cigarette. He was still standing there, seemingly gazing at the shoes on display. The trouble was, they were women's shoes. Bourne gave a hand signal and they both turned to their left, walking away from the shoe store. In a moment Bourne used the available reflective surfaces to glance behind them. The man in the trench coat was nowhere to be seen.

Bourne hefted the gun, which seemed light as air. 'How much?' he said.

Deron shrugged. 'It's a prototype. Let's say this, you name the price based on its use to you. I trust you'll be fair.'

*

When Ethan Hearn had first come to Budapest, it had taken him some time to get used to the fact that Hungarians were as literal as they were deliberate. Accordingly, the bar Underground was situated in Pest at 30 Teréz Körúta, in a cellar beneath a cinema. Being below a movie theater also adhered to the Hungarian idiosyncrasy, for Underground was an homage to the well-known Hungarian film by Emir Kusticura of the same name. As far as Hearn was concerned, the bar was postmodern in the ugliest sense of the word. Steel beams were visible across the ceiling, interspersed with a line of gigantic factory fans that blew the smoke-thickened air down around the drinking and dancing denizens. But what Hearn liked least about Underground was the music – a loud and cacophonous mixture of aggrieved garage rock and sweaty funk.

Oddly, László Molnar did not seem to mind. In fact, he appeared to want to stay out among the hip-swaying crowd, as if reluctant to return home. There was something brittle about his manner, Hearn thought, in his quick abrasive laugh, the way his eyes roamed the room, never alighting on anything or anyone for long, as if he carried a dark and corrosive secret close under his skin. Hearn's occupation caused him to run up against a great deal of money. He wondered, not for the first time, whether so much wealth could have a ruinous effect on the human psyche. Perhaps this was the reason he had never aspired to riches.

Molnar insisted on ordering for both of them, a nastily sweet cocktail called a Causeway Spray that involved whiskey, ginger ale, Triple Sec and lemon. They found a table in a corner where Hearn could barely see the small menu and continued their discussion of opera, which, given the venue, seemed absurd.

It was after his second drink that Hearn spotted Spalko, standing in the haze at the rear of the club. His boss caught his eye, and Hearn excused himself. Two men were loitering near Spalko. They did not look as if they belonged at Underground, but then, Hearn told himself, neither did he or László Molnar. Spalko led him down a dim corridor lit with pin lights like stars. He opened a narrow door into what Hearn imagined was the manager's office. No one was inside.

'Good evening, Ethan.' Spalko smiled as he closed the door behind them. 'It appears you have lived up to your billing. Well done!'

'Thank you, sir.'

'And now,' Spalko said with great bonhomie, 'it is time for me to take over.'

Hearn could hear the bone-jarring thump of the electronic bass through the walls. 'Don't you think I ought to stay around long enough to introduce you?'

'Not necessary, I assure you. Time for you to get some rest.' He looked at his watch. 'In fact, given the late hour, why don't you take tomorrow off.'

Hearn bridled. 'Sir, I couldn't – '

Spalko laughed. 'You can, Ethan, and you will.'

'But you told me in no uncertain terms – '

'Ethan, I have the power to make policy and I have the power to make exceptions to it. When your sleeper-sofa arrives, you can do what you want, but tomorrow you have off.'

'Yes, sir.' The young man ducked his head, grinning sheepishly. He hadn't had a day off in three years. A morning in bed with nothing to do but read the paper, spread orange marmalade on his toast, sounded like heaven to him. 'Thank you. I am most grateful.'

'Go on, then. By the time you're back in the office, I'll have read and made suggestions on your pitch letter.' He guided Hearn out of the overheated office. When he saw the young man mount the steps to the front door, he nodded to the two men flanking him and they set off through the frenetic hubbub of the bar.

László Molnar had begun peering through the fog of smoke and colored lights for his new friend. When Hearn had gotten up, he had been engrossed in the gyrating backside of a young girl in a short skirt, but he'd finally noticed that Hearn had been gone longer than expected. Molnar was taken aback when instead of Hearn the two men sat down on either side of him.

'What is this?' he said, his voice cracking in fright. 'What do you want?'

The men said nothing. The one on his right clamped him with a fearsome strength that made him wince. He was too much in shock to cry out, but even if he had had the presence of mind to do so, the incessant clangor of the club would have drowned him out. As it was, he sat petrified as the man on his left jabbed his thigh with a syringe. It was over so quickly, done so discreetly under the table that no one could possibly notice.

It took but thirty seconds for the drug Molnar had been injected with to take effect. His eyes rolled up in their sockets and his body went limp. The two men were prepared for this, and they held him up as they rose, maneuvering him to a standing position.

'Can't hold his liquor,' one of the men said to a nearby patron. He laughed. 'What can you do with people like that?' The patron shrugged and, grinning, returned to his dancing. No one else gave them a second look as they took László Molnar out of Underground.

Spalko was waiting for them in a long, sleek BMW. They bundled the unconscious Molnar into the trunk of the car, then scrambled into the front, one behind the wheel, the other in the front passenger's seat.

The night was bright and clear. A full moon rode low in the sky. It seemed to Spalko that all he need do was reach out a finger and he could flick it like a marble across the black velvet table of the sky. 'How did it go?' he asked.

'Sweet as honey,' the driver replied as he fired the ignition.

Bourne got out of Tysons Corner as quickly as he could. Though he had deemed it a secure place for his rendezvous with Deron, security for him was now a relative word. He drove to the Wal-Mart on New York Avenue. It was in the belly of the city, a busy enough area for him to feel that he would have some anonymity.

He pulled into the lot between 12th and 13th Streets across the avenue and parked. The sky had begun to fill up with clouds; it was ominously dark on the southern horizon. Inside, he picked out clothes, toiletry items, a battery charger for the cell phone, along with a number of other items. Then he searched for a back-pack in which he could easily stow everything. Waiting on the checkout line, shuffling along with everyone else, he felt his anxiety mounting. He seemed to look at no one, but in reality he was keeping his eye out for any untoward attention directed his way.

Too many thoughts crowded his mind. He was a fugitive from the Agency with what amounted to a price on his head. He was being stalked by a strangely arresting young man of extraordinary talents who just happened to be one of the most accomplished international assassins in the world. He had lost his two best friends, one of whom appeared to be involved in what was clearly an exceedingly dangerous extracurricular activity.

Thus preoccupied, he missed the chief security guard walking behind him. Early this morning a government agent had briefed him on the fugitive, handing him the same photo he'd seen last night on TV, asking him to keep an eagle eye out for the perp. The agent had explained that his visit was part of the dragnet, him and other CIA agents going around to all the major stores, movie theaters and the like, mak-ing sure the security people knew that finding this Jason Bourne should be their number-one priority. The guard felt a combination of pride and fear as he turned right around, went into his office cubicle and dialed the number the agent had given him.

Moments after the guard hung up the phone, Bourne was in the men's room. Using the electric clipper he had bought, he shaved off almost all his hair. Then he changed clothes, pulling on jeans, a red-and-white checked cowboy shirt with pearl-tone buttons and a pair of Nike running shoes. At the mirror in front of the line of sinks, he pulled out the small pots he had purchased at the makeup counter. He applied the contents of these judiciously, deepening the skin tone of his face. Another product thickened his brows, making them more prominent. The contact lenses Deron had provided turned his gray eyes a dull brown. Occasionally, he was obliged to pause as someone entered or washed up, but mainly the men's room was deserted.

When he was finished, he stared at himself in the mirror. Not quite satisfied, he gave himself a mole, prominently displayed high up on one cheek. Now the trans-formation was complete. Donning his backpack, he went out, through the store, heading toward the glass-encased front entrance.

Martin Lindros was in Alexandria, picking up the pieces of the botched termina-tion at Lincoln Fine Tailors when he had gotten the call from the chief security officer at the Wal-Mart on New York Avenue. This morning he had decided that he and Detective Harry Harris would split up, canvassing the area with their respective squads. Lindros knew that Harris was a couple of miles closer than he was because the state policeman had checked in not ten minutes ago. He was in a diabolical quandary. He knew he was going to catch six kinds of hell from the DCI because of the Fine fiasco. If the Old Man found out that he had allowed a state police detective to arrive at Jason Bourne's last-known location before him, he'd never hear the end of it. It was a bad situation, he thought as he gunned his car. But the overriding priority was to get Bourne. All at once he made his decision. *To hell with interdepartmental secrets and jealousies*, he thought. He toggled his phone on, got Harris on the line, gave him the Wal-Mart address.

'Harry, listen carefully, you are to make a silent approach. Your job is to secure the area. You are to make sure Webb does not escape, nothing more. Under no circumstances are you to show yourself or try to apprehend him. Is that clear? I'm only minutes behind you.'

*I'm not as stupid as I look*, Harry Harris thought as he coordinated the three patrol cars he had under his command. *And I'm certainly not as stupid as Lindros thinks I am.* He'd had more than adequate experience with federal types and he had yet to like what he had seen. The feds had ingrained in them this superior attitude, as if the other police forces were clueless, had to be led around like children. This attitude was like a bone stuck in Harris' craw. Lindros interrupted him when he had tried to tell him of his own theories, so why should he bother to share them now? Lindros saw him as nothing more than a pack mule, someone so grateful to be chosen to work with the CIA that he would follow orders unfailingly and unquestioningly. It was clear to Harris now that he was totally out of the loop. Lindros had deliberately failed to inform him of the Alexandria sighting. Harris had only learned about it by accident. As he turned into the Wal-Mart parking lot, he decided to take full control of the situation while he still had the chance. His mind made up, he grabbed his two-way radio, began barking orders to his men.

Bourne was near the entrance to the Wal-Mart when three Virginia State Police cars came barreling down New York Avenue, sirens blaring. He shrank back into shadows. There could be no doubt, they were heading directly for the Wal-Mart. He'd been made, but how? No time to worry about that now. He had to work out an escape plan.

The patrol cars screeched to a halt, blocking traffic, causing immediate irate shouts from motorists. Bourne could think of only one reason why they were out of their jurisdiction. They had been recruited by the Agency. The D.C. Metro Police would be livid.

He pulled out Alex's cell phone, dialed the police emergency line.

'This is Detective Morran of the Virginia State Police,' he said. 'I want to speak to a district commander pronto.'

'This is Third District Commander Burton Philips,' a steely voice said in his ear.

'Listen, Philips, you boys were told in no uncertain terms to keep your noses out of our business. Now I find your cruisers showing up at the Wal-Mart on New York Avenue and I – '

'You're in the heart of the district, Morran. What the hell are you doing poaching on my jurisdiction?'

'That's my business,' Bourne said in his nastiest voice. 'Just get on the horn and pull your goddamned boys out of my hair.'

'Morran, I don't know where you get your shit attitude, but it won't play with me. I swear I'll be there in three minutes to tear your balls off myself!'

By this time the street was swarming with cops. Instead of retreating back to the store, Bourne, keeping his left knee rigid, limped calmly out along with perhaps a dozen other shoppers. Half of the contingent of cops, led by a tall stoop shouldered detective with a haggard face, quickly scanned the faces of the dozen, Bourne included, as they rushed inside the store. The remaining cops fanned out in the parking lot. Some were securing New York Avenue between 12th and 13th Streets, others were busy ensuring that newly arriving patrons remained in their cars; still others were on their walkie-talkies, coordinating traffic.

Instead of heading for his car, Bourne turned to his right, went around the corner toward the loading dock at the rear of the building where the deliveries came in. Up ahead, he could see three or four semis parked, in the process of being unloaded. Diagonally across the street was Franklin Park. He set off in that direction.

Someone shouted at him. He kept on walking as if he hadn't heard. Sirens screamed and he glanced at his watch. Commander Burton Philips was right on time. He was halfway down the side of the building when the shouts came again, more commanding. Then there was a welter of harsh voices, raised in heated expletive-laden argument.

He turned, saw the stoop-shouldered detective, his service revolver out. Behind the detective came running the tall, imposing figure of Commander Philips, silver hair shining, his heavy-jowled face in high color from exertion and rage. In the fashion of dignitaries the world over, he was flanked by a pair of heavyweights armed with scowls as big as their shoulders. They had their right hands on their sidearms, apparently ready to blast to smithereens anyone foolish enough to intervene in their commander's wishes.

'You in charge of these Virginia troopers?' Philips called.

'State police,' the stoop-shouldered detective said. 'And, yeah, I'm in charge.' He frowned as he saw the D.C. Metro uniforms. 'What in hell are you doing here? You'll muck up my operation.'

'*Your* operation!' Commander Philips was apoplectic. 'Get the hell out of my swamp, you fucking hick bastard!'

The detective's narrow face went white. 'Who are you calling a fucking hick bastard?'

Bourne left them to it. The park was out now; having come under the detective's scrutiny, he needed a more immediate means of escape. Slipping to the end of the building, he went down the row of semis until he found one that had already been unloaded. He climbed into the cab. The key was in the ignition and he turned it over. With a basso profundo rumble, the truck started up.

'Hey, where ya think you're goin', dude?'

The driver yanked open the door. He was a huge man with a neck like a tree stump and arms to match. As he swung up, he grabbed a sawed-off shotgun from a hidden berth above his head. Bourne slammed a balled fist into the bridge of his nose. Blood flew, the driver's eyes went out of focus and he lost his grip on the shotgun.

'Sorry, dude,' Bourne said as he delivered a blow designed to render even a man of the trucker's oxlike size unconscious. Hauling him into the passenger's seat by the back of his studded belt, Bourne slammed the door closed and put the semi in gear.

At that moment, he became aware of a new presence on the scene. A youngish man had come between the two law-enforcement antagonists, pushing them roughly apart. Bourne recognized him: Martin Lindros, the Agency's DDCI. So the Old Man had put Lindros in domestic charge of the sanction. That was bad news. Through Alex, Bourne knew that Lindros was exceptionally bright; he would not be so easy to outfox, as evidenced by the tightly designed net in Old Town.

All this was technically moot now because Lindros had spotted the semi moving out of the parking lot and was trying to wave it down.

'No one leaves the area!' he shouted.

Bourne ignored him, depressed the accelerator. He knew he couldn't afford to have a face to face with Lindros; with his field expertise the man might see through his disguise.

Lindros drew his gun. Bourne could see him running toward the galvanized steel gates through which Bourne would have to pass, waving and shouting as he went.

Up ahead, responding to his screamed orders, two Virginia state cops stationed there hastily shut the gates, while an Agency vehicle plowed its way past the blockade of New York Avenue, on an intercept course with the semi.

Bourne jammed his foot down on the gas pedal, and like a wounded behemoth, the semi lurched forward. At the last moment, the cops leaped out of the way as he barreled through the gates, ripping them off their hinges so that they spun high in the air, crashed down on either side of him. He downshifted, turning hard to the right, heading up the street at an ever-increasing speed.

Glancing in the driver's oversized side mirror, he could see the Agency car slowing down. The passenger's door popped open and Lindros leaped in, slamming the door shut after him. The car took off like a rocket, gaining on the semi with little difficulty. Bourne knew that he could not outrun the Agency car with this lumbering beast, but its size, a drawback as far as speed was concerned, could be an asset in other ways.

He allowed the car to tailgate him. Without warning, it accelerated faster, coming up on his side of the cab. He saw Martin Lindros, his lips compressed in a line of concentration, holding his gun in one hand, his arm locked, steadying it with the other. Unlike actors in action films, he knew how to fire a gun from a speeding vehicle.

Just as he was about to pull the trigger, Bourne swerved the semi to the left. The Agency vehicle slammed into its side; Lindros put his gun up as the driver fought to keep the car away from the line of parked cars on the other side.

The moment the driver was able to swerve back into the street, Lindros began firing at the semi's cab. His angle was not good and he was being jolted incessantly, but the fusillade was enough to make Bourne turn the cab to the right. One bullet had smashed his side window and two others had penetrated the backseat, lodging in the trucker's side.

'Goddammit, Lindros,' Bourne said. Dire as his circumstances were, he did not want this innocent man's blood on his hands. He was already heading west; George Washington University Hospital was on 23rd Street, not that far away. He made a right, then a left onto K Street, thundering along, sounding his air horn as he went through traffic lights. A motorist on 18th, possibly half-asleep at the wheel, missed the warning, slammed head-on into the right rear of the semi. Bourne slewed dangerously, fought the truck back to center, kept going. Lindros' car was still behind him, stuck there because K Street, a divided thoroughfare with a planted median, was too narrow for the driver to creep up his side.

By the time he crossed 20th Street, he could see the underpass that would take him beneath Washington Circle. The hospital was a block away from there. Glancing behind him, he saw that the Agency car was no longer behind him. He had been planning to take 22nd Street down to the hospital, but just as he was about to make the left, he saw the Agency car come speeding toward him on 22nd. Lindros leaned out the window and began to fire in his methodical manner.

Bourne tramped on the gas and the truck leaped forward. He was now committed to going through the underpass, coming around to the hospital on the far side. But as he approached the underpass, he realized something was wrong. The tunnel beneath Washington Circle was completely dark; no daylight at all showed at the far end. That could mean only one thing: a roadblock had been set up, a fortress of vehicles set across both lanes of K Street.

He entered the underpass at speed, downshifting, stamping down hard on the air brakes only when he was engulfed in darkness. At the same time, he kept the heel of his hand on the air horn. The screaming noise ricocheted off the stone and concrete until it became deafening, concealing the shriek of the tires as Bourne turned the wheel hard to the left, rolling the cab of the truck over the divider so that the vehicle was turned at right angles to the road. He was out of the cab in an instant, sprinting the north wall behind the protection of the last car to come barreling through in the other direction. It had stopped for a moment as the driver rubbernecked the accident, then as more police arrived it had taken off. The semi was between him and his pursuers, stretched from wall to wall across both lanes of K Street. He scrabbled around for the steel maintenance ladder bolted to the tunnel wall, leaped up it and began to climb just as floodlights were switched on. He turned his head away, closed his eyes and kept climbing.

A few moments later he saw the lights illuminating the truck and the roadbed beneath it. Bourne, almost to the curved top of the underpass, could make out Martin Lindros. He spoke into a walkie-talkie, and floodlights came on from the opposite direction. They had the semi in a pincer grip. Agents were running toward the truck from both ends of K Street, guns at the ready.

'Sir, there's someone in the truck's cab.' The agent moved closer. 'He's been shot; he's bleeding pretty bad.'

Lindros was running, his face bursting into the floodlit field, lined with tension. 'Is it Bourne?'

High above them, Bourne had gained the maintenance hatch. He slid back the bolt, opened it, found himself amidst the decorative trees that lined Washington Circle. All around him, traffic raced, a relentless procession of blurred motion that never ceased. In the tunnel below him, the wounded trucker was being taken to the nearby hospital. Now it was time for Bourne to save himself.

# 9

Khan had accumulated too much respect for David Webb's skill for vanishing to have wasted time trying to find him in the swirling mass of people in Old Town. Instead, he had concentrated on the Agency men, shadowing them back to Lincoln Fine Tailors, where they met with Martin Lindros for the sorry debriefing following the botched termination. He observed them talking to the tailor. In accordance with standard intimidation practices, they had taken him out of his own environment – in this case, his shop – stuffing him into the backseat of one of their cars, where he had been detained without explanation, squeezed between two stone-faced agents. From what he had gathered from the conversation he overheard between Lindros and the agents, they had gotten nothing of substance from the tailor. He claimed the agents had arrived at his shop with such speed that Webb had had no time to tell him why he had come. As a consequence, the agents recommended cutting him loose. Lindros had agreed, but after the tailor had returned to his shop, Lindros had posted two new agents in an unmarked car across the street just in case Webb tried to contact him a second time.

Now, twenty minutes after Lindros had left them, the agents were bored. They'd eaten their donuts and drunk their Cokes and were sitting in their car grumbling about being stuck here on surveillance duty when their brethren were off running down the notorious agent, David Webb.

'Not David Webb,' the heavier of the two agents said. 'The DCI has decreed that we call him by his operational name, Jason Bourne.'

Khan, who was still close enough to hear every word, went rigid. He had, of course, heard of Jason Bourne. For many years, Bourne had had the reputation of being the most accomplished international killer-for-hire on the planet. Khan, knowing his field the way he did, had discounted half the stories as fabrications, the other half as exaggeration. It was simply not possible for one man to have had the daring, the expertise, the sheer animal cunning attributed to Jason Bourne. In fact, a part of him disbelieved in Bourne's existence altogether.

And yet, here were these CIA agents speaking about David Webb as Jason Bourne! Khan felt as if his brain was about to explode. He was shaken to his very foundation. David Webb wasn't simply a college professor of linguistics as Spalko's dossier had claimed, he was one of the field's great assassins. He was the man who Khan had been playing cat-and-mouse with since yesterday. So many things came together for him, not the least of which was how Bourne had made him in the park. Changing his face and hair and even his gait had always been enough to fool people in the past. But now he was dealing with Jason Bourne, an agent whose skills and expertise at, among other things, disguise were legendary and quite possibly the equal of his own. Bourne wasn't going to be gulled by the normal tricks of the trade, clever though they might be. Khan understood that he was going to have to raise the level of his game if he was going to win.

Fleetingly, he wondered if Webb's real identity was another fact Stepan Spalko had known when he had handed Khan the expurgated file. Considering it further, Khan believed that he had to have known. It was the only explanation for why Spalko had arranged to pin the murders of Conklin and Panov on Bourne. It was a classic disinformation technique. As long as the Agency believed that Bourne was responsible, they had no reason to look elsewhere for the real murderer – and surely they would have no chance to uncover the truth about why the two men were killed. Spalko was clearly trying to use Khan as a pawn in some larger game, the way he was using Bourne. Khan had to find out what Spalko was up to – he would not be anyone's pawn.

To unearth the truth behind the murders, Khan knew he had to get to the tailor. Never mind what he had told the Agency. Having followed Webb – it was still difficult for Khan to think of him as Jason Bourne – he knew the tailor Fine had had plenty of time to cough up what information he possessed. Once during his observation of the scene, the tailor Fine had turned his head, staring out the car window, and Khan had taken the opportunity to look into his eyes. He knew him, then, for a proud and obstinate man. Khan's Buddhist nature caused him to look upon pride as an undesirable trait, but in this situation he could see that it had served Fine well because the harder the Agency pushed him, the deeper he had dug in his heels. The Agency would get nothing out of him, but Khan knew how to neutralize pride as well as obstinacy.

Taking off his suede jacket, he ripped part of the lining enough so that the agents on stake-out would see him as nothing more than another Lincoln Fine Tailors customer.

Crossing the street, he entered the shop, the musical bell tinkling behind him. One of the Latina women looked up from reading the newspaper comics pages, her lunch, a Tupperware container of beans and rice, half-eaten in front of her. She came over, asked if she could help him. She was voluptuously built, with a firm, wide brow and large chocolate eyes. He told her that as the ripped jacket was a favorite of his, he'd come to see Mr. Fine himself. The woman nodded. She disappeared into the back and, a moment later, came out and sat down at her position without saying another word to Khan.

Several minutes passed before Leonard Fine appeared. He looked much the worse for his long and thoroughly unpleasant morning. Truth to tell, such close and intimate proximity to the Agency as he had endured seemed to have drained him of vitality.

'How can I help you, sir? Maria tells me you have a jacket in need of restoration.'

Khan spread the suede jacket out on the counter inside out.

Fine touched it with the same delicacy with which a doctor palpates an ill patient. 'Oh, it's just the lining. Lucky for you. Suede is almost impossible to repair.'

'Never mind that,' Khan said in a low whisper. 'I am here on orders from Jason Bourne. I'm his representative.'

Fine did an admirable job of keeping his face closed. 'I've no idea what you're talking about.'

'He thanks you for your part in his successful escape from the Agency,' Khan went on as if Fine hadn't spoken. 'And he wants you to know that even now two agents are spying on you.'

Fine winced slightly. 'I expected as much. Where are they?' His knobby fingers were kneading the jacket anxiously.

'Just across the street,' Khan said. 'In the white Ford Taurus.'

Fine was canny enough not to look. 'Maria,' he said just loud enough for the Latina to hear, 'is there a white Ford Taurus parked across the street?'

Maria turned her head. 'Yes, Mr. Fine.'

'Can you see if anyone's in it?'

'Two men,' Maria said. 'Tall, crew-cut. Very Dick Tracy, like the ones who were in here earlier.'

Fine swore under his breath. His eyes rose to meet Khan's. 'Tell, Mr. Bourne . . . tell him that Leonard Fine says, "May God go with him."'

Khan's expression was impassive. He found thoroughly distasteful the American habit of invoking God in almost any instance one cared to name. 'I need some information.'

'Of course.' Fine nodded gratefully. 'Whatever you want.'

Martin Lindros finally understood the meaning of the phrase 'So angry he could spit blood.' How was he ever going to face the Old Man, knowing that Jason Bourne had evaded him, not once but twice.

'What the hell d'you think you were doing disobeying my direct orders?' he screamed at the top of his lungs. Noises were echoing in the tunnel underneath Washington Circle as DOT personnel were trying to extricate the semi from the position in which Bourne had lodged it.

'Hey, listen, it was me who spotted the subject leaving the Wal-Mart.'

'And subsequently let him get away!'

'That was you, Lindros. I had an irate district commander chewing up my ass!'

'And that's another thing!' Lindros yelled. 'What the fuck was he doing there?'

'You tell me, wise guy, you're the one who fucked things up in Alexandria. If you'd bothered to clue me in, I could've helped you canvass Old Town. I know it like I know my own face. But no, you're the fed, you know better, you're the one running the show.'

'Damn right, I am! I've already directed my people to call all personnel stationed at the airports, train terminals, bus stations, rental car agencies to be on the lookout for Bourne.'

'Don't be absurd, even if you hadn't tied my hands behind my back, I lack the authority to make those kinds of calls. But I do have my men scouring the area and let's not forget that it was my detailed last best description of Bourne you disseminated to all the transportation egress points.'

Even though Harris was right, Lindros continued to fume. 'I demand to know why the hell you dragged the D.C. Metro Police into it? If you needed more backup, you should've come to me.'

'Why the fuck should I come to you, Lindros? Can you give me a reason? Are you my asshole buddy or something? Are we collaborating, anything along that line? Fuck no.' Harris had a disgusted look on his lugubrious face. 'And for the record, I didn't send for the D.C. I told you, he was on my ass from the second he showed up, frothing at the mouth about my poaching on his jurisdiction.'

Lindros barely heard him. The ambulance, its light flashing, its siren screaming, was taking off, ferrying the truck driver he had inadvertently shot to George Washington University Hospital. It had taken them nearly forty-five minutes to secure the area, mark it off as a crime scene and extricate him from the cab. Would he live or die? Lindros didn't want to think about that now. It would be easy to say that his injury was Bourne's fault – he knew the Old Man would see it that way. But the DCI had a crust formed of two parts pragmatism and one part bitterness that Lindros knew he could never match, and thank God for that. Whatever the trucker's fate now, he knew he was responsible, and this knowledge served as the perfect fuel for his antagonism. He may not have had the DCI's cynical crust, but he was not in the market of beating himself up for actions long past remedy. Instead, he spewed the poisonous feeling outward.

'Forty-five minutes!' Harris grunted as an ambulance cut its way through the backed-up traffic. 'Christ, that poor bastard could've died ten times over!'

'Civil servants!'

'You're a civil servant, Harry, if memory serves,' Lindros said nastily.

'And you aren't?'

The venom rose up in Lindros. 'Listen, you over-the-hill fuck, I am made of different cloth than the rest of you. My training – '

'All your training didn't help you to catch Bourne, Lindros! You had two chances and you blew them both!'

'And what did *you* do to help?'

Khan watched Lindros and Harris going at it. In his DOT overalls, he looked like everyone else on the scene. No one questioned his comings or goings. He had been passing close by the rear of the semi, ostensibly examining the damage done by the car that had rammed into it when he had noticed in the shadows the iron ladder that rose along the side of the tunnel. He looked up, craning his neck. He wondered where it led. Had Bourne wondered the same thing, or had he already known? Now, glancing around to make sure no one was looking in his direction, he quickly climbed the ladder, out of the range of the police spotlights, where no one could see him. He found the hatch and was not surprised to discover the slide bolt newly opened. He pushed the hatch open, went up.

From the vantage point of Washington Circle, he turned slowly in a clockwise direction, scanning all things near and far. A gathering wind whipped about his face. The sky had darkened further, looking bruised by the hammerblows of thunder, muffled by distance, that rolled now and again through the canyons and wide European-style avenues of the city. To the west was Rock Creek Parkway, Whitehurst Freeway and Georgetown. To the north rose the modern towers of Hotel Row – the ANA, Grand, Park Hyatt, and Marriott, and Rock Creek beyond. To the west was K Street, running past McPherson Square and Franklin Park. To the south was Foggy Bottom, sprawling George Washington University, the massive monolith of the State Department. Farther out, where the Potomac River bent to the east, widening out to form the placid bywaters of the Tidal Basin, he saw a silver mote, a plane hanging almost motionless, shining like a mirror, caught high up above the thickening clouds by a last bolt of sunlight before it began its descent into Washington National Airport.

Khan's nostrils dilated as if he had caught a scent of his quarry. The airport was where Bourne was going. He was certain of it because, had he been in Bourne's shoes, that was where he would be right now.

The terrible portent of David Webb and Jason Bourne being one and the same man had been marinating in his mind ever since he had heard Lindros and his CIA brethren discussing it. The very idea that he and Bourne were in the same profession felt like an outrage to him, a violation of everything he had painstakingly built for himself. It had been he – and only he – who had drawn himself out of the mire of the jungles. That he had survived those hateful early years was a miracle in itself. But at least those early days had been his and his alone. Now to find himself sharing the stage he had committed himself to conquering with, of all people, David Webb seemed like a cruel jest as well as an intolerable injustice. It was a wrong that must be rectified, the sooner the better. Now he could not wait to confront Bourne, to tell him the truth, to see in his eyes how that revelation would destroy him from the inside out as Khan bled him of life.

# 10

Bourne stood in the glass and chrome shadows of the International Departures building. Washington National Airport was a madhouse, thronged with business-men with laptops and carry-ons, families with multiple suitcases; children with Mickey Mouse, Power Ranger and Teddy bear backpacks; the elderly in wheel-chairs; a group of proselytizing Mormons on their way to the Third World; lovers hand in hand, tickets to paradise. But despite the crowds, there was an emptiness about airports. As a result, Bourne saw nothing but empty stares, the inward look that was the human being's instinctual defense against fearful boredom.

It was an irony not lost on him that in airports, where waiting was an institu-tion, time seemed to stand still. Not for him. Now, every minute counted, bringing him closer to termination by the very people he used to work for.

In the fifteen minutes he had been here he had seen a dozen suspicious plain-clothesmen. Some were prowling the departure lounges, smoking, drinking from big paper cups, as if they could blend in with the civilians. But most were at or near the airline check-in counters, eyeballing the passengers as they queued up to have their bags checked and receive their boarding passes. Bourne saw almost immediately that it was going to be impossible for him to get on a commercial flight. What other choices were there for him? He had to get to Budapest as quickly as possible.

He was wearing tan slacks, a cheap rain shell over a black turtleneck pullover, a pair of Sperry Top-Sider shoes in lieu of the sneakers, which he had dropped in the trash bin, along with a bundle of the other clothes he had on when he walked out of Wal-Mart. Since he had been spotted there, it was vital that he change his profile as quickly as possible. But now that he had assessed the situation at the terminal, he was not at all happy with what he had chosen.

Avoiding the roaming agents, he went outside into a night fizzing with a fine rain, picked up a shuttle bus that would take him to the Cargo Air Terminal. He sat right behind the driver, striking up a conversation with him. His name was Ralph. Bourne had introduced himself as Joe. They shook hands briefly as the shuttle braked at a pedestrian crosswalk.

'Hey, I'm supposed to meet my cousin at OnTime Cargo,' Bourne said, 'but stupid me, I lost the directions he gave me.'

'What's he do?' Ralph said, pulling ahead into the fast lane.

'He's a pilot.' Bourne shifted closer. 'He was desperate to fly with American or Delta, but you know how it goes.'

Ralph nodded his head in sympathy. 'The rich get richer and the poor get shafted.' He had a button nose, a mop of unruly hair and dark circles under his eyes. 'Tell me about it.'

'Anyway, can you direct me?'

'I'll do better than that,' Ralph said with a glance at Bourne in his long mirror. 'My shift's over when I get to the cargo terminal. I'll take you there myself.'

Khan stood in the rain, the crystal lights of the airport all around him, and thought matters through. Bourne would have smelled the Agency suits even before he spotted them. Khan had counted more than fifty, which meant perhaps three times that many sniffing their way throughout other sections of the airport. Bourne would know that he could never get through them onto an overseas flight no matter how he changed his clothing. They had made him at the Wal-Mart, they knew what he looked like now, he'd heard as much in the underpass.

He could feel Bourne close by. Having sat next to him on the park bench, having sensed the weight of him, the spread of his bones, the stretch of his muscles, the play of light over the features of his face. He knew he was here. It was Bourne's face that he had clandestinely studied in their brief moments together. He had been keenly aware of needing to memorize every contour, how each expression changed those contours. What had Khan been searching for in Bourne's expression when he had noted the other's intense interest? Confirmation? Validation? Even he did not know. He only knew that the image of Bourne's face had become part of his consciousness. For better or for worse, Bourne had a hold on him. They were bound together on the wheel of their own desires until the onset of death.

Khan looked around him once more. Bourne needed to get out of the city and possibly country. But the Agency would be adding on personnel, expanding its search even as it sought to tighten its noose. If it was Khan, he'd want to get out of the country as quickly as possible, so he headed toward the International Arrivals building. Inside he stood in front of a huge color-coded map of the airport, traced out the most efficient route to the cargo terminal. With the commercial flights already under such tight security, if Bourne was going to leave from this airport, his best chance would be aboard a cargo plane. Time was a critical factor now for Bourne. It wouldn't be long before the Agency realized that Bourne wasn't going to try to board a regular flight and began to monitor the cargo shippers.

Khan went back out into the rain. Once he determined which flights were departing in the next hour or so, all that remained would be to keep an eye out for Bourne and, should he have guessed correctly, deal with him. He had no more illusions about the difficulty of his task. Much to his shock and chagrin, Bourne had proved to be a clever, determined and resourceful antagonist. He had hurt Khan, had trapped him, slipped away from his grasp more than once. Khan knew that if he was to succeed this time, he would need a way to surprise Bourne, knowing that Bourne would be on the lookout for him. In his mind, the jungle called to him, repeating its message of death and destruction. The end of his long journey was in sight. He would outwit Jason Bourne this one last time.

Bourne was the only passenger by the time they reached their destination. It was raining harder, an early dusk settling in on the afternoon. The sky was indistinct, a blank slate on which any future could now be written.

'OnTime's at Cargo Five, along with FedEx, Lufthansa and Customs.' Ralph pulled the bus over and turned off the ignition. They got out, half-ran across the tarmac to one in a line of huge flat-roofed ugly buildings. 'Right in here.'

They went inside and Ralph shook rain off himself. He was a pear-shaped man, with oddly delicate hands and feet. He pointed now to their left. 'You see where U.S. Customs is? Down the building, two stations past is where you'll find your cousin.'

'Thanks a lot,' Bourne said.

Ralph grinned and shrugged. 'Don't mention it, Joe.' He held out his hand. 'Glad to help.'

As the driver ambled away, hands in his pockets, Bourne headed down toward OnTime's offices. But he had no intention of going there – not yet, anyway. He turned, following Ralph to a door that had affixed to it a sign reading NO ADMIT-TANCE – AUTHORIZED PERSONNEL ONLY. He took out a credit card as he watched Ralph feed his laminated ID card into a metal slot. The door swung open and, as Ralph disappeared inside, Bourne silently darted forward, inserted the credit card. The door shut, just as it should have, but Bourne's maneuver had prevented the lock from engaging. He counted silently to thirty in order to make certain that Ralph was no longer near the door. Then he opened it, pocketing his credit card as he went through.

He found himself in the maintenance locker room. The walls were of white tile; a rubber webbing had been laid on top of the concrete floor to keep the men's bare feet dry as they padded to and from the showers. Eight ranks of standard metal lockers were arrayed in front of him, most with simple combination locks on them. Off to his right was an opening to the showers and sinks. In a smaller space just beyond were the urinals and toilets.

Bourne cautiously peered around the corner, saw Ralph padding toward one of the showers. Closer to hand, another maintenance man was lathering up, his back to both Bourne and Ralph. Bourne looked around, immediately saw Ralph's locker. The door was slightly ajar, the combination lock hanging unhinged on the door handle itself. Of course. In a secure place like this what was there to fear in leaving your locker open for the few minutes it took to shower? Bourne opened the door wider, saw Ralph's ID tag lying atop an undershirt on a metal shelf. He took it. Nearby was the other maintenance man's locker, similarly open. He exchanged the locks, securing Ralph's locker. That should keep the driver from discovering that his ID tag had been stolen for as long as Bourne hoped he'd need.

He grabbed a pair of maintenance overalls from the open cart meant for laundering, making sure the size was more or less right, then quickly changed. Then, with Ralph's ID tag around his neck, he went out, walked quickly down to U.S. Customs, where he obtained the current flight schedule. There was nothing to Budapest, but Rush Service Flight 113 to Paris was leaving from Cargo Four in eighteen minutes. Nothing else was scheduled within the next ninety minutes, but Paris was fine; it was a major hub for intra-European travel. Once there, he would have no trouble getting to Budapest.

Bourne hurried back out to the slick tarmac. The rain was now coming down in sheets, but there was no lightning, and the thunder he had heard earlier was nowhere in evidence. That was good, as he had no desire to see Flight 113 delayed for any reason. He picked up his pace, hurrying to the next building, home to Cargo Three and Four.

He was drenched by the time he arrived inside the terminal. He looked to left and right, hurried toward the Rush Service area. There were few people about, which was not good. It was always easier to blend in with a crowd than with a sparse few. He found the door marked for authorized personnel, slid his ID card into the slot. He heard the gratifying click of the lock opening; he pushed on the door and went through. As he wended his way through the cinder-block corridors, the rooms stacked high with packing crates, the smells of resinous wood, sawdust and cardboard became overpowering. There was about the place an air of impermanence, a sense of constant motion, of lives ruled by schedules and weather, the anxiety of mechanical and human error. There was nothing to sit on, no place to rest.

He kept his eyes straight ahead, walking with the air of authority that no one would question. He soon came to another door, this one steel-clad. Through its small window, he could see planes arrayed on the tarmac, loading and unloading. It did not take him long to spot the Rush Service jet, its cargo bay door open. A fuel line ran from the plane to a tanker truck. A man in a rain slicker, its hood up over his head, was monitoring the gas flow. The pilot and co-pilot were in the cockpit going through their pre-flight instrument check.

Just as he was about to slide Ralph's ID card into the slot, Alex's cell phone rang. It was Robbinet.

'Jacques, it looks as if I'm about to head your way. Can you meet me at the airport in, say, seven hours or so?'

'*Mais oui, mon ami.* Call me when you land.' He gave Bourne his cell phone number. 'I am delighted that I will be seeing you so soon.'

Bourne knew what Robbinet was saying. He was pleased that Bourne was able to slip through from the Agency's noose. *Not yet*, Bourne thought. *Not quite yet.* But his escape was only moments away. In the meantime . . .

'Jacques, what have you discovered? Have you found out what NX 20 is?'

'I am afraid not. No record of any such project exists.'

Bourne's heart sank. 'What about Dr. Schiffer?'

'Ah, there I had a bit more luck,' Robbinet said. 'A Dr. Felix Schiffer works for DARPA – or at least he did.'

A cold hand had wrapped around Bourne's gut. 'What do you mean?'

Bourne could hear a rustling of paper, could imagine his friend reading through the intel he had managed to procure from his sources in Washington. 'Dr. Schiffer is no longer on DARPA's 'active' roster. He left there thirteen months ago.'

'What happened to him?'

'I've no idea.'

'He simply dropped out of sight?' Bourne asked incredulously.

'In this day and age, as unlikely as it seems, that's just what happened.'

Bourne closed his eyes for an instant. 'No, no. He's around somewhere – he has to be.'

'Then what – ?'

'He's been 'disappeared' – by professionals.'

With Felix Schiffer vanished, it was more imperative than ever that he get to

Budapest with all due haste. His only lead was the hotel key from the Danubius Grand Hotel. He glanced at his watch. He was cutting it close. He had to go. Now. 'Jacques, thanks for sticking your neck out.'

'I'm sorry I couldn't be of more help.' Robbinet hesitated. 'Jason . . .'

'Yes?'

'*Bon chance.*'

Bourne pocketed the cell phone, opened the stainless-steel-clad door, headed out into the heavy weather. The sky was low and dark, sheets of rain slanting down, a shimmering silver curtain in the airport's brilliant lights, running in glittering streamers over the depressions in the tarmac. He walked slightly bent over into the wind, walking purposefully, as he had before, a man who knew his job, wanted to get it done quickly and efficiently. Rounding the nose of the jet, he could see the cargo bay door ahead of him. The man fueling the jet had finished and had removed the nozzle from the tank.

Out of the corner of his eye, Bourne saw movement off to his left. One of Cargo Four's doors had burst open and several airport security guards spilled out, weapons drawn. Ralph must have gotten his locker open; Bourne had run out of time. He kept moving at the same deliberate pace. He was almost at the cargo bay door when the fueler said, 'Hey, buddy, got the time? My watch stopped.'

Bourne turned. At the same moment he recognized the Asian features of the face inside the hood; Khan shot a burst of aviation fuel into his face. Bourne's hands came up and he choked, completely blinded.

Khan rushed him, pushing him back against the slick metal skin of the fuselage. He delivered two vicious blows, one to Bourne's solar plexus, one to the side of his head. As Bourne's knees collapsed, Khan shoved him into the cargo hold.

Turning, Khan saw a cargo handler heading toward him. He lifted an arm. 'It's okay, I'll lock up,' he said. Luck was with him, as the rain made it difficult for anyone to see his face or his uniform. The cargo handler, grateful to get out of the rain and wind, returned a salute of thanks. Khan slammed the cargo door shut, locked it. Then he sprinted to the fuel truck, drove it far enough away from the plane so that it would not look suspicious.

The security police that Bourne had spotted before were making their way down the row of jets. They signaled to the pilot. Khan put the jet between himself and the oncoming police. He reached up, unlocked the cargo bay door, swung himself inside. Bourne was on his hands and knees, his head hanging down. Khan, surprised at his recuperative powers, kicked him hard in the ribs. With a grunt, Bourne fell over on his side, his arms wrapped around his waist.

Khan took out a length of cord. He pressed Bourne face-first onto the cargo bay deck, took his arms behind his back and wrapped the wire around his crossed wrists. Over the sound of the rain, he could hear the security police shouting to the pilot and co-pilot for their IDs. Leaving Bourne incapacitated, Khan walked over and quietly pulled the bay door closed.

For a few minutes Khan sat cross-legged in the darkness of the cargo bay. The pinging of the rain on the skin of the fuselage set up an arrhythmic percussion that reminded him of the drums in the jungle. He had been quite ill when he had heard those drums. To his fever-stricken mind, they had sounded like the roaring of aircraft engines, the frantic beating of the air about the outflow vents just before it begins a steep dive. The sound had frightened him because of the memories it brought up, memories he had fought long and hard to keep at the very bottom of his consciousness. Because of the fever, all his senses were heightened to an almost painful pitch. He was aware that the jungle had come alive, that shapes were coming warily toward him in an ominous wedgelike formation. His one conscious action was to bury the small carved stone Buddha he wore around his neck under leaves in a shallow hurriedly dug grave beneath where he lay. He could hear voices, and after a while he became aware that the shapes were asking him questions. He squinted through the fever-sweat to make them out in the emerald twilight, but one of them covered his eyes with a blindfold. Not that it was needed. When they lifted him off the bed of leaves and detritus he had made for himself, he passed out. Waking two days later, he found himself inside a Khmer Rouge encampment. As soon as he was deemed fit by a cadaverous man with sunken cheeks and one watery eye, the interrogation began.

They had thrown him into a pit with writhing creatures which to this day he could not identify. He was cast into a darkness more complete, more profound than any he had ever known before. And it was this darkness, enveloping, constricting, pressing against his temples like a weight growing in baleful proportion to the hours that passed, that terrified him the most.

A darkness not unlike this one, in the belly of Rush Service Flight 113.

. . . *Then Jonah prayed unto the Lord his God out of the fish's belly. And said, I cried by reason of mine affliction unto the Lord, and he heard me; out of the belly of hell cried I, and thou heardest my voice. For thou hadst cast me into the deep, in the midst of the seas; and the floods compassed me about: all thy billows and thy waves passed over me* . . .

He still remembered that section from the frayed and stained copy of the Bible the missionary had made him memorize. Horrible! Horrible! Because Khan, in the midst of the hostile and murderous Khmer Rouge, had been cast quite literally into the belly of hell, and he had prayed – or what passed for prayer in his still unformed mind – for deliverance. This was before the Bible had been pushed on him, before he had understood the teachings of the Buddha, for he had descended into formless chaos at a very early age. The Lord had heard Jonah cry out from the belly of the whale, but no one had heard Khan. He had been utterly alone in the darkness and then, when they felt that they had softened him up sufficiently, they pulled him out and slowly, expertly, with a cold passion it would take him years to acquire, began to bleed him.

Khan snapped on the flashlight he carried with him, sat immobile, staring at Bourne. Unfolding his legs, he kicked out violently, the sole of his shoe catching Bourne on the shoulder so that he rolled over on his side facing Khan. Bourne groaned, and his eyes fluttered open. He gasped, took another shuddering breath, inhaling the fumes from the aviation fuel, and convulsed, vomiting in the space between where he lay in burning pain and misery and where Khan sat serene as Buddha himself.

'I've been down to the bottoms of the mountains; the earth with her bars was about me forever; yet have I brought up my life from the darkness,' Khan said, paraphrasing Jonah. He continued to stare fixedly into Bourne's reddened swollen face. 'You look like shit.'

Bourne struggled to rise onto one elbow. Khan calmly kicked it out from under him. Again Bourne tried to sit up and again Khan thwarted him. The third time, however, Khan did not make a move and Bourne sat up, facing him.

The faint and maddeningly enigmatic smile played across Khan's lips, but there was a sudden spark of flames in his eyes.

'Hello, Father,' he said. 'It's been such a long time I was beginning to think we'd never have this moment.'

Bourne shook his head slightly. 'What the hell are you talking about?'

'I'm your son.'

'My son is ten years old.'

Khan's eyes were glittery. 'Not that one. I'm the one you left behind in Phnom Penh.'

All at once, Bourne felt violated. A red rage rose up inside him. 'How dare you? I don't know who you are, but my son Joshua is dead.' The effort cost him, for he had inhaled more of the fumes, and he bent over suddenly, retching again, but there was nothing left inside him to vomit up.

'I'm not dead.' Khan's voice was almost tender as he leaned forward, pulled Bourne back up to face him. In so doing, the small carved stone Buddha fell away from his hairless chest, swinging a little with his efforts to keep Bourne upright. 'As you can see.'

'No, Joshua *is* dead! I put the coffin in the ground myself, along with Dao and Alyssa! They were wrapped in American flags.'

'Lies, lies and more lies!' Khan held the carved stone Buddha in the palm of his hand, held it toward Bourne. 'Look at this, and remember, Bourne.'

Reality seemed to slip away from Bourne. He heard his rapid pulse thundering in his inner ears, a tidal wave that threatened to pick him up and carry him off. It couldn't be! It couldn't! 'Where – where did you get that?'

'You know what this is, don't you?' The Buddha disappeared behind the curl of his fingers. 'Have you finally recognized your long-lost son Joshua?'

'You're not Joshua!' Bourne was enraged now, his face dark, his lips pulled back from his teeth in an animal snarl. 'Which Southeast Asia diplomat did you kill to get it?' He laughed grimly. 'Yes, I know more about you than you think.'

'Then you're sadly mistaken. This is mine, Bourne. Do you understand?' He opened his hand, revealed the Buddha again, the stone dark with the imprint of his sweat. 'The Buddha is mine!'

'Liar!' Bourne leaped at him, his arms coming around from behind his back. He had flexed his muscles – the cords expanding as Khan had wound the wire around him – then using the slack had worked his way out of the bonds while Khan had been gloating.

Khan was caught out, unprepared for his headlong bull-rush. He tumbled backward, Bourne on top of him. The flashlight struck the deck, rolling back and forth, its potent beam flashing on them, then off, illuminating an expression here, a bulging muscle there. In this eerily striped and stippled darkness and light, so like the dense jungle they had left behind, they fought like beasts, breathing in each other's enmity, struggling for supremacy.

Bourne, his teeth gritted, struck Khan again and again in a maddened attack. Khan managed to gain a grip on Bourne's thigh, pressed in on the nerve bundle there. Bourne lurched, his temporarily paralyzed leg buckling beneath him. Khan struck him hard on the point of the chin, and Bourne staggered further, shaking his head. He grabbed hold of his switchblade just as Khan delivered another massive blow. Bourne dropped the knife and Khan picked it up, flipped open the blade.

He stood over Bourne now, pulled him up by the front of his shirt. A brief tremor passed through him, as a current sizzles through a wire when the switch is thrown. 'I'm your son. Khan is a name I took, just as David Webb took the name Jason Bourne.'

'No!' Bourne fairly shouted this over the rising noise and vibration of the engines. 'My son died with the rest of my family in Phnom Penh!'

'I *am* Joshua Webb,' Khan said. 'You abandoned me. You left me to the jungle, to my death.'

The point of the knife hovered over Bourne's throat. 'How many times I almost died. I would have, I'm sure of it, if I didn't have your memory to hold on to.'

'How dare you use his name! Joshua is dead!' Bourne's face was livid, his teeth bared in animal rage. His vision was clouded with blood-lust.

'Maybe he is.' The knife-blade lay against Bourne's skin. A millimeter more and it would draw blood. 'I'm Khan now. Joshua – the Joshua you knew – is dead. I've come back for revenge, to deliver your punishment for abandoning me. I could've killed you so many times in the last few days, but I stayed my hand because before I killed you I wanted you to know what you had done to me.' Khan's lips opened and a bubble of spittle grew at the corner of his mouth. 'Why did you abandon me? How could you have run away!'

The plane gave a terrific lurch as it began to taxi out onto the runway. The blade sprayed blood as it sliced into Bourne's skin, then it was lifted away as Khan lost his balance. Bourne took the advantage, drove his balled fist into Khan's side. Khan swept his foot back, hooking it behind Bourne's ankle, and Bourne went down. The plane slowed, turning onto the head of the runway.

'I didn't run away!' Bourne shouted. 'Joshua was taken from me!'

Khan pounced on him, the knife flashing down. Bourne twisted and the blade drove past his right ear. He was aware of the ceramic gun secreted at his right hip, but try as he might he wouldn't be able to get to it without leaving himself open to a fatal attack. They struggled, their muscles bulging, their faces engorged with effort and rage. Their breath sawed from between half-open mouths, their eyes and minds searching for the most minute opening as they attacked and defended, counterattacked only to be rebuffed. They were well matched, if not in age, then in speed, strength, skill and cunning. It was as if they knew each other's minds, as if they could anticipate each other's moves a split second beforehand, thus neutralizing whatever advantage had been sought. They did not fight with dispassion and, therefore, they did not fight at peak level. All their emotion had been flushed out of the depths, lay stranded and squirming in the conscious mind, like an oil slick clouding water.

The plane lurched, the fuselage trembling as the plane began its race down the runway. Bourne slipped and Khan used his free hand as a cudgel to draw Bourne's attention away from the knife. Bourne countered, striking the inside of Khan's left wrist. But now the blade-point flashed in on him. He stepped back and to the side, inadvertently unlatching the bay door. The rising motion of the plane caused the unlocked door to swing open.

As the runway blurred by below, Bourne splayed himself out like a starfish to keep himself inside the plane, gripping the doorframe tightly with both hands. Grinning maniacally, Khan leaned in toward Bourne, the knife-blade describing a wicked shallow arc that would cut across the entire width of Bourne's abdomen.

Khan lunged just as the plane was about to lift off the runway. At the last possible instant, Bourne let go with his right hand. His body, driven out and back by gravity, swung so violently away that his shoulder was nearly dislocated. Where his body had been was now a gaping space through which Khan fell, tumbling to the tarmac below. Bourne had one final glimpse of him, nothing more than a gray ball against the black of the runway.

Then the plane was airborne and Bourne was swinging up, farther from the open doorway. He struggled; rain whipped against him like chain-mail. The wind threatened to take his breath away, but it scrubbed the last of the jet fuel from his face, the rain rinsing his stinging red-rimmed eyes, flushing the poison from his skin and tissue. The plane banked to the right and Khan's flashlight rolled across the cargo bay deck, tumbled out after him. Bourne knew that if he did not get himself inside within seconds, he would be lost. The terrible strain on his arm was far too intense for him to hold on much beyond that.

Swinging his leg around, he managed to hook the back of his left ankle into the doorway. Then, with a mighty effort, he heaved himself forward, the back of his knee clamped against the raised frame, giving himself both purchase and leverage enough to turn so that he was facing the fuselage. He got his right hand on the lip of the seal and in this fashion was able to work his way into the interior. His last act was to slam the door shut.

Bourne, bruised, bleeding and in a great deal of pain, collapsed into an exhausted heap. In the frightful, turbulent darkness of the shuddering interior, he saw again the small carved stone Buddha that he and his first wife had given Joshua for his fourth birthday. Dao had wanted the spirit of Buddha to be with their son from the earliest age. Joshua, who had died along with Dao and his little sister when the enemy plane had strafed the river they had been playing in.

Joshua was dead. Dao, Alyssa, Joshua – they were all dead, their bodies ripped asunder by the hail of bullets from the dive-bombing plane. His son could not be alive, he *could not*. To think otherwise would be to invite insanity. Then who was Khan really, and why was he playing this hideously cruel game?

Bourne had no answers. The plane dipped and rose, the pitch of the engines changing as it reached cruising altitude. It grew frigid, his breath clouding as it left his nose and mouth. He wrapped his arms around himself, rocking. It was not possible. It was not!

He gave an inarticulate animal cry, and all at once he was undone by pain and utter despair. His head sank, and he wept bitter tears of rage, disbelief and grief.

# Book 2

# 11

In the full belly of Flight 113, Jason Bourne was asleep, but in his unconscious mind his life – a far-off life he had buried long ago – was once again unspooling. His dreams were filled to overflowing with images, feelings, sights and sounds he had spent the intervening years pushing down as far from his conscious thoughts as they would go.

What had happened that hot summer's day in Phnom Penh? No one knew. At least, no one who was still alive. This much was fact: While he sat bored and restless in his air-cooled office at the American Foreign Services complex, attending a meeting, his wife Dao had taken their two children swimming in the wide, muddy river just outside their house. From out of nowhere, an enemy plane had banked, dropping from the sky. It strafed the river where David Webb's family swam and splashed and played.

How many times had he envisioned the terrible sight? Had Dao seen the plane first? But it had come upon them so swiftly, swooping down in a silent glide. If so, she must have gathered their children to her, pushing them beneath the water, covering them with her own body in a vain attempt to save them even while their screams echoed in her ears, their blood flecked her face, even while she felt the pain of her own impending death. This, in any event, was what he believed, what he dreamed, what had driven him to the edge of madness. For the screams he imagined Dao had heard just before the end were the same screams he heard night after night, starting awake, his heart racing, his blood pounding. Those dreams had forced him to abandon his house, all that he had held dear, for the sight of each familiar object had been like a stab in his guts. He had fled Phnom Penh for Saigon, where Alexander Conklin had taken charge of him.

If only he could have left his nightmares behind in Phnom Penh. In the dripping jungles of Vietnam, they came back to him again and again, as if they were wounds he needed to inflict on himself. Because this truth, above all others, remained: He could not forgive himself for not being there, for not protecting his wife and children.

He cried out now in his tortured dreams thirty thousand feet over the stormy Atlantic. Of what use is a husband and a father, he asked himself as he had a thousand times before, if he failed to protect his family?

The DCI was woken out of a sound sleep at five in the morning by a priority call from the National Security Advisor, summoning him to her office in one hour. Just when did this bitch-woman sleep? he wondered as he put down the phone. He sat on the edge of his bed, facing away from Madeleine. *Nothing disturbed* her *sleep*, he thought sourly. Long ago she had taught herself to sleep through the phone ringing at all hours of the night and morning.

'Wake up!' he said, shaking Madeleine awake. 'There's a flap on and I need coffee.'

Without a note of complaint, she rose, slipped on her robe and slippers and went down the hall to the kitchen.

Rubbing his face, the DCI padded into the bathroom, closed the door. Sitting on the toilet, he called the DDCI. Why the hell should Lindros be sleeping when his superior was not? To his consternation, however, Martin Lindros was wide awake.

'I've been spending all night in the Four-Zero archives.' Lindros was referring to the maximum-security files on CIA personnel. 'I think I know all there is to know about both Alex Conklin and Jason Bourne.'

'Great. Find me Bourne then.'

'Sir, knowing what I know about the two of them, how closely they worked together, how many times they went out on a limb for each other, saved each other's lives, I find it highly improbable that Bourne would murder Alex Conklin.'

'Alonzo-Ortiz wants to see me,' the DCI said irritably. 'After that fiasco at Washington Circle, d'you think I should tell her what you've just told me?'

'Well, no, but – '

'You're goddamned right, sonny boy. I've got to give her facts, facts that add up to *good* news.'

Lindros cleared his throat. 'At the moment, I don't have any. Bourne has vanished.'

'Vanished? Jesus Christ, Martin, what the hell kind of intelligence operation are you running?'

'The man's a magician.'

'He's flesh and blood, just like the rest of us,' the DCI thundered. 'How the hell did he slip through your fingers yet again? I thought you had all the bases covered!'

'We did. He simply – '

'Vanished, I know. This is what you have for me? Alonzo-Ortiz will have my fucking head on a platter, but not before I have yours!'

The DCI cut the connection, flung the phone through the open doorway onto the bed. By the time he had showered, dressed and taken a sip of coffee from the mug Madeleine obediently held out, his car was waiting for him.

Through the pane of bullet-proof glass, he drank in the facade of his house, dark-red brick with pale stone quoins at the corners, working shutters at every window. It had once belonged to a Russian tenor, Maxim something-or-other, but the DCI liked it because it had about it a certain mathematical elegance, an aristocratic air that could no longer be found in buildings of a younger vintage. Best of all was its sense of Old World privacy, owing to a cobbled courtyard screened by leafy poplars and a hand-worked iron fence.

He sat back in the plush seat of the Lincoln Town Car, watching morosely as Washington slept on around him. *Christ, at this hour only the fucking robins are up,* he thought. *Aren't I due the privilege of seniority? After all these years of service, don't I deserve to sleep past five o'clock?*

They sped across the Arlington Memorial Bridge, the Potomac gun-metal gray, looking flat and hard as an airport runway. On the other side, looming over the more or less Doric temple of the Lincoln Memorial, was the Washington Monument, dark and forbidding as the spears the Spartans once used to drive through the hearts of their enemies.

*Each time the water closes over him, he hears a musical sound, as of the bells the monks are sounding, echoing from ridge to ridge in the forested mountains; the monks he hunted when he was with the Khmer Rouge. And the smell of, what is it? cinnamon. The water, swirling with a malevolent current, is alive with sounds and scents from he knows not where. It seeks to drag him down, and once again he's sinking. No matter how hard he struggles, how desperately he strikes out for the surface, he feels himself spiraling down, as if weighted with lead. His hands are scrabbling at the thick rope tied around his left ankle, but it's so slick it keeps sliding through his fingers. What is at the end of the rope? He peers down into the shadowy depths through which he's sinking. It seems imperative to him that he know what is dragging him to his death, as if that knowledge might save him from a horror for which he has no name. He's falling, falling, tumbling into darkness, unable to understand the nature of his desperate predicament. Below him, at the end of the taut rope, he sees a shape – the thing that will cause his death. Emotion sticks in his throat like a mouthful of nettles, and as he tries to define the shape, the musical sound comes to him again, clearer this time, not bells, something else, something at once intimate and barely remembered. At last, he identifies the thing that's causing him to drown: It's a human body. All at once, he begins to weep . . .*

Khan awoke with a start, a whimper caught in his throat. He bit down hard on his lip, looked around the darkened cabin of the plane. Outside, all was black as pitch. He had fallen asleep even though he'd promised himself he wouldn't, knowing that if he did he would be trapped in his recurring nightmare. He rose, went to the lavatory, where he used the paper towels to wipe the sweat off his face and arms. He felt more tired than when the flight had taken off. While he was staring at himself in the mirror, the pilot announced their airtime to Orly Airport: Four hours, fifty minutes. An eternity for Khan.

There was a line of people waiting as he exited. He made his way back to his seat. Jason Bourne had a specific destination in mind; he knew that from the information the tailor, Fine, had provided: Bourne was now in possession of a packet meant for Alex Conklin. Was it possible, he wondered, that Bourne would now take on Conklin's identity? It would be something Khan would consider if he were in Bourne's shoes.

Khan stared out the window at the black sky. Bourne was somewhere in the sprawling metropolis ahead of him, this much was known, but he had no doubt that Paris was just a way station. Bourne's final destination was yet to be learned.

The National Security Advisor's assistant cleared her throat discreetly and the DCI glanced at his watch. Roberta Alonzo-Ortiz, the bitch-woman, had kept him waiting almost forty minutes. Inside the Beltway, playing games of power was standard operating procedure, but Jesus Christ, she was a *woman*. And weren't they both on the National Security Council? But she was the president's direct appointee; she had his ear like no one else. Where the hell was Brent Scowcroft when you needed him? Pasting a smile on his face, he turned away from the window out which he had been gazing while his mind had been engaged.

'She's ready to see you now,' the assistant cooed sweetly. 'Her call with the president just ended.'

*The bitch-woman doesn't miss a trick*, the DCI thought. *How she loves to rub my nose in her power-stink.*

The National Security Advisor was entrenched behind her desk, a huge antique affair she'd had trucked in at her own expense. The DCI thought it absurd, especially since there was nothing on her desk except the brass pen-set the president had given her upon her acceptance of the appointment. He didn't trust people with tidy desks. Behind her, on elaborate gold standards, were the American flag and the flag with the seal of the President of the United States. Between them was a view of Lafayette Park. Two high-backed upholstered chairs sat facing her. The DCI looked at them somewhat longingly.

Roberta Alonzo-Ortiz looked bright and chipper in a dark-blue knit suit and white silk blouse. In her ears were gold-backed enamel earrings of the American flag.

'I just got off the phone with the president,' she said without preamble, not even a 'Good morning' or 'Have a seat.'

'So your assistant told me.'

Alonzo-Ortiz glared at him, a momentary reminder that she hated being interrupted. 'The conversation concerned you.'

Despite his best intentions, the DCI felt his body flush. 'Perhaps I should have been here then.'

'That would not have been inappropriate.' The National Security Advisor went on before he could respond to her verbal slap in the face. 'The terrorism summit will take place in five days. Every element is in place, which is why it pains me to have to reiterate that we are walking on eggshells here. Nothing can disturb the summit, *especially* not a CIA assassin gone criminally insane. The president is anticipating that the summit will be an unqualified success. He expects to make it the cornerstone of his drive for reelection. Even more, it will be his legacy.' She put her hands flat on the highly polished surface of her desk. 'Let me be perfectly clear – I have made the summit my number-one priority. Its success will ensure that this presidency is lauded and revered for generations to come.'

The DCI had been standing throughout this discourse, not having been invited to sit down. The verbal dressing-down was especially humiliating, given its subtext. He did not care for threats, particularly veiled ones. He felt as if he was being given detention in elementary school.

'I had to brief him about the Washington Circle debacle.' She said it as if the DCI had made her deliver a shovelful of shit to the Oval Office. 'There are consequences to failure; there always are. You need to put a stake through the heart of this one so it can be buried as soon as possible. Do you understand me?'

'Perfectly.'

'Because it won't go away on its own,' the National Security Advisor said.

A vein had started to pulse in the DCI's temple. He felt the urge to throw something at her. 'I said I understood perfectly.'

Roberta Alonzo-Ortiz scrutinized him for a moment, as if she was deciding whether he was worthy of being believed. At length, she said, 'Where's Jason Bourne?'

'He's fled the country.' The DCI's fists were clenched and white. It was beyond him to tell the bitch-woman that Bourne had simply vanished. As it was, he could scarcely get the words out. But the moment he saw the look on her face, he realized his error.

'Fled the country?' Alonzo-Ortiz rose. 'Where has he gone?'

The DCI remained silent.

'I see. If Bourne gets anywhere near Reykjavík . . .'

'Why would he do that?'

'I don't know. He's insane, remember? He's gone rogue. He must know that sabotaging the summit security would embarrass us like nothing else.' Her fury was palpable, and for the first time the DCI was truly afraid of her.

'I want Bourne dead,' she said in a voice of steel.

'As much as I do.' The DCI was fuming. 'He's already killed twice, and one of the victims was an old friend.'

The National Security Advisor came around from behind her desk. 'The president wants Bourne dead. An agent gone rogue – and let's be honest here, Jason Bourne is a worst-case scenario – is a wild card we can't afford. Do I make myself clear?'

The DCI nodded. 'Believe me when I tell you that Bourne is as good as dead, *vanished* as if he had never existed at all.'

'From your mouth to God's ear. The president's eye is on you,' Roberta Alonzo-Ortiz said, ending the interview as abruptly and unpleasantly as she had begun it.

Jason Bourne arrived in Paris on a wet, overcast morning. Paris, city of light, was not at its best in the rain. The mansard-roofed buildings looked gray and wan, and the usually gay and lively outdoor cafés that lined the city's boulevards were quite deserted. Life went on in its muted fashion, but the city was not the same as when it sparkled and shone in sunlight, when good conversation and laughter could be heard on almost every corner.

Exhausted both physically and emotionally, Bourne had spent most of the flight on his side, curled in a ball, asleep. His slumber, though now and again interrupted by dark and disturbing dreams, had the benefit of providing a well-needed respite from the pain that had wracked him in the first hour after the plane had taken off. He awoke, chilled and stiff, thinking of the small carved stone Buddha that had hung around Khan's neck. The image seemed to mock him, to be grinning, a mystery yet to be solved. He knew there must be many such carvings – in the shop where he and Dao had chosen the one they would give Joshua there were more than a dozen! He also knew that many Asian Buddhists wore such charms, for both protection and good luck.

In his mind's eye, he saw again Khan's knowing expression, so alight with anticipation and hatred when he had said, '*You know what this is, don't you?*' And then, uttered with such vehemence: '*This is mine, Bourne. Do you understand? The Buddha is mine!*' Khan was not Joshua Webb, Bourne told himself. Khan was clever but cruel – an assassin who had killed many times. He could not be Bourne's son.

Despite a bout of heavy crosswinds as they had left the coastline of the United States behind, Rush Service Flight 113 landed at Charles de Gaulle International Airport more or less on time. Bourne felt the urge to remove himself from the cargo hold while it was still on the runway, but he restrained himself.

Another plane was preparing to land. If he got off now, he would be out in the open, exposed in an area where even airport personnel should not be. And so he waited patiently while the plane taxied onward.

As it slowed, he knew that now was the time to act. While the plane was still moving, the jet engines running, none of the ground crew would approach the plane. He opened the door, jumped out onto the tarmac just as a fuel truck was passing by. He caught a ride on the back of it. Hanging there, he experienced a violent wave of nausea as the fumes triggered the memory of Khan's surprise attack. He leaped off the truck as quickly as was practical, making his way into the terminal building.

Inside, he collided with a baggage handler, apologized profusely in French, with a hand to his head complaining of a migraine. Around the corner of the corridor, he used the ID tag he had swiped from the handler to go through the two sets of doors, out into the terminal proper, which, much to his consternation, was nothing more than a converted hangar. There were precious few people about, but at least he had successfully bypassed Customs and Immigration.

At the first opportunity, he dropped the ID tag into the nearest waste bin. He did not want to be caught wearing it when the handler reported it missing. Standing beneath a large clock, he adjusted his watch. It was just after six in the morning, Paris time. He called Robbinet, described where he was.

The minister seemed puzzled. 'Did you come in on a charter flight, Jason?'

'No, cargo plane.'

'*Bon*, that explains why you are in old Terminal Three. You must have been diverted from Orly,' Robbinet said. 'Stay right where you are, *mon ami*. I will collect you shortly.' He chuckled. 'In the meantime, welcome to Paris. Confusion and ill-fortune to your pursuers.'

Bourne went to wash up. Staring at himself in the men's room mirror, he saw a haggard face, haunted eyes and a bloody throat, someone he barely recognized. Cupping his hands, he threw water over his face and head, sluicing away the sweat, grime and whatever was left of the makeup he had applied earlier. With a damp paper towel, he cleaned the darkened horizontal wound across his throat. He knew he would need to get some antibiotic cream on it as soon as possible.

His stomach was in a knot, and though he didn't feel hungry, he knew he needed to eat. Every once in a while the taste of the jet fuel came back to him and he gagged, eyes tearing with the effort. To get his mind off the sick sensation, he performed five minutes of stretching, five more of calisthenics, ridding his muscles of their cramped and aching condition. He ignored the pain the exercises cost him, concentrating instead on breathing deeply and evenly.

By the time he walked back into the terminal, Jacques Robbinet was waiting for him. He was a tall, extraordinarily fit man, neatly dressed in a dark pinstripe suit, gleaming brogues and a stylish tweed topcoat. He was a bit older and a bit grayer, but otherwise he was the figure out of Bourne's fragmented memory.

He spotted Bourne immediately and a grin broke out on his face, but he made no move toward his old friend. Instead, he used hand signals to indicate that Bourne should walk down the terminal to Bourne's right. Bourne immediately saw why. Several members of the Police Nationale had entered the hangar, were questioning airport personnel, doubtless on the lookout for the suspect who had stolen the baggage handler's ID. Bourne walked at a natural pace. He was almost at the doors when he saw two more Police Nationale, machine pistols slung across their chests, carefully watching everyone who went in and out of the terminal.

Robbinet had seen them as well. Putting a frown on his face, he hurried past Bourne, pushing through the doors and engaging the policemen's attention. As soon as he introduced himself, they told him that they were on the lookout for a suspect – an assumed terrorist – who had stolen a baggage handler's ID tag. They showed him a faxed copy of Bourne's photo.

No, the minister had not seen this man. Robbinet's face assumed an expression of fear. Perhaps – was such a thing possible? – the terrorist was after him, he said. Would they be so kind as to escort him to his car?

As soon as the three men had moved off, Bourne went quickly through the door, out into the gray mist. He saw the policemen accompanying Robbinet to his Peugeot and he walked in the opposite direction. As the minister got into his car, he gave Bourne a furtive glance. He thanked the policemen, who walked back to their post outside the terminal doors.

Robbinet drove off, made a U-turn, coming back to exit the airport. Out of sight of the policemen, he slowed the car, rolled down the off-side window.

'That was close, *mon ami.*'

When Bourne made a move to get in, Robbinet shook his head. 'With the airport on high alert, there is certain to be more Police Nationale about.' He reached down, popped the trunk. 'Not the most comfortable of places.' He looked apologetic. 'But for now surely the safest.'

Without another word, Bourne crawled into the trunk, shutting himself in, and Robbinet took off. It was well the minister had thought ahead; there were two roadblocks to negotiate before they could exit the airport, the first manned by Police Nationale, the second by members of the Quai d'Orsay, the French equivalent of the CIA. With Robbinet's credentials, he got through both without incident, but he was repeatedly shown Bourne's photo, asked if he had seen the fugitive.

Ten minutes after he had turned onto the A1, Robbinet pulled over into a breakdown area, popped the trunk. Bourne got out, slid into the passenger's seat, and Robbinet accelerated onto the motorway, heading north.

'That's him!' The baggage handler pointed to the grainy photo of Jason Bourne. 'That's the man who stole my ID.'

'You're certain, monsieur? Please look again, more closely this time.' Inspector Alain Savoy centered the photo in front of the potential witness. They were in a concrete room inside Terminal Three of Charles de Gaulle Airport, where Savoy had decided to set up temporary headquarters. It was a mean place, smelling strongly of mildew and disinfectant. He was always in such places, it seemed to him. There was nothing permanent in his life.

'Yes, yes,' the baggage handler said. 'He bumped into me, said he had a migraine. Ten minutes later, when I went to go through a secure door, I discovered the tag was gone. He took it.'

'We know he did,' Inspector Savoy said. 'Your presence was electronically reported in two places while your ID tag was missing. Here.' He handed over the tag. He was a short man and sensitive about it. His face looked as rumpled as his longish dark hair. His lips seemed permanently pursed, as if even in repose he was assessing innocence or guilt. 'We found it in a trash bin.'

'Thank you, Inspector.'

'You'll be fined, you know. One day's pay.'

'That's an outrage,' the baggage handler said. 'I'll report this to the union. There may be a demonstration.'

Inspector Savoy sighed. He was used to these threats. Among the union workers, there were always demonstrations. 'Is there anything more you can tell me about the incident?' When the man shook his head, the inspector dismissed him. He stared down at the faxed sheet. Besides Jason Bourne's photo, it contained an American contact. Pulling out a tri-band cell phone, he punched in the number.

'Martin Lindros, Deputy Director of Central Intelligence.'

'Monsieur Lindros, this is Inspector Alain Savoy of the Quai d'Orsay. We have found your fugitive.'

'What?'

A slow smile crept over Savoy's unshaven face. The Quai d'Orsay was always sucking at the CIA teat. There was a great deal of pleasure, not to mention national pride, in having the situation reversed. 'That's right. Jason Bourne arrived at Charles de Gaulle Airport around six this morning, Paris time.' Savoy's heart gladdened at the swift intake of breath at the other end of the line.

'Do you have him?' Lindros asked. 'Is Bourne in custody?'

'Sadly, no.'

'What do you mean? Where is he?'

'This is a mystery.' There ensued a silence so long and deep that Savoy was obliged at length to say, 'Monsieur Lindros, are you still on the line?'

'Yes, Inspector. I'm just going through my notes.' Another silence, briefer this time. 'Alex Conklin had a clandestine contact high up in your government, a man named Jacques Robbinet – do you know him?'

'*Certainement*, Monsieur Robbinet is the Minister of Culture. Surely you don't expect me to believe that a man of his stature is in league with this madman?'

'Of course not,' Lindros said. 'But Bourne has already murdered Monsieur Conklin. If he's in Paris now, it stands to reason that he may be after Monsieur Robbinet.'

'One moment, hold the line, if you please.' Inspector Savoy was certain that he'd heard or read M. Robbinet's name somewhere today. He gestured to a subordinate, who handed him a sheaf of files. Savoy leafed rapidly through the interviews made this morning at Charles de Gaulle by all the various police and security services. Sure enough, there was Robbinet's name. Hurriedly, he got back on the line. 'Monsieur Lindros, it happens that Monsieur Robbinet was here today.'

'At the airport?'

'Yes, and not only that. He was interviewed at the same terminal as the one Bourne was in. In fact, he seemed alarmed when he was told the name of the fugitive. He asked the Police Nationale to accompany him back to his automobile.'

'This proves my theory.' Lindros' voice was slightly breathless with a combination of excitement and alarm. 'Inspector, you've got to find Robbinet, and fast.'

'There's no problem,' Inspector Savoy said. 'I'll simply call the minister's office.'

'That's precisely what you *won't* do,' Lindros said. 'I want to keep this operation absolutely secure.'

'But surely Bourne can't – '

'Inspector, in the brief course of this investigation I've learned never to utter the phrase "Bourne can't" because I know that he *can*. He's an exceedingly clever and dangerous assassin. Anyone who goes near him is in danger of their life, get me?'

'Pardon, monsieur?'

Lindros tried to slow down his speech. 'However you choose to find Robbinet, you'll do it through back channels only. If you surprise the minister, chances are you'll be surprising Bourne as well.'

'*D'accord.*' Savoy stood up and looked for his trench coat.

'Listen closely, Inspector. I'm very much afraid Monsieur Robbinet's life is in imminent danger,' Lindros said. 'Everything now depends on you.'

Concrete high-rises, office buildings, gleaming factories flashed by, squat and blocky by American standards, made even more ugly by the gloomy overcast. Soon enough, Robbinet turned off, driving west on the CD47 into the oncoming downpour.

'Where are we going, Jacques?' Bourne asked. 'I need to get to Budapest as quickly as possible.'

'*D'accord*,' Robbinet said. He'd been periodically glancing in his rear-view mirror, checking for Police Nationale vehicles. The Quai d'Orsay was another matter; their operatives used unmarked cars, switching make and models among their divisions every few months. 'I had booked you on an outboard flight that left five minutes ago, but while you were in the air the game board has changed. The Agency is howling for your blood – and that howl is being heard in all corners of the world where they have leverage, including mine.'

'But there must be a way – '

'Of course there's a way, *mon ami.*' Robbinet smiled. 'There's always a way – a certain someone named Jason Bourne taught me that.' He turned north again, onto the N17. 'While you rested in the boot of my car, I was far from idle. There's a military transport leaving from Orly at sixteen hundred hours.'

'That's not until four this afternoon,' Bourne said. 'What about driving to Budapest?'

'Such a plan is unsafe, too many Police Nationale. And your maddened American friends have pricked the Quai d'Orsay into action.' The Frenchman shrugged. 'It's all arranged. I've all your credentials with me. Under military cover you'll be secure from scrutiny, and in any event it's best to let the incident at Terminal Three die down, *non*?' He swung past some slow-moving traffic. 'Until then, you'll need a place to go to ground.'

Bourne turned his head away, stared out at the dreary industrial landscape. The impact of what had happened during his last encounter with Khan had hit him with the impact of a train derailing. He couldn't help exploring the fierce ache inside himself, much as one keeps pressing a sore tooth, if only to determine just how deep the pain went. The fiercely analytical portion of his mind had already determined that Khan hadn't really said anything that indicated he possessed intimate knowledge of David or Joshua Webb. He had made intimations, innuendoes, yes, but what did they amount to?

Bourne, aware that Robbinet was scrutinizing him, turned further toward the window.

Robbinet, misconstruing the reason for Bourne's brooding silence, said, '*Mon ami*, you will be in Budapest by eighteen hundred hours, have no fear.'

'*Merci*, Jacques.' Bourne momentarily freed himself from his melancholy thoughts. 'Thanks for all your kindness and help. What now?'

'*Alors*, we are going to Goussainville. Not the most scenic town in France, but there's someone there who I suspect will interest you.'

Robbinet said nothing more for the remainder of the trip. He was right about Goussainville. It was one of those French villages that, because of its proximity to the airport, had been transformed into a modern industrial town. The depressing rows of high-rises, glass-fronted offices and giant retailers not unlike Wal-Mart were only slightly alleviated by the roundabouts and curbsides planted with row upon row of colorful flowers.

Bourne noticed the radio unit mounted below the dashboard, presumably used by Jacques' driver. As Robbinet pulled into a gas station, he asked his friend for the frequencies used by the Police Nationale and the Quai d'Orsay. While Robbinet pumped gas into the car, Bourne monitored both frequencies but heard nothing about the incident at the airport, nothing of interest about him. Bourne watched the cars coming and going in and out of the gas station. A woman got out of her car, asked Robbinet his opinion about her front driver's side tire. She was worried it needed air. A vehicle with two young men pulled in. They both got out. One man lounged against the fender of the car while the driver went into the station. The lounging man eyed Jacques' Peugeot, then gazed appreciatively at the woman as she walked back to her car.

'Anything on the air?' Robbinet inquired as he slid in beside Bourne.

'Not a thing.'

'That at least is good news,' Robbinet said as they drove off.

They went down more ugly streets, and Bourne used the mirrors to check that the car with the two young men wasn't tailing them.

'Goussainville had an ancient and royal beginning,' Robbinet said. 'Once upon a time it belonged to Clotaire, wife of Clovis, the king of France early in the sixth century. While we Franks were still considered barbarians, he converted to Catholicism, making us acceptable to the Romans. The emperor made him a consul. Barbarians no longer, we became true champions of the Faith.'

'You'd never know this place was once a medieval city.'

The minister pulled up to a series of concrete apartment buildings. 'In France,' he said, 'history is often hidden in the most unexpected places.'

Bourne looked around. 'This isn't where your current mistress lives, is it?' he said. 'Because the last time you introduced me to your mistress I had to pretend she was my girlfriend when your wife walked into the café where we were having drinks.'

'I recall you having quite a good time that afternoon.' Robbinet shook his head. 'But no, with her Dior this and her Yves Saint Laurent that I'm certain Delphine would rather slit her wrists than live in Goussainville.'

'Then what are we doing here?'

The minister sat staring out at the rain for some time. 'Filthy weather,' he said at last.

'Jacques . . . ?'

Robbinet looked around. 'Ah, yes, forgive me, *mon ami*. My mind wanders. *Alors*, I am taking you to meet Mylene Dutronc.' He cocked his head. 'Have you heard her name?' When Bourne shook his head, Robbinet continued. 'I thought not. Well, now that he's dead, I suppose I can say it. Mlle. Dutronc was Alex Conklin's lover.'

At once, Bourne said, 'Let me guess: light eyes, long wavy hair and a smile with something of the ironic about it.'

'He *did* tell you about her!'

'No, I saw a photo. It's pretty much all he had of a personal nature in his bedroom.' He waited a moment. 'Does she know?'

'I phoned her as soon as I found out.'

Bourne wondered why Robbinet hadn't told her in person. It would have been the decent thing to do.

'Enough talk.' Robbinet grabbed an overnight bag from the footwell of the backseat. 'We'll go see Mylene now.'

Exiting the Peugeot, they went through the rain, along a little flower-flanked walk, and mounted a short flight of poured-concrete stairs. Robbinet pressed the button for 4A and a moment later the buzzer sounded.

The apartment building was as plain and unlovely on the inside as it was on the outside. They walked up the five flights of stairs to the fourth floor and went along a hallway, past rows of identical doors on either side. At the sound of their approach, the door opened. Just inside stood Mylene Dutronc.

She was perhaps a decade older than the image in the photo – in fact, she must have been sixty by now, Bourne thought, though she appeared at least ten years younger – but her light eyes had the same sparkle and her smile had the same enigmatic twist to it. She wore jeans and a man-tailored shirt, an outfit that made her appear feminine because it showed off her full figure. She was in low heels and her hair, a natural-looking ash-blond, was tied back from her face.

'*Bonjour*, Jacques.' She lifted her face for Robbinet to kiss on both cheeks, but she was already looking at his companion.

Bourne could see details that the snapshot hadn't revealed. The color of her eyes, the sculpted flare of her nostrils, the whiteness of her even teeth. Her face was both powerful and compassionate.

'And you must be Jason Bourne.' Her gray eyes appraised him coolly.

'I'm sorry about Alex,' Bourne said.

'You're kind. It's been a shock to all of us who knew him.' She stepped back. 'Please come in.'

As she shut the door behind her, Bourne took in the room. Mlle. Dutronc lived in the middle of a blocky urban landscape, but her apartment was altogether different. Unlike many people her age, she had not continued to surround herself with furniture decades old, relics of the past. Instead, her furnishings were both stylishly modern and comfortable. A scattering of chairs, a matching pair of sofas facing each other on either side of a brick fireplace, patterned curtains. It was a place you would not easily want to leave, Bourne decided.

'I understand you've had a long flight,' she said to Bourne. 'You must be starving.' She made no mention of his disheveled appearance, for which he was grateful. She seated him in the dining room, served him food and drink from a typical

European kitchen, small and dark. When she was finished, she sat down opposite him, put her clasped hands on the table.

Bourne could see now that she had been crying.

'Did he die instantly?' Mlle. Dutronc asked. 'You see, I've been wondering whether he suffered.'

'No,' Bourne said truthfully. 'I very much doubt he did.'

'That's something, at least.' A look of profound relief came over her face. Mlle. Dutronc sat back and, with this movement, Bourne became aware that she had been holding her body tensely. 'Thank you, Jason.' She looked up, her expressive gray eyes locked on his, and he could see all the emotion in her face. 'May I call you Jason?'

'Of course,' he said.

'You knew Alex well, didn't you?'

'As well as one could ever know Alex Conklin.'

For just an instant, her gaze flicked in Robbinet's direction, but it was enough.

'I have some calls to make.' The minister had already pulled out his cell phone. 'You won't mind if I leave you two for a little while.'

She looked bleakly after Robbinet as he headed for the living room. Then she turned back to Bourne. 'Jason, what you told me just now was said as a true friend. Even if Alex had never spoken to me about you, I would say the same thing.'

'Alex talked to you about me?' Bourne shook his head. 'Alex never told civilians about his work.'

There was that smile again; this time the irony in it was quite apparent. 'But I'm not, as you say, a civilian.' There was a pack of cigarettes in her hand. 'Do you mind if I smoke?'

'Not at all.'

'Many Americans do. It's something of an obsession with you, isn't it?'

She had not been seeking an answer and Bourne did not give her one. He watched as she lit up, drew the smoke deep into her lungs, let it out slowly, luxuriously. 'No, I'm definitely not a civilian.' The smoke swirled around her. 'I'm Quai d'Orsay.'

Bourne sat very still. Beneath the table, his hand grasped the butt of the ceramic pistol Deron had given him.

As if reading his mind, Mlle. Dutronc shook her head. 'Calm yourself, Jason. Jacques hasn't led you into a trap. You're among friends here.'

'I don't understand,' he said thickly. 'If you're Quai d'Orsay, Alex would've been doubly sure not to involve you in anything he was working on, so as not to compromise your loyalties.'

'True enough. And this was how it remained for many years.' Mlle. Dutronc took in more smoke, let it drift out of her flared nostrils. She had a habit of raising her head slightly as she exhaled. It made her look like Marlene Dietrich. 'Then, very recently, something happened. I don't know what, he wouldn't tell me, though I begged him to.'

She regarded him through the smoke haze for some moments. Any member of an intelligence organization had to maintain a stone facade that revealed nothing of their inner thoughts or feelings. But through her eyes he could see her mind working, and he knew that she had let her guard down.

'Tell me, Jason, as a long-time friend of Alex's, do you ever remember him being frightened?'

'No,' Bourne said. 'Alex was utterly fearless.'

'Well, that day he *was* frightened. That's why I begged him to tell me what it was, so I could help, or at least convince him to move himself out of harm's way.'

Bourne leaned forward, his body now as tense as Mlle. Dutronc's had been before. 'When was this?'

'Two weeks ago.'

'Did he tell you anything at all?'

'There was a name he mentioned, Felix Schiffer.'

Bourne's pulse began to race. 'Dr. Schiffer worked for DARPA.'

She frowned. 'Alex told me that he worked for the Tactical Non-Lethal Weapons Directorate.'

'That's an Agency adjunct,' Bourne said, half to himself. Now the pieces were starting to fall together. Could Alex have convinced Felix Schiffer to leave DARPA for the Directorate? Surely, it would not have been difficult for Conklin to make Schiffer 'disappear.' But why would he want to? If he was merely poaching on DOD territory, he could've handled the resulting flak. There had to be another reason Alex needed to get Felix Schiffer to ground.

He looked at Mylene. 'Was Dr. Schiffer the reason Alex was frightened?'

'He wouldn't say, Jason. But how could it be otherwise? That day, Alex made and received many calls in a very short period of time. He was terribly tense and I knew he was at the crisis point of a hot field operation. I heard Dr. Schiffer's name mentioned several times. I suspect that he was the subject of the operation.'

Inspector Savoy sat in his Citroën, listening to the scraping sound of his windshield wipers. He hated the rain. It had been raining the day his wife had left him, the day his daughter had gone off to school in America, never to return. His wife was living in Boston now, married to a straight-laced investment banker. She had three children, a house, property, all that she could wish for, while here he was sitting in this shitty town – what was its name? ah, yes, Goussainville – biting his nails down to the quick. And, to top it off, it was raining again.

But today was different because he was closing in on the CIA's most wanted target. Once he got Jason Bourne, his career would skyrocket. Perhaps he'd come to the attention of the president himself. He glanced over at the car across the street – Minister Jacques Robbinet's Peugeot.

From the Quai d'Orsay files, he had retrieved the make, model and license plate of the minister's car. His fellow officers had informed him that upon exiting the airport checkpoint the minister had headed north onto the A1. After having ascertained from headquarters who had been assigned to the northerly section of the dragnet, he had methodically called each car – mindful of Lindros' warning, keeping away from radio transmission, whose frequency wasn't secure. None of his contacts had seen the minister's car, and he was working himself up into a fit of despair when he had gotten to Justine Bérard, who told him that, yes, she had seen Robbinet's car – had spoken to him briefly – at a gas station. She remembered because the minister seemed tense, nervous, even a bit rude.

'Did his behavior strike you as odd?'

'Yes, it did. Though I didn't make much of it at the time,' Bérard had said. 'Though now, of course, my thinking has changed.'

'Was the minister alone?' Inspector Savoy asked.

'I'm not certain. It was raining hard and the window was up,' Bérard said. 'To be candid, my attention was on Monsieur Robbinet.'

'Yes, a handsome specimen,' Savoy said, more dryly than he had intended. Bérard had been a great help. She had seen the direction in which the minister's car had gone, and by the time he had arrived in Goussainville, she had found it sitting outside a block of concrete apartment buildings.

Mlle. Dutronc's eyes strayed to Bourne's throat and she stubbed out her cigarette. 'Your wound has begun bleeding again. Come. We must take care of it.'

She led him into her bathroom, tiled in sea-green and cream. A small window overlooking the street let in the dismal light of day. She sat him down and began to wash the wound with soap and water.

'The bleeding has subsided,' she said as she applied antibiotic to the reddened flesh across his throat. 'This wound wasn't accidental. You were in a fight.'

'It was difficult getting out of the States.'

'You're as tight-lipped as Alex.' She stood a little back, as if she needed to get him in better focus. 'You are sad, Jason. So very sad.'

'Mlle. Dutronc – '

'You must call me Mylene. I insist.' She had fashioned an expert bandage from sterile gauze and surgical tape and now applied it to his wound. 'And you must change the dressing at least every three days, yes?'

'Yes.' He responded to her smile. '*Merci*, Mylene.'

She put a hand gently against his cheek. 'So very sad. I know how close you and Alex were. He thought of you as a son.'

'He said that?'

'He didn't have to; he had a special look on his face when he spoke about you.' She examined the dressing one last time. 'So I know I'm not the only one hurting.'

Bourne felt the urge, then, to tell her everything, that it wasn't just the deaths of Alex and Mo affecting him, but the encounter with Khan. In the end, however, he remained silent. She had her own grief to bear.

Instead, he said, 'What's the deal with you and Jacques? You act as if you hate each other.'

Mylene looked away for a moment, toward the small window with its pebbled glass, running now with rain. 'It was brave of him to bring you here. It must have cost him much to ask for my help.' She turned back, her gray eyes brimming. Alex's death had brought so much emotion to the surface, and at once he intuited that her own past was being churned up by the restless ocean of present events. 'So much sorrow in this world, Jason.' A single tear rolled from her eye, lay quivering on her cheek, before sliding down. 'Before Alex, you see, there was Jacques.'

'You were his mistress?'

She shook her head. 'Jacques was not yet married. We were both very young. We made love like crazy, and because we were both young – and foolish – I became pregnant.'

'You have a child?'

Mylene wiped her eyes. '*Non*, I wouldn't have it. I didn't love Jacques. It took what happened to make me see that. Jacques *did* love me, and he – well, he's so very Catholic.'

She laughed, a little sadly, and Bourne recalled the story Jacques had told him of Goussainville's history and how the barbarian Franks had been won over by the church. King Clovis' conversion to Catholicism had been a shrewd decision, but it had been more a matter of survival and politics than of faith.

'Jacques has never forgiven me.' There was no self-pity in her, making her confession all the more affecting.

He leaned in and tenderly kissed her on both cheeks, and with a small sob she drew him briefly to her.

She left him to shower, and when he was finished, he found a French military uniform piled neatly on the toilet seat. As he dressed, he peered out the window. A linden's branches swung back and forth in the wind. Below him, a handsome woman in her early forties got out of her car, walked down the street to a Citroën in which a man of indeterminate age sat behind the wheel, gnawing obsessively at his fingernails. Opening the passenger's-side door, she slid in.

There was nothing particularly unusual about the scene, except for the fact that Bourne had seen the same woman at the gas station. She had spoken to Jacques about the air pressure in her tire.

Quai d'Orsay!

Quickly, he went back into the living room, where Jacques was still on the phone. The moment the minister saw Bourne's expression, he got off his call.

'What is it, *mon ami*?'

'We've been made,' Bourne said.

'What? How is that possible?'

'I don't know, but there are two Quai d'Orsay agents across the street in a black Citroën.'

Mylene walked in from the kitchen. 'Two more are watching the street behind. But don't worry, they cannot even know which building you're in.'

At that moment, the doorbell rang. Bourne drew his gun but Mylene's eyes flashed their warning. She jerked her head and Bourne and Robbinet moved out of sight. She opened the door, saw a very rumpled inspector in front of her.

'Alain, *bonjour*,' she said.

'I'm sorry to intrude on your vacation,' Inspector Savoy said, a sheepish grin on his face, 'but I was sitting outside and all of a sudden I remembered that you lived here.'

'Would you like to come in, have a cup of coffee?'

'Thank you, no. I can't spare the time.'

Greatly relieved, Mylene said, 'And what were you doing sitting outside my house?'

'We're looking for Jacques Robbinet.'

Her eyes opened wide. 'The Minister of Culture? But why would he be in, of all places, Goussainville?'

'Your guess is as good as mine,' Inspector Savoy said. 'Nevertheless, his car is parked across the street.'

'The inspector is too clever for us, Mylene.' Jacques Robbinet strode into the living room buttoning his white shirt. 'He has found out about us.'

With her back turned to Savoy, Mylene shot Robbinet a look. He returned it, smiling easily.

His lips brushed hers, as he came up beside her.

By this time Inspector Savoy's cheeks had grown warm. 'Minister Robbinet, I had no idea . . . that is, there was no intention to intrude – '

Robbinet raised a hand. 'Apology accepted, but why are you looking for me?'

With an overt show of relief, Savoy handed over the grainy photo of Jason Bourne. 'We're searching for this man, Minister. A known CIA assassin who's turned rogue. We have reason to believe that he means to kill you.'

'But that's terrible, Alain!'

To Bourne, observing this charade from the shadows, Mylene looked shocked indeed.

'I don't know this man,' Robbinet said, 'nor why he would want to take my life. But then who can fathom the minds of assassins, eh?' He shrugged, turned as Mylene handed him his jacket and raincoat. 'But by all means, I'll return to Paris as quickly as possible.'

'With us as an escort,' Savoy said firmly. 'You'll ride with me and my associate will drive your official car.' He held out his hand. 'If you would be so kind.'

'As you wish.' Robbinet delivered the key to his Peugeot. 'I'm in your hands, Inspector.'

Then, he turned, took Mylene in his arms. Savoy discreetly withdrew, saying he would wait in the hallway for Robbinet.

'Take Jason down to the car park,' Robbinet whispered in her ear. 'Take my attaché case with you and give him the contents just before you leave him.' He whispered the combination to her and she nodded.

She stared up at him, then she kissed him hard on the mouth and said, 'Godspeed, Jacques.'

For just an instant, his eyes opened wide in response. Then he was gone, and Mylene went quickly through the living room.

She called softly to Bourne, and he appeared. 'We must make the most of the advantage Jacques has given you.'

Bourne nodded. '*D'accord.*'

Mylene grabbed Robbinet's attaché case. 'Come now. We must hurry!'

She opened the front door, peered out to ensure that the way was clear, then led him down to the underground car park. She stopped just inside the metal-clad door. Peering through the wire-reinforced glass pane, she reported back to him. 'The car park looks clear, but be vigilant, you never know.'

She unlocked the attaché case, held out a packet. 'Here is the money you requested, along with your identity card and your orders. You're Pierre Montefort, a courier due to hand over top-secret documents to the military attaché in Budapest not later than eighteen hundred hours, local time.' She dropped a set of keys into Bourne's palm. 'A military motorcycle is parked in the third rank, next-to-last space on the right.'

For a moment, Bourne and Mylene stood looking at each other. He opened his mouth, but she spoke first, 'Remember, Jason, life is too short for regrets.'

Bourne left then, striding with ramrod-straight back through the door into a grim and gloomy place of naked concrete block and oil-stained macadam. He looked neither to the left nor right as he went down the car ranks. At the third one, he turned right. A moment later, he found the motorcycle, a silver Voxan VB-1, with a huge 996-cubic V2 engine. Bourne strapped his attaché case to the back, where it would be prominently displayed for the Quai d'Orsay to see. He found a helmet in the carry pack, stowed his hat. Climbing on, he walked the machine out of its parking spot, started the engine and wheeled out of the car park into the rain.

Justine Bérard had been thinking about her son, Yves, when she received the call from Inspector Savoy. These days it seemed as if the only way she could relate to Yves was through his video games. The first time she had beaten him in *Grand Theft Auto* by outmaneuvering his car with hers was the moment he had looked at her – and really seen her as a living, breathing human being, rather than the annoyance that cooked him food and washed his clothes. Ever since then, though, he'd been begging her to take him for a spin in her official car. So far, she had been successful in staving him off, but there was no doubt that he was wearing her down, not only because she was proud of her nerveless driving but because she desperately wanted Yves to be proud of her.

Following the call from Savoy, informing her that he had found Minister Robbinet and that they were escorting him back to Paris, she had immediately gotten things rolling, pulling the men off surveillance duty, directing them into standard VIP protection formation. Now she gestured to the Police Nationale standing by as Inspector Savoy escorted the Minister of Culture out the front door of the apartment building. At the same time, she checked the street for any sign of the insane assassin Jason Bourne.

Bérard was elated. It made no difference whether Inspector Savoy had found the minister in this maze of residences through cleverness or good fortune, she would benefit hugely, for it was she who had led Savoy here and it was she who would be in at the end when they brought Jacques Robbinet back to Paris safe and sound.

Savoy and Robbinet had crossed the street under the watchful eyes of the phalanx of policemen, machine pistols at the ready. She had Savoy's car door open, and as he passed her, he handed her the key to the minister's Peugeot.

As Robbinet ducked his head to get into the backseat of Savoy's car, Bérard heard the throaty roar of a powerful motorcycle engine. By the echo, it was coming from the car park below the building in which Savoy had found Minister Robbinet. She cocked her head, recognizing the roar of a Voxan VB-1. A military vehicle.

A moment later, she saw the courier accelerate out of the car park and she grabbed her cell phone. What was a military courier doing in Goussainville? Unconsciously, she was walking toward the minister's Peugeot. She barked out her Quai d'Orsay authorization code, asked to be patched through to Military Liaison. She had reached the Peugeot, unlocked it, slid behind the wheel. With the Code Rouge alert on, it did not take her long to receive the information she was seeking. There was currently no known military courier anywhere near Goussainville.

She started the car, jerked it into gear. Inspector Savoy's shout of query was drowned in the screech of the Peugeot's tires as she stood on the gas pedal, accelerating down the street in pursuit of the Voxan. She could only surmise that Bourne had been on to them, knew that he was trapped here unless he could make a quick escape.

The urgent CIA circular she had read had noted that he was able to change identity and appearance with astonishing rapidity. If he was the courier – and, really, when she thought about it, what other possibility was there? – then appre- hending or killing him would provide her career an entirely new trajectory. She could imagine the minister himself – so grateful for saving his life – interceding on her behalf, even, possibly, offering her the position of chief of his security.

In the meantime, though, she would have to bring down this faux courier. Lucky for her, the minister's car was far from a standard Peugeot sedan. Already she could feel the souped-up engine responding to the pressure she was putting on it as she slewed hard left around a corner, shot through a traffic light, passed a lum- bering truck on the wrong side. She ignored the indignant blare of its air horn. All of her being was concentrated on keeping the Voxan in sight.

At first Bourne couldn't believe that he'd been made so quickly, but as the Peugeot continued its dogged pursuit, he was forced to conclude that something had gone terribly wrong. He had seen the Quai d'Orsay taking Robbinet, knew one of their operatives was driving his car. His assumed identity wouldn't be enough to protect him now; he had to lose this tail permanently. He hunched over, weaving in and out of traffic, varying his speeds, the ways in which he overtook slower traffic. He took turns at dangerously acute angles, aware that at any instant he could go over and send the Voxan screaming onto its side. A glance in the side mirror confirmed that he was unable to shake the Peugeot. More ominously, it appeared to be gaining on him.

Though the Voxan wove in and out of traffic, though her car was less maneuver- able, Bérard kept closing the distance between them. She had flipped the special lever installed in all ministerial cars that made the head- and taillights flash, and this signal caused the more alert motorists to give way. In her head scrolled the increasingly more intricate and hair-raising scenarios of *Grand Theft Auto*. The scrolling of the streets, the vehicles she needed to pass or get around were astonish- ingly similar. Once, in order not to lose the Voxan, she had to make a split-second decision, running up onto the sidewalk. Pedestrians scattered from her path.

All at once, she saw the entrance to the A1 and knew this was where Bourne must be headed. Her best chance of getting him was before he made it onto the motorway. Biting her lip in grim intent, she drew on every last bit of power the Peugeot's engine could give her, closing the gap even more. The Voxan was only two cars away from her. She pulled out to the right, overtook one car, waved the other one back, its driver cowed as much by her aggressive driving as by the Peugeot's flashing lights.

Bérard was not one to waste an opportunity. They were coming up on the entrance; it was now or never. She manhandled the Peugeot up onto the sidewalk, aiming to approach Bourne on the offside so that in order to keep her in sight he would have to take his eyes off the road. At the speed they were both going, she knew he couldn't afford to do that. She rolled down her window, floored the accelerator and the car leaped forward into the wind-driven rain.

'Pull over!' she cried. 'I am Quai d'Orsay! Pull over or risk the consequences!'

The courier ignored her. Drawing her sidearm, she aimed it at his head. Her arm was straight, elbow locked. Tracking him with the gun's sight, she aimed at the leading edge of his silhouette. She squeezed the trigger.

But just as she did so, the Voxan swerved hard to their left, slipped in front of an oncoming car in the next lane, jumped the narrow concrete divider, shot through the oncoming traffic.

'My God!' Bérard breathed. 'He's headed onto the off-ramp!'

Even as she slewed the Peugeot around, she saw the Voxan threading its way between the traffic exiting the A1. Tires screeched, horns blared, terrified drivers shook their fists and cursed. Bérard noted these reactions with only part of her mind. The other part was engaged in driving through the stalled traffic, up over the median, across the street and onto the off-ramp herself.

She made it as far as the top of the ramp before she ran into a virtual wall of vehicles. She raced out into the rain, saw the Voxan accelerating between lanes of the oncoming traffic. Bourne's driving was astounding, but how long could he continue such perilous acrobatics?

The Voxan disappeared behind the silver oval cylinder of a tanker truck. Bérard sucked in her breath as she saw the huge eighteen-wheeler come barreling along in the adjacent lane. She heard the harsh sound of air brakes, then the Voxan struck the semi's massive radiator grille head-on, instantly erupting in a howling ball of oily flame.

# 12

Jason Bourne saw what he liked to call the convergence of opportunity set up right in front of him. He was running between two lanes of oncoming traffic. To his right was a tanker truck; to his left, a bit farther ahead, was a massive eighteen-wheeler. The choice was instinctual, there was no time for second thoughts. He committed his mind and his body to the convergence.

He lifted his legs and, for an instant, he was balanced on the Voxan's seat with only his left hand for support. He aimed the Voxan at the eighteen-wheeler barreling toward him on the left, then let go of the handlebar. Reaching out with his right hand, his fingers grasped hold of a rung of the skeletal metal ladder that rose up the tanker truck's curved side and he was jerked off the bike. Then his grip slipped on the rain-slick metal, and he was on the verge of being swept away like a twig in the wind. Tears welled up in his eyes at the pain that ripped through the same shoulder he'd strained outside the cargo hold of the plane. Both hands on the rung, he tightened his grip. As he swung fully onto the ladder, pressing himself against the tanker, the Voxan slammed into the eighteen-wheeler's radiator.

The tanker truck shuddered, rocking on its shocks as it hurtled through the ball of flame. Then it was past, rolling its way south toward Orly Airport and Bourne's freedom.

There were many reasons for Martin Lindros' swift and unerring rise up the Agency's slippery slope to become DDCI at the age of thirty-eight. He was smart, he came from the right schools, and he had the ability to keep his head even in a crisis. Moreover, his near-eidetic memory gave him a singular edge in keeping the administrative side of the CIA running smoothly. All important assets, no doubt – mandatory, in fact, for any successful DDCI. However, the DCI had chosen Lindros for an even more crucial reason: He was fatherless.

The DCI had known Martin Lindros' father well. For three years they had served together in Russia and Eastern Europe – until the elder Lindros had been killed in a car bomb attack. Martin Lindros had been twenty at the time and the effect on him had been incalculable. It was at the elder Lindros' funeral, while watching the young man's pale and pinched face, that the DCI knew he wanted to draw Martin Lindros into the same web that had so fascinated his father.

Approaching him had been easy; he'd been in a vulnerable place. The DCI had been primed to act, because his unerring instinct had recognized Martin Lindros' desire for revenge. The DCI had seen that the young man went to Georgetown upon his graduation from Yale. This served two purposes: It physically brought

Martin into his orbit, and it ensured he would take the requisite courses for the career path the DCI had chosen for him. The DCI himself had inducted the young man into the Agency, had overseen every phase of his training. And because he wanted to bind the young man to him for all time, he at last provided the revenge Martin so desperately sought – the name and address of the terrorist responsible for constructing the car bomb.

Martin Lindros had followed the DCI's instructions to the letter, showing a commendably steady hand when he had put a bullet between the terrorist's eyes. Had he actually been the one who had made the car bomb? Even the DCI couldn't be certain. But what difference did it make? He *was* a terrorist and in his day had made many car bombs. Now he was dead – one more terrorist disposed of – and Martin Lindros could sleep easy at night, knowing that he had avenged his father's murder.

'You see how Bourne fucked us,' Lindros was saying now. 'He was the one who called D.C. Metro as soon as he saw your cruisers. He knew you had no official jurisdiction in the district, unless you were working with the Agency.'

'Sadly, you've got that fucking-A right.' Detective Harris of the Virginia State Police nodded as he downed his sour mash whiskey. 'But now that the Frogs have him in their sights, maybe they'll have better luck running him to ground than we did.'

'They're Frogs,' Lindros said morosely.

'Even so, they've gotta be able to do something right sometime, no?'

Lindros and Harris were sitting in the Froggy Bottom Lounge on Pennsylvania Avenue. At this hour, the bar was filled with students from George Washington University. For more than an hour Lindros had been watching bare midriffs pierced by navel rings and pert buttocks almost tucked into short skirts nearly twenty years younger than he was. There came a time in a man's life, he thought, when he began looking in the rearview mirror and realizing that he was no longer young. None of these girls would give him a second look; they didn't even know he existed.

'Why is it,' he said, 'that a man can't stay young all his life?'

Harris laughed and called for more drinks.

'You think it's funny?'

They had passed beyond screaming at each other, beyond frosty silence, beyond snide and cutting remarks. In the end, they had said to hell with it and had decided to get drunk.

'Yeah, I think it's damn funny,' Harris said, making room for the new drinks. 'Here you are mooning over pussy, thinkin' life's passed you by. This isn't about pussy, Martin, though to tell you the truth, I never did pass up the opportunity to get laid.'

'Okay, smart guy, what *is* it about?'

'We lost, that's all. We got into Jason Bourne's game and he beat us six ways from Sunday. Not that he didn't have good reason to.'

Lindros sat up a little straighter, paid for the precipitate movement with a brief bout of vertigo. He put a hand to the side of his head. 'What the hell does that mean?'

Harris had a habit of swigging his whiskey around as if it was mouthwash.

His throat clicked when he swallowed. 'I don't think Bourne murdered Conklin and Panov.'

Lindros groaned. 'Jesus, Harry, not that again.'

'I'll say it till I'm blue in the face. What I want to know is why you don't wanna hear it.'

Lindros picked up his head. 'Okay, okay. Tell me why you think Bourne is innocent.'

'What's the point?'

'I'm asking you, aren't I?'

Harris seemed to consider. He shrugged, pulled out his wallet, extracted a slip of paper, which he unfolded on the table. 'Because of this parking ticket.'

Lindros picked the slip up, read it. 'This ticket is made out to a Dr. Felix Schiffer.' He shook his head in confusion.

'Felix Schiffer's a scofflaw,' Harris said. 'I wouldn't've known anything about him, but we're cracking down on scofflaws this month and one of my men couldn't get to first base with tracking him down.' He tapped the ticket. 'It took some doing, but I found out why my guy couldn't find him. Turns out that all of Schiffer's mail is being sent to Alex Conklin.'

Lindros shook his head. 'So?'

'So when I tried to run a database check on this Dr. Felix Schiffer, I ran up against a wall.'

Lindros felt his head starting to clear. 'What kind of a wall?'

'One put up by the United States Government.' Harris finished off his whiskey in a single toss, swish and swallow. 'This Dr. Schiffer's been put on ice with a capital *I*. I don't know what the hell Conklin was into, but it was hidden so deep I'll bet even his own people didn't know nothin' about it.' He shook his head. 'He wasn't killed by a rogue agent, Martin; on that I'll stake my life.'

As Stepan Spalko rode up the private elevator at Humanistas, Ltd., he was in as near to good spirits as he could get. Except for the unexpected development with Khan, everything was now back on track. The Chechens were his; they were intelligent, fearless and willing to die for their cause. As for Arsenov, he was, if nothing else, a dedicated and disciplined leader. This was why Spalko had chosen him to betray Khalid Murat. Murat had not quite trusted Spalko; he'd had a keen nose for duplicity. But now Murat was gone. Spalko had no doubt that the Chechens would perform as he envisioned. On the other front, the damnable Alexander Conklin was dead and the CIA was convinced Jason Bourne was his murderer, two birds with one stone. Still, there was the core issue of the weapon and of Felix Schiffer. He felt the intense pressure of what still needed to be done. He knew that he was running out of time; there was much yet to be accomplished.

He got off at a mid-level floor accessible only with a magnetic key he wore. Letting himself into his sun-splashed living quarters, he crossed to the bank of windows overlooking the Danube, the deep green of Margaret Island, the city beyond. He stood staring out at the Houses of Parliament, thinking of the time to come, when undreamed-of power would be his. Sunlight spun off the medieval facade, the flying buttresses, the domes and spires. Inside, men of power met daily, prattling inconsequentially. His chest filled with air. It was he, Spalko, who knew where the real power in this world resided. He held out his hand, clenched it into a fist. Soon they would all know – the American president in his White House, the Russian president in the Kremlin, the sheiks in their magnificent Arabian palaces. Soon they would all know the true meaning of fear.

Naked, he padded into the large, opulent bathroom whose tiles were the color of lapis lazuli. Beneath eight streaming jets, he took a shower, scrubbing himself until his skin turned red. Then he dried himself with a thick white oversized Turkish towel and changed into jeans and a denim shirt.

At a gleaming stainless-steel wet-bar, he drew a cup of freshly brewed coffee from the automatic maker. He added cream and sugar, a dollop of whipped cream from the half-fridge below. For several moments thereafter, he stood sipping the coffee, allowing his mind to go pleasurably out of focus, allowing the anticipation to build. There were so many wonderful things to look forward to today!

Setting down the coffee cup, he tied on a butcher's apron. He eschewed his loafers, polished to a wicked shine, for a pair of green rubber garden boots.

Sipping the delicious coffee, he crossed to a wood-paneled wall. There was a small table with one drawer, which he pulled open. Inside was a box of latex gloves. Humming to himself, he drew out a pair, snapped them on. Then he pressed a button and two of the wood panels slid aside. He stepped through into a decidedly odd room. The walls were of black concrete; the floor was composed of white tiles, lower in the center where a huge drain was set. A hose on a reel was attached to one wall. The ceiling was heavily baffled. The only furniture was a wooden table, scarred, stained dark in places with blood, and a dentist's chair with modifications made to Spalko's exacting specifications. Beside the chair was a three-tiered cart on which lay a gleaming array of metal implements barbed with ominous-looking ends – straight, hooked and corkscrewed.

In the chair, his wrists and ankles bound in steel cuffs, was László Molnar, as naked as the day he was born. Molnar's face and body were cut, bruised and swollen, his eyes sunk deep within black circles of agony and despair.

Spalko entered the room as briskly and professionally as any doctor. 'My dear László, I must say you're looking the worse for wear.' He stood close enough to see Molnar's nostrils flare at the scent of the coffee. 'It's to be expected, though, isn't it? You've had quite a difficult night. Nothing you could have expected when you set out for the opera, eh? But not to worry, the excitement isn't over yet.' He put down the coffee cup at Molnar's elbow, took up one of the instruments. 'This one, I think, yes.'

'What . . . what are you going to do?' Molnar asked in a cracked voice, thin as parchment.

'Where is Dr. Schiffer?' Spalko asked in a conversational tone of voice.

Molnar's head jerked from side to side, his jaw clamped shut, as if to ensure that no words would pass his lips.

Spalko tested the needlepoint of the instrument. 'I honestly don't know why you hesitate, László. I have the weapon, though Dr. Schiffer is missing – '

'Taken from under your nose,' Molnar whispered.

Spalko, smiling, applied the instrument to his prisoner and in short order Molnar was sufficiently stimulated to scream.

Standing back for a moment, he brought the coffee cup to his lips, swallowed.

'As you've no doubt realized by now, this room is soundproof. You can't be heard – no one is going to save you, least of all Vadas; he doesn't even know that you're missing.'

Taking up another instrument, he spun it into Molnar. 'So you see there is no hope,' he said. 'Unless you tell me what I want to know. As it happens, László, I'm your one and only friend now; I'm the one who can save you.' He grasped Molnar under the chin and kissed his bloody forehead. 'I'm the one who truly loves you.'

Molnar closed his eyes and again shook his head.

Spalko looked directly into Molnar's eyes. 'I don't want to hurt you, László. You know that, don't you?' His voice, unlike his actions, was gentle. 'But your stubbornness troubles me.' He continued his work on Molnar. 'I am wondering whether you understand the true nature of the circumstances into which you've fallen. This pain you feel is Vadas' doing. It's Vadas who got you into these dire straits. Conklin, too, I shouldn't wonder, but Conklin is dead.'

Molnar's mouth opened wide in a terrible scream. There were gaping black holes where his teeth had been slowly and agonizingly pulled.

'Let me assure you that I continue my work most reluctantly,' Spalko said with great concentration. It was important at this stage for Molnar to understand, even through the pain being inflicted on him. 'I'm only the instrument of your own stubbornness. Can't you see that it's Vadas who must pay for this?'

Spalko let up for a moment. Blood had splattered his gloves and he was breathing as hard as if he had just run up three flights of stairs. Interrogation, for all its pleasures, was not easy work. Molnar began to mewl.

'Why do you bother, László? You are praying to a god that doesn't exist and, therefore, can't protect you or help you. As the Russians say, "Pray to God; row to shore."' Spalko's smile was an intimation of a confidence shared between comrades. 'And the Russians ought to know, eh? Their history is written in blood. First the tsars and then the apparatchiks, as if the Party was any better than a line of despots!

'I tell you, László, the Russians may have failed utterly at politics, but when it comes to religion, they have the right idea. Religion – all religion – is false. It's the grand delusion of the weak-willed, the fearful, the sheep of the world, who haven't the strength to lead but want only to be led. Never mind that it's inevitably to their own slaughter.' Spalko shook his head sadly, sagely. 'No, no, the only reality is power, László. Money and power. This is what matters, nothing else.'

Molnar had relaxed somewhat during this discourse, which, in its conversational tone and illusion of camaraderie, had been meant to bind him to his interrogator. Now, however, his eyes opened wide in naked panic as Spalko began again. 'Only you can help yourself, László. Tell me what I want to know. Tell me where Vadas has hidden Felix Schiffer.'

'Stop!' Molnar gasped. 'Please stop!'

'I can't stop, László. Surely by now you can understand that. You're in control of this situation now.' As if to illustrate his point, Spalko applied the instrument. 'Only you can make me stop!'

A look of confusion came over Molnar, and he gazed wildly around as if only now realizing what was happening to him. Studying him, Spalko understood. It often happened this way near the end of a successful interrogation. The subject did not come step by step to the altar of confession, but rather resisted as long as he was able. The mind could manage only so much. As some point, like a stretched rubber band, it reached its limit, and when it snapped back, a new reality – the reality artfully erected by the interrogator – was established.

'I don't – '

'Tell me,' Spalko said in a velvet voice, his gloved hand stroking his victim's sweating brow. 'Tell me and this will all be over, gone like awaking from a dream.'

Molnar's eyes rolled upward. 'Do you promise?' he asked like a small child.

'Trust me. László. I'm your friend. I want what you want, an end to your suffering.'

Molnar was crying now, big tears welling up in his eyes, turning cloudy and pink as they rolled down his cheeks. And then he began to sob as he had not done since he was a small child.

Spalko said nothing. He knew they were at the crucial stage. It was all or nothing now: Either Molnar would step off the precipice to which Spalko had carefully brought him, or he would force himself to drown in the pain.

Molnar's body shook in the storm of emotion the interrogation had unleashed. In time, he put his head back. His face was gray and terribly drawn; his eyes still with their glaze of tears seemed to have shrunk farther back in their sockets. There was no sign of the bright-cheeked, slightly drunk operaphile Spalko's men had drugged in Underground. He had been transformed. He was utterly spent.

'God forgive me,' he whispered hoarsely. 'Dr. Schiffer is in Crete.' He babbled an address.

'There's a good boy,' Spalko said softly. Now the final piece of the puzzle had fallen into place. Tonight, he and his 'staff' would be on their way to retrieve Felix Schiffer and finish the process of extracting from him the information required to launch their assault on the Oskjuhlid Hotel.

Molnar made a small animal noise as Spalko dropped the instrument. His bloodshot eyes rolled in his head; he was on the verge of weeping again.

Slowly, tenderly, Spalko placed the coffee cup to the other's lips, watched with disinterest as he convulsively drank down the hot, sweet coffee. 'At last, deliverance.' Whether he was speaking to Molnar or to himself was an open question.

# 13

At night, Budapest's Parliament resembled a great Magyar shield against the invading hordes of yore. To the average tourist, awestruck at its size as well as its beauty, it appeared solid, timeless, inviolable. But to Jason Bourne, newly arrived from his harrowing passage out of Washington, D.C., and Paris, the Parliament seemed nothing more than a fantasy city straight out of a children's book, a confection of unearthly white stone and pale copper that could at any moment collapse beneath the fall of darkness.

He was in a bleak mood when the taxi dropped him at the glowing dome of the Mammut shopping mall, near Moszkva tér, where he intended to buy himself new clothes. He had entered the country as Pierre Montefort, French military courier, and had therefore been given only the most cursory inspection by Hungarian Immigration. But he needed to get rid of the uniform Jacques had provided for him before he showed up at the hotel as Alex Conklin.

He bought a pair of cords, a Sea Island cotton shirt and black turtleneck sweater, thin-soled black boots and a black leather bomber jacket. He moved through the stores, the crowds of shoppers, gradually absorbing their energy, for the first time in many days feeling part of the world at large. He realized this sudden lightening of mood was because his mind had resolved the enigma of Khan. Of course, he wasn't Joshua; he was a superb con artist. An entity unknown – either Khan or someone who had hired him – wanted to get to Bourne, shake him up so badly that he would lose his concentration and forget about the murders of Alex Conklin and Mo Panov. If they weren't able to kill him, then at least they would make him go off on a wild goose chase searching for his phantom son. How Khan or whoever had hired him knew about Joshua was another question he needed to answer. Still, now that he had reduced the shock to a rational problem, his supremely logical mind could parse the problem into its separate parts and this would lead him to devising a plan of attack.

Bourne needed information that only Khan could provide. He needed to turn the tables on Khan, to draw him into a trap. The first step was to ensure that Khan knew where he was. He had no doubt that Khan would be in Paris by now, having known the destination of the Rush Service flight. Khan might even have heard about Bourne's 'death' on the A1. In fact, from what he knew of Khan, he was, like Bourne, an accomplished chameleon. If Bourne were in his place, the first place he'd look for information was the Quai d'Orsay.

Twenty minutes later Bourne strode out of the mall complex, got into a taxi that was letting off a passenger, and in no time he was in front of the imposing stone portico of the Danubius Grand Hotel on Margaret Island. A uniformed doorman escorted him inside.

Bourne, feeling as if he hadn't slept in a week, crossed the gleaming marble foyer. He introduced himself to the front desk clerk as Alexander Conklin.

'Ah, Mr. Conklin, you're expected. Please wait a moment, won't you?'

The man vanished into an inner office out of which, a moment later, emerged the hotel manager.

'Welcome, welcome! I'm Mr. Hazas and I'm at your disposal.' This gentleman was short, squat and dark, with a pencil mustache and hair parted down the side. He extended a hand, which was warm and dry. 'Mr. Conklin, such a pleasure.' He gestured. 'Would you be so good as to come with me, please?'

He led Bourne through into his office, whereupon he opened a safe, extracting a package roughly the size and shape of a shoebox, which he had Bourne sign for. On the wrapping was printed ALEXANDER CONKLIN. HOLD FOR PICK-UP. There were no stamps.

'The package was hand-delivered,' the manager said in response to Bourne's query.

'By whom?' Bourne asked.

Mr. Hazas spread his hands. 'I'm afraid I don't know.'

Bourne felt a sudden flush of anger. 'What do you mean, you don't know? Surely, the hotel must keep records of delivered packages.'

'Oh, assuredly, Mr. Conklin. As in everything, we are meticulous in this area. However, in this particular case – and I cannot say how – there appears to be no record whatsoever.' He smiled hopefully even as he shrugged helplessly.

After three days of constantly fighting for his life, of having to absorb shock after shock, he found he had no reservoir of patience left. Anger and frustration flared into blind rage. Kicking the door shut, he grabbed Hazas up by his heavily starched shirtfront, slammed him so hard against the wall, the hotel manager's eyes fairly bugged out of his head.

'Mr. Conklin,' he stammered, 'I don't – '

'I want answers!' Bourne shouted, 'and I want them now!'

Mr. Hazas, clearly terrified, was fairly weeping. 'But I have no answers.' His blunt fingers fluttered. 'There . . . there's the ledger! See for yourself!'

Bourne released the hotel manager, whose legs collapsed immediately, depositing him on the floor. Bourne ignored him, went to his desk, took up the ledger. He could see the entries laboriously written out in two distinct handwritings, one crimped, the other fussy – presumably the day and night managers. He was only mildly surprised to learn that he could read Hungarian. Turning the ledger a bit, he ran his eye up and down the columns, looking for any erasures, any hint that the ledger had been tampered with. He found nothing.

He whirled on Mr. Hazas, hauled him up from his curled position. 'How do you account for this package not being logged in?'

'Mr. Conklin, I myself was here when it was delivered.' The hotel manager's eyes showed their whites all around. His skin had gone pale; it crawled with sweat. 'That is to say, I was on duty. I swear to you one moment it was there on the top of the check-in counter. It simply appeared. I didn't see the person who brought it and neither did anyone on my staff. It was noon, check-out time, a very busy period for us. It must have been left anonymously, deliberately – nothing else makes sense.'

He was right, of course. In an instant, Bourne's intense rage drained away, leaving him wondering why he had so terrorized this perfectly harmless man. He let the hotel manager go.

'My apologies, Mr. Hazas. It's been a long day and I've had a number of difficult negotiations.'

'Yes, sir.' Mr. Hazas was doing his best to straighten his tie and jacket, all the while eyeing Bourne as if at any moment he might launch another attack. 'Of course, sir. The business world puts strains on all of us.' He coughed, regaining a semblance of his composure. 'May I suggest a spa treatment – there's nothing like a steam and massage to restore the inner balance.'

'That's very kind of you,' Bourne said. 'Perhaps later.'

'The spa closes at nine o'clock,' Mr. Hazas said, relieved that he had gotten a sane response from this madman. 'But it only takes a call from me to keep it open for you.'

'Another time, thanks very much. Please have a toothbrush and paste sent up to the suite. I forget to bring some,' Bourne said, opening the door and walking out.

The moment he was left alone, Hazas opened a drawer in his desk and, with a hand that trembled terribly, he took out a bottle of schnapps. Filling a shotglass, he spilled some onto his ledger. He didn't care; he swigged it down, felt the liquor burn its fiery path into his stomach. When he had calmed himself sufficiently, he picked up the phone, dialed a local number.

'He arrived not ten minutes ago,' he said to the voice at the other end. There was no need to identify himself. 'My impression? He's a madman. I'll tell you what I mean. He almost choked me to death when I wouldn't tell him who delivered the package.'

The receiver slipped in the sweat of his palm and he switched hands. He poured himself another two fingers of schnapps.

'Of course I didn't tell him, and there's no record of the delivery anywhere. I saw to it myself. He searched carefully enough, I'll give him that.' He listened for a moment. 'He went up to his suite. Yes, I'm sure.'

He put down the phone, then just as quickly dialed another number, delivered the same message, this time to a different and far more terrifying master. Finally, he slumped back in his chair and closed his eyes. *Thank God my part in this is over,* he thought.

Bourne took the elevator up to the top floor. The key opened one of the double doors of solid polished teak, and Bourne walked into a large one-bedroom suite furnished in sumptuous fabrics. Outside the window, the one-hundred-year-old parkland loomed dark and leafy. The island had been named after Margaret, the daughter of King Bela IV who lived in a Dominican convent here during the thirteenth century, the ruins of which were brightly lit on the east bank. He was already undressing as he went through the suite, dropping each article of clothing behind him as he made for the gleaming bathroom. He threw the package down on the bed unopened.

He spent ten blessed minutes naked under a spray of water as hot as he could tolerate, then he soaped up, scrubbing the accumulated grime and sweat off him. Gingerly, he tested his ribs, the muscles of his chest, seeking a final assessment of the damage Khan had inflicted on him. His right shoulder was very sore, and he spent another ten minutes carefully stretching and gently exercising it. He had nearly dislocated it when he had grabbed the tanker truck's rung, and it hurt like hell. He suspected that he had torn some ligaments, but there was nothing he could do about it except try not to overwork the area.

After standing under an icy spray for three minutes, he stepped out of the shower and toweled off. Wrapped in a luxurious bathrobe, he sat on the bed, unwrapped the package. Inside was a gun with extra ammunition. *Alex*, he asked, not for the first time, *what in the world were you involved in?*

For a long time, he sat staring at the weapon. There seemed something evil about it, a darkness seeping out of the barrel. And it was then that Bourne realized that the darkness was bubbling up from the depths of his own unconscious. All at once, he saw that his reality was not at all as he had imagined it at the Mammut mall. It wasn't neat and orderly, rational as a mathematical equation. The real world was chaotic; rationality was merely the system human beings tried to impose on random events in order to make them appear orderly. His explosion of rage was not at the hotel manager, he realized with something of a shock, but at Khan. Khan had shadowed him, bedeviled him, and in the end had tricked him. He wanted nothing less than to pummel that face into the ground, to expunge it from his memory.

The sight of the Buddha had caused the four-year-old Joshua to appear in his mind's eye. It was twilight in Saigon, the sky saffron and greenish-gold. Joshua was running out of the house by the river as David Webb drew up on his return from work. Webb took Joshua up in his arms, swung him around, kissed his cheeks, though the boy shied away. He never did like being kissed by his father.

Bourne now saw his son tucked into bed at night. The crickets and tree frogs were singing and lights from passing boats swept across the far wall of the room. Joshua was listening as Webb read him a story. On a Saturday morning Webb played catch with Joshua, using a baseball he had brought all the way from America. The light struck Joshua's innocent face, turning it incandescent.

Now Bourne blinked and despite himself he saw the small stone Buddha hanging around Khan's neck. He leaped up, and with a guttural cry of utter despair flung the lamp, blotter, writing pad, crystal ashtray off the table. Hands balled into fists, he struck himself repeatedly in the head. With a moan of despair, he fell to his knees, rocking himself. Only the phone ringing brought him around.

Viciously, he willed his head to clear. The phone kept on ringing and for a moment he had the urge to let it ring. Instead, he picked it up. 'It's János Vadas,' came a whispered, smoke-roughened voice. 'Matthias Church. Midnight, not a moment later.' The line clicked dead before Bourne could utter a word.

When Khan learned that Jason Bourne was dead, he felt as if he'd been turned inside out, as if all the nerves inside him had for one instant been exposed to the corrosive outside air. He touched the back of his hand to his forehead, certain that he was burning up from the inside out.

He was in Orly Airport, talking with the Quai d'Orsay. It had been ridiculously easy to get information from them. He was posing as a reporter from *Le Monde*, the French newspaper, whose credentials he had obtained – for an obscene price – from his Parisian contact. Not that it mattered to him; he had more money than he knew what to do with, but the time involved waiting had somehow put him on edge. As the minutes dragged into hours, as the afternoon turned into evening, he had realized that his vaunted patience had been shredded. The moment he had seen David Webb – Jason Bourne – time had been turned inside out, the past had become the present. His hands clenched into fists and a pulse beat strongly in his temple; how many times since sighting Bourne had he felt as if he was losing his mind? The absolute worst moment had been sitting on the bench in Old Town Alexandria, speaking to him as if there was nothing between them, as if the past had been rendered moot and meaningless, as if it had been part of someone else's life, someone Khan had only imagined. The unreality of it – a moment he had dreamed of, prayed for for years – had eviscerated him, leaving him feeling as if every nerve-ending had been rubbed raw, every emotion he had spent years trying to harness and suppress was now rebelling, rising to the surface, sickening him. And now came this news, like a hammerblow from heaven. He felt as if the void inside him he assumed would be filled had only become wider, deeper, threatening to swallow him whole. He could not bear to be here a moment longer.

One moment he was talking, notepad in hand, with the Quai d'Orsay press liaison and the next moment he was hurtled back in time to the jungles of Vietnam, to the wood and bamboo house of Richard Wick, the missionary, a tall, slender man with a somber demeanor who had taken him from out of the wild after he'd escaped from the Vietnamese gunrunner he'd killed. Nevertheless, he was quick to laughter and there was a softness to his brown eyes that spoke of a great sympathy. Wick might have been a tough taskmaster in converting the heathen Khan into a child of Christ, but in the more intimate time of dinner and its quiet aftermath, he was kind and gentle and, in the end, provoked Khan's trust.

So much so, that one evening Khan made up his mind to tell Wick about his past, to lay bare his soul in order that he be healed. Khan desperately wanted to be healed, to vomit up the abscess that had been churning its poison inside him as it grew ever larger. He wanted to confess his rage at his abandonment, he wanted to be rid of it, for he had lately come to understand that he was being held prisoner by his extreme emotions.

He longed to confide in Wick, to describe to him the roil of emotion churning in his guts, but the opportunity never arose. Wick was extremely busy bringing the Word of God to 'this forlorn Godless backwater.' As such, he sponsored Bible study groups of which Khan was ordered to be a part. In fact, one of Wick's favorite pastimes involved calling on Khan to rise in front of this group and recite from memory sections of the Bible, like some form of idiot savant shown off for money at a carnival side show.

Khan hated it, felt humiliated by it. In fact, strange to say, the more proud of him Wick seemed the greater his humiliation. Until, one day, the missionary brought in another young boy. But because the boy was Caucasian, the orphan of a missionary couple of Wick's acquaintance, Wick lavished the love and attention on him that Khan had craved and now saw that he'd never had and, worse, never would have. Still, his abominable recitations continued while the other boy sat and watched, silent, free of the humiliation that racked Khan.

He could never get over the fact of Wick using him, and it was only on the day he ran away that he understood the depths of Wick's betrayal of him. His benefactor, his protector, was not interested in *him* – in Khan – but rather in adding another convert, bringing another savage into the light of God's love.

At that moment, his cell phone rang, and he was dragged back into the awful present. He looked at his phone's screen to see who was calling, then, excusing himself, stepped away from the Quai d'Orsay officer into the swirling anonymity of the concourse proper.

'This is a surprise,' he said into his phone.

'Where are you?' Stepan Spalko's voice sounded curt, as if he had too many things on his mind.

'Orly Airport. I've just learned from the Quai d'Orsay that David Webb is dead.'

'Is that so?'

'It seems he rode a motorcycle into the grille of an oncoming truck.' Khan paused for a moment, waiting for a reaction. 'I must say you don't sound happy. Isn't that what you wanted?'

'It's premature to celebrate Webb's death, Khan,' Spalko said dryly. 'I've heard from my contact at the desk of the Danubius Grand Hotel here in Budapest that Alexander Conklin just checked in.'

Khan was so shocked that he felt his knees begin to give out, and he walked to a wall, leaned against it. 'Webb?'

'It isn't Alex Conklin's ghost!'

To his chagrin, he discovered that he'd broken out into a cold sweat. 'But how can you be sure it's him?'

'I got a description from my contact. I've seen the composite drawing that's been circulated.'

Khan gritted his teeth. He knew the conversation would likely lead to a bad end, and yet he saw himself moving inexorably forward. 'You knew David Webb was Jason Bourne. Why didn't you tell me?'

'I don't see why I needed to,' Spalko said blandly. 'You asked about Webb and I delivered. I'm not in the habit of reading people's minds. But I applaud your initiative.'

Khan was gripped by a spasm of hatred so strong he felt himself shiver. He kept his voice calm, however. 'Now that Bourne's gotten all the way to Budapest, how long do you think it will take him to follow his leads back to you?'

'I've already taken steps to ensure that doesn't happen,' Spalko said. 'But it occurs to me that I wouldn't have needed to go through the trouble if you'd killed the sonuvabitch when you had the chance.'

Khan, distrustful of a man who had lied to him, who had, furthermore, played him for a cat's-paw, felt another devastating stab of anger. Spalko wanted him to kill Bourne, but why? He was going to find that out before he completed his own act of vengeance. When he spoke next, he'd lost a modicum of his icy self-control so that his voice took on a decidedly sharp edge. 'Oh, I'll kill Bourne,' he said. 'But it'll be on *my* terms, according to *my* timetable, not yours.'

*

Humanistas, Ltd. owned three hangars at Ferihegy Airport. In one of them, a container truck was backed up to a small jet on whose curving silver fuselage was painted the Humanistas logo: The green cross held in the palm of a hand. Uniformed men were loading the last of the weapons crates on board while Hasan Arsenov checked the manifest. When he went to talk to one of the workers, Stepan Spalko turned to Zina and in a conversational voice said, 'In just a few hours I'm leaving for Crete. I want you to come with me.'

Zina's eyes opened wide in surprise. 'Shaykh, I am scheduled to return with Hasan to Chechnya in order to make the last-minute preparations for our mission.'

Spalko's eyes did not leave hers. 'Arsenov doesn't need your help with the final touches. In fact, in my estimation he'll be better off without the . . . distraction of having you around.'

Zina, trapped by his gaze, opened her lips.

'I want to make this absolutely clear, Zina.' Spalko saw Arsenov coming back toward them. 'I'm not giving you an order. The decision's entirely up to you.'

Despite the urgency of the moment, he spoke slowly and distinctly, and the import of his words wasn't lost on her. He was offering her an opportunity – for what she had no idea – but it was clear that this was a defining moment in her life. Either choice she made, there was no going back; by the manner in which he'd spoken to her, he'd made that quite clear. The decision might be up to her, but she was certain that if she said no, it would be the end for her in one way or another. The fact was, she didn't want to say no.

'I've always wanted to see Crete,' she whispered as Arsenov came up to them.

Spalko nodded to her. Then turned to the Chechen terrorist leader. 'Everything accounted for?'

Arsenov looked up from his clipboard. 'How could it be otherwise, Shaykh?' He checked his watch. 'Zina and I will be taking off within the hour.'

'Actually, Zina will be accompanying the arms,' Spalko said easily. 'The shipment is due to rendezvous with my fishing boat in the Faeroe Islands. I want one of you there to oversee the transfer and the last leg of the trip to Iceland. You're needed with your unit.' He smiled. 'I've no doubt that you can spare Zina for a few days' time.'

Arsenov frowned, glanced at Zina, who smartly met his gaze with a neutral look, then nodded. 'It will be as you wish, Shaykh, of course.'

Zina found it interesting that the Shaykh had lied to Hasan about his plans for her. She found herself bound inside the little conspiracy he had woven, both excited and nervous with anticipation. She saw the look on Hasan's face and part of her felt a pang, but then she thought of the mystery awaiting her, and the honey of the Shaykh's voice, '*I'm leaving for Crete. I want you to come with me.*'

Standing beside Zina, Spalko held out his arm and Arsenov gripped his forearm in the manner of warriors. '*La illaha ill Allah.*'

'*La illaha ill Allah,*' Arsenov replied, bowing his head.

'There's a limousine waiting outside to take you to the passenger terminal. Until Reykjavík, my friend.' Spalko turned away, walked over to the pilot to speak with him a moment, leaving Zina to say her farewell to her current lover.

Khan felt ravaged by unfamiliar emotions. Forty minutes later, waiting for the flight to Budapest to board, he still had not gotten over the shock he'd received on learning that Jason Bourne was, in fact, alive. He sat, elbows on knees, face in his hands, trying – and failing miserably – to make sense of the world. To someone like him, whose past informed every moment of his present, it was impossible to find a pattern that could make things understandable. The past was a mystery – and his memory of it was a whore that did the bidding of his subconscious, distorting facts, telescoping events or omitting them altogether, all in the service of the sac of poison growing inside him.

But these emotions running rampant through him were even more devastating. He was enraged by the fact that he'd needed Stepan Spalko to tell him that Jason Bourne was still alive. Why hadn't his normally finely tuned instincts told him to check a little deeper? Would an agent of Bourne's skills run into the grille of an oncoming truck? And where was the body? Had there been a proper identification? He'd been told they were still sifting through the remains, that the explosion and subsequent fire had done so much damage that it would take hours more, if not days, to make sense of it all, and even then, there might not be enough found to give them a confirming ID. He should have been suspicious. It was a ploy he would use – in fact, he had employed a variant three years ago when he needed to make a very hot exit from the docks in Singapore.

But there was another question running over and over in his mind, and though he'd been trying to block it out, he couldn't. What had he felt at the precise moment of knowing that Jason Bourne was still alive? Elation? Fear? Rage? Despair? Or was it a melange of all of these – a sickening kaleidoscope that ran the gamut and back again?

He heard his flight being called, and in something of a daze, he joined the line to board.

Spalko, walking past the entrance to the Eurocenter Bio-I Clinic at 75 Hattyu utca, was deep in thought. It appeared as if Khan was going to present a problem. Khan had his uses; he was better than anyone else at eliminating targets, there could be no debate on that score, but even that rare talent faded against the danger he felt Khan was becoming. This very question had been much on his mind ever since the first time Khan had failed to kill Jason Bourne. Something anomalous in the situation had stuck in his craw like a fish bone, and ever since, he'd been trying to cough it up or to swallow it. And yet, there it still sat, refusing to be dislodged. With this last conversation, he was acutely aware that he'd need to see to the final disposition of his former assassin-for-hire without delay. He couldn't afford anyone getting close to his forthcoming operation in Reykjavík. Bourne or Khan, it didn't matter now. In this regard, they were both equally dangerous.

He entered the café around the corner from the ugly modernist structure of the clinic. He smiled into the bland face of the man, tilted slightly up at him now.

'Sorry, Peter,' he said as he slid into a chair at their table.

Dr. Peter Sido raised a hand equably. 'It's of no moment, Stepan. I know how busy you are.'

'Not too busy to find Dr. Schiffer.'

'And thank God for that!' Sido ladled whipped cream into his coffee cup. He shook his head. 'Honestly, Stepan, I don't know how I'd do without you and your contacts. When I discovered that Felix was missing, I was ready to lose my mind.'

'Don't worry, Peter. Every day we're closer to finding him. Trust me.'

'Oh, I do.' Sido was in all ways physically unremarkable. He was of middle height and weight with eyes the color of mud, magnified behind steel-rimmed spectacles, and short brown hair that seemed to fall across his scalp with no design or attention from him. He wore a brown herringbone tweed suit, slightly shabby at the cuffs, white shirt and a brown-and-black tie that was at least a decade out of date. He might have been a salesman or an undertaker, but he was not, for his unremarkable exterior concealed a most remarkable mind.

'The question I have for you,' Spalko said now, 'is whether you have the product for me.'

Sido was apparently expecting the question because he nodded immediately. 'It's all synthesized and ready whenever you need it.'

'Did you bring it?'

'Just the sample. The rest is safely locked away in the Bio-I Clinic's cold room. And don't worry about the sample; it's locked in a travel case I made myself. The product is extremely delicate. You see, up until the moment it's to be used, it must be kept at minus thirty-two degrees Celsius. The case I constructed has its own integrated cooling unit that will last for forty-eight hours.' He reached beneath the table, brought up a small metal box more or less the size of two stacked paperback books. 'Is that long enough?'

'Quite enough, thank you.' Spalko took possession of the box. It was heavier than it looked, no doubt owing to the refrigeration unit. 'It's in the vial I specified?'

'Of course.' Sido sighed. 'I still don't fully understand why you need such a lethal pathogen.'

Spalko studied him for a moment. He took out a cigarette and lit it. He knew that to come up with an explanation too quickly would spoil the effect, and with Dr. Peter Sido effect was everything. Though he was a genius at creating airborne pathogens, the good doctor's people skills left something to be desired. Not that he was much different from most scientists with their noses in their beakers, but in this case, Sido's naïveté suited Spalko's purposes perfectly. He wanted his friend back, nothing else much mattered, which was why he wouldn't listen too carefully to Spalko's explanation. It was his conscience that needed reassuring, nothing more.

Spalko spoke at last. 'As I said, I was contacted by the joint American–British Anti-Terrorist Task Force.'

'Will they be at the summit next week?'

'Of course,' Spalko lied. There was no joint American–British Anti-Terrorist Task Force except for the one he had concocted. 'In any case, they're on the verge of a breakthrough against the threat of bioterrorism, which, as you know better than most, includes lethal airborne pathogens as well as chemical substances. They need to test it, which is why they came to me, and why we've made this agreement. I find Dr. Schiffer for you and you provide the product the task force needs.'

'Yes, I know all that. You explained . . .' Sido's voice trailed off. He played nervously with his spoon, drumming it up and down against his napkin until Spalko asked him to stop.

'Sorry,' he mumbled and pushed his spectacles back up the bridge of his nose. 'But what I still don't understand is what they're going to do with the product. I mean, you mentioned a test of some sort.'

Spalko leaned forward. Now was the crucial time; he had to sell Sido. He looked to his left and right. When he spoke, he lowered his voice considerably. 'Listen very carefully. Peter. I've told you more than I perhaps should have. This is all most top-secret, d'you see?'

Sido, hunched forward in response, nodded his head.

'In fact, I'm afraid that I've violated the confidentiality agreement they made me sign just by telling you this much.'

'Oh, dear.' Sido's expression was mournful. 'I've put you at risk.'

'Please don't worry about that, Peter. I'll be fine,' Spalko said. 'Unless, of course, you tell someone.'

'Oh, but I wouldn't. Never.'

Spalko smiled. 'I know you wouldn't, Peter. I trust you, you see.'

'And I appreciate that, Stepan. You know I do.'

Spalko had to bite his lip in order not to laugh. Instead, he dove deeper into this farce. 'I don't know what the test is, Peter, because they haven't told me,' he said so softly that the other was obliged to lean in so close their noses were almost touching. 'And I wouldn't ask.'

'Of course not.'

'But I believe – and you must also – that these people are doing their utmost to keep us safe in an increasingly unsafe world.' What it always boiled down to, Spalko thought, was a matter of trust. But for the patsy – in this case, Sido – to be taken in, he had to know that *you* had given *him* your trust. After that, you could fleece him of everything he owned and he'd never suspect it was you who'd done it to him. 'I say, whatever they have to do, we must help them in any way we can. This is what I told them when they first approached me.'

'It's what I would've told them, as well.' Sido wiped the perspiration off his unremarkable upper lip. 'Believe me, Stepan, if you can count on anything you can count on that.'

The U.S. Naval Observatory at Massachusetts Avenue and 34th Street was the official source for all standard time in the United States. It was one of the few places in the country where the moon, the stars and the planets were kept under constant observation. The largest telescope on the property was more than one hundred years old and was still in use. Peering through it in 1877, Dr. Asaph Hall discovered the two moons of Mars. Nobody knows why he chose to call them Deimos (Anxiety) and Phobos (Fear), but the DCI knew that when his melancholia lay most deeply about him, he was drawn to the observatory. That was why he'd had an office set up for himself deep in the heart of the building, not far from Dr. Hall's telescope.

It was here that Martin Lindros found him on a closed-circuit teleconference linkup with Jamie Hull, head of the U.S. security detail in Reykjavík.

'Feyd al-Saoud I'm not concerned with,' Hull was saying in his rather supercilious voice. 'The Arabs don't know shit about modern-day security, so they're happy to take our lead.' He shook his head. 'It's the Russian, Boris Illyich Karpov, who's giving me a royal pain in the ass. He questions everything. If I say white, he says black. I think the fucker gets off on arguing.'

'Are you saying you can't handle one goddamn Russian security analyst, Jamie?'

'Uh, what?' Hull's blue eyes looked startled and his ginger mustache jumped up and down. 'No, sir. Not at all.'

'Because I can have you replaced in a heartbeat.' The DCI's voice projected a thorny note of cruelty.

'No, sir.'

'And believe me, I will. I'm in no fucking mood for – '

'That won't be necessary. I'll get Karpov under control.'

'See that you do.' Lindros could hear the sudden weariness in the old warrior's voice, hoped Jamie couldn't detect it through the electronic connection. 'We need a solid front before, during and after the president's visit. Is that clear?'

'Yessir.'

'No sign of Jason Bourne, I suppose.'

'None whatsoever, sir. Believe me, we've been extra vigilant.'

Lindros, aware that the DCI had gotten all the information he required for the moment, cleared his throat.

'Jamie, my next appointment just showed,' the DCI said without turning around. 'I'll be in touch tomorrow.' He toggled off the teleconferencer, sat with his hands steepled, staring at a large color photograph of the planet Mars and its two uninhabitable moons.

Lindros shrugged off his raincoat, came and sat down beside his boss. The room the DCI had chosen was small, cramped and over-hot even in the depths of winter. A portrait of the president was on one wall. Opposite was a single window through which tall pines could be seen, black and white, all detail washed out of them by the brilliant security floodlights. 'The news from Paris is good,' he said. 'Jason Bourne is dead.'

The DCI picked up his head, a certain animation flooding features that had been slack moments ago. 'They got him? How? I hope the bastard died in a world of pain.'

'Chances are he did, sir. He died in a highway collision on the A1 just northwest of Paris. The motorcycle he was driving rammed head-on into an eighteen-wheeler. A Quai d'Orsay officer was an eyewitness.'

'My God,' the DCI breathed. 'Nothing left but an oil slick.' His brows knitted together. 'There can be no doubt?'

'Until we have a confirmed identification, there's always doubt,' Lindros said. 'We forwarded Bourne's dental records and a sample of his DNA, but the French authorities tell me there was a terrific explosion, and in the aftermath the fire burned so hotly that they fear even the bones might not have survived. In any case, it's going to take them a day or two to sift through the scene of the accident. They've assured me that they'll be in touch as soon as they have further information.'

The DCI nodded.

'And Jacques Robbinet is unharmed,' Lindros added.

'Who?'

'The French Minister of Culture, sir. He was a friend of Conklin's and a some-time asset. We were afraid he was Bourne's next target.'

The two men sat very still. The DCI's eyes had turned inward. Perhaps he was thinking of Alex Conklin, perhaps he was contemplating the roles anxiety and fear played in modern life, wondering how Dr. Hall had been so prescient. He had gotten into clandestine work in the mistaken notion that it would help alleviate the anxiety and fear with which he had seemed to have been born. Instead, operating in the twilight had done just the opposite. And yet he had never contemplated leaving his profession. He could not imagine life without it; his very being was defined by who he was and what he had done in the sub-rosa world invisible to civilians.

'Sir, if I may say so, it's late.'

The DCI sighed. 'Tell me something I don't know, Martin.'

'I think it's time you went home to Madeleine,' Lindros said softly.

The DCI passed a hand across his face. All of a sudden he was very tired. 'Maddy's at her sister's in Phoenix. The house is dark tonight.'

'Go home anyway.'

As Lindros rose, the DCI turned his head in his deputy's direction. 'Martin, listen to me, you may think this Bourne business is over, but it isn't.'

Lindros had taken up his raincoat; now he paused. 'I don't understand, sir.'

'Bourne may be dead, but in the last few hours of his life he managed to make monkeys of us.'

'Sir – '

'Public spectacles. We can't have that. In this day and age, there's just too much damn scrutiny. And where there's scrutiny, there are hard questions asked, and these questions unless immediately put to rest inevitably lead to grave consequences.' The DCI's eyes sparked. 'We are lacking only one element to wrap up this sorry episode and consign it to the dustbin of history.'

'What's that, sir?'

'We need a scapegoat, Martin, someone to whom the shit will stick completely, leaving us smelling like rosebuds in May.' He looked hard at his DDCI. 'Do you have someone like that, Martin?'

A cold ball of anxiety had formed in the pit of Lindros' stomach.

'Come, come, Martin,' the DCI said with asperity, 'do speak up.'

Still, Lindros looked at him mutely. He seemed as if he could not get his jaws to work.

'Of course you do, Martin,' the DCI snapped.

'You're loving this, aren't you?'

The DCI winced inside at the accusation. Not for the first time, he was grateful that his boys were safely away from this business where he would have had to hold them down. No one was going to surpass him; he'd make sure of that. 'If you won't name him, I will. Detective Harris.'

'We can't do that to him,' Lindros said tightly. He could feel the anger fizzing in his head like a just-popped can of soda.

'We? Who said anything about we, Martin? This was your assignment. I made that clear from the get-go. Now it's entirely up to you to assign the blame.'

'But Harris didn't do anything wrong.'

The DCI arched an eyebrow. 'I very much doubt that, but even if it's true, who cares?'

'I do, sir.'

'Very well, Martin. Then I suppose you'll be taking the blame for the fiascos in Old Town and Washington Circle yourself.'

Lindros' lips clamped shut. 'This is my choice?'

'I don't see any others, do you? The bitch-woman intends to extract her pound of flesh from me one way or the other. If I have to sacrifice someone, I would damn well rather it be some aging detective in the Virginia State Police than my own DDCI. If you fell on your own sword, how do you suppose that would reflect on me, Martin?'

'Christ,' Lindros said, in a seething rage, 'how in the hell did you manage to survive this snakepit for so long?'

The DCI stood up, drew on his overcoat. 'What makes you think I have?'

Bourne arrived at the Gothic stone edifice of Matthias Church at eleven-forty. He spent the following twenty minutes reconnoitering the area. The air was crisp and chill, the sky clear. But near the horizon a bank of thick clouds roiled and on the freshening wind the damp musk of rain came to him. Now and again a sound or a scent fired something in his damaged memory. He was certain that he had been here before, though when and on what mission he couldn't say. Once again, as he touched the void of loss and longing, he thought of Alex and Mo so strongly he might have been able to conjure them up this very moment.

With a grimace, he went on with his task, securing the area, making sure as best he could that the rendezvous site wasn't under enemy surveillance.

At the stroke of midnight, he approached the enormous southern facade of the church from which rose the eighty-meter Gothic stone tower, laden with gargoyles. A young woman was standing on the lowest step. She was tall, slim, strikingly beautiful. Her long red hair shone in the streetlights. Behind her, over the portal was a fourteenth-century relief of the Virgin Mary. The young woman asked him his name.

'Alex Conklin,' he replied.

'Passport, please,' she said as crisply as an Immigration official.

He handed it over, watched her as she examined it with her eyes and the pad of her thumb. She had interesting hands; they were slender, long-fingered, strong, blunt-nailed. A musician's hands. She could not be more than thirty-five.

'How do I know you're really Alexander Conklin?' she said.

'How does one know anything absolutely?' Bourne said. 'Faith.'

The woman snorted. 'What's your first name?'

'It says right on the pass – '

She gave him a hard look. 'I mean your *real* first name. The one you were born with.'

'Alexsei,' Bourne said, remembering that Conklin was a Russian emigré.

The young woman nodded. She had a well-sculpted face dominated by green Magyar eyes, large and hooded, and wide, generous lips. There was about her a certain sharp-edged primness, but at the same time a fin de siècle sensuality that in its sub-rosa nature hinted intriguingly of a more innocent century when what was kept unspoken was often more important than what was freely expressed. 'Welcome to Budapest, Mr. Conklin. I'm Annaka Vadas.' She lifted a shapely arm, gestured. 'Please come with me.'

She led him across the plaza fronting the church and around the corner. In the shadowed street, a small wooden door with ancient iron bands was barely visible.

She took out a small flashlight, snapped it on. It produced a very powerful beam of light. Taking an old-fashioned key from her purse, she inserted it in the lock, turned it first one way, then the other. The door opened at her touch.

'My father is waiting for you inside,' she said. They entered the vast interior of the church. By the wavering beam of the flashlight, Bourne could see that the plastered walls were iced with colored ornamental design. The frescoes depicted the lives of Hungarian saints.

'In 1541 Buda fell to the invading Turks and for the next one hundred fifty years the church became the main mosque of the city,' she said. Playing the flashlight over her subject. 'In order to serve their needs, the Turks stripped the furnishings and whitewashed the magnificent frescoes. Now, however, everything has been restored to the way it was in the thirteenth century.'

Bourne saw dim light up ahead. Annaka led him into the northern section, where there was a series of chapels. In the one nearest to the chancel the sarcophagi of tenth-century Hungarian king, Bélla III, and his wife, Anne of Châtillon, lay in ghostly precision. In the former crypt, beside a row of medieval carvings, stood a figure in the shadows.

János Vadas extended his hand. As Bourne moved to grasp it, three glowering men appeared from out of the shadows. Bourne, very quick, drew the gun. This only produced a smile from Vadas.

'Look at the firing pin, Mr. Bourne. Did you think I would provide you with a gun that worked?'

Bourne saw that Annaka had a gun trained on him.

'Alexsei Conklin was a long-time friend of mine, Mr. Bourne. And, in any case, your face is on the news.' He had a hunter's calculating face, all dark and brooding brows, a square jaw and glittering eyes. In his youth he had had a distinct widow's peak, but now, in his mid-sixties, time had eroded his hairline, leaving a gleaming triangular promontory on his forehead. 'It's believed you killed Alexsei and another man, a Dr. Panov, I believe. For Alexsei's death alone I would be justified in ordering you killed here and now.'

'He was an old friend, more, even – a mentor.'

Vadas looked sad, resigned. He sighed. 'And you turned on him, I suppose, because you, like everyone else, want what is in Felix Schiffer's mind.'

'I have no idea what you're talking about.'

'No, of course you don't,' Vadas said with a good degree of skepticism.

'How do you think I knew Alex's real name? Alexsei and Mo Panov were friends.'

'Then killing them would have been an act of utter insanity.'

'Exactly.'

'It is Mr. Hazas' considered opinion that you're insane,' Vadas said calmly. 'You remember Mr. Hazas, the hotel manager you almost beat to a pulp. A madman, I believe he called you.'

'So that's how you knew to call me,' Bourne said. 'I may have twisted his arm a little too hard, but I knew he was lying.'

'He was lying for me,' Vadas said with a touch of pride.

Under the watchful gaze of Annaka and the three men, Bourne went across to Vadas, held out the useless gun. The moment Vadas reached for it, Bourne spun him around. At the same instant he drew his ceramic gun, pressed it hard against

Vadas' temple. 'Did you really think I would use an unknown gun without pulling it apart and putting it back together again?'

Directing himself to Annaka, he said in a calm, matter-of-fact voice, 'Unless you want your father's brains spattered all over five centuries of history, put down your gun. Don't look at him; do as I tell you!'

Annaka put down her gun.

'Kick it over here.'

She did as he ordered.

None of the three men had made a move, and now they wouldn't. Bourne kept one eye on them just the same. He took the muzzle away from Vadas' temple, let him go.

'I could have shot you dead, if that had been my wish.'

'And I would have killed you,' Annaka said fiercely.

'I've no doubt you'd have tried,' Bourne said. He put up the ceramic gun, showing her and Vadas' men that had he no intention of using it. 'But these are hostile acts. We'd have to be enemies to make them.' Picking up Annaka's gun, he handed it to her, grips first.

Without a word, she took it, aimed it at him.

'What have you turned your daughter into, Mr. Vadas? She would kill for you, yes, but it also seems as if she would kill too quickly and for no reason at all.'

Vadas stepped between Annaka and Bourne, pushed her gun down with his hand. 'I've enough enemies as it is, Annaka,' he said softly.

Annaka put away her gun, but her flashing eyes still held a hostility Bourne noted.

Vadas turned to Bourne. 'As I said, for you, killing Alexsei would have been an act of insanity, and yet you seem to be the very opposite of a madman.'

'I was set up, made to be the patsy for the killings, so that the real killer would remain free.'

'Interesting. Why?'

'I came here to find that out.'

Vadas stared hard at Bourne. Then he looked around him, raised his arms. 'I would have met Alexsei here, you know, had he lived. You see, this is a place of great significance. Here, at the dawn of the fourteenth century, once stood Buda's first parish church. The huge pipe organ you see up there on the balcony played at the two weddings of King Matthias. The last two kings of Hungary, Francis Joseph I and Charles IV, were crowned on this spot. Yes, there's great history here, and Alexsei and I, we were going to change history.'

'With the help of Dr. Felix Schiffer, wasn't it?' Bourne said.

Vadas had no time to answer. Just then, an echoing roar sounded and he was thrown backward, arms outstretched. Blood oozed from a bullethole in his forehead. Bourne grabbed Annaka, dived onto the stonework paving. Vadas' men turned and, fanning out, began to return fire as they headed for cover. One was shot almost immediately, and he skidded over the marble floor, dead before he collapsed. A second gained the edge of a bench and was desperately trying to get behind it when he, too, was felled by a bullet that entered his spine. He arched back, his weapon crashing to the floor.

Bourne looked from the third man taking cover to Vadas, who lay sprawled face-up in a widening pool of blood. He was unmoving, no respiration visible in his chest. More gunfire brought Bourne's attention back to Vadas' third man, who was now rising out of a crouch, squeezing off a series of shots, his trajectory upward toward the cathedral's great organ. His head flung backward and his arms opened wide as a speck of blood on his chest rapidly widened. He tried to clutch at the fatal wound, but his eyes were already rolling up in his head.

Bourne looked up into the gloom of the organ balcony, saw a darker shadow flitting, and he fired. Stone chips flew. Then he had grabbed Annaka's flashlight, playing the beam over the balcony as he ran toward the spiral stone staircase up to it. Annaka, at last released and able to make sense of the chaos, saw her father and screamed.

'Back!' Bourne shouted. 'You're in danger!'

Ignoring him, Annaka rushed to her father's side.

Bourne covered her, sending more shots into the shadows of the balcony, but he was not surprised at the lack of return fire. The sniper had achieved his aim; in all likelihood he was already on the run.

With no more time to waste, Bourne leaped up the staircase up to the balcony. Seeing a spent shell casing, he kept on going. The balcony appeared deserted. Its floor was stone-flagged, and the wall behind the organ ornately carved wood paneling. Bourne ducked behind the organ, but the space was deserted. He checked the floor around the organ, then the wood wall. The spacing around one of the panels appeared slightly different from the others, one side several millimeters wider as if . . .

Bourne felt around with his fingertips, discovered that the panel was in fact a narrow doorway. He went through it, found himself confronting a steep spiral staircase. With his gun at the ready, he climbed up the treads, which ended at another door. When he pushed it open, he saw that it gave out onto the rooftop of the church. The moment he poked his head out, a shot was fired at him. He ducked back but not before seeing a figure making its way onto the roof tiles, which were pitched at an extreme angle. To make matters worse, it had begun to rain and the tiles were even more treacherous. The positive side to this was that the assassin was too engaged with keeping his balance to risk firing off another shot at Bourne.

Bourne saw immediately that his new boot soles would skid and he pulled them off, dropped them over the side of the parapet. He then went crab-wise across the roof. Thirty meters below him, a dizzying drop away, the square in which the church sat gleamed in the Old World streetlights. Using his fingers and toes to anchor him, he continued his pursuit of the sniper. In the back of his mind was the suspicion that the figure he was pursuing was Khan, but how could he have arrived in Budapest before Bourne and why would he shoot Vadas rather than Bourne?

Lifting his head, he could see the figure was making for the south spire. Bourne scrambled after him, determined not to let him get away. The tiles were old and crumbly. One tile split down the center as he grasped it, coming off in his hand, and for a moment, he flailed about, balancing precariously on the acute pitch. Then he regained his balance, threw the tile away. It shattered on the flat rooftop of the small chapel extension ten feet below him.

His mind was racing ahead. The moment of extreme peril for him was when the sniper reached the safe haven of the spire. If Bourne was still exposed on the roof, the sniper would have a clear shot at him. It was raining harder now, making touch and sight that much more difficult. The south spire was no more than a hazy outline some fifty feet away.

Bourne was three-quarters of the way to the spire when he heard something – the clang of metal against stone – and he threw himself prone onto the tiles. Water sluiced over him and as he felt the zing of the bullet whizz past his ear, the tiles near his right knee exploded and he lost his purchase. He slid down the precipitous slope, tumbling off the edge.

Instinctively, he had relaxed his body, and when his shoulder struck the roof of the chapel below, he rolled himself into a ball, using his own momentum to launch himself across the roof, dissipating the energy of the drop. He fetched up against a stained-glass window, which kept him out of the sniper's line of sight.

Looking up, he could see that he was not that far from the spire. A lesser tower was just in front of him, a narrow slit of a window presenting itself. It was medieval in nature and therefore had no pane of glass in it. He squeezed through, found his way up to the top, which gave out onto a narrow stone parapet that led directly to the south spire.

Bourne had no way of knowing whether he would become visible to the sniper as he crossed the parapet. He took a deep breath, bolted out of the doorway, sprinted along the narrow stone passageway. Ahead of him, he saw the movement of a shadow, and he dove into a ball as a shot rang out. He was up and running again all in one motion, and before the sniper could fire again he had left his feet, this time diving head-first through an open window of the spire.

More shots resounded, and shards of stone flew past him as he scrambled up the spiral staircase at the core of the spire. Above him, he heard the metallic click that told him his adversary had run out of ammo, and he leaped up the stairs three at a time, making the most of his temporary advantage. He heard another metallic sound, and an empty cartridge came bouncing down the stone stairs. Bounding ahead, he bent his back, keeping his profile low. No more shots ensued, increasing the probability that he was gaining on the sniper.

But probability was not good enough; he had to be certain. He aimed Annaka's flashlight up the spiral, flicked the beam on. At once he saw the trace of a shadow on the treads just above him, slipping away almost immediately, and he redoubled his efforts. He switched off the beam before the sniper could get a reading on his position.

They were near the top of the spire now, some eighty meters in the air. There was nowhere else for the sniper to go. He would have to kill Bourne to get himself out of the trap. This desperation would make him both more dangerous and more reckless. It was up to Bourne to use the latter possibility to his advantage.

Up ahead of him, he could see the spire's ending, a circular space surrounded by high arches that let in the rain and wind, and he checked his headlong ascent. He knew that if he continued, the chances were good that he would be met with a fusillade of bullets. And yet he could not stay here. He took his flashlight, set it on a step above him at an angle, then he lay down, and keeping his head down, he reached out, stretching as far as he could, and flicked on the beam.

The resulting hail of bullets was deafening. Even while the noise was still echoing up and down the length of the spire, Bourne had launched himself up the remaining stairs. He had gambled that the sniper's desperation would lead him to empty his entire cartridge at what he assumed was Bourne's final assault.

Out of the haze of stone dust, Bourne bull-rushed the sniper, driving him back across the stone floor, against one of the stone arches. The man slammed his combined fists down on Bourne's back, driving Bourne to his knees. His head went down, exposing his neck, too tempting a target to pass up. As the sniper drove a hand-strike at Bourne's neck, Bourne twisted, grasping the descending arm, using the sniper's own momentum against him, pulling the man off his feet. Bourne struck him in the kidney as he went down.

The sniper brought his ankles together around Bourne's, twisting, so that Bourne fell backward. Immediately, the man leaped at him. They grappled hand-to-hand, the light from the flashlight picked apart by the hail of dust. By its illumination, Bourne saw the sniper's long, hatchet face, blond hair, light eyes. Bourne was briefly taken aback. He realized that he'd expected the sniper to be Khan.

Bourne did not want to kill this man; he wanted to question him. He desperately wanted to know who he was, who had sent him and why Vadas had been marked for death. But the man fought with the strength and tenacity of the damned, and when he struck Bourne on the right shoulder, Bourne's arm went numb. The man was on him before he could shift his stance and protect himself. Three punches in succession sent him reeling through one of the arches until he was backed over the low stone railing. The man came after him, his empty gun reversed in his hand so that he could use the butt as a cudgel.

Shaking his head, Bourne tried to rid himself of the pain in his right side. The sniper was almost upon him, his right arm raised, the heavy butt of the gun gleaming in the lights of the square. There was a murderous look on his face, his lips pulled back in an animal snarl. He swung in a shallow, vicious arc; the butt came down, its clear intention to shatter Bourne's skull. At the last moment, Bourne slid aside just enough and the sniper's own momentum sent him hurtling over the rail.

Bourne reacted instantly, reached down and grabbed the man by his hand, but the rain made the flesh slippery as oil and the fingers slid through his grip. With a scream the man fell away, plummeting to the pavement far below.

# 14

With the fall of night, Khan arrived in Budapest. He took a taxi from the airport and checked into the Danubius Hotel as Heng Raffarin, the name he'd used as a *Le Monde* reporter in Paris. This was how he'd come through Immigration, but he was also carrying other documents, purchased like the other, that identified him as a deputy inspector for Interpol.

'I've flown in from Paris to interview Mr. Conklin,' he said in a harassed tone of voice. 'All these delays! I'm frightfully late. Do you think you could inform Mr. Conklin that I've finally arrived? We're both on rather tight schedules.'

As Khan had foreseen, the desk clerk automatically looked at the cubbyholes behind him, each with a room number printed in gold-leaf. 'Mr. Conklin isn't in his suite at the moment. Would you care to leave a note?'

'I suppose I have no other choice. We'll get a fresh start in the morning.' Khan pretended to write a note for 'Mr. Conklin,' sealed it, gave it to the clerk. Taking his key, he turned away, but out of the corner of his eye he watched as the clerk stuck the envelope in the cubbyhole marked PENTHOUSE 3. Satisfied, he took the elevator up to his room, which was on the floor below the penthouse level.

He washed up, took some implements out of a small bag and went out of his room. He took the stairway up one flight to the penthouse level. He stood in the corridor a very long time, simply listening, accustoming himself to the small noises endemic to any building. He stood, still as stone, waiting for something – a sound, a vibration, a *feel* – that would tell him whether to go forward or to retreat.

In the end, nothing untoward presented itself, and so he moved cautiously forward, reconnoitering the entire corridor, assuring himself that it, at least, was secure. At length, he found himself in front of the polished teak double doors of Penthouse 3. Extracting a pick, he inserted it into the lock. A moment later, the door opened.

Again, he stood for some time in the open doorway, breathing in the suite. Instinct told him that the room was empty. Still, he was wary of a trap. Swaying slightly with the effects of sleeplessness and the rising tide of his emotions, he scanned the room. Besides the remnants of a package the approximate size of a shoebox, there was precious little in the suite to indicate that it was occupied. Judging by the look of the bed, it hadn't been slept in. Where was Bourne now? Khan wondered.

At length, he drew his wandering mind back into his body, crossed to the bathroom, turned on the light. He saw the plastic comb, the toothbrush, toothpaste, tiny bottle of mouthwash the hotel had provided along with soap, shampoo and hand cream. He unscrewed the toothpaste top, squeezed out a bit into the sink, washed it away. Then he pulled out a paper clip and a small silver box. Inside the box were two capsules with shells of quick-dissolving gelatin. One was white, the other black.

'One pill makes your heart beat, the other makes it slow, and the pills that Father gives you don't do anything at all,' he sang to the tune of 'White Rabbit' in a clear tenor as he extracted the white capsule from its bed.

He was about to place it into the open top of the toothpaste tube, tamp it down with the end of the paper clip, when something stopped him. He counted to ten, then replaced the cap, careful to put the tube back precisely as he had found it.

He stood, for a moment, bewildered, staring at the two capsules that he himself had prepared while waiting for his flight out of Paris. He had been clear, then, about what he'd wanted to do – the black capsule was filled with just enough krait venom to paralyze Bourne's body while still allowing his mind to remain conscious and alert. Bourne knew more about what Spalko was planning than Khan did; he had to, having followed his trail of leads all the way back to Spalko's home base. Khan wanted to know what Bourne knew before he killed him. This is what he told himself, at least.

But it was impossible to deny any longer that his mind, so long filled with fevered visions of revenge, had lately made room for other scenarios. No matter how much energy he expended on rejecting them, they persisted. In fact, he realized now, the more violently he dismissed them, the more stubbornly they refused to disappear.

Feeling like a fool, he was standing in the room of his nemesis, unable to follow through on the plan he had meticulously formulated. Instead, in the theater of his mind he was replaying the look on Bourne's face when he had seen the carved stone Buddha that hung by a gold chain around his neck. He clutched at the Buddha now, feeling as he always did a certain sense of solace and safety in its soft shape and singular weight. What was wrong with him?

With a small grunt of anger, he turned and stalked out of the suite. On his way down to his room, he pulled out his cell phone, punched in a local number. After two rings, a voice answered.

'Yes?' said Ethan Hearn.

'How's the job going?' Khan asked.

'Actually, I'm finding it enjoyable.'

'Just as I predicted.'

'Where are you?' Humanistas, Ltd.'s newest development officer asked.

'Budapest.'

'That's a surprise,' Hearn said. 'I thought you had a commission in East Africa.'

'I've declined it,' Khan said. He had reached the lobby and now crossed it, heading to the front door. 'In fact, for the time being I've taken myself off the market.'

'Something pretty important must've brought you here.'

'It's your boss, as a matter of fact. What have you been able to ferret out?'

'Nothing concrete, but he's up to something, I can tell, and it's very, very big.'

'What makes you say that?' Khan asked.

'First, he entertains a pair of Chechens,' Hearn said. 'On the surface, there's nothing strange about that. We have an important initiative in Chechnya. And yet it *was* strange, very strange, because even though they were dressed as Westerners – the man was beardless, the woman without her head scarf – I recognized them, well, *him*, at least. Hasan Arsenov, leader of the Chechen rebels.'

'Go on,' Khan urged, thinking he was getting more than his money's worth from this mole.

'Then, two nights ago, he asked me to go to the opera,' Hearn continued. 'He said he wanted to snag a wealthy prospect by the name of László Molnar.'

'What's so strange about that?' Khan said.

'Two things,' Hearn replied. 'First, Spalko took over midway through the evening. He pretty much ordered me to take the next day off. Second, Molnar's disappeared.'

'Disappeared?'

'Vanished utterly, like he never existed,' Hearn said. 'Spalko thinks I'm too naive not to have checked up.' He laughed softly.

'Don't get overconfident,' Khan warned. 'That's when you make a mistake. And, remember what I told you, don't underestimate Spalko. Once you do, you're as good as dead.'

'I got it, Khan. Christ, I'm not stupid.'

'You wouldn't be on my payroll if you were,' Khan reminded him. 'D'you have this László Molnar's home address?'

Ethan Hearn gave it to him.

'Now,' Khan said, 'all you have to do is keep your ears open and your head down. I want everything of his you can burrow into.'

Jason Bourne watched Annaka Vadas as she exited the morgue, where, he suspected, she had been taken in the company of the police in order to identify her father and the three men who had been gunned down. As for the sniper, he had landed on his face, which ruled out identification by dental records. The police must be running his fingerprints through the EU database. From fragments of the conversation he had overheard at Matthias Church, the police were rightly curious as to why a professional assassin would want to kill János Vadas, but Annaka had no explanation and at length the police had given up and allowed her to go. They, of course, had no inkling of Bourne's involvement. He had stayed away from the investigation by necessity – he was, after all, an internationally wanted man – but he felt some trepidation. He had no idea whether he could trust Annaka. It hadn't been that long ago when she had been intent on putting a bullet through his brain. But he had hoped that his actions following her father's murder would convince her of his good intentions.

Apparently they had, because she had not told the police about him. Instead, he had found his boots in the chapel Annaka had shown him, lying between the crypts of King Bélla III and Anne of Châtillon. Bribing a taxi driver, he'd shadowed her to the police station, and then to the morgue. Now he watched as the police touched their caps, said their goodnights. They had offered to drive her home, but she had refused. Instead, she pulled out her cell phone, in order to call a taxi, he surmised.

When he was certain that she was alone, he quit the shadows in which he had been hiding, walked quickly across the street toward her. She saw him, put her cell phone away. Her look of alarm brought him up short.

'You! How did you find me?' She looked around, rather wildly, he thought. 'Have you been following me all this time?'

'I wanted to make sure you were okay.'

'My father was shot to death in front of me,' she said shortly. 'Why would I be okay?'

He was conscious of the fact that they were standing beneath a streetlight. At night, he always thought in terms of targets and security; it was second nature – he couldn't help it. 'The police here can be difficult.'

'Really? And how would you know that?' Apparently, she wasn't interested in his answer, for she began to walk away from him, her heels click-clacking over the cobbles.

'Annaka, we need each other.'

Her back was very straight, her head held high on her long neck. 'What would make you say such an absurd thing?'

'Because it's true.'

She turned on her heel, confronting him. 'No, it's not true.' Her eyes blazed. 'It's because of you that my father's dead.'

'Now who's being absurd?' He shook his head. 'Your father was murdered because of whatever he and Alex Conklin were into. That's why Alex was murdered in his home, and that's why I'm here.'

She snorted in derision. Bourne understood the source of her brittleness. She had been forced into a male-dominated arena, perhaps by her father, and was now more or less at war. At the very least, she was highly defended.

'Don't you want to know who killed your father?'

'Frankly, no.' Her balled fist was on one hip. 'I want to bury him and forget I ever heard of Alexsei Conklin and Dr. Felix Schiffer.'

'You can't mean that!'

'Do you know me, Mr. Bourne? Do you know anything about me?' Her clear eyes observed him from her slightly cocked head. 'I think not. You're completely in the dark. That's why you came here, posing as Alexsei. A stupid ruse, transparent as plastic. And now that you've blundered your way in, now that blood has been spilled, you think it's your due to find out what my father and Alexsei were up to.'

'Do you know me, Annaka?'

A sardonic smile split her face as she took a step closer to him. 'Oh, yes, Mr. Bourne, I know you well. I've seen your kind come and go, each one thinking in the moments before he is gunned down that he's more clever than the last one.'

'So who am I?'

'You think I won't tell you? Mr. Bourne, I know exactly who you are. You're a cat with a ball of string. Your only thought is to unravel that ball of string no matter the cost. This is all a game to you – a mystery that must be solved. Nothing else matters. You're defined by the very mystery you seek to unravel. Without it, you wouldn't even exist.'

'You're wrong.'

'Oh, no, I'm not.' The sardonic smile widened. 'It's why you can't fathom how I can walk away from this, why I don't want to work with you, help you find out who killed my father. Why should I? Will knowing the answer bring him back? He's dead, Mr. Bourne. He no longer thinks or breathes. He's just a pile of refuse now, waiting for time to finish what it started.'

She turned and began to walk away again.

'Annaka – '

'Go away, Mr. Bourne. Whatever you have to say, I'm not interested.'

He ran to catch up with her. 'How can you say that? Six men have lost their lives because of – '

She gave him a rueful look and he could tell that she was on the verge of tears. 'I begged my father not to get involved, but you know, old friends, the lure of the clandestine, who knows what it was. I warned him that it would all come to an evil end, but he just laughed – yes, laughed – and said I was his daughter and couldn't possibly understand. Well, that put me in my place, didn't it?'

'Annaka, I am being hunted for a double murder I didn't commit. My two best friends were shot to death and I've been framed as the prime suspect. Can you understand – '

'Jesus, have you not heard a word I've said? Has it all gone in one ear and out the other?'

'I can't do this alone, Annaka. I need your help. I've nowhere else to turn. My life is quite literally in your hands. Tell me, please, about Dr. Felix Schiffer. Tell me what you know and I swear you'll never see me again.'

She lived at 106–108 Fo utca in Víziváros, a narrow neighborhood of hills and steep stairs, rather than streets, wedged between the Castle District and the Danube. From her front bay windows you could see Bem tér. It was here, hours before the 1956 Uprising, that thousands congregated, waving Hungarian flags from which they had painstakingly and joyously cut the hammer and sickle, prior to marching on parliament.

The apartment was cramped and crowded, primarily because of the concert grand piano that took up fully half the space of the living room. Books, periodicals and journals on music history and theory, biographies of composers, conductors, musicians, crammed the floor-to-ceiling bookcase.

'Do you play?' Bourne asked.

'Yes,' Annaka said simply.

He sat down on the piano bench, looked at the music chart splayed on the rack. A Chopin Nocturne, Opus 9, No. 1 in B-Flat Minor. *She would have to be quite accomplished to tackle that,* he thought.

From the bay window in the living room there was a view of the boulevard as well as the buildings on the other side. A few lights were on; the sound of fifties jazz – Thelonious Monk – drifted through the night. A dog barked and was still. From time to time, the rattle of traffic intruded.

After turning on the lamps, she went immediately into the kitchen, put on water for tea. From a buttercup-colored cupboard, she took out two sets of cups and saucers, and while the tea was brewing, she uncapped a bottle of schnapps, poured a generous dollop into each cup.

She opened the refrigerator. 'Would you like something to eat? Cheese, a bit of sausage?' Speaking as if to an old friend.

'I'm not hungry.'

'Neither am I.' She sighed and shut the door. It was as if, having made the decision to bring him home, she had also decided to lose the attitude. They made no more mention of János Vadas or Bourne's fruitless pursuit of the killer. That suited him.

She handed him the laced tea and they went into the living room, sat on a sofa old as a dowager.

'My father was working with a professional intermediary named László Molnar,' she said without preamble. 'He was the one who secreted your Dr. Schiffer.'

'Secreted?' Bourne shook his head. 'I don't understand.'

'Dr. Schiffer had been kidnapped.'

Bourne's tension level rose. 'By whom?'

She shook her head. 'My father knew, but I didn't.' She frowned, concentrating. 'That was why Alexsei first contacted him. He needed my father's help in rescuing Dr. Schiffer and spiriting him away to a secret location.'

All at once, he heard Mylene Dutronc's voice in his head: *That day, Alex made and received many calls in a very short period of time. He was terribly tense and I knew he was at the crisis point of a hot field operation. I heard Dr. Schiffer's name mentioned several times. I suspect that he was the subject of the operation.* This was the hot field operation.

'So your father was successful in getting Dr. Schiffer.'

Annaka nodded. The lamplight burnished her hair to a deep copper sheen. Her eyes and half of her forehead were cast in its shadow. She sat with her knees together, slightly hunched over, her hands around the teacup as if she needed to absorb its warmth.

'As soon as my father had Dr. Schiffer, he handed him over to László Molnar. This was strictly for security purposes. Both he and Alexsei were terribly afraid of whoever it was who had kidnapped Dr. Schiffer.'

This, too, jibed with what Mylene had told him, Bourne thought. *That day he was frightened.*

He was thinking furiously. 'Annaka, for all this to start making sense, you have to understand that your father's murder was a setup. That sniper was already at the church when we came in; he knew what your father was up to.'

'What do you mean?'

'Your father was shot before he could tell me what I need to know. Someone doesn't want me to find Dr. Schiffer, and it seems increasingly clear that this is the same someone who kidnapped Schiffer, who your father and Alex were afraid of.'

Annaka's eyes opened wide. 'It is possible now that László Molnar is in danger.'

'Would this mystery man know of your father's involvement with Molnar?'

'My father was extremely careful, very security conscious, so it seems unlikely.' She looked at him, her eyes darkened with fright. 'On the other hand, his defenses were penetrated at Matthias Church.'

Bourne nodded his agreement. 'Do you know where Molnar lives?'

Annaka drove them to Molnar's apartment, which was in the posh embassy district of Rózsadomb, or Rose Hill. Budapest showed itself in jumbled buildings of pale stone, elaborately iced like birthday cakes, carved into ornamental lintels and cornices, quaintly cobbled streets, wrought-iron balconies with flowerpots, coffeehouses illuminated by elaborate chandeliers whose lemon light revealed ruddy wood-paneled walls, brilliant splashes of glass, stained, etched into fin de siècle patterns. Like Paris, it was a city defined first and foremost by the sinuous river that clove it in two, then by the bridges that spanned it. Beyond that, it was a city of etched stone, Gothic spires, sweeping public staircases, lamplit ramparts, copper-encrusted domes, ivied walls, monumental statuary and glittering mosaics. And when it rained, umbrellas, thousands of umbrellas, unfurled like sails along the river.

All these things and more affected Bourne deeply. It was for him like arriving at a place and remembering it from a dream, with a dream's suprareal clarity that stemmed from its direct connection to the unconscious. And yet he could separate no specific remembrance from the tide of emotion that arose from his shattered memory.

'What is it?' Annaka said, as if sensing his unease.

'I've been here before,' he said. 'Remember how I said that the police could be difficult here?'

She nodded. 'You're absolutely right about that. Are you telling me that you don't know how you know?'

He put his head back against the seat rest. 'Years ago I suffered a terrible accident. It wasn't an accident, really. I was shot on a boat and fell overboard. I almost died of shock, blood loss and exposure. A doctor in Ile de Port Noir in France excised the bullet, took care of me. I returned to perfect physical health, but my memory was affected. For some time I had amnesia, and then slowly, painfully, shards of my former life came back to me. The truth I have to live with is that my memory's never fully recovered and it likely never will.'

Annaka drove on, but by the look on her face he could tell that she had been affected by his story.

'You can't imagine what it's like not to know who you are,' he said. 'Unless it's happened to you, there's no way to know or even to explain what it feels like.'

'Unmoored.'

He glanced at her. 'Yes.'

'The sea all around you with no sight of land, no sun or moon or stars to tell you which way you need to go to get back home.'

'It's not unlike that.' He was surprised. He wanted to ask her how she could know something like that, but they were pulling into the curb in front of a large, ornate stone building.

They got out and went into the vestibule. Annaka pressed a button and a low-watt bulb came on, its sickly illumination revealing the mosaic floor, the wall of bell pushes. László Molnar's bell remained unanswered.

'It could mean nothing,' Annaka said. 'More than likely Molnar is with Dr. Schiffer.'

Bourne went to the front door, a wide, thick affair with an etched frosted-glass panel running upward from waist level. 'We'll find out in a minute.'

He bent over the lock and a moment later he had the door open. Annaka hit another button and a light came on for thirty seconds as she led the way up the wide curving staircase to Molnar's second-floor apartment.

Bourne had a bit more difficulty picking this lock, but in the end it gave way. Annaka was about to rush inside, but he held her back. He drew his ceramic gun, pushed the door slowly open. Lamps were lit, but it was very quiet. Moving from the living room into the bedroom to the bathroom, the kitchen, they found the apartment neat as a pin, no evidence of a struggle and no sign of Molnar.

'What bothers me,' Bourne said as he put the gun away, 'is the lights being on. He can't be off with Dr. Schiffer.'

'Then he'll be back any time,' Annaka said. 'We should wait for him.'

Bourne nodded. In the living room he picked up several framed photos off the bookshelves and desk. 'Is this Molnar?' he asked Annaka as he pointed to a heavyset man with a thick mane of slicked-back black hair.

'That's him.' She looked around. 'My grandparents used to live in this building, and as a child, I used to play in the halls. The children who lived here knew all sorts of hiding places.'

Bourne ran his fingers over the spines of old-fashioned 33 1/3 rpm record sleeves stacked next to an expensive stereo with an elaborate turntable. 'I see he's an opera buff as well as an audiophile.'

Annaka peered in. 'No CD player?'

'People like Molnar will tell you that the transfer to digital music takes all the warmth and subtlety out of a recording.'

Bourne turned to the desk, on which sat a notebook computer. He saw that it was plugged in both to an electrical outlet and to a modem. The screen was black, but when he touched the chassis it was warm. He pressed the 'Escape' key and the screen immediately sprang to life; the computer had been in 'sleep' mode – it had never been turned off.

Coming up behind him, Annaka looked at the screen, read from it, 'Anthrax, Argentinean hemorrhagic fever, cryptococcosis, pneumonic plague . . . God in heaven, why was Molnar on a Web site that describes the effects of lethal – what does it call them? – pathogens?'

'All I know is that Dr. Schiffer is the beginning and end to this enigma,' Bourne said. 'Alex Conklin approached Dr. Schiffer when he was in DARPA – that's the advanced weapons program run by the U.S. Department of Defense. Within a year, Dr. Schiffer had transferred to the CIA's Tactical Non-Lethal Weapons Directorate. Shortly after that, he vanished altogether. I have no idea what Schiffer was working on that interested Conklin so much that he would go to the trouble of pissing off the DOD and vanishing a prominent government scientist from the Agency's program.'

'Maybe Dr. Schiffer is a bacteriologist or an epidemiologist.' Annaka shivered. 'The information on this Web site is terrifying.'

She went into the kitchen to get a glass of water while Bourne navigated around the Web page to see if he could get any further clue as to why Molnar would be on this site. Finding nothing, he went to the top of the browser, where he accessed a drop-down menu next to the 'Address' bar that showed the most recent sites Molnar had been on. He clicked on the last one Molnar had accessed. It turned out to be a real-time scientific forum. Navigating to the 'Archives' section, he went back in time to see if he could find out when Molnar had used the forum and what he'd talked about. Approximately forty-eight hours ago, László1647M had logged onto the forum. Bourne, his heart beating fast, spent several minutes reading the dialogue he had had with another forum member.

'Annaka, look at this,' he called. 'It seems Dr. Schiffer is neither a bacteriologist nor an epidemiologist. He's an expert in bacteriological particulate behavior.'

'Mr. Bourne, you'd better come here,' Annaka replied. 'Right now.'

The tightness in her voice brought him into the kitchen at the run. She was standing in front of the sink as if held spellbound. A glass of water was suspended halfway to her lips. She seemed pale, and when she saw him, she licked her lips nervously.

'What is it?'

She pointed to a space between the counter and the refrigerator, where he saw neatly stacked seven or eight white-coated wire racks.

'What the hell are those?' he said.

'They're the refrigerator shelves,' Annaka said. 'Someone took them out.' She turned to him. 'Why would they do that?'

'Maybe Molnar's getting a new refrigerator.'

'This one *is* new.'

He checked behind the refrigerator. 'It's plugged in and the compressor seems to be running normally. You didn't look inside?'

'No.'

He grabbed hold of the handle, opened the door. Annaka gasped.

'Christ,' he said.

A pair of death-clouded eyes stared sightlessly out at them. There in the depths of the shelfless refrigerator was the curled-up, blue-white body of László Molnar.

# 15

The seesaw wail of sirens brought them out of their shock. Racing to the front window, Bourne looked down onto Rose Hill, saw five or six white Opal Astras and Skoda Felicias drawing up, blue-and-white lights flashing. The officers inside tumbled out, making directly for Molnar's building. He had been set up again! The scene was so similar to what had happened at Conklin's house that he knew the same person must be behind both incidents. This was important because it told him two things: First, he and Annaka were being watched. By whom, Khan? He didn't think so. Khan's methodology was increasingly confrontational. Second, Khan may have been telling the truth when he claimed he wasn't responsible for the murders of Alex and Mo. Right now, Bourne couldn't think of a reason why he'd lie about that. That left the unknown person who'd called the police at Conklin's estate. Was the person he was working for based in Budapest? There was a convincing logic to it. Conklin was on his way to Budapest when he was murdered. Dr. Schiffer had been in Budapest, along with János Vadas and László Molnar. Every road led back to this city.

Even as his mind raced through these thoughts, he was yelling to Annaka to wipe off and put away the water glass, wipe down the kitchen faucet. He grabbed Molnar's laptop, wiped down the stereo and the knob on the front door, and they sprinted out of the apartment.

Already, they could hear the police pounding up the stairs. The elevator would be filled with police and so was out of the question.

'They've left us no choice,' Bourne said as they mounted the stairs. 'We have to go up.'

'But why have they come now?' Annaka asked. 'How could they have known we were here?'

'They couldn't,' Bourne said, continuing to lead her upward, 'unless we were under surveillance.' He didn't like the position the police were putting them in. He recalled all too well the fate of the sniper at Matthias Church. When you went up, all too often you came down, hard.

They were a floor from the roof when Annaka tugged on his hand and whispered, 'This way!'

She led him into the corridor. Behind them, the stairwell resounded with the noises any group of men would make, especially one on its way to apprehend a heinous murderer. Three-quarters of the way down the corridor was a door that looked like an emergency exit. Annaka pulled it open. They were in a short hallway, not more than ten feet long, at the end of which was another door, this one made of battered metal plates. Bourne went ahead of her.

He saw that the door was bolted at top and bottom. He slid the slides back, pulled it open. There was only a brick wall, cold as a grave.

'Would you look at that!' Detective Csilla said, ignoring the new recruit who had vomited all over his polished shoes. The academy certainly wasn't turning them out the way they used to, he mused as he studied the victim, curled stiff in his own refrigerator.

'No one in the apartment,' one of his officers said.

'Dust it anyway,' Detective Csilla said. He was a burly, blond-haired man with a broken nose and intelligent eyes. 'I doubt the perpetrator was stupid enough to leave his prints, but you never know,' he said now. Then he pointed. 'Look at those burn marks, would you? And the puncture wounds seem to go very deep.'

'Tortured,' his sergeant, a slim-hipped young man, said, 'by a professional.'

'This one's more than a professional,' Detective Csilla said, leaning in and sniffing as if the corpse were a side of meat he suspected of having begun to rot. 'He enjoys his work.'

'The phone tip said the murderer was here in the apartment.'

Detective Csilla looked up. 'If not the apartment, then surely the building.' He backed away as the forensic team arrived with their kits and flash cameras. 'Have the men fan out.'

'Already done,' his sergeant said in a subtle reminder to his boss that he didn't want to remain a sergeant forever.

'Enough time with the dead,' Detective Csilla said. 'Let's join them.'

As they went down the hallway, the sergeant explained that the elevator had already been secured, as had the floors below. 'The murderer has only one way to go.'

'Get the sharpshooters onto the roof,' Detective Scilla said.

'Already there,' his sergeant replied. 'I put them into the elevator when we entered the building.'

Csilla nodded. 'How many floors above us? Three?'

'Yessir.'

Csilla mounted the stairs two at a time. 'With the roof secured, we can afford to take our time.'

It did not take them long to find the doorway to the short corridor.

'Where does this lead?' Csilla asked.

'I don't know, sir,' his sergeant said, irked that he couldn't provide an answer.

As the two men approached the far end of the corridor, they saw the battered metal door. 'That's this?' Csilla took a look at it. 'Bolts at top and bottom.' He leaned in, saw the gleam of metal. 'They've been recently pulled.' He drew his gun, pulled the door open onto the bricked-up wall.

'Looks like our murderer was as frustrated as we are.'

Csilla was staring at the brickwork, trying to discern if any of it was new. Then he put a hand out, tested one brick after another. The sixth one he touched moved just slightly. Aware that his sergeant was about to exclaim, he clamped a hand across his mouth, gave him a warning look. Then he whispered in his ear, 'Take three of the men and canvass the building next door.'

At first, Bourne, his ears straining to catch the slightest sound in the pitch blackness, thought the noise was one of the rats with whom they were sharing this dank and uncomfortable space between the walls of Molnar's building and the adjacent one. Then it came again, and he knew it for what it was: the scrape of brick against mortar.

'They've found our hiding place,' he whispered as he grabbed hold of Annaka. 'We've got to move.'

The space they occupied was narrow, not more than two feet in width, but it seemed to rise indefinitely into the darkness above their heads. They stood on a floor of sorts, made up of metal pipes. It was not the most secure of floors and Bourne did not care to think about the open space below them into which they would plunge should one or more of the pipes give way.

'Do you know a way out of here?' Bourne whispered.

'I think so,' she said.

She turned to their right, felt her way along the space with the palms of her hands on the wall of the adjacent building.

She tripped once, righted herself. 'It's here somewhere,' she muttered.

They continued onward, putting one foot in front of the other. Then, all at once, a pipe gave way beneath Bourne's weight and his left leg plunged downward. He canted wildly over, his shoulder striking the wall, and Molnar's laptop was thrown from his grip. He tried to catch it even as Annaka was reaching down to grab him, pull him up. Instead, he saw it strike a pipe on edge, then plunge through the gap the rotten pipe had made, lost forever.

'Are you okay?' Annaka said as he regained his feet.

'I'm fine,' he said grimly, 'but Molnar's laptop's gone.'

A moment later he froze. Behind them, he could hear movement, slow and stealthy – someone else was breathing in the space – and he took out his flashlight, his thumb on the slide switch. He put his lips against Annaka's ear, 'He's here with us. No more talking.' He could sense her nod, even as he smelled the scent of her rising off her bare skin, citrus and musk.

Something clanked behind them as the policeman's shoe struck a protrusion of solder where two pipes joined. All of them stood very still. Bourne's heart beat fast. Then Annaka's hand found his, guided it along the wall where a line of grout was missing or had been deliberately gouged away.

But another problem presented itself. As soon as they pushed in the section of wall, the policeman behind them would see the pale patch of light, however feeble, coming in from the other side. He would see them, know where they were going. Bourne took a chance, put his lips against Annaka's ear and whispered, 'You must tell me the moment before you push through the wall.'

She squeezed his hand in response, kept hold of it. When he felt her squeeze it again, he aimed the flashlight directly behind them, snapped on the beam. The burst of glaring light temporarily blinded their pursuer, and Bourne lent his energy to helping her push through the three-foot-by-three-foot section of the wall.

Annaka ducked through while Bourne kept the beam focused on their adversary, but he felt the pipes vibrate under the soles of his boots and an instant later he was struck a terrific blow.

Detective Csilla tried to fight off the light-dazzle. He had been caught totally unprepared, a fact that enraged him, as he prided himself on being prepared for every possibility. He shook his head, but it was no good – the beam of light had temporarily rendered him blind. If he maintained his ground until the light was turned off, he had no doubt the murderer would have already fled. So he used his own advantage of surprise and attacked even though he was blinded. With a grunt of effort, he rushed along the pipes, crashing into the perpetrator, his head down in a street fighter's crouch.

In such close quarters and in the dark, eyesight was of little value, and he proceeded to use his fists, the edges of his hands and the heels of his stout shoes precisely as he had been taught in the academy. He was a man who believed in discipline, in rigor and in the power of advantage. He knew the moment he launched himself that the murderer would never have suspected him of attacking blind, and so he rained down as many blows as he could on the other in as short a space of time as he could manage in order to make the most of the advantage of surprise.

But the man was strong and solidly built. Worse, he was an accomplished hand-to-hand fighter, and almost immediately Csilla knew that in a prolonged fight he would be defeated. He sought, therefore, to end the combat swiftly and surely. In doing so, he made the fatal error of exposing the side of his neck. He felt the surprise of the pressure but no pain. He was already unconscious as his legs buckled under him.

Bourne went through the hole in the wall, helped Annaka slide the square of bricks back into place.

'What happened to you?' she said a little breathlessly.

'A policeman was smarter than he ought to have been.'

They were in another short brick-lined utility corridor. Through a door was the hallway of the building next door to Molnar's, warm light emanating from etched-glass sconces along the flowered-paper walls. Here and there were scattered dark wooden benches.

Annaka had already punched the button for the elevator, but when it rose to their level, Bourne could see through the cage two policemen with their guns drawn.

'Oh, hell!' he said, grabbing Annaka's hand and dragging her to the stairwell. But he heard the heavy tread of footsteps and knew that egress was denied them as well. Behind them, the two policemen had opened the elevator cab gates, were in the hallway, racing toward them. Bourne took her up one flight. In the hallway he quickly picked the lock of the first door they came to, closing the door before the police followed them up the stairs.

Inside, the apartment was dark and still. Whether anyone was home was impossible to say. Crossing to the side window, Bourne opened it, looked out at a stone ledge that overlooked a narrow alley housing a pair of huge green metal trash bins. Illumination came from a streetlamp on Endrodi Street. Three windows over, a fire escape led downward to the alley which, as far as Bourne could see, was deserted.

'Come on,' he said, climbing out onto the ledge.

Annaka's eyes opened wide. 'Are you crazy?'

'Do you want to get caught?' He looked at her levelly. 'This is our only way out.'

She swallowed uneasily. 'I'm afraid of heights.'

'We're not that far up.' He held out a hand, waggled his fingers. 'Come on, there's no time to lose.'

Taking a deep breath, she climbed out and he closed the window behind her. She turned and, glancing down, would have fallen if Bourne hadn't grabbed her, pulled her back against the stone side of the building. 'Jesus Christ, you said we weren't that far up!'

'For me, that's true.'

She bit her lip. 'I'll kill you for this.'

'You've already tried.' He squeezed her hand. 'Just follow me and you'll be fine, I promise.'

They moved to the end of the ledge. He didn't want to push her, but there was good cause for haste. With the police swarming all through the building, it was only a matter of time until they came around to this alley.

'You'll have to let go of my hand now,' he said, and then, because he saw what she was about to do, he added sharply enough to arrest her, 'Don't look down! If you feel yourself getting dizzy, look at the side of the building, concentrate on something small, the carving of the stonework, whatever. Keep your mind occupied with that and your fear will fade.'

She nodded, let go of his hand, and he stepped out, bridging the gap between ledges. His right hand gripped the top of the ledge above the next window and he transferred his weight from his left side to his right side. Lifting his left leg off the ledge on which Annaka was still standing, he moved smoothly across to the next ledge. Then he turned and smiled, held his hand out to her.

'Now you.'

'No.' She shook her head violently from side to side. All the color had drained from her face. 'I can't do it.'

'Yes, you can.' He waggled his fingers again. 'Come on, Annaka, take the first step; after that, the rest is easy. You simply shift your weight from left to right.'

She shook her head mutely.

He continued to smile, showing none of the rising anxiety he felt. Here on the side of the building, they were completely vulnerable. If the police should come into the alley now, they were dead. He had to get them to the fire escape and do it fast. 'One leg, Annaka, reach out with your right leg.'

'Christ!' She was at the end of the ledge, where he had been moments before. 'What if I fall?'

'You won't fall.'

'But what – '

'I'll catch you.' His smile broadened. 'It's time to move now.'

She did as he bade, moving her right leg out and across. He showed her how to grasp the ledge above with her right hand. This she did without hestitation.

'Now shift your weight, left to right, and step across.'

'I'm frozen.'

She was about to look down and he knew it. 'Close your eyes,' he said. 'Do you feel my hand on yours?' She nodded, as if terrified that the vibration of her voice-box would send her spinning down into the void below. 'Shift your weight, Annaka. Just shift it left to right. Good, now lift your left leg and step – '

'No.'

He put his hand around her waist. 'All right, then, just lift your left leg.' As soon as she did, he pulled her, quickly and rather violently, against him onto the next ledge. She fell against him, shivering with fear and the release of tension.

Only two more to go. He moved them to the far end of the ledge, repeated the process. The quicker they got this over with, the better for both of them. She managed the second and third crossings somewhat better, either by sheer nerve or by shutting down her mind completely, following his orders without thinking.

At last, they made it onto the fire escape and began their descent to the street. The lamplight from Endrodi Street spilled long shadows down the alley. Bourne longed to kill it with a shot from his gun, but he didn't dare. Instead, he hurried them onward.

They were one tier from the vertical extending ladder that would take them to within two feet of the cobbles of the alley when out of the corner of his eye Bourne saw the quality of the light change. Shadows moved in the alley from opposing directions; a pair of policemen had entered the alley from either side.

Csilla's sergeant had taken one of their officers out of the building the moment the perpetrator had been spotted. He already knew that he was clever enough to have found his way from building to building. Having successfully escaped from László Molnar's apartment, he didn't now consider that the criminal would allow himself to get trapped in the adjacent building's stairway. That meant he'd find a way out, and the sergeant wanted all bases covered. He had a man on the roof, one each at the front and service entrances. That left the alleyway on the side. He didn't see how the murderer would get to the alley, but he wasn't taking any chances.

Lucky for him, he saw the figure outlined against the fire escape as he turned the building corner and entered the alley. By the light of the streetlamp on Endrodi Street he saw his officer enter the alley from the opposite end. He signed upward to the man, indicating the figure on the fire escape. He had drawn his gun and was steadily advancing toward the vertical ladder that led down from the fire escape when the figure moved, seemed to pull apart as if dividing. The sergeant started in surprise. There were *two* figures on the fire escape!

He raised his gun and fired. Sparks flew off the metal, and he saw one of the figures launch itself into the air, rolling into a ball only to disappear between the two enormous Dumpsters. The officer broke into a run, but the sergeant held back. He saw his officer reach the corner of the Dumpster nearest him, go into a crouch as he approached the space between the two.

The sergeant looked up for the second figure. The feeble illumination made it difficult to pick out details, but he saw no one standing. The fire escape looked clear. Where could the seond one have gone?

He returned his attention to his officer, only to find that the man had vanished. He took several steps forward, called out his name. No response. He pulled out his walkie-talkie, was about to call for reinforcements when something dropped onto him. He stumbled, fell heavily, got up on one knee, shaking his head. Then something emerged from the space between the Dumpsters. By the time he realized that it wasn't his officer, he had been dealt a blow hard enough to cause him to lose consciousness.

'That was really stupid,' Bourne said, stooping to help Annaka up off cobbles of the alley.

'You're welcome,' she said, shaking off his hand, standing on her own power.

'I thought you were afraid of heights.'

'I'm afraid of dying more,' she shot back.

'Let's get out of here before more policemen show up,' he said. 'I think you ought to lead the way.'

The streetlight was in Khan's eyes as Bourne and Annaka ran out of the alley. Although he couldn't see their faces, he recognized Bourne by his shape and his gait. As for his female companion, though his mind registered her in a peripheral way, he did not give her much attention. He, like Bourne, was far more interested in why the police had been drawn to László Molnar's apartment when Bourne had been there. Also, like Bourne, he was struck by the similarity of this scenario to the one at Conklin's estate in Manassas. It had Spalko's thumbprint all over it. The trouble was that unlike in Manassas when he had spotted Spalko's man, he had come across no such person during his thorough recon of the four square blocks around Molnar's apartment building. So who had called the police? Someone had to have been on the scene to tip them off when Bourne and the woman had entered the building.

He started up his rental car and was able to follow Bourne as he got into a taxi. The female continued on. Khan, knowing Bourne, was prepared for the backtracking, the reversal of direction, the changing taxis, and so was able to keep Bourne in sight during the maneuvers meant to shake any tails.

At last Bourne's taxi reached Fo utca. Four blocks north of the magnificent domes of the Kiraly Baths, Bourne stepped out of the taxi and went into the building at 106–108.

Khan slowed his car, pulled it into the curb up the block and across the street – he didn't want to pass by the entrance. He turned off the engine, sank into darkness. Alex Conklin, Jason Bourne, László Molnar, Hasan Arsenov. He thought about Spalko and wondered how all these disparate names were connected. There was a line of logic here, there always was, if only he could see it.

In this manner, five or six minutes passed and then another taxi pulled up in front of the entrance to 106–108. Khan watched a young female get out. He strained to catch a glimpse of her face before she pushed through the heavy front doors, but all he was able to determine was that she had red hair. He waited, watching the facade of the building. No light had gone on after Bourne had entered the lobby, which meant that he must be waiting for the woman – that this was her apartment. Sure enough, within three minutes, lights went on in the fourth – and top – floor bay window.

Now that he knew where they were, he commenced to sink into *zazen*, but after an hour of fruitlessly trying to clear his mind, he gave up. In the darkness, his hand closed around the small carved stone Buddha. Almost immediately thereafter, he fell into a deep sleep, from which he dropped like a stone into the nether world of his recurring nightmare.

*The water is blue-black, swirling restlessly as if alive with malignant energy. He tries to strike out for the surface, stretching up so hard his bones crack with the strain. Still, he continues to sink into the darkness, dragged down by the rope tied around his ankle. His lungs are beginning to burn. He longs to take a breath, but he knows that the moment he opens his mouth, the water will rush in and he'll drown.*

*He reaches down, trying to untie the rope, but his fingers fail to gain a grip on the slick surface. He feels, like an electric current running through him, the terror of whatever waits for him in the darkness. The terror presses in on him like a vise; he forces down an urge to gibber. In that moment he hears the sound rising from the depths – the clangor of bells, of massed monks chanting before they are slaughtered by the Khmer Rouge. Eventually, the sound resolves itself into the song of a single voice, a clear tenor, a repeated ululation not unlike a prayer.*

*And it is as he stares down into the darkness, as he begins to make out the shape tethered to the other rope, the thing that is dragging him inexorably to his doom, that he feels the song he is hearing must be coming from that figure. For he knows the figure twirling in the powerful current below him; it's as familiar to him as his own face, his own body. But now, with a shock that pierces him to the quick, he realizes that the sound isn't coming from the familiar form below him because it's dead, which is why its weight is dragging him down to his doom.*

*The sound is nearer to hand, and now he recognizes the ululation as that of a clear tenor – his own voice coming from deep inside himself. It touches every part of him at once.*

*'Lee-Lee! Lee-Lee!' he is calling just before he drowns . . .*

# 16

Spalko and Zina arrived in Crete before the sun, touching down in Kazantzakis Airport just outside Iráklion. They were accompanied by a surgeon and three men, whom Zina had taken the time to scrutinize during the flight. They were not particularly big men, if only to ensure that they wouldn't stand out in a crowd. Spalko's heightened sense of security dictated that when, as now, he was engaged not as Stepan Spalko, president of Humanistas, Ltd., but as the Shaykh, he maintain the lowest of profiles, not only for himself but for all of his personnel. It was in their motionlessness that Zina recognized their power, for they had absolute control over their bodies, and when they moved, they did so with the fluidity and surety of dancers or yoga masters. She could see the intent in their dark eyes, which came only after years of hard training. Even when they were smiling deferentially at her, she could sense the danger that lurked within them, coiled, waiting patiently for its moment of release.

Crete, the largest island in the Mediterranean, was the gateway between Europe and Africa. For centuries it had lain baking in the hot Mediterranean sun, its southern eye trained on Alexandria in Egypt and Banghazi in Libya. Inevitably, however, an island so blessed in location was also surrounded by predators. At the crossroads of cultures, its history was by necessity bloody. Like waves breaking on the shore, invaders from different lands washed up on Crete's coves and beaches, bringing with them their culture, language, architecture and religion.

Iráklion had been founded by the Saracens in A.D. 824. They had called it Chandax, a bastardization of the Arabic word *kandak*, owing to the moat they dug around it. The Saracens ruled for one hundred forty years, before the Byzantines wrested control away from them. But the pirates were so astoundingly successful that it had taken three hundred boats to carry away all of their amassed booty to Byzantium.

During the Venetian occupation, the city was known as Candia. Under the Venetians, it became the most important cultural center in the Eastern Mediterranean. All of that came to an end with the first Turkish invasion.

This polyglot history was everywhere one looked: in Iráklion's massive Venetian fortress that protected its beautiful harbor from invasion; the town hall, housed in the Venetian Loggia; the 'Koubes,' the Turkish fountain near the former church of the Savior, which the Turks converted into the Valide mosque.

But in the modern, bustling city itself, there remained nothing of Minoan culture, the first and, from an archaeological point of view, the most important Cretan civilization. To be sure, the remnants of the palace of Knossos could be seen outside the city proper, but it was for historians to note that the Saracens had chosen this spot to found Chandax because it had been the main port of the Minoans thousands of years earlier.

At heart, Crete remained an island shrouded in myth, and it was impossible to set foot on it without being reminded of the legend of its birth. Centuries before the Saracens, the Venetians or the Turks existed, Crete had come to prominence from out of the mists of legend. Minos, Crete's first king, was a demigod. His father, Zeus, taking the form of a bull, raped his mother, Europa, and so from the first, the bull became the signifier of the island.

Minos and his two brothers battled for the rule of Crete, but Minos prayed to Poseidon, promising eternal obeisance to the god of the sea if he would use his power to help Minos defeat his brothers. Poseidon heard the prayer and from the churning sea rose a snow-white bull. This animal was meant as a sacrifice for Minos to pledge his subservience to Poseidon, but the greedy king coveted the bull and kept it for himself. Enraged, Poseidon caused Minos' wife to fall in love with it. In secret, she engaged Daedalus, Minos' favorite architect, to build her a hollow cow out of wood in which she hid so that the bull would mate with her. The issue of that sexual congress was the Minotaur – a monstrous man with a bull's head and tail – whose savagery wreaked so much havoc on the island that Minos had Daedalus build an enormous labyrinth, so elaborate that the captured Minotaur could never escape from it.

This legend was much in Stepan Spalko's mind as he and his team drove up the city's steep streets, for he had an affinity for Greek myths – their emphasis on rape and incest, bloodletting and hubris. He saw aspects of himself in many of them, so it was not difficult for him to believe himself a demigod.

Like many Mediterranean island towns, Iráklion was built on the side of a mountain, its stone houses rising up the steep streets mercifully plied by taxis and buses. In fact, the entire spine of the island rose in a chain known as the White Mountains.

The address Spalko had obtained by interrogation from László Molnar was a house perhaps halfway up the city slope. It belonged to an architect by the name of Istos Daedalika, who, as it turned out, was as mythical as his ancient namesake. Spalko's team had determined that the house had been leased by a company associated with László Molnar. They arrived at the address just as the night sky was about to be split open like the hull of a nut, revealing the bloody Mediterranean sun.

After a brief reconnoiter, they all donned tiny headphones, connecting themselves electronically over a wireless network. They checked their weapons, high-powered composite crossbows, excellent for the silence they needed to keep. Spalko synchronized his watch with two of his men, then sent them around to the rear entrance while he and Zina approached the front entrance. The remaining member of the team was ordered to keep watch and warn them of any suspect activity on the street or, alternatively, the approach of the police.

The street was deserted and quiet; no one was stirring. There were no lights on in the house, but Spalko didn't expect there to be any. He glanced at his watch, counting into his microphone as the second hand swept toward sixty.

Inside the house, the mercenaries were astir. It was moving day, the last few hours before they would depart as the others had before them. They moved Dr. Schiffer to a different location on Crete every three days; they did it quickly and quietly, the destination being decided upon only at the last minute. Such security measures required that some of them stay behind to ensure every last vestige of their presence was either taken or destroyed.

At this moment, the mercenaries were dispersed throughout the house. One of them was in the kitchen making thick Turkish coffee, a second was in the bathroom, a third had turned on the satellite TV. He watched the screen disinterestedly for a moment, then went to the front window, pulled aside the curtain, peered out into the street. Everything appeared normal. He stretched like a cat, bending his body this way and that. Then, strapping on his shoulder holster, he went to perform his morning perimeter check.

He unlocked the front door, pulled it open and was promptly shot through the heart by Spalko. He pitched backward, his arms splayed, his eyes rolling upward in their sockets, and was dead before he struck the floor.

Spalko and Zina entered the vestibule at the same moment his men crashed through the back door. The mercenary in the kitchen dropped his coffee cup, drew his weapon and wounded one of Spalko's men before he, too, was shot dead.

Nodding to Zina, Spalko took the stairs three at a time.

Zina had reacted to the shots coming through the bathroom door by ordering one of Spalko's men out the back door. She ordered another of Spalko's team to break down the door. This he did quickly and efficiently. No gunfire greeted them as they burst into the bathroom. Instead, they saw the window out which the mercenary had crawled. Zina had anticipated this possibility, hence her sending a man out the back.

A moment later she heard the telltale *thwok!* of the bolt being loosed, followed by a heavy grunt.

Upstairs, Spalko went from room to room in a crouch. The first bedroom was empty and he moved to the second. As he passed the bed, he caught a movement in the wall mirror above the dresser to his left. Something moved under the bed. At once, he dropped to his knees, shot the bolt. It passed through the dust ruffle and the bed was lifted off its feet. A body thrashed and groaned.

On his knees, Spalko fitted another bolt in his crossbow, began to aim it when he was bowled over. Something hard hit his head, a bullet ricocheted and he felt a weight on him. At once he let go of the crossbow, drew out a hunting knife and stabbed upward into his attacker. When it was buried to the hilt, he turned it, gritting his teeth with the effort, and was rewarded with a heavy gout of blood.

With a grunt, he threw the mercenary off him, retrieved his knife, wiped the blade down on the dust ruffle. Then he shot the second bolt down through the bed. Mattress stuffing flew through the air and the thrashing came to an abrupt halt.

He came back downstairs, after having checked the remaining second-floor rooms, into a living room reeking of cordite. One of his men was entering the open back door with the last remaining mercenary, whom he had seriously wounded. The entire assault had lasted less than three minutes, which suited Spalko's design; the less attention they brought to the house, the better.

There was no trace of Dr. Felix Schiffer. And yet Spalko knew that László Molnar hadn't lied to him. These men were part of the mercenary contingent Molnar had hired when he and Conklin had engineered Schiffer's escape.

'What's the final disposition?' he asked his men.

'Marco is wounded. Nothing major, the bullet went in and out the flesh of his left arm,' one of them said. 'Two opposition dead, one seriously wounded.'

Spalko nodded. 'And two dead upstairs.'

Flicking the snout of his machine pistol at the last remaining mercenary, the man added, 'This one won't last long unless he gets treatment.'

Spalko looked at Zina, nodded. She approached the wounded man and, kneeling, turned him over on his back. He groaned and blood leaked out of him.

'What's your name?' she said in Hungarian.

He looked at her, with eyes darkened by pain and knowledge of his own impending death.

She took out a small box of wooden matches. 'What's your name?' she repeated, this time in Greek.

When there was no reply forthcoming, she said to Spalko's men, 'Hold him still.'

Two of them bent to comply. The mercenary struggled briefly, then was still. He stared up at her with equanimity; he was a professional soldier, after all.

She struck the match. A sharp smell of sulphur accompanied the flare of the flame. With her thumb and forefinger, she pried apart the lids of one eye, brought the flame down toward the exposed eyeball.

The mercenary's free eye blinked maniacally and his breathing became stertorous. The flame, reflected in the curve of his glistening orb, moved ever closer. He felt fear, Zina could see that, but beneath that there was a sense of disbelief. He simply did not believe that she would follow through with her implied threat. A pity, but it made no difference to her.

The mercenary screamed, his body arching up despite the men's efforts to hold him down. He writhed and howled even after the match, guttering, fell smoking onto his chest. His good eyeball rolled around in its socket as if trying to find a safe haven.

Zina calmly lit another match, and all at once the mercenary vomited. Zina wasn't deterred. It was vital now that he understand that there was only one response that would stop her. He wasn't stupid; he knew what it was. Also, no amount of money was worth this torture. Through the tearing of his good eye, she could see his capitulation. Still, she wouldn't let him up, not until he'd told her where they had taken Schiffer.

Behind her, observing the scene from start to finish, Stepan Spalko was impressed despite himself. He'd had no clear idea of how Zina would react when he gave her the assignment of interrogation. In a way, it was a test; but it was more – it was a way to get to know her in the intimate fashion he found so pleasurable.

Because he was a man who used words every day of his life in order to manipulate people and events, Spalko had an innate distrust of them. People lied, it was as simple as that. Some liked to lie for the effect it had; others lied without knowing it, in order to protect themselves from scrutiny; still others lied to themselves. It was only in action, in what people did, especially in extreme circumstances or under duress, that their true natures were revealed. There was no possibility of lying then; you could safely believe the evidence arrayed before you.

Now he knew a truth about Zina he hadn't before. He doubted whether Hasan Arsenov knew it, whether he'd even believe it if told. At her core Zina was hard as a rock; she was tougher than Arsenov himself. Watching her now extracting the information from the hapless mercenary, he knew that she could live without Arsenov, though Arsenov couldn't live without her.

Bourne awoke to the sound of practice arpeggios and the aromatic smell of coffee. For a moment he hung between sleep and consciousness. He was aware that he was lying on Annaka Vadas' sofa, that he had an eiderdown comforter over him and a goose feather pillow beneath his head. At once he rose fully out of sleep into Annaka's sun-drenched apartment. He turned, saw her sitting at the gleaming grand piano, a huge cup of coffee by her side.

'What time is it?'

She continued her chord runs without picking up her head. 'After noon.'

'Christ!'

'Yes, it was time for my practice, time you got up.' She began to play a melody he couldn't place. 'I actually thought you'd have gone back to your hotel by the time I awoke, but I came in here and there you were, sleeping like a child. So I went and made coffee. Would you like some?'

'Absolutely.'

'You know where it is.'

She picked up her head then, refused to turn away, watched him as he peeled off the eiderdown, drew on his cords and shirt. He padded into the bathroom, and when he was finished, he went into the kitchen. As he was pouring himself coffee, she said, 'You have a nice body, scarred though it is.'

He searched for cream; apparently she liked her coffee black. 'The scars give me character.'

'Even the one around your neck?'

Poking through the refrigerator, he didn't answer her but, rather, involuntarily put a hand to the wound, and in so doing felt again Mylene Dutronc's compassionate ministrations.

'That one's new,' she said. 'What happened?'

'I had an encounter with a very large, very angry creature.'

She stirred, abruptly uneasy. 'Who tried to strangle you?'

He had found the cream. He poured in a dollop, then two teaspoonfuls of sugar, took his first sip. Returning to the living room, he said, 'Anger can do that to you, or didn't you know?'

'How would I? I'm not a part of your violent world.'

He looked at her levelly. 'You tried to shoot me, or have you forgotten?'

'I don't forget anything,' she said shortly.

Something he'd said had chafed her, but he didn't know what it was. Part of her was frayed thin. Perhaps it was only the shock of her father's sudden and violent death.

In any case he decided to try another tack. 'There's nothing edible in your refrigerator.'

'I usually go out to eat. There's a sweet café five blocks away.'

'Do you think we could go there?' he said. 'I'm starving.'

'As soon as I'm finished. Our late night delayed my day.'

The piano bench scraped the floor as she settled herself more fully. Then the first bars of Chopin's Nocturne in B-Flat Minor drifted through the room, swirling like leaves falling on a golden autumn afternoon. He was surprised at how much pleasure the music gave him.

After some moments, he got up, went to the small escritoire and opened her computer.

'Please don't do that,' Annaka said without taking her eyes from the music sheet. 'It's distracting.'

Bourne sat, trying to relax, while the gorgeous music swept through the apartment.

While the last of the Nocturne was still echoing, Annaka rose, went into the kitchen. He heard the water in the sink running while she waited for it to get cold. It seemed to run for a long time. She returned then, with a glass of water in one hand, which she drank down in a single long swallow. Bourne, watching her from his position at the escritoire, saw the curve of her pale neck, the curl of several stray strands, a fiery copper, at her hairline.

'You did very well last night,' Bourne said.

'Thank you for talking me down from the ledge.' Her eyes slid away, as if she didn't want any part of his compliment. 'I was never so frightened in my life.'

They were in the café, which was filled with cut-glass chandeliers, velvet-seat cushions and translucent wall sconces affixed to cherrywood walls. They sat across from each other at a window table, overlooking the outdoor portion of the café, which was deserted, it being still too chilly to sit in the pale morning sun.

'My concern now is that Molnar's apartment was under surveillance,' Bourne said. 'There's no other explanation for the police arriving at just that time.'

'But why would anyone be watching the apartment?'

'To see if we showed up. Ever since I've arrived in Budapest, my inquiries have been frustrated.'

Annaka glanced nervously out the window. 'What about now? The thought of someone watching my apartment – watching *us* – gives me the creeps.'

'No one followed us here from your apartment, I made sure of that.' He paused while their food was served. When the waiter had departed, he resumed. 'Remember the precautions I made us take last night after we escaped the police? We took separate taxis, changed twice, reversed direction.'

She nodded. 'I was too exhausted then to question your bizarre instructions.'

'No one knows where we went or even that we're together now.'

'Well, that's a relief.' She released a long-held breath.

Khan had just one thought when he saw Bourne and the woman walk out of her building: Despite Spalko's cocky assurances that he was safe from Bourne's search, Bourne was continuing to circle closer. Somehow Bourne had found out about László Molnar, the man Spalko was interested in. Furthermore, he'd discovered where Molnar lived and, presumably, he'd been inside the apartment when the police showed up. Why was Molnar important to Bourne? Khan had to find out.

He watched from behind as Bourne and the woman walked off. Then he got out of his rental car, went into the entrance of 106–108 Fo utca. He picked the lock on the lobby door and entered the hallway inside. Taking the elevator up to the top floor, he found the staircase up to the roof. Unsurprisingly, the door was alarmed, but for him it was a simple matter to jump the circuit, bypassing the alarm system altogether. He went through the door, onto the roof, crossing immediately to the front of the building.

With his hands on the stone parapet, he leaned over, saw immediately the bay window on the fourth floor just below him. Climbing over the parapet, he eased himself down onto the ledge beneath the window. The first window he tried was locked, but the other wasn't. He opened the window, climbed through into the apartment.

He would dearly have liked to look around, but without knowing how soon they would return, he knew he couldn't risk it. This was a time for business, not indulgences. Looking around for a likely spot, he glanced up at the frosted-glass light fixture hanging from the center of the ceiling. It was as good as any, he quickly determined, and better than most.

Dragging over the piano bench, he positioned it beneath the fixture, then climbed on it. He took out the miniature electronic bug, dropped it over the rim of the frosted-glass bowl. Then he climbed down, put an electronic ear-bud into his ear and activated the bug.

He heard the small noises as he moved the piano bench back into place, heard his own footfalls across the polished wooden floor as he went over to the sofa, where a pillow and down comforter lay. He took up the pillow, sniffed its center. He smelled Bourne, but the scent stirred a previously undisturbed memory. As it began to rise upward in his mind, he dropped the pillow as if it had burst into flame. Quickly now, he exited the apartment as he had come, retracing his steps down to the lobby. But this time he went back through the building, going out the service entrance. One could never be too careful.

Annaka began work on her breakfast. Sunlight streamed in through the window, illuminating her extraordinary fingers. She ate like she played, handling the cutlery as if they were musical instruments.

'Where did you learn to play piano like that?' he said.

'Did you like it?'

'Yes, very much.'

'Why?'

He cocked his head. 'Why?'

She nodded. 'Yes, why did you like it? What did you hear in it?'

Bourne thought a moment. 'A kind of mournfulness, I suppose.'

She put down her knife and fork and, with her hands free, began to sing a section of the Nocturne. 'It's the unresolved dominant sevenths, you see. With them, Chopin expanded the accepted limits of dissonance and key.' She resumed singing, the notes ringing out. 'The result is expansive. And at the same time mournful, because of those unresolved dominant sevenths.'

She paused, her beautiful pale hands hanging suspended over the table, the long fingers arched slightly as if still imbued with the energy of the composer.

'Anything else?'

He gave it some more thought, then shook his head.

She took up her knife and fork, went back to eating. 'My mother taught me to play. It was her profession, teaching piano, and as soon as she felt that I was good enough, she taught me Chopin. He was her favorite, but his music is immensely difficult to play – not only technically but also getting the emotion right.'

'Does your mother still play?'

Annaka shook her head. 'Like Chopin, her health was frail. Tuberculosis. She died when I was eighteen.'

'A bad age to lose a parent.'

'It changed my life forever. I was grief-stricken, of course, but much to my astonishment and shame, beneath that I was angry at her.'

'Angry?'

She nodded. 'I felt abandoned, unmoored, left at sea with no way to find my way back home.'

All at once Bourne understood how she could empathize with the difficulty of his loss of memory.

She frowned. 'But, really, what I regret most is how shabbily I treated her. When she first proposed I take up the piano, I rebelled.'

'Of course you did,' he said gently. 'It was her suggestion. Moreover, it was her profession.' He felt a small *frisson* in the pit of his stomach, as if she had just now played one of Chopin's famous dissonances. 'When I talked to my son about baseball, he turned up his nose, wanted to play soccer instead.' As he dredged up the memory of Joshua, Bourne's eyes turned inward. 'All his friends played soccer, but there was something else. His mother was Thai; he was schooled in Buddhism at a very early age, as was her wish. His "American-ness" wasn't of interest to him.'

Finished, Annaka pushed her plate away.

'On the contrary, I think it was probable that his "American-ness" was very much on his mind,' she said. 'How could it be otherwise? Don't you think he was reminded of it every day at school?'

Unbidden came an image of Joshua in bandages, one eye black-and-blue. When he had asked Dao about it, she had told him that the child had fallen at home, but the following day she had taken Joshua to school herself, had stayed there for several hours. He'd never questioned her; at the time he'd been far too busy at work even to think it through himself.

'It never occurred to me,' he said now.

Annaka shrugged and, without perceptible irony, said, 'Why should it? You're American. The world belongs to you.'

Was that the source of her innate animosity? he wondered. Was it simply generic, the fear of the ugly American that had lately been resurrected?

She asked the waiter for more coffee. 'At least you're able to work things out with your son,' she said. 'With my mother . . .' She shrugged.

'My son's dead,' Bourne said, 'along with his sister and mother. They were killed in Phnom Penh many years ago.'

'Oh.' It appeared that he had finally punctured her cool, steely exterior. 'I'm so sorry.'

He turned his head away; any talk of Joshua felt like salt being rubbed into an open wound. 'Surely you came to terms with your mother before she died.'

'I wish I had.' Annaka stared down at her coffee, a look of concentration on her face. 'It wasn't until she introduced me to Chopin that I understood the full measure of the gift she had given me. How I loved to play the Nocturnes, even when I was far from accomplished!'

'You didn't tell her?'

'I was a teenager; we weren't exactly talking.' Her eyes darkened in sorrow. 'Now that she's gone, I wish I had.'

'You had your father.'

'Yes, of course,' she said. 'I had him.'

# 17

The Tactical Non-Lethal Weapons Directorate was housed in a series of anonymous-looking red-brick buildings covered with climbing ivy that had once been a women's boarding school. The Agency had deemed it more secure to take over an existing site than to build one from scratch. That way they could gut the structures, creating from the inside the warren of labs, conference rooms and testing sites the directorate required, using their own highly skilled personnel rather than outside contractors.

Even though Lindros showed his ID he was taken inside an all-white windowless room where he was photographed, fingerprinted and his retinas scanned. He waited alone.

Finally, after fifteen minutes or so, a CIA suit entered, addressed Lindros, 'Deputy Director Lindros, Director Driver will see you now.'

Without a word, Lindros followed the suit out of the room. They spent another five minutes marching up and down featureless corridors with indirect lighting. For all he knew, he was being led around in a circle.

At length, the suit stopped at a door that, as far as Lindros could tell, was identical to all the others they had passed. As with the others, there was no marking, no identification of any sort anywhere on or near the door, save for two small bulbs. One glowed a deep red. The suit rapped his knuckles three times on the door. A moment later the red light went out and the other bulb glowed green. The suit opened the door, stepped back for him to go through.

On the other side of it, he found Director Randy Driver, a sandy-haired individual with a Marine high-and-tight haircut, a blade-straight nose and narrow blue eyes that gave him a perpetually suspicious look. He had wide shoulders and a muscular torso he liked to show off a bit too much. He sat in a high-tech mesh swivel chair behind a smoked glass and stainless-steel desk. In the center of each white metal wall hung a reproduction of a Mark Rothko painting, each looking like swaths of colored bandages applied to a raw wound.

'Deputy Director, an unexpected pleasure,' Driver said with a tight smile that belied his words. 'I confess I'm not accustomed to snap inspections. I would've preferred the courtesy of an appointment.'

'Apologies,' Lindros said, 'but this isn't a snap inspection. I'm conducting a murder investigation.'

'Alexander Conklin's murder, I presume.'

'Indeed. I need to interview one of your people. A Dr. Felix Schiffer.'

It was as if Lindros had dropped an immobility bomb. Driver sat unmoving behind his desk, the tight smile frozen on his face like a rictus. At last, Driver seemed to regain his composure. 'What on earth for?'

'I just told you,' Lindros said. 'It's part of our ongoing investigation.'

Driver spread his hands. 'I can't see how.'

'It's not required that you do,' Lindros said shortly. Driver had made him sit and wait like a child at detention, now he was being given a verbal runaround. Lindros was rapidly losing patience with him. 'All that's required is that you tell me where Dr. Schiffer is.'

Driver's face closed down entirely. 'The moment you crossed my threshold, you entered my territory.' He stood. 'While you were undergoing our identification procedures, I took the liberty of calling the DCI. His office has no idea why you might be here.'

'Of course not,' Lindros retorted, knowing he'd already lost the battle. 'The DCI debriefs me at the end of each day.'

'I've no interest whatsoever in your operations, Deputy Director. The bottom line is that no one interviews any of my personnel without express written author- ization from the DCI himself.'

'The DCI has empowered me to take this investigation wherever I deem it necessary.'

'I've only your word for that.' Driver shrugged. 'You can see my point of vi – '

'As a matter of fact, I can't,' Lindros said. He knew that continuing on in this vein would get him nowhere. Worse, it wasn't politic, but Randy Driver had pissed him off and he couldn't help himself. 'In my view, you're being obstinate and obstructionist.'

Driver leaned forward, his knuckles cracking as he pushed them down against the desk top. 'Your view is irrelevant. In the absence of official signed documents, I have nothing more to say to you. This interview is at an end.'

The suit must have been listening in on the conversation because just then the door opened and he stood there, waiting to escort Lindros out.

It was while riding down a perp that Detective Harris got the brainstorm. He'd received the all-points radio call about the male Caucasian in a black late model Pontiac GTO, Virginia plates, who'd run a red light outside of Falls Church, heading south on Route 649. Harris, who had been inexplicably banished by Martin Lindros from the Conklin-Panov murders, was in Sleepy Hollow, fol- lowing up on a convenience store robbery-murder when the call came in. Right on 649.

He spun his cruiser around in a ragged U-turn, then had headed off, lights going, siren blaring, heading north on 649. Almost immediately, he saw the black GTO and behind it a string of three Virginia state trooper cars.

He veered across the median in a blare of horns and screeching tires coming from the oncoming traffic and headed straight at the GTO. The driver saw him, changed lanes, and as Harris began to follow him through the jigsaw puzzle of stalled traffic, he veered off the road itself, zipping across the breakdown lane.

Harris, calculating vectors, nosed his cruiser on an intercept course, which forced the plunging GTO onto the apron of a gas station. If he didn't pull up, he'd crash right into the line of pumps.

As the GTO screamed to a halt, rocking on its oversized shocks, Harris scrambled out of his car, his service revolver drawn, headed straight at the driver.

'Get out of the car with your hands in the air!' Harris called.

'Officer – '

'Shut up and do as I say!' Harris said, advancing steadily, his eyes peeled for any sign of a weapon.

'Okay, okay!'

The driver got out of the car just as the other cruisers caught up. Harris could see that the perp was no more than twenty-two, thin as a rail. They found a pint of liquor in the car and, underneath the front seat, a gun.

'I've got a license for it!' the young man said. 'Just look in the glove compartment!'

The gun was, indeed, licensed. The young man was a diamond courier. Why he'd been drinking was another story, one Harris wasn't particularly interested in.

Back at the station, what had caught his attention was that the license didn't check out. He made a call to the store that had supposedly sold the young man the gun. He got a foreign-sounding voice that admitted selling the young man the gun, but something in that voice nagged at Harris. So he'd taken a ride over to the store, only to find that it didn't exist. Instead, he found a single Russian with a computer server. He arrested the Russian and impounded the server.

Now he returned to the station, accessed the gun-permit database for the last six months. He plugged in the name of the bogus gun store and discovered, to his shock, more than three hundred false sales that were used to generate legitimate permits. But there was an even bigger surprise waiting for him when he accessed the files on the server he'd confiscated. When he saw the entry, he grabbed his phone and dialed Lindros' cell.

'Hey, it's Harry.'

'Oh, hello,' Lindros said, as if his attention was elsewhere.

'What's the matter?' Harris asked. 'You sound terrible.'

'I'm stymied. Worse, I just got my teeth figuratively kicked in and now I'm wondering if I have enough ammunition to go to the Old Man with it.'

'Listen, Martin, I know I'm officially off the case – '

'Jesus, Harry, I've been meaning to talk to you about that.'

'Never mind now,' Detective Harris interrupted. He launched into an abbreviated account of the driver of the GTO, his gun, and the scam being run on falsely registered guns. 'You see how it works,' he went on. 'These guys can get guns for anyone they want.'

'Yeah, so?' Lindros said without much enthusiasm.

'So they can also put anyone's name on the registration. Like David Webb's.'

'That's a nice theory, but – '

'Martin, it isn't a theory!' Harris was fairly shouting into the receiver; everyone around him looked up from their work, surprised at the rising sound of his voice. 'It's the real deal!'

'What?!'

'That's right. This same ring 'sold' a gun to one David Webb, only Webb never bought it, because the store on the permit doesn't exist.'

'Okay, but how d'we know Webb didn't know about this ring and used them to get a gun illegally?'

'That's the beauty part,' Harris said. 'I have the electronic ledger from the ring. Every sale is meticulously recorded. Funds for the gun Webb supposedly bought were wired in from Budapest.'

The monastery perched atop a mountain ridge. On the steep terraces far below, it grew oranges and olives, but up above, where the building seemed implanted like a molar in the bedrock itself, there grew only thistle and wild laudanum. *Kri-kri*, the ubiquitous Cretan mountain goat, were the only creatures able to sustain themselves at the level of the monastery.

The ancient stone construction had long been forgotten. Which of the marauding peoples from the island's storied history had built it was difficult for a lay person to say. It had, like Crete itself, passed through many hands, been mute witness to prayers and sacrifice and the spilling of blood. Even from a cursory glance, however, it was clear that it was very old.

From the dawn of time, the issue of security had been of paramount importance to warriors and monastics alike, hence the monastery's place atop the mountain. On one slope were the fragrant terraced groves; on the other was a gorge, not unlike the slash of a Saracen's cutlass, scored deep into the rock, opening up the mountain's flesh.

Having encountered professional resistance at the house in Iraklion, Spalko proceeded to plan this assault with a great deal of care. Making a run at the place in daylight was out of the question. No matter in which direction they might try it, they were certain to be mowed down long before they reached the monastery's thick and crenelated outer walls. Therefore, while his men took their wounded compatriot back to the jet to be tended to by the surgeon and to assemble the needed supplies, Spalko and Zina rented motorcycles so that they could reconnoiter the area surrounding the monastery.

At the edge of the gorge, they left their vehicles and hiked down. The sky was an absorbent blue, so brilliant that it seemed to imbue every other color with its aura. Birds circled and rose on the thermals, and when the breeze picked up, the delicious scent of orange blossoms perfumed the air. Ever since she boarded his personal jet, Zina had been patiently waiting to find out why Spalko wanted to get her alone.

'There's an underground entrance to the monastery,' Spalko said, as they descended the rocky scree into the end of the gorge closest to the structure. The chestnut trees on the lip of the gorge had given way to tougher cypresses, whose twisted trunks extended from the earthen crannies between boulders. They used the flexible branches as impromptu handholds as they continued down the steep slope of the gorge.

Where the Shaykh got his information, Zina could only guess at. In any event, it was clear that he possessed a worldwide network of people with ready access to almost any information he could require.

They rested for a moment, leaning against an outcropping. The afternoon was getting on, and they ate olives, flatbread and a bit of octopus marinated in olive oil, vinegar and garlic.

'Tell me, Zina,' Spalko said now, 'do you think of Khalid Murat – do you miss him?'

'I miss him very much.' Zina wiped her lips with the back of her hand, bit into a wedge of flatbread. 'But Hasan is our leader now; all things must pass. What happened to him was tragic but not unexpected. We're all targets of the savage Russian regime; we all have to live with that knowledge.'

'What if I were to tell you that the Russians had nothing to do with Khalid Murat's death?' Spalko said.

Zina stopped eating. 'I don't understand. I know what happened. Everyone does.'

'No,' Spalko said softly, 'all you know is what Hasan Arsenov has told you.'

She stared at him, and in the dawning of comprehension her knees felt weak.

'How – ' She was so full of emotion her voice failed her and she was obliged to clear her throat, start over again, aware that part of her didn't want to know the answer to the question she was about to ask. 'How d'you know this?'

'I know,' Spalko said levelly, 'because Arsenov contracted with me to assassinate Khalid Murat.'

'But *why*?'

Spalko's eyes bored into hers. 'Oh, you know, Zina – you, of all people – you who's his lover, who knows him better than anyone – you know very well.'

And, sadly, Zina did; Hasan had told her as much many times. Khalid Murat was part of the old order. He couldn't think past the borders of Chechnya; in Hasan's opinion, he was afraid to take on the world when he could not yet see a way for them to hold back the Russian infidels.

'Didn't you suspect?'

And the truly galling thing, she thought, was that she *hadn't* suspected, not for a moment. She had believed Hasan's story from first word to last. She wanted to lie to the Shaykh, to make herself look more clever in his eyes, but under the burden of his gaze, she knew he'd see right through her and know she was lying, and then, she suspected, he'd know she couldn't be trusted and he'd be finished with her.

And so, humiliated, she shook her head. 'He had me fooled.'

'You and everyone else,' he said evenly. 'Never mind.' He smiled suddenly. 'But now you know the truth; you see the power of having information others don't.'

She stood for a moment, her buttocks against the sun-heated rock, rubbing her palms down her thighs. 'What I don't understand,' she said, 'is why you've chosen to tell me.'

Spalko heard the twin notes of fear and trepidation in her voice and decided that was as it should be. She knew she stood on the edge of a precipice. If he was any judge of character, she had suspected as much from the moment he had proposed she come with him to Crete, certainly from the instant she had colluded with him in his lie to Arsenov.

'Yes,' he said, 'you've been chosen.'

'But for what?' She found that she was shaking.

He came and stood close to her. Blocking out the sunlight, he exchanged the sun's warmth for his own. She could smell him, as she had in the hangar, and the male musk of him made her wet.

'You've been chosen for great things.' As he came ever closer, his voice dropped in volume even while it was increasing in intensity.

'Zina,' he whispered, 'Hasan Arsenov is weak. I knew it the moment he came to me with his scheme for assassination. Why should he need me? I asked myself. A strong warrior who believes his leader is no longer fit to lead will undertake to murder the man himself; he will not hire out the deed to others who, if they are clever and patient, will one day use his weakness against him.'

Zina was trembling, both from his words and the force of his physical presence, which was making her feel as if her skin was prickling, her hair standing on end. Her mouth was dry, her throat full with longing.

'If Hasan Arsenov is weak, Zina, of what use is he to me?' Spalko put a hand on her breast and Zina's nostrils flared. 'I'll tell you.' She closed her eyes. 'The mission we'll shortly embark on is fraught with danger every step of the way.' He squeezed gently, pulling upward with agonizing slowness. 'In the event something goes wrong, it's prudent to have a leader who can like a magnet attract the attention of the enemy, drawing them toward him even as the real work goes on unimpeded.' He pressed his body against hers, felt her rising against him in a kind of spasm she was powerless to control. 'Do you see what I mean?'

'Yes,' she whispered.

'You're the strong one, Zina. If you had wanted to dethrone Khalid Murat, you'd never have come to me first. You'd have taken his life yourself and considered it a blessing you'd done for yourself and for your people.' His other hand moved inward along her thigh. 'Isn't that so?'

'Yes,' she breathed. 'But my people will never accept a female leader. It's inconceivable.'

'To them but not to us.' He drew one leg away. 'Think, Zina. How will you make it happen?'

With the hot rush of hormones racing through her, it was hard to think clearly. Part of her realized that that was the point. It wasn't simply that he wanted to take her here in the cleft of the gorge, against the naked rocks, beneath the naked sky. As he had back in the architect's house, he was submitting her to another test. If she lost herself completely now, if she failed to put her mind in gear, if he could make her so beclouded with desire that she couldn't answer his question, then he would be done with her. He would find another candidate to serve his purpose.

Even as he opened her blouse, touched her burning skin, she forced herself to remember how it had been with Khalid Murat, how after his advisors had left their twice-weekly councils, he had listened to what she had to say and often acted on it. She'd never dared tell Hasan the role she'd played, for fear she would be abandoned to the brutality of his jealousy.

But now, splayed out on the rock beneath the Shaykh's advances, she extrapolated forward. Grabbing the back of the Shayhk's head, pulling it down to her neck, she whispered in his ear, 'I'll find someone – someone physically intimidating, someone whose love for me will make him compliant – and I will command through him. It'll be his face the Chechen see, his voice they'll hear, but he'll be doing precisely what I tell him to do.'

He'd pulled his upper torso away for a moment and she looked up into his eyes, saw them glittering as much with admiration as with lust, and with another tremor of exultation she knew that she had passed her second test. And then, opened and all at once impaled, she groaned in a long, drawn-out exclamation of their shared joy.

# 18

The scent of coffee still infused the apartment. They had returned after their meal without dawdling in time-honored tradition over coffee and dessert. Bourne had too much on his mind. But the respite, however brief, had served to revive him, had allowed his subconscious to work on information he needed to process.

They entered the apartment very close together. Citrus and musk rose off her like mist off a river; he couldn't help inhaling it deep into his lungs. In order to distract himself, he grimly turned his mind to the business at hand.

'Did you notice the burns and lesions, the punctures and ligature marks on László Molnár's body?'

She shuddered. 'Don't remind me.'

'He'd been tortured over a period of many hours, perhaps as much as a couple of days.'

She looked at him from beneath straight and serious brows.

'Which means,' he said, 'that he may have given away Dr. Schiffer's location.'

'Or he may not have,' she said, 'which would also be a reason to kill him.'

'I don't think we can afford to make that assumption.'

'What d'you mean "we"?'

'Yes, I know, as of now I'm on my own.'

'Are you trying to make me feel guilty? You forget, I have no interest in finding Dr. Schiffer.'

*'Even if it meant a disaster for the world at large if he fell into the wrong hands?'*

*'What d'you mean?'*

Khan, in his rental car downstairs, pressed the ear-bud. Their words were coming in clearly.

*'Alex Conklin was a master technician – it was his speciality. From what I've learned, he was better at planning and executing complex missions than anyone I ever met. As I told you, he wanted Dr. Schiffer so badly that he poached him off a top-secret Department of Defense program, brought him over to the CIA and then promptly "disappeared" him. That means whatever Schiffer was working on was so important that Alex felt the need to keep him out of harm's way. And as it turned out, he was right, because someone kidnapped Dr. Schiffer. The operation your father ran for him got him away, hidden somewhere only László Molnár knew about. Now your father's dead and so is Molnar. The difference is that Molnar was tortured before he was killed.'*

Khan sat up straighter, his heart beating fast. *Your father?* Could the woman

181

Bourne was with, the one to whom he'd paid no attention – could she really be Annaka?

Annaka stood in a patch of sunlight coming in through her bay window. 'What d'you think Dr. Schiffer was working on that interested all these people so much?'

'I thought you had no interest in Dr. Schiffer,' Bourne said.

'Don't be snide. Just answer the question.'

'Schiffer is the world's foremost expert in bacteriological particulate behavior. That's what I found out from the forum site Molnar had visited. I told you, but you were too busy finding poor Molnar's corpse.'

'That sounds like gibberish to me.'

'Remember the Web site Molnar had accessed?'

'Anthrax, Argentinean hemorrhagic fever . . .'

'Cryptococcosis, pneumonic plague. I think it's possible that the good doctor was working with these lethal biologicals or something similar, maybe something even worse.'

Annaka stared at him for a moment, shook her head.

'I think what got Alex so excited – and frightened – was that Dr. Schiffer has invented a device that could be used as a biological weapon. If so, he holds one of the terrorists' holy grails.'

'Oh, my God! But that's only a guess. How can you be sure you're right?'

'I've just got to keep digging.' Bourne said. 'Still so sanguine about Dr. Schiffer's whereabouts?'

'But I don't see how we can find him.' She turned and went to the piano, as if it were a touchstone or a talisman to keep her safe from harm.

'We,' Bourne said. 'You said "we."'

'A slip of the tongue.'

'A Freudian slip, it would seem.'

'Stop it,' she said crossly, 'right now.'

He had gotten enough of the measure of her to know that she meant what she said. He went and sat down behind the escritoire. He saw the LAN line that connected her laptop computer to the Internet.

'I've got an idea.' he said. That was when he saw the scratches. The sunlight was hitting the highly polished surface of the piano bench in such a way that he could see several marks, freshly made. Someone had been in the apartment while they had been out. For what reason? He looked around for any signs of a disturbance.

'What is it?' Annaka asked. 'What's the matter?'

'Nothing,' he said. But the pillow wasn't in quite the same position in which he'd left it; it was now skewed a bit to the right.

She put her hand on her hip. 'So what's your idea?'

'I need to get something first,' he improvised, 'from the hotel.' He didn't want to alarm her, but he needed to find a way to do some clandestine recon work. It was possible – perhaps even likely – that whoever had been in the apartment was still nearby. After all, they'd been under surveillance at László Molnar's apartment. But how the hell had the watcher trailed them here? he asked himself. He'd been careful in every way that he could imagine. There was a ready answer, of course: Khan had found him.

Bourne grabbed his leather jacket and headed for the door. 'I won't be long, I promise. In the meantime, if you want to be useful, you can go back on that Web site, see what more you can discover.'

Jamie Hull, head of American security at the terrorism summit in Reykjavik, had a thing for Arabs. He didn't like them; he didn't trust them. They didn't even believe in God – at least, not the right one – let alone believe in Christ the Savior, he thought sourly as he strode down the hallway of the vast Oskjuhlid Hotel.

Another reason to dislike them: They had under their control three-quarters of the world's oil. But then, if not for that, no one would've paid them the slightest attention, and all things being equal, they would've wiped themselves out through their indecipherable webs of intertribal warfare. As it was, there were four different Arabic security teams, one for each country present, but Feyd al-Saoud coordinated their work.

As Arabs went, Feyd al-Saoud wasn't so bad. He was a Saudi – or was it Sunni? Hull shook his head. He didn't know. This was another reason he didn't like them; you never could tell who the hell they were or whose arm they'd cut off, given the chance. Feyd al-Saoud was even Western-schooled, somewhere in London, Oxford – or was it Cambridge? Hull asked himself. As if there was any difference! The point was you could speak to the man in plain English without him looking at you as if you'd just grown a second head.

Also, it seemed to Hull, he was a reasonable man, which meant that he knew his place. When it came to the president's needs and desires, he deferred to Hull on almost everything, which was more than you could say for that sonuva-socialist-bitch Boris Illyich Karpov. He regretted bitterly having complained about him to the Old Man and being barked at in return, but, really, Karpov was the most exasperating bastard Hull had ever had the misfortune to work with.

He entered the multitiered conference theater where the summit itself would take place. It was a perfect oval, with a wave-form ceiling made up of blue panels of acoustic baffling. Hidden behind these panels were the large air ducts that allowed in the air filtered by the forum's sophisticated HVAC system, completely separate from the hotel's massive network. For the rest, the walls were of polished teak, the seats blue-cushioned, the horizontal surfaces either bronze or smoked-glass.

Here, every day since he had arrived, he and his two counterparts met in the mornings to refine and argue about details of the elaborate security arrangements. In the afternoons they reconvened with their respective staffs to review the details and to brief their respective personnel on the latest procedures. Ever since they'd arrived, the entire hotel had been closed to the public so that the security teams could do their electronic sweeps and inspections and make the area absolutely secure.

As he walked into the brightly lit forum, he saw his counterparts: Feyd al-Saoud, slim and dark-eyed above his beak of a nose, with a bearing that was almost regal; Boris Illyich Karpov, head of the FSB's elite Alpha Unit, brawny and bull-like, with wide shoulders and narrow hips, a flat Tatar face that seemed brutal beneath heavy brows and thick black hair. Hull had never seen Karpov smile, and as for Feyd al-Saoud, he doubted he knew how.

'Good morning, fellow travelers,' Boris Illyich Karpov said in his ponderous deadpan manner that put Hull in mind of a 1950s newscaster. 'We have but three days until the summit commences and there is still much work to accomplish. Shall we begin?'

'By all means,' Feyd al-Saoud said, taking his accustomed seat on the dais where just thirty-six hours from now the five heads of the leading Arab states would sit side by side with residents of the United States and Russia in order to hammer out the first concerted Arab-Western initiative to stop international terrorism in its tracks. 'I've received instructions from my counterparts in the other attending Islamic nations and will be pleased to relay them to you.'

'Demands, you mean,' Karpov said belligerently. He'd never gotten over their decision to speak English at their briefings; he'd been outvoted two to one.

'Boris, why must you always put a negative spin on things?' Hull said.

Karpov bristled; Hull knew he disliked American informality. 'Demands have a certain stench, Mr. Hull.' He tapped the end of his ruddy nose. 'I can smell them.'

'I'm surprised you can smell anything, Boris, after years of drinking vodka.'

'Drinking vodka makes us strong, makes us real men.' Karpov turned his red lips into a bow of derision. 'Not like you Americans.'

'I should listen to you, Boris? You, a Russian? Your country's an abject failure. Communism proved so corrupt Russia imploded under its weight. And as for your people, they're spiritually bankrupt.'

Karpov leaped up, his cheeks as red as his nose and lips. 'I've had enough of your insults!'

'Too bad.' Hull stood, kicking his chair over, forgetting completely the DCI's admonishment. 'I'm only just warming up.'

'Gentlemen, gentlemen!' Feyd al-Saoud interposed himself between the two antagonists. 'Tell me, please, how these childish arguments are going to further the task we've all been sent here to accomplish.' His voice was calm and even-toned as he looked from one to the other. 'We each have our respective heads of state, whom we serve with unswerving loyalty. Isn't that true? Then we must serve them in the best way we can.' He wouldn't let up until both had agreed.

Karpov sat back down, though with arms crossed over his chest. Hull righted his chair, dragged it back to the table and threw himself into it, a sour expression on his face.

Observing them, Feyd al-Saoud said, 'We may not like one another, but we must learn to work together.'

Dimly, Hull was aware that there was something else about Karpov besides his aggressive intransigence that got under his skin. It took him some moments to locate its origin, but at length he did. Something about Karpov – his smug self-satisfaction – reminded him of David Webb, or Jason Bourne, as all Agency personnel had been ordered to call him. It was Bourne who'd become Alex Conklin's fair-haired boy, despite all the politicking and subtle campaigning Hull had done on his own behalf before he'd given up and gone into the Counterterrorist Center. He'd made a success of his new post, no question, but he never forgot what Bourne had forced him to leave behind. Conklin had been a legend within the Agency. Working with him was all Hull had dreamed about ever since he'd joined the Agency twenty years ago. There are dreams one has as a child; these aren't difficult to let go of. But the dreams one had as an adult, well, that was another matter entirely. The bitterness of what might have been never went away, at least, not in Hull's experience.

He'd actually celebrated when the DCI had informed him that Bourne might be on his way to Reykjavík. The thought of Bourne having turned on his mentor and gone rogue was one that made his blood boil. If only Conklin had chosen him, Hull had thought, he'd be alive today. The thought that he might be the one to terminate Bourne in an Agency sanction was a dream come true. But then he'd got the news that Bourne was dead and his elation had turned to disappointment. He'd become increasingly testy with everyone, including the Secret Service operatives with whom it was vital he keep a close and open relationship. Now, in the absence of any kind of fulfillment, he leveled a murderous look at Karpov and received one in return.

Bourne didn't take the elevator down when he left Annaka's apartment. Instead, he went up the short flight of utility stairs that led to the roof. There, he confronted the alarm system and defeated it quickly and efficiently.

The sun had abandoned the afternoon to slate-gray clouds and a stiff quartering wind. As Bourne gazed south, he could see the four elaborate domes of the Kiraly Turkish Baths. He went to the parapet, leaned over in more or less the same spot that Khan had occupied no more than an hour before.

From this vantage point, he scanned the street, first for anyone standing in a shadowed doorway, then for any pedestrians walking too slowly or stopped altogether. He watched two young women strolling arm in arm, a mother pushing a pram, and an old man he scrutinized, recalling Khan's expert work as a chameleon.

Finding nothing suspicious, he turned his attention to the parked cars, looking for anything out of the ordinary. All rental cars in Hungary were obliged to have a sticker identifying themselves as such. In this residential neighborhood, a rental car was something he'd need to investigate.

He found one on a black Skoda up the block and across the street. He studied its position in detail. Anyone sitting behind the wheel would have an unobstructed view of the front entrance to 106–108 Fo utca. At the moment, however, there was no one behind the wheel or anywhere else inside the car.

He turned and strode back across the rooftop.

Khan, crouched on the stairwell in readiness, watched Bourne coming toward him. This was his chance, he knew. Bourne, his mind no doubt filled with matters of surveillance, was completely unsuspecting. As if in a dream – a dream he'd had in his mind for decades – he saw Bourne heading straight toward him, his eyes clouded with thought. Khan was filled with rage. This was the man who had sat next to him and not recognized him, who even when Khan had identified himself had rejected him for who he was. This only intensified Khan's belief that Bourne had never wanted him, that he was all too ready to run away and abandon him.

Therefore, when Khan rose, it was with righteous fury. As Bourne stepped into the shadow of the doorway, Khan slammed his forehead hard into the bridge of his nose. Blood flew and Bourne staggered backward. Khan, pressing his advantage, moved in, but Bourne kicked out.

'Che-sah!' Bourne exhaled.

Khan absorbed the kick by partially deflecting it, then clamped his left arm against the side of his body, trapping Bourne's ankle in between. Bourne surprised him, then. Instead of being thrown off balance, he rose up, pressing his back and buttocks against the steel door, kicked with his right foot, delivering a sickening blow to Khan's right shoulder, so that Khan was obliged to let go of Bourne's left ankle.

'*Mee-sah!*' Bourne cried softly.

He came at Khan, who shuddered as if in pain even as he delivered a straight-fingered blow to Bourne's sternum. At once he gripped Bourne's head on either side, cracked it against the roof door. Bourne's eyes went out of focus.

'What's Spalko up to?' Khan said harshly. 'You know, don't you?'

Bourne's head was swimming with pain and shock. He tried to focus his eyes and clear his mind at the same time.

'Who's . . . Spalko?' His voice seemed watery, as if it was coming from a long way off.

'Of course you know.'

Bourne shook his head, which produced a fusillade of daggers in his head all digging in at once. He squeezed his eyes shut.

'I thought . . . I thought you wanted to kill me.'

'Listen to me!'

'Who are you?' Bourne whispered hoarsely. 'How d'you know about my son? How d'you know about Joshua?'

'Listen to me!' Khan put his head close to Bourne's. 'Stepan Spalko is the man who ordered Alex Conklin's death, the man who set you up – who set us both up. Why did he do that, Bourne? You know and I need to know!'

Bourne felt as if he were in the grip of an ice floe, everything moving with infinite slowness. He couldn't think, couldn't seem to put two ideas together. Then he noticed something. The oddness of it cut through the strange inertia in which he was gripped. There was something in Khan's right ear. What was it? Under the guise of extreme pain, he moved his head slightly, saw that it was a miniature electronic receiver.

'Who are you?' he said. 'Goddammit, who are you!'

There seemed to be two conversations going on simultaneously, as if the two men were in different worlds, living different lives. Their voices raised, their emotions flamed from embers, and the more they shouted, the further apart they seemed to get.

'I told you!' Khan's hands were covered with Bourne's blood, which had now begun to coagulate in his nostrils. 'I'm your son!'

And with those words, the stasis was broken, their worlds collided once again. The rage that had swept Bourne up in its fist when the hotel manager had frustrated him thundered again in his ears. He screamed, driving Khan backward through the door, out onto the roof.

Ignoring the pain in his head, he hooked his ankle behind Khan, shoved him hard. But Khan grabbed hold of him as he went down, raising his legs as his back struck the roof tiles, lifting Bourne off his feet, and with a powerful kick sent him tumbling head over heels.

Bourne tucked his head under, landed on his shoulders and rolled, dissipating most of the impact. They both regained their feet at the same time, their arms outstretched, their fingers grasping for purchase. Bourne brought his arms down suddenly, striking them hard onto Khan's wrists, breaking his hold, spinning him sideways. Bourne butted him, using his forehead against the nerve bundle just below Khan's ear. Khan's left side went slack, and Bourne, using his advantage, drove his balled fist into Khan's face.

Khan staggered, his knees buckling slightly, but like a punch-drunk heavyweight, he refused to go down. Bourne, a maddened bull, struck him again and again, driving him back with every blow, nearer and nearer the parapet. But in his extreme rage he made a mistake, allowing Khan inside his guard. It surprised him when, instead of staggering back beneath the blow, Khan attacked, driving *forward* off his back foot and, midway through, transferring all his weight to his front foot. The resulting strike rattled Bourne's teeth even as it took him off his feet.

Bourne fell to his knees, and Khan struck him a tremendous blow above his ribs. He began to topple over but Khan grabbed him by the throat and began to squeeze.

'You'd better tell me now,' he said thickly. 'You'd better tell me everything you know.'

Bourne, panting and in intense pain, said, 'Go to hell!'

Khan struck his jaw with the edge of his hand.

'Why won't you listen?'

'Try a little more force,' Bourne said.

'You're completely insane.'

'That's your plan, isn't it?' Bourne shook his head doggedly. 'This whole sick story about you being Joshua – '

'I *am* your son.'

'Listen to yourself – you can't even say his name. You can drop the farce; it'll avail you nothing now. You're an international assassin named Khan. I won't lead you to this Spalko or whoever it is you're planning to get to. I won't be anyone's cat's-paw again.'

'You don't know what you're doing. You don't know – ' He broke off, shook his head violently, changed tacks. He cradled the small carved stone Buddha in his free palm. 'Look at this, Bourne!' He spat out the words as if they were poisonous. '*Look at it!*'

'A talisman anyone in Southeast Asia could pick up – '

'Not *this* one. You gave this one to me – *yes*, you did.' His eyes blazed, and his voice held a tremor that, to his shame, he couldn't control. 'And then you abandoned me to die in the jungles of – '

A gunshot ricocheted off the roof tiles beside Khan's right leg and, releasing Bourne, he jumped back. A second shot nearly struck his shoulder as he scuttled behind the brick wall of the elevator vent.

Bourne turned his head, saw Annaka crouched at the top of the stairwell, her gun gripped tightly in both hands. Cautiously, she came forward. She risked a glance at Bourne.

'Are you all right?'

He nodded, but at the same time Khan, choosing wisely, leaped from his hiding place, bounded to the side of the rooftop, jumped onto the next building. Bourne noted that instead of firing wildly, Annaka put up her gun and turned to him.

'How can you be all right?' she asked. 'There's blood all over you!'

'It's just from my nose.' He felt lightheaded as he sat up. Reacting to her dubious expression, he was compelled to add, 'Really, it looks like a lot of blood, but it's nothing.'

She put a wad of tissues against his nose as he started to bleed again.

'Thank you.'

She brushed away his words with those of her own. 'You said you needed to get something back at your hotel. Why did you come up here?'

Slowly, he rose to his feet but not without her help. 'Wait a minute.' She glanced in the direction Khan had gone, then turned back to Bourne, a look of revelation on her face. 'He's the one who's been watching us, isn't he? The one who called the police when we were at László Molnar's apartment.'

'I don't know.'

She shook her head. 'I don't believe you. It's the only plausible explanation for why you lied to me. You didn't want to alarm me because you'd told me we were safe here. What changed?'

He hesitated for a moment, then realized that he had no choice but to tell her the truth. 'When we came back from the café, there were new scratch marks on your piano bench.'

'What?' Her eyes opened wide and she shook her head. 'I don't understand.'

Bourne thought of the electronic receiver in Khan's right ear. 'Let's go back to the apartment and I'll show you.'

He walked toward the open doorway, but she hesitated. 'I don't know.'

Turning back, he said wearily, 'What don't you know?'

A hard look had come into her face, along with a kind of ruefulness. 'You lied to me.'

'I did it to protect you, Annaka.'

Her eyes were large and glistening. 'How can I trust you now?'

'Annaka – '

'Please tell me, because I really want to know.' She stood her ground, and he knew that she wouldn't take even a step toward the staircase. 'I need to have an answer I can cling to and believe.'

'What d'you want me to say?'

She lifted her arms, let them fall to her side in gesture of exasperation. 'Do you see what you're doing, turning everything I say back on itself?' She shook her head. 'Where did you learn to make people feel like shit?'

'I wanted to keep you out of harm's way,' he said. She had hurt him deeply and, despite his carefully neutral expression, he suspected she knew it. 'I thought I was doing the right thing. I still think so, even if it meant keeping the truth from you, at least for a little while.'

She looked at him for a long time. The gusting wind took her copper hair, floated it out like a bird's wing. Querulous voices drifted up from Fo utca, people wanting to know what those noises were, a car backfiring or something else? There were no answers, and now, save for the intermittent barking of a dog, the neighborhood was quiet.

'You thought you could handle the situation,' Annaka said, 'you thought you could handle *him*.'

Bourne walked stiff-legged over to the front parapet, where he leaned out. Against all odds, the rental car was still there, empty. Maybe it wasn't Khan's, or maybe Khan hadn't fled the scene. With some difficulty, Bourne stood up straight. The pain was coming in waves, breaking harder on the shore of his consciousness as the endorphins released by the shock of the trauma began to dissipate. Every bone in his body seemed to ache, but none more than his jaw and his ribs.

At last, he found it in himself to answer her truthfully. 'I suppose so, yes.'

She lifted a hand, pulled her hair away from her cheek. 'Who *is* he, Jason?'

It was the first time she had called him by his given name, but it scarcely registered on him. At the moment, he was trying – and failing – to give her an answer that would satisfy himself.

Khan, splayed on the stairs of the building onto whose roof he had leaped, stared unseeing at the featureless ceiling of the stairwell. He waited for Bourne to come get him. Or, he wondered with the wandering mind of those in shock, was he waiting for Annaka Vadas to level her gun at him and pull the trigger? He should be in his car now, driving away, and yet here he was, as inert as a fly caught in a spiderweb.

His buzzing mind was swept by shoulds. He should've killed Bourne when he first had him in his sights, but he had a plan then, one that made sense, one that he had meticulously outlined to himself, one that would bring him – so he believed then! – the maximum measure of revenge that was his due. He should've killed Bourne in the cargo hold of the plane bound for Paris. Surely he'd meant to, just as he'd meant to just now.

It would be easy to tell himself that he'd been interrupted by Annaka Vadas, but the blinding, incomprehensible truth was that he'd had his chance before she arrived on the scene and had *made a choice not to exact his revenge.*

Why? He was completely at a loss to say.

His mind, usually as calm as a lake, jumped around from memory to memory, as if it found the present unbearable. He recalled the room in which he was incarcerated during his years with the Vietnamese gunrunner, his brief moment of freedom before being saved by the missionary, Richard Wick. He remembered Wick's house, the sense of space and freedom that gradually eroded, the creeping horror of his time with the Khmer Rouge.

The worst part – the part he kept trying to forget – was that initially, he'd been attracted to the Khmer Rouge philosophy. Ironically enough, because it was founded by a group of young Cambodian radicals trained in Paris, its ethos was based on French nihilism. 'The past is death! Destroy everything to create a new future!' This was the Khmer Rouge mantra, repeated over and over until it ground down all other thought or points of view.

It was hardly surprising that their worldview would initially draw Khan – himself an unwitting refugee, abandoned, marginalized – an outcast by circumstance rather than by design. For Khan the past *was* death – witness his recurring dream. But if he first learned to destroy from them, it was because they had destroyed him first.

Not content to believe his story of abandonment, they'd slowly drained the life, the energy from him as they bled him a little every day. They wanted, so his interlocutor said, to empty his mind of everything; they required a blank slate on which to write their radical version of the new future that awaited them all. They bled him, his smiling interlocutor said, for his own good, to rid him of the toxins of the past. Every day, his interlocutor read to him from their manifesto and then recited the names of those opposing the rebel regime who had been killed. Most, of course, were unknown to Khan, but a few – monks, mainly, as well as a smattering of boys his age – he had known, if only in passing. Some, like the boys, had taunted him, settling the mantle of outcast on his immature shoulders. After a time a new item was added to the agenda. Following the interlocutor's reading of a particular section of the manifesto, Khan was required to repeat it back. This he did, in an ever-increasingly forceful manner.

One day, after the requisite recitation and response, his interlocutor read off the names of those newly killed in furtherance of the revolution. At the end of the list was Richard Wick, the missionary who had taken him in, thinking he'd bring Khan to civilization and to God. What roil of emotion this news elicited within Khan was impossible to say, but the overriding feeling was one of dislocation. His last link to the world at large was now gone. He was completely and utterly alone. In the relative privacy of the latrine, he had wept without knowing why. If there was ever a man he hated, it was the one who'd used and emotionally abandoned him, and now, unaccountably, he was crying over his death.

Later that day his interlocutor led him from the concrete bunker in which he'd been housed ever since being taken prisoner. Even though the sky was low and it was raining heavily, he'd blinked in the light of day. Time had passed; the rainy season had begun.

Lying in the stairwell, it occurred to Khan now that while he was growing up, he'd never been in control of his own life. The truly curious and disturbing thing was that he still wasn't. He'd been under the impression that he was a free agent, having gone to great pains to set himself up in a business where he'd believed – naively, as it turned out – free agents thrived. He could see now that ever since he'd taken on his first commission from Spalko, the man had been manipulating him, and never more so than now.

If he was ever to break free of the chains that bound him, he'd have to do something about Stepan Spalko. He knew he'd been immoderate with him at the end of their last phone conversation, and now he regretted it. In that quick flash of anger, so uncharacteristic of him, he'd accomplished nothing save to put Spalko on his guard. But then, he realized, ever since Bourne had sat down beside him on the park bench in Old Town Alexandria, his usual icy reserve had been shattered, and now emotions he could neither name nor understand kept shooting up to the surface, roiling his consciousness, muddying his intent. He realized with a start that when it came to Jason Bourne, he no longer knew what he wanted.

He sat up, then looked around. He'd heard a sound; he was certain of it. He rose, put one hand on the bannister, his muscles tense, poised for flight. And there it was again. His head turned. What was that sound? Where had he heard it before?

His heart beat fast, his pulse in his throat as the sound rose through the stairwell, echoing in his mind, for he was calling again: *'Lee-Lee! Lee-Lee!'*

But Lee-Lee couldn't answer; Lee-Lee was dead.

# 19

The underground entrance to the monastery lay hidden by shadow and time in the deepest cleft of the northernmost wall of the gorge. The lowering sun had revealed the cleft to be more of a defile, as it must have centuries ago to the monks who had chosen this location for their well-defended home. Perhaps they had been monk-warriors, for the extensive fortifications spoke of battles and bloodshed and the need to keep their home sacrosanct.

Silently the team moved into the defile, following the sun. There was no intimate talk between Spalko and Zina now, no hint whatsoever of what had transpired between them, even though it had been momentous. In a manner of speaking, it could be termed a form of benediction; in any case, it was a transference of allegiance and of power whose silence and secrecy only added to the ramifications of its effect. It was Spalko who once again had metaphorically thrown a pebble in a still pond, only to sit back and watch the effect as the resulting ripples spread outward, altering the basic nature of the pond and all who lived in it.

The sun-splashed rocks vanished behind them as they moved into shadow, and they clicked on their lights. Besides Spalko and Zina, there were two of them – the third having been taken back to the jet at Kazantzakis Airport, where the surgeon awaited. They wore lightweight nylon backpacks, filled with all manner of paraphernalia from canisters of tear gas to balls of twine and everything in between. Spalko didn't know what they'd be up against and he was taking no chances.

The men went first, semiautomatic guns on wide straps slung over their shoulders, held at the ready. The defile narrowed, forcing them to continue on in single-file. Soon, however, the sky vanished beneath a wall of rock and they found themselves in a cave. It was dank and musty, filled with the fetid odors of decay.

'It stinks like an open grave,' one of the men said.

'Look!' the other cried. 'Bones!'

They paused, their lights concentrated on a scattering of small mammal bones, but not a hundred meters on they came upon the thigh-bone of a much larger mammal.

Zina squatted to take up the bone in her hand.

'Don't!' the first man cautioned. 'It's bad luck to handle human bones.'

'What are you talking about? Archaeologists do it all the time.' Zina laughed. 'Besides, this might not be human at all.' Nevertheless, she dropped it back into the dust of the cave floor.

Five minutes later they were clustered around what was unmistakably a human skull. Their lights gleamed off the brow ridge, threw the eye sockets into deepest shadow.

'What d'you think killed him?' Zina asked.

'Exposure, probably,' Spalko said. 'Or thirst.'

'Poor beggar.'

They kept going, deeper into the bedrock upon which the monastery was built. The farther they went, the more numerous the bones became. Now they were all human, and increasingly they were broken or fractured.

'I don't think these people were killed by either exposure or thirst,' Zina said.

'What then?' one of the men asked, but no one had an answer.

Spalko ordered them curtly on. They had, by his calculation, just about reached the spot below the monastery's crenelated outer walls. Up ahead, their lights picked out an odd formation.

'The cave is split in two,' one of the men said, shining his light on first the passageway to the left, then the one to his right.

'Caves don't bifurcate,' Spalko said. He pushed his way ahead of them, stuck his head into the left-hand opening. 'This one's a dead end.' He ran his hand over the edges of the openings. 'These are man-made,' he said. 'Many years ago, possibly when the monastery was first built.' He stepped into the right-hand opening, his voice echoing strangely. 'Yes, this one goes on, but there are twists and turns.'

When he came back out, he had an odd expression on his face. 'I don't think this is a passageway at all,' he said. 'No wonder Molnar chose this place to hide Dr. Schiffer. I believe we're headed into a labyrinth.'

The two men exchanged glances.

'In that case,' Zina said, 'how will we ever find our way back?'

'There's no way of knowing what we'll find in there.' Spalko took out a small rectangular object no larger than a deck of playing cards. He grinned as he showed her how it worked. 'A global positioning system. I've just electronically marked our starting point.' He nodded. 'Let's go.'

It didn't take them long, however, to discover the error of their ways, and not more than five minutes later, they had reconvened outside the labyrinth.

'What's the matter?' Zina asked.

Spalko was frowning. 'The GPS didn't work in there.'

She shook her head. 'What d'you think is wrong?'

'Some mineral in the rock itself must be blocking the signal from the satellite,' Spalko said. He couldn't afford to tell them that he had no idea why the GPS failed to work in the labyrinth. Instead, he opened his backpack, took out a ball of twine. 'We'll take a lesson from Theseus and unwind the twine as we go.'

Zina eyed the ball uncertainly. 'What if we run out of twine?'

'Theseus didn't,' Spalko said. 'And we're almost inside the monastery's walls, so let's hope we don't run out, either.'

Dr. Felix Schiffer was bored. For days now he'd done nothing but follow orders as his cadre of protectors flew him under cover of night to Crete, then proceeded to periodically move him from one location to another. They never stayed in one place for more than three days. He'd liked the house in Iraklion, but that too had proved boring in the end. There was nothing for him to do. They refused to bring him a newspaper or allow him to listen to the radio. As for television, there was none available, but he had to assume they would have kept him away from it, too. Still, he thought glumly, it was a damn sight better than this moldering pile of stone, with only a cot for a bed and a fire for warmth. Heavy chests and sideboards were virtually the only furniture, though the men had brought folding chairs, cots and linens. There was no plumbing; they'd made a privy in the courtyard and its stench reached all the way into the interior of the monastery. It was gloomy and dank, even at noon, and God help them all when darkness fell. Not even a light to read by, if there'd been anything to read.

He longed for freedom. If he'd been a God-fearing man, he would have prayed for his deliverance. So many days since he'd seen Lázló Molnar or spoken to Alex Conklin. When he asked his protectors about that, they invoked the word most sacred to them: Security. Communication was simply not secure. They took pains to reassure him that he would soon be reunited with his friend and his benefactor. But when he asked when, all they did was shrug and go back to their endless card game. He could sense that they were bored as well, at least the ones not on guard duty.

There were seven of them. Originally, there were more, but the others had been left behind in Iraklion. But from what he'd been able to glean, they should have been here by now. Accordingly, there was no card game today – every member of the cadre was on patrol. There was a distinct air of tension that set his teeth on edge.

Schiffer was a rather tall man, with piercing blue eyes and a strong-bridged nose below a mass of salt-and-pepper hair. There was a time before he'd been recruited into DARPA and had been more visible when he'd been taken for Burt Bacharach. Not being good with people, he'd never known how to respond. He'd merely mumble something unintelligible and turn away, but his obvious embarrassment only reinforced the misapprehension.

He got up, walked idly across the room to the window, but he was intercepted by one of the cadre and was turned away.

'Security,' the mercenary said, his tension on his breath if not in his eyes.

'Security! Security! I'm sick to death of that word!' Schiffer exclaimed.

Nevertheless, he was herded back to the chair on which he was meant to sit. It was away from all doors and windows. He shivered in the dampness.

'I miss my lab; I miss my work!' Schiffer looked into the dark eyes of the mercenary. 'I feel like I'm in prison, can you understand that?'

The cadre's leader, Sean Keegan, sensing his charge's unrest, strode swiftly over. 'Please take your seat, Doctor.'

'But I – '

'It's for your own good,' Keegan said. He was one of those black Irishmen, dark of hair and eye, with a rough-hewn face brimming with grim determination, and a street-brawler's lumpy physique. 'We've been hired to keep you safe and we take that responsibility seriously.'

Obediently, Schiffer sat. 'Would *someone* please tell me what's going on?'

Keegan stared down at him for some time. Then, making up his mind, he squatted next to the chair. In a low voice, he said, 'I've avoided keeping you informed, but I suppose it might be best for you to know now.'

'What?' Schiffer's face was pinched and pained. 'What's happened?'

'Alex Conklin's dead.'

'Oh, God, no.' Schiffer wiped his suddenly sweating face with his hand.

'And as for László Molnar, we haven't heard from him in two days.'

'Christ almighty!'

'Calm yourself, Doctor. It's entirely possible Molnar's been out of touch for security reasons.' Keegan's eyes met his. 'On the other hand, the personnel we left at the house in Iraklion have failed to show.'

'I gathered as much,' Schiffer said. 'Do you think something . . . untoward has happened to them?'

'I can't afford not to.'

Schiffer's face shone; he couldn't stop himself from sweating in fear. 'Then it's possible Spalko's found out where I am; it's possible that he's here on Crete.'

Keegan's face was set in stone. 'That's the premise we're going by.'

Schiffer's terror made him aggressive. 'Well,' he demanded, 'what're you doing about it?'

'We have men with machine pistols manning the ramparts, but I very much doubt Spalko's foolish enough to try a ground assault across a treeless terrain.' Keegan shook his head. 'No, if he's here, if he's coming for you, Doctor, he'll have no choice.' He stood, slung his machine-pistol over his shoulder. 'His route will be through the labyrinth.'

Spalko, in the labyrinth with his small party, was becoming more and more apprehensive with every twist and turn they were forced to make. The labyrinth was the only logical approach for an assault on the monastery, which meant they might very well be walking into a trap.

He glanced down, saw the ball of twine was two-thirds behind them. They must be at or near the center of the monastery by now; the trail of twine assured him that the labyrinth hadn't taken them in a circle. At each branching, he believed that he'd chosen well.

He turned to Zina, said under his breath, 'I smell an ambush. I want you to stay here in reserve.' He patted her backpack. 'If we run into trouble, you know what to do.'

Zina nodded, and the three men moved off in a half-crouch. They had only just disappeared when she heard machine-pistol fire coming in quick bursts. Quickly she opened her backpack, drew out a canister of tear gas, headed off after them, following the trail of the twine.

She smelled the stench of cordite before she turned the second corner. She peeked around the corner, saw one of their unit sprawled on the ground in a pool of blood. Spalko and the other man were pinned down by gunfire. From her vantage point, she could tell that it was coming from two different directions.

Pulling the pin on the canister, she tossed it over Spalko's head. It struck the ground, then rolled to the left, exploding in a soft hiss. Spalko had slapped his man's back, and they retreated out of the spread of the gas.

They could hear coughing and retching. By this time they'd all donned their gas masks and were ready to mount a second attack. Spalko rolled another canister to their right, cutting short the gunfire directed at them, but not, regrettably, before his second man caught three bullets in the chest and neck. He went down, blood bubbling from between his slack lips.

Spalko and Zina split, one going right, the other left, killing the incapacitated mercenaries – two each – with efficient bursts from their machine-pistols. They both saw the stairway at the same time and made for it.

Sean Keegan grabbed Felix Schiffer even as he shouted orders for his men on the ramparts to abandon their positions and return to the center of the monastery, where he was now dragging his terrified charge.

He'd begun to act the instant he'd caught a whiff of the tear gas seeping up from the labyrinth below. Moments later he heard the resumption of gunfire, then a deathly ringing silence. Seeing his two men rush in, he directed them toward the stone staircase that led down to where he'd deployed the rest of his men to ambush Spalko.

Keegan had for years been employed by the IRA before going out on his own as a mercenary-for-hire, so he was well acquainted with situations where he was out-manned and outgunned. In fact, he relished such situations, saw them as challenges to overcome.

But there was smoke now in the monastery proper, great billowing wafts of it, and now a hail of machine-gun fire coming out of it. His men had no chance; they were mowed down before they had a chance even to identify their killers.

Keegan didn't wait to identify them either. Hauling on Dr. Schiffer, he took them through the warren of small, dark, stifling rooms, looking for a way out.

As they had planned, Spalko and Zina separated the moment they emerged from the dense clouds of the smoke bomb they had tossed out the door at the head of the stairs they had climbed. Spalko went methodically through the rooms while Zina looked for a door to the outside.

It was Spalko who saw Schiffer and Keegan first, and he called to them, only to be greeted with a burst of gunfire, obliging him to duck behind a heavy wooden chest.

'You've no hope of getting out of this alive,' he called to the mercenary. 'I don't want you; I want Schiffer.'

'It's the same thing,' Keegan shouted back. 'I was given a commission; I intend to carry it out.'

'To what purpose?' Spalko said. 'Your employer, László Molnar, is dead. So is János Vadas.'

'I don't believe you,' Keegan responded. Schiffer was whimpering and he shushed him.

'How d'you think I found you?' Spalko went on. 'I ground it out of Molnar. Come on. You know he's the only one who knew you were here.'

Silence.

'They're all dead now,' Spalko said, inching forward. 'Who'll pay the last of your commission? Hand over Schiffer and I'll pay you whatever you're owed, plus a bonus. How does that sound?'

Keegan was about to answer, when Zina, having come at him from the opposite direction, put a bullet in the back of his head.

The resulting explosion of blood and gore made Dr. Schiffer whimper like a whipped dog. Then, with his last protector pitched over, he saw Stepan Spalko advancing toward him. He turned and ran right into Zina's arms.

'There's nowhere to go, Felix,' Spalko said. 'You see that now, don't you?'

Schiffer stared wide-eyed at Zina. He began to gibber, and she put a hand to his head, stroking his hair back from his damp forehead as if he were a child ill with fever.

'You were mine once,' Spalko said as he stepped over Keegan's corpse. 'And you're mine again.' From out of his backpack he took two items. They were made of surgical steel, glass and titanium.

'Oh, God!' The groan from Schiffer was as heartfelt as it was involuntary.

Zina smiled at Schiffer, kissed him on both cheeks as if they were good friends reunited after a long absence. At once, he burst into tears.

Spalko, enjoying the effect the NX 20 diffuser had on its inventor, said, 'This is the way the two halves fit together, isn't it, Felix?' Whole, the NX 20 was no larger than the automatic weapon slung across Spalko's back. 'Now that I've got a proper payload, you'll teach me the proper use of it.'

'No,' Schiffer said in a quavery voice. 'No, no, no!'

'Don't you worry about a thing,' Zina whispered as Spalko took hold of the back of Dr. Schiffer's neck, sending yet another spasm of terror through the scientist's frame. 'You're in the best of hands now.'

The flight of stairs was short, but, for Bourne, descending them was more painful than he had expected. With every step he took, the trauma he'd received from the blow above his ribs sent jolts of agony through him. What he needed was a hot bath and some sleep, two things he couldn't yet afford.

Back in Annaka's apartment, he showed her the top of the piano bench and she swore under her breath. Together they moved it beneath the light fixture and he stood on it.

'You see?'

She shook her head. 'I haven't the slightest idea what's going on.'

He went to the escritoire, scribbled on a pad: *Do you have a ladder?*

She looked at him oddly but nodded.

*Go get it*, he wrote.

When she brought it back into the living room, he climbed it high enough to look into the shallow frosted-glass bowl of the light fixture. And, sure enough, there it was. Carefully, he reached in, plucked up the tiny item between his fingertips. He climbed down and showed it to her in the palm of his hand.

'What – ?' She broke off at the emphatic shake of his head.

'Do you have a pair of pliers?' he asked.

Again, the curious look as she opened the door of a shallow closet. She handed him the pliers. He put the tiny square between the ribbed ends, squeezed. The square shattered.

'It's a miniature electronic transmitter,' he said.

'What?' Curiosity had turned to bewilderment.

'That's why the man on the roof broke in here, to plant this in the light fixture. He was listening as well as looking.'

She looked around the cozy room and shivered. 'Dear God, I'll never again feel the same way about this place.' Then she turned to Bourne. 'What does he *want*? Why try to record our every move?' Then she snorted. 'It's Dr. Schiffer, isn't it?'

'It may be,' Bourne said, 'I don't know.' All at once, he became dizzy and, near to blacking out, half-fell, half-sat on the sofa.

Annaka hurried to the bathroom to get him disinfectant and some bandages. He put his head back against the cushions, clearing his mind of everything that had just happened. He had to center himself, maintain his concentration, keeping his eye firmly fixed on what had to be done next.

Annaka returned from the bathroom carrying a tray on which were a shallow porcelain bowl of hot water, a sponge, some towels, an ice pack, a bottle of disinfectant and a glass of water.

'Jason?'

He opened his eyes.

She gave him the glass of water, and when he had drained it, she handed him the ice pack. 'Your cheek is starting to swell.'

He put the pack against his face, felt the pain slowly recede into numbness. But when he took a quick breath, his side seized up as he twisted to put the empty glass on a side table. He turned back slowly, stiffly. He was thinking of Joshua, who had been resurrected in his mind if not in reality. Maybe that was why he was so filled with blind rage at Khan, for Khan had raised the specter of the awful past, thrusting into the light a ghost so dear to David Webb he had haunted him in both his personalities.

Watching Annaka as she cleaned his face of dried blood, he recalled their brief exchange at the café when he brought up the subject of her father and she had broken down, and yet he knew that he had to pursue it. He was a father who'd violently lost his family. She was a daughter who'd violently lost her father.

'Annaka,' he began gently, 'I know it's a painful subject for you, but I'd very much like to know about your father.' He felt her stiffen, plowed on. 'Can you talk about him?'

'What d'you want to know? How he and Alexsei met, I suppose.'

She concentrated on what she was doing, but he wondered whether she was deliberately not meeting his gaze.

'I was thinking more along the lines of your relationship with him.'

A shadow flickered across her face. 'That's an odd – and intimate – question to ask.'

'It's my past, you see . . .' Bourne's voice trailed off. He was unable either to lie or to tell the full truth.

'The one you remember only in glimmers.' She nodded. 'I see.' When she wrung out the sponge, the water in the bowl turned pink. 'Ah, well, János Vadas was the perfect father. He changed me when I was an infant, read to me at night, sang to me when I was ill. He was there for all my birthdays and special occasions. Honestly, I don't know how he managed it.' She wrung out the sponge a second time; he'd begun bleeding again. 'I came first. Always. And he never grew tired of telling me how much he loved me.'

'What a lucky child you were.'

'Luckier than any of my friends, luckier than anyone I know.' She was concentrating harder than ever, trying to get the bleeding to stop.

Bourne had sunk into a state of semi-trance, thinking about Joshua – about the rest of his first family – and all the things he would never get to do with them, all the many tiny moments you noted and remembered as your child grew up.

At length, she stanched the flow of blood and now took a peek under the ice pack. Her expression didn't betray what she saw. She sat back on her haunches, hands resting in her lap.

'I think you should take off your jacket and shirt.'

He stared at her.

'So we can take a look at your ribs. I saw you wince when you twisted to put the glass down.'

She held out her hand and he dropped the ice pack into it. She juggled it a little. 'This needs a refill.'

When she returned, he was naked to the waist. A frighteningly large red welt on his left side was already puffed up and very tender as his fingertips probed it.

'My God, you need an ice *bath*,' she exclaimed.

'At least nothing's broken.'

She tossed him the ice pack. He gasped involuntarily as he put it against the swelling. She returned to her haunches, her gaze roving over him once again. He wished he knew what she was thinking.

'I suppose you can't help remembering the son who was killed so young.'

He gritted his teeth. 'It's just that . . . The man on the roof – the one spying on us – has been following me all the way from the States. He says he wants to kill me, but I know he's lying. He wants me to lead him to someone, that's why he's been spying on us.'

Annaka's expression darkened. 'Who does he want to get to?'

'A man named Spalko.'

She registered surprise. 'Stepan Spalko?'

'That's right. Do you know him?'

'Of course I know of him,' she said. 'Everyone in Hungary does. He's the head of Humanistas, Ltd., the worldwide relief organization.' She frowned. 'Jason, now I'm truly worried. This man's dangerous. If he's trying to get to Mr. Spalko, we should contact the authorities.'

He shook his head. 'What would we tell them? That we think a man we know only as Khan wants to contact Stepan Spalko? We don't even know why. And what d'you think they'll say? Why doesn't this Khan just pick up the telephone and call him?'

'Then we should at least call someone at Humanistas.'

'Annaka, until I know what's going on, I don't want to contact anyone. It'll only muddy waters that are already clouded with questions for which I don't have any answers.'

He rose, made his way to the escritoire, sat down in front of her laptop. 'I told you I had an idea. Is it okay if I use your computer?'

'By all means,' she said, rising.

As Bourne turned on the machine, she gathered up the bowl, sponge and other paraphernalia, padded into the kitchen. He heard the sound of running water as he went online. He accessed the U.S. Government net, went from site to site, and by the time she returned, he'd found the one he needed.

The Agency had a whole raft of public sites, accessible to anyone with an Internet connection, but there were a dozen other sites, encrypted, password protected, that were part of the CIA's fabled intranet.

Annaka registered his extreme concentration. 'What is it?' She came around and stood behind him. In a moment, her eyes opened wide. 'What the hell are you doing?'

'Just what it looks like,' Bourne said, 'I'm hacking into the CIA main database.'

'But how d'you – '

'Don't ask,' Bourne said as his fingers flew over the keyboard. 'Trust me, you don't want to know.'

Alex Conklin had always known the way through the front door, but that was because he'd had the updated ciphers delivered to him at six A.M. every Monday morning. It had been Deron, the artist and master forger, who'd taught Bourne the fine art of hacking into U.S Government databases. In his business, it was a necessary skill.

The problem was that the CIA firewall – the software program designed to keep their data secure – was a particular bitch. In addition to its keyword changing every week, it had a floating algorithm tied into the keyword. But Deron had shown Bourne the way to fool the system into thinking you had the keyword when you didn't, so that the program itself would supply it for you.

The way to attack the firewall was through the algorithm, which was a derivation of the core algorithm that encrypted the CIA's central files. Bourne knew this formula because Deron had made him memorize it.

Bourne navigated to the CIA site, where a window popped up in which he was asked to type the current keyword. In this, he typed in the algorithm, which contained a much larger string of numbers and letters than the box was designed to take. On the other hand, after the first three sets of the components, the underlying program recognized it for what it was, and for a moment it was stymied. The trick, Deron had said, was to complete the algorithm before the program figured out what you were doing and shut down, denying you access. The formula string was very long; there was no room for error or even for an instant's hesitation, and Bourne began to sweat because he couldn't believe the software could remain frozen for this long.

In the end, however, he finished entering the algorithm without the program shutting down. The window disappeared, the screen changed.

'I'm inside,' Bourne said.

'Pure alchemy,' Annaka whispered, fascinated.

Bourne was navigating to the Tactical Non-Lethal Weapons Directorate site. He plugged in Schiffer's name but was disappointed in the sparse material that came up. Nothing on what Schiffer was working on, nothing about his background. In fact, if Bourne didn't know better, he could believe that Dr. Felix Schiffer was a minor scientist of no import whatsoever to the TNLWD.

There was another possibility. He used the back-channel hack that Deron had made him memorize, the same one Conklin had used to keep tabs on events occurring behind the scenes at the Department of Defense.

Once in, he went to the DARPA site and navigated to the Archives. Lucky for him the government computer jockeys were notoriously slow at cleaning out old files. There was Schiffer's, which contained some background. He was MIT-trained, was given his own lab right out of grad school by one of the large pharmaceutical firms. He lasted there less than a year, but when he left, he took with him another of their scientists, Dr. Peter Sido, with whom he worked for five years before being recruited by the government and entering DARPA. No explanation was given for his giving up a private position to go into the public sector, but some scientists were like that. They were as unfit for living in society as many prisoners who, when they'd served their time, committed another crime the minute they hit the street, simply to be sent back into a clearly defined world where everything was taken care of for them.

Bourne read on and discovered that Schiffer had been attached to the Defense Sciences Office which, ominously, trafficked in bio-weapons systems. In his time at DARPA, Dr. Schiffer had been working on a way to biologically 'cleanse' a room infected with anthrax.

Bourne paged through, but he couldn't find any more details. What bothered Bourne was that this piece of information wouldn't account for Conklin's intense interest.

Annaka looked over his shoulder. 'Is there any clue we could use to find out where Dr. Schiffer might be hiding?'

'I don't think so, no.'

'All right then.' She squeezed his shoulders. 'The cupboard's bare and we both need to eat something.'

'I think I'd rather stay here, if you don't mind, rest up a bit.'

'You're right. You're in no shape to wander outside.' She smiled as she drew on her coat. 'I'll just pop around the corner, get us some food. Anything you particularly want?'

He shook his head, watched her head for the door. 'Annaka, be careful.'

She turned, pulled her gun partway out of her bag. 'Don't worry, I'll be fine.' She opened the door. 'See you in a few minutes.'

He heard her depart, but he'd already returned his attention to the computer screen. He felt his heart rate increase and tried to calm himself, without success. Even full of intent, he hesitated. He knew he had to go on, but he also recognized that he was terrified.

Watching his hands as if they belonged to someone else, he spent the next five minutes hacking his way through the U.S. Army firewall. At one point, he hit a glitch. The military IT team had upgraded the firewall recently, adding a third layer Deron either hadn't told him about or, more likely, hadn't yet seen. His fingers rose up like Annaka's over the piano keyboard and for a moment they hesitated. It was not too late to turn back, he told himself, there'd be no shame in doing that. For years he'd felt that anything to do with his first family, including the record of them held in the U.S. Army databanks was for him strictly off-limits. He was already tortured enough by their deaths, haunted by the racking guilt that he'd been unable to save them, that he'd been safe at a meeting while the diving jet sent its killing bullets into them. He couldn't help torturing himself anew, conjuring up their last terror-filled minutes. Dao, a child of war, would, of course, have heard the jet engines droning lazily in the hot summer sky. At first she wouldn't have seen it coming out of the white sun, but when its roar grew closer, when its metal bulk became larger than the sun, she would've known. Even while horror gripped her heart, she would've tried to gather her children to her in a vain attempt to protect them from the bullets that would have already begun to pock the surface of the muddy river. *'Joshua! Alyssa! Come to me!'* she would've screamed, as if she could save them from what was to come.

Bourne, sitting in front of Annaka's computer, became aware that he was weeping. For a moment he allowed the tears to flow freely as they hadn't done for so many years. Then he shook himself, wiped his cheeks with his sleeve and, before he had a chance to change his mind, got on with the business at hand.

He found a work-around for the final level of the firewall, and five minutes after beginning the excruciating work, he was logged in. At once, before his nerve could fail again, he navigated to the Death Record Archives, typed in the names and date of death in the required data fields for Dao Webb, Alyssa Webb, Joshua Webb. He stared at the names, thinking, *This was my family, flesh-and-blood human beings who laughed and cried, and who once held me, who called me 'Darling' and 'Daddy.'* Now what were they? Names on a computer screen. Statistics in a databank. His heart was breaking and he felt again that touch of madness that had afflicted him in the first aftermath of their deaths. *I can't feel this again,* he thought. *It'll tear me apart.* Full of a sorrow he found unsupportable, he punched the 'Enter' key. He had no other choice; he could not go back. Never go back, that had been his motto from the moment Alex Conklin had recruited him, turned him into another David Webb and then into Jason Bourne. Then why was it he could still hear their voices? *'Darling, I've missed you!' 'Daddy, you're home!'*

These memories, reaching across the permeable barrier of time, had ensnared them in their web, which was why he did not at first react to what had come up on the screen. He stared at it for several minutes without seeing the terrible anomaly.

He saw in horrifying detail what he'd hoped he'd never see, the photos of his beloved wife Dao, shoulders and chest riddled with bullets, her face grotesquely disfigured by the traumatic wounds. On the second page he saw the photos of Alyssa, her poor body and her head even more disfigured because of their vulnerability, their smaller size. He sat, paralyzed with grief and horror, at what lay before him. He had to go on. One page left, one last set of photos to complete the tragedy.

He scrolled to the third page, bracing himself for the photos of Joshua. Only there weren't any.

Stupefied, he did nothing for a moment. At first, he thought there had been a computer glitch, that he'd been inadvertently directed to another page in the Archives. But, no, there was the name: Joshua Webb. But below it were words that seared through Bourne's consciousness like a hot needle. 'Three articles of clothing, listed below, one shoe, partial (sole and heel missing) found ten meters from the corpses of Dao and Alyssa Webb. After an hour's search, Joshua Webb declared dead. NBF.'

*NBF.* The Army acronym screamed out to him. No Body Found. Bourne was gripped by an icy cold. They searched for Joshua for an hour – *only* an hour? And why hadn't they told him? He'd buried three coffins, his mind excoriated with grief, remorse, and guilt. And all the while they knew, the bastards *knew!* He sat back. His face was white, his hands trembling. In his heart, he felt a rage he could not contain.

He thought of Joshua; he thought of Khan.

His mind was ablaze, overcome by the horror of the terrible possibility that he'd buried from the moment he'd seen the carved stone Buddha around Khan's neck: What if Khan really was Joshua? If so, he'd become a killing machine, a monster. Bourne knew only too well how easy it was to find the path to madness and killing in the jungles of Southeast Asia. But there was, of course, another possibility, one his mind quite naturally gravitated toward and held onto: That the plot to plant Joshua was far more wide-ranging and complex than he'd at first considered. If so, if these records were forged, the conspiracy went all the way up to the highest levels of American government. But, oddly, filling his mind with the usual conspiratorial suspicions only increased his sense of dislocation.

In his mind's eye, he saw Khan holding out the carved stone Buddha, heard him say, *'You gave this one to me* – yes, *you did. And then you abandoned me to die . . .'*

Abruptly, Bourne's gorge rose into his throat and, with his stomach rebelling madly, he launched himself off the sofa, across the room, and, ignoring the pain, ran to the bathroom, where he vomited every last thing left inside him.

In the OpSit room deep in the bowels of CIA HQ, the duty officer, watching a computer screen, picked up the phone and dialed a specific number. He waited a moment while an automated voice said, 'Speak.' The DO asked for the DCI. His voice was analyzed, matched against the list of duty officers. The call was switched, a male voice said, 'Hold, please.' A moment later the clear baritone of the DCI came on the line.

'I thought you should know, sir, that an internal alarm has been tripped. Someone got through the military firewall and accessed death records for the following personnel: Dao Webb, Alyssa Webb, Joshua Webb.'

There was a short, unpleasant pause. 'Webb, son. You're sure it's *Webb.*'

The sudden urgency in the DCI's voice brought out the sweat on the young duty officer's face. 'Yessir.'

'Where's this hacker located?'

'Budapest, sir.'

'Did the alarm do its job? Did it capture the full IP address?'

'Yessir. 106–108 Fo utca.'

In his office the DCI smiled grimly. Totally by coincidence, he'd been leafing through Martin Lindros' latest report. It seemed as if the Frogs had now sifted through all the remains of the accident that was supposed to have killed Jason Bourne without finding a trace of human remains. Not even a molar. So there'd been no definitive confirmation that, despite the Quai d'Orsay officer's eyewitness account, Bourne was actually dead. The DCI's hand clenched into a fist and pounded the desk in anger. Bourne had eluded them again. But despite his ire and frustration, part of him wasn't all that surprised. After all, Bourne had been trained by the best spook the Agency had ever produced. How many times had Alex Conklin faked his own death in the field, though perhaps never in such spectacular fashion.

Of course, the DCI thought, it was always possible that someone other than Jason Bourne had hacked through the U.S. Army firewall in order to get at the moldy death records of a woman and her two children who weren't even military personnel and who were known to only a small handful of people still living. But what were the odds?

No, he thought now with mounting excitement, Bourne hadn't perished in that explosion outside Paris; he was alive and well in Budapest – why there? – and for once he'd made a mistake they could capitalize on. Why he was interested in the death records of his first family the DCI had no idea, nor did he care beyond the fact that Bourne's inquisitiveness had opened the door for finally fulfilling the sanction.

The DCI reached for the phone. He could have assigned the task to a subordinate, but he wanted to feel the joy of ordering this particular sanction himself. He dialed an overseas number, thinking, *I've got you now, you sonuvabitch.*

# 20

For a city founded in the late nineteenth century as a British railroad camp on the Mombasa-to-Uganda line, Nairobi had a depressingly banal skyline filled with sleek modern high-rises. It lay on a flat plain, grasslands that for many years had been the home to the Masai before the coming of Western civilization. It was currently the fastest-growing city in East Africa and, as such, was subject to the usual growing pains as well as the disorienting sight of the old and the new, vast wealth and abject poverty uncomfortably rubbing flanks until sparks flew, tempers flared, and calm needed to be restored. With unemployment high, riots were commonplace as well as late-night muggings, especially in and around Uhuru Park to the west of City Center.

None of these inconveniences were of any interest to the party just arriving from Wilson Airport in a pair of armored limousines, although the occupants noted the signs warning of violence and the private security guards that patrolled City Center and west, where government ministries and foreign embassies resided, as well as along the fringes of Latema and River Roads. They passed along the edge of the bazaar, where virtually every sort of surplus war material, from flame-throwers to tanks to shoulder-mounted ground-to-air missile launchers were on display for sale next to cheap gingham dresses and woven textiles in colorful tribal patterns.

Spalko was in the lead limousine with Hasan Arsenov. Behind them, in the second car, sat Zina and Magomet and Akhmed, two of Arsenov's most senior lieutenants. These men hadn't bothered to shave their thick curling beards. They wore the traditional black outfits and stared at Zina's Western clothes with stupefaction. She smiled at them, studying their expressions carefully for any sign of change.

'Everything's in readiness, Shaykh,' Arsenov said. 'My people are perfectly trained and prepared. They are fluent in Icelandic; they have memorized both the hotel's schematics and the procedures you outlined. They await only my final order of commencement.'

Spalko, staring out at the passing Nairobi parade of natives and foreigners stained red by the setting sun, smiled, if only to himself. 'Do I detect a note of skepticism in your voice?'

'If you do,' Arsenov said quickly, 'it's only from my acute sense of anticipation. I've been waiting all my life for the chance to be free of the Russian yoke. My people have been outcasts too long; they've been waiting for centuries to be welcomed into the community of Islam.'

Spalko nodded abstractedly. For him, Arsenov's opinion had already become irrelevant; the moment he was thrown to the wolves he'd cease to exist altogether.

That evening the five of them convened in a private dining room Spalko had booked on the top floor of the 360 Hotel on Kenyatta Avenue. It, like their rooms, had a view over the city to Nairobi National Park, stocked with giraffes, wildebeest, Thomson's gazelles and rhinos – as well as lions, leopards and water buffalo. During the dinner there was no talk of business, no hint at all as to their purpose here.

After the plates had been cleared, it was a different story. A team from Humanistas, Ltd., that had preceded them to Nairobi had set up a computer-based audiovideo hookup, which was wheeled into the room. A screen was deployed and Spalko commenced to give a Powerpoint presentation, showing the coast of Iceland, the city of Reykjavík and its environs, then aerial views of the Oskjuhlid Hotel, followed by photos outside and inside the hotel. 'There's the HVAC system, which as you can see here and here has been fitted with state-of-the-art motion detectors as well as infrared heat sensors,' he said. 'And here's the control panel, which like every system in the hotel has a security override, electrical in nature but with battery backups.' He continued, running through the plan in the most minute detail, beginning with the moment they arrived and ending with the moment they left. Everything had been planned for; everything was in readiness.

'Tomorrow morning at sunrise,' he said, standing, and the others stood with him. '*La illaha ill Allah.*'

'*La illaha ill Allah*,' the others choroused in solemn reply.

Late at night Spalko lay in bed smoking. One lamp was on, but he was still able to see the glittering lights of the city and, beyond, the forested darkness of the wildlife park. He appeared lost in thought, but in reality he had cleared his mind. He was waiting.

Akhmed heard the distant roaring of the animals and could not sleep. He sat up in bed, rubbed his eyes with the heels of his hands. It was unusual for him not to sleep soundly and he wasn't certain what to do. For a time he lay back down, but he was awake now and, aware of the pounding of his heart, his eyes would not close.

He thought of the impending day and the full flower of its promise. Allah will that it be the start of a new dawn for us, he prayed.

Sighing, he sat up, swung his legs over the side of the bed and rose. He pulled on the odd Western trousers and shirt, wondering if he'd ever get used to them. Allah grant not.

He was just opening the door to his room when he saw Zina passing by. She walked with an uncanny grace, moving silently, her hips swaying provocatively. Often, he'd licked his lips when she passed near him and he'd find himself trying to inhale as much of her scent as he could.

He peered out. She was headed away from her room; he wondered where she was going. A moment later he had his answer. His eyes opened wide as she rapped softly on the Shaykh's door, which opened to reveal the Shaykh. Perhaps he had summoned her for some lapse in discipline Akhmed was not aware of.

Then she said in a tone of voice he'd never heard her use before, 'Hasan's asleep,' and he understood everything.

When the soft knock sounded on his door, Spalko turned, stubbed out his cigarette, then rose, padded across the large room and opened the door.

Zina stood in the hallway. 'Hasan's asleep,' she said as if she was required to explain her presence.

Without a word, Spalko stepped back, and she came in, closing the door softly. He grabbed her, then spun her onto the bed. Within moments she was crying out, her bare flesh slick with their fluids. Their lovemaking contained a certain wildness, as if they had come at last to the end of the world. And when it was over, it wasn't over at all, for she lay astride him, stroking and caressing him, whispering her desires in the most explicit terms until, inflamed, he took her again.

Afterward she lay entwined with him, smoke curling from her half-open lips. The lamp was off, and solely by the pinpoint lights of the Nairobi night, she held him in her gaze. Ever since he had first touched her, she had longed to know him. She knew nothing of his background – to her knowledge, no one did. If he would talk to her, if he would tell her the little secrets of his life, she'd know that he was bound to her as she was bound to him.

She ran her fingertip around the shell of his ear, across the unnaturally smooth skin of his cheek. 'I want to know what happened,' she said softly.

Spalko's eyes came slowly back into focus. 'It was a long time ago.'

'All the more reason to tell me.'

He turned his head, stared into her eyes. 'Do you really want to know?'

'Very much, yes.'

He took a breath, let it out. 'In those days, my younger brother and I were living in Moscow. He was always getting into trouble, not that he could help it; he had an addict's disposition.'

'Drugs?'

'Praise Allah, no. In his case, it was gambling. He couldn't stop betting, even when he'd run out of money. He'd borrow from me, and of course I'd always give him the money because he'd spin a story I chose to believe.'

He turned in her arms, shook out a cigarette, lit it. 'Anyway, there came a time when the plausibility of the stories faltered, or possibly even I could no longer afford to believe him. In any event, I said, 'No more,' believing, again foolishly as it turned out, that he'd stop.' He drew smoke deep into his lungs, let it out with a hiss. 'But he didn't. So what d'you suppose he did? He went to the last people he should've approached, because they were the only ones who'd lend him money.'

'The mob.'

He nodded. 'That's right. He took the money from them knowing that if he lost he'd never be able to pay them back. He knew what they'd do to him, but as I said, he couldn't help himself. He bet and, as almost always happened, he lost.'

'And?' She was on tenterhooks, begging him to go on.

'They waited for him to pay them back, and when he didn't, they came after him.'

Spalko stared at the glowing end of his cigarette. The windows were open. Over the low noise of the traffic and the clattering of the palm fronds, now and again came an animal's booming roar or unearthly howl.

'At first they gave him a beating,' he said, his voice barely above a whisper. 'Nothing too severe because at that point they still assumed he'd come up with the money. When they realized he had nothing and could get nothing, they pursued him in earnest, shot him in the street like a dog.'

He was finished with his cigarette, but he let the butt burn down to where he gripped it between two fingers. He seemed to have forgotten all about it. Beside him, Zina said not a word, so held in thrall was she by his story.

'Six months went by,' he said, flicking the butt across the room and out the window. 'I did my homework; I paid the people who needed to be paid, and at last I got my chance. It happened that the boss who'd ordered my brother killed went to the barbershop at the Metropole Hotel every week.'

'Don't tell me,' Zina said, 'you posed as his barber, and when he sat in your chair, you slit his throat with a straight razor.'

He stared at her for a moment, then he broke into a laugh. 'That's very good, very cinematic.' He shook his head. 'But in real life it wouldn't work. The boss had used the same barber for fifteen years and in all that time he'd never accepted a substitute.' He leaned in, kissed her on the mouth. 'Don't be disappointed; take it as a lesson and learn from it.' He slipped his arm around her, drew her close against him. Somewhere in the park a leopard yowled.

'No, I waited until he was freshly shaved and barbered, relaxed from these tender ministrations. I waited for him in the street outside the Metropole, a place so public only a madman would choose it. When he came out, I shot him and his bodyguards dead.'

'And then you escaped.'

'In a sense,' he said. 'That day I escaped, but six months later, in another city in another country a Molotov cocktail was thrown at me from a passing car.'

She tenderly ran her fingers over his plasticized flesh. 'I like you this way, imperfect. The pain you endured makes you . . . heroic.'

Spalko said nothing, and at length he felt her breathing deepen as she drifted off to sleep. Of course, not a word he'd said was true, though he had to admit it made a good story – very cinematic! The truth – what was the truth? He scarcely knew anymore; he'd spent so much time carefully constructing his elaborate facade that there were days when he became lost in his own fiction. In any event, he'd never reveal the truth to anyone else because it would put him at a disadvantage. When people knew you, they thought they owned you – that the truth you had shared with them in a moment of weakness they called intimacy would bind you to them.

In this Zina was like all the rest, and he found the bitter rind of disappointment in his mouth. But then he was always being disappointed by others. They simply weren't in his sphere; they couldn't understand the nuances of the world as he did.

They were amusing for a while, but only for a while. He took this thought with him down into the bottomless chasm of a deep and untroubled sleep, and when he awoke, Zina was gone, returned to the side of the unsuspecting Hasan Arsenov.

At dawn, the five of them piled into a brace of Range Rovers, which had been provisioned and were driven by members of the Humanistas team, and headed south out of the city toward the great unwashed slum that extended like a festering canker on the flank of Nairobi. No one spoke and they had eaten only lightly, for a pall of hideous tension gripped them all, even Spalko.

Though the morning was clear, a toxic haze hung low over the sprawling slum, ready evidence of the lack of proper sanitation and the ever-present specter of cholera. There were ramshackle structures, mean tin and cardboard huts, some wooden ones, as well as squat concrete buildings that could have been mistaken for bunkers except for the zigzag lines of laundry strung outside, flapping in the gritty air. As well, there were mounds of bulldozed earth, raw and enigmatic until the passing party saw the scorched and charcoaled remains of fire-gutted dwellings, shoes with their soles burned off, tatters of a blue dress. These few artifacts, evidence of recent history, which was all that existed here, lent a particularly forlorn aspect to the ugliness of the grinding poverty. If there was a life to be had here, it was fitful, chaotic, dismal beyond either word or thought. All were struck by the sense of a terminal night that existed here even in the light of a new morning. There was a fatedness to the sprawl that made them recall the bazaar, the black market nature of the city's economy they felt was in some obscure way responsible for the depressing landscape through which they crawled, slowed by the thick crowds that overflowed the cracked sidewalks out into the rutted dirt streets. Traffic lights didn't exist, even if they had, the party would have been stopped by hordes of stinking beggars or merchants hawking their pathetic wares.

At length they arrived at more or less the center of the slum, where they entered a gutted two-story building reeking of smoke. Ash was everywhere inside, white and soft as ground bones. The drivers brought in the provisions, which were contained in what appeared to be two rectangular steamer trucks.

Inside were silver-skinned HAZMAT suits which, at Spalko's direction, they donned. The suits contained their own self-contained breathing systems. Spalko then removed the NX 20 from its case inside one of the trunks, carefully fitted the two pieces together as the four Chechen rebels gathered around to watch. Handing it to Hasan Arsenov for a moment, Spalko drew out the small, heavy box given to him by Dr. Peter Sido. With great care, he unlocked it. They all stared down at the glass vial. It was so small, so deadly. Their breathing slowed, grew labored, as if they were already afraid to draw breath.

Spalko directed Arsenov to hold the NX 20 at arm's length. He flipped open a titanium panel on top, placed the vial into the loading chamber. The NX 20 couldn't be fired yet, he explained. Dr. Schiffer had built in a number of safeguards against accidental or premature dispersal. He pointed out the airtight seal that, with the chamber full, would be activated when he closed and locked the top panel. He did this now, then he took the NX 20 from Arsenov and led them up the interior flight of stairs, still standing, despite the ravages of the fire, only because it was made of concrete.

On the second floor they crowded against a window. Like all the others in the building, its glass had been shattered; all that was left was the frame. Through it, they watched the halt and the lame, the famine-stricken, the diseased. Flies buzzed, a three-legged dog squatted and defecated in an open-air market where used goods were piled in the dust. A child ran naked through the street, crying. An old woman hunching along, hawked and spat.

These sights were of only peripheral interest to the party. They were studying Spalko's every move, listening to his every word with a concentration that bordered on the compulsive. The mathematical precision of the weapon worked like a magical counter-spell to the disease that seemed to have conjured itself into the air.

Spalko showed them the two triggers on the NX 20 – a small one just forward of the larger one. The small one, he told them, injected the payload from the loading chamber into the firing chamber. Once that, too, was sealed by pressing this button, here, on the left side of the weapon, the NX 20 was ready to be fired. He pulled the small trigger, then pressed the button, and could feel within the weapon a slight stirring, the first intimation of death.

The muzzle of the thing was blunt and ugly, but its bluntness was practical as well. Unlike conventional weapons, the NX 20 needed only to be aimed in the most general way, he pointed out. He stuck the muzzle through the window. They all held their breath as his finger curled around the large trigger.

Outside, life went on in its random, disorderly fashion. A young man held a bowl of maize-meal porridge under his chin, scooping up the glop with the first two fingers of his right hand while a group of half-starved people watched with unnaturally large eyes. An impossibly thin girl on a bicycle passed by and a pair of toothless old men stared at the packed earth of the street as if reading there the sad story of their lives.

It was no more than a soft hiss, at least that was how it sounded to each of them secure and safe inside their HAZMAT suits. There was, otherwise, no outward sign of the dispersal. This was as Dr. Schiffer had predicted.

The party watched tensely as the seconds ticked by with agonizing slowness. Every sense seemed heightened. They heard the sonorous tolling of their own pulse in their ears, felt the heavy beat of their hearts. They found that they were holding their breath.

Dr. Schiffer had said that within three minutes they would see the first signs that the disperser had worked properly. It was more or less the last thing he'd said before Spalko and Zina had dropped his near-lifeless body down into the labyrinth.

Spalko, who'd been following the second hand of his watch as it swept toward the three-minute mark, now looked up. He was riveted by what he saw. A dozen people had dropped before the first scream sounded. It was quickly choked off, but others took up the ululating cry, only to drop, writhing, in the street. Chaos and silence as death crept outward in a gathering spiral. There was no hiding from it, no way to avoid it, and no one escaped, even those who tried to run.

He signed to the Chechens and they followed him down the concrete stairs. The drivers were ready and waiting as Spalko broke down the NX 20. The moment he stowed it, they snapped closed the trunks, brought them out to the waiting Range Rovers.

The party took a tour of the street, then the adjacent ones. They walked four blocks in every direction, always seeing the same result. Death and dying, more death and dying. They returned to the vehicles, the taste of triumph in their mouths. The Range Rovers started up the moment they were settled and took them over the entire area of the half-mile-square radius Dr. Schiffer had told Spalko was the NX 20's dispersal range. Spalko was gratified to see that the doctor had neither lied nor exaggerated.

By the time the payload had run its course an hour from now, how many people would be dead or dying? he wondered. He'd stopped counting after a thousand, but he guessed it would be three times that amount, perhaps as much as five times.

Before they left the city of the dead, he gave the order and his drivers started the fires, using a potent accelerant. Immediately, sheets of flame flicked skyward, spreading quickly.

The fire was good to see. It would cover what had happened here this morning, for no one must know, not, at least until after their mission at the Reykjavík summit was completed.

*In just forty-eight hours it would be,* Spalko thought, exultant. Nothing could stop them.

*Now the world is mine.*

# Book 3

# 21

'I think there may be internal bleeding,' Annaka said, looking again at the deeply discolored swelling of Bourne's side. 'We've got to get you to the hospital.'

'You must be joking,' he said. Indeed, the pain was much worse; every time he breathed, he felt as if a couple of ribs had been staved in. But a trip to the hospital was out of the question; he was a wanted man.

'All right,' she conceded. 'A doctor, then.' And raised a hand, anticipating his objection. 'My father's friend, Istvan, is discreet. My father used him from time to time without consequence.'

Bourne shook his head, said, 'Go to a pharmacy if you must, nothing more.'

Before he had a chance to change his mind, Annaka grabbed her coat and purse, promising to be back shortly.

In a way he was glad to be rid of her temporarily, he needed to be alone with his thoughts. Curled up on the sofa, he drew the eiderdown closer around him. His mind seemed to be on fire. He was convinced that Dr. Schiffer was the key. He had to find him, for once he did, he'd find the person who had ordered Alex and Mo's murders, the person who had set him up. The problem was Bourne was quite certain he didn't have much time left. Schiffer had been missing for some time now. Molnar had been dead two days. If, as Bourne feared, he'd disclosed Schiffer's whereabouts under articulated interrogation, then Bourne would have to assume that Schiffer was by now in enemy hands, which would mean that the enemy also had in his possession whatever it was that Schiffer had invented, some sort of biological weapon, code-named NX 20, to which Leonard Fine, Conklin's conduit, had reacted so strongly when he'd mentioned it.

Who *was* the enemy? The only name he had was Stepan Spalko, an internationally renowned humanitarian. And yet, according to Khan, Spalko was the man who had ordered the murders of Alex and Mo and had set Bourne up as the murderer. Khan could be lying, and why not? If he wanted to get to Spalko for his own reasons, he'd hardly announce them to Bourne.

Khan!

The very thought of him caused Bourne to be flooded with unwanted emotion. With effort, he concentrated on his rage against his own government. They'd lied to him – colluded in a coverup to keep him from the truth. Why? What were they trying to hide? Did they believe that Joshua might be alive? If so, why wouldn't they want him to know? *What was it they were doing?* He pressed his hands to his head. His vision seemed to lose its perspective – things that had seemed close at hand a moment ago now appeared far away. He thought he might be losing his mind. With an inarticulate cry, he threw the eiderdown off him and rose, ignoring the flash of pain in his side as he stalked to where he'd hidden his ceramic gun beneath his jacket. He took it up in his hand. Unlike the reassuring heft of a steel gun, this was as light as a feather. He held it by the grips, curled his forefinger through the trigger guard. He stared at it a long time, as if through sheer force of will he could conjure up the officials buried deep inside the military responsible for deciding not to tell him that they'd never found Joshua's body, deciding it was simply easier to declare that he'd been killed when they didn't know for a fact if he was actually dead or alive.

Slowly the pain returned, a universe of agony with every breath he took, forcing him to return to the sofa, where he once again wrapped himself in the eiderdown. And in the quiet of the apartment, the thought, unbidden, came again: What if Khan was telling the truth – what if he was Joshua? And the answer, terrible and unalterable: Then he was an assassin, a brutal murderer without remorse or guilt, utterly disconnected from any human emotion.

All at once Jason Bourne put his head down, as close to tears for the second time since Alex Conklin had created him decades ago.

When Kevin McColl had been assigned the Bourne sanction, he'd been on top of Ilona, a young Hungarian woman of his acquaintance, as uninhibited as she was athletic. She could do wonderful things with her legs, was, in fact, doing them when the call came in.

As it happened, he and Ilona were in the Kiraly Turkish Baths on Fo utca. It being Saturday, a woman's day, she'd had to sneak him in, which, he had to admit, had been part of the excitement. Like everyone else in his position, he'd very quickly gotten used to living beyond the law – to *being* the law.

With a grunt of frustration, he unwound himself from her and picked up his cell phone. There was no question of not answering it; when it rang it was for a sanction. He listened without comment to the voice of the DCI on the other end of the line. He'd have to go now. The sanction was urgent, the target within range.

And so, as he wistfully watched the gleam of Ilona's sweat-slicked skin in the jewel-toned light reflected off the mosaic tiles, he began to dress. He was a huge man, with the physique of a Midwestern football lineman and a flat imperturbable face. He was obsessed with weight training, and it showed. His muscles rippled with every move he made.

'I'm not finished,' Ilona said, her huge dark eyes drinking him in.

'Neither am I,' McColl said, leaving her where she lay.

Two jets stood on the tarmac of Nairobi's Nelson Airport. Both belonged to Stepan Spalko; both had the logo of Humanistas, Ltd. on fuselage and tail. Spalko had flown in from Budapest on the first one. The second had been used by his Humanistas support staff, who were now inside the jet that would return him to Budapest. The other jet would be taking Arsenov and Zina to Iceland where they'd be rendezvousing with the rest of the terrorist cadre flying in from Chechnya by way of Helsinki.

Spalko stood facing Arsenov. Zina was a pace behind Arsenov's left shoulder. He, no doubt, thought her position one of deference, but Spalko knew better. Her eyes smoldered as she drank in the Shaykh.

'You've lived up to the letter of your promise, Shaykh,' Arsenov said. 'The weapon will bring us victory in Reykjavík, of that there can be no question.'

Spalko nodded. 'Soon you'll have everything that's due you.'

'The depth of our gratitude seems quite inadequate.'

'You don't give yourself enough credit, Hasan.' Spalko drew out a leather briefcase, unlocked it. 'Passports, ID tags, maps, diagrams, the latest photos, everything you need.' He handed over the contents. 'The rendezvous with the boat will be at three-hundred hours tomorrow.' He looked at Arsenov. 'May Allah lend you strength and courage. May Allah guide your mailed fist.'

As Arsenov turned away, preoccupied with his precious cargo, Zina said, 'May our next meeting lead to a great future, Shaykh.'

Spalko smiled. 'The past will die,' he said, speaking volumes with his eyes, 'in order to make way for that great future.'

Zina, laughing to herself in silent pleasure, followed Hasan Arsenov as he mounted the metal ladder into the jet.

Spalko watched the door close behind them, then he crossed to his jet, waiting patiently on the tarmac. He pulled out his cell phone, dialed a number and, when he heard the familiar voice on the other end of the line, said without preamble, 'The progress Bourne has been making is an ominous development. I can no longer afford to have Khan kill Bourne in a public way – yes, I know, *if* he ever meant to kill Bourne. Khan's a curious creature, a puzzle I've never been able to solve. But now that he's become unpredictable, I've got to assume he's following his own agenda. If Bourne dies now, Khan will fade into the woodwork and not even I will be able to find him. Nothing must interfere with what will take place in two days' time. Do I make myself clear? Good. Now, listen. There's only one way to neutralize them both.'

McColl had received not only Annaka Vadas' name and address – by an extraordinary stroke of luck, just four blocks north of the baths – but also her photo via a jpg file downloaded to his cell phone. As a result, he had no trouble recognizing her when she came out of the entrance to 106–108 Fo utca. He was immediately stirred by her beauty, the authoritative manner of her gait. He watched as she put away her cell phone, unlocked a blue Skoda and slid in behind the wheel.

Just before Annaka inserted her key into the ignition slot, Khan rose from the backseat of the car and said, 'I should tell Bourne everything.'

She started but made no attempt to turn around; she was that well trained. Staring at him in the rear-view mirror, she replied shortly, 'Tell him what? You don't know anything.'

'I know enough. I know you're the one who brought the police to Molnar's apartment. I know why you did that. Bourne was getting too close to the truth, wasn't he, getting too close to finding out that Spalko was the one who'd set him up. I'd already told him, but it seems he doesn't believe anything I say.'

'Why should he? You have no credibility with him. He's convinced himself you're part of a vast plot to manipulate him.'

Khan whipped a steely hand over the seatback, gripping her arm, which had slowly moved while she spoke. 'Don't do that.' He took her purse, opened it, removed the gun. 'You tried to kill me once. Believe me, you won't get a second chance.'

She stared at his reflected image. Inside her was a constellation of emotions. 'You think I'm lying to you about Jason, but I'm not.'

'What I'd like to know,' he said easily, ignoring her comment, 'was how you convinced him you loved your father when, really, you hated his guts.'

She sat mute, breathing slowly, trying to gather her wits. She knew she was in an extremely perilous situation. The question was how was she going to extricate herself.

'How you must've rejoiced when he was shot to death,' Khan continued, 'though, knowing you as I do, you probably wished you'd been able to shoot him yourself.'

'If you're going to kill me,' she said tersely, 'do it now and spare me your useless chatter.'

With a move like a cobra, he leaned forward, grabbed her by her throat, and at last she looked alarmed, which was, after all, the first thing he was after. 'I don't intend to spare you anything, Annaka. What did you spare me when you had the chance?'

'I didn't think I needed to baby you.'

'You rarely thought when we were together,' he said, 'at least, not about me.'

Her smile was cold. 'Oh, I thought about you constantly.'

'And repeated every one of those thoughts to Stepan Spalko.' His hand tightened on her throat, rattling her head from side to side. 'Isn't that right?'

'Why ask me when you already know the answer?' she said a little breathlessly.

'How long has he been playing me?'

Annaka closed her eyes for a moment. 'From the beginning.'

Khan ground his teeth in fury. 'What's his game? What does he want from me?'

'That I don't know.' She made a wheezing noise as he squeezed so hard he cut off all air to her windpipe. When he released his grip sufficiently, she said in a thin voice, 'Hurt me all you want, you'll still get the same answer, because it's the truth.'

'The truth!' He laughed derisively. 'You wouldn't know the truth if it bit you.' Nevertheless, he believed her, and was disgusted by her uselessness. 'What's your business with Bourne?'

'Keeping him away from Stepan.'

He nodded, recalling his conversation with Spalko. 'That makes sense.'

The lie had come easily to her lips. It had the ring of truth not only because she'd had a lifetime of practice but because up until this last call from Spalko it *had* been the truth. Spalko's plans had changed, and now that she'd had time to think it through, it suited her new purpose to tell this to Khan. Perhaps it was fortuitous that he'd come upon her like this, but only if she managed to get out of the encounter alive.

'Where's Spalko now?' he asked her. 'Here in Budapest?'

'Actually, he's on his way back from Nairobi.'

Khan was surprised. 'What was he doing in Nairobi?'

She laughed, but with his fingers painfully gripping her throat, it sounded more like a dry cough. 'D'you really think he'd tell me? You know how secretive he is.'

He put his lips against her ear. 'I know how secretive *we* used to be, Annaka – only it wasn't secretive at all, was it?'

Her eyes engaged his in the mirror. 'I didn't tell him everything.' How strange it was not to be looking at him directly. 'Some things I kept for myself.'

Khan's lips curled in contempt. 'You don't actually expect me to believe that.'

'Believe what you want,' she said flatly, 'you always have.'

He shook her again. 'Meaning?'

She gasped and bit her lower lip. 'I never understood the depth of my hatred for my father until I spent time with you.' He let up on his grip and she swallowed convulsively. 'But you with your unswerving enmity toward your father, you showed me the light; you showed me how to bide my time, to savor the thought of revenge. And you're right, when he was shot, I felt the bitterness of not having done it myself.'

Though he had no intention of showing it, what she said shook him. Up until a moment ago, he'd had no idea he'd revealed so much of himself to her. He felt ashamed and resentful that she'd been able to get so far under his skin without him being aware of it.

'We were together a year,' he said, 'a lifetime for people like us.'

'Thirteen months, twenty-one days, six hours,' she said. 'I remember the precise moment I walked out on you because it was then I knew I couldn't control you as Stepan wanted me to.'

'And why was that?' His voice was casual, even though his interest was anything but.

Her eyes had engaged his again, refused to let them go. 'Because,' she said, 'when I was with you, I could no longer control myself.'

Was she telling the truth or was she playing him again? Khan, so certain about everything until Jason Bourne had come back into his life, didn't know. Once again he felt ashamed and resentful, even a bit frightened that his vaunted powers of observation and instinct were failing him. Despite his best efforts, emotion had entered the picture, spreading its toxic haze over his mind, clouding his judgment, becalming him on an indistinct sea. He could feel his desire for her rising more strongly than it ever had before. He wanted her so badly that he couldn't help but press his lips against the precious skin at the nape of her neck.

And in so doing he missed the shadow's sudden fall into the interior of the Skoda, the shadow marked by Annaka, who shifted her gaze, saw the burly American wrench open the rear door and bring down the butt end of his gun onto the back of Khan's skull.

Khan's grip relaxed, his hand dropping away as he keeled over onto the backseat, unconscious.

'Hello, Ms. Vadas,' the burly American said in perfectly inflected Hungarian. He smiled as he swept up her gun into his huge hand. 'My name's McColl, but I'd be obliged if you called me Kevin.'

Zina dreamed of an orange sky, beneath which a modern-day horde – an army of Chechens brandishing NX 20s – descended from the Caucuses onto the steppes of Russia to lay waste to their bedeviling nemesis. But such was the power of Spalko's experiment that for her it obliterated time. She was back again, a child in her parents' miserable shell-shocked hovel, her mother staring at her from out of her ruined face, saying, '*I can't get up. Even for our water. I can't go on . . .*'

But someone had to go on. She was then fifteen, the oldest of the four children. When her mother's father-in-law came, he took only her brother Kanti, the male heir of the clan; the Russians had either killed the others, including his own sons, or had sent them away to the dreaded camps in Pobedinskoe and Krasnaya Turbina.

After that, she took over her mother's chores, collecting metal and water. But at night, exhausted as she was, sleep escaped her, fleeing from the vision of Kanti's tear-streaked face, his terror at leaving his family, everything he'd known.

Three times a week she slipped away, crossing terrain littered with unexploded landmines in order to see Kanti, to kiss his pale cheeks and give him news of home. One day she arrived to find her grandfather dead. Of Kanti there was no sign. The Russian Special Forces had come through in a sweep, killing her grandfather and taking her brother to Krasnaya Turbina.

She'd spent the next six months trying to find news of Kanti, but she was young and inexperienced in these matters. Besides, without money she could find no one willing to talk. Three years later, her mother dead, her sisters in foster homes, she joined the rebel forces. She hadn't chosen an easy path: She'd had to endure male intimidation; she'd had to learn to be meek and subservient, to identify what she had then thought of as her meager resources and husband them. But she had always been exceptionally clever and this made her a quick learner of physical skills. It also provided her with a springboard from which to discover how the power game was played. Unlike a man, who rose through the ranks by intimidation, she was obliged to use the physical assets she was born with. A year after enduring the hardships of one handler after another, she managed to convince her controller to mount a night-time raid on Krasnaya Turbina.

This was the sole reason she had joined the rebels, had put herself through hell, but she was frankly terrified of what she might find. And yet she found nothing, no evidence of her brother's whereabouts. It was as if Kanti had simply ceased to exist.

Zina awoke with a gasp. She sat up, looked around, realized that she was in Spalko's jet on the way to Iceland. In her mind's eye, still half in its dream-state, she saw Kanti's tear-streaked face, smelled the acrid stench of lye coming from the killing pits at Krasnaya Turbina. She put her head down. It was the uncertainty that ate at her. If she knew he was dead, she could perhaps put her guilt to rest. But if, by some miracle of chance, he was still alive, she would never know, couldn't come to his rescue, save him from the terrors to which the Russians continued to subject him.

Aware of someone approaching, she looked up. It was Magomet, one of the two lieutenants Hasan had brought with him to Nairobi to bear witness to the gateway to their freedom. Akhmed, the other lieutenant, was studiously ignoring her as he had since he'd seen her comfortable in Western dress. Magomet, a bear of a man with eyes the color of Turkish coffee and a long curling beard he combed with his fingers when he was anxious, stood slightly bent, leaning against the seatback.

'Is everything in order, Zina?' he asked.

Her eyes searched first for Hasan, found him asleep. Then she curved her lips in the ghost of a smile. 'I was dreaming of our coming triumph.'

'It'll be magnificent, won't it? Vindication at last! Our day in the sun!'

She could tell that he was dying to sit next to her, so she said nothing; he would have to be content with her not shooing him away. She stretched, arching her breasts, watching with amusement as his eyes opened slightly. *All that's missing is his tongue hanging out,* she thought.

'Would you like some coffee?' he said.

'I suppose I wouldn't mind.' She kept her voice carefully neutral, knowing that he was questing for hints. Her status, heightened by the important task the Shaykh had given her, the trust implicit in what he'd asked of her, was clearly not lost on him, as it was on Akhmed, who, like most Chechen males, saw her only as an inferior female. For a moment, then, her nerve failed her as she considered the enormous cultural barrier she was attempting to attack. But a moment's clear-eyed concentration returned her to her normal state. The plan she'd formulated with the Shaykh's instigation was sound; it would work – she knew it as surely as she drew breath. Now, as Magomet turned to go, she spoke up in furtherance of that plan. 'And while you're in the galley,' she said, 'bring yourself a cup as well.'

When he returned, she took the coffee from him, sipped it without inviting him to sit. He stood, his elbows on the seatback, holding his cup between his hands.

'Tell me,' Magomet said, 'what's he like?'

'The Shaykh? Haven't you asked Hasan?'

'Hasan Arsenov says nothing.'

'Perhaps,' she said, looking at Magomet over the rim of her cup, 'he jealously guards his favored status.'

'Do you?'

Zina laughed softly. 'No. I don't mind sharing.' She sipped more coffee. 'The Shaykh's a visionary. He sees the world not as it is but as it will be a year from now, five years! It's quite astonishing to be around him, a man who's so in control of every aspect of his self, a man who commands so much power across the globe.'

Magomet made a sound of relief. 'Then we're truly saved.'

'Yes, saved.' Zina put aside her cup, produced a straight razor and cream she'd found in the well-equipped toilet. 'Come sit down here, opposite me.'

Magomet hesitated only an instant. When he sat, he was so close their knees touched.

'You can't deplane in Iceland looking like that, you know.'

He watched her from out of his dark eyes as his fingers combed through his beard. Without taking her eyes off his, Zina grasped his hand in hers, drew it away from his beard. Then she opened the razor, applied cream to his right cheek. The blade scraped against his flesh. Magomet trembled a little, then, as she began to shear him, his eyes closed.

At some point she became aware that Akhmed was sitting up, watching her. By this time, half of Magomet's face was clean-shaven. She continued what she was doing as Akhmed rose and approached her. He said nothing but stared in disbelief as Magomet's beard was peeled away and his face was slowly revealed.

At length he cleared his throat, said to her in a soft voice, 'Do you think I could be next?'

'I wouldn't have expected this guy to be carrying such a mediocre gun,' Kevin McColl said as he hauled Annaka out of the Skoda. He made a noise of contempt as he stowed it away.

Annaka went meekly enough, happy that he'd mistaken her gun for Khan's. She stood on the sidewalk beneath the sullen sky of afternoon, her head bowed, eyes lowered, a secret smile lighting her up inside. Like many men, he couldn't fathom that she'd carry a weapon, let alone might know how to use it. What he didn't know would certainly hurt him – she'd make sure of it.

'First of all, I want to assure you that nothing will happen to you. All you have to do is answer my questions truthfully and obey my commands to the letter.' He used the pad of his thumb on a minor nerve bundle on the inside of her elbow. Just enough to let her know that he was deadly serious. 'Do we understand each other?'

She nodded and cried out briefly as he bore down harder on the nerves.

'I expect you to answer when I ask you a question.'

She said, 'I understand, yes.'

'Good.' He took her into the shadows of the entrance to 106–108 Fo utca. 'I'm looking for Jason Bourne. Where is he?'

'I don't know.'

Her knees buckled in pain as he did something terrible to the inside of her elbow.

'Shall we try it again?' he said. 'Where's Jason Bourne?'

'Upstairs,' she said as tears rolled down her cheeks. 'In my apartment.'

His grip on her loosened noticeably. 'See how easy that was? No fuss, no muss. Now, let's you and me go on up.'

They went inside and she used her key. She turned on the light and they went up the wide staircase. When they reached the fourth floor, McColl reined her in. 'Hear me now,' he said softly. 'As far as you're concerned, nothing's wrong. Got me?'

She almost nodded, caught herself and said, 'Yes.'

He pulled her back against him hard. 'Give him any warning sign and I'll gut you like a large-mouth bass.' He shoved her forward. 'Okay. Get on with it.'

She walked to her door, put her key in the lock and opened it. She saw to her right that Jason was slumped on the sofa, his eyes half closed.

Bourne looked up. 'I thought you were – '

At that instant McColl shoved her, raised his gun. 'Daddy's home!' he cried as he aimed the gun at the recumbent figure and pulled the trigger.

# 22

Annaka, who'd been biding her time, waiting for McColl's first move, drove the point of her cocked elbow into his arm, deflecting his aim. As a result, the bullet entered the wall above Bourne's head where it met the ceiling.

McColl bellowed in rage, reached out with his left hand even as he was swinging his right arm down to aim again at his recumbent target. His fingers sank into Annaka's hair, grabbed tight, jerked her back off her feet. At that moment Bourne brought his ceramic gun from beneath the eiderdown. He wanted to shoot the intruder in the chest, but Annaka was in the way. Altering his aim, he shot the intruder through the meat of his gun arm. The gun fell to the carpet, blood splattered from the wound, and Annaka screamed as the intruder dragged her back against his chest as a shield.

Bourne was up on one knee, the muzzle of his gun roaming, as the intruder, with Annaka braced against him, backed toward the open door.

'This isn't over, not by a long shot,' he said, his gaze on Bourne. 'I've never lost a sanction and I don't intend to start now.' With that ominous pronouncement, he picked Annaka up and hurled her at Bourne.

Bourne, off the sofa, caught Annaka before she had a chance to smash into the side of it. He whirled her around, then sprinted through the open doorway in time to see the elevator door closing. He took the stairs, limping a little. His side felt as if it were on fire and his legs were weak. His breathing became labored and he wanted to stop, if only to be able to get enough oxygen in his lungs, but he kept going, taking the stairs two and three at a time. Rounding the first-floor landing, his left foot slipped on the edge of a tread and he went down, half-falling, half-sliding down the rest of the flight. He groaned as he rose, slammed through the door into the lobby. There was blood on the marble floor but no assassin. He took a step into the lobby, and his legs collapsed out from under him. He sat there, half-stunned, his gun in one hand, the other lying palm up on his thigh. His eyes were glazed with pain and it seemed to him as if he'd forgotten how to breathe.

*I've got to go after the bastard*, he thought. But there was a tremendous noise in his head that he eventually identified as the thudding of his heart working overtime. For the moment, at least, he was incapable of movement. He had just enough time, before Annaka arrived, to reflect that his staged death hadn't fooled the Agency for long.

When she saw him, her face turned white with concern. 'Jason!' She knelt beside him, her arm around him.

'Help me up,' he said.

She took his weight with her canted hip. 'Where is he? Where did he go?'

He should've been able to answer her. Christ, he thought, maybe she was right, maybe he really did need to see a doctor.

Perhaps it was the venom in his heart that had pulled Khan back from unconsciousness so quickly. In any case, he was up and out of the Skoda within minutes of the attack. His head hurt, to be sure, but it was his ego that had taken the brunt of the attack. He replayed the whole sorry scene in his mind, knew with a certainty that caused a sinking feeling in his stomach that it was only his foolish and dangerous feelings for Annaka that had made him vulnerable.

What more proof did he need that emotional attachment was to be shunned at all costs? It had cost him dearly with his parents and, again, with Richard Wick, and now most recently with Annaka, who from the first had betrayed him to Stepan Spalko.

And what of Spalko? *'We're far from strangers. We share secrets of the most intimate nature,'* he'd said that night in Grozny. *'I'd like to think we're more than businessman and client.'*

Like Richard Wick, he'd offered to take Khan in, claimed he wanted to be his friend, to make him part of a hidden – and somehow intimate – world. *'You owe your impeccable reputation in no small part to the commissions I've given you.'* As if Spalko, like Wick, believed he was Khan's benefactor. These people were under the misapprehension that they lived on a higher plane, that they belonged to the elite. Like Wick, Spalko had lied to Khan so that he could use him for his own purposes.

What had Spalko wanted from him? It almost didn't matter; he was past caring. All he wanted was his pound of flesh from Stepan Spalko, a reckoning that would set past injustices to rights. Nothing less than Spalko's death would assuage him now. Spalko would be his first and last commission from himself.

It was then, crouched in the shadows of a doorway, unconsciously massaging the back of his head where a lump had already been raised, that he heard her voice. It rose from the deep, from the shadows in which he sat, dropping down through the depths, pulled under the purling waves.

'Lee-Lee,' he whispered. 'Lee-Lee!'

It was her voice he heard calling to him. He knew what she wanted; she wanted him to join her in the drowned depths. He put his aching head in his hands and a terrible sob escaped his lips like the last bubble of air from his lungs. Lee-Lee. He hadn't thought of her in so long – or had he? He'd dreamed about her almost every night; it had taken him this long to realize it. Why? What was different now that she should come to him so strongly after such a long time gone?

It was then he heard the slam of the front door and his head came up in time for him to see the big man racing out of the entrance to 106–108 Fo utca. He was grasping one hand with the other, and by the trail of blood behind him Khan figured that he'd run into Jason Bourne. A small smile crept across his face, for he knew this must be the man who'd attacked him.

Khan felt an immediate urge to kill him, but with an effort he gained control and came up with a better idea. Leaving the shadows, he followed the figure as he fled down Fo utca.

Dohány Synagogue was the largest synagogue in Europe. On its western side, the massive structure had an intricate Byzantine brickwork facade in blue, red and yellow, the heraldic colors of Budapest. Crowning the entrance was a large stained-glass window. Above this impressive sight rose two Moorish polygonal towers topped by striking copper and gilt cupolas.

'I'll go in and get him,' Annaka said as they got out of her Skoda. Istvan's service had tried to direct her to a covering doctor, but she'd insisted that she needed to see Dr. Ambrus, that she was an old family friend, and at length they'd directed her here. 'The fewer people who see you like this, the better.'

Bourne agreed. 'Listen, Annaka, I'm beginning to lose count of the times you've saved my life.'

She looked at him and smiled. 'Then stop counting.'

'The man who assaulted you.'

'Kevin McColl.'

'He's an Agency specialist.' There was no need for Bourne to have to tell her what sort of specialist McColl was. Yet another thing he liked about her. 'You handled him well.'

'Until he used me as a shield,' she said bitterly. 'I should never have allowed –'

'We got out of it. That's all that matters.'

'But he's still at large, and his threat –'

'The next time I'll be ready for him.'

The small smile returned to her face. She directed him to the courtyard in the rear of the synagogue, where she told him he could wait for them without fear of running into anyone.

Istvan Ambrus, the doctor of János Vadas' acquaintance, was inside at service, but he was amenable enough when Annaka went in and told him of the emergency.

'Of course, I'm pleased to help you in any way I can, Annaka,' he said as he rose from his seat and walked with her through the magnificent chandeliered interior. Behind them was the great five-thousand-tube organ, highly unusual in a Jewish house of worship, on whose keyboard the great composers Franz Liszt and Camille Saint-Saens had once played.

'Your father's death has hit us all very hard.' He took her hand, squeezed it briefly. He had the blunt, strong fingers of a surgeon or a bricklayer. 'How are you holding up, my dear?'

'As well as can be expected,' she said softly, leading him outside.

Bourne was sitting in the courtyard under whose earth lay the corpses of five thousand Jews who had perished in the brutal winter of 1944–45, when Adolph Eichmann turned the synagogue into a concentration point from which he sent ten times that number to camps where they were exterminated. The courtyard, contained between the arches of the inner loggia, was filled with pale memorial stones through which dark-green ivy crept. The trunks of the trees with which it had been planted were similarly wound with the vines. A cold wind ruffled the leaves, a sound that in this place could have been mistaken for distant voices.

It was difficult to sit here and not think of the dead and of the terrible suffering that had gone on here during that dark time. He wondered whether another dark time was gathering itself to overwhelm them once again. He looked up from his contemplation to see Annaka in the company of a round-faced, dapper individual with a pencil mustache and apple cheeks. He was dressed in a brown three-piece suit. The shoes on his small feet were highly polished.

'So you're the disaster in question,' he said after Annaka had made the introductions, assuring him that Bourne could speak their native tongue. 'No, don't get up,' he went on as he sat down beside Bourne and began his examination. 'Well, sir, I don't believe Annaka's description did your injuries justice. You look like you've been put through a wurst-grinder.'

'That's just how I feel, Doctor.' Bourne winced despite himself as Dr. Ambrus' fingers probed a particularly painful spot.

'As I walked out into the courtyard, I saw you deep in thought,' Dr. Ambrus said in a conversational tone. 'In a sense, this is a terrible place, this courtyard, reminding us of those we've lost and, in a larger sense, what humanity as a whole lost during the Holocaust.' His fingers were surprisingly light as well as agile as they roamed over the tender flesh of Bourne's side. 'But the history of that time isn't all so grim, you know. Just before Eichmann and his staff marched in, several priests helped the rabbi remove the twenty-seven scrolls of the Torah from the Ark inside the synagogue. They took them, these priests, and buried them in a Christian cemetery, where they remained safe from the Nazis until after the war was ended.' He smiled thinly. 'So what does this tell us? There remains the potential for light even in the darkest places. Compassion can come from the most unexpected places. And you have two cracked ribs.'

He rose now. 'Come. I have at my house all the equipment necessary to bind you up. In a matter of just a week or so the pain will recede, and you'll be on the mend.' He waggled a thick forefinger. 'But in the interim you must promise me you'll rest. No strenuous exercise for you. In fact, no exercise at all would be best.'

'I can't promise you that, Doctor.'

Dr. Ambrus sighed as he shot Annaka a quick glance. 'Now why doesn't that surprise me?'

Bourne got to his feet. 'In fact, I'm very much afraid I'm going to have to do everything you've just warned me against, in which case I've got to ask you to do what you can in order to protect the damaged ribs.'

'How about a suit of armor?' Dr. Ambrus chuckled at his own joke, but his amusement quickly dropped away as he saw the expression on Bourne's face. 'Good God, man, what do you expect to be going up against?'

'If I could tell you,' Bourne said bleakly, 'I imagine we'd all be better off.'

Though clearly taken aback, Dr. Ambrus was as good as his word, leading them to his house in the Buda Hills where he had a small examining room where others might have had a study. Outside the window were climbing roses, but the geranium pots were still bare, awaiting warmer weather. Inside, were cream walls, white moldings, and on top of the cabinets, framed snapshots of Dr. Ambrus' wife and his two sons.

Dr. Ambrus sat Bourne down on the table, humming to himself as he went methodically through his cabinets, picking out one item here, two more there. Returning to his patient who he'd bade strip to the waist, he swung an armatured light around, snapped it on the field of battle. Then he went to work binding Bourne's ribs tightly in three different layers of material – cotton, spandex and a rubberlike material he said contained Kevlar.

'Better than that no one could do,' he declared when he was finished.

'I can't breathe,' Bourne gasped.

'Good, that means the pain will be kept to a minimum.' He rattled a small brown plastic bottle. 'I'd give you some painkillers, but for a man such as yourself – um, no, I think not. The drug will interfere with your senses, your reflexes will be off, and the next time I see you, you might be on a slab.'

Bourne smiled at the attempt at humor. 'I'll do my best to spare you that shock.' Bourne dug in a pocket. 'How much do I owe you?'

Dr. Ambrus raised his hands. 'Please.'

'How to thank you, then, Istvan?' Annaka said.

'Just to see you again, my dear, is payment enough.' Dr. Ambrus took her face in his hands, kissed her on first one cheek, then the other. 'Promise me you'll come to dinner one night soon. Bela misses you as much as I. Come, my dear. Come. She'll make you her goulash, which you loved as a child.'

'I promise, Istvan. Soon.'

Content at last with this promise of payment, Dr. Ambrus let them go.

# 23

'Something needs to be done about Randy Driver,' Lindros said.

The DCI finished signing a set of papers, pushing them into his outbox before looking up. 'I heard he gave you a sound tongue-lashing.'

'I don't understand. Is this a source of amusement for you, sir?'

'Indulge me, Martin,' he said with a smirk he refused to hide. 'I have few sources of entertainment these days.'

The sun-dazzle that had all afternoon spun off the statue of the three Revolutionary War soldiers outside the window was gone, making the bronze figures appear weary in the shadows shrouding them. The fragile light of another spring day had all too quickly passed into night.

'I want him taken care of. I want access – '

The DCI's face darkened. ' "I want, I want" – what are you, a three-year-old?'

'You put me in charge of the investigation into Conklin's and Panov's murders. I'm only doing what you asked.'

'Investigation?' The DCI's eyes sparked with anger. 'There is no investigation. I told you in no uncertain terms, Martin, that I wanted an end to this. The bleeding is killing us with the bitch-woman. I want it cauterized so it can be forgotten. The last thing I need is for you to be running all over the Beltway, throwing your weight around like a bull in a china shop.' He waved a hand to stave off his deputy's protestations. 'Hang Harris, hang him high and loud enough for the National Security Advisor to be certain we know what we're doing.'

'If you say so, sir, but with all due respect that would be just about the worst mistake we could make right now.' As the DCI stared open-mouth at him, he spun across the desk the computer printout Harris had sent over.

'What is this?' the DCI said. He liked a precis of everything he was given before he had a chance to read it.

'It's part of the electronic record of a ring of Russians providing people with illegal handguns. The gun used to murder Conklin and Panov is there. It was falsely registered to Webb. This proves Webb was set up, that he didn't murder his two best friends.'

The DCI had begun reading the printout, and now his thick white brows furrowed. 'Martin, this proves nothing.'

'Again, with all due respect, sir, I don't see how you can ignore the facts that are right in front of you.'

The DCI sighed, pushed the printout away from him as he sat back in his chair. 'You know, Martin, I've trained you well. But it occurs to me now that you still have a great deal to learn.' He pointed a forefinger at the paper lying on his desk. 'This tells me that the gun Jason Bourne used to shoot Alex and Mo Panov was paid for via a wire transfer from Budapest. Bourne has I don't know how many bank accounts overseas, in Zurich and Geneva mostly, but I don't see why he wouldn't have one in Budapest as well.' He grunted. 'It's a clever trick, one of so many taught to him by Alex himself.'

Lindros' heart had plummeted to his shoes. 'So you don't think – '

'You want me to take this so-called evidence to the bitch-woman?' The DCI shook his head. 'She'd shove it back down my throat.'

Of course, the first thing that had entered the Old Man's mind was that Bourne had hacked into the U.S. Government database from Budapest, which was why he himself had activated Kevin McColl. No point telling Martin that; he'd only get himself all het up. No, the DCI thought obstinately, the money for the murder weapon had originated in Budapest and that was where Bourne had fled. Further damning evidence of his guilt.

Lindros broke in on his musing. 'So you won't authorize going back to Driver – '

'Martin, it's coming up on seven-thirty and my stomach has started to rumble.' The DCI stood. 'To show you that there's no hard feelings, I want you to join me for dinner.'

The Occidental Grill was an insider restaurant at which the DCI had his own table. It was for civilians and low-grade government employees to stand on lines, not for him. In this arena his power rose out of the shadow world he inhabited, made itself known to all of Washington. There were precious few inside the Beltway who possessed this status. After a difficult day, there was nothing like using it.

They valet-parked and mounted the long flight of granite steps to the restaurant. Inside, they went down a narrow passageway hung with photos of the presidents as well as other famous political personages who had dined at the grill. As he always did, the DCI paused in front of the photo of J. Edgar Hoover and his ever-constant shadow, Clyde Tolson. The DCI's eyes bored into the photo of the two men as if he had the power to expunge by fire this duo from the pantheon on the wall of greats.

'I distinctly remember the moment we intercepted the Hoover memo exhorting his senior officers to find the link that tied Martin Luther King, Jr., and the Communist Party to the anti–Vietnam War demonstrations.' He shook his head. 'What a world I've been a party to.'

'It's history, sir.'

'Ignominious history, Martin.'

With that pronouncement, he passed through the half-glass doors into the restaurant itself. The room was all wooden booths, cut-glass partitions and mirrored bar. As usual, there was a line, which the DCI navigated like the Queen Mary sailing through a flotilla of motorboats. He stopped in front of the podium, which was presided over by an elegant silver-haired maître d'.

At the DCI's approach, the man turned with a brace of long menus clutched to his breast. 'Director!' His eyes opened wide. There was an odd paleness to his usually florid skin. 'We had no idea that you'd be dining with us tonight.'

'Since when do you need advance notice, Jack?' The DCI said.

'May I suggest a drink at the bar, Director? I have your favorite sour mash.'

The DCI patted his stomach. 'I'm hungry, Jack. We'll dispense with the bar and go straight to my table.'

The maître d' looked distinctly uncomfortable. 'Please give me a moment, Director,' he said, hurrying away.

'What the hell's the matter with him?' muttered the DCI with some annoyance.

Lindros had already taken a look at the DCI's corner table, saw that it was occupied, and blanched. The DCI saw his expression and he whirled, peering through the throng of waiters and patrons at his beloved table, where the power seat reserved for him was now occupied by Roberta Alonzo-Ortiz, National Security Advisor of the United States. She was deep in conversation with two senators from the Foreign Intelligence Services Committee.

'I'll kill her, Martin. So help me God, I'll rend the bitch-woman limb from limb.'

At that moment the maître d', clearly sweating inside his collar, returned. 'We have a nice table all set up for you, Director, a table for four, just for you gentlemen. And the drinks're on the house, all right?'

The DCI bit back his rage. 'It's quite all right,' he said, aware that he was unable to rid himself of his high color. 'Lead on, Jack.'

The maître d' took them on a route that didn't pass his old table, and the DCI was grateful to Jack for that.

'I told her, Director,' the maître d' said almost under his breath. 'I made it quite clear that that particular corner table was yours, but she insisted. She wouldn't take no for an answer. What could I do? I'll have the drinks over in just a minute.' Jack said all this in a rush as he seated them, presenting the food and wine menus. 'Is there anything else I can do, Director?'

'No, thank you, Jack.' The DCI picked up his menu.

A moment later a burly waiter with muttonchop sideburns brought two glasses of sour mash, along with the bottle and a carafe of water.

'Compliments of the maître d',' he said.

If Lindros had been under any illusion that the DCI was calm, he was disabused of that notion the moment the Old Man took up his glass to sip his sour mash. His hand shook, and now Lindros could see that his eyes were glazed with rage.

Lindros saw his opening and, like the fine tactician he was, took it. 'The National Security Advisor wants the double murders attended to and swept away with as little fuss as possible. But if the basic assumption that underlies this reasoning – mainly that Jason Bourne is responsible – is untrue, then everything else falls apart, including the NSA's extremely vocal position.'

The DCI looked up. He stared shrewdly at his deputy. 'I know you, Martin. You already have some plan in mind, don't you?'

'Yessir, I do, and if I'm right, we'll make the NSA look like fools. But for that to happen, I need Randy Driver's full and complete cooperation.'

The waiter appeared with the chopped salads.

The DCI waited until they were alone and poured them both more sour mash. With a tight smile, he said, 'This business with Randy Driver – you believe it's necessary?'

'More than necessary, sir. It's vital.'

'Vital, eh?' The DCI tucked into his salad, looked at the resulting piece of glistening tomato impaled on the tines of his fork. 'I'll sign the paperwork first thing tomorrow.'

'Thank you, sir.'

The DCI frowned, his gaze sought out that of his deputy, held it captive. 'Only one way to thank me, Martin, bring me the ammunition I need to put the bitch-woman in her place.'

The advantage of having a girl in every port, McColl knew, was that he always had a place to hole up. There was, of course, an Agency safe house in Budapest – in fact, there were several, but with his bleeding arm he had no intention of showing up in an official residence and thereby announcing to his superiors his failure to satisfy the sanction the DCI himself had given him. In his section of the Agency, results were the only thing that mattered.

Ilona was home when, wounded arm at his side, he stumbled up to her door. As always, she was ready for action. He, for once, wasn't, he had business to attend to first. He sent her to make him something to eat – something protein-aceous, he told her, for he needed to regain his strength. Then he went into her bathroom, stripped to the waist, and washed off the blood from his right arm. Then he poured hydrogen peroxide over the wound. The searing pain shot up and down his arm and made his legs tremble so that he was obliged to sit for a moment on the closed toilet lid in order to collect himself. In a moment the pain had subsided to a deep throbbing and he was able to assess the damage done him. The good news was that the wound was clean; the bullet had gone cleanly through the muscle of his arm and exited. Leaning over so that he could rest his elbow on the edge of the sink, he poured more hydrogen peroxide on the wound, whistled softly through his bared teeth. Then he rose, rifled through the cabinets without finding any sterile cotton pads. He did find, under the sink, a roll of duct tape. Using a pair of cuticle scissors, he cut off a length, wrapped it tightly around the wound.

When he returned, Ilona had his meal prepared. He sat, wolfing down the food without tasting it. It was hot and nourishing, which was all he cared about. She stood behind him as he ate, massaging the bunched muscles of his shoulders.

'You're so tense,' she said. She was small and slender with flashing eyes, a ready smile, and curves in all the right places. 'What did you do after you left me at the baths? You were so relaxed then.'

'Work,' he said laconically. He knew by experience that it wasn't politic to ignore her questions, though he had very little desire for small talk. He needed to gather his thoughts, plan for the second, and final, assault on Jason Bourne. 'I've told you my work is stressful.'

Her talented fingers continued to knead the tension out of him. 'I wish you'd quit then.'

'I love what I do,' he said, pushing his empty plate away. 'I'd never quit.'

'And still you're sullen.' She came around, held out her hand. 'Then come to bed now. Let me make it better.'

'You go,' he said. 'Wait for me there. I've some business calls to make. When I'm finished, I'll be all yours.'

*

Morning came in a bevy of shouts to the small, anonymous room in a cheap hotel. The sounds of Budapest stirring penetrated the thin walls as if they were gauze, goading Annaka from her fitful sleep. For a time she lay immobile in the grayish morning illumination, side by side with Bourne on the double bed. At length she turned her head, stared at him.

How her life had changed since she'd met him on the steps of Matthias Church! Her father was dead and now she couldn't return to her own apartment because its location was known to both Khan and the CIA. In truth, there wasn't much about her apartment she'd miss, except for her piano. The pang of yearning she felt for it was akin to what she'd read identical twins experienced when they were separated by a great distance.

And what of Bourne, what did she feel for him? It was difficult for her to tell, since from an early age a certain switch had been thrown inside her that had turned off the spigot of emotion. The mechanism, a form of self-preservation instinct, was a complete mystery, even to experts who purported to study such phenomena. It was buried so deeply inside her mind that she could never reach it – another aspect of its preservation of the self.

As in everything else, she'd lied to Khan when she'd told him that she couldn't control herself around him. She'd walked out on him because Stepan had ordered her to leave. She hadn't minded; in fact, she'd rather relished the look on Khan's face when she'd told him it was over. She'd hurt him, which she liked. At the same time she saw that he'd cared for her, and she was curious about this, not understanding it herself. Of course, long ago and far away she'd cared about her mother, but of what use had that emotion been? Her mother had failed to protect her; worse, she'd died.

Slowly, carefully, she inched away from Bourne until finally she turned and rose. She was reaching for her coat when Bourne, rising from deep sleep to immediate wakefulness, spoke her name softly.

Annaka started, turned. 'I thought you were fast asleep. Did I wake you?'

Bourne watched her, unblinking. 'Where are you going?'

'I . . . we need new clothes.'

He struggled to sit up.

'How are you feeling?'

'I'm fine,' he said. He was in no mood for receiving sympathy. 'Besides clothes, we both need disguises.'

'We?'

'McColl knew who you were, that means he'd been sent a photo of you.'

'But why?' She shook her head. 'How did the CIA know you and I were together?'

'They didn't – at least, they couldn't be sure,' he said. 'I've been thinking, and the only way they could've made you was through your computer's IP address. I must've set off an internal alarm when I hacked into the government's intranet.'

'God in heaven.' She slipped into her coat. 'Still, it's far safer for me out on the streets than it would be for you.'

'Do you know a shop that sells theatrical makeup?'

'There's a district not far from here. Yes, I'm sure I can find a place.'

Bourne grabbed a pad and the stub of a pencil off the desk and made a hurried list. 'This is what I'll need for both of us,' he said. 'I've also written down my shirt, neck and waist sizes. Do you have enough money? I have plenty but it's in American dollars.'

She shook her head. 'Too dangerous. I'd have to go to a bank and change it into Hungarian forint, and that might be noticed. There are ATMs all over the city.'

'Be careful,' he warned.

'Don't worry.' She glanced at the list he'd made. 'I should be back in a couple of hours. Until then, don't leave the room.'

She descended in the tiny creaking elevator. Save for the day clerk behind the desk, the commensurately tiny lobby was deserted. He lifted his head from his newspaper, glanced at her with bored eyes before returning to his reading. She went out into bustling Budapest. The presence of Kevin McColl, a complicating factor, made her uneasy, but Stepan reassured her when she telephoned him with the news. She'd been updating him when she'd telephoned him from her apartment every time she'd run the water in the kitchen.

As she entered the flow of pedestrian traffic, she glanced at her watch. It was just after ten. She had coffee and a sweet roll at a corner café, then proceeded on to an ATM about two-thirds of the way to the shopping district toward which she was headed. She slipped in her debit card, withdrew the maximum amount, put the wad of bills in her purse and, with Bourne's list in hand, set out to shop.

Across town, Kevin McColl strode into the branch of the Budapest Bank that handled Annaka Vadas' account. He flashed his credentials and, in due course, was admitted to the glass-enclosed office of the branch manager, a well-dressed man in a conservatively cut suit. They shook hands as they introduced themselves and the manager indicated that McColl sit in the upholstered chair facing him.

The manager steepled his fingers and said, 'How can I be of assistance, Mr. McColl?'

'We're looking for an international fugitive,' McColl began.

'Ah, and why isn't Interpol involved?'

'They are,' McColl said, 'as well as the Quai d'Orsay in Paris, which was this fugitive's last stop before coming here to Budapest.'

'And the name of this wanted man?'

McColl produced the CIA flyer, which he unfolded and set on the desk in front of the manager.

The bank manager adjusted his glasses as he scanned the flyer. 'Ah, yes, Jason Bourne. I watch CNN.' He glanced up over the gold rim of his glasses. 'You say he's here in Budapest.'

'We've got a confirmed sighting.'

The bank manager set the flyer aside. 'And how may I help?'

'He was in the company of one of your depositors. Annaka Vadas.'

'Really?' The bank manager frowned. 'Her father was killed – shot dead two days ago. Do you think the fugitive murdered him?'

'It's entirely possible.' McColl held tight rein on his impatience. 'I would appreciate your help in finding out if Ms. Vadas has used an ATM anytime in the last twenty-four hours.'

'I understand.' The bank manager nodded sagely. 'The fugitive needs money. He might force her to get it for him.'

'Precisely.' Anything, McColl thought, to get this guy to move off the dime.

The bank manager swiveled around, began to type on his computer keyboard. 'Let's see then. Ah, yes, here she is. Annaka Vadas.' He shook his head. 'Such a tragedy. And now to be subjected to this.'

He was staring at his computer screen when a chirp sounded. 'It seems you were right, Mr. McColl. Annaka Vadas' PIN number was used at an ATM less than a half hour ago.'

'Address,' McColl said, leaning forward.

The manager wrote the address down on a sheet of notepaper, handed it to McColl, who was up and on his way with a 'Thank you' thrown over his shoulder.

Bourne, down in the lobby of the hotel, asked the clerk for directions to the nearest public Internet access point. He walked the twelve blocks to AMI Internet Café at 40 Váci utca. Inside, it was smoky and crowded, people sitting at computer stations, smoking as they read e-mail, did research or simply surfed the Web. He ordered a double-espresso and a buttered roll from a spike-haired young woman, who handed him a time-stamped slip of paper with the number of his station on it and directed him to a free computer that was already logged onto the Internet.

He sat down and began his work. In the 'Search' field, he typed in the name of Peter Sido, Dr. Schiffer's former partner, but found nothing. That, in itself, was both odd and suspicious. If Sido was a scientist of any note at all – which Bourne had to assume he was if he'd worked with Felix Schiffer – then chances were he'd be *somewhere* on the Web. The fact that he wasn't caused Bourne to consider the fact that his 'absence' was deliberate. He'd have to try another path.

There was something about the name Sido that rang a bell in his linguist's brain. Was it Russian in origin? Slavic? He searched these language sites but came up blank. On a hunch he switched to a site on the Magyar language, and there it was.

It turned out that Hungarian family names – what Hungarians called bynames – most always meant something. For instance, they could be patronymic, meaning they used the father's name, or they could be locative, identifying where the person came from. Their family name could also tell you their profession – interestingly, he noted that Vadas meant hunter. Or *what* they were. Sido was the Hungarian word for Jew.

So Peter Sido was a Hungarian, just like Vadas. Conklin had chosen Vadas to work with. Coincidence? Bourne didn't believe in coincidences. There was a connection; he could sense it. Which opened up the following line of thought: All the world-class hospitals and research facilities in Hungary were in Budapest. Could Sido be here?

Bourne's hands flew over the keyboard, accessing the on-line Budapest phone directory. And there he found a Dr. Peter Sido. He noted the address and phone number, then logged off, paid for his time on-line and took his double espresso and roll to the café section, where he sat at a corner table away from other patrons. He chomped on his roll while he took out his cell phone and dialed Sido's number. He sipped his double espresso. After several rings, a female voice answered.

'Hello,' Bourne said in a cheerful voice, 'Mrs. Sido?'

'Yes?'

He hung up without responding, wolfed down the rest of his breakfast while waiting for the taxi he'd called for. One eye on the front door, he scrutinized every-one who walked in, on the lookout for McColl or any other Agency operative who might have been sent into the field. Certain that he was unobserved, he went out into the street to meet the taxi. He gave the driver Dr. Peter Sido's address and not more than twenty minutes later, the taxi drew up in front of a small house with a stone facade, a tiny garden in front, and miniature iron balconies projecting from each story.

He climbed the steps and knocked. The front door was opened by a rather rotund woman of middle years with soft brown eyes and a ready smile. She had brown hair, pulled back in a bun, and was stylishly dressed.

'Mrs. Sido? Dr. Peter Sido's wife?'

'That's right.' She gazed at him inquiringly. 'May I help you?'

'My name is David Schiffer.'

'Yes?'

He smiled winningly. 'Felix Schiffer's cousin, Mrs. Sido.'

'I'm sorry,' Peter Sido's wife said, 'but Felix never mentioned you.'

Bourne was prepared for this. He chuckled. 'That's not surprising. You see, we lost touch with each other. I'm only now just returned from Australia.'

'Australia! My word!' She stepped aside. 'Well, do come in, please. You must think me rude.'

'Not at all,' Bourne said. 'Simply surprised, as anyone would be.'

She showed him into a small sitting room, comfortably, if darkly, furnished and bade him make himself at home. The air smelled of yeast and sugar. When he was seated in an over-upholstered chair, she said, 'Would you like coffee or tea? I have some stollen. I baked it this morning.'

'Stollen, a favorite of mine,' he said. 'And only coffee will do with stollen. Thank you.'

She chuckled and headed for the kitchen. 'Are you sure you're not part Hungarian, Mr. Schiffer?'

'Please call me David,' he said, rising and following her. Not knowing the family background, he was on shaky ground when it came to the Schiffers. 'Is there some-thing I can help you with?'

'Why, thank you, David. And you must call me Eszti.' She pointed at a covered cake platter. 'Why don't you cut us each a piece?'

On the refrigerator door, he saw among several family snapshots, one of a young woman, very pretty, alone. Her hand was pressed to the top of her Scottish tam and her long dark hair was windblown. Behind her was the Tower of London.

'Your daughter?' Bourne said.

Eszti Sido glanced up and smiled. 'Yes, Roza, my youngest. She's at school in London. Cambridge,' she said with understandable pride. 'My other daughters – there they are with their families – are both happily married, thank God. Roza's the ambitious one.' She smiled shyly. 'Shall I tell you a secret, David? I love all my chil-dren, but Roza is my favorite – Peter's too. I think he sees something of himself in her. She loves the sciences.'

Several more minutes of bustling around the kitchen brought a carafe of coffee and plates of stollen on a tray, which Bourne carried back into the sitting room.

'So you're Felix's cousin,' she said when they were both settled, he on the chair, she on the sofa. Between them was a low table on which Bourne had placed the tray.

'Yes, and I'm eager for news of Felix,' Bourne said as she poured the coffee. 'But, you see, I can't find him, and I thought . . . well, I was hoping your husband could help me out.'

'I don't think he knows where Felix is.' Eszti Sido handed him the coffee and a plate of stollen. 'I don't mean to alarm you, David, but he's been quite upset lately. Though they hadn't officially worked together for some time, they'd had a long-distance correspondence going recently.' She stirred cream into her coffee. 'They never stopped being good friends, you see.'

'So this recent correspondence was of a personal nature,' Bourne said.

'I don't know about that.' Eszti frowned. 'I gathered that it had something to do with their work.'

'You wouldn't know what, would you, Eszti? I've come a long way to find my cousin, and, frankly, I've begun to worry a little. Anything you or your husband could tell me, anything at all would be of great help.'

'Of course, David, I understand completely.' She took a dainty bite of her stollen. 'I imagine Peter would be quite happy to see you. At the moment, though, he's at work.'

'D'you think I could have his phone number?'

'Oh, that won't do you any good. Peter never answers his phone at work. You'll have to go to the Eurocenter Bio-I Clinic at 75 Hattyu utca. When you do, you'll first go through a metal detector, after which you'll be stopped at the front desk. Because of the work they do there, they're exceptionally security conscious. They require special ID tags to get into his section, white for visitors, green for resident doctors, blue for assistants and support staff.'

'Thank you for the information, Eszti. May I inquire as to what your husband specializes in?'

'You mean Felix never told you?'

Bourne, sipping his delicious coffee, swallowed. 'As I'm sure you know, Felix is a secretive person, he never spoke to me about his work.'

'Quite so.' Eszti Sido laughed. 'Peter's just the same and, considering the frightening field he's in, it's just as well. I'm sure if I knew what he was into, I'd have nightmares. You see, he's an epidemiologist.'

Bourne's heart skipped a beat. 'Frightening, you say. He must work with some nasty bugs then. Anthrax, pneumonic plague, Argentinian hemorrhagic fever . . .'

Eszti Sido's face clouded over. 'Oh dear, oh dear, please!' She waved a pudgy-fingered hand. 'Those are just the things I know Peter works with but don't want to know about.'

'I apologize.' Bourne leaned forward, poured her more coffee, for which she thanked him in relief.

She sat back, sipping her coffee, her eyes turned inward. 'You know, David, now that I think about it, there was an evening not long ago when Peter came home in a high state of excitement. So much so, in fact, that for once he forgot himself and mentioned something to me. I was cooking dinner and he was unusually late and I was having to juggle six things at once – a roast, you know, doesn't like to be over-cooked, so I'd taken it out, then put it back when Peter finally walked through the door. I wasn't happy with him that night, I can tell you.' She sipped again. 'Now, where was I?'

'Dr. Sido came home very excited,' Bourne prompted.

'Ah, yes, just so.' She took up a tiny piece of the stollen between her fingers. 'He'd been in contact with Felix, he said, who'd had some sort of breakthrough with the – *thing* – he'd been working on for more than two years.'

Bourne's mouth was dry. It seemed odd to him that the fate of the world now lay with a housewife with whom he was cozily sharing coffee and homemade pastry. 'Did your husband tell you what it was?'

'Of course he did!' Eszti Sido said with gusto. 'That was the reason he was so exercised. It was a biochemical disperser – whatever that is. According to Peter, what was so extraordinary about it was that it was portable. It could be carried in an acoustic guitar case, he said.' Her kind eyes gazed at him. 'Isn't that an interesting image to use for a scientific thingy?'

'Interesting, indeed,' Bourne said, his mind furiously clicking into place pieces of the jigsaw puzzle the pursuit of which had more than once almost gotten him killed.

He rose. 'Eszti, I'm afraid I must be going. Thank you so much for your time and your hospitality. Everything was delicious – *especially* the stollen.'

She blushed, smiling warmly as she saw him to the door. 'Do come again, David, under happier circumstances.'

'I will,' he assured her.

Out on the street, he paused. Eszti Sido's information confirmed both his suspicions and his worst fears. The reason everyone wanted to get their hands on Dr. Schiffer was that he had indeed created a portable means of dispersing chemical and biological pathogens. In a big city such as New York or Moscow, that would mean thousands of deaths with no means to save anyone within the radius of the dispersion. A truly terrifying scenario, one that would come true unless he could find Dr. Schiffer. If anyone knew, it would be Peter Sido. The mere fact that he'd become agitated of late confirmed that theory.

There was no doubt that he needed to see Dr. Peter Sido, the sooner the better.

'You realize you're just asking for trouble,' Feyd al-Saoud said.

'I know that,' Jamie Hull replied. 'But Boris forced it on me. You know he's a sonuvabitch as well as I do.'

'First of all,' Feyd al-Saoud said evenly, 'if you insist on calling him Boris, there can be no further discussion. You're doomed to a blood feud.' He spread his hands. 'Perhaps it's my failing, Mr. Hull, so I would ask you to explain to me why you'd want to further complicate an assignment that's already taxing all our security skills.'

The two agents were inspecting the Oskjuhlid Hotel's HVAC system in which they'd installed both heat-sensitive infrared and motion detectors. This foray was quite apart from the daily inspection of the summit's forum HVAC the three agents undertook as a team.

In a little over eight hours the first contingent of the negotiating parties would arrive. Twelve hours after that, the leaders would present themselves and the summit would begin. There was absolutely no margin for error for any of them, including Boris Illyich Karpov.

'You mean you *don't* think he's a sonuvabitch?' Hull said.

Feyd al-Saoud checked a branching against the schematic he seemed to carry with him at all times. 'Frankly, I've had other things on my mind.' Satisfied that the junction was secure, Feyd al-Saoud moved on.

'Okay, let's cut to the chase.'

Feyd al-Saoud turned to him. 'I beg your pardon?'

'What I was thinking was that you and I make a good team. We get along well. When it comes to security, we're on the same page.'

'What you mean is, I follow your orders well.'

Hull looked hurt. 'Did I say that?'

'Mr. Hull, you didn't have to. You, like most Americans, are quite transparent. If you're not in complete control, you tend to either get angry or sulk.'

Hull felt himself flooding with resentment. 'We're not children!' he cried.

'On the contrary,' Feyd al-Saoud said equably, 'there are times when you remind me of my six-year-old son.'

Hull wanted to pull his Glock 31 .357 mm and shove its muzzle in the Arab's face. Where did he get off talking to a representative of the U.S. Government like that? It was like spitting on the flag, for Christ's sake! But what good would a show of force do him now? No, much as he hated to admit it, he needed to go another way.

'So what d'you say?' he said as equably as he could.

Feyd al-Saoud appeared unmoved. 'In all honesty, I'd prefer to see you and Mr. Karpov work out your differences together.'

Hull shook his head. 'Ain't gonna happen, my friend, you know that as well as I do.'

Unfortunately, Feyd al-Saoud did know that. Both Hull and Karpov were entrenched in their mutual enmity. The best that could be hoped for now was that they'd confine hostilities to taking the occasional potshot at each other without an escalation into all-out war.

'I think I could best serve you both by maintaining a neutral position,' he said now. 'If I don't, who's going to keep the two of you from rending each other limb from limb?'

After purchasing everything Bourne needed, Annaka left the men's clothes shop. As she headed toward the theatrical district, she saw the reflection of movement behind her in the shop window. She didn't hesitate or even break stride but slowed her pace enough so that as she strolled she confirmed that she was being followed. As casually as she could, she crossed the street, paused in front of a shop window. In it she recognized the image of Kevin McColl as he crossed the street behind her, ostensibly heading toward a café on the corner of the block. She knew that she had to lose him before she reached the area of theatrical makeup shops.

Making sure he couldn't see, she pulled out her cell phone, dialed Bourne's number.

'Jason,' she said softly, 'McColl's picked me up.'

'Where are you now?' he said.

'The beginning of Váci utca.'

'I'm not far away.'

'I thought you weren't going to leave the hotel. What've you been doing?'

'I've discovered a lead,' he said.

'Really?' Her heart beat fast. Had he found out about Stepan? 'What is it?'

'First, we've got to deal with McColl. I want you to go to 75 Hattyu utca. Wait for me at the front desk.' He continued, giving her details of what she was to do.

She listened intently, then said, 'Jason, are you sure you're up to this?'

'Just do what I tell you,' he said sternly, 'and everything will be fine.'

She disconnected and called a taxi. When it came, she got in and gave the driver the address Bourne had made her repeat back to him. As they drove off, she looked around but didn't see McColl, though she was certain he'd been following her. A moment later a battered dark-green Opel threaded its way through traffic, wedging itself behind her taxi. Annaka, peering into the driver's off-side mirror, recognized the hulking figure behind the wheel of the Opel, and her lips curled in a secret smile. Kevin McColl had taken the bait; now if only Bourne's plan would work.

Stepan Spalko, newly returned to the Humanistas, Ltd. headquarters in Budapest, was monitoring the international clandestine service cipher traffic for news on the summit when his cell phone rang.

'What is it?' he said tersely.

'I'm on my way to meet Bourne at 75 Hattyu utca,' Annaka said.

Spalko turned and walked away from where his technicians were sitting at their deciphering workstations. 'He's sending you to the Eurocenter Bio-I Clinic,' he said. 'He knows about Peter Sido.'

'He said he had an exciting new lead, but he wouldn't tell me what it was.'

'The man's relentless,' Spalko said. 'I'll take care of Sido, but you can't let him anywhere near his office.'

'I understand that,' Annaka said. 'In any event, Bourne's attention is initially going to be directed toward the American CIA agent who's been shadowing him.'

'I don't want Bourne killed, Annaka. He's far too valuable to me alive – at least for the moment.' Spalko's mind was sorting through possibilities, discarding them one by one until he arrived at his desired conclusion. 'Leave everything else to me.'

Annaka, in the speeding taxi, nodded. 'You can count on me, Stepan.'

'I know that.'

Annaka stared out the window at passing Budapest. 'I never thanked you for killing my father.'

'It was a long time coming.'

'Khan thinks I'm angry because I didn't get to do it myself.'

'Is he right?'

There were tears in Annaka's eyes and with some annoyance she wiped them away. 'He was my father, Stepan. Whatever he did . . . still, he was my father. He raised me.'

'Poorly, Annaka. He never really knew how to be a father to you.'

She thought about the lies she'd told Bourne without an iota of compunction, the idealized childhood she'd wished for herself. Her father had never read to her at night or changed her; he'd never once come to one of her graduations – it seemed he was always far away; and as for birthdays, he'd never remembered. Another tear, escaping her vigilance, crawled down her cheek and, at the corner of her mouth, she tasted its salt as if it were the bitterness of memory.

She tossed her head. 'A child can never fully condemn her father, it seems.'

'I did mine.'

'That was different,' she said. 'And, anyway, I know how you felt about my mother.'

'I loved her, yes.' In his mind Spalko conjured up an image of Sasa Vadas: her large, luminous eyes, her creamy skin, the full bow of her mouth when that slow smile brought you close to her heart. 'She was completely unique, a special creature, a princess as her name suggested.'

'She was as much your family as she was mine,' Annaka said. 'She saw right through you, Stepan. In her heart she felt the tragedies you'd suffered without you having to tell her a thing.'

'I waited a long time to take my revenge on your father, Annaka, but I never would've done it if I didn't know it was what you wanted, too.'

Annaka laughed, now fully back to herself. The brief emotional wallow she'd fallen into disgusted her. 'You don't expect me to believe that, do you, Stepan?'

'Now, Annaka – '

'Remember who you're trying to con. I know you, you killed him when it served your purpose. And you were right, he would've told Bourne everything and Bourne would've wasted no time coming after you with everything he had. That I'd wanted my father dead, too, was mere coincidence.'

'Now you're underestimating your importance to me.'

'That may or may not be true, Stepan, but it doesn't matter to me. I wouldn't know how to form an emotional attachment even if I wanted to try.'

Martin Lindros presented his official papers to Randy Driver, Director of the Tactical Non-Lethal Weapons Directorate in person. Driver, who was staring at Lindros as if he had a chance of intimidating him, took the papers without comment and dropped them on his desk.

He was standing as a marine would stand, straight-spined, gut in, muscles taut, as if he were about to go into battle. His close-set blue eyes seemed almost crossed, such was his concentration. A slight antiseptic scent lingered in the white-metal office, as if he'd seen fit to fumigate the place in anticipation of Lindros' arrival.

'I see you've been a busy little beaver since last we met,' he said, looking at no one in particular. Apparently, he'd realized that he wouldn't be able to intimidate Lindros simply with his stare. He was moving on to verbal intimidation.

'I'm always busy,' Lindros said. 'You just forced me into make-work.'

'Happy am I.' Driver's face fairly creaked with the tightness of his smile.

Lindros shifted from one foot to the other. 'Why do you see me as the enemy?'

'Possibly because you *are* the enemy.' Driver finally sat down behind his smoked-glass and stainless-steel desk. 'What else would you call someone who comes in here wanting to dig up my backyard?'

'I'm only investigating – '

'Don't give that bullshit, Lindros!' Driver had leaped up, his face livid. 'I can smell a witch-hunt at a hundred paces! You're the Old Man's bloodhound. You can't fool me. This isn't about Alex Conklin's murder.'

'And why would you think that?'

'Because this investigation is about *me*!'

Now Lindros was really interested. Aware that Driver had given him the advantage, he seized it with a knowing smile. 'Now why would we want to investigate you, Randy?' He'd chosen his words with care, using 'we' to tell Driver that he was operating with the full force of the DCI behind him and his first name to unnerve him.

'You already know why, damnit!' Driver stormed, falling into the trap Lindros had set for him. 'You must've known the first time you ambled in here. I could see it on your face when you asked to talk to Felix Schiffer.'

'I wanted to give you the chance to come clean before I went to the DCI.' Lindros was having fun following the path Driver was laying out, even though he had no idea where it was leading. On the other hand, he had to be careful. One false move on his part, one mistake and Driver would realize his ignorance and, likely as not, clam up, waiting for advice from his lawyer. 'It's not too late for you to do so now.'

Driver stared at him for a moment, before pressing the heel of his hand to his damp forehead. He slumped a little before falling back into his mesh chair.

'Christ Almighty, what a mess,' he mumbled. As if having received a devastating body blow, all the wind had gone out of him. He looked around at the Rothko prints on the wall, as if they might be doorways through which he could flee. At last, finally resigned to his fate, he let his gaze return to the man standing patiently in front of him.

He gestured. 'Sit down, Deputy Director.' His voice was sad. When Lindros had taken his seat, he said, 'It started with Alex Conklin. Well, it always started with Alex, didn't it?' He sighed, as if all at once overcome by nostalgia. 'Almost two years ago Alex came to me with a proposition. He'd befriended a scientist at DARPA; the connection was coincidental, though, to tell you the truth, Alex networked with so many people I doubt if anything in his life was coincidence. I imagine you've worked out that the scientist in question was Felix Schiffer.'

He paused for a moment. 'I'm dying for a cigar. D'you mind?'

'Knock yourself out,' Lindros said. So that explained the smell: air freshener. The building, like all government facilities, was supposed to be smoke-free.

'Care to join me?' Driver asked. 'They were a present from Alex.'

When Lindros declined, Driver pulled out a drawer, extracted a cigar from a humidor, went through the complex ritual of lighting up. Lindros understood; he was calming his nerves. He sniffed as the first puff of blue smoke wafted through the room. It was a Cuban.

'Alex came to see me,' Driver continued. 'No, that's not quite accurate – he took me out to dinner. He told me he'd met this guy who worked at DARPA. Felix Schiffer. He hated the military types there and wanted out. Would I help his friend?'

'And you agreed,' Lindros said, 'just like that?'

'Of course I did. General Baker, the head of DARPA, had poached one of our guys last year.' Driver took a puff on his cigar. 'Payback's a bitch. I leaped at the chance to stick it to that uptight asshole Baker.'

Lindros stirred. 'When Conklin came to you, did he tell you what Schiffer was working on at DARPA?'

'Sure. Schiffer's field was pushing around airborne particulates. He was working on methods to clear indoor areas infected with biologicals.'

Lindros sat up. 'Like anthrax?'

Driver nodded. 'That's right.'

'How far along was he?'

'At DARPA?' Driver shrugged. 'I wouldn't know.'

'But surely you'd gotten updates on his work after he came to work for you.'

Driver glared at him, then pressed some keys on his computer terminal. He swivelled the screen around so they could see.

Lindros leaned forward. 'Looks like gibberish to me, but then I'm no scientist.'

Driver stared at the end of his cigar as if now, at the moment of truth, he couldn't bring himself to look at Lindros. 'It *is* gibberish, more or less.'

Lindros froze. 'What the hell d'you mean?'

Driver was still staring with fascination at the end of his cigar. 'This couldn't be what Schiffer had been working on because it makes no sense.'

Lindros shook his head. 'I don't understand.'

Driver sighed. 'It's possible that Schiffer isn't much of a particulate expert.'

Lindros, who had begun feeling a ball of icy terror form in his gut, said, 'There's another possibility, isn't there?'

'Well, yes, now that you mention it.' Driver ran his tongue around his lips. 'It's possible that Schiffer was working on something else entirely that he wanted neither DARPA nor us to know about.'

Lindros looked perplexed. 'Why haven't you asked Dr. Schiffer about this?'

'I'd very much like to,' Driver said. 'The trouble is I don't know where Felix Schiffer is.'

'If you don't,' Lindros said angrily, 'who the hell does?'

'Alex was the only one who knew.'

'Jesus H. Christ, Alex Conklin's dead!' Lindros rose and, leaning forward, swiped the cigar out of Driver's mouth. 'Randy, how long has Dr. Schiffer been missing?'

Driver closed his eyes. 'Six weeks.'

Now Lindros understood. This was why Driver had been so hostile when he'd first come to him; he was terrified that the Agency suspected his egregious breach of security. He said now, 'How on earth did you allow this to happen?'

Driver's blue gaze rested on him for a moment. 'It was Alex. I trusted him. Why wouldn't I? I knew him for years – he was an Agency legend, for Christ's sake. And then what does he up and do? He disappears Schiffer.'

Driver stared at the cigar on the floor as if it had become a malignant object. 'He used me, Lindros, played me like a fiddle. He didn't want Schiffer in my directorate, he didn't want us, the Agency, to have him. He wanted to get him away from DARPA so he could disappear him.'

'Why?' Lindros said. 'Why would he do that?'

'I don't know. I wish to God I did.'

The pain in Driver's voice was palpable, and for the first time since they'd met, Lindros felt sorry for him. Everything he'd ever heard about Alexander Conklin had turned out to be true. He was the master manipulator, the keeper of all the dark secrets, the agent who trusted no one – no one save Jason Bourne, his protégé. Fleetingly, he wondered what this turn of events was going to do to the DCI. He and Conklin had been close friends for decades; they'd grown up together in the Agency – it was their life. They'd relied on each other, trusted each other, and now this bitterest blow. Conklin had breached just about every major Agency protocol to get what he wanted: Dr. Felix Schiffer. He'd screwed not only Randy Driver but the Agency itself. How was he ever going to protect the Old Man from this news? Lindros wondered. But, even as he thought this, he knew that he had a more pressing problem to deal with.

'Obviously, Conklin knew what Schiffer was really working on and wanted it,' Lindros said. 'But what the hell was it?'

Driver looked at him helplessly.

Stepan Spalko was standing in the center of Kapisztrán tér, within shouting distance of his waiting limo. Above him rose the Mary Magdalene Tower, all that was left of the thirteenth-century Franciscan church, whose nave and chancel were destroyed by Nazi bombs during World War II. As he waited, he felt a gust of chill wind raise the hem of his black coat, insinuating itself against his skin.

Spalko glanced at his watch. Sido was late. Long ago, he'd trained himself not to worry, but such was the significance of this meeting that he couldn't help but experience a twinge of anxiety. At the top of the tower, the twenty-four-piece glockenspiel sounded fifteen minutes after the hour. Sido was *very* late.

Spalko, watching the crowds ebb and flow, was just about to break protocol and call Sido on the cell phone he'd given him when he saw the scientist hurrying toward him from the opposite side of the tower. He was carrying something that looked like a jeweler's sample case.

'You're late,' Spalko said shortly.

'I know, but it couldn't be helped.' Dr. Sido wiped his forehead with the sleeve of his overcoat. 'I had trouble getting the item out of storage. There were staff inside and I had to wait until the cold room was empty so as not to arouse – '

'Not here, Doctor!'

Spalko, who wanted to hit him for talking about their business in public, took Sido firmly by the elbow and all but frog-marched him deep into the desolate shadows thrown by the rather forbidding baroque stone tower.

'You've forgotten to watch your tongue around outsiders, Peter,' Spalko said. 'We're part of an elite group, you and I. I've told you that.'

'I know,' Dr. Sido said nervously, 'but I find it difficult to – '

'You don't find it difficult to take my money, do you?'

Sido's eyes slipped away. 'Here's the product,' he said. 'It's everything you asked for and more.' He held out the case. 'But let's get this over and done with quickly. I have to get back to the lab. I was in the middle of a crucial chemical calculation when you called.'

Spalko pushed Sido's hand away. 'You hold onto that, Peter, at least for a little while longer.'

Sido's spectacles flashed. 'But you said you needed it now – immediately. As I told you, once put in the portable case, the material is alive for only forty-eight hours.'

'I haven't forgotten.'

'Stepan, I'm at a loss. I took a great risk in bringing it out of the clinic during working hours. Now I must get back or – '

Spalko smiled and, at the same time, tightened his grip on Sido's elbow. 'You're not going back, Peter.'

'What?'

'I apologize for not mentioning it before, but, well, for the amount of money I'm paying you, I want more than the product. I want you.'

Dr. Sido shook his head. 'But that's quite impossible. You know that!'

'Nothing is impossible, Peter, you know that.'

'Well, this is,' Dr. Sido said adamantly.

With a charming smile, Spalko produced a snapshot from inside his overcoat. 'What do they say about a picture's worth?' he said, handing it over.

Dr. Sido stared at it and swallowed convulsively. 'Where did you get this photo of my daughter?'

Spalko's smile stayed firmly in place. 'One of my people took it, Peter. Look at the date.'

'It was taken yesterday.' A sudden spasm overtook him and he tore the photo into pieces. 'One can do anything with a photographic image these days,' he said stonily.

'How true,' Spalko said. 'But I assure you this one wasn't doctored.'

'Liar! I'm leaving!' Dr. Sido said. 'Let go of me.'

Spalko did as the doctor asked, but as Sido started to walk away, he said, 'Wouldn't you like to talk with Roza, Peter?' He held out a cell phone. 'I mean right now?'

Dr. Sido halted in midstep. Then he turned to face Spalko. His face was dark with anger and barely suppressed fear. 'You said you were Felix's friend; I thought you were *my* friend.'

Spalko continued to hold out the phone. 'Roza would like to speak to you. If you walk away now . . .' He shrugged. His silence was its own threat.

Slowly, heavily, Dr. Sido came back. He took the cell phone in his free hand, put it up to his ear. He found that his heart was beating so loudly he could scarcely think. 'Roza?'

'Daddy? Daddy! Where am I? What's happening?'

The panic in his daughter's voice sent a lance of terror through Sido. He could never remember being so afraid.

'Darling, what's going on?'

'Men came to my room, they took me, I don't know where, they put a hood over my head, they – '

'That's enough,' Spalko said, taking the phone from Dr. Sido's nerveless fingers. He cut the connection, put the phone away.

'What have you done to her?' Dr. Sido's voice shook with the force of the emotions running through him.

'Nothing yet,' Spalko said easily. 'And nothing will happen to her, Peter, as long as you obey me.'

Dr. Sido swallowed as Spalko resumed possession of him. 'Where . . . where are we going?'

'We're taking a trip,' Spalko said, guiding Dr. Sido toward the waiting limo. 'Just think of it as a vacation, Peter. A well-deserved vacation.'

# 24

The Eurocenter Bio-I Clinic was housed in a modern stone building the color of lead. Bourne entered with the quick authoritative strides of someone who knew where he was going and why.

The interior of the clinic spoke of money, a great deal of it. The lobby was marble-clad. Classical-looking columns were interspersed with bronze statuary. Along the walls were arched niches in which resided the busts of the historical demigods of biology, chemistry, microbiology and epidemiology. The ugly metal detector was particularly offensive in this tranquil and monied setting. Beyond the skeletal structure was a high bank behind which sat three harried-looking attendants.

Bourne passed through the metal detector without incident, his ceramic gun going entirely unnoticed. At the front desk, he was all business.

'Alexander Conklin to see Dr. Peter Sido,' he said so crisply that it was akin to being an order.

'ID, please, Mr. Conklin,' said one of the three female attendants, unconsciously responding and snapping to.

Bourne handed over his false passport, which the attendant glanced at, looking at Bourne's face only long enough to make visual confirmation before returning it to Bourne. She handed over a white plastic tag. 'Please wear this at all times, Mr. Conklin.' Such was Bourne's tone and demeanor that she failed to ask if Sido was expecting him, taking it for granted that 'Mr. Conklin' had an interview with Dr. Sido. She provided the new visitor with directions and Bourne set off.

'*They require special ID tags to get into his section, white for visitors, green for resident doctors, blue for assistants and support staff,*' Eszti Sido had told him, so his immediate task was to find a likely member of the staff.

On his way to the Epidemiological Wing, he passed four men, none of whom were the right somatotype. He needed someone who was more or less his size. Along the way he tried every door that wasn't marked as an office or lab, looking for storage rooms and the like, places that would be infrequently visited by the medical staff. He was unconcerned with members of the cleaning crew, since it was likely that they wouldn't be in until the evening.

At length he saw coming toward him a man in a white lab coat of more or less his height and weight. He wore a green ID tag that identified him as Dr. Lenz Morintz.

'Excuse me, Dr. Morintz,' Bourne said with a deprecating smile, 'I wonder if you could direct me to the Microbiological Wing. I seem to have lost my way.'

'Indeed you have,' Dr. Morintz said. 'You're headed straight for the Epidemiological Wing.'

'Oh, dear,' Bourne said, 'I really have got myself turned around.'

'Not to worry,' Dr. Morintz said. 'Here's all you have to do.'

As he turned to point Bourne in the right direction, Bourne chopped down with the edge of his hand and the bacteriologist collapsed. Bourne caught him before he could hit the floor. Standing him more or less upright, he half-carried, half-dragged the doctor back to the nearest storage room, ignoring the searing pain from his cracked ribs.

Inside, Bourne turned on the light, took off his jacket, and stuffed it into a corner. Then he stripped Dr. Morintz of his lab coat and ID. Using some spare surgical tape, he bound the doctor's hands behind his back, taped his ankles tightly, and wrapped a final piece across his mouth. Then he dragged the body into a corner, stashing it behind a couple of large cartons. He returned to the door, turned off the light and went out into the corridor.

For a time after she arrived at the Eurocenter Bio-I Clinic, Annaka sat in the taxi while the meter ran. Stepan had made it abundantly clear that they were now entering the mission's final phase. Every decision they made, every move they took, was of critical importance. Any mistake now could lead to disaster. Bourne or Khan. She didn't know which was the greater wild card, which one presented the greatest danger. Of the two, Bourne was the more stable, but Khan was without compunction. His similarity to her was an irony she couldn't afford to ignore.

And yet it had occurred to her most recently that there were more differences that she'd once imagined. For a start, he hadn't been able to bring himself to kill Jason Bourne, despite his stated desire to do so. And then, just as startlingly, there was his lapse in her Skoda when he'd leaned down to kiss the nape of her neck. From the moment she'd walked out on him she'd wondered whether what he'd felt for her had been genuine. Now she knew. Khan could feel; he could, if given enough incentive, forge emotional attachments. Frankly, she'd never have believed it of him, not with his background.

'Miss?' the taxi driver's query broke into her thoughts. 'Are you meeting someone here or is there somewhere else you want me to take you?'

Annaka leaned forward, pressing a wad of bills into his hand. 'This will be fine here.'

Still she didn't move, but she looked around, wondering where Kevin McColl was. It was easy for Stepan sitting safe in his office at Humanistas to tell her not to worry about the CIA agent, but she was in the field with a capable and dangerous assassin and the severely wounded man he was determined to kill. When the bullets began to fly, she was the one who was going to be in the line of fire.

She got out at last, her agitation causing her to look up and down the block for the battered green Opel before she caught herself and with a grunt of irritation went through the front door of the clinic.

Inside, the setup was just as Bourne had described it to her. She wondered where he'd gotten his information in such short order. She had to hand it to him; he had a remarkable ability for ferreting out information.

Passing through the metal detector, she was stopped on the other side, was asked to open her purse so the officer could peer through its contents. Following Bourne's instructions to the letter, she approached the high marble bank, smiled at one of the three attendants who looked up long enough to acknowledge her presence.

'My name is Annaka Vadas,' she said. 'I'm waiting for a friend.'

The attendant nodded, went back to her work. The two others were either on the phone or inputting data into a computer workstation. Another phone rang and the woman who'd smiled at Annaka, picked up the receiver, spoke into it for a moment, then, astonishingly, beckoned her over.

When Annaka approached the bank, the attendant said, 'Miss Vadas. Dr. Morintz is expecting you.' She glanced briefly at Annaka's driver's license, then handed her a white plastic ID tag. 'Please wear that at all times, Miss Vadas. The doctor is waiting for you in his laboratory.'

She pointed the way and Annaka, baffled, followed her direction down a corridor. At the first T-junction, she turned left and ran right into a man in a white lab coat.

'Oh, excuse me! What . . . ?' She'd looked up to see Jason Bourne's face. On his lab coat was a green plastic ID tag with the name Dr. Lenz Morintz printed on it, and she started to laugh. 'Oh, I see, a pleasure to meet you, Dr. Morintz.' She squinted. 'Even though you don't look all that much like your photo.'

'You know how those cheap cameras are,' Bourne said, taking her by the elbow and leading her back to the corner she'd just turned. 'They never do you justice.' Peering around the corner, he said, 'Here comes the CIA, right on schedule.'

Annaka saw Kevin McColl showing his credentials to one of the attendants. 'How'd he get his gun past the metal detector?' she asked.

'He didn't,' Bourne said. 'Why d'you think I directed you here?'

Despite herself, she looked at him with admiration. 'A trap. McColl's here without a gun.' He was clever indeed, and this realization caused her a spark of concern. She hoped Stepan knew what he was doing.

'Look, I discovered that Schiffer's former partner, Peter Sido, works here. If anyone knows where Schiffer is, it's Sido. We need to speak with him, but first we've got to take care of McColl once and for all. Are you ready?'

Annaka took a second look at McColl and, shuddering, nodded in assent.

Khan had used a taxi to tail the battered green Opel; he hadn't wanted to use the rental Skoda in case it had been made. He waited for Kevin McColl to pull into a parking space, then he had the taxi go past, and when the CIA agent got out of his Opel, he paid the driver and started after the other on foot.

Last evening, following McColl from Annaka's, he had called Ethan Hearn and read him off the license plate of the green Opel. Within the hour Hearn had gotten him the name and number of the rental car location McColl had used. Posing as an Interpol agent, he'd obtained from the suitably cowed attendant, McColl's name and address in the States. He hadn't left a local address, but as it had turned out, with typical American arrogance, he'd used his real name. It had been a simple matter, then, for Khan to call another number, where a contact of his in Berlin had run McColl's name through his data banks and come up with CIA.

Up ahead, McColl turned the corner onto Hattyu utca, entering a modern gray stone building at 75 that had more than a passing resemblance to a medieval fortress. It was fortunate that Khan waited a moment, as was his habit, because just then McColl ducked out. Khan watched him, curious, as he went to a trash bin. Looking around to make sure no one was paying him any attention, he drew out his gun, placed it quickly and carefully into the bin.

Khan waited until McColl had returned inside, then continued on, passing through the steel and glass door into the lobby. There, he observed McColl throwing around his Agency credentials. Observing the metal detector, Khan realized why McColl had gotten rid of his weapon. Was it coincidence or had Bourne set a trap for him? It's what Khan himself would've done.

As McColl was given an ID tag and went down the corridor, Khan passed through the metal detector, showed the Interpol ID he'd picked up in Paris. This, of course, alarmed the attendant, especially after seeing the Agency man, and she wondered aloud whether she should either alert the clinic's security or call the police, but Khan calmly assured her that they were on the same case and were only here for interview purposes. Any interruption in that process, he warned her sternly, could only lead to unforseen complications, which he knew she didn't want. Still slightly nervous, she nodded and waved him through.

Kevin McColl saw Annaka Vadas up ahead and knew that Bourne had to be close by. He was certain she hadn't made him, but in any event he fingered the small plastic square attached to the wristband of his watch. Inside was a length of nylon line retracted onto a tiny reel hidden within the plastic housing. He'd have preferred to complete the Bourne sanction with a gun because it was quick and clean. The human body, no matter how powerful, couldn't fight off a bullet to the heart or lungs or brain. Other methods using surprise and brute force, which the presence of the metal detector was forcing him into using, took longer and were more often than not messy. He understood the increased risk, as well as the possibility that he would have to kill Annaka Vadas as well. That thought alone caused him a pang of regret. She was a handsome, sexy woman; it went against the grain to kill such beauty.

He saw her now, headed he was quite sure toward a rendezvous with Jason Bourne; there was no other reason he could imagine for her to be here. He hung back, tapping the plastic square lying against the inside of his wrist as he waited for his opportunity.

From his position inside a supply room, Bourne saw Annaka pass by. She knew precisely where he was, but to her credit she didn't even turn her head a fraction as she passed his vantage point. His keen ears detected McColl's tread before he even came into view. Everyone had a way of walking, a certain stride that unless they deliberately altered it became unmistakable. McColl's was heavy and solid, ominous, without doubt the gait of a professional stalker.

The primary issue here, Bourne knew, was timing. If he moved too quickly, McColl would see him and react, negating the element of surprise. If he waited too long, he'd be forced to take a couple of steps to catch up to him and would risk McColl hearing him. But Bourne had taken the measure of McColl's strides and so was able to accurately anticipate when the CIA assassin would be in just the right spot. He pushed from his mind the aches and pains in his body, most especially his cracked ribs. He had no idea what a handicap they would place on him, but he had to be confident in the triple binding Dr. Ambrus had used to protect them.

He could see Kevin McColl now, large and dangerous. Just as the agent passed the partly open door to the supply room, Bourne leaped out and delivered a massive two-handed blow to McColl's right kidney. The agent's body canted over toward Bourne, who grabbed him and began to drag him into the supply room.

But McColl whirled and, with a grimace of pain, exploded a massive fist into Bourne's chest. Pain pinwheeled and, as Bourne staggered back, McColl drew out the nylon line, lunging at Bourne's neck. Bourne used the edge of his hand to land two fierce blows that must have caused McColl a great deal of pain. Still, he came on with reddened eyes and a grim determination. He looped the nylon line around Bourne's neck, pulled so tight that for the first instant Bourne was lifted off his feet.

Bourne fought for breath, which only allowed McColl to tighten the line further. Then Bourne realized his mistake. He ceased to worry about breathing, concentrating on freeing himself. His knee came up, making sharp contact with McColl's genitals. All the breath went out of McColl, and for an instant his grip loosened enough for Bourne to get two fingers between the nylon line and the flesh of his throat.

McColl, though, was a bull of a man, and he recovered more quickly than Bourne could've imagined. With a grunt of rage, he drew all his energy into his arms, jerking the nylon line more tightly than ever. But Bourne had managed to gain the advantage he needed, and his two fingers curled, twisting as the line tightened, and it snapped just as a powerful fish can exert enough torque to break the line on which it's caught.

Bourne used the hand that had been at his neck to strike out and up, catching McColl under the jaw. McColl's head snapped back against the doorjamb, but as Bourne closed with him, he used his elbows, spinning Bourne into the supply room. McColl came after him, snatched up a box cutter, swung with it, slicing through the lab coat. Another swipe and, though Bourne leaped back, the blade cut into his shirt so that it hung open, revealing his bound ribs.

A grin of triumph lit up McColl's face. He knew a vulnerability when he saw it, and he went after it. Switching the box cutter to his left hand, he feinted with it, then lowered a massive blow toward Bourne's rib cage. Bourne wasn't fooled and was able to block the blow with his forearm.

Now McColl saw his opening and swung in with the box cutter, directly toward Bourne's exposed neck.

Having heard the first sounds of engagement, Annaka had turned, but she'd immediately spotted two doctors coming toward the junction in the corridor beyond which Bourne and McColl were locked together. Neatly interposing herself between them and the doctors, she asked the doctors a barrage of questions, all the while moving them along until they were past the junction.

Extricating herself as quickly as she could, she hurried back. By that time she saw that Bourne was in trouble. Remembering Stepan's admonishment to keep Bourne alive, she rushed back down the corridor. By the time she arrived, the two combatants were already inside the supply room. She swung in through the open door just in time to see McColl's vicious attack at Bourne's neck.

She hurled herself at him, knocking him off stride just enough so that the box cutter blade, flashing in the light, flew by Bourne's neck, sparking off the metal corner of a shelf stanchion. McColl, aware of her now in the periphery of his vision, whirled, his left elbow high and cocked, and he smashed it back into her throat.

Annaka gagged, reflexively grabbed at her neck as she began to sink down onto her knees. McColl came at her with the box cutter, slashing at her coat. Bourne took the length of nylon still gripped in one hand and lashed it around McColl's neck from behind.

McColl arched back, but instead of grasping for his throat, he jammed an elbow into Bourne's cracked ribs. Bourne saw stars, but still he held on, inching McColl backward, away from Annaka, hearing his heels dragging on the floor tiles as McColl flailed at his ribs with ever-increasing desperation.

The blood pooled in McColl's head, the cords stood out on the sides of his neck like taut ropes, and soon thereafter, his eyes began to bulge in their sockets. Blood vessels burst in his nose and cheeks and his lips pulled back from his pallid gums. His swollen tongue swirled around his gasping mouth, and still he had it in him to deliver one last blow to Bourne's side. Bourne winced, his grip faltered slightly, and McColl began to regain his balance.

That's when Annaka recklessly kicked him in the stomach. McColl grabbed her raised knee and, twisting violently, brought her back against him. His left arm whipped around her neck, the heel of his right hand positioned itself against the side of her head. He was about to break her neck.

Khan, observing all this from the vantage point of the small darkened office across and slightly down the corridor, watched Bourne, at great risk to himself, let go of the nylon cord he'd so expertly wrapped around McColl's neck. He slammed the assassin's head against a shelf, then drove a thumb into his eye.

McColl, about to scream, found Bourne's forearm between his jaws, and so the sound rattled in his lungs, dying inside him. He kicked out and flailed, refusing to die or even to go down. Bourne withdrew his ceramic gun, smashed the butt into the soft spot over McColl's left ear. Now he was on his knees, his head shaking, his hands moving to press themselves tightly to his ruined eye. But it was only a ruse. He used his hands to trip Annaka, to bring her down to his level. His murderous hands grasped her, and Bourne, without any other recourse, pressed the muzzle of the gun against McColl's flesh and pulled the trigger.

There was very little noise, but the hole in McColl's neck was impressive. Even dead, McColl wouldn't let go of Annaka, and Bourne, putting away the gun, was obliged to pry his fingers one by one off her flesh.

Bourne reached down, pulled her up, but Khan could see his grimace, saw one hand press against his side. Those ribs. Were they bruised, broken, or something in between? he wondered.

Khan moved back into the shadows of the empty office. He'd caused that injury. He could remember in vivid detail the power he'd put behind the blow, the feel of his hand as it made contact, the almost electric jarring that had passed through him, as if from Bourne. But, curiously, the feeling of hot satisfaction never materialized. Instead, he was forced to admire the strength and tenacity of the man to hold on, to continue his titanic struggle with McColl, despite the beating he was taking in his most vulnerable spot.

Why was he even thinking these thoughts? he asked himself angrily. Bourne had done nothing but reject him. In the face of mounting evidence, he adamantly refused to believe that Khan was his son. What did that say about him? For whatever reason, he'd chosen to believe that his son was dead. Didn't that mean that he'd never wanted him in the first place?

'The support staff arrived just a few hours ago,' Jamie Hull said to the DCI over their secure video linkup. 'We've familiarized them with everything. All that's lacking is the principals.'

'The president's in the air even as we speak,' the DCI said as he waved Martin Lindros to a seat. 'In approximately five hours, twenty minutes from now, the President of the United States will be on Icelandic soil. I hope to Christ you're ready for him.'

'Absolutely I am, sir. We all are.'

'Excellent.' But his frown deepened as he glanced down at the notes on his desktop. 'Give me an update on how you're handling Comrade Karpov?'

'Not to worry,' Hull said. 'I have the Boris situation under control.'

'That's a relief. Relations between the president and his Russian counterpart are strained as it is. You've no idea what blood, sweat and tears it took to persuade Aleksandr Yevtushenko to come to the table. Can you imagine the blowup if he hears you and his top security man are ready to slit each other's throats?'

'It'll never happen, sir.'

'Damned straight,' the DCI growled. 'Keep me informed 24-7.'

'Will do, sir,' Hull said, signing off.

The DCI swiveled around, ran his hand through his shock of white hair. 'We're in the final stretch, Martin. Does it pain you as much as it pains me to be stuck here behind a desk while Hull is taking care of business in the field?'

'It does, indeed, sir.' Lindros, keeping his secret close to the vest for all this time, almost lost his nerve then, but duty won out over compassion. He didn't want to wound the Old Man, no matter how badly he'd been treated recently.

He cleared his throat. 'Sir, I've just come from seeing Randy Driver.'

'And?'

Lindros took a deep breath and told the Old Man what Driver had confessed, that Conklin had brought Dr. Felix Schiffer over to the Agency from DARPA for his own dark and unknown reasons, that he had deliberately 'disappeared' Schiffer and that now that Conklin was dead no one knew where Schiffer was.

The Old Man's fist slammed down on his desk. 'Sweet Christ, to have one of our directorate scientists gone missing with the summit about to start is a catastrophe of the first rank. If the bitch-woman should get wind of this, it'll be my ass in a sling, no ifs, ands or buts.'

For a moment nothing stirred in the vast corner office. The photos of world leaders past and present looked back at the two men with mute rebuke.

At last the DCI stirred. 'Are you saying that Alex Conklin stole a scientist out from under DOD's nose and stashed him with us so he could whisk him away to God knows where and for what unknown purpose?'

Lindros, folding his hands in his lap, said nothing, but he knew better than to move his gaze away from the Old Man's.

'Well, that's . . . I mean to say, we don't do that in the Agency, and most especially Alexander Conklin wouldn't do that. He would be breaking every rule in the playbook.'

Lindros stirred, thinking of his research in the top-secret Four-Zero Archives. 'He did it often enough in the field, sir. You know that.'

Indeed, the DCI did, only too well. 'This is different,' he protested. 'This happened here at home. It's a personal affront to the Agency, and to me.' The Old Man shook his craggy head. 'I refuse to believe it, Martin. Goddammit, there must be another explanation!'

Lindros held firm. 'You know there isn't. I'm truly sorry to have been the one to bring you this news, sir.'

At that moment the Old Man's secretary entered the room, handed him a slip of paper, and went out. The DCI unfolded the note.

*'Your wife would like to speak with you,'* he read. *'She says it's important.'*

He crumpled the note, then looked up. 'Of course there's another explanation. Jason Bourne.'

'Sir?'

The DCI looked straight at Lindros and said bleakly, 'This is Bourne's doing, not Alex's. It's the only explanation that makes sense.'

'For the record, I think you're wrong, sir,' Lindros said, gathering himself for the uphill battle. 'With all due respect, I think you've allowed your personal friendship with Alex Conklin to cloud your judgment. After studying the Four-Zero files, I believe that no one alive was closer to Conklin than Jason Bourne, even you.'

A Cheshire cat smile spread across the DCI's face. 'Oh, you're right about that one, Martin. And it's because Bourne knew Alex so well that he was able to capitalize on Alex's involvement with this Dr. Schiffer. Believe me, Bourne smelled something and he went after it.'

'There's no proof – '

'Ah, but there is.' The DCI shifted in his chair. 'As it happens, I know where Bourne is.'

'Sir?' Lindros fairly goggled at him.

'106–108 Fo utca,' the DCI read off a slip of paper. 'That's in Budapest.' The DCI threw his deputy a hard look. 'Didn't you tell me that the gun used to murder Alex and Mo Panov was paid for out of an account in Budapest?'

Lindros' heart contracted. 'Yes, sir.'

The DCI nodded. 'That's why I gave this address to Kevin McColl.'

Lindros' face went white. 'Oh, Christ. I want to talk to McColl.'

'I feel your pain, Martin, really I do.' The DCI nodded toward the phone. 'Call him if you like, but you know McColl's record for efficiency. Chances are Bourne is already dead.'

Bourne kicked the door to the supply room closed, stripped off the bloody lab coat. He was about to drop it over the corpse of Kevin McColl when he noticed a small LED light blinking at McColl's hip. His cell phone. Squatting down, he picked it out of its plastic holster, opened it up. He saw the number and knew who was calling. Rage filled his heart.

Opening the connection, he said to the DCI, 'Keep this up and you'll be paying the undertakers overtime.'

'Bourne!' Lindros cried. 'Wait!'

But he didn't wait. Instead, he threw the cell phone so hard against the wall it split open like an oyster.

Annaka watched him carefully. 'An old enemy?'

'An old fool,' Bourne growled, retrieving his leather jacket. He grunted involuntarily as the pain struck him a hammer blow.

'It appears that McColl gave you quite a beating,' Annaka said.

Bourne slipped on his jacket with its white visitor's ID tag in order to cover his slit shirt. His mind was completely focused on finding Dr. Sido. 'And what about you? How badly did McColl hurt you?'

She refused to rub the red welt at her throat. 'Don't worry about me.'

'We won't worry about each other, then,' Bourne said as he took a bottle of cleaner from the shelf and, using a rag, wiped the blood stains off her coat as best he could. 'We've got to get to Dr. Sido as quickly as possible. Dr. Morintz is bound to be missed sooner or later.'

'Where's Sido?'

'In the Epidemiological Wing.' He gestured. 'Come on.'

He peered around the doorjamb, checking to make sure no one was around. As they emerged into the corridor, he registered that an office door across the way was partially open. He took a step toward it but heard voices approaching from that direction and he hurried them away. He needed a moment to reorient himself, then he took them through a set of swinging doors into the Epidemiological Wing.

'Sido's in 902,' he said, scanning the numbers on the doors they passed.

The wing was in actuality a square with an open space in its center. Doors to labs and offices were set at intervals along the four walls, the only exception being a barred metal exit door, locked from the outside, which was in the center of the far wall. Obviously the Epidemiological Wing was at the back of the clinic because it was clear from the markings on the small storerooms to either side that the door was used to remove hazardous medical waste.

'There's his lab,' Bourne said, hurrying ahead.

Annaka, just behind him, saw the fire alarm box on the wall ahead of her, precisely where Stepan said it would be. As she came abreast of it, she lifted the glass. Bourne was knocking on the door to Sido's lab. Receiving no answer, he opened the door. Just as he stepped into Dr. Sido's lab, Annaka pulled down the handle and the fire alarm went off.

The wing was suddenly filled with people. Three members of the clinic's security force appeared; it was obvious that these were extremely efficient people. Bourne, desperate now, looked around Sido's empty office. He noticed a mug half-filled with coffee, the computer screen lit with a screen saver. He pressed the 'Escape' key, and the upper part of the screen filled with a complex chemical equation. The lower half had the following legend: 'Product must be kept at −32 degrees Celsius as it is extremely fragile. Heat of any kind renders it instantly inert.'

Through the mounting chaos, Bourne was thinking furiously. Though Dr. Sido wasn't here, he had been here not long ago. All evidence pointed to him having left in a hurry.

At that moment Annaka rushed in and pulled at him. 'Jason, the clinic's security is asking questions, checking everyone's ID. We've got to get out of here now.' She led him to the doorway. 'If we can make it to the rear exit, we can escape that way.'

Out in the open space of the wing, chaos reigned. The alarm had triggered sprays of water. As there was a great deal of flammable material in the labs, including oxygen tanks, the staff was understandably panicking. Security, trying to get a grip on who was present, was having to deal with calming the clinic's personnel.

Bourne and Annaka were heading toward the metal exit door when Bourne saw Khan working his way through the stampeding crowd toward them. Bourne grabbed Annaka, interposed himself between her and the oncoming Khan. What was Khan's intention, he wondered. Did he mean to kill them or to intercept them? Did he expect Bourne to tell him everything he'd discovered about Felix Schiffer and the biochemical diffuser? But no, there was something different about Khan's expression, some clockwork calculation that was missing.

'Listen to me!' Khan said, trying to make himself heard above the noise. 'Bourne, you've got to listen to me!'

But Bourne, herding Annaka, had reached the metal exit door and, crashing through it, hurtled into the alley behind the clinic, where a HAZMAT truck was parked. Six men armed with machine-guns stood in front of it. Bourne, instantly recognizing it as a trap, turned and instinctively shouted at Khan, who was coming on behind him.

Annaka, swinging around, saw Khan at last and ordered two of the men to open fire. But Khan, heeding Bourne's warning, leaped aside a split-second before the hail of bullets mowed down the clinic's security detail that had come to investigate. Now all hell broke loose inside the clinic, as staff ran, screaming, through the swinging doors, down the corridor toward the front entrance.

Two of the men grabbed Bourne from behind. He whirled, engaging them.

'Find him,' he heard Annaka shout. 'Find Khan and kill him!'

'Annaka, what – '

Bourne, stunned, watched the pair that had fired race past him, leaping over the wreckage of the bullet-ridden bodies.

Bourne, pushing himself to action, smashed one man in the face, putting him down, but another took his place.

'Careful,' Annaka warned. 'He's got a gun!'

One of the men shackled Bourne's arms behind his back while a second scrabbled for the weapon. He wrestled free, chopped down hard, breaking his would-be captor's nose. Blood gushed and the man fell back, his hands cupping the center of his ruined face.

'What the hell are you doing?'

Then Annaka, armed with a machine pistol, stepped in, slammed him hard with its thick butt in his cracked ribs. All the breath went out of him and he canted over, losing his balance. His knees were like rubber and the agony that racked him was for a moment unbearable. Then they'd grabbed hold of him. One man punched him in the side of the head. Bourne sagged again in their arms.

The two men returned from their recon of the clinic wing. 'No sign of him,' they reported to Annaka.

'No matter,' she said, and pointed to the man writhing on the ground. 'Get him into the vehicle. Hurry now!'

She turned back to Bourne, saw the man with the broken nose was pressing a gun to the side of Bourne's head. His eyes blazed with fury and he seemed intent on pulling the trigger.

Annaka said calmly but firmly. 'Put the gun down. He's to be taken alive.' She stared at him, not moving a muscle. 'Spalko's orders. You know that.' At length the man put the gun up.

'All right,' she said. 'Into the truck.'

Bourne stared at her, his mind was ablaze with her betrayal.

Smirking, Annaka held out a hand and one of the men handed her a hypodermic filled with a clear liquid. With a swift and sure motion, she emptied the hypodermic into Bourne's vein, and slowly his eyes lost focus.

# 25

Hasan Arsenov had put Zina in charge of the physical aspect of the cadre, as if she were a stylist. She took her orders seriously as she always did, though not without a private snicker of cynicism. Like a planet to a sun, she was aligned with the Shaykh now. As was her way, she had mentally and emotionally removed herself from Hasan's orbit. It had begun that night in Budapest – though, in truth, the seeds must have been planted earlier – and had come to fruition under the burning sun of Crete. She clove to their time together on the Mediterranean island as if it were her own private legend, one she shared only with him. They'd been – what? – Theseus and Ariadne. The Shaykh had recounted the myth of the Minotaur's terrible life and bloody death to her. Together, she and the Shaykh had entered a real-life labyrinth and triumphed. In the fever of these newly precious memories, it never occurred to her that this was a Western myth in which she had inserted herself, that in aligning herself with Stepan Spalko, she had moved away from Islam, which had nurtured her, raised her like a second mother, had been her succor, her only solace in the dark days of the Russian occupation. It never occurred to her that to embrace one, she had to let go of the other. And even if it had, with her cynic's nature, she might have made the same choice.

Because of her knowledge and diligence the men of the cadre that arrived in twilit Keflavík Airport were clean-shaven, barbered in the European style, dressed in dark Western business suits, so bland they made themselves virtually anonymous. The women were without traditional *khidzhab*, the scarf that covered their faces. Their bare faces were made up in the European style and they were clothed in sleek Parisian fashions. They passed through Immigration without incident, using the false identities and forged French passports Spalko had provided.

Now, as Arsenov had ordered, they were careful to speak only Icelandic, even when they were alone together. At one of the rental companies' counters in the terminal, Arsenov rented one car and three vans for the cadre, which was composed of six men and four women. While Arsenov and Zina took the car into Reykjavík, the rest of the cadre drove the vans south of the city to the town of Hafnarfjördur, the oldest trading port in Iceland, where Spalko had rented a large clapboard house on a cliff overlooking the harbor. The colorful village of small, quaint clapboard houses was surrounded on the land side by lava flows, filled with mist and a sense of being lost in time. It was possible to imagine among the brightly painted fishing boats lying side by side in the harbor war-shield-bedecked Viking longships readying themselves for their next bloody campaign.

Arsenov and Zina drove through Reykjavík, familiarizing themselves with the streets they'd previously seen only on maps, getting a sense of traffic and travel patterns. The city was picturesque, built on a peninsula so that it was possible to see the white snow-encrusted mountains or the piercing blue-black North Atlantic ocean from almost any place you stood. The island itself was created from the shift of tectonic plates as the American and Eurasian landmasses pulled apart. Because of the relative youth of the island, the crust was thinner than on either of the surrounding continents, which accounted for the remarkable abundance of geothermal activity used to heat Icelandic homes. The entire city was connected to the Reykjavík Energy hot water pipeline.

In City Centre, they cruised past the modern and peculiarly unsettling Hallgrimskirkja Church, looking like a rocket ship out of science fiction. It was by far the tallest structure in what was otherwise a low-rise city. They found the health services building and drove from there to the Oskjuhlid Hotel.

'You're sure this is the route they'll take?' Zina said.

'Absolutely.' Arsenov nodded. 'It's the shortest way and they'll want to get to the hotel as quickly as possible.'

The hotel's periphery was teeming with American, Arab and Russian security.

'They've turned it into a fortress,' Zina said.

'Just as the Shaykh's photos showed us,' Arsenov replied with a small smile. 'How much personnel they have makes no difference to us.'

They parked and went from shop to shop, making their various purchases. Arsenov had been far happier inside the metal shell of their rented car. Mingling with the crowds, he was acutely aware of his own alienness. How different these slim, light-skinned, blue-eyed people were! With his black hair and eyes, his big bones and swarthy skin, he felt as graceless as a Neanderthal among Cro-Magnons. Zina, he discovered, had no such difficulties. She took to new places, new people, new ideas with a frightening zeal. He worried about her, worried about her influence on the children they would one day have.

Twenty minutes after the operation at the rear of the Eurocenter Bio-I Clinic, Khan still wondered when he'd ever felt more strongly the urge to retaliate against an enemy. Even though he'd been outmanned and outgunned, even though the rational part of his mind – usually so in control of every action he took – understood all too well the foolhardiness of launching a counterattack against the men Spalko had sent to get him and Jason Bourne, another part of him had been determined to fight back. Strangely, it was Bourne's warning that had brought out in him the irrational desire to hurl himself into the pitched battle and rend Spalko's men limb from limb. It was a feeling that came from the very core of him, and so powerful was it that it had taken all his rational willpower to pull back, to hide from the men Annaka had sent in to find him. He could have taken those two down, but of what use would it have been? Annaka would only have sent more of them in for him.

He was sitting in Grendel, a café about a mile from the clinic, which was now crawling with police and, probably, Interpol agents. He sipped at his double espresso and thought about the primal feeling in which he still felt gripped. Once again, he saw the look of concern on Jason Bourne's face when he saw Khan about to step into the trap in which he was already ensnared. As if he'd been more concerned with keeping Khan out of danger than with his own safety. But that was impossible, wasn't it?

Khan was not in the habit of replaying recent scenarios, but he found himself doing so now. As Bourne and Annaka had headed for the exit, he'd tried to warn Bourne about her, but he'd been too late. What had motivated him to do that? Certainly, he hadn't planned on it. It was a spur-of-the-moment decision. Or was it? He recalled, with a vividness he found unsettling, his feeling when he'd seen the damage he'd done to Bourne's ribs. Had it been remorse? Impossible!

It was maddening. The thought would not let him be: the moment when Bourne had made the choice between staying safe behind the deadly creature McColl had become or putting himself in harm's way in order to protect Annaka. Up until that moment, he'd been trying to reconcile the notion of David Webb, college professor, being Jason Bourne, international assassin, of being in his line of work. But no assassin he could think of would have endangered himself to protect Annaka.

Who, then, was Jason Bourne?

He shook his head, annoyed at himself. This was a question, though maddening, that he needed to put aside for the time being. At last he understood why Spalko had called him while he was in Paris. He'd been given a test and, to Spalko's way of thinking, he'd failed. Spalko now thought of Khan as an imminent threat to him, just as he thought of Bourne as a threat. For Khan, Spalko had become the enemy. All his life, Khan had only one way of dealing with enemies: He eliminated them. He was very well aware of the danger; he welcomed it as a challenge. Spalko was certain he could defeat Khan. How could Spalko know that that arrogance would only make him burn all the brighter?

Khan drained his small cup and, flipping open his cell phone, punched in a number.

'I was just about to call you but I wanted to wait until I was out of the building,' Ethan Hearn said. 'Something's up.'

Khan checked his watch. It wasn't yet five. 'What, exactly?'

'About two minutes ago I saw a HAZMAT truck approaching and I got down to the basement in time to see two men and a woman bringing a man in on a stretcher.'

'That woman will be Annaka Vadas,' Khan said.

'She's quite the stunner.'

'Listen to me, Ethan,' Khan said forcefully, 'if you run into her, be very careful. She's as dangerous as they come.'

'Too bad,' Hearn mused.

'No one saw you?' Khan wanted to get him off the subject of Annaka Vadas.

'No,' Hearn said. 'I was quite careful about that.'

'Good.' Khan thought a moment. 'Can you find out where they took this man? I mean the exact location?'

'I already know. I watched the elevator when they took him up. He's somewhere on the fourth floor. That's Spalko's personal level; it's accessed only with a magnetic key.'

'Can you get it?' Khan asked.

'Impossible. He keeps it on his person at all times.'

'I'll have to find another way,' Khan said.

'I thought magnetic keys were foolproof.'

Khan laughed shortly. 'Only a fool believes that. There's always a way into a locked room, Ethan, just as there's always a way out.'

Khan rose, threw some money on the table, and walked out of the café. Right now he was loath to stay in one place for too long. 'Speaking of which, I need a way into Humanistas.'

'There are any number – '

'I have reason to believe Spalko is expecting me.' Khan crossed the street, his eyes alert for anyone who might be watching him.

'That's a completely different story,' Hearn said. There was a pause as he considered the problem, then: 'Wait a minute, hang on. Let me look in my PDA. I might have something.'

'Okay, I'm back.' Hearn gave a little laugh. 'I *do* have something, and I think you're going to like it.'

Arsenov and Zina arrived at the house ninety minutes after the others. By that time, the cadre had changed into jeans and workshirts and had pulled the van into the large garage. While the women took charge of the bags of food Arsenov and Zina had bought, the men opened the box of hand weapons waiting for them and helped set up the spray-painters.

Arsenov took out the photos Spalko had given him and they set about spray-painting the van the proper color of an official government vehicle. While the van was drying, they drove the second van into the garage. Using a stencil, they spray-painted *Hafnarfjördur Fine Fruits & Vegetables* onto both sides of the vehicle.

Then they went into the house, which was already perfumed by the meal the women had prepared. Before sitting down to eat, they commenced their prayers. Zina, excitement buzzing through her like an electrical current, was barely present, praying to Allah by rote while she thought of the Shaykh and her role in the triumph that was now only a day away.

At dinner the conversation was spirited, a flux of tension and anticipation animating them. Arsenov, who normally frowned on such loose behavior, allowed this outlet for their nerves, but only for a contained amount of time. Leaving the women to clean up, he led the men back down to the garage, where they applied the official decals and markings to the sides and front of the van. They drove that outside, brought the third one in, spray-painted it the colors of Reykjavík Energy.

Afterward they were all exhausted and ready for sleep, for they would be rising very early. Still, Arsenov made them run through their parts of the plan, insisting they speak Icelandic. He wanted to see what effect mental fatigue would have on them. Not that he doubted them. All of his nine compatriots had long ago proven themselves to him. They were physically strong, mentally tough and, perhaps most important of all, completely without remorse or compunction. However, none of them had ever been involved in an operation of this size, scope or global ramifications; without the NX 20 they'd never had the wherewithal. And so it was particularly satisfying to watch them dredge up the necessary reserves of energy and stamina to run through their roles with flawless precision.

He congratulated them and then, as if they were his blood children, said to them with great love and affection in his heart, *'La illaha ill Allah.'*

*'La illaha ill Allah,'* they chorused in unison with such love burning in their eyes that Arsenov was moved close to tears. In this moment, as they searched one another's faces, the enormity of the task set before them was brought home to them. For Arsenov's part, he saw them all – his family – gathered together in a strange and forbidding land, on the brink of the most glorious moment their people would ever witness. Never had his sense of the future burned so brilliantly, never had his sense of purpose – the righteousness – of their cause been made so manifest to him. He was grateful for the presence of all of them.

As Zina was about to go upstairs, he put a hand on her arm, but as the others passed her, glancing at them, she shook her head. 'I have to help them with the per-oxide,' she said, and he let her go.

'May Allah grant you a peaceful sleep,' she said softly, mounting the stairs.

Later, Arsenov lay in bed unable, as usual, to sleep. Across from him, in the other narrow bed, Akhmed snored with the noise of a buzzsaw. A light wind ruffled the curtains of the open window; as a youth, Arsenov had grown used to the cold; now he liked it. He stared up at the ceiling, thinking as he always did in the dark hours of Khalid Murat, of his betrayal of his mentor and his friend. Despite the necessity of the assassination, his personal disloyalty continued to eat at him. And there was the wound in his leg, a pain no matter how well it was healing that acted as a goad. In the end he'd failed Khalid Murat, and nothing he could do now could change that fact.

He rose, went into the hallway and padded silently down the stairs. He'd slept in his clothes, as he always did. He went out into the chill night air, extracting a ciga-rette and lighting it. Low on the horizon a bloated moon sailed through the star-spangled sky. There were no trees; he heard no insects.

As he walked farther away from the house, his seething mind began to clear, to calm itself. Perhaps, after he'd finished the cigarette he'd even be able to catch a few hours of sleep before the three-thirty rendezvous with Spalko's boat.

He had almost finished his cigarette and was about to turn around when he heard the whisper of low voices. Startled, he drew his gun and looked around. The voices, drifting on the night air, were coming from behind a pair of enormous boulders that rose up like the horns of a monster from the top of the cliff's face.

Dropping his cigarette and grinding its lit end into the ground, he moved toward the rock formation. Though he used caution, he was fully prepared to empty his weapon into the hearts of whoever was spying on them.

But as he peered around the curving face of the rock, it wasn't infidels he saw but Zina. She was talking in low tones to another, larger figure, but from his angle Arsenov could not tell who it was. He moved slightly, drawing closer. He couldn't hear their words, but even before he noticed Zina's hand on the other's arm, he had recognized the voice she used when she was set on seducing him.

He pressed his fist to his temple as if to stop the sudden throbbing in his head. He wanted to scream as he watched the fingers of Zina's hand draw up into what looked to him like spider's legs, her nails scoring the forearm of . . . who was it she was trying to seduce? His jealousy goaded him to action. At the risk of being seen, he moved farther, part of him entering the moonlight, until the face of Magomet came into view.

Blind rage gripped him; he was shaking all over. He thought of his mentor. What would Khalid Murat have done? he asked himself. Doubtless, he would have confronted the pair, heard their separate explanations of what they were doing and then made his judgment accordingly.

Arsenov stood up to his full height and, advancing on the pair, held his right arm out straight in front of him. Magomet, who was more or less turned facing him, saw him and abruptly stepped back, severing the hold Zina had on him. His mouth opened wide, but in his shock and terror, nothing came out.

'Magomet, what is it?' Zina said and, turning, saw Arsenov advancing on them.

'Hasan, no!' she cried just as Arsenov pulled the trigger.

The bullet entered Magomet's open mouth and blew the back of his head off. He was thrown backward in a welter of blood and brains.

Arsenov turned the gun on Zina. Yes, he thought, Khalid Murat would surely have handled the situation differently, but Khalid Murat was dead and he, Hasan Arsenov, the architect of Murat's demise, was alive and in charge, and this was why. It was a new world.

'Now you,' he said.

Staring into his black eyes, she knew that he wanted her to grovel, to get down on her knees and beg him for mercy. He could care less about any explanation she might give him. She knew that he was beyond reason; at this moment he wouldn't know the truth from a clever concoction. She also knew that giving him what he wanted at the moment he wanted it was a trap, a slippery slope once embarked upon impossible to get off. There was only one way to stop him in his tracks.

Her eyes blazed. 'Stop it!' she ordered. 'Right now!' Reaching out, she closed her fingers around the barrel of the gun, drew it upward so that it was no longer pointed at her head. She risked a quick glance at the dead Magomet. That was a mistake she wouldn't make twice.

'What's come over you?' she said. 'So close to our shared goal, have you lost your mind?'

She was clever to have reminded Arsenov of their reason for being in Reykjavík. For the moment, his devotion to her had blinded him to the larger goal. All he'd reacted to was her voice and her hand on Magomet's arm.

With a ragged motion, he put the gun away.

'Now what will we do?' she said. 'Who'll take over Magomet's responsibilities?'

'You caused this,' he said with disgust. 'You figure it out.'

'Hasan.' She knew better than to try to touch him at this moment or even to come closer than she already was. 'You are our leader. It's your decision and yours alone.'

He looked around, as if just coming out of a trance. 'I suspect our neighbors will assume the report of the gunshot was merely a truck backfiring.' He stared at her. 'Why were you out here with him?'

'I was trying to dissuade him from the path he'd chosen,' Zina said carefully. 'Something happened to him when I shaved his beard on the plane. He made overtures.'

Arsenov's eyes blazed anew. 'And what was your response?'

'What d'you imagine it was, Hasan?' she said, her hard voice matching his. 'Are you saying that you don't trust me?'

'I saw your hand on him, your fingers . . .' He could not go on.

'Hasan, look at me.' She reached out. 'Please look at me.'

He turned slowly, reluctantly, and elation rose inside her. She had him; despite her error in judgment, she still had him.

Breathing an inaudible sigh of relief, she said, 'The situation required some delicacy. Surely you can understand that. If I turned him down flat, if I was cold to him, if I angered him, I was afraid of a reprisal. I was afraid his anger would impair his use to us.' Her eyes held his. 'Hasan, I was thinking of the reason we're here. That's my only focus now, as it should be yours.'

He stood immobile for long moments, absorbing her words. The hiss and suck of the waves spending themselves against the cliffs far below seemed unnaturally loud. Then, abruptly, he nodded and the incident was swept away. That was his way.

'All that remains is to dispose of Magomet.'

'We'll wrap him up and take him with us to the rendezvous. The boat crew can dispose of him in deep water.'

Arsenov laughed. 'Zina, really, you're the most pragmatic female I know.'

Bourne awoke to find himself strapped into what appeared to be a dentist's chair. He looked around the black concrete room, saw the large drain in the center of the white tile floor, the hose coiled on the wall, the tiered cart beside the chair on which were arrayed ranks of gleaming stainless-steel implements, all, it seemed, designed to inflict agonizing damage to the human body, and was not reassured. He tried to move his wrists and ankles, but the wide leather straps were secured, he noted, with the same buckles used on straitjackets.

'You can't get out,' Annaka said, coming around from behind him. 'It's useless to try.'

Bourne stared at her for a moment, as if he was struggling to bring her into focus. She was dressed in white leather pants and a black sleeveless silk blouse with a plunging neckline, an outfit she never would have worn while she was playing the role of the innocent classical pianist and devoted daughter. He cursed himself for being gulled by her initial antipathy toward him. He should've known better. She was too available, too conveniently knowledgeable about Molnar's building. Hindsight was useless, however, and he put aside his disappointment in himself and applied himself to the difficult situation at hand.

'What an actress you turned out to be,' he said.

A slow smile broadened her lips, and when she parted them slightly, he could see her white, even teeth. 'Not only with you but with Khan.' She drew up the single chair in the room and sat down close beside him. 'You see, I know him well, your son. Oh, yes, I know, Jason. I know more than you think, much more than you do.' She gave a little laugh, a tinkling, bell-like sound of pure delight as she drank in the expression on Bourne's face. 'For a long time Khan didn't know whether you were alive or dead. Indeed, he made a number of attempts to find you, always unsuccessful – your CIA had done an excellent job of hiding you – until Stepan helped him. But even before he knew you were, in fact, alive, he'd spent all his idle

hours concocting elaborate ways in which he'd seek his revenge on you.' She nodded. 'Yes, Jason, his hatred for you was all-encompassing.' Putting her elbows on
her knees, she leaned toward him. 'How does that make you feel?'

'I applaud your performances.' Despite the potent emotions she had dredged
from him, he was determined not to rise outwardly to her bait.

Annaka made a moue. 'I'm a woman of many talents.'

'And as many loyalties, it seems.' He shook his head. 'Did our saving each other's
lives mean nothing to you?'

She sat back up, her manner brisk now, almost businesslike. 'You and I can agree
on these things, at least. Often life and death are the only things that matter.'

'Then free me,' he said.

'Yes, I've fallen head over heels for you, Jason.' She laughed. 'That's not the way
things work in real life. I saved you for one reason only: Stepan.'

His brow was furrowed in concentration. 'How can you let this happen?'

'How can I not? I have a history with Stepan. For a time he was the only friend
my mother had.'

Bourne was surprised. 'Spalko and your mother knew each other?'

Annaka nodded. Now that he was bound and presented no danger to her, she
seemed to want to talk. Bourne was rightfully suspicious of this.

'He met her after my father had her sent away,' Annaka continued.

'Sent away where?' Bourne was intrigued despite himself. She could charm the
venom out of a snake.

'To a sanatorium.' Annaka's eyes darkened, revealing in a flash a trace of genuine
feeling. 'He had her committed. It wasn't difficult; she was physically frail, unable
to fight him. In those days . . . yes, it was still possible.'

'Why would he do such a thing? I don't believe you,' Bourne said flatly.

'I don't care whether you believe me or not.' She contemplated him for a
moment with the disturbing aspect of a reptile. Then, possibly because she needed
to, she went on. 'She'd become an inconvenience. His mistress demanded it of him;
in this he was abominably weak.' The outpouring of naked hatred had transformed
her face into an ugly mask, and Bourne understood that, at last, she had unleashed
the truth about her past. 'He never knew that I'd discovered the truth, and I never
let on. *Never.*' She tossed her head. 'Anyway, Stepan was visiting the same asylum.
In those days, he went to see his brother . . . the brother who'd tried to kill him.'

Bourne stared at her, dumbfounded. He realized that he had no idea whether
she was lying or telling the truth. He had been correct about one aspect of her, at
least – she *was* at war. The parts she played so masterfully were her offensives, her
raiding parties into enemy territory. He looked into her implacable eyes and knew
that there was something monstrous about the way she chose to manipulate those
she had drawn close to her.

She leaned in, took his chin between her thumb and fingers. 'You haven't seen
Stepan, have you? He's had extensive plastic surgery on the right side of his face and
neck. What he tells people about it varies, but the truth is, his brother threw gasoline on him and then put a lighter to his face.'

Bourne couldn't help but react. 'My God. Why?'

She shrugged. 'Who knows? The brother's dangerously insane. Stepan knew it,
so for that matter did his father, but he refused to acknowledge it until it was too

late. And even afterward, he continued to defend the boy, insisting that it was a tragic accident.'

'All this might be true,' he said. 'But even if it is, it doesn't excuse you conspiring against your own father.'

She laughed. 'How can you, of all people, say that, when you and Khan have tried to kill each other? Such fury in two men, my God!'

'He came after me. I only defended myself.'

'But he hates you, Jason, with a passion I've rarely seen. He hates you just as much as I hated my father. And d'you know why? Because you abandoned him as my father abandoned my mother.'

'You're talking as if he's really my son,' Bourne spat.

'Oh, yes, that's right, you've convinced yourself that he isn't. That's convenient, isn't it? That way you don't have to think about how you left him to die in the jungle.'

'But I didn't!' Bourne knew he shouldn't let her drag him into this emotionally charged subject, but he couldn't help himself. 'I was told he was dead. I had no idea he might've survived. That's what I discovered when I was inside the government database.'

'Did you stay around to look, to check? No, you buried your family without even looking in the coffins! If you had, you would've seen that your son wasn't there. No, you coward, you fled the country instead.'

Bourne tried to pull himself out of his bonds. 'That's rich, you lecturing me on family!'

'That's quite enough.' Stepan Spalko had entered the room with the perfect timing of a ringmaster. 'I have more important matters to discuss with Mr. Bourne than family sagas.'

Annaka obediently stood up. She patted Bourne's cheek. 'Don't look so sullen, Jason. You're not the first man I've fooled, and you won't be the last.'

'No,' he said. 'Spalko will be the last.'

'Annaka, leave us now,' Spalko said, adjusting his butcher's apron with hands covered in Latex gloves. The apron was clean and well pressed. As yet, there wasn't a spot of blood on it.

As Annaka departed, Bourne turned his attention to the man who, according to Khan, had engineered the murders of Alex and Mo. 'And you don't distrust her, not even a little?'

'Yes, she's an excellent liar.' He chuckled. 'And I know a thing or two about lying.' He crossed to the cart, eyed with the connoisseur's intensity the implements arrayed there. 'I suppose it's natural to think that because she betrayed you, she'd do the same to me.' He turned, the light reflecting off the unnaturally smooth skin on the side of his face and neck. 'Or are you trying to drive a wedge between us? That would be standard operating procedure for an operative of your high caliber.' He shrugged and picked up an implement, twirled it between his fingers. 'Mr. Bourne, what I'm interested in is how much you've discovered about Dr. Schiffer and his little invention.'

'Where's Felix Schiffer?'

'You can't help him, Mr. Bourne, even if you could manage the impossible and free yourself. He outlived his usefulness and now he's beyond anyone's power to resurrect.'

'You killed him,' Bourne said, 'just as you killed Alex Conklin and Mo Panov.'

Spalko shrugged. 'Conklin took Dr. Schiffer away from me when I needed him the most. I got Schiffer back, of course. I always get what I want. But Conklin had to pay for thinking he could oppose me with impunity.'

'And Panov?'

'He was in the wrong place at the wrong time,' Spalko said. 'It's as simple as that.'

Bourne thought of all the good Mo Panov had done in his life and felt over-whelmed by the uselessness of his death. 'How can you talk about the taking of two men's lives as if it was as simple as snapping your fingers?'

'Because it was, Mr. Bourne.' Spalko laughed. 'And by tomorrow the taking of those two men's lives will be as nothing to what's coming.'

Bourne tried not to look at the glinting implement. Instead, what came into his mind was an image of László Molnar's blue-white body stuffed into his own refrig-erator. He'd seen first-hand the damage these tools of Spalko's could inflict.

Because he was face to face with the fact that Spalko had been responsible for Molnar's torture and death, he knew that everything Khan had told him about this man was true. And if Khan had told the truth about Spalko, was it not possible that he'd been telling the truth all along, that he was, in fact, Joshua Webb, Bourne's own son? The facts were mounting, the truth was before him, and Bourne felt its crushing weight as if it were a mountain on his shoulders. He couldn't bear to look at . . . what?

It didn't matter now because Spalko had begun wielding his instruments of pain. 'Again, I'll ask you what you know about Dr. Schiffer's invention.'

Bourne stared past Spalko. At the blank concrete wall.

'You've chosen not to answer me,' Spalko said. 'I applaud your courage.' He smiled charmingly. 'And pity the futility of your gesture.'

He applied the whorled end of the implement to Bourne's flesh.

# 26

Khan went into Houdini, a magic and logic games shop at 87 Vaci utca building. The walls and display cabinets of the smallish boutique were crammed with magic tricks, brain teasers and mazes of all kinds, shapes and descriptions, old and new. Children of all ages, their mothers or fathers in tow, prowled the aisles, pointing and staring wide-eyed at the fantastic wares.

Khan approached one of the harried salespeople and told her he wanted to see Oszkar. She asked him his name, then picked up a phone and dialed an interior extension. She spoke into the receiver for a moment, then directed Khan to the back of the store.

He passed through a door at the rear of the shop into a tiny vestibule lit by one bare bulb. The walls were of an indeterminate color; the air smelled of boiled cabbage. He went up an iron circular staircase to the office on the second floor. It was lined with books – mostly first-edition volumes on magic, biographies and autobiographies of famous magicians and escape artists. An autographed photo of Harry Houdini hung on the wall over an antique oak rolltop desk. The old Persian carpet was still on the plank floor, still in desperate need of cleaning, and the huge, thronelike high-backed armchair still sat in its place of honor facing the desk.

Oszkar sat in exactly the same position he'd been in a year ago when Khan last had occasion to visit him. He was a pear-shaped man of middle years with huge side whiskers and a bulbous nose. He rose when he saw Khan and, grinning, came around from behind the desk and shook his hand.

'Welcome back,' he said, gesturing for Khan to take a seat. 'What can I do for you?'

Khan told his contact what he needed. Oszkar wrote as Khan spoke, from time to time nodding to himself.

Then he looked up. 'Is that all?' He seemed disappointed; he loved nothing better than being challenged.

'Not quite,' Khan said. 'There's the matter of a magnetic lock.'

'Now we're talking!' Oszkar was beaming now. He rubbed his hands together as he rose. 'Come with me, my friend.'

He led Khan into a wallpapered hallway lit by what appeared to be gaslamps. He had a way of waddling when he walked, comical as a penguin, but when you saw him escape from three pairs of handcuffs in under ninety seconds, you were exposed to a whole new meaning of the word finesse.

He opened a door and walked into his workshop – a large space evenly divided into areas by workbenches and metal counters. He directed Khan over to one,

263

where he commenced to rummage through a vertical stack of drawers. At length he brought out a small black and chrome square.

'All mag locks work off current, you know that, right?' When Khan nodded, he continued. 'And they're all fail-safe, meaning they need a constant power supply to work. Anyone who installs one of these knows that if you cut the current, the lock will open, so there's certain to be a backup power supply, possibly even two, if the subject's paranoid enough.'

'This one is,' Khan assured him.

'Very well then.' Oszkar nodded. 'So forget about cutting the power supply – it'll take you too long, and even if you had the time you still might not be able to cut the power to all the backups.' He held up a forefinger. 'But, what's not so commonly known is that all magnetic locks work off DC current, so . . .' He rummaged around again, held up another object. 'What you need is a portable AC power supply with enough juice to zap the mag lock.'

Khan took the power pack in his hand. It was heavier than it looked. 'How is it going to work?'

'Imagine a lightning strike on an electrical system.' Oszkar tapped the power supply. 'This baby will scramble the DC current long enough for you to open the door, but it won't short it out completely. Eventually, it'll cycle back on again and the lock will reestablish itself.'

'How long will I have?' Khan asked.

'That depends on the make and model of the mag lock.' Oszkar shrugged his meaty shoulders. 'The best guess I can give you is fifteen minutes, maybe twenty, but no more than that.'

'Can't I just zap it again?'

Oszkar shook his head. 'Chances are good you'll freeze the mag into its locked position, and then you'd have to take the entire door down in order to get out.' He laughed, clapped Khan on the back. 'Not to worry, I have faith in you.'

Khan looked at him askance. 'Since when did you have faith in anything?'

'Quite right.' Oszkar handed him a small zippered leather case. 'Tricks of the trade always trump faith.'

At precisely two-fifteen in the morning, local Icelandic time, Arsenov and Zina placed the carefully wrapped body of Magomet into one of the vans and drove down the coast farther south toward an out-of-the-way cove. Arsenov was behind the wheel. Periodically, Zina, studying a detailed map, gave him directions.

'I sense the nervousness in the others,' he said after a time. 'It's more than simple anticipation.'

'We're on more than a simple mission, Hasan.'

He glanced at her. 'Sometimes I wonder whether icewater runs in your veins.'

She put a smile on her face as she briefly squeezed his leg. 'You know very well what runs in my veins.'

He nodded. 'That I do.' He had to admit that, as much as he was driven by his desire to lead his people, he was happiest being with Zina. He longed for a time when the war would be over, when he could shed his rebel's guise and be a husband to her, a father to their children.

'Zina,' he said as they turned off the road and jounced down the rutted path that descended off the cliff face to their destination, 'we've never talked about us.'

'What d'you mean?' Of course she knew very well what he meant and tried to push away the sudden dread that constricted her. 'Of course we have.'

The way had become steeper and he slowed the van. Zina could see the last turn in the path; beyond that was the rocky cove and the restless North Atlantic.

'Not about our future, our marriage, the children we'll have one day. What better time to pledge our love for each other.'

It was then that she fully understood how intuitive the Shaykh really was. For by his own words, Hasan Arsenov had condemned himself. He was afraid to die. She heard it in his choice of words, if not in his voice or in his eyes.

She saw his doubts, now, about her. If there was one thing she'd learned since joining the rebels, it was that doubt undermined initiative, determination, most especially action. Because of the extreme tension and anxiety, perhaps, he had exposed himself, and his weakness was as repugnant to her as it had been to the Shaykh. Hasan's doubts about her were sure to infect his thinking. She'd made a terrible blunder in seeking so quickly to enlist Magomet, but she was so very eager to embrace the Shaykh's future. Still, judging by Hasan's violent reaction, his doubts about her must have begun earlier. Did he think that he could no longer trust her?

They had arrived at the rendezvous point fifteen minutes ahead of schedule. She turned and took his face in her hands. Tenderly, she said, 'Hasan, long have we walked side by side in the shadow of death. We have survived through the will of Allah, but also because of our unswerving devotion to one another.' She leaned over and kissed him. 'So now we pledge ourselves to one another, because we desire death in the path of Allah more than our enemies desire life.'

Arsenov closed his eyes for a moment. This was what he'd wanted from her, what he'd been afraid she'd never give him. It was why, he realized now, he'd jumped to an ugly conclusion when he'd seen her with Magomet.

'In Allah's eyes, under Allah's hand, in Allah's heart,' he said in a form of benediction.

They embraced, but Zina was, of course, far away across the North Atlantic. She was wondering what the Shaykh was doing at this very moment. She longed to see his face, to be near him. Soon, she told herself. Soon enough everything she wanted would be hers.

Sometime later they got out of the van and stood watching on the shore, hearing the waves rumble and spend themselves against the shingle. The moon had already gone down in the short span of darkness this far north. In another half hour it would grow light and another long day would dawn. They were in more or less the center of the cove, its arms extended on either side so that the tide was stymied, the waves made small and robbed of their usual peril. A chill wind off the black water made Zina shiver, but Arsenov embraced it.

They saw the sweep of the light then, blinking on and off three times. The boat had arrived. Arsenov switched on the flashlight, returning the signal. Faintly, they could see the fishing boat running no lights, nosing in. They went to the back of the van and, together, brought their burden down to the tide line.

'Won't they be surprised to see you again?' Arsenov said.

'They're the Shaykh's men, nothing surprises them,' Zina replied, acutely aware that according to the story the Shaykh told Hasan she was supposed to have met this crew. Of course, the Shaykh would have already apprised them of that fact.

Arsenov switched on his flashlight again and they saw heading toward them an oared boat, heavily laden, lying low in the water. There were two men and a stack of crates; there would be more crates on the fishing boat. Arsenov glanced at his watch; he hoped they could finish before first light.

The two men nosed the prow of the rowboat up onto the shingle and got out. They didn't waste time with introductions, but as they had been ordered to do, they treated Zina as if she was known to them.

With great efficiency, the four of them offloaded the crates, piling them up neatly in the back of the van. Arsenov heard a sound, turned and saw that a second rowboat had pulled up onto the shingle and knew then that they'd beat the dawn.

They loaded Magomet's corpse onto the first rowboat, now otherwise empty, and Zina gave the crew members the order to dump it when they were in the deepest water. They obeyed her without question, which pleased Arsenov. Obviously, she'd made an impression on them when she'd supervised the delivery of the cargo to them.

In short order, then, the six of them moved the rest of the crates into the van. Then the men returned to their boats as silently as they had disembarked from them and, with a push from Arsenov and Zina, began their return journey to the fishing boat.

Arsenov and Zina looked at each other. With the arrival of the cargo, the mission had suddenly taken on a reality it hadn't had before.

'Can you feel it, Zina?' Arsenov said as he put his hand on one of the crates. 'Can you feel the death waiting there?'

She put her hand over his. 'What I feel is victory.'

They drove back to the base where they were met by the other members of the cadre, who through the judicious application of peroxide dye and colored contact lenses had now been utterly transformed. Nothing was said concerning the death of Magomet. He had come to a bad end and this close to their mission none of them wanted to know the details – they had more important things on their minds.

Carefully, the crates were unloaded and opened, revealing compact machine pistols, packs of C4 plastique explosive, HAZMAT suits. Another crate, smaller than the others, contained scallions, bagged, bedded in shaved ice. Arsenov gestured to Akhmed, who donned Latex gloves and removed the crate of scallions to the van that had printed on it *Hafnarfjördur Fine Fruits & Vegetables*. Then the blond and blue-eyed Akhmed climbed into the van and drove off.

The last crate was left for Arsenov and Zina to open. It contained the NX 20. Together, they looked at it, the two halves lying innocently inside their molded foam bed, and thought of what they'd been witness to in Nairobi. Arsenov looked at his watch. 'Very soon now the Shaykh will arrive with the payload.'

The final preparations had begun.

*

Just after nine A.M., a van from Fontana Department Store pulled up at the service entrance on the basement level of Humanistas, Ltd. where it was halted by a pair of security guards. One of them consulted his daily work sheet and even though he saw on it a delivery from Fontana for Ethan Hearn's office, he asked to see the bill of lading. When the driver complied, the guard told him to open the back of the van. The guard climbed in, checked off each item on the list, then he and his partner opened every carton, checking the two chairs, credenza, cabinet and sofa bed. All the doors on the credenza and cabinet were opened, the interiors inspected, the pillows on the sofa and chairs lifted. Finding everything in order, the security guards handed back the bill of lading and gave the driver and his delivery partner directions to Ethan Hearn's office.

The driver parked near the elevator and he and his partner unloaded the furniture. It took them four trips to get everything up to the sixth floor, where Hearn was waiting for them. He was only too pleased to show them where he wanted each piece of furniture, and they were just as pleased to receive the generous gratuity he handed them when their task was completed.

After they left, Hearn closed the door and began to transfer the stacks of files that had built up beside his desk into the cabinet in alphabetical order. The hush of a well-run office fell over the room. After a time, Hearn rose and went to the door. Opening it, he found himself face to face with the woman who had accompanied the man on the stretcher into the building late yesterday.

'You're Ethan Hearn?' When he nodded, she held out a hand. 'Annaka Vadas.'

He took her hand briefly, noting that it was firm and dry. He recalled Khan's warning and he put an innocently quizzical look on his face. 'Do we know each other?'

'I'm a friend of Stepan's.' Her smile was dazzling. 'Do you mind if I come in, or were you just leaving?'

'I do have an appointment in' – he glanced at his watch – 'a little while.'

'I won't take up much of your time.' She walked to the sofa bed and sat, crossing her legs. Her expression, as she stared up at Hearn, was alert and expectant.

He sat in his chair and swiveled it around to face her. 'How may I help you, Ms. Vadas?'

'I think you've got it wrong,' she said brightly. 'The question is how may I help you?'

He shook his head. 'I don't think I understand.'

She looked around the office, humming to herself. Then she leaned forward, her elbows on her knee. 'Oh, but I think you do, Ethan.' That smile again. 'You see, I know something about you even Stepan doesn't.'

He stitched that quizzical look back onto his face, spread his hands in a gesture of helplessness.

'You're trying too hard,' she said shortly. 'I know you're working for someone else as well as for Stepan.'

'I don't – '

But she'd put a forefinger across his lips. 'I saw you yesterday in the garage. You couldn't have been there for your health, and even if you were, you were far too interested in the proceedings.'

He was too stunned even to formulate a denial. And what was the point? he asked himself. She'd made him, even though he thought he'd been so very careful. He stared at her. She was, indeed, beautiful, but she was even more formidable.

She cocked her head. 'It isn't Interpol you work for – you don't have their habits. CIA, no, I don't think so. Stepan would know if the Americans were trying to penetrate his organization. So who then, hmm?'

Hearn wouldn't say; he couldn't. He was only terrified that she already knew – that she knew everything.

'Don't look so ashen, Ethan.' Annaka rose. 'I don't care, really. I simply want an insurance policy in case things turn sour here. That insurance policy is you. For now, let's just call your treachery our little secret.'

She had crossed the room and gone out the door before Hearn could think of a reply. He sat for a moment, immobile with shock. Then, at last he got up and opened the door, looking this way and that up and down the corridor to make certain she was really gone.

Then he closed the door, walked over to the sofa bed and said, 'All clear.'

The cushions lifted up and he put them on the wall-to-wall carpet. When the plywood panels that covered the bed mechanism began to stir, he reached down and lifted them out.

Underneath, instead of the mattress and bed frame, lay Khan.

Hearn realized that he was sweating. 'I know you warned me, but – '

'Quiet.' Khan climbed out of the space that was no larger than a coffin. Hearn cowered, but Khan had more important things on his mind than corporal punishment. 'Just make sure you don't make the same mistake twice.'

Khan walked to the door, put his ear against it. All that could be discerned was the background hum of the offices on the floor. He was dressed in black trousers, shoes, shirt and waist-length jacket. To Hearn, he looked a good deal bulkier in the upper body than he had the last time they'd met.

'Put the sofa bed back together,' Khan ordered, 'then return to work as if nothing had happened. You have a meeting soon? Make sure you go to it and that you're not late. It's imperative that everything appear normal.'

Hearn nodded, dropping the plywood panels into the well of the sofa bed, then replacing the cushions. 'We're on the sixth floor,' he said. 'Your target's on the fourth floor.'

'Let's see the schematics.'

Hearn sat down at his computer terminal and brought up the schematics for the building.

'Let me see the fourth floor,' Khan said, bending over his shoulder.

When Hearn brought it up, Khan studied it carefully. 'What's this?' he asked, pointing.

'I don't know.' Hearn tried zooming in. 'It looks like blank space.'

'Or,' Khan said, 'it could be a room adjacent to Spalko's bedroom suite.'

'Except there isn't a way in or out,' Hearn pointed out.

'Interesting. I wonder if Mr. Spalko made some alterations his architects knew nothing about.'

Having memorized the floor plan, Khan turned away. He'd gotten all he could from the schematic; now he needed to see the place for himself. At the door he turned back to Hearn. 'Remember. Get to your appointment on time.'

'What about you?' Hearn said. 'You can't get in there.'

Khan shook his head. 'The less you know, the better.'

The flags were out in the endless Icelandic morning, filled with brilliant sunshine and the mineral scent of the thermal springs. The elaborate aluminum scaffold of a large dais had been set up and wired for sound at one end of Keflavík Airport, which Jamie Hull, Boris Illyich Karpov and Feyd al-Saoud had determined was the most secure space on the grounds. None of them, even Comrade Boris, it seemed, was happy about their respective leaders appearing in such a public forum, but in this all the heads of state were of a like mind. It was imperative, they felt, not only to show their solidarity in a public manner but also to show their lack of fear. They all knew the risk of assassination when they took their positions, were acutely aware of how that risk had escalated exponentially when they had agreed to the summit. But they all knew the risk of death was a component of their work. If you set out to change the world, inevitably there would be those who would stand in your way.

And so on this morning of the start of the summit, the flags of the United States, Russia and the four most influential Islamic nations rippled and cracked in the biting wind, the front of the dais had been draped with the carefully fought-over logo of the summit, armored security was in place around the perimeter, snipers placed high up at every possible strategic sight line. The press had come from every nation in the world; they had been required to show up two hours in advance of the press conference. Journalists had been methodically screened, their credentials checked, their fingerprints taken and scanned through various data-bases. Photographers had been warned not to load their cameras ahead of time because they needed to be X-rayed on site, each film cannister examined, every one of the photographers themselves observed while they loaded their cameras. As for cell phones, they were confiscated, meticulously tagged and kept outside the perimeter, to be retrieved at the end of the press conference by their respective owners. No detail had been overlooked.

As the president of the United States made his appearance, Jamie Hull was at his side, along with a brace of Secret Service agents. Hull was in constant contact with every member of his contingent as well as the other two heads of security via an electronic earbud. Just behind the U.S. president came Aleksandr Yevtushenko, president of Russia, accompanied by Boris and a cadre of grim-faced FSB agents. Behind him were the leaders of the four Islamic states, with the respective heads of their security services.

The crowd as well as the press surged forward only to be kept back from the front of the dais the dignitaries had now mounted. The microphones were tested, the television cameras went live. The U.S. president took the microphone first. He was a tall, handsome man with a prominent nose and the eyes of a watchdog.

'My fellow citizens of the world,' he began in the strong, declarative voice honed at many a successful primary race, smoothed of any remaining rough edges by numerous press conferences and richly burnished by intimate speeches in the Rose Garden and at Camp David, 'this is a great day for world peace and for the international fight for justice and freedom against the forces of violence and terrorism.

'Today, we once again stand at a crossroads in the history of the world. Will we allow all of humankind to be plunged into the darkness of fear and neverending war or will we band together to strike at the heart of our enemies wherever they may hide?

'The forces of terrorism are arrayed against us. And make no mistake, terrorism is a modern-day hydra, a beast of many heads. We have no illusions about the difficult road ahead of us, but we will not be deterred in our desire to move forward in a single concerted effort. Only united can we destroy the many-headed beast. Only united do we stand a chance of making our world a safe place for each and every citizen.'

At the end of the president's speech there was great applause. Then he yielded the microphone to the Russian president, who said more or less the same things, also to great applause. The four Arab leaders spoke one by one, and though their words were more circumspect, they too reiterated the burning need for a united effort at stamping out terrorism once and for all.

A short question and answer period ensued, after which the six men stood side by side for their photo op. It was an impressive sight, made even more memorable when they grasped one another's hands and raised their arms aloft in an unprecedented display of solidarity between the West and the East.

As the crowd slowly filed out, the mood was jubilant. And even the most jaded journalists and photographers agreed that the summit had gotten off to a sterling start.

'Do you realize that I'm on my third pair of Latex gloves?'

Stepan Spalko was at the scarred and blood-stained table, sitting on the chair Annaka had used the day before. In front of him was a bacon, lettuce and tomato sandwich, for which he'd developed a taste during his long convalescence between operations in the United States. The sandwich was on a plate of fine bone china, and at his right hand was a stemmed glass of finest crystal filled with a vintage Bordeaux.

'No matter. The hour grows late.' He tapped the crystal of the chronometer on his wrist. 'It occurs to me now, Mr. Bourne, that my marvelous entertainment is at an end. I must tell you what a wonderful night you've provided me.' He barked a laugh. 'Which is more than I did for you, I daresay.'

His sandwich had been cut into two equal triangles, exactly to his specifications. He picked one up and bit into it, chewed slowly and luxuriously. 'You know, Mr. Bourne, a bacon, lettuce and tomato sandwich is no good unless the bacon has been freshly cooked and, if possible, thickly sliced.'

He swallowed, put down the sandwich and, grasping the crystal glass, swirled a measure of Bordeaux around in his mouth. Then he pushed back his chair, rose and went over to where Jason Bourne sat strapped into the dentist's chair. His head was lolled on his chest and there were blood spatters in a two-foot radius around him.

Spalko used a knuckle to lift Bourne's head. His eyes, dulled with endless pain, were sunken into dark circles and his face appeared drained of blood. 'Before I go, I must tell you the irony of it all. The hour of my triumph is upon us. It doesn't matter what you know. It doesn't matter whether you talked or not now. All that matters is that I have you here, safe and unable to act against me in any way.' He laughed. 'What a terrible price you've paid for your silence. And for what, Mr. Bourne? Nothing!'

Khan saw the guard standing in the corridor beside the elevator and went cautiously back down toward the door to the staircase. Through the wire-mesh reinforced glass panel he could see a pair of armed guards talking and smoking in the stairwell. Every fifteen seconds one or the other would glance out through the glass panel, checking the sixth-floor corridor. The stairs were too well defended.

He reversed himself. Striding down the corridor at a normal and relaxed pace, he drew the air gun he purchased from Oszkar and held it at his side. The instant the guard saw him, Khan raised the air gun, shot a dart into his neck. The man collapsed where he stood, rendered unconscious by the chemical in the dart's tip.

Khan broke into a run. He began to drag the guard into the men's room when the door opened and a second guard appeared, his machine pistol aimed at Khan's chest.

'Hold it right there,' he said. 'Throw down your weapon and let me see your empty hands.'

Khan did as he was ordered. As he held out his hands for the guard to inspect, he touched a hidden spring-loaded sheath attached to the inner side of his wrist. The guard clapped one hand to his throat. The dart felt like an insect bite. But all at once he found that he couldn't see. That was the last thought he had before he, too, sank into unconsciousness.

Khan dragged both bodies into the men's room, then hit the call button on the wall panel. A moment later the two sets of doors opened as the elevator cab arrived. He got in and pressed the button for the fourth floor. The elevator began to descend, but as it passed the fifth floor, it jolted to a halt, hanging suspended. He pressed several floor buttons to no avail. The elevator was stuck, no doubt deliberately so. He knew he had very little time to escape from the trap Spalko had set for him.

Climbing up onto the handrail that ran around the cab, he stretched upward toward the maintenance hatch. He was about to open it when he stopped and peered more closely. What was that metallic glint? He took out the mini-light from the kit Oszkar had given him, shone it on the screw in the farthest corner. There was a bit of copper wire wrapped around it. It was booby-trapped! Khan knew that the moment he tried to take off the hatch it would detonate a charge placed on top of the cab.

At that moment, a lurch dislodged him from his perch and the elevator cab, shuddering, began to plummet down the shaft.

Spalko's phone rang and he stepped out of the interrogation room. Sunlight spilled through the windows of his bedroom as he walked into it, feeling the warmth on his face.

'Yes?'

A voice spoke in his ear, the words accelerating his pulse. He was here! Khan was here! His hand clenched into a fist. He had them both now. His work here was almost done. He ordered his men onto the third floor, then called the main security desk and ordered them to begin a fire drill that would in short order evacuate all normal Humanistas personnel from the building. Within twenty seconds, the fire alarm shrilled and all through the building, men and women left their offices and proceeded in an orderly fashion to the stairwells, where they were escorted out onto the street. By this time Spalko had called his driver and his pilot, telling the latter to ready the jet that had been waiting for him in the Humanistas hangar at Ferihegy Airport. Per his instructions, it had already been fueled and inspected, a flight plan logged in with the tower.

There was one more call he needed to make before he returned to Jason Bourne.

'Khan's in the building,' he said when Annaka answered the phone. 'He's trapped in the elevator and I've sent men to deal with him if he manages to escape, but you know him better than anyone.' He grunted at her response. 'What you're saying isn't a surprise. Deal with it as you see fit.'

Khan hit the Emergency Stop button with the heel of his hand, but nothing happened, the elevator continued its precipitous descent. With one of the tools from Oszkar's kit, he quickly pried open the display panel. Inside was a nest of wires, but he immediately saw that the wires to the emergency brake had been disconnected. Deftly, he fitted them back into their receptacles, and at once with a squeal of sparking metal the elevator cab lurched to a halt as the emergency brake kicked in. As the cab hung, stalled, between the third and fourth floors, Khan continued to work on the wiring with a breathless intensity.

On the third floor Spalko's armed men reached the outer elevator doors. Employing a fire key, they manually pried open the doors, exposing the shaft. Just above them, they could see the bottom of the stalled elevator cab. They had their orders; they knew what to do. Aiming their machine pistols, they opened fire in a massed fusillade that chewed up the bottom third of the elevator cab. No one could survive such massed firepower.

Khan, spreadeagled, hands and feet pressed hard against the walls of the elevator shaft's setback, watched the lower part of the cab fall away. He was protected from the ricochet of bullets both by the doors of the cab and by the shaft itself. He'd rewired the panel to allow him to open the cab doors just enough to squeeze out. He'd been squirming into position in the setback, climbing to approximately the height of the cab's top when the hail of automatic fire began.

Now, in the echoing aftermath of the percussion, he heard a buzzing as of a swarm of bees loosed from their hive. Looking up, he saw a pair of rappeling lines snaking down from the top of the shaft. Moments later two heavily armed guards in riot gear came down the lines, hand over hand.

One of them saw him and swung his machine pistol toward him. Khan fired his air gun, and the guard's weapon dropped from his numbed fingers. As the second guard aimed his weapon, Khan leaped out, grabbed hold of the unconscious man, who by dint of his rappeling harness was held fast to the line. The second guard, faceless and anonymous in his riot helmet, fired at Khan, who swung his line companion around, using his body as a shield to stop the bullets. He kicked out, snapping the machine pistol out of the second guard's grasp.

They both landed atop the elevator cab together. The small pale square of deadly C4 explosive was taped to the center of the maintenance hatch where it had been hastily wired to set the booby trap. Khan could see that the screws had been loosened; if either of them inadvertently struck the hatch plate, dislodging it even a little, the entire cab would be blown to pieces.

Khan squeezed the trigger on his air gun, but the guard, who had seen how he'd incapacitated his partner, dived out of the way, rolled and kicked upward, knocking the weapon out of Khan's grasp. At the same time he grabbed his partner's machine pistol. Khan trod down hard on his hand, grinding with his heel in an attempt to dislodge the weapon from the guard's grip. But now there were bursts of automatic fire from the guards on the third floor, who were firing up the shaft.

The guard, taking advantage of the distraction, smashed Khan's leg sideways and wrested the machine pistol from him. As he fired, Khan leaped off the cab, sliding down the side of the shaft to the place where the emergency brake was extended. Moving back from the hail of gunfire, he worked on the brake mechanism. The guard on the roof of the cab had followed his progress and was now stretched out on his belly, aiming the machine pistol at Khan. As he began firing, Khan was able to release the emergency brake mechanism. The elevator cab plunged down the shaft, taking the shocked guard with it.

Khan leaped for the nearest rappeling rope and clambered up it. He reached the fourth floor and was applying the AC current to the magnetic lock when the elevator cab impacted with the bottom of the shaft in the sub-basement. The shock dislodged the maintenance hatch and the C4 detonated. The explosion shot up the shaft just as the mag lock circuit was disrupted and Khan tumbled through the door.

The fourth-floor vestibule was clad entirely in café-au-lait marble. Frosted-glass sconces provided soft indirect lighting. As Khan picked himself up, he saw Annaka not five yards from him, fleeing down the hall. Clearly, she was surprised and, quite possibly, he thought, not a little frightened. Obviously, neither she nor Spalko had counted on him making it to the fourth floor. He laughed silently as he set off in pursuit. He couldn't blame them; it was quite a feat he'd performed.

Up ahead, Annaka went through a door. As she slammed it shut behind her, Khan heard the lock click into place. He knew he needed to get to Bourne and Spalko, but Annaka had become a wild card he couldn't afford to ignore. He had a set of picks out even as he reached the locked door. Inserting one, he finessed out the grooves of the tumbler. It took him less than fifteen seconds to open the door, hardly time enough for Annaka to have made it to the other side of the room. She threw him a frightened glance over her shoulder before she slammed the door shut behind her.

In retrospect, he should have been warned by her expression. Annaka never showed fear. He was, however, alerted by the ominous room, which was small and square, as featureless as it was windowless. It appeared unfinished, freshly painted a dead white, even the wide, carved moldings. There was no furniture, nothing at all in the space. But his alarm arrived too late, for the soft hiss had already begun. Peering up, he saw the vents high in the walls, from which a gas was being discharged. Holding his breath, he went to the far door. He picked the lock, but still the door wouldn't open. It must be bolted from the outside, he thought, as he ran back to the door through which he'd entered the room. He turned the knob only to find that it, too, had been bolted from the outside.

The gas was starting to permeate the barred room. He was neatly trapped.

Next to the crumb-spattered bone china plate and the stemmed glass in which remained the dregs of the Bordeaux, Stepan Spalko had arrayed the items he had taken from Bourne: the ceramic gun, Conklin's cell phone, the wad of money and the switchblade knife.

Bourne, battered and bloody, had been deep in delta meditation for hours now, first to survive the waves of agony that had rippled through his body at every new twist and jab of Spalko's implements, then to protect and conserve his inner core of energy, and finally to throw off the debilitating effects of the torture and to build up his strength.

Thoughts of Marie, Alison and Jamie flickered through his emptied mind like fitful flames, but what had come to him most vividly was his years in sun-drenched Phnom Penh. His mind, calmed to the point of complete tranquility, resurrected Dao, Alyssa and Joshua. He was tossing a baseball to Joshua, showing him how to use the glove he'd brought from the States, when Joshua turned to him and said, *'Why did you try to replicate us? Why didn't you save us?'* He became confused for a moment, until he saw Khan's face hanging in his mind like a full moon in a starless sky. Khan opened his mouth and said, *'You tried to replicate Joshua and Alyssa. You even used the same first letters in their names.'*

He wanted to rise out of his enforced meditation, to abandon the fortress he'd erected to protect himself against the worst of the ravages Spalko was visiting upon him, anything to get away from the accusatory face, the crushing guilt.

Guilt.

It was his own guilt that he'd been running away from. Ever since Khan had told him who he really was, he'd run from the truth, just as he'd run from Phnom Penh as fast as he could. He thought he'd been running away from the tragedy that had befallen him, but the truth was he'd run from the burden of his unsupportable guilt. He hadn't been there to protect his family when they'd needed him the most. Slamming the door on the truth, he'd fled.

God help him, in this he was, as Annaka had said, a coward.

As Bourne watched out of bloodshot eyes, Spalko pocketed the money and took up the gun. 'I've used you to keep the hounds of the world's intelligence organizations off my trail. In this you've served me well.' He leveled the gun at Bourne, aiming for a spot just above and between his eyes. 'But, sadly, your use to me is at an end.' His finger tightened on the trigger.

At that moment Annaka came into the room. 'Khan made it onto the floor,' she said.

Despite himself, Spalko registered surprise. 'I heard the explosion. He wasn't killed by it?'

'He somehow managed to crash the elevator. It exploded in the sub-basement.'

'Luckily, the latest delivery of weapons was shipped out.' At last he turned his gaze on her. 'Where's Khan now?'

'He's trapped in the locked room. It's time to leave.'

Spalko nodded. She'd been dead on when it came to Khan's skills. He'd been right to encourage the liaison between them. Duplicitous creature that she was, she's gotten to know Khan better than he himself could've hoped to. Still, he stared at Bourne, certain his business with him was not yet finished.

'Stepan.' Annaka put a hand on his arm. 'The plane is waiting. We need time to leave the building unseen. The fire-circuits have been activated and all the oxygen has been pumped out of the elevator shaft so there's no chance of major damage. Still, there must be flames in the lobby and the fire wagons will be here if they're not already.'

She'd thought of everything. Spalko looked at her admiringly. Then, without any warning, he swept the hand that held Bourne's ceramic gun in an arc, slamming the barrel into the side of Bourne's head.

'I'll just take this as a souvenir of our first and last encounter.'

Then he and Annaka left the room.

Khan, down on his belly, dug furiously, using a small crowbar from the tools he'd requested from Oszkar, at a section of the molding. His eyes burned and teared from the gas, and his lungs were near to bursting from lack of oxygen. He had only a few more seconds left before he passed out and his autonomous nervous system took over, allowing the gas into his system.

But now he'd pried off a section of the molding and immediately he could feel the draft of cool air coming from outside the room he was in. He stuck his nose into the vent he'd made, breathed in the fresh air. Then, taking a deep breath, he quickly set up the small charge of C4 Oszkar had provided. This, above all the items on his list, had told Oszkar the extent of the danger he was heading into, prompting the contact to give Khan the escape kit as added protection.

Putting his nose into the vent, Khan took another deep breath, then he replaced it with the packet of C4, wedging it as far in as he was able. Scrambling to the opposite side of the room, he pressed the remote.

The resulting explosion brought down a section of the wall as it blew a hole right through it. Without waiting for the plastic and wood dust to settle, Khan leaped though the wall into Stepan Spalko's bedroom.

Sunlight slanted through the windows, and the Danube glittered below. Khan threw open all the windows in order to dissipate whatever leakage of gas found its way in. At once he could hear sirens, and glancing down, he saw the fire trucks and the police cars, the frenzied activity on street level. He stepped back from the windows, looked around, orienting himself to the architectural plans Hearn had brought up on his computer screen.

He turned to where the blank space had been, saw the gleaming wooden wall panels. Pressing his ear to each panel in turn, he rapped with his knuckles. In this way the third panel from the left revealed itself as a door. He pressed against the left side of the panel and it swung inward.

Khan stepped into the room of black concrete and white tiles. It stank of sweat and blood. He found himself facing a bloody, battered Jason Bourne. He stared at Bourne, strapped into the dentist's chair, blood spatters in a circle around him. Bourne was bare to the waist. His arms, shoulders, chest and back were a welter of puffy wounds and blistered flesh. The two outer layers that wrapped his ribs had been stripped away, but the underlayer was still intact.

Bourne's head swung around and regarded Khan with the look of a wounded bull, bloody but unbowed.

'I heard the second explosion,' Bourne said, in a reedy voice. 'I thought you had been killed.'

'Disappointed?' Khan bared his teeth. 'Where is he? Where's Spalko?'

'I'm afraid you're too late on that score,' Bourne said. 'He's gone, and Annaka Vadas with him.'

'She was working for him all along,' Khan said. 'I tried to warn you at the clinic, but you didn't want to listen.'

Bourne sighed, closed his eyes against the sharp rebuke. 'I didn't have time.'

'You never seem to have time to listen.'

Khan approached Bourne. His throat seemed constricted. He knew that he should go after Spalko, but something rooted him to the spot. He stared at the damage Spalko had wrought.

Bourne said, 'Will you kill me now.' It was not a question, more a statement of fact.

Khan knew that he would never have a better chance. The dark thing inside him that he had nurtured, that had become his only companion, which daily feasted on his hate, and which daily had spewed its poison back out into his system, refused to die. It wanted to kill Bourne, and it almost took possession of him then. Almost. He felt the impulse coming up from his lower belly into his arm, but it had bypassed his heart and so fell short of impelling him to action.

Abruptly, he turned on his heel and went back into Spalko's luxe bedroom. In a moment he'd returned with a glass of water and a handful of items he'd scavenged from the bathroom. He held the glass to Bourne's mouth, tipping it slowly until it had been drained. As if of their own volition, his hands unstrapped the buckles, freeing Bourne's wrists and ankles.

Bourne's eyes watched him as he went about cleaning and disinfecting the wounds. Bourne didn't lift his hands from the arms of the chair. In a sense, he felt more completely paralyzed now than he had while restrained. He stared hard at Khan, scrutinizing every curve and angle, every feature of his face. Did he see Dao's mouth, his own nose? Or was it all an illusion? If this was his son, he needed to know; he needed to understand what had happened. But he still felt an undercurrent of uncertainty, a ripple of fear. The possibility that he was confronting his own son after so many years of believing him dead was too much for him. On the other hand, the silence into which they had now been plunged was intolerable. And so he fell back to the one neutral topic he knew was of extreme interest to both of them.

'You wanted to know what Spalko was up to,' he said, breathing slowly and deeply as each shock of the disinfectant sent bolts of pain through him. 'He's stolen a weapon invented by Felix Schiffer – a portable bio-diffuser. Somehow Spalko has coerced Peter Sido – an epidemiologist working at the clinic – to provide him with the payload.'

Khan dropped the blood-soaked piece of gauze, picked up a clean one. 'Which is?'

'Anthrax, a designer hemorrhagic fever, I don't know. The only thing for certain is that it's quite lethal.'

Khan continued to clean Bourne's wounds. The floor was now littered with bloody bits of gauze. 'Why are you telling me this now?' he said with undisguised suspicion.

'Because I know what Spalko means to do with this weapon.'

Khan looked up from his work.

Bourne found it physically painful to look into Khan's eyes. Taking a deep breath, he plowed on. 'Spalko's on a very tight time constraint. He needed to get moving now.'

'The terrorism summit in Reykjavík.'

Bourne nodded. 'It's the only possibility that makes sense.'

Khan stood up, rinsing off his hands at the hose. He watched the pink water swirl through the huge grate. 'That is, if I believe you.'

'I'm going after them,' Bourne said. 'After putting the pieces together, I finally realized that Conklin had taken Schiffer and hidden him with Vadas and Molnar because he'd learned of Spalko's threat. I got the code name for the bio-diffuser – NX 20 – from a pad in Conklin's house.'

'And so Conklin was murdered for it.' Khan nodded. 'Why didn't he go to the Agency with his information? Surely, the CIA as a whole would've been better equipped to handle the threat to Dr. Schiffer.'

'There could be many reasons,' Bourne said. 'He didn't think he'd be believed, given Spalko's reputation as a humanitarian. He didn't have enough time; his intel wasn't concrete enough for the Agency's bureaucracy to move on it quickly enough. Also, it wasn't Alex's way. He hated sharing secrets.'

Bourne rose slowly and painfully, one hand supporting himself on the back of the chair. His legs felt like rubber from having been in one position for so long. 'Spalko killed Schiffer, and I have to assume that he has Dr. Sido, alive or dead. I've got to stop him from killing everyone at the summit.'

Khan turned and handed Bourne the cell phone. 'Here. Call the Agency.'

'Do you think they'd believe me? As far as the Agency's concerned, I murdered Conklin and Panov in the house in Manassas.'

'I'll do it then. Even the bureaucracy of the CIA has to take seriously an anonymous call that threatens the life of the president of the United States.'

Bourne shook his head. 'The head of American security is a man named Jamie Hull. He'd be sure to find a way to screw up the intel.' His eyes gleamed. They'd already lost most of their dullness. 'That leaves only one other option, but I don't think I can do it alone.'

'Judging by the look of you,' Khan said, 'you can't do it at all.'

Bourne forced himself to look Khan in the eye. 'All the more reason, then, for you to join me.'

'You're insane!'

Bourne inured himself to the rising hostility. 'You want Spalko as badly as I do. Where's the downside?'

'*All* I see is downside.' Khan sneered. 'Look at you! You're a mess.'

Bourne had detached himself from the chair and was walking around the room, stretching his muscles, gaining strength and confidence in his body with every stride he took. Khan saw this and was, frankly, astonished.

Bourne turned to him and said, 'I promise not to make you do all the heavy lifting.'

Khan didn't reject the offer out of hand. Instead, he made a grudging concession, not at all certain why he was doing it. 'The first thing we have to do is get out of here safely.'

'I know,' Bourne said, 'you managed to start a fire and now the building is swarming with firemen and, no doubt, the police.'

'I wouldn't be here if I hadn't started that fire.'

Bourne could see that his light bantering wasn't easing the tension. If anything, it was doing the opposite. They didn't know how to talk to each other. He wondered whether they ever would. 'Thank you for rescuing me,' he said.

Khan wouldn't meet his eye. 'Don't flatter yourself. I came here to kill Spalko.'

'At last,' Bourne said, 'something to thank Stepan Spalko for.'

Khan shook his head. 'This can't work. I don't trust you and I know you don't trust me.'

'I'm willing to try,' Bourne said. 'Whatever's between us, this is far bigger.'

'Don't tell me what to think,' Khan said shortly. 'I don't need you for that; I never did.' He managed to raise his head and look at Bourne. 'All right, here's how it goes. I'll agree to work together with you on one condition. You find us a way out of here.'

'Done.' Bourne's smile confounded Khan. 'Unlike you, I've had a great many hours to think about escaping from this room. I had assumed that even if I somehow managed to free myself from the chair, I wouldn't get far using conventional methods. At the time I was quite unable to go up against a squadron of Spalko's guards. So I came up with another solution.'

Khan's expression registered annoyance. He hated that this man knew more than he did. 'Which is?'

Bourne nodded in the direction of the grate.

'The drain?' Khan said incredulously.

'Why not?' Bourne knelt beside the grate. 'The diameter is large enough to get through.' He gestured as he snapped open the switchblade and inserted the blade between the grate and its flush housing. 'Why don't you give me a hand?'

As Khan knelt on the opposite side of the grate, Bourne used the knifeblade to raise it slightly. Khan lifted it up. Putting aside the switchblade, Bourne joined him and, together, they heaved the grate all the way up.

Khan could see Bourne wince with the effort. At that moment an eerie sensation rose in him, both strange and familiar, a kind of pride he was able to identify only at length and with considerable pain. It was an emotion he'd felt when he was a boy, before he'd wandered in shock, lost and abandoned, out of Phnom Penh. Since then, he'd so successfully walled it off that it hadn't been a problem for him. Until now.

They rolled the grate aside and Bourne took up some of the bloody bandage that Spalko had ripped off him and wrapped his cell phone. Then he put it and the closed switchblade in his pocket. 'Who'll go first?' he asked.

Khan shrugged, giving no sign that he was in any way impressed. He had a good idea where the drain led, and he believed Bourne did, too. 'It's your idea.'

Bourne levered himself into the circular hole. 'Wait ten seconds, then follow me down,' he said just before he vanished from sight.

Annaka was elated. As they sped toward the airport in Spalko's armor-plated limousine, she knew no one and nothing could stop them. Her last-minute ploy with Ethan Hearn hadn't been necessary, as it turned out, but she didn't regret the overture. It always paid to err on the side of caution, and at the time she'd decided to confront Hearn, Spalko's fate seemed to have hung in the balance. Looking over at him now, she knew that she never should have doubted him. He had the courage, skills and worldwide resources to pull off anything, even this audacious power coup. She had to admit that when he'd first told her what he planned, she'd been skeptical, and she'd remained so until he had engineered their successful emergence on the other side of the Danube through an old air-raid tunnel he'd discovered when he'd bought the building. When he'd started to renovate it, he'd successfully erased any notation of it from the architectural plans so that it remained, up until the moment he'd shown it to her, his personal secret.

The limo and driver had been waiting for them on the far side in the fiery glow of the late afternoon sunshine, and now they were speeding along the motorway toward Ferihegy Airport. She moved closer to Stepan, and when his charismatic face turned toward her, she took his hand briefly in hers. He'd stripped off the bloody butcher's apron and the Latex gloves somewhere in the tunnel. He wore jeans, a crisp white shirt and loafers. You'd never know he'd been up all night.

He smiled. 'I think a glass of champagne is called for, don't you?'

She laughed. 'You think of everything, Stepan.'

He indicated the flutes sitting in their niches on the inside panel of her door. They were crystal, not plastic. As she leaned forward to take them, he removed a split of champagne from a refrigerated compartment. Outside, the high-rises on either side of the motorway sped by, reflecting the orb of the lowering sun.

Spalko ripped off the foil, popped the cork and poured the foaming champagne into first one flute, then the other. He put down the bottle and they clinked glasses in a silent toast. They sipped together and she looked into his eyes. They were like brother and sister, closer even because neither carried with them the baggage of sibling rivalry. Of all the men she had known, she reflected, Stepan came closest to fulfilling her desires. Not that she'd ever longed for a mate. As a girl, a father would have suited her, but it was not to be. Instead, she'd chosen Stepan, strong, competent, invincible. He was everything a daughter would want from her father.

The high-rises were becoming less numerous as they passed through the outermost ring of the city. The light continued to lower as the sun set. The sky was high and ruddy and there was very little wind, conditions ripe for a perfect takeoff.

'How about a little music,' Spalko said, 'to go with our champagne moment?' His hand was raised to the multi-CD player embedded over his head. 'What would please you most? Bach? Beethoven? No, of course. Chopin.'

He chose the corresponding CD and his forefinger pressed a button. But instead of the lyrical melody typical of her favorite composer, she heard her own voice:

*'It isn't Interpol you work for – you don't have their habits. CIA, no, I don't think so. Stepan would know if the Americans were trying to penetrate his organization. So who then, hmm?'*

Annaka, her flute halfway to her partly open lips, froze.

*'Don't look so ashen, Ethan.'*

She saw, to her horror, Stepan grinning at her over the rim of his flute.

*'I don't care, really. I simply want an insurance policy in case things turn sour here. That insurance policy is you.'*

Spalko's finger hit the 'Stop' button, and save for the muffled thrumming of the limo's powerful engine, silence overtook them.

'I imagine you're wondering how I came by your treachery.'

Annaka found that she had temporarily lost the ability to speak. Her mind was frozen in place at the precise moment Stepan had very kindly asked her what music would please her most. More than anything in the world, she wanted to go back to that moment. Her shocked mind could only reflect on the split in her reality that had opened up like a yawning abyss at her feet. There was only her perfect life before Spalko had played the digital recording and the disaster it had become after he'd played it.

Was Stepan still smiling that awful crocodile smile? She found that she was having difficulty focusing. Without thinking, she swiped at her eyes.

'My God, Annaka, are those genuine tears?' Spalko shook his head ruefully. 'You've disappointed me, Annaka, though, to be perfectly honest, I'd been wondering when you'd betray me. On that point, your Mr. Bourne was quite correct.'

'Stepan, I – ' She stopped of her own accord. She hadn't recognized her own voice, and the last thing she would do was beg. Her life was miserable enough as it was.

He was holding something up between thumb and finger, a tiny disk, smaller even than a watch battery. 'An electronic listening device planted in Hearn's office.' He laughed shortly. 'The irony is that I didn't particularly suspect him. One of these is in every new employee's office, at least for the first six months.' He pocketed the disk with the flourish of a magician. 'Bad luck for you, Annaka. Good luck for me.'

Swallowing the rest of his champagne, he set the flute down. She still hadn't moved. Her back was straight, her right elbow cocked. Her fingers surrounded the rim of the flute's flared bottom.

He looked at her tenderly. 'You know, Annaka, if you were anyone else, you'd be dead by now. But we share a history, we share a mother, if you want to stretch a definition to its limit.' He cocked his head, putting the surface of his face in the last of the afternoon's light. The side of his face that was as poreless as plastic shone like the glass windows of the high-rises that were now far behind them. Very little in the way of habitation lay before them until they turned into the airport proper.

'I love you, Annaka.' One hand held her by her waist. 'I love you in a way I could never love anyone else.' The bullet from Bourne's gun made surprisingly little noise. Annaka's torso was thrown back into his welcoming arm and her head came up all at once. He could feel the tremor run through her and knew that the bullet must have lodged near her heart. His eyes never left hers. 'It really is a pity, isn't it?'

He felt the heat of her running over his hand, down onto the leather seat as her blood pooled. Her eyes seemed to be smiling, but there was no expression anywhere else on her face. Even at the point of death, he reflected, she had no fear. Well, that was something, wasn't it?

'Is everything all right, Mr. Spalko?' his driver asked from up front.

'It is now,' Stepan Spalko said.

# 27

The Danube was cold and dark. The grievously injured Bourne hit the river-water first, where the drain emptied out, but it was Khan who had difficulty. The extreme chill of the water was of no import to him, but the darkness brought to him the nightmarish horror of his recurring dream.

The shock of the water, the surface so distant above his head, caused him to feel as if his ankle was tied to the white semi-decomposed body, spinning slowly below him in the depth. Lee-Lee was calling to him, Lee-Lee wanted him to join her . . .

He felt himself tumbling into darkness, even deeper water. And then, quite suddenly and terrifyingly, he was being pulled. By Lee-Lee? he wondered in a panic.

All at once he felt the warmth of another body, large and, despite its wounds, still immensely powerful. He felt Bourne's arm circle his waist, the surge of Bourne's legs as he kicked them out of the swift current into which Khan had fallen, driving them upward toward the surface.

Khan seemed to be crying, or at least crying out, but when they breached the surface and made for the far shore, Khan struck out, as if he wanted nothing more than to punish Bourne, to beat him senseless. But all he could manage at the moment was to tear the encircling arm from around his waist and glare at Bourne as they pulled themselves against the stone embankment.

'What did you think you were doing?' Khan said. 'You almost caused me to drown!'

Bourne opened his mouth to answer him, but apparently thought better of it. Instead, he pointed downriver to where a vertical iron rose out of the water. Across the deep blue water of the Danube, fire trucks, ambulances and police cars still ringed the Humanistas, Ltd. building. Crowds had joined the knots of evacuated employees, surging like surf along the sidewalks, spilling through the streets, hanging out windows, craning their necks for a better angle. Boats sailing up and down the river were converging on the spot and even though members of the police force waved them away, the passengers rushed to the railing to get a closer look at what they thought might be a disaster in the making. But they were too late. It appeared that whatever fires had been started by the explosion in the elevator shaft had been extinguished.

Bourne and Khan, sticking to the shadows of the embankment, made their way to the ladder, which they climbed as quickly as they could. Lucky for them, all eyes were on the commotion at the Humanistas, Ltd. building. Several yards away, a section of the embankment was under repair and they were able to crawl into the sheltering shadows below street level but above the water-line, where the concrete had become undermined and was now shored up with pillars of heavy timber.

'Give me your phone,' Khan said. 'Mine's waterlogged.'

Bourne unwrapped Conklin's cell phone and handed it over.

Khan dialed Oszkar's cell phone and, when he reached him, told him where they were and what they required. He listened for a moment and then said to Bourne.

'Oszkar, my contact here in Budapest, is chartering us a flight. And he's getting you some antibiotics.'

Bourne nodded. 'Now let's see how good he really is. Tell him we need the schematics for the Oskjuhlid Hotel in Reykjavík.'

Khan glared at him and for a moment Bourne was afraid that he was going to hang up simply out of spite. He bit his lip. He'd have to remember to talk to Khan in a less confrontational manner.

Khan told Oszkar what they needed. 'It'll take about an hour,' he said.

'He didn't say "impossible"?' Bourne said.

'Oszkar never says "impossible."'

'My contacts couldn't have done better.'

A chill and fitful wind had sprung up, forcing them to move farther into their makeshift cave. Bourne took the opportunity to assess the damage Spalko had inflicted on him; Khan had done well in ministering to the punctures, which were numerous on his arms, chest and legs. Khan still had on his jacket. He now took it off and shook it out. As he did so, Bourne saw that the inside was composed of a number of pockets, all of which looked filled.

'What d'you have in there?' he asked.

'Tricks of the trade,' Khan said unhelpfully. He retreated into his own world by using Bourne's cell phone.

'Ethan, it's me,' he said. 'Is everything all right?'

'That depends,' Hearn said. 'In the mêlée, I discovered that my office was bugged.'

'Does Spalko know who you work for?'

'I never mentioned your name. Anyway, mostly my calls to you were out of the office.'

'Still, it would be wise for you to leave.'

'My thoughts exactly,' Hearn said. 'I'm happy to hear your voice. After the explosions I didn't know what to think.'

'Have a little faith,' Khan said. 'How much d'you have on him?'

'Enough.'

'Take everything you have and get out now. I will have my revenge on him no matter what happens.'

He heard Hearn take a breath, 'What's that supposed to mean?'

'It means I want a backup. If for some reason you can't get the material to me, I want you to contact – hold on a moment.' He turned to Bourne and said, 'Is there someone at the Agency who can be trusted with intel on Spalko?'

Bourne shook his head, then immediately reconsidered. He thought about what Conklin had told him about the Deputy Director – that he was not only fair-minded but that he was his own man. 'Martin Lindros,' he said.

Khan nodded and repeated the name to Hearn, then he closed the connection and handed back the phone.

Bourne felt in a quandary. He wanted to find some way to connect with Khan, but he didn't know how. Finally, he hit upon the idea of asking him how he had reached the interrogation room. He felt a relief when Khan began to talk. He told Bourne about hiding in the sofa, the explosion in the elevator shaft and his escape from the bolted room. He did not, however, mention Annaka's treachery.

Bourne listened with mounting fascination, but even so, part of him remained detached, as if this conversation was happening to someone else. He was shying away from Khan; the psychic wounds were too raw. He recognized that in his present debilitated state, he was as yet mentally unprepared to tackle the questions and doubts that flooded him. And so the two of them talked fitfully and awkwardly, always skirting the central issue that lay between them like a castle that could besieged but not taken.

An hour later Oszkar arrived in his company van with towels and blankets and new clothes, along with an antibiotic for Bourne. He gave them a Thermos of hot coffee to drink. They climbed into the backseat, and while they changed, he bundled up their torn and sodden clothes, all except Khan's remarkable jacket. Then he gave them bottled water and food, which they wolfed down.

If he was surprised at the sight of Bourne's wounds, he didn't show it, and Khan assumed that he'd worked out that the assault had been a success. He presented Bourne with a lightweight laptop computer.

'The schematics for every system and subsystem in the hotel have been downloaded to the hard drive,' he said, 'as well as maps of Reykjavík and the surrounding area and some basic information I thought might come in handy.'

'I'm impressed.' Bourne said this to Oszkar, but he meant it for Khan, too.

Martin Lindros got the call just after eleven A.M. Eastern Daylight Time. He jumped into his car and made the fifteen-minute drive to George Washington Hospital in just under eight minutes. Detective Harry Harris was in the E.R. Lindros used his credentials to cut through the red tape so that one of the harried residents took him over to the bed. Lindros pulled aside the curtain that ran around three sides of the emergency room station, pulled it shut behind him.

'What the hell happened to you?' he said.

Harris eyed him as best he could from his propped-up position on the bed. His face was puffy and discolored. His upper lip was split and there was a gash under his left eye that had been stitched.

'I got fired – that's what happened.'

Lindros shook his head. 'I don't understand.'

'The National Security Advisor called my boss. Directly. Herself. She demanded I be fired. Dismissed without compensation or pension. This is what he told me when he summoned me to his office yesterday.'

Lindros' hands curled into fists. 'And then?'

'What d'you mean? He fired my ass. Disgraced me after the spotless career I've had.'

'I mean,' Lindros said, 'how did you wind up here?'

'Oh, that.' Harris turned his head to one side, looking at nothing. 'I got drunk, I guess.'

'You guess?'

Harris turned back to him, his eyes blazing. 'I got very drunk, okay? I think it was the least I deserved.'

'But you got more than that.'

'Yah. There was an argument with a couple of bikers, if I remember right, which escalated into something of a brawl.'

'I suppose you think you deserved to get beaten to a pulp.'

Harris said nothing.

Lindros passed a hand across his face. 'I know I promised you I'd take care of this, Harry. I thought I had it under control, even the DCI had come around, more or less. I just didn't figure on the NSA making a preemptive strike.'

'Fuck her,' Harris said. 'Fuck everyone.' He laughed bitterly. 'It's like my ma used to say, "No good deed goes unpunished."'

'Look, Harry, I never would've cracked this Schiffer thing without you. I'm not going to abandon you now. I'll get you out of this.'

'Yeah? I'd like the fuck to know how.'

'As Hannibal, one of my military icons, once famously said, "We will either find a way or make one."'

When they were ready, Oszkar drove them to the airport. Bourne, whose body was racked with pain, was happy to let someone else drive. Still, he remained on operational alert. He was pleased to see that Oszkar was using his mirrors to check for tags. No one appeared to be following them.

Up ahead, he could see the airport's control tower, and a moment later Oszkar turned off the motorway. There were no cops in sight. Nothing seemed out of place. Still, he could feel the vibrations start up inside him.

No one came for them as they cruised through the airport roads, heading toward the charter services airfield. The aircraft was waiting, ready and fueled. They got out of the van. Before he left, Bourne gripped Oszkar's hand. 'Thanks again.'

'No problem,' Oszkar said with a smile. 'It all goes on the bill.'

He drove off and they went up the stairs and into the aircraft.

The pilot welcomed them aboard, then pulled up the stairs and closed and locked the door. Bourne told him their destination and five minutes later they were taxiing down the runway, lifting off for their two-hour, ten-minute flight to Reykjavík.

'We'll be coming up on the fishing boat in three minutes,' the pilot said.

Spalko adjusted the electronic earbud, picked up Sido's refrigerated box and went to the rear of the plane and shrugged himself into the harness. As he tightened the cinches, he stared at the back of Peter Sido's head. Sido was handcuffed to his seat. One of Spalko's armed men was in the seat next to him.

'You know where to take him,' he said softly to the pilot.

'Yessir. It won't be anywhere near Greenland.'

Spalko went to the rear doorway, signaled to his man, who rose and walked back up the narrow aisle to join him.

'Are you all right for fuel?'

'Yessir,' the pilot answered. 'My calculation's right on the money.'

Spalko peered out the small round window in the door. They were lower now, the North Atlantic blue-black, the wave crests a sure sign of its vaunted turbulence.

'Thirty seconds, sir,' the pilot said. 'There's a pretty stiff wind from the north-northeast. Sixteen knots.'

'Roger that.' Spalko could feel the slowing of their airspeed. He was wearing a 7-mm survival dry suit under his clothes. Unlike a diver's wet suit, which relied on a thin layer of water between the body and the neoprene suit to keep body temperature up, this was sealed at the feet and the wrists to keep the water out. Inside the trilaminate shell he wore a Thermal Protection System Thinsulate undersuit for added protection against the cold. Still, unless he timed his landing perfectly, the impact of the freezing water could paralyze him and even with the protection of the suit that would prove fatal. Nothing could go wrong. He attached the box to his left wrist with a locking chain and drew on his dry gloves.

'Fifteen seconds,' the pilot said. 'Wind constant.'

*Good, no gusts,* Spalko thought. He nodded to his man, who pulled down on the huge lever and swung open the door. The howling of the wind filled the interior of the aircraft. There was nothing below him but thirteen thousand feet of air, and then the ocean, which would be as hard as concrete if he hit it at the rate of free fall.

'Go!' the pilot said.

Spalko jumped. There was a rushing in his ears, the wind against his face. He arched his body. Within eleven seconds he was falling at 110 miles per hour, terminal velocity. And yet he didn't feel as if he was falling. Rather, the sensation was one of something softly pressing against him.

He looked down, saw the fishing boat and, using the air pressure, moved himself horizontally to compensate for the sixteen-knot north-by-northeast wind. Aligning himself, he checked his wrist altimeter. At twenty-five hundred feet he pulled the rip cord, felt the gentle tug at his shoulders, the soft rustle of nylon as the canopy deployed above him. All at once the ten square feet of air resistance his body had provided had been transformed into 250 square feet of drag. He was now descending at a leisurely sixteen feet per second.

Above him was the luminous bowl of the sky; below him spread the vastness of the North Atlantic, restless, heaving, sheened to beaten brass by the late afternoon sunlight. He saw the fishing boat bobbing and, far off, the jutting curve of the Icelandic peninsula upon which Reykjavík was built. The wind was a constant tug, and for a time he was busy compensating by repeatedly flaring the canopy. He breathed deeply, relishing the pillowy sensation of the drop.

He seemed suspended, then in a shell of endless blue he thought of the meticulous planning, the years of hard work, maneuvering and manipulation by which he'd reached this point, what he'd come to view as the pinnacle of his life. He thought of his year in America, in tropical Miami, the painful procedures to remake and remodel his ruined face. He had to admit that he'd enjoyed telling Annaka the story of his fictional brother, but then again, how else would he have explained his presence in the asylum? He could never tell her that he was having a passionate affair with her mother. It was a simple matter to bribe the doctors and nurses into giving him private time with their patient. How utterly corrupt human beings are, he reflected. Much of his success had been built on taking advantage of that principle.

What an amazing woman Sasa had been! He'd never met her like before or since. Quite naturally, he'd made the assumption that Annaka would be like her mother. Of course, he'd been much younger then and his foolishness could be forgiven.

What would Annaka have thought, he wondered now, if he'd told her the truth, that years ago he'd slaved for a crime boss, a vindictive, sadistic monster who'd sent him out on a vendetta knowing full well that it could be a trap. It was – and Spalko's face was the result of it. He'd gotten his revenge on Vladimir, but not in the heroic manner he'd painted for Zina. It was shameful what he'd done, but in those days he'd lacked the power to act on his own. But not now.

He was more than five hundred feet in the air when the wind abruptly reversed itself. He began to sail away from the boat, and he worked the canopy to minimize the effect. Still, he was unable to reverse his course. Below him, he could see the flash of reflection on board the fishing boat and knew that the crew was carefully monitoring his descent. The boat began to move with him.

The horizon was higher, and now the ocean was coming up fast, filling the entire world as his perspective changed. The wind suddenly died, and he came down, flaring his canopy at just the right instant, making his landing as soft as possible.

His legs went in first and then he was under the water. Even mentally prepared as he was, the shock of the freezing water struck a hammerblow that drove all the breath from him. The weight of the refrigerated box pulled him quickly under, but he compensated with powerful, practiced scissor-kicks. He surfaced with a swing of his head and took a deep breath while he shed his harness.

He could hear the grinding churn of the fishing boat's engines echoing in the deep, and without even bothering to look, he struck out in that direction. The swells were so high and the current so swift that he soon abandoned the notion of swimming as futile. By the time the boat came alongside, he was near to being spent. Without the protection of the dry suit, he knew he would have gone into hypothermia by now.

A crew member threw him a line and a rope ladder was cast over the side. He grabbed the line and held on with all his strength as they pulled him to the side where the ladder hung down. He climbed up it, the ocean a constant drag on him until the very last instant.

A strong hand reached down, helping him over the side. He looked up, saw a face with piercing blue eyes and thick blond hair.

'*La illaha ill Allah.*' Hasan Arsenov said. 'Welcome aboard, Shaykh.' Spalko stood back while crew members wrapped him in absorbent blankets. '*La illaha ill Allah,*' he replied. 'I almost didn't recognize you.'

'When I first looked at myself in the mirror after I'd bleached my hair,' Arsenov said, 'I didn't either.'

Spalko peered at the terrorist leader's face. 'How do the contact lenses feel?'

'None of us have had a problem.' Arsenov could not take his eyes off the metal box the Shaykh was holding. 'It's here.'

Spalko nodded. He glanced over Arsenov's shoulder and saw Zina standing in the last of the sunlight. Her golden hair streamed out behind her and her cobalt eyes watched his with an avid intensity.

'Head for shore,' Spalko told the crew. 'I want to change into dry clothes.'

He went below into the forward cabin, where clothes had been neatly stacked on a berth. A pair of sturdy black shoes were on the deck beneath. He unlocked the box and set it on the berth. As he stripped off his sopping clothes and peeled off the dry suit, he glanced at his wrist to see how badly the cuff had abraded his skin. Then he rubbed his palms together until he'd returned full circulation to his hands.

While his back was turned, the door opened and just as quickly closed. He did not turn around, did not need to see who'd entered the cabin.

'Let me warm you up,' Zina said in honeyed tones.

A moment later he felt the press of her breasts, the heat from her loins against his back and buttocks. The exhilaration of the jump was still running high through him. It had been heightened by the final denouement to his long relationship with Annaka Vadas, making Zina's advance irresistible.

He turned, sat back on the edge of the berth and allowed her to climb all over him. She was like an animal in heat. He saw the glitter of her eyes, heard the guttural sounds he pulled from her belly. She had lost herself in him, and he was for the moment satisfied.

Approximately ninety minutes later Jamie Hull was below street level, checking the security at the Oskjuhlid Hotel's delivery entrance when he caught sight of Comrade Boris. The Russian security chief evinced surprise at Hull's presence, but Hull wasn't fooled. He'd had a feeling that Boris had been shadowing him of late, but maybe he was just being paranoid. Not that he wouldn't be justified. All the principals were in the hotel. Tomorrow morning at eight A.M. the summit would begin and the time of maximum risk would be upon him. He dreaded the thought that somehow Comrade Boris had gotten wind of what Feyd al-Saoud had discovered, what he and the Arab security chief had concocted.

And so as not to let Comrade Boris get an inkling of the dread in his heart, he put a smile on his face, preparing himself to eat a bite or two of American crow if he had to. Anything now to keep Comrade Boris in the dark.

'Working overtime, I see, my good Mr. Hull,' Karpov said in his booming announcer's voice. 'No rest for the weary, eh?'

'Time enough for rest when the summit's concluded and our job is done.'

'But our job is never done.' Karpov, Hull saw, was wearing one of his very bad serge suits. It looked more like a suit of armor than anything in the least bit fashionable. 'No matter how much we accomplish, there is always more to do. That's one of the charms of what we do, no?'

Hull felt himself wanting to say no just to be argumentative, but he bit his tongue instead.

'And how is security here?' Karpov was looking around with his beady raven's eyes. 'Up to your high American standards, one hopes?'

'I've only just begun.'

'Then you'll welcome some help, no? Two heads are better than one, four eyes are better than two.'

Hull was abruptly weary. He could no longer remember how long he'd been here in this godforsaken country or when he'd last had a decent night's sleep. Not even a single tree to tell you what time of year it was! A kind of disorientation had set in, the sort from which first-time submariners were said sometimes to suffer.

Hull watched the security team stop a food service truck, question the driver and climb into the back to check its load. He could find no fault with either the procedure or the methodology.

'Don't you find this place depressing?' he asked Boris.

'Depressing? This is a fucking wonderland, my friend,' Karpov boomed. 'Spend a winter in Siberia if you want a definition of depressing.'

Hull frowned. 'You were sent to Siberia?'

Karpov laughed. 'Yes, but not in the way you think. I was operational up there several years ago when the tension with China was at its peak. You know, secret military maneuverings, clandestine intelligence gathering, all in the darkest, coldest place you can imagine.' Karpov grunted. 'Or, being American, I suppose you're incapable of imagining such a thing.'

Hull kept the smile stitched to his face, but it cost him in both pent-up anger and self-esteem. Happily, another van was rolling in, the food service vehicle having passed muster. This one was from Reykjavík Energy. For some reason, it seemed to have piqued Comrade Boris' interest, and Hull followed him over to where the van was stopped. Inside were two uniformed men.

Karpov took the call sheet the driver had dutifully handed over to one of the security personnel, glanced down at it. 'What's this all about?' he said in his typically overaggressive manner.

'Quarterly geothermal checkup,' the driver said blandly.

'This has to be done now?' Karpov glared at the blond driver.

'Yes, sir. Our system is interconnected throughout the city. If we don't perform periodic maintenance, we put the entire network at risk.'

'Well, we can't have that,' Hull said. He nodded to one of the security men. 'Check inside. If it's all clear, let them through.'

He walked away from the van and Karpov followed.

'You don't like this work,' Karpov said, 'do you?'

Forgetting himself for a moment, Hull turned on his heel and confronted the Russian. 'I like it just fine.' Then he remembered, and grinned boyishly. 'Nah, you're right. I'd much rather be using my more, shall we say, physical skills.'

Karpov nodded, apparently mollified. 'I understand. There's no feeling like a good kill.'

'Exactly,' Hull said, warming to his task. 'Take this newest sanction, for instance. What I wouldn't give to be the one to find Jason Bourne and put a bullet through his brain.'

Karpov's caterpillar eyebrows lifted. 'For you, this sanction sounds personal. You should beware such emotionalism, my friend. It clouds good judgment.'

'Fuck that,' Hull said. 'Bourne had what I wanted most, what I should've had.'

Karpov considered for a moment. 'It seems that I've misjudged you, my good friend Mr. Hull. It seems that you're more of a warrior than I thought.' He clapped the American on the back. 'What d'you say to trading war stories over a bottle of vodka?'

'I think that sounds doable,' Hull said, as the Reykjavík Energy van rolled inside the hotel.

Stepan Spalko, in a Reykjavík Energy uniform, colored contact lenses in his eyes and a piece of molded Latex making his nose wide and ugly, stepped out of the van and told the driver to wait. With a work order on a clipboard in one hand and a small toolbox in the other, he went through the labyrinth in the hotel's belly. The plan of the hotel floated in his mind like a three-dimensional overlay. He knew his way around the vast complex better than many of the employees whose work confined them to a single area.

It took him twelve minutes to reach the section of the hotel that housed the space that would serve as the summit's venue. In that time, he was stopped four times by security guards even though he was wearing his ID clipped to his overalls. He took the stairs, went down three levels below ground, where he was stopped once again. He was near enough to a thermal heat junction to make his presence there plausible. Still, he was near enough to the HVAC substation that the guard insisted on accompanying him.

Spalko stopped at an electrical junction box and opened it. He could feel the guard's scrutiny like a hand at his throat.

'You've been here how long?' he said in Icelandic as he opened the box he was carrying.

'D'you speak Russian, maybe?' the guard replied.

'As a matter of fact, I do.' Spalko rummaged around in the box. 'You've been here, what, two weeks now?'

'Three,' the guard admitted.

'And in all that time, have you seen anything of my wonderful Iceland?' He found what he wanted in among all the junk and palmed it. 'Do you know anything about it?'

The Russian shook his head, which was Spalko's cue to launch into his discourse. 'Well, let me enlighten you then. Iceland is an island of 103,000 square kilometers at an average height of 500 meters above sea level. Its highest peak, Hvannadalshnúkur, rises to 2,119 meters and over 11 percent of the country is covered by glaciers, including Vatnajökull, the largest in Europe. We're governed by the Althing, whose 63 members are elected every four – '

His voice died out as the guard, unutterably bored by the guidebook babble, turned his back and moved away. Instantly he got to work, taking the small disk and pressing it against two sets of wires until he was sure its four contacts had penetrated the insulation.

'All done here,' he said, slamming the junction box closed.

'Now where? The thermal housing?' the guard said, clearly hoping this stint would be over soon.

'Nah,' Spalko said. 'I've got to check in with my boss first. I'm off to the van.' He waved as he left, but the guard was already walking in the other direction.

Spalko returned to the van, climbed in, and there he sat next to the driver until a security guard wandered up.

'Okay, guys, what's up?'

'We're finished here for the time being.' Spalko smiled winningly as he made some meaningless marks on his bogus worksheet. He checked his watch. 'Hey, we were here longer than I thought. Thanks for checking up.'

'Hey, it's my job.'

As the driver turned on the ignition and put the van in gear, Spalko said, 'Here's the value of making a dry run. We'll have precisely thirty minutes before they come looking for us.'

The chartered jet flung itself through the sky. Across from Bourne sat Khan, staring straight ahead, looking, it seemed, at nothing. Bourne closed his eyes. The overhead lights had been turned off. A few reading lights cast oval pools of illumination in the dark. In an hour they'd be touching down at Keflavík Airport.

Bourne sat very still. He wanted to put his head in his hands and weep bitter tears for the sins of the past, but with Khan across the aisle he couldn't show anything that might be misinterpreted as weakness. The tentative detente they'd managed to achieve seemed as fragile as an eggshell. There were so many things that had the potential to crush it. Emotions churned in his chest, making it difficult to breathe. The pain he felt all through his tortured body was as nothing compared to the anguish that threatened to rend his heart asunder. He grasped the armrests so hard that his knuckles cracked. He knew he had to gain control of himself, just as he knew that he couldn't sit in his seat a moment longer.

He rose and, like a sleepwalker, slipped across the aisle and lowered himself into the seat next to Khan. The young man did not in any way register the fact of Bourne's presence. He might have been deep in meditation, save for the rapid rate of his breathing.

With his heart hammering painfully against his cracked ribs, Bourne said softly, 'If you're my son, I want to know it. If you really are Joshua, I *need* to know it.'

'In other words, you don't believe me.'

'I *want* to believe you,' Bourne said, trying to ignore the by-now familiar knife-edge of Khan's voice. 'Surely you must know that.'

'When it comes to you, I know less than nothing.' Khan turned to him, the hammer of his rage all in his face. 'Don't you remember me at all?'

'Joshua was six, just a child.' Bourne felt his emotions rising again, ready to choke him. 'And then some years ago I suffered amnesia.'

'Amnesia?' This revelation seemed to startle Khan.

Bourne told him what had happened. 'I remember little of my life as Jason Bourne before that time,' he concluded, 'and virtually nothing about my life as David Webb, except when now and again a scent or the sound of a voice dislodges something and I recall a fragment. But that's all it is, discontinuous from a whole that's forever lost to me.'

Bourne tried to find Khan's dark eyes in the low light, searched for the hint of an expression, even the barest clue as to what Khan might be thinking or feeling. 'It's true. We're complete strangers to each other. So before we go on . . .' He broke off, for the moment unable to continue. Then he steeled himself, forcing himself to speak because the silence that was so quick to build between them was worse than the explosion that would surely come. 'Try to understand. I need some tangible proof, something irrefutable.'

'Fuck you!'

Khan stood up, about to step over Bourne into the aisle, but again, as in Spalko's interrogation room, something held him fast. And then, unbidden, he heard Bourne's voice in his head, spoken on a rooftop in Budapest: *'That's your plan, isn't it? This whole sick story about you being Joshua. . . . I won't lead you to this Spalko or whoever it is you're planning to get to. I won't be anyone's cat's-paw again.'*

Khan gripped the carved stone Buddha around his neck and sat back down. They'd both been Stepan Spalko's cat's-paws. It was Spalko who'd brought them together and now, ironically, it was their shared enmity of Spalko that might conceivably keep them together, at least for the time being.

'There *is* something,' he said in a voice he barely recognized. 'A recurring nightmare I have of being underwater. I'm being drowned, pulled deeper because I'm tied to her dead body. She's calling to me, I hear her voice calling to me, or else it's my voice calling to her.'

Bourne recalled Khan's thrashing in the Danube, the panic that had swirled him deeper into the pull of the current. 'What does the voice say?'

'It's *my* voice. I'm saying "Lee-Lee, Lee-Lee."'

Bourne felt his heart skip a beat, for up from the depths of his own damaged memory swam Lee-Lee. For one precious moment only he could see her oval face with his light eyes and Dao's straight black hair. 'Oh, God,' Bourne whispered. 'Lee-Lee was Joshua's nickname for Alyssa. No one else called her that. No one else but Dao knew.'

*Lee-Lee.*

'One of the powerful memories of those days that, with a great deal of help, I've been able to recall is how your sister looked up to you,' Bourne went on. 'She'd always wanted to be close to you. At night, when she went through a bout of night-terrors, you were the only one who could calm her down. You called her Lee-Lee and she called you Joshy.'

*My sister, yes. Lee-Lee.* Khan closed his eyes and immediately he was under the murky water of the river in Phnom Penh. Half-drowned, in shock, he'd seen her tumbling toward him, the shot-up corpse of his little sister. Lee-Lee. Four years old. Dead. Her light eyes – their Daddy's eyes – staring sightlessly at him, accusingly. *Why you?* she seemed to say. *Why was it you and not me?* But he knew that was his own guilt talking. If Lee-Lee could have spoken, she would've said, *I'm glad you didn't die, Joshy. I'm so happy one of us stayed to be with Daddy.*

Khan put his hand to his face, turned away toward the Perspex window. He wanted to die, he wished he *had* died in the river, that it had been Lee-Lee who'd survived. He couldn't stand this life one second more. There was, after all, nothing left for him. In death, at least, he would join her . . .

'Khan.'

It was Bourne's voice. But he couldn't face him, couldn't even look him in the eye. He hated him and he loved him. He couldn't understand how this could be; he was ill equipped to deal with this emotional anomaly. With a strangled sound, he rose and pushed past him, staggering up to the front of the aircraft where he wouldn't have to see Bourne.

With an inexpressible sorrow, Bourne watched his son go. It took an enormous effort to rein in the impulse to pull him back, to put his arms around him and hug him to his chest. He sensed that would be the worst thing he could do now, that, given Khan's history, it might lead to renewed violence between them.

He had no illusions. They both had a hard road to travel before they could accept each other as family. It could even be an impossible task. But because he wasn't in the habit of thinking anything was impossible, he set that frightening thought aside.

In a rush of anguish he realized at last why he'd spent so much time denying that Khan might, in fact, be his son. Annaka, damn her, had nailed it perfectly.

At that moment he looked up. Khan was standing over him, his hands gripping the seatback in front of him as if for dear life.

'You said that you just found out that I was MIA.'

Bourne nodded.

'How long did they look for me?' Khan said.

'You know I can't answer that. No one can.' Bourne had lied on instinct. There was nothing to be gained and much to be lost by telling Khan that the authorities had only searched for one hour. He was acutely conscious of wanting to protect his son from the truth.

An ominous stillness had come over Khan, as if he were preparing for an act of terrible consequence. 'Why didn't *you* check?'

Bourne heard the accusatory tone and sat as if poleaxed. His blood ran cold. Ever since it became clear that Khan could be Joshua, he'd been asking himself the same question.

'I was half-mad with grief,' he said, 'but I don't think now that's a good enough excuse. I couldn't face the fact that I'd failed you all as a father.'

Something in Khan's face shifted, showing what was akin to a spasm of pain, as an ominous thought wormed its way up to the surface. 'You must've had . . . difficulties when you and my mother were together in Phnom Penh.'

'What d'you mean?' Bourne, alarmed by Khan's expression, responded in a tone that was perhaps sharper than it ought to have been.

'You know. Didn't you hear it from your colleagues because you were married to a Thai?'

'I loved Dao with all my heart.'

'Marie isn't Thai, is she?'

'Khan, we don't choose whom we fall in love with.'

There was a short pause, and then, into the charged silence that had sprung up between them, Khan said, as casually as if it were an afterthought, 'And then there was the matter of your two mixed-race children.'

'I never saw it that way,' Bourne said flatly. His heart was breaking, for he heard the silent cry that underlay this line of questioning. 'I loved Dao, I loved you and Alyssa. My God, you were all my life. In the weeks and months afterward, I nearly lost my mind. I was devastated, uncertain whether or not I wanted to go on. If not for meeting Alex Conklin, I might not have. Even so, it took years of agonizingly hard work to recover sufficiently.'

He fell silent for a moment, listening to them both breathe. Then he took a deep breath and said, 'What I've always believed, always struggled with is that I should've been there to protect you.'

Khan regarded him for a long time, but the tension had been broken, some Rubicon had been crossed. 'If you'd been there, you would've been killed, too.'

He turned away without another word, and as he did so, Bourne saw Dao in his eyes and knew that in some profound way the world had changed.

# 28

Reykjavík, like any other civilized place on earth, had its fair share of fast food restaurants. Each day these establishments as well as the more upscale restaurants received shipments of fresh meats, fish, vegetables and fruit. Hafnarfjördur Fine Fruits & Vegetables was one of the main suppliers to the fast-food industry in Reykjavík. The company's van that had pulled up to the Kebab Höllin in City Centre early that morning with a delivery of leaf lettuce, pearl onions and scallions was one of many that had fanned out through the city on their daily rounds. The crucial difference was that, unlike all the others, this particular van had not been dispatched by Hafnarfjördur Fine Fruits & Vegetables.

By early evening all three sites of the Landspitali University Hospital were besieged by people who were increasingly ill. Doctors admitted these patients in alarming numbers even as they ran tests on their blood. By dinnertime the results confirmed that the city had a virulent outbreak of hepatitis A on its hands.

Health department officials frenziedly went to work to deal with the burgeoning crisis. Their job was hampered by several important factors: the quickness and severity of the onset of the particularly virulent strain of the virus, the complexities associated with trying to track which foodstuffs might be involved and where its source might be, and unspoken but much on their minds was the intense world-wide spotlight trained on Reykjavík by the international summit. High on their list of suspect foods were scallions, the culprits in the recent outbreaks of hepatitis A in the United States, but scallions were fairly ubiquitous in the local fast food chains, and of course they couldn't rule out meats or fish.

They worked into the twilit night, interviewing the owners of every company that specialized in fresh vegetables, sending their own staff out to inspect the warehouses, storage containers and vans of each firm, including Hafnarfjördur Fine Fruits & Vegetables. However, much to their surprise and dismay, they found nothing amiss, and as the hours swept by, they were forced to admit that they were no closer to finding the source of the outbreak than when they had started.

Accordingly, just after nine P.M., health department officials went public with their findings. Reykjavík was under a hepatitis A alert. Because they hadn't yet found the source of the infection, they put the city under quarantine. Over all their heads was the specter of a full-blown epidemic, something they could not afford with the terrorism summit beginning and the entire world's attention focused on the capital. In their television and radio interviews, the officials sought to reassure an uneasy public that they were taking every measure to gain control over the virus. To that end, they said repeatedly, the department was devoting its entire staff to the ongoing safety of the public at large.

It was just before ten P.M. when Jamie Hull walked down the hotel corridor to the president's suite in a high state of agitation. First, there was the sudden outbreak of hepatitis A to worry about. Then he was summoned to an unscheduled briefing with the president.

He looked around and saw the Secret Service men who were guarding the president. Farther down the corridor were the Russian FSB and Arab security guarding their leaders, who, for the sake of security and the ease of housing their staffs, had been assigned to one wing of the hotel.

He went through the door guarded by a pair of Secret Service guards, huge and impassive as sphinxes, and into the suite. The president was prowling restlessly back and forth, dictating to a pair of his speechwriters as the press secretary looked on, scribbling hurried notes on a tablet computer. Three more Secret Service men stood by. They were keeping the president away from the windows.

He cooled his heels without protest until the president dismissed the press people, and like mice, they scurried off to another room.

'Jamie,' the president said with a big smile and an extended hand. 'Good of you to come.' He squeezed Hull's hand, gestured for him to sit, then took a seat across from him.

'Jamie, I'm counting on you to help bring this summit off without a hitch,' he said.

'Sir, I can assure you that I have everything under control.'

'Even Karpov?'

'Sir?'

The president smiled. 'I heard that you and Mr. Karpov have been going at it pretty good.'

Hull swallowed hard, wondering if he'd been brought in to be fired. 'There was some minor friction,' he said tentatively, 'but that's all in the past.'

'I'm glad to hear it,' the president said. 'I'm having enough difficulties with Aleksandr Yevtushenko as it is. I don't need him pissed off at me over a slight to his number-one security chief.' He slapped his thighs and rose. 'Well, showtime is eight o'clock this morning. There's still a lot to prepare for.' He stuck out his hand as Hull rose. 'Jamie, no one knows better than I how perilous this situation might become. But I think we're agreed that there's no turning back now.'

Outside in the corridor Hull's cell phone rang.

'Jamie, where are you?' the DCI barked in his ear.

'I just came out of a briefing with the president. He was pleased to hear that I have everything under control, including Comrade Karpov.'

But instead of sounding pleased, the DCI forged on in a tense urgent tone. 'Jamie, listen to me carefully. There's another aspect to this situation, which is given strictly on a need-to-know basis.'

Hull automatically looked around and walked quickly out of earshot of the Secret Service guards. 'I appreciate your confidence in me, sir.'

'It concerns Jason Bourne,' the DCI said. 'He wasn't killed in Paris.'

'What?' For a moment Hull lost his composure. 'Bourne's *alive*?'

'Alive and kicking.'

'Jamie, just so we're on the same page, this call, this conversation, never happened. If you ever mention it to anyone, I'll deny it ever took place and I'll have your ass in a sling, are we clear?'

'Perfectly sir.'

'I have no idea what Bourne is going to do next, but I always believed that he was heading your way. He may or may not have killed Alex Conklin and Mo Panov, but he sure as hell killed Kevin McColl.'

'Jesus. I knew McColl, sir.'

'We all did, Jamie.' The Old Man cleared his throat. 'We can't allow that act to go unpunished.'

All at once Hull's rage vanished, to be replaced by a sense of high elation. 'Leave it to me.'

'Use caution, Jamie. Your first order of business is keeping the president safe.'

'I understand, sir. Absolutely. But you can be sure that if Jason Bourne shows up, he won't leave the hotel.'

'Well, I trust he will,' the Old Man said. 'Feet first.'


Two members of the Chechen cadre were waiting in front of the Reykjavík Energy van when the health services vehicle, dispatched to the Oskjuhlid Hotel, came around the corner. The van was parked crosswise in the street and they had placed orange plastic work cones around and seemed hard at work.

The health services vehicle came to an abrupt halt.

'What are you doing?' one of the health services people said. 'This is an emergency.'

'Fuck you, little man!' one of the Chechen answered in Icelandic.

'What did you say?' The irate health services worker climbed out of his vehicle.

'Are you blind? We have important work here,' the Chechen said. 'Use another fucking route.'

Sensing a situation that could turn ugly, the second man got out of the health services vehicle. Arsenov and Zina, armed and intent, emerged from the back of the Reykjavík Energy van and herded the suddenly cowed health services workers into the van.


Arsenov and Zina and one other member of the cadre arrived at the delivery entrance to the Oskjuhlid Hotel in the hijacked vehicle. The other Chechen had taken the Reykjavík Energy van to pick up Spalko and the remainder of the cadre.

They were dressed as government employees and presented the health department ID tags that Spalko had procured at great expense to the security detail on duty. When queried, Arsenov spoke in Icelandic, then changed to halting English when the American and Arab security people couldn't understand him. He said that they had been sent to ensure that the hotel kitchen was free of hepatitis A. No one – least of all the various security teams – wanted any of the dignitaries to come down with the dread virus. With all due dispatch, they were admitted and directed to the kitchen. This was where the cadre member went, but Arsenov and Zina had other destinations in mind.

Bourne and Khan were still scrutinizing the schematics of the various Oskjuhlid Hotel subsystems when the pilot announced that they were landing at Keflavík Field. Bourne, who had been pacing back and forth while Khan sat with the laptop, reluctantly took his seat. His body ached horribly, which the aircraft's cramped seating had only exacerbated. He'd tried to put on hold the feelings that had come up in connection with finding his son. Their conversations were awkward enough as it was, and he had the distinct impression that Khan would instinctively shy away from any strong emotion he might show.

The process of working toward a reconciliation was immensely difficult for both of them. Still, he suspected, it was worse for Khan. What a son needed from his father was far more complex than what a father needed from his son in order to love him unconditionally.

Bourne had to admit that he was afraid of Khan, not only of what had been done to him, of what he had become, but of his prowess, his cleverness and ingenuity. How he had escaped from the bolted room was a marvel in and of itself.

And there was something else as well, a stumbling block to their accepting each other and perhaps eventually reconciling, which dwarfed all the other obstacles. In order to accept Bourne, Khan had to give up everything his life had been.

In this Bourne was correct. Ever since Bourne had sat down next to him on the park bench in Old Town Alexandria, Khan had been a man at war with himself. He still was, the only difference being that now the war was in the open. As if staring into a rear-view mirror, Khan could see all the opportunities he'd had to kill Bourne, but it was only now that he understood that his decision not to take them had been deliberate. He couldn't harm Bourne, but he couldn't open his heart to him either. He remembered the desperate urge he'd felt to launch himself at Spalko's men at the rear of the clinic in Budapest. The only thing that had stopped him was Bourne's warning. At the time he'd put his feelings down to his desire for revenge against Spalko. But now he knew that it stemmed from another emotion entirely: the devotion one family member has for another.

And yet, to his shame, he realized that he was afraid of Bourne. He was a fearsome man in strength, endurance and intellect. Being near him, Khan felt somehow diminished, as if whatever he'd managed to accomplish in his life was as dust.

With a roll, a bump and a brief squeal of rubber, they were down and taxiing off the active runway toward the far end of the airport, where all private aircraft were directed. Khan was up and heading down the aisle to the door before they had come to a halt.

'Let's go,' he said. 'Spalko already has at least a three-hour start on us.'

But Bourne had also risen and was standing in the aisle to oppose him.

'There's no telling what's waiting for us out there. I'll go out first.'

Immediately, Khan's anger, so near the surface, flared. 'I told you once – don't tell me what to do! I have my own mind; I make my own decisions. I always have and I always will.'

'You're right. I'm not trying to take anything away from you,' Bourne said with his heart in his mouth. This stranger was his son. Everything he said or did around him would have exaggerated consequences for some time to come. 'But consider, up until now you've been alone.'

'And whose fault d'you think that is?'

It was difficult not to take offense, but Bourne did his best to defuse the accusation. 'There's no point in talking of blame,' he said equally. 'Now we're working together.'

'So I should just concede control to you?' Khan answered hotly. 'Why? D'you for a minute think you've earned it?'

They were almost to the terminal. He could see just how fragile their detente was.

'It would be foolish to believe that I've earned anything with you.' He glanced out the window at the bright lights of the terminal. 'I was thinking that if there's a problem – if we're walking into some kind of trap – I'd rather it be me than you who – '

'Have you not listened to anything I've told you?' Khan said as he shouldered past Bourne. 'Have you discounted everything I've done?'

By this time the pilot had appeared. 'Open the door,' Khan ordered him brusquely. 'And stay onboard.'

The pilot dutifully opened the door and dropped the stairs down to the tarmac. Bourne took one step down the aisle. 'Khan – '

But the glare from his son stopped him in his tracks. He watched from the Perspex window as Khan went down the stairs and was met by an Immigration official. He saw Khan show him a passport, then point to the aircraft. The immigration official stamped Khan's passport and nodded.

Khan turned and trotted up the steps. When he came down the aisle, he withdrew a pair of handcuffs from under his jacket, slapped them on Bourne and then on himself.

'My name is Khan LeMarc and I'm a deputy inspector for Interpol.' Khan took the laptop under his arm and began to lead Bourne back down the aisle. 'You're my prisoner.'

'What's my name?' Bourne said.

'You?' Khan pushed him out the door, following closely behind. 'You're Jason Bourne, wanted for murder by the CIA, the Quai d'Orsay and Interpol. It's the only way he'd admit you to Iceland without a passport. Anyway, he, like every other official on the planet, has read the CIA circular.'

The Immigration official stood back, giving them a wide berth as they walked past him. Khan unlocked the cuffs as soon as they were through the terminal. Out front, they got into the first taxi in the queue and gave the driver an address that was within a half-mile of the Oskjuhlid Hotel.

Spalko, the refrigerated box between his legs, sat in the passenger's seat of the Reykjavík Energy van as the Chechen rebel drove through the streets of City Centre toward the Oskjuhlid Hotel. His cell phone rang and he opened it. It wasn't good news.

'Sir, we were successful in closing off the interrogation room before the police or firemen entered the building,' his head of security said from Budapest. 'However, we've just completed an exhaustive sweep of the entire building without finding a sign of either Bourne or Khan.'

'How is that possible?' Spalko said. 'One was strapped down and the other was trapped in a room filled with gas.'

'There was an explosion,' his security chief said, and he went on to describe in detail what they'd found.

'Goddammit!' In a rare display of anger Spalko slammed his fist against the console of the van.

'We're expanding the search perimeter.'

'Don't bother,' Spalko said shortly. 'I know where they are.'


Bourne and Khan walked toward the hotel.

'How are you feeling?' Khan asked.

'I'm fine,' Bourne replied a little too quickly.

Khan glanced at him. 'Not even stiff and sore?'

'All right, I'm stiff and sore,' Bourne conceded.

'The antibiotics Oszkar brought you are state of the art.'

'Don't worry,' Bourne said. 'I'm taking them.'

'What makes you think I'm worried?' Khan pointed. 'Take a look at that.'

The perimeter of the hotel was cordoned off by the local police. Two checkpoints manned both by police and by security personnel of various nationalities were the only ways in and out. As they watched, a Reykjavík Energy van pulled up to the checkpoint at the rear of the hotel.

'That's the only way we're going to get in,' Khan said.

'Well, it's one way,' Bourne said. As the van went through the checkpoint, he saw a pair of hotel employees walking out from behind it.

Bourne glanced at Khan, who nodded. He'd seen them, too. 'What d'you think?' Bourne said.

'Going off-duty, I'd say,' Khan replied.

'That was my thought.'

The hotel employees were talking animatedly to each other and paused only long enough to show their IDs as they went through the checkpoint. Normally, they would have driven into and out of the hotel, using the underground car park, but since the security services had arrived, all hotel personnel were obliged to park on the streets surrounding the hotel.

They shadowed the two men as they turned down a side street, out of sight of the police and guards. Waiting until they neared their cars, they took them down from behind, silently and swiftly. Using the keys, they opened the trunks, placed the unconscious bodies inside, taking the hotel IDs before slamming the trunks closed.

Five minutes later they appeared at the other checkpoint in the front of the hotel so as not to come into contact with the policeman and security people who had checked the two hotel workers as they'd walked out.

They passed through the security ring without incident. At last they were inside the Oskjuhlid Hotel.


The time had come to sever Arsenov, Stepan Spalko thought. The moment had long been brewing, ever since he found that he could no longer bear Arsenov's weakness. Arsenov had once said to him, 'I'm no terrorist. All I want is for my people to receive their due.' Such a childish belief was a fatal flaw. Arsenov could delude himself all he wanted, but the truth was that whether he was asking for money, for prisoners returned, or for his land back, he was marked a terrorist by his methodology not by his aims. He killed people if he didn't get what he wanted. He targeted enemies and civilians – men, women, children – it made no difference to him. What he was sowing was terror; what he would reap was death.

Accordingly, Spalko ordered him to take Akhmed, Karim, and one of the females down to the substation of the HVAC system that supplied the air to the summit's forum. This was a slight change in plan. Magomet had been assigned to go with the three others. But Magomet was dead, and since it had been Arsenov who had killed him, he accepted it without question or complaint. In any event, they were now on a strict timetable.

'We have precisely thirty minutes from the moment we arrived in the Reykjavík Energy van,' he said. 'After that, as we know from the last time, security will come to check up on us.' He consulted his watch. 'Which means we now have twenty-four minutes to accomplish our mission.'

As Arsenov left with Akhmed and the other cadre members, Spalko pulled Zina aside. 'You understand that this will be the last time you see him alive.'

She nodded her blond head.

'You have no misgivings?'

'On the contrary, it'll be a relief,' she replied.

Spalko nodded. 'Come on.' He hurried them down the corridor. 'There's no time to waste.'

Hasan Arsenov took immediate control of his little group. They had a vital function to perform, and he would make certain they performed it. They turned the corner and saw the security guard at his post near the large air discharge grille.

Without breaking stride, they came toward him.

'Hold it right there,' he said, bringing his machine pistol off his chest.

They stopped in front of him. 'We're from Reykjavík Energy,' Arsenov said in Icelandic and then, in response to the guard's blank look, repeated it in English.

The guard frowned. 'There're no heat vents here.'

'I know,' Akhmed said, grabbing the machine pistol with one hand and slamming the guard's head against the wall with the other.

The guard started to go down and Akhmed hit him again, this time with the butt of his own machine pistol.

'Give me a hand here,' Arsenov said, digging his fingers into the air discharge grille. Karim and the female pitched in, but Akhmed kept smashing the butt of his weapon into the guard, even after it was clear that he was unconscious and likely to stay that way for some time.

'Akhmed, give me the weapon!'

Akhmed tossed the machine pistol to Arsenov, then began kicking the fallen guard in the face. Blood was flowing and there was death in the air.

Arsenov forcibly dragged Akhmed away from the security guard. 'When I give you an order, you'll obey it or, by Allah, I'll break your neck.'

Akhmed, his chest heaving, glared at Arsenov.

'We're on a schedule,' Arsenov said fiercely. 'You don't have time to indulge yourself.'

Akhmed bared his teeth and laughed. Shrugging off Arsenov's grip, he went to help Karim take off the grille. They shoved the guard into the air shaft, then, one by one, they crawled in after him. Akhmed, the last in, pulled the grille back in place.

They were obliged to crawl over the guard. As Arsenov did so, he pressed his fingers to the carotid artery. 'Dead,' he said.

'So what?' Akhmed said belligerently. 'Before the morning's over, they'll all be dead.'

On hands and knees, they crawled along the shaft until they came to the junction. Directly ahead of them was a vertical shaft. They deployed their rappeling gear. Placing the aluminum bar across the top of the vertical shaft, they belayed the rope and let it uncoil into the space below them. Taking the lead, Arsenov wrapped the rope around his left thigh and over his right. Moving hand under hand, he descended down the shaft at a steady pace. By the small shivering of the line, he became aware when each member of the cadre began to rappel down after him.

Just above the first junction box, Arsenov stopped. Flicking on a mini-flashlight, he played its concentrated beam over the wall of the shaft, illuminating the vertical lines of trunk cables and electric lines. In the middle of the tangle, something new gleamed.

'Heat sensor,' he called up.

Karim, the electronics expert, was just above him. While Arsenov played his flashlight onto the wall, the man took out pliers and a length of wire with alligator clips on either end. Climbing carefully over Arsenov, he kept going until he hung just above the outer range of the detector. Kicking out with one foot, he swung toward the wall, grabbed a trunk cable and held on. His fingers picked through the nest of wires, cut one, to which he attached one alligator clip. Then he stripped the insulation off the middle of another wire and attached the other alligator clip to it.

'All clear,' he said softly.

He moved down into the range of the sensor, but there was no alarm. He'd successfully bypassed the circuit. So far as the sensor knew, nothing was amiss.

Karim made way for Arsenov, who led them down to the bottom of the shaft. They were in range of the heart of the summit forum's HVAC subsystem.

'Our objective is the summit forum's HVAC subsystem,' Bourne said as he and Khan hurried through the lobby. Khan carried the laptop they'd gotten from Oszkar under his arm. 'That's the logical place for them to activate the diffuser.'

At this hour of the night, the lobby, vast, high-ceilinged and cold, was deserted save for various security and hotel personnel. The dignitaries were in their suites, either sleeping or prepping for the start of the summit, which was only hours away.

'Security has undoubtedly come to the same conclusion,' Khan said, 'which means that we'll be all right until we get near the substation's hub, then they're going to want to know what we're doing in that area.'

'I've been thinking about that,' Bourne said. 'It's time we used my condition to our advantage.'

They went through the main section of the hotel without incident and passed through a decorative inner courtyard of geometric gravel paths, sheared evergreen shrubs, and futuristic-looking stone benches. On the other side was the forum section. Inside, they went down three flights of stairs. Khan activated the laptop and they checked the schematics, reassuring themselves that they were on the right level.

'This way,' Khan said, closing the computer as they moved off.

But they'd gotten only a hundred feet from the stairwell when a harsh voice said, 'Take another step and you're both dead men.'

At the bottom of the vertical air shaft, the Chechen rebels waited, crouched, anxious, their nerves strained to the breaking point. They had been awaiting this moment for months. They were primed, aching to move forward. They shivered as much from the unbearable anticipation as from the chill air, which had grown colder the deeper they went below the hotel. They had only to crawl along a short horizontal shaft to get to the HVAC relays, but they were separated from their objective by the security personnel in the corridor outside by the grillwork. Until the guards moved off on their rounds, they were at bay.

Akhmed checked his watch and saw that they had fourteen minutes to complete their mission and return to the van. Beads of sweat stood out on his forehead and, gathering in his armpits, ran down his side, prickling his skin. His mouth was dry and his breathing shallow. It was always this way on the cusp of a mission. His heart beat fast and his entire body vibrated. He was still seething from Arsenov's rebuke, which had come in front of the others and so was doubly offensive. As he listened, his ears straining, he stared at Arsenov, contempt in his heart. After that night in Nairobi, he'd lost all respect for Arsenov, not only because he was being cuckolded but because he had no idea. Akhmed's thick lips curled into a smile. It felt good to have this power over Arsenov.

At last he heard the voices receding. He sprang forward, eager now to meet his destiny, but Arsenov's powerful arm checked him painfully.

'Not yet.' Arsenov's eyes glowered.

'They've moved off,' Akhmed said. 'We're wasting time.'

'We go when I give the orders.'

This further affront was too much for Akhmed. He spat, his contempt on his face. 'Why should I follow your orders? Why should any of us? You cannot even keep your woman in her place.'

Arsenov lunged at Akhmed and for a moment they grappled indecisively. The others stood by, terrified to interfere.

'I'll tolerate no more of your insolence,' Arsenov said. 'You'll follow my orders or I'll see you dead.'

'Kill me then,' Akhmed said. 'But know this: in Nairobi on the night before the demonstration, Zina entered the Shaykh's room while you were asleep.'

'Liar!' Arsenov said, thinking of the pledge he and Zina had made to each other at the cove. 'Zina would never betray me.'

'Think of where my room was, Arsenov. You made the assignments. I saw her with my own eyes.'

Arsenov's eyes glowed with enmity, but he let Akhmed go. 'I would kill you now except that we all have vital roles to play in the mission.' He gestured to the others. 'Let's get on with it.'

Karim, the electronics expert, went first, then the female and Akhmed, while

Arsenov brought up the rear. Soon enough Karim lifted a hand, bringing them to a halt.

Arsenov heard his soft voice float back to them. 'Motion sensor.'

He saw Karim crouching down, preparing his equipment. He was grateful for the presence of this man. How many bombs had Karim constructed for them over the years? All had worked flawlessly; he never made a mistake.

As before, Karim drew out a length of wire with the alligator clips at either end. With his pliers in one hand, he searched out the proper electrical wires, isolating them, cutting into one and applying an alligator clip to the bare copper end. Then, as before, he stripped away the insulation from the second wire and attached the other alligator clip, creating the bypass loop.

'All clear,' Karim said, and they moved forward into range of the motion sensor.

The alarm went off, shrilling through the corridor, bringing the security guards running, their machine pistols at the ready.

'Karim!' Arsenov cried.

'It's a trap!' Karim wailed. 'Someone crossed the wires!'

Moments before, Bourne and Khan turned slowly to confront the American security guard. He was dressed in army fatigues and riot gear. He came a step closer, peering at their ID tags. He relaxed somewhat, putting the machine pistol up, but the deep frown didn't leave his face.

'What are you guys doing down here?'

'Maintenance checks,' Bourne said. He remembered the Reykjavík Energy truck he'd seen entering the hotel as well as something in the material Oszkar had downloaded to the laptop. 'The thermal heating system's gone offline. We're supposed to be helping the people the energy company sent over.'

'You're in the wrong section,' the guard said, pointing. 'You need to go back the way you came, make a left, then left again.'

'Thanks,' Khan said. 'I guess we got turned around. We're not normally in this section.'

As they turned to leave, Bourne's legs went out from under him. He gave a deep groan and fell.

'What the hell!' the guard said.

Khan knelt beside Bourne, opened his shirt.

'Jesus Christ,' the guard said, leaning over to stare at Bourne's wounded torso, 'what the hell happened to him?'

Khan reached up, jerked down hard on the front of the guard's uniform, slamming the side of his head into the concrete floor. As Bourne rose, Khan stripped the clothes off the guard.

'He's more your size than mine,' Khan said, handing Bourne the fatigues.

Bourne climbed into the guard's uniform while Khan dragged the unconscious form into the shadows.

At that moment the motion sensor alarm screamed and they took off toward the substation at a run.

The security guards were well trained, and, commendably, the Americans and Arabs who were on duty this shift worked together flawlessly. Each kind of sensor had a different-sounding alarm, so they knew immediately that the motion sensor had been tripped and precisely where it was. They were on hair-trigger alert and, this close to the summit, were under orders to shoot first and ask questions later.

As they ran, they opened fire, raking the grillwork with automatic fire. Half of them emptied their magazines into the suspect area. The other half stood back in reserve while the others used crowbars to pry off the ruined grilles. They found three bodies, two men and a woman. One of the Americans notified Hull and one of the Arabs contacted Feyd al-Saoud.

By this time, more security personnel from other sectors on the floor had converged on the site to offer added support.

Two of the personnel held in reserve climbed into the air shaft, and when it was determined that no other hostiles were in evidence, they secured the area. Others dragged the three chewed-up corpses out of the air shaft, along with Karim's paraphernalia for bypassing sensors and what at first glance looked like a time bomb.

Jamie Hull and Feyd al-Saoud arrived almost at the same time. Hull took one look at the situation and called his chief of staff via the wireless network.

'As of this moment, we're on red alert. There's been a breach of security. We have three hostiles down, repeat, three hostiles down. Put the entire hotel on absolute lockdown, no one in or out of the premises.' He continued to bark orders, moving his men into the planned position for a red alert. Then he contacted the Secret Service, who were with the president and his staff in the dignitary wing.

Feyd al-Saoud had squatted down and was studying the corpses. The bodies were pretty well shot up, but their faces, though blood-streaked, were intact. He took out a pen flash, shone it on one of the faces. Then he reached out, put his forefinger against the eye of one of the males. His fingertip came away blue; the corpse's iris was dark brown.

One of the FSB men must have contacted Karpov because the Alpha Unit commander appeared at an ungainly lope. He was out of breath and Feyd al-Saoud guessed that he'd run all the way.

He and Hull briefed the Russian on what had happened. He held up his fingertip. 'They're wearing colored contacts – and look here, they've dyed their hair to pass for Icelanders.'

Karpov's face was grim. 'I know this one,' he said, kicking one of the male corpses. 'His name's Akhmed. He's one of Hasan Arsenov's top lieutenants.'

'The Chechen terrorist leader?' Hull said. 'You'd better inform your president, Boris.'

Karpov stood up, fists on hips. 'What I want to know is where's Arsenov?'

'I would say that we're too late,' Khan said from behind a metal column, as he watched the arrival of the two security chiefs, 'except that I don't see Spalko.'

'It's possible that he wouldn't put himself at risk by coming to the hotel,' Bourne said.

Khan shook his head. 'I know him. He's both an egotist and a perfectionist. No, he's here somewhere.'

'But not here, obviously,' Bourne said thoughtfully. He was watching the

Russian jogging up to Jamie Hull and the Arab security chief. There was something vaguely familiar about that flat, brutal face, the beetling brow and caterpillar eyebrows. When he heard the other's voice, he said, 'I know that man. The Russian.'

'No surprise there. I recognize him, too,' Khan said. 'Boris Illyich Karpov, head of the FSB's elite Alpha Unit.'

'No, I mean I *know* him.'

'How? Where?'

'I don't know,' Bourne said. 'Is he friend or foe?' He beat his fists against his forehead. 'If only I could remember.'

Khan turned to him and clearly saw the anguish that racked him. He felt a dangerous urge to grasp Bourne's shoulder and reassure him. Dangerous because he didn't know where the gesture would lead or even what it would mean. He felt the further disintegration of his life that had begun the moment Bourne sat down beside him and spoke to him. *'Who are you?'* he had said. At the time, Khan had known the answer to that question; now he wasn't sure. Could it be that everything he'd believed, or thought he'd believed, was a lie?

Khan took refuge from these deeply disturbing thoughts by cleaving to what he and Bourne knew best. 'I'm bothered by that object,' he said. 'It's a time bomb. You said that Spalko was planning to use Dr. Schiffer's bio-diffuser.'

Bourne nodded. 'I'd say that this was a classic diversion, except for the fact that it's now just past midnight. The summit isn't scheduled to begin for another eight hours.'

'That's why they've used a time bomb.'

'Yes, but why set it now, so far in advance?' Bourne said.

'Less security,' Khan pointed out.

'True, but there's also more chance of its being discovered during one of security's periodic sweeps.' Bourne shook his head. 'No, we're missing something, I know it. Spalko has something else in mind. But what?'

Spalko, Zina and the remainder of the cadre had reached their objective. Here, far from the section of the hotel housing the summit's forum, security, though tight, had gaps in it that Spalko was able to exploit. Though there were many security people, they couldn't be everywhere at once, and so by taking out two guards, Spalko and his team were soon in position.

They were three levels below the street in a huge concrete windowless space, completely enclosed save for a single open doorway. Masses of huge black pipes ran through the concrete wall on the far side of the space, each labeled with the section of the hotel it served.

The cadre now broke out their HAZMAT suits and put them on, carefully sealing them. Two of the Chechen females went into the passage to stand guard just outside the doorway, and a male rebel backed them up inside.

Spalko opened the larger of the two metal containers he carried. Inside was the NX 20. He carefully fitted the two halves together, checking that all the fittings were securely fastened. He handed it to Zina while he unlocked the refrigerated container Peter Sido had provided. The glass vial it contained was small, almost minuscule. Even after they had seen its effect in Nairobi, it was difficult to believe that such a small amount of the virus could be lethal to so many people.

As he'd done in Nairobi, he opened the loading chamber on the diffuser and placed the vial into it. He closed and locked the chamber, took the NX 20 from Zina's arms and curled his finger around the smaller of the two triggers. Once he squeezed it, the virus, still sealed in its special vial, would be injected into the firing chamber. After that, all that was required was for him to press the button on the left side of the stock, which would lock the firing chamber, and, when it was aimed correctly, pull the main trigger.

He cradled the bio-diffuser in his arms as Zina had done. This weapon needed to be given the proper respect, even from him.

He looked into Zina's eyes, which were shining with her love for him and her patriot's zeal. 'Now we wait,' he said, 'for the sensor alarm.'

They heard it then, the sound faint but its vibrations unmistakable, magnified by the bare concrete corridors. The Shaykh and Zina smiled into each other's faces. He could feel the tension come into the room, fueled by righteous anger and an expectation of redemption long denied.

'Our moment is at hand,' he said, and they all heard him, all reacted. He could almost hear their ululation of victory begin.

With the unstoppable force of destiny propelling him forward, the Shaykh pulled the small trigger, and with an ominous whisper, the payload clicked home into the firing chamber, where it rested, waiting for the moment of its release.

# 29

'They're all Chechens, isn't that right, Boris?' Hull said.

Karpov nodded. 'All, according to the records, members of Hasan Arsenov's terrorist group.'

'This is a coup for the good guys,' Hull exulted.

Feyd al-Saoud, shivering in the damp and chill, said, 'With the amount of C4 in that time bomb, they would've taken out almost the entire weight-bearing substructure. The forum above would've collapsed of its own weight, killing everyone inside.'

'Lucky for us they tripped the motion sensor,' Hull said.

As the minutes passed, Karpov's frown had grown only deeper as he echoed Bourne's query, 'Why set the bomb so far in advance? I think we had a good chance of finding it before the summit started.'

Feyd al-Saoud turned to one of his men. 'Is there some way to turn up the heat down here? We're going to be here for some time and I'm already freezing.'

'That's it!' Bourne said, turning to Khan. He took his laptop, turned it on, scrolling through the schematics until he found the one he wanted. He traced a route from where they were back toward the main section of the hotel. Snapping the computer closed, he said, 'Come on! Let's go!'

'Where are we headed?' Khan asked as they made their way through the maze of the sublevel.

'Think about it. We saw a Reykjavík Energy van pull into the hotel; the entire hotel is heated by the thermal system that services the city as a whole.'

'That's why Spalko sent those Chechens to the HVAC subsystem now,' Khan said as they raced around a corner. 'They were never meant to succeed in planting the bomb. We were right, it *was* a diversion, but not for later this morning when the summit is scheduled to start. He's going to activate the bio-diffuser now!'

'Right,' Bourne said. 'Not through the HVAC subsystem. His target is the main thermal heating system. At this time of night all the dignitaries are in their rooms, right where he's going to release the virus.'

'Someone coming,' one of the female Chechens said.

'Kill them,' the Shaykh commanded.

'But it's Hasan Arsenov!' cried the other female guard.

Spalko and Zina exchanged a bewildered look. What had gone wrong? The sensor had been tripped, the alarm had gone off, and shortly thereafter they'd heard the satisfying bursts of automatic gunfire. How had Arsenov escaped?

'I said kill him!' Spalko shouted.

What haunted Arsenov, what had made him turn tail at the instant he smelled the trap, thus saving himself from the sudden death suffered by his compatriots, was the terror that had been lurking inside him, the thing that had given him nightmares for the past week. He had told himself that it was his guilt at having betrayed Khalid Murat – a hero's guilt at having made the hard choice that would save his people. But the truth of the matter was his terror had to do with Zina. He had not been able to admit to seeing her withdrawal, gradual but inexorable, her emotional distance that, in retrospect, had become glacial. She had been slipping away from him for some time, though even up to a few moments ago he had refused to believe it. But now Akhmed's revelation had thrown it into the light of consciousness. She had lived behind a glass wall, always keeping part of herself aloof and hidden. He couldn't touch that part of her, and it seemed to him now that the harder he'd tried, the further away she pulled herself.

Zina didn't love him – he wondered now whether she ever had. Even if their mission was a complete success, there would be no life with her, no children they could share together. What a farce their last intimate conversation had been!

All at once, he was overcome by shame. He was a coward – he loved her more than he loved his freedom, for without her he knew there would be no freedom for him. In the wake of her betrayal, victory would be like ashes in his mouth.

Now, as he pounded down the cold corridor toward the thermal heating station, he saw one of his own people raise her machine pistol as if she was going to shoot him. Perhaps in the HAZMAT suit she couldn't tell who was coming toward her.

'Wait! Don't shoot!' he cried. 'It's Hasan Arsenov!'

A bullet from her opening volley struck him in the left arm, and half in shock, he spun around, diving around a corner, away from the deadly spray of ricocheting bullets.

In the abrupt frenzy of the present, there was no more time for questions or speculation. He heard renewed gunfire but not in his direction. Peering around the corner, he saw that the two females had turned their backs to him and, crouched, were firing at two figures as they advanced down the passageway.

Arsenov rose and, taking advantage of the diversion, headed for the doorway to the thermal heating station.

Spalko heard the gunfire and said, 'Zina, that can't be just Arsenov.'

Zina swung her machine pistol around, nodded to the guard, who threw her a second one.

Behind them, Spalko went over to the wall of thermal heating pipes. Each one had a valve and, beside it, a gauge that showed the pressure. He found the pipe that corresponded to the dignitaries' wing, began to unscrew the valve.

Hasan Arsenov knew that he'd been meant to die with the others in the HVAC substation. '*It's a trap! Someone crossed the wires!*' Karim had wailed just before he'd died. Spalko had crossed the wires; he'd needed not simply a diversion, as he'd told them, but scapegoats – targets of enough importance that their deaths would occupy the security for a sufficient amount of time for Spalko to reach the real objective and release the virus. Spalko had tricked him and, Arsenov was quite certain now, Zina had conspired with him.

How quickly love turned rancid, its transformation into hate occurring in no more time than it takes a heart to beat. Now they had turned against him, all his compatriots, the men and women he'd fought alongside, whom he'd laughed and cried with, prayed to Allah with, who had the same goals as he did. Chechens! All corrupted now by Stepan Spalko's power and poisonous charm.

In the end Khalid Murat had been right about everything. He hadn't trusted Spalko; he wouldn't have followed him into this folly. Once, Arsenov had accused him of being an old man, of being too cautious, of not understanding the new world that lay before them. But now he knew what Khalid Murat had surely known: that that new world was nothing more than a self-serving illusion created by the man who called himself the Shaykh. Arsenov had believed this pipe dream because he'd wanted to believe it. Spalko had preyed upon that weakness. But no more! Arsenov vowed. No more! If he was to die today, it would be on his own terms, not as a sheep to the slaughter of Spalko's making.

He pressed himself against the edge of the doorway, took a deep breath and when he let it out, he somersaulted past the open doorway. The resulting hail of automatic fire told him all he needed to know. Rolling, he kept to the concrete floor, wriggling on his stomach into the opening. He saw the guard, his machine pistol aimed at waist height, and shot him four times in the chest.

When Bourne saw the two terrorists in HAZMAT suits behind a concrete column, firing their machine pistols in alternate bursts, his blood ran cold. He and Khan took cover around the corner of a T-junction and he fired back.

'Spalko's in that room with the bio-weapon,' Bourne said. 'We've got to get in there now.'

'Not unless those two run out of ammo.' Khan was looking around behind them. 'Do you remember the schematics? Remember what's in the ceiling?'

Bourne, continuing to fire, nodded.

'There's an access panel back about twenty feet. I need a boost.'

Bourne got off one more burst before retreating with Khan.

'Will you be able to see anything up there?' he asked.

Khan nodded, indicating his miraculous jacket. 'I've got a pen light, among other things, up my sleeve.'

Tucking the machine pistol under his arm, Bourne laced his fingers together for Khan to put his foot in. His bones seemed to crack with the weight and the strained muscles in his shoulder seemed to catch fire.

Then Khan slid the panel off and had hoisted himself the rest of the way into the access hatch.

'Time,' Bourne said.

'Fifteen seconds,' Khan replied, disappearing.

Bourne turned. He counted to ten, then turned the corner, his machine pistol blazing. But almost immediately he stopped. He could feel his heart pounding painfully against his ribs. The two Chechens had taken off their HAZMAT suits.

They had emerged from behind the column and now stood facing him. He saw that they were female and that around their waists were a series of linked packets filled with C4 explosive.

'Good Christ,' Bourne said. 'Khan! They're wearing suicide belts!'

At that moment they were plunged into darkness. Khan, in the electrical conduit above his head, had cut the wires.

Arsenov was up and sprinting forward the moment after he fired. He ran into the station, grabbed the guard before he fell. Two other figures were in the room: Spalko and Zina. Using the dead guard as a shield, he fired at the target with a machine pistol in each hand. Zina! But she had squeezed the triggers and even as she staggered back, hit, the massed fury of the automatic fire blew right through the guard's body.

Arsenov's eyes opened wide as he felt the searing pain in his chest, and then an odd kind of numbness. The lights winked out and he lay on the floor, the breath rattling in his blood-filled lungs. As if in a dream, he heard Zina screaming, and he wept for all the dreams he'd had, for a future that would now never come. With a sigh, life left him as it had come upon him, in hardship and brutality and pain.

A terrible, deathly silence had descended on the passage. Time seemed to have stopped. Bourne, his gun aimed into the darkness, heard the soft, shallow breathing of the human bombs. He could feel their fear as well as their determination. If they sensed him take a step toward them, if they became aware of Khan moving in the electrical conduit, they would surely detonate the explosives strapped around their waists.

Then, because he was listening for it, he heard the very faint double tap above his head, the sound, swiftly diminishing, of Khan moving in the electrical conduit. He knew there was an access panel more or less where the doorway to the thermal heating station was, and he had an idea what Khan was going to try. It would require nerves of steel and a very steady hand from both of them. The AR-15 he carried was short-barreled, but it made up for any slight inaccuracy with its awesome firepower. It used .223-caliber ammo which it spit out with a muzzle velocity in excess of 2400 feet per second. He wriggled silently closer, then, aware of a slight shifting ahead of him in the darkness, he froze. His heart was in his throat. Had he heard something, a sibilance, a whisper, footsteps? Utter silence now. He held his breath and concentrated on sighting down the barrel of the AR-15.

Where was Spalko? Had he loaded the bio-weapon yet? Would he stay to finish the mission or would he cut and run? Knowing he had no answers, he put these terrifying questions aside. *Concentrate*, he berated himself. *Relax now, breathe deeply and evenly as you move into alpha rhythm, as you become one with the weapon.*

He saw it then. Khan's penlight flash, the beam illuminating a woman's face, blinding her. There was no time to consider or to think. His finger had been curled on the trigger and now instinct flowed naturally and instantaneously into action. The muzzle flash lit up the corridor, and he watched the woman's head disintegrate in a welter of blood, bone and brains.

He was up then, running forward, looking for the other woman. Then the lights blinked on and he saw the second human bomb, lying beside the other one, her throat slit. An instant later, Khan dropped down from the open access hatch and together they entered the thermal heating station.

Moments before, in the darkness that smelled of cordite and blood and death, Spalko had dropped to his knees, searching blindly for Zina. The darkness had defeated him. Without light, he was unable to make the delicate connection between the muzzle of the NX 20 and the valve into the thermal heating system.

His arm extended, he felt along the floor. He hadn't been paying attention to her, wasn't certain of her position, and in any case, she had moved the moment Arsenov had burst through the doorway. It had been clever of him to use the human shield, but Zina was cleverer still and she had killed him. But she was still alive. He had heard her scream.

Now he waited, knowing that the human bombs he had primed would protect him from whoever was out there. Bourne? Khan? He was ashamed to realize that he was afraid of the unknown presence in the passage. Whoever it was had seen through his diversion, had followed his own reasoning regarding the vulnerability of the thermal heating system. There was a rising panic in him, alleviated for the moment when he heard Zina suck in a ragged breath. Quickly he crawled through a pool of sticky blood to where she lay.

Her hair was wet and stringy as he kissed her cheek. 'Beautiful Zina,' he whispered in her ear. 'Powerful Zina.'

He felt a kind of spasm pass through her and his heart constricted in fear. 'Zina, don't die. You can't die.' Then he tasted the salty wetness running down her cheek and knew that she was weeping. Her breast rose and fell irregularly with her silent sobs.

'Zina' – he kissed away her tears – 'you must be strong, now more than ever before.' He embraced her tenderly and felt her arms slowly come around him.

'This is the moment of our greatest triumph.' He drew away and pressed the NX 20 into her embrace. 'Yes, yes, I choose you to fire the weapon, to bring the future to fruition.'

She couldn't speak. It was all she could do to keep the breath sawing in and out of her lungs. Once again he cursed the darkness, for he couldn't see her eyes, couldn't be certain that he had her. He had to take the chance, however. He took her hands and placed the left one on the barrel of the bio-diffuser, the right one at the guard on the stock. He placed her forefinger on the main trigger.

'All you need do is squeeze,' he whispered in her ear. 'But not yet, not yet. I need time.'

Yes, time was what he needed in order to escape. He was trapped in the darkness, the one contingency for which he hadn't been prepared. And now he couldn't even take the NX 20 with him. He'd have to run and run hard, a condition that Schiffer had made clear, the weapon once loaded was not designed to handle. The payload and its container were far too fragile.

'Zina, you'll do this, won't you?' He kissed her cheek. 'You have enough strength inside you, I know you do.' She was trying to say something, but he put a hand over her mouth, afraid that his unknown pursuers outside would hear her strangled cry. 'I'll be close by, Zina. Remember that.'

Then so slowly and gently that it was imperceptible to her impaired senses, he slithered away. Turning, at last, from her, he stumbled over Arsenov's corpse and his HAZMAT suit ripped. For a moment his new-found terror returned as he imagined himself being trapped in here when Zina pulled the trigger, the virus seeping into the rent, infecting him. In his mind's eye, the city of the dead he had created in Nairobi bloomed in all its vivid, gruesome detail.

Then he'd regained his composure and he stripped off the encumbering suit altogether. Silent as a cat, he made his way to the doorway, swung out into the passage. At once the human bombs became aware of him and shifted slightly, tensing.

'La illaha ill Allah,' he whispered.

'La illaha ill Allah,' they whispered in return.

Then, in the darkness, he stole away.

They both saw it at once, the blunt, ugly snout of Dr. Felix Schiffer's bio-diffuser pointed at them. Bourne and Khan froze.

'Spalko's gone. There's his HAZMAT suit,' Bourne said. 'This station has only one entrance.' He thought of the movement he'd detected, the whisper, the sound of furtive footfalls he thought he'd heard. 'He must've slipped out in the darkness.'

'I know this one,' Khan said. 'It's Hasan Arsenov, but this other, the female holding the weapon, I don't know.'

The female terrorist lay half-propped up on the corpse of another terrorist. How she had managed to drag herself into this position neither of them could say. She was very badly wounded, possibly fatally, though from this distance it was impossible to say for sure. She looked at them from a world filled with pain and, Bourne was quite certain, something else that went beyond mere physical hurt.

Khan had taken a Kalishnikov from one of the human bombs outside and he aimed it now at the female. 'There's no way out for you,' he said.

Bourne, who had been watching only her eyes, stepped forward and pushed the Kalishnikov down. 'There's always a way out,' he said.

Then he squatted down so that he was at the other's level. Without taking his gaze from her, he said, 'Can you speak? Can you tell me your name?'

For a moment there was only silence, and Bourne had to force himself to keep his gaze on her face, not to look at her finger curled and tense on the trigger.

At length her lips opened and began to tremble. Her teeth chattered and a tear slipped free, rolling down her stained cheek.

'What d'you care what her name is?' Khan's voice was filled with contempt. 'She's not human; she's been turned into a machine of destruction.'

'Khan, some might say the same of you.' Bourne's voice was so gentle it was clear that what he said wasn't a rebuke, merely a truth that might not have occurred to his son.

He turned his attention back to the terrorist. 'It's important that you tell me your name, isn't it?'

Her lips opened and with a great effort, she said in a voice somewhere between a rattle and a gurgle, 'Zina.'

'Well, Zina, we're at the endgame,' Bourne said. 'There's nothing left now, except death and life. By the looks of things, it appears as if you've already chosen death. If you pull the trigger, you'll be sent to heaven and in glory will become a *houri*. But I

311

wonder whether that will happen. What is it that you'll be leaving behind? Dead compatriots, at least one of whom you've shot yourself. And then there's Stepan Spalko. Where has he gone, I wonder. No matter. What's important is that at the crucial moment, he abandoned you.

'He's left you to die, Zina, while he's cut and run. So I guess you have to ask yourself, if you pull that trigger, will you go to your glory or will you be cast down, found wanting by Mounkir and Nekir, the Questioners. Given your life, Zina, when they ask you "Who is thy creator? Who is thy Prophet?" will you be able to answer them? Only the righteous remember, Zina, you know that.'

Zina was openly weeping now. But her breast was heaving strangely and Bourne was afraid that a sudden spasm would cause her to pull the trigger in reflex. If he was going to reach her, it had to be now.

'If you pull that trigger, if you choose death, you won't be able to answer them. You know that. You've been abandoned and betrayed, Zina, by those closest to you. And, in turn, you've betrayed them. But it's not too late. There can be redemption; there's always a way out.'

At the moment Khan realized that Bourne was talking as much to him as he was to Zina; he experienced a feeling not unlike an electrical shock. This feeling raced through his body until it sparked both his extremities and his brain. He felt himself stripped naked, revealed at last, and he was terrified of nothing more or less than himself – his own true authentic self that he had buried so many years ago in the jungle of Southeast Asia. It was so long ago that he couldn't remember exactly where or when he'd done it. The truth was that he was a stranger to himself. He hated his father for leading him to that truth, but he could no longer deny that he loved him for it, too.

He knelt, then, beside the man he knew to be his father, and putting the Kalishnikov down where Zina could see it, he extended a hand toward her.

'He's right,' Khan said in an altogether different voice from the one he normally used. 'There is a way to make up for your past sins, for the murders you've committed, for the betrayals to those who've loved you without, perhaps, you even knowing.'

He moved forward inch by inch until his hand closed over hers. Slowly and gently he pried her forefinger away from the trigger. She let go then and allowed him to take the weapon from her useless embrace.

'Thank you, Zina,' Bourne said. 'Khan will take care of you now.' He rose, and giving his son's shoulder a brief squeeze, he turned and went swiftly and silently down the passage after Spalko.

# 30

Stepan Spalko sprinted down the bare concrete passage, Bourne's ceramic gun at the ready. He knew that all the gunfire would bring the security people into the main section of the hotel. Up ahead, he saw the Saudi security chief, Feyd al-Saoud, and two of his men. He ducked out of sight. They hadn't seen him yet and he used this element of surprise, waiting for them to come closer, then shooting them before they had time to react.

For a breathless moment he stood over the downed men. Feyd al-Saoud groaned and Spalko shot him at close range in the forehead. The Saudi security chief flopped once and was still. Quickly Spalko took the ID tags off one of his men, changed into the man's uniform and got rid of his colored contact lenses. As he did so, his thoughts turned inexorably to Zina. She had been fearless, true enough, but the ardor of her loyalty to him had been her fatal flaw. She had protected him from everyone – especially Arsenov. She'd enjoyed that, he could tell. But it struck him that her true passion was for him. It was this love, the repugnant weakness of sacrifice, that had driven him to abandon her.

Swift footfalls behind him brought him back to the present, and he hurried on. The fateful meeting with the Arabs had been a two-edged sword, for while it had provided him with a ready means of disguise, it had slowed him down, and now as he threw a glance over his shoulder, he saw a figure in security fatigues and cursed mightily. He felt like Ahab, who pursued his nemesis until, in an utterly unexpected reversal, his nemesis had come after him. The man in the security fatigues was Jason Bourne.

Bourne saw Spalko, now in an Arab security uniform, open a door and vanish into a stairwell. He leaped over the bodies of the men Spalko had just killed and headed after him. He emerged into the chaos of the lobby. Just a short time ago, when he and Khan had entered the hotel, this vast glassed-in space was tense but hushed, almost deserted. Now it was a welter of security personnel running to and fro. Some were rounding up the hotel personnel, sorting them into groups, depending on their jobs and where they had just been inside the premises. Others had already begun the laborious and time-consuming process of questioning the staff. Each individual had to account for every moment of his whereabouts over the course of the last two days. Still others were on their way down to the subbasement or were being deployed by wireless network to other areas of the hotel. Everyone was hustling; no one had time to question the two men who, one after the other, crossed through the mob scene toward the front door.

It was ironic to watch Spalko walking among them, blending in, becoming one of them. Briefly, Bourne considered trying to alert those around him but immediately thought better of it. Spalko would no doubt call his bluff – it was Bourne who was the internationally wanted murderer still under a CIA sanction. Spalko, of course, knew this, being the clever architect of Bourne's dangerous predicament. And as he followed Spalko out of the front doors, he realized something else. *We're both the same now,* he thought, *both chameleons employing the same marking in order to keep our true identities from being revealed to those around us.* It was odd and disquieting to realize that at the moment this international security force was as much his enemy as it was Spalko's.

The moment he was outside, Bourne realized that the hotel was in absolute lockdown. He watched with fascinated dread as Spalko boldly made his way to the security services car park. Although it was within the limits of the lockdown cordon, it was deserted, as even security personnel weren't allowed in or out.

Bourne went after him but almost immediately lost him in the ranks of vehicles. He broke into a run. There was a shout from behind him. He pulled open the door of the first vehicle he came to – an American Jeep. Yanking out the plastic panel on the bottom of the steering column, he fumbled for the wires. Just then another engine fired up and he saw Spalko in the car he'd stolen, wheeling out of the car park.

There were more shouts now and the pounding of boots against pavement. Several shots were fired. Bourne, concentrating on what needed to be done, got the wires stripped and braided together. The Jeep's engine coughed to life, and he put it in gear. Then with a hard squeal of tires, he turned out of the car park and accelerated through the security checkpoint.

The night was moonless but, then again, it wasn't really night. An insipid darkness lay over Reykjavík as the sun, hanging just below the horizon, turned the sky the color of an oystershell. As Bourne followed Spalko's twists and turns through the city, he realized that Spalko was heading south.

This was something of a surprise, for he'd expected Spalko to make for the airport. Surely he had an escape plan and just as surely it involved an aircraft. But the more Bourne thought about it, the less surprised he was. He was getting to know his adversary better now. Already he understood that Spalko never took the logical way in or out of a situation. His mind was unique, involved as it was in puzzle-logic. He was a man of feints and twists, someone who liked to trap his opponent rather than kill him outright.

So. Keflavík was out. Too obvious and, as Spalko would undoubtedly have foreseen, too well guarded for him to use as an escape route. Bourne oriented himself to the map he'd studied on Oszkar's laptop. What lay south of the city? Hafnarfjördur, a fishing village too small to land the kind of aircraft Spalko would use. The coast! They were on an island, after all. Spalko was going to escape via boat.

At this time of night there was little traffic, especially after they left the city behind them. The roads became narrower, winding through the hillsides that fronted the landward side of the sea cliffs. As Spalko's car went around a particularly sharp curve, Bourne dropped back. Turning off his headlights, he accelerated around the turn. He could see Spalko's vehicle up ahead, but he hoped that Spalko, peering into his rear-view mirror, wouldn't be able to see him. It was a risk, losing sight of the car every time they went around a turn, but Bourne didn't see that he had any alternative. He had to make Spalko believe he'd lost his pursuer.

The utter lack of trees lent the landscape a certain gravity and, with the blue ice mountains as backdrop, a sense of eternal winter as well, made all the more eerie by the intermittent swaths of verdant green. The sky was immense and, in the long false-dawn, filled with the black shapes of shorebirds, soaring and swooping. Seeing them, Bourne felt a certain freedom from his entombment in the death-laden bowels of the hotel. Despite the chill, he rolled down the windows and breathed deeply of the fresh salt-laced air. A sweet smell rose to his nostrils as he flashed past the rolling, flower-dotted carpet of a meadow.

The road narrowed further as it turned toward the sea. Bourne descended through a lushly foliated glen and then zoomed around another curve. The road steepened in its switchback descent of the cliff face. He saw Spalko, then lost him again as another curve loomed. He made the turn and saw the North Atlantic low and spangled dully in the slate-gray dawn.

Spalko's car went around another turn and Bourne followed on. The next turn was so close that the car was already out of sight, and despite the added risk, Bourne pushed the Jeep faster.

He had already committed to the turn when he heard the sound. It was soft and familiar above the flutter of the wind, the noise his ceramic gun made when fired. His front nearside tire blew and he slewed around. He caught a glimpse of Spalko, gun in hand, running to where he'd left his car. Then his view changed, and he was too busy trying to get the Jeep under control as it skidded perilously close to the seaside edge of the road.

He downshifted into neutral, but it wasn't enough. He needed to turn off the ignition, but without the key that was impossible. The rear tires slipped off the road. Bourne unbuckled himself and held on as the Jeep spun off the cliff. It seemed to float, turning over twice. The brash, unmistakable odor of overheated metal came to him, along with the acrid stench of rubber or plastic burning.

He leaped just before the Jeep hit, rolling away as the vehicle bounced off an outcropping of rock and burst open. Flames shot up into the air, and by their light he saw in the cove just below him the fishing boat, nosing in toward the shore.

Spalko drove like a maniac down the road to the dead end at the inner edge of the cove. Throwing a glance back at the flaming Jeep, he said to himself, *To hell with Jason Bourne. He's dead now.* But not, unfortunately, soon forgotten. It was Bourne who had foiled him, and now he had neither the NX 20 nor the Chechens as cat's-paws. So many months of careful planning come to nothing!

He got out of the car and walked across what remained of the wrack-strewn shingle. A rowboat was coming for him, even though it was high tide and the fishing boat was very close to shore. He'd called the captain the moment he'd successfully run the hotel's security checkpoint. Only a skeleton crew of the captain and a mate were onboard. He climbed in as the captain nosed the rowboat onto the shingle, then the mate pushed off with his oar.

Spalko was fuming and not a word was said on the short, unpleasant trip back to the fishing boat. When he was aboard, Spalko said, 'Make ready to leave, Captain.'

'Begging you pardon, sir,' the captain replied, 'but what about the rest of the crew?'

Spalko grabbed the captain by his shirtfront. 'I gave you an order, Captain. I expect you to carry it out.'

'Aye, aye, sir,' the captain grumbled with an evil glint in his eye. 'But with only the two of us to crew, it'll take a little longer to get under way.'

'You'd damn well better get to it then,' Spalko told him, as he headed below.

The water was cold as ice, black as the subbasement of the hotel. Bourne knew that he needed to get onboard the fishing boat as quickly as possible. Thirty seconds after he'd pushed out from the shingle, his fingers and toes had started to go numb; thirty seconds after that, he couldn't feel them at all.

The two minutes it took him to reach the boat seemed like the longest in his life. He reached up for an oiled hawser and hauled himself out of the sea. He shivered in the wind, moving hand over hand up the line.

As he went, he experienced an eerie dislocation. With the scent of the sea in his nostrils, the feel of the brine drying on his skin, it seemed to him as if he wasn't in Iceland at all but in Marseilles, that he wasn't climbing onto a fishing boat in pursuit of Stepan Spalko but was clandestinely boarding a pleasure yacht on his way to execute the international assassin for hire, Carlos. For it was in Marseilles that the nightmare had begun, where the pitched battle with Carlos had ended with him being flung overboard, the shock of being shot and almost drowned robbing him of his memory, of his very life.

As he lifted himself over the gunwale onto the deck of the fishing boat, he felt a stab of fear that was almost paralyzing in its intensity. It was in this very same situation that he'd failed. He felt abruptly exposed, as if he wore this failure on his sleeve. He almost faltered then, but into his mind sprang the image of Khan, and he remembered what he'd said to him when they'd first met in that tension-filled setting. '*Who are you?*' Because it occurred to him now that Khan didn't know, and if Bourne wasn't around to help him find out who he was, he'd have no one. He thought of Khan, on his knees in the thermal heating station, and it seemed to him that it wasn't only the Kalishnikov he'd let go of but also, possibly, something of his own inner rage.

Bourne, taking a deep breath, settled his mind on what was before him and crept along the deck. The captain and his mate were busy in the wheelhouse and he encountered little difficulty in rendering them unconscious. There was plenty of rope around and he was in the process of binding their wrists behind their backs when Spalko said from behind him, 'I think you'd better find a bit of rope for yourself.'

Bourne was crouched down. The two seamen lay on their sides, back to back. Without showing anything to Spalko, Bourne slipped out his switchblade. Immediately, he knew he'd made a fatal mistake. The mate had his back to him, but the captain did not and saw very clearly that he was now armed. His eyes looked into Bourne's but, curiously, he made no sound or movement that would alert Spalko. Instead, he closed his eyes as if in sleep.

'Stand up and turn around,' Spalko ordered.

Bourne did as he was told, keeping his right hand hidden behind the outer edge of his thigh. Spalko, in freshly pressed jeans and a black cable-knit turtleneck sweater, stood spread-legged on the deck, Bourne's ceramic gun in his hand. And again Bourne was subjected to the strange sense of dislocation. As with Carlos years ago, Spalko now had the drop on him. All that remained was for Spalko to pull the trigger, for Bourne to be hit and cast into the water. This time, however, in the bone-chilling North Atlantic, there would be no rescue as there had been in the mild Mediterranean waters. He would quickly freeze and drown.

'You simply will not die, will you, Mr. Bourne?'

Bourne dove at Spalko, the switchblade snapping open. Spalko, startled, squeezed the trigger far too late. The bullet sang out over the water as the blade buried itself in his side. He grunted, clubbed the barrel of the gun down onto Bourne's cheek. Blood spurted from both of them. Spalko's left knee buckled, but Bourne crashed to the deck.

Spalko, remembering, kicked him viciously in his cracked ribs, rendering Bourne nearly unconscious. He pulled the switchblade from his side, threw it into the water. Then he bent and dragged Bourne to the gunwale. As Bourne began to stir, Spalko hit him with the heel of his hand. Then he hauled him more or less upright and bent him over the side.

Bourne was phasing in and out of consciousness, but the sharp tang of the icy black water brought him around enough to know that he was on the brink of annihilation. It was happening again, just as it had so many years ago. He was in so much pain that he could barely draw breath, but there was life to think of – his life now, not the one that had been taken away from him. He wouldn't let himself be robbed again.

As Spalko exerted himself to heave him over the side, Bourne kicked out with all his might. With a sickening snap, the sole of his shoe connected with Spalko's jaw. Spalko, grabbing his broken jaw, staggered backward, and Bourne ran at him. Spalko had no time to use the gun; Bourne was already inside his guard. He slammed the butt down on Bourne's shoulder, and Bourne staggered as more pain flashed through him.

Then he'd reached up, digging his fingers into the broken bones of Spalko's jaw. Spalko screamed and Bourne wrenched the gun from his grip. He jammed the muzzle underneath Spalko's chin and pulled the trigger.

The sound did not amount to much, but the force of the percussion lifted Spalko bodily off the deck and pitched him over the side. He went into the sea headfirst.

For a moment, as Bourne looked on, he floated face down, rocked back and forth by the restless waves. Then he went under as if drawn by something huge and immensely potent beneath the sea.

# 31

Martin Lindros spent twenty minutes on the phone with Ethan Hearn. Hearn had much information about the famous Stepan Spalko, all of it such a stunning revelation it took Lindros some time to absorb and accept. In the end, no item was of more interest to him than the one that showed an electronic transfer from one of Spalko's many shell companies in Budapest to buy a gun from a certain illegal Russian-run company operating out of Virginia until Detective Harris had shut them down.

An hour later he had two hard copies printed out from the electronic files Hearn had e-mailed him. He got into his car and headed over to the DCI's town house. Overnight, the Old Man had been stricken with the flu. It must be bad, Lindros thought now, for him to have left the office at all during the crisis at the summit.

His driver stopped the staff car at the high iron gates, leaned out the open window, and pressed the intercom. In the ensuing silence he began to wonder if the Old Man, feeling better, had summarily taken himself back to the office without informing anyone.

Then the querulous voice crackled over the intercom, the driver announced Lindros, and a moment later, the gates swung soundlessly open. The driver pulled the car up and Lindros got out. He rapped on the door with the brass knocker, and when it opened, he saw the DCI, his face wrinkled and his hair disheveled from lying on a pillow. He was wearing striped pajamas over which he'd wrapped a heavy-looking bathrobe. On his bony feet were carpet slippers.

'Come in, Martin. Come in.' He turned and left the door open without waiting for Lindros to cross the threshold. Lindros entered, closed the door behind him. The DCI had padded into the study, which was off to the left. There were no lights on; there appeared to be none on in the house at all.

He went into the study, a masculine space with hunter green walls, a cream ceiling, and oversize leather chairs and sofa scattered about. A TV, set into a wall of built-in bookcases, was off. Every other time Lindros had been in this room it had been on, tuned to CNN, either with or without the sound.

The Old Man sat heavily down in his favorite chair. The side table at his right elbow was crammed with a large box of tissues and bottles of aspirin, Tylenol Cold & Sinus, NyQuil, Vicks VapoRub, Coricidin, DayQuil, and Robitussin DM cough syrup.

'What is this, sir?' Lindros said, indicating the small drugstore.

'I didn't know what I'd need,' the DCI said, 'so I just took everything out of the medicine chest.'

Then Lindros saw the bottle of bourbon and the old-fashioned glass, and he frowned. 'Sir, what's going on?' He craned his neck to see out the open doorway of the study. 'Where's Madeleine?'

'Ah, Madeleine.' The Old Man picked up his whiskey glass and slugged some down. 'Madeleine has gone to her sister's in Phoenix.'

'And left you on your own?' Lindros reached over and turned on a standing lamp, and the DCI blinked owlishly at him. 'When will she be back, sir?'

'Hmmm,' the DCI said, as if considering his deputy's words. 'Well, the thing of it is, Martin, I don't know when she's coming back.'

'Sir?' Lindros said with some alarm.

'She's left me. At least that's what I think has happened.' The DCI's gaze seemed fixed as he drained his glass of bourbon. He pursed his shining lips as if perplexed. 'How does one know these things, really?'

'Haven't the two of you talked?'

'Talked?' The DCI's gaze snapped back into focus. He looked at Lindros for a moment. 'No. We haven't spoken about it at all.'

'Then how do you know?'

'You think I'm making it up, tempest in a rotunda, eh?' The DCI's eyes came alive for an instant and all at once his voice was clotted with barely suppressed emotion. 'But there are things of hers that're gone, you see – personal things, intimate things. The house is goddamned empty without them.'

Lindros sat down. 'Sir, you have my sympathy, but I have something – '

'Maybe, Martin, she never loved me.' The Old Man reached for the bottle. 'But how is one to know such a mysterious thing?'

Lindros learned forward, gently took the bourbon from his commander. The DCI didn't seem surprised. 'I'll work on it for you, sir, if you'd like.'

The DCI nodded vaguely. 'All right.'

Lindros put the bottle aside. 'But for now we have another pressing matter to discuss.' He set the file he'd gotten from Ethan Hearn down on the Old Man's side table.

'What is that? I can't read anything now, Martin.'

'Then I'll tell you,' Lindros said. When he was done, there was a silence that seemed to echo throughout the house.

After a time the Old Man looked at his deputy with watery eyes. 'Why'd he do it, Martin? Why did Alex break every rule and steal one of our own people?'

'I think he'd gotten a hint of what was coming, sir. He was frightened of Spalko. As it turned out, with very good reason.'

The Old Man sighed and put his head back. 'So it wasn't treason, after all.'

'No, sir.'

'Thank God.'

Lindros cleared his throat. 'Sir, you must rescind the Bourne sanction at once, and someone's going to have to debrief him.'

'Yes, of course. I think you're best equipped to do that, Martin.'

'Yes, sir.' Lindros stood.

'Where are you going?' The querulousness had returned to the Old Man's voice.

'To the Virginia State Police Commissioner. I have another copy of that file to drop into his lap. I'm going to insist that Detective Harris be reinstated, with a commendation from us. And as for the National Security Advisor herself . . . ?'

The DCI took up the file and stroked it lightly. With this bit of animation, some color returned to his face. 'Give me overnight, Martin.' Slowly, the old glint was returning to his eyes. 'I'll think of something deliciously suitable.' He laughed, the first time he'd done so, it seemed, in ages. '"Let the punishment fit the crime," eh?'

Khan was with Zina to the end. He'd hidden the NX 20 and its horribly lethal payload. As far as the security people who were swarming all over the thermal heating station were concerned, he was a hero. They knew nothing about the bio-weapon. They knew nothing about him.

It was a curious time for Khan. He held the hand of a dying young woman who couldn't speak, who could barely breathe, and yet who quite clearly didn't want to let him go. Perhaps it was simply that, in the end, she didn't want to die.

After Hull and Karpov realized that she was on the verge of dying and couldn't provide them with information, they lost interest and so they left her alone with Khan. And he, so inured to death, experienced something wholly unexpected. Each breath she took, labored and painful, was a lifetime. He saw this in her eyes which, like her hand, would not let him go. She was drowning in the silence, sinking down into darkness. He couldn't let that happen.

Unbidden, his own pain was brought to the surface by hers, and he spoke to her of his life: Of his abandonment, his imprisonment by the Vietnamese gunrunner, the religious conversion forced on him by the missionary, the political brainwashing by his Khmer Rouge interlocutor.

And then, most painful of all, was wrenched out of him his feelings about Lee-Lee. 'I had a sister,' he said in a thin, reedy voice. 'She would've been about your age had she lived. She was two years younger than me, looked up to me, and I – I was her protector. I wanted so much to keep her safe, not only because my parents said I should but because I needed to. My father was away a lot. When we were off playing, who would protect her if not me?' Unaccountably, his eyes felt hot and his vision was blurred. Suffused with shame, he was about to turn away, but he saw something in Zina's eyes, a fierce compassion that served as a lifeline for him, and his shame vanished. He continued then, connected to her on an even more intimate level. 'But, in the end, I failed Lee-Lee. My sister was killed along with my mother. I should've been too, but I survived.' His hand found its way to the carved stone Buddha, gaining strength from it as he had done so many times before. 'For such a long time, I used to wonder, what use was my survival? I had failed her.'

When Zina's lips parted slightly, he saw that her teeth were bloody. Her hand, which he held so tightly, squeezed his and he knew that she wanted him to go on. He was not only freeing her from her own agony but he was freeing himself from his own. And the most curious thing was that it worked. Though she couldn't speak, though she was slowly dying, still her brain functioned. She heard what he said, and by her expression, he knew that it meant something to her – he knew that she was transported and that she understood.

'Zina,' he said, 'in a way, we're kindred spirits. I see myself in you – alienated, abandoned, utterly alone. I know this won't make much sense to you, but my own guilt at my failure to protect my sister made me hate my father beyond reason. All I could see was his abandonment of us – of me.' And then, in a moment of astonishing revelation, he realized that he was looking through a glass darkly, that the only way he recognized himself in her was that he had changed. She was, in fact, the way he used to be. It was far easier to plan revenge on his father than to face the full brunt of his own guilt. It was from this knowledge that his desire to help her sprang. He fervently wished that he could rescue her from death.

But he, of all people, understood with uncanny intimacy the coming of death. Its tread, once heard, could not be stopped, even by him. And when the time came, when he heard the tread and saw death's proximity in her eyes, he leaned over and, without being aware of it, smiled down at her reassuringly.

Picking up where Bourne, his father, had left off, he said, 'Remember what to tell the Questioners, Zina. "My God is Allah, my prophet Mohammad, my religion Islam, and my kibla the Holy Kaaba."' There seemed so much that she wanted to tell him and could not. 'You are righteous, Zina. They will welcome you to glory.'

Her eyes flickered once and then, like a flame, the life that animated them was extinguished.

Jamie Hull was waiting for Bourne when he returned to the Oskjuhlid Hotel. It had taken Bourne some time to get back there. Twice he was on the verge of passing out and was obliged to turn off the road, sitting with his forehead pressed against the steering wheel, he was in terrible pain, weary beyond thought; still, his will to see Khan again goaded him on. He did not care about security; he didn't care about anything now but being with his son.

At the hotel, after Bourne had briefly recounted Stepan Spalko's role in the assault on the hotel, Hull insisted on taking him to a medic to see to his fresh wounds.

'Spalko's worldwide reputation is such that even after we recover the body and release the evidence, there will be those who will refuse to believe it,' Hull responded.

The emergency medic's rooms were filled with casualties lying on hastily erected cots. The more seriously wounded had been driven off by ambulance to the hospital. Then there were the dead, of whom no one yet wished to speak.

'We know your part in this, and I must say we're all grateful,' Hull said, as he sat beside Bourne. 'The president wants to speak with you, of course, but that will come later.'

The medic arrived and started to stitch up Bourne's lacerated cheek.

'This won't heal pretty,' she said. 'You might want to consult a plastic surgeon.'

'It won't be my first scar,' Bourne said.

'So I see,' she said dryly.

'One thing we found troubling was the presence of HAZMAT suits,' Hull continued. 'We found no sign of a biological or chemical agent. Did you?'

Bourne had to think fast. He'd left Khan alone with Zina and the bio-weapon. A sudden stab of fear struck him. 'No. We were as surprised as you were. But, afterward, there was no one left alive to ask.'

Hull nodded, and when the medic was finished, he helped Bourne up and out into the corridor. 'I know you'd like nothing better than a hot shower and a change of clothes, but it's important that I debrief you immediately.' He smiled reassuringly. 'It's a matter of national security. My hands are tied. But at least we can do it in a civilized manner over a hot meal, okay?'

Without another word, he delivered a short, sharp kidney punch that dropped Bourne to his knees. As Bourne gasped for breath, Hull drew back his other hand.

In it was a push-dagger, the stubby leaflike blade that emerged from between his second and third fingers dark with a substance that was doubtless poisonous.

As he was about to drive it into Bourne's neck, a shot sounded in the corridor. Bourne, released from Hull's grip, slumped against the wall. Turning his head, he took everything in: Hull lying dead on the maroon carpet, the poisoned push-dagger in his hand, and hurrying up on his slightly bandy legs, Boris Illyich Karpov, director of the FSB's Alpha Unit, a silenced pistol in his hand.

'I must admit,' Karpov said in Russian, as he helped Bourne to his feet, 'I always harbored a secret desire to kill a CIA agent.'

'Christ, thanks,' Bourne gasped in the same language.

'This was a pleasure, believe me.' Karpov stared down at Hull. 'The CIA sanction against you has been rescinded, not that it mattered to him. It seems that you still have enemies inside your own Agency.'

Bourne took several deep breaths, in itself a terribly painful proposition. He waited for his mind to clear sufficiently. 'Karpov, how do I know you?'

The Russian let loose with a booming laugh. '*Gospadin* Bourne, I see the rumors about your memory are true.' He put his arm around Bourne's waist, half support-ing him. 'Do you remember – ? No, of course you don't. Well, the truth is, we've met several times. The last time, you saved my life, in fact.' He laughed again at Bourne's bewildered expression. 'It's a fine tale, my friend. A suitable story to tell over a bottle of vodka. Or maybe two, eh? After a night like this, who knows?'

'I'd be grateful for some vodka,' Bourne acknowledged, 'but there's someone I need to find first.'

'Come,' Karpov said, 'I'll contact my men to clean up this garbage and we'll do together whatever needs to be done.' He grinned hugely, dissolving the brutality of his features. 'You stink like a week-old fish, you know that? But what the hell, I'm used to all sorts of foul odors!' He laughed again. 'What a pleasure to see you again! One doesn't make friends easily, I've discovered, especially in our line of work. And so we must celebrate this event, this reunion, no?'

'Absolutely.'

'And who must you need to find, my good friend Jason Bourne, that you cannot take a hot shower and a well-deserved rest first?'

'A young man named Khan. You've met him, I assume.'

'Indeed,' Karpov said as he led Bourne down another corridor. 'A most remarkable young man. D'you know he never left the dying Chechen's side? And she, for her part, never let go of his hand until the end.' He shook his head. 'Most extraordinary.'

He pursed his ruby lips. 'Not that she deserved his attention. What was she, a murderer, a destroyer? You only have to see what they were attempting here to understand what kind of a monster she was.'

'And yet,' Bourne said, 'she needed to hold his hand.'

'How he put up with it I'll never know.'

'Perhaps he needed something from her, as well.' Bourne gave him a look. 'Still think she was a monster?'

'Oh, yes,' Karpov said, 'but then the Chechens have trained me to think that way.'

'Nothing changes, does it?' Bourne said.

'Not until we wipe them out.' Karpov gave him a sideways glance. 'Listen, my idealistic friend, they have said about us what other terrorists have said about you

Americans, "God has declared war on you." We have learned from bitter experience to take such pronouncements seriously.'

As it happened, Karpov knew just where Khan was – in the main restaurant, which was, after a fashion, up and running again with a severely limited menu.

'Spalko's dead,' Bourne said to cover the rush of feeling he felt when he saw Khan.

Khan put down his hamburger and studied the stitches on Bourne's swollen cheek. 'Are you hurt?'

'More than I already am?' Bourne winced as he sat down. 'It's only minor.'

Khan nodded but didn't take his eyes off Bourne.

Karpov, sitting down beside Bourne, called out to a passing waiter for a bottle of vodka. 'Russian,' he said sharply, 'not that Polish swill. And bring with it large glasses. We're real men here, a Russian and heroes who are almost as good as Russians!' Then he returned his attention to his companions. 'All right, what am I missing?' he said cannily.

'Nothing,' Khan and Bourne said together.

'Is that so?' The Russian agent's caterpillar eyebrows lifted. 'Well, then, there's nothing left but to drink. *In vino, veritas*. In wine, there is truth, so the ancient Romans believed. And who should disbelieve them? They were damn fine soldiers, the Romans, and they had great generals, but they would've been even better if they'd drunk vodka instead of wine!' He laughed raucously until the other two had no choice but to join in.

The vodka came then, along with water glasses. Karpov waved the waiter away.

'One must open the first bottle oneself,' he said. 'It's tradition.'

'Bullshit,' Bourne said, turning to Khan. 'It's a habit from the old days when Russian vodka was so poorly refined there was often fuel oil in it.'

'Don't listen to him.' Karpov pursed his lips, but there was a twinkle in his eye. He filled their glasses and very formally placed them in front of them. 'To share a bottle of fine Russian vodka is the very definition of friendship, fuel oil notwithstanding. Because over that bottle of fine Russian vodka we talk of old times, of comrades and enemies who have passed.'

He lifted up his glass and they followed suit.

'*Na Sdarovye!*' he cried, taking an enormous swallow.

'*Na Sdarovye!*' they echoed, following suit.

Bourne's eyes watered. The vodka burned all the way down, but in a moment a warmth suffused his stomach, reaching out its fingers to assuage the constant pain he'd been in.

Karpov hunkered down, his face slightly flushed from both the fiery liquor and the simple pleasure of being with friends. 'Now we'll get drunk and tell all our secrets. We'll learn what it means to be friends.'

He took another huge swallow and said, 'I'll begin. Here's my first secret. I know who you are, Khan. Though there's never been a photo taken of you, I know you.' He put his finger beside his nose. 'I haven't been in the field for twenty years without honing my sixth sense. And knowing this, I steered you away from Hull, who, had he suspected, would surely have arrested you, hero status or no.'

Khan shifted slightly. 'Why would you do that?'

'Oho, now you would kill me? Here at this amiable table? You think that I kept you isolated for myself? Did I not say that we were friends!' He shook his head. 'You've much to learn about friendship, my young friend.' He leaned forward. 'I kept you safe because of Jason Bourne, who always works alone. You were with him, therefore I knew you were important to him.'

He took another slug of vodka and pointed at Bourne. 'Your turn, my friend.'

Bourne stared down into his vodka. He was acutely aware of Khan's scrutiny. He knew what secret he wanted to divulge, but he was afraid that if he did, Khan would get up and walk away. But a truth was what he needed to tell them. He looked up finally.

'In the end, when I was with Spalko, I almost faltered. Spalko came close to killing me, but the truth is . . . the truth is . . .'

'It will be better for you to say it, yes,' Karpov urged.

Bourne took the vodka into his mouth, swallowed the liquid courage down and turned to his son. 'I thought of you. I thought if I failed now, if I allowed Spalko to kill me, I wouldn't come back. I couldn't abandon you; I couldn't allow that to happen.'

'Good!' Karpov banged his glass on the table. He pointed at Khan. 'Now you, my young friend.'

In the ensuing silence Bourne felt as if his heart was in danger of stopping. Blood pounded in his head and all the pain of his many wounds, so briefly anesthetized, came flooding back.

'Well,' Karpov said, 'has the cat got your tongue? Your friends have given themselves up to you, and now they're waiting.'

Khan looked straight at the Russian and said, 'Boris Illyich Karpov, I'd like to formally introduce myself. My name is Joshua. I'm Jason Bourne's son.'

Many hours and liters of vodka later, Bourne and Khan stood together in the sub-basement of the Oskjuhlid Hotel. It was musty down there and cold, but all they could smell were vodka fumes. There were bloodstains everywhere.

'I suppose you're wondering what happened to the NX 20,' Khan said.

Bourne nodded. 'Hull was suspicious of the HAZMAT suits. He said they didn't find any evidence of biological or chemical weapons.'

'I hid it,' Khan said. 'I was waiting for you to come back so that we could destroy it together.'

Bourne hesitated for a moment. 'You had faith I'd come back.'

Khan turned and looked at his father. 'It seems that I've newly acquired my faith.'

'Or had it restored.'

'Don't tell me – '

'I know, I know, I have no business telling you what you think.' Bourne ducked his head. 'Some acquisitions take more time than others.'

Khan moved to where he'd hidden the NX 20, inside a crumbly niche behind a broken block of concrete obscured from view by one of the huge pipes in the thermal power station. 'I had to leave Zina for a moment to do it,' he said, 'but it couldn't be helped.' He held it with understandable respect as he handed it over to Bourne. He went and took a small metal box out of the niche. 'The vial with the payload is in here.'

'We need a fire,' Bourne said, thinking of the legend he'd read on Dr. Sido's computer. 'Heat will render the payload inert.'

The vast hotel kitchen was spotless. Its gleaming stainless-steel surfaces seemed even colder with the absence of personnel. Bourne had moved the skeleton staff out for the time being while he and Khan went over to the huge floor-to-ceiling ovens. They were gas-powered, and Bourne turned them up to the highest level. At once fierce flames shot through the fire-brick-lined interior. In less than a minute, it was too hot even to get close to.

They donned HAZMAT suits, broke down the weapon and each one threw one half into the flames. The vial went next.

'It's like a Viking funeral pyre,' Bourne said as he watched the NX 20 collapse in on itself. He closed the door and they took off the suits.

Turning to his son, he said, 'I've phoned Marie, but I haven't told her about you yet. I was waiting – '

'I'm not going back with you,' Khan said.

Bourne chose his next words with great care. 'That would not be my choice.'

'I know,' Khan said. 'But I think there was a very good reason you didn't tell your wife about me.'

In the silence that abruptly engulfed them, Bourne was gripped by a terrible sorrow. He wanted to look away, to hide what had rushed to his face, but he could not. He was through hiding his emotions from his son and from himself.

'You have Marie, two small children,' Khan said. 'This is the new life David Webb has made for himself and I'm not a part of it.'

Bourne had learned many things in the few days since the first bullet sang its warning song past his ear on campus, not the least of which was when to keep his mouth shut around his son. He'd made up his mind and that was it. Trying to talk him out of his decision would be useless. Worse, it would reawaken the still-latent anger he would carry around with him for some time. An emotion so toxic, so deep-seated, it couldn't be expunged in a matter of days, weeks or even months.

Bourne understood that Khan had made a wise decision. There was still too much pain, the wound still raw, though the bleeding, at least, had been stopped. And as Khan had astutely pointed out, he knew deep down Khan's entry into the life that David Webb had fashioned for himself made no sense at all. Khan *didn't* belong there.

'Perhaps not now, perhaps not ever. But no matter how you feel about me, I want you to know that you have a brother and a sister who deserve to know you and have an older brother in their life. I hope there will come a time when that will happen – for all our sakes.'

They walked together to the door and Bourne was very much aware that it was for the last time for many months to come. But not forever, no. This, at least, he had to make known to his son.

He moved forward and took Khan into his embrace. They stood together in silence. Bourne could hear the hiss of the gas jets. Inside the ovens, the fire continued to burn fiercely, annihilating the terrible threat to them all.

Reluctantly, he let Khan go, and for the briefest moment, as he stared into his son's eyes, he saw him as he had been, as a little boy in Phnom Penh with the blazing Asian sun on his face and, in the dappled shadows of the palms just beyond, Dao watching, smiling at them both.

'I'm also Jason Bourne,' he said. 'That's something you should never forget.'

# Epilogue

When the President of the United States personally opened the double walnut doors to his West Wing study, the DCI felt as if he was being readmitted to the precincts of heaven after cooling his heels in the seventh circle of hell.

The DCI was still suffering from the godawful malady, but with the telephone summons, he'd managed to drag himself out of his leather chair, had showered, shaved and dressed. He had been expecting the call. In fact, after he had his 'Eyes Only' report delivered to the president, including all the detailed evidence compiled by Martin Lindros and Detective Harris he'd been mentally waiting for the call. And yet he'd waited in his robe and pajamas, sunk in his chair, listening to the oppressive silence of the house as if, within that void, he could discern the ghost of his wife's voice.

Now, as the president ushered him into the royal blue and gold corner office, he felt the desolation of his house even more keenly. Here was his life – the life he'd painstakingly built for himself over decades of faithful service and convoluted manipulation – here is where he understood the rules and knew how to play them, here and nowhere else.

'Good of you to come,' the president said with his high-wattage smile. 'It's been too long.'

'Thank you, sir,' the DCI said. 'I was thinking the same thing.'

'Take a seat.' The president waved him to an upholstered wing-back chair. He was dressed in an impeccably tailored dark-blue suit, white shirt and a red tie with blue polka dots. His cheeks were slightly flushed, as if he'd just come in from running wind sprints. 'Coffee?'

'I think I will. Thank you, sir.'

At that moment, as if in response to an unheard summons, one of the presidential aides came in with a chased silver tray on which sat an ornate coffee pot and china cups in their delicate saucers. With a little thrill of pleasure, the DCI noted that there were only two cups.

'The NSA will be along presently,' the president said, taking a seat opposite the DCI. The flush, the DCI could see now, wasn't from physical exertion but from the full ripening of his power. 'But before that, I wanted to thank you personally for your good work these past several days.'

The aide handed them their coffee and left, closing the heavy door softly behind him.

'I shudder to think of the dire consequences suffered by the civilized world were it not for your man Bourne.'

'Thank you, sir. We never fully believed that he'd murdered Alex Conklin and Dr. Panov,' the DCI said with an earnest and thoroughly hypocritical candor, 'but we were presented with certain evidence – trumped-up, as it turned out – and we were forced to act on it.'

'Of course – I understand.' The president dropped two cubes of sugar into his cup and stirred thoughtfully. 'All's well that ends well, though in our world – as opposed to Shakespeare's – there are consequences to every action.' He sipped his coffee. 'Nevertheless, despite the bloodbath, the summit, as you know, went on as scheduled. And it was an unqualified success. In fact, the threat served to bring us more firmly together. All the heads of state – even, thank God, Aleksandr Yevtushenko – could see clearly the fate the world faced if we didn't put aside our own myopic viewpoints and agree to work together. We now have signed, sealed and delivered a practical framework for going forward in a united front against terrorism. Already, the Secretary of State is on his way to the Middle East to begin the next round of talks. Quite an opening salvo across our enemies' bows.'

*And your reelection is assured*, the DCI thought. *Not to mention the legacy of your presidency.*

At the discreet sound of the intercom, the president excused himself, rose and crossed to his desk. He listened for a moment, then looked up. His penetrating gaze rested on the DCI. 'I've allowed myself to be cut off from someone who could have provided measured and valuable advice. Rest assured I won't allow that to happen again.'

Clearly, the president didn't expect him to respond because he was already saying into the intercom, 'Send her in.'

The DCI, as emotionally vulnerable as he'd ever been, took a moment to collect himself. He looked about the spacious high-ceilinged room with its cream walls, royal blue carpet, dentiled molding and solid, comfortable furniture. Large oil portraits of several Republican presidents hung above a matching pair of Chippendale cherrywood sideboards. An American flag stood half-furled in a corner. Outside the windows, under a downy white haze, was an expanse of closely mowed lawn above which a cherry tree spread its arching branches. Clusters of pale pink blossoms shivered like bells in the spring breeze.

The door opened and Roberta Alonzo-Ortiz was ushered in. The DCI noted with relish that the president didn't budge from his position behind his desk. He stood still, facing the NSA, and, quite pointedly, didn't ask her to sit down. The NSA was wearing a severely cut black suit, steel-gray silk blouse and practical low-heeled pumps. She appeared ready to attend a funeral, which, the DCI thought with no little glee, was entirely appropriate.

She registered a split-instant's surprise at the DCI's presence. A last spark of enmity glowed in her eyes before they turned inward and she drew her face into a rigid mask. Her complexion appeared oddly mottled, as if in reaction to the obvious effort of stifling her emotions. She didn't address him or otherwise acknowledge his presence.

'Ms. Alonzo-Ortiz, I want you to understand some things so that you can put the events of the last several days into some kind of perspective,' the president began in a sonorous voice that brooked no interruption. 'While I acceded to the Bourne sanction, I did so strictly on advice from you. I also agreed when you petitioned me for a quick resolution to the murders of Alex Conklin and Morris Panov and, foolishly, followed your judgment in condemning Detective Harry Harris of the Virginia State Police for the debacle beneath Washington Circle.

'All I can say is that I'm profoundly grateful that the sanction wasn't in the end carried out, but I'm appalled at the damage done to the career of a fine detective. Zeal is a commendable trait but not when it overrides the truth, something you swore to uphold when I asked you to come aboard.'

Through this speech, he had neither moved nor taken his gaze from her. His expression was carefully neutral, but there was a certain clipped cadence to his words that revealed to the DCI, who after all knew him best, both the depth and the breadth of his anger. This was not a man to be made a fool of, this was not a president to forgive and forget. The DCI had counted on this when he prepared his damning report.

'Ms. Alonzo-Ortiz, my administration has no place for political opportunists – at least, not those who are willing to sacrifice the truth in order to cover their own ass. The truth is, you should've aided in the investigation of the murders instead of trying your best to bury those falsely implicated. If you had, we might have uncovered this terrorist, Stepan Spalko, soon enough to have averted the bloodbath at the summit. As it is, we all owe a debt of gratitude to the DCI, especially you.'

At this last, Roberta Alonzo-Ortiz winced, as if the president had dealt her a terrific blow, which, in a sense, he very deliberately had.

He picked up a single sheet of paper off his desk. 'Therefore, I accept your letter of resignation and grant your request to return to the private sector,' effective immediately.'

The former NSA opened her mouth to speak, but the president's laserlike stare froze her in her tracks.

'I wouldn't,' he said shortly.

She blanched, nodded slightly in submission, and turned on her heel.

The moment the door closed behind her the DCI took a deep breath. For a moment the president's gaze intersected his and all was revealed. He knew why his Commander-in-Chief had summoned him to witness the NSA's humiliation. It was his way of making an apology. In all his years toiling as a servant of his country, the DCI had never before been apologized to by the president. He was so overcome he had no idea how to respond.

In a daze of euphoria, he rose. The president was already on the phone, his eyes roving elsewhere. For a brief moment, the DCI paused, savoring his moment of triumph. Then he, too, departed the sanctum sanctorum, striding down the hushed corridors of power that he had made his home.

David Webb had finished hanging the multicolored HAPPY BIRTHDAY sign in the living room. Marie was in the kitchen, putting the finishing touches on the chocolate cake she'd baked for Jamie's eleventh birthday. The smells of pizza and chocolate drifted deliciously through the house. He looked around, wondering if there were enough balloons. He counted thirty – surely, that was more than enough.

Though he'd returned to his life as David Webb, his ribs pained him with every breath he took and the rest of his body ached enough for him to know that he was also Jason Bourne and always would be. For so long he'd been terrified each time that side of his personality resurfaced, but now with Joshua's reemergence, everything had changed. He had a compelling reason to become Jason Bourne again.

But not with the CIA. With Alex's death, he was quits with them, even though the DCI himself had asked him to stay, even though he actually liked and respected Martin Lindros, the man responsible for having the sanction against him lifted. It was Lindros who had admitted him to Bethesda Naval Hospital. In between bouts with a team of Agency-vetted specialists, who had seen to Webb's wounds and had carefully examined his cracked ribs, Lindros had debriefed him. The DDCI had made a difficult task almost easy, allowing Webb precious time to sleep and unwind from his arduous trials.

But after three days Webb wanted nothing more than to return to his students, and he needed time with his family, even though there was now an ache in his heart, a certain void given form and shape by Joshua's return. He'd meant to tell Marie about him, had in fact told her every other detail of what had happened while they'd been out of touch. And yet each time he had come to the subject of his other son, his brain shut down. It wasn't that he was afraid of her reaction – he trusted her too much for that. It was his own reaction he was unsure of. After only a week away he felt estranged from Jamie and Alison. He'd completely forgotten Jamie's birthday until Marie had gently reminded him. Like the proverbial line in the sand, he felt a clear demarcation of his life before Joshua's startling appearance and after. There was the darkness of grief and now there was the light of reconnection. There was death and now, miraculously, there was life. He needed to understand the implications of what had happened. How could he share something so monumental with Marie until he understood it himself?

And so, on this, his young son's birthday, his mind was flooded with thoughts of his older son. Where was Joshua? Shortly after he'd heard from Ozskar that Annaka Vadas' body had been found by the side of the motorway leading to Ferihegy Airport, Joshua had slipped away, vanishing as quickly and completely as he had appeared. Had he returned to Budapest to see Annaka one last time? Webb hoped not.

In any case, Karpov had promised to keep his secret, and Webb believed him. He realized that he had no idea where his son lived or even if he had a real home. It was impossible to imagine where Joshua was or what he might now be doing, and this caused a pain in Webb unlike any other. He felt the lack of him as acutely as if he'd lost a limb. There was so much he wanted to say to Joshua, so much time to make up for. It was difficult being patient, painful not even knowing whether Joshua would choose to come to him again.

The party had begun, the twenty or so kids playing and yelling at the tops of their lungs. And there was Jamie in the center of it all, a born leader, a boy others his own age looked up to. His open face, so like Marie's, was shining with happiness. Webb wondered whether he'd ever see such a look of unalloyed pleasure on Joshua's face. Instantly, as if there was a telepathic link between them, Jamie glanced up and, seeing his father's gaze on him, grinned hugely.

Webb, having drawn greeter duty, once again heard the bell ring. He opened the door to find a FedEx agent with a package for him. He signed for it and at once took it down to the basement, where he unlocked a room to which there was only one key. Inside was a portable X-ray machine Conklin had procured for him. All packages coming to the Webbs were, unbeknownst to the children, run through this machine.

Determining it was clean, Webb opened it. Inside were a baseball and two gloves, one for him and the other just the right size for an eleven-year-old. He unfolded the accompanying note, which read, simply:

```
For Jamie's birthday
– Joshua
```

David Webb stared at the gift, which meant more to him than anyone would ever know. Music drifted down to him from above, along with the intermittent laughter of the children. He thought of Dao and Alyssa and Joshua as they existed in his splintered memory, and this kaleidoscopic image, stimulated by the sharp, earthy scent of the oiled leather, was brought vividly to life. Reaching out, he felt the supple grain of the leather, ran his fingertips over the rawhide stitching. What memories were stirring inside him! His smile, when it came to his face, was bittersweet. He slipped his hand into the larger of the gloves and threw the baseball into the heart of it. Catching it there, he held it as tightly as if it were a will-o'-the-wisp.

He heard a light tread on the top of the stairs, and then Marie's voice calling to him.

'I'll be right up, sweetheart,' he said.

He sat very still for some moments longer, allowing the events of the recent past to swirl around him. Then he exhaled deeply and set aside the past. With Jamie's present cradled in the other hand, he mounted the basement stairs and went to rejoin his family.

# The Bourne Betrayal

In memory of Adam Hall (Elleston Trevor), a literary mentor:
The roses are for you, too

Thanks to

Ken Dorph, my Arabist
Jeff Arbital

And a special thank-you to Victoria,
for the title

# Prologue

The Chinook came beating up into a blood-red sky. It shuddered in the perilous crosscurrents, banking through the thin air. A web of clouds, backlit by the failing sun, streamed by like smoke from a flaming aircraft.

Martin Lindros stared intently out of the military copter carrying him upward into the highest elevations of the Simien mountain range. While it was true that he hadn't been in the field since the Old Man had appointed him to the position of deputy director of Central Intelligence four years ago, he'd made sure that he'd never lost his animal edge. He trained three mornings a week at the CI field agent obstacle course outside Quantico, and every Thursday night at ten he washed away the tedium of vetting electronic intel reports and signing action orders by spending ninety minutes at the firing range, reacquainting himself with every manner of firearm, old, current, and new. Manufacturing action of his own served to assuage his frustration at not being more relevant. All that changed, however, when the Old Man approved his operations proposal for Typhon.

A thin keening knifed through the interior of the CI-modified Chinook. Anders, the commander of Skorpion One, the five-man squad of crack field operatives, nudged him, and he turned. Peering out the window at the shredding clouds, he saw the wind-ravaged north slope of Ras Dejen. There was something distinctly ominous about the forty-five-hundred-meter mountain, tallest in the Simien range. Perhaps that was because Lindros remembered the local lore: legends of spirits, ancient and evil, who supposedly dwelled on its upper reaches.

The sound of the wind rose to a scream, as if the mountain were trying to tear itself from its roots.

It was time.

Lindros nodded and moved forward to where the pilot sat strapped securely into his seat. The deputy director was in his late thirties, a tall, sandy-haired graduate of Brown who had been recruited into CI during his doctorate in foreign studies at Georgetown. He was whip-smart and as dedicated a general as the DCI could ask for. Bending low so he could be heard over the noise, Lindros gave the pilot the final coordinates, which security dictated he keep to himself until the last possible moment.

He had been in the field just over three weeks. In that time, he'd lost two men. A terrible price to pay. Acceptable losses, the Old Man would say, and he had to retrain himself to think that way if he was to have success in the field. But what price do you put on human life? This was a question that he and Jason Bourne had often debated, without an acceptable answer being reached. Privately, Lindros believed there were some questions to which there was no acceptable answer.

Still, when agents were in the field, that was another matter altogether. 'Acceptable losses' had to be accepted. There was no other way. So, yes, the deaths of those two men were acceptable, because in the course of his mission he had ascertained the veracity of the report that a terrorist organization had gotten its hands on a case of triggered spark gaps somewhere in the Horn of Africa. TSGs were small, ultra-high-energy switches, used to turn on and off enormous levels of voltage: high-tech escape valves to protect electronic components such as microwave tubes and medical testing devices. They were also used to trigger nuclear bombs.

Starting in Cape Town, Lindros had followed a twisting trail that led from Botswana, to Zambia, through Uganda, to Ambikwa, a tiny agricultural village – no more than a fistful of buildings, a church and a bar among them – amid alpine pastureland on the slope of Ras Dejen. There he had obtained one of the TSGs, which he had immediately sent back to the Old Man via secure courier.

But then something happened, something extraordinary, something horrifying. In the beaten-down bar with a floor of dung and dried blood, he had heard a rumor that the terrorist organization was transshipping more than TSGs out of Ethiopia. If the rumor was true, it had terrifying implications not only for America, but for the entire world, because it meant the terrorists had in their possession the instrument to plunge the globe into nightmare.

Seven minutes later, the Chinook settled into the eye of a dust storm. The small plateau was entirely deserted. Just ahead was an ancient stone wall – a gateway, so the local legends went, to the fearsome home of the demons that dwelled here. Through a gap in the crumbling wall, Lindros knew, lay the almost vertical path to the giant rock buttresses that guarded the summit of Ras Dejen.

Lindros and the men of Skorpion One hit the ground in a crouch. The pilot remained in his chair, keeping the engine revved, the rotors turning. The men wore goggles to protect them from the swirling dust and hail of small pebbles churned up by their transportation, and tiny wireless mikes and earpieces that curled into their ears, facilitating communication over the roar of the rotors. Each was armed with an XM8 Lightweight Assault Rifle capable of firing a blistering 750 rounds per minute.

Lindros led the way across the rough-hewn plateau. Opposite the stone wall was a forbidding cliff face in which there appeared the black, yawning mouth of a cave. All else was dun-colored, ocher, dull red, the blasted landscape of another planet, the road to hell.

Anders deployed his men in standard fashion, sending them first to check obvious hiding places, then to form a secure perimeter. Two of them went to the stone wall to check out its far side. The other two were assigned to the cave, one to stand at the mouth, the other to make certain the interior was clear.

The wind, rising over the high butte that towered over them, whipped across the bare ground, penetrating their uniforms. Where the rock face didn't drop off precipitously, it towered over them, ominous, muscular, its bare skull magnified in the thin air. Lindros paused at the remnants of a campfire, his attention shifting.

At his side, Anders, like any good commander, was taking readings of the area perimeter from his men. No one lurked behind the stone wall. He listened intently to his second team.

'There's a body in the cave,' the commander reported. 'Took a bullet to the brain. Stone-dead. Otherwise the site's clean.'

Lindros heard Anders's voice in his ear. 'This is where we start,' he said, pointing. 'The only sign of life in this godforsaken place.'

They squatted down. Anders stirred the charcoal with gloved fingers.

'There's a shallow pit here.' The commander scooped out the cindered debris. 'See? The bottom is fire-hardened. Means someone's lit not just one fire but many over the last months, maybe as long as a year.'

Lindros nodded, gave the thumbs-up sign. 'Looks like we might be in the right place.' Anxiety lanced through him. It appeared more and more likely that the rumor he'd heard was true. He'd been hoping against hope that it was just that, a rumor; that he'd get up here and find nothing. Because any other outcome was unthinkable.

Unhooking two devices from his webbed belt, he turned them on, played them over the fire pit. One was an alpha radiation detector, the other a Geiger counter. What he was looking for, what he was hoping not to find, was a combination of alpha and gamma radiation.

There was no reading from either device at the fire site.

He kept going. Using the fire pit as a central point, he moved in concentric circles, his eyes glued to the meters. He was on his third pass, perhaps a hundred meters from the fire pit, when the alpha detector activated.

'Shit,' he said under his breath.

'Find something?' Anders asked.

Lindros moved off axis and the alpha detector fell silent. Nothing on the Geiger. Well, that was something. An alpha reading, at this level, could come from anything, even, possibly, the mountain itself.

He returned to where the detector had picked up the alpha radiation. Looking up, he saw that he was directly in line with the cave. Slowly, he began walking toward it. The reading on the radiation detector remained constant. Then, perhaps twenty meters from the cave mouth, it ramped up. Lindros paused for a moment to wipe beads of sweat off his upper lip. Christ, he was being forced to acknowledge another nail in the world's coffin. Still – *No gamma yet,* he told himself. That was something. He held on to that hope for twelve more meters. Then the Geiger counter started up.

Oh, God, gamma radiation in conjunction with alpha. Precisely the signature he was hoping not to find. He felt a line of perspiration trickle down his spine. Cold sweat. He hadn't experienced anything like that since he'd had to make his first kill in the field. Hand-to-hand, desperation and determination on his face and on that of the man trying his best to kill him. Self-preservation.

'Lights.' Lindros had to force out the word through a mouth full of mortal terror. 'I need to see that corpse.'

Anders nodded and gave orders to Brick, the man who had made the first foray into the cave. Brick switched on a xenon torch. The three men entered the gloom.

There were no dead leaves or other organic materials to leaven the sharp mineral reek. They could feel the deadweight of the rock massif above them. Lindros was reminded of the feeling of near suffocation he had experienced when he'd first entered the tombs of the pharaohs down in the depths of Cairo's pyramids.

The bright xenon beam played over the rock walls. In this bleak setting, the male corpse did not look altogether out of place. Shadows fled across it as Brick moved the light. The xenon beam drained it of any color it might have had, making it seem less than human – a zombie out of a horror film. Its position was one of repose, of utter peace, belied by the neat bullet hole in the center of its forehead. The face was turned away, as if it wished to remain in darkness.

'Wasn't a suicide, that's for sure,' Anders said, which had been the starting point of Lindros's own train of thought. 'Suicides go for something easy – the mouth is a prime example. This man was murdered by a professional.'

'But why?' Lindros's voice was distracted.

The commander shrugged. 'With these people it could be any of a thousand – '

'Get the hell back!'

Lindros shouted so hard into his mike that Brick, who had been circling toward the corpse, leapt back.

'Sorry, sir,' Brick said. 'I just wanted to show you something odd.'

'Use the light,' Lindros instructed him. But he already knew what was coming. The moment they had stepped inside the cave both the rad detector and the Geiger counter had beat a terrifying rat-tat-tat against his eyes.

*Christ,* he thought. *Oh, Christ.*

The corpse was exceedingly thin, and shockingly young, not out of its teens, surely. Did he have the Semitic features of an Arab? He thought not, but it was nearly impossible to tell because –

'Holy Mother of God!'

Anders saw it then. The corpse had no nose. The center of his face had been eaten away. The ugly pit was black with curdled blood that foamed slowly out as if the body were still alive. As if something were feasting on it from the inside out.

*Which,* Lindros thought with a wave of nausea, *is precisely what is happening.*

'What the hell could do that?' Anders said thickly. 'Tissue toxin? Virus?'

Lindros turned to Brick. 'Did you touch it? Tell me, did you touch the corpse?'

'No, I – ' Brick was taken aback. 'Am I contaminated?'

'Deputy Director, begging your pardon, sir, what the hell have you gotten us into? I'm used to being in the dark on black-ops missions, but this has crossed another boundary altogether.'

Lindros, on one knee, uncapped a small metal canister and used his gloved finger to gather some of the dirt near the body. Sealing the container tightly, he rose.

'We need to get out of here.' He stared directly into Anders's face.

'Deputy Director – '

'Don't worry, Brick. You'll be all right,' he said with the voice of authority. 'No more talk. Let's go.'

When they reached the cave mouth and the glare of the blasted, blood-red landscape, Lindros said into his mike, 'Anders, as of now that cave is off limits to you and your men. Not even to take a leak. Got it?'

The commander hesitated an instant, his anger, his concern for his men evident on his face. Then it seemed he shrugged mentally. 'Yessir.'

Lindros spent the next ten minutes scouring the plateau with his rad detector and Geiger counter. He very much wanted to know how the contamination had gotten up here – which route had the men carrying it taken? There was no point in looking for the way they had gone. The fact that the man without a nose had been shot to death told him that the group members had discovered in the most horrifying way that they had a radiation leak. They would surely have sealed it before venturing on. But he had no luck now. Away from the cave, both the alpha and gamma radiation vanished completely. Not a hint of a trace remained for him to determine its path.

Finally, he turned back from the perimeter.

'Evacuate the site, Commander.'

'You heard the man,' Anders shouted as he trotted toward the waiting copter. 'Let's saddle up, boys!'

*'Wa'i,'* Fadi said. He knows.

'Surely not.' Abbud ibn Aziz stirred his position beside Fadi. Crouched behind the high butte three hundred meters above the plateau, they served as advance guard for a cadre of perhaps twenty armed men lying low against the rocky ground behind them.

'With these I can see everything. There was a leak.'

'Why weren't we informed?'

There was no reply. None was needed. They had not been informed because of naked fear. Fadi, had he known, would have killed them all – every last one of the Ethiopian transporters. Such were the wages of absolute intimidation.

Fadi, peering through powerful 12x50 Russian military binoculars, scanned to his right to keep Martin Lindros in his sights. The 12x50s provided a dizzyingly small field of view but more than made up for it in their detail. He had seen that the leader of the group – the deputy director of CI – was using both a rad detector and a Geiger counter. This American knew what he was about.

Fadi, a tall, broad-shouldered man, possessed a decidedly charismatic demeanor. When he spoke, everyone in his presence fell silent. He had a handsome, powerful face, the color of his skin deepened further by desert sun and mountain wind. His beard and hair were long and curling, the inky color of a starless midnight. His lips were full and wide. When he smiled the sun seemed to have come down from its place in the heavens to shine directly on his disciples. For Fadi's avowed mission was messianic in nature: to bring hope where there was no hope, to slaughter the thousands that made up the Saudi royal family, to wipe their abomination off the face of the earth, to free his people, to distribute the obscene wealth of the despots, to restore the rightful order to his beloved Arabia. To begin, he knew, he must delink the symbiotic relationship between the Saudi royal family and the government of the United States of America. And to do that he must strike at America, to make a clear statement that was as lasting as it was indelible.

What he must not do was underestimate the capacity of Americans to endure pain. This was a common mistake among his extremist comrades, this is what got them into trouble with their own people, this more than anything else was the source of a life lived without hope.

Fadi was no fool. He had studied the history of the world. Better, he had learned from it. When Nikita Khrushchev had said to America, 'We will bury you!' he had meant it in his heart as well as in his soul. But who was it that had been buried? The USSR.

When his extremist comrades said, 'We have many lifetimes to bury America,' they were referring to the endless supply of young men who gained their majority each year, from whom they could choose the martyrs to die in battle. But they gave no thought whatsoever to the deaths of these young men. Why should they? Paradise lay waiting with open arms for the martyrs. Yet what, really, had been gained? Was America living without hope? No. Did these acts push America toward a life without hope? Again, no. So what was the answer?

Fadi believed with all his heart and his soul – and most especially with his formidable intellect – that he had found it.

Keeping track of the deputy director through his 12x50s, he saw that the man seemed reluctant to leave. He felt like a bird of prey as he gazed down on the target site. The arrogant American soldiers had climbed into the helicopter, but their commander – Fadi's intel did not extend to his name – would not allow his leader to remain on the plateau unguarded. He was a canny man. Perhaps his nose smelled something his eyes could not see; perhaps he was only adhering to well-taught discipline. In any case, as the two men stood side by side talking, Fadi knew he would not get a better chance.

'Begin,' he said softly to Abbud ibn Aziz without taking his eyes from the lenses.

Beside him, Abbud ibn Aziz took up the Soviet-made RPG-7 shoulder launcher. He was a stocky man, moon-faced with a cast in his left eye, there since birth. Swiftly and surely, he inserted the tapered, finned warhead into the rocket propulsion tube. The fins on the rotating grenade provided stability, assurance that it would hit its target with a high degree of accuracy. When he depressed the trigger, the primary system would launch the grenade at 117 meters per second. That ferocious burst of energy would, in turn, ignite the rocket propulsion system within the trailing tube, boosting the warhead speed to 294 meters per second.

Abbud ibn Aziz put his right eye against the optical sight, mounted just behind the trigger. He found the Chinook, thought fleetingly that it was a pity to lose this magnificent war machine. But such an object of desire was not for him. In any event, everything had been meticulously planned by Fadi's brother, down to the trail of clues that had compelled the deputy director of CI out of his office and into the field, that led him a tortuous route to northwestern Ethiopia, thence here to the upper reaches of Ras Dejen.

Abbud ibn Aziz positioned the RPG-7 so that it was aimed at the helicopter's front rotor assembly. He was now one with the weapon, one with the goal of his cadre. He could feel the absolute resolve of his comrades flowing through him like a tide, a wave about to crash onto the enemy shore.

'Remember,' Fadi said.

But Abbud ibn Aziz, a highly skilled armorist, trained by Fadi's brilliant brother in modern war machinery, needed no reminder. The one drawback of the RPG was that upon firing, it emitted a telltale trail of smoke. They would immediately become visible to the enemy. This, too, had been accounted for.

He felt the tap of Fadi's forefinger on his shoulder, which meant their target was in position. His finger curled around the trigger. He took a deep breath, slowly exhaled.

There came the recoil, a hurricane of superheated air. Then the flash-and-boom of the explosion itself, the plume of smoke, the twisted rotor blades rising together from the opposite camps. Thunderous echoes, like the dull ache in Abbud ibn Aziz's shoulder, were still resounding when Fadi's men rose as one and rushed to the butte, a hundred meters east of where he and Abbud ibn Aziz had been perched and were now scrambling away, where the telltale smoke plume rose. As the cadre had been taught, it fired a massed fusillade of shots, the expressed rage of the faithful.

*Al-Hamdu lil-Allah!* Allah be praised! The attack had begun.

One moment Lindros had been telling Anders why he wanted two more minutes on site, the next he felt as if his skull had been crushed by a pile driver. It took him some moments to realize that he was flat on the ground, his mouth filled with dirt. He lifted his head. Burning debris swung crazily through the smoky air, but there was no sound, nothing at all but a peculiar pressure on his eardrums, an inner whooshing, as if a lazy wind had started up inside his head. Blood ran down his cheeks, hot as tears. The sharp, choking odor of burned rubber and plastics filled his nostrils, but there was something else as well: the heavy underscent of roasting meat.

It was when he tried to roll over that he discovered Anders half lying atop him. The commander had taken the brunt of the blast in an effort to protect him. His face and bared shoulder, where his uniform was burned away, were crisped and smoking. All the hair on his head had been burned off, leaving little more than a skull. Lindros gagged, with a convulsive shudder pushed the corpse off him. He gagged again as he rose to his knees.

A kind of whirring came to him then, strangely muted, as if heard from a great distance. Turning, he saw the members of Skorpion One piling out of the wreckage of the Chinook, firing their semiautomatics as they came.

One of them went down under the withering hail of machine-gun fire. Lindros's next move was instinctual. On his belly, he crawled to the dead man, snatched up his XM8, and began firing.

The battle-hardened men of Skorpion One were both courageous and well trained. They knew when to take their shots and when to take refuge. Nevertheless, as the crossfire started up they were totally unprepared, so concentrated were they on the enemy in front of them. One by one they were shot, most multiple times.

Lindros soldiered on, even after he was the last man standing. Curiously, no one shot at him; not one bullet even came close. He had just begun to wonder about this when his XM8 ran out of ammo. He stood with the smoking assault rifle in his hand, watching the enemy coming down from the butte above him.

They were silent, thin as the ravaged man inside the cave, with the hollow eyes of men who had seen too much blood spilled. Two broke off from the pack and slipped into the smoldering carcass of the Chinook.

Lindros jerked as he heard shots being fired. One of the cadre spun through the open door of the blackened Chinook, but a moment later the other man dragged the bloody pilot out by his collar.

Was he dead or merely unconscious? Lindros longed to know, but the others had enclosed him in a circle. He saw in their faces the peculiar light of the fanatic, a sickly yellow, a flame that could be extinguished only by their own death.

He dropped his useless weapon and they took him, pulling his hands hard behind his back. Men took up the bodies on the ground and dumped them into the Chinook. In their wake, two others advanced with flamethrowers. With unnerving precision, they proceeded to incinerate the helicopter and the dead and wounded men inside it.

Lindros, groggy and bleeding from a number of superficial cuts, watched the supremely coordinated maneuvers. He was surprised and impressed. He was also frightened. Whoever had planned this clever ambush, whoever had trained this cadre was no ordinary terrorist. Out of sight of his captors, he worked the ring he wore off his finger and dropped it into the rocky scree, taking a step to cover it with his shoe. Whoever came after him needed to know that he'd been here, that he hadn't been killed with the rest.

At that moment, the knot of men around him parted and he saw striding toward him a tall, powerful-looking Arab with a bold, desert-chiseled face and large, piercing eyes. Unlike the other terrorists Lindros had interrogated, this one had the mark of civilization on him. The First World had touched him; he had drunk from its technological cup.

Lindros stared into the Arab's dark eyes as they stood, confronting each other.

'Good afternoon, Mr. Lindros,' the terrorist leader said in Arabic.

Lindros continued to stare at him, unblinking.

'Silent American, where is your bluster now?' Smiling, he added: 'It's no use pretending. I know you speak Arabic.' He relieved Lindros of both radiation detector and Geiger counter. 'I must assume you found what you were looking for.' Feeling through Lindros's pockets, he produced the metal canister. 'Ah, yes.' He opened it and poured out the contents between Lindros's boots. 'Pity for you the real evidence is long gone. Wouldn't you like to know its destination.' This last was said as a mocking statement, not as a question.

'Your intel is first-rate,' Lindros said in impeccable Arabic, causing a considerable stir among everyone in the cadre, save two men: the leader himself and a stocky man whom Lindros took to be the second in command.

There came the leader's smile again. 'I return the compliment.'

Silence.

Without warning, the leader hit Lindros so hard across the face his teeth snapped together. 'My name is Fadi, the redeemer, Martin. You don't mind if I call you Martin? Just as well, as we're going to become intimates over the next several weeks.'

'I don't intend to tell you anything,' Lindros said, abruptly switching to English.

'What you intend and what you *will* do are two separate things,' Fadi said in equally precise English. He inclined his head. Lindros winced as he felt the wrench on his arms, so savage it threatened to dislocate his shoulders.

'You have chosen to pass on this round.' Fadi's disappointment appeared genuine. 'How arrogant of you, how truly unwise. But then, after all, you are American. Americans are nothing if they are not arrogant, eh, Martin. And, truly, unwise.'

Again the thought arose that this was no ordinary terrorist: Fadi knew his name. Through the mounting pain shooting up his arms, Lindros fought to keep his face impassive. Why wasn't he equipped with a cyanide capsule in his mouth disguised as a tooth, like agents in spy novels? Sooner or later, he suspected, he'd wish he had one. Still, he'd keep up this front for as long as he was able.

'Yes, hide behind your stereotypes,' he said. 'You accuse us of not understanding you, but you understand us even less. You don't know me at all.'

'Ah, in this, as in most things, you're wrong, Martin. In point of fact I know you quite well. For some time I have – how do American students put it? – ah, yes, I have made you my major. Anthropological studies or realpolitik?' He shrugged as if they were two colleagues drinking together. 'A matter of semantics.'

His smile broadened as he kissed Lindros on each cheek. 'So now we move on to round two.' When he pulled away, there was blood on his lips.

'For three weeks, you have been looking for me; instead, I have found you.'

He did not wipe away Lindros's blood. Instead, he licked it off.

# Book 1

# 1

'When did this particular flashback begin, Mr. Bourne?' Dr. Sunderland asked.

Jason Bourne, unable to sit still, walked about the comfortable, homey space that seemed more like a study in a private home than a doctor's office. Cream walls, mahogany wainscoting, a vintage dark-wood desk with claw feet, two chairs, and a small sofa. The wall behind Dr. Sunderland's desk was covered with his many diplomas and an impressive series of international awards for breakthrough therapy protocols in both psychology and psychopharmacology related to his specialty: memory. Bourne studied them closely, then saw the photo in a silver frame on the doctor's desk.

'What's her name?' Bourne said. 'Your wife.'

'Katya,' Dr. Sunderland said after a slight hesitation.

Psychiatrists always resisted giving out any personal information about themselves and their family. *But in this case,* Bourne thought . . .

Katya was in a ski suit. A striped knit cap was on her head, a pom-pom at its top. She was blond and very beautiful. Something about her suggested that she was comfortable in front of the camera. She was smiling into the camera, the sun in her eyes. The crinkles at their outside corners made her seem peculiarly vulnerable.

Bourne felt tears coming. Once he would have said that they were David Webb's tears. But the two warring personalities – David Webb and Jason Bourne, the day and night of his soul – had finally fused. While it was true that David Webb, sometime professor of linguistics at Georgetown University, was sinking deeper into shadow, it was just as true that Webb had softened Bourne's most paranoid and antisocial edges. Bourne couldn't live in Webb's world of normalcy, just as Webb couldn't survive in Bourne's vicious shadow world.

Dr. Sunderland's voice intruded on his thoughts. 'Please sit down, Mr. Bourne.'

Bourne did so. There was a kind of relief in letting go of the photo.

Dr. Sunderland's face settled into an expression of heartfelt sympathy. 'The flashbacks, Mr. Bourne, they began following your wife's death, I imagine. Such a shock would – '

'Not then, no,' Jason Bourne said quickly. But that was a lie. The memory shards had resurfaced the night he had seen Marie. They had woken him out of sleep – nightmares made manifest, even in the brilliance of the lights he had turned on.

*Blood. Blood on his hands, blood covering his chest. Blood on the face of the woman he is carrying. Marie! No, not Marie! Someone else, the tender planes of her neck pale through the streams of blood. Her life leaking all over him, dripping onto the cobbled street as he runs. Panting through the chill night. Where is he? Why is he running? Dear God, who is she?*

He had bolted up, and though it was the dead of the night he'd dressed and slipped out, running full-out through the Canadian countryside until his sides ached. The bone-white moonlight had followed him like the bloody shards of memory. He'd been unable to outrun either.

Now he was lying to this doctor. Well, why not? He didn't trust him, even though Martin Lindros – the DDCI and Bourne's friend – had recommended him, showed Bourne his impressive credentials. Lindros had gotten Sunderland's name from a list provided by the DCI's office. He didn't have to ask his friend about that: Anne Held's name on the bottom of each page of the document verified his hypothesis. Anne Held was the DCI's assistant, stern right hand.

'Mr. Bourne?' Dr. Sunderland prompted him.

Not that it mattered. He saw Marie's face, pale and lifeless, felt Lindros's presence beside him as he took in the coroner's French-Canadian-accented English: *'The viral pneumonia had spread too far, we couldn't save her. You can take comfort in the fact that she didn't suffer. She went to sleep and never woke up.'* The coroner had looked from the dead woman to her grief-stricken husband and his friend. *'If only she'd come back from the skiing trip sooner.'*

Bourne had bitten his lip. *'She was taking care of our children. Jamie had turned an ankle on his last run. Alison was terribly frightened.'*

*'She didn't seek a doctor? Suppose the ankle was sprained – or broken?'*

*'You don't understand. My wife – her entire family are outdoors people, ranchers, hardy stock. Marie was trained from an early age to take care of herself in the wilderness. She had no fear of it whatsoever.'*

*'Sometimes,'* the coroner had said, *'a little fear is a good thing.'*

*'You have no right to judge her!'* Bourne had cried out in anger and grief.

*'You've spent too much time with the dead,'* Lindros had berated the coroner. *'You need to work on your people skills.'*

*'My apologies.'*

Bourne had caught his breath and, turning to Lindros, said, *'She phoned me, she thought it was just a cold.'*

*'A natural enough conclusion,'* his friend had said. *'In any event, her mind was clearly on her son and daughter.'*

'So, Mr. Bourne, when did the memory flashes begin?' There was the distinct tinge of a Romanian accent to Dr. Sunderland's English. Here was a man, with his high, wide forehead, strong-lined jaw, and prominent nose, that one could easily have confidence in, confide in. He wore steel-rimmed glasses and his hair was slicked back in a curious, old-fashioned style. No PDA for him, no text-messaging on the run. Above all, no multi-tasking. He wore a three-piece suit of heavy Harris tweed, a red-and-white polka-dot bow tie.

'Come, come.' Dr. Sunderland cocked his large head, which made him look like an owl. 'You'll forgive me, but I feel quite sure you're – how shall I put it – hiding the truth.'

At once, Bourne was on the alert. 'Hiding . . . ?'

Dr. Sunderland produced a beautiful crocodile-skin wallet, from which he slipped a hundred-dollar bill. Holding it up, he said, 'I'll wager that the memory flashes began just after you laid your wife to rest. However, this wager will be invalid if you elect not to tell the truth.'

'What are you, a human lie detector?'

Dr. Sunderland wisely kept his own counsel.

'Put your money away,' Bourne said at length. He sighed. 'You're right, of course. The memory flashes began the day I saw Marie for the last time.'

'What form did they take?'

Bourne hesitated. 'I was looking down at her – in the funeral home. Her sister and father had already identified her and had her transferred from the coroner's. I looked down at her and – I didn't see her at all . . .'

'What did you see, Mr. Bourne?' Dr. Sunderland's voice was soft, detached.

'Blood. I saw blood.'

'And?'

'Well, there was no blood. Not really. It was the memory surfacing – without warning – without . . .'

'That's the way it always happens, isn't it?'

Bourne nodded. 'The blood . . . it was fresh, glistening, made bluish by street lamps. The blood covered this face . . .'

'Whose face?'

'I don't know . . . a woman . . . but it wasn't Marie. It was . . . someone else.'

'Can you describe this woman?' Dr. Sunderland asked.

'That's the thing. I can't. I don't know . . . And yet, I know her. I know I do.'

There was a small silence, into which Dr. Sunderland interjected another seemingly unrelated question. 'Tell me, Mr. Bourne, what is today's date?'

'That's not the kind of memory problem I have.'

Dr. Sunderland ducked his head. 'Indulge me, please.'

'Tuesday, February third.'

'Four months since the funeral, since your memory problem began. Why did you wait so long to seek help?'

For a time, there was another silence. 'Something happened last week,' Bourne said at length. 'I saw – I saw an old friend of mine.' Alex Conklin, walking down the street in Alexandria's Old Town where he'd taken Jamie and Alison for the last outing he'd have with them for a long time. They had just come out of a Baskin-Robbins, the two of them loaded with ice-cream cones, and there was Conklin big as life. Alex Conklin: his mentor, the mastermind behind the Jason Bourne identity. Without Conklin, it was impossible to imagine where he'd be today.

Dr. Sunderland cocked his head. 'I don't understand.'

'This friend died three years ago.'

'Yet you saw him.'

Bourne nodded. 'I called his name, and when he turned around he was holding something in his arms – someone, actually. A woman. A bloody woman.'

'*Your* bloody woman.'

'Yes. At that moment I thought I was losing my mind.'

That was when he'd decided to ship the kids off. Alison and Jamie were with Marie's sister and father in Canada, where the family maintained their enormous ranch. It was better for them, though Bourne missed them terribly. It would not be good for them to see him now.

Since then, how many times had he dreamed of the moments he dreaded most: seeing Marie's pale face; picking up her effects at the hospital; standing in the darkened room of the funeral home with the director beside him, staring down at Marie's body, her face still, waxen, made up in a way Marie never would have done herself. He had leaned over, his hand reaching out, and the director had offered a handkerchief, which Bourne had used to wipe the lipstick and rouge off her face. He had kissed her then, the coldness of her lips running right through him like an electric shock: *She's dead, she's dead. That's it, my life with her is over.* With a small sound, he'd lowered the casket lid. Turning to the funeral director, he'd said, *'I've changed my mind. No open casket. I don't want anyone to see her like this, especially the children.'*

'Nevertheless you went after him,' Dr. Sunderland persisted. 'Most fascinating. Given your history, your amnesia, the trauma of your wife's untimely death set off a particular memory flashback. Can you think in what way your deceased friend is connected with the bloody woman?'

'No.' But of course that was a lie. He suspected that he was reliving an old mission – one that Alex Conklin had sent him on years ago.

Dr. Sunderland steepled his fingers together. 'Your memory flashes can be triggered by anything providing it's vivid enough: something you saw, smelled, touched, like a dream resurfacing. Except for you these "dreams" are real. They're your memories; they actually happened.' He took up a gold fountain pen. 'There's no doubt that a trauma such as you've suffered would be at the top of that list. And then to believe you've seen someone you know to be dead – it's hardly surprising the flashbacks have become more numerous.'

True enough, but the escalation of the flashbacks made his mental state that much more unbearable. On that afternoon in Georgetown, he'd left his children. It was only for a moment, but . . . He'd been horrified; he still was.

Marie was gone, in a terrible, senseless moment. And now it wasn't only the memory of Marie that haunted him, but those ancient silent streets, leering at him, streets that possessed knowledge he didn't, that knew something about him, something he couldn't even guess at. His nightmare went like this: The memory flashes would come and he'd be bathed in cold sweat. He'd lie in the darkness, absolutely certain he'd never fall asleep. Inevitably he did – a heavy, almost drugged sleep. And when he rose from that abyss, he'd turn, still in the grip of slumber, searching as he always did for Marie's warm, delicious body. Then it would hit him all over again, a freight train slamming him full in the chest.

*Marie is dead. Dead and gone forever . . .*

The dry, rhythmic sound of Dr. Sunderland writing in his notebook brought Bourne back from his black oblivion.

'These memory flashes are literally driving me crazy.'

'Hardly surprising. Your desire to uncover your past is all-consuming. Some might even term it obsessive – I certainly would. An obsession often deprives those suffering with it of the ability to live what might be termed a normal life – though I detest that term and use it infrequently. In any event, I think I can help.'

Dr. Sunderland spread his hands, which were large and callused. 'Let me begin by explaining to you the nature of your disability. Memories are made when electrical impulses cause synapses in the brain to release neurotransmitters so that the synapses fire, as we say. This creates a temporary memory. To make this permanent a process called consolidation needs to occur. I won't bore you by detailing it. Suffice it to say that consolidation requires the synthesis of new proteins, hence it takes many hours. Along the way the process can be blocked or altered by any number of things – severe trauma, for instance, or unconsciousness. This is what happened to you. While you were unconscious, your abnormal brain activity turned your permanent memories into temporary ones. The proteins that create temporary memories degrade very quickly. Within hours, or even minutes, those temporary memories disappear.'

'But my memories occasionally do surface.'

'That's because trauma – physical, emotional, or a combination of the two – can very quickly flood certain synapses with neurotransmitters, thus resurrecting, shall we say, memories previously lost.'

Dr. Sunderland smiled. 'All this is to prepare you. The idea of full memory erasure, though closer than ever before, is still the stuff of science fiction. However, the very latest procedures are at my disposal, and I can confidently say that I can get your memory to surface completely. But you must give me two weeks.'

'I'm giving you today, Doctor.'

'I highly recommend – '

'Today,' Bourne said more firmly.

Dr. Sunderland studied him for some time, tapping his gold pen contemplatively against his lower lip. 'Under those circumstances . . . I believe I can *suppress* the memory. That's not the same as erasing it.'

'I understand.'

'All right.' Dr. Sunderland slapped his thighs. 'Come into the examination room and I'll do my best to help you.' He lifted a long, cautionary forefinger. 'I suppose I needn't remind you that memory is a terribly slippery creature.'

'No need at all,' Bourne said as another glimmer of foreboding eeled its way through him.

'So you understand there are no guarantees. The chances are excellent that my procedure will work, but for how long . . .' He shrugged.

Bourne nodded as he rose and followed Dr. Sunderland into the next room. This was somewhat larger than the consultation room. The floor was doctor's standard-issue speckled linoleum, the walls lined with stainless-steel equipment, counter, and cabinets. A small sink took up one corner, below which was a red plastic receptacle with a biohazard label prominently affixed to it. The center of the room was taken up by what looked like a particularly plush and futuristic dentist chair. Several articulated arms descended from the ceiling in a tight circle around it. There were two medical devices of unknown origin set on carts with rubber wheels. All in all, the room had the efficient, sterile look of an operating theater.

Bourne sat on the chair and waited while Dr. Sunderland adjusted its height and inclination to his satisfaction. From one of the rolling carts, the doctor then affixed eight electronic leads to different areas of Bourne's head.

'I'm going to perform two series of tests of your brain waves, one when you're conscious, one when you're unconscious. It's crucial that I be able to evaluate both states of your brain activity.'

'And then what?'

'It depends on what I find,' Dr. Sunderland said. 'But the treatment will involve stimulating certain synapses in the brain with specific complex proteins.' He peered down at Bourne. 'Miniaturization is the key, you see. That's one of my specialties. You cannot work with proteins, on that minuscule level, without being an expert in miniaturization. You've heard of nanotechnology?'

Bourne nodded. 'Manufactured electronic bits of microscopic size. In effect, tiny computers.'

'Precisely.' Dr. Sunderland's eyes gleamed. He appeared very pleased by the scope of his patient's knowledge. 'These complex proteins – these neurotransmitters – act just like nanosites, binding and strengthening synapses in areas of your brain to which I will direct them, to block or make memories.'

All at once Bourne ripped off the electronic leads, rose, and, without a word, bolted out of the office. He half ran down the marble-clad hall, his shoes making small clicking sounds as if a many-legged animal were pursuing him. What was he doing, allowing someone to tinker with his brain?

The two bathroom doors stood side by side. Hauling open the door that said men, he rushed inside, stood with his arms rigid on either side of the white porcelain sink. There was his face, pallid, ghostly in the mirror. He saw reflected the tiles behind him, so like those in the funeral home. He saw Marie – lying still, hands crossed on her flat, athlete's belly. She floated as if on a barge, as if on a swift river, taking her away from him.

He pressed his forehead against the mirror. The floodgates opened, tears welled up in his eyes, rolled freely down his cheeks. He remembered Marie as she had been, her hair floating in the wind, the skin at the nape of her neck like satin; when they'd whitewater-rafted down the Snake River, her strong, sun-browned arms digging the paddle into the churning water, the big Western sky reflected in her eyes; when he'd asked her to marry him, on the stolid granite grounds of Georgetown University, she in a black spaghetti-strap dress beneath a Canadian shearling coat, holding hands, laughing on the way to a faculty Christmas party; when they'd said their vows, the sun sliding behind the jagged snowcapped peaks of the Canadian Rockies, their newly ringed hands linked, their lips pressed together, their hearts beating as one. He remembered when she'd given birth to Alison. Two days before Halloween, she was sitting at the sewing machine, making a ghost pirate costume for Jamie, when her water broke. Alison's birth was hard and long. At the end, Marie had begun to bleed. He'd almost lost her then, holding on tight, willing her not to leave him. Now he had lost her forever . . .

He found himself sobbing, unable to stop.

And then, like a ghoul haunting him, the unknown woman's bloody face once again rose from the depths of his memory to blot out his beloved Marie. Blood dripped. Her eyes stared sightlessly up at him. What did she want? Why was she haunting him? He gripped his temples in despair and moaned. He desperately wanted to leave this floor, this building, but he knew he couldn't. Not like this, not being assaulted by his own brain.

Dr. Sunderland was waiting with pursed lips, patient as stone, in his office. 'Shall I?'

Bourne, the bloody face still clogging his senses, took a breath and nodded. 'Go ahead.'

He sat in the chair, and Dr. Sunderland reattached the leads. He flipped a switch on the movable cart and began to ramp up dials, some quickly, others slowly, almost gingerly.

'Don't be apprehensive,' Dr. Sunderland said gently. 'You will feel nothing at all.'

Bourne didn't.

When Dr. Sunderland was satisfied, he threw another switch and a long sheet of paper much like the one used in an EEG machine came rolling out of a slot. The doctor peered at the printout of Bourne's waking brain waves.

He made no notations on the printout but nodded to himself, his brow roiled like an oncoming thunderhead. Bourne could not tell whether any of this was a good sign or a bad one.

'All right then,' Dr. Sunderland said at length. He switched off the machine, rolled the cart away, and replaced it with the second one.

From a tray on its gleaming metal top he picked up a syringe. Bourne could see that it was already loaded with a clear liquid.

Dr. Sunderland turned to Bourne. 'The shot won't put you all the way out, just into a deep sleep – delta waves, the slowest brain waves.' In response to the practiced movement of the doctor's thumb, a bit of the liquid squirted out the end of the needle. 'I need to see if there are any unusual breaks in your delta wave patterns.'

Bourne nodded, and awoke as if no time had passed.

'How do you feel?' Dr. Sunderland asked.

'Better, I think,' Bourne said.

'Good.' Dr. Sunderland showed him a printout. 'As I suspected, there was an anomaly in your delta wave pattern.' He pointed. 'Here, you see? And again here.' He handed Bourne a second printout. 'Now here is your delta wave pattern after the treatment. The anomaly is vastly diminished. Judging by the evidence, it is reasonable to assume that your flashbacks will disappear altogether over the course of the next ten or so days. Though I have to warn you there's a good chance they might get worse over the next forty-eight hours, the time it takes for your synapses to adjust to the treatment.'

The short winter twilight was skidding toward night when Bourne exited the doctor's building, a large Greek Revival limestone structure on K Street. An icy wind off the Potomac, smelling of phosphorus and rot, whipped the flaps of his overcoat around his shins.

Turning away from a bitter swirl of dust and grit, he saw his reflection in a flower shop window, a bright spray of flowers displayed behind the glass, so like the flowers at Marie's funeral.

Then, just to his right, the brass-clad door to the shop opened and someone exited, a gaily wrapped bouquet in her arms. He smelled . . . what was it, wafting out from the bouquet? Gardenias, yes. That was a spray of gardenias carefully wrapped against winter's chill.

Now, in his mind's eye, he carried the woman from his unknown past in his arms, felt her blood warm and pulsing on his forearms. She was younger than he had assumed, in her early twenties, no more. Her lips moved, sending a shiver down his spine. She was still alive! Her eyes sought his. Blood leaked out of her half-open mouth. And words, clotted, distorted. He strained to hear her. What was she saying? Was she trying to tell him something? Who *was* she?

With another gust of gritty wind, he returned to the chill Washington twilight. The horrific image had vanished. Had the scent of the gardenias summoned her from inside him? Was there a connection?

He turned around, about to go back to Dr. Sunderland, even though he had been warned that in the short run he might still be tormented. His cell phone buzzed. For a moment, he considered ignoring it. Then he flipped open the phone, put it to his ear.

He was surprised to discover that it was Anne Held, the DCI's assistant. He formed a mental picture of a tall, slim brunette in her middle twenties, with classic features, rosebud lips, and icy gray eyes.

'Hello, Mr. Bourne. The DCI wishes to see you.' Her accent was Middle Atlantic, meaning that it lay somewhere between her British birthplace and her adopted American home.

'I have no wish to see him,' Bourne responded coldly.

Anne Held sighed, clearly steeling herself. 'Mr. Bourne, next to Martin Lindros himself nobody knows your antagonistic relationship with the Old Man – with CI in general – better than I do. God knows you have ample cause: They've used you countless times as a stalking horse, and then they were sure you'd turned rogue on them. But you really must come in now.'

'Eloquently said. But all the eloquence in the world won't sway me. If the DCI has something to say to me, he can do it through Martin.'

'It's Martin Lindros the Old Man needs to talk to you about.'

Bourne realized he was holding the phone with a death grip. His voice was ice cold when he said: 'What about Martin?'

'That's just it. I don't know. No one knows but the Old Man. He's been closeted in Signals since before lunchtime. Even I haven't seen him. Three minutes ago, he called me and ordered me to have you brought in.'

'That's how he put it?'

'His precise words were, "I know how close Bourne and Lindros are. That's why I need him." Mr. Bourne, I implore you, come in. It's Code Mesa here.'

*Code Mesa* was CI-speak for a Level One emergency.

While Bourne waited for the taxi he'd called, he had time to think about Martin Lindros.

How many times in the past three years had he spoken of the intimate, often painful subject of his memory loss with Martin. Lindros, the deputy director of CI – the least likely confidant. Who would have expected him to become Jason Bourne's friend? Not Bourne himself, who had found his suspicion and paranoia coming to the fore when Lindros had shown up at Webb's campus office nearly three years ago. Surely, Bourne had figured, he was there to once more try to recruit Bourne into CI. It wasn't such an odd notion. After all, Lindros was using his newfound power to reshape CI into a leaner, cleaner organization with the expertise to take on the worldwide threats that radical, fundamentalist Islam presented.

Such a change would have been all but unthinkable five years ago, when the Old

Man ruled CI with an iron hand. But now the DCI truly was an old man – in reality as well as in name. Rumors swirled that he was losing his grip; that it was time for him to retire honorably before he was fired. Bourne would wish this were so, but chances were that these particular rumors had been started by the Old Man himself to flush out the enemies he knew were hiding in the Beltway brush. He was a wily old bastard, better connected to the old-boy network that was the bedrock of Washington than anyone else Bourne had ever come across.

The red-and-white taxi pulled to a halt at the curb; Bourne got in and gave an address to the driver. Settling himself into the backseat, his thoughts returned inward.

To his complete surprise, the subject of recruitment had never come up in the conversation. Over dinner, Bourne began to get to know Lindros in an entirely different way from their time in the field together. The very fact of his changing CI from the inside had turned him into a loner within his own organization. He had the absolute, unshakable trust of the Old Man, who saw in Lindros something of his own younger self, but the heads of the seven directorates feared him because he held their futures in the palm of his hand.

Lindros had a girlfriend named Moira, but otherwise had no one close to him. And he had a particular empathy for Bourne's situation. *'You can't remember your life,'* he had said over that first of many dinners. *'I have no life to remember . . .'*

Perhaps what drew them unconsciously was the deep, abiding damage each of them had suffered. From their mutual incompleteness came friendship and trust.

Finally, a week ago, he'd taken a medical leave from Georgetown. He'd called Lindros, but his friend was unavailable. No one would tell him where Lindros was. Bourne missed his friend's careful, rational analysis of Bourne's increasingly irrational state of mind. And now his friend was at the center of a mystery that had caused CI to go into emergency lockdown mode.

The moment Costin Veintrop – the man who called himself Dr. Sunderland – received confirmation that Jason Bourne had, indeed, left the building, he neatly and rapidly packed his equipment into the gusseted outside compartment of a black leather briefcase. From one of the two main sections he produced a laptop computer, which he fired up. This was no ordinary laptop; Veintrop, a specialist in miniaturization, an adjunct to his study of human memory, had customized it himself. Plugging a high-definition digital camera into the Firewire port, he brought up four photo enlargements of the laboratory room taken from different angles. Comparing them with the scene in front of him, he went about ensuring that every item was as he had found it when he'd entered the office fifteen minutes before Bourne had arrived. When he was through, he turned off the lights and went into the consult room.

Veintrop took down the photos he'd put up, giving a lingering look at the woman he'd identified as his wife. She was indeed Katya, his Baltic Katya, his wife. His ingenuous sincerity had helped him sell himself to Bourne. Veintrop was a man who believed in verisimilitude. This was why he'd used a photo of his wife and not a woman unknown to him. When taking on a legend – a new identity – he felt it crucial to mix in bits of things he himself believed. Especially with a man of Jason Bourne's expertise. In any event, Katya's photo had had the desired effect on Bourne. Unfortunately, it had also served to remind Veintrop of where she was and why he could not see her. Briefly, his fingers curled, making fists so tight his knuckles went pale.

Abruptly he shook himself. Enough of this morbid self-pity; he had work to do. Placing the laptop on the corner of the real Dr. Sunderland's desk, he brought up enlargements of the digital photos he'd made of this room. As before, he was meticulous in his scrutiny, assuring himself that every single detail of the consult room was as he had found it. It was essential that no trace of his presence remain after he'd left.

His quad-band GSM cell phone buzzed, and he put it to his ear.

'It's done,' Veintrop said in Romanian. He could have used Arabic, his employer's native language, but it had been mutually decided that Romanian would be less obtrusive.

'To your satisfaction?' It was a different voice, somewhat deeper and coarser than the compelling voice of the man who'd hired him, belonging to someone who was used to exhorting rabid followers.

'Most certainly. I have honed and perfected the procedure on the test subjects you provided for me. Everything contracted for is in place.'

'The proof of it will occur shortly.' The dominant note of impatience was soured by a faint undertone of anxiety.

'Have faith, my friend,' Veintrop said, and broke the connection.

Returning to his work, he packed away his laptop, digital camera, and Firewire connector, then slipped on his tweed overcoat and felt fedora. Grasping his brief-case in one hand, he took one final look around with exacting finality. There was no place for error in the highly specialized work he did.

Satisfied, he flipped the light switch and, in utter darkness, slipped out of the office. In the hallway he glanced at his watch: 4:46 pm. Three minutes over, still well within the time-frame tolerance allotted to him by his employer. It was Tuesday, February 3, as Bourne had said. On Tuesday, Dr. Sunderland had no office hours.

# 2

CI headquarters, located on 23rd Street NW, was identified on maps of the city as belonging to the Department of Agriculture. To reinforce the illusion, it was surrounded by perfectly manicured lawns, dotted here and there with ornamental shade trees, divided by snaking gravel paths. The building itself was as nondescript as was possible in a city devoted to the grandeur of monumental Federal architecture. It was bounded to the north by huge structures that housed the State Department and the Navy Bureau of Medicine and Surgery, and on the east by the National Academy of Sciences. The DCI's office had a sobering view of the Vietnam Veterans Memorial, as well as a slice of the shining, white Lincoln Memorial.

Anne Held hadn't been exaggerating. Bourne had to go through no less than three separate security checkpoints before he gained admittance to the inner lobby. They took place in the bomb- and fireproof public lobby, which was, in effect, a bunker. Hidden behind decorative marble slabs and columns were half-meter-thick meta-concrete blast walls, reinforced with a mesh of steel rods and Kevlar webbing. There was no glass to shatter, and the lighting and electrical circuits were heavily shielded. The first checkpoint required him to repeat a code phrase that changed three times a day; at the second he had to submit to a fingerprint scanner. At the third, he put his right eye to the lens of a sinister-looking matte-black machine, which took a photo of his retina and digitally compared it with the photo already on file. This added layer of high-tech security was crucial since it was now possible to fake fingerprints with silicone patches affixed to the pads of the fingers. Bourne ought to know: He'd done it several times.

There was another security check just before the elevator bank, and still another – a jury-rigged affair as per Code Mesa regs – just outside the DCI's suite of offices on the fifth floor.

Once through the thick, steel-plated, rosewood-clad door he saw Anne Held. Uncharacteristically, she was accompanied by a whey-faced man with muscles rippling beneath his suit jacket.

She gave him a small, tight smile. 'I saw the DCI a few moments ago. He looks like he's aged ten years.'

'I'm not here for him,' Bourne said. 'Martin Lindros is the only man in CI I care about and trust. Where is he?'

'He's been in the field for the last three weeks, doing God alone knows what.' Anne was dressed in her usual impeccable fashion in a charcoal-gray Armani suit, a fire-red silk blouse, and Manolo Blahniks with three-inch heels. 'But I'll wager high money that whatever signals the DCI has received today are what's caused the extraordinary flap around here.'

The whey-faced man escorted them wordlessly down one corridor after another – a deliberately bewildering labyrinth through which visitors were led via a different route every time – until they arrived at the door to the DCI's sanctum sanctorum. There his escort stood aside, but did not leave. Another marker of Code Mesa, Bourne thought as he smiled thinly up at the tiny eye of the security camera.

A moment later, he heard the electronic lock clicking open remotely.

The DCI stood at the far end of an office as large as a football field. He held a file in one hand, a lit cigarette in the other, defying the building's federally mandated ban. *When did he start smoking again?* Bourne wondered. Standing beside him was another man – tall, beefy, with a long scowling face, light brush-cut hair, and a dangerous stillness about him.

'Ah, you've come at last.' The Old Man strode toward Bourne, the heels of his handmade shoes clicking across the polished wood floor. His shoulders were up around his ears, hunched as if against heavy weather. As he approached, the floodlights from outside illuminated him, the moving images of his past exploits written like soft white explosions across his face.

He looked old and tired, his cheeks fissured like a mountainside, his eyes sunken into their sockets, the flesh beneath them puddled and yellow, a candle burned too low. He jammed the cigarette between his liver-colored lips, underscoring the fact that he would not offer to shake hands.

The other man followed, clearly and deliberately at his own pace.

'Bourne, this is Matthew Lerner, my new deputy director. Lerner, Bourne.'

The two men shook hands briefly.

'I thought Martin was DDCI,' Bourne said to Lerner, puzzled.

'It's complicated. We – '

'Lerner will brief you following this interview,' the Old Man interrupted.

'If there is to be a briefing after this.' Bourne frowned, abruptly uneasy. 'What about Martin?'

DCI hesitated. The old antipathy was still there – it would never disappear. Bourne knew that and accepted it as gospel. Clearly the current situation was dire enough for the Old Man to do something he'd sworn never to do: ask for Jason Bourne's help. On the other hand, the DCI was the ultimate pragmatist. He'd have to be to keep the director's job for so long. He had become immune to the slings and arrows of difficult and, often, morally ambiguous compromise. This was, simply, the world in which he existed. He needed Bourne now, and he was furious about it.

'Martin Lindros has been missing for almost seven days.' All at once the DCI seemed smaller, as if his suit were about to fall off him.

Bourne stood stock-still. No wonder he hadn't heard from Martin. 'What the hell happened?'

The Old Man lit another cigarette from the glowing end of the first, grinding out the butt in a cut-crystal ashtray. His hand shook slightly. 'Martin was on a mission to Ethiopia.'

'What was he doing in the field?' Bourne asked.

'I asked the same question,' Lerner said. 'But this was his baby.'

'Martin's people have gotten a sudden increase in chatter on particular terrorist frequencies.' The DCI pulled smoke deep into his lungs, let it out in a soft hiss. 'His analysts are expert at differentiating the real stuff from the disinformation that has counterterrorist divisions at other agencies chasing their tails and crying wolf.'

His eyes locked with Bourne's. 'He's provided us with credible evidence that the chatter is real, that an attack against one of three major cities in the United States – D.C., New York, L.A. – is imminent. Worse still, this attack involves a nuclear bomb.'

The DCI took a package off a nearby sideboard and handed it to Bourne.

Bourne opened it. Inside was a small, oblong metallic object.

'Know what that is?' Lerner spoke as if issuing a challenge.

'It's a triggered spark gap. It's used in industry to switch on tremendously powerful engines.' Bourne looked up. 'It's also used to trigger nuclear weapons.'

'That's right. Especially this one.' The DCI's face was grim as he handed Bourne a file marked deo – Director's Eyes Only. It contained a highly detailed spec sheet on this particular device. 'Usually triggered spark gaps use gases – air, argon, oxygen, $SF_6$, or a combination of these – to carry the current. This one uses a solid material.'

'It's designed to be used once and once only.'

'Correct. That rules out an industrial application.'

Bourne rolled the TSG between his fingers. 'The only possible use, then, would be in a nuclear device.'

'A nuclear device in the hands of terrorists,' Lerner said with a dark look.

The DCI took the TSG from Bourne, tapped it with a gnarled forefinger. 'Martin was following the trail of an illicit shipment of these TSGs, which led to the mountains of northwestern Ethiopia where he believed they were being transshipped by a terrorist cadre.'

'Destination?'

'Unknown,' the DCI said.

Bourne was deeply disturbed, but he chose to keep the feeling to himself. 'All right. Let's hear the details.'

'At 17:32 local time, six days ago, Martin and the five-man team of Skorpion One choppered onto the upper reaches of the northern slope of Ras Dejen.' Lerner passed over a sheet of onionskin. 'Here are the exact coordinates.'

The DCI said, 'Ras Dejen is the highest peak in the Simien Range. You've been there. Better yet, you speak the language of the local tribespeople.'

Lerner continued. 'At 18:04 local time, we lost radio contact with Skorpion One. At 10:06 am Eastern Standard Time, I ordered Skorpion Two to those coordinates.' He took the sheet of onionskin back from Bourne. 'At 10:46 EST today, we got a signal from Ken Jeffries, the commander of Skorpion Two. The unit found the burned-out wreckage of the Chinook on a small plateau at the correct coordinates.'

'That was the last communication we had from Skorpion Two,' the DCI said. 'Since then, nothing from Lindros or anyone else in the party.'

'Skorpion Three is stationed in Djibouti and ready to go,' Lerner said, neatly sidestepping the Old Man's look of disgust.

But Bourne, ignoring Lerner, was turning over possibilities in his mind, which helped him put aside his anxiety regarding his friend's fate. 'One of two things has happened,' he said firmly. 'Either Martin is dead or he's been captured and is undergoing articulated interrogation. Clearly, a team is not the way.'

'The Skorpion units are made up of some of our best and brightest field agents – battle-hardened in Somalia, Afghanistan, and Iraq,' Lerner pointed out. 'You'll need their firepower, believe me.'

'The firepower of two Skorpion units couldn't handle the situation on Ras Dejen. I go in alone, or not at all.'

His point was clear, but the new DDCI wasn't buying it. 'Where you see "flexibility," Bourne, the organization sees irresponsibility, unacceptable danger to those around you.'

'Listen, you called me in here. You're asking a favor of me.'

'Fine, forget Skorpion Three,' the Old Man said. 'I know you work alone.'

Lerner closed the file. 'In return, you'll get all the intel, all the transportation and support you need.'

The DCI took a step toward Bourne. 'I know you won't pass up the chance to go after your friend.'

'In that you're right.' Bourne walked calmly to the door. 'Do whatever the hell you want with the people you command. For myself, I'm going after Martin without your help.'

'Wait.' The Old Man's voice rang out in the huge office. There was a note to it like a whistle on a train passing through a dark and deserted landscape. Sadness and cynicism venomously mixed. 'Wait, you bastard.'

Bourne took his time turning around.

The DCI glared at him with a bitter enmity. 'How Martin gets along with you is a goddamn mystery.' Hands clenched behind his back, he strode in full military fashion to the window, stood staring out at the immaculate lawn and, beyond, the Vietnam Veterans Memorial. He turned back and fixed Bourne in his implacable gaze. 'Your arrogance disgusts me.'

Bourne met his gaze mutely.

'All right, no leash,' the DCI snapped. He was shaking with barely suppressed rage. 'Lerner will see that you have everything you need. But I'm telling you, you'd damn well better bring Martin Lindros home.'

# 3

Lerner led Bourne out of the DCI's suite, down the hall, into his own office. Lerner sat down behind his desk. When he realized that Bourne had chosen to stand, he leaned back.

'What I'm about to tell you cannot under any circumstances leave this room. The Old Man has named Martin director of a black-ops agency code-named Typhon, dealing exclusively with countering Muslim extremist terrorist groups.'

Bourne recalled that *Typhon* was a name out of Greek mythology: the fearsome hundred-headed father of the deadly Hydra. 'We already have a Counterterrorist Center.'

'CTC knows nothing about Typhon,' Lerner said. 'In fact, even inside CI, knowledge of it is on a strict need-to-know basis.'

'So Typhon is a *double-blind* black op.'

Lerner nodded. 'I know what you're thinking: that we haven't had anything like this since Treadstone. But there are compelling reasons. Aspects of Typhon are – shall we say – extremely controversial, so far as powerful reactionary elements within the administration and Congress are concerned.'

He pursed his lips. 'I'll cut to the chase. Lindros has constructed Typhon from the ground up. It's not a division, it's an agency unto itself. Lindros insisted that he be free of administrative red tape. Also, it's by necessity worldwide – he's already staffed up in London, Paris, Istanbul, Dubai, Saudi Arabia, and three locations in the Horn of Africa. And it's Martin's intention to infiltrate terrorist cells in order to destroy the networks from the inside out.'

'Infiltration,' Bourne said. So that's what Martin had meant when he'd told Bourne that save for the director, he was completely alone inside CI. 'That's the holy grail of counterterrorism, but so far no one's been able to even come close.'

'Because they have few Muslims and even fewer Arabists working for them. In all of the FBI, only thirty-three out of twelve thousand have even a limited proficiency in Arabic, and none of those works in the sections of the bureau that investigate terrorism within our borders. With good reason. Leading members of the administration are still reluctant to use Muslims and Western Arabists – they're simply not trusted.'

'Stupid and shortsighted,' Bourne said.

'But these people exist, and Lindros has been quietly recruiting them.' Lerner stood up. 'So much for orientation. Your next stop, I believe, will be Typhon ops itself.'

Because it was a double-blind counterterrorist agency, Typhon was down in the depths. The CI building sub-basement had been recast and remodeled by a construction firm whose every worker had been extensively vetted even before they had been made to sign a confidentiality agreement that would assure them a twenty-year term in a federal maximum-security facility if they were foolish or greedy enough to break their silence. The supplies that had been filling up the sub-basement had been exiled to an annex.

On his way out of the DCI's office, Bourne briefly stopped by Anne Held's domain. Armed with the names of the two case officers who had eavesdropped on the conversation that had sent Martin Lindros halfway around the world on the trail of transshipped TSGs, he took the private elevator that shuttled between the DCI's floor and the sub-basement.

As the elevator sighed to a stop, an LCD panel on the left-hand door activated, an electronic eye scanning the shiny black octagon Anne had affixed to the lapel of his jacket. It was encoded with a number invisible save to the scanner. Only then did the steel doors slide open.

Martin Lindros had reimagined the sub-basement as, basically, one gigantic space filled with mobile workstations, each with a braid of electronic leads spiraling up to the ceiling. The braids were on tracks so they could move with the workstations and the personnel as they relocated from assignment to assignment. At the far end, Bourne saw, was a series of conference rooms, separated from the main space by alternating frosted-glass and steel panels.

As befitted an agency named after a monster with two hundred eyes, the Typhon office was filled with monitors. In fact, the walls were a mosaic of flat-panel plasma screens on which a dizzying array of digital images were displayed: satellite chartings, closed-circuit television pictures of public spaces, transportation hubs such as airports, bus depots, train stations, street corners, cross sections of snaking highways and suburban rail lines, metropolitan underground platforms worldwide – Bourne recognized metros in New York, London, Paris, Moscow. People of all shapes, sizes, religions, ethnicities walking, milling mindlessly, standing undecided, lounging, smoking, getting on and off conveyances, talking to one another, ignoring one another, plugged into iPods, shopping, eating on the run, kissing, cuddling, exchanging bitter words, oblivious, cell phones slapped to their ears, accessing e-mail or porno, slouched, hunched, drunk, stoned, fights breaking out, first-date embarrassments, skulking, mumbling to themselves. A chaos of unedited video from which the analysts were required to find specific patterns, digital omens, electronic warning signs.

Lerner must have alerted the case officers to his arrival, because he saw a striking young woman whom he judged to be in her midthirties detach herself from a view screen and come toward him. He at once knew that she was or had been, at any rate, a field agent. Her stride was not too long, not too short, not too fast, not too slow. It was, to sum it up in one word, anonymous. Because an individual's stride was as distinctive as his fingerprints, it was one of the best ways to cull an adversary out of a swarming pack of pedestrians, even one whose disguise was otherwise first-rate.

She had a face that was both strong and proud, the chiseled prow of a sleek ship knifing through seas that would capsize inferior vessels. The large, deep blue eyes were set like jewels in the cinnamon dusk of her Arabian face.

'You must be Soraya Moore,' he said, 'the senior case officer.'

Her smile showed for a moment, then was quickly hidden behind a cloud of confusion and abrupt coolness. 'That's right, Mr. Bourne. This way.'

She led him down the length of the vast, teeming space to the second conference room from the left. Opening the frosted-glass door, she watched him pass with that same odd curiosity. But then considering his often adversarial relationship with CI, perhaps it wasn't odd after all.

There was a man inside, younger than Soraya by at least several years. He was of middling height, athletic, with sandy hair and a fair complexion. He was sitting at an oval glass conference table working on a laptop. The screen was filled with what looked to be an exceptionally difficult crossword puzzle.

He glanced up only when Soraya cleared her throat.

'Tim Hytner,' he said without rising,

When Bourne took a seat between the two case officers, he discovered that the crossword Hytner was trying to solve was, in fact, a cipher – and quite a sophisticated one at that.

'I have just over five hours until my flight to London departs,' Bourne said. 'Triggered spark gaps – tell me what I need to know.'

'Along with fissionable material, TSGs are among the most highly restricted items in the world,' Hytner began. 'To be precise, they're number two thousand six hundred forty-one on the government's controlled list.'

'So the tip that got Lindros so excited he couldn't help going into the field himself concerned a transshipment of TSGs.'

Hytner was back to trying to crack the cipher, so Soraya took over. 'The whole thing began in South Africa. Cape Town, to be exact.'

'Why Cape Town?' Bourne asked.

'During the apartheid era, the country became a haven for smugglers, mostly by necessity.' Soraya spoke quickly, efficiently, but with an unmistakable detachment. 'Now that South Africa is on our "white list," it's okay for American manufacturers to export TSGs there.'

'Then they get "lost,"' Hytner chimed in without lifting his head from the letters on the screen.

'Lost is right.' Soraya nodded. 'Smugglers are more difficult to eradicate than roaches. As you can imagine, there's still a network of them operating out of Cape Town, and these days they're highly sophisticated.'

'And the tip came from where?' Bourne said.

Without looking at him, Soraya passed over sheets of computer printouts. 'The smugglers communicate by cell phone. They use "burners," cheap phones available in any convenience store on pay-as-you-go plans. They use them for anywhere from a day to, maybe, a week, if they can get their hands on another SIM card. Then they throw them away and use another.'

'Virtually impossible to trace, you wouldn't believe.' Hytner's body was tense. He was putting all he had into breaking the cipher. 'But there is a way.'

'There's always a way,' Bourne said.

'Especially if your uncle works in the phone company.' Hytner shot a quick grin at Soraya.

She maintained her icy demeanor. 'Uncle Kingsley emigrated to Cape Town thirty years ago. London was too grim for him, he said. He needed a place that was still full of promise.' She shrugged. 'Anyway, we got lucky. We caught a conversation regarding this particular shipment – the transcript is on the second sheet. He's telling one of his people the cargo can't go through the usual channels.'

Bourne noticed Hytner looking at him curiously. 'And what was special about this "lost" shipment,' Bourne said, 'was that it coincided with the specific threat to the U.S.'

'That and the fact that we have the smuggler in custody,' Hytner said.

Bourne ran his finger down the second page of the transcript. 'Was it wise to bring him in? Chances are you'll alert his customer.'

Soraya shook her head. 'Not likely. These people use a source once, then they move on.'

'So you know who bought the TSGs.'

'Let's say we have a strong suspicion. That's why Lindros went into the field himself.'

'Have you heard of Dujja?' Hytner said.

Bourne accessed the memory. 'Dujja has been credited with at least a dozen attacks in Jordan and Saudi Arabia, the most recent being last month's bombing that killed ninety-five people at the Grand Mosque in Khanaqin, 144 kilometers northeast of Baghdad. If I remember right, it was also allegedly responsible for the assassinations of two members of the Saudi royal family, the Jordanian foreign minister, and the Iraqi chief of internal security.'

Soraya took back the transcript. 'It sounds implausible, doesn't it, that one cadre could be responsible for so many attacks? But it's true. One thing links them all: the Saudis. There was a secret business meeting going on in the mosque that included high-level Saudi emissaries. The Jordanian foreign minister was a personal friend of the royal family; the Iraqi security chief was a vocal supporter of the United States.'

'I'm familiar with the classified debrief material,' Bourne said. 'Those were all sophisticated, highly engineered attacks. Most of them didn't include suicide bombers, and none of the perpetrators has been caught. Who's the leader of Dujja?'

Soraya put the transcript back in its folder. 'His name is Fadi.'

'Fadi. The redeemer, in Arabic,' Bourne said. 'A name he must have taken.'

'The truth is we don't know anything else about him, not even his real name,' Hytner said sourly.

'But we do know some things,' Bourne said. 'For one, Dujja's attacks are so well coordinated and sophisticated, it's safe to assume that Fadi either has been educated in the West or has had considerable contact with it. For another, the cadre is unusually well armed with modern-day weaponry not normally associated with Arab or Muslim fundamentalist terror groups.'

Soraya nodded. 'We're all over that angle. Dujja is one of the new generation of cadres that has joined forces with organized crime, drug traffickers out of South Asia and Latin America.'

'If you ask me,' Hytner chipped in, 'the reason Deputy Director Lindros got the Old Man to approve Typhon so quickly was that he told him our first directive is to find out who Fadi is, flush him out, and terminate him.' He glanced up. 'Each year,

Dujja's become stronger and more influential among Muslim extremists. Our intel indicates that they're flocking to Fadi in unprecedented numbers.'

'Still, as of today no agency has been able to get to first base, not even us,' Soraya said.

'But then, we've only recently been organized,' Hytner added.

'Have you contacted the Saudi secret service?' Bourne asked.

Soraya gave him a bitter laugh. 'One of our informants swears the Saudi secret service is pursuing a lead on Dujja. The Saudis deny it.'

Hytner looked up. 'They also deny their oil reserves are drying up.'

Soraya closed her files, stacked them neatly. 'I know there are people in the field who call you the Chameleon because of your legendary skill at disguising yourself. But Fadi – whoever he is – is a true chameleon. Though we have corroborating intel that he not only plans the attacks but is also actively involved in many of them, we have no photo of him.'

'Not even an Identi-Kit drawing,' Hytner said with evident disgust.

Bourne frowned. 'What makes you think Dujja bought the TSGs from the supplier?'

'We know he's holding back vital information.' Hytner pointed to the screen of his laptop. 'We found this cipher on one of the buttons of his shirt. Dujja is the only terrorist cadre we know of that uses ciphers of this level of sophistication.'

'I want to interrogate him.'

'Soraya's the AIC – the agent in charge,' Hytner said. 'You'll have to ask her.'

Bourne turned to her.

Soraya hesitated only a moment. Then she stood and gestured toward the door. 'Shall we?'

Bourne rose. 'Tim, make a hard copy of the cipher, give us fifteen, then come find us.'

Hytner glanced up, squinting as if Bourne were in a glare. 'I won't be near finished in fifteen minutes.'

'Yes, you will.' Bourne opened the door. 'At least, you'll sell it that way.'

The holding cells were accessed via a short, steep flight of perforated steel stairs. In stark contrast with Typhon's light-drenched ops room, the space here was small, dark, cramped, as if the bedrock of Washington itself were reluctant to give up any more of its domain.

Bourne stopped her at the bottom of the stairs. 'Have I done something to offend you?'

Soraya stared at him for a moment as if she couldn't believe what she was seeing. 'His name is Hiram Cevik,' she said, pointedly ignoring Bourne's question. 'Fifty-one, married, three children. He's of Turkish descent, moved to Ukraine when he was eighteen. He's been in Cape Town for the last twenty-three years. Owns an import-export firm. For the most part, the business is legit, but every once in a while, it seems, Mr. Cevik gets a whole other thing going.' She shrugged. 'Maybe his mistress has a taste for diamonds, maybe it's his Internet gambling.'

'It's so hard to make ends meet these days,' Bourne said.

Soraya looked like she wanted to laugh, but didn't.

'I rarely do things by the book,' he said. 'But whatever I do, whatever I say, goes. Is that clear?'

For a moment she stared deep into his eyes. What was she looking for? he wondered. What was the matter with her?

'I'm familiar with your methods,' she said in an icy tone.

Cevik was leaning against one wall of his cage, smoking a cigarette. When he saw Bourne approaching with Soraya, he blew out a cloud of smoke and said, 'You the cavalry or the inquisitor?'

Bourne watched him as Soraya unlocked the cage door.

'Inquisitor, then.' Cevik dropped the cigarette butt and ground it beneath his heel. 'I should tell you that my wife knows all about my gambling – and about my mistress.'

'I'm not here to blackmail you.' Bourne stepped into the cage. He could feel Soraya behind him as if she were a part of him. His scalp began to tingle. She had a weapon and was prepared to use it on the prisoner before the situation got out of hand. She was a perfectionist, Bourne sensed that about her.

Cevik came off the wall and stood with his hands at his side, fingers slightly curled. He was tall, with the wide shoulders of a former rugby player and gold cat's eyes. 'Judging by your extreme fitness, it's to be physical coercion, then.'

Bourne looked around the cage, getting a feel for what it was like to be pent up in it. A flare of something half remembered, a feeling of sickness in the pit of his stomach. 'That would get me nowhere.' He used the words to bring himself out of it.

'Too true.'

It wasn't a boast. The simple statement of fact told him more about Cevik than an hour of vigorous interrogation. Bourne's gaze resettled on the South African.

'How to resolve this dilemma?' Bourne spread his hands. 'You need to get out of here. I need information. It's as simple as that.'

Cevik let a thin laugh escape his lips. 'If it were that simple, my friend, I'd be long gone.'

'My name is Jason Bourne. You're talking to me now. I'm neither your jailor nor your adversary.' Bourne paused. 'Unless you wish it.'

'I doubt I'd care for that,' Cevik said. 'I've heard of you.'

Bourne gestured with his head. 'Walk with me.'

'That's not a good idea.' Soraya planted herself between them and the outside world.

Bourne gave her a curt hand signal.

She pointedly ignored him. 'This is a gross breach of security.'

'I went out of my way to warn you,' he said. 'Step aside.'

She had her cell phone to her ear as he and Cevik went past. But it was Tim Hytner she was calling, not the Old Man.

Though it was night, the floodlights turned the lawn and its paths into silver oases amid the many-armed shadows of the leafless trees. Bourne walked beside Cevik. Soraya Moore followed five paces behind them, like a dutiful duenna, a look of disapproval on her face, a hand on her holstered gun.

Down in the depths, Bourne had been gripped by a sudden compulsion, fired by the lick of a memory – an interrogation technique used on subjects who were particularly resistant to the standard techniques of torture and sensory deprivation. Bourne was suddenly quite certain that if Cevik tasted the open air, experienced the space after being holed up in the cage for days, it would bring home to him all he had to gain from answering Bourne's questions truthfully. And all he had to lose.

'Who did you sell the TSGs to?' Bourne asked.

'I've already told this one behind us. I don't know. It was just a voice on the telephone.'

Bourne was skeptical. 'Do you normally sell TSGs over the phone?'

'For five mil, I do.'

Believable, but was it the truth?

'Man or woman?' Bourne said.

'Man.'

'Accent?'

'British, like I told them.'

'Do better.'

'What, you don't believe me?'

'I'm asking you to think again, I'm asking you to think harder. Take a moment, then tell me what you remember.'

'Nothing, I . . .' Cevik paused in the crisscross shadows of an Adams flowering crab apple. 'Hang on. Maybe, just maybe, there was a hint of something else, something more exotic, maybe Eastern European.'

'You lived for a number of years in Ukraine, didn't you?'

'You have me.' Cevik screwed up his face. 'I want to say possibly he was Slavic. There was a touch . . . maybe southern Ukraine. In Odessa, on the northern Black Sea coast, where I've spent time, the dialect is somewhat different, you know.'

Bourne, of course, did know, but he said nothing. In his mind, he was on a countdown to the moment when Tim Hytner would arrive with the 'decoded' cipher.

'You're still lying to me,' Bourne said. 'You must've seen your buyer when he picked up the TSGs.'

'And yet I didn't. The deal was done through a dead drop.'

'From a voice on the phone? Come on, Cevik.'

'It's the truth. He gave me a specific time and a specific place. I left half the shipment and I returned an hour later for half the five mil. The next day, we completed the deal. I saw no one, and believe me when I tell you I didn't want to.'

Again, plausible – and a clever arrangement, Bourne thought. If it was true.

'Human beings are born curious.'

'That may be so,' Cevik said with a nod. 'But I have no desire to die. This man . . . his people were watching the dead drop. They would have shot me on sight. You know that, Bourne. This situation is familiar to you.'

Cevik shook out a cigarette, offered Bourne one, then took one himself. He lit it with a book of matches that was almost empty. Seeing the direction of Bourne's gaze, he said, 'Nothing to burn in the hole so they let me keep it.'

Bourne heard an echo in his mind, as if a voice were speaking to him from a great distance. 'That was then, this is now,' he said, taking the matchbook from Cevik.

Cevik, having made no move to resist, pulled the smoke into his lungs, let it out with a soft hiss, the sound of the cars rolling by beyond the moat of grass.

*Nothing to burn in the hole.* The words bounced around in Bourne's head as if his brain were a pinball machine.

'Tell me, Mr. Bourne, have you ever been incarcerated?'

*Nothing to burn in the hole.* The sentence, once evoked, kept repeating, blocking out thought and reason.

With a grunt almost of pain, Bourne pushed Cevik on and they resumed walking; Bourne wanted him in the light. Out of the corner of his eye, he saw Tim Hytner hurrying their way.

'Do you know what it means to have your freedom taken from you?' Cevik flicked a bit of tobacco off his underlip. 'All your life to live in poverty. Being poor is like watching pornography: Once you start, there's no way out. It's addictive, d'you see, this life without hope. Don't you agree?'

Bourne's head was hurting now, each repetition of each word falling like a hammer blow on the inside of his skull. It was with extreme difficulty that he realized Cevik was merely trying to regain a measure of control. It was a basic rule of the interrogator never to answer a question. Once he did, he lost his absolute power.

Bourne frowned. He wanted to say something; what was it? 'Make no mistake. We have you where we want you.'

'I?' Cevik's eyebrows lifted. 'I'm nothing, a conduit, that's all. It's my buyer you need to find. What do you want with me?'

'We know you can lead us to the buyer.'

'No I can't. I already told you – '

Hytner was approaching through inky shadow and glazed light. Why was Hytner here? Through the pounding in his head, Bourne could scarcely remember. He had it; it slipped away like a fish, then reappeared. 'The cipher, Cevik. We've broken it.'

Right on cue, Hytner came up and handed the paper to Bourne, who almost dropped it, such was his preoccupation with the ringing in his brain.

'It was a bitch all right,' Hytner said a bit breathlessly. 'But I finally got it licked. The fifteenth algorithm I used proved to be – '

The last part of what he was going to say turned into a ragged shout of shock and pain as Cevik jammed the glowing end of his cigarette into Hytner's left eye. At the same time he spun the agent around in front of him, locking his left forearm across his throat.

'Take one step toward me,' he said low in his throat, 'and I'll break his neck.'

'We'll take you down, right enough.' Soraya, with a quick glance at Bourne, was advancing, her gun arm straight out, her other hand cupped beneath the gun butt, its barrel aimed, questing. Waiting for an opening. 'You don't want to die, Cevik. Think of your wife and three children.'

Bourne stood as if poleaxed. Cevik, seeing this, showed his teeth.

'Think of the five mil.'

His golden eyes flicked toward her for an instant. But he was already backing away from her and from Bourne, his bleeding human shield held tight to his chest.

'There's nowhere to go,' Soraya said in a most reasonable tone. 'Not with all the agents we have around. Not with him slowing you down.'

'I'm thinking of the five mil.' He kept edging away from them, away from the glare of the sodium lights. He was heading toward 23rd Street, beyond which rose the National Academy of Sciences.

More people there – tourists especially – to hamper the agents' pursuit.

'No more prisons for me. Not one more day.'

*Nothing to burn in the hole.* Bourne wanted to scream. And then a sudden explosion of memory obliterated even those words: He was running across ancient cobblestones, a sharp mineral wind in his nostrils. The weight in his arms seemed suddenly too heavy to bear. He looked down to see Marie – no, it was the unknown woman's bloody face! Blood everywhere, streaming from her though he frantically tried to stanch the flow . . .

'Don't be an idiot,' Soraya was saying to Cevik. 'Cape Town? You'll never be able to hide from us. There or anywhere else.'

Cevik cocked his head. 'But look what I've done to him.'

'He's maimed, not dead,' she said through gritted teeth. 'Let him go.'

'When you hand me your gun.' Cevik's smile was ironic. 'No? See? I'm already a dead man in your eyes, isn't that true, Bourne?'

Bourne seemed to be coming very slowly out of his nightmare. He saw Cevik step into 23rd Street now with Hytner skidding off the curb like a recalcitrant child.

Just as Bourne lunged at him, Cevik pitched Hytner at them.

Then everything happened at once. Hytner staggered pitifully. Brakes screeched from a black Hummer close by. Just behind it a trailer-truck filled with new Harley-Davidson motorcycles swerved to avoid a collision. Air horns blaring, it almost struck a red Lexus, whose driver spun in terror into two other cars. In the first fraction of a second it appeared as if Hytner had stumbled over the curb, but then a plume of blood spat out of his chest and he twisted with the impact of the bullet.

'Oh, God!' Soraya moaned.

The black Hummer, rocking on its shocks, had pulled up. Its front window was partly open, the ugly gleam of a silencer briefly glimpsed. Soraya squeezed off two shots before answering fire sent her and Bourne diving for cover. The Hummer's rear door flew open and Cevik ducked inside. It sped off even before he'd pulled the door closed behind him.

Putting up her gun, Soraya ran to her partner, cradling his head in her lap.

Bourne, hearing the echo of the gunshot in his memory, felt himself released from a velvet prison where everything around him was muffled, dim. He leapt past Soraya and the crumpled form of Hytner, ran out onto 23rd Street, one eye on the Hummer, the other on the trailer-truck. The truck's driver had recovered and sent his gears clashing as he resumed speed. Bourne sprinted toward the back of the trailer, grabbed the chain across the lifted ramp, and hauled himself aboard.

His mind was racing as he clambered up onto the platform on which the motorcycles were chained in neat, soldierly rows. The guttering flame in the darkness, the flare of the match: Cevik lighting his cigarette had two purposes. The first, of course, was to provide him with a weapon. The second was as a signal. The black Hummer had been waiting, prepared. Cevik's escape had been meticulously planned.

By whom? And how could they have known where he'd be, and when?

No time for answers now. Bourne saw the Hummer just ahead. It was neither speeding nor weaving in and out of the traffic; its driver secure in the assumption that he and his passengers had made a clean escape.

Bourne unchained the motorcycle closest to the rear of the trailer and swung into the saddle. Where were the keys? Bending over and shielding it from the wind, he lit a match from the matchbook Cevik had tossed to him. Even so, the flame lasted only a moment, but in that time it revealed the keys taped to the underside of the gleaming black tank console.

Jamming the key into the ignition, Bourne fired up the Twin Cam 88B engine. He gunned the engine, shifted his weight to the rear. The front end of the motorcycle rose up as it shot forward off the rear edge of the trailer.

While he was still in free fall the cars behind the trailer jammed on their brakes, their front ends slewing dangerously. Bourne hit the pavement, leaned forward as the Harley bounced once, gaining traction as both wheels bit into the road. In a welter of squealing tires and stripped rubber, he made an acute U-turn and sped off after the black Hummer.

After a long, anxiety-filled moment, he spotted it going through the traffic-clogged square where 23rd Street intersected with Constitution Avenue, heading south toward the Lincoln Memorial. The Hummer's profile was unmistakable. Bourne kicked the motorcycle into high gear, blasting into the intersection on the amber, zigzagging through it to more squeals and angry horn blasts.

He shadowed the Hummer as it followed the road to the right, describing a quarter of a circle around the arc-lit memorial slowly enough that he made up most of the distance between them. As the Hummer continued on around toward the on-ramp to the Arlington Memorial Bridge, he gunned up, nudged its passenger-side rear bumper. The vehicle shrugged off the motorcycle's maneuver like an elephant swatting a fly. Before Bourne could drop back, the driver stamped on his brakes. The Hummer's massive rear end collided with the motorcycle, sending Bourne toward the guardrail and the black Potomac below. A VW came up on him, horn blaring, and almost finished the job the Hummer had started – but at the last instant Bourne was able to regain control. He swerved away from the VW, snaking back through traffic after the accelerating Hummer.

Above his head he heard the telltale *thwup-thwup-thwup* and, glancing up, saw a dark insect with bright eyes: a CI helicopter. Soraya had been busy on her cell phone again.

As if she were in his mind, his cell phone rang. Answering it, he heard her deep-toned voice in his ear.

'I'm right above you. There's a rotary on the center of Columbia Island just ahead. You'd better make sure the Hummer gets there.'

He swerved around a minivan. 'Did Hytner make it?'

'Tim's dead because of you, you sonovabitch.'

The chopper landed on the island rotary, and the infernal noise level dropped abruptly as the pilot cut the motor. The black Hummer kept on going as if nothing were amiss. Bourne, threading his way through the last of the traffic between him and his quarry, once again drew close to the vehicle.

He saw Soraya and two other CI agents emerge from the body of the helicopter with police riot helmets on their heads and shotguns in their hands. Swerving abruptly, he drew alongside the Hummer. With his cocked elbow, he smashed the driver's-side window.

'Pull over!' he shouted. 'Pull over onto the rotary or you'll be shot dead!'

A second helicopter appeared over the Potomac, angling in very fast toward their position. CI backup.

The Hummer gave no indication of slowing. Without taking his eyes off the road, Bourne reached behind him and opened the custom saddlebag. His scrabbling fingers found a wrench. He'd have one chance, he knew. Calculating vectors and speed, he threw the wrench. It slammed into the front of the driver's-side rear-wheel well. The wheel, revolving at speed, went over the wrench, launched it up with sickening power into the rear-wheel assembly.

At once the Hummer began to wobble, which only jammed the wrench deeper into the assembly. Then something cracked, an axle possibly, and the Hummer decelerated in a barely controlled spin. Mostly on its own momentum, it ran up over the curb onto the rotary and came to a stop, its engine ticking like a clock.

Soraya and the other agents spread out, moving toward the Hummer with drawn guns aimed at the passenger cabin. When she was close enough, Soraya shot the two front tires flat. One of the other agents did the same with the rear tires. The Hummer wasn't going anywhere until a CI tow truck hauled it back to HQ for forensics.

'All right!' Soraya shouted. 'Out of the vehicle, all of you! Out of the vehicle now!'

As the agents closed the circle around the Hummer, Bourne could see that they were wearing body armor. After Hytner's death, Soraya wasn't taking any chances.

They were within ten meters of the Hummer when Bourne felt his scalp begin to tingle. Something was wrong with the scene, but he couldn't quite put his mental finger on it. He looked again: Everything seemed right – the target surrounded, the approaching agents, the second helicopter hovering above, the noise level rising exponentially . . .

Then he had it.

*Oh, my God,* he thought, and viciously twisted the handlebar accelerator. He yelled at the agents, but over the noise of the two copters and his own motorcycle there was no chance they could hear him. Soraya was in the lead, closing in on the driver's door as the others, spread apart, hung back, providing her with a crossfire of cover should she need it.

The setup looked fine, perfect, in fact, but it wasn't.

Bourne leaned forward as the motorcycle sped across the rotary. He had a hundred meters to cover, a route that would take him just left of the Hummer's gleaming flank. He took his right hand off the handlebar grip, gesturing frantically at the agents, but they were properly concentrated on their target.

He gunned the engine, its deep, guttural roar at last cutting through the heavy vibrational *thwup-thwup-thwup* of the hovering copter. One of the agents saw him coming, watched him gesturing. He called to the other agent, who glanced at Bourne as he roared past the Hummer.

The setup looked right out of the CI playbook, but it wasn't, because the Hummer's engine was ticking over – cooling – *while it was still running.* Impossible.

Soraya was less than five meters from the target, her body tense, in a semi-crouch. Her eyes opened wide as she became aware of him. Then he was upon her.

He swept her up in his extended right arm, swung her back behind him as he raced off. One of the other agents, now flat on the ground, had alerted the second chopper, because it abruptly rose into the spangled night, swinging away.

The ticking Bourne had heard hadn't come from the engine at all. It was from a triggering device.

The explosion took the Hummer apart, turned its components into smoking shrapnel, shrieked behind them. Bourne, with the motorcycle at full speed, felt Soraya's arms wrap around his ribs. He bent low over the handlebars, feeling her breasts pressing softly against his back as she molded herself to him. The howling air was blast-furnace hot; the sky, bright orange, then clogged with oily black smoke. A hail of ruptured metal whirred and whizzed all around them, plowed into the ground, struck the roadway, fizzed into the river, shriveling.

Jason Bourne, with Soraya Moore clinging tightly to him, accelerated into the light-glare of monument-laden D.C.

# 4

Jakob Silver and his brother appeared from out of the dinner-time night, when even cities such as Washington appear deserted or, at least, lonely, a certain indigo melancholy robbing the streets of life. When the two men entered the hushed luxury of the Hotel Constitution on the northeast corner of 20th and F Streets, Thomas, the desk clerk on duty, hurried past the fluted marble columns and across the expanse of luxurious carpeting to meet them.

He had good reason to scurry. He, as well as the other desk clerks, had been given a crisp new hundred-dollar bill by Lev Silver, Jakob Silver's brother, when he had checked in. These Jewish diamond merchants from Amsterdam were wealthy men, this much the desk clerk had surmised. The Silvers were to be treated with the utmost respect and care, befitting their exalted status.

Thomas, a small, mousy, damp-handed man, could see that Jakob Silver's face was flushed as if in victory. It was Thomas's job to anticipate his VIP clients' needs.

'Mr. Silver, my name is Thomas. It's a pleasure to meet you, sir,' he said. 'Is there anything I might get for you?'

'That you may, Thomas,' Jakob Silver replied. 'A bottle of your best champagne.'

'And have the Pakistani,' Lev Silver added, 'what's his name – ?'

'Omar, Mr. Silver.'

'Ah, yes, Omar. I like him. Have him bring up the champagne.'

'Very good.' Thomas all but bowed from the waist. 'Right away, Mr. Silver.'

He hurried away as the Silver brothers entered the elevator, a plush cubicle that silently whisked them up to the executive-level fifth floor.

'How did it go?' Lev Silver said.

And Jakob Silver answered, 'It worked to perfection.'

Inside their suite, he shrugged off his coat and jacket, went directly into the bathroom, and turned on all the lights. Behind him, in the sitting room, he heard the TV start up. He stripped off his sweat-stained shirt.

In the pink-marble bathroom, everything was prepared.

Jakob Silver, naked to the waist, bent over the marble sink and took out his gold eyes. Tall, with the build of a former rugby player, he was as fit as an Olympian: washboard abdomen, muscular shoulders, powerful limbs. Snapping closed the plastic case in which he had carefully placed the gold contact lenses, he looked into the bathroom mirror. Beyond his reflection, he could see a good chunk of the cream-and-silver suite. He heard the low drone of CNN. Then the channel was switched to Fox News, then MSNBC.

'Nothing.' Muta ibn Aziz's vibrant tenor voice emerged from the other room.

Muta ibn Aziz had picked his cover name – Lev – himself. 'On any of the all-news stations.'

'And there won't be,' Jakob Silver said. 'CI is extremely efficient in manipulating the media.'

Now Muta ibn Aziz appeared in the mirror, one hand gripping the door frame to the bathroom, the other out of sight behind him. Dark hair and eyes, a classic Semitic face, a zealous and inextinguishable resolve, he was Abbud ibn Aziz's younger brother.

Muta dragged a chair behind him, which he set down opposite the toilet. After glancing at himself in the mirror, he said: 'We look naked without our beards.'

'This is America.' He gestured curtly with his head. 'Go back inside.'

Alone again, Jakob Silver allowed himself to think like Fadi. He had jettisoned the identity of Hiram Cevik the moment he and Muta had exited the black Hummer. Muta, as previously instructed, had left the Beretta semiautomatic pistol with its ugly M9SD Suppressor on the front seat as they had tumbled onto the sidewalk. His aim had been true, but then he'd never had a doubt about Muta ibn Aziz's marksmanship.

They had run out of sight as the Hummer sped up again, slipped around a corner, and walked quickly up 20th Street to F Street, vanishing like wraiths inside the warmly glowing facade of the hotel.

Meanwhile, not a mile away, Ahmad, with his load of C-4 explosives that had filled up the front foot well of the Hummer's cabin, was already martyred, already in Paradise. A hero to his family, his people.

'*Your objective is to take out as many of them as you can,*' Fadi had told him when Ahmad had volunteered to martyr himself. In truth, there had been many volunteers, with very little difference among them. All were absolutely reliable. Fadi had chosen Ahmad because he was a cousin. One of a great many, admittedly, but Fadi had owed his uncle a small favor, which this decision repaid.

Fadi dug into his mouth and removed the porcelain tooth sheaths he'd used to widen Hiram Cevik's jaw. Washing them with soap and water, he returned them to the hard-sided case that merchants used to transport gems and jewelry. Muta had thoughtfully placed it on the generous rim of the bathtub so that everything in it would be within easy reach: a warren of small trays and custom compartments filled with every manner of theatrical makeup, removers, spirit gums, wigs, colored contact lenses, and various prosthetics for noses, jaws, teeth, and ears.

Squeezing a solvent onto a broad cotton pad, he methodically wiped the makeup off his face, neck, and hands. His natural, sun-darkened skin reappeared in streaks, a good decade peeled away, until the Fadi he recognized was whole again. A short time as himself, precious as a jewel, in the center of the enemy camp. Then he and Muta ibn Aziz would be gone, lifting through the clouds to their next destination.

He dried his face and hands on a towel and went back into the sitting room of the suite where Muta stood, watching *The Sopranos* on HBO.

'I find myself repelled by this creature Carmela, the leader's wife,' he said.

'As well you should. Look at her bare arms!'

Carmela was standing at the open door to her obscenely huge house, watching her obscenely huge husband get into his obscenely huge Cadillac Escalade.

'And their daughter has sex before her marriage. Why doesn't Tony kill her, as the law dictates. An honor killing, so that he and his family's honor won't be dragged through the mud.' In a fit of disgust, Muta ibn Aziz went over to the TV, switched it off.

'We strive to inculcate in our women the wisdom of Muhammad, the Quran, the true faith as their guides,' Fadi said. 'This American woman is an infidel. She has nothing, she is nothing.'

There came then a discreet knock on the door.

'Omar,' Muta said. 'Let me.'

Fadi gave his silent assent before he slipped back into the bathroom.

Muta crossed the plush carpet and drew open the door for Omar to enter. He was a tall, broad-shouldered man of no more than forty, with a shaven head, a quick smile, and a penchant for telling incomprehensible jokes. On his shoulder was a silver tray laden with a bottle in an enormous ice bucket, two flutes, and a plate of freshly sliced fruit. Omar filled the doorway, Muta thought, much as Fadi would, for the two men were of the same approximate height and weight.

'Your champagne,' Omar said superfluously. Crossing the room, he set his burden down on the glass top of the cocktail table. The ice made a shivery sound as he pulled the bottle free.

'I'll open it,' Muta said, grasping the heavy champagne bottle from the waiter.

When Omar proffered the leather-bound folder with the chit to sign, Muta called, 'Jakob, the champagne's here. You must sign.'

'Tell Omar to come into the bathroom.'

Even so, Omar looked at the other questioningly.

'Go on.' Muta ibn Aziz smiled winningly. 'I assure you, he won't bite.'

With the small leather folder held before him like an offering, Omar plodded toward the sound of Fadi's voice.

Muta dropped the bottle back into its bed of shaved ice. He had no idea what champagne tasted like and wasn't in the least interested. When he heard the sudden loud noise from the bathroom, he used the remote to turn the TV back on, cranking up the volume. Switching channels because *The Sopranos* was over, he stopped when he recognized the face of Jack Nicholson. The actor's voice filled the room.

'Here's Johnny!' Nicholson crowed through the rent in the bathroom door he'd made with an ax.

Omar, his hands tied behind his back, was bound to the chair in the bathtub. His large brown liquid eyes were staring up at Fadi. There was an ugly bruise on his jaw just beginning to inflate.

'You're not Jewish,' Omar said in Urdu. 'You're Muslim.'

Fadi ignored him and went about his business, which, at the moment, was death.

'You're Muslim, just like me,' Omar repeated. To his utter surprise, he wasn't frightened. He seemed to be in something of a dream state, as if from the moment he was born he was fated for this encounter. 'How can you do this?'

'In a moment, you will be martyred to the cause,' Fadi said in Urdu, which his father had made certain he learned as a child. 'What is your complaint?'

'The cause,' Omar said calmly, 'is your cause. It isn't mine. Islam is a religion of peace, and yet here you are waging a terrible, bloody war that devastates families, whole generations.'

'We are given no choice by the American terrorists. They suck at our oil tit, but that isn't enough for them. They want to *own* the oil tit. So they make up lies and use them to invade our land. The American president claims, of course falsely, that his god has spoken to him. The Americans have revived the era of the Crusades. They are the world's chief infidels – where they lead Europe follows, either willingly or grudgingly. America is like a colossal engine rolling across the world, its citizens grinding whatever they find into shit that all looks the same. If we don't stop them, they will be the end of us. They want nothing less. Our backs are against the wall. We have been driven into this war of survival, unwilling. They have systematically stripped us of power, of dignity. Now they want to occupy all of the Middle East.'

'You speak with a terrible hatred.'

'A gift of the Americans. Cleanse yourself of all Western corruption.'

'And I say that as long as your focus is hatred, you're doomed. Your hatred has blinded you to any possibility but the one you have created.'

A tremor of barely suppressed rage rippled through Fadi. 'I have created nothing! I am defending what *must* be defended. Why can you not see that our very way of life hangs in the balance.'

'It is you who cannot see. There is another way.'

Fadi threw his head back, his voice corrosive. 'Ah, yes, now you have opened my eyes, Omar. I shall renounce my people, my heritage. I will become like you, a servant waiting on the decadent whims of pampered Americans, dependent on the crumbs left on their table.'

'You see only what you want to see.' Omar's expression was sad. 'You've only to look at the Israeli model to know what can be done with hard work and – '

'The Israelis have the money and the military might of America behind them,' Fadi hissed into Omar's face. 'They also have the atomic bomb.'

'Of course, that is what you see. But Israelis themselves are Nobel laureates in physics, economics, chemistry, literature; prizewinners in quantum computing, black-hole thermo-dynamics, string theory. Israelis were founders of Packard Bell, Oracle, SanDisk, Akamai, Mercury Interactive, Check Point, Amdocs, ICQ.'

'You're talking gibberish,' Fadi said, dismissively.

'To you, yes. Because all you know how to do is destroy. These people created a life for themselves, for their children, for their children's children. This is the model you need to follow. Turn inward, help your people, educate them, allow them to make something of themselves.'

'You're insane,' Fadi said in fury. 'Never. Finished. The end.' The flat of his hand cut through the air. It held a shining blade that slit Omar's throat from side to side. With a last look at Nicholson's manically grinning face, Muta ibn Aziz followed Omar into the grotesque pink-marble bathroom, which looked to him like flesh after the skin had been stripped off. There was Omar, sitting on the chair he had placed in the bathtub. There was Fadi bent over, studying Omar's face as if to memorize it. Fadi's makeup case had been overturned when Omar had kicked it during his death throes. Small jars, broken bottles, prosthetics were all over the place. Not that it mattered.

'He looks so sad, slumped there on the chair,' Muta said.

'He's beyond sadness,' Fadi said. 'He's beyond all pain and pleasure.'

Muta stared into Omar's glassy eyes, the pupils fixed and dilated in death. 'You broke his neck. So neat, so precise.'

Fadi sat down on the lip of the tub. After a moment's hesitation, Muta retrieved an electric hair shearer from the tile floor. Fadi had affixed a mirror to the wall at the back of the tub by means of suction cups. He stared into this, scrutinizing every motion, as Muta began to take off his hair.

When the task was done, Fadi rose. He stared at himself in the mirror over the sink, then back at Omar. He turned to one side, and Muta moved Omar's head so the same side was visible. Then the other side.

'A little more here – ' Fadi pointed at a spot on the top of his own scalp. ' – where Omar is already bald.'

When he was satisfied, he began to give himself Omar's nose, Omar's slight overbite, Omar's elongated earlobes.

Together they stripped Omar of his uniform, socks, and shoes. Fadi did not forget the man's underwear, putting those on first. The idea was to be absolutely authentic.

'La ilaha ill allah.' Muta grinned. 'You look every inch the Pakistani servant.'

Fadi nodded. 'Then it's time.'

As he went through the suite, he picked up the tray Omar had brought. Out in the corridor, he took the service elevator to the basement. He drew out a handheld video device, brought up the schematics for the hotel. Locating the room housing the electronic panels for the HVAC, electrical power, and sprinkler systems took less than three minutes. Inside, he removed the cover to the sprinkler panel and replaced the wires for the fifth floor. The color coding would look correct to anyone who checked, but the wires were now shorted out, rendering the fifth-floor sprinklers inoperable.

He returned to the fifth floor the way he had come. Encountering a maid who entered the service lift on the second floor, he tried out his imitation of Omar's voice. She got out on the fourth floor without suspecting a thing.

Returning to the Silvers' suite, he went into the bathroom. From the bottom drawer of his case, he pulled out a small spray can and two metal containers of carbon disulfide. He emptied one container into Omar's accommodating lap, the odor of rotten eggs pervading the air. Back in the living room, he poured out the second just below the window, where the hem of the thick curtains fell. Then he sprayed the curtains with a substance that would turn the fabric from fire-retardant to flammable.

In the sitting room, he said, 'Do you have everything you need?'

'I have forgotten nothing, Fadi.'

Fadi ducked back into the bathroom and lit the accelerant in Omar's lap. Virtually no trace of him, not a recognizable bone nor a bit of flesh, would survive the intense heat of the inferno the accelerants would generate. With Muta watching, Fadi lit the bottom of the curtains in the living room, and they left the suite together. They parted almost immediately, Muta ibn Aziz to the stairwell, Fadi once again to the service elevator. Two minutes later, he exited the side entrance: Omar on a cigarette break. Forty-three seconds later, Muta joined him.

They had just turned off 20th Street onto H Street, protected by the bulk of one of the buildings at George Washington University, when, with a thunderous roar, the fire blew out the fifth-floor window, on its way to completely incinerating all three rooms of the Silvers' suite.

They strolled down the street to the sounds of shouts, cries, the mounting wail of sirens. A flickering red heat rose into the night, the heartbreaking light of disaster and death.

Both Fadi and Muta ibn Aziz knew it well.

A world away from both luxury and international terrorism, Northeast quadrant was rife with its own homegrown disasters arising from poverty, inner-city rage, and disenfranchisement – toxic ingredients of existence so familiar to Fadi and Muta ibn Aziz.

Gangs owned much of the territory; drug- and numbers-running were the commerce that fed the strong, the amoral. Vicious turf wars, drive-by shootings, raging fires were nightly occurrences. There wasn't a foot patrolman on the Metro D.C. Police who would venture onto the streets without armed backup. This held true for the squad cars as well, which were without exception manned by two cops; sometimes, on particularly bloody-minded nights or when the moon was full, by three or four.

Bourne and Soraya were racing through the night along these mean streets when he noted for the second time a black Camaro behind them.

'We picked up a tail,' he said over his shoulder.

Soraya didn't bother looking back. 'It's Typhon.'

'How d'you know?'

Over the sighing wind he heard the distinct metallic *snik!* of a switchblade. Then the edge of the blade was at his throat.

'Pull over,' she said in his ear.

'You're crazy. Put the knife away.'

She pressed the blade into his skin. 'Do as I tell you.'

'Don't do this, Soraya.'

'You're the one who needs to think about what he's done.'

'I don't know what you – '

She gave him a shove in the back with the heel of her hand. 'Dammit! Pull over now!'

Obediently, he slowed down. The black Camaro came roaring up on his left to trap him between it and the curb. Soraya noted this with satisfaction and, as she did so, Bourne jammed his thumb into the nerve on the inside of her wrist. Her hand opened involuntarily and he caught the falling switchblade by the handle, closed it, and stuck it into his jacket.

The Camaro, following procedure to the letter, had now angled in to the curb just in front of him. The passenger door swung open even as it rocked on its shocks, and an armed agent leapt out. Bourne twisted the handlebars and the motorcycle's engine screamed as he turned to his right, cutting across a burned-out lawn, slipping into a narrow alley between two houses.

He could hear shouts behind him, the slamming of a door, the angry roar of the Camaro, but it was no use. The alley was too narrow for the car to be able to follow the motorcycle. It might try to find him on the other side, but Bourne had an answer for that as well. He was intimate with this part of Washington, and he was willing to bet everything that they weren't.

On the other hand, he had Soraya to contend with. He might have stripped her of her knife, but she could still use every part of her body as a weapon. This she did with an economy of movement and an efficiency of application. She dug knuckles into his kidneys, repeatedly slammed her elbow into his ribs, even tried to gouge out an eye with her thumb, in obvious retaliation for what had happened to poor Tim Hytner.

All these assaults Bourne suffered with a grim stoicism, fending her off as best he could while the motorcycle rocketed through the narrow lane between the stained building walls on either side. Garbage cans and passed-out drunks were only the most frequent obstacles he had to negotiate at speed.

Then three teens appeared at the end of the alley. Two had baseball bats, which they brandished with chop-licking menace. The third, just behind the others, leveled a Saturday-night special at him as the motorcycle neared.

'Hang on!' he shouted at Soraya. Feeling her arms wrapped tightly around his waist, he leaned back, shifting their center of gravity sharply, at the same time gunning the engine. The front end of the motorcycle lifted off the ground. They rushed at the thugs reared up like a lion on the attack. He heard a shot fired, but the underside of the motorcycle protected them. Then they were in the midst of it. He snatched a bat from the grip of the thug on the left, slammed it down onto the wrist of the third teen, and the gun went flying.

They burst out of the end of the alley. Bourne leaned forward, guiding the motorcycle back onto two wheels just in time for the sharp turn to the right, down a street seething with garbage and stray dogs, yelping at the Harley's thunderous passage.

Bourne said, 'Now we can straighten – '

He never finished. Soraya had locked the crook of her arm across his windpipe and was bringing to bear a lethal pressure.

# 5

'Damn you, damn you, damn you!' Soraya chanted like an exorcist.

Bourne scarcely heard her. He was far too busy trying to stay alive. The motorcycle was hurtling at a hundred kilometers an hour down the street, the wrong way, as it happened. He managed to swerve out of the way of an old Ford, horn blaring, a deep voice shouting obscenities. But in the process he sideswiped a Lincoln idling at the opposite curb. The motorcycle hit, bouncing off the long dented slash in the Continental's front fender. Bourne's windpipe, almost entirely blocked by the choke hold Soraya had on him, was allowing next to no air into his lungs. Stars twinkled at the periphery of his vision, and he was blacking out for micro-seconds at a time.

Even so, he was aware that the Lincoln had awakened and, making a sharp U-turn, was now in fast pursuit of the motorcycle that had done it damage. Up ahead, a truck lumbered toward him, taking up most of the street.

Putting on a shocking burst of speed, the Continental came abreast of him, its blackened window rolled down and a moon-faced black man scowling and howling a string of curses. Then the voracious snout of a sawed-off shotgun showed itself.

'This'll teach yo, muthafucka!'

Before Moon-face had a chance to pull the trigger, Soraya kicked upward with her left leg. The edge of her boot struck the shotgun barrel; it swung wildly upward, the blast exploding into the treetops lining the street. Taking advantage, Bourne twisted the handlebars to full speed and took off down the street directly toward the huge truck. The driver saw their suicide maneuver and panicked, turning the wheel hard over as he simultaneously downshifted and stood on the air brakes. The truck, howling in protest, slewed broadside across the road.

Soraya, seeing death approaching with appalling speed, cried out in Arabic. She relinquished her choke hold to once again swing her arms tight around Bourne's waist.

Bourne coughed, sucked sweet air into his burning lungs, leaned all the way over to his right, cut the engine an instant before they were sure to slam into the truck.

Soraya's scream was cut short. The motorcycle went down on its side in a welter of sparks and blood from skin flayed off Bourne's right leg as they slid between the truck's madly spinning axles.

On the other side Bourne brought the engine to life, using the momentum and the weight of their combined bodies to return the motorcycle to its normal upright position.

Soraya, too dazed to immediately resume her attack, said, 'Stop, please stop now.'

Bourne ignored her. He knew where he was going.

*

The DCI was in conference with Matthew Lerner, being debriefed on the particulars of Hiram Cevik's escape and its fiery aftermath.

'Hytner aside,' Lerner said, 'the damage was light. Two agents with cuts and abrasions – one of those also with a concussion from the blast. A third agent missing. Minor damage to the bird on the ground' – he meant the helicopter – 'none to the one that had been hovering.'

'That was a public arena,' the Old Man said. 'It was fucking amateur hour out there.'

'What the hell was Bourne thinking, bringing Cevik out into the open?'

The director's gaze rose to the portrait of the president that hung on one wall of the conference room. On the other wall was a portrait of his predecessor. *You only get your portrait painted after they've hung you out to dry,* he thought sourly. The years had piled up on him, and some days – like today – he could feel every grain of sand in the hourglass burying him slowly, surely. Atlas with bowed shoulders.

The DCI shuffled through some papers, held one to the light. 'The chief of D.C. Metro's called, ditto the FB fucking I.' His eyes bored into Lerner's. 'You know what they wanted, Matthew? They wanted to know if they could help. Can you beat that? Well, I can.

'The president phoned to ask what the hell was going on, if we were under attack by terrorists, if he should head for Oz.' Another name for the Hidden Seat of Power, the secret place from which the president and his staff could run the country during a full-fledged emergency. 'I told him everything was under control. Now I'm asking you the same question, and by God I'd better get the answer I want.'

'In the end, we return to Bourne,' Lerner said, reading from the hastily prepared research notes his chief of staff had thrust into his fist just moments before the meeting convened. 'But then the recent history of CI is riddled with snafus and disasters that somehow always have their origin with Jason Bourne.

'It pains me to say I told you so, but this whole mess could've been avoided had you kept Lindros here at HQ. I know he was once a field operative, but that was some time ago. The animal edge is quickly dulled by administrative concerns. He's got his own shop to run. Who's going to run it if he's dead? The Cevik debacle was the direct result of Typhon being without a head.'

'Everything you say is true, dammit. I never should've allowed Martin to talk me into this. Then disaster upon disaster at Ras Dejen. Well, at least this time Bourne won't disappear off the grid.'

Lerner shook his head. 'But I have to wonder whether that's enough.'

'What d'you mean?'

'There's more than a fair chance that Bourne had a hand in Cevik's escape.'

The Old Man's eyebrows knit together. 'You have proof of this?'

'I'm working on it,' Lerner said. 'But it stands to reason. The escape was planned in advance. What Cevik's people needed to do was to get him out of the cage, and Bourne accomplished that quite efficiently. He's nothing if not efficient, this we already knew.'

The Old Man slammed his hand on the table. 'If he's behind Cevik's escape, I swear I'll skin him alive.'

'I'll take care of Bourne.'

'Patience, Matthew. For the moment we need him. We must get Martin Lindros back, and Bourne is now our only hope. After due consideration, the Operations Directorate sent the Skorpion Two team in after Skorpion One, and we lost them both.'

'With my contacts, I told you I could gather a small unit – '

'Of freelancers, former NSA operatives now in the private sector.' The DCI shook his head. 'That idea was DOA. I could never sanction a bunch of mercenaries, men I don't know, men not under my command, for such a sensitive mission.'

'But Bourne – dammit, you know his history, and now history is repeating itself. He does whatever the hell he wants whenever it suits him and fuck anyone else.'

'Everything you say is true. Personally, I despise the man. He represents everything that I've been taught is a menace to an organization like CI. But one thing I know about him is that he's loyal to the men he bonds with. Martin is one of those. If anyone can find him and extract him, it's Bourne.'

At that moment, the door swung open and Anne Held poked her head in.

'Sir, we have an internal problem. My clearance has been busted. I called Electronic Security and they said it wasn't a mistake.'

'That's right, Anne. It's part of Matthew's reorganization plan. He felt you didn't need top clearance to do the work I give you.'

'But, sir – '

'Clerical staff has one set of clearance priorities,' Lerner said. 'Operational staff another. Neat and clean, no ambiguities.' He looked at her. 'Still a problem, Ms. Held?'

Anne was furious. She looked to the Old Man, but realized at once that she'd get no help from that quarter. She saw his silence, his complicity, as a betrayal of the relationship she'd worked so long and hard to forge with him. She felt compelled to defend herself, but knew this was the wrong time and place to do it.

She was about to close the door when a messenger from Ops Directorate came up behind her. She turned, took a sheet of paper from him, turned back.

'We just got a read on the missing agent,' she said.

The DCI's mood had darkened considerably in the last few minutes. 'Who is it?' he snapped.

'Soraya Moore,' Anne told him.

'You see,' Lerner said sternly, 'another one of our people transferred out of my jurisdiction. How am I expected to do my job when people I have no control over slide off the grid? This is directly attributable to Lindros, sir. If you would give me control of Typhon at least until he's either found or confirmed dead – '

'Soraya's with Bourne,' Anne Held said to her boss before Lerner could say another word.

'Goddamm it!' the DCI exploded. 'How the hell did that happen?'

'No one seems to know,' Anne said.

The DCI was standing, his face empurpled with rage. 'Matthew, I do believe Typhon needs an acting director. As of now, you're it. Go forth and get the fucking job done ASAP.'

'Stop the motorcycle,' Soraya said in his ear.

Bourne shook his head. 'We're still too close to the – '

'Now.' She put the blade of a knife against his throat. 'I mean it.'

Bourne turned down a side street, pulled the cycle over to the curb, engaged the kickstand. As they both got off, he turned to her. 'Now what the hell is this all about?'

Her eyes blazed with an ill-contained fury. 'You killed Tim, you sonovabitch.'

'What? How could you even think – ?'

'You told Cevik's people where he'd be.'

'You're insane.'

'Am I? It was your idea to take him out of the cell block. I tried to stop you, but – '

'I didn't have Hytner killed.'

'Then why did you just stand there while he was shot?'

Bourne didn't give her an answer because he had none to give. He recalled that at the time he'd been assaulted by sound, and – he rubbed his forehead – a debilitating headache. Soraya was right. Cevik's escape, Hytner's death. How had he allowed it all to happen?

'Cevik's escape was meticulously planned and timed. But how?' Soraya was saying. 'How could Cevik's people know where he was? How *could* they know, unless you told them?' She shook her head. 'I should've listened more closely to the stories about you going rogue. There were only two men in all of CI you were able to buffalo: One's dead and the other's missing. Clearly you can't be trusted.'

With an effort, Bourne willed his head to clear. 'There's another possibility.'

'This should be good.'

'I didn't call anyone while we were down in the cells or outside – '

'You could've used hand signs, anything.'

'You're right about the method, wrong about the messenger. Remember when Cevik struck the match?'

'How could I forget?' she said bitterly.

'That was the final signal for the waiting Hummer.'

'That's just the *point*, the Hummer was *already* waiting. You *knew* because it was your setup.'

'If it was my setup, would I be telling you about it? Think, Soraya! You called Hytner to tell him we were going outside. It was *Hytner* who called Cevik's people.'

Her laugh was harsh and derisive. 'What, so then one of Cevik's people shot Tim to death? Why on earth would they do that?'

'To cover their tracks absolutely. With Hytner dead, there was no chance of him being caught and giving them up.'

She shook her head stubbornly. 'I knew Tim a long time; he was no traitor.'

'Those are usually the guilty ones, Soraya.'

'Shut up!'

'Maybe he wasn't a willing traitor. Maybe they got to him in some way.'

'Don't say one more thing against Tim.' She brandished the knife. 'You're just trying to save your own skin.'

'Look, you're absolutely right that Cevik's escape was planned in advance. But I didn't know where Cevik was being held – I didn't even know you were holding *anyone* until you told me not ten minutes before you took me to see Cevik.'

This stopped her in her tracks. She looked at him oddly. It was the same look she'd given him when he'd first seen her down in the Typhon ops center.

'If I was your enemy, why would I save you from the explosion?'

A little shiver went through her. 'I don't pretend to have all the -answers – '

Bourne shrugged. 'If your mind's made up, maybe I shouldn't confuse you with the truth.'

She took a breath, her nostrils flared. 'I don't know what to believe. Ever since you came down to Typhon – '

In a flash he reached out, disarmed her. She stared at him wide-eyed as he reversed the knife, handing it back to her butt-first.

'If I was your enemy . . .'

She looked at it a long time, then up at him as she took it, slid it back into its neoprene sheath at the small of her back.

'Okay, so you're not the enemy. But neither was Tim. There's *got* to be another explanation.'

'Then we'll find it together,' he said. 'I have my name to clear, you have Hytner's.'

'Give me your right hand,' she said to Bourne.

Gripping Bourne's wrist, she turned the hand over so that the palm was face up. With her other hand, she laid the flat of the blade on the tip of Bourne's forefinger.

'Don't move.'

With one deft motion she flicked the blade forward, along his skin. Instead of drawing blood, she lifted off a minute oval of translucent material so thin Bourne had not felt or noticed it.

'Here we go.' She held it up in the fitful glow of the streetlight for Bourne to see. 'It's known as a NET. A nano-electronic tag, according to the tech boys from DARPA.' She meant the Defense Advanced Research Projects Agency, an arm of the Department of Defense. 'It uses nanotechnology – microscopic servers. This is how I tracked you with the copter so quickly.'

Bourne had fleetingly wondered how the CI copter had picked him up so quickly, but he'd assumed it was the Hummer's distinctive profile they'd spotted. He considered for a moment. Now he recalled with vivid clarity the curious look Tim Hytner had given him when he had handled the transcript of Cevik's phone conversation: That was how they'd planted the NET on him.

'Sonovabitch!' He eyed Soraya as she slid the NET into a small oval plastic case and screwed down the lid. 'They were going to monitor me all the way to Ras Dejen, weren't they?'

She nodded. 'DCI's orders.'

'So much for the promise to keep me off the leash,' Bourne said bitterly.

'You're off now.'

He nodded. 'Thanks.'

'How about returning the favor?'

'Which would be . . . ?'

'Let me help you.'

He shook his head. 'If you knew me better, you'd know I work alone.'

Soraya looked as if she was about to say something, then changed her mind. 'Look, as you said yourself, you're already in hot water with the Old Man. You're going to need someone on the inside. Someone you can trust absolutely.' She took a step back toward the motorcycle. 'Because you know as sure as we're both standing here that the Old Man's going to find ways to fuck you every which way from Sunday.'

# 6

Kim Lovett was tired. She wanted to go home to her husband of six months. He was too new to the district and they were too new to each other for him to have yet succumbed to the crushing separation dictated by his wife's job.

Kim was always tired. The D.C. Fire Investigation Unit knew no typical hours or workdays. As a consequence, agents like Kim, who were clever, experienced, and knew what they were doing, were called on to labor hours akin to those of an ER surgeon in a war zone.

Kim had caught the call from DCFD during a brief lull in the mind-numbing drudgery of filling out paperwork on a phalanx of arson investigations, one of the few moments during the past weeks when she'd allowed herself to think about her husband – his wide shoulders, his strong arms, the scent of his naked body. The reverie didn't last long. She had picked up her kit and was on her way to the Hotel Constitution.

She engaged the siren as she headed out. From Vermont Avenue and 11th Street to the northeast corner of 20th and F took no more than seven minutes. The hotel was surrounded by police cars and fire engines, but by now the fire had been contained. Water streamed down the facade from the open wound at the end of the fifth floor. The EMT vehicles had come and gone, and there was about the scene the brittle, jittery aftermath of cinders and draining adrenaline Kim's father had described to her so well.

Chief O'Grady was waiting for her. She got out of the car and, displaying her ID, was admitted past the police barricades.

'Lovett,' O'Grady grunted. He was a big, beefy man with short but unruly white hair and ears the size and shape of a thick slice of pork tenderloin. His sad, watery eyes watched her guardedly. He was one of the majority who felt that women had no place in the DCFD.

'What've we got?'

'Explosion and fire.' O'Grady lifted his chin in the direction of the gaping wound.

'Any of our men killed or injured?'

'No, but thanks for asking.' O'Grady wiped his forehead with a dirty paper towel. 'There was a death, however – probably the occupant of the suite, though with the tiny fragments I've found I can tell you it will be impossible to make an ID. Also, the cops say one employee is missing. Damn lucky for a fireworks display like this one.'

'You said *probably* the guest.'

'That's right. The fire was unnaturally hot, and it was one bitch to put out. That's why FIU was called in.'

'Any idea what caused the explosion?' she asked.

'Well, it wasn't the fucking boiler,' the chief said shortly. He stepped closer to her, the burned rubber-and-cinder smell coming off him in waves. When he spoke again, his voice was low, urgent. 'You've got about an hour up there before Metro Police hand everything over to Homeland Security. And you know what's gonna happen when those boyos start tramping through our crime scene.'

'Gotcha.' Kim nodded.

'Okay. Go on up. A Detective Overton is waiting.'

He strode off in his rolling, slightly bandy-legged gait.

The lobby was filled with cops and firemen milling around. The cops were taking the temperature of the staff and guests, huddled in separate corners like plotting factions. The firefighters were busy dragging equipment across the blackened runner and marble floor. The place smelled of anxiety and frustration, like a stalled subway car at rush hour.

Kim rode the elevator up, stepping out into a charred and ruined fifth-floor corridor that, except for her, was utterly deserted. Just inside the suite, she found Overton, a stoop-shouldered detective with a long, mournful face, squinting at his notes.

'What the hell happened?' she said after introducing herself. 'Any ideas?'

'Possibly.' Detective Overton flipped open a notebook. 'The occupants of this corner suite were Jakob and Lev Silver. Brothers. Diamond merchants from Amsterdam. They came in at seven forty-five or thereabouts. We know that because they had a brief conversation with a concierge – ' He flipped a page. ' – named Thomas. One of them ordered a bottle of champagne, some kind of celebration. After that, Thomas didn't see them. He swears they didn't leave the hotel.'

They went into the suite proper.

'Can you give me the lowdown on what caused the explosion?'

'That's what I'm here for.' She snapped on latex gloves, went to work. Twenty minutes went by as she hunted down the epicenter of the blast and worked her way outward from there. Normally she'd take carpet samples – if an accelerant had been used, it was most likely to be a highly inflammable hydrocarbon-based liquid, such as turpentine, acetone, naphtha, or the like. Two telltale signs: The liquid would have seeped into the carpet, even into the underlayer. Also, there would be what was commonly called headspace – short for headspace gas chromatography – which would pick up the traces of the gases released when the accelerants ignited. Since each compound released a unique fingerprint, the headspace could determine not only if an accelerant had been used but also which one.

Here, however, the fire was of such intensity that it had eaten through the carpet and the underlayer. No wonder O'Grady and his men had had difficulty putting it out.

She examined every scrap of metal, splinter of wood, fiber of cloth, and pile of ash. Opening her kit, she exposed parts of this detritus to myriad tests. The rest she carefully put into glass containers, sealed them with airtight lids, and placed each container in its foam padding in her kit.

'I can tell you now that an accelerant was definitely used,' she said as she continued to stow evidence. 'I won't know what it was precisely until I get back to the lab, but I'll say this much: It wasn't your garden-variety accelerant. This heat, this level of destruction – '

Detective Overton interrupted her. 'But the explosion – '

'There's no trace of explosive residue,' she said. 'Accelerants have flashpoints that often cause explosions in and of themselves. But again, I won't be sure until I can conduct tests back at the lab.'

By this time, she had moved on in an ever-widening circle surrounding the point of explosion.

All at once, she sat back on her haunches and said, 'Have you found out why the sprinklers didn't come on?'

Overton flipped through his notes. 'As it happens, the sprinklers engaged on every floor of the hotel but this one. When we went down to the basement, we discovered that the system had been tampered with. I had to call in an electrician to find out, but the bottom line is that the sprinklers on this floor were disabled.'

'So the entire episode was deliberate.'

'Jakob and Lev Silver were Jews. The waiter who brought him the bottle of champagne – the one employee who's missing – is Pakistani. Hence my duty to turn this sucker over to Homeland Security.'

She looked up from her work. 'You think this waiter is a terrorist?'

Overton shrugged. 'My bet's on a business vendetta against the Silvers, but I sure as hell want to know before Homeland Security does.'

She shook her head. 'This setup is too sophisticated by half for a terrorist attack.'

'Diamonds are forever.'

She rose. 'Let's see the body.'

'*Body* would be the wrong word for what we got left.'

He took Kim into the bathroom, and together they stared down at the bits of charred bone scattered about the porcelain tub.

'Not even a skeleton.' Lovett nodded to herself. She did a complete 360. 'Here lies either Jakob or Lev Silver, fair enough. But where's the other brother?'

'Could be cindered. No?'

'In this heat, a definite possibility,' Kim said. 'It'll take me days, if not weeks to sift through the debris for any human ash. But then again I might not find anything at all.'

She knew he'd combed the entire suite, but she went through every nook and cranny herself.

He glanced nervously at his watch as they returned to the bathroom. 'This gonna take much longer? Time's running out on me.'

Kim climbed into the bathtub with the bits and pieces of charred bone. 'What's with you and Homeland Security?'

'Nothing, I just . . .' He shrugged. 'I've tried five times to make it as an HS agent. Five times they turned me down. That's my stake in this case. If I show them what I can do, they'll have to take me when I reapply.'

She crawled around with her equipment. 'There was accelerant here,' she said, 'as well as in the other room. You see, porcelain, which is created in fierce heat, tolerates it better than anything else, even some metals.' She moved down. 'Accelerants are heavy, so they tend to seep. That's why we look for them in the underlayer of a carpet or between the cracks of a wood floor. Here an accelerant would seek the lowest point in the tub. It would seep down into the drain.'

She swabbed out the drain, moving deeper with each separate swab she produced from her kit. All at once she stopped. She withdrew the swab, bagged it, put it away. Then she shone the xenon beam of a pencil flash into the hole.

'Ah, what have we here?'

She lowered a pair of needle-nose pliers into the drain. A moment later, she withdrew it. Clamped between its steel tips was something that looked quite familiar to both of them.

Detective Overton leaned forward until his head and torso were over the bathtub. 'A pair of one of the Silver brothers' teeth.'

Kim was scrutinizing them as she turned them in the cool, penetrating light of her pencil flash. 'Maybe.' She was frowning. *Then again maybe not*, she thought.

The olive-colored house just off 7th Street NE looked much like its neighbors – dingy, time-worn, in desperate need of a new front porch. The skeleton of the house to its right was still standing, more or less, but the rest of it had been gutted by arson long ago. The worn stoop to its right was inhabited by a clutch of teens, jangly with hard-core hip-hop roaring from a battered ghetto blaster. They were illuminated by a buzzing streetlight in desperate need of refitting.

As one, the teens came off the stoop as the motorcycle drew up to the curb in front of the olive-colored house, but Bourne waved them off as he and Soraya climbed slowly off.

Bourne, ignoring the ripped right leg of his trousers and the blood seeping through it, touched knuckled fist with the tallest of the teens. 'How's it going, Tyrone.'

'It goin',' Tyrone said. 'Yo know.'

'This is Soraya Moore.'

Tyrone gave Soraya the once-over with his large black eyes. 'Deron, he gonna be pissed. Ain't no one should be here 'cept yo.'

'It's on me,' Bourne said. 'I'll make it right with Deron.'

At that moment, the front door of the olive-colored house opened. A tall, slim, handsome man with skin the color of light cocoa stepped out onto the front porch.

'Jason, what the hell?' Deron frowned deeply as he came down off the porch toward them. He was dressed in jeans and a chambray work shirt with the sleeves rolled up to expose his forearms. He seemed impervious to the cold. 'You know the rules. You made them yourself with my father. No one but yourself comes here.'

Bourne stepped between Deron and Soraya. 'I've got just over two hours to make my flight to London,' he said in a low tone. 'I'm in a pile of it. I need her help as much as I do yours.'

Deron came on in his long, languid strides. He was close enough now for Soraya to see that he had a gun in his hand. And not just any gun: a .357 Magnum.

As she began to take an involuntary step backward, Deron said, *'Ah, who is nigh? come to me, friend or foe, And tell me who is victor, York or Warwick?'* in a very fine British accent. *'Why ask I that? my mangled body shows, My blood, my want of strength, my sick heart shows, That I must yield my body to the earth And, by my fall, the conquest to my foe.'*

Soraya replied, '*See who it is: and, now the battle's ended, If friend or foe, let him be gently used.*'

'I see you know your Shakespeare,' Deron said.

'*Henry the Sixth, Part Three,* one of my favorites at school.'

'But is the battle truly ended?'

'Show him the NET,' Bourne said.

She handed over the small oval case.

Stashing the Magnum in the waistband of his jeans, Deron extended the delicate long-fingered hand of a surgeon, or a pickpocket, to open the case.

'Ah.' His eyes lit up as he plucked out the beacon to study.

'The newest CI leash,' Bourne said. 'She dug that little devil off me.'

'DARPA-engineered,' Deron said. You could almost see him smack his lips in delight. There was nothing he liked better than new technology.

Deron was neither a surgeon nor a pickpocket, Bourne informed Soraya as they followed him into the olive-colored house. He was one of the world's foremost forgers. Vermeers were a specialty – Deron had a knack with light – but in truth he could reproduce virtually anything, and often did, for an astronomically high price. Every one of his clients said his work was worth the money. He prided himself on satisfied customers.

Deron led them into the entryway, shut the front door behind them. The unexpected heavy clangor startled Soraya. This was no ordinary door, though that was how it appeared from the outside. From this side, the metal sheathing reflected the warm lamplight.

She looked around, astonished. Directly ahead was a curving tiger-oak staircase; to the left, a corridor. To her right was a large living room. The polished wood floors were covered in costly Persian carpets, the walls hung with masterpieces out of the storied history of fine art: Rembrandt, Vermeer, van Gogh, Monet, Degas, many others. Of course, they were all forgeries, weren't they? She peered at them closely, and while she was no expert she thought them all brilliant. She was certain that if she had viewed them at a museum or auction she would have had no doubt as to their authenticity. She squinted harder. Unless some of them *were* the originals.

Turning back, she saw that Deron had clasped Bourne in a warm embrace.

'I never had a chance to thank you for coming to the funeral,' Bourne said. 'That meant a lot to me. I know how busy you are.'

'My dear friend, there are things in life that outweigh commerce,' Deron said with a sad smile, 'no matter how pressing or lucrative.' Then he pushed Bourne away. 'First thing, we take care of the leg. Upstairs, first door on the right. You know the drill. Get cleaned up. New duds for you up there as well.' He grinned. 'Always the finest selection at Deron's.'

Soraya followed Deron down a yellow enameled hallway, through a large kitchen, into what must once have been the house's washroom and pantry. Here were waist-high cabinets topped by zinc-wrapped counters, banks of computers, and stacks of incomprehensible electronic instruments.

'I know what he's looking for,' Deron said as if Soraya had ceased to exist. Methodically he began to open cabinet doors and drawers, taking out an item here, a handful there.

Soraya, looking over his shoulder, was startled to see noses, ears, and teeth. Reaching out, she picked up a nose, turning it over in her hand.

'Don't worry,' Deron said. 'They're made of latex and porcelain.' He picked up what looked like a piece of dental bridgework. 'Lifelike, though, don't you think?' He showed her one edge. 'Reason being, there's little difference between this prosthetic and the real thing, except here on the inside. The real thing would have a small recess in order to fit over the ground-down tooth. This, as you can see, is just a porcelain shell, meant to fit over normal teeth.'

Soraya couldn't help herself – she put on the latex nose, making Deron laugh. He rummaged around another drawer, handing her a much smaller model. This did feel better. Just for demonstration, he used some theatrical gum to mold it on.

'Of course, in real life you'd use another kind of glue, and makeup, to hide the edges of the prosthetic.'

'Isn't that a problem when you sweat or – I don't know, swim, maybe?'

'This isn't makeup from Chanel,' Deron said with a laugh. 'Once you apply it, you need a special solvent to get it off.'

Bourne returned just as Soraya was peeling off the fake nose. His leg wound was cleaned and bandaged, and he was dressed in new trousers and shirt.

Bourne said, 'Soraya, you and I need to talk.'

She followed him into the kitchen, where they stood by a huge stainless-steel refrigerator against the wall farthest from Deron's lab.

Bourne turned to her. 'You and Deron have a pleasant visit while I was gone?'

'You mean did he try to pump me for information?'

'You mean did I ask him to pump you.'

'Right.'

'As a matter of fact, I didn't.'

She nodded. 'He didn't.' Then she waited.

'There's no good way to get into this.' Bourne searched her face. 'Were you and Tim close?'

She turned her head away for a moment, bit her lip. 'What d'you care? To you he's a traitor.'

'Soraya, listen to me, it's either Tim Hytner or me. I know it's not me.'

Her expression was deliberately confrontational. 'Then tell me why you took Cevik outside?'

'I wanted him to get a taste of the freedom he no longer had.'

'That's it? I don't believe you.'

Bourne frowned. It wouldn't be the first time since Marie's death that he'd wondered if his latest trauma had somehow impaired his judgment. 'I'm afraid it's true.'

'Forget about my believing you,' she snapped. 'How d'you think that's going to play with the Old Man?'

'What does it matter? The Old Man hates loose cannons.'

She looked at her boots, shook her head. She took a breath, let it all out. 'I nominated Tim for Typhon, now he's dead.'

Bourne was silent. He was a warrior, what did she expect? Tears and regret? No, but would showing a smidgen of emotion kill him? Then she remembered his wife's recent death, and she felt immediately ashamed.

She cleared her throat, but not her emotions. 'We were in school together. He was one of those boys girls made fun of.'

'Why not you?'

'I wasn't like the other girls. I could see he was sweet and vulnerable. I sensed something.' She shrugged. 'He liked to talk about his younger childhood; he was born in rural Nebraska. To me, it was like hearing about another country.'

'He was wrong for Typhon,' Bourne said bluntly.

'He was wrong for the field, that's no lie,' she said just as bluntly.

Bourne put his hands in his pockets. 'So where does all this leave us?'

She started as if he'd pricked her with the business end of her switchblade. 'All what?'

'We've saved each other's lives, you've tried to kill me twice. Bottom line: We don't trust each other.'

Her eyes, large and liquid with incipient tears, bored into his. 'I gave up the NET; you brought me here to Deron's. What's *your* definition of trust?'

Bourne said, 'You took photos of Cevik when he was detained.'

She nodded, waiting for the ax to fall. What would he require of her now? What, exactly, did she require of him? She knew, of course, but it was too painful to admit to herself, let alone tell him.

'Okay, call Typhon. Get them to upload the photos to your phone.' He began to walk down the corridor, and she paced him step for step. 'Then have them upload the cipher Hytner took off Cevik.'

'You forget that all of CI is still locked down. That includes data transfers.'

'You can get me what I want, Soraya. I have faith in you.'

The curious look came back into her eyes for a moment, then vanished as if it had never existed. She was on the phone to Typhon by the time they entered Deron's workroom, an L-shaped space carved out of the old kitchen and pantry. His artist's studio was upstairs, in the room that gathered the most daylight. As for Deron himself, he was bent over a worktable, poring over the NET.

No one in Typhon save its director had the clearance to upload sensitive data during lockdown. She knew she'd have to search elsewhere to get what Bourne needed.

She heard Anne Held's voice and identified herself.

'Listen, Anne, I need your help.'

'Really? You won't even tell me where you are.'

'It's not important. I'm not in any danger.'

'Well, that's a relief. Why did the beacon stop transmitting?'

'I don't know.' Soraya was careful to keep her voice level. 'Maybe it's defective.'

'Since you're still with Bourne, it shouldn't be too difficult to find out.'

'Are you crazy? I can't get that close to him.'

'And yet you need a favor. Tell me.'

Soraya did.

Silence. 'Why is it you never ask for anything easy.'

'I can ask other people for those things.'

'Too true.' Then, 'If I get caught . . .'

'Anne, I think we have a lead to Cevik, but we need the intel.'

'Okay,' Anne said. 'But in return you've got to find out what happened to that beacon. I've got to tell the Old Man something that'll satisfy him. He's out for blood and I want to make certain it's not mine.'

Soraya thought for a moment, but couldn't come up with another alternative. She'd just have to come back to Anne with something more detailed, something plausible. 'All right. I think I can work something out.'

'Good. By the way, Soraya, when it comes to the new DDCI, I'd watch my back if I were you. He's no friend of Lindros, or of Typhon.'

'Thanks, Anne. Thanks very much.'

'It's done,' Soraya said. 'The data's been uploaded successfully.'

Bourne took her cell and handed it to Deron, who dragged himself away from his new toy to plug the phone into his computer network and download the files.

Cevik's face popped up on one of the many monitors.

'Knock yourself out.' Deron went back to studying the NET.

Bourne sat down in a task chair and studied the photos for a long time. He could feel Soraya leaning over his right shoulder. He felt – what? – the ghost of a memory. He rubbed his temples, willing himself to remember, but the sliver of light eeled away into darkness. With some disquiet, he returned to his scrutiny of Cevik's face.

There was something about it – not any single feature, but an overall impression – that swam in his memory like the shadow of a fish out of sight beneath the surface of a lake. He zoomed in on one area of Cevik's face after another – mouth, nose, brow, temple, ears. But this only served to push the impressionistic memory farther into the unknown recesses of his mind. Then he came to the eyes – the golden eyes. There was something about the left one. Zooming in closer, he saw a minute crescent of light at the outer edge of the iris. He zoomed in again, but here the resolution failed him and the image began to blur. He zoomed out until the crescent of light sharpened. It was tiny. It could be nothing – a reflection of the illumination in the cell. But why was it at the edge of the iris? If it was a reflection off the iris, the light would be a mote nearer the center, where the eyeball was most prominent, and therefore most likely to pick up the light. This was at the edge where . . .

Bourne laughed silently.

At that moment Soraya's cell phone buzzed. He heard her on it briefly. Then she said: 'The prelim from forensics indicates that the Hummer was packed with a shitload of C-Four.'

He turned to her. 'Which is why they wouldn't respond.'

'Cevik and his crew were suicide bombers.'

'Maybe not.' Bourne turned back to the photo, pointing at the tiny crescent of light. 'See that? It's a reflection off the edge of a contact lens, because it's slightly raised above the surface of the iris and has caught the light. Now look here. Notice this tiny fleck of the gold intruding on the curving left edge of the pupil? The only way that's possible is if Cevik was wearing colored contacts.'

He peered up into her face. 'Why would Cevik disguise himself unless he wasn't Cevik at all.' He waited for her response. 'Soraya?'

'I'm thinking.'

'The disguise, the meticulous planning, the deliberate bomb attack.'

'In the jungle,' she said, 'only a chameleon can spot another chameleon.'

'Yes,' Bourne said, staring at the photo. 'I think we had Fadi under our thumb.'

Another pause, this one shorter. Her brain was working so fiercely he could hear it.

'Chances are, then, Cevik didn't die in the blast,' she said at length.

'That would be a good bet.' Bourne thought a moment. 'He wouldn't have had much time to get out of the Hummer. The only time I didn't have it in sight was when I was starting up the motorcycle. That means before the Twenty-third and Constitution intersection.'

'He might have had another car waiting.'

'Check it out, but, frankly, I doubt it,' Bourne said. Now he understood why Fadi had used the high-profile Hummer. He *wanted* it followed and, finally, surrounded by CI personnel. He wanted to inflict maximum damage. 'There was no way for him to predict where he needed to bail.'

Soraya nodded. 'I'll grid it out from the point the Hummer picked Fadi up.' She was already dialing Typhon. 'I'll start a couple of teams canvassing right away.' She gave her instructions, listened gravely for a moment, then disconnected. 'Jason, I have to tell you there's a growing internal rift. The DCI's gone ballistic over the Cevik fiasco. He's blaming you.'

'Naturally.' Bourne shook his head. 'If it wasn't for Martin, I'd have nothing more to do with CI or Typhon. But he's my friend – he believed in me, fought for me when the agency was out for my blood. I won't turn my back on him. Still. I swear this is my last mission for CI.'

For Martin Lindros, the shadows resolved themselves into the undersides of clouds, reflected in the still waters of the lake. There was a vague sensation of pain – what you might feel if a dentist drilled into a partially Novocained tooth. The pain, far off on the horizon, failed to disturb him. He was far too concentrated on the trout at the business end of his fishing line. He reeled in, lifted the rod high so that it bent like a bow, then reeled in more line. Just as his father had taught him. This was the way to tire out a fish, even the most vigorous fighter. With discipline and patience, any hooked fish could be landed.

The shadows seemed to cluster right above him, blotting out the sun. The growing chill caused him to concentrate on this fish even harder.

Lindros's father had taught him many other things besides how to fish. A man of singular talents, Oscar Lindros had founded Vaultline, turning it into the world's foremost private security firm. Vaultline's clients were the super-conglomerates whose businesses often took their personnel into dangerous parts of the world. Oscar Lindros or one of his personally trained operatives was there to protect them.

Lindros, bending over the side of the boat, could see the flashing rainbow-and-silver of the trout. It was a big one, all right. Bigger than any he'd caught to date. Despite the fish's thrashing, Lindros could see the triangular head, the bony mouth opening and closing. He hauled up on the rod and the trout came halfway out of the water, spraying him with droplets.

Early on, Martin Lindros had developed an interest in being a spy. It went without saying that this desire had thrilled his father. And so Oscar Lindros had set about teaching his son everything he knew about the business of clandestine work. Chief among this knowledge was how to survive any form of capture or torture. It was all in the mind, Oscar Lindros told his son. You had to train your mind to withdraw from the outside world. Then you had to train it to withdraw from those sections of the brain that transmitted pain. To do this, you needed to conjure up a time and a place, you needed to make this place real – as real as anything you could experience with your five senses. You had to go there and you had to stay there for the duration. Otherwise, either your will would eventually be broken or you would go mad.

This was where Martin Lindros was, where he had been ever since he had been taken by Dujja, brought to this place where his body now lay twitching and bleeding.

Out on the lake, Lindros finally landed the trout. It flopped and gasped in the bottom of the boat, its eye fixed on him even as it grayed over. Bending down, he removed the barbed hook from the hard cartilage around the trout's mouth. How many fish had he landed since he'd been out on the lake? It was impossible to know since they'd never stayed around long afterward; they were of no use to him once they were off the hook.

He baited the hook, cast out the line. He had to keep going, he had to keep fishing. Otherwise the pain, a dim cloudbank on the horizon, would rush at him with the fury of a hurricane.

Sitting in the business-class section of the overnight flight to London, Bourne put up the do not disturb sign and took out the Sony PS3 Deron had given him, modified with expanded memory and ultra-high-resolution screen. The hard drive was preloaded with a bunch of new goodies Deron had concocted. Art forgeries might pay the rent, but his real love was dreaming up new miniaturized gadgets – hence his interest in the NET, which Bourne now had safely tucked away in its case.

Deron had provided Bourne with three separate passports beyond his diplomatic-CI passport. In each of the photos Deron had on file, Bourne looked completely different. He had with him makeup, colored contact lenses, and the like, along with one of Deron's new-generation guns made of rubber-wrapped plastic. According to Deron, the Kevlar-coated rubber bullets could bring down a charging elephant if put in the right spot.

Bourne brought up the photo of Hiram Cevik. Fadi. How many other identities had this mastermind assumed over the years? It seemed probable that surveillance cameras, closed-circuit TV cameras, in public places, had recorded his image, but he'd doubtless looked different every time. Bourne had advised Soraya to go over all the tapes or still photos available of the areas just before and after the Dujja attacks, comparing the faces etched there with this photo of Cevik, although he had little hope she'd find anything. He himself had had his photo taken by surveillance cameras and CCTV over the years. He had no worries because the Chameleon had looked different in every one. No one could spot any similarities; he'd made damn sure of that. So Fadi, the chameleon.

He stared at the face for a long time. Though he fought it, exhaustion overtook him, and he slept . . .

. . . *Marie comes to him, in a place of mature acacia trees and cobbled streets. There is a sharp mineral tang in the air, as of a restless sea. A humid breeze lifts her hair off her ears, and it streams behind her like a banner.*

*He speaks to her. 'You can get me what I want. I have faith in you.'*

*There is fear in her eyes, but also courage and determination. She will do what he asks of her, no matter the danger, he knows it. He nods in farewell, and she vanishes . . .*

*He finds himself on the same street of looming acacias that he's summoned up before. The black water is in front of him. And then he's descending, floating through air as if from a parachute. He's sprinting across a beach at night. On his left is a dark line of kiosks. He's carrying . . . there is something in his arms. No, not something. Someone. Blood all over, a pounding in his veins. A pale face, eyes closed, one cheek on his left biceps. He sprints along the beach, feeling terribly exposed. He's violated his covenant with himself and because of that they'll all die: him, the figure in his arms . . . the young woman covered in blood. She's saying something to him, but he can't hear what. Running footsteps behind him, and the thought, clear as the moon riding low in the sky:* We've been betrayed . . .

When Matthew Lerner walked into the outer office of the DCI's suite, Anne Held took a moment before she looked up. She had been working on nothing special. Nothing, in fact, that required her attention, yet it was important that Lerner think so. Privately, Anne likened the Old Man's outer office to a moat around a castle keep; she, the large-toothed carnivore that swam in it.

When she deemed that Lerner had waited long enough, she looked up, smiled coolly.

'You said the DCI wants to see me.'

'In point of fact, *I* want to see you.' Anne stood up, running her hands down her thighs to flatten any wrinkles that might have developed while she had been sitting. Pearly light spun off her perfectly manicured nails. 'D'you fancy a cup of coffee?' she added as she crossed the room.

Lerner arched his eyebrows. 'I thought it was tea you Brits liked.'

She held the door open for him to pass through. 'Just one of the many misconceptions you have about me.'

In the metal-clad elevator going down to the CI commissary, silence reigned. Anne looked straight ahead while Lerner, no doubt, tried to figure out what this was all about.

The commissary was unlike that of any other governmental agency. Its atmosphere was hushed, the floors carpeted with deep pile in presidential blue. The walls were white, the banquettes and chairs red leather. The ceiling was constructed of a series of acoustic baffles that dampened all sound, especially voices. Waistcoated waiters glided expertly and soundlessly up and down the generous aisles between tables. In short, the CI dining room was more like a gentlemen's club than a commissary.

The captain, recognizing Anne instantly, showed the pair to the DCI's round corner table, almost entirely surrounded by one of the high-backed banquettes. She and Lerner slid in, coffee was served, then they were discreetly left alone.

Lerner stirred sugar into his cup for a moment. 'So what's this all about?'

She took a sip of the black coffee, rolled the liquid around in her mouth as if it were a fine wine, then, satisfied, swallowed and put down her cup.

'Drink up, Matthew. It's single-estate Ethiopian. Strong and rich.'

'Another new protocol I've instituted, Ms. Held. We do not address each other by our Christian names.'

'The problem with some strong coffee,' she said, ignoring him, 'is that it can be quite acidic. Too much acid will turn the strength against itself, upset the entire digestive system. Even burn a hole in the stomach. When that happens, the coffee must be thrown out.'

Lerner sat back. 'Meaning?' He knew she wasn't talking about coffee.

She allowed her eyes to rest on his face for a moment. 'You were named DDCI, what, six months ago? Change is difficult for everyone. But there are certain protocols that cannot be – '

'Get to the point.'

She took another sip of coffee. 'It's not a good idea, Matthew, to be bad-mouthing Martin Lindros.'

'Yeah? What makes him so special?'

'If you'd been at this level longer, you wouldn't need to ask.'

'Why are we talking about Lindros? Chances are he's dead.'

'We don't know that,' Anne said shortly.

'Anyway, we're not really talking about Lindros's territory, are we, Ms. Held?'

She flushed then, despite herself. 'You had no good cause to lower my clearance level.'

'Whatever you might think your title entitles you to, it doesn't. You're still support personnel.'

'I'm the DCI's right hand. If he needs intel, I fetch it for him.'

'I'm transferring in Reilly from Ops Directorate. He'll be handling all the Old Man's research from now on.' Lerner sighed. 'I see the look on your face. Don't take these changes personally. It's standard operational procedure. Besides, if you get special treatment, the other support personnel start to resent it. Resentment breeds distrust, and that we cannot tolerate.'

He pushed his coffee cup away. 'Whether you choose to believe it or not, Ms. Held, CI is moribund. It has been for years. What it needs most is a high colonic. I'm it.'

'Martin Lindros has been put in charge of revamping CI,' she said icily.

'Lindros is the Old Man's weakness. His way isn't the right way. Mine is.' He smiled as he rose. 'Oh, and one other thing. Don't ever mislead me again. Support staff have no business wasting the deputy director's time with coffee and opinions.'

Kim Lovett, in her lab at FIU headquarters on Vermont Avenue, was at the most crucial stage of her tests. She had to transfer the solid material she'd collected on the fifth-floor suite of the Constitution Hotel from its airtight vials for the head-space gas chromatography. The theory was this: Since all known fire accelerants were highly volatile liquid hydrocarbons, the gases that the compounds gave off often remained at the scene for hours afterward. The idea was to capture the gases in the headspace above the solid material that had been impregnated with the accelerants: bits of charred wood, carpet fibers, lines of grout she'd dug out with a dentist's tool. She would then take a chromatogram of each of the gases based on its individual boiling point. In this way, a fingerprint of the accelerant emerged to be identified.

Kim stuck a long needle into the lid of each container, drew out the gas that had formed above the solid material, and injected it into the cylinder of the gas chromatograph without exposing it to the air. She ensured that the settings were correct, then slipped the switch that would begin the process of separation and analysis.

She was making notes as to the date, time, and sample number when she heard the lab door whoosh open and, turning, saw Detective Overton enter. He wore a fog-gray overcoat and carried two paper coffee cups in his hands. He set one down in front of her. She thanked him.

He seemed more morose than before. 'What news?'

Kim savored the hot, sweet burn of the coffee in her mouth and her throat. 'We'll know in a minute what accelerant was used.'

'How's that going to help me?'

'I thought you were handing the case over to Homeland Security?'

'Magnificent bastards. Two agents were in my captain's office this morning, demanding my notes,' Overton said. 'Not that I wasn't expecting it. So I made two sets, because I mean to break this case and shove it in their faces.'

A beep sounded.

'Here we go.' Kim swiveled around. 'The results are ready.' She peered at the chromatograph's readout. 'Carbon disulfide.' She nodded. 'This is interesting. Typically, we don't see this particular accelerant in arson cases.'

'Then why choose this one?'

'Good question. My guess is because it burns hotter and has an explosive limit of fifty percent – way higher than other accelerants.' She swiveled around again. 'You remember I found accelerants in two places – in the bathroom and under the windows. This interested me, and now I know why. The chromagraph gave me two separate readouts. In the bathroom, all that was used was the carbon disulfide. But at the other spot, the one in the living room near the windows, I found another compound, a rather complex and odd one.'

'Like what?'

'Not an explosive. Something more unusual. I had to do some checking, but I discovered that it's a hydrocarbon compound that counteracts fire retardants. This explains how the curtains caught fire, this explains why the explosion blew out the windows. Between the oxygen feeding the flames and the sprinklers being disabled, the maximum amount of damage in the minimum amount of time was virtually ensured.'

'Which is why we were left with nothing, not even an intact skeleton or a set of teeth from which to make a definite ID of the body.' He rubbed the blue stubble on his chin. 'The perps thought of everything, didn't they?'

'Maybe not everything.' Kim held up the two porcelain teeth she'd extracted from the bathtub drain. She had cleaned them of the coating of ash, so that they gleamed an ivory color.

'Right,' said Overton. 'We're trying to find out through channels in Amsterdam whether Jakob or Lev Silver wore a dental bridge. At least then we could make a positive ID.'

'Well, the thing of it is,' Kim said, 'I'm not at all sure this is a dental bridge.'

Overton plucked it out of her hand, studied it under a high-intensity lamp. So far as he could see, there wasn't anything out of the ordinary. 'What else could it be?'

'I've got a call in to a friend of mine. Maybe she can tell us.'

'Oh, yeah? What's she do?'

Kim looked at him. 'She's a spook.'

Bourne traveled from London to Addis Ababa; Addis Ababa to Djibouti. He rested very little, slept even less. He was too busy poring over the intel of Lindros's known movements that Soraya had provided him. Unfortunately, much of it was lacking details. Not altogether surprising. Lindros had been tracking the world's most deadly terrorist cadre. Communications of any kind would have been exceedingly difficult and would have compromised security.

When he wasn't memorizing the data, Bourne was reviewing the video intel Anne Held had uploaded to Soraya's cell, which now resided in the PS3, most especially Tim Hytner's attempt to break the cipher Typhon had found on Cevik's person. But now Bourne had to wonder about that cipher itself: Was it an authentic Dujja communication or was it a fake, planted, for some reason, for Typhon to find and decode? A bewildering labyrinth of duplicity had opened in front of him. From now on, each step he took was fraught with peril. A single false assumption could drag him under like quicksand.

It was at this moment that Bourne realized that he was up against a foe of extraordinary intelligence and will, a mastermind to rival his old nemesis Carlos.

He closed his eyes for a moment and immediately Marie's image came to him. It was she who had been his rock, who had helped him get through the tortures of the past. But Marie was gone. Every day that passed, he felt her fading. He tried to hold on, but the Bourne identity was relentless; it would not allow him to dwell on sentimentality, on sorrow and despair. All these emotions dwelled in him, but they were shadows, held at bay by Bourne's exceptional concentration and relentless need to solve deadly puzzles no one else could tackle. Of course, he understood the wellspring of his singular ability; he'd known it even before Dr. Sunderland had so succinctly summed it up: he was driven by his burning need to unravel the enigma of who he was.

In Djibouti a CI copter, fueled and ready, was waiting for him. He ran across the wet tarmac beneath an angry sky filled with bruised clouds and a humid, swirling wind, and climbed in. It was the morning of the third day since he'd set out from D.C. His limbs felt cramped, muscles bunched tight. He longed for action and was not looking forward to the hour-long flight to Ras Dejen.

Breakfast was served on a metal tray, and he dug in as the copter took off. But he tasted nothing and saw nothing, for he was totally inside his mind. He was, for the thousandth time, running Fadi's cipher, looking at it as a whole, because he'd gotten nowhere following the algorithm route that Tim Hytner had chosen. If Fadi had, indeed, turned Hytner – and Bourne could not come up with another reasonable conclusion – Hytner would have no incentive to actually break the cipher. This was why Bourne had wanted the cipher and Hytner's work. If he saw that Hytner's work was bogus, he'd have his proof of the man's culpability. But of course, that wouldn't answer the question of whether the cipher contained real intel or disinformation meant to confuse and misdirect Typhon.

Unfortunately, he was no closer to solving the cipher's algorithm or even knowing whether Hytner had been on the right track. He had, however, spent two restless nights filled not with dreams, but memory shards. He was disappointed that Dr. Sunderland's treatment had had such a short-term effect, but he couldn't say he hadn't been warned. Worse, by far, was the sense of impending calamity. All the shards revolved around the tall trees, the mineral scent of the water, the desperate flight across sand. Desperate not only for him, but for someone else as well. He'd violated one of his own cardinal rules, and now he was going to pay for it. Something had set off this series of memory fragments, and he had a strong suspicion that this origin was the key to understanding what had happened to him before. It was maddening to have no – or at best limited – access to his past. His life was a blank slate, each day like the day he'd been born. Knowledge denied – essential knowledge. How could he begin to know himself when his past had been taken away from him?

The copter, soaring below the thick cloud layer, swung northwest, heading toward the Simien mountain range. When Bourne finished his breakfast, he climbed into an extreme-weather jumpsuit and specially made snow boots with extra-thick soles studded with metal blades meant to give him support on icy and rocky terrain.

As he stared out the curved window, his thoughts turned inward again, this time toward his friend Martin Lindros. He'd met Lindros after his old mentor, Alex Conklin, was found murdered. It was Lindros who'd stood behind Bourne, believed in him when the Old Man had put out a worldwide sanction against him. Ever since, Lindros had been his faithful backup at CI. Bourne steeled himself. Whatever had happened to Lindros – whether he was alive or dead – Bourne was determined to bring him home.

Just over an hour later, he arrived on the north slope of Ras Dejen. Brilliant sunlight made shadows sharp as razor blades on the mountainside, which seemed to exist in a curling sea of cloud through which, now and again, vultures could be seen, soaring on the thermals.

Bourne was just behind Davis's right shoulder when the young pilot pointed down. There was the wreckage of both Chinooks, pillowed in fresh snow, streaked with black, metal stripped back, twisted off as if with a mammoth can opener wielded by a maniacal demon.

'Damage is consistent with ground-to-air missiles,' Davis said.

So Soraya had been right. This kind of war matériel was expensive, a high cost only an alliance with organized crime could pay for. Bourne peered more closely as they neared the site. 'But there's a difference. The one on the left – '

'From what's left of the markings, the chopper carrying Skorpion One.'

'Look at the rotors. That one was shot as it was about to take off. The second chopper hit the ground with a great deal of force. It must've been hit as it was coming in for a landing.'

Davis nodded. 'Roger that. The opposition's well armed, all right. Odd for this neck of the woods.'

Bourne couldn't have agreed more.

Taking up a pair of field glasses, he directed Davis to circle the site. The moment the terrain came into focus, he was gripped with an intense feeling of déjà vu. He'd been to this part of Ras Dejen before, he was certain of it. But when? And why? He knew, for instance, where to look for hiding enemies. Directing the pilot, he searched every nook and crevice, every shadowed place around the periphery of the landing site.

He knew also that Ras Dejen, the highest peak in the Simien mountain chain, was within Amhara, one of the nine ethnic divisions within Ethiopia. The Amhara people made up 30 percent of the country's population. Amharic was Ethiopia's official language. In fact, after Arabic, it was the world's second most spoken Semitic language.

He was familiar with the Amhara mountain tribes. None of them had the means – either financially or technically – to inflict such sophisticated damage. 'Whoever it was isn't here now. Take her down.'

Davis brought the copter to rest just north of the wreckage. It slipped sideways a bit on the ice beneath the layer of fresh powder; then he had it under control. The moment they were on solid ground, he handed Bourne a Thuraya satellite phone. Just slightly larger than a normal cell phone, it was the only kind that would work in this mountainous terrain, where normal GSM signals were unavailable.

'Stay here,' Bourne said as the pilot began to unstrap himself. 'No matter what, wait for me. I'll check in every two hours. Six hours go by without hearing from me, you take off.'

'Can't do that, sir. I've never left a man behind.'

'This time is different.' Bourne gripped his shoulder. 'Under no circumstances are you to go after me, got it?'

Davis looked unhappy. 'Yessir.' He took up an assault rifle, opened the chopper door. Bitter-cold air shouldered its way in.

'You want something to do? Cover that cave mouth. Anything unknown to you moves or comes out, shoot first. We'll ask questions later.'

Bourne leapt out. It was frigid. The high terrain of Ras Dejen was no place to be in winter. The snow was thick enough, but so dry that the constant wind had pushed it about, causing high dunes of Saharan proportions. In other areas, the plateau had been swept clean, revealing patches of burned-out grass and rocks irregularly spaced like the rotting teeth of an old man.

Even though he'd done a 360 visual from the air, Bourne moved cautiously toward the wreckage of the two Chinooks. He was most concerned about the cave. It could hold good news – wounded survivors of either of the crashes – or bad news, namely members of the cadre that had taken out the two Skorpion units.

As he came abreast of the Chinooks, he saw bodies inside – nothing more than charcoaled skeletons, bits of singed hair. He resisted the urge to look inside the hulks for any sign of Lindros. Securing the site came first.

He reached the cave without incident. The wind, slithering through knuckles of rock, sent up an eerie, keening cry that sounded like someone being tortured. The cave mouth leered at him, daring him to enter. He stood against the bone-chilling rock face for a moment, taking deep, controlled breaths. Then he leapt, rolling into darkness.

Switching on a powerful flashlight, he sent the beam into niches and corners where those lying in wait were sure to secrete themselves. No one. Rising to his feet, he took a step, then, nostrils flared, came to an abrupt halt.

Once, in Egypt, he'd been led through an underground maze by a local conduit. There had come to him an odd scent – at once sweet and spicy – something utterly beyond his previous experience. When he'd voiced his question, the conduit had switched on a battery-powered flashlight for perhaps ten seconds, and Bourne saw the bodies, dark skin stretched like leather, drying, awaiting burial.

'*What you smell,*' his conduit had said as he switched off the flashlight, '*is human flesh after all the fluids are gone.*'

This was what Bourne smelled now in the cave punched into the north slope of Ras Dejen. Desiccated human flesh, and something else: the nauseating stench of decomposition trapped in the rear of the cave like swamp gas.

Fanning the high-intensity beam out in front of him, he moved forward. There came from underfoot a sharp, crunching sound. Redirecting the beam, he discovered that the floor was covered in bones – animal, bird, human alike. He continued, until he saw something stuck up from the rock bed. A body sat with its back against the rear wall.

Hunkering down on his haunches brought him to eye level with the head. Or what was left of it. A pit had begun in the center of the face, fountaining its poison outward like a volcano spewing lava, obliterating first the nose, then the eyes and cheeks, peeling away the skin, eating the flesh beneath. Now even parts of the skull – the bone itself – was pitted and scarred by the same force that had feasted on the softer human materials.

Bourne, his heart thudding hard against his rib cage, realized that he was holding his breath. He'd seen this particular kind of necrosis before. Only one thing could cause it: radiation.

This answered many questions: what had so suddenly, compellingly brought Martin Lindros into the field; why this area was so important, it had been defended by ground-to-air missiles and God only knew what other ordnance. His heart sank. Everyone from Skorpion One and Two – including Martin – would have to have been killed to protect the mind-numbing secret. Someone was transshipping more than triggered spark gaps via this route; someone had in their possession uranium ore. That was what this person had died of: radiation poisoning from a leak in the uranium container he was transporting. By itself, yellowcake uranium ore meant nothing: It was cheap, fairly easy to obtain, and impossible to refine into HEU unless you had a facility more than a kilometer square and four floors high, not to mention almost unlimited funds.

Also, yellowcake would not have left this radiation signature. No, without doubt, what Dujja had somehow gotten its hands on was uranium dioxide powder, only one easy step away from weapons-grade HEU. The question he was asking himself now was the same one that must have launched Lindros so precipitously into harm's way: What would a terrorist cadre be doing with uranium dioxide and triggered spark gaps *unless it had a facility somewhere with the personnel and the capability of manufacturing atomic bombs?*

Which could mean only one thing: Dujja was more extraordinary than anyone at Typhon realized. It was at the heart of a covert international nuclear network. Just such a network had been shut down in 2004, when Pakistani scientist Abdul Qadeer Khan admitted selling atomic technology to Iran, North Korea, and Libya. Now the terrifying specter had been resurrected.

Dizzied by this revelation, Bourne rose and backed out of the cave. He turned, took several deep breaths, even though the wind knifed into his lungs, and shivered. Giving the all-clear sign to Davis, he made his way back to the crash site. He could not stop his mind from buzzing. The threat to America that Typhon had intercepted was not only real, it was of a scope and consequence that was absolutely devastating.

He recalled the single-use triggered spark gap – the smoking gun of Martin's recent investigation. Unless he could stop Fadi, a nuclear attack would be carried out on a major American city.

# 7

Anne Held corralled Soraya the moment she appeared back at CI headquarters.

'Ladies,' she said under her breath. 'Now.'

Once inside the ladies' room in the lobby, Anne went through the cubicles one by one, making sure they were alone.

'My part of the bargain,' Soraya began. 'The NET came in contact with fire, which destroyed half of the circuits.'

'Well, that's something I can give the Old Man,' Anne said. 'He's out for Bourne's blood – and so is Lerner.'

'Because of what happened with Cevik.' Soraya frowned. 'But what's Lerner's involvement?'

'That's why I called you in here,' Anne said sharply. 'While you were with Bourne, Lerner staged a coup.'

'He did what?'

'He convinced the Old Man to name him acting director of Typhon.'

'Oh, Jesus,' Soraya said. 'As if things aren't screwed up enough as it is.'

'I have a feeling you haven't seen anything yet. He's hell-bent on reorganizing everything in CI, and now that he's got his claws into Typhon he's going to shake that up as well.'

Someone tried to come in, but Anne discouraged the intrusion. 'There's a flood in here,' she said with authority. 'Try upstairs.'

When they were alone again, she continued: 'Lerner's going to come after everyone he doesn't trust. And because of your association with Bourne, I'd bet the house you're at the top of his list.' She went to the door. 'Heads up, poppet.'

Bourne sat, head in hands, trying to think his way out of this growing nightmare. The trouble was, he didn't have enough information. There was nothing he could do other than keep going, trying to find Lindros or, failing that – if his friend was already dead – continue his mission to find and stop Fadi and Dujja before they made good on their threat.

At length, he rose. After inspecting the outside of the Chinooks, he bypassed the one closest to the cave and clambered into the copter that had brought Lindros.

The interior looked surreal, like a painting by Dalí: plastic melted into puddles, metal fused to metal. Seared beyond anything he could have imagined. This interested him. At this high elevation, there wasn't enough oxygen to support a fire of such intensity for long, certainly not long enough to do this kind of damage. The fire must have come from another source – a flamethrower.

Bourne saw Hiram Cevik's face in his mind's eye. Fadi was behind the ambush. The advanced weaponry, the precise coordination of the attacks, the high level of tactics that had caused two of CI's crack field teams to be killed: All evidence pointed to it.

But another question gnawed at him. Why had Fadi allowed himself to be captured by CI? Several answers presented themselves. The most likely one was that he was sending CI a message: *You think you have me in your sights, but you don't know who you're dealing with.* To some extent, Bourne knew that Fadi was correct: They knew next to nothing about him. But it was exactly this act of bravado that might provide Bourne with the opening he needed. Bourne's success had come from being able to get inside his adversaries' heads. Experience had taught him that it was impossible to do this with someone who remained in the shadows. Now, however, Fadi had emerged into the light of Bourne's vision. He'd shown his face. For the first time, Bourne had a template – rough and imprecise as it might be – from which to begin his pursuit.

Bourne returned his full attention to the interior of the Chinook. He counted four skeletons. This was nothing short of a revelation. Two people were missing from the dead. Could they be alive? Was Martin one of them?

The CI's Skorpion units were run military-style. All the men wore dog tags that identified them as being attached to an Army Ranger unit that didn't exist. As quickly as he could, he collected the four dog tags. He rubbed off the snow, ash, and soot to read their names, which he'd memorized from the packet of intel he'd gotten from Typhon. Martin wasn't here! The pilot – Jaime Cowell – was also unaccounted for.

Moving to the final resting place of Skorpion Two, he discovered the five skeletons of the Skorpion complement. Judging by the number of limb bones strewn about, it was safe to say none of them was in operational condition when the Chinook crashed. They'd been sitting ducks. Bourne hunted around, gathering up their dog tags.

All at once there came the hint of movement in the shadows of the interior, then the brief glitter of eyes before a head turned away. Bourne reached into the recessed space beneath the instrument panel. He felt a sharp pain in his hand, then a blur rushed him, knocking him backward.

Regaining his feet, he followed the figure out of the shell of the Chinook and took off after it, all the while waving at Davis to hold his fire. He glimpsed the bloody semicircle of tooth marks on the back of his hand just as the figure slipped over the low stone wall on the northeast side of the site.

Bourne flung himself into the air, came down feet-first on the top of the wall, and, orienting himself, leapt off it onto the back of the figure.

They both went down, rolling, but Bourne kept a firm grip on the hair, yanking it back to see the face. He was confronted with a boy of no more than eleven.

'Who are you?' Bourne said in the local Amharic dialect. 'What are you doing here?'

The boy spat into his face, clawed him, trying to get away. Holding his crossed wrists behind his back, Bourne sat him down in the lee of the wall, out of the howling wind. The boy was thin as a spike, the bones prominent in his cheeks, shoulders, and hips.

'When was the last time you ate?'

No response. At least the boy didn't spit at him again, but possibly that was because he was as dry inside as the snow crunching beneath their feet. With his free hand, Bourne unhooked a canteen, opened it with his teeth.

'I want to let you go. I've no wish to hurt you. Would you like some water?' The boy opened his mouth wide like a chick in the nest.

'Then you must promise to answer my questions. Is that fair?'

The boy looked at him for a moment with his black eyes, then nodded. Bourne let go of his wrists, and he reached out for the canteen, tipped it, drank the water in great, convulsive gulps.

While he drank, Bourne built up snow walls on either side of them, to reflect back their own heat. He took back the canteen.

'First question: Do you know what happened up here?'

The boy shook his head.

'You must've seen the flash of weapons, the balls of smoke rising up over the mountain.'

A small hesitation. 'I saw them, yes.' He had the high voice of a girl.

'And naturally enough, you were curious. You climbed up here, didn't you?'

The boy looked away, bit his lip.

This wasn't working. Bourne knew he had to find another way to get the boy to open up.

'My name is Jason,' he said. 'What's yours?'

Again that hesitation. 'Alem.'

'Alem, did you ever lose anyone? Someone you cared about a great deal?'

'Why?' Alem asked suspiciously.

'Because I've lost someone. My best friend. That's why I'm here. He was in one of the burned-out birds. I need to know if you saw him or know what happened to him.'

Alem was already shaking his head.

'His name is Martin Lindros. Have you heard it spoken by anyone?'

Alem bit his lip again, which had begun to tremble slightly, but not, Bourne thought, from the chill. He shook his head.

Bourne reached down, scooped snow onto the back of his hand where Alem had bitten it. He saw Alem's eyes following his every movement.

'My older brother died six months ago,' Alem said after a time.

Bourne went on with packing the snow. *Best to act casual,* he reasoned. 'What happened to him?'

Alem drew his knees up to his chest, crossed his arms over them. 'He was buried in a rockslide that crippled my father.'

'I'm sorry,' Bourne said, meaning it. 'Listen, about my friend. What if he's alive? Would you want him to die?'

Alem was trailing his fingers in the icy rubble at the base of the wall. 'You'll beat me,' he muttered.

'Why would I do that?'

'I scavenged something.' He jerked his head in the direction of the crash site. 'From there.'

'Alem, I promise you. All I care about is finding my friend.'

Without another glance at Bourne, Alem produced a ring. Bourne took it, held it in the sunlight. He recognized the shield with an open book in each quadrant: the coat of arms of Brown University.

'This is my friend's ring.' Carefully, he gave it back to Alem. 'Will you show me where you found it?'

Alem took him over the wall, then tromped through the snow to a spot several hundred meters away from the crash site. He knelt down, Bourne with him.

'Here?'

Alem nodded. 'It was under the snow, half buried.'

'As if it had been ground into the dirt,' Bourne finished for him. 'Yet you found it.'

'I was up here with my father.' Alem's wrists rested on his bony knees. 'We were scavenging.'

'What did your father find?'

Alem shrugged.

'Will you take me to him?'

Alem stared down at the ring in his grimy palm. He curled his fingers over it, put it back in his pocket. Then he looked up at Bourne.

'I won't tell him,' Bourne said quietly. 'I promise.'

Alem nodded, and they rose together. From Davis, Bourne got antiseptic and a bandage for his hand. Then the boy led him down from the small, bleak alpine meadow via a heart-stoppingly steep path that twisted along the iced rock face of Ras Dejen.

Anne wasn't kidding about Lerner being out for blood. There were two glowering agents waiting for Soraya at Typhon level as she stepped out of the elevator. Even to be here, she knew, they had to have Typhon-issued ID. Bad news, getting worse every second.

'Acting Director Lerner wants a word,' the one on the left said.

'He asks that you come with us,' the one on the right said.

She used her lightest, flirtatious voice. 'D'you think I could freshen up first, boys?'

The one on the left, the taller one, said: '"ASAP." That was the acting director's order.'

Stoics, eunuchs, or both. Soraya shrugged and went with them. In truth, there wasn't much else she could do. As she marched down the corridors between the two animated pillars, she tried not to worry. The best thing she could do now was to keep her head while those around her were losing theirs. Lerner would no doubt needle her, do his best to drive her to the wall. She'd heard stories about him, and he had been at CI, what, all of six months? He'd know she resented him, and he'd work on that like a sadistic dentist clamped onto her molar.

At the end of the corridor, she confronted the corner office. The taller agent beat a brief military tattoo on the door with his callused knuckles. Then he opened the door and stood aside for her to enter. But he and his doppelgänger didn't leave. They stepped into the office behind her, closed the door, and took a step back, as if holding the wall up with their brawny shoulders.

Soraya's heart sank. In the blink of an eye, Lerner had taken over Lindros's office, swept all of Lindros's personal mementos into God only knew where. The photos were down, their faces turned to the wall, as if already in exile.

The acting director was sitting behind Lindros's desk, his beefy ass in Lindros's chair, leafing through a pale green folder, a CAD – a current action dossier – while he fielded Lindros's calls as if they were his own. They *were* his own, Soraya reminded herself, and was instantly depressed. She longed for Lindros to return, prayed for Bourne to find him and bring him back alive. What other outcome should she hope for?

'Ah, Ms. Moore.' Lerner hung up the phone. 'Good of you to join us.' He smiled but did not offer her a seat. Clearly he wanted her to stand, like a pupil brought before the vice principal for disciplinary action.

'Just where have you been?'

She knew he knew because she'd checked in via her cell. Apparently, it was a personal confession he wanted. He was a man, she saw, for whom the world existed as a series of boxes, all the same size, into which he could fit everything and everyone, each to its own neat cubbyhole. In that way he fooled himself into believing that he could control the chaos of reality.

'I've been consoling Tim Hytner's mother and sisters in Maryland.'

'There are certain procedures,' Lerner said stiffly. 'They're there for a reason. Or didn't that occur to you?'

'Tim was my friend.'

'You were presumptuous to assume CI incapable of caring for its own.'

'I know his family. It was better the news came from me. I made it easier for them.'

'By lying, by telling them Hytner was a hero, instead of an inept bungler who allowed himself to be used by the enemy?'

Soraya was desperately trying to keep herself on an even keel. She hated herself for feeling intimidated by this man.

'Tim wasn't a field op.' At once, she knew she'd made a tactical error.

Lerner picked up the CAD. 'And yet your own written report states that Hytner was drawn into the field directly by Jason Bourne.'

'Tim was working to decode the cipher we found on Cevik – the man we now know was Fadi. Bourne wanted to use that fact to make him talk.'

Lerner's face grew hard and tight as a drumhead. His eyes seemed to her like bullet holes – black, deadly, ready to erupt. Other than that he seemed to her quite ordinary. He could have been a shoe salesman, a middle-aged office drone of any flavor. Which, she supposed, was just the point. A good field agent needed to be forgotten almost as soon as he was seen.

'Let me get this straight, Ms. Moore. You're defending Jason Bourne?'

'It was Bourne who identified Fadi. He's given us a starting point to –'

'Curious that he made this so-called ID *after* Hytner was killed, *after* he allowed Cevik to escape.'

Soraya was incredulous. 'Are you saying you don't think Cevik was Fadi?'

'I'm saying all you have is the say-so of a rogue agent, whose word is as far from gospel as it's possible to get. It's damn dangerous to allow your personal feelings to get in the way of your professional judgment.'

'I'm sure that's not the – '

'You cleared this little excursion to Hytner's family with whom?'

Soraya tried to keep her equilibrium through his abrupt shifts of topics. 'There was no one to clear it with.'

'There is now.' With a flourish, he closed the CAD. 'Here's a bit of advice, Ms. Moore: Don't wander off the reservation again. Are we clear on that point?'

'Quite clear,' she said shortly.

'I wonder. You see, you haven't been here the last several days, so you missed an important staff meeting. Would you care to hear the gist of it?'

'Very much,' she said through gritted teeth.

'Here it is in a nutshell,' Lerner said amiably. 'I'm changing Typhon's mission.'

'You're doing *what*?'

'You see, Ms. Moore, what this agency needs is less navel-gazing and more action. It doesn't matter in the least what the Islamic extremists think or feel. They want us dead. Therefore, we're going to go out and kick their butts into the Red Sea. It's as simple as that.'

'Sir, if I may say, there's nothing simple about this war. It's not like other – '

'Now you've been brought up to speed, Ms. Moore,' Lerner said sharply.

An acid churning had begun in Soraya's guts. This couldn't be happening. All of Lindros's planning, all of their hard work, was going down the drain. Where was Lindros when they all needed him? Was he even alive? She had to believe that he was. But for the moment, at least, it was this monster from the field who was calling the shots. At least this interrogation was over.

Elbows on the desk, Lerner steepled his fingers. 'I wonder,' he said, once again turning on a dime, 'if you could clear up a matter for me.' He wagged the CAD up and down as if it was an admonishing finger. 'How on earth did you fuck things up so royally?'

She stood stock-still, despite the rage running through her. He'd led her to believe the interview was over. In fact, it was just starting. She knew that he was just getting around to the real reason he'd called her in.

'You allowed Bourne to take Hiram Cevik out of the cage. You were on site when Cevik made his escape. You ordered the choppers into action.' He dropped the dossier onto the desktop. 'What have I gotten wrong so far?'

Soraya briefly thought about remaining mute, but she didn't want to give him that measure of satisfaction. 'Nothing,' she said dully.

'You were the agent in charge for Cevik. You were responsible.'

Nothing for it now. She squared her shoulders. 'Yes, I was.'

'Grounds for firing, Ms. Moore, isn't it?'

'I wouldn't know.'

'That's just the trouble. You *should* know. Just as you should've known better than to let Cevik out of his cage.'

No matter what she said, he found a way to turn it against her. 'Begging your pardon, but I had orders from the DCI's office to accommodate Bourne in every way.'

Lerner stared at her for a long moment. Then he gestured in an almost avuncular fashion. 'Why the hell are you standing?' he said.

Soraya settled into a chair facing him.

'On the subject of Bourne.' His eyes locked on hers. 'You would seem to be something of an expert.'

'I wouldn't say that.'

'Your file says that you worked with him in Odessa.'

'I suppose you could say I know Jason Bourne better than most agents.'

Lerner sat back. 'Surely, Ms. Moore, you don't think you've learned all there is to know about your craft.'

'I don't. No.'

'Then I have full confidence that we'll get along, that eventually you'll be as loyal to me as you were to Martin Lindros.'

'Why are you talking as if Lindros is dead?'

Lerner ignored her. 'For the moment, I have to respond to the unfolding situation. As AIC, the fiasco with Cevik was your responsibility. Therefore, I have no recourse but to ask for your resignation.'

Soraya's heart leapt up into her throat. 'Resignation?' she barely got out.

Lerner, gimlet-eyed, said, 'A resignation will look better on your records. Even you should be able to understand that.'

Soraya jumped up. He'd played her cruelly and beautifully, which infuriated her all the more. She hated this man and she wanted him to know it. Otherwise nothing would be left of her self-esteem. 'Who the hell are you to come in here and throw your weight around?'

'That's it, we're done here, Ms. Moore. Clear out your things. You're fired.'

# 8

The narrow path, treacherous with ice, down which Alem led him went on so long that Bourne felt it would never end. All at once, however, it did, winding inward from the dizzying face of the mountain to emerge into an alpine meadow many times the size of the one onto which the two Chinooks had been brought down. Much of this one was clear of snow.

The village was little more than a grouping of ramshackle structures, none of them very large. A gridwork of streets appeared to be made of tramped-down manure. A flock of brown goats lifted their triangular heads as the two approached but, apparently recognizing Alem, shortly returned to munching clumps of brittle brown grasses. Farther away, horses whinnied, shaking their heads as the men's scents reached them.

'Your father is where?' Bourne said.

'In the bar, as usual.' Alem looked up at him. 'But I won't take you to him. You must go alone. You can't let him know that I said anything to you about his scavenging.'

Bourne nodded. 'I promised you, Alem.'

'Or even that you met me.'

'How will I recognize him?'

'By his leg – his left leg is thin, and you can see it's shorter than his right. His name is Zaim.'

Bourne was about to turn away when Alem pressed Lindros's ring into his hand.

'You found this, Alem – '

'It belongs to your friend,' the boy said. 'If I return it to you maybe he won't be dead.'

It was time to eat. Again. No matter how else you resisted, Oscar Lindros had told his son, you could not refuse to eat. You needed to keep up your strength. Your captors could starve you, of course, but only if they wanted to kill you, which quite clearly Dujja didn't. They could drug your food, of course, and after the torture proved fruitless Martin Lindros's captors had done just that. To no avail. Ditto for sensory deprivation. His mind was vaulted up; his father had seen to that. Sodium Pentothal, for instance, had made him babble like a baby, but about nothing useful. Everything they wanted to know was inside the vault, unavailable to them.

They were on a timetable, so now they more or less left him alone. They did feed him regularly, though sometimes his jailers spat in his food. One of them would not clean him up when he soiled himself. When the stink became unbearable, they pulled out a hose. The resulting blast of ice-cold water lifted him off his feet, slammed him against the rock wall. There he would lie for hours, blood and water mingling in pink rivulets, while he reeled trout out of the peaceful lake, one by one.

But that was weeks ago – at least he thought so. He was better now. They'd even had a doctor look at him, stitch up the worst of the cuts, bandage him, feed him antibiotics for the fever that had raged through him.

Now he could let go of the lake for longer and longer periods of time. He could take in his surroundings, understand that he was in a cave. Judging by the chill, the howling of the wind that swirled in the cave mouth, he was high up, presumably still somewhere on Ras Dejen. He did not see Fadi, but from time to time he saw Fadi's chief lieutenant, the man called Abbud ibn Aziz. This man had been his chief interrogator after Fadi had failed to break him in the first few days of his incarceration.

For Lindros, Abbud ibn Aziz was a familiar type. He was essentially feral – that is to say, he was a stranger to civilization. He always would be. His comfort came from the trackless desert, where he had been born and raised. This much Lindros surmised from the form of Arabic he spoke – Abbud ibn Aziz was a Bedouin. His understanding of right and wrong was perfectly black-and-white, carved in stone. In this sense, he was exactly like Oscar Lindros.

Abbud ibn Aziz seemed to enjoy talking with Lindros. Perhaps he relished the prisoner's helplessness. Perhaps he felt that if they talked long enough Lindros would come to see him as a friend – that the Stockholm syndrome would set in, making Lindros identify with his captor. Perhaps he was simply being the Good Cop, because it was he who always toweled Lindros off after the hose attacks, it was he who changed Lindros's clothes when Lindros was too weak or out of it to do it himself.

Lindros was not a person to be affected by the temptation to reach out from his isolation, to become friends. Lindros had never made friends easily; he found that it was far easier to be a loner. In fact, his father had encouraged it. Being a loner was an asset if you aspired to be a spy, Oscar had said. This tendency had also been noted in Lindros's personnel file when he'd gone through the grueling month long vetting process thought up by the sadistic CI psych wonks just before his acceptance into the agency.

By now he knew very well what Abbud ibn Aziz wanted from him. It had come as something of a mystery to him that the terrorist sought information on a mission CI had mounted years ago against Hamid ibn Ashef. What did Hamid ibn Ashef have to do with Abbud ibn Aziz?

They had wanted more from him, of course. Much more. And despite Abbud ibn Aziz's apparent single-mindedness, Lindros had noted with interest that the interrogation about the CI mission against Hamid ibn Ashef occurred only when Abbud was alone with him.

From this, he had deduced that this particular line of questioning was a private agenda that had nothing at all to do with Dujja's reason for kidnapping him.

'How are you feeling today?'

Abbud ibn Aziz stood in front of him. He had brought two identical plates of food. He put one in Lindros's hands. When it came to food, Lindros knew his way around the Quran. All food fell into one of two categories: *haram* or *halal*, forbidden or allowed. All the food here was, of course, strictly *halal*.

'No coffee today, I'm afraid,' Abbud said. 'But the dates and buttermilk curds are fine.'

The dates were a bit on the dry side, and the curds had a strange taste. These things were small but, in Lindros's world, significant. The dates were drying up, the curds turning, and the coffee was gone. No more supplies were being delivered. Why?

They both ate with their right hands, their teeth bared as they bit into the dark flesh of the dates. Lindros's mind was racing.

'How is the weather?' he asked at length.

'Cold, and the constant wind makes it colder still.' Abbud shivered. 'Another front is coming in.'

Lindros knew that he was used to hundred-plus-degree temperatures, sand in his food, the molten-white glare of the sun, the blessed cool relief of a star-strewn night. This endless deep freeze was intolerable, to say nothing of the altitude. His bones and his lungs must be protesting like old men on a forced march. Lindros watched as he switched his Ruger semiautomatic in the crook of his left arm.

'Being here must be painful for you.' Lindros's question was not mere banter.

Abbud's shrug ended as another shiver.

'It's more than the desert you miss.' Lindros put his plate aside. Taking an almost constant beating day after day did terrible things to the appetite. 'It's the world of your fathers that you miss, isn't it?'

'Western civilization is an abomination,' Abbud said. 'Its influence on our society is like an infectious disease that needs to be wiped out.'

'You're afraid of Western civilization, because you don't understand it.'

Abbud spat out a date pit, white as a baby's bottom. 'I would say the same of you Americans.'

Lindros nodded. 'You wouldn't be wrong. But where does that leave us?'

'At each other's throats.'

Bourne surveyed the interior of the bar. It was much like the outside: the walls bare stone and wood, mortared together by wattle. The floor was hard-pressed dung. It smelled of fermentation, of both the alcoholic and human variety. A dung fire roared in the stone hearth, adding heat and a particular odor. There were a handful of Amhara inside, all in varying degrees of drunkenness. Otherwise Bourne's appearance in the doorway would have kicked up more of a stir. As it was, it caused barely a ripple.

He tromped up to the bar, trailing snow. He ordered a beer, which, promisingly, came in a bottle. While he drank the thin, oddly brackish brew, he took the measure of the place. In truth, there wasn't much to see: just a rectangular room with a scattering of rude tables and backless chairs more like stools. Nevertheless, he marked them all in his memory, making of the area a sort of map in his head, should danger raise its head or he need a quick escape. Not long after that, he spied the man with the maimed leg. Zaim was sitting by himself in a corner, a bottle of rotgut in one hand and a filthy glass in the other. He was beetle-browed, with the burned, crusty skin of the mountain native. He looked at Bourne vaguely as the other approached his table.

Bourne hooked a boot around one of the stool legs, pulled it out, sat down across from Alem's father.

'Get away from me, you fucking tourist,' Zaim muttered.

'I'm no tourist,' Bourne responded in the same dialect.

Alem's father opened his eyes wide, turned his head, spat on the floor. 'Still, you must want something. No one dares summit Ras Dejen in winter.'

Bourne took a long swig of his beer. 'You're right, of course.' Noticing that Zaim's bottle was nearly empty, he said, 'What are you drinking?'

'Dust,' Alem's father replied. 'That's all there is to drink up here. Dust and ash.'

Bourne went and got him another bottle, set it down on the table. As he was about to fill the glass, Zaim stayed his hand.

'There won't be time,' he muttered under his breath. 'Not when you have brought your enemy with you.'

'I didn't know I had an enemy.' There was no point in telling this man the truth.

'You came from the Site of Death, did you not?' Zaim stared hard at Bourne with watery eyes. 'You climbed into the metal carcasses of the warbirds, you sifted through the bones of the warriors berthed inside. Don't bother to deny it. Anyone who does gathers enemies the same way a rotting corpse gathers flies.' He flicked his free hand. His heavily callused palms and fingers were tattooed with dirt so ingrained, it could never be washed away. 'I can smell it on you.'

'This enemy,' Bourne said, 'is at the moment unknown to me.'

Zaim grinned, showing many dark gaps between what teeth were left in his mouth. His breath was as rank as the grave. 'Then I have become valuable to you. More valuable, surely, than a bottle of liquor.'

'My enemies were in hiding, watching the Site of Death?'

'How much is it worth to you,' Zaim said, 'to be shown the face of your enemy?'

Bourne slid money across the table.

Zaim took it with a practiced swipe of his clawlike hand. 'Your enemy keeps watch on the Site, day and night. It's like a spiderweb, you see? He wants to see what insects it attracts.'

'What's it to him?'

Zaim shrugged. 'Very little.'

'So there's someone else.'

Zaim leaned closer. 'We are pawns, you see. We are born pawns. What else are we good for? How else are we to scratch out a living?' He shrugged again. 'Even so, one can keep the evil times at bay only so long. Sooner or later, grief comes in whatever guise will be most painful.'

Bourne thought of Zaim's son, buried alive in the landslide. But he could say nothing; he'd promised Alem.

'I'm looking for a friend of mine,' he said softly. 'He was carried onto Ras Dejen by the first warbird. His body is not at the Site of Death. Therefore, I believe he's alive. What do you know of this?'

'I? I know nothing. Except for snatches overheard here and there.' Zaim scratched at his beard with gnarly black nails. 'But there is perhaps someone who could help.'

'Will you bring me to him?'

Zaim smiled. 'That is entirely up to you.'

Bourne pushed another wad of money across the stained table. Zaim took it, grunted, folded it away.

'On the other hand,' he said, 'we can do nothing while your enemy watches.' He pursed his lips reflectively. 'The eye of your enemy sits spread-legged over your left shoulder – a foot soldier, we would say, no one higher up.'

'Now you're involved,' Bourne said, nodding to where the other had put the money.

Alem's father shrugged. 'I am unconcerned. I know this man; I know his people. Nothing evil will come of me talking to you, believe me.'

'I want him off my back,' Bourne said. 'I want the eye to sleep.'

'Of course you do.' Zaim rubbed his chin. 'Anything can be arranged, even such a difficult wish.'

Bourne slid over more money, and Zaim nodded, apparently satisfied, at least for the moment. He reminded Bourne of a Vegas slot machine: he wasn't going to stop taking money from Bourne until Bourne walked away.

'Wait exactly three minutes – no more, no less – then follow me out the front door.' Zaim stood. 'Walk a hundred paces down the main street, then turn left into an alley, then take the first right. Of course, I cannot risk being seen to help you in this. In any event, I trust you'll know what to do. Afterward you'll walk away without retracing your steps. I'll find you.'

'There's a message for you,' Peter Marks said when Soraya returned to Typhon to clean out her desk.

'You take it, Pete,' she said dully. 'I've been bounced out of here.'

'What the hell – ?'

'The acting director has spoken.'

'He's gonna kill everything that Lindros wanted Typhon to be.'

'That seems to be the idea.'

As she was about to turn away, he took hold of her arm, swung her back. He was a young man, stocky, with deep-set eyes, hair the color of corn, a faint dry Nebraska twang. 'Soraya, I just want to say for me – well, for all of us, really – no one blames you for what happened to Tim. Shit happens. In this business it's, unfortunately, all really bad.'

Soraya took a breath, let it out slowly. 'Thanks, Pete. I appreciate that.'

'I figured you'd been beating yourself up for letting Bourne run roughshod all over you and Tim.'

She was silent for a moment, unsure what she was feeling. 'It wasn't Bourne,' she said at last, 'and it wasn't me. It just happened, Pete. That's all.'

'Sure, okay. I only meant that, you know, Bourne is another outsider forced on us by the Old Man. Like that sonovabitch Lerner. If you ask me, the Old Man's losing his grip.'

'Not my worry anymore,' Soraya said, beginning to move toward her office.

'But this message – '

'Come on, Pete. Handle it yourself.'

'But it's marked urgent.' He held it out. 'It's from Kim Lovett.'

After Zaim left, Bourne went into the WC, which stank like the inside of a zoo. Using the Thuraya phone, he checked in with Davis.

'I have new intel that the site is being watched,' he said. 'So keep a sharp lookout.'

'You, too,' Davis said. 'There's a weather front moving in.'

'I know. Is our exit strategy going to be compromised?'

'Don't worry,' Davis assured him. 'I'll take care of things on this end.'

Exiting the filthy pit, Bourne paid his bill at the bar. Under cover of the transaction, he caught a glimpse of the 'eye of his enemy,' as Zaim called him, and knew at once that he was Amhara. The man didn't bother lowering his gaze, instead glowered at Bourne with undisguised enmity. This was his territory, after all. He was confident on his home ground and, under normal circumstances, would have every right to be.

Bourne, who'd started the three-minute clock running in his head the moment Zaim had walked out the door, realized it was time to go. He chose a path that took him directly past the Eye. He was gratified to see the man's muscles bunch up in tension as he neared. His left hand went to his right hip, to whatever weapon he had there out of Bourne's sight. Bourne knew then what was required of him.

He went out of the bar. As he silently measured off the hundred paces, he became aware that the Eye had followed him out onto the street. Quickening the pace so that his tail would have to hurry to catch up, he reached the corner Zaim had described to him and turned left without warning into a narrow alley clogged with snow. Almost immediately he saw the next right, and rounded it at a brisk clip.

He'd only taken two steps when he turned around, flattened himself against the icy wall, and waited until the Eye came into view. Bourne grabbed him, slammed him against the corner of the building so that his teeth clacked together sharply. A blow to the side of the head rendered him unconscious.

A moment later Zaim darted lopsidedly into the alley. 'Quickly now!' he said breathlessly. 'There are two others I hadn't counted on.'

He led Bourne to the nearest intersection of alleys, turned left. At once they found themselves on the outskirts of the village. The snow lay thickly, its crust brittle. Zaim was having difficulty negotiating the terrain, especially at the pace he had set. But quite soon they came to a ramshackle outbuilding behind which three horses stood grazing.

'How are you at bareback riding?' he said.

'I'll manage.'

Bourne put his hand on the muzzle of a gray horse, looked him in the eye, then vaulted up. Leaning over, he grabbed Zaim above the elbow, assisted him onto a brown horse. Together they turned their steeds into the wind and took off at a canter.

The wind was rising. Bourne did not need to be a native to know that a storm was coming in from the northwest, laden with the bitter taste of serious snow. Davis was going to have a hell of a time digging the copter out. He'd have to, though; there was no other way to get off the mountain quickly.

Zaim was making directly for the tree line but, glancing behind him, Bourne saw that it was already too late. The riders – no doubt the two Amhara whom Zaim was worried about – were pounding along behind them, closing the gap.

Bourne, making a quick calculation, discovered that the Amhara would overtake them several hundred meters before they'd have a chance to lose themselves in the forest. Putting his head against the horse's mane, he kicked it hard in the sides.

The gray horse leapt forward, racing toward the trees. Startled for an instant, Zaim kneed his mount, taking off after Bourne.

Halfway there, Bourne realized they weren't going to make it. Without another thought, he squeezed his knees against the horse's flanks and jerked its mane to the right. Without breaking stride, the gray wheeled around, and before their pursuers had time to react Bourne was galloping full-out directly at them.

They split apart, as he had foreseen. Leaning to his right, he drew his left leg back and kicked out from the hip. His thick-soled boot slammed into the chest of one of the Amhara, knocking him off his horse. By this time, the other Amhara had had time to wheel around. He'd drawn a handgun – an old but deadly 9mm PM Makarov – and was aiming it at Bourne.

A shot rang out, lifting the Amhara from his blanket saddle. Bourne turned to see Zaim rising up, a gun in his hand. He waved his free hand, and they headed as fast as they could for the outlying stand of firs.

Another shot snipped off branches above their heads as they galloped into the forest. The Amharan whom Bourne had kicked off his horse had remounted and was coming after them.

Zaim threaded them through the fir trees. It had turned markedly colder and wetter. Even here, in the shelter of the forest, the icy wind cut through them, shaking periodic snowfalls from the upper branches. Bourne, thinking of their pursuer, could not rid himself of the itching along his spine, but he kept going in the brown horse's wake.

The ground began to fall away, at first gradually, then more steeply. The horses put their heads down, snorting, as if to more carefully feel the buried stones, their curved surfaces slick with ice, which made the footing alarmingly treacherous.

Bourne heard a cracking behind them, and he urged the gray on. He wanted to ask Zaim where they were headed and how close they were to it, but raising his voice would only serve to reveal their location in the maze of the forest. Just as he was thinking this, he glimpsed a clearing through the trees, then the heavy glitter of a sheet of ice. They were coming to a river that wound steeply from the edge of one alpine meadow to a lower one.

At that moment he heard a shot; an instant later Zaim's horse collapsed from under him. Zaim went tumbling. Urging the gray on, Bourne reached down, dragging Zaim up behind him.

They were almost at the bank of the frozen river. Another shot, snapping nearby branches.

'Your gun!' Bourne said.

'I lost it when my horse was shot,' Zaim replied unhappily.

'We'll be picked off like wooden ducks.'

Bourne handed Zaim down to the snowpack, then slid off the gray. A smart slap to its rump sent it crashing through the forest on a more or less parallel course to the river.

'Now what?' Zaim slapped his bum leg. 'With this, we'll be helpless out here.'

'Let's go.' Grabbing him by his thick wool jacket, Bourne began to run down the bank to the river.

'What are you doing?' Zaim's eyes were wide with fear.

Bourne half lifted him off his feet an instant before they hit the ice on the run.

415

Compensating for the other man's weight, Bourne began the long back-and-forth strides of an ice skater. Using the blades embedded in his boot soles as skates, he built up speed with the natural downward slope of the river.

He took the snaking turns expertly, but he had almost no control over his speed, and he was racing along faster and faster as the rivercourse steepened.

They flashed around another bend and Zaim uttered an inarticulate cry. A moment later Bourne saw why. Not a thousand meters away the river broke sharply downward into a waterfall, now frozen in place like a stop-motion photo.

'How high?' Bourne called over the howling of the wind in his face.

'Too high,' Zaim moaned in terror. 'Oh, too, too high!'

# 9

Bourne tried to veer to the left or right, but he couldn't. He was flying along a fold in the ice that would not allow him to change direction. At any rate, it was too late now. The ruffled top of the waterfall was upon them, so he did the only thing he could think of: He steered for the exact center, where the water was deepest and the ice thinnest.

They hit it at speed, which combined with their weight to shatter the thin crust of ice that had formed over the streaming water. Into the waterfall they plunged, tumbling down and down, the icy water taking their breath away, freezing them from their limbs inward.

As he fell from the heights, Bourne struggled against becoming disoriented, which was his primary concern. If he lost his sense of direction, he'd either freeze to death or drown before he could break through the ice at the base of the water-fall. There was another concern: If he allowed himself to get too far from the base area, the ice would quickly thicken into a layer he'd likely find unbreakable.

Light and shadow, blue-black, gray-opal spun across his vision as he was tossed and tumbled through the churning water. Once, his shoulder smashed into a rock outcropping. Pain leapt through him like a surge of electricity, and as his downward momentum abruptly ceased, he searched for the light in the jumble of darkness. There was none! His head was spinning, his hands almost completely numb. His heart was laboring from both the physical pounding and the lack of oxygen.

He struck out with his arms. At once he realized that Zaim's body was almost against him; as he drew it to one side, he saw pearlescent light shining behind it and knew which way was up. Zaim seemed to be unconscious. Blood plumed from the side of his head, and Bourne guessed that he, too, had struck a rock.

With one arm around the limp form, Bourne kicked out hard for the surface, banging the top of his head sooner than he had anticipated against the ice sheet. It didn't give.

His head was pounding, and the ribbons of blood leaking from Zaim's wound were obscuring his vision. He clawed against the ice, but could find no purchase. He slid along the underside, searching for a crack, a flaw he could exploit. But the ice was thicker than he'd imagined, even here at the waterfall's base. His lungs were burning and the headache caused by the lack of oxygen was fast becoming intolerable. Perhaps Zaim was already dead. Surely he himself would be if he couldn't break through to the surface.

A strong eddy caught him, threatening to send them swirling out to certain death in the darkness where the ice sheet was thickest. As he struggled against it, his nails bit into something – not a crack precisely, but a stress flaw in the sheet. He could see that one side was allowing more light in, and there he concentrated his efforts. But his fists, numbed into clumsy weights, were of no use.

Only one chance now. He let go of Zaim and dove down into the darkness until he felt the river bottom. Reversing himself, he coiled his legs, launching himself upward in a straight line. The top of his head struck the stress flaw and he heard it crack, then splinter apart as his shoulders followed his head into the blessed air. Bourne drew air into his lungs once, twice, three times. Then he dove back down. Zaim wasn't where he had left him. He had been caught in the powerful eddy and was now being launched into the darkness.

Bourne kicked, fighting the current, stretching out full-length to grab Zaim by the ankle. Slowly, surely he drew him back to the light, bringing him up through the ragged hole in the ice, laying him out on the frozen riverbed before he levered himself out of the water.

They had come through just to the east of the falls, at the edge of a thick slice of the fir forest that continued unabated to the north and east.

He spent a moment hunkered down in the shadows of the trees, catching his breath. But that was all the time he could spare. He checked Zaim's vital signs – his pulse, his breathing, his pupils. The man was alive. An examination of the wound showed it to be superficial. Zaim's hard skull had done its job, protecting him from serious injury.

Bourne's problem now, apart from stanching the flow of blood from Zaim's wound, was drying him off so he wouldn't freeze to death. Bourne himself had been partially protected by his extreme-weather jumpsuit, though he saw now that it had been abraded badly in several places during his violent tumble down the falls. Water was already freezing against his skin. Unzipping the suit for a moment, he stripped off a sleeve of his shirt, packed it with snow, and wrapped it around Zaim's wound. Then he hoisted the still-unconscious man over his unbruised shoulder, stumbling up the treacherous bank into the forest. He could feel the cold slowly seeping in at his elbows and shoulder, where the outer layer of his jumpsuit had been shredded.

Zaim was becoming heavier and heavier, but Bourne pushed on, angling north and east away from the river. A vague memory surfaced – a flash akin to the one he'd had when he'd first alit on Ras Dejen, but more detailed. If he was right, there was another village – larger than the one where he'd found Zaim – several kilometers ahead.

All at once he was brought up short by a familiar sound: the snorting of a horse. Carefully putting Zaim down against the bole of a tree, he moved cautiously toward the sound. Perhaps five hundred meters ahead, he came upon a small clearing. In it, he saw the gray, its muzzle picking through the snowpack for something to eat. Apparently the animal had followed the course of the river down to this patch of open space. It was just what Bourne needed to carry him and Zaim to safety.

Bourne was about to move into the glade when the gray's head came up and its nostrils dilated. What had it smelled? The wind was swirling, bringing with it the scent of danger.

Bourne thought he understood, and he silently thanked the gray. Moving back into the firs, he began to circle to his left, keeping the clearing in sight as he went, keeping the wind in his face. Perhaps a quarter of the way around, he saw a spot of color, then a slight movement. Heading obliquely toward it, he saw that it was the Amhara whom he had kicked off his horse. This man must have brought the gray down here as bait, to lure them if one or both had survived the waterfall.

Keeping low, Bourne came at him fast, blindsiding him. He went down with a grunt, got his left hand free as Bourne pummeled him, drew out a curving knife. It slashed down, heading straight for Bourne's exposed side just above his kidney. Bourne rolled, his torso flicking out of range. At the same time, he locked his ankles around the tribesman's neck, back and front. With a swift, violent twist Bourne snapped the Amhara's neck.

He rose, took from the corpse the knife, sheath, and 9mm Makarov. Then he loped into the clearing, bringing the gray back to where Zaim lay. Slinging the other over the horse's sturdy back, Bourne swung up and set off through the firs, down the mountainside, heading by memory for the village.

When Soraya Moore strode into the FIU lab, Kim Lovett was still kicking around forensic evidence with Detective Overton.

Kim, having taken care of the introductions, got right down to business by bringing Soraya up to date on their case. Then she handed her the set of two porcelain teeth.

'I found these in the suite's bathtub drain,' she said. 'At first glance, it could easily be mistaken for a dental bridge, but I don't think it is.'

Soraya, looking at the interior hollows, knew that she had seen something very similar in Deron's lab. Examining it more closely, she recognized the high quality of the workmanship. No doubt this was part of a world-class chameleon's arsenal. She had no doubt what she was holding, and to whom it belonged. She'd thought she was through with all this when Lerner kicked her butt out of Typhon, but now she knew the truth. Maybe she'd known it all along. She wasn't through with Fadi, not by a long shot.

'You're right, Kim,' she said. 'It's a prosthetic.'

'Prosthetic?' Overton echoed. 'I'm not following.'

'This is a shell,' Soraya told him, 'used to slip over perfectly good teeth, not as a substitute for nonviable ones, but to alter the shape of the mouth and cheek line.' She slipped the prosthetic on. Though it was too big for her, both Kim and Overton were astonished to see how much it changed the shape of her mouth and lips. 'Which means your Jakob Silver and his brother were using aliases,' she said as she spat out the teeth. To Kim, she said, 'Do you mind if I borrow this?'

'Go on,' Kim said. 'But I'll have to log it out.'

Overton shook his head. 'None of this makes sense.'

'It makes perfect sense if you know all the facts.' Soraya shared with them the incident outside CI headquarters. 'This man who passed as a Cape Town entrepreneur named Hiram Cevik is, in actuality, a Saudi who calls himself Fadi, a terrorist leader with high-level connections to what seems to be an enormous amount of money. What his real name might be we have no idea. He disappeared within blocks of where the Hummer picked him up.' She held up the prosthetic. 'Now we know where he went.'

Kim considered everything Soraya had told them. 'Then the remains we found aren't either brother.'

'I very much doubt it. The fire seems like a diversion for him slipping out of D.C. Out of the country, for that matter.' Soraya went over to the shallow metal pan in which Kim had placed the bones found in the bathtub. 'I do believe we're looking at all that's left of Omar, the Pakistani waiter.'

'Jesus Christ!' *At last we're getting somewhere,* Overton thought. 'Then which brother was Fadi?'

Soraya turned to him. 'Jakob, undoubtedly. It was Lev who checked into the suite. Fadi was in Cape Town, and then in our custody.'

Overton was elated. At last his luck was changing. He'd hit the mother lode with these two. Very soon now, he'd have enough intel to bring to Homeland Security. He'd become their newest recruit and their newest hero in one fell swoop.

Soraya turned back to Kim. 'What else did you find?'

'Very little. Except the accelerant.' Kim picked up a sheaf of computer readouts. 'It was carbon disulfide. I can't remember the last time I encountered it. Arsonists typically use acetone, kerosene, something easily attainable like that.' She shrugged. 'On the other hand, in this case carbon disulfide makes a certain kind of sense. It's more dangerous than the others because of its low flashpoint and the probability of an explosion once it's ignited. Fadi wanted the windows blown out so that the flames could feed on the added oxygen. But you'd have to be a real professional to use it without blowing yourself up.'

Soraya took a look at the printout Kim handed her. 'That's Fadi all over. Where would you get it?'

'You'd have to have access to a manufacturing plant or one of their sources,' Kim said. 'It's used in the manufacture of cellulose, carbon tetrachloride, and other organic sulfur compounds.'

'Can I borrow your computer?'

'Help yourself,' Kim said.

Soraya sat down at Kim's workstation and brought up the Internet browser. Navigating to the Google Web site, she typed in 'carbon disulfide.'

'Cellulose is used in the manufacture of rayon and cellophane,' she called out to them as she read the text on the screen. 'Carbon tet used to be a key ingredient in fire extinguishers and refrigeration, though it's been abandoned because of its toxicity. Dithiocarbamates, dmit, xanthate are flotation agents in mineral processing. It's also used to make metham sodium, a soil fumigant.'

'One thing's for sure,' Kim said. 'You won't find it in your neighborhood hardware store. You've got to go searching for it.'

Soraya nodded. 'And it presupposes prior knowledge of the compound and its specific characteristics.' She made a few quick notes in her PDA, then got up. 'Okay, I'm out of here.'

'Mind if I tag along?' Overton said. 'Until you showed up, this case was a brick wall in my face.'

'I don't think so.' Soraya's glance slid over to Kim. 'I was going to tell you when I came in. I've been fired.'

'What?' Kim was aghast. 'Why?'

'The new acting director doesn't appreciate my streak of rebelliousness. I think he's out to establish his authority. Today I'm the one he decided to piss on.'

Kim came over and hugged her in sympathy. 'If there's anything I can do.'

Soraya smiled. 'I know who to call. Thanks.'

She was too preoccupied to notice the scowl of displeasure that had darkened Detective Overton's face. He wasn't going to be thwarted, not when he was so close to his goal.

Snow had begun to fall by the time Bourne and Zaim reached the village. It was there, nestled in a narrow valley like a ball in a cupped palm, just as Bourne remembered it. The clouds, low and heavy, made the mountains seem small and insignificant, as if they were about to be crushed in a clash of titans. The steeple of the church was the most prominent structure, and Bourne made for it.

Zaim stirred and groaned. Some time ago, he had awakened, and Bourne had gotten him off the horse just in time for him to vomit copiously among the whistling firs. Bourne made the Amhara eat some snow in order to hydrate him. He was dizzy and weak, but he understood completely when Bourne filled him in on what had happened. Their destination, he had informed Bourne, was a camp just outside the village in Bourne's memory.

Now they had arrived at the village. Though Bourne was eager to link up with the person Zaim claimed could take him to Lindros, Zaim's clothes had already frozen; unless he could be warmed up reasonably quickly, the cloth would take his skin with it when it was removed.

The gray, which Bourne had urged on at full gallop through knee-high snowbanks, was just about done in by the time they reached the outskirts of the camp. Three Amhara appeared as if out of nowhere, brandishing curved knives similar to the one Bourne had taken off the man whose neck he'd broken.

Bourne had been expecting them. No campsite would be left unguarded. He sat very still atop the panting, snorting gray while the Amhara drew Zaim down. When they saw who it was, one of them ran into a tent at the center of the campsite. He returned within minutes with an Amhara who was quite obviously the tribal chieftain, the *nagus*.

'Zaim,' he said, 'what happened to you?'

'He saved my life,' Zaim muttered.

'And he, mine.' Bourne slid off the horse. 'We were attacked on our way here.'

If the *nagus* was surprised that Bourne spoke Amharic, he gave no outward sign of it. 'Like all Westerners, you brought your enemies with you.'

Bourne shivered. 'You're only half right. We were attacked by three Amhara soldiers.'

'You know who is paying them,' Zaim said weakly.

The *nagus* nodded. 'Take them both inside to my hut, where it is warm. We will build up the fire slowly.'

Abbud ibn Aziz stood squinting up at the noxious sky that swirled around Ras Dejen's north face, listening for the sound of rotors slicing the thin air.

Where was Fadi? His helicopter was late. Abbud ibn Aziz had been monitoring the weather all morning. With the front moving in, he knew the pilot had an extremely narrow window in which to make his landing.

In truth, though, he knew it wasn't the cold or the thin air he silently railed against. It was the fact that he and Fadi were here in the first place. The plan. He knew who was behind it. Only one man could have dreamed up such a high-risk, volatile scheme: Fadi's brother, Karim al-Jamil. Fadi might be the firebrand face of Dujja, but Abbud ibn Aziz, alone of all of Fadi's many followers, knew that Karim al-Jamil was the heart of the cadre. He was the chess master, the patient spider spinning multiple webs into the future. Even thinking about what Karim al-Jamil might be planning sent Abbud ibn Aziz's head spinning. Like Fadi and Karim al-Jamil, he had been educated in the West. He knew the history, politics, and economics of the non-Arab world – a prerequisite, so far as Fadi and Karim al-Jamil were concerned, in stepping up the ladder of command.

The problem for Abbud ibn Aziz was that he didn't altogether trust Karim al-Jamil. For one thing, he was reclusive. For another, so far as he knew Karim al-Jamil spoke only to Fadi. That this might not be the case at all – that he knew less than he suspected about Karim al-Jamil – made him all the more uneasy.

This was his bias against Karim al-Jamil: that he, Fadi's second in command, his most intimate comrade, was shut out from the inner workings of Dujja. This seemed to him eminently unjust, and though he was utterly loyal to Fadi, still he chafed to be kept on the outside. Of course, he understood that blood was thicker than water – who among the desert tribesmen wouldn't? But Fadi and Karim al-Jamil were only half Arab. Their mother was English. Both had been born in London after their father had moved his company base there from Saudi Arabia.

Abbud ibn Aziz was haunted by several questions that part of him did not want answered. Why had Abu Sarif Hamid ibn Ashef al-Wahhib left Saudi Arabia? Why had he taken up with an infidel? Why had he compounded his error by marrying her? Abbud ibn Aziz could find no earthly reason why a Saudi would do such a thing. In truth, neither Fadi nor Karim al-Jamil was of the desert, as he was. They had grown up in the West, been schooled in the ceaselessly throbbing metropolis of London. What did they know of the profound silence, the severe beauty, the clean scents of the desert? The desert, where the grace and wisdom of Allah could be seen in all things.

Fadi, as befit an older brother, was protective of Karim al-Jamil. This, at least, was something Abbud ibn Aziz could understand. He himself felt the same way about his younger brothers. But in the case of Karim al-Jamil, he had been asking himself for some time into what dark waters he was leading Dujja. Was it a place that Abbud ibn Aziz wanted to go? He had come this far without raising his voice because he was loyal to Fadi. It was Fadi who had indoctrinated him into the terror war they had been forced into by the West's incursions into their lands. It was Fadi who had sent him to Europe to be schooled, a time in his life he had despised but had nevertheless proved of benefit. To know the enemy, Fadi had told him many times, is to defeat him.

He owed Fadi everything; where Fadi led, he would follow. On the other hand, he wasn't deaf, dumb, and blind. If at some future date when he had more information, he felt that Karim al-Jamil was leading Dujja – and, therefore, Fadi – into ruin, he would speak up, no matter the consequences.

A harsh, dry wind broke against his cheek. The whirring of the helicopter's rotors came to him as if from a dream. But it was his own reverie from which he needed to free himself. He looked up, feeling the first snowflakes on his cheeks and lashes.

He picked out the black dot against the roiled grays of the sky. It bloomed quickly. Swinging his arms back and forth over his head, he stepped back from the landing site. Three minutes later, the helicopter had landed. The door swung open, and Muta ibn Aziz jumped out into the snow and ice.

Abbud ibn Aziz waited for Fadi to appear, but only his brother came to where he stood, outside the slowing swing of the rotor blades.

'All went well.' His embrace of his brother was stiff, formal. 'Fadi has contacted me.'

Muta stood silent in the harsh wind.

For some time, a dispute had carved itself into the frontier of their lives. Like the rift created by an earthquake, the issue had separated them more than either of them would admit. Like an earthquake it had spit up festering sores that now, years later, had turned to scoria – hard, dry, twisted as scar tissue.

Muta squinted. 'Brother, where did Fadi go after he and I parted?'

Abbud could not keep the superior edge out of his voice. 'His business lies elsewhere.'

Muta grunted. A bitter taste, all too familiar, had flooded his mouth. *It is as it has always been. Abbud uses his power to keep me away from Fadi and Karim al-Jamil, the centers of our universe. Thus does he lord it over me. Thus has he sworn me to keep our secret. He is my elder brother. How can I fight him?* His teeth ground together. *As always, I must obey him all things.*

Muta shivered mightily, moved out of the wind, into the lee of a rock formation. 'Tell me, brother, what has been happening here?'

'Bourne arrived on Ras Dejen this morning. He's making progress.'

Muta ibn Aziz nodded. 'Then we must move Lindros to a safe location.'

'It is about to be done,' Abbud said with an icy edge to his voice.

Muta, his heart full of bile, nodded. 'It's almost over now. Within the next few days, Jason Bourne's use to us will be at an end.' He smiled deeply, but it was completely self-contained. 'As Fadi has said, revenge is sweet. How pleasurable it will be for him to see Jason Bourne dead!'

The *nagus's* hut was surprisingly spacious and comfortable, especially for a structure that was more or less portable. The floor consisted of overlapping rugs. Skins hung on the walls, helping keep in the warmth provided by a fire fueled with dried bricks of dung.

Bourne, wrapped in a rough wool blanket, sat cross-legged by the fire while the *nagus's* men slowly and gingerly undressed Zaim. When that was done, they wrapped him as well, made him sit beside Bourne. Then they served both men steaming cups of hot, strong tea.

Other men tended to Zaim's wound, cleaning it, packing it with an herbal poultice, rebandaging it. As this was happening, the *nagus* sat down next to Bourne. He was a small man, unprepossessing save for the black eyes that burned like twin lamps in his burnished bronze skull. His body was thin and wiry, but Bourne was not fooled. This man would be skilled in the many ways, offensive and defensive, to keep himself and his men alive.

'My name is Kabur,' the *nagus* said. 'Zaim tells me your name is Bourne.' He pronounced it in two syllables: *Boh-orn.*

Bourne nodded. 'I've come to Ras Dejen to find my friend, who was on one of the warbirds that were shot down nearly a week ago. You know of this?'

'I do,' Kabur said.

His hand moved to his chest, and he held out something silver for Bourne to see. It was the pilot's dog tags.

'He has no more need of them,' Kabur said simply.

Bourne's heart sank. 'He's dead?'

'As close as can be.'

'What about my friend?'

'They took him along with this man.' The *nagus* offered Bourne a wooden bowl of heavily spiced stew into which a rough semicircle of unleavened bread had been stuck. While Bourne ate, using the bread as a spoon, Kabur went on. 'Not by us, you understand. We are nothing in this, though, as you have already witnessed, some have taken money from them in return for service.' He shook his head. 'But it is evil, a form of enslavement for which some have paid the ultimate price.'

'They.' Bourne, having eaten his fill, put the bowl aside. 'Who, precisely, are they?'

Kabur tilted his head. 'I feel surprise. I would have expected you to know far more about them than I. They come to us from across the Gulf of Aden. From Yemen, I imagine. But they aren't Yemeni, no. God alone knows where they make their base. Some are Egyptian, others Saudi, still others Afghani.'

'And the leader?'

'Ah, Fadi. He is Saudi.' The *nagus*'s fierce black eyes had gone opaque. 'We are, to a man, afraid of Fadi.'

'Why?'

'Why? Because he is powerful, because he is cruel beyond imagining. Because he carries death in the palm of his hand.'

Bourne thought of the uranium transshipments. 'You have seen evidence of the death he carries.'

The *nagus* nodded. 'With my own eyes. One of Zaim's sons – '

'The boy in the cave?'

Kabur swung toward Zaim, in whose eyes was a sea of pain. 'A wayward son who could not hold advice in his head. Now we cannot touch him, even to bury him.'

'I can do that,' Bourne said. Now he understood why Alem was hiding out in the Chinook closest to the cave: He wanted to be near his brother. 'I can bury him up there, near the summit.'

The *nagus* was silent. But Zaim's eyes had turned liquid as they reengaged Bourne's. 'That would be a true blessing – for him, for me, for my family.'

'It will be done, this I swear,' Bourne said. He turned back to Kabur. 'Will you help me find my friend?'

The *nagus* hesitated a moment while he studied Zaim. At length, he sighed. 'Will finding your friend hurt Fadi?'

'Yes,' Bourne said. 'It will hurt him badly.'

'This is a very difficult journey you ask us to take with you. But because of my friend, because of his bond to you, because of your promise to him, I am honor-bound to grant your request.'

He raised his right hand and a man brought a device similar to a hookah. 'We will smoke together, to seal the bargain we have made.'

Soraya had every intention of going home, but somehow she found herself driving into the Northeast quadrant of D.C. It was only when she turned onto 7th Street that she knew why she had come here. Making one more turn, she arrived outside Deron's house.

For a moment, she sat, listening to the engine ticking. Five or six of the tough-looking crew infested the stoop of the house to the left but, though they observed her with gimlet eyes, they made no move to stop her as she got out of the car and went up the steps to Deron's front door.

She knocked on the front door several times. Waited, then knocked again. There was no answer. Hearing someone coming up the walk, she turned, expecting Deron. Instead she encountered a tall, lean young man, one of the crew.

'Yo, Miss Spook, name's Tyrone. What yo doin' here?'

'Do you know where Deron is?'

Tyrone kept a neutral expression. 'Yo could see me instead, Miss S.'

'I would, Tyrone,' she said carefully, 'if you could instruct me on the uses of carbon disulfide.'

'Huh, yo think I'm a useless nigga, doantcha?'

'To be honest, I don't know anything about you.'

Without a change in expression, he said, 'Walk wid me.'

Soraya nodded. Instinctively she knew that any hesitation on her part would reflect badly on her.

Together they went down the walk and turned right, past the stoop where members of the crew were perched like a murder of crows.

'Deron, he down wid his daddy. Won't be back for coupla days.'

'No lie?'

'True dat.' Tyrone pursed his lips. 'So. What yo want ta know 'bout me? Maybe my druggie mama? Is it my daddy you're interested in, rottin' away in prison? Or my younger sister nursin' a baby when she should be in high school? My older brother makin' shit-per-week working for the man as a motorman in the Metro? Shee-it, yo mustave heard all that sob stuff before, so yo doan need t'hear it again.'

'It's your life,' Soraya said. 'That makes it different from anything I've heard.'

Tyrone snorted, but by his look she knew he was pleased.

'Me, though I was trained for the street, I was born with an engineer's mind. What's that mean?' He shrugged and pointed into the distance. 'Down Florida, they puttin' up a shitload a high-rises. I go there every chance I get, see how it all goin' up, y'know?'

Soraya met his eyes for a moment. 'Will you think me a fool if I say there're ways for you to take advantage of your mind.'

'Fo yo maybe.' A slow smile spread across his face, an expression considerably older than his years. 'We walkin' in my prison, girl.'

Soraya considered answering that, but decided she'd pushed him far enough for the moment. 'I gotta go.'

Tyrone pursed his lips. 'Yo, just so you know, yo. It's about the car that followed you here.'

Soraya stopped in her tracks. 'Tell me you're putting me on.'

His head swiveled, and he looked at her as a cobra stares down its prey. 'Straight dope, like before.'

Soraya was furious with herself. She'd been so wrapped up in her own personal fog, she hadn't even considered that someone might tail her. She had failed to check, which was usually second nature to her. Obviously she was more upset about that sonovabitch Lerner benching her than she'd realized. Now she'd paid the price for her lack of vigilance.

'Tyrone, I owe you one.'

He shrugged. 'It's what Deron pays me t'do. Protection doan come cheap, but loyalty ain't got no price.'

She looked at him, but for the first time seemed to really see him. 'Where is it? The car that tailed me?'

They began to walk again. 'Up ahead, at the corner of Eighth,' Tyrone said. 'Far side, so the driver get a good look at what yo up to.' He shrugged. 'My crew'll take care a him.'

'Not that I don't appreciate the offer, Tyrone.' She gave him a serious look. 'But I brought him here. It's on me.'

'Yo, I admire that, yo.' He stopped, stood facing her for a minute. His expression was as serious as hers. There was no mistaking the grim determination in it. Around here, he was the immovable object. 'Understand, it's gotta be done 'fore he get any idea 'bout Deron. Afta that, nuthin can save him. Even yo.'

'I'll take care of it right now.' She ducked her head, abruptly shy. 'Thanks.'

Tyrone nodded, headed back to his crew. Taking a deep breath, she kept on the way she had been going, down to the corner of 8th Street, where Detective Overton sat in his car, scribbling on a slip of lined paper.

She rapped her knuckles on the glass. He looked up, hastily jammed the paper into his shirt's breast pocket.

When the window whispered down, she said, 'What the hell d'you think you're doing?'

He put away his pen. 'Making sure you don't get hurt. This a helluva neighborhood.'

'I can take care of myself, thank you very much.'

'Listen, I know you're on to something – something important Homeland Security doesn't have a clue about. I gotta have the info.'

She glared down at him. 'What you have to do is leave. Now.'

All at once his face turned into a granite mask. 'I want what you know soon's you know it.'

Soraya felt the heat of combat in her cheeks. 'Or what?'

Without warning, he swung the door open, catching her in the stomach. Down she went to her knees, gasping.

Slowly, Overton climbed out of the car and stood over her. 'Don't fuck with me, little lady. I'm older'n you. I don't play by the book. I've forgotten more tricks than you'll ever learn.'

Soraya closed her eyes for a moment, to show him that she was trying to regain both her wind and her composure. Meanwhile her left hand had pulled a compact no-snag ASP pistol from its slim holster at the small of her back, aimed it at Overton. 'This is loaded with nine-by-nineteen-millimeter Parabellum bullets,' she said. 'At this range, one of them will most likely tear you in two.' She took two deep breaths. Her gun hand was steady. 'Get the hell out of here. Now.'

He backed up slowly and deliberately, sitting down behind the wheel without taking his eyes off her. He shook out a cigarette, stuck it between his bloodless lips, lit it with a languid motion, drew down on it.

'Yes, ma'am.' There was nothing in his voice; all the venom was in his eyes. He slammed the door shut.

He watched her regain her feet as the engine roared to life and he pulled out. Glancing in the rearview mirrors, he saw her aiming the ASP squarely at his rear window until the car disappeared into traffic.

When he lost sight of her, he pulled out his cell phone, pressed a speed-dial key. The moment he heard Matthew Lerner's voice, he said, 'You were right, Mr. Lerner. Soraya Moore's still nosing around, and to tell you the truth she's just become a clear and present danger.'

Kabur directed them to the church whose steeple had guided Bourne to the village. It was, like all the churches in the country, part of the Ethiopian Orthodox Tewahedo Church. The religion was old, and with more than thirty-six million members, it was the world's largest Oriental Orthodox church. In fact, it was the only pre-colonial Christian church in its part of Africa.

There was a moment, in the watery light of the church, when Bourne thought Kabur had played him for a fool. That not only Zaim's radiation-eaten son but also the *nagus* himself was in Fadi's employ; that he had been led into a trap. He whipped out the Makarov. Then the shadows and patches of light resolved themselves and he saw a figure beckoning wordlessly to him.

'It's Father Mihret,' Zaim whispered. 'I know him.'

Zaim, though still recovering from his wound, had insisted on coming along. He was attached to Bourne now. They had saved each other's lives.

'My sons,' Father Mihret said softly, 'I fear you've come too late.'

'The pilot,' Bourne said. 'Please take me to him.'

As they hastily made their way through the church, Bourne said, 'Is he still alive?'

'Barely.' The priest was tall and thin as a post. He possessed the large eyes and emaciated look of an ascetic. 'We've done everything we can for him.'

'How did he come to you, Father?' Zaim asked.

'He was found by herders on the outskirts of the village, within a clump of firs near the river. They came to me and I ordered him moved here on a litter, but I fear it did him little good.'

'I have access to a warbird,' Bourne said. 'I can airlift him out.'

Father Mihret shook his head. 'He has fractures of the neck and spinal cord. There is no way to successfully immobilize him. He would never survive another move.'

The pilot, Jaime Cowell, was in Father Mihret's own bed. Two women tended to him, one salving his flayed skin, the other squeezing water from a cloth into his half-open lips. A flicker appeared in Cowell's eyes when Bourne came into his line of sight.

Bourne briefly turned his back to him. 'Can he talk?' he said to the priest.

'Very little,' Father Mihret replied. 'When he moves at all, the pain is excruciating.'

Bourne stood over the bed so that his face was in Cowell's direct line of sight. 'I've come to take you home, Jaime. D'you understand me?'

Cowell's lips moved, a soft hiss emanating from between them.

'Look, I'll make this short,' Bourne said. 'I need to find Martin Lindros. You two were the only ones to survive the attacks. Is Lindros alive?'

Bourne had to bend down, his ear almost touching Cowell's lips.

'Yes. When I . . . last saw him.' Cowell's voice was like sand slithering across a dune.

Though his heart leapt, Bourne was appalled by the stench. The priest wasn't wrong: Death was already in the room, stinking up the place.

'Jaime, this is very important. Do you know where Lindros is?'

Again, the terrible stench as Bourne leaned in.

'Three klicks west by southwest . . . across the . . . river.' Cowell was sweating with the effort and the pain. 'Camp . . . heavily defended.'

Bourne was about to move away when Cowell's rasp began again. His chest, rising and falling with unnatural rapidity, began to shudder, as his already overstressed muscles began to spasm. Cowell's eyes closed, tears leaking out from under the lids.

'Take it easy,' Bourne urged. 'Rest now.'

'No! Oh, God!'

Cowell's eyes flew open, and when he stared up into Bourne's the darkness of the abyss could be seen moving closer.

'This man . . . the leader . . .'

'Fadi.' Bourne supplied his name.

'He's tortur . . . torturing Lindros.'

Bourne's stomach rolled up into a ball of ice. 'Is Lindros holding out? Cowell! Cowell can you answer me?'

'He's beyond all questions now.' Father Mihret stepped forward, put his hand on Cowell's sweat-soaked forehead. 'God has granted him blessed relief from his suffering.'

They were moving him. Martin Lindros knew this because he could hear Abbud ibn Aziz barking out a multitude of orders, all in the service of getting them the hell out of the cave. There came the clangor of booted feet, the clash of metal weapons, the grunting of men lifting heavy loads. Then he heard the rattling engine of the truck as it backed up to the cave mouth.

A moment later, Abbud ibn Aziz himself came to blindfold him.

He squatted down beside Lindros. 'Don't worry,' he said.

'I'm beyond worry,' Lindros said in a cracked voice he barely recognized as his own.

Abbud ibn Aziz fingered the hood he was about to place over Lindros's head. It was sewn of black cloth and had no eyeholes. 'Whatever you know about the mission to murder Hamid ibn Ashef, now would be the time.'

'I've told you repeatedly, I don't know anything. You still don't believe me.'

'No.' Abbud ibn Aziz placed the hood over his head. 'I don't.'

Then, quite unexpectedly, his hand briefly gripped Lindros's shoulder.

*What is this,* Lindros wondered, *a sign of empathy?* It was amusing in a way that was currently beyond him to appreciate. He could observe it as he observed everything these days, from behind a sheet of bulletproof glass of his own manufacture. That the pane was figurative made it no less effective. Ever since he'd returned from his private vault, Lindros had found himself in a semi-dissociative state, as if he couldn't fully inhabit his own body. Things his body did – eating, sleeping, eliminating, walking for exercise, even talking occasionally with Abbud ibn Aziz – seemed to be happening to someone else. Lindros could scarcely believe that he had been captured. That the dissociation was an inevitable consequence of being locked up for so long in his mental vault – that the state would slowly dissolve and, finally, vanish – seemed at the moment to be a pure pipe dream. It seemed to him that he would live out the rest of his life in this limbo – alive, but not truly living.

He was pulled roughly to his feet, feeling as if he were in a dream imagined over and over during his time out on the placid lake. Why was he being moved with this kind of haste? Had someone come after him? He doubted that it was CI; from snippets he'd overheard days ago, he knew that Dujja had destroyed the second helicopter of agents sent to find him. No. There was only one person who had the knowledge, tenacity, and sheer skill to get to the summit of Ras Dejen without being killed: Jason Bourne! Jason had come to find him and bring him home!

Matthew Lerner sat in the rear of Golden Duck. Though it was in Chinatown, the small restaurant was featured in many D.C. guidebooks, which meant it was frequented by tourists and shunned by locals, including members of Lerner's peculiar covert fraternity of spies and government agents. This, of course, suited him just fine. He had a good half a dozen meeting places he'd ferreted out around the district, randomizing his rendezvous with conduits and certain other individuals whose services he found useful.

The place, dim and dingy, smelled of sesame oil, five-spice powder, and the bubbling contents of a deep fryer from which egg rolls and breaded chicken parts were periodically lifted.

He was nursing a Tsingtao, drinking it out of the bottle because he found the oily smudges on the water glasses disturbing. Truth to tell, he'd much rather have been swigging Johnnie Walker Black, but not now. Not with this particular rendezvous.

His cell phone buzzed and, opening it, he saw a text message: 'out the back onto 7 st. five minutes.'

Deleting it at once, he pocketed the phone and returned to polishing off his Tsingtao. When he'd finished, he plunked some bills onto the table, got his coat, and walked to the men's room. He was, of course, familiar with the restaurant's layout, as he was with the sites of all his rendezvous. After urinating, he turned right out of the men's room, went past a kitchen clouded with steam, alive with shouted Cantonese and the angry sizzle of huge iron woks over open flames.

Pulling the rear door open, he slipped through onto 7th Street. The late-model Ford was as anonymous as you could get in D.C., where all government agencies were mandated to buy American when it came to transportation. With a quick look in either direction, he opened the rear door and slid inside. The Ford began to roll.

Lerner settled back into the seat. 'Frank.'

'Hello, Mr. Lerner,' the driver said. 'How's tricks?'

'Tricky,' Lerner replied drily. 'As usual.'

'I hear you,' Frank nodded. He was a beefy, bullnecked man, carrying the air of one who slavishly worked out in the gym.

'How's the secretary this pm?'

'You know.' Frank snapped his fingers. 'What's the word?'

'Angry? Pissed off? Homicidal?'

Frank gave him a glance in the rearview mirror. 'Sounds about right.'

They went over the George Mason Memorial Bridge, then swung southeast onto the Washington Memorial Parkway. Everything in the district, Lerner observed, seemed to have *memorial* attached to it. Pork-barrel politics at its worst. Just the kind of crap to piss off the secretary.

The stretch limousine was waiting for him on the outskirts of Washington National Airport's cargo terminal, its colossal engine purring like an aircraft about to take off. As Frank slid the Ford to a stop, Lerner got out and made the transfer, as he'd done so many times in recent years.

The interior bore no resemblance to any vehicle Lerner had ever heard of, save Air Force One, the president's airplane. Walls of polished burlwood covered the windows when need be – as now. A walnut desk, a state-of-the-art wi-fi communications center, a plush sofa that doubled as a bed, a pair of equally plush swivel chairs, and a half-size refrigerator completed the picture.

A distinguished man pushing seventy, with a halo of close-cut silver hair, sat behind the desk, his fingers roving over the keyboard of a laptop. His large, slightly bulging eyes were as alert and intense as they had been in his youth. They belied his sunken cheeks, the paleness of his flesh, the loose wattle beneath his chin.

'Secretary,' Lerner said, with a potent combination of respect and awe.

'Take a pew, Matthew.' Secretary of Defense Halliday's clipped Texas accent marked him as a man born and raised in the urban wilds of Dallas. 'I'll be with you momentarily.'

As Lerner chose one of the chairs, the stretch started up. Bud Halliday grew anxious if he remained in one place for long. What Lerner responded to most about him was that he was a self-made man, having been raised far from the rural oil fields that had spawned many of the men Lerner had come across during his time in the district. The secretary had earned his millions the old-fashioned way, which made him his own man. He was beholden to no one, not even the president. The deals he parlayed on behalf of his constituents and himself were so shrewd and politically deft, they invariably added to his clout, while rarely putting him in any of his colleagues' debt.

Finishing his work, Secretary Halliday looked up, tried to smile, and didn't quite make it. The only evidence of the minor stroke he'd suffered some ten years ago was the left corner of his mouth, which didn't always work as he wished it to.

'So far, so good, Matthew. When you came to me with the news that the DCI had proposed your transfer, I couldn't believe my good fortune. In one backdoor way or another, I've been trying to get control of CI for several years. The DCI is a dinosaur, the last remaining Old Boy still in service. But he's old now, and getting older by the minute. I've heard the rumors that he's beginning to lose his grip. I want to strike now, while he's beset on all sides. I can't touch him publicly; there are other dinosaurs who still have plenty of muscle inside the Beltway, even though they're retired. That's why I hired you and Mueller. I need to be at arm's length. Plausible deniability when the shit hits the fan.

'Still and all, bottom line, he's got to go; his agency needs a thorough house-cleaning. They've always taken the lead in the so-called human intelligence, which is just Beltway-speak for spying. The Pentagon, which I control, and NSA, which the Pentagon controls, have always taken a backseat. We were responsible for the recon satellites, the eavesdropping – preparing the battlefield, as Luther LaValle, my strong right arm in the Pentagon, likes to say.

'But these days we are at war, and it's my firm belief that the Pentagon needs to take control of human intelligence as well. I want to control all of it, so that we become a more efficient machine in destroying every goddamn terrorist network and cell working both outside our borders and inside toward our destruction.'

Lerner watched the secretary's face, though such was the long and intimate nature of their relationship that he could sense what was coming. Anyone else would have been satisfied with his progress, but not Halliday. Lerner mentally braced himself, because whenever he got a compliment from the secretary, it was followed by a demand for the all but impossible. Not that Halliday gave a shit. He was made in the leathery mold of Lyndon Johnson: one tough sonovabitch.

'Mind telling me what you mean by that?'

Halliday eyed him for a moment. 'Now that you've confirmed my suspicion that CI has become newly infested with Arabs and Muslims, your first act after we take care of the DCI is to purge them.'

'Which ones?' Lerner said. 'D'you have a list?'

'List? I don't need a fucking list,' Halliday said sharply. 'When I say purge, I *mean* purge. I want them *all* gone.'

Lerner nearly winced. 'That will take some time, Mr. Secretary. Like it or not, we're living in religiously sensitive times.'

'I don't want to hear that bullshit, Matthew. I've had a pain in my right buttock for close to ten years. You know what's causing that pain?'

'Yessir. Religious sensitivity.'

'Damn right. We're at war with the goddamn Muslims. I won't tolerate any of 'em undermining our security agencies from the inside, got me?'

'I do indeed, sir.'

It was like a stand-up routine between them, though Lerner doubted the secretary would agree. If he had a sense of humor, it was buried as deep as a Neanderthal's bones.

'While we're on the subject of pains in the ass, there's the matter of Anne Held.'

Lerner knew the real show was about to commence. All of this other stuff was part of the secretary's preliminary dance. 'What about her?'

Halliday plucked a manila folder off the desk, spun it into Lerner hands. Lerner opened it and leafed quickly through the sheets. Then he looked up.

Halliday nodded. 'That's right, my friend. Anne Held has started her own personal investigation into your background.'

'That bitch. I thought I had her under control.'

'She's whip-smart, Matthew, and she's intensely loyal to the DCI. Which means she will never tolerate your move up the CI ladder. Now she's become a clear threat to us. QED.'

'I can't just terminate her. Even if I made it look like a break-in or an accident – '

'Forget it. The incident would be investigated so thoroughly, it would tie you up till kingdom come.' Halliday tapped the cap of a fountain pen against his lips 'That's why I propose you find a way to sever her in a manner that will be most embarrassing and painful to her and to him. Another embarrassment in a string of others. Stripped of his loyal right hand, the DCI will be all the more vulnerable. Your star will rise even more quickly, hastening the dinosaur's demise. I'll see to it.'

# 10

Once they crossed the frozen river, heading west by southwest, the darkness of the steeply rising mountain overtook them. Bourne and Zaim were in the company of three of Kabur's foot soldiers, who were more familiar with the terrain than Zaim.

Bourne was uneasy to be traveling in what was, for him, a large pack. His methodology depended on stealth and invisibility – both of which were made extremely difficult in the present circumstances. Still, as they moved briskly along, he had to admit that Kabur's men were silent and concentrated on their mission, which was to get him and Zaim to Fadi's camp alive.

After rising gradually from the western bank of the river, the terrain leveled off for a time, indicating that they had mounted a forested plateau. The mountain loomed up in an ever-more-forbidding formation: an almost sheer wall that, thirty meters up, abruptly jutted out in a massive overhang.

The snow, which had begun to fall in earnest as they set out, had now abated to a gentle shower that did nothing to impede their progress. Thus they covered the first two and a half kilometers without incident. At this point, one of Kabur's men signaled them to halt while he sent his comrade out on a scouting foray. They waited, hunkered down amid the sighing firs, as snow continued to drift down on them. A terrible silence had come down with the vanguard of the storm, which now overstretched the area as if the massive overhanging shelf had sucked all sound out of the mountainside.

The Amhara returned, signaling that all was clear ahead, and they moved out, trudging through the snow, eyes and ears alert. As they drew nearer the overhang, the plateau steadily rose, the way becoming simultaneously rockier and more densely forested. It made perfect sense to Bourne that Fadi would pitch his camp on the high ground.

When they had gone another half a kilometer, Kabur's commander called another halt and once again sent a comrade to scout ahead. He was gone for longer this time, and when he returned he huddled with his superior in a heated conference. Kabur's man broke away and approached Bourne and Zaim.

'We have confirmation of the enemy up ahead. There are two of them to the east of us.'

'We must be close to their camp now,' Bourne said.

'These aren't guards. They're actively searching the forest, and they're coming this way.' The commander frowned. 'I'm wondering if they somehow know we're coming.'

'There's no way to know,' Zaim said. 'In any case, we need to kill them.'

The commander's frown deepened. 'These are Fadi's men. There will be consequences.'

'Forget it,' Bourne said brusquely. 'Zaim and I will go on alone.'

'Do you take me for a coward?' The commander shook his head. 'Our mission is to get you to Fadi's camp. This we will do.'

He signaled to his men, who set out heading due east. 'The three of us will keep to our original course. Let my brothers do their work.'

They were climbing in earnest, the mountain reaching upward as if trying to touch the massive overhang. It had stopped snowing for the moment, and now the sun broke out behind a rent in the streaming clouds.

All at once a flurry of gunshots echoed and reechoed. The three of them stopped, crouching down within the trees. A second flurry came on its heels, then all was silent again.

'We must hurry now,' the commander said, and they rose, resuming their course west-southwest.

Within moments, they heard a bird trill. Soon thereafter, the commander's two soldiers rejoined them. One was wounded, but not badly. They continued on grimly, a tight-knit unit, with the scout in the lead.

Almost immediately the rising ground began to level out, the trees becoming sparser. When the scout went to his knees it seemed as if he'd stumbled over a rock or a tree root. Then blood spattered the snow as the second soldier was shot through the head. The rest of the group took cover. They'd been unprepared, Bourne thought, because the shots had come from the west. The two-man scouting party coming from the east was a feint, part of a hidden pincer movement from both east and west. Bourne now learned something else about Fadi. He had accepted the risk of losing two men in order to ambush the entire party.

More shots were being fired, a veritable fusillade, so that it was impossible to determine how many of Fadi's men opposed them. Bourne broke away from Zaim and the commander, both of whom were firing back from behind whatever makeshift cover they could find. Heading off to his right, he scrambled up a steep slope, rough enough for him to find hand- and footholds through the snow. He knew it had been a mistake to allow Kabur's men to come – he didn't even want Zaim's assistance – but the culture made it impossible to refuse these gifts.

Reaching a high point, he crawled to the far edge where the wave of rock fell sharply away. From the vantage point he saw four men, carrying rifles and handguns. Even at this distance it was impossible to mistake them for Amhara. They had to be part of Fadi's terrorist cadre.

The problem now was one of logistics. Armed only with handguns, Bourne was at a distinct disadvantage opposing an enemy with rifles. The only way to negate that was to move into close quarters. This plan had its own dangers, but there was no help for it.

Circling, Bourne came at them from the rear. Very soon he realized that a simple rear assault was out of the question. The terrorists had posted a man to watch their backs. The guard sat on a rock he'd cleared of snow, holding a German-made sniper rifle – a Mauser SP66. It used 7.62 x 51mm ammo and was equipped with a precision Zeiss Diavari telescopic sight. All of this detail was vital to Bourne's next move. Though the Mauser was an excellent weapon for bringing down a long-range target, it was heavy-barreled and manually bolt-operated. It was a poor weapon if you needed to fire it in a hurry.

He crept within fifteen meters of the man, drew out the curved knife he'd taken off the Amhara soldier. Breaking cover, he stood in full view of the terrorist, who jumped up off the rock, providing Bourne with a maximum target. He was still trying to aim the Mauser when Bourne sent the knife whistling through the air. It struck the man just below the sternum, burying itself to the hilt. The curved blade sliced through tissue and organ alike. Even before the terrorist hit the snow, he was drowning in his own blood.

Bourne retrieved the knife as he stepped over the corpse, wiped the blade in the snow, slipped it into its sheath. Then he took up the Mauser and went in search of a place of concealment.

He heard shots being fired in short and long bursts, like Morse code spelling out the deaths of the combatants. He began to run toward the terrorists' position, but they had begun to move. He threw down the Mauser, drew out the Makarov.

Breaking out along the high ridge, he saw just below him the commander sprawled in the snow amid a cloud of blood. Then, as he inched forward, two terrorists came into view. He shot one in the heart from the back. The second turned and fired back. Bourne dove behind a rock.

More shots were being fired, ragged bursts, a peppering of sound taken up by the overhang, rocketed back into Bourne's ears. Bourne rose to his knees and three shots spanged off a nearby rock, sending sparks into the air.

He made a show of moving to his right, drawing fire, then slithered on his belly to his left until one shoulder of the terrorist came into view. Bourne fired twice, heard a grunt of pain. He made a show of rising up, coming forward, and when the terrorist popped up, Makarov aimed directly at him, Bourne shot the man cleanly between the eyes.

Moving on, Bourne searched for the third terrorist. He found him writhing in the snow, one hand clutching his stomach. His eyes flashed as he saw Bourne and, curiously, the ghost of a smile crossed his face. Then, in a final spasm, blood erupted from his mouth and his eyes clouded over.

Bourne ran on, then. Not more than thirty meters along he found Zaim. The Amhara was on his knees. He'd been shot twice in the chest. His eyes were crossed in pain. Nevertheless, as Bourne came to him, he said, 'No, leave me. I'm finished.'

'Zaim – '

'Go on. Find your friend. Bring him home.'

'I can't leave you.'

Zaim arranged his lips in a smile. 'You still don't understand. I have no regrets. Because of you my son will be buried. This is all I ask.'

With a long, rattling sigh, he fell sideways and did not move again.

Bourne approached him at last and, kneeling down, closed his companion's eyes. Then he went on toward Fadi's camp. Fifteen minutes later, after wending his way through thickening stands of firs, he saw it: a military array of tents pitched on a patch of flat ground that had been cleared some time ago, judging by the healed-over tree stumps.

Hunkered down beside the bole of a tree, he studied the camp: nine tents, three cook fires, a latrine. The trouble was that he could see no one. The camp appeared deserted.

He rose, then, and began to make his surveillance circuit around the camp's periphery. The moment he left the sanctuary of the fir's low-hanging branches, bullets kicked up snow all around him. He glimpsed at least half a dozen men.

Bourne began to run.

'Up here! This way! Quickly!'

Bourne, looking up, saw Alem lying prone on a shelf of snow-laden rock. He found a foothold, vaulted up onto the ledge. Alem slithered back from the edge beside Bourne, who was on his belly, watching Fadi's men fan out to search for him.

Following Alem's lead, Bourne pushed himself farther back onto the ledge. When they were far enough to gain their feet, Alem said: 'They've moved your friend. There are caves beneath the overhang. This is where they've taken him.'

'What are you doing here?' Bourne said as they began to climb upward.

'Where is my father? Why isn't he with you?'

'I'm sorry, Alem. He was shot to death.'

Bourne reached out to the boy, but Alem flinched away. The boy hung off the rock, his gaze turned inward.

'He gave as good as he got, if that makes a difference.' Bourne crouched next to Alem. 'He was at peace at the end. I promised to bury your brother.'

'You can do that?'

Bourne nodded. 'I think so. Yes.'

Alem's dark eyes roved over Bourne's face. Then he nodded and, silently, they resumed their ascent. It had begun to snow again – a heavy white curtain coming down, putting them at a remove from the rest of the world. It also muffled all sound, which was both good for them and bad. While it would hide the sounds of their movement, it would do the same for their pursuers.

Nevertheless, Alem led them on fearlessly. He was using a channel that ran diagonally across the bulge of the overhang. He was sure-footed, didn't miss a step. Within fifteen minutes, they had gained the top.

Alem and Bourne crept the irregular surface. 'There are chimneys that go all the way down to the caves,' he said. 'Many times I played hide-and-seek here with my brother. I know which chimney to use to get to your friend.'

Even through the snow, Bourne could see that the overhang was pocked with the holes that marked vertical chimneys, indications of glacial ice powerful enough to excavate through the mountain's granitic material.

Bent over one of these, Bourne wiped away the accumulated snow and peered down. Light didn't quite make it all the way down to the bottom, but the shaft looked to be several hundred meters in height.

Beside him, Alem said, 'Your enemies were watching.'

'Your father told me this.'

Alem nodded. Clearly he was not surprised. 'Your friend was then moved out of the camp so you would not find him.'

Bourne sat back, contemplating the boy. 'Why are you telling me this now? Assuming it is the truth.'

'They killed my father. I think now that was always what they intended. What do they care for us, how many of us are killed or maimed, so long as they gain what they want. But they assured me that he would be safe, that he'd be protected, and I was stupid enough to believe them. So now I say fuck them. I want to help you rescue your friend.'

Bourne said nothing, made no move.

'I know I must prove myself to you, so I'll go first down the chimney. If it is a trap, if your suspicion is right, if they think you'll use the chimney, then they will shoot me dead. You will be safe.'

'No matter what you've done, Alem, I don't want to see you hurt.'

Confusion flitted across the boy's face. Clearly, it was the first time a stranger had expressed interest in his welfare.

'I've told you the truth,' Alem said. 'The terrorists have no knowledge of these chimneys.'

After a moment's hesitation, Bourne said, 'You can prove your loyalty to me and to your father, but not this way.' He dug in his pocket, taking out a small octagonal object made of a dark gray rubbery plastic compound in the center of which were two buttons, one black and one red.

As he put it into Alem's hand, he said, 'I need you to go back down the overhang, heading south. You'll no doubt come across some of Fadi's men. As soon as you see them, press the black button. When you're within a hundred meters of them, press the red button, then throw this at them as hard as you can. Do you have all that?'

The boy looked down at the octagon. 'Is this an explosive?'

'You know it is.'

'You can count on me,' Alem said solemnly.

'Good. I'm not going to make a move until I hear the explosion. Then I'll go down the chimney.'

'The explosion will draw them.' Alem rose to leave. 'Two-thirds of the way down, the chimney branches. Take the right branch. When you reach the end, turn right. You'll be fifty meters from where they're holding your friend.'

Bourne watched as the boy scrambled across the top of the overhang, vanishing into the swirling snow as he went over the south side. At once, he called Davis on the Thuraya satellite phone.

'Your position is compromised,' he said. 'Has there been any activity? Anything at all?'

'Quiet as a tomb,' the pilot said. 'You have an ETA? There's a helluva front forming to the northwest.'

'So I've heard. Listen, I need you to get out of there. I passed through an alpine meadow thirteen or fourteen klicks northwest of your current position. Head for that. But first, I want you to bury the body in the cave. You won't be able to get anywhere with the ground, so use rocks. Make a cairn. Say a prayer over it. Oh, and one other thing – wear the radiation suit I saw in the cockpit.'

Bourne turned back to the job at hand. He had to trust that Alem was now telling him the truth. And yet he needed to take precautions in the event he was wrong. Instead of waiting for the detonation, as he'd told Alem he would, he lowered himself at once into the chimney, slithering his way down. At this moment, the boy might be handing the grenade over to one of Fadi's men. At least Bourne wouldn't be where Alem thought he'd be.

Knees, ankles, and elbows were the means of locomotion as Bourne descended the rock chimney. The pressure he put on them was the only thing stopping him from plummeting the full length of the channel to the rock floor below.

Just as Alem had said, the chimney diverged approximately two-thirds of the way down. Bourne hung for a moment above the crux, pondering the imponderable. Either he believed Alem or he didn't, it was as simple as that. But of course it wasn't simple at all. When it came to human motivations and impulses, nothing was simple.

Bourne took the right fork. Within a short distance, the way narrowed slightly, so that at points he had to force himself through. Once, he had to turn forty-five degrees in order to get his shoulders through. Eventually, though, he emerged onto the cave floor. Makarov in hand, he looked both ways. No terrorist lurked in ambush. But a meter-and-a-half stalagmite rose from the cavern floor, a calcite deposit caused by mineral-rich water washed down the chimney.

Bourne kicked out, snapping the stalagmite a foot above its base. Taking it up in his free hand, he headed right along the cavern. It wasn't long before the passageway curved to the left. Bourne slowed his pace, then dropped down to knee level.

What he saw when he first took a look around the corner was one of Fadi's men standing with a Ruger semiautomatic rifle on his hip. Bourne waited, breathing slowly and deeply. The terrorist moved, and Bourne could see Martin Lindros. Bound and gagged, he was propped up against a canvas pack of some kind. Bourne's heart beat hard in his chest. Martin was alive!

He had no time to fully assess his friend's condition because at that moment the echo of an explosion ricocheted in the cave. Alem had proved himself; he'd lobbed Deron's grenade, just as he'd promised.

The terrorist moved once again, cutting off Bourne's view of Lindros. Now he could see two more terrorists as they huddled with the first, who was speaking in rapid Arabic on a satellite phone, deciding their course of action. So Fadi had left three men to guard his prisoner. Bourne now had a crucial bit of information.

The three terrorists, having come to a decision, arrayed themselves in a triangular defensive formation: one man on point, near the cave mouth, two spread out behind Lindros, near where Bourne crouched.

Bourne put away the Makarov. He couldn't afford to use a firearm. The noise would surely bring the rest of Fadi's men to the cave at a run. He rose, planting his feet. Holding the stalagmite in one hand, he drew out the curved blade knife. He threw that first, strong and true, so that it buried itself to the hilt in the back of the left-facing rear guard. As the other one turned, Bourne hurled the stalagmite like a spear. It struck the terrorist in the throat, piercing clean through. The man clawed briefly at it as he toppled over. Then he slumped over his comrade.

The terrorist on point had spun around and was aiming his Ruger at Bourne, who immediately raised his hands and came walking toward the other.

The terrorist said, 'Halt!' in Arabic.

But Bourne had already broken into a sprint. He reached the terrorist while the man's eyes were still wide in shock. Shoving the muzzle of the Ruger to the side, Bourne slammed the heel of his hand into the terrorist's nose. Blood and bits of cartilage sprayed outward. Bourne chopped down on the man's clavicle, breaking it. The terrorist was on his knees now, swaying groggily. Jason ripped the Ruger out of his hands and mashed the butt into his temple. The man pitched over, unmoving.

Bourne was already striding away. He slit the ropes that bound Lindros hand and ankle. As he pulled his friend to his feet, he stripped off the gag.

'Easy,' he said. 'Are you okay?'

Lindros nodded.

'Okay. Let's get you the hell out of here.'

As he hustled Lindros back the way he had come, Bourne untied his friend's wrists. Martin's face was puffy and discolored, the most easily visible effects of his torture. What agonies of mind and body had Fadi put him through? Bourne had been a victim of articulated torture more than once. He knew that some people stood up to it better than others.

Skirting the stub of the stalagmite Bourne had broken off, they arrived at the chimney.

'We have to go up,' Bourne said. 'It's the only way out.'

'I'll do what I have to do.'

'Don't worry,' Bourne said. 'I'll help you.'

As he was about to hoist himself up into the chimney, Lindros put a hand on his arm.

'Jason, I never lost hope. I knew you'd find me,' he said. 'I owe you a debt I can never adequately repay.'

Bourne squeezed his arm briefly. 'Now come on. Follow me up.'

The ascent took longer than the descent. For one thing, the climb up was far more difficult and tiring. For another, there was Lindros. Several times, Bourne was obliged to stop and move back a meter or two to help his friend get through a particularly rough spot in the chimney. And he had to haul Lindros bodily through one of the narrow places.

At last, after a harrowing thirty minutes, they emerged onto the top of the overhang. While Martin regained his breath, Bourne took a reading of the weather. The wind had swung around. It was now coming out of the south. The light pattering of snow was all that was coming down – and clearly all that would come down: The front had shifted away. The ancient demons of Ras Dejen had been merciful this time.

Bourne pulled Lindros to his feet, and they began the trek to the waiting helicopter.

# 11

Anne Held lived in a two-story Federal redbrick house a stone's throw from Dumbarton Oaks in Georgetown. It had black shutters, a slate roof, and a neat privet hedge out front. The house had belonged to her late sister, Joyce. She and her husband, Peter, had died three years ago when their small plane had gone down in fog as they headed toward Martha's Vineyard. Anne had inherited the house, which she never could have afforded on her own.

Most nights, returning home from CI, Anne didn't miss her Lover. For one thing, the DCI invariably kept her late. He'd always been a tireless worker, but after his wife had walked out on him two years ago, he had absolutely no reason to leave the office. For another, once she was home she kept herself busy up until the moment she took an Ambien, slipped beneath the covers, and snapped off the bedside lamp.

But there were other nights – like this one – when she could not turn her thoughts away from her Lover. She missed the scent of him, the feel of his muscled limbs, the flutter of his flat belly against hers, the exquisite sensation as he took her – or she took him. The emptiness inside her his absence caused was a physical pain, the only anodyne more work or drugged sleep.

Her Lover. He had a name, of course. And a thousand love-names she had given him over the years. But in her mind, in her dreams, he was her Lover. She had met him in London, at a festive consular party – the ambassador of somewhere-or-other was celebrating his seventy-fifth birthday, and all of his six-hundred-odd friends had been invited, she among them. She had been working then for the director of MI6, an old and trusted friend of the DCI.

At once, she had grown dizzy and a little afraid. Dizzy at his proximity, afraid of his profound effect on her. She was, at twenty, not without experience when it came to the opposite sex. However, her experience had been with callow boys. Her Lover was a man. She missed him now with an ache that left a knot in her breast.

Her throat was parched. She crossed the entryway and entered the library, on the other side of which was the hallway to the kitchen. She had taken no more than three or four steps into the room when she stopped dead in her tracks.

Nothing was as she had left it. The sight snapped her out of the emotional pit she'd fallen into. Without taking her eyes from the scene, she opened her handbag and took out her Smith & Wesson J-frame. She was a good shot; she practiced twice a month at the CI firing range. Not that she was a big fan of guns, but the training was mandatory for all office personnel.

Thus armed, she took a closer look around. It wasn't as if a sneak thief had broken in and rifled the place. This job was neat and tidy. In fact, if she hadn't been such an anal retentive she might never have noticed the changes – that's how minute most of them were. Papers on her desk not quite as neatly stacked as they had been, an old-fashioned chrome stapler at more of an angle than she had left it, her colored pencils in a slightly different order, the books on the shelves not precisely aligned as she had ordered them.

The first thing she did was go through every room and closet in the house to make sure she was alone. Then she checked all the doors and windows. None had been broken or damaged in any way. Which meant someone either had a set of keys or had picked the lock. Of the two possibilities, the second seemed far more probable.

Next, she returned to the library and slowly and methodically examined every single item there. It was important to her to get a sense of who had invaded her house. As she moved from shelf to shelf, she imagined him stalking her, poking, prodding in an attempt to ferret out her innermost secrets.

In a sense, considering the business she was in, it seemed inevitable that this would happen. However, that knowledge did not assuage the dread she felt at this rape of her private world. She was defended, of course, heavily so. And as scrupulously careful here as she was at the office. Whoever had been here had found nothing of value, of this she was certain. It was the act itself that gnawed at her. She had been attacked. Why? By whom? Questions without immediate answers.

*Forget that glass of water now,* she thought. Instead she poured herself a stiff single-malt Scotch and, sipping it, went upstairs to her bedroom. She sat on the bed, kicked off her shoes. But the adrenaline still racing through her body would not allow her respite. She got up, padded over to her dresser, set her old-fashioned glass down. Standing before the mirror, she unbuttoned her blouse, shrugged it off. She went into the closet, swept a line of other blouses out of the way to get to the free hanger. Reaching up, she stopped in midmotion. Her heart beat like a trip-hammer and she felt a wave of nausea wash over her.

There, swinging from the chrome hanger rod, was a miniature hangman's noose. And caught in that noose, pulled tight as if around the condemned's neck, was a pair of her underpants.

'They wanted to know what I knew. They wanted to know why I was following them.' Martin Lindros sat with his head against the specially configured airplane seat's back, eyes half closed. 'I could've kicked myself. They made me in Zambia, my interrogator told me. I never knew it.'

'No use beating yourself up,' Bourne said. 'You aren't used to fieldwork.'

Lindros shook his head. 'No excuse.'

'Martin,' he said gently, 'what's happened to your voice?'

Lindros winced. 'I must have been screaming for days. I don't remember.' He tried to twist away from the memory. 'I never saw what it was.'

His friend was still in a kind of post-rescue shock, that was clear enough to Bourne. He'd asked twice about the fate of Jaime Cowell, his pilot, as if he hadn't heard Bourne the first time or had not been able to absorb the news. Bourne had chosen not to tell him about the second helicopter; time for that later. So much had happened so quickly, they'd hardly been able to say another word to each other, until now. The moment they'd taken off from Ras Dejen, Davis had radioed Ambouli airport in Djibouti for a CI physician. For that choppy flight, Lindros had been lying down on a stretcher, moving in and out of a fitful sleep. He was thinner than Bourne had ever seen him, his face haggard and gray. The beard altered his appearance in an unsettling way: it made him look like one of his captors.

Davis, a hotshot pilot if ever there was one, had wrestled the helicopter into the air, raced through the eye of a needle: a rent in the howling wind at the side edge of the front. He skillfully followed it down the mountain, out into clear weather. Beside him, Lindros lay, white-faced, the mask feeding him oxygen clamped firmly in place.

During the pulse-quickening flight, Bourne tried to keep the ruined, pitted face of Alem's brother out of his mind. He wished he could have buried the boy himself. That had proved impossible, so he'd done the next best thing. Imagining the stone cairn Davis had erected, he said a silent prayer for the dead, as he'd done months ago over Marie's grave.

In Djibouti, the CI physician had clambered aboard the moment they touched down. He was a young man with a stern countenance and prematurely graying hair. After spending close to an hour examining Lindros, he and Bourne stood outside the chopper and spoke.

'Clearly, he's been badly mistreated,' the doctor had said. 'Bruises, contusions, a cracked rib. And of course, dehydration. The good news is there's no sign of internal bleeding. I have him on saline and antibiotic drips, so for the next hour or so he can't be moved. Clean up, get yourself something proteinaceous to eat.'

He had given Bourne the ghost of a smile. 'Physically, he'll be fine. What I can't quantify is what was done to him mentally and emotionally. The official evaluation will have to wait until we get back to D.C., but in the meantime you can do your bit. Engage his mind, when you can, during the trip back. I understand the two of you are good friends. Talk to him about the times you've spent together, see if you can get a sense of what changes – if any – have occurred.'

'Who interrogated you?' Bourne said now to Lindros as they sat side by side in the CI jet.

His friend's eyes closed briefly. 'Their leader: Fadi.'

'So Fadi himself was there on Ras Dejen.'

'Yes.' A slight shudder went through Lindros like a gust of wind. 'This shipment was too important to leave in the hands of a lieutenant.'

'So you found out before they captured you.'

'Uranium, yes. I had taken radiation detectors with me.' Lindros's gaze slid away to the shrieking darkness outside the jet's Perspex window. 'I started out by thinking Dujja was after TSGs. But really, that didn't make sense. I mean, *why* would they want triggered spark gaps unless . . .' His body was racked by another small spasm. 'We have to assume they have it all, Jason. The TSGs and, far worse, the means to enrich the uranium. We have to assume they're constructing a nuclear bomb.'

'That was my conclusion as well.'

'And it's none of this "dirty bomb" crap that would impact a couple of square blocks. This is the real thing, power enough to devastate a major city, irradiate the surrounding areas. For the love of God, we're talking millions of lives!'

Lindros was right. In Djibouti, Bourne had called the Old Man while the doctor was assessing Martin's condition, giving him an abbreviated briefing on Lindros, their current status, and, especially, what they'd discovered about Dujja's threat and its capacity to carry it out. For now, however, all he could do was try to assess his friend's mental condition. 'Tell me about your time in captivity.'

'There's not much to tell, really. Most of the time I had a hood over my head. Believe it or not, I came to dread the times it would be removed, because that was when Fadi interrogated me.'

Bourne knew he was now skating on thin ice. But he had to get at the truth, even if it wasn't what he wanted to hear. 'Did he know you were CI?'

'No.'

'Did you tell him?'

'I told him I was NSA, and he believed me. He had no reason not to. One American spy agency is like another to these people.'

'Did he want information on NSA personnel deployment or mission objectives?'

Lindros shook his head. 'As I said, what interested him was how I came to be following him and how much I knew.'

Bourne hesitated fractionally. 'Did he find that out?'

'I know what you're getting at, Jason. I had a strong conviction that if I broke, he'd kill me.'

Bourne said nothing more for the moment. Lindros's breathing was coming quick and fast, cold sweat breaking out across his forehead. The doctor had warned him that if he went too far, too fast with Lindros, a reaction might set in.

'Should I call the doctor?'

Lindros shook his head. 'Give me a minute. I'll be okay.'

Bourne went back to the galley, made plates of food for them both. There were no attendants on board, just the doctor, a CI pilot, and an armed copilot up front. Returning to his seat, he handed a plate to his friend, sat down with the other. For some time, Bourne ate in silence. Presently, he could see that Lindros had calmed down enough to begin picking at his food.

'Tell me what's been happening while I've been gone.'

'I wish I had some good news. But the fact is your people caught that Cape Town dealer who sold the TSGs to Dujja.'

'Hiram Cevik, yes.'

Bourne produced the PS3, brought up the photo of Cevik, showed it to Lindros. 'This him?'

'No,' Lindros said. 'Why?'

'This is the man picked up in Cape Town and brought to D.C. He escaped, but not before one of his people shot Tim Hytner to death.'

'Dammit all. Hytner was a good man.' Lindros tapped the PS3 screen. 'So who is this?'

'I think it's Fadi.'

Lindros was incredulous. 'We had him, and lost him?'

'I'm afraid so. On the other hand, this is the first lead we have to what Fadi actually might look like.'

'Let me see that.' Lindros stared hard at the photo. After a long time, he said, 'Christ, that *is* Fadi!'

'You're sure?'

Lindros nodded. 'He was there when they took us. He's got a load of makeup on here, but I recognize the shape of the face. And those eyes.' He nodded, handing back the PS3. 'That's Fadi, all right.'

'Can you make a sketch of him for me?'

Lindros nodded. Bourne rose, then came back a moment later with a pad and a fistful of pencils he'd gotten from the copilot.

While Lindros went to work, Bourne spoke of something he had noticed in his friend. 'Martin, you look like there's something else you want to tell me.'

Lindros looked up from the sketch. 'It's probably nothing, but . . .' He shook his head. 'When I was alone with another of my interrogators – a man named Abbud ibn Aziz, who by the way is Fadi's right hand – a name kept coming up. Hamid ibn Ashef.'

'I don't know him.'

'Really? I thought I saw his name in your file.'

'If so, it must have been a mission set up by Alex Conklin. But if it involved me, I have no memory of it.'

'I was just wondering why Abbud ibn Aziz wanted information on that particular mission. I guess now I'll never know.' Lindros took a long drink of water. He was following the doctor's orders to rest and rehydrate. 'Jason, I may still be somewhat out of it, but I'm no longer in shock. I know the powers that be are going to run a complete battery of tests to determine my fitness.'

'You're going to return to duty, Martin.'

'I hope you know you're going to play a major role in that decision. After all, you know me best. CI will have to be guided by your opinion.'

Bourne couldn't help laughing. 'Now, that will be a switch.'

Lindros took a deep breath, let it out, along with a little whistle of pain. 'Irrespective of all this, I want you to promise me something.'

Bourne searched his shadowed face for any sign that he knew what the powers that be would really be looking for: whether he had been brainwashed, turned into a ticking time bomb, a human weapon to be used against CI. It had always been in the back of Bourne's mind as he'd gone after his friend. What would be the worse horror, he'd wondered. To find his friend dead, or to discover that he'd been turned into the enemy?

'Dujja's rigid, almost businesslike, organization, its seemingly unending supply of modern armament, the fact that Fadi is obviously Western-educated – all these factors taken together make this cadre unlike any other terrorist network we've ever been up against,' Lindros continued. 'The construction of a uranium enrichment plant is massively expensive. Who has that kind of money to throw around? My guess is a crime cartel. Drug money from crops in Afghanistan or Colombia. Turn off that spigot – the money men – and you cut off its ability to enrich uranium, to get more up-to-date weapons. There's no surer way of sending it all the way back into the Iron Age.' His voice lowered. 'In Botswana, I unearthed what I believe to be Dujja's money trail, which runs back to Odessa. I have a name: Lemontov. Edor Vladovich Lemontov. The intel I gathered in Uganda is that Lemontov is based there.'

His eyes gleamed, the old excitement returning. 'Think of it, Jason! Up until now, the only realistic way to destroy an Islamic terrorist network was to try to infiltrate it. A tactic that is so difficult, it's never succeeded. Now, for the first time, we have another option. A tangible means to dismantle the world's most lethal terrorist network from the outside in.

'I can take care of that end. But as for this money man, I don't trust anyone else the way I trust you. I need you to go to Odessa as soon as possible, track down Lemontov, and terminate him.'

The rambling fieldstone house had been built more than a hundred years before. Since then, it'd had ample time to settle into the rolling hills of Virginia. It had dormer windows, slate-tile roof, and a high stone wall around the property, with iron gates that opened electronically. It was said by neighbors that the estate was owned by an old recluse of a writer who, if anyone were to take the trouble to look at a copy of the deed housed in the municipal building fifty kilometers away, had bought the estate twenty-two years ago for the sum of $240,000 after the county had closed the insane asylum. This writer was something of a paranoid, it was said. Why else would his wall be electrified? Why else would the pair of lean and perpetually hungry Dobermans roam the grounds, sniffing and growling ominously?

In fact, the estate was owned by CI. Veteran agents, those in the know, had given it the name of Bleak House, because it was here that CI enacted its formal debriefs. They made macabre jokes about it because its very existence filled them with anxiety. It was to here that Bourne and Lindros were driven, on a joint-cracking winter's morning, upon their arrival at Dulles airport.

'Place your head just there. That's right.'

The CI agent cupped his hand to the back of Martin Lindros's head as, moments before, he had done with Jason Bourne.

'Look straight ahead, please,' the agent continued, 'and try not to blink.'

'I've done this a thousand times before,' Lindros growled.

The agent ignored him, switching on the retinal reader and watching the read-out as it scanned the center of Lindros's right eye. Having taken its picture, the reader automatically compared the retinal pattern with the one on file. The match was perfect.

'Welcome home, Deputy Director.' The agent grinned, extending his hand. 'You're cleared to enter Bleak House. Second door on your left. Mr. Bourne, you're the third door on the right.'

He nodded them to the elevator that had been installed when CI bought the estate. Since it was controlled by him, the doors were open, the car waiting patiently for them. Inside the shining stainless-steel cab, there was no need for numbers or buttons to push. This elevator went only to the sub-basement, where the warren of rough concrete corridors, claustrophobic windowless rooms, and mysterious laboratories staffed by a veritable phalanx of medical and psychological experts awaited like a medieval chamber of horrors.

Everybody in CI knew that being taken to Bleak House meant something had gone horribly wrong. It was the temporary home of defectors, double agents, incompetents, and traitors.

After that, these people were never heard from again, their fate a source of endless grisly rumor within the agency.

Bourne and Lindros reached the sub-basement and stepped out into the corridor, which smelled vaguely of cleaning fluid and acid. They stood facing each other for a moment. There was nothing more to say. They gripped each other's hand like gladiators about to enter the bloody arena, and parted.

In the room behind the third door on the right, Bourne sat on a ladder-backed metal chair bolted to the concrete floor. The long fluorescent tubes of an industrial overhead light, covered by a steel grille, buzzed like a horsefly against a windowpane. It revealed a metal table and another metal chair, both also bolted to the floor. There was a stainless-steel toilet in one corner, prison-style, and a tiny sink. The room was otherwise bare save for a mirror on one wall, through which he could be observed by whoever was assigned to his interrogation.

For two hours he waited with only the company of the fluorescent tube's angry buzzing for company. Then abruptly the door opened. An agent walked in, sat down on the other side of the table. He set out a small tape recorder, turned it on, opened a file on the tabletop, and began his questioning.

'Tell me in as much detail as you remember what happened from the moment you arrived on the north face of Ras Dejen to the moment you took off with the subject on board.'

While Bourne spoke, the interrogator never took his eyes off his face. He himself was a man of middle years, of medium height, with a high domed forehead and thin, receding hair. He had a receding chin but the eyes of a fox. He never once looked at Bourne directly, instead he studied him from the corners of his eyes, as if this might give him the advantage of insight, or at least intimidation.

'What was the subject's condition when you found him?'

The interrogator was asking Bourne to repeat what he'd already said. This was standard operating procedure, a way to ferret out the lies from the truth. If a subject was lying, his story would change sooner or later. 'He was bound and gagged. He appeared very thin – much as he does now – as if his captors had fed him minimally.'

'I imagine he had great difficulty managing the ascent back to the helicopter.'

'The beginning was the most difficult for him. I thought I might have to carry him. His muscles were cramped and his stamina was virtually nil. I fed him a couple of protein bars and that helped. Within an hour, he was walking more steadily.'

'What was the first thing he said?' the interrogator said with a false mildness.

Bourne knew that the more casually a question was asked, the more important it was to the interrogator. '"I'll do what I have to do."'

The interrogator shook his head. 'I mean when he first saw you. When you removed the gag.'

'I asked him if he was okay – '

The interrogator regarded the ceiling as if he was bored. 'And he said what, precisely?'

Bourne remained stone-faced. 'He nodded. He didn't say a word.'

The interrogator looked puzzled, a sure sign that he was trying to trip Bourne up. 'Why not? You'd think after more than a week in captivity, he'd say something.'

'It was insecure. The less we spoke at that moment, the better. He knew that.'

Bourne was in the corners of the interrogator's eyes again. 'So his first words to you were . . .'

'I told him we needed to climb the rock chimney in order to escape and he said "I'll do what I have to do."'

The interrogator appeared unconvinced. 'All right, passing over that. In your opinion, what was his mental state at that time?'

'He seemed okay. Relieved. He wanted out of there.'

'He wasn't disoriented, didn't exhibit any lapses of memory? He didn't say anything odd, out of place?'

'No, none of that.'

'You seem very sure of yourself, Mr. Bourne. Don't you yourself have a memory problem?'

Bourne knew he was being baited, and he relaxed inside. Baiting was the method of last resort, when every other avenue to break a story apart had been exhausted. 'Of events in the past. My memories of yesterday, last week, last month are crystal clear.'

Without a moment's hesitation the interrogator said, 'Has the subject been brainwashed, has he been turned?'

'The man across the hall is Martin Lindros as he's always been,' Bourne replied. 'On the plane ride home, we talked of things only he and I knew about.'

'Please be more specific.'

'He confirmed the identity of the terrorist Fadi. He made a sketch for me. A huge breakthrough for us. Before that, Fadi was just a cipher. Martin also gave me the name of Fadi's right-hand man, Abbud ibn Aziz.'

The interrogator asked him another dozen questions, many of which he'd asked before with different wording. Bourne patiently answered them all. Nothing was going to ruffle his calm.

As abruptly as it had started, the session came to an end. Without either acknowledgment or explanation, the interrogator turned off the tape recorder, then took it and his notes with him out of the room.

Another period of waiting ensued, interrupted only by another agent, younger, bringing in a tray of food. He left without saying a word.

It was just after six in the evening, according to Bourne's watch – an entire day spent in interrogation – when the door next opened.

Bourne, who thought he was ready for anything, was very much surprised to see the DCI walk in. He stood, regarding Bourne for a long time. In his face, Bourne recognized the conflicting emotions that clogged the Old Man's throat. It had cost him something to come in here at all, and now what he'd come to say stuck in his craw like a fish bone.

At last he said, 'You made good on your promise. You brought Martin home.'

'Martin's my friend. I wasn't about to fail him.'

'You know, Bourne, it's no secret I wish I'd never met you.' The Old Man shook his head. 'But really, you're a fucking enigma.'

'Even to myself.'

The DCI blinked several times. Then he turned on his heel and strode out, leaving the door open. Bourne rose. He supposed he was free to leave, and so was Martin. That's all that mattered. Martin had passed the exhausting battery of physical and psychological tests. They had both survived Bleak House.

Matthew Lerner, sitting in the Typhon director's chair, behind the Typhon director's desk, knew something was amiss the moment he heard the applause. He turned away from the computer terminal, where he had been devising a new system of cataloging Typhon e-files.

He rose, crossed the director's office, and opened the door. There he was greeted by the sight of Martin Lindros being surrounded by the members of his Typhon cadre, all of whom were smiling, laughing, and pumping his hand enthusiastically when they weren't egging him on with their applause.

Lerner could scarcely believe his eyes. *Here comes Caesar,* he thought bitterly. *And why didn't the DCI see fit to tell me he'd returned?* With a mixture of repulsion and envy, he watched the prodigal general making his slow, triumphal way toward him. *Why are you here? Why aren't you dead?*

With no small pain, he screwed a smile onto his face and held out his hand.

'All hail the returning hero.'

Lindros reflected back the smile in all its steel-clad irony. 'Thanks for keeping my chair warm, Matthew.'

He swept by Lerner and into his office. There he stood stock-still, taking inventory. 'What, no new coat of paint?' As Lerner followed him in, he added: 'A verbal debriefing will do, before you go upstairs.'

Lerner did as he was asked while he went about gathering his personal items. When he was finished, Lindros said, 'I'd appreciate getting the office back as I left it, Matthew.'

Lerner glared at him for a microsecond, then carefully put back all the photos, prints, and memorabilia he had put away, hoping never to see again. As an accomplished commander, he knew when to leave the field of battle. It was with the certain knowledge that this was a war, and it had just begun.

Three minutes after Lerner had left the Typhon offices, Lindros's phone rang. It was the Old Man.

'I bet it feels good to be sitting behind that desk.'

'You have no idea,' Lindros said.

'Welcome back, Martin. And I mean that most sincerely. The confirmation of Dujja's intentions you obtained is invaluable.'

'Yes sir. I've already worked up a step-by-step plan to interdict them.'

'Good man,' the DCI said. 'Assemble your team and press forward with the mission, Martin. Until the crisis has been dealt with, your mission is CI's mission. From this moment, you have unlimited access to all of CI's resources.'

'I'll get the job done, sir.'

'I'm counting on you, Martin,' the DCI said. 'You'll be able to deliver your first briefing at dinner tonight. Eight sharp.'

'I'll look forward to it, sir.'

The DCI cleared his throat. 'Now, what do you propose to do about Bourne?'

'I don't understand, sir.'

'Don't play games with me, Martin. The man's a menace, we both know it.'

'He brought me home, sir. I doubt anyone else could have done it.'

The Old Man shook off Lindros's words. 'We're in the midst of a national crisis of unprecedented proportion and gravity. The last thing we need is a loose cannon. I want you to get rid of him.'

Lindros shifted in his chair, staring out the window at the silver pellets of freezing rain. He made a mental note to check whether Bourne's flight would be delayed. Into the mounting silence, he said: 'I'm going to need clarification on that.'

'Oh, no, no, nothing like that. Anyway, the man is cursed with nine lives.' The DCI paused a moment. 'I know you two have formed some sort of bond, but it's unhealthy. Trust me, I know. Consider that we buried Alex Conklin three years ago. It's dangerous for anyone to get too close to him.'

'Sir – '

'If it helps, I'm giving you one last loyalty test, Martin. Your continuation at Typhon depends on it. I don't have to remind you there's someone snapping at your heels. As of this moment, you are to sever all ties with Jason Bourne. He gets no information – none at all – from your office or any other in the building. Are we clear?'

'Yessir.' Lindros severed the connection.

Carrying the cordless phone, he rose and stood by the window, resting his cheek against the pane, felt the cold wash over him. His bone-deep aches and pains remained, along with a headache he'd neglected to mention to the CI physicians, which never quite left him – all vivid reminders of what had happened to him, how long his journey here had been.

Dialing a number, he held the phone to his ear. 'Is Bourne's flight on time?' He nodded at the reply. 'Good. He's at Washington National? You've made visual contact? Excellent, come on home. That's right.' He severed the connection. Whatever might transpire here, Bourne was on his way to Odessa.

Returning to his desk, he opened the intercom and told his secretary to set up an immediate phone conference with all of Typhon's overseas agents. When that had been accomplished, he activated the speakerphone in the conference room where he had assembled an emergency meeting of all D.C. Typhon personnel. There he gave them what details he had of the threat, then outlined his plan. Dividing his people into four-man teams, he meted out assignments that, he told them, were to begin immediately.

'As of this moment, all other missions are frozen,' he told them. 'Finding and stopping Dujja is our first and only priority. Until that's accomplished, all leaves are hereby canceled. Get used to these walls, folks. We're going on a day-and-night emergency schedule.'

Once he saw that his orders were being carried out to his satisfaction, he left to go to Soraya's apartment to straighten out whatever it was Matthew Lerner had fucked up with her. In the car, he opened his quad-band GSM cell phone and dialed a number in Odessa.

When the familiar male voice answered, Lindros said, 'It's done. Bourne will be arriving at 4:40 local time tomorrow afternoon, from Munich.' He ran a red light, made a right turn. Soraya's apartment building was three blocks ahead. 'You will keep him on a short leash, as we discussed . . . No, I simply want to make sure you haven't decided to make changes to the plan on the fly. All right, then. He'll find his way to the kiosk because that's where he'll think Lemontov is headquartered. Before he can find out the truth, you'll kill him.'

# Book 2

# 12

*In Odessa, there is a kiosk, one among many on the beach fronting the Black Sea. It is weathered, gray as the water that rolls into the tide line. Bourne picks the lock of a side door in the kiosk, steals his way inside. Where is the person he was carrying? He doesn't remember, but he sees that his hands are covered with blood. He smells violent death on himself. What happened? he wonders. No time, no time! Somewhere a clock is ticking; he has to move on.*

*The kiosk, which should be filled with life, is as still as a boneyard. At the back, a windowed kitchen, garishly lit by fluorescent tubes. He sees movement through the glass and, crouching, makes his way between the crates of beer and soda piled up like columns in a cathedral. He sees the silhouette of the man he was sent here to kill, who has done his best to confuse and elude him.*

*To no avail.*

*He's about to make the final approach to his target when movement to his left causes him to spin around. A woman comes toward him out of the shadows – Marie! What is she doing in Odessa? How did she know where he was?*

*'Darling,' she says. 'Come with me, come away from here.'*

*'Marie.' He feels panic constrict his chest. 'You can't be here. It's too dangerous.'*

*'Marrying you was dangerous, darling. That didn't stop me.'*

*A high keening begins, reverberating through the empty space inside him. 'But now you're dead.'*

*'Dead? Yes, I suppose I am.' A frown momentarily fractures the beauty of her face. 'Why weren't you there, darling? Why weren't you protecting me and the children? I would be alive now if you hadn't been halfway across the globe, if you hadn't been with* her.'

*'Her?' Bourne's heart is beating like a trip-hammer, and his panic grows exponentially.*

*'You're an expert at lying to everyone, except me, darling.'*

*'What do you mean?'*

*'Look at your hands.'*

*He stares down at the blood drying into the crevasses of his palms. 'Whose blood is this?'*

*Wanting – needing – an answer, he looks up. But Marie is gone. There is nothing but the lurid light spilling out onto the floor like blood from a wound.*

*'Marie,' he calls softly. 'Marie, don't leave me!'*

Martin Lindros and his retinue of captors had been traveling for quite some time. He had flown in a helicopter and, after a short wait, on a small jet, which had stopped at least once for refueling. He wasn't sure because either he had slept or they had given him something to make him sleep. Not that it mattered. He knew he was off Ras Dejen, out of northwest Ethiopia, out of the continent of Africa altogether.

Jason. What had happened to Jason? Was he dead or alive? Clearly Jason had failed to find him in time. He didn't want to think about Jason being dead. He wouldn't believe it even if Fadi himself told him so. He knew Bourne too well. He always had a way of turning over the newly shoveled earth to climb out of his grave. Jason was alive, Lindros knew it.

But he wondered whether it even mattered. Did Jason suspect that Karim al-Jamil had taken Lindros's place? If he'd been fooled, then even if he'd survived the rescue attempt on Ras Dejen he'd have abandoned the rescue. An even worse scenario made him break out into a cold sweat. What if Jason had found Karim al-Jamil, brought him back to CI headquarters. God in heaven, was that what Fadi had planned all along?

His body swayed and juddered as the plane hit a pocket of turbulence. To steady himself, he leaned against the plane's chill concave bulkhead. After a moment, he put his hand over the bandage that covered half his face. Underneath was the excavation where his right eye had been. This had become a habit of his. His head throbbed with an unspeakable pain. It was as if his eye were on fire – only his eye was no longer his. It belonged to Fadi's brother, Karim al-Jamil ibn Hamid ibn Ashef al-Wahhib. At first, this thought had made him sick to his stomach; he would vomit often and rackingly, like a junkie going cold turkey. Now it simply made him sick at heart.

The violation of his body, the harvesting of his organ while he was still alive, was a horror from which he would never recover. At several points, while he was out on the silver lake fishing for rainbow trout, the thought of killing himself crossed his mind, but he had never actually considered it. Suicide was the coward's way out.

Besides, he very much wanted to live, if only to exact his revenge on Fadi and Karim al-Jamil.

Bourne awoke with a violent twitch. He looked around him, momentarily disoriented. Where was he? He saw a bureau, a night table, curtains drawn against the light. Anonymous furniture, heavy, threadbare. A hotel room. Where?

Sliding out of bed, he padded across the mottled carpet, pulled back the thick curtains. A sudden glare struck him a clean blow across his face and chest. He squinted at the tiny scimitars of sunlight, gold against the deep gray of the water. The Black Sea. He was in Odessa.

Had he been dreaming of Odessa, or remembering Odessa?

He turned, his mind still filled with the dream-memory, stretched like taffy into the blue morning. Marie in Odessa? Never! Then what was she doing in his memory shard of . . .

Odessa!

It was in this city that his memory shard had been born. He'd been here before. He'd been sent to kill . . . someone. Who? He had no idea.

He sat back down on the bed, rubbing the heels of his hands against his eyes. He still heard Marie's voice.

'*I would be alive now if you hadn't been halfway across the globe, if you hadn't been with* her.' Not accusatory. Sad.

What did it matter where he was, what he was doing? He hadn't been with her. Marie had phoned him. She thought she had a cold, that's all. Then the second call, which had sent him half out of his mind with grief. And guilt.

He should have been there to protect his family, just as he should have been there to protect his first family. History had repeated itself, if not exactly, then tragically close enough. Ironically, this far away in kilometers from the scene of the disaster had brought him closer, to the very brink of the black void inside him. Staring into it, he felt that old, overwhelming despair well up inside him – a need to punish himself, or to punish someone else.

He felt totally, absolutely alone. For him, this was a deeply disturbing state, as if he had stepped outside himself, as one does in a dream. Only this was no dream; this was waking life. Not for the first time he wondered whether his judgment was being impaired by his current emotional turmoil. He could find no other logical explanation for certain anomalies: his bringing Hiram Cevik out of the CI cell; his waking up here and not knowing where he was. For a brief, despairing moment, he wondered if Marie's death had ripped him completely asunder, if the delicate threads that held his multiple identities together had snapped. *Am I losing my mind?*

His cell phone buzzed.

'Jason, where are you?' It was Soraya.

'In Odessa,' he said thickly. His mouth felt wadded with cotton.

There was a quick catch to her breathing. Then: 'What on earth are you doing there?'

'Lindros sent me here. I'm following up a lead he gave me. He thinks a man named Lemontov is funding Dujja. Edor Vladovich Lemontov. Criminal cartel – drugs, most likely. Does the name ring a bell?'

'No. But I'll check the CI database.'

Briefly, she told him about the events at the Hotel Constitution. 'The one true oddity is that a highly unusual accelerant was used – carbon disulfide. According to my friend, she's never encountered it before.'

'What's it used in?'

'Mainly the manufacture of cellulose, carbon tet, all kinds of sulfur compounds. It's also used in soil fumigants, a flotation agent in mineral processing. In the past, it was a component of refrigerants and fire extinguishers. She said she thought it was used because it has a low flashpoint.'

Bourne nodded as he stared at an oil tanker chugging in empty from Istanbul. 'Turning it into an explosive.'

'Very effective. Blew out the suite. A complete firestorm. We were lucky with the prosthesis, which was protected by the bathtub catch basin. Nothing else of value was left, not even enough of a body to ID.'

'Fadi's luck seems to be going down the drain,' Bourne said drily.

Soraya laughed. 'The Lemontov lead interests me, because I thought of the old refrigerants and fire extinguishers that had been banned in the States, but probably not elsewhere, like Eastern Europe, Ukraine, Odessa.'

'That's a thought worth following up on,' Bourne said, breaking the connection.

*

Although it was after 1 A.M. Martin Lindros was at his computer terminal entering information. CI was still in Code Mesa. There was a crisis on, all leaves canceled. Sleep was a luxury none of them could afford.

A soft knock on the door, then Soraya poked her head in, gave him a questioning look. He raised a beckoning hand, and she shut the door behind her. Taking a seat in front of the desk, she placed something on the desktop.

'What's this?' Lindros said.

'It's a prosthetic. A friend of mine – an arson expert with the Fire Investigation Unit – called me in.' Soraya had previously filled him in on the events at the Hotel Constitution. 'She found something in the Silvers' suite at the Constitution she couldn't explain. That. It's used in highly sophisticated disguises.'

He picked up the prosthetic. 'Yes. Jason showed me something like this once. It's meant to change your appearance.'

Soraya nodded. 'There's enough evidence to conclude that Jakob Silver was, in fact, Fadi, that his brother was another terrorist, that they were responsible for the fire.'

'Wasn't there a body found in the suite? Wasn't it Silver's?'

'Yes, and no. It seems more than likely that the body was that of a Pakistani waiter. There never were a pair of Mr. Silvers.'

'Ingenious,' Lindros mused as he turned the prosthetic between his fingertips. 'But not of much use to us now.'

'On the contrary.' Soraya took it back. 'I'm going to see if I can find out who manufactured it.'

Lindros was lost in thought for a moment.

'I talked to Bourne less than an hour ago,' Soraya continued.

'Oh?'

'He wanted me to dig up whatever I can on a drug lord by the name of Edor Vladovich Lemontov.'

Lindros set his elbows on his desk, steepled his fingers. This was a situation that could quickly spiral out of control if he let it. Keeping his voice neutral, he said, 'And what have you discovered?'

'Nothing yet. I wanted to bring you up to date on the prosthetic first.'

'You did well.'

'Thanks, boss.' She rose. 'Now I've got hours of eyestrain ahead of me.'

'Forget research. I couldn't find anything on this sonovabitch. Whoever he is, he's securely shielded. Just the sort Dujja would use as a money man.' Lindros had already turned back to his computer screen. 'I want you on the next plane to Odessa. I want you to back Bourne up.'

Soraya was clearly surprised. 'He won't like that.'

'He's not required to,' Lindros said shortly.

When Soraya reached for the prosthetic, Lindros swept it up in his hand. 'I'll take care of this myself.'

'Sir, if you don't mind my saying, you've got a lot on your plate as it is.'

Lindros searched her face. 'Soraya, I wanted to be the one to tell you this. We've had a mole inside Typhon.' He could hear her sharply indrawn breath and was pleased. Opening a drawer, he spun across a thin dossier he'd prepared.

Soraya picked it up, flipped back the cover. As soon as she started reading, she felt hot tears distorting her vision. It was Tim Hytner. Bourne had been right, after all. Hytner had been working for Dujja.

She looked up at Lindros. 'Why?'

He shrugged. 'Money. It's all in there. The electronic trail back to an account in the Caymans. Hytner was born dirt-poor, wasn't he? His father is in a long-term care medical facility his insurance won't pay for, isn't that right? His mother has no money to speak of. Everyone's got a weakness, Soraya. Even your best friend.'

He took the file from her. 'Forget Hytner, he's yesterday's news. You've got work to do. I want you in Odessa ASAP.'

When he heard the door sigh shut, Lindros stared after her as if he could see her walking away. *Yes, indeed,* he thought. *In Odessa, you'll be killed before you can find out who made this prosthetic.*

# 13

Bourne was booked into the Samarin Hotel, a rather shambling mammoth of a place on the seaport directly across from the Passenger Sea Terminal, where ferries went to and fro on a regular schedule. The sleek ultramodern Odessa Hotel had risen from the massive sea terminal pier since the last time he'd been here. To him, it seemed as out of place as a Dolce & Gabbana suit on a homeless man.

Shaved, bathed, and dressed, he walked down to the vast somnolent lobby, which was as ornate as an early nineteenth-century Easter bonnet. In fact, every-thing about the hotel reeked of early nineteenth century, from the massive frayed velvet furniture to the floral-patterned wallpapered walls.

He ate breakfast amid florid-faced businessmen in the sun-filled dining room overlooking the harbor. It smelled vaguely of burned butter and beer. When his waiter brought the check, he said, 'At this time of year, where does one go here to have a good time?'

Bourne spoke in Russian. Though this was Ukraine, Russian was Odessa's official language.

'Ibitza is closed,' the waiter said, 'as are all the clubs in Arkadia.' Arkadia was the beachside district; in summer the strands swarmed with young, affluent Russian women and male tourists on the prowl. 'It depends. What is your preference, female or male?'

'Neither,' Bourne said. He put his fingertip to his nose, inhaled noisily.

'Ah, that trade is open year-round,' the waiter said. He was a thin man, stoop-shouldered, prematurely old. 'How much do you need?'

'More than you can get for me. I'm in wholesale.'

'Another story entirely,' the waiter said warily.

'Here's all you have to know.' Bourne pushed over a roll of American money.

Without hesitation, the waiter vacuumed up the bills. 'You know the Privoz Market?'

'I'll find it.'

'Egg Row, third stall from the east end. Tell Yevgeny Feyodovich you want brown eggs, only brown.'

The Samarin, like all of old Odessa, was built in the neo-classical style, which meant it was Frenchified. This was hardly surprising, since one of the founding fathers of Odessa was the duc de Richelieu, who had been the city's chief architect and designer during the eleven years he was governor in the early 1800s. It was the

Russian poet Aleksander Pushkin, living in exile here, who said that he could smell Europe in Odessa's shops and coffeehouses.

On shadowy, linden-lined Primorskaya Street, Bourne was immediately greeted by a chill, damp wind that slapped his face and reddened his skin. To the south, far out on the water, low clouds hung dense and dark, dispensing a sleety rain onto goosefleshed waves.

The salt tang from the sea brought memory back with breathless ferocity. Night in Odessa, blood on his hands, a life hanging in the balance, a desperate search for his target, leading to the kiosk where he'd found his target.

His gaze turned inland, toward the terraced levels that rose into the hills guarding the scimitar-shaped harbor. Consulting a map he'd been given by the hotel's ancient concierge, he leapt onto a slowing tram that would take him to the railway station on Italiansky Boulevard.

The Privoz farmers' market, a stone's throw from the station, was a colossal array of live food and produce under a corrugated tin roof. The stalls were set up behind waist-high concrete slabs that made Bourne think of the antiterrorist blockades in D.C. Makeshift shanties and bedrolls surrounded the market. Farmers came from near and far, and those who were obliged to travel a great distance invariably slept here overnight.

Inside, it was a riot of sounds, smells, cries in different languages – butchered Russian, Ukrainian, Romanian, Yiddish, Georgian, Armenian, Turkish. The scents of cheese mingled with those of fresh meat, root vegetables, pungent herbs, and plucked fowl. Bourne saw huge, linebacker-like women with moth-eaten sweaters and head scarves manning the booths at Turkey Row. For the uninitiated, the market presented a thoroughly bewildering array of stalls against which hordes of stout shoppers pressed their impressive bellies.

After asking directions from several people, Bourne made his way through the clamor and throb to Egg Row. Orienting himself, he moved to the third stall from the east end, which was typically crowded. A red-faced woman and a burly man – presumably Yevgeny Feyodovich – were busily exchanging eggs for money. He waited on the man's side of the stall, and when his turn came he said, 'You are Yevgeny Feyodovich?'

The man squinted at him. 'Who wants to know?'

'I'm looking for brown eggs, only brown. I was told to come here and ask for Yevgeny Feyodovich.'

Yevgeny Feyodovich grunted, leaned over, said something to his female partner. She nodding without breaking her practiced rhythm of packing eggs and shoveling money into the outsize pockets of her faded dress.

'This way,' Yevgeny said with a flick of his head. He pulled on a ratty wool pea-coat, came out from behind the concrete barrier, led Bourne out the eastern side of the market. They crossed Srednefontanskaya Street and entered Kulikovo Pole Square. The sky was white now, as if a colossal cloud had come down from the heavens to blanket the city. The light, flat and shadowless, was a photographer's dream. It revealed everything.

'As you can see, this square is very Soviet, very ugly, retro, but not in a good way,' Yevgeny Feyodovich said with a good bit of ironic humor. 'Still, it serves to remind us of the past – of starvation and massacres.'

He kept walking until they arrived at a ten-meter-high statue. 'My favorite place to transact business: at Lenin's feet. In the old days, the communists used to rally here.' His meaty shoulders lifted and fell. 'What better place, eh? Now Lenin watches over me like a bastard patron saint who, I trust, has been banished to the lowest fiery pit of hell.'

His eyes squinted again. He smelled the way a baby smells, of curdled milk and sugar. He had a beetling brow below a halo of brown hair that curled every which way like a wad of used steel wool.

'So it's brown eggs you desire.'

'A large amount,' Bourne said. 'Also, a constant supply.'

'That so?' Yevgeny parked a buttock on the limestone plinth of the Lenin statue, shook out a black Turkish cigarette. He lit it in a slow, almost religious ritual, drawing a goodly amount of smoke into his lungs. Then he held it there like a hippie enjoying a doobie of Acapulco Gold. 'How do I know you're not Interpol?' he said in the soft hiss of an exhale. 'Or an undercover operative of SBU?' He meant the Security Service of Ukraine.

'Because I'm telling you I'm not.'

Yevgeny laughed. 'You know the ironic thing about this city? It's smack up against the Black Sea but has always been short of drinking water. That in itself wouldn't be of much interest, except it's how Odessa got its name. They spoke French in Catherine's imperial court, see, and some wag suggested she name the city Odessa, because that's what it sounds like when you say *assez d'eau* backward. 'Enough water,' see? It's a fucking joke the French played on us.'

'If we're through with the history lesson,' Bourne said, 'I'd like to meet Lemontov.'

Yevgeny squinted up at him through the acrid smoke. 'Who?'

'Edor Vladovich Lemontov. He owns the trade here.'

Yevgeny started, rose from the plinth, his eyes looking past Bourne. He led them around the plinth.

Without turning his head, Bourne could see in the periphery of his vision a man walking a large Doberman pinscher. The dog's long, narrow face swung around, its yellow eyes staring at Yevgeny as if sensing his fear.

When they reached the other side of the statue of Lenin, Yevgeny said, 'Now, where were we?'

'Lemontov,' Bourne says. 'Your boss.'

'Are you telling me he is?'

'If you work for someone else, tell me now,' Bourne said shortly. 'It's Lemontov I want to do business with.'

Bourne sensed another man stealing up behind him but didn't move, giving Yevgeny Feyodovich no sign that he knew until the frigid muzzle of the gun pressed the flesh just behind his right ear.

'Meet Bogdan Illiyanovich.' Stepping forward, Yevgeny Feyodovich unbuttoned Bourne's overcoat. 'Now we'll get at the truth, *tovarich*.' With minimum effort, his fingers lifted the wallet and passport from the inside pocket.

Stepping back, Yevgeny opened the passport first. 'Moldavian, are you? Ilias Voda.' He stared hard at the photo. 'Yes, that's you, all right.' He flipped a page. 'Came here straight from Bucharest.'

'The people I represent are Romanian,' Bourne said.

Bourne watched Yevgeny Feyodovich paw through the wallet, sifting through three different kinds of identification, including a driver's license and an import-export license. That last was a nice touch, Bourne thought. He'd have to thank Deron when he got back.

At length, Yevgeny handed back the wallet and the passport. Keeping his eye on Bourne, he took out a cell phone, punched in a local number.

'New business,' he said laconically. 'Ilias Voda, representing Romanian interests, he says.' He put the cell phone aside for a moment, said to Bourne, 'How much?'

'Is that Lemontov?'

Yevgeny's face darkened. *'How much?'*

'A hundred kilos now.'

Yevgeny stared at him, entranced.

'Twice as much next month if everything pans out.'

Yevgeny walked a bit away, putting his back to Bourne while he spoke again into the phone. A moment later, he came back. The cell was already in his pocket.

Another flick of his head caused Bogdan Illiyanovich to remove the gun from Bourne's head, stow it away beneath the long wool coat that flapped around his ankles. He was a thick-necked man with very black hair that was pomaded across his scalp from right to left in a style vaguely reminiscent of the one Hitler had favored. His eyes were like agates, glimmering darkly at the bottom of a well.

'Tomorrow night.'

Bourne looked at him steadily. He wanted to get on with it; time was of the essence. Every day, every hour brought Fadi and his cadre closer to unleashing their nuclear weapon. But he saw in Yevgeny's face the cold expression of the hardened professional. It was no good trying to see Lemontov sooner. He was being tested to determine if he was as hardened as they were. Bourne knew that Lemontov wanted time to observe him before he allowed him an audience. Protesting that would be more than foolhardy; it would make him seem weak.

'Give me the time and place,' Bourne said.

'After dinner. Be ready. Someone will call your room. The Samarin, yes?'

The waiter who had given him Yevgeny's name, Bourne thought. 'I needn't give you my room number, then.'

'Indeed not.'

Yevgeny Feyodovich held out his hand. As Bourne gripped it, he said, '*Gospadin,* Voda, I wish you good fortune in your quest.' He did not immediately release his ferocious clamp on Bourne's hand. 'Now you are within our orbit. Now you are either friend or enemy. I beg you to remember that if you try to communicate with anyone by any means for any reason whatsoever, you are enemy. There will be no second chance.' His yellow teeth appeared as his lips drew back from them. 'For such a betrayal, you will never leave Odessa alive, you have my assurance on this.'

# 14

Martin Lindros, dossiers in hand, was on his way to the Old Man's office for a hastily called briefing when his cell buzzed. It was Anne Held.

'Good afternoon, Mr. Lindros. There's been a change of plan. Please meet the DCI down in the Tunnel.'

'Thank you, Anne.'

Lindros disconnected, punched the down button. The Tunnel was the underground parking facility where the pool of agency cars was housed and maintained, and where service people on CI-approved lists came and went under the scrutiny of armed agents wearing body armor.

He rode the elevator down to the Tunnel, where he showed his ID to one of the agents on duty. The place was in effect an enormous reinforced concrete bunker: both bomb- and fireproof. There was only one ramp that led up to the street, which could be sealed on both ends at a moment's notice. The Old Man's armored Lincoln limousine sat purring on the concrete, its rear door open. Lindros ducked as he entered, sitting beside the DCI on the plush leather seats. The door closed without his help, electronically locking itself. The driver and his shotgun nodded to him, then the privacy window slid up, sealing the passengers in the spacious rear compartment. The windows in the rear compartment were specially tinted so no one could see in, but the passengers could see out.

'You've brought both dossiers?'

'Yessir.' Lindros nodded as he handed over the folders.

'That was good work, Martin.' The Old Man scrunched up his face. 'I've been summoned by the POTUS.' *POTUS* was the preferred acronym among security people in the district for the president of the United States. 'Judging by the crises we're in – external and internal – the question is how bad this interview is going to be.'

As it turned out, the meeting was very bad indeed. For one thing, the Old Man was conducted not to the Oval Office, but to the War Room, three floors underground. For another, the president was not alone. There were six people ranged around the oval table in the center of the concrete-reinforced room. It was lit solely by the giant screens that flickered on all four walls, showing shifting scenes of military bases, jet recon missions, digital war simulations in a dizzying array.

The Old Man knew some of the players confronting him; the president introduced him to the others. From left to right, the group started with Luther LaValle, the Pentagon's intelligence czar, a big, boxy man with a creased dome of a forehead and a thin bristle of gunmetal-gray hair. On his left, the president introduced Jon Mueller, a ranking official from the Department of Homeland Security, a gimlet-eyed specimen whose utter stillness spoke to the DCI of his extreme danger. The man to his left needed no introduction: Bud Halliday, secretary of defense. Then came the president himself, a slight, dapper man with silver hair, a forthright face, and a keen mind. To his left was the national security adviser, dark-haired, round-shouldered, with the restless and overly bright eyes, the Old Man had always thought, of a large rodent. The last person on the right was a bespectacled man by the name of Gundarsson, who worked for the International Atomic Energy Agency.

'Now that we're all assembled,' the president began without the usual protocol or oratory preamble, 'let's get down to it.' His eyes came to rest on the DCI. 'We are in the midst of a crisis of unprecedented proportions. We've all been briefed on the situation, but as it's in a highly fluid state, bring us up to date, would you, Kurt?'

The Old Man nodded, opened the Dujja dossier. 'Having Deputy Director Lindros back with us has brought us added intel on Dujja's movements, as well as significantly boosting morale within the agency. We now have confirmation that Dujja was in the Simien mountain range of northwest Ethiopia, and that they were transporting uranium as well as the TSGs used to trigger a nuclear device. From analysis of the latest translations of Dujja's phone traffic, we're beginning to home in on the place where we believe they're enriching uranium.'

'Excellent,' LaValle said. 'As soon as you confirm actual coordinates, we'll order a surgical air strike that will bomb the sons-of-bitches back into the Stone Age.'

'Director,' Gundarsson said, 'how certain are we that Dujja possesses the capacity to enrich uranium? After all, it takes not only specialized know-how but also a facility stocked with, among other things, thousands of centrifuges to get the form of enriched uranium needed for even a single nuclear weapon.'

'We're not certain at all,' the director said crisply, 'but we now have eyewitness accounts from both Deputy Director Lindros and the agent who brought him back that Dujja is trafficking in both uranium and TSGs.'

'All well and good,' LaValle said, 'but we all know that yellowcake uranium is both plentiful and inexpensive. It's also a long, long way from weapons grade.'

'I agree. Trouble is, the residual signature leads us to believe Dujja is transshipping uranium dioxide powder,' the DCI said. 'Unlike yellowcake, $UO_2$ is only one simple step removed from weapons-grade uranium. It can be converted to the metal in any decent lab. As a consequence, we have to take extremely seriously anything Dujja is planning.'

'Unless it's all disinformation,' LaValle said doggedly. He was a man who often used his undeniable power to rub people the wrong way. Worse, he appeared to enjoy it.

Gundarsson cleared his throat portentously. 'I agree with the director. The idea of a terrorist network possessing uranium dioxide is terrifying. When it comes to the direct threat of a nuclear device, we cannot afford to dismiss it as disinformation.' He reached into a briefcase at his side and took out a sheaf of papers, which he distributed to everyone. 'A nuclear device, whether it's a so-called dirty bomb or not, has a certain size, specifications, and unvarying components. I have taken the liberty of drawing up a list, along with detailed drawings showing size, specs, and possible markers for detection. I would suggest getting these out to all law enforcement entities in every large city in America.'

The president nodded. 'Kurt, I want you to coordinate the distribution.'

'Right away, sir,' the DCI said.

'Just a moment, Director,' LaValle said. 'I want to go back to that other agent you mentioned. That would be Jason Bourne. He was the agent involved in the debacle of the escaped terrorist. He was the one who took your prisoner out of his cell without proper authorization, correct?'

'This is strictly an internal matter, Mr. LaValle.'

'In this room, at least, I think the need to be candid outweighs any sense of interagency rivalry,' the Pentagon intelligence czar said. 'Frankly, I question whether anything Bourne says can be believed.'

'You've run into difficulty before with him, haven't you, Director?' This from Secretary Halliday.

The DCI looked as if he was half asleep. In fact, his brain was running at full speed. He knew the moment he'd been waiting for had arrived. He was under a carefully coordinated attack. 'What of it?'

Halliday smiled thinly. 'With all due respect, Director, I'd submit that this man is an embarrassment to your agency, to the administration, to all of us. He allowed a high-level suspect to escape from CI custody and in the process endangered the lives of I don't know how many innocent citizens. I submit that he needs to be dealt with, the sooner the better.'

The DCI swiped the secretary's words away with the back of his hand. 'Can we get back to the issue at hand, Mr. President? Dujja – '

'Secretary Halliday is right,' LaValle persisted. 'We are at war with Dujja. We cannot afford to lose control of one of their assets. That being the case, kindly tell us what steps your agency is taking against Jason Bourne.'

'Mr. LaValle's point is well taken, Director,' Secretary Halliday said in his oiliest Texan imitation of Lyndon Johnson. 'That very public screwup on the Arlington Memorial Bridge gave us all a black eye and our enemy a moral lift just when we can least afford it. Following the collateral death of one of your own – ' He snapped his fingers. 'What was his name?'

'Timothy Hytner,' the DCI supplied.

'That's right. Hytner,' the secretary continued as if confirming the DCI's response. 'With all due respect, Director, if I were you, I'd be far more concerned with internal security than you seem to be.'

This was what the DCI had been waiting for. He opened the thinner of the two dossiers that Martin Lindros had turned over to him in the Tunnel. 'In point of fact, we have just concluded our internal investigation into those matters you just brought up, Mr. Secretary. Here is our irrefutable conclusion.' He spun the top sheet across the tabletop, watched Halliday take cautious possession of it.

'While the Defense Secretary is reading, I'll summarize the conclusions for the rest of you.' The DCI laced his fingers, bent forward like a professor addressing his students. 'We discovered that we had a mole inside CI. His name? Timothy Hytner. It was Hytner who caught Soraya Moore's call informing him that the prisoner was being taken out of his cell. It was Timothy Hytner who called the prisoner's cohorts to effect his escape. Unfortunately for him, a shot meant for Ms. Moore struck him instead, killing him.'

The DCI looked from face to face around the War Room. 'As I said, our internal security is under control. Now we can direct our full attention to where it belongs: stopping Dujja in its tracks and bringing its members to justice.'

His gaze fell upon Secretary Halliday last, lingered there significantly. Here was the origin of the attack, he was certain of it. He'd been warned that Halliday and LaValle wanted to move into the sphere traditionally controlled by CI, which was why he'd concocted the rumors about himself. Over the last six months, during meetings up on Capitol Hill, lunches and dinner with both colleagues and rivals, he'd put in some strenuous acting time, pretending bouts of vagueness, depression, momentary disorientation. His aim was to give the impression that his advanced age was taking its toll on him; that he wasn't the man he'd once been. That he was, at long last, vulnerable to political attack.

In response, as he had hoped, the cabal had come out of the shadows at last. One thing concerned him, however: Why hadn't the president intervened to stop the attack against him? Had he done too good a job? Had the cabal convinced the president that he was on the verge of becoming incompetent to continue as DCI?

The call came at precisely twelve minutes after midnight. Bourne picked up the phone and heard a male voice give him a street corner three blocks from the hotel. He'd had hours to prepare. He grabbed his overcoat and went out the door.

The night was mild, with very little breeze. Now and again, a wisp of cloud scudded across the three-quarter moon. The moon was quite beautiful: very white, very clear, as if seen through a telescope.

He stood at the corner, arms hanging loosely at his side. In the day and a half since his meeting with Yevgeny, he'd done nothing but sightsee. He'd walked endlessly, the activity allowing him the opportunity to check on who was following him, how many there were, how long their shifts were. He'd memorized their faces, could have picked them out of a crowd of a hundred or a thousand, if need be. He'd also had ample time to observe their methodology, as well as their habits. He could imitate any of them. With a different face, he could have been one of them. But that would have taken time, and time was in short supply. One thing disturbed him: There were times when he was certain his followers weren't around – they were between shifts or, as an amusement to pass the time, he'd given them the slip. During those intervals, animal instincts honed on stone and steel told him that he was being observed by someone else. One of Lemontov's bodyguards? He didn't know, since he could never catch a glimpse of him.

The throaty gurgle of a diesel engine rose from behind him. He didn't turn around. With an awful grinding of gears, a *marshrutka* – a routed minibus – pulled up in front of him. Its door opened from the inside, and he climbed in.

He found himself staring into the agate eyes of Bogdan Illiyanovich. He knew better than to ask him where they were going.

The *marshrutka* let them out at the foot of French Boulevard. They walked across the cobblestones beneath towering acacia trees, so familiar to him in memory. At the end of the cobbled street rose the terminus of a cable car that ran down to the beach. He'd been here before, he was certain of it.

Bogdan made his way toward the terminus. Bourne was about to follow him when some sixth sense caused him to turn. He noted that their driver hadn't backed away. He slouched in his seat with his cell phone to his cheek. His eyes flicked left and right, but never lit on either Bourne or Bogdan.

The cable car, like a ride in an amusement park, comprised candy-colored two-person gondolas that hung vertically from the creaking steel cable overhead. The cable was strung high above the green zone, trees and dense shrubbery through which narrow paths and steep steps zigzagged before giving out onto Otrada Beach. In the height of summer, this beach was filled with bronzed bathers and sun worshippers, but at this time of year, this time of day, with an onshore wind whipping up the damp sand, it was nearly deserted. Craning his neck over the iron railing, Bourne could see a large brindled boxer romping in the pale green moonlit foam while its master – a slim man, wide-brimmed hat on his head, hands jammed into the huge pockets of his oversize tweed coat – paced the dog along the beach. A blast of chaotic Russian pop blasted through a pair of tinny speakers, then abruptly was cut off.

'Turn around. Arms at shoulder height.'

Bourne did as Bogdan ordered. He felt the other man's big hands patting him down, searching for weapons or a wire with which to tape the transaction, trap Lemontov. Bogdan grunted, stood back. He lit a cigarette and his eyes went dead.

As they entered the cable car terminus, Bourne saw a black car pull up. Four men got out. Businessmen dressed in cheap Eastern European suits. Except these men looked uncomfortable in their outfits. They looked around, stretched and yawned, then took another look around, during which time they all fastened their gaze on Bourne. Another shock of recognition raced through Bourne. This, too, had happened before.

One of the businessmen took out a digital camera and started snapping photos of the others. Laughter ensued, along with a certain amount of manly banter.

While the businessmen joked and made like sightseers, Bourne and Bogdan waited for the candy-apple-red gondola to reach the concrete terminus. Bourne stood with his back to the fist of men.

'Bodgan Illiyanovich, we're being followed.'

'Of course we're being followed, I'm only surprised you mention it.'

'Why?'

'Do you take me for a fool?' Bogdan took out his Mauser and aimed it casually at Bourne. 'They're your men. You were warned. No second chances. Here is the gondola. Climb in, *tovarich*. When we're out over the green zone, I will kill you.'

At precisely 5:33 pm, the DCI was up in the Library, which was where Lerner found him. The Library was a large, roughly square room with double-height ceilings. It did not, however, contain any books. Not one volume. Every bit of data, history, commentary, strategy, tactic – in sum, the collected wisdom of CI directors and officers past and present – was digitized, housed on the enormous linked hard drives of a special computer server. Sixteen terminals were arrayed around the periphery of the room.

The Old Man had accessed the files on Abu Sarif Hamid ibn Ashef al-Wahhib, the mission instituted by Alex Conklin, the only one in the DCI's knowledge that Bourne had failed to execute. Hamid was owner of a multinational conglomerate refining oil, manufacturing chemicals, iron, copper, silver, steel, and the like. The company, Integrated Vertical Technologies, was based in London, where the Saudi had emigrated when he'd married for the second time, an upper-class Brit named Holly Cargill, who had borne him two sons and a daughter.

CI – specifically Conklin – had targeted Hamid ibn Ashef. In due course, Conklin had sent Bourne to terminate him. Bourne had run him down in Odessa, but there had been complications. Bourne had shot the Saudi but failed to kill him. With the vast network of operatives at Hamid ibn Ashef's disposal, he'd gone to ground; Bourne had barely made it out of Odessa alive.

Lerner cleared his throat. The Old Man turned around.

'Ah, Matthew, have a seat.'

Lerner dragged over a chair, sat. 'Dredging up old wounds, sir?'

'The Hamid ibn Ashef affair? I was trying to find out what happened to the family. Is the old man alive or dead? If he's alive, where is he? Soon after the Odessa hit cracked open, his younger son, Karim al-Jamil, took over the company. Some time after that, the elder son, Abu Ghazi Nadir al-Jamuh, vanished, possibly to take care of Hamid ibn Ashef. That would be in keeping with Saudi tribal tradition.'

'What about the daughter?' Lerner asked.

'Sarah ibn Ashef. She's the youngest of the siblings. As secular as her mother, so far as we know. For obvious reasons, she's never been on our radar.'

Lerner inched forward. 'Is there a reason you're looking at the family now?'

'It's a loose end that sticks in my craw. It's Bourne's lone failure, and in light of recent events failure is much on my mind these days.' He sat for a moment, his eyes in the middle distance, ruminating. 'I told Lindros to sever all ties with Bourne.'

'That was a wise decision, sir.'

'Was it?' The DCI regarded him darkly. 'I think I made a mistake. One I want you to rectify. Martin is working night and day mobilizing Typhon in tracking down Fadi. You have a different mission. I want you to find Bourne and terminate him.'

'Sir?'

'Don't play coy with me,' the DCI said sharply. 'I've watched you rise up the CI ladder. I know how successful you were in the field. You've done wet work. Even more important, you can get intel out of a stone.'

Lerner said nothing, which was, in its way, an acknowledgment. His silence didn't mean his mind wasn't working a mile a minute. *So this is the real reason he promoted me,* he thought. *The Old Man doesn't care about reorganizing CI. He wants my particular expertise. He wants an outsider to do the one piece of wet work he can't entrust to one of his own.*

'Let's continue then.' The Old Man held up a forefinger. 'I've had a bellyful of this insolent sonovabitch. He's had his own agenda from the moment he first came to us. Sometimes I think we work for him. Witness his taking Cevik out of the cells. He had his reasons, you can bet on it, but he'll never willingly tell us what they were. Just like we know nothing of what happened in Odessa.'

Lerner was taken aback. He was wondering whether he'd underestimated the Old Man.

'You can't mean that Bourne was never fully debriefed.'

The DCI looked aggrieved. 'Of course he was debriefed, along with everyone involved. But he claimed he could remember nothing – not a fucking thing. Martin believed him, but I never did.'

'Give me the word. I can get the truth out of him, sir.'

'Don't fool yourself, Lerner. Bourne will kill himself before he'll give up intel.'

'One thing I learned in the field, anyone can be broken.'

'Not Bourne. Trust me on this. No, I want him dead. That will have to suffice for my pound of flesh.'

'Yessir.'

'Not a word to anyone, including Martin. He's saved Bourne from the executioner more times than I can count. Not this time, dammit. He said he's severed Bourne. Now go find him.'

'I understand.' Lerner briskly rose.

The DCI lifted his head. 'And Matthew, do yourself a favor. Don't come back without the intel.'

Lerner met his gaze unflinchingly. 'And when I do?'

The Old Man recognized a challenge better than the next man. He sat back, steepled his fingers, tapped the pads together as if in deep contemplation. 'You may not get what you want,' he said. 'But you just might get what you need.'

Bourne climbed into the narrow cabin, and Bogdan followed close behind. The gondola left the terminus and swung out over the steeply dropping limestone cliff.

Bourne said: 'I assumed those men were yours.'

'Don't make me laugh.'

'I'm here alone, Bogdan Illiyanovich. I want only to make a deal with Lemontov.'

The two men's eyes locked for a moment. Between them there was a kind of animus so strong it could actually be felt as a third party. Bogdan's woolen coat stank of mildew and cigarette smoke. There were dandruff flakes on his lapels.

The cable groaned as the steel wheels above the gondola ground along. At the last moment, the four men leapt into the last two gondolas. They continued to make noise, as if they were drunk.

'You wouldn't survive a fall from this height,' Bogdan observed mildly. 'No one would.'

Bourne watched the men behind them.

The sea was restless. Tankers shambled across the harbor, but the ferries, like the gulls, were at rest. Farther out, moonlight frosted the tips of the waves.

On the beach, the boxer was scampering. As it made its way across the gray sand, it lifted its head. Its square muzzle was grizzled with foam and bits of sea kelp. It barked once and was hushed by its master, who patted its flank as they passed under a wooden pier, its greenish pilings creaking in the tide. To the left was a skeletal labyrinth of wooden beams; they held up a part of the green area that at some time in the past had been undermined by the sea. Past that was the line of darkened kiosks, bars, and restaurants that serviced the summer crowds. Down the gentle curve of the beach, perhaps a kilometer to the south, was the yacht club, where lights were burning like the glow from a small village.

The four men from the cable car had arrived on the beach.

Bogdan said, 'Something has to be done.'

The moment he said it, Bourne knew this was another test. A glance told him that the men had disappeared, just like that. But of course he knew they must still be on the beach. Perhaps they were in the wooden framework that held up part of the hillside, or in one of the refreshment kiosks.

He held out his hand. 'Give me the Mauser and I'll go after them.'

'Do you imagine that I'd trust you with a gun? Or trust you to actually shoot them?' Bogdan spat. 'If it's going to be hunting, we'll both do it.'

Bourne nodded. 'I've been here before, I know my way around. Just follow me.' They were crossing the sand, moving diagonally away from the surf. He ducked into the labyrinth, picked up a length of wood, banged it against a pole to judge its sturdiness. He looked at Bogdan to see if the other man would protest, but Bogdan only shrugged. He had the Mauser, after all.

They moved through the shadows in the labyrinth, ducking here and there so as not to hit their heads on low-bolted beams.

'How close are we to our rendezvous with Lemontov?' Bourne whispered.

Bogdan laughed silently. The suspicion hadn't left his eyes.

Bourne had a feeling it was to be on one of the boats anchored in the yacht basin. He returned his attention to peering into the shadows. Ahead of him, he knew, was the first of the kiosks – the place where he'd been before.

They crept ahead, Bourne a pace in front of Bogdan. Moonlight, reflected off the sand, stretched pale fingers into this subterranean world of four-square spars, massive trusses, and crossbeams. They were more or less parallel with the pier, very close to the kiosk now, Bourne knew.

Out of the corner of his eye, he saw a movement, furtive and indistinct. He didn't change direction, didn't turn his head, only moved his eyes. At first, he saw nothing but a jumbled crisscross of shadows. Then, out of the architectural angles, he saw an arc – a curve that could only belong to a human. One, two, three. He identified them all. The men were waiting for them, spread like a spider web in the shadows, placed perfectly.

They knew he was heading here, just as if they could read his mind. But how? Was he going mad? It was as if his memories were leading him into making choices that led to mistakes and danger.

What could he do now? He stopped, started to back up, but at once felt the muzzle of Bogdan's gun in his side, urging him forward. Was Bogdan in on this? Was the Ukrainian part of the conspiracy meant to trap him?

All at once, Bourne broke to his left, toward the beach. He twisted his torso as he ran, threw the length of wood at Bogdan's head. Bogdan dodged it easily, but it delayed his firing, allowing Bourne to dodge behind a spar an instant before a bullet from the Mauser shredded a corner of it.

Bourne feinted right, sprinted left, taking longer strides with his right leg than with his left in order to keep Bogdan from predicting his pace. Another shot, this one a bit wider of the mark.

A third shot made a ragged hole in his overcoat, which was flared out by his flight. But then he'd reached the pier's first piling and he slipped into shadow.

Bogdan Illiyanovich's breathing increased as he raced after the man calling himself Ilias Voda. His lips were pulled back, baring teeth clenched with the effort of running through sand that became increasingly boggy as he neared the pier. His shoes were coated with sand inside and out, the ends of his overcoat blistered with clumps of it.

The water was frigid. He didn't want to go any deeper, but all at once he caught a glimpse of his prey, and he pressed on. The water rose to his knees, then slapped against his thighs. The tide was coming in, slowing his progress considerably. It was becoming a struggle to –

A sudden sharp noise to his left caused him to wheel around. But the damnable water clawed at his ankle-length woolen coat, slowing him, and at the same time the incoming tide threw him off balance. He stumbled and, in that moment of being physically out of control, he realized why Voda had run this way. It was to deliberately lure him into the water, where his coat would limit his maneuverability.

He began a string of curses, but bit it off as if it were his tongue. In the moonlight, he saw three of the businessmen, guns drawn, sprinting full-tilt toward him.

As he ran on, the lead man aimed and fired.

Bourne saw the men coming before Bogdan did. He was almost upon the Ukrainian when the first shot took a chunk out of the nearest piling. Bogdan was in the process of turning toward him when he slipped. Bourne pulled him back up, swung him around so he was between Bourne and the armed men.

Another of them aimed and fired. A bullet plowed into Bogdan's left shoulder, jerking his body back and to the left. Bourne was ready – he had, in fact, braced himself in the stance of a martial artist: feet at hip width, knees slightly flexed, torso loose and, therefore, ready for the next move. His strength fountained up from his lower belly. He hauled Bogdan's body back around, keeping him as a shield. The three men were quite close now, almost in the surf, spread out in a triangle. Bourne could see them very clearly in the cool moonlight.

Another bullet struck the Ukrainian in the abdomen, almost doubling him over. Bourne brought him back up, aiming Bogdan's Mauser with his own arm, his own hand. He pulled the trigger, his forefinger over Bogdan's. The man on the right, the one closest to him, buckled and went down headfirst. A third bullet struck Bogdan in the thigh, but by that time Bourne had squeezed off another shot. The man in the middle flew backward, his arms spread wide.

Bourne dragged Bogdan to the right. Two more bullets missed the Ukrainian's head by centimeters. Then Bourne squeezed off another shot, missed. The third man came on in a wild zigzag pattern, firing as he neared, but he was in the increasingly rough surf now and his balance was off. Bourne shot him between the eyes.

In the ringing aftermath, Bourne became aware of an animal stirring, a faint wriggling as Bogdan drew a second gun strapped beneath his overcoat. He'd lost the first one somewhere in the water, which was black and full of the seaweedy plumes of his own blood. Bourne chopped down with the edge of his hand, and the gun flew from the Ukrainian's hand, vanishing into the restless sea.

He reached up and with the strength of the damned closed his hands around Bourne's neck. An incoming wave brought Bourne to his knees. Bogdan groped with his thumbs to crush the cartilage of Bourne's throat. Bourne jammed the heel of his hand into one of the bullet wounds. Bogdan's head went back as he screamed.

Bourne rose, staggering, delivered a final blow that took Bogdan off his feet, hurled him backward. The side of his head slammed against a piling, and blood spewed out of his mouth.

He looked at Bourne for a moment. A little smile curled the corners of his mouth. 'Lemontov,' he said.

There was now no other sound on the beach save for the waves running hard at the pilings. No thrum of a ship's engine, no other earthly noise, until the boxer gave a whining bark, as if in distress.

Then Bogdan began a gurgling laugh.

Bourne grabbed him. 'What's so damn funny, Bogdan Illiyanovich?'

'Lemontov.' The Ukrainian's voice was thin, insubstantial, like air being released from a balloon. His eyes were rolling up, yet still he fought to say this one last thing. 'There is no Lemontov.'

Bourne, letting the corpse sink into the water, sensed someone coming at him fast out of the shadows. He whirled to his left. The fourth man!

Too late. He felt a searing pain in his side, then a gush of warmth. His assailant began to twist the knife. He shoved the man away with both his hands and the knife the man had buried in his side released, spewing a line of blood.

'He was right, you know,' the man said. 'Lemontov is a ghost we conjured up for you to chase.'

'We?'

His assailant came forward. Moonlight, creeping between the planks of the pier, revealed a face, strangely familiar.

'You don't recognize me, Bourne.' His grin was as feral as it was venomous.

But with a shock, recalling the face Martin Lindros had sketched for him, Bourne did.

'Fadi,' he said.

# 15

'I've waited a long time for this moment,' Fadi said. He held a Makarov in one hand, a bloody snake-bladed knife in the other.

'A long time to look you in the face again.'

Bourne felt the tide sucking and drawing around his thighs. He held his left arm hard against his side in an effort to stanch the bleeding.

'A long time to exact my revenge.'

'Revenge,' Bourne echoed. There was a metallic taste in his mouth, and all at once he was possessed with a burning thirst. 'For what?'

'Don't pretend you don't know. You couldn't have forgotten – not that.'

The tide was strengthening as it came in, bringing with it larger clumps of kelp and seaweed. Without taking his eyes off Fadi's, Bourne's right hand dipped beneath the water, scooped up a fistful of the floating morass. Giving no warning at all, he threw the soaked ball directly at Fadi's head. Fadi fired blindly at almost the same instant the seaweed-kelp mass struck him in the face.

Bourne was already moving, but the tide that had been his ally against Bogdan and Fadi's men now betrayed him as a strong wave struck him obliquely. He stumbled, pain lanced through him, his left arm came away from his wound, and the blood began to flow again.

By this time, Fadi had recovered. As he held Bourne square in the Makarov's sights, he loped toward him through the waves, flicking the serpent-bladed knife with which he clearly meant to carve Bourne up.

Bourne struggled to recover, to keep moving to his right, away from Fadi's attack, but another wave struck him full in the back, pitching him directly toward the oncoming blade.

At that moment he heard a guttural animal growl close by. The brindled boxer leapt through the water, slamming its muscular body into Fadi's right side. Taken completely by surprise, Fadi went down, pitched into the water, the boxer on top of him, snapping its jaws, raking him under with its forepaws.

'Come on, come on!'

Bourne heard the whispered voice in the darkness beneath that pier. Then he felt an arm, slim but strong, come around him, urging him off to his left, a winding, shadowy path between the mossy pilings, out into the moonlight.

He gasped. 'I have to go back and – '

'Not now.' The whispered voice was firm. It came from the slender man with the wide-brimmed hat he'd seen on the beach – the boxer's master. The man gave a whistle and the dog came bounding out from under the pier, paddling through the water toward them.

And then Bourne heard the wail of sirens. Someone from the nearby yacht club must have heard the repeated sound of gunfire and called the police.

So he lumbered on, the helping arm around him, the pain throbbing hotly and agonizingly with every step he took, as if the blade were still being twisted inside him. And with every beat of his heart, he lost more blood.

When Fadi, choking and sputtering, broke the surface, the first thing he saw through reddened eyes was Abbud ibn Aziz, who was leaning over the low rail of a sailboat running without lights. The boat, heeled over slightly, had taken advantage of the onshore breeze to move in closer to land than many powerboats could without running aground.

Abbud ibn Aziz held out a strong, browned arm. His forehead was furrowed in concern. As Fadi clambered onto the deck, Abbud ibn Aziz called out. The mate, who was already at the sheets, hauled the yardarm, causing the sailboat to tack away from the shore.

Just in time. As they turned, Fadi could see what had caused Abbud ibn Aziz's concern. Three police launches had just turned the headland to the north and were speeding toward the area surrounding the pier.

'We'll make for the yacht club,' Abbud ibn Aziz said in Fadi's ear. 'By the time they're close enough to scrutinize the area, we'll be safely berthed.' He said nothing of the three men. They weren't here, clearly they weren't coming. They were dead.

'Bourne?' he asked.

'Wounded, but still alive.'

'How bad?'

Fadi lay on his back, wiping blood off his face. That damn dog had bitten him in three places, including his right biceps, which felt as if it were on fire. His eyes glowed like a wolf's in the moonlight. 'Bad enough, perhaps, that he'll end up as damaged as my father.'

'A just fate.'

The lights from the yacht club were coming up fast on the bow. 'The documents.'

Abbud ibn Aziz handed over a packet wrapped in waterproof oilskin.

Fadi took possession of the packet, turned on his side, spat into the water. 'But is it a just revenge?' His head moved from side to side as he answered his own question. 'I don't think so, no. Not yet.'

This way, this way!' the urgent voice said in Bourne's ear. 'Don't slacken now, it's not far.'

*Not far?* he thought. Every three steps he took felt like a kilometer. His breathing was labored and his legs felt like stone columns. It was becoming more and more difficult to keep them moving. Waves of exhaustion swept over him and from time to time he lost his balance, pitching forward. The first time took his companion by surprise. He was face down in the water before he was hauled back into the humid Odessa night. Thereafter, he was saved from the same watery fate.

He tried to lift his head, to see where they were, where they were headed. But keeping himself moving through the water was struggle enough. He was aware of his companion, aware of a peculiar familiarity that spread across the surface of his mind like an oil slick. Yet like an oil slick he couldn't see beneath it, couldn't decide who this person was. Someone from his past. Someone . . .

'Who are you?' he gasped.

'Come on now!' the whispered voice urged him. 'We must keep on. The police are behind us.'

All at once he became aware of lights dancing in the water. He blinked. No, not in the water, *on* the water. The wave-smeared reflections of electric lights. Somewhere in the back of his head a bell rang, and he thought, *Yacht club.*

But his curiously familiar companion turned them toward land before they got to the northern end of the network of piers, berths, and slatted walkways. With immense effort, they staggered into the surf. Once, Bourne went to his knees. Furious, he was about to hurl himself to his feet when his companion kept him in position. He felt something soft being wrapped around his torso so tight it nearly took his breath away. Around and around until he lost count. The pressure did its job. He stopped bleeding, but the moment he got to his feet and they continued up the sideline and onto the sand, a small stain appeared, spreading slowly, soaking into the material. Still, he wouldn't leave a bloody trail on dry land. Whoever his companion was, he was both clever and brave.

On the beach, he became aware of the boxer, a huge brindled male with the magnificent face of royalty. They had passed the end of the line of kiosks. At the land side of the beach, bare rock towered over them, silent, frowning. Directly in front of them he saw a waist-high wooden shed, painted dark green, closed and padlocked, where beach umbrellas were stored.

The boxer emitted a short, sharp whine, and his rear end began to twitch anxiously.

'Quickly now! Quickly!'

Half bent over, they scrambled forward. From the water rose the thrumming of powerful marine engines, and all at once the beach to their right was ablaze with the intense glare of spotlights, directed from the police launches. The beams swept the beach, coming directly toward them. In a moment, they'd be revealed.

They tumbled to the landward side of the umbrella lockbox, crouched, pressing their bodies against it. Here came the beams, swiping back and forth across the sand. For a nerve-racking moment, the lockbox was caught square in the nexus of the spotlights. Then they had moved on.

But there was shouting from the police launches, and now Bourne could see that another police unit had begun to infiltrate the yacht club. The men wore steel helmets, flak vests. They carried semiautomatic rifles.

His companion pulled urgently on him, and they ran on toward the base of the cliff. Bourne felt naked and vulnerable as they crossed the upper portion of the beach. He knew he lacked the strength to defend himself, let alone both of them.

Then a push on his back took him off his feet. Face down in the sand, his companion beside him, he saw more beams of light bobbing through the night, perpendicular to the searchlights from seaside. Several policemen at the yacht club were scanning the beach with their flashlights. The beams passed over the two prone bodies with scarcely twenty centimeters to spare. There was movement in the periphery of his vision. A contingent of policemen were jumping down from the wharves onto the sand. They were coming this way.

Acting on a silent signal from his companion, Bourne crawled painfully into the shadow of the naked cliff face where the dog crouched, waiting. Turning back, he saw that his companion had taken off his overcoat and was using its skirt behind him to cover the tracks they had made in the sand.

He stood, panting, weaving on his feet like a wrestler who'd gone one too many rounds against a superior opponent.

He saw his companion on his knees, gripping the thick iron bars of what appeared to be a sewage outlet. The shouting increased in volume. The police were moving closer.

He bent over to help and together they pulled out the grille. He saw that some-one had already removed the bolts.

His companion shoved him inside, the boxer loping excitedly at his side. He watched his companion follow. As the man ducked down, his wide-brimmed hat came off. He twisted to retrieve it and moonlight shone on the face.

Bourne sucked in a sharp breath, which caused an explosion of pain.

'You!'

For the person who'd saved him, whose manner was so familiar to him, wasn't a man at all.

It was Soraya Moore.

# 16

At 6:46 pm, Anne Held's PDA began to vibrate. This was her personal PDA, a gift from her Lover, not the one issued to her by CI. When she grabbed it, the black housing was warm from the outside of her thigh, where she had it strapped. On its screen appeared this message, like the writing of a genie: twenty minutes. his apartment.

Her heart raced, her blood sang, because the message was from a genie of sorts: her Lover. Her Lover had returned.

She told the Old Man she had an appointment with her gynecologist, which made her laugh inside. In any event, he took it in stride. HQ was like a hospital ER: They'd all been working nonstop for hours, ever since Lindros had placed them on emergency status.

She exited the building, called for a taxi, took it to within six blocks of Dupont Circle. From there, she walked. The high moonlit sky, without any clouds to speak of, brought with it a knifing wind that intensified the cold. Anne, hands jammed in her pockets, felt warm inside, despite the weather.

The apartment was on 20th Street, in a historic four-story nineteenth-century house in the Colonial Revival style, designed by Stanford White. She was buzzed through a wood-framed beveled-glass door. Beyond was a wainscoted hallway that ran straight through the center of the building, ending in a rear glass-and-wood-framed door that looked out onto a narrow, minimally landscaped area between buildings used as a private parking lot.

She stopped at the bank of mailboxes, her fingertips running over the vertically hinged brass door with 401: MARTIN LINDROS stenciled on it.

On the fourth landing, in front of the cream-colored door, she paused, one hand on the thick wood. It seemed to her that she could feel a subtle vibration, as if the apartment, so long vacant, was humming with newfound life. Her Lover's body, warm and electric, inhabited the rooms beyond the door, flooding them with energy and a magnified heat, like sunlight through glass.

Into her mind came the moment of their last parting. It carried with it the same pain, sharp as an indrawn breath on a freezing night that shot between her ribs, inflicting another wound to her heart. And yet this time the pain had also been different, because she'd been certain not to see him for a minimum of nine months. In fact, today would make it just shy of eleven. Yet it wasn't only the matter of time – bad enough – but also the knowledge of the changes that would be effected.

Of course she had put that fear away in a cupboard in the far recesses of her mind, but now, here in front of the apartment door, she understood that it was a weight she had been carrying like an unwanted child for all these months.

She leaned forward, pressing her forehead against the painted wood, remembering their parting.

'*You look so troubled,*' he had said. '*I've told you not to worry.*'

'*How can I not?*' she'd replied. '*It's never been done before.*'

'*I've always thought of myself as something of a pioneer.*' He smiled encouragement. Then, seeing that fail, he enfolded her in his arms. '*Extreme times require extreme measures. Who better than you to understand this.*'

'*Yes, yes. Of course.*' She had shuddered. '*Still, I can't help but wonder what will happen to us on . . . the other side.*'

'*Why should anything change?*'

She had pushed away from him just enough so that she could look into his eyes. '*You know why,*' she had whispered.

'*No, I don't. I will be the same, just the same inside. You must trust me, Anne.*'

Now here she was – here they both were – on the other side. This was the moment of truth, when she would discover what changes had been wrought in him by those eleven months. She did trust him, she did. Yet the fear she'd been living with now unleashed itself, slithered in her lower belly. She was about to enter the great unknown. There was no precedent, and she was genuinely frightened that she would find him so altered, he would no longer be her Lover.

With a low growl of self-disgust, she turned the brass knob of the door and pushed it open. He'd left it unlatched for her. Walking into the entryway, she felt like a Hindu, as if her path had been set for her long ago and she lived in the grip of a destiny that outstripped her, that outstripped even him. How far she was from the privileged upbringing her parents had foisted upon her. She had her Lover to thank for that. She had come partway, it was true, but her rebelliousness had been reckless. He had tamed that, turned it into a focused beam of light. She had nothing to fear.

She was about to call out when she heard his voice, the ululating song she had come to know so well floating to her as if on a personal current of air. She found him in the master bedroom on one of Lindros's carpets because of course he could not carry one of his own.

He was on his knees, feet bare, head covered with a white skullcap, his torso bent over so that his forehead pressed against the low nap of the carpet. He was facing toward Mecca, praying.

She stood very still, as if any movement would disturb him, and let the Arabic flow over her like a gentle rain. She was fluent in the language – in a number of the many dialects, a fact that had intrigued him when they'd first met.

At length, the prayer came to an end. He rose and, seeing her, smiled with Martin Lindros's face.

'I know what you want to see first,' he said softly in Arabic, pulling his shirt over his head.

'Yes, show me all of it,' she answered in the same language.

There was the body she knew so well. Her eyes took in his abdomen, his chest. Traveling up, they met his eyes – his altered right eye with its new retina. Martin Lindros's face, complete with Lindros's right retina. It was she who had provided the photos and retinal scans that had made the transformation possible. Now she studied the face in a way she hadn't been able to at work on those two occasions when he'd passed by her on his way in and out of the Old Man's office. Then they had acknowledged each other with a brief nod, exchanging hellos, as she would have done with the real Martin Lindros.

She marveled. The face was perfect – Dr. Andursky had done a magnificent job. The transformation was everything he'd promised, and then some.

He put his hands up to his face, laughing softly as he touched the bruises, abrasions, and cuts. He was very pleased with himself. 'You see, the "rough treatment" I received from my "captors" was calculated to conceal what little remains of the scars Andursky's scalpel made.'

'Jamil,' she whispered.

His name was Karim al-Jamil ibn Hamid ibn Ashef al-Wahhib. *Karim al-Jamil* meant 'Karim the beautiful.' He allowed Anne to call him Jamil because it gave her so much pleasure. No one else would even think of such a thing, let alone dare to say it.

Without ever taking her eyes off his face, she shrugged off her coat and jacket, unbuttoned her shirt, unzipped her skirt. In the same slow, deliberate manner, she unhooked her bra, rolled down her underpants. She stood in high heels, shimmering stockings, lacy garter belt, her heart thrilling to see his eyes drinking her in.

She stepped out of the soft puddle her clothes made and walked toward him.

'I've missed you,' he said.

She came into his arms, fit her bare flesh against him, moaned low in her throat as her breasts flattened against his chest. She ran the palms of her hands along the largest of his muscles, her fingertips tracing the small hillocks and hollows she had memorized the first night they'd spent together in London. She was a long time at it. He didn't rush her, knowing she was like a blind person assuring herself that she had entered familiar territory.

'Tell me what happened. What did it feel like?'

Karim al-Jamil closed his eyes. 'For six weeks it was terribly painful. Dr. Andursky's biggest fear was infection while the grafted skin and muscles healed. No one could see me, except him and his team. They wore rubber gloves, a mask over their mouths and noses. They fed me one antibiotic after another.

'After the retinal replacement, I couldn't open my right eye for many days. A cotton ball was taped over the lowered lid, and then a patch over that. I was immobilized for a day, my movements severely limited for ten days after that. I couldn't sleep, so they had to sedate me. I lost track of time. No matter what they injected into my veins, the pain wouldn't stop. It was like a second heart, beating with mine. My face felt like it was on fire. Behind my right eye was an ice pick I couldn't remove.

'That's what happened. That's what it felt like.'

She was already climbing him, as if he were a tree. His hands came down to grasp her buttocks. He backed her against the wall, pressing her against it, her legs wrapped tightly, resting on his hipbones. Fumbling at his belt, he pushed down his pants. He was so hard it hurt. She cried out as he bit her, cried out again as his pelvis tilted, thrust upward.

*

In the kitchen, Anne, her bare skin pleasantly raised in goose bumps, poured champagne into a pair of crystal flutes. Then she dropped a strawberry into each, watching the drizzle of fizz as they bobbed. The kitchen was on the western side of the building. Its windows looked out onto a courtyard between buildings.

She handed him one of the flutes. 'I can still see your mother in the coloring of your skin.'

'Allah be praised. Without her English blood I would never have been able to pass for Martin Lindros. His great-grandfather came from a town in Cornwall not eighty kilometers from my mother's family estate.'

Anne laughed. 'Now, that's irony.' It felt as if, so long deprived of the feel of his flesh, her hands could caress him for all eternity. Putting her flute on the granite counter, she grabbed him, pushed him playfully backward until he was against the window. 'I can't believe we're both here together. I can't believe you're safe.'

Karim al-Jamil kissed her forehead. 'You had doubts about my plan.'

'You know I did. Doubts and fears. It seemed to be so . . . reckless, so difficult to pull off.'

'It's all a matter of perception. You must think of it as a clock. A clock performs a simple function, measuring off the seconds and minutes. And when the hour strikes, it lets forth a chime. Simple, yet reliable. That's because inside are a set of carefully conceived parts, honed and polished, so that when they are set in motion, they mesh perfectly.'

It was at this moment that he saw her gaze shift beyond him. A terrible light came into her eyes.

He turned, stared out the window at the parking lot between the buildings. Two late-model American cars were side by side, headed in opposite directions. The north-facing car was idling. Both drivers' windows were rolled down. It was clear two men were talking.

'What is it?'

'The two cars,' she whispered. 'That's a cop formation.'

'Or any two drivers who want to chat.'

'No, there's something – '

Anne bit off her words. One of the men was leaning out of the window enough for her to recognize him.

'That's Matthew Lerner. Dammit!' She shivered. 'I haven't had a chance to tell you, but he broke into my house, went through it, and left a noose in my closet strangling a pair of my underpants.'

Karim al-Jamil choked off a bitter laugh. 'He's got a sense of humor, I'll give him that. Does he suspect?'

'No. He would have gone to the DCI if he had even an inkling. What he wants is me out of the way. I strongly suspect it's so he can take an uncontested shot at the Old Man's job.'

Down in the parking lot, whatever had needed to be said between the two men was finished. Lerner, in the north-facing car, drove away, leaving the other man sitting behind the wheel of his vehicle. He made no move to turn on his engine. Instead, he lit a cigarette.

Karim al-Jamil said, 'In either case, he's having you followed. Our security has been compromised.' He turned away from the window. 'Get dressed. We have work to do.'

The moment the sailboat pulled into the yacht club, police jumped aboard and, as was typical of them, began to swarm. The captain and mates, including Abbud ibn Aziz, looking suitably cowed, produced their identity documents for the officious lieutenant. Then he turned to Fadi.

Without a word, without looking in the least bit intimidated, Fadi handed over the documents Abbud ibn Aziz had given him. They identified him as Major General Viktor Leonidovich Romanchenko, counterintelligence SBU. His orders, attached, were signed by Colonel General Igor P. Smeshko, chief of SBU.

It amused Fadi to see this smug police lieutenant come so smartly to attention, all the blood draining from his face. It was an instant transformation: The overlord had become the servant.

'I'm here to track down a murderer, a high-priority fugitive from justice,' Fadi said, repossessing his cunningly forged papers. 'The four men on the sideline were murdered by him, so you see for yourself how dangerous, how highly skilled he is.'

'I am Lieutenant Kove. We are at your full command, Major General.'

Fadi led the lieutenant and his men off the sailboat at a fast trot. 'A word of caution,' he said over his shoulder. 'I will personally execute anyone who kills the fugitive. Inform all your men. This criminal is mine.'

Detective Bill Overton sat in his car, smoking. He was relaxed, happier than he'd been in a year. This off-the-books job he'd taken on for Lerner had been a godsend. When it was over, Lerner had guaranteed him he'd have that position in Homeland Security he so desperately wanted. Overton knew Lerner wasn't yanking his chain. This was a man of devious power. He said what he meant and he meant what he said. All that the detective had to do was whatever Lerner ordered without asking the whys and wherefores. Easy for him; he didn't give a rat's ass what Lerner was up to. He cared only that the man was his ticket to HS.

Overton chewed on his cigarette. HS meant everything to him. What else did he have? A wife he was indifferent to, a mother with Alzheimer's, an ex-wife he hated, and a couple of kids poisoned by her into disrespecting him. If he didn't have his work, he had nothing of value.

Which, he supposed, was the way it worked best in law enforcement.

He might be smoking and musing, but he hadn't forgotten his training. He had been checking the environment every fifteen seconds like clockwork. He was positioned so that he had a clear view of the building's hallway through the reinforced glass-and-wood rear door, all the way to the front entrance. It was a beautiful setup, which he'd exploited to the max.

Now he saw Anne Held coming out of the elevator. She turned, heading down the hall toward the rear door. She was hurrying, a frown of concern on her face. He watched as she swept out of the rear door. She looked as if she'd been crying. As she neared, he noticed that her face was red and puffy looking. What had happened to her?

Not that it mattered to him. His mandate was to follow her wherever she went, at some point give her a scare – sideswiping her car, a quick mugging on an otherwise deserted street. Something she wouldn't soon forget, Lerner had told him. Cold bastard, Overton thought. He admired that.

As Anne strode past, he got out of his car, ditched his cigarette, and with hands jammed into the pockets of his overcoat followed her at a safe distance. Between the buildings, there was no one about. Just the woman and him. He couldn't possibly lose her.

Up ahead, his target had reached the end of the area between the buildings. She turned the corner onto Massachusetts Avenue NW, and Overton lengthened his stride so as not to lose her.

Just then something knocked him sideways so hard he was taken off his feet. His head slammed into the brick wall of the neighboring building. He saw stars. Even so, instinct made him reach for his service revolver. But his right wrist was struck with such a blow that the hand was rendered useless. Blood covered one side of his face. One ear was half torn off. He turned, saw a male figure looming over him. On hands and knees, he tried to reach his revolver. But a powerful kick to his ribs turned him over like a tortoise in the dust.

'What . . . what . . . ?'

It was all a blur. An instant later his assailant was pointing a gun, affixed with an air-baffled silencer.

'No.' He blinked up into the pitiless face of his killer. He was ashamed to discover he wasn't above begging. 'No, please.'

A sound filled his ears, as if his head had been submerged in water. To anyone else it was as soft as a discreet cough; to him it was loud enough to make him believe that the world had been torn apart. Then the bullet entered his brain and there was nothing but a terrible, all-encompassing silence.

The problem now,' Soraya said as she and Bourne fit the grille back into place, 'is how to get you to a doctor.'

On the beach, they could hear the shouts of the policemen. There were more of them now. Possibly the police launches had tied up at the yacht club so their personnel could join in the hunt. Powerful searchlights crisscrossed the area visible to them through the grille. In that rather poor illumination, Soraya took her first close look at the wound.

'It's deep, but seems clean enough,' she told him. 'Clearly, it hasn't punctured an organ. Otherwise you'd be flat on your back.' The question that plagued her, that she couldn't answer, was how much blood he had lost, therefore how much his stamina might be affected. On the other hand, she'd seen him go full-out for thirty-six hours with a bullet lodged in his shoulder.

'It was Fadi,' he said.

'What? He's here?'

'Fadi was the one who stabbed me. The boxer – '

'Oleksandr.' At the sound of his name, the dog's ears pricked up.

'Fadi was the one you sicced him on.'

They were alone, isolated in a hostile environment, Soraya thought. Not only was the beach crawling with Ukrainian police, but now Fadi was stalking them as well. 'What is Fadi doing here?'

'He said something about revenge. For what, I don't know. He didn't believe me when I told him I couldn't remember.'

Bourne was white-faced and sweating. But she had witnessed the depth of his inner strength, his determination not only to survive but to succeed at all costs. She gathered strength from him, leading him away from the grille. With only the fast-diminishing cone of pale moonlight to guide them, they hurried, stumbling down the tunnel.

The air was gritty. It smelled as lifeless as a snake's shed skin. All around them were little creaks and moans, as if spirits in distress were trying to make themselves heard. Packed earth filled in spots where the sandstone had been partially quarried or had split beneath the crushing weight from above. Massive six-by-six rough-hewn beams, bound with iron, black with mold, here and there sporting a dark reddish crust, rose at intervals, bolted to joists and headers. The passageways smelled of rot and decomposition, as if the earth through which they wound were in the process of slowly dying.

Soraya's stomach clenched painfully. What had the police found? What had she forgotten? Dear God, let it be nothing. Odessa was the site of her worst mistake, a nightmare that had haunted her day and night. Now fate had put her and Bourne here together again. She was bound and determined to make up for what had gone before.

Oleksandr roamed ahead of them, muzzle to the ground, as if following his nose. Bourne followed without complaint. His entire torso felt as if it had burst into flame. He had to reach back for his training, maintain slow deep breaths even when it seemed most painful. He had assumed Soraya had found an outlet of the city's sewer, but there was neither the stench nor the seepage associated with such a system. Besides, they were moving steeply downward. Then he remembered that much of Odessa had been built with blocks of the underlying sandstone, resulting in an immense network of catacombs. During World War II, partisans used the catacombs as a base when launching guerrilla raids against the invading German and Romanian armies.

Soraya had come prepared: She now switched on a strong battery-powered xenon light strapped to her wrist. Bourne was not reassured at what he saw. The catacombs were very old. Worse, they were in disrepair, in desperate need of shoring up. Here and there, the two of them were obliged to climb over a fall of rock and debris, which slowed their progress considerably.

From behind them they heard a grinding sound of metal against metal, as if an enormous rusted wheel was being forced into use. They stopped in their tracks, half turned.

'They've found the grate,' Soraya whispered. 'There was no way to replace the screws that fastened it in place. The police are in the tunnel.'

'He's a cop.' Karim al-Jamil was holding Overton's open wallet in his hand. 'A detective, no less, in the Metro Police.'

Anne had driven Overton's car to where he lay slumped against the wall of the building. The pallid brick was discolored with his blood.

'Clearly he was on Lerner's payroll,' she said. 'He might've been the one who broke into my house.' She regarded his crude, horsey face. 'I'll bet he got off on it.'

481

'The question we need to answer,' Karim al-Jamil said as he rose, 'is how many more individuals does Matthew Lerner have on his payroll?'

He gestured with his head, and Anne popped the trunk. Stooping down, Karim al-Jamil picked Overton up, grunting. 'Too many doughnuts and Big Macs.'

'Like all Americans,' Anne said, watching him dump the body into the trunk, slam down the lid. She slid out from behind the wheel, went over to the garden hose on its reel bolted to the brick. Turning on the spigot, she played the stream of water over the wall, sluicing it free of Overton's blood. She had felt no remorse at his death. On the contrary, the spilling of his blood made her feel inside her chest the beating of a second heart, filled with hatred for Western society: the waste, the selfishness of the moneyed, the privileged, the American celebristocracy so self-involved in reproducing themselves they were deaf, dumb, and blind to the world's poorest. This feeling, she supposed, had always been with her. Her mother had, after all, been first a model, then an editor for *Town & Country*. Her father had been born into money and aristocracy. No surprise that Anne had been embedded in a life filled with chauffeurs, butlers, personal assistants, private jets, skiing in Chamonix, clubbing in Ibiza, all within the boundaries set by her parents' body-guards. Someone to do everything for you that you ought to be doing for yourself. It was all so artificial, so out of touch with reality. Life as a prison she couldn't wait to flee. Her pointed rebelliousness had been her way of expressing that hatred. But it had taken Jamil to make her brain understand what her emotions had been telling her. The clothes she wore here – expensive designer fashions – were part of her cover. Inside them, her skin itched as if she were covered in fire ants. At night, she threw them off as quickly as she could, never looked at them again until she donned them in the morning.

With these thoughts boiling in her head, she got back into the car. Karim al-Jamil slid in beside her. Without hesitation, she pulled out onto Massachusetts Avenue.

'Where to?' she asked.

'You ought to go back to CI,' Karim al-Jamil said.

'So should you,' she pointed out. Then she looked him in the eye. 'Jamil, when you recruited me I was no starry-eyed idealist, wanting to wage war on inequality and injustice. That's what you thought of me at first, I know. I doubt you realized then that I had a brain that could think for itself. Now I hope you know better.'

'You have doubts.'

'Jamil, orthodox Islam works against women. Men like you are brought up believing that woman should cover their heads, their faces. That they shouldn't be educated, shouldn't think for themselves, and Allah help them if they begin to think of themselves as independent.'

'I wasn't brought up that way.'

'Thank your mother, Jamil. I mean it. It was she who saved you from believing that it was all right to stone a woman to death for imagined sins.'

'The sin of adultery is not imagined.'

'It is for men.'

He was silent, and she laughed softly. But it was a sad laugh, tinged with disap-pointments and disillusionment dredged up from the core of her. 'There is more than a continent that separates us, Jamil. Is it any wonder I'm terrified when the two of us are apart?'

Karim al-Jamil eyed her judiciously. For some reason he found it impossible to be angry with her. 'This is not the first time we've had this discussion.'

'And it won't be the last.'

'Yet you say you love me.'

'I *do* love you.'

'Despite what you see as my sins.'

'Not sins, Jamil. We all have our blind spots, even you.'

'You're dangerous,' he said, meaning it.

Anne shrugged. 'I'm not any different from your Islamic women, except I recognize the strength inside me.'

'This is precisely what makes you dangerous.'

'Only to the status quo.'

There was silence for a moment. She had pushed him farther than anyone else would dare. But that was all right. She'd never fed him bullshit like most of the others circling him to gain a measure of his influence and power. It was times like these that she wished she could crawl inside his mind, because he'd never willingly tell her what he was thinking, even by his expression or body language. He was something of an enigma, which in part was why she had been drawn to him in the first place. Men were usually so transparent. Not Jamil.

At length, she put a hand lightly over his. 'You see how much like a marriage this is? For better or for worse, we're in it together. All the way to the end.'

He contemplated her for a moment. 'Drive east by southeast. Eighth Street, Northeast, between L and West Virginia Avenue.'

Fadi would have been happy to put a bullet through Lieutenant Kove's head, but that would have led to all manner of complications he couldn't afford. Instead he contented himself with playing his part to the hilt.

This was hardly difficult; he was a born actor. His mother, recognizing his talent with a mother's unerring instinct, had enrolled him in the Royal Theatrical Academy when he was seven. By nine, he was an accomplished performer, which stood him in good stead when he became radicalized. Gathering followers – winning the hearts and minds of the poor, the downtrodden, the marginalized, the desperate – was, at bedrock, a matter of charisma. Fadi understood the essential nature of being a successful leader: It didn't matter what your philosophy was; all you needed to concern yourself with was how well you sold it. That was not to say Fadi was a cynic – no radical worth his salt could be. It simply meant he had learned the crucial lesson of market manipulation.

These thoughts brought the ghost of a smile to his full lips as he followed the bobbing police searchlights.

'These catacombs are two thousand kilometers long,' Lieutenant Kove said, trying to be helpful. 'A honeycomb all the way to the village of Nerubaiskoye, half an hour's drive from here.'

'Surely not all of the catacombs are passable.' Fadi had taken in the cracked and rotting wooden beams, walls that bulged alarmingly in places, offshoots blocked by debris falls.

'No, sir,' Lieutenant Kove said. 'They run short tours out of the museum in

Nerubaiskoye, but of those who venture down here on their own the percentage of dead and missing is exceedingly high.'

Fadi could feel the anxiety mounting in the contingent of three policemen Lieutenant Kove had chosen to accompany them. He realized that Kove continued to talk in order to damp down on his own nervousness.

Anyone else would have picked up this agitation from his companions, but Fadi was incapable of feeling fear. He approached new and perilous situations with the steely confidence of a mountain climber. The possibility of failure never entered his mind. It wasn't that he didn't value life; it wasn't only that he didn't fear death. In order to feel alive, it was necessary to drive himself to extremes.

'If the man is wounded, as you told me, he can't get far,' Lieutenant Kove said – though whether this was for Fadi's benefit or that of his jumpy men wasn't entirely clear. 'I have some expertise in this place. This close to the water, the catacombs are particularly susceptible to falls and cave-ins. We must also watch out for slurry pits. The seepage in some spots is so bad that it has undermined the integrity of the floor. These pits are particularly dangerous because they act like quicksand. A man can be pulled under in less than a minute.'

The lieutenant broke off abruptly. Everyone in their contingent was standing stock-still. The point man was half turned toward them. He made a gesture indicating that he'd heard something from up ahead. They waited, sweating.

Then it came again: a soft scraping sound as of leather against stone. A boot heel?

The lieutenant's expression had changed. It now resembled a hunting dog that had scented its prey. He nodded, and silently they moved forward.

Anne drove Detective Overton's car through increasingly destitute neighborhoods, cruising past intersections with burned-out traffic lights and lewdly defaced street signs. It was fully dark now, winter's ashy twilight having fallen by the wayside, along with neat row houses, clean streets, museums, and monuments. This was another city on another planet, but it was one with which Karim al-Jamil was all too familiar and in which he felt comfortable.

They drifted down 8th Street until Karim al-Jamil pointed out a double-width cement block building on which a faded sign was still affixed: m&n bodywork. At his direction, Anne swung onto a cracked cement apron, stopping in front of the metal doors.

He jumped out. As they walked up the apron, he took a long, lingering look around. The shadows were deep here where few streetlights remained. Illumination came in fits and starts from the headlights of cars passing on L Street NE to the north and West Virginia Avenue to the south. There were only two or three cars parked on this block, none of them near where they stood. The sidewalks were clear; the windows of the houses dark and blank.

He opened a large padlock with a key taken from beneath a small section of cracked concrete. Then he rolled up the door and signaled Anne.

She put the car in gear. When she was abreast of him, she rolled down her window.

'Last chance,' he said. 'You can walk away now.'

She said nothing, didn't budge from behind the wheel.

He searched her eyes in the firefly light of the passing cars, looking for the truth. Then he waved her into the abandoned body shop. 'Roll up your sleeves, then. Let's get to work.'

'I hear them,' Soraya whispered. 'But I can't see their lights yet. That's a good sign.'

'Fadi knows I'm wounded,' Bourne said. 'He knows I can't outrun them.'

'He doesn't know about me,' Soraya said.

'Just what do you intend?'

She rubbed Oleksandr's brindled coat, and he nuzzled her knee. They had come to a division, where the passable catacomb branched into a Y. Without hesitation, she led them into the left-hand tunnel.

'How did you find me?'

'The way I'd shadow any target.'

So it was Soraya he'd sensed following him, even when Yevgeny Feyodovich's men were off duty.

'Besides,' she went on, 'I know this city inside and out.'

'How?'

'I was chief of station here when you arrived.'

'When I . . . ?'

Instantly his mind filled with memory . . .

. . . *Marie comes to him, in a place of mature acacia trees and cobbled streets. There is a sharp mineral tang in the air, as of a restless sea. A humid breeze lifts her hair off her ears, and it streams behind her like a banner.*

*He speaks to her. 'You can get me what I want. I have faith in you.'*

*There is fear in her eyes, but also courage, and determination. 'I'll be back soon,' she says. 'I won't let you down.' . . .*

Bourne staggered under the assault of the memory. The acacia trees, the cobbled street: It was the approach to the cable car terminal. The face, the voice: It wasn't Marie he was speaking with. It was . . .

'Soraya!'

She gripped him now, fearing he'd lost so much blood that he couldn't continue.

'It was you! When I was in Odessa years ago, I was here with you!'

'I was the agent in place. You wanted nothing to do with me, but in the end you had no choice. It was my conduit who was funneling the intel you needed to get to your target.'

'I remember talking to you under the acacia trees on French Boulevard. Why was I here? What the hell happened? It's driving me crazy.'

'I'll fill in the blanks.'

He stumbled. With a strong hand, she pulled him upright.

'Why didn't you tell me we'd worked together when I first walked into the Typhon ops center?'

'I wanted to – '

'That look on your face – '

'We're almost there,' Soraya said.

'Where?'

'The place where you and I holed up before.'

They were now perhaps a thousand meters down the left-hand fork. Conditions looked particularly bad here. Cracked beams and seeping water were everywhere. The catacomb itself seemed to emit a terrible groaning sound, as if forces were threatening to pull it apart.

He saw that she had led him toward a gap in the left wall. It wasn't an offshoot at all, but a section that had been worn away by seepage, as the tide will create a cove over time. But quickly they were confronted by a debris fall that filled the space almost to the top.

He watched as Soraya climbed the mound, slithering on her belly through the space between the top of the fall and the ceiling. He followed her, each step, each reach upward bringing a fresh stabbing pain to his side. By the time he wormed through, his entire body seemed to throb with the beat of his heart.

Soraya led him on, down a dogleg to the right, where they came upon what could only be called a room, with a raised plank platform for a bed, a thin blanket. Opposite were three smaller planks nailed between two wooden pillars on which several bottles of water and tins of food were arrayed.

'From the last time,' Soraya said as she helped him onto the plank bed.

'I can't stay here,' Bourne protested.

'Yes, you can. We have no antibiotics and you need a full dose, the sooner the better. I'm going to get some from the CI doctor. I know and trust her.'

'Don't expect me to just lie here.'

'Oleksandr will stay with you.' She rubbed the boxer's shiny muzzle. 'He'll guard you with his life, won't you, my little man?' The dog seemed to understand. He came and sat by Bourne, the tiny pink tip of his tongue showing between his incisors.

'This is crazy.' Bourne swung his legs over the side of the makeshift bed. 'We'll go together.'

She watched him for a moment. 'All right. Come on.'

He pushed himself off the planks, and got to his feet. Or rather he tried to, his knees buckling as soon as he let go his grip on the plank. Soraya caught him, pushed him back onto the bed.

'Let's can that idea, okay?' She rubbed her knuckles absently between Oleksandr's triangular ears. 'I'm going back to the fork in the catacombs. I need to take the right fork to get to the doctor, but I'll do it with just enough noise that they'll follow me, assuming it's the two of us. I'll lead them away from you.'

'It's too dangerous.'

She waited a moment. 'Any other ideas?'

He shook his head.

'Okay, I won't be long, I promise. I won't leave you behind.'

'Soraya?'

She faced him in profile, her body already half turned to go.

'Why didn't you tell me?'

She hesitated for a split second. 'I figured it was better all around that you couldn't remember how badly I'd fucked up.'

He watched her leave, her words echoing in his head.

A rugged fifteen-minute march brought them to a crossroads.

'We're at a major juncture,' Lieutenant Kove said as their searchlights probed the beginnings of the Y.

Fadi didn't like hesitation. To him, indecision was a sign of weakness. 'Then we need an educated guess, Kove, as to which fork he took.' His eyes bored into the policeman's. 'You're the expert. You tell me.'

In Fadi's presence, it was nearly impossible either to disagree or to remain inactive. Kove said, 'The right fork. That's the one I'd choose if I were in his position.'

'Very well,' Fadi said.

They entered the right fork. It was then that they heard the sound again, the scrape of leather on stone, more distinct this time and repeated at regular intervals. There could be no doubt that they were hearing footfalls echoing down the shaft. They were gaining on their quarry.

With a grim determination, Kove urged his men on. 'Quickly, now! In a moment we'll overtake him.'

'One moment.'

They were brought up short by the cold voice of authority.

'Sir?'

Fadi thought for a moment. 'I need one of those searchlights. You continue on the course you laid out. I'm going to see what I can find down the left fork.'

'Sir, I hardly think that wise. As I told you – '

'I never need to be told anything twice,' Fadi said shortly. 'This criminal is devilishly clever. The sounds might be a feint, a way to throw us off their scent. In all probability, with the man having lost so much blood, you'll overtake him in the right fork. But I can't leave this other possibility unexplored.'

Without another word, he took the light one of Kove's men offered and, backtracking several paces to the juncture of the Y, headed down the left-hand fork. A moment later, his snake-bladed knife was in his hand.

# 17

Karim al-Jamil, in thick rubber apron and heavy work gloves, pulled the cord that started the chain saw. Under cover of its horrific noise, he said, 'Our objective to detonate a nuclear device in a major American city has been a decade in conception and planning.' Not that he suspected there to be a microphone in sight, but his training would not allow him to relax his strict code of security.

He approached the corpse of Detective Overton, which lay on a zinc-topped table inside the eerie hollow interior of M&N Bodywork. A trio of purplish fluorescent lights sizzled above their heads.

'But to ensure that we'd have the highest percentage for success,' Anne Held said, 'you needed Jason Bourne to be able to vouch for you when you became Martin Lindros. Of course, he'd never do that willingly, so we needed to find a way to manipulate and use him. Since I had access to Bourne's file, we were able to exploit his one weakness – his memory – as well as his many strengths, like loyalty, tenacity, and a highly intelligent, paranoid mind.'

Anne was also bound into an apron. She gripped a hammer in one gloved hand, a wide-headed chisel in the other. As Karim al-Jamil went to work on Overton's feet and legs, she placed the chisel into the crease on the inner side of the left elbow, then brought the hammer down in a quick, accurate strike onto the chisel's head. The body shop was once again alive with industry, as it had been in its happy heyday.

'But what was the trigger mechanism that would allow you access to Bourne's weakness?' she asked.

He gave her a thin smile as he concentrated on his grisly work. 'My research on the subject of amnesiacs provided the answer: Amnesiacs react most strongly to emotionally charged situations. We needed to give Bourne a nasty shock, one that would jar his memory.'

'Is that what you did when I told you that Bourne's wife had died suddenly and unexpectedly?'

With his forearm, Karim al-Jamil wiped a thick squirt of blood off his face. 'What do we Bedouins say. Life is but Allah's will.' He nodded. 'In his grief, Bourne's sickness of memory threatened to overwhelm him. So I instructed you to present him with a cure.'

'Now I see.' She turned away momentarily from an eruption of gas. 'Naturally, it had to come from his friend Martin Lindros. I gave Lindros the name and address of Dr. Allen Sunderland.

'But in fact the phone call came to us,' Karim said. 'We set up Bourne's appointment for a Tuesday, the day of the week when Sunderland and his staff aren't there. We substituted our own Dr. Costin Veintrop, who posed as Sunderland.'

'Brilliant, my darling!' Anne's eyes were shining with her admiration.

There was a large oval tub made of galvanized steel into which the body parts were dropped, one by one, like the beginnings of an experiment in Dr. Frankenstein's laboratory. Karim al-Jamil kept one eye on Anne, but she neither flinched nor blanched at what she was doing. She was going about her business in a matter-of-fact manner that both pleased and surprised him. One thing she was right about: He had underestimated her right down the line. The fact was, he was unprepared for a woman who exhibited the attributes of a man. He had been used to his sister, meek and subservient. Sarah had been a good girl, a credit to the family; in her slim form, all their honor had resided. She had not deserved to die young. Now revenge was the only way to win back the family honor that had been buried with her.

In the culture of his father, women were excluded from anything a man had to do. Of course, Karim al-Jamil's mother was an exception. But she hadn't converted to Islam. Mysteriously to Karim al-Jamil, his father had neither cared nor forced her to convert. He seemed to take great pleasure in his secular wife, though she had made for him a great many enemies among the imams and the faithful. Even more mysteriously to Karim al-Jamil, he didn't care about that, either. His mother mourned for their lost daughter, and he, the crippled old man, engulfed every day by her grief, was forced to mourn, too.

'What exactly did Veintrop do to Bourne?' Anne asked.

Happily bisecting a knee joint, Karim replied, 'Veintrop is an unheralded genius in memory loss. It was he whom I consulted regarding Bourne's amnesiac state. He used an injection of certain chemically engineered proteins he designed to stimulate synapses in parts of Bourne's brain, subtly altering their makeup and function. The stimulation acts as a trauma, which Veintrop's research revealed can alter memories. Veintrop's protein injection is able to affect *specific* synapses, thus creating *new* memories. Each individual memory is designed to be triggered in Bourne's head by certain outside stimuli.'

'I'd call that brainwashing,' Anne said.

Karim nodded. 'In a sense, yes. But in a whole new sphere that doesn't involve physical coercion, weeks of sensory deprivation, and articulated torture.'

The oval basin was almost full. Karim signaled to Anne. Together they laid their tools on Overton's chest – which, other than his head, was about all that was left whole.

'Give me an example,' she said.

Together they hoisted the basin by its oversize handles and moved it over to a large dry well that in earlier times had been used to illegally dump used motor oil.

'The sight of Hiram Cevik triggered an "added" memory in Bourne – the tactic of showing a prisoner the freedom he'd lost as a means of getting him to talk. Otherwise he would never have taken Fadi out of the cells for any reason whatsoever. His action accomplished two things at once: It allowed Fadi to escape, and it put Bourne under suspicion by his own organization.'

They tipped the basin. Out tumbled the contents, vanishing down the dry well.

'But I didn't feel that a single added memory was enough to slow Bourne down,'

Karim said, 'so I had Veintrop add an element of physical discomfort – a debilitating headache whenever an added memory is triggered.'

As they were carrying the receptacle back to the table, Anne said, 'This much is clear. But wasn't it unconscionably dangerous for Fadi to allow himself to be captured in Cape Town?'

'Everything I design and do is by default dangerous,' said Karim al-Jamil. 'We're in a war for the hearts, minds, and future of our people. There's no action too perilous for us. As for Fadi, first of all he was posing as the arms dealer Hiram Cevik. Second of all, he knew that we had arranged for Bourne to unwittingly rescue him.'

'And what if Dr. Veintrop's procedure hadn't worked, or hadn't worked properly?'

'Well, then, we always had you, my darling. I would have provided you with instructions that would have extracted my brother.'

He switched on the chain saw, made short shrift of the remains. Into the dry well they went. 'Fortunately, we never had to implement that part of the plan.'

'We assumed Soraya Moore would call the DCI to clear Bourne's request to release Fadi,' Anne said. 'Instead she called Tim Hytner to inform him that he should meet her outside on the grounds. She told him exactly where Fadi would be. Since I was monitoring all her calls, you were able to set the rest of the escape plan in motion.'

Karim picked up a can of gasoline, unscrewed the cap, poured a third of the contents into the dry well. 'Allah even provided us with the perfect scapegoat: Hytner.'

Pulling off the car's gas cap, he splashed most of what was left in the can into the car's interior. No forensics team was going to get anything out of what would be left. Pointing to the rear entrance, he backed away from the car, pouring a trail from the can as he went.

They both bellied up to the oversize soapstone sink, stripped off their gloves, and washed the blood off their arms and cheeks. Then they untied their aprons and dropped them onto the floor.

When they were at the door, Anne said, 'There's still Lerner to consider.'

Karim al-Jamil nodded. 'You'll have to watch your back until I decide how to handle him. We can't deal with him the way we did Overton.'

He lit a match and dropped it at his feet. With a whoosh, blue flame sprang up, rushed headlong toward the car.

Anne opened the door, and they walked out into ghetto darkness.

Way before M&N Bodywork burst into flames, Tyrone had the man and woman in his sights. He'd been crouched on a stone wall, deep in the shadows of an old oak that spread its gnarled branches in a domed Medusa's nest. He had on black sweats, and his hoodie was up over the back of his head. He'd been hanging, waiting for DJ Tank to bring a pair of gloves because, damn, it was cold.

He'd been blowing on his hands when the car had drawn up in front of the ruins of M&N Bodywork. For months, he'd had his eye on the place: He was hoping it had been abandoned, and he coveted it as a base for his crew. But six weeks ago, he'd been told of some activity there, late at night when any legitimate business was shut down, and he'd taken DJ Tank over for a look-see.

Sure enough, people were inside. Two bearded men. Even more interestingly, there was another bearded man posted outside. When he'd turned, Tyrone had clearly seen the glint of a gun at the man's waist. He knew who wore beards like that: either Orthodox Jews or Arab extremists.

When he and DJ Tank had sneaked around to the side and peered in through a grimy window, the men were outfitting the place with canisters, tools, and some kind of machinery. Though the electricity had been restored, clearly no renovations were being contemplated, and when the men left, they'd locked the front door with an immense padlock that Tyrone's expert eye knew was unbreakable.

On the other hand, there was the back door, hidden in a narrow back alley, which hardly anyone knew about. Tyrone did, though. There wasn't hardly anything in his turf he didn't know about or could get info on at a moment's notice.

After the men had left, Tyrone had picked the lock on the back door, and they went in. What did he find? A mess of power tools, which told him nothing about the men and their intentions. But the canisters, now they were another story entirely. He inspected them one by one: trinitrotoluene, penthrite, carbon disulfide, octogen. He knew what TNT was, of course, but he'd never heard of the others. He'd called Deron, who'd told him. Except for carbon disulfide, they were all high-level explosives. Penthrite, also known as PETN, was used as the core in detonator fuses. Octogen, also known as HMX, was a polymer-bonded explosive, a solid like C-4. Unlike TNT, it wasn't sensitive to motion or vibration.

From that night on the incident had sat in his mind like a squalling baby. Tyrone wanted to understand what that baby was saying, so he'd staked out M&N Bodywork, and tonight his vigilance was rewarded.

Lookee here: a body on the zinc-topped table in the center of the floor. And a man and a woman in aprons and work gloves were cutting the damn thing up as if it were the carcass of a steer. What some people got up to! Tyrone shook his head as he and DJ Tank peered through the smeared glass of the side window. And then he felt a small shock ping the back of his neck. He recognized the face of the corpse on the table! It was the man who had followed Miss S a couple of days ago, the one she said she'd take care of.

He watched the man and the woman at their work, but after the shock of recognition he paid no attention to what they were doing. Instead he spent his time more advantageously memorizing their faces. He had a feeling Miss S would be very interested in what these two were up to.

Then the night lit up, he felt an intense heat on his cheek, and flames gushed out of the building.

Fire – or more accurately arson – was no stranger to Tyrone, so he couldn't say he was shocked, merely saddened. He'd lost the use of M&N Bodywork for sure. But then a thought occurred to him, and he whispered something to DJ Tank.

When they'd snuck into the place the first time, the interior had been stocked with all manner of explosives and accelerants. If the chemicals had still been inside, the explosion would have taken out the entire block, him and DJ Tank with it.

Now he asked himself: If the explosives weren't inside, where the fuck were they?

Secretary of Defense E. R. 'Bud' Halliday took his meals at no fixed time of the day or night. But unless summoned by the president for a policy skull session or to take the current temperature of the Senate, unless jawboning with the vice president or the Joint Chiefs, he took his meals in his limousine. Save for certain necessary pit stops of various sorts, the limousine, like a shark, was never at rest, but continued to roll through the streets and avenues of D.C. undisturbed.

Matthew Lerner enjoyed certain privileges in the secretary's company, not the least of which was to break bread with Bud, as he was about to do this evening. In the world outside the tinted-glass windows, the hour was early for dinner. But this was the secretary's world; dinner was bang on time.

After a short prayer, they dug into their plates of Texas barbeque – massive beef ribs, a deep, glossy red; baked beans with bits of fiery chile peppers in them; and, in the lone concession to the vegetable kingdom, steak fries. All of this was washed down with bottles of Shiner Blonde, proudly brewed, as Bud would say, in Fort Worth.

Finished in jig time, the secretary wiped his hands and mouth, then grabbed another bottle of Blonde and sat back. 'So the DCI hired you to be his personal assassin.'

'Looks that way,' Lerner said.

The secretary's cheeks were flushed, gleaming with a lovely sheen of beef fat. 'Any thoughts about that?'

'I've never backed down from either a job or a dare,' Lerner said.

Bud glanced down at the sheet of paper Lerner had handed him as he'd climbed into the limo. He'd already read it, of course; he did it for effect, something at which the secretary was very good.

'It took some doing, but I found out where Bourne is. His face came up on the closed-circuit security cameras at Kennedy International.' Bud looked up, sucked a shred of charred beef from between his molars. 'This assignment's going to take you to Odessa. That's quite a far piece from CI headquarters.'

Lerner knew the secretary meant it was going to take him away from the mission Bud had sent him on in the first place. 'Not necessarily,' he said. 'I do this for the Old Man and he owes me big time. He'll know it and I'll know it. I can leverage that.'

'What about Held?'

'I've put someone I can trust on Anne Held.' Lerner mopped the last of the thick, spicy sauce with a slice of Wonder Bread. 'He's a dogged sonovabitch. You'd have to kill him to get him to let go.'

Bourne dreamed again. Only this time, he knew it was no dream. He was reliving a shard of memory, another piece of the puzzle clicking into place: *In a filthy Odessa alleyway, Soraya is kneeling over him. He hears the bitter regret in her voice. 'That bastard Tariq ibn Said had me fooled from the outset,' she says. 'He was Hamid ibn Ashef's son, Nadir al-Jamuh. He gave me the information that led us into this trap. Jason, I fucked up.'*

*Bourne sits up. Hamid ibn Ashef. He had to find his target, shoot him dead. Orders from Conklin. 'Do you know where Hamid ibn Ashef is now?'*

*'Yes, and this time the intel's straight,' Soraya says. 'He's at Otrada Beach.'*

Oleksandr stirred, nudging Bourne's thigh with his blunt black muzzle. Bourne, blinking the memory from in front of his eyes, struggled to concentrate on the present. He must have fallen asleep, even though he'd meant to stay vigilant. Oleksandr had been vigilant for him.

Propped up on the planks in the tiny underground cell, he saw the ominous pearling of the darkness. The boxer's neck fur bristled. Someone was coming!

Ignoring the flood of pain, Bourne swung his legs over the side. It was too soon for Soraya to be coming back. Leaning against the wall, he levered himself to his feet, stood for a moment, feeling Oleksandr's warm, muscular form against him. He was still weak, but he'd spent his time productively, going into energizing meditation and deep breathing. His forces might be weakened by blood loss, but he was still able to marshal them.

The change in the light was still faint, but now he could confirm that it wasn't coming from a fixed source. It was bobbing up and down, which meant that it was being held by someone coming toward him down the tunnel.

Beside him, Oleksandr, the fur at the ruff of his neck standing straight up, licked his lips in anticipation. Bourne rubbed the place between his ears, as he'd seen Soraya do. Who was she, really? he asked himself. What had she meant to him? The little reactions to him she'd had when he'd first come into the Typhon offices, seeming odd then, now made sense. She'd expected him to remember her, to remember their time here. What had they done? Why had it taken her out of the field?

The light was no longer formless. He had no more time to ponder his fractured memory. It was time to act. But as he began to move, a wave of vertigo caused him to stagger. He grasped the stone wall as his knees buckled. The light brightened and there was nothing he could do.

Fadi, moving along the left-hand branch, kept his ears open for even the smallest sound. Each time he heard something, he swung the light in its direction. All he saw were rats, red-eyed, skittering away with a flick of their tails. There was an acute sense in him of unfinished business. The thought of his father – his brilliant, robust, powerful father – reduced to a drooling shell, bound into a wheelchair, staring at a gray infinity, was like a fire in his gut. Bourne had done that, Bourne and the woman. Not so far from here, and so close to being shot to death by him. He had no illusions when it came to Jason Bourne. The man was a magician – changing his appearance, materializing as if out of nowhere, vanishing just as mysteriously. In fact, it was Bourne who had inspired his own chameleon-like changes of identity.

His life's work had changed the moment the shot Bourne had fired lodged in his father's spine. The bullet had caused instant paralysis. Worse, the trauma had brought on a stroke, robbing his father of the ability to speak, or to think coherently.

Fadi had internalized his radical philosophy. As far as his followers were concerned, nothing had changed. But inside, he knew it had. Since his father's maiming at the hands of Jason Bourne, he had his own personal agenda, which was to inflict the worst possible damage on Bourne and Soraya Moore before he killed them. A quick death for them was intolerable. He knew that, and so did his brother, Karim al-Jamil. The living death of their father had bonded them in a way nothing else could. They became one mind in two bodies, dedicated to the revenge they would wreak. And so they had applied their prodigious minds to the task.

Fadi – born Abu Ghazi Nadir al-Jamuh ibn Hamid ibn Ashef al-Wahhib – passed a hole in the passageway on his left. Up ahead, his light picked out passageways left and right. He went several meters down each of them without finding a sign of anyone.

Deciding he'd been wrong after all, he turned back, heading toward the fork. He was hurrying now to catch up with Lieutenant Kove and his men. He desperately needed to be in on the kill. There was always the chance that in the heat of battle, his express orders to keep Bourne alive would be forgotten.

He'd just passed the hole in the passageway when he paused. Turning, he probed the darkness with his light. He saw nothing out of the ordinary, but he ventured in anyway. Quite soon, he came to the debris fall. He saw the bulging walls, the substantial cracks in the stone, the groaning wooden beams. The place was a mess, undoubtedly unsafe.

Playing the beam of light over the debris, he saw that there was a small gap between the top of it and the ceiling of the chamber. He was just contemplating whether it was wide enough for a man to slither through when he heard the gunfire echoing through the catacombs.

*They've found him!* he thought. Turning on his heel, he emerged into the main passageway, heading for the fork at a dead run.

# 18

Soraya, flying down the passageway, felt stone fragments from the ricochets whiz by her. One struck her shoulder, almost made her cry out. She pulled it out of her on the run, dropped it for her pursuers to find. She was determined to protect Bourne, to atone for the dreadful mistake in judgment she'd made the last time they'd been in Odessa.

She had switched off her light and was traveling by memory alone, which was far from the ideal way to make her way through these catacombs. Still, she knew she had no choice. She had been counting her strides. By her calculations, rough though they might be, she was five kilometers from the fork. Another two klicks to the access nearest Dr. Pavlyna's house.

But first she'd have to negotiate three turns, another branching. She heard something. An instant later the catacombs behind her were briefly, though dimly, lit. Someone had picked up her trail! Taking advantage of the light to orient herself, she dashed into a tunnel on her right. Blackness, the sounds of pursuit for the moment muted.

Then the toe of her right shoe struck something. She stumbled, pitched forward onto hands and knees. She could feel the ground rise irregularly just in front of her, and her heart clenched. It could only mean a new debris fall. But how extensive was it? She'd have to risk turning on her light, if only for a second or two.

This she did, clambering up and over the new fall, continuing on. She heard no more sounds of pursuit. It was entirely possible that she'd eluded the police, but she couldn't count on it.

She kept going, pushing herself. Around the second turn to the left she went, then the third. Approximately a kilometer ahead, she knew, was the second branching. After that, she was home free.

Fadi discovered that the police had not only caught sight of Bourne but fired at him. Without asking Kove's permission, he struck the offending officer a terrible blow that nearly cracked his skull. Kove stood red-faced, biting his lip. He said nothing, even when Fadi ordered them on. Several hundred meters farther, Fadi spotted a stone shard, shiny with blood in the floodlights. He picked it up, closed his fist around it, and was heartened.

But now, this far into the catacombs, he knew that following in a pack made no sense. He turned to Kove and said, 'The longer he stays in the catacombs, the greater his chance of eluding us. Split up the men, let them fan out singly as they would in a forest in enemy territory.'

He could see that Kove's men were rapidly losing their nerve – and that their anxiety was spreading to their commander. He had to get them moving now or it would happen not at all.

He drew close to Kove, whispering in the lieutenant's ear: 'We're losing the race against time. Give the order now, or I will.'

Kove jerked as if coming in contact with a live wire. He retreated a pace, licked his lips. For a moment, he seemed mesmerized by Fadi. Then, with a minute shiver, he turned to his men and delivered the order for them to fan out, one man to a passageway or arm.

Soraya sensed the branching up ahead. A wisp of fresh air brushed her cheek like a lover's caress: the access point. Darkness behind her. It was very damp. She could smell the rot as the underground water worked on the earth and wood, decomposing it bit by bit. She risked another flicker of light. She ignored the weeping walls, because she saw the Y juncture less than twenty meters directly ahead. Here she needed to take the left branch.

At that moment a splinter of light probed the passage behind her. At once she extinguished her light. Her pulse throbbed in her temples; her heart raced. Had her pursuer seen the light up ahead and realized she was here? Though she needed to continue, she nevertheless could not allow Dr. Pavlyna to be compromised. The doctor was CI, under deep cover.

She stood still, turned so that she could see the way she had come. The light was gone. No, there it was again, a tiny beacon in the pitch blackness, less diffuse now. Someone was, indeed, coming down this part of the catacombs.

Slowly, she began to back up, edging away from her pursuer, moving cautiously toward the Y juncture, never taking her eyes from the bobbing stab of light. She kept moving, trying to decide what to do. Then it was too late.

Her back foot broke the soft surface of the catacomb floor. She tried to shift her weight forward, but the suck of the disintegrated floor pulled her backward, and down. She flung out her arms for balance, but it wasn't enough. She had already sunk into the ooze to the level of her thighs. She began to struggle.

A sharp brightening brought the passageway into sudden focus. A black blob resolved itself into a familiar shape: a Ukrainian policeman, massive-looking in the confined space.

He saw her, his eyes widened, and he drew his gun.

At precisely 10:45 pm Karim al-Jamil's computer terminal chimed softly, reminding him that the second of his twice-daily briefings with the DCI was fifteen minutes away. This concerned him less than the mysterious disappearance of Matthew Lerner. He'd asked the Old Man, but the bastard had only said that Lerner was 'on assignment.' That could mean anything. Like all the best schemers, Karim al-Jamil hated loose ends, which was precisely what Matthew Lerner had become. Even Anne didn't know where the man was, an oddity in itself. Normally, she would have booked Lerner's itinerary personally. The DCI was up to something. Karim al-Jamil could not discount the possibility that Lerner's sudden disappearance had something to do with Anne. He'd have to find out, as quickly as possible. That meant dealing directly with the DCI.

The monitor chimed again: time to go. He scooped up the translations of the latest Dujja chatter the Typhon team had compiled, picking up a couple more as he stepped out of his office. He read them on his way up to the DCI's suite.

Anne was waiting for him, sitting behind her desk in her usual formal pose. Her eyes lit up for a tenth of a second when he appeared. Then she said, 'He's ready for you.'

Karim al-Jamil nodded, strode past her. She buzzed him into the enormous office. The DCI was on the phone, but he waved Karim al-Jamil in.

'That's right. All stations to remain on highest alert.'

It seemed clear he was talking to the chief of Operations Directorate.

'The director of the IAEA was briefed yesterday morning,' the DCI continued, after listening for a moment to the voice on the other end. 'Their personnel have been mobilized and are temporarily under our aegis. Yes. The chief problem now is keeping Homeland Security from screwing up the works. No, as of now we're maintaining a strict news blackout on all of this. The last thing we need is the media instigating a panic among the civilian population.' He nodded. 'All right. Keep me informed, night or day.'

He put down the receiver, motioned for Karim al-Jamil to take a seat. 'What d'you have for me?'

'A break, finally.' Karim al-Jamil handed over one of the sheets he'd been given on exiting his office. 'There's unusual activity with Dujja's signature coming out of Yemen.'

The DCI nodded as he studied the intel. 'Specifically Shabwah, in the south, I see.'

'Shabwah is mountainous, sparsely populated,' Karim al-Jamil said. 'Perfect for building an underground nuclear facility.'

'I agree,' the Old Man said. 'Let's get Skorpion units there ASAP. But this time I want ground assist.' He grabbed the phone. 'There are two battalions of Marine Rangers stationed in Djibouti. I'll get them to send in a full company to coordinate with our personnel.' His eyes were alight. 'Good work, Martin. Your people may have provided us with the means to nip this nightmare in the bud.'

'Thank you, sir.'

Karim al-Jamil smiled. The Old Man would have been right, had the intel not been disinformation his people at Dujja had put out into the airwaves. Though the wilds of Shabwah did indeed make an excellent hiding place – one that he and his brother had once considered – the actual location of Dujja's underground nuclear facility was, in fact, nowhere near South Yemen.

Soraya was lucky in one sense, though at first blush it failed to impress her: Veins of metal in the walls of the catacombs made it impossible for the policeman to contact the rest of his contingent. He was on his own.

Regaining her composure, she ceased to move. Her struggling had only served to work her body deeper into the slurry pit in the catacombs' floor. She was up to her crotch in muck, and the Ukrainian policeman was strutting toward her.

It was only when he neared her that she realized just how frightened he was. Maybe he'd lost a brother or a daughter to the catacombs, who knew? In any event, it was clear that he was all too aware of the multiple dangers that lurked in every corner of the tunnels. He saw her now where he'd been imagining himself ever since he'd been ordered inside.

'For the love of God, please help me!'

The policeman, as he approached the edge of the pit, played the beam of light over her. She had one arm in front of her, the other behind her back.

'Who are you? What are you doing here?'

'I'm a tourist. I got lost down here.' She began to cry. 'I'm afraid. I'm afraid I'll drown.'

'A tourist, no. I've been told who you are.' He shook his head. 'For you and your friend, it's too late. You're both in too deep.' He drew his gun, leveled it at her. 'Anyway, you're both going to die tonight.'

'Don't be so sure,' Soraya said, shooting him through the heart with the ASP pistol.

The policeman's eyes opened wide, and he fell backward as if he were a cardboard target on a firing range. He dropped the light, which rang onto the floor and immediately went out.

'Shit,' she said under her breath.

She stowed the ASP back in its shoulder holster. She'd drawn it the moment she'd regained her equilibrium, had been holding it behind her back as the policeman approached. Now her first order of business was to reach his feet. She lowered her upper torso into the muck, trying to splay herself out horizontally. This maneuver also had the effect of moving her closer to her objective.

*Float*, she thought. *Float, dammit!*

She let her legs go slack, using the strength in her upper body only to inch forward, arms stretched out in front of her to their farthest extent. She could feel the muck sucking at her, reluctant to release her legs and hips. She fought down another wave of panic, set her mind firmly on moving one inch at a time. In the darkness, it was more difficult. Once or twice she thought she was already under, already dead.

Then her fingers encountered rubber: boot soles! Squirming another centimeter or two brought her enough purchase to grasp the policeman's boots. She took a deep breath, hauled with all her might. She didn't move, but he did. His feet and legs angled down into the pit. That was it, though; his huge body wouldn't budge another millimeter.

It was all she needed. Using his corpse as a makeshift ramp, she slowly but surely pulled herself hand over hand up his legs until she could grasp his wide belt with both her palms. In this way, she slowly pulled herself the rest of the way out of the slurry pit.

For a moment, she lay atop him, feeling the thunder of her heart, hearing the breath sigh in and out of her lungs. At length, she rolled away, onto the damp floor of the catacombs, and regained her feet.

As she feared, his light was beyond repair. Wiping off her own, she prayed that it still worked. A feeble beam flickered on, off, on again. Now that she had more leverage, she was able to roll the policeman into the pit. She scuffed at the floor, kicking dirt and debris over whatever blood had leaked from him.

Knowing the light's batteries were running down, she hurried into the left-hand fork, heading toward the access point nearest Dr. Pavlyna's house.

\*

At the second refueling stop, the plane carrying Martin Lindros took on a new passenger. This individual sat down next to Lindros and said something in the Bedouin-inflected Arabic of Abbud ibn Aziz.

'But you are not Abbud ibn Aziz,' Lindros said, turning his head in the way of a blind man. He still wore the black cloth hood.

'No, indeed. I am his brother, Muta ibn Aziz.'

'Are you as good at maiming human beings as your brother is?'

'I leave such things to my brother,' Muta ibn Aziz said rather sharply.

Lindros, whose sense of hearing had been honed by his lack of sight, heard the note; he thought he could exploit the emotion behind it. 'Your hands are clean, I imagine.' He sensed the other studying him, as if he'd just stumbled upon a new species of mammal.

'My conscience is clear.'

Lindros shrugged. 'It doesn't matter to me that you're lying.'

Muta ibn Aziz struck him across the face.

Lindros tasted his own blood. He wondered dimly if his lip could swell any more than it already had. 'You have more in common with your brother than you seem to think,' he said thickly.

'My brother and I could not be more different.'

There was an awkward silence. Lindros realized that Muta had revealed something he regretted. He wondered what dispute lay between Abbud and Muta, and whether there was a way to exploit it.

'I've spent some weeks with Abbud ibn Aziz,' Lindros said. 'He has tortured me then, when that didn't work, he tried to become my friend.'

'Hah!'

'That was my response also,' Lindros said. 'All he wanted was how much I knew about the shooting of Hamid ibn Ashef.'

He could hear Muta's body shift, could feel him moving closer. When Muta spoke again, his voice was barely audible over the drone of the engines. 'Why would he want to know about *that*? Did he tell you?'

'That would have been stupid.' Lindros's internal antenna was focused now on what had just happened. The mention of the Hamid ibn Ashef incident was obviously of extreme importance to both brothers. Why? 'Abbud ibn Aziz may be many things, but stupid isn't one of them.'

'No, he's not stupid.' Muta's voice had hardened into steel. 'But a liar and a deceiver, now that is another matter.'

Karim al-Jamil bin Hamid ibn Ashef al-Wahhib, the man who for the past few days had passed for Martin Lindros, was in the process of worming his way into the CI mainframe, where every iota of sensitive data was stored. The problem was, he didn't know the access code that would unlock the digital gateway. The real Martin Lindros had failed to cough up his access code. No surprise there. He'd devised an alternative that was as elegant as it was efficient. Trying to hack into the CI mainframe was useless. People more talented than he was at geek-logic had tried and failed. The CI firewall – known as Sentinel – was notorious for its vault-like properties.

The problem was then how to get into a hackproof computer for which you lacked an access code. Karim knew that if he could shut down the CI mainframe, the CI tech people would issue everyone – including him – new access codes. The only way to do that was to introduce a computer virus into the system. Since that couldn't be done from the outside – because of Sentinel – it had to be done from the inside.

Therefore, he had needed an absolutely foolproof way to get the computer virus into the CI building. Far too dangerous for him or Anne to smuggle it in; and there were too many safeguards for it to be done another way. No. It could not even be brought into the building by a CI agent. This was the problem he and Fadi had spent months trying to solve.

Here was what they had come up with: The cipher on the button the CI agents had found on Fadi's shirt wasn't a cipher at all, which was why Tim Hytner had gotten nowhere in trying to break it. It was step-by-step instructions on how to reconstruct the virus using ordinary computer binary code – a string of root-level commands that worked in the background, totally invisible. Once reconstructed on a CI computer, the root-level commands attacked the operating system – in this case, UNIX – corrupting its basic commands. The process would create wholesale havoc, rendering the CI terminals inoperative in the space of six minutes.

There was a safeguard, too, so that even if by some fluke of luck Hytner tumbled to the fact that it wasn't a cipher, he couldn't inadvertently begin the chain of instructions – because they were reversed.

He brought up the computer file Hytner was working on, typed in the binary string in reverse, saved it to a file. Then he exited the Linux OS and went into C++ computer language. Pasting the chain of instructions into this set up the steps he needed to build the virus in C++.

Karim al-Jamil, staring at the virus, needed only to depress one key to activate it. In a tenth of a second it would insinuate itself into the operating system – not simply the main pathways, but also the byways and cross-connections. In other words, it would clog and then corrupt the data streams as they entered and exited the CI mainframe, thus bypassing Sentinel altogether. This could only be accomplished on a networked computer *inside* CI, because Sentinel would stop any extra-network attack, no matter how sophisticated, dead in its tracks.

First, however, there was one more matter that required his attention. On another screen, he brought up a personnel file and began affixing to it a string of irrefutable artifacts, including the cipher he was using to create the virus.

This done, he made hard copies of the file, put the pages in a CI dossier, locked it away. With one fingertip, he cleared the screen, brought up the program that had been patiently awaiting its birth. Exhaling a small sigh of satisfaction, he depressed the key.

The virus was activated.

# 19

Abbud ibn Aziz, alone with the waves and his darkening thoughts, was the first to see Fadi emerge from the hole where the grate had been. It had been more than three hours since he and the police contingent had gone in. Attuned to the facial expressions and body language of his leader, he knew at once that Bourne hadn't been found. This was very bad for him, because it was very bad for Fadi. Then the policemen stumbled out, gasping for breath.

Abbud ibn Aziz heard Lieutenant Kove's plaintive voice. 'I've lost a man in this operation, Major General Romanchenko.'

'I've lost far more than that, Lieutenant,' Fadi snapped. 'Your man failed to detain my objective. He was killed for his incompetence, a just punishment, I should say. Instead of whining to me, you should use this incident as a learning experience. Your men are not hard enough – not by a long shot.'

Before Kove could respond, Fadi turned on his heel and strode down the beach to the jetty at which the sailboat was tied up.

'Get under way,' he snapped as he came aboard.

He was in such a foul mood, sparks seemed to fly off him. At such times, Fadi was at his most volatile, as Abbud ibn Aziz knew better than anyone, save perhaps Karim al-Jamil. It was about Karim al-Jamil that he needed to talk to his leader now.

He waited until they had cast off, the sails trimmed. Gradually, they left the police contingent behind, plowing through the Black Sea night on their way to a dockage where Abbud ibn Aziz had a car waiting to take them to the airport. Sitting with Fadi in the bow, away from the two-man crew, he offered food and drink. For some time, they ate together with only the whooshing of the water purling in a symmetrical bow wave and the occasional hoot of a ship's horn, mournful as the cry of a lost child.

'While you were gone, I had a disturbing communication from Dr. Senarz,' Abbud ibn Aziz said. 'It is his contention that Dr. Veintrop is ready for the final series of procedures to complete the nuclear device, even though Veintrop denies this.'

'Dr. Veintrop is stalling,' Fadi said.

Abbud ibn Aziz nodded. 'That's Dr. Senarz's contention, and I'm inclined to believe him. He's the nuclear physicist, after all. Anyway, it wouldn't be the first time we had a problem with Veintrop.'

Fadi considered a moment. 'All right. Call your brother. Have him fetch Katya Veintrop and bring her to Miran Shah, where we will meet him. I think once Dr. Veintrop gets a look at what we can do to his wife, he'll become compliant again.'

Abbud ibn Aziz looked pointedly at his watch. 'The last flight took off hours ago. The next one isn't scheduled until this evening.'

Fadi sat rigid, his gaze unmoving. Once again, his consciousness had removed itself, Abbud ibn Aziz knew, back to the time when his father had been shot. His guilt over the incident was enormous. Many times, Abbud ibn Aziz had tried to counsel his leader and friend to keep his mind and energies in the present. But the incident had been complicated with the deep pain of betrayal, of murder. Fadi's mother had never forgiven him for the death of her only daughter. Abbud ibn Aziz's mother would never have placed such a terrible burden on him. But then she was Islamic; Fadi's mother was Christian, and this made all the difference. He himself had met Sarah ibn Ashef innumerable times, but he'd never given her a second thought until that night in Odessa. Fadi, on the other hand, was half English; who could fathom what he thought or felt about his sister, or why?

Abbud ibn Aziz felt the muscles of his abdomen tighten. He licked his lips and began the speech he'd been practicing.

'Fadi, this plan of Karim al-Jamil's has begun to worry me.' Fadi still said nothing; his gaze never wavered. Had he even heard Abbud ibn Aziz's words? Abbud ibn Aziz had to assume so. He continued: 'First, the secretiveness. I ask you questions, you refuse to answer. I try to check security, but I am obstructed by you and your brother. Second, there is the extreme danger of it. If we are thwarted, the entire Dujja network will be threatened, the major source of our funding exposed.'

'Why bring this up now?' Fadi had not moved, had not removed his gaze from the past. He sounded like a ghost, making Abbud ibn Aziz shudder.

'It has been in my mind from the start. But now, I have discovered the identity of the woman Karim al-Jamil is seeing.'

'His mistress,' Fadi said. 'What of it?'

'Your father took an infidel as a mistress, Fadi. She became his wife.'

Fadi's head swung around. His dark eyes were like those of a mongoose that has set its sights on a cobra. 'You go too far, Abbud ibn Aziz. You speak now of my mother.'

Abbud ibn Aziz had no choice but to shudder again. 'I speak of Islam and of Christianity. Fadi, my friend, we live with the Christian occupation of our countries, the threat to our way of life. This is the battle we have vowed to fight, and to win. It is our cultural identity, our very essence that hangs in the balance.

'Now Karim al-Jamil sleeps with an infidel, plants his seed in her, confides in her – who knows? If this were to become known among our people, they would rise up in anger, they would demand her death.'

Fadi's face darkened. 'Is this a threat I hear from your lips?'

'How could you think that? I would never say a word.'

Fadi rose, his feet planted wide against the rocking of the sailboat, and looked down at his second. 'Yet you sneak around, spying on my brother. Now you speak to me of this, you hold it over my head.'

'My friend, I seek only to protect you from the influence of the infidel. I know, though the others do not, that this plan was conceived by Karim al-Jamil. Your brother consorts with the enemy. I know, because you yourself placed me in the enemy citadel. I know how many distractions and corruptions Western culture provides. The stink of them turned my stomach. But there are others for whom that may not be so.'

'My brother?'

'It may be so, Fadi. For myself, I cannot say, since there is an impenetrable wall between him and me.'

Fadi shook his fists. 'Ah, now the truth comes out. You resent being kept in the dark, even though this is my brother's wish.' Leaning over, he landed a stinging blow to his second's face. 'I know what this is about. You want to be elevated above the others. You crave knowledge, Abbud ibn Aziz, because knowledge is power, and more power is what you're after.'

Abbud ibn Aziz, quaking inside, did not move, did not dare raise a hand to his inflamed cheek. He knew only too well that Fadi was quite capable of kicking him overboard, leaving him to drown without an ounce of remorse. Still, he had embarked on a course. If he failed to see it through, he would never forgive himself.

'Fadi, if I show you a fistful of sand, what do you see?'

'You ask me riddles now?'

'I see the world. I see the hand of Allah,' Abbud ibn Aziz hurried on. 'This is the tribal Arab in me. I was born and raised in the desert. The pure and magnificent desert. You and Karim al-Jamil were born and raised in a Western metropolis. Yes, you must know your enemy in order to defeat him, as you have rightly told me. But Fadi, answer me this: What happens when you begin to identify with the enemy? Isn't it possible that you *become* the enemy?'

Fadi rocked from side to side on the balls of his feet. He was close to erupting entirely. 'You dare imply – '

'I imply nothing, Fadi. Believe me. This is a matter of trust – of faith. If you do not trust me, if you do not have faith in me, turn me out now. I will go without another word. But we have known each other all our lives. I owe everything to you. As you strive to protect Karim al-Jamil, my wish is to protect you from all dangers, both within and without Dujja.'

'Then your obsession has made you mad.'

'That possibility exists, certainly.' Abbud ibn Aziz sat as he had before, without cowering or wincing, which would surely induce Fadi to kick him into the water. 'I say only that Karim al-Jamil's self-imposed isolation has made him a force unto himself. You cannot argue with the point. Perhaps this is solely to your advantage, as you both believe. But I submit that the relationship has a serious drawback. You feed off each other. There is no intermediary, no third party to provide balance.'

Abbud ibn Aziz risked gaining his feet, slowly and carefully. 'Now I give you a case in point. I beg you to ask yourself: Are your motives and Karim al-Jamil's motives pure? You know the answer: They are not. They have been clouded, corrupted by your obsession with revenge. I say to you that you and Karim al-Jamil must forget Jason Bourne, forget what your father has become. He was a great man, no question. But his day is gone; yours has dawned. This is the way of life. To stand in its path is pure arrogance; you risk getting plowed under.

'The future must be your focus, not the past. You must think of your people now. You are our father, our protector, our savior. Without you, we are dust in the wind, we are nothing. You are our shining star. But only if your motives are once again pure.'

For a long time, then, no sound issued from either of them. For his part, Abbud ibn Aziz felt as if an enormous weight had been lifted off his shoulders. He believed in his argument, every word of it. If this was to be the end of him, so be it. He would die knowing that he had fulfilled his duty to his leader and his friend.

Fadi, however, was no longer glaring at him, no longer aware of the sea or the lights of Odessa twinkling in the darkness. His gaze had turned inward again, his essence fleeing down into the depths, where, Abbud ibn Aziz suspected – no, hoped with all his might – not even Karim al-Jamil was allowed entry.

With all of CI's computers down, all hell had broken loose within its headquarters complex. Every available member of the Signals and Codes Directorate had been ordered to tackle the problem of the computer virus. A third of them had taken Sentinel – the CI firewall – offline in order to run a series of level-three diagnostics. The rest of the agents were using hunt-and-destroy software to stalk through every vein and artery of the CI intranet. This software, designed by DARPA for CI, used an advanced heuristic algorithm, which meant that it was a problem-solving code. It changed, continually adapting depending on which form of virus it encountered.

The premises were in full lockdown mode – no one in or out. In the soundproof oval conference room across from the Old Man's suite of offices, nine men sat around a burnished burlwood table. At each seat was a computer terminal, sunk into the tabletop, plus bottles of chilled water. The man to the DCI's immediate left, the director of the Signals and Codes Directorate, was being continually updated on the progress of his feverish legions. These updates appeared on his own terminal, were cleaned up – made intelligible to the nongeeks in the room – and bloomed on one of half a dozen flat-panel screens affixed to the matte-black felt-clad walls.

'Nothing leaks outside these walls,' the DCI said. Today he was feeling all of his sixty-eight years. 'What's happened here today remains here.' History pressed down on him with the weight of Atlas's burden. One of these days, he knew, it was going to break his back. But not today. Not today, dammit!

'Nothing has been compromised.' This from the director of S&C, scanning the raw data scrolling across his terminal. 'This virus, it appears, did not come from outside. The diagnostics on Sentinel have been completed. The firewall was doing its job, just as it was programmed to do. It was not breached. I say again, it was not breached.'

'Then what the hell happened?' the DCI barked. He was already thanking his lucky stars that the defense secretary would never know anything about this unmitigated disaster.

The S&C director lifted his shining, bald head. 'As far as we can determine at this stage, we were attacked from inside.'

'*Inside?*' Karim al-Jamil said, incredulously. He was sitting at the Old Man's right hand. 'Are you saying we have a traitor inside CI?'

'It would seem that way,' said Rob Batt, the chief of operations, most influential of the Seven – as the directors were known internally.

'Rob, I want you all over this angle ASAP,' the Old Man said. 'Confirm it, or assure us we're clean.'

'I can handle that,' Karim said, and immediately regretted it.

Rob Batt's snakelike gaze was turned in his direction. 'Don't you have enough on your plate as it is, Martin?' he said softly.

The DCI cleared his throat. 'Martin, I need you to concentrate all your resources on stopping Dujja.' The last thing he needed now, he thought sourly, was an inter-directorate turf war. He turned to the director of S&C. 'I need an ETA for the computers to be restored.'

'Could be a day or more.'

'Unacceptable,' the Old Man snapped. 'I need a solution so we'll be up and running within two hours.'

The S&C director scratched his bald dome. 'Well, we could switch to the backup net. But that would entail distributing new access codes to everyone in the build – '

'Do it!' the DCI said sharply. He slapped the table with the flat of his hand. 'All right, gentlemen. We all know what we have to do. Let's get this shit off our shoes before it starts to stink!'

Bourne, slipping in and out of consciousness, was revisited by the events from his past that had been haunting him ever since Marie's death.

*. . . He is in Odessa, running. It is night; a chill mineral wind coming in off the Black Sea skids him along the cobbled street. She is in his arms – the young woman leaking blood at a terrific rate. He sees the gunshot wound, knows she is going to die. Even as this thought comes to him, her eyes open. They are pale, the pupils dilated in pain. She is trying to see him in the darkness at the end of her life.*

*He can do nothing, nothing but carry her from the square where she was gunned down. Her mouth moves. She cannot project her voice. His ear is bloodied as he presses it to her open mouth.*

*Her voice, fragile as glass, reverberates against his eardrum, but what he hears is the sound of the sea rushing in, pulling back. Breath fails her. All that remains is the unsteady beat of his shoes against the cobbles . . .*

*He falters, falls. He crawls until his back is against a slimy brick wall. He cannot relinquish his hold on the woman. Who is she? He stares down at her, trying to concentrate. If he can bring her back to life, he can ask her who she is.* I could have saved her, *he thinks in despair.*

*And now, in a flash, it is Marie he's holding in his arms. The blood is gone, but life has not returned. Marie is dead.* I could have saved her, *he thinks in despair . . .*

He woke, crying for his lost love, for his lost life. 'I should have saved you!' And all at once he knew why the fragment of his past returned at the moment of Marie's death.

Guilt was crippling him. Guilt at not being there to save Marie. Then it must follow that he'd had a chance to save the bloody woman, and didn't.

'Martin, a word.'

Karim al-Jamil turned to see Rob Batt watching him. The director of operations had not risen like everyone else in the conference room. Now only he and Karim remained in the darkened space.

Karim regarded him with a deliberately neutral expression. 'As you said, Rob, I have a great deal on my plate.'

Batt had hands like meat cleavers. The palms were unnaturally dark, as if they had been permanently stained by blood. He spread them, normally a conciliatory gesture – but now there was something distinctly menacing in the display of raw animal power, as if he were a silverback gorilla preparing to charge.

'Indulge me. This won't take but a minute.'

Karim went back, sat down at the table across from him. Batt was one of those people for whom an office environment was almost intolerable. He wore his suit as if it had bristles on the inside. His leathery, deeply scored, sun-crisped face could have come from either skiing in Gstaad or taking lives in the Afghani mountains. Karim found all this interesting, as he had spent so much time in fine tailor shops being fitted in fine Western clothes that a Savile Row suit felt as natural to him as a burnoose.

He steepled his fingers, stitched the ghost of a smile onto his face. 'What can I do for you, Rob?'

'Frankly, I'm a little concerned.' Batt apparently did not care to beat around the bush, but perhaps conversation wasn't his forte.

Karim, his heart beating fast, kept his tone polite. 'In what way?'

'Well, you've had a helluva difficult time. To be honest, I felt strongly that you should take a few weeks off – relax, be evaluated by other doctors.'

'Shrinks, you mean.'

Batt went on as if the other hadn't responded. 'I was overruled by the DCI. He said your work was too valuable – especially in this crisis.' His lips pulled back in what in someone else might have been a smile.

'But then, just now, you wanted in on my investigation into whoever the hell it was set the virus loose on us.' Those snakelike eyes, black as volcanic soil, ran over Karim as if he were mentally frisking the DDCI. 'You've never poached on my territory before. In fact, we made a pact never to poach.'

Karim said nothing. What if the statement was a trap? What if Lindros and Batt had never made such a pact?

'I'd like to know why you've reneged,' Batt said. 'I'd like to know why, in your current state, you'd want to take on even more work.' His voice had dropped in volume and, at the same time, had slowed like cooling honey. If he were an animal, he'd be circling Karim now, waiting for a moment to his advantage.

'Apologies, Rob. I just wanted to help, that's all. There was no – '

Batt's head lunged forward so sharply that Karim had to keep himself in check, lest he recoil.

'See, I'm concerned about you, Martin.' Batt's lips, already thin, were compressed into bloodless lines. 'But unlike our peerless leader, who loves you like a son, who forgives you anything, my concern is more like that of an older brother for his younger sibling.'

Batt spread his enormous clublike hands on the table between them. 'You lived with the enemy, Martin. The enemy tried to fuck you up. I know it and you know it. You know how I know it? Do you?'

'I'm sure my test results – '

'Fuck the test results,' Batt said shortly. 'Test results are for academics, which you and I most certainly are not. Those boys are still debating the results; they'll be in that hole till hell freezes over. To boot, we've been forced to take the opinion of Jason Bourne, a man who is at best unstable, at worst a menace to CI protocol and discipline. But he's the one person who knows you best. Ironic, no?' He cocked his head. 'Why the hell do you maintain your relationship with him?'

'Take a look at his file,' Karim said. 'Bourne is more valuable to me – to *us* – than a handful of your Ways and Means agents.' *Me singing Jason Bourne's praises, now that's irony,* he thought.

Batt would not be deterred. 'See, it's your *behavior* I'm worried about, Martin. In some ways it's fine – just as it always was. But in other, smaller, more subtle ways . . .' He shook his head. 'Well, let's just say it doesn't track. God knows you were always a reclusive sonovabitch. "Too good for the rest of us," the other directorate chiefs said. Not me. I had you pegged. You're an idea tank; you have no need for the idle chitchat that passes for friendship in these hallways.'

Karim wondered whether the time had come – a possibility he had, of course, factored into his plan – when one of Lindros's colleagues would become suspicious. But he'd calculated that the probability of this was low – his time at CI was a matter of days, no more. And as Batt himself had said, Lindros had always been something of a loner. Despite the odds, here he was on the precipice of having to decide how to neutralize a directorate chief.

'If you've noticed anything erratic in my behavior, I'm quite certain it's due to the stress of the current situation. One thing I'm a master of is compartmentalizing my life. I assure you that the past isn't an issue.'

There was silence for a moment. Karim had the impression of a very dangerous beast passing him by, so close he could smell its rank musk.

Batt nodded. 'Then we're done here, Martin.' He rose, extended his hand. 'I'm glad we had this little heart-to-heart.'

As Karim walked out, he was grateful that he had planted convincing evidence as to the identity of the 'traitor.' Otherwise Batt's teeth would be sinking into the back of his neck.

'Hello, Oleksandr. Good boy.'

Soraya, a heavily laden satchel slung over one shoulder, returned with a terrible intimation of death to the hidey-hole where she had left Bourne. In the light of the oil lamp she lit, she found Bourne, not dead, but unconscious from blood loss. The boxer sat steadfastly by his side. His liquid brown eyes sought hers, as if pleading for help.

'Don't worry,' she said both to Bourne and the dog. 'I'm here now.'

She produced from the satchel the bulk of the paraphernalia she had obtained from Dr. Pavlyna: plastic bags filled with a variety of fluids. She felt Bourne's forehead to assure herself he wasn't running a fever, recited to herself the protocol Dr. Pavlyna had made her memorize.

Tearing open a plastic envelope, she took out a needle and inserted it into a vein on the back of his left hand. She attached a port and fit the end of the tube leading to the first bag of fluid into the open end of the port, beginning the drip of two wide-spectrum antibiotics. Next, she removed the blood-soaked makeshift bandage and irrigated the wound with a large amount of sterile saline solution. An antiseptic, the doctor told her, would only retard the healing process.

Bringing the lamp closer, she probed for foreign bodies – threads, bits of cloth, whatever. She found none, much to her relief. But there was some devitalized tissue at the edges that she had to snip away with surgical scissors.

Taking up the tiny curved needle by its holder, she pierced the skin, pulling the nylon suture material through. Very carefully, she drew the two sides of the wound together, using a rectangular stitch, just as Dr. Pavlyna had showed her. Gently, gently, making sure she didn't pull the skin too tightly, which would increase the risk of infection. When she was done, she tied off the last suture and cut away the rest of the nylon still attached to the needle. Lastly, she placed a sterile gauze pad over her handiwork, then wound a bandage around and around, fixing the pad in place.

By this time, the bag of antibiotics was empty. She unhooked it, replacing the tube with the one from the bag of hydrating and nourishing fluids.

Within an hour, Bourne was sleeping normally. An hour after that, he began to come around.

His eyes opened.

She smiled down at him. 'Do you know where you are?'

'You came back,' he whispered.

'I said I would, didn't I?'

'Fadi?'

'I don't know. I killed one of the policemen, but I never saw anyone else. I think they've all given up.'

His eyes closed for a moment. 'I remember, Soraya. I remember.'

She shook her head. 'Rest now, we'll talk later.'

'No.' His expression was one of grim concentration. 'We need to talk. Now.'

What had happened to him? He woke up and felt immediately different, as if his mind had been removed from a vise. It was as if he had been freed from the endless defile in which he had been existing, filled with the smoke of voices, compulsions. The pounding headaches were gone, the repeating phrases. With perfect clarity, he recalled what Dr. Sunderland had told him about how memories were formed, how abnormal brain activity brought on by trauma or extreme conditions could affect their creation and resurrection.

'For the first time, I realize how stupid I was to even contemplate taking Cevik out of the Typhon cells,' he said. 'And there have been other odd things. For instance, a blinding headache paralyzed me while Fadi was making his escape.'

'When Tim was shot.'

'Yes.' He tried to sit up, winced in pain.

Soraya moved toward him. 'No, you don't.'

He would not be deterred. 'Help me sit up.'

'Jason – '

'Just do it,' he said sharply.

She reached around him, pushing as he rose, scooting him so that his back pressed against the wall.

'These odd compulsions have led me into dangerous situations,' he continued. 'In every case, the compulsions have led to behavior that has benefited Fadi.'

'But surely that's a coincidence,' she said.

His smile was almost painful. 'Soraya, if my life has taught me anything it's that coincidence is most often a symptom of a conspiracy.'

Soraya laughed softly. 'Spoken like a true paranoid.'

'There's a case to be made that it's my paranoia that's kept me alive.' Bourne stirred. 'What if I'm on to something?'

Soraya crossed her arms over her breast. 'Like what?'

'Okay, let's start with the premise that these coincidences, as you call them, have their roots in a conspiracy. As I said, all of them have way benefited Fadi in a material way.'

'Go on.'

'The headaches began after I saw Dr. Sunderland, the memory expert Martin recommended.'

Soraya frowned. All of a sudden, there was nothing funny in what Bourne was saying. 'Why did you go see him?'

'I was being driven crazy by the memory fragments of my first visit here, to Odessa. But at the time, I didn't even know it was Odessa, let alone what I was doing there.'

'But how could that memory be part of this conspiracy you're constructing?'

'I don't know,' Bourne conceded.

'It *can't* be part of it.' Soraya realized that she was pleading a case against him.

Bourne waved a hand. 'Let's leave that aside for the moment. When I was bringing Martin home, he told me that I needed to come here – *no matter what* – to find a man named Lemontov who, he said, was Dujja's banker. His reasoning was that if I got Lemontov, Dujja's money flow would dry up.'

Soraya nodded. 'Acute thinking.'

'It would have been if Lemontov existed. He doesn't.' Bourne's expression was perfectly unreadable. 'Not only that, but Fadi *knew* about Lemontov. *He knew Lemontov was fiction!*'

'So?'

Bourne pushed off the wall, faced her squarely. 'So by what possible means could Fadi know about Lemontov?'

'You forget that Lindros was interrogated by Dujja. Maybe they fed him disinformation.'

'That would presuppose they knew he was going to be rescued.'

Soraya considered for a moment. 'This Lemontov thing interests me. Lindros told me about him as well. He's the reason I'm here. But why? Why did he send us both here?'

'To chase a ghost,' Bourne said. 'Chasing Lemontov was just a ruse. Fadi was waiting for us. He *knew* we were coming. He was prepared to kill me – in fact, if I'm any judge, he *needed* to. I could see it in his eyes, hear it in his voice. He'd been waiting a long time to catch up to me.'

Soraya looked shaken.

'One other thing,' Bourne pressed on. 'On the plane ride home, Martin said that his interrogators kept asking about a mission targeting Hamid ibn Ashef. A mission of mine. He kept asking if I'd remembered it.'

'Jason, why would Lindros want to know about a mission dreamed up by Alex Conklin?'

'You know why,' Bourne said. 'Fadi and Martin are somehow connected.'

'*What?*'

'As is Dr. Sunderland.' There was a relentless logic to his theory. 'Sunderland's treatment did something to me, something that caused me to make mistakes at crucial moments.'

'How is that possible?'

'A technique in brainwashing is to use a color, a sound, a key word or phrase to trigger a certain response in the subject at a later date.'

*Nothing to burn in the hole.* The words had bounced around in Bourne's head until he thought he'd go mad.

Bourne repeated the phrase to Soraya. 'Fadi used it. That phrase is what set off the headache. Fadi had the trigger phrase Sunderland set up in my brain.'

'I remember the look on your face when he said it,' Soraya said. 'But do you also remember that he said he'd spent time in Odessa?'

'The Odessa mission to kill Hamid ibn Ashef is the key, Soraya. Everything points back to it.' His skin was gray; he seemed abruptly weary. 'The conspiracy is in place. But what's its ultimate purpose?'

'Just as impossible to fathom is how they coerced Lindros into helping them.'

'They didn't. I know Martin better than anyone. He couldn't be coerced to turn traitor.'

She spread her hands. 'What other explanation is there?'

'What if the man I saved from Dujja, the man I brought back to CI, the man I vouched for, isn't Martin Lindros?'

'Okay, stop right there.' Her hands came up, palms outward. 'You've just crossed the line from paranoia into full-blown psychosis.'

He ignored her outburst. 'What if the man I brought back, the man who is right now running Typhon, is an impostor?'

'Jason, that's impossible. He looks like Lindros, talks like Lindros. For God's sake, he passed the retinal scanner test.'

'The retinal scanner can be fooled,' Bourne pointed out. 'It's extremely rare and difficult to do – it requires a retinal or a full eye implant. But then if this impostor went to the trouble of having his face remade, the retinal implant would have been a piece of cake.'

Soraya shook her head. 'Do you have any idea of the ramifications of what you're saying? An impostor in the center of CI, controlling more than a thousand agents worldwide. I say again it's impossible, utterly insane.'

'That's precisely why it's worked. You, me, everyone in Typhon and CI – all of us are being manipulated, misdirected. That was the plan all along. While we trot all around the globe, Fadi has been free to smuggle his people into the United States, to ship the nuclear device – in pieces, no doubt – to the location where they mean to detonate it.'

'What you're saying is monstrous.' Soraya was near shock. 'No one's going to believe you. I can't even get my head around it.'

She sank onto the edge of the planks. 'Look, you've lost a lot of blood. You're exhausted, not thinking clearly. You need to sleep and then – '

'There's one sure way to verify whether or not the Martin Lindros I brought back is real or an impostor,' Bourne continued, ignoring her. 'I need to find the real Martin Lindros. If I'm right about all this, it means he's still alive. The impostor needs him alive.' He began to slide off the bed. 'We've got to – '

A powerful wave of dizziness forced him to stop and slump back against the wall. Soraya levered him back down to a prone position. His eyelids grew heavy with fatigue.

'Whatever we decide to do, right now you must get some rest,' she said with newfound firmness. 'We're both exhausted, and you need to heal.'

A moment later, sleep overtook him. Soraya rose and settled herself on the floor next to the planks. She opened her arms; Oleksandr curled up against her breasts. She was filled with foreboding. What if Bourne was right? The consequences of such a scheme were unthinkable. And yet she found herself thinking about nothing else.

'Oh, Oleksandr,' she whispered. 'What are we to do?'

The boxer turned his muzzle up to her, licked her face.

She closed her eyes, deepened her breathing. Gradually, feeling the comforting *thump-thump* of Oleksandr's heartbeat, she gave in to the stealthy approach of sleep.

# 20

Matthew Lerner and Jon Mueller had met ten years ago by fortuitous accident in a whorehouse in Bangkok. The two men had a lot in common besides whoring, drinking, and killing. Like Lerner, Mueller was a loner, a self-taught genius at tactical operation and strategic analysis. The moment they met, they recognized something in each other that drew them, even though Lerner was CI and Mueller, at the time, NSA.

Lerner, walking through the air terminal in Odessa, moving closer to his target, had cause to think of Jon Mueller and all Mueller had taught him when his cell phone rang. It was Weller at D.C. Metro Police, where Lerner had a number of men on his payroll.

'What's up?' Lerner asked as soon as he'd recognized the desk sergeant's voice.

'I thought you'd want to know. Overton's missing.'

Lerner stood still, jostled as other arriving and departing passengers strode by him. 'What?'

'Didn't show for his shift. Not answering his cell. Hasn't been home. He's dead gone, Matt.'

Lerner, his mind churning, watched a pair of policemen pass. They stopped for a moment to talk to a comrade who was coming in the opposite direction, then moved on, their eyes alert.

Into the significant silence, Weller ventured a postscript. 'Overton was working on a case for you, wasn't he?'

'That was awhile ago,' Lerner lied. What Overton was doing for him was none of Weller's business. 'Hey, thanks for the heads-up.'

'It's what you pay me for,' Weller said before hanging up.

Lerner grabbed his small suitcase and moved to the side of the terminal passageway. Instinct told him that Overton was more than missing – he was dead. The question he asked himself now was: How had Anne Held had him killed? Because he knew as sure as he was standing in the Odessa air terminal that Held was behind Overton's death.

Perhaps he'd seriously underestimated the bitch. Clearly she hadn't been intimidated by Overton's house break-in. Just as clearly, she had decided to fight back. Too bad he was so far away. He'd relish butting heads with her. But at the moment, he had bigger fish to fillet.

He opened his cell, dialed an unlisted Washington number. He waited while the call went through the usual security switching. Then a familiar voice answered.

'Hey, Matt.'

'Hey, Jon. I've got an interesting one for you.'

Jon Mueller laughed. 'All your jobs are interesting, Matt.'

That was true. Briefly, Lerner described Anne Held, bringing Mueller up to date on the situation.

'The escalation caught you by surprise, didn't it?'

'I underestimated her,' Lerner admitted. He and Jon had no secrets from each other. 'Don't you do the same.'

'Gotcha. I'll take her out.'

'I mean it, Jon. This is one serious bitch. She's got resources I know nothing about. I never imagined she could have Overton offed. But don't make a move before you talk to the secretary. This is his game, it's his decision whether or not to roll the dice.'

Dr. Pavlyna was waiting for him just past the line of Customs and Immigration kiosks. Lerner hadn't thought about it, but with a name like that he should've realized she'd be a woman. She was now CI chief of station in Odessa. A woman. Lerner made a mental note to do something about that as soon as he got back to D.C.

Dr. Pavlyna was a rather handsome woman, tall, deep-breasted, imposing, her thick, dark hair streaked with gray, though to look at her face she couldn't be past forty.

They walked through the terminal, out into an afternoon warmer than he'd imagined. He'd never been to Odessa before. He'd been expecting Moscow weather, which he'd unhappily endured several times.

'You're in luck, Mr. Lerner,' Dr. Pavlyna said as they crossed a road on the way to the parking lot. 'I've had contact with this man Bourne you need to find. Not direct contact, mind you. It seems he's been injured. A knife wound to the side. No vital organs pierced, but a deep wound nonetheless. He's lost a lot of blood.'

'How d'you know all this if you've had no direct contact with him?'

'Fortunately, he's not alone. He's with one of us. Soraya Moore. She appeared at my door last night. Bourne was too badly hurt to accompany her, she said. I gave her antibiotics, sutures, and the like.'

'Where are they?'

'She didn't say, and I didn't ask. SOP.'

'That's a pity,' Lerner said, meaning it. He wondered what the hell Soraya was doing here. How had she known Bourne was here unless Martin Lindros had sent her? But why would he do that – Bourne notoriously worked alone . . . the assignment made no sense. Lerner would dearly have liked to call Lindros on his decision, but of course he couldn't. His own presence here was a secret, a point made clear to Dr. Pavlyna when the Old Man had called her.

They'd stopped at a new silver Skoda Octavia RS, a small but neat sports wagon. Dr. Pavlyna opened the doors, and they got in.

'The DCI himself told me to give you all the assistance I could organize.' Dr. Pavlyna drove through the lot, paid her ticket. 'There have been some newer developments. It seems Bourne is wanted by the police for the killing of four men.'

'That means he's going to have to get out of Odessa as quickly and as stealthily as possible.'

'That's certainly what I would do.' She waited for an opening in the traffic flow and pulled out.

Lerner's practiced eye took in everything around him. 'This is a relatively big city. I'm sure there are a number of ways to get out.'

'Naturally.' Dr. Pavlyna nodded. 'But very few of them will be open to him. For instance, the heightened police presence at the airport. He can't get out that way.'

'Don't be so sure. The guy's a fucking chameleon.'

Dr. Pavlyna, moved left, accelerating into the passing lane. 'You forget that he's badly wounded. Somehow the police know this. It would be too much of a risk.'

'What then?' Lerner said. 'Train, car?'

'Neither. The railway system won't get him out of Ukraine; driving would take too long and prove too hazardous – roadblocks and the like. Especially in his condition.'

'That leaves boat.'

Dr. Pavlyna nodded. 'There's a passenger ferry from Odessa to Istanbul, but it only runs once a week. He'd have to hole up for four days before the next one sails.' She considered for a moment as she put on more speed. 'Odessa's lifeblood is commerce. Freight and rail ferries run several times a day between here and a number of destinations: Bulgaria, Georgia, Turkey, Cyprus, Egypt. Security is relatively slack. In my opinion, that's far and away his best bet.'

'Then you'd better get us there first,' Lerner said, 'or we'll lose him for sure.'

Yevgeny Feyodovich strode purposely into the Privoz farmers' market. He headed directly toward Egg Row without his usual stops to smoke and gab with his circle of buddies. This morning, he had no time for them, no time for anything but getting the hell out of Odessa.

Magda, the partner with whom he owned the kiosk, was already there. It was Magda's farm from which the eggs came. He was the one with the capital.

'Had anyone come around asking for me?' he said as he came around behind the counter.

She was uncrating the eggs, separating the colors and sizes. 'Quiet as a churchyard.'

'Why did you use that phrase?'

Something in the tone of his voice made her stop what she was doing, look up. 'Yevgeny Feyodovich, whatever is the matter?'

'Nothing.' He was busy gathering up personal items.

'Huh. You look like you've seen the sun at midnight.' She put her fists on her ample hips. 'And where d'you think you're going? We'll be swamped here morning till sunset today.'

'I have a business matter to attend to,' he said hurriedly.

She barred his way. 'Don't think you can leave me like this. We have an agreement.'

'Get your brother to help you.'

Magda puffed her chest out. 'My brother's an idiot.'

'Then he's tailor-made for the job.'

He shouldered her roughly out of the way while her face was filling with blood. Putting his back to the whole scene, he strode quickly away, ignoring her indignant screeches, the stares of nearby vendors.

This morning on his way to the market, he'd received a call with the chilling news that Bogdan Illiyanovich had been shot to death on his way to leading the Moldavian

Ilias Voda into the trap set for him by Fadi, the terrorist. Yevgeny had been paid well to be the roper, the one who brought the mark – in this case Voda – to the access point. Until he'd received a call from one of his friends in the police, he'd had no idea what Fadi wanted with Ilias Voda or that it would involve multiple murders. Now Bogdan Illiyanovich was dead, along with three of Fadi's men and, worst of all, a police officer.

Yevgeny knew that if anyone got caught, his name would be the first one to pop up. He was about the last person in Odessa able to withstand a full-on police investigation. His livelihood – his very life – depended on him being anonymous, clinging to the shadows. Once the spotlight was shone on him, he was a dead man.

That was why he was on the run, why he was obliged in the most urgent terms to leave his past behind and relocate, hopefully outside Ukraine altogether. He was thinking Istanbul, of course. The man who had hired him for this godforsaken job was in Istanbul. Since Yevgeny was the only one who'd come out of this fiasco alive, perhaps the man would give him a job. Going to one of Yevgeny's current drug sources was out of the question. That entire chain of custody was in jeopardy now. Best to sever his ties to them completely, start over. In Yevgeny's chosen field, Istanbul was a more hospitable base than many he could think of, especially those closer to hand.

He hurried through the crowds that had begun to clog the access points. He was impelled by an uncomfortable prickling at the back of his neck, as if he was already in the crosshairs of an unknown assassin.

He was just passing a stack of crates in which beakless chickens were roiling as though they'd already lost their heads when he saw a pair of policemen threading their way through the pedestrian traffic. He didn't have to ask anyone why they were there.

Just as he was shying away, a woman stepped out from between two stacks of crates. Already on edge, he took an involuntary step back, his fingers curled around the grip of his gun.

'The police are here, they've set a trap,' the woman said.

She looked slightly Arabian to him, but that could mean anything. Half of his world was part Arabian.

She gestured urgently. 'Come with me. I can get you out of here.'

'Don't make me laugh. For all I know you're working for the SBU.'

He started to move away from her, away from the two policemen he'd seen. Soraya shook her head. 'They're waiting for you that way.'

He continued on. 'I don't believe you.'

She went with him, shouldering her way through the thick stream of people until she was slightly ahead of him. All at once she stopped, indicated with her head. An unpleasant ball of ice formed in Yevgeny's lower belly.

'I told you it was a trap, Yevgeny Feyodovich.'

'How do you know my name? How do you know the police are after me?'

'Please. There's no time.' She plucked at his sleeve. 'This way, quickly! It's your only hope of evading them.'

He nodded. What else could he do? She took him back to the city of chicken crates, then through them. They had to walk sideways to make it through the narrow lanes. On the other hand, the crate stacks, rising above their heads, kept them invisible to the police moving through the market.

At last, they broke out onto a street, hurried across it against traffic. He could see that they were heading toward a battered old Skoda.

'Please get in back,' she said curtly as she slid behind the wheel.

In something of a blind panic, Yevgeny Feyodovich did as she ordered, wrenching open the door, climbing in. He slammed the door shut, and she pulled out from the curb. That was when he became aware of someone sitting unmoving on the seat next to him.

'Ilias Voda!' His voice sounded bleak.

'You've stepped in it this time.' Jason Bourne relieved him of gun and knife.

'What?' Yevgeny Feyodovich, shocked to be unarmed, was even more so to see how white and drawn Voda was.

Bourne turned to him. 'In this town you're thoroughly fucked, *tovarich*.'

Deron had often said that Tyrone could be like a dog with a bone. He'd get certain ideas stuck in his head and he couldn't – or wouldn't – let them go until they were resolved. He was like this with the two people he'd seen chopping up the cop's body then burning down M&N Bodywork. He followed the inevitable aftermath like the most rabid fan of *American Idol*. The fire department came, and then the cops. But nothing remained inside the concrete-block building except ash and cinders. Moreover, it was District NE, which meant nobody really gave a shit. Inside an hour, Five-O had given up and, with a collective sigh of relief, had hightailed it to safety in the white parts of the city.

But Tyrone knew what had happened. Not that anyone had asked him. Not that he would have told them shit had they bothered to interview him. In fact, he didn't even call his friend Deron in Florida to tell him.

In his world, you took the knife off your hoop enemy when you beat him to a pulp for dissing you, or your sister, or your girlfriend, whatever. So at ten or eleven, you gained a measure of respect, which increased exponentially when your Masta Blasta slipped you a Saturday-night special with a taped butt and the serial numbers filed off.

Then, of course, you had to use it, because you didn't want to be a hop-along, a wannabe nobody would hang with or, worse, a mentard. It wasn't so difficult, really, because you already had some experience blowing people's heads off playing Postal 2 and Soldier of Fortune. As it turned out, the real thing wasn't much different. Just that you had to be careful afterward so the kill wouldn't turn into a career-ending move.

And yet there was something inside him, some nagging sense that this was not the only way it could be. There was Deron, of course, who'd been born and raised in the hood. But he'd had a momma who was straight and a father who'd loved him. In some way Tyrone couldn't understand, let alone articulate, he suspected those things counted for something. Then Deron had gone away to be educated in the white world and everyone in the hood – including Tyrone – had instantly hated his guts. But when he'd returned they forgave him everything because they saw he hadn't abandoned them, as they'd feared. For that, they loved him all the more, and rallied round to protect him.

Now Tyrone, sitting under the tree opposite the burned-out hulk of M&N Bodywork, faced both the destruction of his dream to make it his crew's crib, and the terrible notion that the dream was not what he'd wanted after all. He stared at the blank, blackened wall of cinder block, and it looked not much different than his life.

He drew out his cellie. He didn't have Miss S's number. How to contact her, how to let her know he had the 411 – what did Deron call it? intel, yeah – for her? Him and only him. If she'd meet him, if she'd walk with him again. He forced himself to believe that's all he wanted from her. The real truth he couldn't face yet.

He called 411. The only listed number for CI was the so-called public relations office. Tyrone knew what a joke that was, but he dialed it anyway. Once again, his life had refused to allow him a choice.

'Yes? How can I help?' a young white male voice said in clipped fashion.

'I'm tryin' t'reach a agent I spoke to coupla days ago,' Tyrone said, for once self-conscious about his ghetto slur.

'The agent's name?'

'Soraya Moore.'

'Just a moment, please.'

Tyrone heard some clicking, all at once became paranoid. He got up from his perch, began to walk down the street.

'Sir? May I have your name and number, please?'

Paranoia in full flower. He began to walk faster, as if he could outrun the inquiry. 'I just want to speak to – '

'If you give me your name and number, I'll see that Agent Moore gets the message.'

At this, Tyrone felt completely boxed in by a world he knew nothing about. 'Just tell her I know who put the salt on her tail.'

'Pardon me, sir, you know *what*?'

Tyrone felt that his own ignorance was being used as a weapon against which he was powerless. By design, his world was hidden within the larger one. Once, he'd been proud of that. Now, all at once, he knew it was a failing.

He repeated what he'd said, disconnected. Disgusted, he threw the cellie into the gutter, made a mental note to have DJ Tank get him another burner. His old one had just gotten too hot.

'So who are you, really?' Yevgeny Feyodovich asked with world weariness.

'Does it matter?' Bourne said.

'I suppose not.' Yevgeny stared out the window as they passed through the city. Every time he saw a police car or a policeman on foot, his muscles tensed. 'You're not even Moldavian, are you?'

'Your pal, Bogdan Illiyanovich, tried to kill me.' Bourne, watching the other's face carefully, said: 'You don't seem surprised.'

'Today,' Yevgeny Feyodovich replied, 'nothing surprises me.'

'Who hired you?' Bourne said sharply.

Yevgeny's head swung around. 'You don't expect me to tell you.'

'Was it the Saudi, Fadi?'

'I don't know a Fadi.'

'But you knew Edor Vladovich Lemontov, a fictitious drug lord.'

'I never actually said I knew him.' Yevgeny Feyodovich looked around. Judging by the sun, they were heading southwest. 'Where are we going?'

'A killing field.'

Yevgeny affected nonchalance. 'I should say my prayers then.'

'By all means.'

Soraya drove hard and fast, always staying within the speed limit. The last thing any of them needed was to attract the attention of a cruising police car. At length, they left the urban sprawl of Odessa behind, only to be confronted by rows of huge factories, transfer depots, and rail yards.

A bit farther on, there was a break of perhaps three or four kilometers where a village had sprung up, stores and houses looking tiny and incongruous amid the gargantuan structures on either side. Near the far end, Soraya turned down a side street that was soon fleshed out with foliage, both natural and artificial.

Oleksandr was waiting for them in the front yard of his owner and trainer – a friend of Soraya – who was, at the moment, nowhere to be seen. The boxer lifted his head as the battered Skoda turned into the driveway. The dacha behind him was of moderate size, set in a shallow dell, protected from its neighbors by thick stands of fir and cypress.

As Soraya rolled to a halt, Oleksandr rose, trotting toward them. He barked in greeting as he saw Soraya emerge from the car.

'My God, that's a huge beast,' Yevgeny Feyodovich said under his breath.

Bourne smiled at him. 'Welcome to the killing ground.' He grabbed the Ukrainian by his collar and dragged him off the backseat, out into the yard.

Oleksandr, seeing an unfamiliar face, raised his ears, sat back on his haunches, growled low in his throat. He bared his teeth.

'Let me introduce you to your executioner.' Bourne shoved Yevgeny toward the dog.

The Ukrainian appeared thunderstruck. 'The dog?'

'Oleksandr chewed Fadi's face off,' Bourne said. 'And hasn't eaten since then.'

Yevgeny Feyodovich shuddered. He closed his eyes. 'All I want is to be somewhere else.'

'Don't we all,' Bourne said, meaning it. 'Just tell me who hired you.'

Yevgeny Feyodovich wiped his sweating face. 'He'll kill me, no doubt.'

Bourne swept his hand toward the boxer. 'At least that way you'll have a head start.'

At that moment, just as they'd planned, Soraya gave Oleksandr a hand command. The dog leapt forward directly toward Yevgeny, who let out with a high, almost comical yelp.

At the last instant Bourne reached down and grabbed the dog's collar, pulling him up short. The maneuver took more out of Bourne than it should have, sending shock waves of pain radiating from the wound in his side. He gave no outward sign of his distress. Nevertheless, he was aware of Soraya's eyes reading his face as if it were today's newspaper.

'Yevgeny Feyodovich,' Bourne said, straightening up, 'as you can plainly see, Oleksandr is big and powerful. My hand is getting tired. You have five seconds before I let go.'

Yevgeny, his mind functioning off the adrenaline of terror, made up his mind in three. 'All right, keep that dog away from me.'

Bourne began to walk toward him, a straining Oleksandr in tow. He saw Yevgeny's eyes open wide enough to see the whites all around.

'Who hired you, Yevgeny Feyodovich?'

'A man named Nesim Hatun.' The Ukrainian could not take his eyes off the boxer. 'He works out of Istanbul – the Sultanahmet District.'

'Where in Sultanahmet?' Bourne said.

Yevgeny cringed away from Oleksandr, whom Bourne had allowed to rise up on his hind legs. He was as tall as the Ukrainian. 'I don't know,' Yevgeny said. 'I swear. I've told you everything.'

The moment Bourne let go of Oleksandr's collar, the dog sprang forward like an arrow from a drawn bow. Yevgeny Feyodovich screamed. A stain appeared at the crotch of his trousers as he was plowed under.

A moment later, Oleksandr was sitting on his chest, licking his face.

'As far as freight ports are concerned, you basically have two choices,' Dr. Pavlyna said. 'Odessa and Ilyichevsk, some seven kilometers to the southwest.'

'What's your take?' Matthew Lerner said. They were in her car, heading toward the northern end of Odessa, where the shipyards were located.

'Odessa is, of course, closer,' she said. 'But the police are sure to have at least some surveillance there. On the other hand, Ilyichevsk is appealing simply because it's farther away from the center of the manhunt; there's sure to be less of a police presence – if any. Also, it's a larger, busier facility, with ferries on more frequent schedules.'

'Ilyichevsk it is, then.'

She changed lanes, preparing to make a turn, so that they could head south. 'The only problem for them will be roadblocks.'

Leaving the main road behind, Soraya drove through back streets, even some alleys she could squeeze the Skoda through.

'Even so,' Bourne said, 'I wouldn't rule out hitting one roadblock between here and Ilyichevsk.'

They had left Yevgeny Feyodovich in the front yard of Soraya's friend, guarded for the time being by Oleksandr. Three hours from now, when his release would be meaningless to them, Soraya's friend would let him go.

'How are you feeling?' Soraya drove through narrow streets lined with warehouses. Here and there in the distance, they could see the portal and floating cranes at the port of Ilyichevsk rising like the necks of dinosaurs. It was slower going along this route, but it was also safer than taking the main road.

'I'm fine,' he said, but she could tell he was lying. His face was still pale, stitched with pain, his breathing ragged, not as deep as it ought to be.

'Glad to hear it,' she said with heavy irony. 'Because like it or not, we're going to come up against that roadblock in about three minutes.'

He looked up ahead. There were several cars and trucks stopped, lined up to be funneled through a gap between two armored police vehicles parked perpendicular to the street, so that their formidable tanklike sides were presented to the oncoming traffic. Two policemen in riot gear were questioning the cars' occupants, peering into their trunks or – in the case of the trucks – checking the rear and underneath the carriage. With faces clamped tight, they worked slowly, methodically, thoroughly. Clearly, they were leaving nothing to chance.

Soraya shook her head. 'There's no way out of this, no alternate route I can take. The water's on our right, the main highway on our left.' She glanced in her side mirror, at the traffic building behind her, another police car. 'I can't even turn around without the risk of being stopped.'

'Time for Plan B,' Bourne said grimly. 'You watch the cops in back of us; I'll keep my eye on the ones in front.'

Valery Petrovich, having just emptied his bladder against the brick side of a building, walked back to his position. He and his partner had been assigned to check that no vehicle lined up for the roadblock tried to turn around. He was thinking with some disgust about this bottom-of-the-barrel assignment, worrying that he'd been hit with it because he'd pissed off his sergeant, because, true, he'd beaten him at dice and at cards, taking six hundred rubles off him each time. Also true, the man was a vindictive bastard. Look what he'd done to poor Mikhail Arkanovich for mistakenly eating the sergeant's pierogi, vile though they'd been, so he'd heard from a very bitter Mikhail Arkanovich.

He was considering methods for remedying his deteriorating situation when he saw someone slip out of a battered Skoda seven cars from the front of the queue. His curiosity piqued, Valery Petrovich walked forward along the fronts of the warehouses, keeping his eye on the figure. He had just made out that it was a man when the figure slipped into a refuse-strewn alley between two buildings. Glancing front and back, the officer realized that no one else had noticed the man.

For half a second, he thought about using his walkie-talkie to alert his partner to the suspicious figure. That's all the time it took for him to realize that this was his ticket to returning to his sergeant's good graces. He sure as hell wasn't going to let the opportunity slip through his fingers by allowing someone else to capture what might very possibly be the fugitive they'd been sent to capture. He had no intention of becoming the next Mikhail Arkanovich, so, pistol drawn, licking his chops like a wolf about to rend its unsuspecting prey, he hurried eagerly on.

Taking a quick visual survey behind the line of warehouses, Bourne had already determined the best route to work his way around the roadblock. Under normal circumstances, there would have been no problem. Trouble was, he now found himself in anything but normal circumstances. Certainly he'd been injured before in the field – many times, in fact. But rarely this severely. On the car ride out to the dog handler's, he'd begun to feel feverish. Now he felt chills running through him. His forehead was hot, his mouth dry. He was in need not only of rest but also of more antibiotics – a full course – to fully pull himself out of the weakness inflicted by the knife wound.

Rest was, of course, out of the question. Where he was going to get antibiotics was problematic. If he didn't have an urgent reason to get out of Odessa immediately, he could have gone to the CI doctor. But that, too, was now out of the question.

He was in the open area behind the warehouses. A wide paved road gave access to the row of loading docks. Here and there were scattered refrigerated trucks and semis, either backed up to the docks or pulled to the far side of the road, where they sat idle, waiting for their drivers to return.

As he moved toward the area parallel to the roadblock on the other side of the buildings on his left, he passed a couple of forklifts, dodging several others loaded with large crates that scooted from one loading dock to another.

He saw his pursuer – a policeman – as a reflection in a forklift. Without breaking stride, he clambered painfully onto a loading dock and passed between two stacks of boxes into the warehouse interior. All the men, he noticed, were wearing port ID tags.

He found his way to the locker room. It was past the beginning of the shift, and the tiled room was deserted. He went along the lines of lockers, picking the locks at random. The third locker provided what he was looking for: a maintenance uniform. He donned it, not without a series of hot stitches of pain radiating out from his side. A thorough search turned up no ID tag. He knew how to take care of that. On the way out, he brushed against a man coming in, mumbling a hasty apology. As he hurried back onto the loading dock, he clipped on the tag he'd lifted.

Checking the immediate environment, he could find no sign of his pursuer. He set out on foot, skirting the empty steel cabs of the trucks whose cargo was being unloaded onto the concrete docks, where each crate, barrel, or container was checked against a manifest or bill of lading.

'Halt!' came a voice behind him. 'Stop right there!' He saw the policeman behind the wheel of one of the empty forklifts. The policeman put the vehicle in gear and drove it straight at him.

Though the forklift wasn't fast, Bourne nevertheless found himself at a distinct disadvantage. Because of the path the forklift was taking, he was imprisoned within a relatively narrow space, bordered on one side by the parked trucks, on the other by a strip of bunkerlike raw concrete buildings that housed the offices of the warehouse companies.

For the moment, the traffic was dense, and everyone was too busy at their jobs to notice the wayward forklift and its prey, but that might change at any moment.

Bourne turned and ran. With every stride the forklift gained on him, not only because it was in high gear but also because Bourne was in crippling agony. He dodged the machine once, twice, the tips of its forks releasing a shower of sparks as they scraped along a concrete wall.

He was near the end of the loading docks closest to the roadblock. There was an enormous semi backed into the last bay. Bourne's only chance was to run directly at the side of the cab, ducking under it at the last minute. He would have made it, too, but at almost the last instant, the overworked muscles of his left leg buckled under the pain.

He stumbled, slamming his side against the cab. A heartbeat later the ends of the forks punctured the painted steel on either side of Bourne, pinning him in place. He tried to duck down but he couldn't; he was held fast on either side by the forks.

He struggled to recover, to disengage himself from a pain so debilitating it made all thought difficult. Then the policeman crashed the gears, and the forklift ground forward. The tines buried themselves deeper into the side of the semi, thrusting him forward toward the truck.

A moment more and he would be crushed between the forklift and the semi.

# 21

Bourne exhaled and twisted his body. At the same time, he jammed his hands against the tops of the horizontal forks, levering his torso, then his legs up above the level of the tines. He spread his feet on the metal sill in front of the cab and levered himself onto the windshield.

The policeman threw the forklift into reverse in an attempt to dislodge Bourne, but the forks had pierced into the core of the cab and now something there was holding them fast.

Seeing his opening, Bourne swung around to the open side. The policemen drew his gun, aimed it at Bourne, but before he could pull the trigger Bourne kicked out, the toe of his shoe colliding with the side of the policeman's face. The jawbone dislocated, cracking apart.

Bourne grabbed the policeman's pistol and drove another fist into the man's solar plexus, doubling him over. He turned, jumped to the ground, the jarring force running right up into his left side like a spear thrust.

Then Bourne was off and running, past the line of the roadblock into a small woods, then out again on the other side. By the time he reached the side of the road several thousand meters beyond the police presence, he was winded and spent. But there was the battered Skoda, its passenger door open, Soraya's face, drawn and anxious, peering across the car's interior, watching him all the way as he climbed aboard. He slammed the door shut, and the Skoda lurched forward as she put it in gear.

'Are you all right?' she said, her eyes flicking from him to the road ahead. 'What the hell happened?'

'I had to go to Plan C,' Bourne said. 'And then to Plan D.'

'There were no Plans C and D.'

Bourne put his head against the seat. 'That's what I mean.'

Arriving at Ilyichevsk under gathering clouds, Lerner said, 'Take me to the ferry slips. I want to check the first outgoing ferry, because that's where he's headed.'

'I disagree.' Dr. Pavlyna drove the car through the byways of the port with the assurance of someone who'd done it many times before. 'The facility maintains its own Polyclinic. Believe me when I tell you that by now Bourne is going to need what only the clinic has got.'

Lerner, who'd never taken an order from a woman in his life, disliked the idea of taking Dr. Pavlyna's suggestion. In fact, he disliked having her driving him around. But for the time being, it served its purpose. That didn't mean her competence didn't put him in a surly mood.

Ilyichevsk was vast, a cityscape of low, flat, ugly buildings, vast warehouses and silos, cold storage facilities, container terminals, and monstrously tall TAKRAF cranes floating on barges. To the west, fishing trawlers lay at berth being off-loaded or refitted. The port, built in a kind of arc around a natural inlet to the Black Sea, comprised seven cargo-handling complexes. Six specialized in areas such as steel and pig iron, tropical oils, timber, vegetables and liquid oils, fertilizer. One was an immense grain silo reloader. The seventh was for ferries and ro-ro vessels. *Ro-ro* was short for 'roll on–roll off,' meaning that the central space housed enormous containers from both rail lines and tractor-trailers that were driven onto the ferry and stacked in its bowels. Above this space was the area housing the passengers, captain, and much of the crew. The main drawback to the design was its inherent instability. With only a centimeter or two of water penetrating the cargo deck, the ferry would start to roll over and sink. Nevertheless, no other craft could serve its purpose as efficiently, so ro-ros continued to be used all over Asia and the Middle East.

The Polyclinic lay more or less midway between Terminals Three and Six. It was in an unremarkable three-story building with strictly utilitarian lines. Dr. Pavlyna drew her car up to the side of the Polyclinic and switched off the engine.

She turned to Lerner. 'I'll go in myself. That way, there won't be any questions with security.'

As she moved to open her door, Lerner grasped her arm. 'I think it would be better if I went with you.'

She glanced down at his hand for a moment before saying, 'You're making things difficult. Let me take the lead in this; I know the people here.'

Lerner tightened his grip. His grin revealed a set of very large teeth. 'If you know the people, Doctor, there won't be any questions with security, will there?'

She gave him a long appraising look, as if seeing him for the first time. 'Is there a problem?'

'Not from my end.'

Dr. Pavlyna wrested her arm from his grasp. 'Because if there is, we should settle it now. We're in the field – '

'I know precisely where we are, Doctor.'

' – where misconceptions and misunderstandings can lead to fatal errors.'

Lerner got out of the car and began walking toward the front door of the Polyclinic. A moment later, he heard Dr. Pavlyna's boots crunch against the gravel before she caught up with him on the tarmac.

'You may have been sent by the DCI, but I'm the COS here.'

'For the time being,' he said blithely.

'Is that a threat?' Dr. Pavlyna didn't hesitate. Men of one sort or another had been trying to intimidate her ever since she was a little girl. She'd taken her early knocks before learning how to fight back with her arsenal of weapons. 'You're under my command. You understand that.'

He paused for a moment in front of the door. 'I understand that I have to deal with you while I'm here.'

'Lerner, have you ever been married?'

'Married, and divorced. Happily.'

'Why am I not surprised.' As she tried to brush past him, he grabbed her again.

Dr. Pavlyna said, 'You don't like women much, do you?'

'Not the ones who think they're men, I don't.'

Having made his point, he dropped his hand from her arm.

She opened the door, but for the moment barred his entry with her body. 'For God's sake keep your mouth shut, otherwise you'll compromise my security.' She stepped aside. 'Even someone as crude as you can understand that.'

Under the pretext of a mission briefing update, Karim al-Jamil wangled himself an invitation to breakfast with the Old Man. Not that he didn't have an update, but the mission was bullshit, so anything he had to say about it was bullshit. On the other hand, it felt fine to feed the DCI bullshit for breakfast. Anyway, he had his own intel update to digest. The memories Dr. Veintrop implanted had led Bourne to the ambush point. Somehow the man had recovered enough to shoot four men to death and escape Fadi. But not before Fadi had knifed him in the side. Was Bourne dead or alive? If Karim al-Jamil were allowed to bet, he'd put his money on alive.

But now that he had reached the top floor of CI headquarters, he forced his mind back into its role of Martin Lindros.

Even during a crisis, the Old Man took his meals where he always did.

'Being chained to the same desk, staring at the same monitor day in, day out, is enough to drive a man mad,' he said as Karim al-Jamil sat down opposite him. The floor was divided in two. The west wing was devoted to a world-class gym and Olympic-size swimming pool. The walled-off east wing, where they were now, housed quarters off limits to everyone except the Old Man.

This was the room to which the seven heads of directorates had from time to time been invited. It had the look and feel of a greenhouse, with a thick terracotta tile floor and a high humidity level, the better to accommodate a wide variety of tropical greenery and orchids. Who tended them was the stuff of much speculation and fanciful urban legends. The bottom line was that no one knew, just as no one knew who – if anyone – occupied the east wing's ten or twelve securely locked off-limits offices.

This was, of course, Karim al-Jamil's first time in the Gerbil Circuit, as it was referred to internally. Why? Because the DCI kept three gerbils in side-by-side cages. In each cage, one gerbil was confined to a wheel on which it ran endlessly. Much like the agents of CI.

Those few directorate heads who spoke of their breakfasts with the Old Man claimed he found watching the gerbils at their labor relaxing – like staring at fish in a tank. Speculation among the agents, however, was that the DCI perversely enjoyed being reminded that, like the ancient Greek Sisyphus, CI's task was without either praise or end.

'On the other hand,' the Old Man was saying now, 'the job itself can drive a man mad.'

The table was set with a starched white cloth, two bone-china settings, a basket of croissants and muffins, and two carafes, one of strong, freshly brewed coffee, the other of Earl Grey tea, the Old Man's favorite.

Karim al-Jamil helped himself to coffee, which he sipped black. The DCI liked his tea milky and sweet. There was no sign of a waiter, but a metal cart stood tableside, keeping its contents warm for the diners.

Digging out his papers, Karim al-Jamil said, 'Should I start the briefing now or wait for Lerner?'

'Lerner won't be joining us,' the DCI said enigmatically.

Karim al-Jamil began. 'The Skorpion units are three-quarters of the way to their destination in the Shabwah region of South Yemen. The marines have been mobilized out of Djibouti.' He glanced at his watch. 'As of twenty minutes ago, they were on the ground in Shabwah, awaiting orders from our Skorpion commanders.'

'Excellent.' The DCI refilled his teacup, stirred in cream and sugar. 'What progress on pinning down the specific location of the transmissions?'

'I put two separate Typhon teams onto parsing different packets of data. Right now we're reasonably certain the Dujja facility is somewhere within the eighty-kilometer target radius.'

The DCI was staring into the cages at the busy gerbils. 'Can't we pin it down more accurately?'

'The chief problem is the mountains. They tend to distort and reflect the signals. But we're working on it.'

The Old Man nodded absently.

'Sir, if I might ask, what's on your mind?'

For a moment it appeared as if the older man hadn't heard. Then the DCI's head swung around, his canny eyes engaging those of Karim al-Jamil. 'I don't know, but I feel as if I'm missing something . . . something important.'

Karim al-Jamil kept his breathing even, arranged his expression into one of mild concern. 'Is there anything I can help you with, sir? Perhaps it's Lerner – '

'Why d'you mention him in particular?' the DCI said a trifle too sharply.

'We've never spoken about his taking over my position in Typhon.'

'You were gone; Typhon was leaderless.'

'And you put an outsider into the breach?'

The DCI set down his cup with an ungainly clatter. 'Are you second-guessing my judgment, Martin?'

'Of course not.' *Be careful,* Karim al-Jamil thought. 'But it was damn strange to see him in my chair when I got back.'

The Old Man frowned. 'Yes, I can see that.'

'And now in the middle of this ultimate crisis, he's nowhere to be found.'

'Get us our breakfast, would you, Martin,' the DCI said. 'I'm hungry.'

Karim al-Jamil opened the food cart, taking out two plates of fried eggs and bacon. It was all he could do not to gag. He'd never gotten used to pork products or, for that matter, eggs fried in butter. As he set a plate down in front of the DCI, he said, 'If there's still a bit of distrust after my ordeal, I certainly understand.'

'It's not that,' the Old Man said, again a bit too sharply.

Karim al-Jamil set his own plate down. 'Then what is it? I'd appreciate knowing. These mysterious incidents with Matthew Lerner make me feel as if I've been cut out of the loop.'

'Seeing how much it means to you, Martin, I'll make you a proposition.'

The Old Man paused to chew a mouthful of bacon and eggs, swallow, and wipe his glistening lips in a fair imitation of gentlemanly fashion.

Karim al-Jamil almost felt sorry for the real Martin Lindros, who'd had to put up with this insulting behavior. *And they call us barbarians.*

'I know you have a great deal on your plate at the moment,' the DCI finally continued. 'But if you could find your way to make some discreet inquiries for me – '

'Who or what?'

The DCI sliced into his eggs and neatly piled a third of a strip of bacon on top. 'It has lately come to my attention through certain back channels that I have an enemy inside the Beltway.'

'After all these years,' Karim al-Jamil observed, 'there has to be a list of some size.'

'Of course there is. But this one's special. I ought to warn you to be exceedingly careful; he's as powerful as they come.'

'I trust it's not the president,' Karim al-Jamil said, joking.

'No, but damn close.' The Old Man was perfectly serious. 'Secretary of Defense Ervin Reynolds Halliday, known as Bud to everyone who kisses his ass. I very much doubt he has anything approaching real friends.'

'Who does, in this town?'

The DCI emitted a rare chuckle. 'Just so.' He stuffed the forkful of food into his mouth, transferred it to one cheek in order to continue talking. 'But you and I, Martin, we're friends. Close as, anyway. So this little deal is between us.'

'You can count on me, sir.'

'I know I can, Martin. The best thing I've done in the past decade is bring you along to the top of the CI ladder.'

'I appreciate your trust in me, sir.'

The DCI gave no indication he'd heard the other's remark. 'After Halliday and his faithful pit bull, LaValle, tried to ambush me in the War Room, I made some inquiries. What I've discovered is that the two of them have been quietly setting up parallel intelligence units. They're moving into our turf.'

'Which means we have to stop them.'

The Old Man's eyes narrowed. 'Yes, it does, Martin. And unfortunately they're making their overt move at the worst possible time: when Dujja is attempting a major attack.'

'Maybe that's deliberate, sir.'

The DCI thought about the ambush in the War Room. There was no doubt that both Halliday and LaValle were trying to embarrass him in front of the president. He thought again of the president sitting back, watching the thrust and parry unfold. Was he already on the defense secretary's side? Did he want CI taken over by the Pentagon? The Old Man shuddered at the thought of the military in control of human intelligence. There was no telling what liberties LaValle and Halliday would take with their newfound power. There was a good reason for the separation of power of the Pentagon and CI. Without it, a police state was just a shot away.

'What are you looking for?'

'Dirt.' The DCI swallowed. 'The more the merrier.'

Karim al-Jamil nodded. 'I'll need someone – '

'Anyone. Just say the name.'

'Anne Held.'

The DCI was taken aback. 'My Anne Held?' He shook his head. 'Choose someone else.'

'You said discreet. I can't use an agent. It's Anne or nothing.'

The DCI eyed him to see if he could spot the hint of a bluff. Apparently, he couldn't. 'Done,' he conceded.

'Now tell me about Matthew Lerner.'

The Old Man looked him in the eye. 'It's Bourne.'

After a long, awkward moment during which all that could be heard was the whirring of wheels propelled by twelve tiny gerbil feet, Karim al-Jamil said quietly, 'What does Jason Bourne have to do with Matthew Lerner?'

The DCI put down his knife and fork. 'I know what Bourne has meant to you, Martin. You have a certain, though inexplicable, rapport with him. But the simple fact is that he's the worst kind of poison for CI. Consequently, I've dispatched Matthew Lerner to terminate him.'

For a moment, Karim al-Jamil could not believe what he was hearing. The DCI had sent an assassin to kill Bourne? To take from him and his brother the satisfaction of a long-held and meticulously plotted revenge? No. He wouldn't have it.

The killing rage – what his father had called the Desert Wind – took possession of his heart, heated it, beat it down until it was like a forged blade. All that could be discerned of this grave inner turmoil was the briefest flare of his nostrils – which in any event his companion, having taken up his cutlery, failed to notice.

Karim al-Jamil cut into his eggs, watched the yolks run. One of them had a blood spot on its glassy surface.

'That was a radical move,' he said when he was in full control of his emotions. 'I told you I'd severed him.'

'I thought about it and decided it wasn't the proper solution.'

'You should have come to me.'

'You'd only have tried to talk me out of it,' the DCI said briskly. Clearly he was pleased with how well he'd handled a tricky situation. 'Now it's too late. You can't stop it, Martin, so don't even try.' He wiped his lips. 'The good of the group supersedes the desires of the individual. You know that as well as anyone.'

Karim al-Jamil considered the extreme danger of what the DCI had set in motion. In addition to being a threat to their personal revenge, Lerner's presence in the field was a wild card, one that he and Fadi hadn't taken into consideration. The altered scenario menaced the execution of their plan. He had learned from Fadi – via a scrambled channel piggybacked onto CI's own overseas communications – that he had knifed Bourne. If not dealt with, Lerner could become aware of this, and he'd quite naturally become interested in finding out the identity of who had done it. Alternatively, if he discovered that Bourne had already been killed, he'd want to know who the killer was. Either way, it would lead to dangerous complications.

Pushing back from the table, Karim al-Jamil said, 'Have you considered the possibility of Bourne killing Lerner?'

'I brought Lerner aboard because of his rep.' The Old Man picked up his cup, saw that the tea had gone cold, set it back down. 'They don't make men like him anymore. He's a born killer.'

*So is Bourne,* Karim al-Jamil thought with a bitterness that burned like acid.

Soraya, noticing the drip of fresh blood on the car seat, said, 'It looks as if you popped a stitch or two. You're never going to make it without immediate medical attention.'

'Forget it,' Bourne said. 'We both need to get out of here now. The police cordon is only going to draw tighter.' He looked around the port. 'Besides, where am I going to get medical attention here?'

'The port maintains a Polyclinic.'

Soraya drove through Ilyichevsk and parked at the side of a three-story building, next to the late-model Skoda Octavia RS. She was aware of how badly Bourne winced as he got out of the car. 'We'd better use the side entrance.'

'That's not going to take care of security,' he said. Opening up the lining of his coat, he took out a small packet sealed in plastic. Ripping it open, he produced another set of ID documents. He leafed through them briefly, though on the plane ride he'd memorized all the documents Deron had forged for him. 'My name is Mykola Petrovich Tuz. I'm a lieutenant general in DZND, the SBU's Department for National Statehood Protection and Combating Terrorism.' He came up to her, took her arm. 'Here's the drill. You're my prisoner. A Chechnyan terrorist.'

'In that case,' Soraya said, 'I'd better put this cloth over my head.'

'No one will even look at you, let alone ask you questions,' Bourne said. 'They'll be dead afraid of you.'

He opened the door and pushed her rudely ahead of him. Almost at once an orderly called for a security guard.

Bourne held out his DZND credentials. 'Lieutenant General Tuz,' he said brusquely. 'I've been knifed, and am in need of a doctor.' He saw the guard's eyes slide toward Soraya. 'She's my prisoner. A Chechnyan suicide bomber.'

The security guard, his face drained of color, nodded. 'This way, Lieutenant General.'

He spoke into his walkie-talkie, then led them down several corridors into a spare examination room typical of hospital ERs.

He indicated the examination table. 'I've contacted the Polyclinic's administrator. Make yourself comfortable, Lieutenant General.' Clearly unnerved by both Bourne's status and Soraya's presence, he drew his pistol. Aimed it at Soraya. 'Stand over there, so the lieutenant general can be seen to.'

Bourne let go of Soraya's arm, giving her an almost imperceptible nod. She went to the corner of the room and sat on a metal-legged chair as the guard tried to keep an eye on her without actually looking at her face.

'A lieutenant general in SBU,' the Polyclinic administrator said from behind his desk. 'This can't be your man.'

'We'll be the judge of that,' Matthew Lerner said in passable Russian.

Dr. Pavlyna shot him a wicked look before turning to the administrator. 'You did say he's suffering from a knife wound.'

The administrator nodded. 'That's what I've been told.'

Dr. Pavlyna rose. 'Then I think I should see him.'

'We'll both go,' Lerner said. He'd been standing near the door, a kind of invisible electricity coming off him in waves, like a racehorse in the starting gate.

'That wouldn't be wise.' The deliberateness with which Dr. Pavlyna said this held significant emphasis for Lerner.

'I agree.' The administrator got up and came around his desk. 'If the patient really is who he says he is, I'll take the brunt of the breach in protocol.'

'Nevertheless,' Lerner said. 'I'm going to accompany the doctor.'

'You'll force me to call security,' the administrator said sternly. 'The lieutenant general won't know who you are or why you're there. In fact, he could order you held or even shot. I won't have anything like that in my facility.'

'Stay here,' Dr. Pavlyna said. 'I'll call you as soon as I've determined his identity.'

Lerner said nothing as Dr. Pavlyna and the administrator left the office, but he had no intention of cooling his heels while the doctor took charge. She had no idea why he was in Odessa, why he was after Jason Bourne. He didn't for a minute believe that the patient was anyone but Bourne. A lieutenant general of the Ukrainian secret police here with a knife wound in his side? No chance.

He wasn't going to allow Dr. Pavlyna to fuck things up. The first thing she would tell Bourne was that Lerner had been dispatched from D.C. to find him. That would set off instant alarm bells in Bourne's head. He'd be gone before Lerner could get to him. And this time, he'd be far more difficult to locate.

The immediate problem was that he didn't know where the patient was. He went out the door, accosted the first person he saw, asked where the lieutenant general was being treated. The young woman pointed the way. He thanked her and walked on down the corridor with such concentration that he failed to see her pick up the receiver of an intraclinic phone on the wall, asking to speak to the administrator.

'Good afternoon, Lieutenant General. I'm Dr. Pavlyna,' she said the moment she entered the examination room. To the administrator, she added, 'This is not our man.'

Bourne, sitting on the examination table, saw nothing in her eye to tell him she was lying, but when he saw her glance over at Soraya, he said, 'Stay away from my prisoner, Doctor. She's dangerous.'

'Please lie back, Lieutenant General.' As Bourne complied, Dr. Pavlyna donned surgeon's gloves, slit open Bourne's bloody shirt, and began to peel back the bloody bandage. 'Is she the one who gave you the knife wound?'

'Yes,' Bourne said.

She palpated around the wound, judging Bourne's pain level. 'Whoever sutured you did a first-rate job.' She looked into Bourne's eyes. 'Unfortunately, you've been a bit too active. I'll have to resuture the part that's torn open.'

On cue, the administrator showed her where the paraphernalia was, opening the locked cupboard where the drugs were stored. She selected a box from the second shelf, counted out fourteen pills, wrapped them in a twist of sturdy paper. 'Also, I want you to take this. One twice a day for a week. It's a powerful wide-spectrum antibiotic to guard against infection. Please take them all.'

Bourne accepted the packet, stowed it away.

Dr. Pavlyna brought a bottle of liquid disinfectant, gauze pads, a needle, and suture material to the table. Then she loaded up a syringe.

'What's that?' Bourne said warily.

'Anesthesia.' She inserted the needle into his side, depressed the plunger. Once again, her eyes caught Bourne's. 'Don't worry, Lieutenant General, it's just a local. It'll take the pain away but will in no way impair your physical or mental acuity.'

As she began the procedure, the phone on the wall burred discreetly. The administrator picked up the receiver and listened for a moment. 'All right, I understand. Thank you, Nurse.' He put back the receiver.

'Dr. Pavlyna,' he said. 'It seems your friend couldn't contain his impatience. He's on his way here.' He went to the door. 'I'll take care of him.' Then he slipped out.

'What friend?' Bourne said.

'Nothing to worry about, Lieutenant General,' Dr. Pavlyna said. She gave him another significant look. 'A friend of yours from headquarters.'

On his way to the room where the patient was being treated, Lerner passed three examination rooms. He took the time to peer into each one. Having determined that they were identical, he memorized the layout: where the examining table was, chairs, cabinets, sink . . . Knowing Bourne's reputation, he didn't think he'd get more than one chance to blow his brains out.

He took out his Glock, screwing the silencer onto the end of the barrel. He would have preferred not to use it, because it cut down on both the range and the accuracy of the gun. But in this environment he didn't have a choice. If he was to accomplish his mission and get out of the building alive, he had to kill Bourne in the quietest way possible. From the moment the DCI had given him his assignment, he knew he'd never be able to torture intel out of him – not in a hostile environment, and possibly not at all. Besides, the best way to take Bourne out was to kill him as quickly and efficiently as possible, giving him no possibility of a counterattack.

At that moment, the administrator rounded the corner up ahead, carrying a disapproving look on his face.

'Excuse me, but you were asked to stay in my office until called,' he said as he confronted Lerner. 'I must ask you to return to – '

The heavy blow from the end of the silencer struck him square on the left temple, sending him to the floor in a heap, insensate. Lerner took him by the back of his collar, dragged him back to one of the empty examination rooms, and stowed him behind the door.

Without another thought, he returned to the corridor and walked the rest of the way to his destination without further interference. Standing outside the closed door, he settled his mind into the clear quiet of the kill. Grasping the doorknob with his free hand, he slowly turned it as far as he could, held it in place. The kill-state surrounded him, entered him.

Simultaneously, he let go of the knob, kicked the door open and, taking a long stride across the threshold, squeezed off three shots into the figure on the examination table.

# 22

Lerner's brain took a moment to make sense of what his eyes saw. It recognized the rolls of material on the examination table; as a result, he began to turn.

But that lag between action and reaction was just enough to allow Bourne, standing to one side, to drive the syringe loaded with a general anesthetic into Lerner's neck. Still, Lerner was far from finished. He had the constitution of a bull, the determination of the damned. Breaking the syringe before Bourne had a chance to deliver the full dose, he drove his body against Bourne's.

As Bourne delivered two blows, Lerner squeezed off a shot that ripped open the security guard's chest.

'What are you doing?' Dr. Pavlyna screamed. 'You told me – '

Lerner, driving an elbow into Bourne's bloody wound, shot her in the head. Her body flew backward into Soraya's arms.

Bourne dropped to his knees, pain weakening every muscle, firing every nerve ending. As Lerner grabbed him by the neck, Soraya threw the chair she'd been sitting on into his face. His death grip on Bourne broken, he staggered back, firing still, though wildly. She saw the guard's gun across the room, thought momentarily of making a run for it, but Lerner, recovering with frightening speed, made that impossible.

Instead she lunged for Bourne, dragged him to his feet, and got both of them out of there. She heard the *phut! phut!* of silenced bullets splinter the wall at her elbow, and then they were racing around a corner, down the corridor, retracing their route to the side door.

Outside, she half threw, half stuffed Bourne into the passenger seat of the battered Skoda, slid behind the wheel, fired the ignition, and in a squeal of tires and spray of gravel reversed them out of there.

Lerner, half leaning against the examination table, staggered to his feet. He shook his head, trying to clear it, failed. Reaching up, he pulled the needle from the broken syringe out of his neck. What the hell had Bourne injected him with?

He stood for a moment, weaving like a landlubber on a boat in heavy weather. He gripped the countertop to steady himself. Groggily, he went over to the sink and splashed cold water on his face. The only thing that did was blur his vision even further. He found he had trouble breathing.

Moving his hand along the counter, he discovered a small glass container with one of the rubber tops that allows needles through. He picked it up, put it in front of his face. It took him a moment for his eyes to focus on the small print.

531

Midazolam. That's what this was. A short-term anesthetic meant to induce twilight sleep. Knowing that, he knew what he needed to counteract its effects. He went through the cabinets until he found a vial of epinephrine, the main chemical in adrenaline. Locating the syringes, he loaded one up, zipped a little of the liquid out the end of the needle to get rid of any air bubbles that might have formed, then injected himself.

That was the end of the midazolam. The cotton-wool haziness went up in a blaze of mental fire. He could breathe again. He knelt over the corpse of the late unlamented Dr. Pavlyna and fished out her ring of keys.

Minutes later, finding his way to the side door, he was out of the Polyclinic. As he approached Dr. Pavlyna's car, he saw fresh skid marks in the gravel by a vehicle that had been parked beside it. The driver had been in a hurry. He piled into the Skoda Octavia. The skid marks led in the direction of the ferry terminal.

Having been thoroughly briefed on Ilyichevsk's workings by Dr. Pavlyna, Lerner knew precisely where Bourne was headed. Up ahead, he saw a huge ro-ro loading. He squinted. What was its name? *Itkursk.*

He grinned fiercely. It looked as if he was going to get a second shot at Bourne after all.

The captain of the ro-ro *Itkursk* was more than happy to accommodate Lieutenant General M. P. Tuz of the DZND and his assistant. In fact, he gave them the stateroom reserved for VIPs, a cabin with windows and its own bathroom. The walls were white, curved inward like the hull of the ship. The floor was much-scuffed wooden boards. There was a bed, a slim desk, two chairs, doors that revealed a narrow clothes closet and the bathroom.

Shaking off his coat, Bourne sat on the bed. 'Are you all right?'

'Lie down.' Soraya threw her overcoat onto a chair, held up a curved needle and a string of suture material. 'I've got work to do.'

Bourne, grateful, did as she asked. His entire body was on fire. With a professional sadist's expertise, Lerner had landed the blow to his side so as to inflict maximum pain. He gasped as she began the resuturing process.

'Lerner really did a number on you,' Soraya said as she worked. 'What is he doing here? And what the hell does he think he's doing coming after you?'

Bourne stared at the low ceiling. By now he was used to CI betrayals, its attempts to terminate him. In some ways, he had made himself numb to the agency's calculated inhumanity. But another part of him found it difficult to fathom the depth of its hypocrisy. The DCI was all too ready to use him when he had no other recourse, but his enmity toward Bourne was unshakable.

'Lerner is the Old Man's personal pit bull,' Bourne said. 'I can only guess he's been sent to fulfill a termination order.'

Soraya stared down at him. 'How can you say that so calmly?'

Bourne winced as the needle went in, the suture pulled through. 'Calmly is the only way to assess the situation.'

'But your own agency –'

'Soraya, what you have to understand is that CI was never my agency. I was brought in through a black-ops group. I worked with my handler, not the Old

Man, not anyone else in CI. The same goes for Martin. By CI's strict code, I'm a maverick, a loose end.'

She left him for a moment to go into the bathroom. A moment later, she returned with a washcloth she'd soaked in hot water. She pressed this over the newly restitched wound and held it there, waiting for the bleeding to stop.

'Jason,' she said. 'Look at me. Why don't you look at me?'

'Because,' he said, directing his gaze into her beautiful uptilted eyes, 'when I look at you I don't see you at all. I see Marie.'

Soraya, abruptly deflated, sat down on the edge of the bed. 'Are we so alike, then?'

He resumed his study of the stateroom ceiling. 'On the contrary. You're nothing like her.'

'Then why – '

The deep booming of the ro-ro's horn filled the stateroom. A moment later, they felt a small lurch, then a gentle rocking. They were moving out of the port, on their journey across the Black Sea to Istanbul.

'I think you owe me an explanation,' she said softly.

'Did we . . . I mean before?'

'No. I would never have asked that of you.'

'And me? Did I ask it of you?'

'Oh, Jason, you know yourself better than that.'

'I wouldn't have taken Fadi out of his cell, either. I wouldn't have been led into a trap on the beach.' His gaze slid down to her patiently waiting face. 'It's bad enough not being able to remember.' He remembered the confetti of memories – his and . . . someone else's. 'But having memories that lead you astray . . .'

'But how? Why?'

'Dr. Sunderland introduced certain proteins into the synapses of the brain.' Bourne struggled to sit up, waving off her help. 'Sunderland is in league with Fadi. The procedure was part of Fadi's plan.'

'Jason, we've talked about this. It's insane. For one thing, how could Fadi possibly know you'd need a memory specialist? For another, how would he know which one you'd go to?'

'Both good questions. Unfortunately, I still don't have any answers. But consider: Fadi had enough information about CI to know who Lindros was. He knew about Typhon. His information was so extensive, so detailed, it allowed him to create an impostor who fooled everyone, even me, even the sophisticated CI retinal scan.'

'Could he be part of the conspiracy?' she said. 'Fadi's conspiracy?'

'It sounds like a paranoid's dream. But I'm beginning to believe that all these incidents – Sunderland's treatment, Martin's kidnapping and replacement, Fadi's revenge against me – are related, parts of a brilliantly designed and executed conspiracy to bring me down, along with all of CI.'

'How do we discover whether or not you're right? How do we make sense of it all?'

He regarded Soraya for a moment. 'We need to go back to the beginning. Back to the first time I came to Odessa, when you were COS. But in order to do that, I need you to fill in the missing parts of my memory.'

Soraya stood and moved to the window, staring out at the widening swatch of water, the curving haze-smeared coastline of Odessa they were leaving behind.

Painful as it was, he swung his legs around and got gingerly to his feet. The local anesthetic was wearing off; a deeper pain pulsed through him as the full extent of the damage from Lerner's calculated blow hit him like a freight train. He staggered, almost fell back in the bed, but caught himself. He deepened his breathing, slowing it. Gradually, the pain receded to a tolerable level. Then he walked across the stateroom to stand beside her.

'You should be back in bed,' she said in a distant voice.

'Soraya, why is it so difficult to tell me what happened?'

For a moment, she said nothing. Then: 'I thought I'd put it all behind me. That I'd never have to think of it again.'

He gripped her shoulders and spun her around. 'For the love of God, what happened?'

Her eyes, dark and luminous, brimmed with tears. 'We killed someone, Jason. You and I. A civilian, an innocent. A young woman barely out of her teens.'

*He is running down the street carrying someone in his arms. His hands are covered in blood. Her blood . . .*

'Who?' he said sharply. 'Who did we kill?'

Soraya was trembling as if with a terrible chill. 'Her name was Sarah.'

'Sarah who?'

'That's all I know.' Tears overflowed her eyes. 'I know that because you told me. You told me that before she died, her last words were, "My name is Sarah. Remember me."'

*Where am I now?* Martin Lindros wondered. He had felt the heat, the gritty dust against his skin as he was led off the plane, still blinded by the hood. But he'd been exposed to neither the heat nor the dust for very long. A vehicle – a jeep or possibly a light truck – had rumbled him down a peculiarly smooth incline. Greeted by an air-cooled environment, he had walked for perhaps a thousand meters. He heard a bolt being thrown, a door opened, and then he was shoved in. After he heard the door slam, the lock bolted into place, he stood for a moment, trying to do nothing more than breathe deeply and evenly. Then he reached up and plucked the hood from his head.

He stood in more or less the center of a room, perhaps five meters on a side, constructed solidly but rather crudely of reinforced concrete. It contained a rather dated doctor's examining table, a small stainless-steel sink, a row of low cabinets on top of which were neatly lined boxes of latex gloves, cotton swabs, bottles of disinfectant, various liquids and implements.

The infirmary was windowless, which did not surprise him, since he surmised that they were underground. But where? Certainly he was in a desertlike climate, but not an actual desert – building anything underground in the desert was impossible. So, a hot, mountainous country. From the echoes that had reached him as he and his guards had made their way here, the facility was quite large. Therefore, it had to be situated in a place hidden from prying eyes. He could think of half a dozen such areas – such as Somalia – but he dismissed most of them as too close to Ras Dejen. He moved around the room in a counterclockwise motion, the better to see out of his left eye. If he had to guess, he'd say he was somewhere on the border between Afghanistan and Pakistan. A rugged, utterly lawless swath of real estate controlled from top to bottom by ethnic tribes whose patrons were legions of the world's most deadly terrorists.

He would have enjoyed asking Muta ibn Aziz about that, but Abbud's brother had debarked some hours before the plane had arrived here.

Hearing the bolt slide back, the door open, he turned and saw a slim, bespectacled man with bad skin and a shocking pompadour of sandy gray hair walk in.

With a guttural growl, he rushed at the man, who stepped neatly aside, revealing the two guards behind him. Their presence hardly deterred his rage-filled heart, but the butts of their semiautomatics put him on the floor.

'I don't blame you for wanting to do me harm,' Dr. Andursky said from his vantage point safely standing over Lindros's prone body. 'I might feel the same way if I were in your shoes.'

'If only you were.'

This response produced in Dr. Andursky a smile that fairly radiated insincerity. 'I came here to see to your health.'

'Is that what you were doing when you took out my right eye?' Lindros shouted.

One of the guards pressed the muzzle of his semiautomatic to Lindros's chest, to make his point.

Dr. Andursky appeared unruffled. 'As you well know, I needed your eye; I needed the retina to transplant into Karim al-Jamil's. Without that part of you, he never would have fooled the CI retinal scanner. He never would have passed for you, no matter how good a job I did on his face.'

Lindros brushed away the gun muzzle as he sat up. 'You make it sound so cut and dried.'

'Science *is* cut and dried,' Dr. Andursky pointed out. 'Now, why don't you go over to the examining table so I can take a look at how your eye is healing.'

Lindros rose, walked back, lay down on the table. Dr. Andursky, flanked by his guards, used a pair of surgeon's scissors to cut through the filthy bandages over Lindros's right eye. He clucked to himself as he peered into the still-raw pit where Martin's eye used to be.

'They could have done better than this.' Dr. Andursky was clearly miffed. 'All my good work . . .'

He washed up at the sink, snapped on a pair of the latex gloves, and got to work cleaning the excavation. Lindros felt nothing more than the dull ache he'd become accustomed to. It was like a houseguest who showed up unexpectedly one night and never left. Now, like it or not, the pain was a permanent fixture.

'I imagine you've already adjusted to your monovision.' As was his wont, Dr. Andursky worked quickly and efficiently. He knew what he needed to do, and how he wanted to do it.

'I have an idea,' Lindros said. 'Why don't you take Fadi's right eye and give it to me?'

'How very Old Testament of you.' Dr. Andursky rebandaged the excavation. 'But you're alone, Lindros. There's no one here to help you.'

Finished, he snapped off his gloves. 'For you, there is no escape from this hell-pit.'

*

Jon Mueller caught up with Defense Secretary Halliday as he was coming out of the Pentagon. Halliday was, of course, not alone. He had with him two aides, a bodyguard, and several pilot fish – lieutenant generals eager to ingratiate themselves with the great man.

Halliday, seeing Mueller out of the corner of his eye, made a hand gesture Mueller knew well. He hung back, at the bottom of the stairs, at the last minute allowing himself to be swept up into the secretary's retinue as he ducked into his limo. They said nothing to each other until the two aides had been dropped off near the secretary's office. Then the privacy wall came down between passengers in the rear, and driver and bodyguard in front. Mueller brought Halliday up to date.

Storm clouds of displeasure raced across the secretary's broad forehead. 'Lerner assured me everything was under control.'

'Matt made the mistake of farming out the job. I'll take care of the Held woman myself.'

The secretary nodded. 'All right. But be warned, Jon. Nothing can be traced back to me, you understand? If something goes wrong, I won't lift a finger. In fact, I may be the one to prosecute you. From this moment on, you're on your own.'

Mueller grinned like a savage. 'No worries, Mr. Secretary, I've been on my own for as long as I can remember. It's bred in the bone.'

'Sarah. Just Sarah. You never followed it up?'

'There was nothing to follow up. I couldn't even remember her face clearly. It was night, everything happened so fast. And then you were shot. We were on the run, pursued. We holed up in the catacombs, then got out. Afterward, all I had was a name. There was no official record of her body; it was as if we'd never been in Odessa.' Soraya put her head down. 'But even if there had been some way, the truth is I . . . couldn't. I wanted to forget her, forget her death ever happened.'

'But I remember running down a cobbled street, holding her in my arms, her blood everywhere.'

Soraya nodded. Her face was heavy with sorrow. 'You saw her moving. You picked her up. That's when you were shot. I returned fire and suddenly there was a hail of bullets. We got separated. You went to find the target, Hamid ibn Ashef. From what you told me later, when we rendezvoused in the catacombs, you found him and shot him, but were unsure whether you'd killed him.'

'And Sarah?'

'By then she was long dead. You left her on the way to kill Hamid ibn Ashef.'

For a long time, there was silence in the stateroom. Bourne turned, went to the water jug, poured himself half a glass. He opened the twist of paper Dr. Pavlyna had given him, swallowed one of the antibiotic pills. The water tasted flat, slightly bitter.

'How did it happen?' He had his back to her. He didn't want to see her face when she told him.

'She appeared at the spot where we met my conduit. He told us where Hamid ibn Ashef was. In return, we gave him the money he'd asked for. We were finishing the transaction when we saw her. She was running. I don't know why. Also, she had her mouth open as if shouting something. But the conduit was shouting, too. We thought he'd betrayed us – which, it turned out, he had. We shot at her. Both of us. And she fell.'

Bourne, abruptly tired, sat down on the bed.

Soraya took a step toward him. 'Are you all right?'

He nodded, took a deep breath. 'It was a mistake,' he said.

'Do you think that makes any difference to her?'

'You may not even have hit her.'

'And then again I may have. In any event, would that absolve me?'

'You're drowning in your own guilt.'

She gave a sad little laugh. 'Then I guess we both are.'

They regarded each other across the small space of the stateroom. The *Itkursk*'s horn sounded again, muffled, mournful. The ro-ro rocked them as it plowed south across the Black Sea, but it was so quiet in the stateroom that she imagined she could hear the sound of his mind working through a deep and tangled mystery.

He said, 'Soraya, listen to me, I think Sarah's death is the key to everything that's happened, everything that's happening now.'

'You can't be serious.' But by the expression on his face she knew he was, and she was sorry for her response. 'Go on,' she said.

'I think Sarah is central. I think her death set everything in motion.'

'Dujja's plan to detonate a nuclear bomb in a major American city? That's a stretch.'

'Not the plan per se. I have no doubt that was already being discussed,' Bourne said. 'But I think the timing of it changed. I think Sarah's death lit the fuse.'

'That would mean that Sarah is connected with your original mission to terminate Hamid ibn Ashef.'

He nodded. 'That would be my guess. I don't think she was at the rendezvous point by accident.'

'Why would she be there? How would she have known?'

'She could have found out from your conduit. He betrayed us to Hamid ibn Ashef's people,' Bourne said. 'As to why she was there, I have no idea.'

Soraya frowned. 'But where's the link between Hamid ibn Ashef and Fadi?'

'I've been thinking about that bit of intel you got from your forensics friend at the Fire Investigation Unit.'

'Carbon disulfide – the accelerant Fadi used at the Hotel Constitution.'

'Right. One of things you told me carbon disulfide is used for is flotation – a method for the separation of mixtures. Flotation was developed in the late twentieth century on a commercial scale mainly for the processing of silver.'

Soraya's eyes lit up. 'One of Integrated Vertical Technologies' businesses is silver processing. IVT is owned by Hamid ibn Ashef.'

Bourne nodded. 'I think IVT is the legitimate entity that's been bankrolling Dujja all these years.'

'But Sarah – '

'As for Sarah, or anything else, for that matter, we're dead in the water until we reach Istanbul and can connect to the Internet. Right now, our cell phones are useless.'

Soraya rose. 'In that event, I'm going to get us something to eat. I don't know about you, but I'm starving.'

'We'll go together.'

Bourne began to rise, but she pushed him back onto the bed. 'You need your rest, Jason. I'll get food for both of us.'

She smiled at him before turning and going out the door.

Bourne lay back for a moment, trying to recall more of the abortive mission to terminate Hamid ibn Ashef. He imagined the young woman Sarah as she ran into the square, mouth open. What was she shouting? Who was she shouting at? He felt her in his arms, strained to hear her failing voice.

But it was Fadi's voice he heard, echoing beneath the pier in Odessa:

*'I've waited a long time for this moment. A long time to look you in the face again. A long time to exact my revenge.'*

So there was a significant personal element to Fadi's plan. Because Fadi had come after him, leading him carefully, craftily into the web of a conspiracy of unprecedented proportions. It was he who had come after the man posing as Lindros; he who had vouched for the impostor at Bleak House. That, too, was part of the plan. Fadi had used him to infiltrate CI on the highest level.

No longer able to lie still, Bourne levered himself off the bed, not without some pain and stiffness. He stretched as much as he could, then padded into the bathroom: a sheet-metal shower, tiny metal sink, porcelain toilet, hexagonal mirror. On a rack were a pair of thin, almost threadbare towels, two large oblong cakes of soap, probably mostly lye.

Reaching up, he turned on the shower, waited for the spray of water to run hot, stepped in.

The afternoon, waning, had turned gray, the sun having lowered beneath dark clouds holding what would soon be a deluge. With the premature darkness a humid wind had sprung up from the southwest, bringing with it imagined hints of the pungent scents of sumac and oregano from the Turkish shore.

Matthew Lerner, standing amidships at the *Itkursk*'s starboard rail, was smoking a cigarette when he saw Soraya Moore emerge from one of the two VIP staterooms on the flagship deck.

He watched her moving away from the stateroom, down a metal stairway to one of the lower decks. He felt the impulse to go after her, to bury the ice pick he carried into the nape of her neck. That would have made him personally happy, but professionally it was suicide – just as it would be to use his gun in the enclosed environment of the ship. He was after Bourne. Killing Soraya Moore would complicate a situation that had already jumped the tracks. He was having to improvise, not the best of scenarios, though in the field improvisation was almost inevitable.

Swiveling adroitly, he faced the rolling waves as she came to the midway landing, for a moment facing in his direction. He pulled on the harsh Turkish cigarette then spun the butt over the side.

He turned back. Soraya Moore had disappeared. There were no colors here. The sea was gunmetal gray, the ship itself painted black and white. Moving quickly across the deck, he climbed the staircase to the flagship deck and the door to the VIP stateroom.

Bourne, careful of his wound, soaped up. Aches and muscle tightness sluiced away, along with the layers of sweat and grime. He wished he could stay under the hot water, but this was a working ship, not a luxury liner. The cold water came too quickly, and then the spray stopped altogether, with his skin still partially soap-slicked.

At almost the same moment he saw a blur of movement out of the corner of his eye. Turning, he went into a crouch. His reflexes and the slickness of his skin saved him from having the ice pick wielded by Lerner puncture his neck. As it was, he lurched hard against the back wall of the shower as Lerner rushed him.

Using the heavily callused edge of his hand, Lerner delivered two quick blows to Bourne's midsection. Designed to incapacitate him so that Lerner could strike again with the ice pick, they landed hard, but not hard enough. Bourne countered a third blow, using the added leverage of the stall back to slam the heel of his left foot into Lerner's chest just as Lerner was stepping into the shower. Instead of hemming Bourne in, Lerner shot backward, skidding across the tile of the bathroom floor.

Bourne was out of the stall in an instant. He grabbed a new bar of soap, placed it squarely in the center of the towel. Holding the towel at either end, he spun it around, securely embedding the cake. With the two ends of the towel in his right hand, he swung it back and forth. He blocked a vicious edge-hand strike with his left forearm, lifting Lerner's right arm up and away, creating an opening. He lashed his homemade weapon into Lerner's midsection.

The towel-wrapped bar of soap delivered a surprisingly wicked blow for which Lerner was unprepared. He staggered backward into the stateroom. Nevertheless, with his body in peak condition, it slowed him only momentarily. Set back on his heels, he waited for Bourne's attempt to maneuver inside his defense. Instead Bourne whipped his weapon in low, forcing Lerner to take a swipe at it with the ice pick.

At once Bourne stamped down with his left foot on Lerner's right wrist, trapping it against the stateroom carpet. But Bourne was barefoot; moreover, his foot was still wet and somewhat slick, and Lerner was able to wrench his wrist free. Lerner slashed upward with the ice pick, barely missed impaling Bourne's foot. He feinted right, drove his right knee into the left side of Bourne's rib cage.

The pain reverberated through Bourne, his teeth bared in a grimace. The iron-hard knuckles of Lerner's fist struck him on the opposite shoulder. He sagged and, as he did so, Lerner hooked his heel behind Bourne's ankle, then jerked him off his feet.

He fell on Bourne, who struck upward. Blood spattered them both as Bourne landed a direct hit on Lerner's nose, breaking it. As Lerner wiped the blood out of his eyes, Bourne upended him, jamming his fingertips into the spot just at the bottom of Lerner's rib cage. Lerner grunted in surprise and pain as he felt two of his ribs give.

He roared, letting go with such a flurry of powerful blows that even with both hands free Bourne couldn't protect himself from all of them. Only a third got through his defenses, but those were enough to seriously weaken his already compromised stamina.

Without knowing how it happened, he found Lerner's ham-like hand around his throat. Pinned to the floor, he saw the point of the ice pick sweep down toward his right eye.

Only one chance now. He ceded all conscious control to the killer instinct of the Bourne identity. No thought, no fear. He slammed the palms of his hands against Lerner's ears. The twin blows not only disoriented Lerner but also created a semi-airtight seal, so that when Bourne swung his hands apart the resulting pressure ruptured Lerner's eardrums.

The ice pick stopped in midstrike, trembling in Lerner's suddenly palsied hand. Bourne swept it aside, grabbed Lerner by the front of his shirt, jerked him down as he brought his head up. The bone of his forehead impacted Lerner's face just where the bridge of his nose met his forehead.

Lerner reared back, his eyes rolling up. Still he grasped the ice pick. Half unconscious, his superbly developed survival instinct kicked in. His right hand swept down, passing through the skin on the outside of Bourne's right arm as Bourne twisted away.

Then Bourne delivered a two-handed blow to the carotid artery in the right side of Lerner's neck. Lerner, on his knees, fell back, swaying. Forming his fingers into a tight wedge, Bourne drove his fingertips into the soft spot beneath Lerner's jaw. He felt the shredding of skin, muscle, viscera.

The stateroom turned red.

Bourne felt a sudden blackness imposing itself on his vision. All at once, he felt his strength desert him, ebbing like the tide. He shivered, toppled over, unconscious.

# 23

Muta ibn Aziz, his fingers gripping Katya Veintrop's shapely upper arm, rode the stainless-steel elevator down to Dujja's Miran Shah nuclear facility.

'Will I see my husband now?' Katya asked.

'You will,' Muta ibn Aziz said, 'but the reunion won't make either of you happy, this I promise.'

The elevator door slid open. Katya shuddered as they stepped out.

'I feel like I'm in the bowels of hell,' she said, looking around at the bare concrete corridors.

The infernal lighting did nothing to disfigure her beauty, which Muta ibn Aziz, like any good Arab, had done his best to cover with the utmost modesty. She was tall, slender, full-breasted, blond, light-eyed. Her skin, free of blemishes, seemed to glow, as if she'd recently buffed it. A small constellation of freckles rode the bridge of her nose. None of this mattered to Muta ibn Aziz, who ignored her with an absoluteness born and bred in the desert.

During the dusty, monotonous eight-hour trip by Land Rover to Miran Shah, he had turned his mind to other matters. He had been to this spot once before, three years ago. He had come with his brother Abbud ibn Aziz; with them was the brilliant and reluctant Dr. Costin Veintrop. They had been sent by Fadi to escort Veintrop from his laboratory in Bucharest to Miran Shah because the good doctor appeared incapable of making the trip on his own.

Veintrop had been in a depressed and bitter mood, having been summarily severed from Integrated Vertical Technologies for crimes he claimed he'd never committed. He was right, but that was beside the point. The charges themselves had been enough to blackball him from any legitimate corporation, university, or grant program to which he applied.

Along had come Fadi with his seductive offer. He hadn't bothered to sugar-coat the goal of what he was proposing; what would be the point? The doctor would realize it soon enough. Veintrop was, naturally, dazzled by the money. But as it happened, he possessed scruples as well as brilliance. So Fadi had abandoned the carrot for the stick. This particular stick being Katya. Fadi had learned quickly enough that Veintrop would do virtually anything to keep Katya safe.

'Your wife is safe with me, Doctor,' Fadi had said when Muta ibn Aziz and his brother had appeared at Miran Shah with Veintrop in tow. 'Safer than she'd be anywhere else on the planet.' And to prove it, he'd shown Veintrop a video of Katya made just days before. Katya weeping, imploring her husband to come for her.

Veintrop, too, had wept. Then, wiping his eyes, he had accepted Fadi's offer. But in his eyes they all recognized the shadow of trouble.

After Dr. Senarz had taken Veintrop away to begin his work at the Miran Shah labs, Fadi had turned to Muta ibn Aziz and Abbud ibn Aziz. 'Will he do what we want? What is your opinion?'

The two brothers spoke up at once, agreeing. 'He'll do everything asked of him as long as we beat him with the stick.'

But it was the last thing they agreed on during that four-day sojourn in the concrete city deep below the wild, bare-knuckled mountains that formed the border between western Pakistan and Afghanistan. A man could get killed in those mountain passes – many men, in fact, no matter how well trained, how heavily armed. Miran Shah was the lethal badlands into which no representative of the Pakistani government or army dared venture. Taliban, al-Qaeda, World Jihad, Muslim fundamentalists of every stripe and flavor – Miran Shah was crawling with terrorists, many of whom were hostile to one another, for it was one of the more successful American lies that all terrorist groups were coordinated and controlled by one or two men, or even a handful. This was ludicrous: There were so many ancient enmities among sects, so many different objectives that interfered with one another. Still, the myth remained. Fadi, schooled in the West, master of the principles of mass communication, used the American lie against them, to build Dujja's reputation, along with his own.

As Muta ibn Aziz marched Katya along the corridors for her interview with Fadi and with her husband, he could not help but reflect on the fundamental splinter that had driven him and his brother apart. They had disagreed on it three years ago, and time had only hardened their respective positions. The splinter had a name: Sarah ibn Ashef, Fadi and Karim al-Jamil's only sister. Her murder had changed all their lives, spawning secrets, lies, and enmity where none had existed before. Her death had destroyed two families, in ways both obvious and obscure. After that night in Odessa when her arms had flung out and she had pitched to the cobbles of the square, Muta ibn Aziz and his brother were finished. Outwardly they acted as if nothing had happened, but inside their thoughts never again ran down parallel tracks. They were lost to each other.

Turning a corner, Muta ibn Aziz saw his brother step out of an open doorway, beckon to him. Muta hated when he did that. It was the gesture of a professor to a pupil, one who was due for a reprimand.

'Ah, you're here,' Abbud ibn Aziz said, as if his brother had taken a wrong turn and was now late.

Muta ibn Aziz contrived to ignore Abbud ibn Aziz, brushing past him as he manhandled Katya over the threshold.

The room was spacious, though by necessity low-ceilinged. It was furnished in strictly utilitarian fashion: six chairs made of molded plastic, a zinc-topped table, cabinets along the left-hand wall, with a sink and a single electric burner.

Fadi was standing, facing them. His hands were on the shoulders of Dr. Veintrop, who was sitting, clearly not of his own volition, on one of the chairs.

'Katya!' he cried when he saw her. His face lit up, but the light in his eyes was quickly extinguished as he tried, and failed, to go to her.

Fadi, exerting the requisite pressure on Veintrop to keep him from moving, nodded to Muta ibn Aziz, who released the young woman. With an inarticulate cry, she ran to her husband, knelt in front of him.

Veintrop caressed her hair, her face, his fingers moving over every contour as if he needed to reassure himself that she wasn't a mirage or a doppelgänger. He'd seen what Dr. Andursky had done with Karim al-Jamil's face. What would prevent him from doing the same with some other Russian woman, turning her into a Katya who would lie to him, do their bidding?

Ever since Fadi had 'recruited' him, his paranoia threshold was exceedingly low. Everything revolved around the plot to enslave him. In this, he wasn't far wrong.

'Now that you've been reunited, more or less,' Fadi said to Dr. Veintrop, 'I'd like you to stop procrastinating. We have a specific timetable, and your foot-dragging is doing us no good.'

'I'm not procrastinating,' Veintrop said. 'The microcircuits – ' He broke off, wincing, as Fadi applied more pressure to his shoulders.

Fadi nodded to Abbud ibn Aziz, who stepped out of the room. When he returned, it was with Dr. Senarz, the nuclear physicist.

'Dr. Senarz,' Fadi said, 'please tell me why the nuclear device I ordered you to construct is not yet complete.'

Dr. Senarz stared directly at Veintrop. He had trained under the notorious Pakistani nuclear scientist Abdul Qadeer Khan. 'My work is complete,' he said. 'The uranium dioxide powder you delivered to me has been converted to HEU, the metal form needed for the warhead. In other words, we have the fissionable material. The casing is also complete. We are now only waiting on Dr. Veintrop. His work is crucial, as you know. Without it, you won't have the device you requested.'

'So Costin, here we come to the crux of the matter at hand.' Fadi's voice was calm, soft, neutral. 'With your help my plan succeeds, without your help my plan is doomed. An equation as simple as it is elegant, to put it in scientific terms. Why aren't you helping me?'

'The process is more difficult than I had anticipated.' Veintrop could not keep his eyes off his wife.

Fadi said, 'Dr. Senarz?'

'Dr. Veintrop's miniaturization work has been complete for days now.'

'What does he know of miniaturization?' Veintrop said sharply. 'It simply isn't true.'

'I don't want opinions, Dr. Senarz,' Fadi said with equal sharpness.

When Senarz produced the small notebook with a dark red leather cover, Veintrop let out an involuntary moan. Katya, alarmed, gripped him tighter.

Dr. Senarz held out the notebook. 'Here we have Dr. Veintrop's private notes.'

'You have no right!' Veintrop shouted.

'Ah, but he has every right.' Fadi accepted the notebook from Dr. Senarz. 'You belong to me, Veintrop. Everything you do, everything you think, write, or dream of is mine.'

Katya groaned. 'Costin, what did you do?'

'I sold my soul to the devil,' Veintrop muttered.

Abbud ibn Aziz must have received a silent signal from Fadi, because he tapped Dr. Senarz on the shoulder and led him out of the room. The sound of the door closing behind them made Veintrop jump.

'All right,' Fadi said in his gentlest voice.

At once, Muta ibn Aziz grabbed Katya's clothes at the nape of her neck and at her waist, wrenching her away from her husband. At the same time, Fadi resumed his two-handed grip on the doctor, slamming him back down onto the chair, from which he struggled to rise.

'I won't ask you again,' Fadi said in that same gentle tone, a father to a beloved child who has misbehaved.

Muta ibn Aziz struck Katya a tremendous blow on the back of her head.

'No!' Veintrop screamed as she sprawled face-first on the floor.

No one paid him the slightest attention. Muta ibn Aziz hauled her up to a sitting position, came around, punched her so hard he broke her perfect nose. Blood gushed forth, spattering them both.

'No!' Veintrop screamed.

Gripping the back of her blond hair, Muta ibn Aziz drove his knuckles into Katya's beautiful left cheek. Tears rolled down Katya's bloated face as she sobbed.

'Stop!' Veintrop shouted. 'For the love of God, stop! I beg you!'

Muta ibn Aziz drew back his bloody fist.

'Don't make me ask you again,' Fadi said in the doctor's ear. 'Don't make me distrust you, Costin.'

'No, all right.' Veintrop was himself sobbing. His heart was breaking into ten thousand pieces he would never be able to fit back together. 'I'll do what you want. I'll have the miniaturization finished in two days.'

'Two days, Costin.' Fadi grabbed his hair, jerked his head back so that his eyes looked up directly into his captor's. 'Not a moment more. Understood?'

'Yes.'

'Otherwise, what will be done to Katya not even Dr. Andursky will be able to fix.'

Muta ibn Aziz found his brother in Dr. Andursky's operating theater. It was here that Karim al-Jamil had been given Martin Lindros's face. It was here that Karim al-Jamil had been given a new iris, a new pupil, and, most important, a retina that would prove to CI's scanners that Karim al-Jamil was Lindros.

To Muta ibn Aziz's relief, the theater was currently empty save for his brother.

'Now surely we must tell Fadi the truth.' Muta ibn Aziz's voice was low, urgent.

Abbud ibn Aziz, staring at the battery of gleaming equipment, said, 'Don't you think of anything else? This is precisely what you said to me three years ago.'

'Circumstances have changed, radically. It's our duty to tell him.'

'I disagree, in the strongest possible terms, just as I did then,' Abbud ibn Aziz replied. 'In fact, it's our duty to keep the truth from Fadi and Karim al-Jamil.'

'There's no logic to your argument now.'

'Really? The central issue now is the same at it was in the beginning. With Sarah ibn Ashef's death, they have suffered an unsupportable loss. Should there be more? Sarah ibn Ashef was Allah's flower, the repository of the family's honor, the beautiful innocent destined for a life of happiness. It is vital that her memory be kept sacrosanct. Our duty is to insulate Fadi and Karim al-Jamil from outside distractions.'

'Distraction,' Muta ibn Aziz cried. 'You call the truth about their sister a distraction?'

'What would you call it?'

'A full-scale disaster, a disgrace beyond anything – '

'And you would be the one to deliver this terrible truth to Fadi? Toward what end? What would you seek to accomplish?'

'Three years ago, I answered that question by saying I wanted simply to tell the truth,' Muta ibn Aziz said. 'Now their plan includes taking revenge on Jason Bourne.'

'I see no reason to stop them. Bourne is a menace to us – you included. You were there that night, as was I.'

'Their obsession with revenging their sister's death has warped both of them. What if they've overreached?'

'With one man?' Abbud ibn Aziz laughed.

'You were with Fadi both times in Odessa. Tell me, brother, was he successful in killing Bourne?'

Abbud ibn Aziz reacted to his brother's icy tone. 'Bourne was wounded, very badly. Fadi hounded him into the catacombs beneath the city. I very much doubt he survived. But really, it's of no consequence. He's incapacitated; he cannot harm us now. It's Allah's will. Whatever happened, happened. Whatever happens, will happen.'

'And I say that as long as there's the slightest possibility of Bourne being alive, neither of them will rest. The distraction will continue. Whereas if we tell them – '

'Silence! It is Allah's will!'

Abbud ibn Aziz had never before spoken to his younger brother with such venom. Between them, Muta ibn Aziz knew, lay the death of Sarah ibn Ashef, a topic about which both thought but never, ever spoke. The silence was an evil thing, Muta ibn Aziz knew, a poisoning of the well of their fraternal bond. He harbored a strong conviction that one day, the deliberately invoked silence would destroy him and his older brother.

Not for the first time he felt a wave of despair roll over him. In these moments, it seemed to him that he was trapped; that no matter which way he turned, no matter what action he took now, he and his brother were condemned to the hell-fire reserved for the wicked. *La ilaha ill allah! May Allah forbid the Fire from touching us!*

As if to underscore Muta's dark thoughts, Abbud reiterated the stance he had taken from the night of her death: 'In the matter of Sarah ibn Ashef, we keep our own counsel,' he said flatly. 'You will obey me without question, just as you've always done. Just as you must do. We are not individuals, brother, we are links in the family chain. *La ilaha ill allah!* The fate of one is the fate of all.'

The man sitting cross-legged at the head of a low wooden table laden with para-phernalia regarded Fadi with a jaundiced eye. Doubtless, this was because he had the use of only one eye – his left. The other, beneath its white Egyptian cotton patch, was a blackened crater.

Kicking off his shoes, Fadi padded across the poured concrete floor. Every floor, wall, and ceiling in Miran Shah was of poured concrete, looked identical. He sat at a ninety-degree angle from the other.

From a glass jar, he shook out a fistful of coffee beans that had been roasted hours ago. He dropped them into a brass mortar, took up the pestle, ground them to a fine powder. A copper pot sat atop the ring of a portable gas burner. Fadi poured water from a pitcher into the pot, then lit the burner. A circle of blue flame licked at the bottom of the pot.

'It's been some time,' Fadi said.

'Do you actually expect me to drink with you?' said the real Martin Lindros.

'I expect you to behave like a civilized human being.'

Lindros laughed bitterly, touched the center of his eye patch with the tip of his forefinger. 'That would make one of us.'

'Have a date,' Fadi said, pushing an oval plate piled high with the dried fruit in front of Lindros. 'They're best dipped in this goat butter.'

The moment the water began to boil, Fadi upended the mortar, spilling the coffee powder into the pot. He drew to him a small cup, whose contents were fragrant with the scent of freshly crushed cardamom seeds. Now all his concentration was on the roiling coffee. An instant before it would have foamed up, he took the pot off the burner, with the fingers of his right hand he dropped a few crushed cardamom seeds into the coffee, then poured it into what looked like a small teapot. A fragment of palm fiber stuffed into the spout served to keep the grounds out of the liquid. Setting the pot aside, Fadi poured the *qahwah 'Arabiyah* – the Arabic coffee – into a pair of tiny cups without handles. He served Lindros first, as any Bedouin would his honored guest, though never before had a Bedouin sat cross-legged in such a tent – immense, subterranean, fashioned of concrete half a meter thick.

'How's your brother doing? I hope seeing with my eye will give him a different perspective. Perhaps he won't be so hell-bent on the destruction of the West.'

'Do you really wish to speak of destruction, Martin? We shall speak then of America's forced exportation of a culture riddled with the decadence of a jaded populace that wants everything immediately, that no longer understands the meaning of the word *sacrifice*. We shall speak of America's occupation of the Middle East, of its willful destruction of ancient traditions.'

'Then those traditions must include the blowing up of religious statues, as the Taliban did in Afghanistan. Those traditions must include the stoning of women who commit adultery, while their lovers go without punishment.'

'I – a Saudi Bedouin – have as much to do with the Taliban as you do. And as for adulterous women, there is Islamic law to consider. We are not individuals, Martin, but part of a family unit. The honor of the family resides in its daughters. If our sisters are shamed, that shame reflects on all in the family until the woman is excised.'

'To kill your own flesh and blood? It's inhuman.'

'Because it's not your way?' Fadi made a gesture with his head. 'Drink.'

Lindros raised his cup to his lips, downed the coffee in one gulp.

'You must sip it, Martin.' Fadi refilled Lindros's cup, then drank his coffee in three small, savory sips. With his right hand, he took up a date, dipped it in the fragrant butter, then popped it into his mouth. He chewed slowly, thoughtfully, and spat out the long, flat pit. 'It will do you good to try one. Dates are delicious, and ever so nutritious. Do you know that Muhammad would invariably break his fast with dates? So do we, because it brings us closer to his ideals.'

Lindros stared at him, stiff and silent, as if on vigil.

Fadi wiped his right hand on a small towel. 'You know, my father made coffee from morning to night. That's the highest compliment I could pay him – or any

Bedouin. It means he's a generous man.' He refilled his coffee cup. 'However, my father can no longer make coffee. In fact, he can do nothing at all but stare into space. My mother speaks to him, but he cannot answer. Do you know why, Martin?' He drained his cup in three more sips. 'Because his name is Abu Sarif Hamid ibn Ashef al-Wahhib.'

At this, Lindros's good eye gave a slight twitch.

'Yes, that's right,' Fadi said. 'Hamid ibn Ashef. The man you sent Jason Bourne to kill.'

'So that's why you captured me.'

'You think so?'

'That wasn't my mission, you fool. I didn't even know Jason Bourne then. His handler was Alex Conklin, and Conklin's dead.' Lindros began to laugh.

Without any warning Fadi lunged across the table and grabbed Lindros by his shirtfront. He shook him so violently that Lindros's teeth chattered.

'You think you're so clever, Martin. But now you're going to pay for it. You and Bourne.'

Fadi gripped Lindros's throat as if he wanted to rip out his windpipe. He took visible pleasure in the man's gasps.

'Bourne is still alive, I'm told, though just barely. Still and all, I know he'll move heaven and earth to find you, especially if he thinks I'll be here as well.'

'What . . . what are you going to do?' Lindros could barely spit the words through his labored breathing.

'I'm going to give him the information he needs, Martin, to find you here in Miran Shah. And when he does, I'll disembowel you in front of his eyes. Then I'll go to work on him.'

Fadi put his face against Lindros's, peering into his left eye as if to find all the things Lindros was hiding from him. 'In the end, Bourne will want to die, Martin. Of this there is no question. But for him, death will be a long time coming. Before he dies, I'll make certain he witnesses the nuclear destruction of the American capital.'

# Book 3

# 24

*The coffin is being lowered into the ground. Dull reflections spin off the handles, the inscribed panel set into its lid creating tiny dizzying whorls of light. In response to an emphatic gesture from the minister, the coffin hangs motionless in midair. The minister, dapper and trim in his European-cut suit, leans over the grave so far that Bourne is certain he'll fall in. But he does not. Instead, with an astonishing burst of super-human strength, he wrenches off the coffin lid.*

*'What are you doing?' Bourne asks.*

*The minister turns to him, beckons as he drops the heavy mahogany lid into the grave, and Bourne sees that it isn't the minister at all. It's Fadi.*

*'Come on,' Fadi says in Saudi Arabic. He lights up a cigarette, hands Bourne the matchbook. 'Take a look.'*

*Bourne takes a step forward, peers into the open coffin . . .*

*. . . and finds himself sitting in the backseat of a car. He looks out the window and sees a familiar landscape that he nevertheless cannot identify. He shakes the driver's shoulder.*

*'Where are we going?'*

*The driver turns around. It's Lindros. But there's something wrong with his face. It's shadowed, or scarred: It's the Lindros he brought back to CI headquarters. 'Where do you think?' the Lindros impostor says, increasing their speed.*

*Leaning forward, Bourne sees a figure standing by the side of the road. They come up on it fast. A young woman, a hitchhiker with her thumb out: Sarah. They're almost abreast of her when she takes a step into the path of the speeding car.*

*Bourne tries to shout a warning, but he is mute. He feels the car lurch and buck, sees Sarah's body flung into the air, blood streaming from her. In a rage, he reaches for the driver . . .*

*. . . and finds himself aboard a bus. The passengers, blank-faced, ignore him completely. Bourne moves forward along the aisle between the sets of seats. The driver is wearing a neat suit of European manufacture. He is Dr. Sunderland, the D.C. memory specialist.*

*'Where are we going?' Bourne asks him.*

*'I already told you.' Dr. Sunderland points.*

*Through the huge pane of the windshield, Bourne sees the beach at Odessa. He sees Fadi smoking a cigarette, smiling, waiting for him.*

*'It's all been arranged,' Dr. Sunderland says, 'from the beginning.'*

*The bus slows. There is a gun in Fadi's hand. Dr. Sunderland opens the door for him; he swings aboard, aims the gun at Bourne, then pulls the trigger . . .*

*

Bourne awoke to the sound of a reverberating gunshot. Someone stood over him. A man with a blue stubble of beard, deeply embedded eyes, and a low, simian hairline. Gauzy light slanted in through the window, illuminating the man's long, somber face. Behind him, the sky was striped blue and white.

'Ah, Lieutenant General Mykola Petrovich Tuz. You're awake at last.' His atrocious Russian was further slurred by heavy drinking. 'I'm Dr. Korovin.'

For a moment Bourne couldn't remember where he was. The bed rocking gently beneath him made his heart skip a beat. He'd been here before – had he lost his memory again?

Then everything came flooding back. He took in the tiny medical infirmary, realized he was on the *Itkursk,* that he was Lieutenant General Mykola Petrovich Tuz, and said in a voice thick with cotton wool, 'I require my assistant.'

'Of course.' Dr. Korovin took a step back. 'She's right here.'

His face was replaced by that of Soraya Moore's. 'Lieutenant General,' she said crisply. 'You're feeling better.'

He could clearly see the concern in her eyes. 'We need to talk,' he whispered.

She turned to the doctor. 'Please leave us,' she said curtly.

'Certainly,' Dr. Korovin said. 'In the meantime, I'll inform the captain that the lieutenant general is on his way to recovery.'

As soon as the door closed behind him, Soraya sat on the edge of the bed. 'Lerner has been deep-sixed,' she said softly. 'When I identified him as a foreign spy, the captain was only too happy to oblige. In fact, he's relieved. He doesn't want any adverse publicity, and that goes double for the freight company, so over the side Lerner went.'

'Where are we?' Bourne said.

'About forty minutes from Istanbul.' Soraya gripped his arm gently as he sought to sit up. 'As for Lerner being aboard ship, we both missed that.'

'I think I missed something else, something even more important,' Bourne said. 'Hand me my trousers.'

They were hanging neatly over the back of a chair. Soraya passed them to Bourne. 'We need to get some food into you. The doctor pumped you full of fluids while he fixed you up. He tells me you should be feeling much better in a couple of hours.'

'In a minute.' He could feel the dull ache of the knife wound and the place where Lerner had kicked him. There was a bandage around his right biceps where the ice pick had pierced him, but he felt no pain there. He closed his eyes, but that only brought back his dream of Fadi, the impostor, Sarah, and Dr. Sunderland.

'Jason, what is it?'

He opened his eyes. 'Soraya, it isn't only Dr. Sunderland who's been playing around inside my head.'

'What do you mean?'

Rummaging through his pockets, he found a matchbook. *Fadi lights up a cigarette, hands Bourne the matchbook.* That image had been in Bourne's dream, but it had happened in real life. Bourne, under the influence of Sunderland's implanted memories, had taken Fadi out of the Typhon cell. Outside, Fadi had lit a cigarette with a matchbook – '*Nothing to burn in the hole so they let me keep it,*' he'd said. Then he'd handed Bourne the matchbook.

Why had he done that? It had been such a simple gesture, barely noticed or recorded in memory, especially with what had come after. Fadi had been counting on that.

'A matchbook?' Soraya said.

'The matchbook Fadi handed me outside CI headquarters.' Bourne opened it. It was all but ruined, creased, the corners bent, the writing nearly unintelligible from the soaking Bourne had endured in the Black Sea.

Virtually the only thing left intact were the bottom layers, from which the matches themselves were torn off. Using a thumbnail, Bourne pried off the metal staples that had held the matches in place. Underneath he found a tiny oblong of metal and ceramic.

'My God, he bugged you.'

Bourne examined it closely. 'It's a tracer.' He handed it to her. 'I want you to throw it overboard. Right now.'

Soraya took it, left the cabin. In a moment she was back.

'Now to other matters.' He looked at her. 'It's clear that Tim Hytner provided Fadi with all the inside knowledge.'

'Tim wasn't the mole,' Soraya said firmly.

'I know he was your friend – '

'That's not it, Jason. Lindros's impostor went out of his way to show me documented evidence that Tim was the mole.'

Bourne took a deep breath and, ignoring the pain it caused him, slid his feet onto the floor. 'Then the odds are good that Hytner wasn't the mole after all.'

Soraya nodded. 'Which means it's likely a mole is still at work inside CI.'

They sat in the Kaktüs Café, half a block south of Istiklal Caddesi – Independence Avenue – in the chicly modern Beyoglu District of Istanbul. Their table was piled with small *meze* plates, tiny cups of thick, strong Turkish coffee. The interior was filled with chatter in many different languages, which suited their purpose.

Bourne had eaten his fill and, on his third cup of coffee, had begun to feel halfway human again. At length, he said, 'It's clear we can't trust anyone at CI. If you get on a computer here can you hack past the Sentinel firewall?'

Soraya shook her head. 'Even Tim couldn't get through it.'

Bourne nodded. 'Then you have to go back to D.C. We've got to ID the mole. With him still in place, nothing inside CI is secure, including the investigation into Dujja's plan. You'll need to keep an eye on the impostor. Since they're both working for Fadi, he might lead you to the mole.'

'I'll go to the Old Man.'

'That's precisely what you *won't* do. We have no concrete evidence. It would be your word against the impostor's. You're already tainted by your association with me. And the Old Man loves Lindros, trusts him completely. It's what makes Fadi's plan so damn brilliant.' He shook his head. 'No, you'll never get anywhere accusing Lindros. The best course is to keep your eyes and ears open and your mouth shut. I don't want the impostor to get the idea you're on to him. He's already going to be suspicious of you. He sent you to keep an eye on me, after all.'

A grim smile came over Bourne's battered face. 'We'll give him what he wants.

You'll tell him that you witnessed the struggle between me and Lerner on this ferry, during which we killed each other.'

'That's why you had me throw the tracer overboard.'

Bourne nodded. 'Fadi will confirm that it's at the bottom of the Black Sea.'

Soraya laughed. 'Now we're getting somewhere.'

Down the block from the Kaktüs was an Internet café. Soraya paid for their time while Bourne took a seat in front of a terminal in the back. He was already looking up Dr. Allen Sunderland when Soraya dragged over a chair. It seemed Sunderland had been the recipient of a number of awards and books. One of the sites Bourne pulled up contained a photo of the eminent memory specialist.

'This isn't the man who treated me,' Bourne said, staring at the photo. 'Fadi used a substitute. A doctor he had bought or coerced to screw with the synapses of my brain introduced neurotransmitters. They suppressed certain memories, but they also created false ones. Memories meant to help me accept Martin's impostor, memories meant to lead me to my death.'

'It's horrible, Jason. Like someone has crawled inside your head.' Soraya put a hand on his shoulder. 'How do you fight something like that?'

'The fact is I can't. Not unless I find the man who did this to me.'

His mind went back to his conversation with the false Sunderland. The photo on the desk of the beautiful blonde Sunderland had called Katya. Was that part of the cover? Bourne opened his mind, listened to the tone of Sunderland's voice. No, he was being sincere about the woman. She, at least, was real to the man who had passed himself off as Allen Sunderland.

And then there was the doctor's accent. Bourne remembered he'd pinned it as Romanian. So this much was legitimate: The man was a doctor – a specialist in memory reconstruction; he was Romanian; he was married to a woman named Katya. Katya, who was so relaxed in front of a camera that she might be a model or an ex-model. These bits and pieces didn't amount to much, he thought, but a little knowledge was better than none at all.

'Now let's go back to our beginning.' His fingers flew over the keyboard. A moment later, he brought up information on Abu Sarif Hamid ibn Ashef al-Wahhib, founder of Integrated Vertical Technologies. 'He was married thirty-three years ago to Holly Cargill, youngest daughter of Simon and Jacqui Cargill of Cargill and Denison, top-tier solicitors. The Cargills are an important part of London society. They claim to trace their lineage back to the time of Henry the Eighth.' His fingers continued their dance; the screen continued to spew out information. 'Holly gave Hamid ibn Ashef three children. The first was Abu Ghazi Nadir al-Jamuh bin Hamid bin Ashef al Wahhib. Then his younger brother, Jamil bin Hamid bin Ashef al Wahhib – who, by the way, assumed the presidency of IVT the same year you and I were first in Odessa.'

'Two weeks after you shot Hamid ibn Ashef,' Soraya said from over his shoulder. 'What about the third child?'

'I'm coming to that.' Bourne scrolled down the page. 'Here we go. The youngest sibling is a daughter.' He stopped, his heart pounding in his throat. He said her name in a strangled voice. 'Sarah ibn Ashef. Deceased.'

'Our Sarah,' Soraya breathed in his ear.

'It would seem so.' All at once, everything fell into place. 'My God, Fadi is one of Hamid ibn Ashef's sons.'

Soraya looked stunned. 'The elder, I'd surmise, since Karim assumed the presidency of IVT.'

Bourne recalled his violent encounter with Fadi in the Black Sea surf. *'I've waited a long time for this moment,'* Fadi had said. *'A long time to look you in the face again. A long time to exact my revenge.'* When Bourne had asked him what he meant, Fadi had snarled, *'You couldn't have forgotten – not that.'* He could only have been talking about one thing.

'I killed their sister,' Bourne said, sitting back. 'That's why they wove me into their plan for destruction.'

'We're still no closer to finding out the identity of the man impersonating Martin Lindros,' Soraya said.

'Or to whether they've kept Martin alive.' Bourne returned his attention to the computer terminal. 'But maybe we can find out something about the other impostor.' Bourne had brought up the International Vertical Technologies Web site. On it was listed the conglomerate's personnel, including its R&D staff, far-flung over a dozen countries.

'If you're searching for the man who impersonated Dr. Sunderland, it'll be like looking for a needle in a haystack.'

'Not necessarily,' Bourne said. 'Don't forget, this man was a specialist.'

'In memory restoration.'

'That's right.' Then Bourne remembered another part of his conversation with Sunderland. 'Also miniaturization.'

There were ten doctors in fields that were related or seemed likely. Bourne looked them up on the Net, one by one. None was the man who had performed the procedure on him.

'Now what?' Soraya said.

He quit the IVT site and switched to historical news listings for the conglomerate. Fifteen minutes of wading through articles on announcements of mergers, spin-offs, quarterly P&L reports, personnel hirings and firings finally led him to an item on Dr. Costin Veintrop, a specialist in biopharmaceutical nanoscience, scanning force microscopy, and molecular medicine.

'It seems that Dr. Veintrop was summarily sacked from IVT for alleged intellectual property theft.'

'Wouldn't that strike him off the list?' Soraya said.

'Just the opposite. Consider. A public sacking like that got Veintrop blackballed from every legitimate laboratory job, every university professorship. He went from the top of the heap to oblivion.'

'Just the kind of situation Fadi's brother could fabricate. Then it was work for Fadi or nothing.'

Bourne nodded. 'It's a theory that bears checking out.' He typed in Dr. Costin Veintrop's name, and out popped a curriculum vitae. All very interesting, but conclusive it was not. The photo link was, however. It showed the doctor posing at an awards ceremony. By his side was his trophy wife: the tall beautiful blonde whose photo he'd seen at Sunderland's office. She was a former Perfect Ten model. Her name was Katya Stepanova Vdova.

*

Marlin Dorph, CI field commander in charge of Skorpion units Five and Six, had been given a legitimate military rank of captain, which held him in good stead when, just before dawn, he and his team had rendezvoused with the marine detachment just outside the town of al-Ghaydah, in the Shabwah region of South Yemen.

Dorph was the man for the job. He knew the Shabwah like the back of his hand. Its bloody history was tattooed into his flesh both by numerous victories and by defeats. Despite the assurances of Yemen's government, Shabwah was still infested with an unsavory stew of Islamic terrorist militant groups. During the Cold War, the Soviet Union, East Germany, and Cuba had developed a network of training facilities tucked away in this inhospitable mountainous region. During that time, al-Ghaydah, staffed by Cuban terrorist instructors, had become notorious for training and arming the People's Front for the Liberation of Oman. In a nearby town, East Germans were busy preparing key members of the Saudi Communist Party and the Bahrain Liberation Front for destabilizing activities, including the manipulation of the mass media for the purpose of spreading the groups' ideologies into every corner of their respective countries, thus undermining the spiritual lives of their peoples. Though the Soviets and their satellites left South Yemen in 1987, the terrorist cells did not, finding renewed vigor in the leadership of the venomous al-Qaeda.

'Anything yet?'

Dorph turned to find Captain Lowrie, commander of the marine forces who would be accompanying Skorpions Five and Six to the Dujja nuclear facility. Lowrie was tall, fair-haired, big as a bear, and twice as nasty-looking.

Dorph, who had seen his kind perform heroics and die in battle, hefted his Thuraya satellite phone. 'Waiting for confirmation now.'

They had rendezvoused on a sun-blasted plateau east of al-Ghaydah. The town shimmered in the dawn light, scoured by the restless wind, surrounded by mountains and desert. High clouds, shredded by winds aloft, streamed across the deep blue bowl of the sky. The mud-plastered buildings, ten and twelve stories high, were boxlike with oblong windows that lent the facades the appearance of ancient temples. Time seemed to have stopped here, as if history had never progressed.

On the plateau, the two military groups were silent, tense, spring-loaded, ready for the deployment they knew was imminent. They understood what was at stake; every man there was ready to lay down his life to ensure the safety of his country.

While they waited, Dorph pulled out his GPS, showing his marine counterpart the tentative target site. It was less than a hundred kilometers south-southwest of their present position.

The Thuraya buzzed. Dorph put it to his ear and listened while the man he believed to be Martin Lindros confirmed the coordinates he had marked out on his GPS.

'Yessir,' he said softly into the Thuraya's mouthpiece. 'ETA twenty minutes. You can count on us, sir.'

Breaking the connection, he nodded to Lowrie. Together they gave orders to their men, who silently climbed into the four Chinook helicopters. A moment later the rotors swung into motion, revolving faster and faster. The Chinook war machines took off two at a time, lifting massive clouds of dirt and sand that whirled upward in a fine mist, partially obscuring the aircraft until they reached altitude. Then they tipped forward slightly and shot ahead on a south by southwest course.

The War Room, forty-five meters beneath the ground floor of the White House, was a hive of activity. The flat-panel plasma screens showed satellite photos of South Yemen in differing degrees of detail, from an overview to specific topographic landmarks, details of the terrain around al-Ghaydah. Others presented 3-D-rendered displays of the target area and the progress of the four Chinook helicopters.

Those present were more or less the same contingent that had convened for the Old Man's skewering: the president; Luther LaValle, the Pentagon intelligence czar, plus two lower-ranking generals; Defense Secretary Halliday; the national security advisor; and Gundarsson from the IAEA. The only missing member was Jon Mueller.

'Ten minutes to contact,' the Old Man said. He had a headphone on, patched in to Commander Dorph's scrambled communication net.

'Remind me again what weaponry the strike force is carrying,' Secretary Halliday drawled from his seat on the president's left.

'These Chinooks are specially designed for us by McDonnell Douglas,' the Old Man said evenly. 'In fact, they have more in common with the Apache attack helis McD makes than regulation Chinooks. Like the Apache, they're equipped with target acquisition designation sights and laser range finder/designators. Our Chinooks have the capacity to withstand hits from rounds up to twenty-three millimeters. As for offensive weaponry, they're carrying a full complement of Hellfire antitank missiles, three M230 thirty-millimeter chain guns, and twelve Hydra 70 rockets, which are fired from the M261 nineteen-tube rocket launcher. The rockets are fitted with unitary warheads with impact-detonating fuzes or remote-set multi-option fuzes.'

The president laughed somewhat too loudly. 'That kind of detail should satisfy even you, Bud.'

'Pardon my confusion, Director,' Halliday persisted, 'but I'm baffled. You haven't mentioned the severe breach of CI security at your headquarters.'

'What breach?' The president looked bewildered, then, his face filling with blood, angry. 'What's Bud talking about?'

'We were hit with a computer virus,' the DCI said smoothly. *How in hell did he find out about the virus?* 'Our IT people assure us the integrity of the core mainframe wasn't breached. Our Sentinel firewall ensured that. They're purging the system even as we speak.'

'If I were in your shoes, Director,' Secretary Halliday pressed on, 'I sure as shootin' wouldn't be downplaying any electronic breach of agency security. Not with these goddamn terrorists breathing down our necks.'

As any loyal vassal would, LaValle picked up the interrogation. 'Director, you're telling us that your people are purging the virus. But the fact remains that your agency was electronically attacked.'

'It isn't the first time,' the DCI said. 'Believe me, it won't be the last.'

'Still,' LaValle continued, 'an attack from the outside – '

'It wasn't from the outside.' The DCI fixed the Pentagon intelligence czar in his formidable gaze. 'Due to the alert sleuthing of my deputy, Martin Lindros, we discovered an electronic trail that led back to the mole – the late Tim Hytner. His last action was to insert the virus into the system under the guise of "decrypting" a Dujja cipher that turned out to be the binary code culprit.'

The Old Man's gaze swung to the president. 'Now please, let's return to the grave matter at hand.' *How many more unsuccessful attacks must I endure from these two before the president puts an end to it?* he wondered sourly.

The atmosphere in the War Room was tense as the images flickered across multiple screens. Every mouth was dry, every eye glued to the plasma screen that showed the progress of the four CI Chinooks over the mountainous terrain. The graphics were the same as those of a video game, but once the engagement began all similarities to a game would end.

'They've overflown the westernmost wadi,' the DCI reported. 'Now all that separates them from the Dujja facility is a minor mountain chain. They're taking the gap just to the southwest of their current position. They'll go in two by two.'

'We've got RF,' Marlin Dorph reported to the DCI. He meant radiation fog, an odd phenomenon that sometimes occurred at dawn or during the night, arising from the radiational cooling of the earth's surface, when a layer of relatively moist air was trapped just above surface level by drier air aloft.

'Do you have visual on the target?' the DCI's voice, thin and metallicized, buzzed in his ear.

'Negative, sir. We're heading in for a closer look, but two of the Chinooks are holding back in perimeter formation.' He turned to Lowrie, who nodded. 'Norris,' he said to the pilot in the heli on their left wing, 'take 'er down.'

He watched as the accompanying Chinook dove down, its rotors beating the RF, dissipating it.

'There!' Lowrie yelled.

Dorph could see a group of perhaps six armed men. Startled, they looked up. He allowed his eyes to follow the path they were taking, saw a cluster of low, bunkerlike buildings. They looked like structures typical of the terrorist training camps, but that's just how Dujja would camouflage its base.

The low-flying Chinook was loosing its M230 chains: The ground erupted with a hail of 30mm rounds. The men fell, fired back, scattered, fired again, were mowed down.

'Let's go!' Dorph spoke into his mike. 'The complex is half a klick dead ahead.' The Chinook began its dive. Dorph could hear the racket increase as the other two helis left their perimeter patrol, heading in after him.

'Hellfires up!' he called. 'I want one missile from each ship launched on my signal.' The different angles would cause even the most heavily reinforced walls to collapse.

He could see the other three helis as they converged on the target. 'On my mark,' Dorph barked. 'Now!'

Four Hellfire missiles were loosed from the undercarriages of the Chinooks. They homed in on the building complex, detonating within seconds of one another. A ball of flame erupted. The shock wave juddered through the heli as great gouts of oily black smoke rose from the target.

Then all hell broke loose.

Soraya Moore, waiting in line to board at Atatürk International Airport for her flight to D.C., took out her cell phone. Ever since she'd left Bourne, she'd been thinking about the situation at headquarters. Bourne was right: The false Lindros had set himself up in a perfect position. But why had he taken all this trouble to infiltrate CI? For its intel? Soraya didn't think so. Fadi was smart enough to know that there was no way his man could smuggle the data past CI's watertight security. He could only be there to deter Typhon's efforts to stop Dujja. To her, that meant an offensive plan. Active disinformation. Because if CI personnel were off on a wild goose chase, Fadi and his team could sneak into the United States under the radar. It was classic misdirection, the conjuror's oldest trick. But it was often the most effective.

She knew that Bourne had said they couldn't approach the DCI, but she could do the next best thing: contact Anne Held. She could tell Anne anything; Anne would find a way to approach the Old Man without anyone else knowing. That effectively cut out the mole, whoever he might be.

Soraya moved forward in the line. The flight was boarding. She thought through her idea again, then dialed Anne's private number. It rang and rang, and she found herself praying that Anne would answer. She didn't dare leave a voice-mail message, not even for Anne to call her back. On the seventh ring Anne answered.

'Anne, thank God.' The line was moving in earnest now. 'It's Soraya. Listen, I have very little time. I'm on my way back to D.C. Don't say anything until I've finished. I've discovered that the Martin Lindros whom Bourne brought back from Ethiopia is an impostor.'

'An impostor?'

'That's what I said.'

'But that's impossible!'

'I know it sounds crazy.'

'Soraya, I don't know what's happened to you over there, but believe me, Lindros is who he says he is. He even passed the retinal scan.'

'Please, let me finish. This man – whoever he is – is working for Fadi. He's been planted to throw us off Dujja's trail. Anne, I need you to tell the Old Man.'

'Now I know you've gone crackers. I tell the Old Man that Lindros is a plant and he'll have me institutionalized.'

Soraya was almost up to the boarding gate. She'd run out of time. 'Anne, you've got to believe me. You have to find a way to convince him.'

'Not without some proof,' Anne said. 'Anything of substance will do.'

'But I don't – '

'I've got a pen. Give me your flight info. I'll meet you at the airport myself. We'll figure something out before we get to HQ.'

Soraya gave Anne her flight number and arrival time. She nodded to the attendant at the head of the gate as she handed over her boarding pass.

'Thanks, Anne, I knew I could count on you.'

*

The Sidewinder missiles came out of nowhere.

'Our right flank!' Dorph yelled, but the alarms were shrieking through the interior of the Chinook. He saw a missile make a direct hit on the lowest-flying heli. The Chinook burst into a fireball, at once engulfed in the fierce stream of smoke rising from the ruined buildings. A second heli, in the process of taking evasive maneuvers, was struck in its tail. The entire rear section flew apart; the rest lurched over on its side and spiraled down into the raging inferno.

Dorph forgot about the remaining heli; he needed to concentrate on his own. He staggered over to the pilot just as the Chinook heeled over in the first of its evasive maneuvers.

'Incoming locked, Skip,' the pilot said. 'It's right on our tail.' As he twisted and turned the joystick, the Chinook made a series of stomach-churning loops and dives.

'Keep on it,' Dorph said. He signed to the ordnance officer. 'I need you to remote-set a multi-option fuze for five seconds.'

The officer's eyes opened. 'That's cutting it mighty close, Skip. We could be caught up in the blast.'

'That's what I'm hoping for,' Dorph said. 'Sort of.'

He glanced out the window as the officer went to work. Not a hundred meters from him another Sidewinder missile found its target, detonating amidships. The third Chinook dropped like a stone. That left only them.

'Skip, ordnance closing on us,' the pilot said. 'I can't keep this up for much longer.'

*Hopefully you won't have to,* Dorph thought. He slapped the pilot on the shoulder. 'On my mark, veer to the left and down, steep as you can make it. Got it?'

The pilot nodded. 'Roger that, Skip.'

'Keep a firm hand,' Dorph told him. He could hear the shrill scream as the Sidewinder tore up the air in its attempt to get to them. They were running out of time.

The ordnance officer nodded to Dorph. 'All set, Skip.'

'Let 'er rip,' Dorph said.

There was a small chirrup as the Hydra 70 rocket was fired. Dorph counted: 'One-two.' He slapped the pilot. 'Now!'

At once the heli dove sharply to its left, then down. The ground was coming up fast when the Hydra detonated. The blast threw everyone forward and to their right. Dorph could feel the heat even through the armored skin of the Chinook. That was the bait, and the Sidewinder – an air-to-air weapon guided by a heat-seeking mechanism – headed straight into the heart of it, blowing itself to smithereens.

The Chinook shuddered, hesitated as the pilot struggled to pull it out of the dive, then – swinging like a pendulum – righted itself.

'Nicely done.' Dorph squeezed the pilot's shoulder. 'Everyone okay?' He saw the nods and uptilted thumbs out of the corner of his eye. 'Okay, now we go after the hostile aircraft that shot our guys down.'

After Soraya left for the airport, Bourne began to make his plans to find and interrogate Nesim Hatun, the man who had hired Yevgeny Feyodovich. According to Yevgeny, Hatun worked out of the Sultanahmet District, which was some distance from where he was now.

He was almost dead on his feet. He hadn't let himself think about it, but the knife wound Fadi had inflicted was seriously sapping his strength. His fight with Matthew Lerner had done more damage to his body. He knew it would be foolish, possibly suicidal, to seek out Nesim Hatun in his present condition.

Therefore, he went looking for an El Achab. Strictly speaking, these traditional herbalists were centered in Morocco. However, Turkey's many microclimates nurtured more than eleven thousand plant species, so it was hardly surprising that there should be among the many shops in Istanbul an apothecary overseen by a Moroccan expert in phytochemistry.

After forty-five minutes of wandering and asking passers-by and shopkeepers, he found just such a place. It was in the middle of a bustling market, a tiny storefront with narrow, dusty windows and a certain flyblown air.

Inside, El Achab sat on a stool grinding herbs into powder with a mortar and pestle. He looked up as Bourne came toward him, his eyes watery and myopic.

The atmosphere was dense, almost suffocatingly so, with the sharp, unfamiliar odors of dried herbs, grasses, stalks, mushrooms, leaves, spoors, flower petals, and more. The walls were lined from floor to ceiling with wooden drawers and cubbyholes that held the herbalist's vast stock. What light penetrated the dusty windows was defeated by the aromatic dust accumulated by years of grinding.

'Yes?' El Achab said in Moroccan-inflected Turkish. 'How may I help?'

By way of reply, Bourne stripped to the waist, revealing his bandaged wounds, his livid bruises, his cuts etched in dried blood.

El Achab crooked a long forefinger. He was a small man, thin to the point of emaciation, with the dark, leathery skin of a desert dweller. 'Closer, please.'

Bourne did as he asked.

The herbalist's watery eyes blinked heavily. 'What do you require?'

'To keep going,' Bourne said in Moroccan Arabic.

El Achab rose, went to a drawer, and took out what looked like a handful of goat hair. '*Huperzia serrata*. A rare moss found in northern China.' He sat down at his stool, set aside his mortar and pestle, began to tear the dried moss into small bits. 'Believe it or not, everything you need is in here. The moss will counteract the inflammation that is draining your body of energy. At the same time, it will vastly heighten your mental acuity.'

He turned, took a kettle off a hot plate, poured some water just under the boiling point into a copper teapot. Then he dropped the tufts of moss into the pot, poured more water in, set the lid on the teapot, and placed the kettle beside the mortar and pestle.

Bourne, rebuttoning his shirt, sat on a wooden stool.

They waited in companionable silence for the herbal 'tea' to steep. El Achab's eyes might have been watery and myopic, but they nevertheless took in every feature of Bourne's face. 'Who are you?'

Bourne replied, 'I don't know.'

'Perhaps one day you will.'

The steeping was done. El Achab used his long fingers to pour a precise amount into a glass. It was thick, dark, impenetrable, and from it issued the odor of a bog.

'Now drink.' He held out the glass. 'All of it. At once, please.'

The taste was unspeakable. Nevertheless, Bourne swallowed every last drop.

'Within an hour your body will feel stronger, your mind more vibrant,' El Achab said. 'The process will continue for several days.'

Bourne rose, thanking the man as he paid. Back outside in the market, he went first into a clothing store and bought himself a traditional Turkish outfit, right down to the thin-soled shoes. The proprietor directed him back to Istiklal Caddesi, across the Golden Horn from Sultanahmet. There he entered a theatrical supply shop where he chose a beard, along with a small metal can of spirit gum. In front of the shop's mirror, he affixed the beard.

He then rummaged through the shop's other offerings, buying what he needed, stuffing everything into a small, battered secondhand leather satchel. All the while he shopped, he was filled with an implacable rage. He couldn't get out of his mind what Veintrop and Fadi had done to him. His enemy had insinuated himself inside his head, subtly influencing Bourne's thoughts, destabilizing his decisions. How had Fadi planted Veintrop in the real Sunderland's office?

Taking out his cell, he scrolled down to Sunderland's number and punched in the overseas codes, then the eleven-digit number. The office wasn't open at this hour, but a recorded voice asked if he wanted to make an appointment, wanted Dr. Sunderland's office hours, wanted directions from Washington, Maryland, or Virginia. He wanted the second option, definitely. The recorded voice told him the doctor's hours were from 10 am to 6 pm Monday, and Wednesday through Friday. The office was closed on Tuesday. Tuesday was the day he'd seen Sunderland. Who had made the appointment for him?

Sweat broke out along his hairline as his heart beat faster. How had Fadi's people known that he was taking Fadi out of the cage? Soraya had made the call to Tim Hytner, which was why Bourne had suspected him of being the mole. But Hytner wasn't. Who had access to CI-net cell calls? Who could possibly be eavesdropping except the mole? That would be the same person who had made his appointment with Sunderland on the day the doctor wouldn't be at his office.

Anne Held!

*Oh, Christ,* he thought. The Old Man's right hand. It couldn't be. And yet it was the only explanation that made sense of the recent history. Who better for Fadi, for anyone wanting to know what took place in the center of the CI web?

His fingers worked his cell phone. He needed to warn Soraya before she boarded the plane. But her voice mail picked up immediately, which meant her phone was already off. She'd boarded, was on her way to D.C., to disaster.

He left a message, telling her that Anne Held must be the mole inside CI.

# 25

'Come in, Martin.' The DCI waved to Karim, who stood in the doorway to his inner sanctum. 'I'm glad Anne caught you.'

Karim took the long walk to the chair in front of the DCI's immense desk. The walk reminded him of the gauntlet of rock throwers a Bedouin traitor was forced to tread. If he made it to the end alive, he received a swift, merciful death. If not, he was left in the desert for the vultures to feed on.

Sounds came to him. Throughout the building, a strange atmosphere of celebration and mourning had gripped CI following the news that the Dujja nuclear facility in South Yemen had been obliterated, though men were killed in the raid. The DCI had been in contact with Commander Dorph. He and his complement of Skorpions and marines had been the only ones to survive the attack. There had been many casualties – three Chinooks filled with marines and CI Skorpions. The facility had been heavily protected by two Soviet MiGs armed with Sidewinder missiles. Dorph's heli had taken them both down following the destruction of the target.

Karim sat. His nerves were always on edge when he sat in this chair. 'Sir, I know we paid a heavy price, but you seem peculiarly gloomy given the success of our mission against Dujja.'

'I've done my grieving for my people, Martin.' The Old Man grunted as if in pain. 'It's not that I don't feel relief – and no little vindication after the grilling I got in the War Room.' His heavy brows knitted together. 'But between you and me, something doesn't feel right.'

Karim felt a jolt of anxiety travel down his spine. Unconsciously, he moved to the edge of the chair. 'I don't follow, sir. Dorph confirmed that the facility suffered four direct hits, all from different angles. There's no doubt that it was completely destroyed, as were the two hostile jet fighters defending it.'

'True enough.' The DCI nodded. 'Still . . .'

Karim's mind was racing, extrapolating possibilities. The DCI's instincts were well known. He hadn't kept his job for so long solely because he'd learned to be a good politician, and Karim knew it would be unwise simply to placate him. 'If you could be more specific . . .'

The Old Man shook his head. 'I wish I could be.'

'Our intel was right on the money, sir.'

The DCI sat back, rubbed at his chin. 'Here's what sticks in my craw. Why did the MiGs wait to launch the missiles until after the facility was destroyed?'

'Perhaps they were late in scrambling.' Karim was on delicate ground, and he knew it. 'You heard Dorph – there was radiation fog.'

'The fog was low to the ground. The MiGs came in from above; the RF wouldn't have affected them. What if they *deliberately* waited until the facility had been destroyed?'

Karim tried to ignore the buzzing in his ears. 'Sir, that makes no sense.'

'It would if the facility was a dummy,' the Old Man said.

This line of inquiry was one that Karim could not allow the DCI – or anyone in CI – to pursue. 'You may be right, sir, now that I think of it.' He stood. 'I'll look into it right away.'

The Old Man's keen eyes peered up at him from beneath heavy brows. 'Sit down, Martin.'

Silence engulfed the office. Even the dim sounds of celebration had faded as the CI personnel got back to their grim work.

'What if Dujja wanted us to believe we'd destroyed their nuclear facility?'

Of course that was exactly what had happened. Karim struggled to keep his heart rate under control.

'I know I sold Secretary Halliday on Tim Hytner being the mole,' the DCI went on doggedly. 'That doesn't mean I believe it. If my hunch on the signal disinformation proves correct, here's another set of theories: Either Hytner was framed by the real mole, or he wasn't the only rotten apple in our barrel.'

'Those are all big ifs, sir.'

'Then eliminate them, Martin. Make it a priority. Use all necessary resources.'

The Old Man put his hands on his desk, levered himself up. His face was pale and pasty-looking. 'Christ on a crutch, Martin, if Dujja's misdirected us, it means we haven't stopped them. To the contrary, they're close to launching their attack.'

Muta ibn Aziz arrived in Istanbul just after noon and went immediately to see Nesim Hatun. Hatun ran the Miraj Hammam, a Turkish bath, in the Sultanahmet District. It was in an old building, large and rambling, on a side street not five blocks from the Hagia Sophia, the great church created by Justinian in AD 532. As such, the *hammam* was always well attended, its prices higher than those in less touristed sections of the city. It had been a *hammam* for many years – since well before Hatun had been born, in fact.

Hatun was proud of the fact that he'd bribed the right people so that his business was well written up in all the best guidebooks. The *hammam* made him a good living, especially by Turkish standards. But what had made him a millionaire many times over was his work for Fadi.

Hatun, a man of immense appetites, had a roly-poly body and the cruel face of a vulture. Looking into his black eyes, it was clear there was venom in his soul – a venom that Fadi had identified, coaxed out, and lovingly fed. Hatun had had many wives, all of them either dead or exiled to the countryside. On the other hand, his twelve children, whom he loved and trusted, happily ran the *hammam* for him. Hatun, his heart like a closed fist, preferred it that way. So did Fadi.

'*Merhaba, habibi!*' Hatun said by way of greeting when Muta ibn Aziz crossed his threshold. He kissed his guest on both cheeks and led him through the heavily mosaiced public rooms of the *hammam* into the rear section, which surrounded a small garden in the center of which grew Hatun's prized date palm. He'd brought it all the way from a caravanserai in the Sahara, though at the time it was only a seedling, hardly bigger than his forefinger. He lavished more attention on that one tree than he had on any of his wives.

They sat on cool stone benches in filtered sunlight while they were served sweet tea and tiny cakes by two of Hatun's daughters. Afterward, one of them brought an ornate *nargilah* – a traditional water pipe – which the two men shared.

These rituals and the time it took to perform them were a necessary part of life in the East. They served to cement friendship by showing the proper politeness and respect as observed by civilized people. Even today there were men like Nesim Hatun who observed the old ways, dedicated as they were to keeping the lamp of tradition burning through the neon glare of the electronic age.

At length, Hatun pushed the *nargilah* away. 'You have come a long way, my friend.'

'Sometimes, as you know only too well, the oldest forms of communication are the most secure.'

'I understand completely.' Hatun nodded. 'I myself use a new cell phone each day, and then speak only in the most general terms.'

'We have heard nothing from Yevgeny Feyodovich.'

Hatun's eyebrows knit together. 'Bourne survived Odessa?'

'This we do not know. But Feyodovich's silence is disturbing. Understandably, Fadi is unhappy.'

Hatun spread his hands. They were surprisingly small, the fingers delicate as a girl's. 'As am I. Please be assured that I will see to Yevgeny Feyodovich myself.'

Muta ibn Aziz nodded his acceptance. 'In the meantime, we must assume that he has been compromised.'

Nesim Hatun considered for a moment. 'This man Bourne, they say that he is like a chameleon. If he is still alive, if he does find his way here, how will I know?'

'Fadi knifed him in the left side. Badly. His body will be battered. If he does come, it will be shortly, possibly even later today.'

Nesim Hatun sensed the messenger's nervousness. *The fruition of Fadi's plan must be terribly close,* he surmised.

They rose, passed through the private rooms, silent, lush as the garden outside.

'I will stay here for the remainder of the day and night. If, by then Bourne hasn't shown, he won't. And even if he does, it will be too late.'

Hatun nodded. He was right, then. Fadi's attack against the United States was imminent.

Muta ibn Aziz pointed. 'There is a screen at the far end of the garden, just there. This is where I will wait. If it happens that Bourne comes, he will want to see you. That you will allow, but in the middle of the interview I will send one of your sons to fetch you, and you and I will have a conversation.'

'So Bourne can overhear it. I understand.'

Muta ibn Aziz took a step closer, his voice reduced to a papery whisper. 'I want Bourne to know who I am. I want him to know that I am returning to Fadi.'

Nesim Hatun nodded. 'He will follow you.'

'Precisely.'

Right from the outset, Jon Mueller could see where Lerner's man, Overton, had gotten himself into trouble. Shadowing Anne Held, he discovered her surveillance without too much difficulty. There was a difference between surveillance and shadowing: He was looking not to follow Held but to unearth the people who were protecting her from outside surveillance. As such, he was far back and high up. In the beginning, he used his own eyes rather than binoculars because he needed to see Held's immediate environment in the widest range possible. Binoculars would home in on only narrow sections of it. They were useful, however, once he had IDed the man surveilling her.

In fact, there were three men, working in eight-hour shifts. That they were on twenty-four-hour alert hardly surprised him. Overton's botched surveillance had surely made them both more fearful and more wary. Mueller had anticipated all this, and had a plan for countering it.

For twenty-four hours, he had observed Held's complement of protectors. He noted their habits, quirks, predilections, methods of operation, all of which varied slightly. The one on the night shift needed a constant supply of coffee to keep him alert, while the one on the early-morning shift used his cell phone constantly. The one on the late-afternoon shift smoked like a fiend. Mueller chose him because his innate nervousness made him the most vulnerable.

He knew he would only get one shot, so he made the most of the opportunity he knew would sooner or later come his way. Hours ago, he'd stolen a utility truck off the back of the Potomac Electric Power Company lot on Pennsylvania Avenue. He drove this now, as Anne Held got into a waiting taxi outside CI headquarters.

As the cab pulled out into traffic, Mueller waited, patient as death. Quite soon, he heard an engine cough into life. A white Ford sedan edged out from its spot across the street as the afternoon man took up his position two vehicles behind the taxi. Mueller followed in the heavy traffic.

Within ten minutes, the Held woman had exited the taxi and had begun to walk. Mueller knew this MO well. She was on her way to a rendezvous. The traffic was such that the afternoon man couldn't follow her in the car. Mueller had deduced this before her protector did, and so he'd pulled the truck over and parked on 17th Street NW, in a no-parking zone, knowing that no one would question someone in a public service utility truck.

Swinging out of the truck, he walked quickly to where the afternoon man had pulled over to the curb. Striding up, he tapped on the driver's-side window. When the man slid down the glass, Mueller said, 'Hey, buddy,' then sucker-punched him just below his left ear.

The traumatic disruption to the nerve bundle put him down for the count. Mueller set the unconscious man upright behind the wheel, then stepped up onto the sidewalk, keeping the Held woman in sight as she walked up the street.

Anne Held and Karim were strolling through the Corcoran Gallery on 17th Street, NW. The impressive collection of artwork was housed in a magnificent white Georgian marble structure that Frank Lloyd Wright had once called the best-designed building in Washington. Karim paused in front of a large canvas of the San Francisco painter Robert Bechtel, a photorealist whose artistic worth he could not fathom.

'The DCI suspects that the raid target was bogus,' Karim was saying, 'which means he suspects that the Dujja intel Typhon intercepted and decoded is disinformation.'

Anne was shocked. 'Where are these suspicions coming from?'

'The MiG pilots made a crucial mistake. They waited until *after* the American Chinooks leveled the abandoned complex before firing their missiles. Their orders were to allow the bombing so the Americans would believe the raid had been successful, but they were to come on the scene minutes later than they did. They thought the fog would hide them from the Chinooks, but the Americans found a way to dissipate it with their rotors. Now the Old Man wants me to look for a leak inside CI.'

'I thought you sold everyone on Hytner being the mole.'

'Everyone, it appears, except him.'

'What are we going to do?' Anne said.

'Move up the timetable.'

Anne looked around covertly, but nervously.

'Not to worry,' Karim said. 'After we incinerated Overton, I put safeguards in place.' He looked at his watch and headed for the entrance. 'Come. Soraya Moore is due to land in three hours.'

Jon Mueller, behind the wheel of the Potomac Electric truck, was just down the block from the Corcoran. He was now certain that Anne Held was making a rendezvous. That would have occupied Lerner, but not him. It wouldn't matter who she was meeting after he took her out.

As soon as he saw Held come out the front entrance, he pulled out into traffic. Up ahead was the light at the junction of Pennsylvania Avenue. It was still green as she came down the stairs, but as he approached, it changed to amber. There was one car ahead of him. With a crash of gears and a roar of the truck's engine, he pulled out, sideswiping the car as he barreled past it and jumped the red light, driving straight through the intersection to a chorus of curses, angry shouts, and horn blasts.

Mueller stamped the accelerator to the floor as he bore down on Anne Held.

The high-velocity bullet breaking the glass of the truck's side window sounded like a far-off chime. Mueller had no time to consider that it might be anything else because the bullet tore into one side of his head and blew out the opposite, taking half his skull with it.

A moment before the Potomac Electric truck went out of control, Karim took Anne's arm and dragged her back onto the curb. As the truck slammed into the two cars ahead of it, he began to walk with her very fast away from the scene of the deadly pileup.

'What happened?' she said.

'The man driving the truck was intent on making you the victim of a hit-and-run.'

'What?'

He had to squeeze her arm hard to get her not to look back. 'Keep walking,' he said. 'Let's get away from this place.'

Three blocks down, a black Lincoln Aviator with diplomatic plates was idling at the curb. With a single fluid motion, Karim opened the rear door and urged Anne inside. He followed after her, slamming the door, and the Aviator took off.

'Are you all right?' he asked.

Anne nodded. 'Just a bit shaken up. What happened?'

'I made arrangements to have you covertly watched.'

Up front were a driver and his sidekick. Both appeared to be Arab diplomatic officials. For all Anne knew they *were* Arab diplomatic officials. She didn't know, didn't want to know. Just as she didn't want to know where they were going. In her business, too much information, just like curiosity about the wrong things, could get you killed.

'I had read up on Lerner, so the moment the Old Man told me he'd sent him to Odessa, I suspected that someone even higher up on the intelligence food chain would be put on you. I was right. A man named Jon Mueller from Homeland Security. Mueller and Lerner were whoring buddies. The interesting thing is that Mueller is on the payroll of Defense Secretary Halliday.'

'Which means, chances are that Lerner's also under the defense secretary's control.'

Karim nodded, leaned forward, and told the driver to slow down as the wail of the sirens from police, EMTs, and fire department vehicles rose, then fell away. 'Halliday seems intent on increasing the Pentagon's power. Taking over CI, remaking it in its own image. We can use the chaos caused by this inter-agency warfare to our advantage.'

By this time, the Aviator had reached the far northern precincts of the city. Skirting the northeastern edge of Rock Creek Park, they at last came to the rear of a large mortuary run by a Pakistani family.

The family also owned the building, courtesy of money from International Vertical Technologies, funneled through one of the independent companies in the Bahamas and the Caymans that Karim had set up over the years since he'd taken over the corporation from his father. As a result, they had gutted the structure, rebuilding it to the specifications Karim had provided.

One of those specs had provided for what appeared to be the hall's own loading bay in the rear. In fact, it *was* a loading bay as far as the hall's suppliers were concerned. As the driver of the Aviator turned into the bay, the concrete 'wall' at the rear slid into a niche in the floor, revealing a ramp down which the vehicle rolled. It stopped in the vast sub-basement, and they all got out.

Barrels and crates lined the wall closest to them, the former contents of M&N Bodywork. To the left of the explosives stood a black Lincoln limousine with familiar plates.

Anne walked over to it, running her fingertips across its gleaming surface. She turned to Jamil. 'Where did you get the Old Man's car?'

'It's an exact replica, down to the armor plating and special bulletproof glass.' He opened a rear door. 'Except for one thing.'

The courtesy light had gone on when the door was opened. Peering in, Anne marveled that the interior was a perfect match, down to the plush royal-blue carpet. She watched as he pulled up a corner of the carpet that hadn't yet been glued down. Using the blade of a pocketknife, he pried up the floorboard far enough for her to see what was underneath.

The entire bottom of the replica was packed tight with neat rectangles of a light gray clay-like substance.

'That's right,' he said, reacting to her sharply indrawn breath. 'There's enough C-Four explosive here to take out the entire reinforced foundation of CI headquarters.'

# 26

The district where Nesim Hatun plied a trade as yet unknown to Bourne was named after Sultan Ahmet I who, during the first decade of the seventeenth century, built the Blue Mosque in the heart of what nineteenth-century Europeans called Stamboul. This was the center of the once immense Byzantine Empire that, at its height, extended from southern Spain to Bulgaria to Egypt.

Modern-day Sultanahmet had lost neither its spectacular architecture nor its power to awe. The center was a hillock called the Hippodrome, with the Blue Mosque on one side and the Hagia Sophia, built a century earlier, on the other. The two were linked by a small park. Nowadays the social center of the district was nearby Akbiyik Caddesi, the Avenue of the White Mustache, whose northernmost end gave out onto Topkapi Palace. This wide thoroughfare was lined with shops, bars, cafés, groceries, restaurants, and, on Wednesday mornings, a street market.

Bourne, appearing among the loudly chattering hordes packing Akbiyik Caddesi, was barely recognizable. He wore the traditional Turkish outfit, his jaw hidden behind the full beard.

He stopped at a street cart to buy *simit* – sesame bread – and pale yellow yogurt, eating them as he took in his surroundings. Hustlers plied their shady trade, merchants shouted out the prices of their wares, locals haggled over prices, tourists were systematically fleeced by clever Turks. Businessmen on cell phones, kids taking pictures of one another with cell phones, teens playing raucous music they'd just downloaded into their cell phones. Laughter and tears, lovers' smiles, combatants' angry shouts. The boiling stew of human emotion and life lit up the avenue like a neon sign, blazing through the clouds of aromatic smoke billowing from braziers over which sizzling lamb and vegetable kebabs browned.

After finishing his makeshift meal, he headed straight for a rug shop, where he picked out a prayer rug, haggling good-naturedly with the owner on the price. When he left, both were satisfied with the bargain they had made.

The Blue Mosque to which Bourne now walked, his prayer rug tucked under one arm, was surrounded by six slender minarets. These had come from a mistake. Sultan Ahmet I had told his architect he wanted the mosque to have a gold minaret. *Altin* is the Turkish word for 'gold,' but the architect misheard him and instead built *alti* – six – minarets. Still, Ahmet I was pleased with the result, because at that time no other sultan had a mosque with so many minarets.

As befit such a magnificent edifice, the mosque had multiple doors. Most visitors went in through the north side, but Muslims entered from the west. It was through this door that Bourne walked. Just inside, he stopped, took off his shoes, and set them aside in a plastic bag handed to him by a young boy. He covered his head, then at a stone basin washed his feet, face, neck, and forearms. Padding into the mosque proper, he set out his prayer rug on the rug-strewn marble floor and knelt on it.

The interior of the mosque was, in true Byzantine fashion, covered with intricate artwork, filigreed carvings, halos of metalwork lamps, immense columns painted blue and gold, four stories of magnificent stained-glass windows reaching up into the heavens of the central dome. The power of it all was as moving as it was undeniable.

Bourne said the Muslim prayers, his forehead pressed to the carpet he had just bought. He was perfectly sincere in his prayers, feeling the centuries of history etched into the stone, marble, gold leaf, and lapis from which the mosque had been constructed and fervently embellished. Spirituality came in many guises, was called by many names, but they all spoke directly to the heart in a language as old as time.

When he was finished, he rose and rolled up his rug. He lingered in the mosque, allowing the reverberating near silence to wash over him. The sibilant rustle of silk and cotton, the soft hum of muttered prayers, the undercurrent of whispered voices, every human sound and movement gathered up into the mosque's great dome, swirled like granules of sugar in rich coffee, subtly altering the taste.

In fact, all the while he seemed lost in holy contemplation he was covertly watching those finishing their prayers. He spotted an older man, his beard shot through with white, roll up his rug and walk slowly over to the lines of shoes. Bourne arrived at his shoes at the same time the older man was putting on his.

The old man, who had one withered arm, regarded Bourne as he stepped into his shoes. 'You're new here, sir,' he said in Turkish. 'I haven't seen your face before.'

'I just arrived, sir,' Bourne replied with a deferential smile.

'And what brings you to Istanbul, my son?'

They moved out through the western door.

'I'm searching for a relative,' Bourne said. 'A man by the name of Nesim Hatun.'

'Not so uncommon a name,' the old man said. 'Do you know anything about him?'

'Only that he runs his business, whatever that may be, here in Sultanahmet,' Bourne said.

'Ah, then perhaps I can be of help.' The old man squinted in the sunlight. 'There is a Nesim Hatun who, along with his twelve children, runs the Miraj Hammam on Bayramfirini Sokak, a street not so far from here. The directions are simple enough.'

Bayramfirini Sokak – the Street of the Festival Oven, midway along Akbiyik Caddesi – was a shade calmer than the frantic avenues of Istanbul. Nevertheless, the sharp, raised calls of merchants, the chanting of itinerant food sellers, the particular bleat-and-squeal, a product of negotiating a sale, collected in the narrow street like a dense fog. Bayramfirini Sokak, as severely pitched as a mountainside, ran all the way down to the Sea of Marmara. It was home to a number of small guesthouses and the *hammam* of Nesim Hatun, the man who had hired Yevgeny Feyodovich at the behest of Fadi to help lead Bourne to the killing ground on the Odessa beach.

The *hammam*'s door was a thick, dark wooden affair, carved with Byzantine designs. It was flanked by a pair of colossal stone urns, originally used to store oil for lamps. The whole made for an impressive entrance.

Bourne stashed his leather satchel behind the left-hand urn. Then he opened the door and entered the dimly lit forecourt. At once the constant bawling of the city vanished, and Bourne was enfolded in the silence of a snow-cloaked forest. It took a moment for the ringing in his ears to settle. He found himself in a hexagonal space in the center of which was a marble fountain gracefully spewing water. There were graven arches held up by fluted columns on four sides, beyond which were a combination of lush enclosed gardens and hushed, lamplit corridors.

This could have been the vestibule of a mosque or a medieval monastery. As in all important Islamic buildings, the architecture was paramount. Because Islam forbade the use of images of Allah or, indeed, of any living thing, the Islamic artisan's desire to carve was channeled into the building itself and its many embellishments.

It was no coincidence that the *hammam* was reminiscent of a mosque. Both were places of reverence as well as of community. Since much of the religion was based on the purification of the body, a special place was reserved for the *hammam* in the lives of Muslims.

Bourne was met by a *tellak* – a masseur – a slim young man with the face of a wolf. 'I would very much like to meet Nesim Hatun. He and I have a mutual business associate. Yevgeny Feyodovich.'

The *tellak* did not react to the name. 'I will see if my father is available.'

Soraya, striding past the security area of Washington National Airport, was about to thumb on her cell phone when she saw Anne Held wave to her. Soraya felt a flood of relief when she embraced the other woman.

'It's so good to have you back,' Anne said.

Soraya craned her neck, looked around. 'Were you followed?'

'Of course not. I made certain of that.'

Soraya fell into step with Anne as they headed out of the terminal. Her nerves were twanging unpleasantly. It was one thing to be in the field working against the enemy, quite another to be coming home to a viper in your nest. She began to work her emotions as any good actor would, thinking of a tragedy long ago: the day her dog, Ranger, got run over in front of her. *Ah, good,* she thought, *here come the tears.*

Anne's face clouded with concern. 'What is it?'

'Jason Bourne is dead.'

'What?' Anne was so shocked she stopped them in the midst of the bustling concourse. 'What happened?'

'The Old Man sent Lerner after Bourne, like a personal assassin. The two fought. They ended up killing each other.' Soraya shook her head. 'The reason I came back was to keep an eye on the man posing as Martin Lindros. Sooner or later, he's bound to make a mistake.'

Anne held her at arm's length. 'Are you certain about your intel about Lindros? He just masterminded an all-out attack on the Dujja nuclear facility in South Yemen. It's been totally destroyed.'

Blood flushed Soraya's face. 'My God, I was right! It's why Dujja went to all this trouble to infiltrate CI. If Lindros spearheaded it, you can be damn sure the facility was a decoy. CI is dead wrong if they believe they've averted the threat.'

'In that case, the sooner we get back to headquarters, the better, don't you think?' Anne threw an arm around Soraya's shoulders, hurrying her through the electric doors into the damp chill of the Washington winter. Glow from the floodlit monuments engraved a majestic pattern on the dark, low clouds. Anne guided Soraya into a CI-issue Pontiac sedan, then slid behind the wheel.

They joined the long line of vehicles circling like fish around a reef, heading toward the exit. On the way into Washington, Soraya, leaning slightly forward, glanced in the side mirror. It was habit, long ago ingrained in her. She did it as a matter of course, whether or not she was on a field mission. She saw the black Ford behind them, thought nothing of it, until her second glance. It was now one car behind them, but keeping pace in the right-hand lane. Not enough to say anything yet, but when it was still in place on her third look, she felt under the circumstances she had enough evidence to consider that they were being followed.

She turned to Anne to tell her, then saw her glance in the rearview mirror. No doubt she'd seen the black Ford as well. But when she didn't mention it or execute any evasive maneuvers, Soraya felt her stomach slowly clench. She tried to calm down by telling herself that after all Anne was the Old Man's assistant. She was office-trained, unaccustomed to even the rudiments of fieldwork.

She cleared her throat. 'Anne, I think we're being followed.'

Anne signaled, moving them into the right-hand lane. 'I'd better slow down.'

'What? No. What are you doing?'

'If they slow down, then we'll know – '

'No, you've got to speed up,' Soraya said. 'Get away from them as quickly as possible.'

'I want to see who's in that car,' Anne said, slowing even more as she steered toward the shoulder.

'You're crazy.'

Soraya reached for the wheel, abruptly reared back as she saw the Smith & Wesson J-frame compact gun in Anne's hand.

'What the hell d'you think you're doing?'

They were rolling across the shoulder, toward the low metal fence. 'After everything you told me, I didn't want to leave headquarters unarmed.'

'Do you even know how to use that?'

The black Ford followed them off the road, pulling up behind them. Two men with dark complexions got out, came toward them.

'I take shooting practice twice a month,' Anne said, pressing the muzzle of the S&W against Soraya's temple. 'Now get out of the car.'

'Anne, what are you – ?'

'Just do as I say.'

Soraya nodded. 'All right.' Edging away, she pushed down on the door handle. As she saw Anne's eyes move toward the door, she struck upward with her left arm, deflecting Anne's right arm upward. The gun exploded, the bullet tearing a hole in the Pontiac's roof.

Soraya slammed her cocked elbow into the side of Anne's face. Galvanized by the gunshot, the men ran toward the Pontiac. Soraya, seeing them coming, quickly leaned across Anne's slumped torso, opened the door, pushed her out.

Just as the men, guns drawn, reached the rear of the Pontiac, Soraya slid behind the wheel, threw it into gear, and stepped on the accelerator. She bounced along the shoulder for a moment then, finding a potential gap in the traffic, pulled out, tires squealing and smoking. Her last glimpse of the men was of them running back to the black Ford, but what made her hands tremble on the wheel was the sight of Anne Held supported between them, helped into the back of their car.

Nesim Hatun was reclining on a carved wooden bench softened by a marshmallow mound of silk pillows beneath the clattering green fronds of his beloved date palm. He was popping fresh dates into his mouth, one by one, chewing thoughtfully, swallowing the sweet flesh, spitting out the white spear-point pits into a shallow dish. Beside his right elbow was a small octagonal table on which stood a chased silver tray filled with a teapot and a pair of small glass tumblers.

As his son brought Bourne – who had peeled off his beard before entering the Turkish bath – into the shade of the date palm, Hatun's head swung around, his vulture's face impassive. His olive eyes did not hide his curiosity, however.

'*Merhaba,* my friend.'

'*Merhaba,* Nesim Hatun. My name is Abu Bakr.'

Hatun scratched at his tiny, pointed beard. 'Named after the companion of our Prophet Muhammad.'

'A thousand apologies for disturbing the tranquility of your magnificent garden.'

Nesim Hatun nodded at his guest's good manners. 'My garden is but a miserable patch of earth.' Dismissing his son, he gestured. 'Please join me, my friend.'

Bourne rolled out the prayer rug so that its silk threads shimmered in the golden shots of sunlight that found their way between the palm fronds.

Hatun slipped off one slipperlike shoe and placed his bare foot on the rug. 'A beautiful example of the weaver's art. I thank you, my friend, for this unexpected largesse.'

'A token altogether unworthy of you, Nesim Hatun.'

'Ah, well, Yevgeny Feyodovich never presented me with such a gift.' His eyes rose to impale Bourne's. 'And how is our mutual friend?'

'When I left him,' Bourne said, 'he'd made rather a mess of things.'

Hatun's face froze into stone. 'I have no idea what you're talking about.'

'Then let me enlighten you,' Bourne said softly. 'Yevgeny Feyodovich did precisely what you paid him to do. How do I know? Because I took Bourne to Otrada Beach, I led him into the trap Fadi had prepared for him. I did what Yevgeny Feyodovich hired me to do.'

'Here is my problem, Abu Bakr.' Hatun pitched his torso forward. 'Yevgeny Feyodovich never would have hired a Turk for this particular piece of work.'

'Of course not. Bourne would have been suspicious of such a man.'

Hatun scrutinized Bourne with his vulture's face. 'So. The question remains: Who are you?'

'My name is Bogdan Illiyanovich,' he said, identifying himself as the man he'd killed at Otrada Beach. He had inserted the prosthetics he'd purchased in the theatrical supply store in Beyoglu. As a result, the shapes of jawline and cheeks were significantly altered. His front teeth slightly splayed.

'You speak excellent Turkish, for a Ukrainian.' Hatun said this with a certain amount of contempt. 'And now I suppose your boss wants the second half of his payment.'

'Yevgeny Feyodovich isn't in any condition to receive anything. As for me, I want what I have earned.'

Some unnamed emotion seemed to come over Nesim Hatun. He poured them both hot sweet tea, handing one of the glasses to Bourne.

When they had both sipped, he said, 'Perhaps that wound on your left side should be looked after.'

Bourne glanced down at the specks of blood on his clothes. 'A scratch. It's nothing.'

Nesim Hatun was about to reply when the son who had brought Bourne to see him appeared, gave a silent signal.

He rose. 'Please excuse me for a moment. I have a bit of unfinished business to attend to. I assure you I won't be long.' Following his son through an archway, he disappeared behind a filigreed wooden screen.

After a short interval, Bourne rose, strolling through the garden as if admiring it. In this fashion, he made his way through the same archway, stood on the garden side of the screen. He could hear two men speaking in hushed voices. One was Nesim Hatun. The other . . .

' – using a messenger, Muta ibn Aziz,' Nesim Hatun said. 'As you have said, this late in the plan it would not do to have any cell phone communication intercepted. And yet now you tell me that just such a thing has happened.'

'The news was vital to both of us,' Muta ibn Aziz said. 'Fadi has been in communication with his brother. Jason Bourne is dead.' Muta ibn Aziz took a step toward the other. 'That being the case, your role in this matter is now ended.'

Muta ibn Aziz embraced Hatun, kissed him on both cheeks. 'I leave tonight at twenty hundred hours. I go straight to Fadi. With Bourne dead, there will be no further delay. The endgame has begun.'

'*La ilaha ill allah!*' Hatun breathed. 'Now come, my friend, I will lead you out.'

Bourne turned, went silently back through the garden, swiftly down the side corridor and out of the *hammam*.

Soraya, her foot pressed against the accelerator, knew she was in trouble. Keeping one eye in the rearview mirror for the Ford, she pulled out her cell phone and thumbed it on. There was a soft chime. She had a message. She dialed in, got Bourne's message about Anne.

There was a bitter taste in her mouth. So Anne was the mole after all. *The bitch! How could she?* Soraya pounded her fist against the steering wheel. *Goddamn her to hell.*

As she was putting the phone away, she heard the crunch of metal against metal, felt a sickening jar, had to struggle to keep the Pontiac from screeching over into a truck in the next lane.

'What the – !'

A Lincoln Aviator, looking as big and menacing as an M1 Abrams tank, had sideswiped her. Now it was ahead of her. Without warning, it decelerated and she banged into it. Its brake lights weren't working – or they had been deliberately disconnected.

She swerved, switching lanes, then came abreast of the Aviator. She tried to peer in, to see who was driving, but the windows were tinted so darkly she couldn't even make out a silhouette.

The Aviator lurched toward her, its side smashing the Pontiac's passenger doors. Pressing the window buttons repeatedly, Soraya found them stuck fast. Replacing her right foot on the gas pedal with her left, she kicked at the ruined door with the heel of her right foot. It didn't budge; it, too, was jammed shut. With a burst of anxiety, she returned to her normal driving position. Her heart was racing, her pulse pounding in her ears.

Now the Aviator sprinted ahead, weaving as she had through the traffic until she lost sight of it. She had to get off the highway. She began to look for signs for the next exit. It was three kilometers away. Sweating profusely, she moved over into the right-hand lane so she'd be in position to take the upcoming exit ramp.

That was when the Aviator roared up on her left and swerved hard into her, crumpling the doors on that side. Clearly it had dropped back in the traffic flow so that it could come up on her from behind. She hit the window button, tried to turn the inside handle, but this window and door were jammed shut as well. Now none of them would open. She was effectively trapped, a prisoner inside the speeding Pontiac.

# 27

Bourne retrieved his satchel from behind the urn then walked quickly, silently around the side of the *hammam,* searching for the street onto which the rear door to Nesim Hatun's establishment opened. He found it without difficulty, saw a man walking away from the *hammam's* rear door.

The messenger Muta ibn Aziz, who would lead him back to Fadi.

As he walked, Bourne opened the satchel, found the can of spirit gum, and reapplied his beard. Returned to his Semitic disguise, he followed Muta ibn Aziz out of the alley into the clamorous bustle of Sultanahmet. For close to forty minutes, he kept pace with his quarry, who neither paused nor looked around him. It was clear he knew where he was headed. In the overcrowded heart of the district, with the flow of pedestrians moving toward all points of the compass, it was not easy keeping Muta ibn Aziz in sight. On the other hand, the relentless crowds also worked to Bourne's benefit, for it was easy to keep himself anonymous. Even if his target was using the reflective surfaces of vehicle and shop windows, he'd never spot his tail. They crossed from Sultanahmet into Eminonu.

At length, the domed mass of Sirkeci Station loomed up in front of him. Was Muta ibn Aziz taking a train to where Fadi was located? But no, Bourne saw him bypass the main entrance, walk briskly on, as he threaded his way through the throng.

He and Bourne skirted a huge knot of tourists that had formed a semicircle around three *Mevlevi,* Whirling Dervishes, their long white dresses unfurled around them as they spun in their ecstatic *sema* to the drone of ancient Islamic hymns. As they whirled, the *Mevlevi* threw off sprays of saffron- and myrrh-scented sweat. The air around them seemed alive with the mystic unknown, another world glimpsed in the blink of an eye before vanishing again.

Opposite the station was the Adalar Iskelesi dock. Bourne loitered inconspicuously with a clutch of German tourists while he watched Muta ibn Aziz purchase a one-way ticket to Büyükada. He must be leaving from there, Bourne thought, most likely by boat. But to where? It didn't matter, because Bourne was determined to be on whatever mode of transport Muta ibn Aziz chose to take him to Fadi.

For the time being, exiting her mashed Pontiac was the least of Soraya's problems. Topping the list was the Aviator hard on her tail. The sign for the next exit blurred by overhead, and she prepared herself. She saw the two-lane off-ramp, took the left-hand lane. The Aviator, half a car length away, followed her. There were cars ahead of her in both lanes, but a quick check in her rearview mirror showed her the break in the exiting traffic she was hoping for. Now if only the

Pontiac's transmission wouldn't fall out from the punishment she was about to give it.

She swung the wheel hard over. The Pontiac veered into the right-hand lane of the off-ramp. Before the Aviator's driver could fully react, Soraya slammed the Pontiac into reverse and stepped on the gas pedal.

She shot past the Aviator, which was just now swinging into her lane. Its rear end took out the headlight on her side. Then she was accelerating away, back up the off-ramp. There was a dissonant clamor of horns, shouts, along with the squeal of tires as the cars behind her got out of her way.

With an insistent warning from its horn, the Aviator itself reversed, following her. Near the top of the ramp a motorist in a gray Toyota panicked, slamming into the car behind it. Chrome and plastic hanging from its front, it slewed around blocking both lanes, effectively cutting off the Aviator.

Soraya backed onto the breakdown lane of the highway, then shifted the Pontiac into drive and took off, heading into Washington proper.

'It will be easy to ram the Toyota out of the way,' the driver of the Aviator said.

'Don't bother,' the man in the backseat replied. 'Let her go.'

Though they were diplomats stationed at the Saudi embassy, they also belonged to Karim's Washington sleeper cell. As the Aviator reached the city streets, the man in the backseat activated a GPS. At once, a grid of downtown D.C. appeared, along with a moving pinpoint of light. He punched a number into his cell phone.

'The subject slipped the noose,' the man in the backseat said. 'She's driving the Pontiac we fitted with the electronic tracking device. It's heading in your direction. Judging from the speed, it should be in range within thirty seconds.'

He waited patiently until the driver of the black Ford said, 'Got her. It looks like she's heading toward the northeast.'

'Follow her,' the man in the backseat said. 'You know what to do.'

During the ferry ride to the island of Büyükada, Bourne stayed with a family of Chinese tourists with whom he struck up a conversation. He talked with them in Mandarin, joking with the children, pointing out the important buildings as they left Istanbul behind, recounting the city's storied history. All the while, he kept Muta ibn Aziz in view.

Fadi's messenger stood by himself, leaning against the ferry's railing, staring out across the water toward the smudge of land toward which they were headed. He neither moved nor looked around.

When Muta ibn Aziz turned and walked inside, Bourne excused himself from the Chinese family and followed. He saw the messenger ordering tea at the onboard café. Bourne wandered over, poring through a rack of picture postcards and maps. Choosing a map of Büyükada and vicinity, he managed to reach the cashier just ahead of Muta ibn Aziz. He spoke to the cashier in Arabic. The mustachioed man with a gold cross hanging from a chain around his neck shook his head, replying in Turkish. Bourne gestured that he didn't understand.

Muta ibn Aziz leaned over, said, 'Pardon me, friend, but the filthy infidel is asking for payment.'

Bourne showed a handful of coins. Muta ibn Aziz plucked up the right change and gave it to the cashier. Bourne waited until he had paid for his own tea, then said, 'Thank you, friend. I'm afraid Turkish sounds like pig grunts to me.'

Muta ibn Aziz laughed. 'An apt phrase.' He gestured, and together they walked out onto the deck.

Bourne followed the messenger to his spot at the rail. The sun was strong, counteracting the chill of the wind coming in off the Sea of Marmara. The feathery fingertips of cirrus clouds dotted the deep blue of the winter sky.

'The Christians are the swine of the world,' Muta ibn Aziz said.

'And the Jews are the apes,' Bourne replied.

'Peace be upon you, brother. I see we read the same schoolbooks.'

'Jihad in the path of God is the summit of Islam,' Bourne said. 'I needed no schoolmaster to explain this to me. It seems to me that I was born knowing it.'

'Like me, you are Wahhabi.' Muta ibn Aziz gave him a considered sidelong glance. 'Just as we were successful in the past when we came together with the Muslims to evict the Christian crusaders from Palestine, so will we emerge victorious against the latter-day crusaders who occupy our lands.'

Bourne nodded. 'We think alike, brother.'

Muta ibn Aziz sipped his tea. 'Do these righteous beliefs move you to act, brother? Or are they the philosophy of the café and coffeehouse?'

'In Sharm el-Sheikh and in Gaza I have drawn the blood of the infidel.'

'Individual endeavors are to be applauded,' Muta ibn Aziz mused, 'but the greater the organization, the more damage can be inflicted on our enemies.'

'Just so.' *Time to bait the hook,* Bourne thought. 'Again and again I have thought of joining Dujja, but always the same consideration has stopped me.'

The paper cup of tea paused halfway to Muta ibn Aziz's lips. 'And what is that?'

*Slowly, slowly,* Bourne cautioned himself. 'I don't know whether I can say, brother. After all, we have just met. Your intentions – '

'Are the same as yours,' Muta ibn Aziz said with a newfound quickness. 'Of this I assure you.'

Still Bourne held back, appearing undecided.

'Brother, is it not true that we have spoken of a like philosophy? Is it not true that we share a certain outlook on the world, on its future?'

'Indeed, yes.' Bourne pursed his lips. 'All right then, brother. But I warn you, if you have been untrue about your intentions, then I swear I will find out, and I will mete out the proper punishment.'

'*La ilaha ill allah.* Every word I have spoken is the truth.'

Bourne said: 'I went to school in London with Dujja's leader.'

'I don't know – '

'Please, I have no intention of mentioning Fadi's real name. But knowing it myself gives me knowledge of the family others do not have.'

Muta ibn Aziz's curiosity, once feigned, now became real. 'Why is that a deterrent to becoming one with Dujja?'

'Ah, well, it's the father, you see. Or, more specifically, his second wife. She is English. Worse, she is Christian.' Bourne shook his head, his fierce expression reinforcing the edge to his words. 'It is forbidden for a true Muslim to be a loyal friend to someone who does not believe in God and His Prophet. Yet this man married the infidel, mated with her. Fadi is the spawn. Tell me, brother, how can I follow such a creature? How can I believe a word he says, when the devil lurks inside him?'

Muta ibn Aziz was taken aback. 'And yet Fadi has done so much for our cause.'

'This can hardly be denied,' Bourne said. 'But it seems to me, speaking in terms of blood – which, as we know, can be neither ignored nor disowned – Fadi is like the tiger taken from the jungle, brought into a new environment, lovingly domesticated by a foster family. It's merely a matter of time before the tiger reverts to his true nature, turns on those who have adopted him and destroys them.' He shook his head again, this time in perfectly believable sorrow. 'It is a mistake to try to change the tiger's nature, brother. Of this there can be no doubt.'

Muta ibn Aziz turned his head to stare morosely out to sea, where the image of Büyükada rose from the sea like Atlantis or the island of a long-forgotten caliph, stuck in time. He wanted to say something that would refute the other's contention, but somehow he couldn't find it in him to do so. *Doubly depressing*, he thought, *to have the truth come from the mouth of this man.*

Soraya's mind was reeling, not only from the violence of her flight from the Lincoln Aviator but also from Anne Held's betrayal. Her blood ran cold. My God, what had she and everyone else told her over the years? How many secrets had they given away to Dujja?

She drove her rolling coffin without conscious thought. The colors of the day seemed supersaturated, vibrating with a strange pulse that made the passing cars, the streets, the buildings, even the roiling clouds overhead seem unfamiliar, menacing, venomous. Her entire being was trapped within the horror of the ugly truth.

Her head ached with the doomsday possibilities, her body trembled in the aftermath of her adrenaline rush.

She needed to go to ground until she could regroup, figure out her next step. She needed an ally here in D.C. She immediately thought of her friend Kim Lovett, but almost as quickly dismissed the notion. For one thing, her situation was too precarious, too dangerous to get Kim involved. For another, people within CI, most especially Anne, knew of the friendship.

She needed someone unknown to anyone at CI. She activated her phone, punched in Deron's number. She prayed that he was back from visiting his father in Florida, but her heart sank as she heard his recorded voice-mail message come on.

*Where to now?* she asked herself in desperation. She needed a port in this gathering storm, and she needed it now. Then, just before the panic set in, she remembered Tyrone. He was only a teenager, of course, but Deron had enough faith in him to use him for protection. Tyrone had also been the one to tell her that she'd been followed to Deron's house. Still, even if Tyrone might consent to help her, even if she took the chance to trust him, how on earth would she get in touch with him?

Then she remembered him telling her that he hung out at a construction site. Where was it? She racked her brain.

*'Down Florida, they puttin' up a shitload a high-rises. I go there every chance I get, see how it all goin' up, y'know?'*

For the first time, she actually looked at where she was. In the Northeast quadrant, right where she needed to be.

\*

Büyükada was the largest of the Princes' Islands, so called because in ancient times the Byzantine emperors exiled the princes who had displeased or offended them to this chain of islands off Istanbul's coast. For three years, Büyükada had been home to Leon Trotsky, who wrote *The History of the Russian Revolution* there.

Because of their unsavory history, the islands remained deserted for years, one of the many boneyards of the Ottoman Empire's bloody history. Nowadays, however, Büyükada had been turned into a lushly landscaped playground for the wealthy, strewn with masses of flowers, tree-shaded lanes, and villas in the ornamentally baroque Byzantine style.

Bourne and Muta ibn Aziz walked off the ferry together. On the dock they embraced, wished each other Allah's grace and protection.

'*La ilaha ill allah,*' said Bourne.

'*La ilaha ill allah,*' said Fadi's messenger as they parted.

Bourne waited to see which way he went, then opened his map of the island. Turning his head a bit, he could see his target out of the corner of his eye. He had just rented a bicycle. Because no automotive traffic was allowed on the island, there were three modes of transportation: bicycles, horse and carriage, one's own feet. The island was large enough that walking all the time was prohibitive.

Now that Bourne knew which mode Muta ibn Aziz had chosen, he returned his attention to the map. He knew that the messenger was leaving here at eight o'clock this evening, but the exact location and the means were still a mystery.

Entering the bike rental shop, he chose a model with a basket in front. It wouldn't be as fast as the one Muta ibn Aziz had, but he needed the basket to hold his satchel. Paying the proprietor in advance, he set off in the direction the messenger had taken, ascending toward the interior of the island.

When he was out of sight of the dock, he pulled over and, beneath the shade of a palm, rummaged in the satchel for the transponder that went with the NET, the nano-electronic tag that Soraya had planted on him to track his movements. He'd transferred the NET itself to Muta ibn Aziz when they had embraced on the dock. In a place like this without cars, it would be impossible to shadow the messenger on a bicycle without being seen.

Switching on the transponder, he keyed in his location, saw the blip that represented his position appear on the screen. He pressed another key and, soon enough, located the signal. He got back on the bike and set off, ignoring the pain in his side, building speed until he was going at a fairly rapid clip, even though the road ahead of him wound steeply uphill.

Soraya rolled along the southern edge of the immense construction site bounded by 9th Street and Florida Avenue. The housing project that would replace the neighborhood's rotten teeth with towering steel-and-glass implants was well under way. The metal skeletons of two of the towers were almost complete. The site was filled with gigantic cranes swinging steel beams through the air as if they were lollipop sticks. Bulldozers shoved rubble; semis were being unloaded next to a line of trailer offices to which a fistful of electrical lines ran.

Soraya drove her heap slowly along the periphery of the site. She was looking for Tyrone. In her desperation, she had remembered that this was his favorite spot. He came here every day, he'd told her.

The Pontiac's engine wheezed like an asthmatic in Bangkok, then returned to normal. For the past ten minutes, the noises emanating from the engine had been getting louder and more frequent. She was praying that it wouldn't give out before she found Tyrone.

Having traveled the length of the southern perimeter, she now turned north, heading toward Florida Avenue. She was looking for likely vantage points where Tyrone might hide himself in shadow so as not to be seen by the several hundred workmen at the site. She found a couple, but at this time of the morning none were in shadow. No Tyrone. She realized that she'd have to get to the northern border before she might find him.

Florida Avenue was five hundred meters ahead when she heard a loud clank. The wounded Pontiac lurched, then shuddered pathetically. It had ended not with a roar, but with a whimper. The engine was dead. Soraya swore and slammed the dash with the heel of her hand, as if the car were a television whose reception required clearing.

It was when she unstrapped her seat belt that she saw the black Ford. It had turned the corner and was now headed directly toward her.

'God help me,' she whispered to herself.

Putting her back onto the seat, she rolled herself into a ball and slammed both feet into her side window. It was made of safety glass, of course, difficult to shatter. She drew her legs, uncoiled them again. Her soles struck the glass without effect.

She made the mistake of peeking up over the dash. The Ford was now so close that she could see the two men inside. With a little sound, she slid back down and returned to her task. Two more strikes with her feet and the glass shattered. But the pieces were held in place by the central sheet of plastic.

All at once the window cracked with the sound of thunder. Small sheets of the shattered pieces fell in on her. Someone had cracked the glass from the outside. Then one of the men from the black Ford reached in. She launched herself at him, but as soon as she grabbed hold of his arm the second man zapped her with a Taser.

Her body went limp. Together the men hauled her roughly out of the Pontiac. Through the awful buzzing in her head, she heard a gout of rapid-fire Arabic. An explosion of laughter. Their hands were all over her helpless body.

Then one of them put a gun to her head.

# 28

Martin Lindros, standing in the windowless cell deep underground in Dujja's Miran Shah complex, ran his hand over the walls. He had done this so many times since he'd been brought here he could feel the rebar like bones that crisscrossed beneath the rough concrete, reinforcing them.

Precisely fifteen paces to a side, each side equal, the only break a pallet hinged to one wall and, opposite, a stainless steel sink and toilet. Back and forth he paced, like a caged animal going quietly mad from its confinement. Three sets of purple-blue fluorescent lights were embedded into the ceiling. They were unguarded by wire mesh, being too high up for him to reach, even with his best to the hoop leap, therefore, they glared mercilessly down sixteen hours a day.

When they were turned off, when he lay down to sleep, they had the uncanny habit of snapping on just as he was sinking down into sleep, jerking him awake like a hooked fish. From these occurrences Lindros quickly determined that he was under continuous surveillance. After some detective work, he'd discovered a tiny hole in the ceiling between two of the sets of lights – another reason for the glare, no doubt – through which a fiber-optic eye observed him with all the dispassion of a god. All this possessed a level of sophistication befitting Dujja. It was confirmation, if he needed any, that he was at the heart of the terrorist network.

It was difficult not to believe that Fadi himself was keeping an eye on him, if not always in person, then by periodically reviewing the video tapes of him in his cell. How the terrorist must gloat every time he saw Lindros prowling back and forth. Was he looking forward to the moment when he imagined Lindros would make the break from human being to animal? Lindros was certain of it, and his fists turned white as they trembled at his side.

The door to his cell banged open, admitting Fadi, his face dark with fury. Without a word he strode to Lindros and struck him a massive blow to the side of the head. Lindros fell to the concrete floor, stunned and sickened. Fadi kicked him.

'Bourne is dead. Do you hear me, Lindros? Dead!' There was a terrifying edge to Fadi's voice, a slight tremor that spoke of being pushed to the edge of an emotional abyss. 'The unthinkable has happened. I have been cheated of the revenge I meticulously planned. All undone by the unforeseen.'

Lindros, recovering, hauled himself up on one elbow. 'The future is unforeseen,' he said. 'It's unknowable.'

Fadi squatted down, his face almost touching Lindros's. 'Infidel. Allah knows the future; He shows it to the righteous.'

'Fadi, I pity you. You can't see the truth even when it's staring you in the face.'

His face a twisted fist of rage, Fadi grabbed Lindros and threw him to the floor of the cell. His hands closed over the other man's throat, cutting off his breath.

'I may not be able to kill Jason Bourne with my bare hands, but here you are. I will kill you instead.' His eyes fairly bulging with fury, he squeezed Lindros's neck in a death grip. Lindros kicked and thrashed, but he had neither the strength nor the leverage to throw Fadi off him or to displace his hands.

He was losing consciousness, his good eye rolling up in its socket, when Abbud ibn Aziz appeared in the cell's open doorway.

'Fadi – '

'Get out of here!' Fadi cried. 'Leave me alone!'

Nevertheless, Abbud ibn Aziz took a step into the cell. 'Fadi, it's Veintrop.'

Fadi's eyes showed white all around. The Desert Wind – the killing rage – had taken possession of him.

'Fadi,' Abbud persisted. 'You must come now.'

Letting go of his hold, Fadi rose, turned on his second in command. 'Why? Why must I come now? Tell me this instant before I kill you as well.'

'Veintrop is finished.'

'All the safeguards are in place?'

'Yes,' Abbud said. 'The nuclear device is ready to be deployed.'

Tyrone was munching on a quarter-pound burger while watching with a self-taught engineer's eye the steady climb of a massive I-beam when the severely battered Pontiac came under attack. Two men in slick business suits ran out of a black Ford that had met the Pontiac head-on. They spoke to each other, but over the construction noise he couldn't make out the words.

He rose from a crate, his impromptu bench, and began to walk toward the men. One of them held a weapon: neither a gun nor a knife, Tyrone saw, but a Taser.

Then, as one of the men bashed in the driver's side window of the Pontiac, Tyrone recognized him as a guard he'd seen outside M&N Bodywork. These people were invading his turf.

Throwing aside his burger, he began to walk quickly toward the Pontiac, which looked as if some monster twenty-wheeler had tried its best to crush it. Having bashed in the safety glass, one of the men reached through it. Then the man with the Taser thrust his right arm through the opening, using the weapon on whoever was inside. A moment later, both men began to haul out the incapacitated driver.

Tyrone was close enough now to see that the victim was a woman. They man-handled her roughly to her feet, turned her so that he saw her face. He broke out into a cold sweat. Miss Spook! His mind racing, he began to run.

With the constant din of the construction site, the men did not become aware of him until he was almost upon them. One of them took the gun from Miss S's head, aimed it at Tyrone. Tyrone, his hands in the air, came to an abrupt halt a pace away from them. It was all he could do not to look at Miss S. Her head was hanging down on her chest; her legs looked rubbery. They had zapped her but good.

'Get the fuck out of here,' the man with the gun said. 'Turn around and keep walking.'

Tyrone put a frightened look on his face. 'Yessir,' he said meekly.

As he began to turn away, his hands sank to his sides. The switchblade slid into his right hand; he *snikked* it open and, as he whirled back, drove the blade to the hilt between the man's ribs, as he had been taught to handle the close-on street fights of turf wars.

The man dropped his gun. His eyes rolled up and his legs gave out. The other man groped for his Taser, but he had Miss S to consider. He threw her back against the crumpled side of the Pontiac just as Tyrone's fist shattered the cartilage in his nose. Blood flew out, blinding him. Tyrone drove a knee into his groin, then took his head between his hands, slamming it into the Pontiac's side mirror.

As the man crumpled to the ground, Tyrone delivered a vicious kick to his side, stoving in a handful of ribs. He bent, retrieved his switchblade. Then he hoisted Miss S over his shoulder, took her to the idling Ford, laid her carefully on the backseat. As soon as he slid behind the wheel, he once again checked out the construction site. Luckily, the Pontiac had blocked the workmen's view. They'd seen nothing of the incident.

He spat out of the side window in the direction of the fallen men. Putting the SUV into gear, he drove off, careful not to exceed the speed limit. The last thing he needed now was for a cop to pull him over for a traffic violation.

Snaking up the hillside, Bourne passed one wooden villa after another, built in the nineteenth century by Greek and Armenian bankers. Today they were owned by the billionaires of Istanbul, whose businesses, like those of their Ottoman ancestors, spanned the known world.

While he rode, keeping track of Muta ibn Aziz, he thought about Fadi's brother, Karim, the man who had taken Martin Lindros's face, his right eye, his identity. On the surface, he was just about the last person anyone would expect to be directly involved in Dujja's plan. He was, after all, the scion of the family, the man who had stepped in to run Integrated Vertical Technologies when his father had been incapacitated by Bourne's bullet. He was the legitimate brother, the businessman, just like the businessmen who had built these modern-day palaces.

And now, for the first time, Bourne understood the depth of the obsession the two brothers felt in avenging their sister's murder. Sarah had been the family's shining star, the repository of the Hamid ibn Ashef al-Wahhib honor that stretched back over the centuries, over the endless wastes of the Arabian desert, over time itself. Theirs was an honor embedded in the three-thousand-year history of the Arabian peninsula, of the Sinai, of Palestine. Their ancestors had come out of the desert, had come back from defeat after defeat, erasing ignominious retreat to take back the Arabian peninsula from their enemies. Their patriarch, Muhammad ibn Abd-al-Wahhab, was one of the great Islamic reformists. In the middle 1700s, he had joined forces with Muhammad ibn Saud to create a new political entity. A hundred fifty years later, the two families captured Riyadh, and modern Saudi Arabia was born.

Difficult as it was for a Westerner to understand, Sarah ibn Ashef embodied all of that. Of course her brothers would move heaven and earth to kill her murderer. This was why they had taken the time to weave Bourne's utter destruction – first of mind, then of body. Because it would not be enough for them merely to seek him out and put a bullet through the back of his head. No, the plan was to break him, then to have Fadi kill him with bare hands. Nothing less would do.

Bourne knew that the news of his death would send both brothers into a frenzy. In this unstable state they were more apt to make a mistake. All the better for him.

He needed to tell Soraya the identity of the man who was pretending to be Martin Lindros. Pulling out his cell phone, he punched in the country and city code, then her number. The act of dialing brought home to him that he hadn't heard from her. He glanced at his watch. Unless it had been badly delayed, her flight would have landed in Washington by now.

Once again, she wasn't answering, and now he began to worry. For security reasons he didn't leave another message. After all, he was supposed to be dead. He prayed that she hadn't fallen into enemy hands. But if the worst had happened, he had to protect himself from Karim, who would no doubt check her cell for incoming and outgoing calls. He made a mental note to try her again in an hour or so. That would be just after seven, less than an hour before Muta ibn Aziz was due to leave Büyükada to wherever Fadi was now.

'The endgame has begun,' the messenger had told Hatun. Bourne felt a chill run down his spine. So little time to find Fadi, to stop him from detonating the nuclear device.

According to the map he had purchased on the ferry, the island consisted of two hills separated by a valley. He was now climbing the southern hill, Yule Tepe, on top of which sat the twelfth-century St. George's Monastery. As he rose in elevation, the road turned into a path. By this time, the palm trees had given way to thick, pine-forested swaths, shadowed, mysterious, deserted. The villas, too, had fallen away.

The monastery consisted of a series of chapels over three levels, along with several outbuildings. The blip that represented Muta ibn Aziz's position had remained stationary for some minutes. The way became too rocky and uneven for the bike. Plucking his satchel from the basket, Bourne set the bicycle aside, continuing on foot.

He saw no tourists, no caretakers; no one at all. But then the hour was growing late; darkness had descended. Skirting the ramshackle main building itself, he made his way farther up the hillside. According to the transponder, Muta ibn Aziz was inside the small building dead ahead. Lamplight glowed through the windowpanes.

As he approached, the blip started to move. Shrinking back under the protection of a towering pine, he watched as Fadi's messenger, holding an old-fashioned oil lantern, came out of the building and headed off between two colossal chunks of stone into the thicket of the pine forest.

Bourne made a quick recon of the area, assuring himself that no one was watching the building. Then he slipped in through the scarred wooden door into the cool interior. Oil lamps had been lit against the darkness. His map identified this building as having once been used as an asylum for the criminally insane. The interior was fairly bare; clearly it was unused now. However, evidence of its grisly past was evident. The stone floor was studded with iron rings, which presumably had been used to bind the inmates when they became violent. An open doorway to the left led into a small room, empty save for some tarps and various workers' implements.

He returned to the main room. Against a line of windows facing north toward the woods was a long refectory table of dark wood. On the table, within a generous oval of lamplight, lay unfolded a large sheet of thick paper. Going over to it, Bourne saw that it was a map with a flight plan plotted on it. He studied it, fascinated. The air route led southeast across almost the entire length of Turkey, the southernmost tip of Armenia and Azerbaijan, out over the Caspian Sea, then, transversing a section of Iran, diagonally across the width of Afghanistan, with a landing in the mountainous region just across the border, in terrorist-infested western Pakistan.

So it wasn't a boat Muta ibn Aziz was going to use to leave Büyükada. It was a private jet with permission to enter Iran-ian airspace and enough fuel capacity to make the thirty-five-hundred-kilometer trip without refueling.

Bourne looked out the window at the dense pine forest into which Muta ibn Aziz had disappeared. He was wondering where in that mass a landing strip suitable for a jet could be hidden when he heard a noise. He was in the process of turning around when pain exploded in the back of his head. He had the sensation of falling. Then blackness.

# 29

Anne had never seen Jamil so angry. He was angry at the DCI. He was angry at her. He didn't hit her or scream at her. He did something far worse: He ignored her.

As she went about her work, Anne grieved inside with a desperation she had thought she had left behind. There was a certain mind-set to being a mistress, something you had to get used to, like the dull pain of a dying tooth. You had to learn to be without your lover on birthdays, Valentine's Day, Christmas, the anniversary of your meeting, the first time you slept together, the first time he stayed the night, the first breakfast, eaten with the naked delight of children. All these things were denied a mistress.

At first, Anne had found this peculiar aloneness intolerable. She tried to call him when he could not be with her on the days – and nights! – she craved him the most. Until he explained to her carefully but firmly that she could not. When he wasn't physically with her, she was to forget he existed. *How can I do that?* she had wailed inside her head while she smiled, nodding her assent. It was vital, she knew, that he believe she understood. Instinct warned her that if he didn't, he would turn away from her. If he did, she would surely die.

So she pretended for him, for her own survival. And gradually she learned how to cope. She didn't forget he existed, of course. That was impossible. But she came to see her time with him as if it were a movie she went to see now and again. In between, she could keep the movie in her head, as anyone does with the movies they adore, ones they long to see again and again. In this way, she was able to live her life in a more or less normal manner. Because deep down where she dared to look only infrequently, she knew that without him at her side her life was only half lived.

And now, because she had allowed Soraya to escape, he wasn't speaking to her at all. He passed by her desk on his way to and from meetings with the Old Man as if she didn't exist, ignored the swelling of her left cheek where Soraya's elbow had connected. The worst had happened, the one thing that had terrified her from the moment she had fallen deeply, madly, irretrievably in love with him: She had failed him.

She wondered whether he had gotten the goods on Defense Secretary Halliday. For a moment, she had been dead certain that he had, but then the Old Man had asked her to set up an appointment with Luther LaValle, the Pentagon intelligence czar, not Secretary Halliday. What was he up to?

She was in the dark, too, about Soraya's fate. Had she been captured? Killed? She didn't know because Jamil had cut her out of the loop. She didn't share his confidence. She could no longer tuck herself into his body, hot as the desert wind. In her heart, she suspected that Soraya was still alive. If Jamil's cell had caught Soraya, surely he would have forgiven her the sin of allowing her to get away. She felt chilled. Soraya's knowledge was like a guillotine hovering over her neck. Anne's whole life would be revealed as a lie. She'd be tried for treason.

Part of her mind went through the motions of her daily routine. She listened to the Old Man when he summoned her into his office; she input his memos and printed them out for him to sign. She made his calls, scheduled his long day with the precision of a military campaign. She protected his phone lines as fiercely as ever. But another part of her mind was frantically trying to figure out how she could reverse the fatal mistake she had made.

She needed to win Jamil back. And she had to have him, she knew that. Redemption came in many guises, but not for Jamil. He was Bedouin; his mind was locked in the ancient ways of the desert. Exile or death, those were the choices. She would have to find Soraya. Her bloodied hands were the only things that would bring him back to her. She would have to kill Soraya herself.

Bourne awoke. He tried to move, but found himself bound by ropes tied to two of the iron rings bolted to the asylum's floor. A man was crouched over him, a Caucasian with a lantern jaw and eyes pale as ice. He was wearing a leather flight jacket and a cap with a silver pin in the shape of a pair of wings stuck on it.

The pilot of the jet. From the look of him, Bourne knew he was one of those flyboys who fancied himself a cowboy of the sky.

He grinned down at Bourne. 'Whatcha doing here?' He spoke in very poor Arabic, reacting to Bourne's disguise. 'Checking out my flight plan. Spying on me.' He shook his head in a deliberately exaggerated fashion, like a nanny admonishing her charge. 'That's forbidden. Got that? For-bid-den.' He pursed his lips. 'You savvy?' he added in English.

Then he showed Bourne what he was holding: the NET transponder. 'What the fuck is this, you rat bastard? Huh? Who the fuck are you? Who sent you?' He pulled a knife, bringing the long blade close to Bourne's face. 'Answer me, goddammit, or I'll carve you up like a Christmas goose! You savvy Christmas? Huh?'

Bourne stared up at him with blank eyes. He opened his mouth, spoke a sentence very softly.

'What?' The pilot leaned closer to Bourne. 'What did you say?'

Using the power in his lower belly, Bourne brought his legs straight up in the air, scissoring them so that his ankles crossed behind the pilot's neck. His lower legs locked and he spun the pilot over and down. The side of the man's head struck the marble floor with such force, his cheekbone shattered. Immediately he passed out.

Twisting his neck, Bourne could see the knife on the floor behind his head. It was on the other side of the iron rings. Drawing his legs up, his body rolled into a ball, he rocked back and forth, gaining momentum. When he judged that he had enough force, he rocked backward with all his might. Though anchored by the rings to which his wrists were tied, he flew through the air in a backflip, passing over the rings, landing on his knees on the other side.

Extending one leg, he hooked the knife with the top of his shoe, kicked it so that the hilt clacked against the ring to which his right hand was bound. By moving the ring down until it was almost parallel with the floor, he was able to grab the knife. Laying the edge of the blade against the rope, he began to saw through it.

It was hard, cramped work. He couldn't apply the kind of pressure he'd have liked, so progress was frighteningly slow. From where he knelt, he couldn't see the transponder's screen; he had no idea where Muta ibn Aziz was. For all he knew, at any moment the messenger would walk in on him.

At length, he'd sawed through the rope. Quickly, he cut the rope binding his left hand, and he was free. Lunging for the transponder, he looked at the screen. Muta ibn Aziz's blip was still some way distant.

Bourne rolled the pilot over and methodically stripped off his clothes, which he donned piece by piece, though the shirt was too small, the pants too big. When he had arranged the pilot's outfit on his frame as best he could, he drew over his satchel and took out the various items he'd bought at the theatrical shop in Istanbul. Setting a small square mirror down on the floor where he could easily see the reflection of his face, he removed the prosthetics from his mouth. Then he began the process of transforming himself into the pilot.

Bourne trimmed and restyled his hair, changed the complexion of his face, added a pair of prosthetics to give his jaw a longer appearance. He had no colored lenses, but in the darkness of the night the disguise would have to do. Luckily, he could keep the pilot's cap low on his forehead.

He took another glance at the transponder, then went through the pilot's wallet and papers. His name was Walter B. Darwin. An American expat, with passports identifying him as a citizen of three different countries. Bourne could relate to that. He had a military tattoo on one shoulder, the words fuck you, too on the other. What he was doing ferrying terrorists around the globe was anyone's guess. Not that it mattered now. Walter Darwin's flyboy career was over. Bourne dragged his naked body into a back room, covered it in a dusty tarp.

Back in the main room, he went to the table, gathered up the flight plan. It was twenty minutes to eight. Keeping an eye on the blip on the transponder screen, he stuffed the plan in his satchel, took up one of the lamps, and went in search of the airstrip.

Anne knew that Soraya was too smart to come anywhere near her apartment. Pretending to be Kim Lovett, Soraya's friend in the DCFD's Fire Investigation Unit, she called both Tim Hytner's mother and sister. Neither of them had seen or heard from Soraya since she had visited to break the news that Tim had been shot to death. If Soraya had gone there now, she would have warned them about a woman named Anne Held. But surely she'd want to talk to her best friend. Anne was about to call Kim Lovett herself when she thought better of it. Instead, when she left the office that evening, she took a taxi straight to the FIU labs on Vermont Avenue and 11th Street.

Finding her way to Kim's lab, she went in.

'I'm Anne Held,' she said. 'Soraya works with me.'

Kim rose from her work: two metal trays filled with ash, charred bits of bone, and half-burned cloth. She stretched like a cat, stripped off her latex gloves, held out her hand for a firm shake.

'So,' Kim said, 'what brings you down to this grim place?'

'Well, actually, it's Soraya.'

Kim was instantly alarmed. 'Has something happened to her?'

'That's what I'm trying to find out. I was wondering whether you'd heard from her.'

Kim shook her head. 'But that's hardly unusual.' She considered a moment. 'It may be nothing, but a week or two ago there was a police detective who was interested in her. They met here at the lab. He wanted her to take him with her on some investigation or other, but Soraya said no. I had the feeling, though, that his interest in her was more than professional.'

'Do you remember the date, and the detective's name?'

Kim gave her the date. 'As for his name, I did write it down somewhere.' She rummaged through one of several stacks of files on the countertop. 'Ah, here it is,' she said, pulled out a torn-off strip of paper. 'Detective William Overton.'

*How small the world is,* Anne thought as she exited the FIU building. *How full of coincidence.* The cop who had been following her had been after Soraya as well. He was dead now, of course, but perhaps he could still tell her where to find Soraya.

Using her cell phone, Anne quickly found Detective William Overton's precinct, its address, and the name of his commanding officer. Arriving there, she produced her credentials, told the desk sergeant she needed to see Captain Morrell on a matter of some urgency. When he balked, as she knew he would, she invoked the Old Man's name. The desk sergeant picked up the phone. Five minutes later a young uniform was escorting her into Captain Morrell's corner office.

He dismissed the uniform, offered Anne a seat, then closed the door. 'What can I do for you, Ms. Held?' He was a small man with thinning hair, a bristling mustache, and eyes that had seen too much death and accommodation. 'My desk sergeant said it was a matter of some urgency.'

Anne got right to the point. 'CI is investigating Detective Overton's disappearance.'

'Bill Overton? *My* Bill Overton?' Captain Morrell looked bewildered. 'Why – ?'

'It's a matter of national security,' Anne said, using the surefire catchall phrase that no one could refute these days. 'I need to see all his logs for the past month, also his personal effects.'

'Sure. Of course.' He stood. 'The investigation's ongoing, so we have everything here.'

'We'll keep you personally informed every step of the way, Captain,' she assured him.

'I appreciate that.' He opened the door, bawled 'Ritchie!' into the corridor. The same young uniform dutifully appeared. 'Ritchie, give Ms. Held access to Overton's effects.'

'Yessir.' Ritchie turned to Anne. 'If you'll follow me, ma'am.'

*Ma'am.* God, that made her feel old.

He led her farther along the corridor, down a set of metal stairs to a basement room guarded by a floor-to-ceiling fence with a locked door in it. Using a key, he unlocked the door, then took her down an aisle lined on both sides with utilitarian metal shelves. They were packed with cartons in alphabetical order, identified with typewritten labels.

He pulled down two boxes and carried them to a table pushed up against the back wall. 'Official,' he said, pointing to the carton on the left. 'This other's his personal stuff.'

He looked at her, expectant as a puppy. 'Can I be of any help?'

'That's all right, Officer Ritchie,' Anne said with a smile. 'I can take it from here.'

'Right. Well, I'll leave you to it, then. I'll be in the next room, if you need me.'

When she was alone, Anne turned to the carton on the left, laying out everything in a grid. The files with Overton's logs she put to one side. As soon as she had assured herself that there was nothing of value to her in the grid, she turned her attention to the logs. She examined each item carefully and methodically, giving special attention to entries on and after the date Kim Lovett had given her, when Overton had met Soraya at FIU. There was nothing.

'Bollocks!' she muttered, turned her attention to the carton on her right, filled with Overton's personal effects. These turned out to be even more pathetic than she had expected: a cheap comb and brush sporting a thin mat of hairs; two packs of TUMS, one opened; a blue dress shirt, soiled down the placket with what looked like marinara sauce; a hideous blue-and-red-striped polyester tie; a photo of a goofily grinning young man in a football outfit, probably Overton's son; a box of Raisinets, and another of nonpareils, both unopened. That was it.

*'Merde!'*

With a convulsive gesture, she swept the gutter leavings of Overton's life off the table. She was about to turn away when she saw a bit of white sticking out of the breast pocket of the blue shirt. Bending down, she pulled it out with extended fingertips. It was a square of lined paper, folded in quarters. She opened it up, saw scribbled in blue ballpoint ink:

*S. Moore – 8 & 12 NE (ck)*

Anne's heart beat fast. This was what she was looking for. *S. Moore* was undoubtedly Soraya; *(ck)* could mean 'check.' Of course, 8th Street didn't cross 12th Street in Northeast – or in any quadrant of the district, for that matter. Still, it was clear that Overton had followed Soraya into Northeast. What the hell was she doing there? Whatever it was, she'd kept it secret from CI.

Anne stood staring at the memo Overton had made to himself, trying to work it out. Then it hit her, and she began to laugh. The twelfth letter of the alphabet was *L*. Eighth and L NE.

If Soraya was alive, it was more than likely she'd gone to ground there.

When Bourne passed between the two hulking chunks of stone, the lamplight revealed the path Muta ibn Aziz had taken. It went west for perhaps a kilometer before veering sharply to the northeast. He ascended a slight rise, after which the path headed almost directly north, down into a shallow swale that gradually rose onto the beginning of what appeared to be a plateau of considerable size.

All the while, he had been drawing closer to Muta ibn Aziz, who for the last minute or so hadn't moved. The pine forest was still dense, the thatch of brown needles underfoot deeply aromatic, deadening sound.

Within five minutes, however, the forest simply ended. Clearly it had been cut down here to make room for a landing strip long enough to accommodate the jet he saw sitting at one end of the packed-dirt runway.

And there was Muta ibn Aziz, at the foot of the folding stairs. Bourne strode out from the path through the forest, heading directly for the plane, a Citation Sovereign. The pitch-black sky was strewn with stars, glittering coolly like diamonds on a jeweler's velvet pad. A breeze, dense with sea minerals, played across the cleared hilltop.

'Time to leave,' Muta ibn Aziz said. 'Everything in order?'

Bourne nodded. Muta ibn Aziz pressed a button on a small black object in his hand, and the runway lights flashed on. Bourne followed him up the stairway, retracting it as soon as he was inside. He went down the cabin to the cockpit. He was familiar with the Citation line. The Sovereign had a range of more than 4,500 kilometers and a top speed of 826 kph.

Seating himself in the pilot's chair, he flipped switches, turned dials as he went through the intricate pre-takeoff checklist. Everything was as it should be.

Releasing the brakes, he pushed the throttle forward. The Sovereign responded at once. They taxied down the runway, gathering speed. Then they lifted off into the inky, spangled sky, climbing steadily, leaving the Golden Horn, the gateway to Asia, behind.

# 30

'Why do they do it?' Martin Lindros said in very fine Russian.

Lying flat on his back in the infirmary in Miran Shah, he gazed up into the bruised face of Katya Stepanova Vdova, Dr. Veintrop's stunning young wife.

'Why do they do what?' she said dully as she rather ineptly administered to the abrasions on his throat. She had been training to be a physician's assistant after Veintrop had made her quit Perfect Ten modeling.

'The doctors here: your husband, Senarz, Andursky. Why have they hired out their services to Fadi?' Speaking of Andursky, the plastic surgeon who had remade Karim's face with his eye, Lindros wondered, *Why isn't he tending to me instead of this clumsy amateur?* Almost as soon as he had posed the question, he had the answer: He was no longer of any use either to Fadi or to his brother.

'They're human,' Katya said. 'Which means they're weak. Fadi finds their weakness and uses it against them. For Senarz, it was money. For Andursky, it was boys.'

'And Veintrop?'

She made a face. 'Ah, my husband. He thinks he's being noble, that he's being forced to work for Dujja because Fadi holds my own well-being over his head. He's fooling himself, of course. The truth is he's doing it to get his pride back. Fadi's brother sacked him from IVT on false allegations. He needs to work, my husband. That's his weakness.'

She sat back, her hands in her lap. 'You think I don't know how bad I am at this? But Costin insists, you see, so what choice do I have?'

'You have a choice, Katya. Everyone does. You have only to see it.' He glanced at the two guards just outside the infirmary door. They were talking to each other in low tones. 'Don't you want to get out of here?'

'What about Costin?'

'Veintrop's finished his work for Fadi. A smart woman like you should know that he's now a liability.'

'That's not true!' she said.

'Katya, we all have the capacity for fooling ourselves. That's where we get into trouble. Look no further than your husband.'

She sat very still, staring at him with an odd look in her eyes.

'We also all have the capacity to change, Katya. It only takes us deciding that we have to in order to keep going, in order to survive.'

She looked away for a moment, as people do when they're afraid, when they've made up their minds but need encouragement.

'Who did that to you, Katya?' he said softly.

Her eyes snapped back to him, and he saw the shadow of her fear lurking there. 'Fadi. Fadi and his man. To persuade Costin to complete the nuclear device.'

'That doesn't make sense,' Lindros said. 'If Veintrop knew Fadi had you, that should have been enough.'

Katya bit her lip, kept her eyes focused on her work. She finished up, then rose.

'Katya, why won't you answer me?'

She didn't look back as she walked out of the infirmary.

Anne Held, standing in a chill rain on the corner of 8th and L NE, felt the presence of the S&W J-frame compact handgun in the right-hand pocket of her trench coat as if it were some terrible disfigurement with which she had just been diagnosed.

She knew she would risk anything, do anything to rid herself of the feeling that she no longer belonged anywhere, that there was nothing left inside her. The only thing to do was to prove herself worthy again. If she shot Soraya dead, Jamil would surely welcome her back. She would belong again.

Pulling up her collar against the wind-driven rain, she began to walk. She should have been afraid in this neighborhood – the police certainly were – but strangely she was not. Then again, perhaps it wasn't strange at all. She had nothing left to lose.

She turned the corner onto 7th Street. What was she looking for? What kinds of clues would tell her whether she had deduced correctly that this was where Soraya had gone to ground? A car went by, then another. Faces – black, Hispanic, hostile, strange – glared at her as the vehicles cruised by. One driver grinned, waggled his tongue obscenely at her. She put her right hand in her pocket and closed it around the S&W.

As she walked, she kept her eye on the houses she passed – torn up, beaten down, singed by poverty, neglect, and flames. Rubble and rubbish filled their tiny front yards, as if the street were inhabited by junkmen displaying their woebegone wares for sale. The air was fouled by the stench of rotting garbage and urine, defeat and despair. Gaunt dogs ran here and there, baring their yellow teeth at her.

She was like a drowning woman, clutching at the only thing that could save her from going under. Her palm felt sweaty against the grip of the handgun. The day had finally arrived, she thought vaguely, when all her hours on the firing range would stand her in good stead. She could hear the deep, crisp voice of the CI firearms instructor correcting her stance or her grip while she reloaded the agency-issue S&W.

She thought again of her sister, Joyce, remembering the pain of their shared childhood. But surely there had been pleasure, too, hadn't there, on the nights they had slept in one bed, telling each other ghost stories, seeing which one of them would be the first to scream in fear? Anne felt like a ghost now, drifting through a world she could only haunt. She crossed the street, passing an open lot with weeds as high as her waist, tenacious even in winter. Tires, worn as an old man's face, empty plastic bottles, syringes, used condoms and cell phones, one red sock with the toe cap gone. And a severed arm.

Anne jumped, her heart pounding against the cage of her chest. A doll's arm only. But her heart rate didn't come down. She stared in grim fascination at that severed arm. It was like Joyce's aborted future, lying in a slag-heap of dead weeds.

What exactly was the difference between Joyce's future and her own present? she asked herself. She hadn't cried in the longest time. Now it seemed that she had forgotten how.

Day had descended into the grave of night, icy rain had turned to clammy fog. Moisture seemed to congeal on her hair, the backs of her hands. Now and again a siren rose in distress, only to fall again into uneasy silence.

From behind her came the grumble of an engine. She paused, her heart hammering, waiting for the car to pass. When it didn't, she began to walk again, more quickly. The car, emerging from the fog, kept pace just behind her.

All at once she reversed course and, with her hand gripping the S&W, walked back toward the car. As she did so, it stopped. The driver's-side window rolled down, revealing a long, withered face the color of old shoe leather, the bottom half of which was whiskery and gray.

'You look like you're lost,' the driver said in a voice gravelly with a lifetime of tar and nicotine. 'Gypsy cab.' He tipped his baseball cap. 'I thought you might need a ride. There's a crew down the end a the block lickin' their chops at the thought a you.'

'I can take care of myself.' Sudden fear caused her to sound defensive.

The cabbie eyed her with a downtrodden expression. 'Whatever.'

As he put the car in gear, Anne said, 'Wait!' She passed a hand across her damp brow. She felt as if a raging fever had broken. Who was she kidding? She didn't have it in her to shoot Soraya, let alone kill her.

Grabbing the rear door handle, she slid into the gypsy cab and gave the driver her address. She didn't want to go back to CI headquarters. She couldn't face either Jamil or the Old Man. She wondered whether she'd ever be able to face them again.

Then she noticed that the cabbie had turned around to scrutinize her face.

'What?' Anne said, a bit too defensively.

The cabbie grunted. 'You goddamn good lookin'.'

Opting for forbearance, she took out a clutch of bills, waving them in his face. 'Are you going to give me a ride or not?'

The cabbie licked his lips, put the car in gear.

As the car started off, she leaned forward. 'Just so you know,' she said, 'I've got a gun.'

'So do I, sister.' The grizzled cabbie leered at her. 'So do fuckin' I.'

The DCI met Luther LaValle at Thistle, a trendy restaurant on 19th and Q NW. He'd had Anne book a center table, because when he talked to LaValle he wanted them to be surrounded by raucous diners.

The Pentagon's intelligence czar was already seated when the Old Man arrived from out of the dense winter fog into the restaurant's roar. In a navy-blue suit, crisp white shirt, and red-and-blue-striped regimental tie pierced by an American flag enamel pin, LaValle looked out of place surrounded by young men and women of the next generation.

LaValle's boxer's torso ballooned the suit in the way of all overly muscled men. He looked like Bruce Banner in the process of transforming into the Hulk. Smiling thinly, he rose from his Scotch and soda to give the DCI's proffered hand a perfunctory squeeze.

The Old Man took the chair across from him. 'Good of you to meet me at such short notice, Luther.'

LaValle spread his brutal, blunt-fingered hands. 'What are you having?'

'Oban,' the Old Man said to the waiter who had appeared at his elbow. 'Make it a double, one ice cube, but only if it's large.'

The waiter gave a little nod, vanished into the crowd.

'Large ice cubes are best for liquor,' the DCI said to his companion. 'They take longer to melt.'

The intelligence czar said nothing, but looked at the Old Man expectantly. When the single-malt Scotch arrived, the two men raised their glasses and drank.

'The traffic tonight is insufferable,' the DCI said.

'It's the fog,' LaValle responded vaguely.

'When was the last time we got together like this?'

'You know, I can't recall.'

Both seemed to be talking to the young couple at the next table. Their neutral words sat between them like pawns, already sacrificed on the field of battle. The waiter returned with menus. They opened them, made their choices, and once again were left to their own devices.

The DCI pulled a dossier from his slim briefcase and set it on the table, unopened. His palms came down heavily on it. 'I assume you've heard about the utility truck that went out of control outside the Corcoran.'

'A traffic accident?' LaValle shrugged. 'Do you know how many of those occur in the district each hour?'

'This one is different,' the Old Man said. 'The truck was trying to run down one of my people.'

LaValle took a sip of his Scotch and soda. The Old Man thought he drank like a lady.

'Which one?'

'Anne Held, my assistant. Martin Lindros was with her. He saved her.'

LaValle leaned down, came back with his own dossier. It had the Pentagon's seal on its cover. He opened it and, without a word, reversed it, passing it across the table.

As the Old Man began to read, LaValle said, 'Someone inside your headquarters is sending and receiving periodic messages.'

The Old Man was shocked in more ways than one. 'Since when is the Pentagon monitoring CI communications? Dammit, that's a gross breach of inter-agency protocol.'

'I ordered it, with the president's okay. We thought it necessary. When Secretary Halliday became aware of a mole inside CI – '

'From Matthew Lerner, his creature,' the DCI said heatedly. 'Halliday has no business creeping into my shorts. And without me, the president is getting improperly briefed.'

'It was done for the agency's own good.'

Thunderclouds of indignation cracked open across the DCI's face. 'Are you implying that I no longer know what's good for CI?'

LaValle's finger stabbed out. 'You see, there. The electronic signal is piggyback-ing on CI carrier waves. It's encrypted. We haven't been able to break it. Also, we don't know who's doing the communicating. But from the dates it clearly can't be Hytner, the agent you IDed as the mole. He was already dead.'

The Old Man shifted aside the Pentagon dossier, opened his own. 'I'll take care of this leak, if that's what it is,' he said. Likely as not what these idiots had picked up was a clandestine Typhon communiqué with one of its deep-cover overseas operatives. Of course Martin's black-ops department wouldn't use normal CI channels. 'And you'll take care of the defense secretary.'

'I beg your pardon?' For the first time since they had sat down together, LaValle appeared nonplussed.

'That utility van I mentioned earlier, the one that tried to run over Anne Held.'

'To be candid, Secretary Halliday shared with me that he suspected Anne Held of being the mole inside – '

The appetizers arrived: colossal pink prawns dipped in blood-red cocktail sauce.

Before LaValle could pick up his tiny fork, the DCI held out a single sheet of paper he'd plucked from the dossier Martin had provided him. 'The van that almost killed her was driven by the late Jon Mueller.' He waited a beat. 'You know Mueller, Luther, don't bother pretending otherwise. He was with Homeland Security, but he was trained by NSA. He knew Matthew Lerner. The two were whoring and drinking buddies, in fact. Both Halliday's creatures.'

'Do you have any hard proof of this?' LaValle said blandly.

The Old Man was fully prepared for this question. 'You already know the answer to that. But I have enough to start an investigation. Unexplained deposits in Mueller's bank account, a Lamborghini that Lerner couldn't possibly afford, trips to Las Vegas where both dropped bundles of cash. Arrogance begets stupidity; it's an axiom old as time.' He took back the sheet of paper. 'I assure you that once the investigation gets to the Senate, the net that'll be thrown out will catch not only Halliday but those close to him.'

He folded his arms. 'Frankly, I don't fancy a scandal of this grave a scope. It would only help our enemies abroad.' He lifted a prawn. 'But this time, the secretary's gone too far. He believes he can do anything he wants, even sanctioning a murder using our government's men.'

He paused here to let these words sink in. As the intelligence czar's eyes rose to meet his, the Old Man said, 'Here is where I make my stand. I cannot condone such a recklessly unlawful act. Neither, I think, can you.'

Muta ibn Aziz sat brooding, watching the sky outside the jet's Perspex window glowing blue-black. Below him was the unruffled skin of the Caspian Sea, obscured now and again by streaks of clouds the color of a gull's wing.

He inhabited a dark corner of Dujja, performing the demeaning task of messenger boy, while his brother basked in the limelight of Fadi's favor. And all because of that one moment in Odessa, the lie they had told Fadi and Karim that Abbud had forbidden him to correct. Abbud had said he must keep quiet for Fadi's sake, but now, when Muta looked at the situation from a distance, he realized that this was yet another lie perpetrated by his brother. Abbud insisted on hiding the truth about Sarah ibn Ashef's death for his own sake, for the consolidation of his own power within Dujja.

Rousing himself, Muta saw the dark smudge of land coming into view. He glanced at his watch. Right on schedule. Rising, he stretched, hesitating. His thoughts went to the man piloting the jet. He knew this wasn't the real pilot; he'd failed to give the recognition sign when he'd emerged from the woods. Who was he then? A CI agent, certainly; Jason Bourne, most probably. But then he had received a cell phone text message three hours ago that Jason Bourne was dead, according to an eyewitness and the electronic tracker, which now resided at the bottom of the Black Sea.

But what if the eyewitness lied? What if Bourne, discovering the tracker, had thrown it into the ocean? Who else could this pilot be but Jason Bourne, the Chameleon?

He went up the central aisle, into the cockpit. The pilot kept his attention focused on the neat rows of dials in front of him.

'We're coming up on Iranian airspace,' Muta said. 'Here's the code you need to radio in.'

Bourne nodded.

Muta stood, his legs spread slightly apart, gazing at the back of the pilot's head. He drew out his Korovin TK.

'Call in the code,' he said.

Ignoring him, Bourne continued to fly the plane into Iranian airspace.

Muta ibn Aziz took a step forward, put the muzzle of the Korovin at the base of Bourne's skull. 'Radio in the code immediately.'

'Or what?' Bourne said. 'You'll shoot me? Do you know how to fly a Sovereign?'

Of course Muta didn't, which was why he'd gotten on board with the impostor. Just then the radio squawked.

An electronically thinned voice said in Farsi, '*Salām aleikom. Esmetān chī st?*'

Bourne picked up the mike. '*Salām aleikom,*' he responded.

'*Esmetān chī st?*' the voice said. What is your name?

Muta said, 'Are you insane? Give him the code at once.'

'*Esmetān chī st!*' came the voice from the radio. It was no longer a question. '*Esmetān chī st!*' It was a command.

'Damn you, radio the code!' Muta was shaking with rage and terror. 'Otherwise they'll shoot us out of the sky!'

# 31

Bourne put the Sovereign into such a sudden, steep bank to the left that Muta ibn Aziz was thrown across the cockpit, fetching up hard against the starboard bulkhead. As Muta ibn Aziz struggled to regain his footing, Bourne sent the jet into a dive, simultaneously banking it to the right. Muta ibn Aziz slipped backward, banging his head on the edge of the doorway.

Bourne glanced back. Fadi's messenger was unconscious.

The radar was showing two fighter planes coming up fast from beneath him. The hair-trigger Iranian government had wasted no time in scrambling its air defense. He brought the Sovereign around, caught a visual fix. What the Iranians had sent to intercept him were a pair of Chinese-built J-6s, reverse-engineered copies of the old MiG-19 used in the mid-1950s. These jets were so out of date, the Chengdu plant had stopped manufacturing them more than a decade ago. Even so, they were armed and the Sovereign wasn't. He needed to do something to negate that enormous advantage.

They'd expect him to turn tail and run. Instead he lowered the Sovereign's nose and put on a burst of speed as he headed directly toward them. Clearly startled, the Iranian pilots did nothing until the last moment, when they each peeled away from the Sovereign's path.

As soon as they'd done so, Bourne pulled back on the yoke and brought the Sovereign's nose to the vertical, performing a loop that set him behind both of them. They turned, describing paths like cloverleafs, homing in on him from either side.

They began to fire at him. He dipped below the crossfire, and it ceased immediately. Choosing the J-6 on the right because it was slightly closer, he banked sharply toward it. He allowed it to come under him, allowed the pilot to assume he'd made a tactical error. Taking evasive maneuvers as the chatter of the machine gun sprang up again, he waited until the J-6 had locked on to his tail, then he tipped the Sovereign's nose up again. The Iranian pilot had seen the maneuver before and was ready, climbing steeply just behind the Sovereign. He knew what Bourne would do next: put the Sovereign into a steep dive. This Bourne did, but he also banked sharply to the right. The J-6 followed, even as Bourne punched in every ounce of the Sovereign's speed. The plane began to chatter in the powerful shearing force. Bourne steepened both the bank and the dive.

Behind him, the old J-6 was shuddering and jerking. All at once a handful of rivets were sucked off the left wing. The wing crumpled as if punched by an invisible fist. The wing ripped from its socket in the fuselage. The two sections of the J-6 blew apart in a welter of stripped and shredded metal, plummeting end-over-end downward to the earth.

Bullets ripped through the Sovereign's skin as the second J-6 came after them. Now Bourne lit out for the border to Afghanistan, crossing it within seconds. The second Iranian J-6, undeterred, came on, its engines screaming, its guns chattering.

Just south of the position where he had crossed into Afghani airspace was a chain of mountains that began in northern Iran. The mountains didn't rise to significant height, however, until they reached Bourne's current position, just northwest of Koh-i-Markhura. With a compass heading of east by southeast, he dipped the Sovereign toward the highest peaks.

The J-6 was shuddering and shrieking as it flattened out the curve of its descent. Having seen what had happened to his companion, the Iranian pilot had no intention of getting that close to the Sovereign. But it shadowed Bourne's plane, dogging it from behind and just above, now and again firing short bursts at his engines.

Bourne could see that the pilot was trying to herd him into a narrow valley between two sharp-edged mountains that loomed ahead. In the confined space, the pilot sought to keep the Sovereign's superior maneuverability to a minimum, catch it in the chute, and shoot it down.

The mountains rose up, blocking out light on either side. The massive rock faces blurred by. Both planes were in the chute now. The Iranian pilot had the Sovereign just where he wanted it. He began to fire in earnest, knowing that his prey was limited in the evasive maneuvers it could take.

Bourne felt several more hits judder through the Sovereign. If the J-6 hit an engine, he was finished. The end would come before he had a chance to react. Turning the plane on its right wingtip, he waggled out of the line of fire. But the maneuver would help him only temporarily. Unless he could find a more permanent solution, the J-6 would shoot him out of the sky.

Off to his left he saw a jagged rift in the sheer mountain wall, and immediately headed for it. Almost at once he saw the danger: a spire of rock splitting the aperture in two.

The defile they were in was now so narrow that behind him, the J-6 had assumed the same sideways position. Bourne maneuvered the Sovereign ever so slightly, keeping the profile of his plane between the J-6 and the rock spire.

As far as the Iranian pilot knew, they were both going to fly through the aperture. He was so hell-bent on blowing the Sovereign away that when, at the last moment, his prey moved slightly to the right in order to pass through the rift, he had no chance to react. The spire came up on him, froze him with its frightful proximity, and then his plane smashed into the rock spire, sending up a fireball out of which a column of black smoke shot upward into the arid sky. The J-6 and its pilot, now no more than a hail of white-hot debris, vanished as if by a conjuror's hand.

Soraya awoke to the sound of a baby crying. She tried to move, groaned as her traumatized nerves rebelled in pain. As if her sound antagonized it, the baby started to scream. Soraya looked around. She was in a grimy room, filled with grimy light. The smells of cooking and closely packed human beings clogged the air. A cheap print of Christ on the cross hung at a slant on the grimy wall across from her. Where was she?

'Hey!' she called.

A moment later, Tyrone appeared. He was holding an infant in the crook of his left arm. The baby's face was so scrunched up in rage, all its features were sucked into its wrinkled center. It looked like a fist.

'Yo, how yo feelin' yo?'

'Like I just went fifteen rounds with Lennox Lewis.' Soraya made another, more concerted effort to sit up. As she struggled, she said, 'Man, do I owe you.'

'Take yo up on dat sumtime.' He grinned as he came into the room.

'What happened to the guys from the black Ford? They didn't follow you – ?'

'They fuckin' dead, girl. Sure as shit, they won't bother yo no mo.'

The squalling baby turned her head, staring right into Soraya's eyes with that pure vulnerability only very young children had. Her screams subsided to gulping sobs.

'Here.' Soraya held out her arms. Tyrone transferred the baby to her. At once she laid her head against Soraya's breast, gave a tiny squawk. 'She's hungry, Tyrone.'

He left the room, returning several moments later with a bottle full of milk. He turned it over, tested the temperature on the inside of his wrist.

'S'okay,' he said, handing it to her.

Soraya looked at him for a moment.

'What?'

She put the bottle's nipple to the infant's lips. 'I never thought of you as being domesticated.'

'Yo evah thought a me havin' a kid?'

'This baby's yours?'

'Nah. Belongs t'my sis.' He half turned and called: 'Aisha!'

The doorway remained empty for a time, but Tyrone must have detected movement, because he said, 'C'mon, yo.'

Soraya saw a shadow of movement, then a thin little girl with big coffee-colored eyes stood framed in the doorway.

'Doan yo go bein' shy, girl.' Tyrone's voice had softened. 'This here's Miss Spook.'

Aisha crunched up her face. 'Miss Spook! Are you scary?'

Her father laughed good-naturedly. 'Nah. Looka how she holdin' Darlonna. Yo woan bite, will ya, Miss Spook?'

'Not if you call me Soraya, Aisha.' She smiled at the little girl, who was quite beautiful. 'Think you can do that?'

Aisha stared at her, winding a braid around her tiny forefinger. Tyrone was about to admonish her again, but Soraya headed him off by saying, 'You have such a pretty name. How old are you, Aisha?'

'Six,' the girl said very softly. 'What do your name mean? Mine means "alive and well."'

Soraya laughed. 'I know, that's Arabic. *Soraya* is a Farsi word. It means "princess."'

Aisha's eyes opened wider, and she took several steps into the room. 'Are you a real princess?'

Soraya, trying to keep the laughter down, said to her with exaggerated solemnity, 'Not a real princess, no.'

'She a *kind* a princess.' Tyrone contrived to ignore Soraya's curious glance. 'Only she not allowed to say so.'

'Why?' The child, fully engaged now, tripped over to them.

'Because bad people are after her,' Tyrone said.

The girl looked up at him. 'Like the ones you shot, Daddy?'

In the ensuing silence, Soraya could hear raucous sounds from the street: the sudden throaty roar of motorcycles, the teeth-rattling blare of hip-hop, the clangor of heated conversations.

'Go play wid yo aunt Libby,' he said, not unkindly.

Aisha gave one last glance toward Soraya, then whirled, skipped out of the room.

Tyrone turned to Soraya, but before he could say anything he took off one shoe, threw it hard and expertly into a corner. Soraya turned and saw the large rat lying on its side. The heel of Tyrone's shoe had nearly decapitated it. Wrapping the rat in some old newspaper, he wiped off his shoe, then took the rat out of the room.

When he returned, Tyrone said, 'About Aisha's mother, it's a old story hereabouts. She got hit in a drive-by. She was wid two a her cousins who pissed off some gangstas inna hood, skimmin' an shit off a drug run.' His face clouded. 'I couldn't let that go, yo.'

'No,' Soraya said. 'I don't imagine you could.'

The baby had drifted off, draining the bottle. She lay in Soraya's arms breathing deeply and evenly.

Tyrone fell silent, abruptly shy. Soraya cocked her head.

'What is it?'

'Yo, I got sumpin important to tell yo, leastways I think it's important.' He sat on the edge of the bed. 'Ain't a short story, but I'll try'tell it dat way.'

He told her about M&N Bodywork, how he and DJ Tank had been staking it out to use as the crew's new crib. He told her about seeing the armed men there one night and how he and DJ Tank had sneaked in after the men had left, what they'd found, 'the plastic explosive an shit.' He told her about coming upon the couple – the man and the woman – sawing up a man's body.

'My God.' Soraya stopped him there. 'Can you describe the man and woman?'

He began, painting frighteningly accurate word pictures of the false Lindros and Anne Held. *How little we know people,* Soraya thought bitterly. *How easily they fool us.*

'Okay,' she said at length, 'what happened then?'

'They set fire to the building. Burn it to the fuckin' ground.'

Soraya considered. 'So by that time the explosives had been moved.'

'True dat.' Tyrone nodded. 'There's sumpin else, too. Those two shitbirds I pulled offa you over Ninth and Florida? I recognized one a them. He were a guard that night outside that body shop.'

# 32

Muta ibn Aziz had begun to stir during the latter part of the aerial dogfight. Now Bourne became aware that he had regained his feet. He couldn't relinquish the controls in order to engage the terrorist, so he had to find another way to deal with Muta.

The Sovereign was nearing the end of the mountain chasm. As Muta ibn Aziz put the muzzle of the gun against his right ear, Bourne directed the Sovereign toward the mountain peak at the end of the chasm.

'What are you doing?' Muta said.

'Put the gun away,' Bourne said while focusing on the peak rising up in front of them.

Muta stared out the windshield, mesmerized. 'Get us out of here.'

Bourne kept the nose of the Sovereign headed directly for the peak.

'You're going to kill us both.' Muta licked his lips nervously. All at once he lifted the gun away from Bourne's head. 'All right, all right! Just – '

They were terrifyingly close to the mountain.

'Throw the gun across the cockpit,' Bourne ordered.

'You've left it too late,' Muta ibn Aziz cried. 'We'll never make it!'

Bourne kept his hands steady on the yoke. With a shout of disgust, Muta tossed his gun across the floor.

Bourne pulled back on the yoke. The Sovereign whooshed upward. The mountain rushed at them with appalling speed. It was going to be close, very close. At the last instant Bourne saw the gap in the right side, as if the hand of God had reached down and cracked off half the mountaintop. He banked a precise amount; any farther and the passing crag would snap off the right wingtip. They passed just above the mountaintop, then, still climbing, pulled free of the chasm, blasting into blue sky.

Muta, on hands and knees, went scrabbling after the gun. Bourne was ready for this. He'd already engaged the auto-pilot. Unstrapping himself, he leapt onto the terrorist's back, delivered a savage kidney punch. With a muted scream, Muta collapsed onto the cockpit floor.

Quickly, Bourne took possession of the gun, then bound the terrorist in a coil of wire he found in the engineer's locker. Dragging him back across the cockpit, he returned to the pilot's chair, disengaged the autopilot, adjusted the heading a bit more south. They were halfway across Afghanistan now, heading for Miran Shah, just across the eastern border in Pakistan, the place circled on the pilot's map Bourne had studied.

Muta ibn Aziz expelled a long string of Bedouin curses.

'Bourne,' he added, 'I was right. You manufactured the story of your own death.'

Bourne grinned at him. 'Shall we call *everyone* by their real name? Let's start with Abu Ghazi Nadir al-Jamuh ibn Hamid ibn Ashef al-Wahhib. But *Fadi* is so much shorter and to the point.'

'How could you possibly know – ?'

'I also know that his brother, Karim, has taken Martin Lindros's place.'

The shock showed in Muta's dark eyes.

'And then there's the sister, Sarah ibn Ashef.' With grim satisfaction, Bourne watched the messenger's expression. 'Yes, I know about that, too.'

Muta's face was ashen. 'She told you her name?'

At once Bourne understood. 'You were there that night in Odessa when we had the rendezvous set up with our contact. I shot Sarah ibn Ashef as she ran into the square. We barely managed to escape the trap with our lives.'

'You took her,' Muta ibn Aziz said. 'You took Sarah ibn Ashef with you.'

'She was still alive,' Bourne said.

'Did she say anything?'

Muta said this so quickly, Bourne knew that he was desperate for the answer. Why? There was more here than Bourne knew. What was he missing?

He was at the very end of what was known to him. But it was vital that he keep his opponent believing that he knew more than he did. He decided the best course was to say nothing.

The silence worked on Muta, who became extremely agitated. 'She said my name, didn't she?'

Bourne kept his voice neutral. 'Why would she do that?'

'She did, didn't she?' Muta was frantic now, twisting this way and that in a vain attempt to free himself. 'What else did she say?'

'I don't remember.'

'You *must* remember.'

He had Muta ibn Aziz. All that remained was to reel him in. 'I saw a doctor once who said that descriptions of things I'd forgotten – even fragments – could unlock those memories.'

They were nearing the border. He started the gradual descent that took them down to the hogback ridges of the mountain chain that did such an expert job at hiding many of the world's most dangerous terrorist cadres.

Muta stared at him incredulously. 'Let me get this straight. You want me to help you.' He gave a joyless laugh. 'I don't think so.'

'All right.' Bourne turned his full attention on the topography as it began to reveal its gross details. 'It was you who asked. I don't care one way or another, really.'

Muta's face contorted first one way, then another. He was under some form of terrible pressure, and Bourne wondered what it was. Outwardly he gave no sign that he cared, but he felt he needed to up the ante, so he said, 'Six minutes to landing, maybe a little less. You'd better brace yourself as best you can.' Glancing over at Muta ibn Aziz, he laughed. 'Oh, yeah, you're already strapped in.'

And then Muta said, 'It wasn't an accident.'

*

Unfortunately,' Karim said, 'LaValle was right.'

The DCI flinched. Clearly he didn't want to hear more bad news. 'Typhon routinely piggybacks on CI transmissions.'

'True enough, sir. But after some backbreaking electronic spadework, I discovered three piggybacked communiqués I can't account for.'

They sat side by side in the sixth pew on the right arm of the arc inside the Foundry Methodist Church on 16th Street NW. Behind them, affixed to the back, was a plaque that read: in this pew, side by side, sat president franklin d. roosevelt and prime minister winston churchill at the national christmas service in 1941. Which meant that the service had taken place just three weeks after the Japanese attack on Pearl Harbor – dark days, indeed, for America. As for Britain, it had gained, through a painful disaster, an important ally. This spot, therefore, held great meaning for the Old Man. It was where he came to pray, to gain insight, the moral strength to do the dark and difficult deeds he was often required to do.

As he stared down at the dossier his second in command had handed him, he knew without a shadow of a doubt that another of those deeds lay dead ahead of him.

He let out a long breath, opened the dossier. And there it was in black and white: the fearsome truth. Still, he raised his head, said in an unsteady voice, 'Anne?'

'I'm afraid so, sir.' Karim was careful to keep his hands palms up in his lap. He needed to seem as devastated as the Old Man clearly was. The news had shaken the DCI to his roots. 'All three communiqués came from a PDA in her possession. One not CI-authorized, one we had no knowledge of until now. It seems she was also able to replace and doctor intel, falsely implicating Tim Hytner.'

For a long time, the DCI said nothing. They had kept their voices down because of the church's astoundingly fine acoustics, but when he spoke again his companion was obliged to lean forward in order to hear him.

'What was the nature of the three communiqués?'

'They were sent via an encrypted band,' Karim said. 'I have my best people working on a deciphering solution.'

The Old Man nodded absently. 'Good work, Martin. I don't know what I'd do without you.'

Today, at this moment, he looked every year of his age and then some. With his trusted Anne's terrible betrayal, a vital spark had gone out of him. He sat hunched over, his shoulders up around his ears, as if anticipating further psychic blows.

'Sir,' Karim said softly. 'We have to take immediate action.'

The DCI nodded, but his gaze was lost in the middle distance, focused on thoughts and memories his companion could not imagine.

'I think this should be handled privately,' Karim continued. 'Just you and me. What do you say?'

The Old Man's rheumy eyes swung around to take in his second's face. 'Yes, a private solution, by all means.' His voice was whispery. It cracked on the word *solution*.

Karim stood. 'Shall we go?'

The DCI looked up at him, a black terror swimming behind his eyes. 'Now?'

'That would be best, sir – for everyone.' He helped the Old Man to his feet. 'She's not at headquarters. I imagine she's home.'

Then he handed the DCI a gun.

Within several hours, Katya returned to the infirmary to check on the swelling of Lindros's throat. She knelt by the side of the low cot on which he lay. Her fingers stumbled over her previous handiwork so badly that tears came to her eyes.

'I'm no good at this,' she said softly, as if to herself. 'I'm no good at all.'

Lindros watched her, remembering the end of their last conversation. He wondered whether he should say something or whether opening his mouth would just push her farther away.

After a long, tense silence, Katya said, 'I've been thinking about what you said.'

Her eyes found his at last. They were an astonishing shade of blue-gray, like the sky just before the onset of a storm.

'And now I believe that Costin wanted Fadi to hurt me. Why? Why would he want someone to do that? Because he was afraid I would leave him? Because he wanted me to see how dangerous the world outside his world was? I don't know. But he didn't have to . . .' She put a hand up to her cheek, winced at the touch of her own delicate fingertips. 'He didn't have to let Fadi hurt me.'

'No, he didn't,' Lindros said. 'He shouldn't have. You know that.'

She nodded.

'Then help me,' Lindros went on. 'Otherwise, neither of us is getting out of here alive.'

'I . . . I don't know whether I can.'

'Then *I'll* help *you*.' Lindros sat up. 'If you let me, I'll help you change. But it has to be what you want. You have to want it badly enough to risk everything.'

'Everything.' She gave him a smile so filled with remorse, it nearly broke his heart. 'I was born with nothing. I grew up with nothing. And then, through a chance encounter, I was given everything. At least, that's what I was told, and for a time I believed it. But in a way that life was worse than having nothing. At least the nothing was real. And then Costin came. He promised to take me away from the unreality. So I married him. But his world was just as false as the one I'd made for myself, and I thought, *Where do I belong? Nowhere.*'

Lindros was moved to briefly touch the back of her hand. 'We're both outsiders.'

Katya turned her head slightly to glance at the guards. 'Do you know a way out of here?'

'Yes,' Lindros said, 'but it will take both of us.' He saw the fear in her eyes, but also the spark of hope.

At length, she said, 'What must I do?'

Anne was in the midst of packing when she heard a car's large engine thrumming on the street outside her house. As she picked her head up, it stopped. She almost went back to her packing, but some sixth sense or paranoia caused her to cross her second-floor bedroom and peer out the window.

Below her, she saw the DCI's long black armored car. The Old Man stepped out of it, followed by Jamil. Her heart skipped a beat. What was happening? Why had they come to her house? Had Soraya somehow got through to the Old

Man, told him of her treachery? But no, Jamil was with him. Jamil would never let Soraya anywhere near CI headquarters, let alone allowing her access to the Old Man.

But what if . . . ?

Running purely on instinct now, she went to her dresser, opened the second drawer, scrabbled in it for the S&W she had returned to its customary hiding place when she'd returned home from the Northeast quadrant.

The bell rang downstairs, making her jump, even though she had been expecting it. Slipping the S&W into her waistband at the small of her back, she left her bedroom and descended the polished wood stairs to the front door. Through the diamonds of translucent yellow glass, she could see the silhouettes of the two men, both so important to her throughout her adult life.

With a slow exhalation of breath, she grabbed the brass handle, painted a smile on her face, opened the door.

'Hello, Anne.' The Old Man seemed to reflect her own lacquered smile back at her. 'I'm sorry to disturb you at home, but something rather pressing . . .' At this point he faltered.

'It's no bother at all,' Anne replied. 'I could use the company.'

She stepped back, and they entered the small marble-floored vestibule. A spray of hothouse lilies rose from a slender cloisonné vase on a small oval table with delicate cabriolet legs. She led them into the living room with its facing silk-covered sofas on either side of a red-veined white-stone fireplace, above which was a wooden mantelpiece. Anne offered them a seat, but everyone seemed inclined to remain standing. The men did not take off their coats.

She dared not look at Jamil's face for fear of what she might find there. On the other hand, the Old Man's face was no bargain. It was drained of blood, the skin hanging loosely on the bones. When had he grown so old? she wondered. Where had the time gone? It seemed like just yesterday that she had been a wild child at college in London, with nothing ahead of her but a bright, endless future.

'I expect you'd like some tea,' she said to his mummy's face. 'And I have a tin of your favorite ginger biscuits in the larder.' But her attempt to retain a degree of normalcy fell flat.

'Nothing, thank you, Anne,' the DCI said. 'For either of us.' He looked truly pained now, as if he was fighting the effects of a kidney stone or a tumor. He took from his overcoat a rolled-up dossier. Spreading it out on one of the soft sofa backs, he said, 'I'm afraid we've been presented with something of an unpleasant realization.' His forefinger moved over the computer printout as if it were a Ouija board. 'We know, Anne.'

Anne felt as if she had been delivered a death blow. She could scarcely catch her breath. Nevertheless, she said in a perfectly normal voice, 'Know what?'

'We know all about you.' He could not yet bring himself to meet her eyes. 'We know that you've been communicating with the enemy.'

'What? I don't –'

At last, the DCI lifted his gaze, impaled her with his implacable eyes. She knew that terrifying look; she's seen it directed at others the Old Man had crossed off his list. She'd never seen or heard from any of them again.

'We know that you *are* the enemy.' His voice was full of rage and loathing. She knew there was nothing he despised more than a traitor.

Automatically, her eyes went to Jamil. What was he thinking? Why wasn't he coming to her defense? And then, looking into his blank face, she understood everything – she understood how he had seduced her with both his physical presence and his philosophical manifesto. She understood how he had used her. She was cannon fodder, as expendable as anyone in his cadre.

The thing that upset her most was that she should have known – from the very beginning, she should have seen through him. But she had been so sure of herself, so willing to rebel against the fussy old-line aristocracy from which she was descended. He had seen how eager she was to throw a bag of shit in her parents' faces. He'd taken advantage of her zeal, as well as of her body. She had committed treason for him; so many people would lose their lives because of her complicity. My God, my God!

She turned to Jamil now, said, 'Fucking me was the least of it, wasn't it?'

That was the last thing she ever said, and she never got to hear his reply, if he'd ever meant to give one, because the DCI had his gun out, and shot her three times in the head. He was still a crack shot, even after all these years.

Anne's blind eyes were on Jamil as her body collapsed from under her.

'Damn her.' The Old Man turned away. His voice was full of venom. 'Goddamn her.'

'I'll take care of the disposition of the body,' Karim said. 'Also, a news release with an appropriate cover story. And I'll call her parents myself.'

'No,' the DCI said dully. 'That's my job.'

Karim walked over to where his former lover lay curled in a pool of blood. He looked down at her. What was he thinking? That he needed to go upstairs, open the second drawer of her dresser. Then, as he turned the corpse over with the toe of his shoe, he saw that luck was still very much with him. He wouldn't have to go into her bedroom after all. He said a silent prayer of thanks to Allah.

Snapping on a pair of latex gloves, he pulled the S&W from its place at the small of her back. He noted the fact she'd had the presence of mind to arm herself. Staring down at her face for a moment, he tried to summon up even the tiniest bit of emotion for this infidel. Nothing came. His heart beat in the same rhythm it always did. He couldn't say that he'd miss her. She had served her purpose, even helping him dismember Overton. Which meant, simply, that he had chosen well. She was an instrument he had trained to use against his enemies, nothing more.

He rose, stood straddling Anne's crumpled form. The DCI's back was still to him. 'Sir,' he said. 'There's something here you need to see.'

The Old Man took a deep breath. He wiped eyes that had been wet with tears. 'What is it, Martin?' he said, turning.

And Karim shot him quite neatly through the heart with Anne Held's S&W.

'It wasn't an accident.'

Bourne, concentrating more than he had to on his pre-landing routine, contrived to ignore this bombshell. They were overflying Zhawar Kili, a known al-Qaeda hotbed until the U.S. military bombed it in November 2001. At length, he said, 'What wasn't an accident?'

'Sarah ibn Ashef's death. It wasn't an accident.' Muta ibn Aziz was breathless, terrified, and liberated all at once. How he'd wanted to tell his abominable secret to someone! It had grown around his heart as the shell of an oyster excretes, layer by layer, over time becoming something humped and ugly.

'Of course it was,' Bourne insisted. He had to insist now; it was the only way to keep the spell going, keep Muta ibn Aziz talking. 'I should know. I shot her.'

'No, you didn't.' Muta ibn Aziz began to worry his lower lip with the ends of his upper teeth. 'You and your partner were too far away to make accurate shots. My brother, Abbud ibn Aziz, and I shot her.'

Bourne did turn to him now, but with a deeply skeptical look. 'You're making this up.'

Muta ibn Aziz appeared hurt. 'Why would I do that?'

'Let's go down the list, shall we? You're continuing to screw with my head. You did it to get Fadi and his brother to come after me.' He frowned. 'Have we met before? Do I know you? Do you and your brother harbor a grudge against me?'

'No, no, and no.' He was annoyed, just as Bourne wanted him to be. 'The truth is . . . I can hardly say it . . .'

He turned away for a moment, and Bourne was listening closely for what was to come. The final approach to Miran Shah the pilot had laid out was coming up. It was in the center of a narrow valley – *defile* would be the more accurate term, now that Bourne saw it – between two mountains just inside the wild and woolly western border of Pakistan.

The sky was clear – a deep, piercing blue – and at this time of day the sun glare was minimal. The gray-brown mountains of altered volcanic rock from the Kurram River group – limestone, dark chert, green shale – looked stripped, barren, devoid of life. Automatically, he studied the vicinity. He scrutinized the furrowed mountainsides to the south and west for cave openings, east the length of the defile for bunkers, north through ruffled hillsides broken by a deeply shadowed, rock-strewn ravine. But there were no signs of Dujja's nuclear complex, nothing man-made, not even a hut or a campsite.

He was coming in a trifle hot. He slowed the Sovereign's speed, saw the runway in front of him. Unlike the one he'd taken off from, this was made of tarmac. Still no sign of habitation, let alone a modern laboratory complex. Had he come to the wrong place? Was this another in Fadi's endless bag of tricks? Was it, in fact, a trap?

Too late now to worry about that. Wheels and flaps were down. He'd reduced speed into the green zone.

'You're coming in too low,' Muta ibn Aziz said in sudden agitation. 'You'll hit the runway too soon. Pull up! For God's sake pull up!'

Bourne overflew the first eighth of the runway, guiding the Sovereign down until the wheels struck the tarmac. They were down, taxiing along the runway. Bourne cut the engines, much of the interior power. That was when he saw a rush of shadows coming from his right side.

He had only time to realize that Muta ibn Aziz must have phoned Bourne's identity to the people at Miran Shah before the starboard bulkhead blew inward with a horrific roar. The Sovereign shuddered and, like a wounded elephant, fell to its knees, its front wheels and struts blown out.

Flying debris made mincemeat of almost everything in the cockpit. Dials were shattered, levers sheared off. Wires dangled from ripped-apart bays in the ceiling.

The trussed Muta ibn Aziz, who'd been on the side of the plane that was now crumpled in on itself, was lying underneath a major piece of the fuselage. Bourne, strapped in on the far side of the cockpit, had escaped with a multitude of minor cuts, bruises, and what felt to his dazed brain like a mild concussion.

Instinct forced him to push the blackness from the periphery of his vision, reach up, and release his harness. He staggered over to Muta ibn Aziz, a frozen tundra of shattered glass crunching underfoot. He choked on air full of broken needles of metal, fiberglass, and superheated plastic.

Seeing that Muta was breathing, he hauled the twisted wreckage, charred and scored and still burning hot, off to the side. But when he knelt down, he saw that a shard of metal, roughly the size and shape of a sword blade, had lodged itself in Muta's gut.

He peered down at the man, then slapped his face hard. Muta's eyes fluttered open, focusing with difficulty.

'I wasn't making it up,' he said in a thin, reedy voice. Blood was leaking out of his mouth, down his chin. It pooled in the hollow of his throat, dark, throwing off the scent of copper.

'You're dying,' Bourne said. 'Tell me what happened with Sarah ibn Ashef.'

A slow smile spread across Muta's face. 'So you *do* want to know.' His breath sawing in and out of his punctured lungs sounded like the scream of a prehistoric beast. 'The truth is important to you, after all.'

'Tell me!' Bourne shouted at him.

He grabbed Muta ibn Aziz, hauled him up by the front of his shirt in an attempt to rattle the answer out of him. But at that moment a cadre of Dujja terrorists swarmed through the rent in the fuselage. They hauled him off Fadi's messenger, who lay coughing up the last of his life.

Chaos ensued – a rushing of bodies, a jumble of spoken Arabic, clipped orders and even more clipped responses – as they dragged him half conscious across the bloody floor, out into the arid wastes of Miran Shah.

# Book 4

# 33

Soraya Moore, on the corner of 7th Street NE, a well-armed Tyrone standing look-out beside her, called CI headquarters – from a pay phone, not from her cell.

When Peter Marks heard it was her, his voice lowered to a whisper.

'Jesus Christ,' he said, 'what the hell have you done?'

'I haven't done anything, Peter,' she replied hotly.

'Then why is there an all-department directive posted to report any appearance, any phone call, any contact whatsoever with you immediately and directly to Director Lindros?'

'Because Lindros isn't Lindros.'

'He's an impostor, right?'

Soraya's heart lifted. 'Then you know.'

'What I know is that Deputy Director Lindros called a meeting, told us you'd gone over the edge, completely lost it. It was Bourne's death, right? Anyway, he said you were making insane accusations about him.'

*Oh, my God,* Soraya thought. *He's turned everyone at CI against me.*

She heard the naked suspicion in Marks's voice, but plowed gamely on anyway. 'He's lied to you, Peter. The truth is too complicated to get into now, but you've got to listen to me. Terrorists have put into motion a plan to blow up headquarters.' She knew she sounded breathless, even a little bit mad. 'Please, I'm begging you. Go to the Old Man, tell him it's going to happen in the next twenty-four hours.'

'The Old Man and Anne are at the White House, meeting with the president. They'll be there for some time, Deputy Director Lindros said.'

'Then contact one of the directorate chiefs – better yet, *all* of them. Anyone but Lindros.'

'Listen, come in. Give yourself up. We can help you.'

'I'm not crazy,' Soraya said, though increasingly she felt as if she was.

'Then this conversation is over.'

As Katya turned toward the two guards outside the infirmary, her delicate fingers undid the top two buttons of her blouse. She had never worn a bra. She had beautiful breasts, and she knew it.

The guards were playing the same game they always did, the rules of which she could never fathom. Of course, no money changed hands; that would make it gambling, which was forbidden by Islamic law. The object seemed to be to sharpen their reaction time.

To turn her mind away from her present situation, she conjured up the rush of her old life, the one Costin had insisted she give up. As the guards became aware of her, she stood in profile, as she would on a Perfect Ten shoot, her back slightly arched, her breasts thrust out.

Then slowly, disarmingly, she turned toward them. Their eyes were nailed to her body.

She felt the ache in her breastbone, where she had instructed Lindros to hit her. She opened her blouse wide enough so that they could see the bruise, so new that the skin was bright red, just starting to puff up.

'Look,' she said, quite unnecessarily. 'Look what that bastard has done to me.'

With these words, the guards roused themselves sufficiently to rush past her into the infirmary. They saw Lindros flat on his back, his eyes closed. There was blood on his face. He seemed to be scarcely breathing.

The taller of the two guards turned to Katya, who was standing directly behind him. 'What have *you* done to *him*?'

At that precise moment, Lindros drew back his right leg, opened his eyes, and slammed the heel of his right foot as hard as he could into the shorter guard's crotch. The guard gave a little grunt of surprise as he collapsed in on himself.

The taller guard, slow in turning back, received the tightly curled edge of Lindros's knuckles in his throat. He coughed, his eyes going wide, his fingers scrabbling for his sidearm. Katya, as Lindros had instructed her, kicked the back of his left knee. As he pitched over, the side of his head made violent contact with Lindros's fist.

The two of them spent the next five minutes stripping the guards, then tying and gagging them. Lindros dragged first one, then the other to the utility closet, stowing them away like so much rubbish. He and Katya climbed into their clothes, she in the smaller guard's outfit, Lindros in the taller one's.

As they dressed, he smiled at her. She reached out and wiped the blood from his pricked finger off his cheek.

'How was that?' he said.

'We're a long way from being free.'

'How right you are.' Lindros gathered up the guards' weapons – sidearms and semiautomatic machine guns. 'Do you know how to use these?'

'I know how to pull a trigger,' she said.

'That'll have to do.'

He took her hand, and together they fled the infirmary.

Bourne was not treated as roughly by the terrorists as he had expected. In fact, once they'd dragged him out of the wrecked Sovereign, he wasn't treated harshly at all. They were all Saudis, this cadre. He could tell not only by the way they looked, but by the Arabic dialect they spoke as well.

As soon as his shoe soles hit the scorched earth of the runway, they stood him up straight and frog-marched him onto the shale, where two armored military all-terrain vehicles, veiled in heavy camouflaging, stood waiting. No wonder he'd missed seeing them from the air.

They took him around to the larger of the two vehicles, which on close inspection looked like a mobile command center. The rear doors banged open, two burly arms extended, and he was hauled bodily up and in. Immediately the metal doors slammed shut.

From out of the inky darkness, a familiar voice in a beautiful clipped British accent said, 'Hello, Jason.'

Red lights flickered on, making Bourne blink as his eyes adjusted. By the odd illumination he could see banks of electronic equipment, silently emitting mysterious readouts, like communications from another planet. To one side, a young bearded Saudi sat hunched over an islet of equipment. He had on a pair of professional earphones. Occasionally, he jotted a sentence or two from whatever he was listening to.

To his left, close to where Bourne stood, was the huge, overmuscled man who must have hoisted Bourne into the mobile command center. He stared at Bourne without any emotion whatsoever. With his shaved head, his rocklike arms crossed over his equally muscular chest, he might have been a eunuch guarding a sultan's harem.

However, this one was guarding the third person in the truck, who sat at the command console. He must have swiveled the chair around as soon as Bourne had been hoisted aboard. He grinned from ear to ear, which belied his regal bearing.

'We must stop meeting like this, Jason.' His ruby-red lips pursed. 'Or no, perhaps it is kismet that we do so at the most propitious times.'

'Goddammit,' Bourne said, recognizing the slim, dark-eyed man with the beak of a nose. 'Feyd al-Saoud!'

The chief of the Saudi secret police fairly jumped out of his chair and rushed to embrace Bourne, kissing him happily and moistly on both cheeks.

'My friend, my friend. Thank Allah you're still alive! We had no idea you were inside. How could we? It's Fadi's plane!' Waggling an admonishing forefinger, he said with mock anger, 'And in any event, you never tell me what you're up to.'

Bourne and Feyd al-Saoud had known each other for some time. They had worked together once, in Iceland.

'I'd heard a rumor that the Saudis had a line on Fadi, though they vehemently denied it.'

'Fadi is Saudi,' Feyd al-Saoud said, sobering quickly. 'He is a Saudi problem.'

'You mean he's a Saudi embarrassment,' Bourne said. 'I'm afraid he's made himself everyone's problem.'

He went on to brief his friend on Fadi's identity, as well as on what he and his brother, Karim al-Jamil, had planned, including the infiltration of CI. 'You may think you've homed in on Dujja's main camp,' Bourne said in conclusion, 'but I can assure you this isn't it. What is here, somewhere, is the nuclear facility that's enriching the uranium and manufacturing the nuclear device they plan to detonate somewhere in the United States.'

Feyd al-Saoud nodded. 'Now things are starting to make sense.' He swung around, brought up a tactical pilotage chart of the area in order to orient Bourne. Next, he switched to a series of close-up IKONOS satellite images.

'These were taken last week, at two-minute intervals,' he said. 'You'll notice that in the first image we see Miran Shah as we do now – barren, desolate. But here, in image two, we see two jeeplike vehicles. They're heading more or less northwest. Now what do we see in image three? Miran Shah is once again barren, desolate. No people, no vehicles. In two minutes, where did they go? They could not possibly have driven out of the IKONOS range.' He sat back. 'Given your intel, what must be our conclusion?'

'Dujja's nuclear facility is underground,' Bourne said.

'One must believe so. We have been monitoring terrorist communications. From whence, we had no idea – until now. It's coming from beneath the rocks and sand. Interestingly, it's from *within* the facility. There have been no communications from the outside world for the three hours we've been here.'

'Just how many men did you bring with you?' Bourne asked.

'Including myself, twelve. As you've discovered, we had to pose as members of Dujja ourselves. This is North Waziristan, the most deeply conservative of Pakistan's western provinces. The local Pashtun tribespeople have profound religious and ethnic ties to the Taliban, which is why they welcome al-Qaeda and Dujja alike. I couldn't afford to bring more of my people in without awkward questions being raised.'

At that moment the man with the headphones tore off the top sheet of paper on which he'd been frantically scribbling. He handed it to his chief.

'Something in the rock or perhaps the facility's lead shielding is interfering with the monitoring.' Feyd al-Saoud scanned the sheet quickly, then handed it to Bourne. 'I think you'd better have a look at this.'

Bourne read the Arabic transcription:

'*[?] both missing. We found the guards in [?] closet.*'
'*How long?*'
'*[?] twenty minutes. [?] couldn't say for sure.*'
'*Mobilize [?] you can spare. Send [?] to the entrance. Find them.*'
'*And then?*'
'*Kill them.*'

Lindros and Katya sprinted through the modern catacomb under Miran Shah. The alarm was blaring from loudspeakers spaced along the walls of the facility. The entrance had been in sight when the alarm had gone off, and immediately Lindros had reversed course. Now they were heading deeper into the facility.

From snatches of overheard conversations as well as his own observations, Lindros had deduced that the Dujja facility was on two levels. The upper contained living quarters, kitchens, communications, and the like. The infirmary was on this floor. But the surgical facilities where Dr. Andursky had taken Lindros's right eye, where he had remade Karim's face, were below, along with the laboratories: the cavernous centrifuge room where the enriched uranium was concentrated even further, the double-walled fusion lab, and so on.

'They know we're missing,' Katya said. 'What now?'

'Plan B,' Lindros replied. 'We have to get to the communications room.'

'But that's farther away from the entrance,' Katya said. 'We'll never get out.'

They raced around a corner, were confronted by a long corridor that ran down the spine of the facility. Everything in the place – the rooms, corridors, stairwells, elevators – was oversize. No matter where you stood, you felt insignificant. There was something inherently terrifying about such a facility, as if it were designed not for people, but for a machine army. Humanity had been excluded from the premises.

'We have to think first about survival, then escape,' Lindros said. 'That means letting my people know where we are.'

Though he was nervous, he slowed them down to a fast walk. He didn't like this long, wide corridor stretching out in front of them. If they got trapped here, there was nowhere to hide or to run.

As if reading his worst fear, two men appeared at the far end of the corridor. Seeing their quarry, they drew their weapons. One of them advanced down the corridor while the other held his position. His semiautomatic swung up to aim at them.

'I've got to find a way to warn everyone inside CI headquarters,' Soraya said.

'But yo heard fo yoself they be illin' on yo,' Tyrone replied. 'Ain't gonna get no props from them no matter what yo do.'

'I can't stop trying, can I?'

Tyrone nodded. 'True dat.'

Which was why they were hid out, as Tyrone would say, in a tobacco shop where an old, grizzled Salvadoran was hand-rolling Cuban-seed shit he grew himself into Partagas, Montecristos, and Coronas, selling them to eager customers at a premium price over the Internet. As it happened, Tyrone owned the place, so to him went the lion's share of the profits. It was just a ratty hole-in-the-wall on 9th Street NE, but at least it was legit.

In any event, today its grease-streaked window afforded them a more or less clear view of the black Ford that Tyrone had stolen from the two Arabs he'd offed at the construction site. Tyrone had parked it directly across from the tobacco shop, where it now sat, waiting along with them.

They had come up with the idea together. Since Soraya could no longer simply walk through the doors of CI headquarters, couldn't even call anyone there without the threat of it being traced back to her, she needed another way in.

'I know my vehicles, girl,' Tyrone had said, 'an that some tricked-out beast. Them shitbirds know by now they two ain't comin' home. Think they just let that go? Shit, no. They be comin' afta it an you. Ain't gon let either a yo be. Sure as shit they be comin' here to Northeast 'cause that's the last place they knowd you be.' He'd grinned, wide and handsome. 'When they get here, we on 'em like flies on shit.'

It was a dangerous plan, but a good one for all that, Soraya had to admit. Besides, she couldn't think of any alternative that wouldn't get her either thrown in a CI cage or, more likely, killed.

'Fadi has taken prisoners,' Feyd al-Saoud said.

'I might know one of them,' Bourne said. 'My friend Martin Lindros.'

'Ah, yes.' The security chief nodded. 'The man whom Fadi's brother is impersonating. He may still be alive, then. And the other?'

'I've no idea,' Bourne said.

'In any case, we must hurry if we're to have any chance of saving them.' He frowned. 'But we still have no idea how to gain entrance.'

'Those vehicles on the IKONOS imagery,' Bourne said. 'They had to go somewhere. Somewhere within a radius of a thousand meters of where we are now.' He pointed at the screen. 'Can you make a printout of that?'

'Of course.' Feyd al-Saoud tapped a computer keyboard. There came a soft whirring sound; then a sheet of paper was spewed out of the printer slot. The security chief handed it over.

Bourne exited the mobile command post, followed by Feyd al-Saoud and his immense bodyguard, whose name, the security chief had told Bourne, was Abdullah.

He stood on the southeast side of the runway, staring at the topography and comparing it with the IKONOS map.

'The trouble is, there's nothing here.' Feyd al-Saoud's fists were on his hips. 'As soon as we arrived, I sent out a recon of three men. After an hour, they returned without success.'

'And yet,' Bourne said, 'those vehicles must have gone *somewhere.*'

He walked straight ahead, onto the runway. To his right was the wreck of the Sovereign, which would never fly again. To his left was the beginning of the strip. In his mind's eye, he could see the Sovereign coming in too hot.

All at once Muta ibn Aziz came into his mind. *'You're coming in too low,'* he'd said. *'You'll hit the runway too soon.'* Why had he become so agitated? The worst that would have happened was that the Sovereign's wheels would have struck the tarmac at its near end. Why would that concern Muta ibn Aziz? Why would he even care?

Bourne began to walk to his left, along the tarmac toward its beginning. He kept his eyes on the landing strip. He was now at the near end, the place Muta ibn Aziz was adamant he avoid. What would he be afraid of? Three things occurred when a jet touched down: high-level applications of friction, heat, and weight. Which one had worried him?

Bourne crouched down, put his fingertips on the runway. It looked like tarmac, felt like tarmac. Except for one crucial thing.

'Feel this,' Bourne said. 'The tarmac should be burning hot from the strong sunlight.'

'It's not.' Feyd al-Saoud moved his hand around. 'It's not hot at all.'

'Which means,' Bourne said, 'it's not tarmac.'

'What could Dujja be using?'

Bourne rose. 'Don't forget that they have access to IVT's technology.'

He walked farther down the runway. When he reached the place where marks showed he'd set the Sovereign down, he knelt again, put his hand to the tarmac. And snatched it away quickly.

'Hot?' Feyd al-Saoud said.

'This is tarmac.'

'Then what's back there?'

'I don't know, but the man I was with – Fadi's messenger – didn't want me to land there.'

Returning to the end of the runway, Bourne traced a route across the full width of it. In the back of his mind he was furiously working on a plan. They needed to gain access to the underground facility, get to Fadi before his men found the prisoners. If there was any chance that one of them was Lindros . . .

Once again, he scanned the IKONOS topographic readout, compared it with the visual survey he'd taken on his way in. A facility enriching uranium required water – a lot of it. Which was where that deeply shadowed, rock-strewn ravine came in. He'd noted it from the air, and it had stayed in his mind like a beacon.

What he was considering might work, but he knew Feyd al-Saoud wasn't going to like it. And if he couldn't sell his friend on the plan, it wasn't going to work. It might not work even *with* the security chief's cooperation, but he didn't see any viable alternative.

Reaching the near side of the runway, he once again knelt down, scrutinizing the edge. Then he said to Abdullah, 'Can you help me with this?'

Together Bourne and Abdullah heaved up, curling their fingertips around the end. With a titanic effort, they began to peel the surface back.

'What we have here,' Bourne said, 'is a strip of landing material.'

Feyd al-Saoud came forward, bending his body from the waist. He was looking at the material, which was perhaps six centimeters thick and the precise color and texture of tarmac. Clearly, it wasn't tarmac. What it was, exactly, there was no way of telling. Not that it mattered in the least. What was of intense interest to them, what they were all studying with a fierce concentration of joy and triumph, was what lay beneath the peeled-back layer.

A metal hatch, large as the door of a two-car garage, set flush with the ground.

# 34

What are you doing here?' the lead terrorist shouted. He was clearly agitated, which meant he was on hair-trigger alert.

'We've been sent to the – '

'Turn into the light! You're not one of us! Put your weapons down now!'

At once Lindros raised his hands. Having a semiautomatic rifle leveled at you was a threat that needed to be taken very seriously.

'Don't shoot!' he said in Arabic. 'Don't shoot!' To Katya, he muttered, 'Walk in front of me. Do exactly as I say. And for God's sake, whatever happens, keep your hands in the air.'

They began to walk toward the front man, who was in a semi-crouch. While keeping him in the periphery of his vision, Lindros watched the cover man farther down the corridor. At this moment, he was the real problem.

'Halt!' the terrorist said when they were several paces from him. 'Turn around!'

Katya obeyed. As she was turning, Lindros drew out a bottle of alcohol he'd taken from the infirmary, opened the top, and threw the contents in the terrorist's face.

'Down!' he shouted.

Lindros leapt over Katya as she dropped to the floor. Lunging for the recoiled terrorist, he grabbed his semiautomatic and pressed the trigger, spraying the corridor with bullets. Several struck the cover man in the arm and leg, spinning him back against a wall. He returned fire, but his aim was wild. With a short, precise burst, Lindros brought him down.

'Come on!'

He slammed the butt of the semiautomatic into the base of the skull of the terrorist, still clawing at his face, then went roughly through his clothes for other weapons. He found a handgun and a thick-bladed knife. With Katya behind him he sprinted down the corridor, snatched up the cover man's semiautomatic, handed it to Katya.

They made their way to the communications room, which according to Katya was around to the left at the far end of the corridor.

Two men were inside, busy at their equipment. Lindros stepped up behind the one on the right, put his hand under his chin, and, as shocked tension came into the frame, quickly brought his head up and back, slashing his throat. As the second man turned, coming up out of his seat, Lindros threw the knife into his chest. With a small gurgle, he arched backward, his lungs already filling up with blood. Even as he slid, lifeless, onto the floor, Lindros took his seat, began to work the communications system.

'Don't just stand there whimpering,' he ordered. 'Guard the door. Shoot at anything that moves, and keep shooting till it stops!'

Feyd al-Saoud's earpiece crackled. He put a hand up to it to press it more firmly into his ear canal. In a moment, he nodded. 'I understand.' To Bourne, he said, 'We must return to the command center. At once.'

The three men covered the several hundred meters to the vehicle in very little time. Inside, they found the communications officer gesticulating wildly. When he saw them, he ripped off his headphone and pressed a cup to his left ear, so he could hear them and what was coming out of the earphones simultaneously.

'We're receiving a signal from inside the facility,' he said in rapid Arabic. 'The man says his name is Martin Lindros. He says that – '

Lunging, Bourne ripped the headphones out of his hand, slipped them on.

'Martin?' he said into the mike. 'Martin, it's Bourne.'

'Jason . . . are alive?'

'Very much so.'

'Fadi thinks . . . dead.'

'Just what I want him to think.'

'. . . are you now?'

'Right here, above you.'

'. . . God. I'm here with a woman named Katya.'

'Katya Veintrop?'

There came a short bark that might have been a laugh, during which Fadi, monitoring the conversation via the auxiliary comm system, signed to Abbud ibn Aziz. Fadi resumed listening, his heart like a trip-hammer. Bourne was alive! Alive and here! O, sweet revenge. What could be better?

'I should have known.'

'Martin, what's . . . situation?'

'. . . hostiles down. We're well armed. So far, so good.'

Abbud ibn Aziz, Fadi saw, was already ordering the men to the comm room.

'Martin, listen . . . coming in after you.'

'We have to find a safer place right now.'

'. . . kay, but . . . hold on until I get in.'

'Will do.'

'Martin, headquarters isn't . . . without you. Maddy keeps asking . . . haven't forgotten her, have you?'

'Maddy? How could I forget her.'

'Right. Hang on. Out.'

Fadi touched the wireless transceiver in his right ear that connected him with his team leaders. 'Now we know the fate of the Sovereign,' he said to Abbud ibn Aziz. 'Bourne's presence here explains the communication I've had from our people in Riyadh. Two jets were scrambled over northern Iran when a plane answering the Sovereign's signature failed to give the flyover code. The two fighters haven't been heard from since.'

Fadi strode into the corridor. 'All of which means that Bourne somehow commandeered the flight. We must assume that Bourne has killed both Muta ibn Aziz and the pilot.'

He embraced his companion. 'Courage, my friend. Your brother died a martyr – in the way we all wish to die. He is a hero.'

Abbud ibn Aziz nodded soberly. 'I will miss him.' He kissed Fadi on both cheeks. 'The contingency plan has been activated,' he said. 'When the plane failed to check in, I myself loaded the nuclear device into the helicopter. The second jet is standing by in Mazar-i-Sharif. I have sent the signal to your brother. Now that you cannot fly directly from here, it's imperative that you get under way immediately. The deadline comes in precisely twelve hours, when Karim al-Jamil ignites the C-Four charges.'

'What you say is true enough. But I cannot ignore the fact that Bourne is alive. He's *here now*.'

'Leave. I'll take care of Bourne. You have a far more important agenda – '

A blind rage boiled through Fadi. 'Do you imagine that I can allow the cold-blooded murder of my sister to go unavenged? Bourne must die by my hands – my hands, do you understand?'

'Of course, yes.'

Abbud ibn Aziz felt a violent fizzing in his brain, a sense that his worst fears were being confirmed: There was a disconnect in Fadi between Dujja's mission and the private revenge of him and his brother. That he, Abbud ibn Aziz, was at the heart of this twisted course of events had played havoc with his mind for some time. For this he blamed Muta ibn Aziz, whose voice he still heard, admonishing him for the lie he had built around Sarah ibn Ashef's death.

He had no sense of the disconnect inside himself. His lack of reaction to the likelihood of his brother's death was due to the crisis of the moment. It was his responsibility, he kept telling himself like a mantra, to focus Fadi on the endgame, the nuclear card that Dujja – and only Dujja, of all terrorist organizations – was able to play. The amount of time, energy, money, and connections they had all spent on this one, single outcome was incalculable. To have it put in jeopardy now by Fadi's obsessive need for personal revenge was intolerable.

A sudden hail of semiautomatic gunfire from the interior of the facility brought them to an abrupt halt.

'Lindros!' Fadi listened to the crackle of his in-ear headset. 'Six more men down.' He ground his teeth in fury. 'See to him and Veintrop's wife.'

But instead of heading back, Abbud ibn Aziz sprinted toward the entrance ramp. If he couldn't talk Fadi out of his madness, he needed to take the cause of the madness away. He needed to find Jason Bourne and kill him.

'An there they be,' Tyrone said.

He and Soraya watched as a white Chevy cruised by the Ford for the second time. Near the far corner of the block it stopped and double-parked. Two men got out. To Tyrone, they looked nearly identical in face and physique to the Arabs he'd cooked. This pair was younger, however. Both wore Phat Farm clothes.

One hung back, probing between his teeth with a toothpick, while the other ambled over to the Ford. He took a thin, flat strip of metal out of his pocket. Standing very close to the black vehicle, he jammed it down between the driver's window and the outer metal panel. Two or three quick jabs of the strip unlocked the door. In one fluid motion he opened it and slid behind the wheel.

'Aight,' Tyrone said. 'Time to get our grind on.'

'Someone's coming,' Katya said.

Lindros sprinted, took her by the hand, and raced out of the comm room. He could hear shouts from behind.

'Go on,' he urged her. 'Wait for me around the corner.'

'What are you doing? Why stop?'

'Jason gave me a coded signal. That means two things. One, that he felt certain our conversation was being monitored. Two, that he has a specific plan in mind. I've got to give him a chance to get in here,' he said. 'What he needs most now is a diversion.'

She nodded, her eyes wide with fear. When she had disappeared, Lindros turned and saw the first terrorist appear. He suppressed his desire to shoot, instead waiting, still as death. When the group of them were in the corridor, creeping toward the comm room, he opened fire, mowing them down beneath a blistering fusillade.

Then, before more of them could appear, he turned, raced after Katya. The expression of relief when she saw him was palpable.

'Where will we go now?' she asked as they ran toward a flight of rough concrete stairs.

'Away from where they're searching,' Lindros said.

They had reached the lower level, where all the laboratories and surgeries were laid out in a neat grid. Each lab, he saw, was double-walled, and there were two sets of thick doors between the surgeries and the nuclear workshops.

'We have to find a place to hide.'

Because it was so well hidden, the hatch had no need of a lock.

Bourne stood alone, at the edge of the hatch. Of course, Feyd al-Saoud had protested vehemently, but in the end he came around to Bourne's point of view. Frankly, Bourne didn't see that he had any choice. A full frontal assault with his men would be tantamount to suicide. But following Bourne's plan – well, then there was a chance.

The hatch was perfectly smooth. There were no handles or any other visible means of opening it. For vehicles to enter and exit, then, there must be an electric-powered opener that could be activated remotely from the vehicles themselves. That meant that there must be a receiver located on or near the hatch.

It took him a few short moments to find the junction box housing the receiver. Pulling off its cover, he traced the circuits and hot-wired the one he wanted. Hydraulics were involved. The hatch opened upward smoothly and silently, revealing an oil-stained concrete ramp – the very ramp, he was certain, down which those vehicles caught in the IKONOS satellite eye had disappeared. He swung the semiautomatic off his shoulder, holding it at the ready as he began to descend.

Illumination from reflected daylight soon petered out, leaving him in twilight. There was no good way to go about this, he knew. Assuming Fadi had been monitoring his communications with Martin, somewhere near the end of the ramp a trap was waiting for him.

He heard the gunfire then, and knew that Lindros had been able to create a diversion. He threw himself forward onto the concrete then curled into a ball, rolling the rest of the way down the ramp.

Fetching up against a wall, he lifted the semiautomatic as he scanned the low-lit corridor yawning in front of him. He saw no one, no motion whatsoever. This did not necessarily surprise him, but it did make him warier than ever.

He moved forward, crouched against the wall. Ahead, low-watt electric light-bulbs in niches spaced along both walls provided enough illumination for him to make out the layout of this part of the facility.

Immediately to his right, the corridor branched into the entrance to the under-ground parking area. Dimly, he could make out the silhouette of a number of all-terrain vehicles parked in neat rows, military-fashion. Dead ahead was a slightly narrower corridor that seemed to run down the center of the facility.

As he continued to move forward, he saw something out of the corner of his eye. A slight metallic glint, as of a weapon. He veered to his right, diving into the parking lot.

At once a spray of bullets sent chips of the concrete floor into his cheek. The fire was coming from *inside* the lot. Headlights came on, dazzling him into immobility. At the same time, an engine gave a deep, throaty cough and, with a screech of tires, one of the all-terrain vehicles came hurtling at him.

# 35

Bourne ran straight at the oncoming vehicle, leapt off his feet, and landed on its hood. Using a combination of the vehicle's momentum and his own strength, he lowered his shoulder as his entire body was driven into the windshield.

The glass shattered from the force, and Bourne used his leading elbow and forearm to sweep aside the remaining shards. Scrambling through the rent, he found himself in the seat next to a man who, given his close facial similarity to Muta ibn Aziz, could only be his brother, Abbud.

Abbud ibn Aziz had a gun at the ready, but Bourne lunged at the wheel, turning it hard to the right. Centrifugal force slammed his body into the terrorist's. The gun fired, deafening them both, but the bullet went awry, embedding itself in the doorpost. Abbud ibn Aziz squeezed off two more shots before the vehicle slammed into the concrete wall.

Bourne, who had prepared for the impact by willing his body to go completely slack, was slammed forward, then back against the seat. Beside him, Abbud ibn Aziz smashed into the top of the steering wheel, causing a great bloody gash in his forehead as well as a fracture in the bone over his right eye.

Wresting the gun from his slack fingers, Bourne slapped him hard across the cheek. He knew he had little time, but he was determined to get to the bottom of the mystery of Sarah ibn Ashef's death.

'What happened that night in Odessa, Abbud?'

He deliberately left off the last half of the terrorist's name, a clear sign of contempt.

Abbud ibn Aziz's head lolled against the back of the seat. Blood, coming from several places, leaked from him. 'What d'you mean?'

'You shot Sarah ibn Ashef to death.'

'You're insane.'

'Muta told me. He *told* me, Abbud. You shot Fadi's sister, not me. This whole vendetta could have been avoided if only you'd told the truth.'

'The truth?' Abbud spat blood. 'In the desert, there is no such thing as the truth. The sands shift constantly, like the truth.'

'Why did you lie?'

He began to cough, blood vomiting out of his mouth.

'Tell me why you lied about Sarah ibn Ashef's death.'

Abbud ibn Aziz spat again, almost choked on his own blood. When he'd recovered sufficiently, he muttered, 'Why should I tell you anything?'

'It's over for you, Abbud. You're dying. But you already knew that, didn't you?

Your death from a car accident won't get you to heaven. But if I kill you, you will have a martyr's death, filled with glory.'

Abbud looked away, as if in that way he could escape the fate awaiting him. 'I lied to Fadi because I had to. The truth would have destroyed him.'

'Time's running out.' Bourne held a knife to his throat. 'I'm the only one who can help you now. In a moment, it will be too late. You will have lost your chance at *shahada*.'

'What do you, an infidel, know of *shahada*?'

'I know that without jihad there can be no martyrdom. I know that jihad is the inclusive struggle for truth. Without your confession of the truth, there can be no jihad, there can be no *shahada* for you.

'Without my help, you won't be able to stand witness to the truth that is Allah. Therefore, your holy struggle in the cause of Allah – your entire existence – will be meaningless.'

Wholly unbidden, Abbud ibn Aziz felt tears stinging his eyes. His enemy was right. He needed him now. Allah had placed this final terrible choice in front of him: testify to the truth, or be condemned to the eternal fires of damnation. In this way, at this moment, he understood that Muta ibn Aziz had been right. It was the shifting sands of the truth that had buried him. If only he had spoken the truth at once. For now, in order to die righteously, in order to be clean in the eyes of Allah and all that he held holy, he would have to betray Fadi.

He closed his eyes for a moment, all the defiance drained out of him. Then he stared up into his enemy's face.

'I shot Sarah ibn Ashef, not Muta ibn Aziz. I *had* to shoot her. Six days before the evening of her death, I discovered that she was carrying on a love affair. I took her aside and confronted her. She didn't bother denying it. I told her that the law of the desert dictated that she commit suicide. She laughed at me. I told her that committing suicide would relieve her brothers of the stress of killing her themselves. She told me to get out of her sight.'

Abbud paused for a moment. Clearly, reliving the shock of the confrontation had robbed him of his remaining strength. Presently, however, he gathered himself. 'That night, she was late, hurrying across town to meet her lover. She had ignored me. Instead she was continuing to betray her own family. I was shocked, but not surprised. I had lost count of the times she had told me that we inverted Islam, that we twisted Allah's holy words to further our cause, to justify our . . . what did she call it? . . . Ah, yes, our death dealing. She had turned her back on the desert, on her Bedouin heritage. Now the only thing she could bring her family was shame and humiliation. I shot her. I'm proud of it. It was a virtue killing.'

Bourne, sick at heart, had heard enough. Without another word, he slashed the blade of the knife across Abbud ibn Aziz's throat, slipping out of the vehicle as the gout of blood flooded the front seat.

The moment Abbud ibn Aziz had taken off against his orders, Fadi drew out a gun, aimed it at his back. Truly, if it hadn't been for the hail of gunfire, he'd have shot his second dead. So far as he was concerned, there was no excuse for insubordination. Orders were to be obeyed without either thought or question. This was not the UN; others did not get their moment to wade in with options.

As he ran toward the comm room, this last thought rolled around his head, raising echoes he didn't want to hear. In his opinion, the Aziz brothers had been acting strangely for some time. Their verbal battles had long since become legendary – so much so that they were now expected, never remarked upon by the others. Lately, however, their fights had occurred behind closed doors. Afterward, neither wanted to talk about the subject, but Fadi had noted that the growing friction between them was beginning to interfere with their work. Which was why, at this crucial juncture, he had sent Muta ibn Aziz off to Istanbul. He needed to break the brothers up, give them both space to work out their enmity. Now Muta ibn Aziz was dead, and Abbud ibn Aziz had disobeyed orders. For one reason or another, he could no longer rely on either of them.

He saw the carnage the moment he turned the corner to the comm room. Soberly, angrily, he high-stepped between the corpses like a jittery Arabian horse. He checked each body, as well as the room itself. Eight men down in total, all dead. Lindros must have taken more weapons.

Cursing under his breath, he was about to return to the ramped entrance when his earpiece sizzled.

'We've sighted the fugitives,' one of his men said in his ear.

Fadi's body tensed. 'Where?'

'Lower level,' his man said. 'They're heading for the uranium labs.'

*The nuke,* Fadi thought.

'Shall we close in?'

'Keep them in sight but under no circumstances are you to engage them, is that clear?'

'Yes sir.'

This conversation had driven all considerations of revenge clear out of his head. If Lindros should find the nuke and the heli, he would have it all. After all this time, all the sacrifice, all the endless work and bloodshed, he would be left with nothing.

He ran down the corridor, turned left, then left again. The open door to a freight elevator yawned in front of him. He stepped smartly in, punching the bottom button on the panel. The doors slid shut, and he began to descend.

At some point, as they advanced along the warren of lower-level labs, Lindros became aware that they were under surveillance. This disturbed him, of course, but it also frightened him. Why weren't these watchers closing in, as the first group had?

As they ran, he could see that Katya was crying. The violence and the death she'd been exposed to would have shaken anyone up, especially a civilian inexperienced with incarceration and violence. But to her credit, she kept pace with him.

All at once she pulled away and lunged out for an open doorway then, leaning over, vomited up whatever was in her stomach. Lindros put one arm around her to try to hold her steady, the butt of the semiautomatic on his opposite hip. That was when he glanced into the lab they had come to. It was the surgery where Dr. Andursky had carved out his eye, where he had transformed Karim into a terrifying doppelgänger. When he was finished with his infernal business, Andursky had trotted Lindros out to see his handiwork, so the new Martin Lindros could ask the original Martin Lindros to populate his mind with Lindros's memories – enough, anyway, to fool the CI interrogators and Jason Bourne. That's when Lindros had devised a code he hoped would reach Jason.

At first the surgery looked deserted, but then he saw cowering behind one of the two surgical tables the thin, weasely face of Dr. Andursky.

Soraya, her arms wrapped tightly around Tyrone's rock-hard waist, sat behind him on his Passion Red Kawasaki Ninja ZX-12R. The motorcycle was on 5th Street NE, following both the reappropriated black Ford and the white Chevy. They were turning northwest onto Florida Avenue.

Tyrone was a superb driver who, Soraya could see, knew his way around D.C., not just his neighborhood. He wove in and out of traffic, never staying in the same position. One moment he was three car lengths behind their quarry, the next five. But Soraya never felt that they were in danger of losing their targets.

On Florida Avenue, they crossed over into the Northwest quadrant, turned right onto Sherman Ave NW, heading due north. At the junction of Park Road NW, they made a slight jog to the right onto the beginning of New Hampshire, then almost an immediate left onto Spring Road, which, in turn, led to 16th Street NW, onto which they made a right.

They were traveling due north once again, more or less paralleling the eastern edge of Rock Creek Park. Skirting the park's northeastern boundary, the two cars pulled into the loading bay of a large mortuary. Tyrone turned off the Ninja's engine, and they dismounted. As they watched, the inner wall of the right side of the loading bay began to slide down.

Once they crossed the street, they saw the closed-circuit TV guarding the loading bay. The camera was on a wall mount that moved it slowly back and forth to cover the entire area.

Both vehicles drove through the aperture and slowly down the concrete ramp. Soraya, one eye on the CCTV, calculated that if they followed the vehicles the camera would immediately pick them up. It was rotating away, but slowly, so slowly. The concrete wall was rising up from its slot in the floor.

They edged closer, closer. Then, with the wall halfway up, she clapped Tyrone on the back. Sprinting for the disappearing aperture, they leapt through the opening at the last instant. After landing on the concrete ramp, they picked themselves up.

Behind them, the wall slid home, encasing them in fumy darkness.

Feyd al-Saoud stood at the southwestern end of the rock-filled ravine. At last his men were in place, the charges set. Incredible as it seemed, Dujja had the technology to tap into the underground river. His men had discovered three huge pipes, clearly with wheelcocks inside the facility, to regulate the water flow. It was these wheelcocks they had to destroy.

He moved back several hundred meters and saw that his splendidly disciplined men ringed the ravine. Lifting his arm, he caught the attention of his two explosives experts.

In the heat and utter stillness of the moment, his mind flashed back to the moment when Jason Bourne had described the plan to him. His initial response had been incredulity. He had told Bourne that the plan was an insane one. He'd said, 'We'll go in the old-fashioned way. With a frontal assault.'

'You'll be committing your men to certain death,' Bourne had told him. 'I'm reasonably sure that Fadi monitored my conversation with Lindros, which would argue for him having monitored your communication with your recon party earlier.'

'But what about you?' Feyd al-Saoud had said. 'If you go in by yourself, his men will mow you down as soon as you show your face.'

'That's where you're wrong,' Bourne had replied. 'Fadi needs to kill me himself. Anything else is unacceptable to him. Besides, his weakness is that he thinks he's gotten inside my mind. He's expecting a diversion. Lindros will give him one, to lure him into a false sense of complacency. He'll convince himself he's gotten my tactic right, that the situation is under control.'

'Which is where we come in.' Feyd al-Saoud nodded. 'You're right. The plan is unorthodox enough that it just might work.'

He glanced at his watch. Now that he was committed, he itched to get started. But Bourne had insisted they stick to the plan. 'You have to give me fifteen minutes to do what must be done,' he said.

Ninety seconds left.

Feyd al-Saoud stared at the jumbled bottom of the ravine, which, as it turned out, was not a ravine at all. Bourne had been right: It was a dry riverbed whose bottom was slowly collapsing into the underground waterway that had once, along ago, been on the surface. The underground river was where the Dujja facility was getting its needed supply of running water for the nuclear manufacturing. His men had set their charges at the facility end of the riverbed. The attack would serve two purposes: It would either drown or flush out every member of Dujja, and it would render the canisters of enriched uranium safe until a full complement of CI and Saudi experts could take over the facility permanently.

Fifteen seconds to go. Feyd al-Saoud took one long look around at each of his men. They'd been briefed; they knew what the stakes were. They knew what to do.

His arm swept down. The detonators were activated. The twin blasts exploded several seconds apart, but to Feyd al-Saoud and his men they sounded like one long percussion, a ripping wind, a hailstorm of rocky debris, and then the sound they were all waiting for: the deep, earthbound roar of water rushing along the course it had carved out of the bedrock.

Down in the Dujja facility, the mighty blasts felt like earthquake temblors. Everything on the shelves of the surgery smashed to the floor. Cupboard doors flew open, their contents exploding out into the room, coating the floor with a lake of liquids, shards of glass, twisted ribbons of plastic, a pickup-sticks welter of metal surgical instruments.

Katya, clinging both to Lindros and the door frame, wiped her mouth and said, 'Come on! We've got to get out of here!'

Lindros knew she was right. They had very little time now to get to a place of safety where they could stay until the worst was over.

And yet he couldn't budge. His eyes were riveted on the face of Dr. Andursky. How many times during his recovery from the surgical rape Andursky had subjected him to had he dreamed of killing this man. Not simply killing. My God! The *methods* he had devised for Andursky's end! Some days, those increasingly elaborate fantasies were the only things that kept him from going insane. Even so, time and again he'd awaken from a dream of ravens plucking at the man, his flesh peeled back, exposing the bones of his skeleton for the windborne sand to scour clean of whatever mocking semblance of life he still clung to. This dream was so detailed, so keenly felt, so *real* that sometimes Lindos couldn't help feeling he'd crossed the line into insanity.

Even now, though he felt the imperative to get to safety, he knew there would be no solace for him as long as Andursky lived. And so he said to Katya, 'You go. Get as close to the nuclear lab as possible, then climb up into the nearest HVAC vent and stay there.'

'But you're coming with me.' Katya tugged at his arm. 'We're going together.'

'No, Katya, there's something I have to do here.'

'But you promised. You said you'd help me.'

He swung around, fixed her with his one good eye. 'I have helped you, Katya. But you must understand, if I don't stay here and do this, I will be like the walking dead.'

She shivered. 'Then I'll stay with you.'

The entire facility gave a great shudder, moaning as if in terrible pain. Somewhere not so far ahead, he could hear the shriek of a wall splitting apart.

'No,' he said sharply, returning his attention to her. 'That's not an option.'

She hefted the semiautomatic. 'And I say it is.'

Lindros nodded. What else could he do? They'd run out of time. He could hear a distant roaring, becoming louder, harsher, closer with each beat of his heart. *Water!* he thought. *Good Lord, Jason's flooding the facility!*

Without another word he strode into the surgery, Katya following several paces behind, her rifle at the ready. In the last few minutes since they'd left the comm room, she'd studied Lindros, thought she had a semblance of knowledge of how to use this instrument of death.

Lindros advanced on Dr. Andursky who, through all of this, had remained in the same position, cowering behind the table on which he had taken out Lindros's eye. His gaze was locked on Martin much as a rabbit will crouch, mesmerized, as the owl swoops silently down out of the twilight to snatch it up in its powerful talons.

As he went through the surgery, Lindros had to struggle to keep his gorge down, to keep the sickly sweet scent of the anesthetic from clogging his nostrils. He had to fight all over again the terror of helplessness and rage that had all but paralyzed him upon awakening to discover what had been stolen from him.

And yet here was Dr. Andursky in front of him, here he was gripped by Lindros's taloned fingers, scoring the flesh of his chest.

'Hello, Doctor,' Lindros said.

'No, please don't. I didn't want to. They made me.'

'Please enlighten me, Doctor. After all the little boys they supplied you – they made you pluck out my eye? They insisted you do it – or what? They would refuse to service you?'

'Martin,' Katya called, wide-eyed with fear. 'Our time has run out. Come on now! Please, for the love of God!'

'Yes, yes, listen to her. Have mercy.' Andursky was actually weeping now, his body quaking in much the same way as the walls around them had begun to quake. 'You don't understand. I'm weak.'

'And I,' Lindros said, 'gather strength with every breath I take.' He drew Andursky to him, until they stood intimate as lovers. Now it was different. The end would not be the same.

Drawing on an enormous wellspring of strength, Lindros pressed his thumbs into Andursky's eyes.

Andursky shrieked and thrashed about, desperately trying to get away. But Lindros had him in an unbreakable death grip. Every fiber of his being was directed toward one end. In a kind of ecstatic semi-trance, he felt the soft, springy tissue of the eyeballs beneath the pads of his thumbs. He drew in a breath, expelled it as he drove his thumbs slowly, inexorably into Andursky's eye sockets.

The surgeon shrieked again, a sharp inhuman noise abruptly cut off as Lindros shoved his thumbs all the way in. Andursky danced for a little, his autonomous nervous system flickering with whatever galvanic energy remained inside his body. Then that, too, was gone and, released from Lindros's grip, he slithered to the floor as if all his bones had dissolved.

# 36

Fadi heard the screams of pain from the facility he had designed and helped build, saw the cracks shoot through the reinforced concrete as if lightning was streaking through it. Then a throaty roar echoed through the corridors and he knew the water was coming, gallons of water, tons of it flooding the labs, and all he could think of was the nuclear device.

He tore along the corridors past the elevator. He pushed past milling guards, who looked to him for guidance. He ordered them to the front entrance to find Bourne, then he forgot about them. They were all cannon fodder anyway. What did it matter if they died? There were more where they came from, an endless supply of young men clamoring to follow him, eager to die for him, to martyr themselves for the cause, the dream that one day they would live in a world of righteousness, a world without the infidel.

That this frankly brutal outlook had been forced on him by his enemies was a given, a watchword by which he'd lived his entire adult life. He told himself as much several times a day, although it never occurred to him that he needed to justify to himself any of his decisions or actions. His mind, his heart, and his hand were guided by Allah; this he believed absolutely. The possibility that their plan might not succeed had until now never entered his mind. Now that thought superseded all others, even his obsessive need to revenge himself for the crippling of his father or the death of his sister.

Racing down the stairs, he found the lower level already calf-deep in water. He pulled his Glock 36, checked the .45 to make sure it was fully loaded. The water lapped at his legs, rising with every step he took. He felt as if he were walking against the tide, the sensation bringing him back to the encounter with Bourne under the pier in Odessa. How he wished he'd finished him off there. Except for the damn dog, he felt certain he would have.

But this was no time for recriminations, and he was not a man who dwelled on what-ifs. He was a pragmatist, which dictated that he get to the heli with its all-important payload. What was unfortunate was that the secret exit to the camouflaged helipad was at the rear of the lower level. This location had been deliberate, for the exit was nearest the nuclear facilities where, Fadi had surmised, he would need to be if the facility was ever discovered and raided.

What he hadn't counted on was the raiding party discovering the underground river. The section of the facility he sought was also where the water was gushing in at the fastest rate. Once he got to his destination, however, he'd be all right, since the helipad had wide drainage apertures all around its perimeters. This thought occupied him as he ran past the open door to the surgery and saw Katya. Ludicrously, she held one of his own semiautomatics in both hands. But it wasn't Veintrop's wife that so arrested him. Rather, it was the sight of Martin Lindros standing, bloody-handed, over the corpse of the man who had maimed him, Dr. Andursky.

The singsong lilt of Arabic threaded through the darkness beneath the mortuary. Karim's men were praying, their bodies bowed toward Mecca. From the bottom of the ramp illumination spread upward like the fingers of a hand. Tyrone was wearing sneakers, but Soraya had taken off her shoes to silence her footfalls.

Moving cautiously toward the lower end of the ramp, Soraya and Tyrone peered into the basement. The first thing Soraya saw were the two vehicles they had been following: the white Chevy and the black Ford. Behind them was what looked to be a gleaming black limo. On the left side of the Ford, four men were lined up, kneeling on small prayer rugs, their foreheads to the low nap. To the right was a glass-paned door. Soraya craned her neck but could not get a good angle at which to see through the door's glass.

They waited. At length, the prayers ended. The men rose, rolled their rugs, and stowed them away. Then the group broke up. Two of the men disappeared up a stainless-steel spiral staircase to the mortuary proper. The remaining pair snapped on latex gloves, opened the Ford's doors, and proceeded to go over it as thoroughly and meticulously as a professional forensics team.

Soraya, curious about what lay behind the glass-paned door, signed to Tyrone to stay put and cover her, if necessary. He nodded, produced a Saturday-night special, the grips wrapped in black elecrician's tape, and stepped back into deep shadow. Not for the first time in the last several hours, Soraya felt comforted to have him with her. He was street-savvy, knew the district in far more detail than she did.

Watching the two men examine the Ford, she waited until both their backs were turned to the mouth of the ramp, then ran silently to the door. Twisting the knob, she opened it and slipped through.

At once she was suffused with a deep chill that emanated from the cold rooms where the corpses were kept. She was confronted with a short, wide corridor off which six open doorways presented themselves. Peeking around the corner of the first one, she came upon the bodies of the two men who had attacked her at the construction site. In accordance with austere Saudi Islamic tradition, they had been placed on bare wooden slabs and were draped in the simplest cloth robes. There would be no embalming of these men.

Her heart leapt. The corpses were the first hard evidence she had that Karim was working with a cadre of Dujja terrorists inside the district. How had they all missed this Dujja sleeper cell right under their noses? State-of-the-art surveillance equipment was all well and good, but even the best electronic net couldn't catch every human being who slipped inside America's borders.

The second and third rooms she came to were empty, but in the fourth a dark-complected man with his back to her was bent over an embalming table. He wore latex gloves and was using a machine to pump the body laid out on the table with the ghastly pink embalming fluid. He would stop every so often, put aside the probe, then use his hands to knead the fish-white flesh in order to effect the even circulation of fluids through the corpse's veins and arteries.

As he moved from the corpse's right side to its left, Soraya was able to see the head, then the face of the deceased. As soon as her brain passed though its shock phase and was able to process the image, she was compelled to bite her lip in order to stop herself from screaming.

*No,* she thought. Fear and panic fought for dominance inside her. *It can't be.* And yet it was.

Here in the mortuary owned and operated by Dujja was the corpse of the DCI. The Old Man was dead, a bullet hole drilled through his heart.

The moment he had memorized the schematic of the facility affixed to the wall, Bourne ran out of the parking area. At once he saw a group of armed Dujja running his way. Ducking back away from their fire, he climbed into the smallest vehicle. Fortunately it, like all the others, had the key already in it; there was no need to waste time hot-wiring the ignition.

He roared into the corridor, then pressed the accelerator to the floor, shooting the vehicle ahead like a bolt released from a crossbow. It plowed into the clutch of terrorists, flinging them under it or to either side. He sped down the spine of the facility until he came to the freight elevator.

As the doors opened, he drove in, crushing four more armed men. Climbing out, he pushed the button for the lower level. He grabbed one of the semiautomatics as the oversize cab began to descend.

Reaching its destination, the elevator came to a halt, but its doors refused to open. Water was leaking in from the corridor outside. Opening the panel in the side wall, he pressed the manual release. This, too, was inoperative.

Bourne climbed onto the vehicle's roof. Bracing himself, he slammed the butt of the semiautomatic repeatedly against the small square door in the cab's roof. Finally it gave. He shoved it out of the way and, slinging the weapon across his back, hoisted himself up. On top of the cab, he knelt down by the side of an oblong control box and opened it. Inside he found the circuit that operated the doors. He took its wires and diverted them to the lift mechanism's power source. The doors slid open, a heavy slosh of water roiling into the elevator.

Back behind the wheel, he put the vehicle in gear, then screeched out into the waterlogged lower level. He headed toward the nuclear labs, gunning the engine as the water level rose. In a moment it would be high enough to flood the engine. Unless he kept going it would conk out altogether, and his advantage would disappear.

But a moment later, the vehicle's use ran its course anyway. Dead ahead of him he saw Fadi standing in the center of the corridor, blocking his way. Held in front of him in the crook of Fadi's powerful left arm was Martin Lindros. In Fadi's right hand was a Glock 36, the muzzle pressed to Martin's temple.

'My pursuit of you ends here, Bourne!' Fadi shouted over the roar of the incoming water and the noise of the vehicle's engine. 'Turn off the ignition! Out of the car! Now!'

Bourne did as Fadi ordered. Now, closer, he saw something in Fadi's right ear. A wireless earpiece. He *had* been monitoring the communications.

'Get rid of that rifle! All your weapons! Now, keeping your hands where I can see them, walk very slowly toward me.'

Bourne sloshed through the water, his eyes on Martin's ruined face. His one eye glared at Bourne with a fierce pride. He intuited that Lindros was going to make a move, and wanted to warn him against it; Bourne had his own plan for dealing with Fadi. But Lindros had always wanted to be a hero.

Sure enough, a scalpel appeared in Martin's left hand. As he drove it into the meat of Fadi's thigh, Fadi fired the Glock. He'd been aiming for Lindros's brain, but the stab caused an involuntary spasm of shock and pain so that, instead, the bullet ran along Lindros's jaw. Still, it was a .45. Martin's body was launched through the doorway, into the surgery beyond.

Bourne leapt. His leading shoulder struck Fadi in the solar plexus as the terrorist was wrestling the scalpel out of his muscle. Both of them fell backward into the water, now as high as their knees. Bourne got his hand on the Glock and wrestled it upward, so that it fired harmlessly into the air. At the same time Fadi wrenched the scalpel out of his thigh and, seeking to finishing what he had started, stabbed it toward Bourne's left side.

Bourne was ready. He lifted the Glock, and Fadi's right hand with it, so that the blade skimmed off the gun's thick barrel. Fadi realized the gun was useless in the water, released it, and, grabbing Bourne by the shirtfront, flipped him over onto his back. Using his right elbow, he kept Bourne's head under the water while he stabbed downward again and again with the point of the scalpel.

Twisting and writhing his torso, Bourne sought to keep the keen-edged blade away from him. At the same time he reached up so that his hands and forearms were out of the water. Marshaling all the power of his shoulders, he slammed the heels of his hands against Fadi's ears. The terrorist arched back, his hands clutching his right ear. Bourne's blow had driven the wireless transceiver through his eardrum, rupturing it and the canal behind it.

Fadi lost the scalpel, then his balance. Bourne, sensing this, scissor-kicked, twisting himself onto one hip as he did so. The maneuver threw Fadi off far enough for him to rise up above the waterline.

He reached for Fadi. As he did so, he heard a ferocious roar from farther down the corridor. Fadi appeared to be trying to shake off the effects of his ruptured eardrum, blood leaking out of his right ear. Bourne reached for him, felt the bite of Fadi's serpent-bladed knife as it drew blood along the back of his hand.

Tearing off his belt, Bourne wrapped it around and around his knuckles, using the layers of leather to fend off Fadi's knife thrusts. Inevitably, however, the struck leather began to come apart. A moment more and he would be defenseless.

The roaring increased to a howl. What was coming? Fadi, seeing his advantage, stepped up his attack with precise swipes, lent unnatural power by his desperation. Bourne was forced back toward the surgery.

Then out of the corner of his eye he saw a blurred movement. Someone had darted from the doorway to the surgery. A woman: Katya. Tears were streaming down her face. Her hands were red with blood – Martin's blood. It was she who had attempted to escape with Martin. But then Fadi had found them. Why hadn't Martin led her to shelter as Bourne had warned him to do? Too late now.

'Look what they've done to him!' Katya wailed.

Bourne saw something metallic gleaming in her hand.

Wading out into the corridor, Katya came toward him. At that moment the roar reached a fever pitch. Katya turned her head to stare down along the corridor. Bourne, following her gaze, saw a wall of water filling the corridor from floor to ceiling, heading toward them.

Fadi's knife blade swept across his makeshift shield one last time. All the layers fell away, baring his bloody knuckles.

'Get back!' he shouted to Katya. 'Take shelter!'

Instead she continued to wade toward him. But now the water was waist-deep, the rush of it so powerful that she could no longer make headway. Fadi tried for a killing stab, but Bourne kicked out through the rushing water, throwing him off balance. The blade turned; Bourne's bruised defensive forearm struck the flat of it, sending it up and away.

Katya, realizing she was stymied, tossed the metallic object toward Bourne.

He reached out, caught the metallic implement at its midsection – a Collins twenty-two-centimeter amputating knife. In one smooth motion he reversed it, plunged the wicked blade into the soft spot at the base of Fadi's throat, then drove it downward through his collarbone, into his chest.

Fadi stared at him, openmouthed. At the moment of his death, he was paralyzed, helpless, without thought. Frozen in time. His eyes, in the process of glazing over, revealed that he was trying to understand something. In this, too, he failed.

The roiling wall of water was almost upon them. There was nothing else Bourne could do except clamber up Fadi's split upper torso. He locked his curled fingers through the holes in the HVAC vent in the ceiling, levered himself up. Then he reached back for Katya. Afterward, he never knew whether she could have made it to him. She stood there, staring at nothing while he shouted to her.

He was about to go after her when the water struck him with the fury of a giant's fist, knocking all the breath out of him. Howling like the demon that lived atop Ras Dejen, it ripped Fadi's corpse from under him and swept Katya into its furious heart. It roared and foamed through the Dujja facility like Noah's flood, drowning all in its wake, scouring everything clean.

# 37

There was in Feyd al-Saoud's brave heart a rising conviction that one day – not soon, perhaps not even in his lifetime – the war against the tribespeople intent on setting the world on fire in order to destroy his country would be won. It would take great sacrifice, stern conviction, an iron will, as well as unconventional alliances with infidels like Jason Bourne, who had caught a glimpse of the Arab mind and understood what they had witnessed. Most of all, it would take patience and perseverance during the inevitable setbacks. But the reward would be days such as this one.

Having used a second set of C-4 charges to divert the underground river, his men entered the Dujja facility via the blast hole. He stood on the edge of the camouflaged helipad, which looked like the bed of a flat-bottomed well. Above him the opening in the rock widened as it neared the top, which had over it the specially designed camouflage material that made it indistinguishable from the rock around it.

The waters had receded, swallowed at last by the huge drains built into the facility's lower level.

Directly in front of Feyd al-Saoud, in a raised platform undamaged by the flood, squatted the helicopter meant, he was certain, to take Fadi to his rendezvous with the nuclear device. Another of his men held the pilot under guard.

Though he very much wanted to know how Bourne had made out, he was understandably reluctant to leave the device to anyone else's care. Besides, the fact that he was standing here, rather than watching the copter lifting off as Fadi made his escape, spoke eloquently of Bourne's victory. Still, he'd sent his men in to find his friend. He very much wanted to share this moment with him.

However, the individual they brought back was an older man with a high, wide forehead, prominent nose, and steel-rimmed glasses, one lens of which was cracked.

'I ask you for Jason Bourne and you bring me this.' Feyd al-Saoud's annoyance masked his alarm. Where was Jason? Was he lying injured somewhere in the washed-out bowels of this hellhole? Was he still alive?

'The man says his name is Costin Veintrop,' the team leader said.

Hearing his name amid the blur of fast-paced Arabic, the newcomer said, '*Doctor* Veintrop.' He followed this up with something in such poor Arabic as to be incomprehensible.

'Speak English, please,' Feyd al-Saoud said in his impeccably accented British.

Looking visibly relieved, Veintrop said: 'Thank God you're here. My wife and I have been held prisoner.'

Feyd al-Saoud stared at him, mute as the Sphinx.

Veintrop cleared his throat. 'Please let me go. I need to find my wife.'

'You tell me you're Dr. Costin Veintrop. You tell me that you and your wife were being held prisoner here.' Feyd al-Saoud's growing anxiety as to his friend's fate was making him ever more testy. 'I know who was being held prisoner here, and it wasn't you.'

Veintrop, properly cowed, turned to the man who'd brought him here. 'My wife, Katya, is in the facility. Can you tell me if you've found her?'

The group leader, taking his cue from his chief, stared at Veintrop in stony silence.

'Ah, God,' Veintrop moaned, lapsing in shock and worry into his native Romanian. 'My God in heaven.'

Completely unmoved, Feyd al-Saoud gave him a look of disdain before turning at the sound of movement behind him.

'Jason!'

At the sight of his friend, he rushed to the entrance of the helipad. With Bourne was another of Feyd al-Saoud's detachment. They were supporting between them a tall, well-built man whose face and head looked as if they had been put through a meat grinder.

'Allah!' Feyd al-Saoud cried. 'Is Fadi dead or alive?'

'Dead,' Bourne said.

'Who is this, Jason?'

'My friend Martin Lindros,' Bourne said.

'Ah, no!' At once, the security chief called for his group surgeon. 'Jason, the nuclear device is in the heli. Incredibly, it's contained within a slim black briefcase. How did Fadi manage that?'

Bourne stared at Veintrop balefully for a moment. 'Hello, Dr. Sunderland – or I should say Costin Veintrop.'

Veintrop winced.

Feyd al-Saoud raised his eyebrows. 'You know this man?'

'We've met once before,' Bourne said. 'The doctor is an extremely talented scientist with a number of specialities. Including miniaturization.'

'So he was the one who built the circuits that allowed the nuke to fit into the briefcase.' Feyd al-Saoud's expression was dark, indeed. 'He claimed that he and his wife were prisoners.'

'I *was* a prisoner,' Veintrop insisted. 'You don't understand, I – '

'Now you know about him.' Bourne talked over his response. 'As for his wife – '

'Where is she?' Veintrop gasped. 'Do you know? I want my Katya!'

'Katya is dead.' Bourne said this bluntly, almost brutally. He had no sympathy to spend on the man who had connived with Fadi and Karim to destroy him from the inside out. 'She saved me. I tried to save her, but the wall of water took her.'

'That's a lie!' Veintrop, white-faced, fairly shouted. 'You have her! You have her!'

Bourne grabbed him and took him into the chamber from which he'd first come. In the aftermath of the deluge, the Saudi team was lining up the corpses they'd found. Next to Fadi's was Katya's. Her head lay at an unnatural angle.

Veintrop gave out a low moan that seemed almost inhuman. Bourne, watching him sink to his knees, felt a pang for the beautiful young woman who had sacrificed herself so that he could kill Fadi. She had wanted Fadi's death, it seemed, as much as he did.

His gaze slid over to Fadi. The eyes, still open, seemed to stare at Bourne with a hateful fury. Bourne took out his cell. Crouched down, he took several shots of Fadi's face. When he was finished, he rose and dragged Veintrop back to the helipad.

Bourne addressed Feyd al-Saoud. 'Is the pilot inside the heli?'

The security chief nodded. 'He's under guard.' He pointed. 'And here is the case.'

'Are you certain that is the device?' Veintrop said.

Feyd al-Saoud looked to his expert, who nodded. 'I've opened the case. It's a nuclear bomb, all right.'

'Well, then,' Veintrop said with an oddly vibrant note to his voice, 'I'd open it again if I were you. Perhaps you haven't seen everything inside.'

Feyd al-Saoud glanced at Bourne, who nodded. 'Open it,' the security chief said to his man.

The man laid the case carefully down on the concrete floor and snapped the lid open.

'Look on the left side,' Veintrop said. 'No, nearer the rear.'

The Saudi craned his neck, then recoiled involuntarily. 'A timer's been activated.'

'That happened when you opened the case without using the code.'

Bourne recognized the note in his voice: It was triumph.

'How much time?' Feyd al-Saoud said.

'Four minutes, thirty-seven seconds.'

'I created the circuit,' Veintrop said. 'I can stop it.' He looked from one man to the other. 'In return, I want my freedom. No prosecution. No negotiation. A new life, paid in full.'

'Is that all?' Bourne hit him so hard that Veintrop bounced off the wall. He caught him on the rebound. 'Knife,' he said.

Feyd al-Saoud knew what was required now. He handed one to Bourne.

The moment Bourne took possession of the knife he buried the blade just above Veintrop's kneecap.

Veintrop screamed. 'What have you done?' Then he began to weep uncontrollably.

'No, Doctor, it's what *you've* done.' Bourne crouched down beside him, holding the bloody blade in his line of vision. 'You've got just under four minutes to disable the timer.'

Veintrop, holding his ruined knee, rocked back and forth on his backside. 'What . . . what about my terms?'

'Here are *my* terms.' Bourne flicked the blade and Veintrop screamed again.

'All right, all right!'

Bourne looked up. 'Put the open case in front of him.'

When that had been done, Bourne said, 'It's all yours, Doctor. But rest assured I'm going to be watching every move you make.'

Bourne stood, saw Feyd al-Saoud staring at him, his heavy lips pushed out in a silent whistle of relief.

Bourne watched while Veintrop worked on the timer. It took him just over two minutes, by Bourne's wristwatch. At the end of that time, he sat back, arms folded protectively around his ruined knee.

Feyd al-Saoud signed for his man to take a look.

'The wires are cut,' the man said. 'The timer's dead. There's no chance of detonation.'

Veintrop had returned to his mindless rocking. 'I need a painkiller,' he said dully.

Feyd al-Saoud called for his surgeon, then went to take possession of the nuclear device. Bourne got to it before him.

'I'm going to need this to get to Karim.'

The security chief frowned deeply. 'I don't understand.'

'I'm taking the route Fadi would have taken to Washington,' Bourne said in a tone that brooked no interference.

Even so, Feyd al-Saoud said, 'Do you think that's wise, Jason?'

'I'm afraid at this juncture wise doesn't enter into it,' Bourne replied. 'Karim has put himself into a position of such power inside CI he's all but untouchable. I've got to go another route.'

'I expect you have a plan, then.'

'I always have a plan.'

'All right. My surgeon will take charge of your friend.'

'No,' Bourne said. 'Martin comes with me.'

Again, Feyd al-Saoud recognized Bourne's steely tone of voice. 'Then my surgeon will accompany you.'

'Thank you,' Bourne said.

Feyd al-Saoud helped his friend load Martin Lindros into the helicopter. While Bourne laid down the law to Fadi's pilot, the security chief sent his man off the copter, then knelt to help his surgeon make Lindros as comfortable as possible.

'How long does he have?' Feyd al-Saoud said softly, for it was clear Lindros was dying.

The surgeon shrugged. 'An hour, give or take.'

Bourne was finished talking to the pilot, who now slipped into his chair. 'I need you to do something for me.'

Feyd al-Saoud rose up. 'Anything, my friend.'

'First, I need a phone. Mine is fried.'

The security chief was handed a cell by one of his men. Bourne transferred the chip that held all his phone numbers into the new model.

'Thanks. Now I want you to phone your contacts in the U.S. government, tell them that the plane I'll be taking is a Saudi diplomatic mission. As soon as I speak with the pilot, I'll send you the flight plan. I don't want any problems with Customs and Immigration.'

'Consider it done.'

'Then I want you to call CI, tell them the same thing. Only give them an ETA forty minutes later than the actual one I'll give you when the pilot has checked the weather.'

'My call to CI will alert the impostor – '

'Yes,' Bourne said. 'It will.'

Feyd al-Saoud's face was wreathed in concern. 'You play a terribly deadly game, Jason.'

Having delivered this warning, he embraced his friend warmly.

'Allah has given you wings. May He protect you on your mission.'

He kissed Bourne on both cheeks then, bending over, stepped out of the heli. The pilot threw a switch that retracted the camouflaged top of the helipad. When he was certain that all ground personnel were well clear of the rotor, he started the engine.

Bourne knelt beside Lindros and took his hand. Martin's good eye fluttered open. He stared up at Bourne, smiled with what was left of his mouth, and gripped Bourne's hand all the tighter.

Bourne felt tears come to his eyes. With an effort, he held them back. 'Fadi's dead, Martin,' he said over the mounting noise. 'You've got your wish. You're a hero.'

# 38

Karim was deliberately late to the directorate admin meeting. He wanted all seven of the directorate chiefs around the table when he walked in. The conference room was by design located adjacent to the DCI's office suite. In fact, there was a connecting door from the Old Man's suite into the conference room. Also by design, it was through this door that Karim made his entrance. He wanted to reiterate to the Seven, without having to utter a word, where he stood vis-à-vis them in the CI hierarchy.

'The DCI sends his regrets,' he said briskly, taking the Old Man's seat around the table. 'Anne, who's with him, tells me that he's still closeted with the president and the Joint Chiefs.'

Karim opened a thick dossier, only the first five pages of which were real – if you could call real disinformation he had carried in his head for months.

'Now that the imminent threat posed by Dujja has been eliminated, now that Dujja itself is a shell of itself, it's time we moved on to other matters.'

'One moment, Martin,' cut in the steely voice of Rob Batt, chief of operations. 'If I may, before we close the door on this one there's still the matter of Fadi himself to consider.'

Karim sat back, twisting a pen through his fingers. The worst thing he could do, he knew, was cut off this line of inquiry. As the meeting several days ago had indicated, he was on Batt's shit list. He wasn't about to do anything to raise Batt's level of distrust.

'By all means,' Karim said, 'let's discuss going after Fadi.'

'I agree with Rob,' Dick Symes, chief of the Intelligence Directorate, said. 'I'm in favor of committing a significant percentage of personnel to his capture.'

There were nods from several of the other chiefs arrayed around the table.

In the face of this rising wave, Karim said, 'In the absence of the Old Man, we'll naturally implement what the majority thinks best. However, I'd like to point out several things. First, having wiped out Dujja's most important base of operations, we have no idea whether Fadi is alive or dead. If he was in or near the facility in South Yemen, there's no doubt that he was incinerated along with everyone else. Second, if he was elsewhere at the time of the raid, we have no idea where he might be. For sure, he will have gone to ground. I say we allow time to pass, see what we pick up on the Dujja network. Let the terrorist world believe we've turned our attention elsewhere. If Fadi is alive, he'll begin to stir, and then we'll get a line on him.'

Karim looked from face to face. There were no frowns, no dissenting shakes of the head, no covert glances among the Seven.

'Third, and perhaps most important, we have to get our own house in order,' he continued. 'I can confirm the rumors that the Old Man has been under attack by Defense Secretary Halliday and his Pentagon lackey, Luther LaValle. Halliday knew about our mole, and he knew about the computer virus attack. It turns out that the late Matthew Lerner was also Halliday's man.'

This caused quite a stir around the table. Karim held up his hands, palms outward. 'I know, I know, we've all felt the turmoil caused by Lerner's attempt to realign CI. And now we know why the changes felt so alien to us – they were mandated by Halliday and his henchmen at NSA.

'Well, Lerner's dead. Whatever clandestine influence the defense secretary had here is gone. And now that the mole has been dispatched, we're free to do what should have been done years ago. We need to remake CI into an agency better equipped than any other to wage war on global terrorism.

'That's why my first proposal is to hire the uniquely qualified Arabs and Muslims drummed out of the various agencies in the wake of September 11. If we have any chance of winning this new war, we have to understand the terrorists who make up our patchwork enemy. We have to stop confusing Arab with Muslim, Saudi with Syrian, Azerbaijani with Afghani, Sunni with Shia.'

'Hard to argue with any of that,' Symes said.

'We can still take a vote on Rob's suggestion,' Karim said smoothly.

As all eyes turned to the chief of operations. 'That won't be necessary,' Batt said. 'I hearby withdraw my suggestion in favor of Martin's.'


Bourne sat on the floor of the helicopter facing the Saudi surgeon and his large black bag. Between them lay the bloody body of Martin Lindros. The doctor was continuing to give Martin something intravenously for the pain.

'The best I can do,' the surgeon had said as they had sped away from Miran Shah, 'is to make him as comfortable as I can.'

Bourne stared down into Lindros's ruined face, conjuring up an image of his friend as he had been. He wasn't entirely successful. The .45 bullet from Fadi's gun had exploded along the right side of his head, destroying the eye socket and half the brow ridge. The surgeon had been able to stop the bleeding, but because the gun had been fired from close range, the damage had been massive enough to cause the shutdown of Martin's vital organs. According to the surgeon, the cascade effect had progressed far enough as to make any attempt at saving Martin's life fruitless.

Martin was in a period of uneasy sleep now. Watching him, Bourne felt a combination of rage and despair. Why had this happened to Martin? Why wasn't he able to keep him alive? He knew his distress came from helplessness. It was the same feeling he'd had on seeing Marie for the last time. Helplessness was the one emotion Bourne could not abide. It got under his skin, buried itself in his psyche like an itch he couldn't scratch, a mocking voice he couldn't silence.

With a guttural growl, he turned away. They had reached a high enough altitude to be clear of the mountains, so he opened his cell phone, tried Soraya again. It rang, which was a good sign. Once again, she didn't answer, which wasn't. This time, he left a brief voice-mail message that evoked Odessa. It would be cryptic to anyone but Soraya herself.

Then he called Deron's cell. He was still down in Florida.

'I've got a problem only you can handle,' Bourne said without preamble.

'Shoot.'

This kind of abbreviated conversation was typical with them.

'I need a full kit.'

'No problem. Where are you?'

'About ten hours out of Washington.'

'Kay. Tyrone's got my keys. He'll get it all together. Dulles or Reagan International?'

'Neither. We're scheduled to set down eighteen kilo-meters south of Annandale,' Bourne said, giving Deron the coordinates in Virginia he'd gotten from the pilot. 'It's on the extreme eastern edge of property owned by Sistain Labs.' Sistain was a subsidiary of IVT. 'Thanks, Deron.'

'No biggie, my man. I just wish I was there myself.'

As Bourne disconnected, Martin stirred.

'Jason.'

Martin's reedy whisper caused him to put his head beside his friend's. The odor of lacerated flesh, of impending death, was nauseating.

'I'm here, Martin.'

'The man who took my place – '

'Karim. Fadi's brother, I know. I worked it all out, Martin. It started with the Odessa mission Conklin gave me. I was with Soraya at the meet with her contact. A young woman came running toward us. It was Sarah ibn Ashef, Karim and Fadi's sister. I shot at her, but I didn't hit her as I assumed I had. It was one of Fadi's men. He shot her dead because she was having an affair.'

Martin's one remaining eye, red-rimmed, burning still with life, fixed on Bourne. 'It's Karim . . . you have . . . to get, Jason.' He was wheezing, his breath coming in herky-jerky gasps, clotted with pink phlegm and blood. 'He's the wily one, the . . . chess player . . . the spider sitting at the . . . center of the . . . Jesus, of the . . . web.'

His eye was open wide, moving to the spasms of pain racking him. 'Fadi . . . Fadi was just the . . . front, the rallying . . . point. Karim is the . . . truly . . . dangerous one.'

'Martin, I heard every word you said, and it's time to rest now,' Bourne said.

'No, no . . .' Lindros seemed to have been seized by a peculiar frenzy. The energy of a small star radiated from him, bathing Bourne in its glow. 'Plenty of time to . . . rest when . . . I'm . . . dead.'

He had started to bleed again. The surgeon leaned over, wiped the blood away with a gauze pad that soon enough was soaked through.

'For Karim it isn't . . . simply America, Jason. It's CI itself. He hates us – all of us with . . . every fiber of his . . . being. That . . . that's why he . . . was willing to . . . gamble . . . everything, his entire . . . life and soul to . . . get . . . inside.'

'What does he mean to do? Martin, what does he mean to do?'

'Destroy CI.' Martin looked up at Bourne. 'I wish I knew more. Christ, Jason, how I fucked up.'

'It wasn't your fault, Martin.' Bourne's expression was stern. 'If you blame yourself for any of this, I'll be extremely angry with you.'

Lindros tried to laugh, but with all the blood he brought up he didn't quite make it. 'We can't have that, now, can we?'

Bourne wiped his mouth.

Like a momentary loss of electricity through a power grid, something flickered across Lindros's face – a window to a dark, cold place. He began to shiver.

'Jason, listen, when this . . . is all . . . over, I want you to send a dozen red roses to Moira. You'll find her address in . . . my cell phone at home. Cremate my body. Take my ashes to the Cloisters in New York City.'

Bourne felt a burning behind his eyes. 'Of course, I'll do whatever you want.'

'I'm glad you're . . . here.'

'You're my best friend, Martin. My *only* friend.'

'It's sad, then, for . . . both of us.' Lindros tried to smile again, gave up, exhausted. 'You know . . . the thing . . . between us, Jason . . . what bound us? You . . . can't remember your past and . . . I can't . . . bear to remember . . . mine.'

The moment came, then, and Bourne could feel it. An instant ago Martin's good eye was regarding him with grave intelligence; now it was fixed in the middle distance, staring at something Bourne had sensed many times, but never seen.

Soraya, horrified not only by what she saw but also by its implications, stood transfixed, staring at the half-embalmed corpse of the Old Man. It was like seeing your father dead, she thought. You knew it had to happen someday, but when that day came you couldn't wrap your mind around it. To her, as to everyone else at CI, he had seemed indestructible as well as invincible. He had been their moral compass, the font of their worldwide power for so long that now with him gone she felt naked and horribly vulnerable.

In the wake of the first shock, she felt a cold panic grip her. With the Old Man dead, who was running CI? Of course, there were the directorate chiefs, but everyone from the upper echelons on down knew that Martin Lindros was the DCI's anointed successor.

Which meant that the false Lindros was heading up CI. *God in heaven,* she thought. *He's going to take CI down – this was part of the plan all along.* What a coup for Fadi and Dujja to be able to destroy America's most effective espionage agency just before they detonated a nuclear bomb on American soil.

In the blink of an eye, she saw it all. The barrels of C-4 Tyrone had seen were meant for CI headquarters. But how on earth was Dujja going to get the explosives past security? She knew Fadi had devised a method to do so. Perhaps it would be easy now that the false Lindros had effected a coup.

All at once Soraya snapped back into the here and now. Given the Old Man's murder, it was imperative she gain access to CI headquarters. She had to inform the seven directorate chiefs of the truth, her own safety be damned. But how? The false Lindros would have her picked up the moment she showed her ID to CI security. And there was absolutely no way to sneak into HQ undetected.

As the helicopter descended through the clouds toward the private airstrip in Mazar-i-Sharif, Bourne sat beside Martin Lindros, his head bowed. His mind was filled with connections, some to memories, others that went nowhere because the memories were lost to him. In that very important respect, connections were of paramount importance to him. Now a key one was gone. It was only now, in the aftermath, that Bourne understood how important Martin had been to him.

Amnesia could engender many things in the mind, including insanity – or at least the semblance of it, which more or less amounted to the same thing.

Being able to connect with Martin after Conklin was murdered had been a lifeline. Now Martin was dead. He no longer had Marie to come home to. When the stress level became too great, what would prevent him from slipping into the madness that came from the forest of broken connections within his brain?

He held on to the briefcase as the pilot set the helicopter down on the tarmac.

'You're coming with us,' Bourne said to the pilot. 'I need your help for a bit longer.'

The pilot rose and, together with Bourne, picked up Lindros's body. With some difficulty, they maneuvered it off the helicopter. A larger high-speed jet was sitting on the tarmac, fueled and ready. The two men made the transfer, and Bourne spoke with the jet's pilot. Then Bourne ordered the copter pilot to ferry the surgeon back to Miran Shah. Bourne warned him that Feyd al-Saoud's team would be monitoring both his flight progress and his communications.

Ten minutes later, with the two men and the corpse on board, the jet rolled down the runway. Gathering speed, it lifted off into the slate-gray clouds of an oncoming storm.

Ever since he'd taken the call from Soraya, Peter Marks had found it impossible to concentrate on his work. The encrypted communications from Dujja seemed like so much Martian to him. Feigning a migraine, he finally had to hand them off to a colleague.

For some time, he sat at his desk, brooding. He couldn't help but examine every aspect of that call, as well as his response to it. At first, he'd had to get over his anger. How dare Soraya try to get him involved in whatever mess she had made for herself? That was the moment he'd almost picked up the phone and punched Lindros's extension, to report her call.

But with his hand halfway to the receiver, something had stopped him. What was it? On the face of it, Soraya's story was so outlandish that it didn't even rate considering. First, they all knew that the Dujja nuclear threat had been averted. Second, Lindros himself had warned everyone that Soraya had been unhinged by Jason Bourne's death. And she certainly had sounded nuts on the phone.

But then there was her warning about the danger to the CI headquarters building. With all his years of training, it would be remiss of him to ignore that part of her story. For the second time, he almost punched Lindros's extension. What stopped him was the hole in his reasoning. Namely, why would one part of her story be true and the other made up? He couldn't believe anyone – let alone Soraya – would be that unhinged.

Which meant that he was back to square one. What to do about her call? His fingers drummed a tattoo on the desktop. Of course, he could do nothing, simply forgetting the conversation had ever taken place. But then if something did happen to headquarters, he'd never be able to forgive himself. Assuming, of course, he was still alive to feel the insupportable guilt.

Before he could second-guess himself into inaction, he grabbed the receiver and dialed his contact at the White House.

'Hey, Ken. Peter here,' he said when the other answered. 'I've got an urgent message for the DCI. Could you scare him up for me? He's in with the POTUS.'

'No, he's not, Peter. The POTUS is meeting with the Joint Chiefs.'

Peter's heart skipped a very small beat. 'When did the DCI leave?'

'Hold on, I'll access the log.' A moment later, Ken said, 'You sure about your intel? The DCI hasn't been here today, and he isn't on the POTUS's or anyone else's schedule.'

'Thanks, Ken,' Peter said in a strangled voice. 'My mistake.'

*Oh, dear God,* he thought. *Soraya is as sane as I am.* He looked through the open door to his cubicle. He could just see a corner of Lindros's office. *If it isn't Lindros, who the hell is running Typhon?*

He lunged for his cell phone. As soon as he could get his fingers to work properly, he punched in Soraya's number.

# 39

Tyrone was waiting patiently for Soraya when she poked her head out of the glass-paned door. As she did so, she felt her cell phone vibrate. Tyrone signaled to her and she ran silently into the shadows at the ramp's mouth.

'The two shitbirds finished,' he said in a low voice. 'They upstairs now wit they peeps.'

'We'd better go,' she said.

But before she could move back up the ramp, he took hold of her arm. 'We ain't finished here, girl.' He pointed. 'See that past the Ford?'

'What is it?' She craned her neck. 'A limo?'

'Not jus' any limo. This one got government plates on her.'

'Government plates?'

'Not ony that, they's CI plates.'

Catching her sharp glance, he said, 'Deron taught me t'look out for 'em.' He motioned with his head. 'Yo, check it out, yo.'

Soraya stole around the flank of the Ford. Immediately she saw the gleaming expanse of the limo and its license plates. She almost gasped out loud. Not only were they CI plates, they were the plates on the Old Man's limo. All at once she understood why they had taken the trouble to embalm the DCI. They needed the body, which meant two things: It had to be malleable, and it must not stink.

Her cell buzzed again. She pulled it out, looked at the screen. It was Peter Marks. What the hell did he want? Crab-walking her way back to Tyrone, she said, 'They've killed the director of CI. That's his limo.'

'Yeah, but what they doing wit it?'

'Maybe that's where they killed him.'

'Mebbe.' Tyrone scratched his chin. 'But I seen 'em foolin' wit the inside.'

For the third time her cell buzzed. This time, it was Bourne. She needed desperately to tell him what was going on, but she couldn't risk a prolonged conversation now. 'We've got to get out of here now, Tyrone.'

'Mebbe you,' he said, his eye on the limo. 'But I'm gonna stay here awhile longer.'

'It's too dangerous,' Soraya said. 'We're both leaving now.'

Tyrone raised his gun. 'Doan give me no orders. I done tol yo what I was doin'. You make yo own choice.'

Soraya shook her head. 'I'm not leaving you here. I don't want you any more involved than you already are.'

'Yo, I killed two men fo yo, girl. How much more involved could I get?'

She had to admit he had a point. 'What I don't get is why you got involved in the first place.'

He gave her a grin because he knew she was done fighting him. 'Yo mean what in it fo me? Hood where Deron an I brought up, homeboys only do things f'two reasons: t'make money or t'fuck sumbody over. Hopefully both. Now I watch Deron for a while. He pull hisself outta the shit; he make sumpin of his bad self. I admire that, but I always thought: That him, not me. Now wit this shit, I see I got a shot at a future.'

'You've also got a shot at getting killed.'

Tyrone shrugged. 'Yo, ain't no more than every day inna hood, yo.'

At that moment, he pulled out a PDA.

'I didn't know you had anything but a burner,' she said, referring to the throw-away cell phones she'd seen him carry.

'Only one person knows bout this PET. One who give it t'me.'

'PET?'

'Yeah. Personal Electronic Thingy.'

He checked the PET, obviously reading an e-mail. 'Shit.' Then he glanced up. 'What a we waitin' fo? Let's get the fuck outta Dodge.'

They walked back up the ramp to the panel they'd found for the lights and the automatic door opener. 'What changed your mind?'

Tyrone put a disgusted expression on his face. 'Deron say I gotta split right this fuckin' minute. I got yo man Bourne's back.'

Peter Marks, lurking in the corridor near the elevator, caught Rob Batt's eye as the Seven emerged from the conference room. Marks had worked for Batt before being chosen by Martin Lindros for Typhon. In fact, metaphorically speaking, he'd cut his eyeteeth on Batt's methodology; he still considered the chief of operations his rabbi within CI.

So it was not surprising that Marks, having caught the older man's eye, got his attention immediately. Batt peeled off from the others and turned a corner into the corridor where Marks stood.

'What are you doing here, Peter?'

'Waiting for you, actually.' Marks glanced nervously around. 'We need to talk.'

'Can it wait?'

'No, sir, it can't.'

Batt frowned. 'Okay. My office.'

'Outside would be best, sir.'

The chief of operations gave him a curious glance, then shrugged.

They took the elevator down together and walked across the lobby, then out the front door. There was a rose garden on the east side of the property, which is where Marks led them. When they were a reasonably safe distance from the building, he told Batt word for word what Soraya Moore had told him.

'I didn't believe it, either, sir,' he said, seeing the look on Batt's face. 'But then I called a buddy of mine at the White House. The Old Man isn't there, never was there today.'

Batt rubbed his blue jowls with one hand. 'Then where the fuck is he?'

'That's just the thing, sir.' Marks, already ill at ease, was getting more nervous with every moment that passed. 'I've spent the last forty minutes on the phone. I don't know where he is, and neither does anyone else.'

'Anne?'

'Also AWOL.'

'Christ Jesus.'

Marks rechecked their immediate environment. 'Sir, incredible as it might seem on the face of it, I think we have to take Soraya's story seriously.'

'Incredible is right, Peter. Not to mention insane. Don't tell me you believe this –' Batt shook his head as words failed him. 'Where the hell is she?'

'That I don't know,' Marks conceded. 'I've put in a couple of calls to her cell, but she hasn't gotten back to me. She's terrified of Lindros finding her.'

'I should hope to fuck she is. We need to get her in here, pronto, process this crap out of her before she causes a panic inside the agency.'

'If she's wrong, then where's the Old Man and Anne?'

Batt headed back out of the rose garden. 'That's what I'm going to find out,' he said over his shoulder.

'What about Soraya – ?'

'When she calls you, make her believe you're on her side. Get her in here, pronto.'

As the chief of operations disappeared inside headquarters, Marks's phone sang. He checked the incoming call. Punching a button, he said, 'Hi, Soraya. Look, I was thinking about what you said, and I checked at the White House. Both the Old Man and Anne are missing.'

'Of course they are,' he heard her say in his ear. 'I've just seen the Old Man. He's laid out on a mortuary slab with a bullet hole in his heart.'

Along with the Seven, Karim sat in the conference room adjacent to the Old Man's suite. They were all listening to the message from the Saudi secret service informing them of the takeover of the Dujja nuclear facility in Miran Shah. Unlike the others, however, he received the communiqué with equal parts confusion and trepidation. Was this a ploy by his brother because of the heightened terror alert, or had something gone horribly wrong?

He knew there was only one way to find out. He left the conference room, but on the way to the elevator he glimpsed Peter Marks out of the corner of his eye. This was the second time he'd noticed Marks up here where he didn't belong. A warning bell went off in his head and, instead of entering the elevator with some of the other chiefs, he turned to his left. The corner behind which he stood gave him a view of the conference room door. As Rob Batt emerged, Marks approached him. They spoke for a moment. Batt, initially cool, nodded, and together they walked back into the conference room, shutting the door behind them.

Karim walked very quickly into the DCI's suite, past the desk where a young man from Signals was filling in for Anne. The man nodded to him as he went into the Old Man's office.

Once behind the desk, he toggled on a switch. Two voices from the conference room became audible.

'. . . *from Soraya,*' Marks was saying. '*She claims to have seen the DCI's body in a morgue with a bullet hole through his heart.*'

'*What is this woman on? I spoke to Martin. He's heard from the Old Man.*'

'*Where is he?*'

'*On personal business, with Anne,*' Batt said, with what sounded like a yawn.

'*Soraya's also heard from Bourne.*'

'*Bourne's dead.*'

'*He isn't. He found the real nuclear facility. It's in Miran Shah, on the border of—*'

'*I know where Miran Shah is, Peter,*' Batt snapped. '*What is this crap?*'

'*She said you can verify everything with Feyd al-Saoud.*'

'*That's just what I need, go crawling to the chief of Saudi security for our own intel.*'

'*She also said Bourne killed Fadi. He's on his way here in Fadi's jet.*'

There was more to the conversation, but Karim had heard enough. His skin felt as if ants were crawling all over it. He wanted to scream, to tear himself limb from limb.

Bolting from the office, he took the elevator down. But instead of picking up a CI vehicle in the basement parking area, for which he'd have to sign, he hurried out the front door and walked off the grounds.

The night was well advanced in the district. The low sky, full of glowering clouds, seemed to absorb the spangle of lights from the city. Shadows rose to monument height.

He stopped at the corner of 21st and Constitution and called a taxi service. Seven agonizing minutes later, the cab pulled up and he got in.

Thirteen minutes after that, he alit in front of an Avis rental and began to walk away from it. When the taxi had disappeared, he reversed course, went into the Avis office, and rented a car, using false ID. He paid cash, took possession of the GM car, asked for directions to Dulles airport, then drove off.

In fact, he had no intention of going to Dulles. His destination was the Sistain Labs airstrip south of Annandale.

The jet, banking low over Occoquan Bay, turned north heading toward the airstrip on the fist-shaped peninsula that jutted out into the water. The pilot, following the glide path of the lights, brought the jet down in a whisper of a landing. As they taxied along the runway, losing speed with every meter, Bourne saw Tyrone astride his Ninja, a hard-sided black leather case strapped across his back. He glanced at his watch. They were right on time, which meant he had approximately thirty-five minutes to prepare himself for Karim.

En route, he'd spoken to Soraya several times. They had brought each other up to date with news that was both shocking and gratifying. Fadi was dead, Dujja's nuclear threat thwarted, but Karim had killed the Old Man, consolidating his power inside CI. Now he was planning to destroy CI headquarters and everyone in it, coordinating the devastating attack with the detonation of the nuke. Soraya had one ally inside CI – the Typhon agent named Peter Marks, but Marks wasn't a rebel by nature. She didn't know how far he would bend the regs for her.

As for the Old Man's death, Bourne had mixed feelings. He had been made to feel like the prodigal grandson, a wayward who, on returning home, was subject to his grandfather's spiteful wrath. More than once, the DCI had tried to have him killed. But then he'd never understood Bourne, and so had been deeply frightened of him. Bourne could blame the Old Man for many things, but not for that. Bourne had never fit into the CI scheme – he'd been shoehorned into an agency that despised individualists. He'd never asked for the association, but there it was. Or rather, there it had been.

Now he turned his attention to Karim.

The plane had come to a stop on the tarmac; the engines whined down. Bourne, taking the pilot with him, went down the cabin aisle, opened the door, and lowered the stairs for Tyrone, who had driven up beside the jet.

Tyrone came up the stairway, dropping the black leather case at Bourne's feet.

'Hey, Tyrone. Thanks.'

'Yo, need some light in here, yo. Can't see a thing.'

'That's the point.'

Tyrone was peering at him. 'Yo look like a fuckin' Arab.'

Bourne laughed. He pulled the bag up, went over to a set of facing seats, opened it up. Tyrone became aware of the Arab pilot, a dark-skinned, bearded man who glowered at him, half defiant, half fearful.

'Who the fuck is this?'

'Terrorist,' Bourne said simply. He paused in unloading the bag long enough to drink in the situation. 'You want to get a taste?'

Tyrone laughed. 'Killed two of 'em was about to do for Miss Spook.'

'Now, who would that be?'

Tyrone's dark eyes flashed. 'I know yo an Deron are close, but doan fuck wid me.'

'I'm not fucking with you, Tyrone. Excuse me for this, but I'm on a deadline.' Bourne turned on one of the overhead seat lights, opened his cell, and brought up the photos he'd taken of Fadi's face. Then he set about opening small pots, jars, tubes, and various oddly shaped prosthetics. 'Would you please tell me what you're talking about?'

Tyrone hesitated for a minute, studying Bourne to see if he was still fucking with him. Apparently, he decided he'd been wrong. 'Talkin' 'bout Miss Spook. Soraya.'

Bourne, glancing at the photos of Fadi, placed several prosthetics in his mouth and worked his jaws around experimentally. 'Then I owe you a thank-you.'

'Yo, what the fuck happened to yo voice, man?'

Bourne said: 'As you can see, I'm becoming a new man.' He continued with his transformation, finding a thick beard from the pile inside the case, shaping it with a scissors so that it was the exact replica of Fadi's. He applied the beard, took a look at himself in the magnifying mirror he pulled from the case.

He handed his cell to Tyrone. 'Do me a favor, would you? How much do I look like the man in these photos?'

Tyrone blinked, as if he couldn't believe what Bourne had asked of him. Then he looked at the photos one by one. Before moving on to the next one, he studied Bourne's face.

'Fuck me,' he said finally. 'Yo, how yo do that shit, man?'

'It's a gift,' Bourne said, meaning it. 'Now, look. I need you to do me another favor.' He glanced at his watch. 'In just over eleven minutes, this bastard Soraya's been after is going to be coming here. I want you out of the way. I need you to take care of something for me. Something important. In the next cabin is my friend, Martin Lindros. He's dead. I want you to contact a mortuary. His remains need to be cremated. Okay? Will you do that for me?'

'Got my cycle, so I gots t'sling him across my lap, that okay?'

Bourne nodded. 'Treat him with respect, Tyrone, okay? Now take off. And don't use the front entrance.'

'Never do.'

Bourne laughed. 'I'll see you on the other side.'

Tyrone looked at him. 'The otha side a what?'

# 40

Driving into Virginia, Karim called Abd al-Malik at the mortuary.

'I need three men at the Sistain Labs location at once.'

'That will leave us with no one to spare.'

'Do it,' Karim said shortly.

'One moment, sir.' After a slight pause. 'They're on their way.'

'Is the DCI's body prepared?'

'Forty minutes, possibly a bit more, sir. This isn't your normal embalming job.'

'How does he look? That's what's most important.'

'Indeed, sir. His cheeks are rosy.' Abd al-Malik made a pleased sound in the back of his throat. 'Believe me, security will be convinced he's still alive.'

'Good. As soon as you're finished, get him into the limo. The timetable has been accelerated. Fadi wants the CI building taken out as soon as humanly possible. Call me when you're in position.'

'It will be done,' Abd al-Malik said.

Karim knew it would. Abd al-Malik, the most accomplished member of his sleeper cell in the district, and its leader, had never failed him.

Traffic was light. It took him thirty-eight minutes to arrive at the main entrance, on the western side of the Sistain Labs property. The place was deserted. He'd had to restrain himself twice on the drive down here – once when a kid in what the Americans called a muscle car cut him off; again when a trucker had come up behind him, sounding his air horn. Both times, he'd pulled out his Glock, was ready to pull the trigger, when he'd caught himself.

It was Bourne, not these poor fools, he wanted to kill. His rage – the Desert Wind he'd inherited from his grandfather – was running high, giving him hair-trigger responses to stimuli. But this wasn't the desert; he wasn't among Bedouins who would know better than to antagonize him.

It was Bourne; it was always Bourne. Bourne had murdered innocent Sarah, the pride of the family. Karim had forgiven her her impious views, her unexplained absences, her wanting her independence, putting those things down to the same English blood that pulsed through her veins. He'd overcome his Western blood, which was why he had embarked on a program to reeducate her in the ways of the desert, the Saudi ethos that was her true heritage.

Now Bourne had killed Fadi, the public figurehead. Fadi, who had relied so heavily on the planning and the funds of his older brother, just as Karim had counted on his younger brother to protect him. He'd forgiven Fadi his hot blood, his excesses, because these traits were vital to a public leader, who drew the faithful to him with both his fiery rhetoric and his incendiary exploits.

They were both gone now – the innocent and the commander, one the tower of moral strength, the other of physical. He, of all of Abu Sarif Hamid ibn Ashef al-Wahhib's children, remained. Alive, but alone. All that was left were the memories he held close to him of Fadi and Sarah ibn Ashef. The same memories held by his father – maimed, paralyzed, helplessly bound to his bed, needing a special harness to get into the wheelchair he despised.

This was the end for Bourne, he vowed. This was the end for all the infidels.

He made his way through the long, curving drives that skirted the low, sleek green-glass and black-brick lab buildings. A final swing around to the left brought the airfield into sight. Just beyond the parked jet was the fat gray-blue crescent of water adjacent to Occoquan Bay.

Nearing the landing strip, he slowed, took a long, careful survey of the area. The jet sat alone on the tarmac, near the far end of the runway. No vehicles were in sight. No boat plied the wintry waters of Belmont Bay. No helicopters hovered anywhere in the vicinity. Yet Fadi was dead, and Bourne sat inside the jet in his place.

Of course there wouldn't be anyone here. Unlike him, Bourne had no support to back him up. He pulled the car over out of sight of the jet, lit a cigarette, waited. Quite soon the black Ford carrying his men arrived, pulling up alongside him.

He got out and gave them their instructions, telling them what to expect and what they should do. Then he leaned against the front fender of the car, smoking still as the Ford drove onto the tarmac.

When it reached the plane, the door swung inward and the stairway was lowered. Two of the three men got out, trotted up the stairs.

Karim spat the butt from his mouth, ground it beneath the heel of his shoe. Then he climbed into the rental car and headed back along the drive to the lab building hunkered eerily alone, on the northern fringe of the property, hard against the waste dump.

I can help you, Soraya,' Peter Marks said, his cell to his ear, 'but I think we should meet.'

'Why? You have to be my eyes and ears at HQ. I need you to keep track of the impostor.'

'I don't know where Lindros is,' Peter said. 'He isn't in his office. In fact, he's nowhere in the building. He didn't check out with his assistant. Is this an epidemic?'

He heard the sharpness of Soraya's indrawn breath. 'What is it?'

'Okay,' Soraya said. 'I'll meet you, but I pick the place.'

'Whatever you want.'

She gave him the address of the mortuary on the northeast edge of Rock Creek Park. 'Get there,' she said, 'fast as you can.'

Marks checked out a CI vehicle, making the trip in record time. He pulled up across the street and down the block from the rear of the mortuary, then sat in his car as Soraya had directed. Before leaving headquarters, he'd toyed with the idea of contacting Rob Batt, of getting permission to take several agents with him, but the urgency of the meet made it imperative that he not take the time to persuade Batt to divert personnel.

Soraya tapping on the glass of the passenger window caused him to jump. He'd been so wrapped up in his thoughts that he hadn't seen her approach. This made him doubly nervous, because he was out in the field where she had the distinct advantage over him. He'd been nothing but a desk jockey his entire career – which, he supposed, was the real reason he hadn't wanted to take anyone with him. He had something to prove to his rabbi.

He unlocked the doors and she slipped into the passenger's seat. She certainly didn't look as if she'd cracked.

'I wanted you to come here,' she said a bit breathlessly, 'because this is the mortuary where the Old Man is.'

He listened to these words as if they were part of a dream he was having. He had wrapped his hand around his gun when she was opening the door and he was out of sight to her. Now, as if he himself were in a dream, he brought the gun to her head and said, 'Sorry, Soraya, but you're coming back to headquarters with me.'

The two terrorists who boarded the jet blinked in the semidarkness. They looked stunned when they recognized him.

'Fadi,' the taller of the men said. 'Where is Jason Bourne?'

'Bourne is dead,' Bourne said. 'I killed him in Miran Shah.'

'But Karim al-Jamil said he would be on board.'

Bourne held up the briefcase with the nuclear device. 'As you can see, he was mistaken. There's been a change in plan. I need to see my brother.'

'At once, Fadi.'

They didn't search the plane, didn't see the pilot Bourne had tied and gagged.

As they led Bourne to the black Ford, the tall man said, 'Your brother is nearby.'

They all got into the Ford, Bourne in the backseat with one of the men. Bourne kept his face averted from the runway lights, the only light source. As long as he kept his face in semi-shadow, he'd be fine. These men were reacting to a familiar voice, familiar body language. These were a mimic's most powerful weapons. You needed to convince the mind, not the eye.

The driver left the airfield, looped around to the north, stopped at the side of a black-brick building that stood some distance away from the others. Bourne could see the slag pit as they opened a huge corrugated-iron door and led him inside.

The interior was huge and empty. There were no interior walls. Oil stains on the concrete floor indicated that it was, in fact, an airplane hangar. Light came in through the door, as well as through square windows set high up in the walls, but it soon dissipated in the vastness, swallowed up by great swaths of shadow.

'Karim al-Jamil,' the tall man called, 'it was your brother who was on the plane, not Jason Bourne. He's with us, and he has the device.'

A figure appeared out of the shadows.

'My brother is dead,' Karim said.

Behind Bourne, the men tensed.

*

'I'm not going anywhere with you,' Soraya said.

Marks was about to reply when the wall at the back of the mortuary loading bay slid down.

'What the hell – ?' he said.

Soraya took advantage of his surprise and bolted out of the car. Marks was about to go after her when he saw the DCI's limo emerge, then head down the street away from him. He forgot all about Soraya. He put his car in gear, peeling out after the limo. The Old Man was supposed to be away on personal business. What was he doing here?

As he raced after the limo, he dimly heard Soraya shouting for him to turn back. He ignored her. Of course she'd say that; she was sure the Old Man was dead.

Up ahead, the limo stopped at a red light. He pulled up alongside it, scrolled down his window.

'Hey!' he called. 'Peter Marks, CI! Open up!'

The driver's window remained in place. Marks put the car in park, got out, pounded on the window.

He pulled out his ID. 'Open up, dammit! Open up!'

The window slid down. He caught an instant's glimpse of the Old Man sitting bolt upright in the back. Then the driver aimed a Luger P-08 at his face and pulled the trigger.

The detonation burst his eardrums. He flew backward, arms outstretched, dead before he hit the pavement.

The limo's window slid back up and, as the light turned green, it rolled swiftly down the street.

Karim stood staring intently at Bourne. 'It can't be. Brother, I was told you were dead.'

Bourne raised the briefcase. 'And yet,' he said in Fadi's voice, 'I come in the guise of destruction.'

'Let the infidel beware!'

'Truly.' Even though Bourne knew he was looking at Karim, it was unnerving to face this man who was a dead ringer for his best friend. 'We're together again, brother!'

Martin had warned him that Karim was the dangerous one. *He's the chess player,* Martin had said, *the spider sitting at the center of the web.* Bourne held no illusions. The moment Karim asked him an intimate question, one only his brother would know, the masquerade would be over.

It didn't take that long.

Karim beckoned. 'Come into the light, brother, that I may once more look upon you after so many months.'

Bourne took a step forward; light flooded his face.

Karim stood stock-still. His head rocked a little, as if he had developed a palsy. 'You're as much a chameleon as Fadi was.'

'Brother, I've brought the device. How could you mistake me?'

'I overheard a CI agent say – '

'Not Peter Marks.' Bourne took a shot because it was all he had left. Marks was the only one in CI Soraya had contacted.

Confused again, Karim frowned. 'What about him?'

'Marks is Soraya Moore's conduit. He's repeating the disinformation we fed her.'

Karim gave a wolfish grin; the doubt cleared from his eyes. 'Wrong answer. CI believes my brother was killed in the raid on the false Dujja facility in South Yemen. But you wouldn't have known that, Bourne, would you?'

He gave a sign and the three men behind Bourne grabbed him, then held his arms at his sides. Without taking his eyes from Bourne's, Karim stepped forward, wrenched the briefcase out of his hand.

Soraya was running to where Peter Marks lay dead, spread-eagled on the curb, when she heard the deep-throated roar of a motorcycle approaching from behind. Pulling her gun, she swung around and saw Tyrone on his Ninja. He had just dropped Lindros's corpse at the mortuary.

Slowing, he allowed her to climb aboard, then took off.

'You saw what happened. They killed Peter.'

'We gotta stop them.' Tyrone jumped a red light. 'You put alla pieces t'gether – C-Four explosive, a replica of yo boss's limo, yo boss hisself lyin' flat-out on a embalming table, whattaya got?'

'That's how they're going to get in!' Soraya said. 'Security will take one look at the Old Man in the backseat and wave the limo through into the underground parking lot.'

'Where the foundation of the building is.'

Tyrone, bending low over the Ninja's handlebars, put on a burst of speed.

'We can't shoot at the limo,' Soraya said, 'without running the risk of setting off the C-Four and killing who knows how many bystanders.'

'An we can't allow it t'get to CI headquarters,' Tyrone said. 'So what d'we do?'

The answer was provided for them as one of the limo's rear windows slid down and someone began firing at them.

Bourne stood without trying to move. He tried to clear his mind of the image of Martin Lindros's ruined face, but in fact he found he didn't want to. Martin was with him, speaking to him, demanding retribution for what had been done to him. Bourne felt him; Bourne heard him.

*Patience,* he whispered silently.

Centering himself, he felt where each of the three men was in relation to himself. Then he said: 'My one regret is that I never finished what I started in Odessa. Your father is still alive.'

'Only you would call that kind of existence living,' Karim snapped. 'Every time I'm in his presence, I vow anew that I'll make you pay for what you did to him.'

'Too bad he can't see you as you are today,' Bourne said. 'He'd take a gun and shoot you himself. If only he was able.'

'I understand you, Bourne, better than you think.' Karim stood barely a pace away from Bourne. 'Look at you. To everyone but ourselves you're Fadi and I'm Lindros. We're in our own separate world, locked in our circle of revenge. Isn't that what you're thinking? Isn't that how you planned it? Isn't that why you've made yourself up to look like my brother?'

He shifted the briefcase from one hand to the other. 'It's also why you're trying to bait me. An angry man is easier to defeat, isn't that how the Tao of Bourne goes?' He laughed. 'But in fact, with this last chameleon act of yours you've done me an incalculable service. You think I'm going to shoot you dead, here and now. How wrong you are! Because after I detonate the nuclear device, after I destroy CI head-quarters, I'm going to take you back to whatever is left of CI. I'll shoot you there. And so, having killed Fadi, the world's most notorious terrorist, Martin Lindros will become a national hero. And now that I've killed the DCI, who do you think a grateful president will elevate to the post?'

He laughed again. 'I'll be running the agency, Bourne. I'll be able to remake it in my own image. How's that for irony?'

At the mention of the fate of CI headquarters, Bourne felt Martin's voice stir-ring inside him. *Not yet,* he thought. *Not yet.*

'What I find ironic,' he said, 'is what happened to Sarah ibn Ashef.'

Fire leapt into Karim's eyes. He backhanded Bourne across the face. 'You who murdered her are not fit to speak my sister's name!'

'I didn't murder her,' Bourne said slowly and distinctly.

Karim spat in Bourne's face.

'I couldn't have shot her. Both Soraya and I were too far away. We both were using Glock 21s. Sarah ibn Ashef was all the way across the plaza when she was shot dead. As you well know, the Glock is accurate up to twenty-five meters. Your sister was at least fifty meters away when she was killed. I didn't realize it at the time; everything happened too quickly.'

His face a taut mask, Karim struck Bourne again.

Bourne, having expected the blow, shook it off. 'Muta ibn Aziz refreshed my memory, however. He and his brother were in the right position that night. They were at the right distance.'

Karim grabbed Bourne by the throat. 'You dare to make a mockery of my sis-ter's death?' He was fairly shaking with rage. 'The brothers were like family. To even insinuate – '

'It's precisely because they *were* like family that Abbud ibn Aziz shot your sister to death.'

'I'll kill you for that!' Karim screamed as he began to strangle Bourne. 'I'll make you wish you'd never been born!'

Tyrone zigzagged the Ninja through the streets, following the limo. He could hear the bullets whizzing past them. He knew what it was like to be shot at; he knew the agony of having a loved one shot dead in a drive-by. His only defense was study. He knew bullets the way his crew knew gangsta rappers or porn stars. He knew the characteristics of every caliber, every Parabellum, every hollow-point. His own Walther PPK was loaded with hollow-cavity bullets – like hollow-points on steroids. When they impacted with a soft target – human flesh, for instance – they expanded to the point of disintegration. The target felt like he had been hit by an M-80. Needless to say, the internal damage was extreme.

The man was shooting .45s at them, but his range was limited, his accuracy low. Still, Tyrone knew he needed to find a way to stop the shooting altogether.

'Look up ahead,' Soraya urgently said into his ear. 'See that black-glass building six blocks away? That's CI headquarters.'

Putting on another burst of speed, Tyrone brought the Ninja up very fast on the limo's left flank. This brought them within range of the Luger, but the distance was also of benefit to him.

Drawing her ASP pistol, Soraya aimed and fired in one motion. The hollow-core struck the terrorist full in the face. There was an explosion of blood and bone out the open window.

'They killed Sarah ibn Ashef and covered up their complicity,' Bourne managed to get out. 'They did it to protect you and Fadi. Because sweet, innocent Sarah ibn Ashef was carrying on a torrid love affair.'

'Liar!'

Bourne was having trouble breathing, but he had to keep talking. He'd known going into this that psychology was his best weapon against a man like Karim, the only one that might bring him victory. 'She hated what you and Fadi had become. She made her decision. She turned her back on her Bedouin heritage.'

He saw something explode onto Karim's face.

'Shut up!' Karim cried. 'These are the foulest of lies! Of course they are!'

But Bourne could sense that he was unsuccessfully trying to convince himself. He had finally put all the pieces of Sarah's death together, and it was killing him.

'My sister was the moral core of my family! The core you destroyed! Her murder set my brother and me on this course. You brought this death and destruction on yourself!'

Bourne was already on the move. He stepped backward and planted his heel hard onto the instep of the man directly behind him. As he did so, he twisted his torso, breaking the hold of the man on his right. Burying a cocked elbow into the solar plexus of the man on his left, he struck outward with the edge of his other hand, slashing it into the side of the third man's neck.

He heard the crack as the vertebrae fractured. The man went down. By this time the man directly behind him had thrown his arms around Bourne, gripping him tight. Bourne bent double, sending the man head over heels into Karim.

The man on his left was still bent over, trying to catch his breath. Scooping up a Luger that had fallen to the floor, Bourne slammed the butt into the crown of his head. The man he'd sent tumbling into Karim had drawn his gun. Bourne shot him and he collapsed in a heap.

That left Karim. He was on his knees, the attaché case directly in front of him. His eyes were red with a kind of madness that sent a shiver down Bourne's spine. Once or twice before, Bourne had seen a man teetering on the edge of madness, and he knew that Karim was capable of anything.

As he was thinking of this, Karim produced a small stainless-steel square. Bourne recognized it instantly as a remote detonator.

Karim held the device aloft, his thumb pressed against a black button. 'I know you, Bourne. And knowing you, I own you. You won't shoot me, not while I can detonate twenty kilos of C-Four in the parking ramp under CI headquarters.'

There was no time for thought, no time for second guesses. Bourne heard Martin's ghostly whisper in his mind. He pointed the Luger and shot Karim in the throat. The bullet passed through the soft tissue, then severed the spinal column.

In near-paralyzing pain, Karim sat down hard. He stared at Bourne, disbelieving. He tried to work his fingers, but they wouldn't respond.

His eyes, the light in them fading, found the knuckles of one of his downed men. Bourne, understanding what was about to happen, lunged toward him, but with one last effort, Karim toppled over.

The detonator slammed against the bared knuckles.

At last, Bourne was able to let Karim go. At last, Martin's voice in his head was silent. Bourne stared down at Karim's right eye – Martin's eye – and thought about his dead friend. Soon enough he'd send a dozen red roses to Moira, soon enough he'd take Martin's ashes to the Cloisters in New York.

One thing lingered in his mind, like an angler's unbaited hook. When he had the chance, why hadn't Karim tried to detonate the nuke? Why the limo, which would have a far more limited effect?

He turned, saw the attaché case lying on the concrete floor. The snaps were open. Had Karim done that in the vain hope of engaging the timer? He crouched down, about to close the snaps, when a chill passed through him, the force of it making his teeth chatter.

He opened the case. Peering inside, he searched for the timer, seeing that it was indeed inactive. The LED was dark, the wires disconnected. Then what . . . ?

Probing beneath the nest of wires, he looked closer and saw something that injected the chill into his bones. A secondary timer had been activated when Karim had popped the snaps. A secondary timer that Veintrop had installed, but deliberately never told them about.

Bourne sat back on his haunches, beads of sweat rolling down his spine. It looked as if Dujja – and the doctor – were going to get their revenge after all.

# 41

Four minutes and one second. That was the amount of time Bourne had left, according to the readout of the secondary timer.

He closed his eyes, conjured up an image of Veintrop's hands working on the timer. He could see every move the doctor had made, every twist of the wrist, every curl of a finger. He'd needed no tools. There were six wires: red, white, black, yellow, blue, green.

Bourne remembered where they had been attached to the primary timer and in what order Veintrop had disconnected them. Twice, Veintrop had reattached the black wire – first to the terminal on which the end of the white one had been wound, then on the terminal for the red.

Remembering what Veintrop had done wasn't Bourne's problem. Though he saw that the secondary timer, like the primary, was powered by another set of six color-coded wires, the two were physically different. As a consequence, none of the terminals to which the wires were attached was in the same place.

Pulling out his cell, Bourne called Feyd al-Saoud's number in the hope that he could get Veintrop to tell him the truth about deactivating the secondary timer. There was no answer. Bourne wasn't surprised. Miran Shah, mountainous as it was, was a disaster for cell service. Still, it had been worth a try.

3:01.

Veintrop had started with the blue wire, then the green. Bourne's fingertips gripped the blue wire, about to unwind it from its terminal. Still, he hesitated. Why, he asked himself, would the secondary timer deactivate in the same way? Veintrop had designed this ingenious trap. The secondary timer would come into play only if the primary had been disabled. Therefore, it would make no sense to design it to be disabled in the same way.

Bourne lifted his hands free of the secondary timer.

2:01.

The question here was not how to deactivate the timer; it was how Veintrop's fiendish mind worked. If the primary had been disabled, it would mean that someone had known the right order in which to detach the wires. In the secondary, the order in which the wires needed to be detached could be reversed, or even scrambled in so many possible combinations it would be virtually impossible to stumble upon the right one before inadvertently detonating the nuclear device.

1:19.

The time for speculation had passed. He had to make a decision, and it had to be the right one. He decided to reverse the order; he grasped the red wire, about to

661

unwind it when his keen eye spotted something. He leaned in closer, studying the secondary timer in a different way. Pushing aside the nest of colored wires, he discovered that the timer was attached to the main part of the device in a wholly different way than was the primary.

:49.

Bourne tipped the primary out of its niche, the better to see what was underneath. Then he pulled it free of the detonator, to which it was attached by a single wire. Now he saw the secondary timer unimpeded. It was resting directly against the detonator. The trouble was, he couldn't see where the two were attached.

:27.

He moved the wires away, careful not to detach any of them. Using a fingernail, he lifted the right edge of the secondary timer up and away from the detonator. Nothing.

:18.

He slipped his nail beneath the left edge. It wouldn't budge. He applied more pressure and slowly, up it came. There, beneath, he saw the wire, coiled like a tiny snake. His finger touched it, moved it slightly, and like a snake, it uncoiled. He couldn't believe his eyes.

The wire wasn't attached to the detonator!

:10.

He heard the voice of Dr. Veintrop. '*I was a prisoner,*' he'd said. '*You don't understand, I . . .*' Bourne hadn't allowed him to finish his thought. Again, the problem was to solve the riddle of Veintrop's mind. He was a man who enjoyed playing mind games – his research proved as much. If Fadi had held him against his will, if Fadi had used Katya against him, Veintrop would have tried to gain a measure of vengeance against him.

Bourne took up the primary, checked the wire dangling from it. The insulation was intact, but the bare copper core at the end felt loose. It came away in his fingers, no more than a couple of centimeters in length. The wire was a fake. He removed his hands from the device, sat back, watched the timer face count down its final seconds. His heart beat painfully against the cage of his chest. If he was wrong . . .

:00.

But he wasn't wrong. Nothing happened. There was no detonation, no nuclear holocaust. There was only silence. Veintrop had gained his revenge against his captors. Under Fadi's nose, he'd secretly disarmed the device.

Bourne began to laugh. Veintrop had been made to accurately rig the primary trigger, but with the backup he'd somehow cleverly fooled Fadi and Dujja's other scientists. He closed the attaché case, took it as he rose. He laughed all the way out of the building.

# 42

In the aftermath of the C-4 explosion, Soraya invoked the power of her CI credentials. The surrounding buildings, thick, hulking government edifices, had sustained superficial damage, but nothing structural. The street, however, was a disaster. An enormous hole had been blown out of it, into which the incinerated remains of the limo had dropped like a flaming meteor. The one saving grace was that at this time of the evening, there were no pedestrians in the general vicinity.

Dozens of police cars, fire engines, ambulances, and various emergency and utility agency personnel were swarming over the area, which had been cordoned off. Power was out in a two-and-a-half-square-kilometer radius, and the immediate area was without water, as the mains were ruptured.

Soraya and Tyrone had given statements to the police, but already she saw Rob Batt and Bill Hunter, chief of the Security Directorate, on the scene, taking over. Batt saw her and gave her a *sit tight* nod as he spoke to the police captain nominally in charge of the scene.

'All this official shit make me nervous as a priest wid the clap,' Tyrone said.

Soraya laughed. 'Don't worry. I'm here to protect you.'

Tyrone gave a snort of derision, but she saw that he stayed close to her. With the din of workers moving equipment, shouting to one another, vehicles pulling up, they seemed to be engulfed in a web of sound.

Above them, a news helicopter hovered. Soon it was joined by another. With a roar, air force jets, scrambled and weapons loaded, did a flyby. Their wingtips waggled, then they were gone into the clear blue sky.

New York was fogbound the morning Bourne arrived at the gates of the Cloisters. He passed through, holding the bronze urn containing Martin Lindros's remains close against his chest. He'd sent the dozen roses to Moira, then discovered when she'd called him that they were a silent good-bye from Martin to her.

He'd never met Moira. Martin had only mentioned her once, when he and Bourne had gotten very, very drunk.

Bourne saw her now, a slim, shapely figure in the mist, dark hair swirled about her face. She was standing where she said she would be, in front of the tree that had been trained to spread against the stone blocks of a building wall. She had been overseas on business; had arrived home, she said, only hours before Bourne's call. She had, it seemed, done her weeping in private.

Dry-eyed, she nodded to him, and together they walked to the south parapet. Below them were trees. Off to the right, he could see the flat surface of the

Hudson River. It looked dull and sluggish, as if it were the skin of a serpent about to be shed.

'We each knew him in different ways.' Moira said this carefully, as if fearful of giving away too much of what she and Martin had had together.

Bourne said, 'If you can know anyone at all.'

The flesh around her eyes was puffy. No doubt she had spent the last several days crying. Her face was strong, sharp-featured, her deep brown eyes wide apart and intelligent. There was an uncommon serenity about her, as if she was a woman content with herself. She would have been good for Martin, Bourne thought.

He opened the top of the urn. Inside was a plastic bag filled with carbon dust, the stuff of life. Moira used her long, slender fingers to open the bag. Together they lifted the urn over the top of the parapet, tipped it, watched as the gray matter floated out, became one with the mist.

Moira stared into the indistinct shapes below them. 'What matters is we both loved him.'

Bourne supposed that was the perfect eulogy, one that brought a kind of peace to all three of them.

# The Bourne Sanction

For Dan and Linda Jariabka,
with thanks and love.

My thanks to:
The intrepid reporters at *The Exile*.
Bourne's adventures in Moscow
and Arkadin's history in Nizhny Tagil
would not have existed without their help.

Gregg Winter for turning me on to the logistics of transporting LNG.

Henry Morrison for clutch ideating at all hours.

A note to my readers:
I try to be as factual as possible in my novels,
but this is, after all, a work of fiction.
In order to make the story as exciting as possible,
I've inevitably taken artistic license
here and there, with places, objects, and,
possibly, even time.
I trust readers will overlook these small anomalies
and enjoy the ride.

# Prologue

While the four inmates waited for Borya Maks to appear, they lounged against filthy stone walls whose cold no longer affected them. Out in the prison yard where they smoked expensive black-market cigarettes made from harsh black Turkish tobacco, they talked among themselves as if they had nothing better to do than to suck the acrid smoke into their lungs, expel it in puffs that seemed to harden in the freezing air. Above their heads was a cloudless sky whose glittering starlight turned it into a depthless enamel shell. Ursa Major, Lynx, Canes Venatici, Perseus – these same constellations burned the heavens above Moscow, six hundred miles to the southwest, but how different life was here from the gaudy, overheated clubs of Trehgorny val and Sadovnicheskaya street.

By day the inmates of Colony 13 manufactured parts for the T-90, Russia's formidable battle tank. But at night what do men without conscience or emotion talk to one another about? Strangely, family. There was a stability to coming home to a wife and children that defined their previous lives like the massive walls of High Security Colony 13 defined their present ones. What they did to earn money – lie, cheat, steal, extort, blackmail, torture, and kill – was all they knew. That they did these things well was a given, otherwise they would have been dead. Theirs was a life outside civilization as most people knew it. Returning to the warmth of a familiar woman, to the homey smells of sweet beets, boiled cabbage, stewed meat, the fire of peppery vodka, was a comfort that made them all nostalgic. The nostalgia bound them as securely as the tattoos of their shadowy profession.

A soft whistle cut through the frosty night air, evaporated their reminiscences like turpentine on oil paint. The night lost all its imagined color, returned to blue and black as Borya Maks appeared. Maks was a big man – a man who lifted weights for an hour, followed by ninety minutes of skipping rope every single day he'd been inside. As a contract killer for Kazanskaya, a branch of the Russian *grupperovka* trafficking in drugs and black-market cars, he held a certain status among the fifteen hundred inmates of Colony 13. The guards feared and despised him. His reputation preceded him like a shadow at sunset. He was not unlike the eye of a hurricane, around which swirled the howling winds of violence and death. The latest being the fifth man in the group that was now four. Kazanskaya or no Kazanskaya, Maks had to be punished, otherwise all of them knew their days in Colony 13 were numbered.

They smiled at Maks. One of them offered him a cigarette, another lit it for him as he bent forward, cupping a hand to keep the tiny flame alive in the wind. The other two men each grabbed one of Maks's steel-banded arms, while the man who had offered the cigarette drove a makeshift knife he'd painstakingly honed in the prison factory toward Maks's solar plexus. At the last instant Maks slapped it away with a superbly attuned flick of his hand. Immediately the man with the burned match delivered a vicious uppercut to the point of Maks's chin.

Maks staggered back into the chests of the two men holding his arms. But at the same time, he stomped the heel of his left boot onto the instep of one of the men holding him. Shaking his left arm free, he swung his body in a sharp arc, driving his cocked elbow into the rib cage of the man holding his right arm. Free for the moment, he put his back against the wall deep in shadow. The four closed ranks, moving in for the kill. The one with the knife stepped to the fore, another slipped a curved scrap of metal over his knuckles.

The fight began in earnest with grunts of pain and effort, showers of sweat, smears of blood. Maks was powerful and canny; his reputation was well deserved, but though he delivered as good as he got, he was facing four determined enemies. When Maks drove one to his knees another would take his place, so that there were always two of them beating at him while the others regrouped and repaired themselves as best they could. The four had had no illusions about the task ahead of them. They knew they'd never overcome Maks at the first or even the second attack. Their plan was to wear him down in shifts; while they took breaks, they allowed him none.

And it appeared to be working. Bloody and bruised, they continued their relentless assault, until Maks drove the edge of his hand into the throat of one of the four – the one with the homemade knife – crushing his cricoid cartilage. As the man staggered back into the arms of his compatriots, gasping like a hooked fish, Maks grabbed the knife out of his hand. Then his eyes rolled up and he became a deadweight. Blinded by rage and bloodlust, the remaining three charged Maks.

Their rush almost succeeded in getting inside Maks's defenses, but he dealt with them calmly and efficiently. Muscles popped along his arms as he turned, presenting his left side to them, giving them a smaller target, even as he used the knife in short, flicking thrusts and stabs to inflict a picket line of wounds that, though not deep, produced a welter of blood. This was deliberate, Maks's counter to their tactic of trying to wear him out. Fatigue was one thing, loss of blood quite another.

One of his assailants lunged forward, slipped on his own blood, and Maks hammered him down. This created an opening, and the one with the makeshift knuckle-duster moved in, slamming the metal into the side of Maks's neck. Maks at once lost breath and strength. The remaining men beat an unholy tattoo on him and were on the verge of plowing him under when a guard emerged out of the murk to drive them methodically back with a solid wood truncheon whose force was far more devastating than any piece of scrap metal could be.

A shoulder separated, then cracked under the expertly wielded truncheon; another man had the side of his skull staved in. The third, turning to flee, was struck flush on his third sacral vertebra, which shattered on impact, breaking his back.

'What are you doing?' Maks said to the guard between attempts to regain control of his breathing. 'I assumed these bastards bribed all the guards.'

'They did.' The guard grabbed Maks's elbow. 'This way,' he indicated with the glistening end of the truncheon.

Maks's eyes narrowed. 'That's not the way back to the cells.'

'Do you want to get out of here or not?' the guard said.

Maks nodded his conditional assent, and the two men loped across the deserted yard. The guard kept his body pressed against the wall, and Maks followed suit. They moved at a deliberate pace, he saw, that kept them out of the beams of the roving spotlights. He would have wondered who this guard was, but there was no time. Besides, in the back of his mind he'd been expecting something like this. He knew his boss, the head of the Kazanskaya, wasn't going to let him rot in Colony 13 for the rest of his life, if only because he was too valuable an asset to let rot. Who could possibly replace the great Borya Maks? Only one, perhaps: Leonid Arkadin. But Arkadin – whoever he was; no one Maks knew had ever met him or seen his face – wouldn't work for Kazanskaya, or any of the families; he was a freelancer, the last of a dying breed. If he existed at all, which, frankly, Maks doubted. He'd grown up with stories of bogeymen with all manner of unbelievable powers – for some perverse reason Russians delighted in trying to scare their children. But the fact was, Maks never believed in bogeymen, was never scared. He had no reason to be scared of the specter of Leonid Arkadin, either.

By this time the guard had pulled open a door midway along the wall. They ducked in just as a searchlight beam crawled across the stones against which, moments before, they had been pressed.

After several turnings, he found himself in the corridor that led to the communal men's shower, beyond which, he knew, was one of the two entries to the wing of the prison. How this guard meant to get them through the checkpoints was anyone's guess, but Maks wasted no energy trying to second-guess him. Up to now he'd known just what to do and how to do it. Why should this be any different? The man was clearly a professional. He'd researched the prison thoroughly, he obviously had major juice behind him: first, to have gotten in here, second, to have the apparent run of the place. That was Maks's boss all over.

As they moved down the corridor toward the opening to the showers, Maks said, 'Who are you?'

'My name is unimportant,' the guard said. 'Who sent me is not.'

Maks absorbed everything in the unnatural stillness of the prison night. The guard's Russian was flawless, but to Maks's practiced eye he didn't look Russian, or Georgian, Chechen, Ukrainian, or Azerbaijani, for that matter. He was small by Maks's standards, but then almost everyone was small by his standards. His body was toned, though, its responses finely honed. He possessed the preternatural stillness of properly harnessed energy. He made no move unless he needed to and then used only the amount of energy required, no more. Maks himself was like this, so it was easy for him to spot the subtle signs others would miss. The guard's eyes were pale, his expression grim, almost detached, like a surgeon in the OR. His light hair thick on top, spiked in a style that would have been unfamiliar to Maks had he not been an aficionado of international magazines and foreign films. In fact, if Maks didn't know better he'd say the guard was American. But that was impossible. Maks's boss didn't employ Americans; he co-opted them.

'So Maslov sent you,' Maks said. Dimitri Maslov was the head of Kazanskaya.

'It's about fucking time, let me tell you. Fifteen months in this place feels like fifteen years.'

At that moment, as they came abreast of the showers, the guard, without turning fully around, swung the truncheon into the side of Maks's head. Maks, taken completely by surprise, staggered onto the bare concrete floor of the shower room, which reeked of mildew, disinfectant, and men lacking proper hygiene.

The guard came after him as nonchalantly as if he were out for the evening with a girl on his arm. He swung the truncheon almost lazily. He struck Maks on his left biceps, just hard enough to herd him backward toward the line of showerheads protruding from the moist rear wall. But Maks refused to be herded, by this guard or by anyone else. As the truncheon whistled down from the apex of its arc, he stepped forward, broke the trajectory of the blow with his tensed forearm. Now, inside the guard's line of defense, he could go to work in the way that suited the situation best.

The homemade knife was in his left hand. He thrust it point-first. When the guard moved to block it, he slashed upward, ripping the edge of the blade against flesh. He'd aimed for the underside of the guard's wrist, the nexus of veins that, if severed, would render the hand useless. The guard's reflexes were as fast as his own, though, and instead the blade scored the arm of the leather jacket. But it did not penetrate the leather as it should have. Maks only had time to register that the jacket must be lined with Kevlar or some other impenetrable material before the callused edge of the guard's hand struck the knife from his grip.

Another blow sent him reeling back. He tripped over one of the drain holes, his heel sinking into it, and the guard smashed the sole of his boot into the side of Maks's knee. There was an awful sound, the grinding of bone against bone as Maks's right leg collapsed.

As the guard closed in he said, 'It wasn't Dimitri Maslov who sent me. It was Pyotr Zilber.'

Maks struggled to extricate his heel, which he could no longer feel, from the drain hole. 'I don't know who you're talking about.'

The guard grabbed his shirtfront. 'You killed his brother, Aleksei. One shot to the back of the head. They found him facedown in the Moskva River.'

'It was business,' Maks said. 'Just business.'

'Yes, well, this is personal,' the guard said as he drove his knee into Maks's crotch.

Maks doubled over. When the guard bent to haul him upright, he slammed the top of his head against the point of the guard's chin. Blood spurted from between the guard's lips as his teeth cut into his tongue.

Maks used this advantage to drive his fist into the guard's side just over his kidney. The guard's eyes opened wide – the only indication that he felt pain – and he kicked Maks's ruined knee. Maks went down and stayed down. Agony flowed in a river through him. As he struggled to compartmentalize it, the guard kicked again. He felt his ribs give way, his cheek kissed the stinking concrete floor. He lay dazed, unable to rise.

The guard squatted down beside him. Seeing the grimace the guard made gave Maks a measure of satisfaction, but that was all he was destined to receive in the way of solace.

'I have money,' Maks gasped weakly. 'It's buried in a safe place where no one will find it. If you get me out of here, I'll lead you to it. You can have half. That's over half a million American dollars.'

This only made the guard angry. He struck Maks hard on his ear, making sparks fly behind his eyes. His head rang with a pain that in anyone else would have been unendurable. 'Do you think I'm like you? That I have no loyalty?' He spat into Maks's face.

'Poor Maks, you made a grave error killing this boy. People like Pyotr Zilber never forget. And they have the means to move heaven and earth to get what they want.'

'All right,' Maks whispered, 'you can have it all. More than a million dollars.'

'Pyotr Zilber wants you dead, Maks. I came here to tell you that. And to kill you.' His expression changed subtly. 'But first.'

He extended Maks's left arm, trod on the wrist, pinning it securely against the rough concrete. He then produced a pair of thick-bladed pruning shears.

This procedure roused Maks from his pain-induced lethargy. 'What are you doing?'

The guard grasped Maks's thumb, on the back of which was a tattoo of a skull, mirroring the larger one on his chest. It was a symbol of Maks's exalted status in his murderous profession.

'Besides wanting you to know the identity of the man who ordered your death, Pyotr Zilber requires proof of your demise, Maks.'

The guard settled the shears at the base of Maks's thumb, then he squeezed the handles together. Maks made a gurgling sound, not unlike that of a baby.

As a butcher would, the guard wrapped the thumb in a square of waxed paper, snapped a rubber band around it, then sealed it in a plastic bag.

'Who are you?' Maks managed to get out.

'My name is Arkadin,' the guard said. He opened his shirt, revealing a pair of candlestick tattoos on his chest. 'Or, in your case, Death.'

With a movement full of grace Arkadin broke Maks's neck.

Crisp Alpine sunlight lit up Campione d'Italia, a tiny exquisite Italian enclave of two-thirds of a square mile nestled within the clockwork-perfect setting of Switzerland. Owing to its prime position on the eastern edge of Lake Lugano, it was both stupendously picturesque and an excellent place to be domiciled. Like Monaco, it was a tax haven for wealthy individuals who owned magnificent villas and gambled away idle hours at the Casino di Campione. Money and valuables could be stored in Swiss banks, with their justly famous reputation for discreet service, completely shielded from international law enforcement's prying eyes.

It was this little-known, idyllic setting that Pyotr Zilber chose for the first face-to-face meeting with Leonid Arkadin. He had contacted Arkadin through an intermediary, for various security reasons opting not to contact the contract killer directly. From an early age Pyotr had learned that there was no such thing as being too security-minded. There was a heavy burden of responsibility being born into a family with secrets.

From his lofty perch on the overlook just off Via Totone, Pyotr had a breathtaking panorama of the red-brown tile roofs of the chalets and apartment houses, the palm-lined squares of the town, the cerulean waters of the lake, the mountains, their shoulders mantled with capes of mist. The distant drone of powerboats, leaving frothy scimitars of white wake, came to him intermittently while he sat in his gray BMW. In truth, part of his mind was already on his imminent trip. Having gotten the stolen document, he had sent it on the long journey along his network to its ultimate end.

Being here excited him in the most extraordinary way. His anticipation of what was to come, of the accolades he would receive, especially from his father, sent an electric charge through him. He was on the brink of an unimaginable victory. Arkadin had called him from the Moscow airport to tell him that the operation had been successful, that he had in his possession the physical proof Pyotr required.

He had taken a risk going after Maks, but the man had murdered Pyotr's brother. Was he supposed to turn his cheek and forget the affront? He knew better than anyone his father's stern dictum to keep to the shadows, to remain hidden, but he thought this one act of vengeance was worth the risk. Besides, he'd handled the matter via intermediaries, the way he knew his father would have.

Hearing the deep growl of a car engine, he turned, saw a dark blue Mercedes come up the rise toward the overlook.

The only real risk he was taking was going to happen right now, and that, he knew, couldn't be helped. If Leonid Arkadin was able to infiltrate Colony 13 in Nizhny Tagil and kill Borya Maks, he was the man for the next job Pyotr had in mind. One his father should have taken care of years ago. Now he had a chance to finish what his father was too timid to attempt. To the bold belonged the spoils. The document he'd procured was proof positive that the time for caution was at an end.

The Mercedes drew to a stop beside his BMW, a man with light hair and even lighter eyes emerging with the fluidity of a tiger. He was not a particularly large man, he wasn't overmuscled like many of the Russian *grupperovka* personnel; nevertheless something inside him radiated a quiet menace Pyotr found impressive. From a very young age Pyotr had been exposed to dangerous men. At the age of eleven he had killed a man who had threatened his mother. He hadn't hesitated in the slightest. If he had, his mother would have died that afternoon in the Azerbaijani bazaar at the hands of the knife-wielding assassin. That assassin, as well as others over the years, had been sent by Semion Icoupov, Pyotr's father's implacable nemesis, the man who at this moment was safely ensconced in his villa on Viale Marco Campione, not a mile from where Pyotr and Leonid Arkadin now stood.

The two men did not greet each other, did not address each other by name. Arkadin took out the stainless-steel briefcase Pyotr had sent him. Pyotr reached for its twin inside the BMW. The exchange was made on the hood of the Mercedes. The men put the cases down side by side, unlocked them. Arkadin's contained Maks's severed thumb, wrapped and bagged. Pyotr's contained thirty thousand dollars in diamonds, the only currency Arkadin accepted as payment.

Arkadin waited patiently. As Pyotr unwrapped the thumb he stared out at the lake, perhaps wishing he were on one of the powerboats slicing a path away from land. Maks's thumb had withered slightly on the journey from Russia. A certain odor emanated from it, which was not unfamiliar to Pyotr Zilber. He'd buried his share of family and compatriots. He turned so the sunlight struck the tattoo, produced a small magnifying glass through which he peered at the marking.

At length, he put the glass away. 'Did he prove difficult?'

Arkadin turned back to face him. For a moment he stared implacably into Pyotr's eyes. 'Not especially.'

Pyotr nodded. He threw the thumb over the side of the overlook, tossed the empty case after it. Arkadin, taking this to be the conclusion of their deal, reached for the packet filled with diamonds. Opening it, he took out a jeweler's loupe, plucked a diamond at random, examined it with an expert's aplomb.

When he nodded, satisfied as to the clarity and color, Pyotr said, 'How would you like to make three times what I paid you for this assignment?'

'I'm a very busy man,' Arkadin said, revealing nothing.

Pyotr inclined his head deferentially. 'I have no doubt.'

'I only take assignments that interest me.'

'Would Semion Icoupov interest you?'

Arkadin stood very still. Two sports cars passed, heading up the road as if it were Le Mans. In the echo of their throaty exhausts, Arkadin said, 'How convenient that we happen to be in the tiny principality where Semion Icoupov lives.'

'You see?' Pyotr grinned. 'I know precisely how busy you are.'

'Two hundred thousand,' Arkadin said. 'The usual terms.'

Pyotr, who had anticipated Arkadin's fee, nodded his agreement. 'Conditional on immediate delivery.'

'Agreed.'

Pyotr popped the trunk of the BMW. Inside were two more cases. From one, he transferred a hundred thousand in diamonds to the case on the Mercedes's hood. From the other, he handed Arkadin a packet of documents, including a satellite map, indicating the precise location of Icoupov's villa, a list of his bodyguards, and a set of architectural blueprints of the villa, including the electrical circuits, the separate power supply, and details of the security devices in place.

'Icoupov is in residence now,' Pyotr said. 'How you make your way inside is up to you.'

'I'll be in touch.' After paging through the documents, asking a question here and there, Arkadin placed them in the case on top of the diamonds, snapped the lid shut, slung the case into the passenger's seat of the Mercedes as easily as if it were filled with balloons.

'Tomorrow, same time, right here,' Pyotr said as Arkadin slid behind the wheel.

The Mercedes started up, its engine purring. Then Arkadin put it in gear. As he slid out onto the road, Pyotr turned to walk to the front of the BMW. He heard the squeal of brakes, the slewing of a car, and turned to see the Mercedes heading directly toward him. He was paralyzed for a moment. *What the hell is he doing?* he asked himself. Belatedly, he began to run. But the Mercedes was already on top of him, its front grille slammed into him, pinned him to the side of the BMW.

Through a haze of agony he saw Arkadin get out of his car, walk toward him. Then something gave out inside him and he passed into oblivion.

He regained consciousness in a paneled study, gleaming with polished brass fixtures, lush with jewel-toned Isfahan carpets. A walnut desk and chair were within his field of vision, as was an enormous window that looked out on the sparkling water of Lake Lugano and the veiled mountains behind it. The sun was low in the west, sending long shadows the color of a fresh bruise over the water, up the white-washed walls of Campione d'Italia.

He was bound to a plain wooden chair that seemed to be as out of place in the surroundings of wealth and power as he was. He tried to take a deep breath, winced with shocking pain. Looking down, he saw bandages wrapped tightly around his chest, realized that he must have at least one cracked rib.

'At last you have returned from the land of the dead. For a while there you had me worried.'

It was painful for Pyotr to turn his head. Every muscle in his body felt as if it were on fire. But his curiosity would not be denied, so he bit his lip, kept turning his head until a man came into view. He was rather small, stoop-shouldered. Glasses with round lenses were fitted over large, watery eyes. His bronzed scalp, lined and furrowed as pastureland, was without a single hair, but as if to make up for his bald pate his eyebrows were astonishingly thick, arching up over the skin above his eye sockets. He looked like one of those wily Turkish traders from the Levant.

'Semion Icoupov,' Pyotr said. He coughed. His mouth felt stiff, as if it were stuffed with cotton. He could taste the salt-copper of his own blood, and swallowed heavily.

Icoupov could have moved so that Pyotr didn't have to twist his neck so far in order to keep him in view, but he didn't. Instead he dropped his gaze to the sheet of heavy paper he'd unrolled. 'You know, these architectural plans of my villa are so complete I'm learning things about the building I never knew before. For instance, there is a sub-basement below the cellar.' He ran his stubby forefinger along the surface of the plan. 'I suppose it would take some doing to break into it now, but who knows, it might prove worthwhile.'

His head snapped up and he fixed Pyotr with his gaze. 'For instance, it would make a perfect place for your incarceration. I'd be assured that not even my closest neighbor would hear you scream.' He smiled, a cue for a terrible focusing of his energies. 'And you *will* scream, Pyotr, this I promise you.' His head swiveled, the beacons of his eyes searching out someone else. 'Won't he, Leonid?'

Now Arkadin came into Pyotr's field of view. At once he grabbed Pyotr's head with one hand, dug into the hinge of his jaw with the other. Pyotr had no choice but to open his mouth. Arkadin checked his teeth one by one. Pyotr knew that he was looking for a false tooth filled with liquid cyanide. A death pill.

'All his,' Arkadin said as he let go of Pyotr.

'I'm curious,' Icoupov said. 'How in the world did you procure these plans, Pyotr?'

Pyotr, waiting for the proverbial shoe to drop, said nothing. But all at once he began to shiver so violently his teeth chattered.

Icoupov signaled to Arkadin, who swaddled Pyotr's upper body in a thick blanket. Icoupov brought a carved cherry chair to a position facing Pyotr, sat down on it.

He continued just as if he hadn't expected an answer. 'I must admit that shows a fair amount of initiative on your part. So the clever boy has grown into a clever young man.' Icoupov shrugged. 'I'm hardly surprised. But listen to me now, I know who you really are – did you think you could fool me by continually changing your name? The truth of the matter is you've prodded open a wasps' nest, so *you* shouldn't be surprised to get stung. And stung and stung and stung.'

He inclined his upper body toward Pyotr. 'However much your father and I despise each other, we grew up together; once we were as close as brothers. So. Out of respect for him, I won't lie to you, Pyotr. This bold foray of yours won't end well. In fact, it was doomed from the start. And d'you want to know why? You needn't answer; of course you do. Your earthly needs betrayed you, Pyotr. That delicious girl you've been bedding for the past six months belongs to me. I know you're thinking that's not possible. I know you vetted her thoroughly; that's your MO. I anticipated all your inquiries; I made certain you received the answers you needed to hear.'

Pyotr, staring into Icoupov's face, found his teeth chattering again, no matter how tightly he clamped his jaw.

'Tea, please, Philippe,' Icoupov said to an unseen person. Moments later, a slender young man set an English silver tea service onto a low table at Icoupov's right hand. Like a favorite uncle, Icoupov went about pouring and sugaring the tea. He put the porcelain cup to Pyotr's bluish lips, said, 'Please drink, Pyotr. It's for your own good.'

Pyotr stared implacably at him until Icoupov said, 'Ah, yes, I see.' He sipped the tea from the cup himself to assure Pyotr it was only tea, then offered it again. The rim chattered against Pyotr's teeth, but eventually Pyotr drank, slowly at first, then more avidly. When the tea was drained, Icoupov set the cup back on its matching saucer. By this time Pyotr's shivering had subsided.

'Feeling better?'

'I'll feel better,' Pyotr said, 'when I get out of here.'

'Ah, well, I'm afraid that won't be for some time,' Icoupov said. 'If ever. Unless you tell me what I want to know.'

He hitched his chair closer; the benign uncle's expression was now nowhere to be found. 'You stole something that belongs to me,' he said. 'I want it back.'

'It never belonged to you; you stole it first.'

Pyotr replied with such venom that Icoupov said, 'You hate me as much as you love your father, this is your basic problem, Pyotr. You never learned that hate and love are essentially the same in that the person who loves is as easily manipulated as the person who hates.'

Pyotr screwed up his mouth, as if Icoupov's words left a bitter taste in his mouth. 'Anyway, it's too late. The document is already on its way.'

Instantly, there was a change in Icoupov's demeanor. His face became as closed as a fist. A certain tension lent his entire small body the aspect of a weapon about to be launched. 'Where did you send it?'

Pyotr shrugged, but said nothing more.

Icoupov's face turned dark with momentary rage. 'Do you think I know nothing about the information and matériel pipeline you have been refining for the past three years? It's how you send information you stole from me back to your father, wherever he is.'

For the first time since he'd regained consciousness, Pyotr smiled. 'If you knew anything important about the pipeline, you'd have rolled it up by now.'

At this Icoupov regained the icy control over his emotions.

'I told you talking to him would be useless,' Arkadin said from his position directly behind Pyotr's chair.

'Nevertheless,' Icoupov said, 'there are certain protocols that must be acknowledged. I'm not an animal.'

Pyotr snorted.

Icoupov eyed his prisoner. Sitting back, he fastidiously pulled up his trouser leg, crossed one leg over the other, laced his stubby fingers on his lower belly.

'I give you one last chance to continue this conversation.'

It was not until the silence was drawn out into an almost intolerable length that Icoupov raised his gaze to Arkadin.

'Pyotr, why are you doing this to me?' he said with a resigned tone. And then to Arkadin, 'Begin.'

Though it cost him in pain and breath, Pyotr twisted as far as he was able, but he couldn't see what Arkadin was doing. He heard the sound of implements on a metal cart being rolled across the carpet.

Pyotr turned back. 'You don't frighten me.'

'I don't mean to frighten you, Pyotr,' Icoupov said. 'I mean to hurt you, very, very badly.'

With a painful convulsion, Pyotr's world contracted to the pinpoint of a star in the night sky. He was locked within the confines of his mind, but despite all his training, all his courage, he could not compartmentalize the pain. There was a hood over his head, drawn tight around his neck. This confinement magnified the pain a hundredfold because, despite his fearlessness, Pyotr was subject to claustrophobia. For someone who never went into caves, small spaces, or even underwater, the hood was the worst of all possible worlds. His senses could tell him that, in fact, he wasn't confined at all, but his mind wouldn't accept that input – it was in the full flight of panic. The pain Arkadin was inflicting on him was one thing, its magnification was quite another. Pyotr's mind was spinning out of control. He felt a wildness enter him – the wolf caught in a trap that begins to frantically gnaw its leg off. But the mind was not a limb; he couldn't gnaw it off.

Dimly, he heard someone asking him a question to which he knew the answer. He didn't want to give the answer, but he knew he would because the voice told him the hood would come off if he answered. His crazed mind only knew it needed the hood off; it could no longer distinguish right from wrong, good from evil, lies from truth. It reacted to only one imperative: the need to survive. He tried to move his fingers, but in bending over him his interrogator must have been pressing down on them with the heels of his hands.

Pyotr couldn't hang on any longer. He answered the question.

The hood didn't come off. He howled in indignation and terror. *Of course it didn't come off*, he thought in a tiny instant of lucidity. If it did, he'd have no incentive to answer the next question and the next and the next.

And he would answer them – all of them. He knew this with a bone-chilling certainty. Even though part of him suspected that the hood might never come off, his trapped mind would take the chance. It had no other choice.

But now that he could move his fingers, there was another choice. Just before the whirlwind of panicked madness overtook him again, Pyotr made that choice. There was one way out and, saying a silent prayer to Allah, he took it.

\*

Icoupov and Arkadin stood over Pyotr's body. Pyotr's head lay on one side; his lips were very blue, and a faint but distinct foam emanated from his half-open mouth. Icoupov bent down, sniffed the scent of bitter almonds.

'I didn't want him dead, Leonid, I was very clear on the point.' Icoupov was vexed. 'How did he get hold of cyanide?'

'They used a variation I've never encountered.' Arkadin did not look happy himself. 'He was fitted with a false fingernail.'

'He would have talked.'

'Of course he would have talked,' Arkadin said. 'He'd already begun.'

'So he took it upon himself to shut his own mouth, forever.' Icoupov shook his head in distaste. 'This will have significant fallout. He's got dangerous friends.'

'I'll find them,' Arkadin said. 'I'll kill them.'

Icoupov shook his head. 'Even you can't kill them all in time.'

'I can contact Mischa.'

'And risk losing everything? No. I understand your connection with him – closest friend, mentor. I understand the urge to talk to him, to see him. But you can't, not until this is finished and Mischa comes home. That's final.'

'I understand.'

Icoupov walked over to the window, stood with his hand behind his back contemplating the fall of darkness. Lights sparkled along the edges of the lake, up the hillside of Campione d'Italia. There ensued a long silence while he contemplated the face of the altered landscape. 'We'll have to move up the timetable, that's all there is to it. And you'll take Sevastopol as a starting point. Use the one name you got out of Pyotr before he committed suicide.'

He turned around to face Arkadin. 'Everything now rides on you, Leonid. This attack has been in the planning stages for three years. It has been designed to cripple the American economy. Now there are barely two weeks left before it becomes a reality.' He walked noiselessly across the carpet. 'Philippe will provide you with money, documents, weaponry that will escape electronic detection, anything you need. Find this man in Sevastopol. Retrieve the document, and when you do, follow the pipeline back and shut it down so that it will never again be used to threaten our plans.'

# Book 1

# 1

'Who is David Webb?'

Moira Trevor, standing in front of his desk at Georgetown University, asked the question so seriously that Jason Bourne felt obliged to answer.

'Strange,' he said, 'no one's ever asked me that before. David Webb is a linguistics expert, a man with two children who are living happily with their grandparents' – Marie's parents – 'on a ranch in Canada.'

Moira frowned. 'Don't you miss them?'

'I miss them terribly,' Bourne said, 'but the truth is they're far better off where they are. What kind of life could I offer them? And then there's the constant danger from my Bourne identity. Marie was kidnapped and threatened in order to force me to do something I had no intention of doing. I won't make that mistake again.'

'But surely you see them from time to time.'

'As often as I can, but it's difficult. I can't afford to have anyone following me back to them.'

'My heart goes out to you,' Moira said, meaning it. She smiled. 'I must say it's odd seeing you here, on a university campus, behind a desk.' She laughed. 'Shall I buy you a pipe and a jacket with elbow patches?'

Bourne smiled. 'I'm content here, Moira. Really I am.'

'I'm happy for you. Martin's death was difficult for both of us. My anodyne is going back to work full-bore. Yours is obviously here, in a new life.'

'An old life, really.' Bourne looked around the office. 'Marie was happiest when I was teaching, when she could count on me being home every night in time to have dinner with her and the kids.'

'What about you?' Moira asked. 'Were you happiest here?'

A cloud passed across Bourne's face. 'I was happy being with Marie.' He turned to her. 'I can't imagine being able to say that to anyone else but you.'

'A rare compliment from you, Jason.'

'Are my compliments so rare?'

'Like Martin, you're a master at keeping secrets,' she said. 'But I have doubts about how healthy that is.'

'I'm sure it's not healthy at all,' Bourne said. 'But it's the life we chose.'

'Speaking of which.' She sat down on a chair opposite him. 'I came early for our dinner date to talk to you about a work situation, but now, seeing how content you are here, I don't know whether to continue.'

Bourne recalled the first time he had seen her, a slim, shapely figure in the mist, dark hair swirling about her face. She was standing at the parapet in the Cloisters, overlooking the Hudson River. The two of them had come there to say good-bye to their mutual friend Martin Lindros, whom Bourne had valiantly tried to save, only to fail.

Today Moira was dressed in a wool suit, a silk blouse open at the throat. Her face was strong, with a prominent nose, deep brown eyes wide apart, intelligent, curved slightly at their outer corners. Her hair fell to her shoulders in luxuriant waves. There was an uncommon serenity about her, a woman who knew what she was about, who wouldn't be intimidated or bullied by anyone, woman or man.

Perhaps this last was what Bourne liked best about her. In that, though in no other way, she was like Marie. He had never pried into her relationship with Martin, but he assumed it had been romantic, since Martin had given Bourne standing orders to send her a dozen red roses should he ever die. This Bourne had done, with a sadness whose depth surprised even him.

Settled in her chair, one long, shapely leg crossed over her knee, she looked the model of a European businesswoman. She had told him that she was half French, half English, but her genes still carried the imprint of ancient Venetian and Turkish ancestors. She was proud of the fire in her mixed blood, the result of wars, invasions, fierce love.

'Go on.' He leaned forward, elbows on his desk. 'I want to hear what you have to say.'

She nodded. 'All right. As I've told you, NextGen Energy Solutions has completed our new liquid natural gas terminal in Long Beach. Our first shipment is due in two weeks. I had this idea, which now seems utterly crazy, but here goes. I'd like you to head up the security procedures. My bosses are worried the terminal would make an awfully tempting target for any terrorist group, and I agree. Frankly, I can't think of anyone who'd make it more secure than you.'

'I'm flattered, Moira. But I have obligations here. As you know, Professor Specter has installed me as the head of the Comparative Linguistics Department. I don't want to disappoint him.'

'I like Dominic Specter, Jason, really I do. You've made it clear that he's your mentor. Actually, he's David Webb's mentor, right? But it's Jason Bourne I first met, it feels like it's Jason Bourne I've been coming to know these last few months. Who is Jason Bourne's mentor?'

Bourne's face darkened, as it had at the mention of Marie. 'Alex Conklin's dead.'

Moira shifted in her chair. 'If you come work with me there's no baggage attached to it. Think about it. It's a chance to leave your past lives behind – both David Webb's and Jason Bourne's. I'm flying to Munich shortly because a key element of the terminal is being manufactured there. I need an expert opinion on it when I check the specs.'

'Moira, there are any number of experts you can use.'

'But none whose opinion I trust as much as yours. This is crucial stuff, Jason. More than half the goods shipped into the United States come through the port at Long Beach, so our security measures have to be something special. The US government has already shown it has neither the time nor the inclination to secure commercial traffic, so we're forced to police it ourselves. The danger to this terminal is real and it's serious. I know how expert you are at bypassing even the most arcane security systems. You're the perfect candidate to put nonconventional measures into place.'

Bourne stood. 'Moira, listen to me. Marie was David Webb's biggest cheerleader. Since her death, I've let go of him completely. But he's not dead, he's not an invalid. He lives on inside me. When I fall asleep I dream of his life as if it was someone else's, and I wake up in a sweat. I feel as if a part of me has been sliced off. I don't want to feel that way anymore. It's time to give David Webb his due.'

Veronica Hart's step was light and virtually carefree as she was admitted past checkpoint after checkpoint on her way into the bunker that was the West Wing of the White House. The job she was about to be handed – director of Central Intelligence – was a formidable one, especially in the aftermath of last year's twin debacles of murder and gross breach of security. Nevertheless, she had never been happier. Having a sense of purpose was vital to her; being singled out for daunting responsibility was the ultimate validation of all the arduous work, setbacks, and threats she'd had to endure because of her gender.

There was also the matter of her age. At forty-six she was the youngest DCI in recent memory. Being the youngest at something was nothing new to her. Her astonishing intelligence combined with her fierce determination to ensure that she was the youngest to graduate from her college, youngest to be appointed to military intelligence, to central army command, to a highly lucrative Black River private intelligence position in Afghanistan and the Horn of Africa where, to this day, not even the heads of the seven directorates within CI knew precisely where she had been posted, whom she commanded, or what her mission had been.

Now, at last, she was steps away from the apex, the top of the intelligence heap. She'd successfully leapt all the hurdles, sidestepped every trap, negotiated every maze, learned who to befriend and who to show her back to. She had endured relentless sexual innuendo, rumors of conduct unbecoming, stories of her reliance on her male inferiors who supposedly did her thinking for her. In each case she had triumphed, emphatically putting a stake through the heart of the lies and, in some instances, taking down their instigators.

She was, at this stage of her life, a force to be reckoned with, a fact in which she justifiably reveled. So it was with a light heart that she approached her meeting with the president. In her briefcase was a thick file detailing the changes she proposed to make in CI to clean up the unholy mess left behind by Karim al-Jamil and the subsequent murder of her predecessor. Not surprisingly, CI was in total disarray, morale had never been lower, and of course there was resentment across the board from the all-male directorate heads, each of whom felt he should have been elevated to DCI.

The chaos and low morale were about to change, and she had a raft of initiatives to ensure it. She was absolutely certain that the president would be delighted not only with her plans but also with the speed with which she would implement them. An intelligence organization as important and vital as CI could not long endure the despair into which it had sunk. Only the anti-terrorist black ops, Typhon, brainchild of Martin Lindros, was running normally, and for that she had its new director, Soraya Moore, to thank. Soraya's assumption of command had been seamless. Her operatives loved her, would follow her into the fires of Hades should she ask it of them. As for the rest of CI, it was for herself to heal, energize, and give a refocused sense of purpose.

She was surprised – perhaps *shocked* wasn't too strong a word – to find the Oval Office occupied not only by the president but also by Luther LaValle, the Pentagon's intelligence czar, and his deputy, General Richard P. Kendall. Ignoring the others, she walked across the plush American blue carpet to shake the president's hand. She was tall, long-necked, and slender. Her ash-blond hair was cut in a stylish fashion that fell short of being masculine but lent her a business-like air. She wore a midnight-blue suit, low-heeled pumps, small gold earrings, and a minimum of makeup. Her nails were cut square across.

'Please have a seat, Veronica,' the president said. 'You know Luther LaValle and General Kendall.'

'Yes.' Veronica inclined her head fractionally. 'Gentlemen, a pleasure to see you.' Though nothing could be farther from the truth.

She hated LaValle. In many ways he was the most dangerous man in American intelligence, not the least because he was backed by the immensely powerful E. R. 'Bud' Halliday, the secretary of defense. LaValle was a power-hungry egotist who believed that he and his people should be running American intelligence, period. He fed on war the way other people fed on meat and potatoes. And though she had never been able to prove it, she suspected that he was behind several of the more lurid rumors that had circulated about her. He enjoyed ruining other people's reputations, savored standing impudently on the skulls of his enemies.

Ever since Afghanistan and, subsequently, Iraq, LaValle had seized the initiative – under the typically wide-ranging and murky Pentagon rubric of 'preparing the battlefield' for the troops to come – to expand the purview of the Pentagon's intelligence-gathering initiatives until now they encroached uncomfortably on those of CI. It was an open secret within American intelligence circles that he coveted CI's operatives and its long-established international networks. Now, with the Old Man and his anointed successor dead, it would fit LaValle's MO to try to make a land grab in the most aggressive manner possible. This was why his presence and that of his lapdog set off the most serious warning bells inside Veronica's mind.

There were three chairs ranged in a rough semicircle in front of the president's desk. Two of them were, of course, filled. Veronica took the third chair, acutely aware that she was flanked by the two men, doubtless by design. She laughed inwardly. If these two thought to intimidate her by making her feel surrounded, they were sorely mistaken. But then as the president began to talk she hoped to God her laugh wouldn't echo hollowly in her mind an hour from now.

Dominic Specter hurried around the corner as Bourne was locking the door to his office. The deep frown that creased his high forehead vanished the moment he saw Bourne.

'David, I'm so glad I caught you before you left!' he said with great enthusiasm. Then, turning his charm on Bourne's companion, he added, 'And with the magnificent Moira, no less.' As always the perfect gentleman, he bowed to her in the Old World European fashion.

He returned his attention to Bourne. He was a short man full of unbridled energy despite his seventy-odd years. His head seemed perfectly round, surmounted by a halo of hair that wound from ear to ear. His eyes were dark and inquisitive, his skin a deep bronze. His generous mouth made him look vaguely and amusingly like a frog about to spring from one lily pad to another. 'A matter of some concern has come up and I need your opinion.' He smiled. 'I see that this evening is out of the question. Would dinner tomorrow be inconvenient?'

Bourne discerned something behind Specter's smile that gave him pause; something was troubling his old mentor. 'Why don't we meet for breakfast?'

'Are you certain I'm not putting you out, David?' But he couldn't hide the relief that flooded his face.

'Actually, breakfast is better for me,' Bourne lied, to make things easier for Specter. 'Eight o'clock?'

'Splendid! I look forward to it.' With a nod in Moira's direction he was off.

'A firecracker,' Moira said. 'If only I'd had professors like him.'

Bourne looked at her. 'Your college years must've been hell.'

She laughed. 'Not quite as bad as all that, but then I only had two years of it before I fled to Berlin.'

'If you'd had professors like Dominic Specter, your experience would have been far different, believe me.' They sidestepped several knots of students gathered to gossip or to trade questions about their last classes.

They strode along the corridor, out the doors, descended the steps to the quad. He and Moira walked briskly across campus in the direction of the restaurant where they would have dinner. Students streamed past them, hurrying down the paths between trees and lawns. Somewhere a band was playing in the stolid, almost plodding rhythm endemic to colleges and universities. The sky was steeped in clouds, scudding overhead like clipper ships on the high seas. A dank winter wind came streaming in off the Potomac.

'There was a time when I was plunged deep in depression. I knew it but I wouldn't accept it – you know what I mean. Professor Specter was the one who connected with me, who was able to crack the shell I was using to protect myself. To this day I have no idea how he did it or even why he persevered. He said he saw something of himself in me. In any event, he wanted to help.'

They passed the ivy-covered building where Specter, who was now the president of the School of International Studies at Georgetown, had his office. Men in tweed coats and corduroy jackets passed in and out of the doors, frowns of deep concentration on their faces.

'Professor Specter gave me a job teaching linguistics. It was like a life preserver to a drowning man. What I needed most then was a sense of order and stability. I honestly don't know what would have happened to me if not for him. He alone understood that immersing myself in language makes me happy. No matter who I've been, the one constant is my proficiency with languages. Learning languages is like learning history from the inside out. It encompasses the battles of ethnicity, religion, compromise, politics. So much can be learned from language because it's been shaped by history.'

By this time they had left campus and were walking down 36th Street, NW, toward 1789, a favorite restaurant of Moira's, which was housed in a Federal town house. When they arrived, they were shown to a window table on the second floor in a dim, paneled, old-fashioned room with candles burning brightly on tables set with fine china and sparkling stemware. They sat down facing each other and ordered drinks.

Bourne leaned across the table, said in a low voice, 'Listen to me, Moira, because I'm going to tell you something very few people know. The Bourne identity continues to haunt me. Marie used to worry that the decisions I was forced to make, the actions I had to take as Jason Bourne would eventually drain me of all feeling, that one day I'd come back to her and David Webb would be gone for good. I can't let that happen.'

'Jason, you and I have spent quite a bit of time with each other since we met to scatter Martin's ashes. I've never seen a hint that you've lost any part of your humanity.'

Both sat back, silent as the waiter set the drinks in front of them, handed them menus. As soon as he left, Bourne said, 'That's reassuring, believe me. In the short time I've known you I've come to value your opinions. You're not like anyone else I've ever met.'

Moira took a sip of her drink, set it down, all without taking her eyes from his. 'Thank you. Coming from you that's quite a compliment, particularly because I know how special Marie was to you.'

Bourne stared down at his drink.

Moira reached across the starched white linen for his hand. 'I'm sorry, now you're drifting away.'

He glanced at her hand over his but didn't pull away. When he looked up, he said, 'I relied on her for many things. But I find now that those things are slipping away from me.'

'Is that a bad thing, or a good thing?'

'That's just it,' he said. 'I don't know.'

Moira saw the anguish in his face, and her heart went out to him. It was only months ago that she'd seen him standing by the parapet in the Cloisters. He was clutching the bronze urn holding Martin's ashes as if he never wanted to let it go. She'd known then, even if Martin hadn't told her, what they'd meant to each other.

'Martin was your friend,' she said now. 'You put yourself in terrible jeopardy to save him. Don't tell me you didn't feel anything for him. Besides, by your own admission, you're not Jason Bourne now. You're David Webb.'

He smiled. 'You have me there.'

Her face clouded over. 'I want to ask you a question, but I don't know whether I have the right.'

At once, he responded to the seriousness of her expression. 'Of course you can ask, Moira. Go on.'

She took a deep breath, let it go. 'Jason, I know you've said that you're content at the university, and if that's so, fine. But I also know you blame yourself for not being able to save Martin. You must understand, though, if you couldn't save him, no one could. You did your best; he knew that, I'm sure. And now I find myself wondering if you believe you failed him – that you're not up to being Jason Bourne anymore. I wonder if you've ever considered the idea that you accepted Professor Specter's offer at the university in order to turn away from Jason Bourne's life.'

'Of course I've considered it.' After Martin's death he'd once again decided to turn his back on Jason Bourne's life, on the running, the deaths, a river that seemed to have as many bodies as the Ganges. Always, for him, memories lurked. The sad ones he remembered. The others, the shadowed ones that filled the halls of his mind, seemed to have shape until he neared them, when they flowed away like a tide at ebb. And what was left behind were the bleached bones of all those he'd killed or had been killed because of who he was. But he knew just as surely that as long as he drew breath, the Bourne identity wouldn't die.

There was a tormented look in his eyes. 'You have to understand how difficult it is having two personalities, always at war with each other. I wish with every fiber of my being that I could cut one of them out of me.'

Moira said, 'Which one would it be?'

'That's the damnable part,' Bourne said. 'Every time I think I know, I realize that I don't.'

# 2

Luther LaValle was as telegenic as the president and two-thirds his age. He had straw-colored hair slicked back like a movie idol of the 1930s or 1940s and restless hands. By contrast, General Kendall was square-jawed and beady-eyed, the very essence of a ramrod officer. He was big and beefy; perhaps he'd been a fullback at Wisconsin or Ohio State. He looked to LaValle the way a running back looks to his quarterback for instructions.

'Luther,' the president said, 'seeing as how you requested this meeting I think it appropriate that you begin.'

LaValle nodded, as if the president deferring to him was a fait accompli. 'After the recent debacle of CI being infiltrated at its highest level, culminating with the murder of the former DCI, firmer security and controls need to be set in place. Only the Pentagon can do that.'

Veronica felt compelled to jump in before LaValle got too much of a head start. 'I beg to differ, sir,' she said, aiming her remarks at the president. 'Human intelligence gathering has always been the province of CI. Our on-the-ground networks are unparalleled, as are our armies of contacts, who have been cultivated for decades. The Pentagon's expertise has always been in electronic surveillance. The two are separate, requiring altogether different methodologies and mind-sets.'

LaValle smiled as winningly as he did when appearing on Fox TV or *Larry King Live*. 'I'd be remiss if I didn't point out that the landscape of intelligence has changed radically since 2001. We're at war. In my opinion this state of affairs is likely to last indefinitely, which is why the Pentagon has recently expanded its field of expertise, creating teams of clandestine DIA personnel and special-ops forces who are conducting successful counterintelligence ops in Iraq and Afghanistan.'

'With all due respect, Mr. LaValle and his military machine are eager to fill any perceived vacuum or create one, if necessary. Mr. LaValle and General Kendall need us to believe that we're in a perpetual state of war whether or not it's the truth.' From her briefcase Veronica produced a file, which she opened and read from. 'As this evidence makes clear, they have systematically directed the expansion of their human intelligence-gathering squads, outside of Afghanistan and Iraq, into other territories – CI's territories – often with disastrous results. They've corrupted informers and, in at least one instance, they've jeopardized an ongoing CI deep-cover operation.'

After the president glanced at the pages Veronica handed him, he said, 'While this is compelling, Veronica, Congress seems to be on Luther's side. It has provided him with twenty-five million dollars a year to pay informants on the ground and to recruit mercenaries.'

'That's part of the problem, not the solution,' Veronica said emphatically. 'Theirs is a failed methodology, the same one they've used all the way back to the OSS in Berlin after World War Two. Our paid informants have had a history of turning on us – working for the other side, feeding us disinformation. As for the mercenaries we recruited – like the Taliban or various other Muslim insurgent groups – they, to a man, eventually turned against us to become our implacable enemies.'

'She's got a point,' the president said.

'The past is the past,' General Kendall said angrily. His face had been darkening with every word Veronica had said. 'There's no evidence whatsoever that either our new informants or our mercenaries, both of which are vital to our victory in the Middle East, would ever turn on us. On the contrary, the intel they've provided has been of great help to our men on the field of battle.'

'Mercenaries, by definition, owe their allegiance to whoever pays them the most,' Veronica said. 'Centuries of history from Roman times forward have proved this point over and over.'

'All this back-and-forth is of little moment.' LaValle shifted in his seat uncomfortably. Clearly he hadn't counted on such a spirited defense. Kendall handed him a dossier, which he presented to the president. 'General Kendall and I have spent the better part of two weeks putting together this proposal for how to restructure CI going forward. The Pentagon is prepared to implement this plan the moment we get your approval, Mr. President.'

To Veronica's horror, the president looked over the proposal, then turned it over to her. 'What do you say to this?'

Veronica felt suffused with rage. She was already being undermined. On the other hand, she observed, this was a good object lesson for her. Trust no one, not even seeming allies. Up until this moment she'd thought she had the full support of the president. The fact that LaValle, who was, after all, basically the mouthpiece for Defense Secretary Halliday, had the muscle to call this meeting shouldn't have surprised her. But that the president was asking her to consider a takeover from the Pentagon was outrageous and, quite frankly, frightening.

Without even glancing at the toxic papers, she squared her shoulders. 'Sir, this proposal is irrelevant, at best. I resent Mr. LaValle's flagrant attempt to expand his intelligence empire at CI's expense. For one thing, as I've detailed, the Pentagon is ill suited to direct, let alone win the trust of our vast array of agents in the field. For another, this coup would set a dangerous precedent for the entire intelligence community. Being under the control of the armed forces will not benefit our intelligence-gathering potential. On the contrary, the Pentagon's history of flagrant disregard for human life, its legacy of illegal operations combined with well-documented fiscal profligacy, makes it an extremely poor candidate to poach on anyone else's territory, especially CI's.'

Only the presence of the president forced LaValle to keep his ire in check. 'Sir, CI is in total disarray. It needs to be turned around ASAP. As I said, our plan can be implemented today.'

Veronica drew out the thick file detailing her plans for CI. She rose, placed it in the president's hands. 'Sir, I feel duty-bound to reiterate one of the main points of our last discussion. Though I've served in the military, I come from the private sector. CI is in need not only of a clean sweep but of a fresh perspective untainted by the monolithic thinking that got us into this insupportable situation in the first place.'

Jason Bourne smiled. 'To be honest, tonight I don't know who I am.' He leaned forward and said very softly, 'Listen to me. I want you to take your cell phone out of your handbag without anyone seeing. I want you to call me. Can you do that?'

Moira kept her eyes on his as she found her cell in her handbag, hit the appropriate speed-dial key. His cell phone chimed. He sat back, answered the call. He spoke into the phone as if someone was on the other end of the line. Then he closed the phone, said, 'I have to go. It's an emergency. I'm sorry.'

She continued to stare at him. 'Could you act even the least bit upset?' she whispered.

His mouth turned down.

'Do you really have to go?' she said in a normal tone of voice. 'Now?'

'Now.' Bourne threw some bills on the table. 'I'll be in touch.'

She nodded a bit quizzically, wondering what he'd seen or heard.

Bourne went down the stairs and out of the restaurant. Immediately he turned right, walked a quarter block, then entered a store selling handmade ceramics. Positioning himself so that he had a view of the street through the plate-glass window, he pretended to look at bowls and serving dishes.

Outside, people passed by – a young couple, an elderly man with a cane, three young women, laughing. But the man who'd been seated in the back corner of their room precisely ninety seconds after they sat down did not appear. Bourne had marked him the moment he'd come in, and when he'd asked for a table in back facing them, he'd had no doubt: Someone was following him. All of a sudden he'd felt that old anxiety that had roiled him when Marie and Martin had been threatened. He'd lost Martin, he wasn't about to lose Moira as well.

Bourne, whose interior radar had swept the second-floor dining room every few minutes or so, hadn't picked up anyone else of a suspicious nature, so he waited now inside the ceramics shop for the tail to amble by. When this didn't occur after five minutes, Bourne went out the door and immediately strode across the street. Using streetlights and the reflective surfaces of windows and car mirrors, he spent another few minutes scrutinizing the area for any sign of the man at the table in back. After ascertaining he was nowhere to be found, Bourne returned to the restaurant.

He went up the stairs to the second floor, but paused in the dark hallway between the staircase and the dining room. There was the man at his rear table. To any casual observer he seemed to be reading the current issue of *The Washingtonian*, like any good tourist, but every once in a while his gaze flicked upward for a fraction of a second, focused on Moira.

Bourne felt a little chill go through him. This man wasn't following him; he was following Moira.

As Veronica Hart emerged through the outermost checkpoint to the West Wing, Luther LaValle emerged from the shadows, fell into step beside her.

691

'Nicely done,' he said icily. 'Next time I'll be better prepared.'

'There won't be a next time,' Veronica said.

'Secretary Halliday is confident there will be. So am I.'

They had reached the hushed vestibule with its dome and columns. Busy presidential aides strode purposefully past them in either direction. Like surgeons, they exuded an air of supreme confidence and exclusivity, as if theirs was a club you desperately wanted to belong to, but never would.

'Where's your personal pit bull?' Veronica asked. 'Sniffing out crotches, I shouldn't wonder.'

'You're terribly flip for someone whose job is hanging by a thread.'

'It's foolish – not to mention dangerous, Mr. LaValle – to confuse confidence with being flip.'

They pushed through the doors, went down the steps to the grounds proper. Floodlights pushed back the darkness to the edges of the premises. Beyond, streetlights glittered.

'Of course, you're right,' LaValle said. 'I apologize.'

Veronica eyed him with no little skepticism.

LaValle gave her a small smile. 'I sincerely regret that we've gotten off on the wrong foot.'

*What he really regrets,* Veronica thought, *is my pulling him and Kendall to pieces in front of the president. Understandable, really.*

As she buttoned her coat, he said, 'Perhaps both of us have been coming at this situation from the wrong angle.'

Veronica knotted her scarf at her throat outside her collar. 'What situation?'

'The collapse of CI.'

In the near distance, beyond the flotilla of heavy reinforced concrete anti-terrorist barriers, tourists strolled by, chatting animatedly, paused briefly to take snapshots, then went on to their dinners at McDonald's or Burger King.

'It seems to me that more can be gained by us joining forces than by being antagonists.'

Veronica turned to him. 'Listen, buddy, you take care of your shop and I'll take care of mine. I've been given a job to do and I'm going to do it without interference from you or Secretary Halliday. Personally, I'm sick and tired of you people extending the line in the sand farther and farther so your empire can grow bigger. CI is off limits to you now and forever, got it?'

LaValle made a face as if he were about to whistle. Then he said, very quietly, 'I'd be a bit more careful if I were you. You're walking across a knife-edge. One false step, one hesitation, and when you fall no one's going to be there to catch you.'

Her voice turned steely. 'I've had my fill of your threats, too, Mr. LaValle.'

He turned up his collar against the wind. 'When you get to know me better, Veronica, you'll realize I don't make threats. I make predictions.'

# 3

The violence of the Black Sea fit Leonid Arkadin down to his steel-tipped shoes. In a tumultuous rain, he drove into Sevastopol from Belbek Aerodrome. Sevastopol inhabited a coveted bit of territory on the southwestern edge of the Crimean peninsula of Ukraine. Because the area was blessed with subtropical weather, its seas never froze. From the time of its founding by Greek traders as Chersonesus in 422 BC, Sevastopol was a vital commercial and military outpost for fishing fleets and naval armadas alike. Following the decline of Chersonesus – 'peninsula,' in Greek – the area fell into ruin until the modern-day Sevastopol was founded in 1783 as a naval base and fortress on the southern boundaries of the Russian Empire. Most of the city's history was linked to its military glory – the name *Sevastopol* translated from Greek means 'august, glorious.' The name seemed justified: The city survived two bloody sieges during the Crimean War of 1854–1855 and World War Two, when it withstood Axis bombing for 250 days. Although the city was destroyed on two different occasions, it had risen from the ashes both times. As a result, the inhabitants were tough, no-nonsense people. They despised the Cold War era, dating to roughly 1960 when, because of its naval base, the USSR ordered Sevastopol off limits to visitors of all kinds. In 1997 the Russians agreed to return the city to the Ukrainians, who opened it again.

It was late afternoon when Arkadin arrived on Primorskiy Boulevard. The sky was black, except for a thin red line along the western horizon. The port bulged with round-hulled fishing ships and sleek steel-hulled naval vessels. An angry sea lashed the *Monument to Scuttled Ships,* commemorating the 1855 last-ditch defense of the city against the combined forces of the British, French, Turks, and Sardinians. It rose from a bed of rough granite blocks in a Corinthian column three yards high, crowned by an eagle with wings spread wide, its proud head bent, a laurel wreath gripped in its beak. Facing it, embedded in the thick seawall, were the anchors of the Russian ships that were deliberately sunk to block the harbor from the invading enemy.

Arkadin checked into the Hotel Oblast where everything, including the walls, seemed to be made of paper. The furniture was covered in fabric of hideous patterns whose colors clashed like enemies on a battlefield. The place seemed a likely candidate to go up like a torch. He made a mental note not to smoke in bed.

Downstairs, in the space that passed for a lobby, he asked the rodent-like clerk for a recommendation for a hot meal, then requested a telephone book. Taking it, he retired to an understuffed upholstered chair by a window that overlooked Admiral Nakhimov Square. And there he was on a magnificent plinth, the hero of

693

the first defense of Sevastopol, staring stonily at Arkadin, as if aware of what was to come. This was a city, like so many in the former Soviet Union, filled with monuments to the past.

With a last glance at slope-shouldered pedestrians hurrying through the driving rain, Arkadin turned his attention to the phone book. The name that Pyotr Zilber had given up just before he'd committed suicide was Oleg Shumenko. Arkadin dearly would have loved to have gotten more out of Zilber. Now Arkadin had to page through the phone book looking for Shumenko, assuming the man had a landline, which was always problematic outside Moscow or St. Petersburg. He made note of the five Oleg Shumenkos listed, handed the book back to the clerk, and went out into the windy false dusk.

The first three Oleg Shumenkos were of no help. Arkadin, posing as a close friend of Pyotr Zilber's, told each of them that he had a message from Pyotr so urgent it had to be transmitted in person. They looked at him blankly, shook their heads. He could see in their eyes they had no idea who Pyotr Zilber was.

The fourth Shumenko worked at Yugreftransflot, which maintained the largest fleet of refrigerated ships in Ukraine. Since Yugreftransflot was a public corporation, it took Arkadin some time just to get in to see Shumenko, who was a transport manager. Like everywhere in the former USSR, the red tape was enough to grind all work to a near halt. How anything got done in the public sector was beyond Arkadin.

At length, Shumenko appeared, led Arkadin to his tiny office, apologizing for the delay. He was a small man with very dark hair and the small ears and low forehead of a Neanderthal. When Arkadin introduced himself, Shumenko said, 'Obviously, you have the wrong man. I don't know a Pyotr Zilber.'

Arkadin consulted his list. 'I only have one more Oleg Shumenko left.'

'Let me see.' Shumenko consulted the list. 'Pity you didn't come to me first. These three are my cousins. And the fifth, the one you haven't seen yet, won't be of any use to you. He's dead. Fishing accident six months ago.' He handed back the list. 'But all isn't lost. There's one other Oleg Shumenko. Though we're not related, people are always getting us confused because we have the same patronymic, Ivanovich. He doesn't have a landline, which is why I'm constantly getting his calls.'

'Do you know where I can find him?'

Oleg Ivanovich Shumenko checked his watch. 'At this hour, yes, he'd be at work. He's a winemaker, you see. Champagne. I understand the French say you're not allowed to use that term for any wine not produced in their Champagne region.' He chuckled. 'Still, the Sevastopol Winery turns out quite a fine champagne.'

He led Arkadin from his office out through dull corridors into the enormous main vestibule. 'Are you familiar with the city, *gospadin* Arkadin? Sevastopol is divided into five districts. We're in the Gagarinskiy district, named after the world's first astronaut, Yuri Alexeevich Gagarin. This is the western section of the city. To the north is the Nakhimovskiy district, which is where the mammoth dry docks are. Perhaps you've heard of them. No? No matter. In the eastern section, away from the water, is the rural area of the city – pasturelands and vineyards, magnificent even at this time of the year.'

He crossed the marble floor to a long bank behind which sat half a dozen functionaries looking as if they'd had little to do in the past year. From one of them Shumenko received a city map, which he drew on. Then he handed it to Arkadin, pointing at a star he'd marked.

'There's the winery.' He glanced outside. 'The sky's clearing. Who knows, by the time you get there, you may even see some sun.'

Bourne walked the streets of Georgetown securely hidden within the crowds of college and university kids prowling the cobbles, looking for beer, girls, and guys. He was discreetly shadowing the man in the restaurant, who was, in turn, following Moira.

Once he had determined that the man was her tail, he'd backed away and returned to the street, where he'd called Moira.

'Can you think of anyone who wants to keep tabs on you?'

'I guess several,' she said. 'My own company, for one. I told you they've become paranoid ever since we started to build the LNG station in Long Beach. NoHold Energy might be another. They've been waving a vice president's job at me for six months. I could see them wanting to know more about me so they can sweeten their offer.'

'Other than those two?'

'No.'

He'd told her what he wanted her to do, and now in the Georgetown night she was doing it. They always had habits, these watchers in the shadows, little peculiarities built up from all the boring hours spent at their lonely jobs. This one liked to be on the inside of the sidewalk so he could duck quickly into a doorway if need be.

Once he had the shadow's idiosyncrasies down, it was time to take him out. But as Bourne worked his way through the crowds, moving closer to the shadow, he saw something else. The man wasn't alone. A second tail had taken up a parallel position on the opposite side of the street, which made sense. If Moira decided to cross the street in this throng, the first shadow might run into some difficulty keeping her in sight. These people, whoever they were, were leaving little to chance.

Bourne melted back, matching his pace to that of the crowd's. At the same time, he called Moira. She'd put in her Bluetooth earpiece so she could take his call without being conspicuous. Bourne gave her detailed instructions, then broke off following her shadows.

Moira, the back of her neck tingling as if she were in the crosshairs of an assassin's rifle, crossed the street, walked over to M Street. The main thing for her to keep in mind, Jason said, was to move at a normal pace, neither fast nor slow. Jason had alarmed her with the news that she was being followed. She had merely maintained the illusion of being calm. There were many people from both present and past who might be following her – a number of whom she hadn't mentioned when Jason had asked. Still, so close to the opening of the LNG terminal it was an ominous sign. She had desperately wanted to share with Jason the intel that had come to her today about the possibility of the terminal being a terrorist target, not in theory, but in reality. However, she couldn't – not unless he was an employee of the company. She was bound by her ironclad contract not to tell anyone outside the firm any confidential information.

At 31st Street, NW, she turned south, walking toward the Canal Towpath. A third of the way down the block, on her side, was a discreet plaque on which the word JEWEL was etched. She opened the ruby-colored door, entered the high-priced new restaurant. This was the kind of place where dishes were accessorized with kaffir lime foam, freeze-dried ginger, and ruby grapefruit pearls.

Smiling sweetly at the manager, she told him that she was looking for a friend. Before he could check his reservation book, she said her friend was with a man whose name she didn't know. She'd been here several times, once with Jason, so she knew the layout. At the rear of the second room was a short corridor. Against the right-hand wall were two unisex bathrooms. If you kept on going, which she did, you came to the kitchen, all bright lights, stainless-steel pans, copper pots, huge stovetops raging at high heat. Young men and women moved around the room in what seemed to her like military precision – sous-chefs, line cooks, expediters, the pastry chef and her staff, all performing under the stern commands of the chef de cuisine.

They were all too concentrated on their respective tasks to give Moira much notice. By the time her figure did register she'd already disappeared out the rear door. In a back alley filled with Dumpsters, a White Top cab was waiting, its engine purring. She climbed in and the cab took off.

Arkadin drove through the hills of rural Nakhimovskiy district, lush even in winter. He passed checkered farmland, bounded by low forested areas. The sky was lightening, the dark, rain-laden clouds already disappearing, replaced by high cumulus that glowed like embers in the sunlight that broke through everywhere. A golden sheen covered the acres of vineyards as he approached the Sevastopol Winery. At this time of year there were no leaves or fruit, of course, but the twisted, stunted boles, like the trunks of elephants, bore a life of their own that gave the vineyard a certain mystery, a mythic aspect, as if these sleeping vines needed only the spell of a wizard to come awake.

A burly woman named Yetnikova introduced herself as Oleg Ivanovich Shumenko's immediate supervisor – there was, apparently, no end to the tiers of supervisors in the winery. She had shoulders as wide as Arkadin's, a red, round, vodka face with features as curiously small as those of a doll. She wore her hair tied up in a peasant babushka, but she was all bristling business.

When she demanded to know Arkadin's business, he whipped out one of many false credentials he carried. This one identified him as a colonel in the SBU, the Security Service of Ukraine. Upon seeing the SBU card, Yetnikova wilted like an unwatered plant and showed him where to find Shumenko.

Arkadin, following her direction, went down corridor after corridor. He opened each door he came to, peering inside offices, utility closets, storerooms, and the like, apologizing to the occupants as he did so.

Shumenko was working in the fermentation room when Arkadin found him. He was a reed-thin man, much younger than Arkadin had imagined – no more than thirty or so. He had thick hair the color of goldenrod that stood up from his scalp like a series of cockscombs. Music spilled out from a portable player – a British band, the Cure. Arkadin had heard the song many times in Moscow clubs, but it seemed startling here in the hind end of the Crimea.

Shumenko stood on a catwalk four yards in the air, bent over a stainless-steel apparatus as large as a blue whale. He seemed to be sniffing something, possibly the latest batch of champagne he was concocting. Rather than turn down the music, Shumenko gestured for Arkadin to join him.

Without hesitation Arkadin mounted the vertical ladder, climbed swiftly up to the catwalk. The yeasty, slightly sweet odors of fermentation tickled his nostrils, causing him to rub the end of his nose vigorously to stave off a sneezing fit. His practiced gaze swept the immediate vicinity taking in every last detail, no matter how minute.

'Oleg Ivanovich Shumenko?'

The reedy young man put aside a clipboard on which he was taking notes. 'At your service.' He wore a badly fitting suit. He placed the pen he had been using in his breast pocket, where it joined a line of others. 'And you would be?'

'A friend of Pyotr Zilber's.'

'Never heard of him.'

But his eyes had already betrayed him. Arkadin reached out, turned up the music. 'He's heard of you, Oleg Ivanovich. In fact, you're quite important to him.'

Shumenko plastered a simulated smile on his face. 'I have no idea what you're talking about.'

'There was a grave mistake made. He needs the document back.'

Shumenko, smiling still, jammed his hands in his pockets. 'Once again, I must tell you –'

Arkadin made a grab for him, but Shumenko's right hand reappeared, gripping a GSh-18 semiautomatic that was pointed at Arkadin's heart.

'Hmm. The sights are acceptable at best,' Arkadin said.

'Please don't move. Whoever you are – and don't bother to give me a name that in any case will be false – you're no friend of Pyotr's. He must be dead. Perhaps even by your hand.'

'But the trigger pull is relatively heavy,' Arkadin continued, as if he hadn't been listening, 'so that'll give me an extra tenth of a second.'

'A tenth of a second is nothing.'

'It's all I need.'

Shumenko backed up, as Arkadin wanted him to, toward the curved side of a container to keep a safer distance. 'Even while I mourn Pyotr's death I will defend our network with my life.'

He backed up farther as Arkadin took another step toward him.

'It's a long fall from here so I suggest you turn around, climb back down the ladder, and disappear into whatever sewer you crawled out of.'

As Shumenko retreated, his right foot skidded on a bit of yeast paste Arkadin had noted earlier. Shumenko's right knee went out from under him, the hand holding the GSh-18 raised in an instinctive gesture to help keep him from falling.

In one long stride Arkadin was inside the perimeter of his defense. He made a grab for the gun, missed. His fist struck Shumenko on the right cheek, sending the reedy man lurching back into the side of the container in the space between two protruding levers. Shumenko slashed his arm in a horizontal arc, the sight on the barrel of the GSh-18 raking across the bridge of Arkadin's nose, drawing blood.

Arkadin made another lunge at the semiautomatic and, bent back against the curved sheet of stainless steel, the two men grappled. Shumenko was surprisingly strong for a thin man, and he was proficient in hand-to-hand combat. He had the proper counter for every attack Arkadin threw at him. They were very close now, not a hand's span separating them. Their limbs worked quickly, hands, elbows, forearms, even shoulders used to produce pain or, in blocking, minimize it.

Gradually, Arkadin seemed to be getting the better of his adversary, but with a double feint Shumenko managed to get the butt of the GSh-18 lodged against Arkadin's throat. He pressed in, using leverage in an attempt to crush Arkadin's windpipe. One of Arkadin's hands was trapped between their bodies. With the other, he pounded Shumenko's side, but he lacked Shumenko's leverage, and his blows did no damage. When he tried for Shumenko's kidney, the other man twisted his hips away, so his hand glanced off the hip bone.

Shumenko pressed his advantage, bending Arkadin over the railing, trying with the butt of his gun and his upper body to shove Arkadin off the catwalk. Ribbons of darkness flowed across Arkadin's vision, a sign that his brain was becoming oxygen-starved. He had underestimated Shumenko, and now he was about to pay the price.

He coughed, then gagged, trying to breathe. Then he moved his free hand up against the front of Shumenko's jacket. It would seem to Shumenko – concentrating on killing the interloper – as if Arkadin was making one last futile attempt to free his trapped hand. He was taken completely off guard when Arkadin slipped a pen out of his breast pocket, stabbed it into his left eye.

Immediately Shumenko reared back. Arkadin caught the GSh-18 as it dropped from the stricken man's nerveless hand. As Shumenko slid to the catwalk, Arkadin grabbed him by the shirtfront, knelt to be on the same level with him.

'The document,' he said. And when Shumenko's head began to loll, 'Oleg Ivanovich, listen to me. Where is the document?'

The man's good eye glistened, running with tears. His mouth worked. Arkadin shook him until he moaned with pain.

'Where?'

'Gone.'

Arkadin had to bend his head to hear Shumenko's whisper over the loud music. The Cure had been replaced by Siouxsie and the Banshees.

'What d'you mean gone?'

'Down the pipeline.' Shumenko's mouth curled in the semblance of a smile. 'Not what you wanted to hear, 'friend of Pyotr Zilber,' is it?' He blinked tears out of his good eye. 'Since this is the end of the line for you, bend closer and I'll tell you a secret.' He licked his lips as Arkadin complied, then lunged forward and bit into the lobe of Arkadin's right ear.

Arkadin reacted without thinking. He jammed the muzzle of the GSh-18 into Shumenko's mouth, pulled the trigger. Almost at the same instant, he realized his mistake, said 'Shit!' in six different languages.

# 4

Bourne, sunk deep into the shadows opposite the restaurant Jewel, saw the two men emerge. By the annoyed expressions on their faces he knew they'd lost Moira. He kept them in sight as they moved off together. One of them began to speak into a cell phone. He paused for a moment to ask his colleague a question, then returned to his conversation on the phone. By this time the two had reached M Street, NW. Finished with his call, the man put his cell phone away. They waited on the corner, watching the nubile young girls slipping by. They didn't slouch, Bourne noted, but stood ramrod-straight, their hands in view, at their sides. It appeared that they were waiting to be picked up; a good call on a night like this when parking was at a premium and traffic on M Street as thick as molasses.

Bourne, without a vehicle, looked around, saw a bicyclist coming up 31st Street, NW, from the towpath. He was cycling along the gutter to avoid the traffic. Bourne walked smartly toward him and stepped in front of him. The cyclist stopped short, uttering a sharp exclamation.

'I need your bike,' Bourne said.

'Well, you bloody well can't have it, mate,' the cyclist said with a heavy British accent.

At the corner of 31st and M, a black GMC SUV was pulling into the curb in front of the two men.

Bourne pressed four hundred dollars into the cyclist's hand. 'Like I said, right now.'

The young man stared down at the money for a moment. Then he swung off, said, 'Be my guest.'

As Bourne mounted up, he handed over his helmet. 'You'll be wanting this, mate.'

The two men had already vanished into the GMC's interior, the SUV was pulling out into the thick traffic flow. Bourne took off, leaving the cyclist to shrug behind him as he climbed onto the sidewalk.

Reaching the corner, Bourne turned right onto M Street. The GMC was three cars ahead of him. Bourne wove his way around the traffic, moving into position to keep up with the SUV. At 30th Street, NW, they all hit a red light. Bourne was forced to put one foot down, which was why he got a late start when the GMC jumped the light just before it turned green. The SUV roared ahead of the other vehicles, and Bourne launched himself forward. A white Toyota was coming from 30th into the intersection, heading right for him at a ninety-degree angle. Bourne put on a burst of speed, swerved up onto the corner sidewalk, backing a clutch of pedestrians into those behind them, to a round of curses. The Toyota, horn blaring angrily, just missed him as it jounced across M Street.

Bourne was able to make good headway, as the GMC had been slowed by the sludgy traffic up ahead, splitting off where M Street and Pennsylvania Avenue, NW, intersected at 29th Street. Just as he neared the light he saw the GMC take off and knew he had been spotted. The problem with a bicycle, especially one that had caused a minor uproar lunging through a red light, was that the cyclist became conspicuous, exactly the opposite of what was intended.

Making the best of a worsening situation, Bourne threw caution to the wind, following the accelerating GMC into the fork as it took Pennsylvania Avenue. The good news was that the congestion prevented the GMC from keeping up speed. More good news: Another red light loomed. This time Bourne was ready for the GMC to plow right through. Swerving in and out between vehicles, he put on another burst of speed, running the red light with the big SUV. But just as he was coming abreast of the far crosswalk, a gaggle of drunk teenagers stumbled off the curb on their way across the avenue. They closed off the lane behind the GMC and were so raucous they either didn't hear Bourne's warning shout or didn't care. He was forced to swerve sharply to the right. His front tire struck the curb, the bike lifted up. People scattered out of its way as it became, in effect, a missile. Bourne was able to keep it going after it landed, but there was simply nowhere for him to steer it without plowing into another group of kids. He applied the brakes without enough effect. Leaning to the right, he forced the bike down on its side, ripping his right trouser leg as it skidded along the cement.

'Are you all right?'

'What were you trying to do?'

'Didn't you see the red light?'

'You could have killed yourself – or someone else!'

A welter of voices as pedestrians surrounded him, trying to help him out from under the bicycle. Bourne thanked them as he scrambled to his feet. He ran several hundred yards down the avenue, but as he feared the GMC was long gone.

Expelling a string of bawdily colorful curses, Arkadin rummaged through the pockets of Oleg Ivanovich Shumenko, who lay twitching in the bloodstained catwalk deep inside the Sevastopol Winery. As he did so, he wondered how he could have been such a fool. He'd done precisely what Shumenko had wanted him to do, which was to kill him. He'd rather have died than divulge the name of the next man in Pyotr Zilber's network.

Still, there was a chance that something he had on his person would lead Arkadin farther along. Arkadin had already made a small pile of coins, bills, toothpicks, and the like. He unfolded each scrap of paper he came across, but none of them contained either a name or an address, just lists of chemicals, presumably those the winery required for fermentation or the periodic cleaning of its vats.

Shumenko's wallet was a sad affair – sliver-thin, containing a faded photo of an older couple smiling into the sun and the camera Arkadin took to be Shumenko's parents, a condom in a worn foil pouch, a driver's license, car registration, ID badge for a sailing club, an IOU chit for ten thousand hryvnia – just under two thousand American dollars – two receipts, one for a restaurant, the other for a nightclub, an old photo of a young girl smiling into the camera.

In pocketing the receipts, the only reasonable leads he'd found, he inadvertently flipped over the IOU. On the reverse was the name DEVRA, written in a sharp, spiky feminine hand. Arkadin wanted to look for more, but he heard an electronic squawk, then the bawl of Yetnikova's voice. He looked around, saw an old-fashioned walkie-talkie hanging by its strap from the railing. Stuffing the papers into his pocket, he hurried along the catwalk, slid down the ladder, made his way out of the champagne fermentation room.

Shumenko's boss, Yetnikova, marched toward him down the labyrinthine corridors as if she were in the forefront of the Red Army entering Warsaw. Even at this distance, he could see the scowl on her face. Unlike his Russian credentials, his Ukrainian ones were paper-thin. They'd pass a cursory test, but after any kind of checking he'd be busted.

'I called the SBU office in Kiev. They did some digging on you, Colonel.' Yetnikova's voice had turned from servile to hostile. 'Or whoever you are.' She puffed herself up like a porcupine about to do battle. 'They never heard of – '

She gave a little squeak as he jammed one hand over her mouth while he punched her hard in the solar plexus. She collapsed into his arms like a rag doll, and he dragged her along the corridor until he came to the utility closet. Opening the door, he shoved her in, went in after her.

Sprawled on the floor, Yetnikova slowly came to her senses. Immediately she began her bluster – cursing and promising dire consequences for the outrages perpetrated on her person. Arkadin didn't hear her; he didn't even see her. He attempted to block out the past, but as always the memories flattened him. They took possession of him, taking him out of himself, producing like a drug a dreamlike state that over the years had become as familiar as a twin brother.

Kneeling over Yetnikova, he dodged her kicks, the snapping of her jaws. He withdrew a switchblade from a sheath strapped to the side of his right calf. When he *snikk*ed open its long, thin blade, fear finally twisted Yetnikova's face. Her eyes opened wide and she gasped, raising her hands instinctively.

'Why are you doing this?' she cried. 'Why?'

'Because of what you've done.'

'What? What did I do? I don't even know you!'

'But I know you.' Slapping her hands aside, Arkadin went to work on her.

When, moments later, he was done, his vision came back into focus. He took a long, shuddering breath as if shaking off the effects of an anesthetic. He stared down at the headless corpse. Then, remembering, he kicked the head into a corner filled with filthy rags. For a moment, it rocked like a ship on the ocean. The eyes seemed to him gray with age, but they were only filmed with dust, and the release he sought eluded him once again.

'Who were they?' Moira asked.

'That's the difficulty,' Bourne told her. 'I wasn't able to find out. It would help if you could tell me why they're following you.'

Moira frowned. 'I have to assume it has something to do with the security on the LNG terminal.'

They were sitting side by side in Moira's living room, a small, cozy space in a Georgetown town house of red-brown brick on Cambridge Place, NW, near Dumbarton Oaks. A fire was crackling and licking in the brick hearth; espresso and brandy sat on the coffee table in front of them. The chenille-covered sofa was deep enough for Moira to curl up on. It had big roll arms and a neck-high back.

'One thing I can tell you,' Bourne said, 'these people are professionals.'

'Makes sense,' she said. 'Any rival of my firm would hire the best people available. That doesn't necessarily mean I'm in any danger.'

Nevertheless, Bourne felt another sharp pang at the loss of Marie, then carefully, almost reverently, put the feeling aside.

'More espresso?' Moira asked.

'Please.'

Bourne handed her his cup. As she bent forward, the light V-neck sweater revealed the tops of her firm breasts. At that moment, she raised her gaze to his. There was a mischievous glint in her eyes.

'What are you thinking about?'

'Probably the same thing you are.' He rose, looked around for his coat. 'I think I'd better go.'

'Jason . . .'

He paused. Lamplight gave her face a golden glow. 'Don't,' she said. 'Stay. Please.'

He shook his head. 'You and I both know that's not a good idea.'

'Just for tonight. I don't want to be alone, not after what you discovered.' She gave a little shiver. 'I was being brave before, but I'm not you. Being followed gives me the willies.'

She offered the cup of espresso. 'If it makes you feel any better, I'd prefer you sleep out here. This sofa's quite comfortable.'

Bourne looked around at the warm chestnut walls, the dark wooden blinds, the jewel-toned accents here and there in the form of vases and bowls of flowers. An agate box with gold legs sat on a mahogany sideboard. A small brass ship's clock ticked away beside it. The photos of the French countryside in summer and autumn made him feel both mournful and nostalgic. For precisely what, he couldn't say. Though his mind fished for memories, none surfaced. His past was a lake of black ice. 'Yes, it is.' He took the cup, sat down beside her.

She pulled a pillow against her breast. 'Shall we talk about what we've been avoiding saying all evening?'

'I'm not big on talking.'

Her wide lips curved in a smile. 'Which one of you isn't big on talking, David Webb or Jason Bourne?'

Bourne laughed, sipped his espresso. 'What if I said both of us?'

'I'd have to call you a liar.'

'We can't have that, can we?'

'It wouldn't be my choice.' She rested one cheek on her hand, waiting. When he said nothing further, she continued. 'Please, Jason. Just talk to me.'

The old fear of getting close to someone reared its head again, but at the same time he felt a kind of melting inside him, as if his frozen heart were beginning to thaw. For some years, he'd made it an ironclad rule to keep his distance from other people. Alex Conklin had been murdered, Marie had died, Martin Lindros hadn't made it out of Miran Shah. All gone, his only friends and first love. With a start, he realized that he hadn't felt attracted to anyone except Marie. He hadn't allowed himself to feel, but now he couldn't help himself. Was that a function of the David Webb personality or of Moira herself? She was strong, self-assured. In her he recognized a kindred spirit, someone who viewed the world as he did – as an outsider.

He looked into her face, said what was in his mind. 'Everyone I get close to dies.'

She sighed, put a hand briefly over his. 'I'm not going to die.' Her dark brown eyes glimmered in the lamplight. 'Anyway, it's not your job to protect me.'

This was another reason he was drawn to her. She was fierce, a warrior, in her own way.

'Tell me the truth, then. Are you really happy at the university?'

Bourne thought a moment, the conflict inside him becoming an unholy din. 'I think I am.' After a slight pause, he added: 'I thought I was.'

There'd been a golden glow to his life with Marie, but Marie was gone, that life was in the past. With her gone, he was forced to confront the terrifying question: What was David Webb without her? He was no longer a family man. He'd been able to raise his children, he saw now, only with her love and help. And for the first time he realized what his retreat into the university really meant. He'd been trying to regain that golden life he'd had with Marie. It wasn't only Professor Specter he didn't want to disappoint, it was Marie.

'What are you thinking?' Moira said softly.

'Nothing,' he said. 'Nothing at all.'

She studied him for a moment. Then she nodded. 'All right, then.' She rose, leaned over, kissed him on the cheek. 'I'll make up the sofa.'

'That's all right, just tell me where the linen closet is.'

She pointed. 'Over there.'

He nodded.

'Good night, Jason.'

'See you in the morning. But early. I've got – '

'I know. Breakfast with Dominic Specter.'


Bourne lay on his back, one arm behind his head. He was tired; he was sure he'd fall asleep immediately. But an hour after he'd turned off the lights, sleep seemed a thousand miles away. Now and again, the red-and-black remnants of the fire snapped and softly fell in on themselves. He stared at the stripes of light seeping in through the wide wooden blinds, hoping they'd take him to far-off places, which, in his case, meant his past. In some ways he was like an amputee who still felt his arm even though it had been sawed off. The sense of memories just beyond his ability to recall was maddening, an itch he couldn't scratch. He often wished he would remember nothing at all, which was one reason Moira's offer was so compelling. The thought of starting fresh, without the baggage of sadness and loss, was a powerful draw. This conflict was always with him, a major part of his life, whether he was David Webb or Jason Bourne. And yet, whether he liked it or not, his past was there, waiting for him like a wolf at night, if only he could reach through the mysterious barrier his brain had raised. Not for the first time, he wondered what other terrible traumas had befallen him in the past to cause his mind to protect itself from it. The fact that the answer lurked within his own mind turned his blood cold because it represented his own personal demon.

'Jason?'

The door to Moira's bedroom was open. Despite the dimness, his keen eyes could make out her form moving slowly toward him on bare feet.

'I couldn't sleep,' she said in a throaty voice. She stopped several paces from where he lay. She was wearing a silk paisley bathrobe, belted at the waist. The lush curves of her body were unmistakable.

For a moment, they remained in silence.

'I lied to you before,' she said quietly. 'I don't want you to sleep out here.'

Bourne rose on one elbow. 'I lied, too. I was thinking about what I once had and how I've been desperate to hang on to it. But it's gone, Moira. All gone forever.' He drew up one leg. 'I don't want to lose you.'

She moved minutely, and a bar of light picked out the glitter of tears in her eyes. 'You won't, Jason. I promise.'

Another silence engulfed them, this one so profound they seemed to be the only two people left in the world.

At last, he held out his hand, and she came toward him. He rose from the sofa, took her in his arms. She smelled of lime and geranium. He ran his hands through her thick hair, grabbed it. Her face tilted up to him and their lips came together, and his heart shivered off another coating of ice. After a long time, he felt her hands at her waist and he stepped back.

She undid the belt and the robe parted, slid off her shoulders. Her naked flesh shone a dusky gold. She had wide hips and a deep navel; there seemed nothing about her body he didn't love. Now it was she who took his hand, leading him to her bed, where they fell upon each other like half-starved animals.

Bourne dreamed he was standing at the window of Moira's bedroom, peering through the wooden blinds. The streetlight fell across the sidewalk and street, casting long, oblique shadows. As he watched, one of the shadows rose up from the cobbles, walked directly toward him as if it were alive and could somehow see him through the wide wooden slats.

Bourne opened his eyes, the demarcation between sleep and consciousness instantaneous and complete. His mind was filled with the dream; he could feel his heart working in his chest harder than it should have been at this moment.

Moira's arm was draped over his hip. He moved it to her side, rolled silently out of bed. Naked, he padded into the living room. Ashes lay in a cold, gray heap in the hearth. The ship's clock ticked toward the fourth hour of the night. He went straight toward the bars of streetlight, peered out just as he had in his dream. As in his dream the light cast oblique shadows across the sidewalk and street. No traffic passed. All was quiet and still. It took a minute or two, but he found the movement, minute, fleeting, as if someone standing had begun to shift from one foot to the other, then changed his mind. He waited to see if the movement would continue. Instead a small puff of exhaled breath flared into the light, then almost immediately vanished.

He dressed quickly. Bypassing both the front and rear doors, he slipped out of the house via a side window. It was very cold. He held his breath so it wouldn't steam up and betray his presence, as it had the watcher.

He stopped just before he reached the corner of the building, peered cautiously around the brick wall. He could see the curve of a shoulder, but it was at the wrong height, so low Bourne might have taken the watcher for a child. In any event, he hadn't moved. Melting back into the shadows, he went down 30th Street, NW, turned left onto Dent Place, which paralleled Cambridge Place. When he reached the end of the block, he turned left onto Cambridge, on Moira's block. Now he could see just where the watcher was situated, crouched between two parked cars almost directly across the street from Moira's house.

A gust of humid wind caused the watcher to huddle down, sink his head between his shoulders, like a turtle. Bourne seized the moment to cross the street to the watcher's side. Without pausing, he advanced down the block swiftly and silently. The watcher became aware of him far too late. He was still turning his head when Bourne grabbed him by the back of his jacket, slammed him back across the hood of the parked car.

This threw him into the light. Bourne saw his black face, recognized the features all in a split second. At once he hauled the young man up, hustled him back into the shadows, where he was certain they wouldn't be seen by other prying eyes.

'Jesus Christ, Tyrone,' he said, 'what the hell are you doing here?'

'Can't say.' Tyrone was sullen, possibly from having been discovered.

'What d'you mean, you can't say?'

'I signed a confidentiality agreement is why.'

Bourne frowned. 'Deron wouldn't make you sign something like that.' Deron was the art forger Bourne used for all his documents and, sometimes, unique new technologies or weapons Deron was experimenting with.

'Doan work fo Deron no more.'

'Who made you sign the agreement, Tyrone?' Bourne grabbed him by his jacket front. 'Who are you working for? I don't have time to play games with you. Answer me!'

'Can't.' Tyrone could be damn stubborn when he wanted to be, a by-product of growing up on the streets of the northeast Washington slums. 'But, okay, I guess I can take yo where yo can see fo yoself.'

He led Bourne around to the unnamed alley behind Moira's house, stopped at an anonymous-looking black Chevy. Leaving Bourne, he used his knuckle to knock on the driver's window. The window lowered. As he bent down to speak to whoever was inside, Bourne came up, pulled him aside so he could look in. What he saw astonished even him. The person sitting behind the wheel was Soraya Moore.

# 5

'We've been surveilling her for close to ten days now,' Soraya said.

'CI?' Bourne said. 'Why?'

They were sitting in the Chevy. Soraya had turned on the engine to get some heat up. She'd sent Tyrone home, even though it was clear he wanted to be her protector. According to Soraya, he was now working for her in a strictly off-the-record capacity – a kind of personal black-ops unit of one.

'You know I can't tell you that.'

'No, Tyrone can't tell me. You can.'

Bourne had worked with Soraya when he'd put together his mission to rescue Martin Lindros, the founder and director of Typhon. She was one of the few people with whom he'd worked in the field, both times in Odessa.

'I suppose I could,' Soraya admitted, 'but I won't, because it appears that you and Moira Trevor are intimate.'

She sat staring out the window at the blank sheen of the street. Her large, deep blue eyes and her aggressive nose were the centerpieces of a bold Arabian face the color of cinnamon.

When she turned back, Bourne could see that she wasn't happy at being forced to reveal CI intel.

'There's a new sheriff in town,' Soraya said. 'Her name is Veronica Hart.'

'You ever hear of her?'

'No, and neither have any of the others.' She shrugged. 'I'm quite sure that was the point. She comes from the private sector: Black River. The president decided on a new broom to sweep out the hash we'd all made of the events leading up to the Old Man's murder.'

'What's she like?'

'Too soon to tell, but one thing I'm willing to bet on: She's going to be a whole helluva lot better than the alternative.'

'Which is?'

'Secretary of Defense Halliday has been trying to expand his domain for years now. He's moving through Luther LaValle, the Pentagon's intel czar. Rumor has it that LaValle tried to pry away the DCI job from Veronica Hart.'

'And she won.' Bourne nodded. 'That says something about her.'

Soraya produced a packet of Lambert & Butler cigarettes, knocked one out, lit up.

'When did that begin?' Bourne said.

Soraya rolled down her window partway, blew the smoke into the waning night. 'The day I was promoted to director of Typhon.'

'Congratulations.' He sat back, impressed. 'But now we have even more of a mystery. Why is the director of Typhon on a surveillance team at four in the morning? I would've thought that would be a job for someone farther down the CI food chain.'

'It would be, in other circumstances.' Soraya inhaled, blew smoke out the window again. What was left of the cigarette followed. Then she turned her body toward Bourne. 'My new boss told me to handle this myself. That's what I'm doing.'

'What does all this clandestine work have to do with Moira? She's a civilian.'

'Maybe she is,' Soraya said, 'and maybe she isn't.' Her large eyes studied Bourne's for a reaction. 'I've been digging through the masses of interoffice e-mails and cell phone records going back over the last two years. I came upon some irregularities and handed them over to the new DCI.' She paused for a moment, as if unsure whether to continue. 'The thing is, the irregularities concern Martin's private communications with Moira.'

'You mean he told her CI classified secrets?'

'Frankly, we're not sure. The communications weren't intact; they had to be pieced together and enhanced electronically. Some words were garbled, others were out of order. It was clear, however, that they were collaborating on something that bypassed the normal CI channels.' She sighed. 'It's possible he was merely helping her with security issues for NextGen Energy Solutions. But especially after the multiple security breaches CI recently suffered, Hart has made it clear that we can't afford to overlook the possibility that she's working clandestinely for some other entity Martin knew nothing about.'

'You mean she was milking him for intel. I find that hard to believe.'

'Right. Now you know why I didn't want to tell you about it.'

'I'd like to see these communications for myself.'

'For that you'll have to see the DCI, which, quite honestly, I wouldn't recommend. There are still high-level operatives in CI who blame you for the Old Man's death.'

'That's absurd,' Bourne said. 'I had nothing to do with his death.'

Soraya ran a hand through her thick hair. 'It was you who brought Karim al-Jamil back to CI thinking he was Martin Lindros.'

'He looked exactly like Martin, spoke exactly like him.'

'You vouched for him.'

'So did a phalanx of CI shrinks.'

'You're an easy target around CI. Rob Batt, who's just been promoted to deputy director, is the ringleader of a group who are convinced you're a schizophrenic, unreliable rogue agent. I'm just saying.'

Bourne closed his eyes for a moment. He'd heard these allegations leveled against him time and again. 'You've left off another reason why I'm an easy target. I'm a legacy left over from the Alex Conklin era. He had the Old Man's confidence but hardly anyone else's, mainly because no one knew what he was doing, especially with the program that created me.'

'All the more reason for you to stay in the shadows.'

Bourne glanced out the window. 'I've got an early breakfast meeting.'

As he was about to get out of the car, Soraya put a hand on his arm. 'Stay out of this, Jason. That's my advice.'

'And I appreciate the concern.' He leaned toward her, kissed her lightly on the cheek. Then he was crossing the street. A moment later he'd vanished into shadow.

As soon as he was out of her sight, Bourne flipped open the cell phone he'd lifted from her when he'd leaned in to kiss her. Quickly he scrolled through to Veronica Hart's number, connected with it. He wondered if he'd be pulling her out of sleep, but when she answered she sounded wide awake.

'How's the surveillance going?' She had a rich, mellow voice.

'That's what I want to talk with you about.'

There was the briefest of silences before she answered. 'Who is this?'

'Jason Bourne.'

'Where is Soraya Moore?'

'Soraya is fine, Director. I simply needed a way to contact you once I'd broken the surveillance, and I was quite certain Soraya wouldn't give it to me willingly.'

'So you stole her phone.'

'I want to meet with you,' Bourne said. He didn't have much time. At any moment, Soraya might reach for her phone, would know he'd hijacked it and come after him. 'I want to see the evidence that led you to order the surveillance on Moira Trevor.'

'I don't take kindly to being told what to do, especially by a rogue agent.'

'But you will meet with me, Director, because I'm the only one with access to Moira. I'm your fast track to finding out if she's really rotten or whether you're on a wild goose chase.'

'I think I'll stick to the proven way.' Veronica Hart, sitting in her new office with Rob Batt, mouthed the words *Jason Bourne* to her DDCI.

'But you can't,' Bourne said in her ear. 'Now that I've broken the surveillance I can ensure that Moira vanishes off your grid.'

Hart stood up. 'I also don't respond well to threats.'

'I have no need to threaten you, Director. I'm simply telling you the facts.'

Batt studied her expression as well as her responses, trying to get a reading of the conversation. They had been working nonstop since she'd returned from her meeting with the president. He was exhausted, on the point of leaving, but this call interested him intensely.

'Look,' Bourne said, 'Martin was my friend. He was a hero. I don't want his reputation tarnished.'

'All right,' Hart said, 'come to my office later this morning, say around eleven.'

'I'm not setting foot inside CI headquarters,' Bourne said. 'We'll meet this evening at five at the entrance to the Freer Gallery.'

'What if I – ?'

But Bourne had already severed the connection.

Moira was up, clad in her paisley robe, when Bourne returned. She was in the kitchen, making fresh coffee. She glanced at him without comment. She had more sense than to ask about his comings and goings.

Bourne took off his coat. 'Just checking the area for tails.'

She paused. 'And did you find any?'

'Quiet as the grave.' He didn't believe that Moira had been pumping Martin for CI intel, but the inordinate sense of security – of secretiveness – instilled in him by Conklin warned him not to tell her the truth.

She relaxed visibly. 'That's a relief.' Setting the pot on the flame, she said, 'Do we have time for a cup together?'

Gray light filtered through the blinds, brightening by the minute. An engine coughed, traffic started up on the street. Voices rose briefly, and a dog barked. The morning had begun.

They stood side by side in the kitchen. Between them on the wall was a Kit-Cat Klock, its raffish kitty eyes and tail moving back and forth as time passed.

'Jason, tell me it wasn't just mutual loneliness and sorrow that motivated us.'

When he took her in his arms he felt a tiny shiver work its way through her. 'One-night stands are not in my vocabulary, Moira.'

She put her head against his chest.

He pulled her hair back from her cheek. 'I don't feel like coffee right now.'

She moved against him. 'Neither do I.'


Professor Dominic Specter was stirring sugar into the strong Turkish tea he always carried with him when David Webb walked into the Wonderlake diner on 36th Street, NW. The place was lined with wooden boards, the tables reclaimed wooden slabs, the mismatched chairs found objects. Photographs of loggers and Pacific Northwest vistas were ranged around the walls, interspersed with real logging tools: peaveys, cant hooks, pulp hooks, and timberjacks. The place was a perennial student favorite because of its hours, the inexpensive food, and the inescapable associations with Monty Python's 'The Lumberjack Song.'

Bourne ordered coffee as soon as he sat down.

'Good morning, David.' Specter cocked his head like a bird on a wire. 'You look like you haven't slept.'

The coffee was just the way Bourne liked it: strong, black, sugarless. 'I had a lot to think about.'

Specter cocked his head. 'David, what is it? Anything I can help with? My door is always open.'

'I appreciate that. I always have.'

'I can see something's troubling you. Whatever it is, together we can work it out.'

The waiter, dressed in red-checked flannel shirt, jeans, and Timberland boots, set the menus down on the table and left.

'It's about my job.'

'Is it wrong for you?' The professor spread his hands. 'You miss teaching, I imagine. All right, we'll put you back in the classroom.'

'I'm afraid it's more serious than that.'

When he didn't continue, Professor Specter cleared his throat. 'I've noticed a certain restlessness in you over the past few weeks. Could it have anything to do with that?'

Bourne nodded. 'I think I've been trying to recapture something that can't be caught.'

'Are you worried about disappointing me, my boy?' Specter rubbed his chin. 'You know, years ago when you told me about the Bourne identity, I counseled you to seek professional help. Such a serious mental schism inevitably builds up pressure in the individual.'

'I've had help before. So I know how to handle the pressure.'

'I'm not questioning that, David.' Specter paused. 'Or should I be calling you Jason?'

Bourne continued to sip his coffee, said nothing.

'I'd love you to stay, Jason, but only if it's the right thing for you.'

Specter's cell phone buzzed but he ignored it. 'Understand, I only want what's best for you. But your life's been in upheaval. First, Marie's death, then the demise of your best friends.' His phone buzzed again. 'I thought you needed sanctuary, which you always have here. But if you've made up your mind to leave . . .' He looked at the number lit up on his phone. 'Excuse me a moment.'

He took the call, listening.

'The deal can't be closed without it?'

He nodded, held the phone away from his ear, said to Bourne, 'I need to get something from my car. Please order for me. Scrambled eggs and dark toast.'

He rose, went out of the restaurant. His Honda was parked directly across 36th Street. He was in the middle of the street when two men came out of nowhere. One grabbed him while the other struck him several times about the head. As a black Cadillac screeched to a halt beside the three men, Bourne was up and running. The man struck Specter again, yanked open the rear door of the car.

Bourne grabbed a pulp hook off the wall, sprinted out of the restaurant. The man bundled Specter into the backseat of the Cadillac and jumped in beside him, while the first man ducked into the front passenger's seat. The Cadillac took off just as Bourne reached it. He barely had time to swing the pulp hook into the car before he was jerked off his feet. He'd been aiming for the roof, but the Cadillac's sudden acceleration had caused it to pierce the rear window instead. The pointed end managed to embed itself in the top of the backseat. Bourne swung his trailing legs onto the trunk.

The rear pane of safety glass was completely crazed, but the thin film of plastic sandwiched between the glass layers kept it basically intact. As the car began to swerve insanely back and forth, the driver trying to dislodge him, chips of the safety glass came away, giving Bourne an increasingly tenuous hold on the Cadillac.

The car accelerated ever more dangerously through building traffic. Then, so abruptly it took his breath away, it whipped around a corner and he slid off the trunk, his body now banging against the driver's-side fender. His shoes struck the tarmac with such force, one of them was ripped off. Sock and skin were flayed off his heel before he could regain a semblance of balance. Using the fulcrum of the pulp hook's turned wooden handle, he levered his legs back up onto the trunk, only to have the driver slew the Cadillac so that he was almost thrown completely clear of the car. His feet struck a trash can, sending it barreling down the sidewalk as shocked pedestrians scattered helter-skelter. Pain shot through him and he might have been finished, but the driver could not keep the Cadillac in its spin any longer. Traffic forced him to straighten out the car's trajectory. Bourne took advantage to swing himself back up onto the trunk. His right fist plunged through the shattered rear window, seeking a second, more secure hold. The car was accelerating again as it bypassed the last of the bunched-up local traffic, gained the ramp onto

Whitehurst Freeway. Bourne tucked his legs up under him, braced on his knees.

As they passed into shadow beneath the Francis Scott Key Bridge the man who had shoved Specter into the backseat thrust a Taurus PT140 through the gap in the broken glass. The handgun's muzzle turned toward Bourne as the man prepared to fire. Bourne let go with his right hand, gripped the man's wrist, and jerked hard, bringing the entire forearm into the open air. The motion pushed back the sleeve of the man's coat and shirt. He saw a peculiar tattoo on the inside of the forearm: three horses' heads joined by a central skull. He slammed his right knee into the inside of the man's elbow, at the same time pushed it back against the frame of the car. With a satisfying crack, it broke, the hand opened, the Taurus fell away. Bourne made a grab for it, but missed.

The Cadillac swerved into the left lane and the pulp hook, ripping through the fabric of the backseat, was forced out of Bourne's hand. He gripped the gunman's broken arm with both hands, used it to lever himself through the ruined rear window feet first.

He landed between the man with the broken arm and Specter, who was huddled against the left-hand door. The man in the front passenger's seat was kneeling on the seat, turned toward him. He also had a Taurus, which he aimed at Bourne. Bourne grabbed the body of the man beside him, shifted him so that the shot plowed into the man's chest, killing him instantly. At once Bourne heaved the corpse against the gunman in the front bench seat. The gunman swiped the corpse in the shoulder in an attempt to move him away, but this only brought the corpse in contact with the driver, who had put on a burst of speed and who seemed to be focused solely on weaving in and out of the traffic.

Bourne punched the gunman in the nose. Blood spattered as the gunman was thrown off his knees, jolted back against the dashboard. As Bourne moved to follow up his advantage, the gunman aimed the Taurus at Specter.

'Get back,' he shouted, 'or I'll kill him.'

Bourne judged the moment. If the men had wanted to kill Specter they'd have gunned him down in the street. Since they grabbed him, they must need him alive.

'All right.' Unseen by the gunman, his right hand scraped along the cushion of the backseat. As he raised his hands, he flicked a palmful of glass chips into the gunman's face. As the man's hands instinctively went up, Bourne chopped him twice with the edge of his hand. The gunman drew out a push dagger, the wicked-looking blade protruding from between his second and third knuckles. He jabbed it directly at Bourne's face. Bourne ducked; the blade followed him, moving closer until Bourne slammed his fist into the side of the gunman's head, which snapped back against the rear doorpost. Bourne heard the crack as his neck broke. The gunman's eyes rolled up and he slumped against the door.

Bourne locked his crooked arm around the driver's neck, pulled back hard. The driver began to choke. He whipped his head back and forth, trying to free himself. As he did so, the car swerved from one lane to another. The car began to swerve dangerously as he lost consciousness. Bourne climbed over the seat, pushing the driver off, down into the passenger's-side foot well, so that he could slide behind the wheel. The trouble was though Bourne could steer, the driver's body was blocking the pedals.

The Cadillac was now out of control. It hit a car in the left lane, bounced off to the right. Instead of fighting against the resulting spin, Bourne turned into it. At the same time, he shifted the car into neutral. Instantly the transmission disengaged; the engine was no longer being fed gas. Now its immediate momentum was the issue. Bourne, struggling to gain control, found his foot blocked from the brake by part of a leg. He steered right, jouncing over the divider and into an enormous parking lot that lay between the freeway and the Potomac.

The Cadillac sideswiped a parked SUV, careened farther to the right toward the water. Bourne kicked the unconscious driver's inert body with his bare left foot, at last finding the brake pedal. The car finally slowed, but not enough – they were still heading toward the Potomac. Whipping the wheel hard to the right caused the Cadillac's tires to shriek as Bourne tried to turn the car away from the low barrier that separated the lot from the water. As the front end of the Cadillac went up over the barrier, Bourne jammed the brake pedal to the floor, and the car came to a halt partway over the side. It teetered precariously back and forth. Specter, still huddled in the backseat behind Bourne, moaned a little, the right sleeve of his Harris Tweed jacket spattered with blood from his captor's broken nose.

Bourne, trying to keep the Cadillac out of the Potomac, sensed that the front wheels were still on the top of the barrier. He threw the car into reverse. The Cadillac shot backward, slamming into another parked car before Bourne had a chance to shift back into neutral.

From far away he could hear the seesaw wail of sirens.

'Professor, are you all right?'

Specter groaned, but at least his voice was more distinct. 'We have to get out of here.'

Bourne was freeing the pedals from the strangled man's legs. 'That tattoo I saw on the gunman's arm – '

'No police,' Specter managed to croak. 'There's a place we can go. I'll tell you.'

Bourne got out of the Caddy, then helped Specter out. Limping over to another car, Bourne smashed the window with his elbow. The police sirens were coming closer. Bourne got in, hot-wired the ignition, and the car's engine coughed to life. He unlocked the doors. The instant the professor slid into the passenger's seat Bourne took off, heading east on the freeway. As quickly as he could he moved into the left-hand lane. Then he turned abruptly to his left. The car jumped the central divider and he accelerated, heading west now, in the opposite direction the sirens were coming from.

# 6

Arkadin took his evening meal at Tractir on Bolshaya Morsekay, halfway up the steep hill, a typically unlovely place with roughly varnished wooden tables and chairs. Almost one entire wall was taken up by a painting of three-masted ships in Sevastopol harbor circa 1900. The food was unremarkable, but that wasn't why Arkadin was here. Tractir was the restaurant whose name he'd found in Oleg Ivanovich Shumenko's wallet. No one here knew anyone named Devra, so after the borscht and the blini, he moved on.

Along the coast was a section called Omega, filled with cafés and restaurants. As the hub of the city's nightlife culture, it featured every variety of club one could want. Calla was a club a short stroll from the open-air car park. The night was clear and brisk. Pinpoints dotted the Black Sea as well as the sky, making for a dizzying vista. Sea and sky seemed to be virtually interchangeable.

Calla was several steps down from the sidewalk, a place filled with the sweet scent of marijuana and an unearthly din. A roughly square room was divided between a jam-packed dance floor and a raised section filled with minuscule round tables and metal café chairs. A grid of colored lights pulsed in time with the house music the straw-thin female DJ was spinning. She stood behind a small stand on which was set an iPod hooked up to a number of digital mixing machines.

The dance floor was packed with men and women. Bumping hips and elbows was part of the scene. Arkadin picked his way over to the bar, which ran along the front of the right wall. Twice he was intercepted by young, busty blondes who wanted his attention and, he assumed, his money. He brushed past them, made a beeline for the harried bartender. Three tiers of glass shelves filled with liquor bottles were attached to a mirror on the wall behind the bar so patrons could check out the action or admire themselves while getting polluted.

Arkadin was obliged to wade through a phalanx of revelers before he could order a Stoli on the rocks. When, some time later, the bartender returned with his drink, Arkadin asked him if he knew a Devra.

'Yah, sure. Over there,' he said, nodding in the direction of the straw-thin DJ.

It was 1 A.M. before Devra took a break. There were other people waiting for her to finish – fans, Arkadin presumed. He intended to get to her first. He used the force of his personality rather than his false credentials. Not that the rabble here would challenge them, but after the incident at the winery, he didn't want to leave any trail for the real SBU to follow. The state police alias he'd used there was now dangerous to him.

Devra was blond, almost as tall as he was. He couldn't believe how thin her arms were. They had no definition at all. Her hips were no wider than a young boy's, and he could see the bones of her scapulae when she moved. She had large eyes and dead-white skin, as if she rarely saw the light of day. Her black jumpsuit with its white skull and crossbones across the stomach was drenched in sweat. Perhaps because of her DJing, her hands were in constant motion even if the rest of her stayed relatively still.

She eyed him up and down while he introduced himself. 'You don't look like a friend of Oleg's,' she said.

But when he dangled the IOU in front of her face her skepticism evaporated. *Thus is it ever,* Arkadin thought as she led him backstage. *The venality of the human race cannot be overestimated.*

The green room where she relaxed between sets was better off left to the wharf rats that were no doubt shuttered behind the walls, but right now that couldn't be helped. He tried not to think of the rats; he wouldn't be here long anyway. There were no windows; the walls and ceiling were painted black, no doubt to cover up a multitude of sins.

Devra turned on a lamp with a mean forty-watt bulb and sat down on a wooden chair damaged by knife scars and cigarette burns. The difference between the green room and an interrogation cell was negligible. There were no other chairs or furniture, save for a narrow wooden table against one wall on which was a jumble of makeup, CDs, cigarettes, matches, gloves, and other piles of debris Arkadin didn't bother to identify.

Devra leaned back, lit a cigarette she nimbly swiped from the table without offering him one. 'So you're here to pay off Oleg's debt.'

'In a sense.'

Her eyes narrowed, making her look a lot like a stoat Arkadin had once shot outside St. Petersburg.

'Meaning what, exactly?'

Arkadin produced the bills. 'I have the money he owes you right here.' As she reached out for it, he pulled it away. 'In return I'd like some information.'

Devra laughed. 'What do I look like, the phone operator?'

Arkadin hit her hard with the back of his hand, so that she crashed into the table. Tubes of lipstick and mascara went rolling and tumbling. Devra put a hand out to steady herself, fingers clutching through the morass.

When she pulled out a small handgun Arkadin was ready. His fist hammered her delicate wrist and he plucked the handgun from her numb fingers.

'Now,' he said, setting her back on the chair, 'are you ready to continue?'

Devra looked at him sullenly. 'I knew this was too good to be true.' She spat. 'Shit! No good deed goes unpunished.'

Arkadin took a moment to process what she was really saying. Then he said, 'Why did Shumenko need the ten thousand hryvnia?'

'So I was right. You're not a friend of his.'

'Does it matter?' Arkadin emptied the handgun, broke it down without taking his eyes off her, tossed the pieces onto the table. 'This is between you and me now.'

'I think not,' a deep male voice said from behind him.

'Filya,' Devra breathed. 'What took you so long?'

Arkadin did not turn around. He'd heard the click of the switchblade, knew what he was up against. He eyeballed the mess on the table, and when he saw the double half-moon grips of scissors peeping out from under a small pyramid of CD cases, he fixed their location in his mind, then turned around.

As if startled by the big man with heavily pocked cheeks and new hair plugs, he retreated up against the edge of the table.

'Who the hell're you? This is a private discussion.' Arkadin spoke more to distract Filya from his left hand moving behind him along the tabletop.

'Devra is mine.' Filya brandished the long, cruel blade of the handmade switchblade. 'No one talks to her without my permission.'

Arkadin smiled thinly. 'I wasn't talking to her so much as threatening her.'

The idea was to antagonize Filya to the point that he'd do something precipitous and, therefore, stupid, and Arkadin succeeded admirably. With a growl, Filya rushed him, knife blade extended, tilted slightly upward.

With only one shot at a surprise maneuver, Arkadin had to make the most of it. The fingers of his left hand had gripped the scissors. They were small, which was just as well; he had no intention of again killing someone who might provide useful information. He lifted them, calculating their weight. Then as he brought the scissors around the side of his body, he flicked his wrist, a deceptively small gesture that was nevertheless all power. Released from his grip, the scissors flew through the air, embedding in the soft spot just below Filya's sternum.

Filya's eyes opened wide as his headlong rush faltered two paces from Arkadin, then he resumed his advance, brandishing the knife. Arkadin ducked away from the sweeping arc of the blade. He grappled with Filya, wanting only to wear him out, let the wound in his chest sap his strength, but Filya wasn't having any. Being stabbed had only enraged him. With superhuman strength he broke Arkadin's grip on the wrist that held the switchblade, swung it from a low point upward, breaking through Arkadin's defense. The point of the blade blurred toward Arkadin's face. Too late to stop the attack, Arkadin reacted instinctively, managing to deflect the stab at the last instant, so that the point drove through Filya's own throat.

An arcing veil of blood caused Devra to scream. As she stumbled backward, Arkadin reached for her. Clamping one hand over her mouth, he shook his head. Her ashen cheeks and forehead were spattered with blood. Arkadin supported Filya in the crook of one arm. The man was dying. Arkadin had never meant this to happen. First Shumenko, now Filya. If he had believed in such things, he would have said that the assignment was cursed.

'Filya!' He slapped the man, whose eyes had turned glassy. Blood leaked out of the side of Filya's slack mouth. 'The package. Where is it?'

For a moment, Filya's eyes focused on him. When Arkadin repeated his question a curious smile took Filya down into death. Arkadin held him for a moment more before propping him up against a wall.

As he returned his attention to Devra he saw a rat glowering from a corner, and his gorge rose. It took all his willpower not to abandon the girl to go after it, rip it limb from limb.

'Now,' he said, 'it's just you and me.'

*

Making certain he wasn't being followed, Rob Batt pulled into the parking lot adjacent to the Tysons Corner Baptist Church. He sat waiting in his car. From time to time, he checked his watch.

Under the late DCI, he had been chief of operations, the most influential of CI's seven directorate heads. He was of the Beltway old school with connections that ran directly back to Yale's legendary Skull & Bones Club, of which he'd been an officer during his college days. Just how many Skull & Bones men had been recruited into America's clandestine services was one of those secrets its keepers would kill to protect. Suffice it to say it was many, and Batt was one of them. It was particularly galling for him to play second fiddle to an outsider – and a female, at that. The Old Man would never have tolerated such an outrage, but the Old Man was gone, murdered in his own home reportedly by his traitorous assistant, Anne Held. Though Batt – and others of his brethren – had his doubts about that.

What a difference three months made. Had the Old Man still been alive he'd never have considered even consenting to this meet. Batt was a loyal man, but his loyalty, he realized, extended to the man who had reached out to him in grad school, recruited him to CI. Those were the old days, though. The new order was in place, and it wasn't fair. He hadn't been part of the problem caused by Martin Lindros and Jason Bourne – he'd been part of the solution. He'd even been suspicious of the man who'd turned out to be an impostor. He would have exposed him had Bourne not interfered. That coup, Batt knew, would have scored him the inside track with the Old Man.

But with the Old Man gone, his lobbying for the directorship had been to no avail. Instead, the president had opted for Veronica Hart. God alone knew why. It was such a colossal mistake; she'd just run CI into the ground. A woman wasn't constructed to make the kinds of decisions necessary to captain the CI ship. The priorities and ways of approaching problems were different with women. The hounds of the NSA were circling CI, and he couldn't bear watching this woman turn them all, the entire company, into carrion for the feast. At least Batt could join the people who would inevitably take over when Hart fucked up. Even so, it pained him to be here, to embark upon this unknown sea.

At 10:30 A.M. the doors to the church swung open, the parishioners came down the stairs, stood in the wan sunshine, turning their heads up like sunflowers at dawn. The ministers appeared, walking side by side with Luther LaValle. LaValle was accompanied by his wife and teenage son. The two men stood chatting while the family grouped loosely around. LaValle's wife seemed interested in the conversation, but the son was busy ogling a girl more or less his age who was prancing down the stairs. She was a beauty, Batt had to admit. Then, with a start, he realized that she was one of General Kendall's three daughters, because here Kendall was with his arm around his stubby wife. How the two of them could have produced a trio of such handsome girls was anyone's guess. Even Darwin couldn't have figured it out, Batt thought.

The two families – the LaValles and the Kendalls – gathered in a loose huddle as if they were a football team. Then the kids went their own ways, some in cars, others on bicycles because the church wasn't far from their homes. The two wives chastely kissed their husbands, piled into a Cadillac Escalade, and took off.

That left the two men, who stood for a moment in front of the church before coming around to the parking lot. Not a word had been exchanged between them. Batt heard a heavyweight engine cough to life.

A long black armored limousine came cruising down the aisle like a sleek shark. It stopped briefly while LaValle and Kendall climbed inside. Its engine, idling, sent small puffs of exhaust into the cool, crisp air. Batt counted to thirty and, as he'd been instructed, got out of his car. As he did so, the rear door of the limo popped open. Ducking his head, he climbed into the dim, plush interior. The door closed behind him.

'Gentlemen,' he said, folding himself onto the bench seat opposite them. The two men sat side by side in the limo's backseat: Luther LaValle, the Pentagon's intel czar, and his second, General Richard P. Kendall.

'So kind of you to join us,' LaValle said.

Kindness had nothing to do with it, Batt thought. A convergence of objectives did.

'The pleasure's all mine, gentlemen. I'm flattered and, if I may be frank, grateful that you reached out to me.'

'We're here,' General Kendall said, 'to speak frankly.'

'We've opposed the appointment of Veronica Hart from the start,' LaValle said. 'The secretary of defense made his opinion quite clear to the president. However, others, including the national security advisor and the secretary of state – who, as you know, is a personal friend of the president – both lobbied for an outsider from the private security sector.'

'Bad enough,' Batt said. 'And a woman.'

'Precisely.' General Kendall nodded. 'It's madness.'

LaValle stirred. 'It's the clearest sign yet of the deterioration of our defense grid that Secretary Halliday has been warning against for several years now.'

'When we start listening to Congress and the people of the country all hope is lost,' Kendall said. 'A mulligan stew of amateurs all with petty axes to grind and absolutely no idea of how to maintain security or run the intelligence services.'

LaValle gave off an icy smile. 'That's why the secretary of defense has labored mightily to keep the workings clandestine.'

'The more they know, the less they understand,' General Kendall said, 'and the more inclined they are to interfere by means of their congressional hearings and threats of budget cuts.'

'Oversight is a bitch,' LaValle agreed. 'Which is why areas of the Pentagon under my control are working without it.' He paused for a moment, studying Batt. 'How does that sound to you, Deputy Director?'

'Like manna from heaven.'

'Oleg had screwed up big time,' Devra said.

Arkadin took a stab. 'He got in over his head with loan sharks?'

She shook her head. 'That was last year. It had to do with Pyotr Zilber.'

Arkadin's ears pricked up. 'What about him?'

'I don't know.' Her eyes opened wide as Arkadin raised his fist. 'I swear it.'

'But you're part of Zilber's network.'

She turned her head away from him, as if she couldn't stand herself. 'A minor part. I shuffle things from here to there.'

'Within the past week Shumenko gave you a document.'

'He gave me a package, I don't know what was in it,' Devra said. 'It was sealed.'

'Compartmentalization.'

'What?' She looked up at him. Blood beads on her face looked like freckles. Tears had caused her mascara to run, giving her dark half circles under her eyes.

'The first principle of putting together a cadre.' Arkadin nodded. 'Go on.'

She shrugged. 'That's all I know.'

'What about the package?'

'I passed it on, as I was instructed to do.'

Arkadin bent over her. 'Who did you give it to?'

She glanced at the crumpled form on the floor. 'I gave it to Filya.'

LaValle had paused a moment to reflect. 'We never knew each other at Yale.'

'You were two years ahead of me,' Batt said. 'But in Skull and Bones you were notorious.'

LaValle laughed. 'Now you flatter me.'

'Hardly.' Batt unbuttoned his overcoat. 'The stories I heard.'

LaValle frowned. 'Are never to be repeated.'

General Kendall let loose with a guffaw that filled the compartment. 'Should I leave you two girls alone? Better not; one of you could wind up pregnant.'

The comment was meant as a joke, of course, but there was a nasty undercurrent to it. Did the military man resent his exclusion from the elite club, or the connection the other two had through Skull & Bones? Possibly it was a bit of both. In any event, Batt noted the second's tone of voice, tucked the possible implications into a place where he could examine them later.

'What d'you have in mind, Mr. LaValle?'

'I'm looking for a way to convince the president that his more immoderate advisors made a mistake in recommending Veronica Hart for DCI.' LaValle pursed his lips. 'Any ideas?'

'Off the top of my head, plenty,' Batt said. 'What's in it for me?'

As if on cue LaValle produced another smile. 'We're going to require a new DCI when we can get Hart's ass out of the District. Who would be your first choice?'

'The current deputy director seems the logical one,' Batt said. 'That would be me.'

LaValle nodded. 'Our thought precisely.'

Batt tapped his fingertips against his knee. 'If you two are serious.'

'We are, I assure you.'

Batt's mind worked furiously. 'It seems to me unwise at this early juncture to have attacked Hart directly.'

'How about you don't tell us our business,' Kendall said.

LaValle held up a hand. 'Let's hear what the man has to say, Richard.' To Batt, he added, 'However, let me make something crystal clear. We want Hart out as soon as possible.'

'We all do, but you don't want suspicion thrown back at you – or at the defense secretary.'

LaValle and General Kendall exchanged a quick and knowing look. They were like twins, able to communicate with each other without uttering a word. 'Indeed not,' LaValle said.

'She told me how you ambushed her at that meeting with the president – and the threats you made to her outside the White House.'

'Women are more easily intimidated than men,' Kendall pointed out. 'It's a well-known fact.'

Batt ignored the military man. 'You put her on notice. She took your threats very personally. She had a killer's rep in Black River. I checked through my sources.'

LaValle seemed thoughtful. 'How would you have handled her?'

'I would have made nice, welcomed her to the fold, let her know you're there for her whenever she needs your help.'

'She'd never have bought it,' LaValle said. 'She knows my agenda.'

'It doesn't matter. The idea is not to antagonize her. You don't want her knives out when you come for her.'

LaValle nodded, as if he saw the wisdom in this approach. 'So how do you suggest we proceed from here?'

'Give me some time,' Batt said. 'Hart's just getting started at CI, and because I'm her deputy I know everything she does, every decision she makes. But when she's out of the office, shadow her, see where she goes, who she meets. Using parabolic mikes you can listen in to her conversations. Between us, we'll have her covered twenty-four/seven.'

'Sounds pretty vanilla to me,' Kendall said skeptically.

'Keep it simple, especially when there's so much at stake, that's my advice,' Batt said.

'What if she cottons on to the surveillance?' Kendall said.

Batt smiled. 'So much the better. It'll only bolster the CI mantra that the NSA is run by incompetents.'

LaValle laughed. 'Batt, I like the way you think.'

Batt nodded, acknowledging the compliment. 'Coming from the private sector Hart's not used to government procedure. She doesn't have the leeway she enjoyed at Black River. I can already see that, to her, rules and regs are meant to be bent, sidestepped, even, on occasion, broken. Mark my words, sooner rather than later, Director Hart is going to give us the ammunition we need to kick her butt out of CI.'

# 7

'How is your foot, Jason?'

Bourne looked up at Professor Specter, whose face was swollen and discolored. His left eye was half closed, dark as a storm cloud.

'Yes,' Specter said, 'after what just happened I'm compelled to call you by what seems like your rightful name.'

'My heel is fine,' Bourne said. 'It's me who should be asking about you.'

Specter put fingertips gingerly against his cheek. 'In my life I've endured worse beatings.'

The two men were seated in a high-ceilinged library filled with a large, magnificent Isfahan carpet, ox-blood leather furniture. Three walls were fitted floor-to-ceiling with books neatly arrayed on mahogany shelves. The fourth wall was pierced by a large leaded-glass window overlooking stands of stately firs on a knoll, which sloped down to a pond guarded by a weeping willow, shivering in the wind.

Specter's personal physician had been summoned, but the professor had insisted the doctor tend to Bourne's flayed heel first.

'I'm sure we can find you a pair of shoes somewhere,' Specter said, sending one of the half a dozen men in residence scurrying off with Bourne's remaining shoe.

This rather large stone-and-slate house deep in the Virginia countryside to which Specter had directed Bourne was a far cry from the modest apartment the professor maintained near the university. Bourne had been to the apartment numerous times over the years, but never here. Then there was the matter of the staff, which Bourne noted with interest as well as surprise.

'I imagine you're wondering about all this,' Specter said, as if reading Bourne's mind. 'All in good time, my friend.' He smiled. 'First, I must thank you for rescuing me.'

'Who were those men?' Bourne said. 'Why did they try to kidnap you?'

The doctor applied an antibiotic ointment, placed a gauze pad over the heel, taped it in place. Then he wrapped the heel in cohesive bandage.

'It's a long story,' Specter said. The doctor, finished with Bourne, now rose to examine the professor. 'One I propose to tell you over the breakfast we were unable to enjoy earlier.' He winced as the doctor palpated areas of his body.

'Contusions, bruises,' the doctor intoned colorlessly, 'but no broken bones or fractures.'

He was a small swarthy man with a mustache and dark slicked-back hair. Bourne made him as Turkish. In fact, all the staff seemed of Turkish origin.

He gave Specter a small packet. 'You may need these painkillers, but only for the next forty-eight hours.' He'd already left a tube of the antibiotic cream, along with instructions, for Bourne.

While Specter was being examined, Bourne used his cell phone to call Deron, the art forger whom he used for all his travel documents. Bourne recited the license tag of the black Cadillac he'd commandeered from the professor's would-be kidnappers.

'I need a registration report ASAP.'

'You okay, Jason?' Deron said in his sonorous London-accented voice. Deron had been Bourne's backup through many hair-raising missions. He always asked the same question.

'I'm fine,' Bourne said, 'but that's more than I can say for the car's original occupants.'

'Brilliant.'

Bourne pictured him in his lab in the northeast section of DC, a tall, vibrant black man with the mind of a conjuror.

When the doctor departed, Bourne and Specter were left alone.

'I already know who came after me,' Specter said.

'I don't like loose ends,' Bourne replied. 'The Cadillac's registration will tell us something, perhaps something even you don't know.'

The professor nodded, clearly impressed.

Bourne sat on the leather sofa with his leg up on the coffee table. Specter eased himself into a facing chair. Clouds chased each other across the windblown sky, setting patterns shifting across the Persian carpet. Bourne saw a different kind of shadow pass across Specter's face.

'Professor, what is it?'

Specter shook his head. 'I owe you a most sincere and abject apology, Jason. I'm afraid I had an ulterior motive in asking you to return to university life.' His eyes were filled with regret. 'I thought it would be good for you, yes, that's true enough, absolutely. But also I wanted you near me because . . .' He waved a hand as if to clear the air of deceit. 'Because I was fearful that what happened this morning would happen. Now, because of my selfishness, I'm very much afraid that I've put your life in jeopardy.'

Turkish tea, strong and intensely aromatic, was served along with eggs, smoked fish, coarse bread, butter, deep yellow and fragrant.

Bourne and Specter sat at a long table covered with a white hand-finished linen cloth. The china and silverware were of the highest quality. Again, an oddity in an academic's household. They remained mute while a young man, slim and sleek, served their perfectly cooked, elegantly presented breakfast.

When Bourne began to ask a question, Specter cut him off. 'First we must fill our stomachs, regain our strength, ensure our minds are working at full capacity.'

The two men did not speak again until they were finished, the plates and cutlery were cleared, and a fresh pot of tea had been poured. A small bowl of gigantic Medjool dates and halved fresh pomegranates lay between them.

When they were again alone in the dining room, Specter said without preamble, 'The night before last I received word that a former student of mine whose father was a close friend was dead. Murdered in a most despicable fashion. This young man,

Pyotr Zilber, was special. Besides being a former student he ran an information network that spanned several countries. After a number of difficult and perilous months of subterfuge and negotiation he had managed to obtain for me a vital document. He was found out, with the inevitable consequences. This is the incident I've been dreading. It may sound melodramatic, but I assure you it's the truth: The war I've been engaged in for close to twenty years has reached its final stage.'

'What sort of a war, Professor?' Bourne said. 'Against whom?'

'I'll get to that in a moment.' Specter leaned forward. 'I imagine you're curious, shocked even, that a university professor should be involved in matters that are more the province of Jason Bourne.' He lifted both arms briefly to encompass the house. 'But as you've no doubt noted there is more to me than meets the eye.' He smiled rather sadly. 'This makes two of us, yes?'

'As someone who also leads a double life I understand you better than most others. I need one personality when I step onto campus, but here I'm someone else entirely.' He tapped a stubby forefinger against the side of his nose. 'I pay attention. I saw something familiar in you the moment I met you – how your eyes took in every detail of the people and things around you.'

Bourne's cell buzzed. He flipped it open, listened to what Deron had to say, then put the phone away.

'The Cadillac was reported stolen an hour before it appeared in front of the restaurant.'

'That is entirely unsurprising.'

'Who tried to kidnap you, Professor?'

'I know you're impatient for the facts, Jason. I would be, too, in your place. But I promise they won't have meaning without some background first. When I said there's more to me than meets the eye, this is what I meant: I'm a terrorist hunter. For many years, from the camouflage and sanctuary my position at the university affords me, I have built up a network of people who gather intelligence just like your own CI. However, the intelligence that interests me is highly specific. There are people who took my wife from me. In the dead of night, while I was away, they snatched her from our house, tortured her, killed her, then dumped her on my doorstep. As a warning, you see.'

Bourne felt a prickling at the back of his neck. He knew what it felt like to be driven by revenge. When Martin died all Bourne could think about was destroying the men who'd tortured him. He felt a new, more intimate connection with Specter, even as the Bourne identity rose inside him, riding a cresting wave of pure adrenaline. All at once the idea of him working at the university struck him as absurd. Moira was right: He was already chafing at the confinement. How would he feel after months of the academic life, bereft of adventure, stripped of the adrenaline rush for which Bourne lived?

'My father was taken because he was plotting to overthrow the head of an organization. They call themselves the Eastern Brotherhood.'

'Doesn't the EB espouse a peaceful integration of Muslims into Western society?'

'That's their public stance, certainly, and their literature would have you believe it's so.' Specter put down his cup. 'In fact, nothing could be farther from the truth. I know them as the Black Legion.'

'Then the Black Legion has finally decided to come after you.'

'If only it were as simple as that.' He halted at a discreet knock on the door. 'Enter.'

The young man he'd sent on the errand strode in carrying a shoe box, which he set down in front of Bourne.

Specter gestured. 'Please.'

Taking his foot off the table, Bourne opened the box. Inside were a pair of very fine Italian loafers, along with a pair of socks.

'The left one is half a size larger to accommodate the pad that will protect your heel,' the young man said in German.

Bourne pulled on the socks, slipped on the loafers. They fit perfectly. Seeing this, Specter nodded to the young man, who turned and, without another word, left the room.

'Does he speak English?' Bourne asked.

'Oh, yes. Whenever the need arises.' Specter's face was wreathed in a mischievous smile. 'And now, my dear Jason, you're asking yourself why he's speaking German if he's a Turk?'

'I assume it's because your network spans many countries including Germany, which is, like England, a hotbed of Muslim terrorist activity.'

Specter's smile deepened. 'You're like a rock. I can always count on you.' He raised a forefinger. 'But there is yet another reason. It has to do with the Black Legion. Come. I've something to show you.'

Filya Petrovich, Pyotr's Sevastopol courier, lived in an anonymous block of crumbling housing left over from the days the Soviets had reshaped the city into a vast barracks housing its largest naval contingent. The apartment, frozen in time since the 1970s, had all the charm of a meat locker.

Arkadin opened the door with the key he'd found on Filya. He pushed Devra over the threshold, stepped in. Turning on the lights, he closed the door behind him. She hadn't wanted to come, but she had no say in the matter, just as she'd had no say in helping him drag Filya's corpse out the nightclub's back door. They set him down at the end of the filthy alley, propped up against a wall damp with unknown fluids. Arkadin poured the contents of a half-empty bottle of cheap vodka over him, then pressed the man's fingers around the bottle's neck. Filya became one drunk among many other drunks in the city. His death would be swept away on an inefficient and overworked bureaucratic tide.

'What're you looking for?' Devra stood in the middle of the living room, watching Arkadin's methodical search. 'What d'you think you'll find? The document?' Her laugh was a kind of shrill catcall. 'It's gone.'

Arkadin glanced up from the mess his switchblade had made of the sofa cushions. 'Where?'

'Far out of your reach, that's for sure.'

Closing his knife, Arkadin crossed the space between the two of them in one long stride. 'Do you think this is a joke, or a game we're playing here?'

Devra's upper lip curled. 'Are you going to hurt me now? Believe me, nothing you could do would be worse than what's already been done to me.'

Arkadin, the blood pounding in his veins, held himself in check to consider her words. What she said was probably the truth. Under the Soviet boot, God had forsaken many Ukrainians, especially the young attractive females. He needed to take another tack entirely.

'I'm not going to hurt you, even though you're with the wrong people.' He turned on his heel, sat down on a wood-framed chair. Leaning back, he ran his fingers through his hair. 'I've seen a lot of shit – I've done two stints in prison. I can imagine the systematic brutalization you've been through.'

'Me and my mother, God rest her soul.'

The headlights of passing cars shone briefly through the windows, then dwindled away. A dog barked in an alleyway, its melancholy voice echoing. A couple passing by outside argued vehemently. Inside the shabby apartment the patchy light cast by the lamps, their shades either torn or askew, caused Devra to look terribly vulnerable, like a wisp of a child. Arkadin rose, stretched mightily, strolled over to the window, looked out onto the street. His eyes picked out every bit of shadow, every flare of light no matter how brief or tiny. Sooner or later Pyotr's people were going to come after him; it was an inevitability that he and Icoupov had discussed before he left the villa. Icoupov had offered to send a couple of hard men to lie low in Sevastopol in the event they were needed, but Arkadin refused, saying he preferred to work alone.

Having assured himself that the street was for the moment clear, he turned away from the window, back to the room. 'My mother died badly,' he said. 'She was murdered, brutally beaten, left in a closet for the rats to gnaw on. At least that's what the coroner told me.'

'Where was your father?'

Arkadin shrugged. 'Who knows? By that time, the sonovabitch could've been in Shanghai, or he could've been dead. My mother told me he was a merchant marine, but I seriously doubt it. She was ashamed of having been knocked up by a perfect stranger.'

Devra, who had sat down on the ripped-apart arm of the sofa during this recitation, said, 'It sucks not knowing where you came from, doesn't it? Like always being adrift at sea. You'll never recognize home even if you come upon it.'

'Home,' Arkadin said heavily. 'I never think of it.'

Devra caught something in his tone. 'But you'd like to, wouldn't you?'

His expression went sour. He checked the street again with his usual thoroughness. 'What would be the point?'

'Because knowing where we come from allows us to know who we are.' She beat softly at her chest with a fist. 'Our past is part of us.'

Arkadin felt as if she'd pricked him with a needle. Venom squirted through his veins. 'My past is an island I've sailed away from long ago.'

'Nevertheless, it's still with you, even if you're not aware of it,' she said with the force of having mulled the question over and over in her own mind. 'We can't outrun our past, no matter how hard we try.'

Unlike him, she seemed eager to talk about her past. He found this curious. Did she think this subject was common ground? If so, he needed to stay with it, to keep the connection with her going.

'What about your father?'

'I was born here, grew up here.' She stared down at her hands. 'My father was a naval engineer. He was thrown out of the shipyards when the Russians took it over. Then one night they came for him, said he was spying on them, delivering technical information on their ships to the Americans. I never saw him again. But the Russian security officer in charge took a liking to my mother. When he'd used her up, he started on me.'

Arkadin could just imagine. 'How did it end?'

'An American killed him.' She looked up at him. 'Fucking ironic, because this American was a spy sent to photograph the Russian fleet. When the American had completed his assignment he should've gone back home. Instead he stayed. He took care of me, nursed me back to health.'

'Naturally you fell in love with him.'

She laughed. 'If I was a character in a novel, sure. But he was so kind to me; I was like a daughter to him. I cried when he left.'

Arkadin found that he was embarrassed by her confession. To distract himself, he looked around the ruined apartment one more time.

Devra watched him warily. 'Hey. I'm dying for something to eat.'

Arkadin laughed. 'Aren't we all?'

His hawk-like gaze took in the street once more. This time the hairs on the back of his neck stirred as he stepped to the side of the window. A car he'd heard approaching had pulled up in front of the building. Devra, alerted by the sudden tension in his body, moved to the window behind him. What caught his attention was that though its engine was still running, all its lights had been extinguished. Three men exited the car, headed for the building entrance. It was past time to leave.

He turned away from the window. 'We're going. Now.'

'Pyotr's people. It was inevitable they'd find us.'

Much to Arkadin's surprise she made no protest when he hustled her out of the apartment. The hallway was already reverberating with the tribal beat of heavy shoes on the concrete floor.

Bourne found walking unpleasant but hardly intolerable. He'd put up with a lot worse than a flayed heel in his time. As he followed the professor down a metal staircase into the basement, he reflected that this was proof again that there were no absolutes when it came to people. He had assumed that Specter's life was neat, tidy, dull, and quiet, restricted by the dimensions of the university campus. Nothing could be farther from the truth.

Halfway down, the staircase changed to stone treads, worn by decades of use. Their way was guided by plenty of light from below. They entered a finished basement made up of movable walls that separated what looked like office cubicles outfitted with laptop computers attached to high-speed modems. All of them were staffed.

Specter stopped at the last cubicle, where a young man appeared to be decoding text that scrolled across his computer screen. The young man, becoming aware of Specter, pulled a sheet of paper out of the printer hopper, handed it to him. As soon as the professor read it a change came over his demeanor. Though he kept his expression neutral, a certain tension stiffened his frame.

'Good work.' He gave the young man a nod before he led Bourne into a room that appeared to be a small library. Specter crossed to one section of the shelves, touched the spine of a compilation of haiku by the master poet Matsuo Bashō. A square section of the books opened to reveal a set of drawers. From one of these Specter pulled out what looked like a photo album. All the pages were old, each one wrapped in archival plastic to preserve them. He showed one of them to Bourne.

At the top was the familiar war eagle, gripping a swastika in its beak, the symbol of Germany's Third Reich. The text was in German. Just below was the word OSTLEGIONEN, accompanied by a color photo of a woven oval, obviously a uniform insignia, of a swastika encircled by laurel leaves. Around the central symbol were the words TREU, TAPIR, GEHORSAM, which Bourne translated as 'loyal, brave, steadfast.' Below that was another color photo of a woven rampant wolf's head, under which was the designation: OSTMANISCHE SS-DIVISION.

Bourne noted the date on the page: 14 December 1941.

'I never heard of the Eastern Legions,' Bourne said. 'Who were they?'

Specter turned the page and there, pinned to it, was a square of olive fabric. On it had been sewn a blue shield with a black border. Across the top was the word BERGKAUKASIEN – Caucasus Mountains. Directly beneath it in bright yellow was the emblem of three horses' heads joined to what Bourne now knew was a death's head, the symbol of the Nazi Schutzstaffel, the Protective Squadron, known colloquially as the SS. It was exactly the same as the tattoo on the gunman's arm.

'Not were, *are.*' Specter's eyes glittered. 'They're the people who tried to kidnap me, Jason. They want to interrogate me and kill me. Now that they've become aware of you, they'll want to do the same to you.'

# 8

'The roof or the basement?' Arkadin said.

'The roof,' she said at once. 'There's only one way in and out of the basement itself.'

They ran as fast as they could to the stairway, then took the steps two at a time. Arkadin's heart pounded, his blood raced, the adrenaline pumped into him with every leap upward. He could hear his pursuers laboring up below him. The noose was tightening around him. Racing to the far end of the narrow hallway, he reached up with his right hand, pulled down the metal ladder that led to the roof. Soviet structures of this era were notorious for their flimsy doors. He knew he'd have no trouble breaking out onto the roof. From there, it was a short jump to the next building and the next, then down to the streets, where it would be easy to elude the enemy.

Boosting Devra's body through the square hole in the ceiling, he clambered up. Behind him, the shouted calls of the three men: Filya's apartment had been searched. All of them were coming after him. Gaining the tiny landing, he now faced the door to the roof, but when he tried to push against the horizontal metal bar nothing happened. He pushed harder, with the same result. Fishing a ring of slender metal picks out of his pocket, he inserted one after another into the lock, fiddling it up and down, getting nowhere. Looking more closely, he could see why: The interior of the cheap lock was rusted shut. It wouldn't open.

He turned back, staring down the ladder. Here came his pursuers. He had nowhere to go.

On June 22, 1941, Germany invaded Soviet Russia,' Professor Specter said. 'As they did so they came upon thousands upon thousands of enemy soldiers who either surrendered without a fight or were flat-out deserting. By August of that year the invading army had interned half a million Soviet prisoners of war. Many of them were Muslims – Tatars from the Caucasus, Turks, Azerbaijani, Uzbek, Kazakhs, others from the tribes in the Ural Mountains, Turkestan, Crimea. The one thing all these Muslims had in common was their hatred of the Soviets, Stalin in particular. To make a very long story short, these Muslims, taken as prisoners of war, offered their services to the Nazis to fight alongside them on the Eastern Front, where they could do the most damage both by infiltration and by decoding Soviet intelligence transmissions. The Führer was elated; the Ostlegionen became the particular interest of Reichsführer SS Heinrich Himmler, who saw Islam as a masculine, war-like religion that featured certain key qualities in common with his SS philosophy, mainly blind obedience, the willingness for self-sacrifice, a total lack of compassion for the enemy.'

Bourne was absorbing every word, every detail of the photos. 'Didn't his embrace of Islam fly in the face of the Nazi racial order?'

'You know humans better than most, Jason. They have an infinite capacity for rationalizing reality to fit their personal ideas. So it was with Himmler, who had convinced himself that the Slavs and the Jews were subhuman. The Asian element in the Russian nation made those people who were descended from the great war-riors Attila, Genghis Khan, Tamerlane fit his criteria of superiority. Himmler embraced the Muslims from that area, descendants of the Mongols.

'These men became the core of the Nazi Ostlegionen, but the cream of the crop Himmler reserved for himself, training them in secret with his best SS leaders, honing their skills not simply as soldiers, but as the elite warriors, spies, and assas-sins it was widely known he'd yearned to command. He called this unit the Black Legion. You see, I've made an exhaustive study of the Nazis and their Ostlegionen.' Specter pointed to the shield of three horses' heads joined by the death's head. 'This is their emblem. From 1943 on it became more feared than even the SS's own twin lightning bolts, or the symbol of its adjunct, the Gestapo.'

'It's a little late in the day for Nazis to be a serious threat,' Bourne said, 'don't you think?'

'The Black Legion's Nazi affiliation has long since vanished. It's now the most powerful and influential Islamic terrorist network no one has heard of. Its anonymity is deliberate. It is funded through the legitimate front, the Eastern Brotherhood.'

Specter took out another album. This one was filled with newspaper clippings of terrorist attacks all over the world: London, Madrid, Karachi, Fallujah, Afghanistan, Russia. As Bourne paged through the album, the list grew.

'As you can see, other, known terrorist networks claimed responsibility for some of these attacks. For others, no claim was made, no terrorists were ever linked to them. But I know through my sources that all were perpetrated by the Black Legion,' Specter said. 'And now they're planning their biggest, most spectacular attack. Jason, we think that they're targeting New York. I told you Pyotr Zilber, the young man the Black Legion murdered, was special. He was a magician. He'd somehow managed to steal the plans for the target of the Legion's attack. Normally, of course, the planning would all be oral. But apparently the target of this attack is so complex, the Black Legion had to obtain the actual plans of the structure. That's why I believe it to be a large building in a major metropolitan area. It's absolutely imperative that we find that document. It's the only way we'll know where the Black Legion intends to strike.'

Arkadin sat on the floor of the small landing, his legs on either side of the opening down to the top residential floor.

'Shout to them,' he whispered. Now that he was situated on the high ground, so to speak, he wanted to draw them to him. 'Go on. Let them know where you are.'

Devra screamed.

Now Arkadin heard the hollow ring of someone climbing the metal ladder. When a head popped up, along with a hand holding a gun, Arkadin slammed his ankles into the man's ears. As his eyes began to roll up, Arkadin snatched the gun from his hand, braced himself, and broke the man's neck.

The moment he let go the man vanished, clattering back down the ladder. Predictably, a hail of gunfire shot through the square opening, the bullets embedding themselves in the ceiling. The moment that abated, Arkadin shoved Devra through the opening, followed her, sliding down with the insides of his shoes against the outside of the ladder.

As Arkadin had hoped, the remaining two men were stunned by the fall of their compatriot and held their fire. Arkadin shot one through the right eye. The other retreated around a corner as Arkadin fired at him. Arkadin gathered the girl, bruised but otherwise fine, ran to the first door, and pounded on it. Hearing a querulous man's voice raised in protest, he pounded on the opposite door. No answer. Firing his gun at the lock, he crashed open the door.

The apartment was unoccupied, and from the looks of the piles of dust and filth no one had been in residence in quite some time. Arkadin ran to the window. As he did so, he heard familiar squeals. He stepped on a pile of rubbish and out leapt a rat, then another and another. They were all over the place. Arkadin shot the first one, then got hold of himself and slid the window up as far as it would go. Icy rain struck him, sluiced down the side of the building.

Holding Devra in front of him, he straddled the sash. At that moment he heard the third man calling for reinforcements, and fired three shots through the ruined door. He manhandled her out onto the narrow fire escape and edged them to his left, toward the vertical ladder bolted to the concrete that led to the roof.

Save for one or two security lights, the Sevastopol night was darker than Hades itself. The rain slanted in needled sheets, beating against his face and arms. He was close enough to reach out for the ladder when the wrought-iron slats on which he was walking gave way.

Devra shrieked as the two of them plummeted, landing against the railing of the fire escape below. Almost immediately this rickety affair gave way beneath their weight and they toppled over the end. Arkadin reached out, grabbed a rung of the ladder with his left hand. He held on to Devra with his right. They dangled in the air, the ground too far for him to risk letting go. Plus there was no convenient fully loaded Dumpster to break their fall.

He began to lose his grip on her hand.

'Draw yourself up,' he said. 'Put your legs around me.'

'What?'

He bellowed the command at her and, flinching, she did as he ordered.

'Now lock your ankles tight around my waist.'

This time she didn't hesitate.

'All right,' Arkadin said, 'now reach up, you can just make the lowest rung – no, hold on to it with both hands.'

The rain made the metal slippery, and on the first attempt Devra lost her grip.

'Again,' Arkadin shouted. 'And this time don't let go.'

Clearly terrified, Devra closed her fingers around the rung, held on so tightly her knuckles turned white. As for Arkadin, his left arm was being slowly dislocated from its socket. If he didn't change his position soon, he'd be done for.

'Now what?' Devra said.

'Once your grip on the rung is secure, uncross your ankles and pull yourself up the ladder until you can stand on a rung.'

'I don't know if I have the strength.'

He lifted himself up until he'd wedged the rung in his right armpit. His left arm was numb. He worked his fingers, and bolts of pain shot up into his throbbing shoulder. 'Go ahead,' he said, pushing her up. He couldn't let her see how much pain he was in. His left arm was in agony, but he kept pushing her.

Finally, she stood on the ladder above him. She looked down. 'Now you.'

His entire left side was numb; the rest of him was on fire.

Devra reached down toward him. 'Come on.'

'I've got nothing much to live for, I died a long time ago.'

'Screw you.' She crouched down so when she reached down again she grabbed onto his arm. As she did so, her foot slipped off the rung, slid downward and against him with such force she almost dislodged them both.

'Christ, I'm going to fall!' she screamed.

'Wrap your legs back around my waist,' he shouted. 'That's right. Now let go of the ladder one hand at a time. Hold on to me instead.'

When she'd done as he said, he commenced to climb up the ladder. Once he was high enough to get his shoes onto the rungs the going was easier. He ignored the fire burning up his left shoulder; he needed both hands to ascend.

They made the roof at last, rolling over the stone parapet, lying breathless on tar streaming with water. That was when Arkadin realized the rain was no longer hitting his face. He looked up, saw a man – the third of the trio – standing over him, a gun aimed at his face.

The man grinned. 'Time to die, bastard.'

Professor Specter put the albums away. Before he closed the drawer, however, he took out a pair of photos. Bourne studied the faces of two men. The one in the first photo was approximately the same age as the professor. Glasses almost comically magnified large, watery eyes, above which lay remarkably thick eyebrows. Otherwise, his head was bald.

'Semion Icoupov,' Specter said, 'leader of the Black Legion.'

He took Bourne out of the basement library, up the steps, out the back of the house into the fresh air. A formal English garden lay before them, defined by low boxwood hedges. The sky was an airy blue, high and rich, full of the promise of an early spring. A bird fluttered between the bare branches of the willow, unsure where to alight.

'Jason, we need to stop the Black Legion. The only way to do that is to kill Semion Icoupov. I've already lost three good men to that end. I need someone better. I need you.'

'I'm not a contract killer.'

'Jason, please don't take offense. I need your help to stop this attack. Icoupov knows where the plans are.'

'All right. I'll find him and the plans.' Bourne shook his head. 'But he doesn't have to be killed.'

The professor shook his head sadly. 'A noble sentiment, but you don't know Semion Icoupov like I do. If you don't kill him, he'll surely kill you. Believe me when I tell you I've tried to take him alive. None of my men has returned from that assignment.'

He stared out across the pond. 'There's no one else I can turn to, no one else who has the expertise to find Icoupov and end this madness once and for all. Pyotr's murder signals the beginning of the endgame between me and the Black Legion. Either we stop them here or they will be successful in their attack on this target.'

'If what you say is true –'

'It is, Jason. I swear to you.'

'Where is Icoupov?'

'We don't know. For the last forty-eight hours we've been trying to track him, but everything's turned up a blank. He was in his villa in Campione d'Italia, Switzerland. That's where we believe Pyotr was killed. But he's not there now.'

Bourne stared down at the two photos he held in his hand. 'Who's the younger man?'

'Leonid Danilovich Arkadin. Up until a few days ago we believed he was an independent assassin for hire among the families of the Russian *grupperovka*.' Specter tapped a forefinger between Arkadin's eyes. 'He's the man who brought Pyotr to Icoupov. Somehow – we're still trying to establish how – Icoupov discovered that it was Pyotr who had stolen his plans. In any event, it was Arkadin who, along with Icoupov, interrogated Pyotr and killed him.'

'Sounds as if you've got a traitor in your organization, Professor.'

Specter nodded. 'I've reluctantly come to the same conclusion.'

Something that had been bothering Bourne now rose to the surface of his mind. 'Professor, who called you when we were having breakfast?'

'One of my people. He needed verification of information. I had it in my car. Why?'

'Because it was that call that drew you out into the street just as the black Cadillac came by. That wasn't a coincidence.'

A frown creased Specter's brow. 'No, I don't suppose it could have been.'

'Give me his name and address,' Bourne said, 'and we'll find out for certain.'

The man on the rooftop had a mole on his cheek, black as sin. Arkadin concentrated on it as the man pulled Devra off the tar, away from Arkadin.

'Did you tell him anything?' he said without taking his eyes off Arkadin.

'Of course not,' Devra shot back. 'What d'you take me for?'

'A weak link,' Mole-man said. 'I told Pyotr not to use you. Now, because of you, Filya is dead.'

'Filya was an idiot!'

Mole-man took his eyes off Arkadin to sneer at Devra. 'He was your fucking responsibility, bitch.'

Arkadin scissored his legs between Mole-man's, throwing him off balance. Arkadin, quick as a cat, leapt on him, pummeling him. Mole-man fought back as best he could. Arkadin tried not to show the pain in his left shoulder, but it was already dislocated and it wouldn't work correctly. Seeing this, Mole-man struck a blow as hard as he could flush into the shoulder.

All the breath went out of Arkadin. He sat back, dazed, almost blacked out with pain. Mole-man scrabbled for his gun, found Arkadin's instead, and swung it up. He was about to pull the trigger when Devra shot him in the back of the head with his own gun.

Without a word, he pitched over onto his face. She stood, wide-legged, in the classic shooter's stance, one hand supporting the other around the grips. Arkadin, on his knees, for the moment paralyzed with agony, watched her swing the gun around, point it at him. There was something in her eyes he couldn't identify, let alone understand.

Then, all at once, she let out the long breath she'd been holding inside, her arms relaxed, and the gun came down.

'Why?' Arkadin said. 'Why did you shoot him?'

'He was a fool. Fuck me, I hate them all.'

The rain beat down on them, drummed against the rooftop. The sky, utterly dark, muffled the world around them. They could have been standing on a mountaintop on the roof of the world. Arkadin watched her approach him. She put one foot in front of the other, walking stiff-legged. She seemed like a wild animal – angry, bitter, out of her element in the civilized world. Like him. He was tied to her, but he didn't understand her, he couldn't trust her.

When she held out her hand to him he took it.

# 9

'I have this recurring nightmare,' Defense Secretary Ervin Reynolds 'Bud' Halliday said. 'I'm sitting right here at Aushak in Bethesda, when in comes Jason Bourne and in the style of *The Godfather Part II* shoots me in the throat and then between my eyes.'

Halliday was seated at a table in the rear of the restaurant, along with Luther LaValle and Rob Batt. Aushak, more or less midway between the National Naval Medical Center and the Chevy Chase Country Club, was a favorite meeting place of his. Because it was in Bethesda and, especially, because it was Afghani, no one he knew or wanted to keep secrets from came here. The defense secretary felt most comfortable in off-the-beaten-path places. He was a man who despised Congress, despised even more its oversight committees, which were always mucking about in matters that didn't concern them and for which they had no understanding, let alone expertise.

The three men had ordered the dish after which the restaurant was named: sheets of pasta, filled with scallions, drenched in a savory meat-infused tomato sauce, the whole crowned by rich Middle Eastern yogurt in which flowered tiny bits of mint. The aushak, they all agreed, was a perfect winter meal.

'We'll soon have that particular nightmare laid to rest, sir,' LaValle said with the kind of obsequiousness that set Batt's teeth on edge. 'Isn't that so, Rob?'

Batt nodded emphatically. 'Quite right. I have a plan that's virtually foolproof.'

Perhaps that wasn't the correct thing to say. Halliday frowned. 'No plan is foolproof, Mr. Batt, especially when it involves Jason Bourne.'

'I assure you, no one knows that better than I do, Mr. Secretary.'

Batt, as the seniormost of the seven directorate heads, did not care for being contradicted. He was a linebacker of a man with plenty of experience beating back pretenders to his crown. Still, he was aware that he was treading terra incognita, where a power struggle was raging, the outcome unknown.

He pushed his plate away. In dealing with these people he knew he was making a calculated gamble; on the other hand, he felt the spark that emanated from Secretary Halliday. Batt had entered the nation's true power grid, a place he'd secretly longed to be, and a powerful sense of elation shot through him.

'Because the plan revolves around DCI Hart,' Batt said now, 'my hope is that we'll be able to bring down two clay pigeons with one shot.'

'Not another word' – Halliday held up his hand – 'to either of us. Luther and I must maintain plausible deniability. We can't afford this operation coming back to bite us on the ass. Is that clear, Mr. Batt?'

'Perfectly clear, sir. This is my operation, pure and simple.'

Halliday grinned. 'Son, those words are music to these big ol' Texan ears.' He tugged at the lobe of his ear. 'Now, I assume Luther here told you about Typhon.'

Batt looked from the secretary to LaValle and back again. A frown formed on his face. 'No, sir, he didn't.'

'An oversight,' LaValle said smoothly.

'Well, no time like the present.' A smile continued to light Halliday's expression.

'We believe that one of CI's problems is Typhon,' LaValle said. 'It's become too much for the director to properly rehabilitate and manage CI, *and* keep tabs on Typhon. As such, responsibility for Typhon will be taken off your shoulders. That section will be controlled directly by me.'

The entire topic had been handled smoothly, but Batt knew he'd been deliberately sandbagged. These people had wanted control of Typhon from the beginning. 'Typhon is home-grown CI,' he said. 'It's Martin Lindros's brainchild.'

'Martin Lindros is dead,' LaValle pointed out needlessly. 'Another female is the director of Typhon now. That needs to be addressed, along with many other decisions that will affect Typhon's future. You will also need to be making crucial decisions, Rob, about all of CI. You don't want more on your plate than you can handle, do you.' It wasn't a question.

Batt felt himself losing traction on a slippery slope. 'Typhon is part of CI,' he said as a last, feeble attempt to win back control.

'Mr. Batt,' Halliday interjected. 'We have made our determination. Are you with us or shall we recruit someone else for DCI?'

The man whose call had drawn Professor Specter out into the street was Mikhail Tarkanian. Bourne suggested the National Zoo as a place to meet, and the professor had called Tarkanian. The professor then contacted his secretary at the university to tell her that he and Professor Webb were each taking a personal day. They got in Specter's car, which had been driven to the estate by one of his men, and headed toward the zoo.

'Your problem, Jason, is that you need an ideology,' Specter said. 'An ideology grounds you. It's the backbone of commitment.'

Bourne, who was driving, shook his head. 'As far back as I can remember I've been manipulated by ideologues. So far as I can tell, all ideology does is give you tunnel vision. Everything that doesn't fit within your self-imposed limits is either ignored or destroyed.'

'Now I know I'm truly speaking to Jason Bourne,' Specter said, 'because I tried my best to instill in David Webb a sense of purpose he lost somewhere in his past. When you came to me you weren't just cast adrift, you were severely maimed. I sought to help heal you by helping you turn away from whatever it was that hurt you so deeply. But now I see I was wrong –'

'You weren't wrong, Professor.'

'No, let me finish. You're always quick to defend me, to believe I'm always right. Don't think I don't appreciate how you feel about me. I wouldn't want anything to change that. But occasionally I do make mistakes, and this was one of them. I don't know what went into the making of the Bourne identity, and believe me when I tell you that I don't want to know.

'What seems clear to me, however, is that however much you don't want to believe it, something inside you, something innate and connected with the Bourne identity, sets you apart from everyone else.'

Bourne felt troubled by the direction of the conversation. 'Do you mean that I'm Jason Bourne through and through – that David Webb would have become him no matter what?'

'No, not at all. But I do think from what you've shared with me that if there had been no intervention, if there had been no Bourne identity, then David Webb would have been a very unhappy man.'

This idea was not a new one to Bourne. But he'd always assumed the thought occurred to him because he knew so damnably little about who he'd been. David Webb was more of an enigma to him than Jason Bourne. That realization itself haunted Bourne, as if Webb were a ghost, a shadowing armature into which the Bourne identity had been hung, fleshed out, given life by Alex Conklin.

Bourne, driving up Connecticut Avenue, NW, crossed Cathedral Avenue. The entrance to the zoo appeared up ahead. 'The truth is, I don't think David Webb would have lasted to the end of the school year.'

'Then I'm pleased I decided to involve you in my real passion.' Something seemed to have been settled inside Specter. 'It's not often a man gets a chance to rectify his mistakes.'

The day was mild enough that the gorilla family had been let out. Schoolchildren clustered noisily at the end of the area where the patriarch sat, surrounded by his brood. The silverback did his level best to ignore them, but when their incessant chatter became too much for him, he walked to the other end of the compound, trailed by his family. There he sat while the same annoyances spiraled out of control. Then he plodded back to the spot where Bourne had first seen him.

Mikhail Tarkanian was waiting for them beside the silverback gorilla area. He looked Specter up and down, clucking over his black eye. Then he took him in his arms, kissed him on both cheeks. 'Allah is good, my friend. You are alive and well.'

'Thanks to Jason here. He rescued me. I owe him my life.' Specter introduced the two men.

Tarkanian kissed Bourne on both cheeks, thanking him effusively.

There came a shuffling of the gorilla family as some grooming got under way.

'Damn sad life.' Tarkanian hooked his thumb at the silverback.

Bourne noted that his English was heavily accented in the manner of the tough Sokolniki slum of northeast Moscow.

'Look at the poor bastard,' Tarkanian said.

The gorilla's expression was glum – resigned rather than defiant.

Specter said, 'Jason's here on a bit of a fact-finding mission.'

'Is he now?' Tarkanian was fleshy in the way of ex-athletes – neck like a bull, wary eyes sunk in yellow flesh. He kept his shoulders up around his ears, as if to ward off an expected blow. Enough hard knocks in Sokolniki to last a lifetime.

'I want you to answer his questions,' Specter said.

'Of course. Anything I can do.'

'I need your help,' Bourne said. 'Tell me about Pyotr Zilber.'

Tarkanian, appearing somewhat taken aback, glanced at Specter, who had retreated a pace in order to center his man's full attention on Bourne. Then he shrugged. 'Sure. What d'you want to know?'

'How did you find out he'd been killed?'

'The usual way. Through one of our contacts.' Tarkanian shook his head. 'I was devastated. Pyotr was a key man for us. He was also a friend.'

'How d'you figure he was found out?'

A gaggle of schoolgirls pranced by. When they had passed out of earshot, Tarkanian said, 'I wish I knew. He wasn't easy to get to, I'll tell you that.'

Bourne said casually, 'Did Pyotr have friends?'

'Of course he had friends. But none of them would betray him, if that's what you're asking.' Tarkanian pushed his lips out. 'On the other hand . . .' His words trailed off.

Bourne found his eyes, held them.

'Pyotr was seeing this woman. Gala Nematova. He was head-over-heels about her.'

'I assume she was properly vetted,' Bourne said.

'Of course. But, well, Pyotr was a bit, um, headstrong when it came to women.'

'Was that widely known?'

'I seriously doubt it,' Tarkanian said.

That was a mistake, Bourne thought. The habits and proclivities of the enemy were always for sale if you were clever and persistent enough. Tarkanian should have said, *I don't know. Possibly.* As neutral an answer as possible, and closer to the truth.

'Women can be a weak link.' Bourne thought briefly of Moira and the cloud of uncertainty that hovered over her from the CI investigation. The idea that Martin could have been seduced into revealing CI secrets was a bitter pill to swallow. He hoped when he read the communication between her and Martin that Soraya had unearthed, he could lay the question to rest.

'We're all sick about Pyotr's death,' Tarkanian offered. Again the glance at Specter.

'No question.' Bourne smiled rather vaguely. 'Murder's a serious matter, especially in this case. I'm talking to everyone, that's all.'

'Of course. I understand.'

'You've been extremely helpful.' Bourne smiled, shook Tarkanian's hand. As he did so, he said in a sharp tone of voice, 'By the way, how much did Icoupov's people pay you to call the professor's cell this morning?'

Instead of freezing Tarkanian seemed to relax. 'What the hell kind of question is that? I'm loyal, I always have been.'

After a moment, he tried to extricate his hand, but Bourne's grip tightened. Tarkanian's eyes met Bourne's, held them.

Behind them, the silverback made a noise, growing restive. The sound was low, like the sudden ripple of wind disturbing a field of wheat. The message from the gorilla was so subtle, Bourne was the only one who picked up on it. He registered movement at the extreme edge of his peripheral vision, tracked for several seconds. He leaned back to Specter, said in a low, urgent voice. 'Leave now. Go straight through the Small Mammal House, then turn left. A hundred yards on will be a small food kiosk. Ask for help getting to your car. Go back to your house and stay there until you hear from me.'

As the professor walked swiftly away, Bourne grabbed Tarkanian, pushed him in the opposite direction. They joined a Home Sweet Habitat scavenger hunt comprising a score of rowdy kids and their parents. The two men Bourne was tracking hurried toward them. It was this pair and their rushed anxiety that had aroused the suspicion of the silverback, alerting Bourne.

'Where are we going?' Tarkanian said. 'Why did you leave the professor unprotected?'

A good question. Bourne's decision had been instantaneous, instinct-driven. The men headed toward Tarkanian, not the professor. Now, as the group moved down Olmsted Walk, Bourne dragged Tarkanian into the Reptile Discovery Center. The lights were low here. They hurried past glass cases that held dozing alligators, slit-eyed crocodiles, lumbering tortoises, evil-looking vipers, and pebble-skinned lizards of all sizes, shapes, and dispositions. Up ahead, Bourne could see the snake cases. At one of them, a handler opened a door, prepared to set out a feast of rodents for the green tree pythons, which, in their hunger, had emerged from their stupor, slithering along the case's fake tree branches. These snakes used infrared heat sensors to target their prey.

Behind them, the two men wove their way through the crowd of children. They were swarthy but otherwise unremarkable in feature. They had their hands plunged into the pockets of their wool overcoats, surely gripping some form of weapon. They weren't hurrying now. There was no point in alarming the visitors.

Passing the European glass lizard, Bourne hauled Tarkanian into the snake section. It was at that moment that Tarkanian chose to make a move. Twisting away as he lunged back toward the approaching men, he dragged Bourne for a step, until Bourne struck him a dizzying blow to the side of the head.

A workman knelt with his toolbox in front of an empty case. He was fiddling with the ventilation grille at the base. Bourne swiped a short length of stiff wire from the box.

'The cavalry's not going to save you today,' Bourne said as he dragged Tarkanian toward a door set flush in the wall between cases that led to the work area hidden from the public. One of the pursuers was closing in when Bourne jimmied the lock with the bit of wire. He opened the door, stepped through. He slammed it shut behind him, set the lock.

The door began to shudder on its hinges as the men pounded on it. Bourne found himself in a narrow utility corridor, lit by long fluorescent tubes, that ran behind the cases. Doors and, in the cases of the venomous snakes, feeding windows appeared at regular intervals along the right-hand wall.

Bourne heard a soft *phutt!* and the lock popped out of the door. The men were armed with small-caliber handguns fitted with suppressors. He pushed the stumbling Tarkanian ahead of him as one of the men stepped through. Where was the other one? Bourne thought he knew, and he turned his attention to the far end of the corridor, where any moment now he expected the second man to appear.

Tarkanian, sensing Bourne's momentary shift of attention, spun, slamming the side of his body into Bourne's. Thrown off balance, Bourne skidded through the open doorway into the tree python case. With a harsh bark of laughter, Tarkanian rushed on.

A herpetologist in the case to check on the python was already protesting

Bourne's appearance. Bourne ignored him, reached up, unwound one of the hungry pythons from the branch nearest him. As the snake, sensing his heat, wrapped itself around his outstretched arm, Bourne turned and burst out into the corridor just in time to drive a fist into the gunman's solar plexus. When the man doubled over, Bourne slid his arm out of the python's coils, wrapped its body around the gunman's chest. Seeing the python, the man screamed. It began to tighten its coils around him.

Bourne snatched the handgun with its suppressor from his hand, took off after Tarkanian. The gun was a Glock, not a Taurus. As Bourne suspected, these two weren't part of the same team that had abducted the professor. Who were they then? Members of the Black Legion, sent to extract Tarkanian? But if that was the case, how had they known he'd been blown? No time for answers: The second man had appeared at the far end of the corridor. He was in a crouch, motioning to Tarkanian, who squeezed himself against the side of the corridor.

As the gunman took aim at him Bourne covered his face with his folded forearms, dived headfirst through one of the feeding windows. Glass shattered. Bourne looked up to see that he was face-to-face with a Gaboon viper, the species with the longest fangs and highest venom yield of any snake. It was black and ocher. Its ugly, triangular head rose, its tongue flicked out, sensing, trying to determine if the creature sprawled in front of it was a threat.

Bourne lay still as stone. The viper began to hiss, a steady rhythm that flattened its head with each fierce exhalation. The small horns beside its nostrils quivered. Bourne had definitely disturbed it. Having traveled extensively in Africa, he knew something of this creature's habits. It was not prone to bite unless severely provoked. On the other hand, he couldn't risk moving his body at all at this point.

Aware that he was vulnerable from behind as well as in front, he slowly raised his left hand. The hissing's steady rhythm didn't change. Keeping his eyes on the snake's head, he moved his hand until it was over the snake. He'd read about a technique meant to calm this kind of snake but had no idea whether it would work. He touched the snake on the top of its head with a fingertip. The hissing stopped. It did work!

He grasped it at its neck. Letting go of the gun, he supported the viper's body with his other hand. The creature didn't struggle. Walking gingerly across the case to the far end, he set it carefully down in a corner. A group of kids were staring, openmouthed, from the other side of the glass. Bourne backed away from the viper, never taking his eyes from it. Near the shattered feeding window he knelt down, grasped the Glock.

A voice behind him said, 'Leave the gun where it is and turn around slowly.'

'The damn thing's dislocated,' Arkadin said.

Devra stared at his deformed shoulder.

'You'll have to reset it for me.'

Drenched to the bone, they were sitting in a late-night café on the other side of Sevastopol, warming themselves as best they could. The gas heater in the café hissed and hiccupped alarmingly, as if it were coming down with pneumonia. Glasses of steaming tea sat before them, half empty. It was barely an hour after their hair's-breadth escape, and both of them were exhausted.

'You're kidding,' she said.

'Absolutely, you will,' he said. 'I can't go to a proper doctor.'

Arkadin ordered food. Devra ate like an animal, shoving dripping pieces of stew into her mouth with her fingertips. She looked as if she hadn't eaten in days. Perhaps she hadn't. Seeing how she laid waste to the food, Arkadin ordered more. He ate slowly and deliberately, conscious of everything he put into his mouth. Killing did that to him: All his senses were working overtime. Colors were brighter, smells stronger, everything tasted rich and complex. He could hear the acrid political argument going on in the opposite corner between two old men. His own fingertips on his cheek felt like sandpaper. He was acutely aware of his own heartbeat, the blood rushing behind his ears. He was, in short, a walking, talking exposed nerve.

He both loved and hated being in this state. The feeling was a form of ecstasy. He remembered coming across a dog-eared paperback copy of *The Teachings of Don Juan* by Carlos Castaneda, had learned to read English from it, a long, torturous path. The concept of ecstasy had never occurred to him before reading this book. Later, in emulation of Castaneda, he thought of trying peyote – if he could find it – but the idea of a drug, any drug, set his teeth on edge. He was already lost quite enough. He held no desire to find a place from which he could never return.

Meanwhile the ecstasy he was in was a burden as well as a revelation, but he knew he couldn't long stand being that exposed nerve. Everything from a car backfiring to the chirrup of a cricket crashed against him, as painful as if he'd been turned inside out.

He studied Devra with an almost obsessive concentration. He noticed something he hadn't seen before – likely, with her gesticulating, she'd distracted him from noticing. But now she'd let down her guard. Perhaps she was just exhausted or had relaxed with him. She had a tremor in her hands, a nerve that had gone awry. Clandestinely, he watched the tremor, thinking it made her seem even more vulnerable.

'I don't get you,' he told her now. 'Why have you turned against your own people?'

'You think Pyotr Zilber, Oleg Shumenko, and Filya were my own people?'

'You're a cog in Zilber's network. What else would I think?'

'You heard how that pig talked to me up on the roof. Shit, they were all like that.' She wiped grease off her lips and chin. 'I never liked Shumenko. First it was gambling debts I had to bail him out of, then it was drugs.'

Arkadin's voice was offhand when he said, 'You told me you didn't know what the last loan was for.'

'I lied.'

'Did you tell Pyotr?'

'You're joking. Pyotr was the worst of the lot.'

'Talented little bugger, though.'

Devra nodded. 'So I thought when I was in his bed. He got away with an awful lot of shit because he was the boss – drinking, partying, and, Jesus, the girls! Sometimes two and three a night. I got thoroughly sick of him and asked to be reassigned back home.'

So she'd been Pyotr's squeeze for a short time, Arkadin thought. 'The partying was part of his job, though, forging contacts, ensuring they came back for more.'

'Sure. Trouble was he liked it all too much. And inevitably, that attitude infected those who were close to him. Where d'you think Shumenko learned to live like that? From Pyotr, that's who.'

'And Filya?'

'Filya thought he owned me, like chattel. When we'd go out together he'd act as if he was my pimp. I hated his guts.'

'Why didn't you get rid of him?'

'He was the one supplying Shumenko with coke.'

Quick as a cat, Arkadin leaned across the table, looming. 'Listen, *lapochka*, I don't give a fuck who you like or don't like. But lying to me, that's another story.'

'What did you expect?' she said. 'You blew in like a fucking whirlwind.'

Arkadin laughed then, breaking a tension that was stretched to the breaking point. This girl had a sense of humor, which meant she was clever as well as smart. His mind had made a connection between her and a woman who'd once been important to him.

'I still don't understand you.' He shook his head. 'We're on different sides of this conflict.'

'That's where you're wrong. I was never part of this conflict. I didn't like it; I only pretended I did. At first it was a goal I set for myself: whether I could fool Pyotr, and then the others. When I did, it just seemed easier to keep going. I got paid well, I learned quicker than most, I got perks I never would have gotten from being a DJ.'

'You could've left anytime.'

'Could I?' She cocked her head. 'They would've come after me like they're coming after you.'

'But now you've made up your mind to leave them.' He cocked his head. 'Don't tell me it's because of me.'

'Why not? I like sitting next to a whirlwind. It's comforting.'

Arkadin grunted, embarrassed again.

'Besides, the last straw came when I found out what they're planning.'

'You thought of your American savior.'

'Maybe you can't understand that one person can make a difference in your life.'

'Oh, but I can,' Arkadin said, thinking of Semion Icoupov. 'In that, you and I are the same.'

She gestured. 'You look so uncomfortable.'

'Come on,' he said, standing. He led her back past the kitchen, poked his head in for a moment, then took her into the men's room.

'Get out,' he ordered a man at the sink.

He checked the stall to make sure they were alone. 'I'll tell you how to fix this damnable shoulder.'

When he gave her the instructions, she said, 'Is it going to hurt?'

In answer, he put the handle of the wooden spoon he'd swiped from the kitchen between his teeth.

With great reluctance Bourne turned his back on the Gaboon viper. Many things flitted through his mind, not the least of which was Mikhail Tarkanian. He was the mole inside the professor's organization. Who knew how much intel he had about Specter's network; Bourne couldn't afford to let him get away.

The man before him now was flat-faced, his skin slightly greasy. He had a two-day growth of beard and bad teeth. His breath stank from cigarettes and rotting food. He pointed his suppressed Glock directly at Bourne's chest.

'Come out of there,' he said softly.

'It won't matter whether or not I comply,' Bourne answered. 'The herpetologist down the corridor has surely phoned security. We're all about to be put into custody.'

'Out. Now.'

The man made a fatal error of gesturing with the Glock. Bourne used his left forearm to knock the elongated barrel aside. Slamming the gunman back against the opposite wall of the corridor, Bourne drove a knee into his groin. As the gunman gagged, Bourne chopped the gun out of his hand, grabbed him by his overcoat, flung him headlong into the Gaboon viper's case with such force that he skidded along the floor toward the corner where the viper lay coiled.

Bourne, imitating the viper, made a rhythmic hissing sound, and the snake raised its head. At the same moment it heard the hissing of a rival snake, it sensed something living thrust into its territory. It struck out at the terrified gunman.

Bourne was already pounding down the corridor. The door at the far end gaped open. He burst out into daylight. Tarkanian was waiting for him, in case he escaped the two gunmen; he had no stomach to prolong the pursuit. He drove a fist into Bourne's cheek, followed that up with a vicious kick. But Bourne caught his shoe in his hands, twisted his foot violently, spinning him off his feet.

Bourne could hear shouts, the slap and squeak of cheap soles against concrete. Security was on its way, though he couldn't see them yet.

'Tarkanian,' he said, and cold-cocked him.

Tarkanian went down heavily. Bourne knelt beside him and was giving him mouth-to-mouth when three security guards rounded the corner, came pounding up to him.

'My friend collapsed just as we saw the men with the guns.' Bourne gave an accurate description of the two gunmen, pointed toward the open door to the Reptile Discovery Center. 'Can you get help? My friend is allergic to mustard. I think there must have been some in the potato salad we had for lunch.'

One of the security guards called 911, while the other two, guns drawn, vanished into the doorway. The guard stayed with Bourne until the paramedics arrived. They took Tarkanian's vitals, loaded him onto the gurney. Bourne walked at Tarkanian's side as they made their way through the gawking crowds to the ambulance waiting on Connecticut Avenue. He told them about Tarkanian's allergic reaction, also that in this state he was hypersensitive to light. He climbed into the back of the ambulance. One of the paramedics closed the doors behind him while the other prepared the IV drip of phenothiazine. The vehicle took off, siren wailing.

Tears streamed down Arkadin's face, but he made no noise. The pain was excruciating, but at least the arm was back in its socket. He could move the fingers of his left hand, just barely. The good news was that the numbness was giving way to a peculiar tingling, as if his blood had turned to champagne.

Devra held the wooden spoon in her hand. 'Shit, you almost bit this in two. It must've hurt like a bitch.'

Arkadin, dizzy and nauseous, grimaced in pain. 'I could never get food down now.'

Devra tossed aside the spoon as they left the men's room. Arkadin paid their check, and they went out of the café. The rain had stopped, leaving the streets with that slick, just-washed look so familiar to him from old American films from the 1940s and 1950s.

'We can go to my place,' Devra offered. 'It's not far from here.'

Arkadin shook his head. 'I think not.'

They walked, seemingly aimlessly, until they came to a small hotel. Arkadin booked a room. The flyblown night clerk barely looked at them. He was only interested in taking their money.

The room was mean, barely furnished with a bed, a hard-backed chair, and a dresser with three legs and a pile of books propping up the fourth corner. A circular threadbare carpet covered the center of the room. It was stained, pocked with cigarette burns. What appeared to be a closet was the toilet. The shower and sink were down the hall.

Arkadin went to the window. He'd asked for a room in front, knowing it would be noisier, but would afford him a bird's-eye view of anyone coming. The street was deserted, not a car in sight. Sevastopol glowed in a slow, cold pulse.

'Time,' he said, turning back into the room, 'to get some things straight.'

'Now? Can't this wait?' Devra was lying crosswise on the bed, her feet still on the floor. 'I'm dead on my feet.'

Arkadin considered a moment. It was deep into the night. He was exhausted but not yet ready for sleep. He kicked off his shoes, lay down on the bed. Devra had to sit up to make room for him, but instead of lying down parallel to him, she resumed her position, head on his belly. She closed her eyes.

'I want to come with you,' she said softly, almost as if in sleep.

He was instantly alert. 'Why?' he said. 'Why would you want to come with me?'

She said nothing in reply; she was asleep.

For a time, he lay listening to her steady breathing. He didn't know what to do with her, but she was all he had left of this end of Pyotr's network. He spent some time digesting what she had told him about Shumenko, Filya, and Pyotr, looking for holes. It seemed improbable to him that Pyotr could be so undisciplined, but then again he'd been betrayed by his girlfriend of the moment, who worked for Icoupov. That spoke of a man out of control, whose habits could indeed filter down to his subordinates. He had no idea if Pyotr had daddy issues, but given who his daddy was it certainly wasn't out of the question.

This girl was strange. On the surface she was so much like other young girls he'd come across: hard-edged, cynical, desperate, and despairing. But this one was different. He could see beneath her armor plating to the little lost girl she once had been and perhaps still was. He put his hand on the side of her neck, felt the slow pulse of her life. He could be wrong, of course. It could all be a performance put on for his benefit. But for the life of him he couldn't figure out what her angle might be.

And there was something else about her, connected to her fragility, her deliberate vulnerability. She needed something, he thought, as, in the end, we all did, even those who fooled themselves into thinking they didn't. He knew what he needed; it was simply that he chose not to think about it. She needed a father, that was clear enough. He couldn't help suspecting there was something about her he was missing, something she hadn't told him but wanted him to find. The answer was already inside him, dancing like a firefly. But every time he reached out to capture it, it just danced farther away. The feeling was maddening, as if he'd had sex with a woman without reaching an orgasm.

And then she stirred, and in stirring said his name. It was like a bolt of lightning illuminating the room. He was back on the rainy rooftop, with Mole-man standing over him, listening to the conversation between him and Devra.

'He was your responsibility,' Mole-man said, referring to Filya.

Arkadin's heart beat faster. *Your responsibility.* Why would Mole-man say that if Filya was the courier in Sevastopol? As if of their own accord, his fingertips stroked the velvet flesh of Devra's neck. The crafty little bitch! Filya was a soldier, a guard. *She* was the courier in Sevastopol. She'd handed the document off to the next link. She knew where he had to go next.

Holding her tightly, Arkadin at last let go of the night, the room, the present. On a tide of elation, he drifted into sleep, into the blood-soaked clutches of his past.

Arkadin would have killed himself, this was certain, had it not been for the intervention of Semion Icoupov. Arkadin's best and only friend, Mischa Tarkanian, concerned for his life, had appealed to the man he worked for. Arkadin remembered with an eerie clarity the day Icoupov had come to see him. He had walked in, and Arkadin, half crazed with a will to die, had put a Makarov PM to his head – the same gun he was going to use to blow his own brains out.

Icoupov, to his credit, didn't make a move. He stood in the ruins of Arkadin's Moscow apartment, not looking at Arkadin at all. Arkadin, in the grip of his sulfurous past, was unable to make sense of anything. Much later, he understood. In the same way you didn't look a bear in the eye, lest he charge you, Icoupov had kept his gaze focused on other things – the broken picture frames, the smashed crystal, the overturned chairs, the ashes of the fetishistic fire Arkadin had lit to burn his clothes.

'Mischa tells me you're having a difficult time.'

'Mischa should keep his mouth shut.'

Icoupov spread his hands. 'Someone has to save your life.'

'What d'you know about it?' Arkadin said harshly.

'Actually, I know nothing about what's happened to you,' Icoupov said.

Arkadin, digging the muzzle of the Makarov into Icoupov's temple, stepped closer. 'Then shut the fuck up.'

'What I am concerned about is the here and now.' Icoupov didn't blink an eye; he didn't move a muscle, either. 'For fuck's sake, son, look at you. If you won't pull back from the brink for yourself, do it for Mischa, who loves you better than any brother would.'

Arkadin let out a ragged breath, as if he were expelling a dollop of poison. He took the Makarov from Icoupov's head.

Icoupov held out his hand. When Arkadin hesitated, he said with great gentleness, 'This isn't Nizhny Tagil. There is no one here worth hurting, Leonid Danilovich.'

Arkadin gave a curt nod, let go of the gun. Icoupov called out, handed it to one of two very large men who came down the hallway from the far end where they had been stationed, not making a sound. Arkadin tensed, angry at himself for not sensing them. Clearly, they were bodyguards. In his current condition, they could have taken Arkadin anytime. He looked at Icoupov, who nodded, and an unspoken connection sprang up between them.

'There is only one path for you now,' Icoupov said.

Icoupov moved to sit on the sofa in Arkadin's trashed apartment, then gestured, and the bodyguard who had taken possession of Arkadin's Makarov held it out to him.

'Here, now, you will have witnesses to your last spasm of nihilism. If you wish it.'

Arkadin for once in his life ignored the gun, stared implacably at Icoupov.

'No?' Icoupov shrugged. 'Do you know what I think, Leonid Danilovich? I think it gives you a measure of comfort to believe that your life has no meaning. Most times you revel in this belief; it's what fuels you. But there are times, like now, when it takes you by the throat and shakes you till your teeth rattle in your skull.' He was dressed in dark slacks, an oyster-gray shirt, a long black leather coat that made him look somewhat sinister, like a German SS-Stürmbannführer. 'But I believe to the contrary that you are searching for the meaning of your life.' His dark skin shone like polished bronze. He gave the appearance of a man who knew what he was doing, someone, above all, not to be trifled with.

'What path?' Arkadin said dully, taking a seat on the sofa.

Icoupov gestured with both hands, encompassing the self-inflicted whirlwind that had torn apart the rooms. 'The past for you is dead, Leonid Danilovich, do you not agree?'

'God has punished me. God has abandoned me,' Arkadin said, regurgitating by rote a lament of his mother's.

Icoupov smiled a perfectly innocent smile, one that could not possibly be misinterpreted. He had an uncanny ability to engage others one-on-one. 'And what God is that?'

Arkadin had no answer because this God he spoke of was his mother's God, the God of his childhood, the God that had remained an enigma to him, a shadow, a God of bile, of rage, of split bone and spilt blood.

'But no,' he said, 'God, like heaven, is a word on a page. Hell is the here and now.'

Icoupov shook his head. 'You have never known God, Leonid Danilovich. Put yourself in my hands. With me, you will find God, and learn the future he has planned for you.'

'I cannot be alone.' Arkadin realized that this was the truest thing he'd ever said.

'Nor shall you be.'

Icoupov turned to accept a tray from one of the bodyguards. While they had been talking, he'd made tea. Icoupov poured two glasses full, added sugar, handed one to Arkadin.

'Drink with me now, Leonid Danilovich,' he said as he lifted his steaming glass. 'To your recovery, to your health, to the future, which will be as bright for you as you wish to make it.'

The two men sipped their tea, which the bodyguard had astutely fortified with a considerable amount of vodka.

'To never being alone again,' said Leonid Danilovich Arkadin.

That was a long time ago, at a way station on a river that had turned to blood.

Was he much changed from the near-insane man who had put the muzzle of a gun to Semion Icoupov's head? Who could say? But on days of heavy rain, ominous thunder, and twilight at noon, when the world looked as bleak as he knew it to be, thoughts of his past surfaced like corpses in a river, regurgitated by his memory. And he would be alone again.

Tarkanian was coming around, but the phenothiazine that had been administered to him was doing its job, sedating him mildly and impairing his mental functioning enough so that when Bourne bent over him and said in Russian, 'Bourne's dead, we're in the process of extracting you,' Tarkanian dazedly thought he was one of the men at the reptile house.

'Icoupov sent you.' Tarkanian lifted a hand, felt the bandage the paramedics had used to keep light out of his eyes. 'Why can't I see?'

'Lie still,' Bourne said softly. 'There are civilians around. Paramedics. That's how we're extracting you. You'll be safe in the hospital for a few hours while we arrange the rest of your travel.'

Tarkanian nodded.

'Icoupov is on the move,' Bourne whispered. 'Do you know where?'

'No.'

'He wants you to be most comfortable during your debriefing. Where should we take you?'

'Moscow, of course.' Tarkanian licked his lips. 'It's been years since I've been home. I have an apartment on the Frunzenskaya embankment.' More and more he seemed to be speaking to himself. 'From my living room window you can see the pedestrian bridge to Gorky Park. Such a peaceful setting. I haven't seen it in so long.'

They arrived at the hospital before Bourne had a chance to continue the interrogation. Then everything happened very quickly. The doors banged open and the paramedic leapt into action, getting the gurney down, rushing it through the automatic glass doors into a corridor leading to the ER. The place was packed with patients. One of the paramedics was talking to a harried overworked intern, who directed him to a small room, one of many off the corridor. Bourne saw that the other rooms were filled.

The two paramedics rolled Tarkanian into the room, checked the IV, took his vitals again, unhooked him.

'He'll come around in a minute,' one of them said. 'Someone will be in shortly to see to him.' He produced a practiced smile that was not unlikable. 'Don't worry, your friend's going to be fine.'

After they'd left, Bourne went back to Tarkanian, said, 'Mikhail, I know the Frunzenskaya embankment well. Where exactly is your apartment?'

'He's not going to tell you.'

Bourne whirled just as the first gunman – the one he'd wrapped the python around – threw himself on top of him. Bourne staggered back, bounced hard against the wall. He struck at the gunman's face. The gunman blocked it, punched Bourne hard on the point of his sternum. Bourne grunted, and the gunman followed up with a short chop to Bourne's side.

Down on one knee, Bourne saw him pull out a knife, swipe the blade at him. Bourne shrank back. The gunman attacked with the knife point-first. Bourne landed a hard right flush on his face, heard the satisfying crack of the cheekbone fracturing. Enraged, the gunman closed, the blade swinging through Bourne's shirt, bringing out an arc of blood like beads on a string.

Bourne hit him so hard he staggered back, struck the gurney on which Tarkanian was stirring out of his drugged stupor. The man took out his handgun with the suppressor. Bourne closed with him, grabbing him tightly, depriving him of space to aim the gun.

Tarkanian ripped off the bandage the paramedics had used to keep light out of his eyes, blinked heavily, looking around. 'What the hell's going on?' he said drowsily to the gunman. 'You told me Bourne was dead.'

The man was too busy fending off Bourne's attack to answer. Seeing his firearm was of no use to him he dropped it, kicked it along the floor. He tried to get the knife blade inside Bourne's defense, but Bourne broke the attacks, not fooled by the feints the gunman used to distract him.

Tarkanian sat up, slid off the gurney. He found it difficult to talk, so he slipped to his knees, crawled across the cool linoleum to where the gun lay.

The gunman, one hand gripping Bourne's neck, was working the knife free, prepared to stab downward into Bourne's stomach.

'Move away from him.' Tarkanian was aiming the gun at the two men. 'I'll have a clear shot.'

The gunman heard him, shoved the heel of his hand into Bourne's Adam's apple, choking him. Then he moved his upper body to one side.

Just as Tarkanian was about to squeeze the trigger Bourne rabbit-punched the gunman in the kidney. He groaned and Bourne hauled him between himself and Tarkanian. A coughing sound announced the bullet plowing into the gunman's chest.

Tarkanian cursed, moved to get Bourne back in his sights. As he did so, Bourne wrested the knife away from the gunman's limp hand, threw it with deadly accuracy. The force of it lifted Tarkanian backward off his feet. Bourne pushed the gunman away from him, crossed the room to where Tarkanian lay in a pool of his own blood. The knife was buried to the hilt in his chest. By its position, Bourne knew it had pierced a lung. Within moments Tarkanian would drown in his own blood.

Tarkanian stared up at Bourne. He laughed even as he said, 'Now you're a dead man.'

# 10

Rob Batt made his arrangements through General Kendall, LaValle's second in command. Through him, Batt was able to access certain black-ops assets in the NSA. No congressional oversight, no fuss, no muss. As far as the federal government was concerned, these people didn't exist, except as auxiliary staff seconded to the Pentagon; they were thought to be pushing papers in a windowless office somewhere in the bowels of the building.

*Now, this is the way the clandestine services should run,* Batt said to himself as he laid out the operation for the eight young men ranged in a semicircle in a Pentagon briefing room Kendall had provided for him. No supervision, no snooping congressional committees to report to.

The plan was simple, as all his plans tended to be. Other people might like bells and whistles, but not Batt. Vanilla, Kendall had called it. But the more that was involved, the more that could go wrong was how he looked at it. Also, no one fucked up simple plans; they could be put together and executed in a matter of hours, if need be, even with new personnel. But the fact was he liked these NSA agents, perhaps because they were military men. They were quick to catch on, quicker even to learn. He never had to repeat himself. To a man, they seemed to memorize everything as it was presented to them.

Better still, because of their military background, they obeyed orders unquestioningly, unlike agents in CI – Soraya Moore a case in point – who always thought they knew a better way to get things done. Plus, these bad boys weren't afraid of rendition; they weren't afraid to pull the trigger. If given the appropriate order they'd kill a target without either question or regret.

Batt felt a certain exhilaration at the knowledge that no one was looking over his shoulder, that he wouldn't have to explain himself to anyone – not even the new DCI. He'd entered an altogether different arena, one all his own, where he could make decisions of great moment, devise field operations, and carry them out with the confidence that he would be backed to the hilt, that no operation would ever boomerang on him, bring him face-to-face with a congressional committee and disgrace. As he wrapped up the pre-mission briefing, his cheeks were flushed, his pulse accelerated. There was a heat building inside him that could almost be called arousal.

He tried not to think of his conversation with the defense secretary, tried not to think of Luther LaValle heading up Typhon while he looked helplessly on. He desperately didn't want to give up control of such a powerful weapon against terrorism, but Halliday hadn't given him a choice.

One step at a time. If there was a way to foil Halliday and LaValle, he was confident he'd find it. But for the moment, he returned his attention to the job at hand. No one was going to fuck up his plan to capture Jason Bourne. He knew this absolutely. Within hours Bourne would be in custody, down so deep even a Houdini like him would never get out.

Soraya Moore made her way to Veronica Hart's office. Two men were emerging: Dick Symes, the chief of intelligence, and Rodney Feir, chief of field support. Symes was a short, round man whose red face appeared to have been applied directly to his shoulders. Feir, several years Symes's junior, was fair-haired, with an athletic body, an expression as closed as a bank vault.

Both men greeted her cordially, but there was a repellent condescension to Symes's smile.

'Bearding the lioness in her den?' Feir said.

'Is she in a bad mood?' Soraya asked.

Feir shrugged. 'Too soon to tell.'

'We're waiting to see if she can carry the weight of the world on those delicate shoulders,' Symes said. 'Just like with you, *Director*.'

Soraya forced a smile through her clenched jaws. 'You gentlemen are too kind.'

Feir laughed. 'Ready, willing, and able to oblige, ma'am.'

Soraya watched them leave, two peas in a pod. Then she poked her head into the DCI's inner sanctum. Unlike her predecessor, Veronica Hart maintained an open-door policy when it came to her upper-echelon staff. It engendered a sense of trust and camaraderie that – as she'd told Soraya – had been sorely lacking at CI in the past. In fact, from the vast amount of electronic data she'd pored over the last couple of days it was becoming increasingly clear to her that the previous DCI's bunker mentality had led to an atmosphere of cynicism and alienation among the directorate heads. The Old Man came from the school of letting the Seven vie with one another, complete with duplicity, backstabbing, and, so far as she was concerned, outright objectionable behavior.

Hart was a product of a new era, where the primary watchword was cooperation. The events of 2001 had proved that when it came to the intelligence services, competition was deadly. So far as Soraya was concerned that was all to the good.

'How long have you been at this?' Soraya asked.

Hart glanced out the window. 'It's morning already? I ordered Rob home hours ago.'

'Way past morning.' Soraya smiled. 'How about lunch? You definitely need to get out of this office.'

She spread her hands to indicate the queue of dossiers loaded onto her computer. 'Too much work –'

'It won't get done if you pass out from hunger and dehydration.'

'Okay, the canteen –'

'It's such a fine day, I was thinking of walking to a favorite restaurant of mine.'

Hearing a warning note in Soraya's otherwise light voice, Hart looked up. Yes, there was definitely something her director of Typhon wanted to talk to her about outside the confines of the CI building.

Hart nodded. 'All right. I'll get my coat.'

Soraya took out her new cell, which she'd picked up at CI this morning. She'd found her old one in the gutter by her car at the Moira Trevor surveillance site, had disposed of it at the office. Now she texted a message.

A moment later Hart's cell buzzed. The text from Soraya read: VAN X ST. Van across the street.

Hart folded her cell away and launched into a long story at the end of which both women laughed. Then they talked about shoes versus boots, leather versus suede, and which Jimmy Choos they'd buy if they were ever paid enough.

Both women kept an eye on the van without seeming to look at it. Soraya directed them down a side street where the van couldn't go for fear of becoming conspicuous. They were moving out of the range of its electronics.

'You came from the private sector,' Soraya said. 'What I don't understand is why you'd give up that payday to become DCI. It's such a thankless job.'

'Why did you agree to be director of Typhon?' Hart asked.

'It was a huge step up for me, both in prestige and in pay.'

'But that's not really why you accepted it, was it?'

Soraya shook her head. 'No. I felt a strong sense of obligation to Martin Lindros. I was in at the beginning. Because I'm half Arab, Martin sought out my input both in the creation of Typhon and in its recruitment. He meant Typhon to be a very different intelligence-gathering organization, staffed with people who understood both the Arab and the Muslim mind-set. He felt – and I wholeheartedly agree – that the only way to successfully combat the wide array of extremist terrorist cells was to understand what motivates them. Once you were in sync with their motivation, you could begin to anticipate their actions.'

Hart nodded, her long face in a neutral set as she sank deeper in thought. 'My own motivations were similar to yours. I grew sick of the cynical attitude of the private security firms. All of them, not just Black River where I worked, were focused on how much money they could milk out of the mess in the Middle East. In times of war, the government is a mighty cash cow, throwing newly minted money at every situation, as if that alone will make a difference. But the fact is, everyone involved has a license to plunder and steal to their heart's content. What happens in Iraq stays in Iraq. No one's going to prosecute them. They're indemnified against retribution for profiting from other people's misery.'

Soraya took them into a clothes store, where they made a pretense of checking out camisoles to cover the seriousness of the conversation.

'I came to CI because I couldn't change Black River, but I felt I could make a difference here. The president gave me a mandate to change an organization that was in disarray, that long ago had lost its way.'

They went out the back, across the street, hurrying now, down the block, turning left for a block, then right for two blocks, left again. They went into a large restaurant boiling with people. Perfect. The high level of ambient noise, the multiple crosscurrents of conversations would make their own conversation undetectable.

At Hart's request they were seated at a table near the rear where they had excellent sight lines of the interior as well as the front door. Everyone who came in would be visually vetted by them.

'Well executed,' Hart said when they were seated. 'I see you've done this before.'

'There were times – especially when I was working with Jason Bourne – when I was obliged to lose a CI tail or two.'

Hart scanned the large menu. 'Do you think that was a CI van?'

'No.'

Hart looked at Soraya over the menu. 'Neither do I.'

They ordered brook trout, Caesar salads to start, mineral water to drink. They took turns checking out the people who came into the restaurant.

Halfway through the salads Soraya said, 'We've intercepted some unconventional chatter in the last couple of days. I don't think *alarming* would be too strong a word.'

Hart put down her fork. 'How so?'

'It seems possible that a plan for a new attack on American soil is in its final stages.'

Hart's demeanor changed instantly. She was clearly shaken. 'What the hell are we doing here?' she said angrily. 'Why aren't we in the office where I can mobilize the forces?'

'Wait until you hear the whole story.' Soraya said. 'Remember that the lines and frequencies Typhon monitors are almost all overseas, so unlike the chatter other intelligence agencies scan, ours is more concentrated, but from what I've seen it's also far more accurate. As you know, there's always an enormous amount of disinformation in the regular chatter. Not so with the terrorists we keep an ear on. Of course, we're checking and rechecking the accuracy of this intel, but until proven otherwise we're going on the assumption that it's real. We have two problems, however, which is why mobilizing CI now isn't the wisest course.'

Three women came in, chatting animatedly. The manager greeted them like old friends, showed them to a round table near the window, where they settled in.

'First, we have an immediate time frame, that is to say within a week, ten days at the outside. However, we have almost nothing on the target, except from the intercepts we know it's large and complex, so we're thinking a building. Again, because of our Muslim expertise we believe it will be a structure of both economic and symbolic importance.'

'But no specific location?'

'East Coast, most probably New York.'

'Nothing's crossed my desk, which means none of our sister agencies has a clue about this intel.'

'That's what I'm telling you,' Soraya said. 'This is ours alone. Typhon's. This is why we were created.'

'You haven't yet told me why I shouldn't inform Homeland Security and mobilize CI.'

'Because the source of this intel is entirely new. Do you seriously think HS or NSA would take our intel at its face value? They'd need corroboration – and A, they wouldn't get it from their own sources, and, B, their mucking about in the bush would jeopardize the inroads we've made.'

'You're right about that,' Hart said. 'They're about as subtle as an elephant in Manhattan.'

Soraya hunched forward. 'The point is the group planning the attack is unknown to us. That means we don't know their motivation, their mind-set, their methodology.'

Two men came in, one after the other. They were dressed as civilians, but their military bearing gave them away. They were seated at separate tables on opposite sides of the restaurant.

'NSA,' Hart said.

Soraya frowned. 'Why would NSA be shadowing us?'

'I'll tell you in a minute. Let's continue with what's most immediately pressing. You mean we're dealing with a complete unknown, an unaffiliated terrorist organization that is capable of planning a large-scale attack? That sounds far-fetched.'

'Imagine how it'll sound to your directorate heads. Plus, our operatives have determined that keeping our information secret is the only way to get more intel. The moment this group catches wind of our mobilizing they'll postpone the operation for another time.'

'Assuming the current time frame is correct, could they abort or postpone at this late stage?'

'*We* couldn't, that's for sure.' Soraya gave her a sardonic smile. 'But terrorist networks have no infrastructure or bureaucracy to slow them down, so who knows? Part of the difficulty in locating them and taking them down is their infinite flexibility. This superior methodology is what Martin wanted for Typhon. That's my mandate.'

The waiter took their half-eaten salads away. A moment later, their main courses arrived. Hart asked for another bottle of mineral water. Her mouth was dry. Now she had NSA on one side, an off-the-grid terrorist organization about to carry out an attack on a large East Coast building on the other. Scylla and Charybdis. Either one could wreck her career at CI before it even began. She couldn't allow that to happen. She wouldn't.

'Excuse me a moment,' she said, getting up.

Soraya scanned the restaurant, but kept at least one of the agents in her peripheral vision. She saw him tense when the DCI went off to the ladies' room. He had risen and was making his way toward the rear when Hart returned. He reversed course, sat back down.

When the DCI had settled herself in her chair she looked Soraya in the eye. 'Since you decided to deliver this intel here instead of the office I assume you have a specific idea as to how to proceed.'

'Listen,' Soraya said, 'we have a red-hot situation, and we don't have enough intel to mobilize, let alone act. We have less than a week to find out everything on this terrorist organization based God only knows where with who knows how many members.'

'This isn't the time or place for the usual protocols. They're not going to avail us anything.' She glanced down at her fish as if it were the last thing she wanted to put in her mouth. When her gaze rose again, she said, 'We need Jason Bourne to find this terrorist group. We'll take care of the rest.'

Hart looked at her as if she were out of her mind. 'Out of the question.'

'Given the urgency of the mission,' Soraya said, 'he's the only one who has a chance of finding them and stopping them.'

'I wouldn't last a day in the job once it got out that I was using Jason Bourne.'

'On the other hand,' Soraya said, 'if you don't follow through on this intel, if this group executes their attack, you'll be out of CI before you can catch your breath.'

Hart sat back, produced a short laugh. 'You really are a piece of work. You want me to authorize the use of a rogue agent – a man who's unstable at best, who many powerful people in this organization feel is dangerous to CI in particular – for a mission that could have dire consequences for this country, for the continuation of CI as you and I know it?'

A jolt of anxiety ran down Soraya's spine. 'Wait a minute, back that up. What do you mean the continuation of CI as we know it?'

Hart glanced from one of the NSA agents to the other. Then she expelled a deep breath and told Soraya everything that had happened from the moment she'd been summoned into the Oval Office to meet with the president and had found herself confronting Luther LaValle and General Kendall.

'After I managed to prevail with the president, LaValle accosted me outside for a chat,' Hart concluded. 'He told me that if I didn't play nice with him he'd come after me with everything he has. He wants to take over CI, Soraya, wants it as part of his ever-enlarging intelligence services domain. But it isn't just LaValle we're fighting, it's his boss, the secretary of defense. The plan is Bud Halliday's through and through. Black River had some dealings with him when I was there, none of them pleasant. If he succeeds in bringing CI into the Pentagon fold, you can be sure the military will come in, ruin everything with their usual war-like mentality.'

'Then there's even more reason to let me bring Jason in for this.' Soraya's voice had taken on added urgency. 'He'll get the job done where a company of agents can't. Believe me, I've worked with him in the field twice. Whatever's said about him within CI is totally false. Sure, lifers like Rob Batt hate his guts, why wouldn't they? Bourne's got a freedom they wish they had. Plus, he's got abilities they never dreamed of.'

'Soraya, it's been implied in several evaluations that you once had an affair with Bourne. Please tell me the truth – I need to know if you're being swayed by anything other than what you think will be best for the country and for CI.'

Soraya knew this was coming and was prepared. 'I thought Martin had laid that office scuttlebutt to rest. There's absolutely no truth to it. We became friends when I was chief of station in Odessa. That was a long time ago; he doesn't remember. When he came back last year to rescue Martin he had no idea who I was.'

'Last year you were in the field with him again.'

'We work well together. That's all,' Soraya said firmly.

Hart was still clandestinely watching the NSA agents. 'Even if I thought what you were proposing would work, he'd never consent. From everything I've read and heard since coming to CI, he hates the organization.'

'True enough,' Soraya said. 'But once he understands the nature of the threat I think I can convince him to sign on one more time.'

Hart shook her head. 'I don't know. Even talking to him is a damn huge gamble, one I'm not sure I'm willing to take.'

'Director, if you don't seize this opportunity, you'll never be able to. It'll be too late.'

Still, Hart was unsure which direction to take: the tried and true or the unorthodox. *No*, she thought, *not unorthodox, insane.*

'I think this place has outlived its usefulness,' she said abruptly. She signaled the waiter. 'Soraya, I believe you have to powder your nose. And while you're there, please call the Metro DC Police. Use the pay phone; it's in working order, I checked. Tell Metro that there are two armed men at this restaurant. Then come right back to the table and be ready to move quickly.'

Soraya gave her a small conspiratorial smile, then rose, threading her way back to the ladies' room. The waiter approached the table, frowning.

'Is there something wrong with the brook trout, ma'am?'

'It's fine,' Hart said.

As the waiter gathered up the plates Hart took out five twenty-dollar bills, slipped them in his pocket. 'You see that man over there, the one with the wide face and football player's shoulders?'

'Yes, ma'am.'

'How about you trip when you get to his table.'

'If I do that,' the waiter said, 'I'm liable to dump these brook trouts in his lap.'

'Precisely,' Hart said with a winning smile.

'But it could mean my job.'

'Don't worry.' Hart took out her ID, showed it to him. 'I'll square things with your boss.'

The waiter nodded, turned away. Soraya reappeared, made her way to the table. Hart threw some bills onto their table but didn't stand up until the waiter bumped into a busboy. He staggered, the plates tipped. As the NSA shadow leapt up, Hart rose. Together she and Soraya walked to the door. The NSA shadow was berating the waiter, who was brushing him down with several napkins; everyone was looking, gesticulating. A couple of people closest to the accident were shouting their versions of what happened. Amid the escalating chaos, the second NSA shadow had gotten up to come to his compatriot's aid, but when he saw his target heading toward him he changed his mind.

Hart and Soraya had reached the door, were stepping out into the street. The second NSA shadow began to follow them, but a pair of burly Metro cops burst into the restaurant detaining him. 'Hey! What about them!' he shouted at the two women.

Two more patrol cars screeched to a halt, cops raced out. Hart and Soraya already had their IDs out. The cops checked them.

'We're late for a meeting,' Hart said briskly and authoritatively. 'National security.'

The phrase was like *open sesame*. The cops waved them on.

'Sweet,' Soraya said, impressed.

Hart nodded her head in acknowledgment, but her expression was grim. Winning such a small skirmish meant nothing to her, save a bit of immediate gratification. It was the war she had her gaze set on.

When they were several blocks away and had determined that they were clean of LaValle's tags, Soraya said, 'At least let me set up a meet with Bourne so we can pick his brain.'

'I very much doubt this will work.'

'Jason trusts me. He'll do the right thing,' Soraya said with absolute conviction. 'He always does.'

Hart considered for some time. Scylla and Charybdis still loomed large in her thought process. Death by water or fire, which was it to be? But even now she didn't regret taking the director's position. If there was anything she was up for at this stage in her life it was a challenge. She couldn't imagine a bigger one than this.

'As you no doubt know,' she said, 'Bourne wants to see the files on the conversations between Lindros and Moira Trevor.' She paused in order to judge Soraya's reaction to the woman Bourne was now linked with. 'I agreed.' There wasn't even a tremor in Soraya's face. 'I'm meeting him this evening at five,' she said slowly, as if still chewing the idea over. Then, all at once, she nodded decisively. 'Join me. We'll hear his take on your intel then.'

# 11

'Splendidly done,' Specter said to Bourne. 'I can't tell you how impressed I am with how you handled the situations at the zoo and at the hospital.'

'Mikhail Tarkanian is dead,' Bourne said. 'I never meant that to happen.'

'Nevertheless it did.' Specter's black eye wasn't quite as swollen, but it was beginning to turn lurid colors. 'Once again I'm deeply in your debt, my dear Jason. Tarkanian was quite clearly the traitor. If not for you, he would have been the instigator of my torture and eventual death. You'll pardon me if I don't grieve for him.'

The professor clapped Bourne on the back as the two men walked down to the weeping willow on Specter's property. Out of the corner of his eye, Bourne could see several young men, armed with assault rifles, flanking them. Following the events of today, Bourne didn't begrudge the professor his armed guards. In fact, they made him feel better about leaving Specter's side.

Under the nebula of delicate yellow branches the two men gazed out at the pond, its surface as perfectly flat as if it were a sheet of steel. A brace of skittish grackles lifted up from the willow, cawing angrily. Their feathers gleamed in brief rainbow hues as they banked away from the swiftly lowering sun.

'How well do you know Moscow?' Specter asked. Bourne had told him what Tarkanian had said, and they'd agreed that Bourne should start there in his search for Pyotr's killer.

'Well enough. I've been there several times.'

'Still and all, I'll have a friend, Lev Baronov, meet you at Sheremetyevo. Whatever you require, he'll provide. Including weapons.'

'I work alone,' Bourne said. 'I don't want or need a partner.'

Specter nodded understandingly. 'Lev will be there for support only, I promise he won't be a hindrance.'

The professor paused a moment. 'What worries me, Jason, is your relationship with Ms. Trevor.' Turning so that he faced away from the house, he spoke more softly. 'I have no intention of prying into your personal life, but if you're going overseas –'

'We both are. She's off to Munich this evening,' Bourne said. 'I appreciate your concern, but she's as tough a woman as I've come across. She can take care of herself.'

Specter nodded, clearly relieved. 'All right, then. There's just the matter of the information on Icoupov.' He drew out a packet. 'In here are your plane tickets to Moscow, along with the documentation you'll need. There's money waiting for you. Lev has the details as to which bank, the account number attached to the safe-deposit box, and a false identity. The account has been established in that name, not in yours.'

'This took some planning.'

'I had it done last night, in the hope that you'd agree to go,' Specter said. 'All that remains is for us to take a picture of you for the passport.'

'And if I'd said no?'

'Someone else had already volunteered.' Specter smiled. 'But I had faith, Jason. And my faith was rewarded.'

They turned back and were heading for the house when the professor paused.

'One more thing,' he said. 'The situation in Moscow vis-à-vis the *grupperovka* – the criminal families – is at one of its periodic boiling points. The Kazanskaya and the Azeri are vying for sole control of the drug trade. The stakes are extraordinarily high – in the billions of dollars. So don't get in their way. If there is any contact with you, I beg you not to engage them. Instead, turn the other cheek. It's the only way to survive there.'

'I'll remember that,' Bourne said, just as one of Specter's men came hurrying out of the back of the house.

'A woman, Moira Trevor, is here to see Mr. Bourne,' he said in German-inflected Turkish.

Specter turned to Bourne, his eyebrows raised in either surprise or concern, if not both.

'I had no other choice,' Bourne said. 'I need to see her before she leaves, and after what happened today I wasn't about to leave you until the last moment.'

Specter's face cleared. 'I appreciate that, Jason. Indeed, I do.' His hand swept up and away. 'Go see your lady friend, and then we'll make our last preparations.'

'I'm on my way to the airport,' Moira said when Bourne met her in the hallway. 'The plane takes off in two hours.' She gave him all the pertinent information.

'I'm on another flight,' he said. 'I have some work to do for the professor.'

A flicker of disappointment crossed her face before vanishing in a smile. 'You have to do what you think is best for you.'

Bourne heard the slight distance in her voice, as if a glass partition had come down between them. 'I'm out of the university. You were right about that.'

'Another bit of good news.'

'Moira, I don't want my decision to cause any problems between us.'

'That could never happen, Jason, I promise you.' She kissed him on the cheek. 'I have some interviews lined up when I get to Munich, security people I've been able to contact through back channels – two Germans, an Israeli, and a German Muslim, who may be the most promising of the lot.'

As two of Specter's young men came through the door, Bourne took Moira into one of the two sitting rooms. A ship's brass clock on the marble mantel chimed the change in watch.

'Quite a grand palace for the head of a university.'

'The professor comes from money,' Bourne lied. 'But he's private about it.'

'My lips are sealed,' Moira said. 'By the way, where's he sending you?'

'Moscow. Some friends of his have gotten into a bit of trouble.'

'The Russian mob?'

'Something like that.'

Best that she believe the simplest explanation, Bourne thought. He watched the play of lamplight reveal her expression. He was certainly no stranger to duplicity, but his heart constricted at the thought that Moira might be playing him as she was suspected of playing Martin. Several times today he had considered bypassing the meet with the new DCI, but he had to admit to himself that seeing the questioned communication between her and Martin had become important to him. Once he saw the evidence he'd know how to proceed with Moira. He owed it to Martin to discover the truth about his relationship with her. Besides, it was no use fooling himself: He now had a personal stake in the situation. His newly revealed feelings for her complicated matters for everyone, not the least himself. Why was there a price to pay for every pleasure? he wondered bitterly. But now he stood committed; there was no turning back, either from Moscow or from discovering who Moira really was.

Moira, moving closer to him, put a hand on his arm. 'Jason, what is it? You look so troubled.'

Bourne tried not to look alarmed. Like Marie, she had the uncanny ability to sense what he was feeling, though with everyone else he was adept at keeping his expression neutral. The important thing now was not to lie to her; she'd pick that up in a heartbeat.

'The mission is extremely delicate. Professor Specter has already warned me that I'm jumping into the middle of a blood feud between two Moscow *grupperovka* families.'

Her grip on him tightened briefly. 'Your loyalty to the professor is admirable. And after all, your loyalty is what Martin admired most about you.' She checked her watch. 'I've got to go.'

She lifted her face to his, her lips soft as melting butter, and they kissed for what seemed a long time.

She laughed softly. 'Dear Jason, don't worry. I'm not one of those people who ask about when I'll see you again.'

Then she turned and, walking into the foyer, saw herself out. A moment later Bourne heard the cough of a car starting up, the crunch of its tires as it performed a quarter circle back down the gravel drive to the road.

Arkadin awoke grimy and stiff. His shirt was still damp with sweat from his nightmare. Gray light sifted in through the skewed blinds on the window. Stretching his neck by rolling his head in a circle, he thought what he needed most was a good long soak, but the hotel had only a shower in the hallway bathroom.

He rolled over to find that he was alone in the room; Devra had gone. Sitting up, he slid out of the damp, rumpled bed, scrubbed his rough face with the heels of his hands. His shoulder throbbed. It was swollen and hot.

He was reaching for the doorknob when the door opened. Devra stood on the threshold, a paper bag in one hand.

'Did you miss me?' she said with a sardonic smile. 'I can see it in your face. You thought I'd skipped out.'

She came inside, kicked the door shut. Her eyes, unblinking, met his. She put her free arm up. Her hand squeezed his left shoulder, gently but firmly enough to cause him pain.

'I brought us coffee and fresh rolls,' she said evenly. 'Don't manhandle me.'

Arkadin glared at her for a moment. The pain meant nothing to him, but her defiance did. He was right. There was much more to her than what she presented on the surface.

He let go and so did she.

'I know who you are,' he said. 'Filya wasn't Pyotr's courier. You are.'

That sardonic smile returned. 'I was wondering how long it would take you to figure it out.' She crossed to the dresser, lined up the paper cups of coffee, set the rolls on the flattened bag. She took out a small bag of ice and tossed it to him.

'They're still warm.' She bit into one, chewed thoughtfully.

Arkadin placed the ice on his left shoulder, sighed inwardly at the relief. He wolfed down his roll in three bites. Then he poured the scalding coffee down his throat.

'Next I suppose you're going to hold your palm over an open flame.' Devra shook her head. 'Men.'

'Why are you still here?' Arkadin said. 'You could've just run off.'

'And go where? I shot one of Pyotr's own men.'

'You must have friends.'

'None I can trust.'

Which implied she trusted him. He had an instinct she wasn't lying about this. She'd washed off the heavy mascara that had run and smudged last night. Oddly, this made her eyes seem even larger. And her cheeks held a blush now that she'd scrubbed off what had to be white theatrical makeup.

'I'll take you to Turkey,' she said. 'A small town called Eskişehir. That's where I sent the document.'

Given what he knew, Turkey – the ancient gateway between East and West – made perfect sense.

The bag of ice slipped off as Arkadin grabbed the front of her shirt, crossed to the window, threw it wide open. Though the action cost him in pain to his shoulder, he hardly cared. The early-morning sounds of the street rose up to him like the smell of baking bread. He bent her backward so her head and torso were out the window. 'What did I tell you about lying to me?'

'You might as well kill me now,' she said in her little-girl voice. 'I won't tolerate your abuse anymore.'

Arkadin pulled her back inside the room, let go of her. 'What are you going to do,' he said with a smirk, 'jump out the window?'

No sooner had the words come out of his mouth than she walked calmly to the window and sat on the sash, staring at him all the time. Then she tipped herself backward, through the open window. Arkadin grabbed her around the legs and hauled her up from the brink.

They stood glaring at each other, breathing fast, hearts pumping with excess adrenaline.

'Yesterday, while we were on the ladder, you told me that you had nothing much to live for,' Devra said. 'That pretty much goes for me, too. So here we both are, brothers under the skin, with nothing but each other.'

'How do I know the next link in the network is Turkey?'

She drew her hair back from her face. 'I'm tired of lying to you,' she said. 'It's like lying to myself. What's the point?'

'Talk is cheap,' he said.

'Then I'll prove it to you. When we get to Turkey I'll take you to the document.'

Arkadin, trying not to think too much about what she said, nodded his acknowledgment of their uneasy truce. 'I won't lay a hand on you again.'

*Except to kill you*, he thought.

# 12

The Freer Gallery of Art stood on the south side of the Mall, bounded on the west by the Washington Monument and on the east by the Reflecting Pool, gateway to the immense Capitol building. It was situated on the corner of Jefferson Drive and 12th Street, SW, near the western edge of the Mall.

The building, a Florentine Renaissance palazzo faced with Stony Creek granite imported from Connecticut, had been commissioned by Charles Freer to house his enormous collection of Near East and East Asian art. The main entrance on the north side of the building where the meet was to take place consisted of three arches accented by Doric pilasters surrounding a central loggia. Because its architecture looked inward, many critics felt it was a rather forbidding façade, especially when compared with the nearby exuberance of the National Gallery of Art.

Nevertheless, the Freer was the preeminent museum of its kind in the country, and Soraya loved it not only for the depth of art it housed but also for the elegant lines of the palazzo itself. She especially loved the contained open space at its entrance, and the fact that even, as now, when the Mall was agitated with hordes of tourists heading to and from the Smithsonian Metro rail stop on 12th Street, the Freer itself was an oasis of calm and tranquility. When things boiled over in the office during the day, it was to the Freer she came to decompress. Ten minutes with Sung dynasty jades and lacquers acted like a soothing balm to her soul.

Approaching the north side of the Mall, she searched past the crowds outside the entrance to the Freer and thought she saw – among the sturdy men with their hard, clipped Midwestern accents, the scampering children and their laughing mothers, the vacant-eyed teenagers plugged into their iPods – Veronica Hart's long, elegant figure walking past the entrance, then doubling back.

She stepped off the curb, but the blare of a horn from an oncoming car startled her back onto the sidewalk. It was at that moment that her cell phone buzzed.

'What exactly do you think you're doing?' Bourne said in her ear.

'Jason?'

'Why are you coming to this meet?'

Foolishly, she looked around; she'd never be able to spot him, and she knew it.

'Hart invited me. I need to talk to you. The DCI and I both do.'

'About what?'

Soraya took a deep breath. 'Typhon's listening posts have picked up a series of disturbing communications pointing to an imminent terrorist attack on an East Coast city. The trouble is, that's all we have. Worse, the communications are between two cadres of a group about which we have no intel whatsoever. It was my idea to recruit you to find them and stop the attack.'

'Not much to go on,' Bourne said. 'Doesn't matter. The group's name is the Black Legion.'

'In grad school I studied the link between a branch of Muslim extremism and the Third Reich. But this can't be the same Black Legion. They were either killed or disbanded when Nazi Germany fell.'

'It can and it is,' Bourne said. 'I don't know how it managed to survive, but it did. Three of their members tried to kidnap Professor Specter this morning. I saw their device tattooed on the gunman's arm.'

'The three horses' heads joined by the death's head?'

'Yes.' Bourne described the incident in detail. 'Check the body at the morgue.'

'I'll do that,' Soraya said. 'But how could the Black Legion remain so far underground all this time without being detected?'

'They have a powerful international front,' Bourne said. 'The Eastern Brotherhood.'

'That sounds far-fetched,' Soraya said. 'The Eastern Brotherhood is in the forefront of Islamic–Western relations.'

'Nevertheless, my source is unimpeachable.'

'God in heaven, what've you been doing while you've been away from CI?'

'I was never in CI,' Bourne said brusquely, 'and here's just one reason why. You say you want to talk with me but I doubt you need half a dozen agents to do that.'

Soraya froze. 'Agents?' She was on the Mall itself now, and she had to restrain herself from looking around again. 'There are no CI agents here.'

'How d'you know that?'

'Hart would've told me –'

'Why should she tell you anything? We go way back, you and I.'

'That's true enough.' She kept walking. 'But something happened earlier today that makes me believe the agents you've spotted are NSA.' She described the way she and Hart had been shadowed from CI HQ to the restaurant. She told him about Secretary Halliday and Luther LaValle, both of whom were gunning to make CI a part of the Pentagon clandestine service.

'That might make sense,' Bourne said, 'if there were only two of them. But six? No, there's another agenda, one neither of us knows about.'

'Such as?'

'The agents are vectored perfectly, triangulated on the entrance to the Freer,' Bourne said. 'This means that they must have had foreknowledge of the meet. It also means the six weren't sent to shadow Veronica Hart. If they aren't here for her, they must have been sent for me. This is Hart's doing.'

Soraya felt a chill crawl down her spine. What if the DCI was lying to her? What if she meant all along to lead Bourne into a trap? It would make sense for one of her first official acts as DCI to be the capture of Jason Bourne. It certainly would put her in solidly with Rob Batt and the others who despised and feared Bourne, and who resented her. Plus, capturing Jason would score her big points with the president and prevent Secretary Halliday from building on his already considerable influence. Still, why would Hart have allowed Soraya to possibly muck up her first field op by coming along? No, she had to believe this was an NSA initiative.

'I don't believe that,' she said emphatically.

'Let's say you're right. The other possibility is just as dire. If Hart didn't set the trap, then there's someone highly placed in CI who did. I went to Hart directly with the request.'

'Yes,' she said, 'using my cell, thank you very much.'

'Did you find it? You're on a new one now.'

'It was in the gutter where you tossed it.'

'Then stop complaining,' Bourne said, not unkindly. 'I can't imagine Hart told too many people about this meet, but one of them is working against her, and if that's the case chances are he's been recruited by LaValle.'

If Bourne was right . . . But of course he was. 'You're the grand prize, Jason. If LaValle can take you down when no one in CI could, he'll be a hero. Taking over CI will be a cakewalk for him after that.' Soraya felt perspiration break out at her hairline. 'Under the circumstances,' she continued, 'I think you ought to withdraw.'

'I need to see the correspondence between Martin and Moira. And if Hart is instigating this trap, then she'll never give me access to the files at another time. I'll have to take my chances, but not until you're certain Hart has the material.'

Soraya, who was almost at the entrance, expelled a long breath. 'Jason, I found the conversations. I can tell you what's in them.'

'Do you think you could quote them to me verbatim?' he said. 'Anyway, it's not that simple. Karim al-Jamil doctored hundreds of files before he left. I know the method he used to alter them. I have to see them myself.'

'I see there's no way I can talk you out of this.'

'Right,' Bourne said. 'When you've made sure the material is genuine, beep my cell once. Then I need you to move Hart into the loggia, away from the entrance proper.'

'Why?' she said. 'That'll only make it more difficult for you to – Jason?'

But Bourne had already disconnected.

From his vantage point on the roof of the Forrestal Building on Independence Avenue, Bourne tracked his high-powered night-vision glasses from Soraya as she moved toward the DCI, past clots of tourists hurrying about, to the agents in place around the west end of the Mall. Two lounged, chatting, at the northeast corner of the Department of Agriculture North Building. Another, hands in the pockets of his trench coat, was crossing diagonally southwest from Madison Drive toward the Smithsonian. A fourth was behind the wheel of an illegally parked car on Constitution Avenue. In fact, he was the one who'd given the game away. Bourne had spotted the car illegally parked just before a Metro police cruiser stopped parallel to it. Windows were rolled down, a conversation ensued. ID was briefly flashed by the driver of the illegally parked car. The cruiser rolled on.

The fifth and sixth agents were east of the Freer, one approximately midway between Madison and Jefferson Drives, the other in front of the Arts Industries Building. He knew there had to be at least one more.

It was almost five o'clock. A short winter twilight had descended, aided by the twinkling lights wound festively around lampposts. With the location of each agent memorized Bourne returned to the ground, using the window ledges for hands and feet.

The moment he showed himself the agents would start moving. Estimating the distance they were from where the DCI and Soraya stood, he calculated he'd have no more than two minutes with Hart to get the files.

Hidden in shadows, waiting for Soraya's signal, he strained to pick out the remaining agents. They couldn't afford to leave Independence Avenue unguarded. If Hart didn't in fact have the files, then he'd do as Soraya first suggested and get out of the area without being spotted.

He imagined her at the entrance to the Freer, talking with the DCI. There would be the first nervous moment of acknowledgment, then Soraya would have to direct the conversation around to the files. She'd have to find a way for Hart to show them to her, to make sure they were authentic.

His phone beeped once and was still. The files were authentic.

He accessed the Internet, navigating to the DC Metro site, checked the up-to-the-minute transit schedules, checking his options. This procedure took longer than he would have liked. The very real and immediate danger was that one of the six agents was in contact with home base – either CI or the Pentagon – whose sophisticated electronic telemetry could pinpoint his phone and, worse, spy on what he was pulling up from the Net. Couldn't be helped, however. Access had to be made on site and at the immediate moment in case of unforeseen transit delays. He put the worry out of his head, concentrated on what he'd have to do. The next five minutes were crucial.

Time to go.

Moments after Soraya secretly contacted Bourne she said to Veronica Hart, 'I'm afraid we may have a problem.'

The DCI's head whipped around. She'd been scanning the area for any sign of Bourne's presence. The crowds around the Freer had thickened as many made their way to the Smithsonian Metro station around the corner, returning to their hotels to prepare for dinner.

'What kind of problem?'

'I think I saw one of the NSA shadows we picked up at lunch.'

'Hell, I don't want LaValle knowing I'm meeting with Bourne. He'll have a fit, go running to the president.' She turned. 'I think we ought to leave before Bourne gets here.'

'What about my intel?' Soraya said. 'What chance are we going to have without him? I say let's stay and talk to him. Showing him the material will go a long way toward winning his trust.'

The DCI was clearly on edge. 'I don't like any of this.'

'Time is of the essence.' Soraya took her by the elbow. 'Let's move back here,' she said, indicating the loggia. 'We'll be out of the shadow's line of sight.'

Hart reluctantly walked into the open space. The loggia was especially crowded with people milling about, discussing the art they'd just seen, their plans for dinner and the next day. The gallery closed at five thirty, so the building was starting to clear out.

'Where the hell is he, anyway?' Hart said testily.

'He'll be here,' Soraya assured her. 'He wants the material.'

'Of course he wants it. The material concerns his friend.'

'Clearing Martin's name is extremely important to him.'

'I was speaking of Moira Trevor,' the DCI said.

Before Soraya could form a reply, a group of people spewed out of the front doors. Bourne was in the middle of them. Soraya could see him, but he was shielded from anyone across the street.

'Here he is,' she muttered as Bourne came quickly and silently up behind them. He must have somehow gotten into the Independence Avenue entrance at the south side of the building, closed to the public, made his way through the galleries to the front.

The DCI turned, impaling Bourne with a penetrating gaze. 'So you came after all.'

'I said I would.'

He didn't blink, didn't move at all. Soraya thought that he was at his most terrifying then, the sheer force of his will at its peak.

'You have something for me.'

'I said you could read it.' The DCI held out a small manila envelope.

Bourne took it. 'I regret I haven't the time to do that here.'

He whirled, snaking through the crowd, vanishing inside the Freer.

'Wait!' Hart cried. 'Wait!'

But it was too late, and in any event three NSA agents came walking rapidly through the entrance. Their progress was slowed by the people exiting the gallery, but they pushed many of them aside. They trotted past the DCI and Soraya as if they didn't exist. A fourth agent appeared, took up position just inside the loggia. He stared at them and smiled thinly.

Bourne moved as quickly as he thought prudent through the interior. Having memorized it from the visitors' brochure and come through it once already, he did not waste a step. But one thing worried him. He hadn't seen any agents on his way in. That meant, more than likely, he'd have to deal with them on the way out.

Near the rear entrance, a guard was checking galleries just before closing time. Bourne was obliged to detour around a corner with an outcropping of a fire call box and extinguisher. He could hear the guard's soft voice as he herded a family toward the exit in front. Bourne was about to slip out when he heard other voices sharper, clipped. Moving into shadow, he saw a pair of slim, white-haired Chinese scholars in pin-striped suits and shiny brogues arguing the merits of a Tang porcel-ain vase. Their voices faded along with their footsteps as they headed toward Jefferson Drive.

Without losing another instant Bourne checked the bypass he'd made on the alarm system. So far it showed everything as normal. He pushed out the door. Night wind struck his face as he saw two agents, sidearms drawn, hurrying up the granite stairs. He had just enough time to register the oddness of the guns before he ducked back inside, went directly to the fire call box.

They came through the door. The leading one got a face full of fire-smothering foam. Bourne ducked a wild shot from the second agent. There was virtually no noise, but something pinged off the Tennessee white marble wall near his shoulder, then clattered to the floor. He hurled the fire extinguisher at the shooter. It struck him on the temple and he went down. Bourne broke the call box's glass, pulled hard on the red metal handle. Instantly the fire alarm sounded, piercing every corner of the gallery.

\*

Out the door, Bourne ran diagonally down the steps, heading west, directly for 12th Street, SW. He expected to find more agents at the southwest corner of the building, but as he turned off Independence Avenue onto 12th Street he encountered a flood of people drawn to the building by the alarm. Already the sirens of fire trucks could be heard floating through the rising chatter of the crowd.

He hurried along the street toward the entrance down to the Smithsonian Metro stop. As he did so, he accessed the Internet through his cell. It took longer than he would have liked, but at last he pressed the FAVORITES icon, was returned to the Metro site. Navigating to the Smithsonian station, he scrolled down to the hyperlink to the next train arrival, which was refreshed every thirty seconds. Three minutes to the Orange line 6 train to Vienna/Fairfax. Quickly he composed a text mail 'FB,' sent it to a number he'd prearranged with Professor Specter.

The Metro entrance, clogged with people stopped on the stairs to watch the unfolding scenario, was a mere fifty yards away. Bourne heard police sirens now, saw a number of unmarked cars heading down 12th Street toward Jefferson. They turned east when they got to the junction – all except one, which headed due south.

Bourne tried to run, but he was hampered by the press of people. He broke free, into a small area blessedly empty of the gigantic jostle, when the driver's window of a cruising car slid down. A burly man with a grim face and a nearly bald head aimed another one of those strange-looking handguns at him.

Bourne twisted, putting one of the Metro entrance posts between himself and the gunman. He heard nothing, no sound at all – just as he hadn't back inside the Freer – and something bit into his left calf. He looked down, saw the metal of a mini dart lying on the street. It had grazed him, but that was all. With a controlled swing, Bourne went around the post, down the stairs, pushing his way through the gawkers into the Metro. He had just under two minutes to make the Orange 6 to Vienna. The next train didn't leave for four minutes after that – too much time in the platform, waiting for the NSA agents to find him. He had to make the first train.

He bought his ticket, went through. The crowds thinned and thickened like waves rushing to shore. He began to sweat. His left foot slipped. Rebalancing himself, he guessed that whatever was in that mini dart must be having an effect despite only grazing him. Looking up at the electronic signs, he had to work to focus in order to find the correct platform. He kept pushing forward, not trusting himself to rest, though part of him seemed hell-bent on doing just that. *Sit down, close your eyes, sink into sleep.* Turning to a vending machine, he fished in his pockets for change, bought every chocolate bar he could. Then he entered the line for the escalator.

Partway down he stumbled, missed the riser, crashed into the couple ahead of him. He'd blacked out for an instant. Gaining the platform, he felt both shaky and sluggish. The concrete-paneled ceiling arched overhead, deadening the sounds of the hundreds crowding the platform.

Less than a minute to go. He could feel the vibration of the oncoming train, the wind it pushed ahead of it.

He'd gobbled down one chocolate bar and was starting on the second when the train pulled into the station. He stepped in, allowing the surge of the crowd to take him. Just as the doors were closing, a tall man with broad shoulders and a black trench coat sprinted into the other end of Bourne's car. The doors closed and the train lurched forward.

# 13

As he saw the man in the black trench making his way toward him from the end of the train car, Bourne felt an unpleasant form of claustrophobia. Until they reached the next station, he was trapped in this finite space. Moreover, despite the initial chocolate hit, he was starting to feel a lassitude creeping up from his left leg as the serum entered his bloodstream. He tore off the wrapping on another chocolate bar, wolfed it down. The faster he could get the sugar and the caffeine into his system, the better able his body would be to fight off the effects of the drug. But that would only be temporary, and then his blood sugar would plummet, draining the adrenaline out of him.

The train reached Federal Triangle and the doors slid open. A mass of people got off, another mass got on. Black Trench used the brief slackening of passengers to make headway toward where Bourne stood, hands clasped around a chromium pole. The doors closed, the train accelerated. Black Trench was blocked by a huge man with tattoos on the backs of his hands. He tried to push by, but the tattooed man glared at him, refusing to budge. Black Trench could have used his federal ID to move people out of the way, but he didn't, no doubt so as not to cause a panic. But whether he was NSA or CI was still a mystery. Bourne, struggling to stop his mind from going in and out of focus, stared into the face of his newest adversary, looking for clues to his affiliation. Black Trench's face was blocky, bland, but with the particular dry cruelty the military demanded in its clandestine agents. He must be NSA, Bourne decided. Through the fog in his brain, he knew he had to deal with Black Trench before the rendezvous point at Foggy Bottom.

Two children swung into Bourne as the train lurched around a bend. He held them upright, returning them to their place beside their mother, who smiled her thanks at him, put a protecting arm around their narrow shoulders. The train rolled into Metro Center. Bourne saw a brief glare of temporary spotlights where a work crew was busy fixing an escalator. On the other side of him a young blonde with earbuds leading to an MP3 player pressed her shoulder against his, took out a cheap plastic compact, checked the state of her makeup. Pursing her lips, she slid the compact back in her bag, dug out flavored lip gloss. While she was applying it, Bourne lifted the compact, palming it immediately. He replaced it with a twenty-dollar bill.

The doors opened and Bourne stepped out within a small whirlwind of people. Black Trench, caught between doors, rushed down the car, made it onto the platform just in time. Weaving his way through the hurrying throngs, he followed Bourne toward the elevator. The majority of people headed for the stairs.

Bourne checked the position of the temporary spotlights. He made for them, but not at too fast a pace. He wanted Black Trench to make up some of the distance between them. He had to assume that Black Trench was also armed with a dart gun. If a dart struck Bourne anywhere, even in an extremity, it would mean the end. Caffeine or no caffeine, he'd pass out, and NSA would have him.

There was a wall of elderly and disabled people, some of them in wheelchairs, waiting for the elevator. The door opened. Bourne sprinted ahead as if making for the elevator, but the moment he reached the glare of the spotlights, he turned and aimed the mirror inside the compact at an angle that reflected the dazzle into Black Trench's face.

Momentarily blinded, Black Trench halted, put up his hand palm-outward. Bourne was at him in a heartbeat. He drove his hand into the main nerve bundle beneath Black Trench's right ear, wrested the dart gun out of his hand, fired it into his side.

As the man listed to one side, staggering, Bourne caught him, dragged him to a wall. Several people turned their heads to gape, but no one stopped. The pace of the crowd hurrying by barely flickered before returning to full force.

Bourne left Black Trench there, eeled his way through the almost solid curtain of people back to the Orange line. Four minutes later, he'd eaten through two more chocolate bars. Another Orange 6 to Vienna rolled in and, with a last glance thrown over his shoulder, he got on. His head didn't feel any deeper in the mist, but he knew what he needed most now was water, as much as he could get down his throat, to flush the chemical out of his system as quickly as possible.

Two stops later, he exited at Foggy Bottom. He waited at the rear of the platform until no more passengers got off. Then he followed them up, taking the stairs two at a time in an attempt to further clear his head.

His first breath of cool evening air was a deep and exhilarating one. Except for a slight nausea, perhaps caused by a continuing vertigo, he felt better. As he emerged from the Metro exit a nearby engine coughed to life; the headlights of a dark blue Audi came on. He walked briskly to the car, opened the passenger's-side door, slid in.

'How did it go?' Professor Specter nosed the Audi out into the heavy traffic.

'I got more than I bargained for,' Bourne said, leaning his head against the seat rest. 'And there's been a change of plan. People are sure to be looking for me at the airport. I'm going with Moira, at least as far as Munich.'

A look of deep concern crossed the professor's face. 'Do you think that's wise?'

Bourne turned his head, stared out the window at the passing city. 'It doesn't matter.' His thoughts were of Martin, and of Moira. 'I passed wise some time ago.'

# Book 2

# 14

'It's amazing,' Moira said.

Bourne looked up from the files he'd snatched from Veronica Hart. 'What's amazing?'

'You sitting here opposite me in this opulent corporate jet.' Moira was wearing a sleek black suit of nubbly wool, shoes with sensible heels. A thin gold chain was around her neck. 'Weren't you supposed to be on your way to Moscow tonight?'

Bourne drank water from the bottle on his side tray table, closed the file. He needed more time to ascertain whether Karim al-Jamil had doctored these conversations, but he had his suspicions. He knew Martin was far too canny to tell her anything that was classified – which covered just about everything that happened at CI.

'I couldn't stay away from you.' He watched a small smile curl Moira's wide lips. Then he dropped the bomb. 'Also, the NSA is after me.'

It was as if a light went out in her face. 'Say again?'

'The NSA. Luther LaValle has decided to make me a target.' He waved a hand to forestall her questions. 'It's political. If he can bag me when the CI hierarchy can't, he'll prove to the powers that be that his thesis that CI should come under his jurisdiction makes sense, especially after the turmoil CI has been in since Martin's death.'

Moira pursed her lips. 'So Martin was right. He was the only one left who believed in you.'

Bourne almost added Soraya's name, then thought better of it. 'It doesn't matter now.'

'It matters to me,' she said fiercely.

'Because you loved him.'

'We both loved him.' Her head tilted to one side. 'Wait a minute, are you saying there's something wrong in that?'

'We live on the outskirts of society, in a world of secrets.' He deliberately included her. 'For people like us there's always a price to pay for loving someone.'

'Like what?'

'We've spoken about it,' Bourne said. 'Love is a weakness your enemies can exploit.'

'And I've said that's a horrid way to live one's life.'

Bourne turned to stare out the Perspex window at the darkness rushing by. 'It's the only one I know.'

'I don't believe that.' Moira leaned forward until their knees touched. 'Surely you see you're more than that, Jason. You loved your wife; you love your children.'

'What kind of a father can I be to them? I'm a memory. And I'm a danger to them. Soon enough I'll be a ghost.'

'You can do something about that. And what kind of friend were you to Martin? The best kind. The only kind that matters.' She tried to get him to turn back to her. 'Sometimes I'm convinced you're looking for answers to questions that have none.'

'What does that mean?'

'That no matter what you've done in the past, no matter what you'll do in the future, you'll never lose your humanity.' She watched his eyes engage hers slowly, enigmatically. 'That's the one thing that frightens you, isn't it?'


'What's the matter with you?' Devra asked.

Arkadin, behind the wheel of a rental car they had picked up in Istanbul, grunted irritably. 'What're you talking about?'

'How long is it going to take you to fuck me?'

There being no flights from Sevastopol to Turkey, they'd spent a long night in a cramped cabin of the *Heroes of Sevastopol*, being transported southwest across the Black Sea from Ukraine to Turkey.

'Why would I want to do that?' Arkadin said as he headed off a lumbering truck on the highway.

'Every man I meet wants to fuck me. Why should you be any different?' Devra ran her hands through her hair. Her raised arms lifted her small breasts invitingly. 'Like I said. What's the matter with you?' A smirk played at the corners of her mouth. 'Maybe you're not a real man. Is that it?'

Arkadin laughed. 'You're so transparent.' He glanced at her briefly. 'What's your game? Why are you trying to provoke me?'

'I like to extract reactions in my men. How else will I get to know them?'

'I'm not your man,' he growled.

Now Devra laughed. She wrapped slender fingers around his arm, rubbing back and forth. 'If your shoulder's bothering you I'll drive.'

He saw the familiar symbol on the inside of her wrist, all the more fearsome for being tattooed on the porcelain skin. 'When did you get that?'

'Does it matter?'

'Not really. What matters is *why* you got it.' Faced with open highway, he put on speed. 'How else will I get to know you?'

She scratched the tattoo as if it had moved beneath her skin. 'Pyotr made me get it. He said it was part of the initiation. He said he wouldn't go to bed with me until I got it.'

'And you wanted to go to bed with him.'

'Not as much as I want to go to bed with you.'

She turned away then, stared out the side window, as if she was suddenly embarrassed by her confession. Perhaps she actually was, Arkadin thought as he signaled, moving right through two lanes as a sign for a rest stop appeared. He turned off the highway, parked at the far end of the rest stop, away from the two vehicles that occupied parking slots. He got out, walked to the edge, and, with his back to her, took a long satisfying pee.

The day was bright and warmer than it had been in Sevastopol. The breeze coming off the water was laden with moisture that lay on his skin like sweat. On the way back to the car he rolled up his sleeves. His coat was slung with hers across the car's backseat.

'We'd better enjoy this warmth while we can,' Devra said. 'Once we get onto the Anatolian Plateau, the mountains will block this temperate weather. It'll be colder than a witch's teat.'

It was as if she'd never made the intimate statement. But she'd caught his attention, all right. It seemed to him now that he understood something important about her – or, more accurately, about himself. It went through Gala, as well, now that he thought of it. He seemed to have a certain power over women. He knew Gala loved him with every fiber of her being, and she wasn't the first one. Now this slim tomboyish *dyevochka*, hard-bitten, downright nasty when she needed to be, had fallen under his spell. Which meant he had the handle on her he was searching for.

'How many times have you been to Eskişehir?' he asked.

'Enough to know what to expect.'

He sat back. 'Where did you learn to answer questions without revealing a thing?'

'If I'm bad, I learned it at my mother's breast.'

Arkadin looked away. He seemed to have trouble breathing. Without a word, he opened the door, bolted outside, stalking in small circles like a lion in the zoo.

'I cannot be alone,' Arkadin had said to Semion Icoupov, and Icoupov had taken him at his word. At Icoupov's villa where Arkadin was installed, his host provided a young man. But when, a week later, Arkadin had beaten his companion nearly into a coma, Icoupov switched tactics. He spent hours with Arkadin, trying to determine the root of his outbursts of fury. This failed utterly, as Arkadin seemed at a loss to remember, let alone explain these frightening episodes.

'I don't know what to do with you,' Icoupov said. 'I don't want to incarcerate you, but I need to protect myself.'

'I would never harm you,' Arkadin said.

'Not knowingly, perhaps,' the older man said ruminatively.

The following week a stoop-shouldered man with a formal goatee and colorless lips spent every afternoon with Arkadin. He sat in a plush upholstered chair, one leg crossed over the other, writing in a neat, crabbed hand in a tablet notebook he protected as if it were his child. For his part, Arkadin lay on his host's favorite chaise longue, a roll pillow behind his head. He answered questions. He spoke at length about many things, but the things that shadowed his mind he kept tucked away in a black corner of the deepest depths of his mind, never to be spoken of. That door was closed forever.

At the end of three weeks, the psychiatrist handed in his report to Icoupov and vanished as quickly as he had appeared. No matter. Arkadin's nightmares continued to haunt him in the dead of night when, upon awakening with a gasp and a start, he was convinced he heard rats scuttling, red eyes burning in the darkness. At those moments, the fact that Icoupov's villa was completely vermin-free was of no solace to him. The rats lived inside him squirming, shrieking, feeding.

The next person Icoupov employed to burrow into Arkadin's past in an attempt to cure him of his fits of rage was a woman whose sensuality and lush figure he felt would keep her safe from Arkadin's outbursts of fury. Marlene was adept at handling men of all kinds and kinks. She possessed an uncanny ability to sense the specific thing a man desired from her, and provide it.

At first Arkadin didn't trust Marlene. Why should he? He couldn't trust the psychiatrist. Wasn't she just another form of analyst sent to coax out the secrets of his past? Marlene of course noted this aversion in him and set about countering it. The way she saw it, Arkadin was living under a spell, self-induced or otherwise. It was up to her to concoct an antidote.

'This won't be a short process,' she told Icoupov at the end of her first week with Arkadin, and he believed her.

Arkadin observed Marlene walking on little cat feet. He suspected she was smart enough to know that even the slightest misstep on her part might strike him as a seismic shift, and then all the progress she'd made in gaining his trust would evaporate like alcohol over a flame. She seemed to him wary, acutely aware that at any moment he could turn on her. She acted as if she were in a cage with a bear. Day by day you could track the training of it, but that didn't mean it wouldn't unexpectedly rip your face off.

Arkadin had to laugh at that, the care with which she was treating every aspect of him. But gradually something else began to creep into his consciousness. He suspected that she was coming to feel something genuine for him.

Devra watched Arkadin through the windshield. Then she kicked open her door, went after him. She shaded her eyes against a white sun plastered to a high, pale sky.

'What is it?' she said when she'd caught up to him. 'What did I say?'

Arkadin turned a murderous look her way. He appeared to be in a towering rage, just barely holding himself together. Devra found herself wondering what would happen if he let himself go, but she also didn't want to be in his way when it happened.

She felt an urge to touch him, to speak soothingly until he returned to a calmer state of mind, but she sensed that would only inflame him further. So she went back to the car to wait patiently for him to return.

Eventually he did, sitting sideways on the seat, his shoes on the ground as if he might bolt again.

'I'm not going to fuck you,' he said, 'but that doesn't mean I don't want to.'

She felt he wanted to say something else, but couldn't, that whatever it was was too bound up in what had happened to him a long time ago.

'It was a joke,' she said softly. 'I was making a stupid joke.'

'There was a time when I would've thought nothing of it,' he said, as if talking to himself. 'Sex is unimportant.'

She sensed that he was speaking about something else, something only he knew, and she glimpsed just how alone he was. She suspected that even in a crowd, even with friends – if he had any – he'd feel alone. It seemed to her that he'd walled himself off from sexual melding because it would underscore the depth of his apartness. He seemed to her to be a moonless planet with no sun to revolve around. Just emptiness everywhere as far as he could see. In that moment she realized that she loved him.

*

'How long has he been in there?' Luther LaValle asked.

'Six days,' General Kendall replied. He was in his shirtsleeves, which were turned up. That precaution hadn't been enough to protect them from spatters of blood. 'But I guarantee that to him it feels like six months. He's as disoriented as it's possible for a human being to be.'

LaValle grunted, peering at the bearded Arab through the one-way mirror. The man looked like a raw piece of meat. LaValle didn't know or care whether he was Sunni or Shi'a. They were the same to him – terrorists bent on destroying his way of life. He took these matters very personally.

'What's he given up?'

'Enough that we know the copies of the Typhon intercepts Batt has given us are disinformation.'

'Still,' LaValle said, 'it comes straight from Typhon.'

'This man's very highly placed, there's no question whatsoever of his identity, and he knows of no plans moving into their final stages to hit a major New York building.'

'That in itself could be disinformation,' LaValle said. 'These bastards are masters of that kind of shit.'

'Right.' Kendall wiped his hands on a towel he'd thrown over his shoulder like a chef at the stove. 'They love nothing better than to see us running around in circles, chasing our tails, which is what we'll be doing if we put out an alert.'

LaValle nodded, as if to himself. 'I want our best people to follow up on it. Confirm the Typhon intercepts.'

'We'll do our best, but I feel it my duty to report that the prisoner laughed in my face when I asked him about this terrorist group.'

LaValle snapped his fingers several times. 'What are they called again?'

'The Black Lesion, the Black Legion, something like that.'

'Nothing in our database about this group?'

'No, or at any of our sister agencies, either.' Kendall threw the soiled towel into a basket whose contents were incinerated every twelve hours. 'It doesn't exist.'

'I tend to agree,' LaValle said, 'but I'd like to be certain.'

He turned from the window, and the two men went out of the viewing room. They walked down a rough concrete corridor painted an institutional green, the buzzing fluorescent tubes that hurled purple shadows on the linoleum floor as they passed. He waited patiently outside the locker room for Kendall to change his clothes; then they proceeded down the corridor. At the end of it they climbed a flight of stairs to a reinforced metal door.

LaValle pressed his forefinger onto a fingerprint reader. He was rewarded by the clicking of bolts being shot, not unlike a bank vault opening.

They found themselves in another corridor, the polar opposite of the one they were leaving. This one was paneled in polished mahogany; wall sconces produced a soft, buttery glow between paintings of historical naval engagements, phalanxes of Roman legions, Prussian Hussars, and English light cavalry.

The first door on the left brought them into a room straight out of a high-toned men's club, replete with hunter-green walls, cream moldings, leather furniture, antique breakfronts, and a wooden bar from an old English pub. The sofas and chairs were well spaced, the better to allow occupants to speak of private matters. Flames cracked and sparked comfortingly in a large fireplace.

A liveried butler met them before they'd taken three steps on the thick, sound-deadening carpet. He guided them to their accustomed spot, in a discreet corner where two high-backed leather chairs were arranged on either side of a mahogany pedestal card table. They were near a tall, mullioned window flanked by thick drapes, which overlooked the Virginia countryside. This club-like room, known as the Library, was in an enormous stone house that the NSA had taken over decades ago. It was used as a retreat as well as for formal dinners for the generals and directors of the organization. Its lower depths, however, were used for other purposes.

When they had ordered drinks and light refreshments, and were alone again, LaValle said, 'Do we have a line on Bourne yet?'

'Yes and no.' Kendall crossed one leg over the other, arranging the crease in his trousers. 'As per our previous briefing, he came onto the grid at six thirty-seven last night, passing through Immigration at Dulles. He was booked on a Lufthansa flight to Moscow. Had he showed we could've put McNally onto the flight.'

'Bourne's far too clever for that,' LaValle grumbled. 'He knows we're after him now. The element of surprise has been neutralized, dammit.'

'We managed to discover that he boarded a NextGen Energy Solutions corporate jet.'

Like a hunting dog on alert, Lavalle's head came up. 'Really? Explain.'

'An executive by the name of Moira Trevor was on it.'

'What is she to Bourne?'

'A question we're trying to answer,' Kendall said unhappily. He hated disappointing his boss. 'In the meantime, we obtained a copy of the flight plan. The destination was Munich. Shall I activate a point man there?'

'Don't waste your time.' LaValle waved a hand. 'My money's on Moscow. That's where he meant to go, that's where he's going.'

'I'll get right on it.' Kendall opened his cell phone.

'I want Anthony Prowess.'

'He's in Afghanistan.'

'Then pull him the fuck out,' LaValle said shortly. 'Get him on a military chopper. I want him on the ground in Moscow by the time Bourne gets there.'

Kendall nodded, punched in a special encrypted number, and typed the coded text message to Prowess.

LaValle smiled at the approaching waiter. 'Thank you, Willard,' he said as the man snapped out a starched white tablecloth, arranged the glasses of whiskey, small plates of nibbles, and cutlery on the table, then departed as silently as he'd come.

LaValle stared at the food. 'It seems we've backed the wrong horse.'

General Kendall knew he meant Rob Batt. 'Soraya Moore witnessed the debacle. She's put two and two together in short order. Batt told us he knew about Hart's meet with Bourne because he was in her office when Bourne's call came in. Other than the Moore woman, who else is she likely to have told? No one. That'll lead Hart right back to the deputy director.'

'Hang him out to dry.'

Picking up his glass, Kendall said. 'Time for Plan B.'

LaValle stared into the chestnut liquid. 'I always thank God for Plan B, Richard. Always.'

Their glasses clinked together. They drank in studied silence while LaValle ruminated. When, half an hour later, they'd drained their whiskeys and new ones were in their hands, LaValle said, 'On the subject of Soraya Moore, I do believe it's time to bring her in for a chat.'

'Private?'

'Oh, yes.' LaValle added a dollop of water to his whiskey, releasing its complex scent. 'Bring her here.'

# 15

'Tell me about Jason Bourne.'

Harun Iliev, in an American Nike jogging suit identical to the one worn by his commander, Semion Icoupov, rounded the turn of the natural ice-skating rink in the heart of Grindelwald village. Harun had spent more than a decade as Icoupov's second in command. As a boy he'd been adopted by Icoupov's father, Farid, after his parents had drowned when a ferry taking them from Istanbul to Odessa had capsized. Harun, at the age of four, was visiting his grandmother there. The news of the deaths of her daughter and son-in-law sent her into cardiac arrest. She died almost instantly – which everyone involved felt was a blessing, for she lacked both the strength and the stamina to care for a four-year-old. Farid Icoupov stepped in, because Harun's father had worked for him; the two were close.

'There's no easy answer,' Harun said now, 'principally because there's no one answer. Some swear he's an agent of the American CI, others claim he's an international assassin for hire. Clearly he can't be both. What is indisputable is that he was responsible for foiling the plot to gas the attendees of the International Anti-Terrorist Conference in Reykjavik three years ago and, last year, the very real nuclear threat to Washington, DC, posed by Dujja, the terrorist group that was run by the two Wahhib brothers, Fadi and Karim al-Jamil. Rumor has it Bourne killed them both.'

'Impressive, if true. But just the fact that no one can get a handle on him is of extreme interest.' Icoupov's arms chugged up and down in perfect rhythm to his gliding back and forth. His cheeks were apple red and he smiled warmly at the children skating on either side of them, laughing when they laughed, giving encouragement when one of them fell. 'And how did such a man get involved with Our Friend?'

'Through the university in Georgetown,' Harun said. He was a slender man with the look of an accountant, which wasn't helped by his sallow skin and the way his olive-pit eyes were sunk deep in his skull. Ice-skating did not come naturally to him as it did to Icoupov. 'Besides killing people, it seems Bourne is something of a genius at linguistics.'

'Is he now?'

Even though they'd skated for more than forty minutes, Icoupov wasn't breathing hard. Harun knew he was just getting warmed up. They were in spectacular country. The resort of Grindelwald was just under a hundred miles southeast of Bern. Above them towered three of Switzerland's most famous mountains – Jungfrau, Mönch, and Eiger – glittering white with snow and ice.

'It seems that Bourne's weak spot is for a mentor. The first was a man named Alexander Conklin, who – '

'I knew Alex,' Icoupov said curtly. 'It was before your time. Another lifetime, it often seems.' He nodded. 'Please continue.'

'It seems Our Friend has made a play to become his new mentor.'

'I must interject here. That seems improbable.'

'Then why did Bourne kill Mikhail Tarkanian?'

'Mischa.' Icoupov's pace faltered for a moment. 'Allah preserve us! Does Leonid Danilovich know?'

'Arkadin is currently out of contact.'

'What's his progress?'

'He's come and gone from Sevastopol.'

'That's something, anyway.' Icoupov shook his head. 'We're running out of time.'

'Arkadin knows this.'

'I want Tarkanian's death kept from him, Harun. Mischa was his best friend; they were closer than brothers. Under no circumstances can he be allowed to be distracted from his present assignment.'

A lovely young woman held out her hand as she skated abreast of them. Icoupov took it and for a time was swept away in an ice dance that made him feel as if he were twenty again. When he returned, he resumed their skate around the rink. Something about the easy gliding motion of skating, he'd once told Harun, helped him to think.

'Given what you've told me,' Icoupov said at length, 'this Jason Bourne may very well cause an unforeseen complication.'

'You can be sure Our Friend has recruited Bourne to his cause by telling him that you caused the death of – '

Icoupov shot him a warning look. 'I agree. But the question we must answer is how much of the truth he's risked telling Bourne.'

'Knowing Our Friend,' Harun said, 'I would say very little, if at all.'

'Yes.' Icoupov tapped a gloved forefinger against his lips. 'And if this is the case we can use the truth against him, don't you think?'

'If we can get to Bourne,' Harun said. 'And if we can get him to believe us.'

'Oh, he'll believe us. I'll make sure of that.' Icoupov executed a perfect spin. 'Your new assignment, Harun, is to ensure we get to him before he can do any more damage. We could ill afford to lose our eye in Our Friend's camp. Further deaths are unacceptable.'

Munich was full of cold rain. It was a gray city on the best of days, but in this windswept downpour it seemed to hunker down. Like a turtle, it pulled in its head into its concrete shell, turning its back on all visitors.

Bourne and Moira sat inside the cavernous NextGen 747. Bourne was on his cell, making a reservation on the next flight to Moscow.

'I wish I could authorize the plane to take you,' Moira said after he'd folded away the phone.

'No, you don't,' Bourne said. 'You'd like me to stay here by your side.'

'I already told you why I think that would be a bad idea.' She looked out at the wet tarmac, rainbow-streaked with droplets of fuel and oil. Raindrops trickled down the Perspex window like racing cars in their lanes. 'And I find myself not wanting to be here at all.'

Bourne opened the file he'd taken from Veronica Hart, turned it around, held it out. 'I'd like you to take a look at this.'

Moira turned back, put the file on her lap, paged through it. All at once she looked up. 'Was it CI that had me under surveillance?' When Bourne nodded, she said, 'Well, that's a relief.'

'How is it a relief?'

She lifted the file. 'This is all disinformation, a setup. Two years ago, when bidding for the Long Beach LNG terminal was at its height, my bosses suspected that AllEn, our chief rival, was monitoring our communications in order to get a handle on the proprietary systems that make our terminal unique. As a favor to me, Martin went to the Old Man for permission to set up a sting. The Old Man agreed, but it was imperative that no one else know about it, so he never told anyone else at CI. It worked. By tracking our cell conversations we discovered that AllEn was, indeed, monitoring the calls.'

'I recall the settlement,' Bourne said.

'Because of the evidence Martin and I provided, AllEn had no incentive to go to trial.'

'NextGen got a mid-eight-figure settlement, right?'

Moira nodded. 'And won the rights to build the LNG terminal in Long Beach. That's how I got my promotion to executive vice president.'

Bourne took back the file. He, too, was relieved. For him, trust was like an ill-made boat, springing leaks at every turn, threatening at any moment to sink him. He'd ceded part of himself to Moira, but the loss of control was like a knife in his heart.

Moira looked at him rather sadly. 'Did you suspect me of being a Mata Hari?'

'It was important to make sure,' he said.

Her face closed up. 'Sure. I understand.' She began to stuff papers into a slim leather briefcase more roughly than was needed. 'You thought I'd betrayed Martin and was going to betray you.'

'I'm relieved it's not true.'

'I'm so very happy to hear that.' She shot him an acid stare.

'Moira . . .'

'What?' She pulled hair off her face. 'What is it you want to say to me, Jason?'

'I . . . This is hard for me.'

She leaned forward, peering at him. 'Just tell me.'

'I trusted Marie,' Bourne said. 'I leaned on her, she helped me with my amnesia. She was always there. And then, suddenly, she wasn't.'

Moira's voice softened. 'I know.'

He looked at her at last. 'There is no good thing about being alone. But for me it's all a matter of trust.'

'I know you think I haven't told you the truth about Martin and me.' She took his hands in hers. 'We were never lovers, Jason. We were more like brother and sister. We supported each other. Trust didn't come easily to either of us. I think it's important for both of us that I tell you that now.'

Bourne understood that she was also talking about the two of them, not her and

Martin. He'd trusted so few people in his life: Marie, Alex Conklin, Mo Panov, Martin, Soraya. He saw all the things that had been keeping him from moving on with his life. With so little past, it was difficult letting go of the people he'd known and cared about.

A pang of sorrow shot through him. 'Marie is dead. She's in the past now. And my children are far better off with their grandparents. Their life is stable and happy. That's best for them.'

He rose, needing to get moving.

Moira, aware he was ill at ease, changed the subject. 'Do you know how long you'll be in Moscow?'

'The same amount of time you'll be in Munich, I imagine.'

That got a smile out of her. She stood, leaned toward him. 'Be well, Jason. Stay safe.' She gave him a lingering, loving kiss. 'Remember me.'

# 16

Soraya Moore was ushered cordially into the hushed sanctuary of the Library where less than twenty-four hours before, Luther LaValle and General Kendall had had their post-rendition fireside chat. It was Kendall himself who had picked her up, chauffeured her to the NSA safe house deep in the Virginia countryside. Soraya had, of course, never been here.

LaValle, in a midnight-blue chalk-striped suit, blue shirt with white collar and cuffs, a striped tie in the Yale colors, looked like a merchant banker. He rose as Kendall brought her over to the area by the window. There were three chairs grouped around the antique card table.

'Director Moore, having heard so much about you, it's a genuine pleasure to meet you.' Smiling broadly, LaValle indicated a chair. 'Please.'

Soraya saw no point in refusing the invitation. She didn't know whether she was more curious or alarmed by the abrupt summons. She did, however, glance around the room. 'Where is Secretary Halliday? General Kendall informed me that the invitation came from him.'

'Oh, it did,' LaValle said. 'Unfortunately, the secretary of defense was called into a meeting in the Oval Office. He phoned me to convey to you his apologies and to insist that we carry on without him.'

All of which meant, Soraya knew, that Halliday had never had any intention of attending this little tête-à-tête. She doubted he even knew about it.

'Anyway,' LaValle said as Kendall sat in the third chair, 'now that you're here you might as well enjoy yourself.' He raised his hand, and Willard appeared as if by prestidigitation. 'Something to drink, Director? I know as you're Muslim you're forbidden alcohol, but we have a full range of potions for you to choose from.'

'Tea, please,' she said directly to Willard. 'Ceylon, if you have it.'

'Of course, ma'am. Milk? Sugar?'

'Neither, thank you.' She'd never formed the British habit.

Willard seemed to bow before he vanished without a sound.

Soraya redirected her attention to the two men. 'Now, gentlemen, in what way can I help you?'

'I rather think it's the other way around,' General Kendall said.

Soraya cocked her head. 'How d'you figure that?'

'Frankly, because of the turmoil at CI,' LaValle said, 'we think Typhon is working with one hand tied behind its back.'

Willard arrived with Soraya's tea, the men's whiskeys. He set the japanned tray down with the cup, glasses, and tea service, then left.

LaValle waited until Soraya had poured her tea before he continued. 'It seems to me that Typhon would benefit immensely from taking advantage of all the resources at NSA's disposal. We could even help you expand beyond the scope of CI's reach.'

Soraya lifted her cup to her lips, found the fragrant Ceylon tea exquisitely delicious. 'It seems that you know more about Typhon than any of us at CI were aware.'

LaValle let go with a soft laugh. 'Okay, let's stop beating around the bush. We had a mole inside CI. You know who it is now. He made a fatal mistake in going after Jason Bourne and failing.'

Veronica Hart had relieved Rob Batt of his position that morning, a fact that must have come to LaValle's attention, especially since his replacement, Peter Marks, had been one of Hart's most vocal supporters from day one. Soraya knew Peter well, had suggested to Hart that he deserved the promotion.

'Is Batt now working for NSA?'

'Mr. Batt has outlived his usefulness,' Kendall said rather stiffly.

Soraya turned her attention to the military man. 'A glimpse of your own fate, don't you think, General?'

Kendall's face closed up like a fist, but following an almost imperceptible shake of LaValle's head he bit back a rejoinder.

'While it's certainly true that life in the intelligence services can be harsh, even brutal,' LaValle interjected, 'certain individuals within it are – shall we say – inoculated against such unfortunate eventualities.'

Soraya kept her gaze on Kendall. 'I suppose I could be one of those certain individuals.'

'Yes, absolutely.' LaValle put one hand over the other on his knee. 'Your knowledge of Muslim thought and custom, your expertise as Martin Lindros's right hand as he put Typhon together are invaluable.'

'You see how it is, General,' Soraya said. 'One day an invaluable asset like me is bound to take over your position.'

LaValle cleared his throat. 'Does that mean you're on board?'

Smiling sweetly, Soraya put her teacup down. 'I'll say this for you, Mr. LaValle, you certainly know how to make lemonade from lemons.'

LaValle returned her smile as if it were a tennis serve. 'My dear Director, I do believe you've hit upon one of my specialities.'

'What makes you think I'd abandon CI?'

LaValle put a forefinger beside his nose. 'My reading of you is that you're a pragmatic woman. You know better than we do what kind of a mess CI is in. How long do you think it's going to take the new DCI to right the ship? What makes you think she even can?' He raised his finger. 'I'm exceedingly interested in your opinion, but before you answer think about how little time we might have before this unknown terrorist group is going to strike.'

Soraya felt as if she'd been rabbit-punched. How in the hell had NSA gotten wind of the Typhon terrorist intercepts? At the moment, however, that was a moot point. The important thing was how to respond to this breach of security.

Before she could formulate a counter, LaValle said, 'I'm curious about one thing, though. Why is it that Director Hart saw fit to keep this intel to herself, rather than bringing in Homeland Security, FBI, and NSA?'

'That was my doing.' *I'm in it now*, Soraya thought. *I might as well go all the way.* 'Until the incident at the Freer, the intel was sketchy enough that I felt the involvement of other intelligence agencies would only muddy the waters.'

'Meaning,' Kendall said, glad of the opportunity to get in a dig, 'you didn't want us rooting around in your carrot patch.'

'This is a serious situation, Director,' LaValle said. 'In matters of national security – '

'If this Muslim terrorist group – which we now know calls itself the Black Legion – gets wind that we've intercepted their communications we'll be sunk before we even start trying to counter their attack.'

'I could have you shit-canned.'

'And lose my invaluable expertise?' Soraya shook her head. 'I don't think so.'

'So what do we have?' Kendall snapped.

'Stalemate.' LaValle passed a hand across his brow. 'Do you think it would be possible for me to see the Typhon intercepts?' His tone had changed completely. He was now in conciliatory mode. 'Believe it or not, we're not the Evil Empire. We actually might be able to be of some assistance.'

Soraya considered. 'I think that can be arranged.'

'Excellent.'

'It would have to be Eyes Only.'

LaValle agreed at once.

'And in a controlled, highly restricted environment,' Soraya added, following up her advantage. 'The Typhon offices at CI would be perfect.'

LaValle spread his hands. 'Why not here?'

Soraya smiled. 'I think not.'

'Under the current climate I think you can understand why I'd be reluctant to meet you there.'

'I take your point.' Soraya thought for a moment. 'If I did bring the intercepts here I'd have to have someone with me.'

LaValle nodded vigorously. 'Of course. Whatever makes you feel comfortable.' He seemed far more pleased than Kendall, who looked at her as if he had caught sight of her from a battlefield trench.

'Frankly,' Soraya said, 'none of this makes me feel comfortable.' She glanced around the room again.

'The building is swept three times a day for electronic bugs,' LaValle pointed out. 'Plus, we have all the most sophisticated surveillance systems, basically a computerized monitoring system that keeps track of the two thousand closed-circuit video cameras installed throughout the facility and grounds, compares them from second to second for any anomalies whatsoever. The DARPA software compares any anomalies against a database of more than a million images, makes real-time decisions in nanoseconds. For instance, a bird in flight would be ignored, a running figure wouldn't. Believe me, you have nothing to worry about.'

'Right now, the only thing I worry about,' Soraya said, 'is you, Mr. LaValle.'

'I understand completely.' LaValle finished off his whiskey. 'That's what this exercise is all about, Director. To engender trust between us. How else could we be expected to work together?'

*

General Kendall sent Soraya back to the district with one of his drivers. She had him drop her where she'd arranged to meet Kendall, outside what had once been the National Historical Wax Museum on E Street, SW. She waited until the black Ford had been swallowed up in traffic, then she turned away, walked all the way around the block at a normal pace. By the end of her circuit she was certain she was free of tags, NSA or otherwise. At that point, she sent a three-letter text message via her cell. Two minutes later, a young man on a motorcycle appeared. He wore jeans, a black leather jacket, a gleaming black helmet with the smoked faceplate lowered. He slowed, stopped just long enough for her to climb on behind him. Handing her a helmet, he waited for her to don it, then he zoomed off down the street.

'I have several contacts within DARPA,' Deron said. DARPA was an acronym for the Defense Advanced Research Projects Agency, an arm of the Department of Defense. 'I have a working knowledge of the software architecture at the heart of the NSA's surveillance system.' He shrugged. 'This is one way I keep my edge.'

'We gotta find a way around it or through it,' Tyrone said.

He was still wearing his black leather jacket. His black helmet was on a table alongside the one he'd given Soraya for the high-speed trip here to Deron's house-lab. Soraya had met both Deron and Tyrone when Bourne had brought her to this nondescript olive-colored house just off 7th Street, NE.

'You must be joking, right?' Deron, a tall, slim, handsome man with skin the color of light cocoa, looked from one to the other. 'Tell me you're joking.'

'If we were joking we wouldn't be here.' Soraya rubbed the heel of her hand against her temple as she sought to ignore the fierce headache that had begun after her terrifying interview with LaValle and Kendall.

'It's just not possible.' Deron put his hands on his hips. 'That software is state-of-the-art. And two thousand CCTV cameras! Fuck me.'

They sat on canvas chairs in his lab, a double-height room filled with all manner of monitors, keyboards, electronic systems whose functions were known only to Deron. Ranged around the wall were a number of paintings – all masterpieces by Titian, Seurat, Rembrandt, van Gogh. *Water Lilies, Green Reflection, Left Part* was Soraya's favorite. That all of them were painted by Deron in the atelier in the next room had stunned her the first time she was here. Now they simply filled her with wonder. How he had reproduced Monet's exact shade of cobalt blue was beyond her. It was hardly surprising that Bourne used Deron to forge all his ID documents, when in this day and age it was becoming increasingly difficult to do. Many forgers had quit, claiming governments had made their job impossible, but not Deron. It was his stock in trade. Little wonder that he and Bourne were so close. Birds of a feather, Soraya thought.

'What about mirrors?' Tyrone said.

'That would be simplest,' Deron said. 'But one of the reasons they've installed so many cameras is to give the system multiple views of the same area. That negates mirrors right there.'

'Too bad Bourne killed dat fucker Karim al-Jamil. He could probably write a worm t'screw with the DARPA software like he did with the CI database.'

Soraya turned to Deron. 'Can it be done?' she said. 'Could you do it?'

'Hacking's not my thing. I leave that to my old lady.'

Soraya didn't know Deron had a girlfriend. 'How good is she?'

'Please,' Deron snorted.

'Can we talk to her?'

Deron looked dubious. 'This is the NSA we're talking about. Those fuckers don't fool around. To be frank, I don't think you ought to be messing with them in the first place.'

'Unfortunately, I have no choice,' Soraya said.

'They fuckin' wid us,' Tyrone said, 'and unless we get all medieval on they ass, they gonna walk all over us an' own us forever.'

Deron shook his head. 'You sure put some interesting notions in this man's head, Soraya. Before you came along he was the best street protection I ever had. Now look at him. Messing with the big boys in the bad world outside the ghetto.' He didn't hide the pride he felt for Tyrone, but his voice held a warning, too. 'I hope to hell you know what you're getting yourself into, Tyrone. If this thing comes apart in any way you're in the federal slammer till Gabriel comes calling.'

Tyrone crossed his arms over his chest, stood his ground.

Deron sighed. 'All right, then. We're all adults here.' He reached for his cell. 'Kiki's upstairs in her lair. She doesn't like to be interrupted, but in this case I think she'll be intrigued.' He spoke briefly into the cell, then put it down. Moments later a slim woman with a beautiful African face and deep chocolate skin appeared. She was as tall as Deron, with the upright carriage of proud and ancient royalty.

Her face split into a ferocious grin when she saw Tyrone. 'Hey,' they said to each other. That one word seemed all that was needed.

'Kiki, this is Soraya,' Deron said.

Kiki's smile was wide and dazzling. 'My name's actually Esiankiki. I'm Masai. But in America I'm not so formal; everyone calls me Kiki.'

The two women touched hands. Kiki's grip was cool and dry. She regarded Soraya out of large coffee-colored eyes. She had the smoothest skin Soraya had ever seen, which she instantly envied. Her hair was very short, marvelously cut like a cap to fit her elongated skull. She wore a brown ankle-length dress that clung provocatively to her slim hips and small breasts.

Deron briefly outlined the problem while he brought up the DARPA software architecture on one of his computer terminals. While Kiki checked it out, he filled her in on the basics. 'We need something that can bypass the firewall, and is undetectable.'

'The first isn't all that difficult.' Kiki's long, delicate fingers were flying over the keyboard as she experimented with the computer code. 'The second, I don't know.'

'Unfortunately, that's not the end of it.' Deron positioned himself so he could peer over her shoulder at the terminal. 'This particular software controls two thousand CCTV cameras. Our friends here need to get in and out of the facility without being detected.'

Kiki stood up, turned around to face them. 'In other words all two thousand cameras have to be covered.'

'That's right,' Soraya said.

'You don't need a hacker, dear. You need the invisible man.'

'But you can make them invisible, Kiki.' Deron slid his arm around her slender waist. 'Can't you?'

'Hmm.' Kiki peered again at the code on the terminal. 'You know, there looks like there may be a recurring variance I might be able to exploit.' She hunkered down on a stool. 'I'm going to transfer this upstairs.'

Deron winked at Soraya, as if to say, *I told you so.*

Kiki routed a number of files to her computer, which was separate from Deron's. She spun around, slapped her hands on her thighs, and got up. 'Okay, then, I'll see you all later.'

'How much later?' Soraya said, but Kiki was already taking the stairs three at a time.

Moscow was wreathed in snow when Bourne stepped off the Aeroflot plane at Sheremetyevo. His flight had been delayed forty minutes, the jet circling while the runways were de-iced. He cleared Customs and Immigration and was met by a small, cat-like individual wrapped in a white down coat. Lev Baronov, Professor Specter's contact.

'No luggage, I see,' Baronov said in heavily accented English. He was as wiry and hyperactive as a Jack Russell terrier as he elbowed and barked at the small army of gypsy cab drivers vying for a fare. They were a sad-faced lot, plucked from the minorities in the Caucasus, Asians and the like whose ethnicity prevented them from getting a decent job with decent pay in Moscow. 'We'll take care of that on the way in to town. You'll need proper clothes for Moscow's winter. It's a balmy minus two Celsius today.'

'That would be most helpful,' Bourne replied in perfect Russian.

Baronov's bushy eyebrows rose in surprise. 'You speak like a native, *gospadin* Bourne.'

'I had excellent instructors,' Bourne said laconically.

Amid the bustle of the flight terminal, he was studying the flow of passengers, noting those who lingered at a newsagent or outside the duty-free shop, those who didn't move at all. Ever since he emerged into the terminal he'd had the unshakable feeling that he was being watched. Of course there were CCTV cameras all over, but the particular prickling of his scalp that had developed over the years of fieldwork was unerring. Someone had him under surveillance. This fact was both alarming and reassuring – that he'd already picked up a tag meant someone knew he was scheduled to arrive in Moscow. NSA could have scanned the departing flight manifests back at New York and picked up his name from Lufthansa; there'd been no time to take himself off the list. He looked only in short touristic glances because he had no desire to alert his shadow that he was on to him.

'I'm being followed,' Bourne said as he sat in Baronov's wheezing Zil. They were on the M10 motorway.

'No problem,' Baronov said, as if he was used to being tailed all the time. He didn't even ask who was following Bourne. Bourne thought of the professor's pledge that Baronov wouldn't get in his way.

Bourne paged through the packet Baronov had given him, which included new ID, a key, and the box number to get money out of the safe-deposit vault in the Moskva Bank.

'I need a plan of the bank building,' Bourne said.

'No problem.' Baronov exited the M10. Bourne was now Fyodor Ilianovich

Popov, a midlevel functionary of GazProm, the gargantuan state-run energy conglomerate.

'How well will this ID hold up?' Bourne asked.

'Not to worry.' Baronov grinned. 'The professor has friends in GazProm who know how to protect you, Fyodor Ilianovich Popov.'

Anthony Prowess had come a long way to keep the ancient Zil in sight and he wasn't about to lose it, no matter what evasive maneuvers the driver took. He'd been waiting at Sheremetyevo for Bourne to come through Immigration. General Kendall had sent a recent surveillance photo of Bourne to his cell. The photo was grainy and two-dimensional because of the long telephoto lens used, but it was a close-up; there was no mistaking Bourne when he arrived.

For Prowess, the next few minutes were crucial. He had no illusions that he could remain unnoticed by Bourne for any length of time; therefore, in the short moments while his subject was still unselfconscious, he needed to drink in every tic and habit, no matter how minuscule or seemingly irrelevant. He knew from bitter experience that these small insights would prove invaluable as the surveillance ground on, especially when it came time to engage the subject and terminate him.

Prowess was no stranger to Moscow. He'd been born here to a British diplomat and his cultural attaché wife. Not until Prowess was fifteen did he understand that his mother's job was a cover. She was, in fact, a spy for MI6, Her Majesty's Secret Service. Four years later Prowess's mother was compromised, and MI6 spirited them out of the country. Because his mother was now a wanted woman, the Prowesses were sent to America, to begin a new life with a new family name. The danger had been ground so deeply into Prowess that he'd actually forgotten what they were once called. He was now simply Anthony Prowess.

As soon as he'd built up qualified academic credits, he applied to the NSA. From the moment he'd discovered that his mother was a spy, that was all he'd wanted to do. No amount of pleading from his parents could dissuade him. Because of his ease with foreign languages and his knowledge of other cultures, the NSA sent him abroad, first to the Horn of Africa to train, then to Afghanistan, where he liaised with the local tribes fighting the Taliban in rough mountain terrain. He was a hard man, no stranger to hardship, or to death. He knew more ways to kill a human being than there were days in the year. Compared with what he'd been through in the past nineteen months, this assignment was going to be a piece of cake.

# 17

Bourne and Baronov sped down Volokolamskoye Highway. Crocus City was an enormous high-end mall. Built in 2002, it was a seemingly endless array of glittering boutiques, restaurants, car showrooms, and marble fountains. It was also an excellent place to lose a tail.

While Bourne shopped for suitable clothes, Baronov was busy on his cell phone. There was no point in going to the trouble of losing the tail inside the maze of the mall only to have him pick them up again when they returned to the Zil. Baronov was calling a colleague to come to Crocus City. They'd take his car, and he'd drive the Zil into Moscow.

Bourne paid for his purchases and changed into them. Baronov took him to the Franck Muller Café inside the mall, where they had coffee and sandwiches.

'Tell me about Pyotr's last girlfriend,' Bourne said.

'Gala Nematova?' Baronov shrugged. 'Not much to tell, really. She's just another one of those pretty girls one sees around all the latest Moscow nightclubs. These women are a ruble a dozen.'

'Where would I find her?'

Baronov shrugged. 'She'll go where the oligarchs cluster. Really, your guess is as good as mine.' He laughed good-naturedly. 'For myself, I'm too old for places like that, but I'll be glad to take you on a round-robin tonight.'

'All I need is for you to lend me a car.'

'Suit yourself, *miya droog*.'

A few moments later, Baronov went to the men's room, where he'd agreed to make the switch of car keys with his friend. When he returned he handed Bourne a folded piece of paper on which was the plan for the Moskva Bank building.

They went out a different direction from the way they'd come in, which led them to a parking lot on the other side of the mall. They got into a vintage black Volga four-door sedan that, to Bourne's relief, started up immediately.

'You see? No problem.' Baronov laughed jovially. 'What would you do without me, *gospadin* Bourne?'

The Frunzenskaya embankment was located southwest of Moscow's inner Garden Ring. Mikhail Tarkanian had said that he could see the pedestrian bridge to Gorky Park from his living-room window. He hadn't lied. His apartment was in a building not far from Khlastekov, a restaurant serving excellent Russian food, according to Baronov. With its two-story, square-columned portico and decorative concrete balconies, the building itself was a prime example of the Stalinist

Empire style that raped and beat into submission a more pastoral and romantic architectural past.

Bourne instructed Baronov to stay in the Volga until he returned. He went up the stone steps, under the colonnade, and through the glass door. He was in a small vestibule that ended in an inner door, which was locked. On the right wall was a brass panel with rows of bell pushes corresponding to the apartments. Bourne ran his finger down the rows until he found the push with Tarkanian's name. Noting the apartment number, he crossed to the inner door and used a small flexible blade to fool the lock's tumblers into thinking he had a key. The door clicked open, and he went inside.

There was a small arthritic elevator on the left wall. To the right, a rather grand staircase swept up to the first floor. The first three treads were in marble, but these gave way to simple concrete steps that released a kind of talcum-like powder as the porous treads wore away.

Tarkanian's apartment was on the third floor, down a dark corridor, dank with the odors of boiled cabbage and stewed meat. The floor was composed of tiny hexagonal tiles, chipped and worn as the steps leading up.

Bourne found the door without trouble. He put his ear against it, listening for sounds within the apartment. When he heard none, he picked the lock. Turning the glass knob slowly, he pushed open the door a crack. Weak light filtered in past half-drawn curtains framing windows on the right. Behind the smell of disuse was a whiff of a masculine scent – cologne or hair cream. Tarkanian had made it clear he hadn't been back here in years, so who was using his apartment?

Bourne moved silently, cautiously through the rooms. Where he'd expected to find dust, there was none; where he expected the furniture to be covered in sheets, it wasn't. There was food in the refrigerator, though the bread on the counter was growing mold. Still, within the week, someone had been living here. The knobs to all the doors were glass, just like the one on the front door, and some looked wobbly on their brass shafts. There were photos on the wall: high-toned black-and-whites of Gorky Park in different seasons.

Tarkanian's bed was unmade. The covers lay pulled back in unruly waves, as if someone had been startled out of sleep or had made a hasty exit. On the other side of the bed, the door to the bathroom was half closed.

As Bourne stepped around the end of the bed, he noticed a five-by-seven framed photo of a young woman, blonde, with a veneer of beauty cultivated by models the world over. He was wondering whether this was Gala Nematova when he caught a blurred movement out of the corner of his eye.

A man hidden behind the bathroom door made a run at Bourne. He was armed with a thick-bladed fisherman's knife, which he jabbed at Bourne point-first. Bourne rolled away, the man followed. He was blue-eyed, blond, and big. There were tattoos on the sides of his neck and the palms of his hands. Mementos of a Russian prison.

The best way to neutralize a knife was to close with your opponent. As the man lunged after him, Bourne turned, grabbed the man by his shirt, slammed his forehead into the bridge of the man's nose. Blood spurted, the man grunted, cursed in guttural Russian, '*Blyad!*'

He drove a fist into Bourne's side, tried to free his hand with the knife. Bourne applied a nerve block at the base of the thumb. The Russian butted Bourne in the sternum, drove him back off the bed, into the half-open bathroom door. The glass knob drilled into Bourne's spine, causing him to arch back. The door swung fully open and he sprawled on the cold tiles. The Russian, regaining use of his hand, pulled out a Stechkin APS 9mm. Bourne kicked him in the shin, so he went down on one knee, then struck him on the side of the face, and the Stechkin went flying across the tiles. The Russian launched a flurry of punches and hand strikes that battered Bourne back against the door before grabbing the Stechkin. Bourne reached up, felt the cool octagon of the glass doorknob. Grinning, the Russian aimed the pistol at Bourne's heart. Wrenching off the knob, Bourne threw it at the center of the Russian's forehead, where it struck full-on. His eyes rolled up and he slumped to the floor.

Bourne gathered up the Stechkin and took a moment to catch his breath. Then he crawled over to the Russian. Of course, he had no conventional ID on him, but that didn't mean Bourne couldn't find out where he'd come from.

Stripping off the big man's jacket and shirt, Bourne took a long look at a constellation of tattoos. On his chest was a tiger, a sign of an enforcer. On his left shoulder was a dagger dripping blood, a sign that he was a killer. But it was the third symbol, a genie emerging from a Middle Eastern lamp, that interested Bourne the most. This was a sign that the Russian had been put in prison for drug-related crimes.

The professor had told Bourne that two of the Russian Mafia families, the Kazanskaya and the Azeri, were vying for sole control of the drug market. *Don't get in their way*, Specter had warned. *If they have any contact with you, I beg you not to engage them. Instead, turn the other cheek. It's the only way to survive there.*

Bourne was about to get up when he saw something on the inside of the Russian's left elbow: a small tattoo of a figure with a man's body and a jackal's head. Anubis, Egyptian god of the underworld. This symbol was supposed to protect the wearer from death, but it had also latterly been appropriated by the Kazanskaya. What was a member of such a powerful Russian *grupperovka* family doing in Tarkanian's apartment? He'd been sent to find him and kill him. Why? That was something Bourne needed to find out.

He looked around the bathroom at the sink with its dripping faucet, pots of eye cream and powder, makeup pencils, the stained mirror. He pulled back the shower curtain, plucked several blond hairs from the drain. They were long; from a woman's head. Gala Nematova's head?

He made his way to the kitchen, opened drawers, pawed through them until he found a blue ballpoint pen. Back in the bathroom, he took one of the eyeliner pencils. Crouching down beside the Russian, he drew a facsimile of the Anubis tattoo on the inside of his left elbow; when he got a line wrong, he rubbed it off. When he was satisfied, he used the blue ballpoint pen to make the final 'tattoo.' He knew it wouldn't withstand a close inspection, but for a flash of identification he thought it would suffice. At the sink, he delicately rinsed off the makeup pencil, then shot some hair spray over the ink outline to further fix it on his skin.

He checked behind the toilet tank and in it, favorite hiding places for money, documents, or important materials, but found nothing. He was about to leave when his eyes fell again on the mirror. Peering more closely, he could see a trace of red here and there. Lipstick, which had been carefully wiped off, as if someone –

possibly the Kazanskaya Russian – had sought to erase it. Why would he do that?

It seemed to Bourne the smears formed a kind of pattern. Taking up a pot of face powder, he blew across the top of it. The petroleum-based powder sought its twin, clung to the ghost image of the petroleum-based lipstick.

When he was done, he put the pot down, took a step backward. He was looking at a scrawled note:

Off to the Kitaysky Lyotchik. Where R U? Gala.

So Gala Nematova, Pyotr's last girlfriend, did live here. Had Pyotr used this apartment while Tarkanian was away?

On his way out, he checked the Russian's pulse. It was slow but steady. The question of why the Kazanskaya sent this prison-hardened assassin to an apartment where Gala Nematova had once lived with Pyotr loomed large in his mind. Was there a connection between Semion Icoupov and the *grupperovka* family?

Taking another long look at Gala Nematova's photo, Bourne slipped out of the apartment as silently as he'd entered it. Out in the hallway he listened for human sounds, but apart from the muted wailing of a baby in an apartment on the second floor, all was still. He descended the stairs and went through the vestibule, where a little girl holding her mother's hand was trying to drag her upstairs. Bourne and the mother exchanged the meaningless smiles of strangers passing each other. Then Bourne was outside, emerging from under the colonnade. Save for an old woman gingerly picking her way through the treacherous snow, no one was about. He slipped into the passenger's seat of the Volga and shut the door behind him.

That was when he saw the blood leaking from Baronov's throat. At the same instant a wire whipped around his neck, digging into his windpipe.

Four times a week after work, Rodney Feir, chief of field support for CI, worked out at a health club a short walk from his house in Fairfax, Virginia. He spent an hour on the treadmill, another hour weight training, then took a cold shower and headed for the steam room.

This evening General Kendall was waiting for him. Kendall dimly saw the glass door open, cold air briefly sucked in as tendrils of steam escaped into the men's locker room. Then Feir's trim, athletic body appeared through the mist.

'Good to see you, Rodney,' General Kendall said.

Feir nodded silently, sat down beside Kendall.

Rodney Feir was Plan B, the backup the general had put in place in the event the plan involving Rob Batt blew up. In fact, Feir had been easier to land than Batt. Feir was someone who'd drifted into security work not for any patriotic reason, not because he liked the clandestine life. He was simply lazy. Not that he didn't do his job, not that he didn't do it damn well. It was just that government life suited him down to his black wing-tip shoes. The key fact to remember about him was that whatever Feir did, he did because it would benefit him. He was, in fact, an opportunist. He, more than any of the others at CI, could see the writing on the wall, which is why his conversion to the NSA cause had been so easy and seamless. With the death of the Old Man, the end of days had arrived. He had none of Batt's loyalty to contend with.

Still, it didn't do to take anyone for granted, which is why Kendall met him here occasionally. They would take a steam, then shower, climb into their civvies, and go to dinner at one of several grungy barbecue joints Kendall knew in the southeast section of the district.

These places were no more than shacks. They were mainly the pit out back, where the pitmaster lovingly smoked his cuts of meat – ribs, brisket, burnt ends, sweet and hot sausages, sometimes a whole hog – for hours on end. The old, scarred wooden picnic tables, topped with four or five sauces of varying ingredients and heat, were a kind of afterthought. Most folk had their meat wrapped up to take out. Not Kendall and Feir. They sat at a table, eating and drinking beer, while the bones piled up along with the wadded-up napkins and the slices of white bread so soft, they disintegrated under a few drops of sauce.

Now and again Feir stopped eating to impart to Kendall some bit of fact or scuttlebutt currently going around the CI offices. Kendall noted these with his steel-trap military mind, occasionally asking questions to help Feir clarify or amplify a point, especially when it came to the movements of Veronica Hart and Soraya Moore.

Afterward, they drove to an old abandoned library for the main event. The Renaissance-style building had been bought at fire sale prices by Drew Davis, a local businessman familiar in SE but otherwise unknown within the district, which was precisely how he liked it. He was one of those people savvy enough to fly under the Metro police radar. Not so simple a matter in SE, because like almost everyone else who lived there he was black. Unlike most of those around him, he had friends in high places. This was mainly due to the place he ran, The Glass Slipper.

To all intents and purposes it was a legit music club, and an extremely successful one to boot, attracting many big-name R&B acts. But in the back was the real business: a high-end cathouse that specialized in women of color. To those in the know, any flavor of color, which in this case meant ethnicity, could be procured at The Glass Slipper. Rates were steep but nobody seemed to mind, partly because Drew Davis paid his girls well.

Kendall had frequented this cathouse since his senior year in college. He'd come with a bunch of well-connected buddies one night as a hoot. Didn't want to but they'd dared him, and he knew how much he'd be ridiculed if he failed to take them up on it. Ironically he stayed, over the years having developed a taste for, as he put it, walking on the wild side. At first he told himself that the attraction was purely physical. Then he realized he liked being there; no one bothered him, no one made fun of him. Later, his continued interest was a reaction to his role as outsider when it came to working with the power junkies like Luther LaValle. Christ, even the fallen Rob Batt had been a member of Skull & Bones at Yale. *Well, The Glass Slipper is my Skull & Bones*, Kendall thought as he was ushered into the back room. This was as clandestine, as outré as things got inside the Beltway. It was Kendall's own little hideaway, a life that was his alone. Not even Luther knew about The Glass Slipper. It felt good to have a secret from LaValle.

Kendall and Feir sat in purple velvet chairs – the color of royalty, as Kendall pointed out – and were treated to a soft parade of women of all sizes and colors. Kendall chose Imani, one of his favorites, Feir a dusky-skinned Eurasian woman who was part Indian.

They retired to spacious rooms, furnished like bedrooms in European villas, with four-poster beds, tons of chintz, velvet, swags, drapes. There Kendall watched as, in one astonishing shimmy, Imani slid out of her chocolate silk spaghetti-strap dress. She wore nothing underneath. The lamplight burnished her dark skin.

Then she opened her arms and, with a deep-felt groan, General Richard P. Kendall melted into the sinuous river of her flawless body.

The moment Bourne felt his air supply cut off, he levered himself up off the front bench seat, arching his back so that he could put first one foot, then the other on the dashboard. Using his legs, he launched himself diagonally into the backseat, so that he landed right behind the ill-fated Baronov. The strangler was forced to turn to his right in order to keep the wire around Bourne's throat. This was an awkward position for him; he now lacked the leverage he had when Bourne was directly in front of him.

Bourne planted the heel of his shoe in the strangler's groin and ground down as hard as he could, but his strength was depleted from the lack of oxygen.

'Die, fucker,' the strangler said in a hard-edged Midwestern accent.

White lights danced in his vision, and a blackness was seeping up all around him. It was as if he were looking down a tunnel through the wrong end of a telescope. Nothing looked real; his sense of perspective was skewed. He could see the man, his dark hair, his cruel face, the unmistakable hundred-mile stare of the American soldier in combat. In the back of his mind, he knew the NSA had found him.

Bourne's lapse of concentration allowed the strangler to free himself, jerk the ends of the wire so that it dug deeper into Bourne's throat. Bourne's windpipe was totally cut off. Blood was running down into his collar as the wire bit through his skin. Strange animal noises bubbled up from deep inside him. He blinked away tears and sweat, used his last ounce of strength to jam his thumb into the agent's eye. Keeping up the pressure despite blows to his midsection gained him a temporary respite: The wire slackened. He gasped in a railing breath, and dug deeper with his thumb.

The wire slackened further. He heard the car door open. The strangler's face wrenched away from him, and the car door slammed shut. He heard running feet, dying away. By the time he managed to unwind the wire, to cough and gasp air into his burning lungs, the street was empty. The NSA agent was gone.

Bourne was alone in the Volga with the corpse of Lev Baronov, dizzy, weak, and sick at heart.

# 18

'I can't simply contact Haydar,' Devra said. 'After what happened in Sevastopol they'll know you'll be going after him.'

'That being the case,' Arkadin said, 'the document is long gone.'

'Not necessarily.' Devra stirred her Turkish coffee, thick as tar. 'They chose this backwater because it's so inaccessible. But that works both ways. Chances are Haydar hasn't yet been able to pass the document along.'

They were sitting in a tiny dust-blown café in Eskişehir. Even for Turkey this was a backward place, filled with sheep, the smells of pine, dung, and urine, and not much else. A chill wind blew across the mountain pass. There was snow on the north side of the buildings that made up the village, and judging by the lowering clouds more was on its way.

'*Godforsaken* is too good a word for this hellhole,' Arkadin said. 'For shit's sake, there isn't even a cell phone signal.'

'That's funny coming from you.' Devra downed her coffee. 'You were born in a shithole, weren't you?'

Arkadin felt an almost uncontrollable urge to drag her around the back of the rickety structure and beat her. But he held his hand and his rage, husbanding them both for another day when he would gaze down at her as if from a hundred miles away, whisper into her ear, *I have no regard for you. To me, your life is without meaning. If you have any hope of staying alive even a little longer, you'll never again ask where I was born, who my parents were, anything of a personal nature whatsoever.*

As it turned out, among her other talents Marlene was an accomplished hypnotist. She told him she wanted to hypnotize him in order to get at the root of his rage.

'I've heard there are people who can't be hypnotized,' Arkadin said. 'Is that right?'

'Yes,' Marlene said.

It turned out he was one of them.

'You simply will not take suggestion,' she said. 'Your mind has put up a wall it's impossible to penetrate.'

They were sitting in the garden behind Semion Icoupov's villa. Owing to the steep lay of the land it was the size of a postage stamp. They sat on a stone bench beneath the shade afforded by a fig tree, whose dark, soon-to-be-luscious fruit was just beginning to curl the branches downward to the stony earth.

'Well,' Arkadin said, 'what are we to do?'

'The question is what are *you* going to do, Leonid.' She brushed a fragment of leaf off her thigh. She was wearing American designer jeans, an open-necked shirt, sandals on her feet. 'The process of examining your past is designed to help you regain control over yourself.'

'You mean my homicidal tendencies,' he said.

'Why would you choose to say it that way, Leonid?'

He looked deeply into her eyes. 'Because it's the truth.'

Marlene's eyes grew dark. 'Then why are you so reluctant to talk to me about the things I feel will help you?'

'You just want to worm your way inside my head. You think if you know everything about me you can control me.'

'You're wrong. This isn't about control, Leonid.'

Arkadin laughed. 'What is it about then?'

'What it's always been – it's about helping you control yourself.'

A light wind tugged at her hair, and she smoothed it back into place. He noticed such things and attached to them psychological meaning. Marlene liked everything just so.

'I was a sad little boy. Then I was an angry little boy. Then I ran away from home. There, does that satisfy you?'

Marlene tilted her head to catch a bit of sunlight that appeared through the tossed leaves of the fig tree. 'How is it you went from being sad to being angry?'

'I grew up,' Arkadin said.

'You were still a child.'

'Only in a manner of speaking.'

He studied her for a moment. Her hands were crossed on her lap. She lifted one of them, touched his cheek with her fingertips, traced the line of his jaw until she reached his chin. She turned his face a bit farther toward her. Then she leaned forward. Her lips, when they touched his, were soft. They opened like a flower. The touch of her tongue was like an explosion in his mouth.

Arkadin, damping down the dark eddy of his emotion, smiled winningly. 'Doesn't matter. I'm never going back.'

'I second that emotion.' Devra nodded, then rose. 'Let's see if we can get proper lodgings. I don't know about you but I need a shower. Then we'll see about contacting Haydar without anyone knowing.'

As she began to turn away, he caught her by the elbow.

'Just a minute.'

Her expression was quizzical as she waited for him to continue.

'If you're not my enemy, if you haven't been lying to me, if you want to stay with me, then you'll demonstrate your fidelity.'

'I said, yes, I would do what you asked of me.'

'That might entail killing the people who are surely guarding Haydar.'

She didn't even blink. 'Give me the fucking gun.'

Veronica Hart lived in an apartment complex in Langley, Virginia. Like so many other complexes in this part of the world, it served as temporary housing for the thousands of federal government workers, including spooks of all stripes, who were often on assignment overseas or in other parts of the country.

Hart had lived in this particular apartment for just over two years. Not that it mattered; since coming to the district seven years ago she'd had nothing but temporary lodgings. By this point she doubted she'd be comfortable settling down and nesting. At least, those were her thoughts as she buzzed Soraya Moore into the lobby. A moment later a discreet knock sounded, and she let the other woman in.

'I'm clean,' Soraya said as she shrugged off her coat. 'I made sure of that.'

Hart hung her coat in the foyer closet, led her into the kitchen. 'For breakfast I have cold cereal or' – she opened the refrigerator – 'cold Chinese food. Last night's leftovers.'

'I'm not one for conventional breakfasts,' Soraya said.

'Good. Neither am I.'

Hart grabbed an array of cardboard cartons, told Soraya where to find plates, serving spoons, and chopsticks. They moved into the living room, set everything on a glass coffee table between facing sofas.

Hart began opening the cartons. 'No pork, right?'

Soraya smiled, pleased that her boss remembered her Muslim strictures. 'Thank you.'

Hart returned to the kitchen, put up water for tea. 'I have Earl Grey or oolong.'

'Oolong for me, please.'

Hart finished brewing the tea, brought the pot and two small handleless cups back to the living room. The two women settled themselves on opposite sides of the table, sitting cross-legged on the abstract patterned rug. Soraya looked around. There were some basic prints on the wall, the kind you'd expect to find at any midlevel hotel chain. The furniture looked rented, as anonymous as anything else. There were no photos, no sense of Hart's background or family. The only unusual feature was an upright piano.

'My only real possession,' Hart said, following Soraya's gaze. 'It's a Steinway K-52, better known as a Chippendale hamburg. It's got a sounding board larger than many grand pianos, so it lets out with a helluva sound.'

'You play?'

Hart went over, sat down on the stool, began to play Frédéric Chopin's Nocturne in B-Flat Minor. Without missing a beat she segued into Isaac Albéniz's sensuous 'Malagueña,' and, finally, into a raucous transposition of Jimi Hendrix's 'Purple Haze.'

Soraya laughed and applauded as Hart rose, came back to sit opposite her.

'My absolute only talent besides intelligence work.' Hart opened one of the cartons, spooned out General Tso's chicken. 'Careful,' she said as she handed it over, 'I order it extra hot.'

'That's okay by me,' Soraya said, digging deep into the carton. 'I always wanted to play the piano.'

'Actually, I wanted to play electric guitar.' Hart licked oyster sauce off her finger as she passed over another carton. 'My father wouldn't hear of it. According to him, electric guitar wasn't a "lady's" instrument.'

'Strict, was he?' Soraya said sympathetically.

'You bet. He was a full-bird colonel in the air force. He'd been a fighter pilot back in his salad days. He resented being too old to fly, missed that damn oily-smelling cockpit something fierce. Who could he complain to in the force? So he took his frustration out on me and my mother.'

Soraya nodded. 'My father is old-school Muslim. Very strict, very rigid. Like many of his generation he's bewildered by the modern world, and that makes him angry. I felt trapped at home. When I left, he said he'd never forgive me.'

'Did he?'

Soraya had a faraway look in her eyes. 'I see my mom once a month. We go shopping together. I speak to my father once in a while. He's never invited me back home; I've never gone.'

Hart put down her chopsticks. 'I'm sorry.'

'Don't be. It is what it is. Do you still see your father?'

'I do, but he doesn't know who I am. My mother's gone now, which is a blessing. I don't think she could've tolerated seeing him like that.'

'It must be hard for you,' Soraya said. 'The indomitable fighter pilot reduced like that.'

'There's a point in life where you have to let go of your parents.' Hart resumed eating, though more slowly. 'Whoever's lying in that bed isn't my father. He died a long time ago.'

Soraya looked down at her food for a moment. Then she said, 'Tell me how you knew about the NSA safe house.'

'Ah, that.' Hart's face brightened. Clearly, she was happy to be on a work topic. 'During my time at Black River we were often hired by NSA. This was before they trained and deployed their own home-grown black-ops details. We were good for them because they never had to specify to anyone what we'd been hired to do. It was all 'fieldwork,' priming the battlefield for our troops. No one on Capitol Hill was going to look farther than that.'

She dabbed her mouth, sat back. 'Anyway, after one particular mission, I caught the short straw. I was the one from my squad who brought the findings back to the NSA. Because it was a black-ops mission, the debriefing took place at the safe house in Virginia. Not in the fine library you were taken to, but in one of the base-ment-level cubicles – windowless, featureless, just gritty reinforced concrete. It's like a war bunker down there.'

'And what did you see?'

'It wasn't what I saw,' Hart said. 'It was what I heard. The cubicles are sound-proof, except for the doors, I assume so the guards in the corridors know what's going on. What I heard was ghastly. The sounds were barely human.'

'Did you tell your bosses at Black River?'

'What was the point? They didn't care, and even if they did, what were they going to do? Start a congressional investigation on the basis of sounds I heard? The NSA would have cut them off at the knees, put them out of business in a heartbeat.' She shook her head. 'No, these boys are businessmen, pure and simple. Their ideol-ogy revolves around milking as much money from the government as possible.'

'So now we have a chance to do what you couldn't before, what Black River wouldn't do.'

'That's right,' Hart said. 'I want to get photos, videos, absolute proof of what NSA is doing down there so I can present the evidence myself to the president. That's where you and Tyrone come in.' She shoved her plate away. 'I want Luther LaValle's head on a platter, and by God I'm going to get it.'

# 19

Because of the corpse and all the blood on the seats Bourne was forced to abandon the Volga. Before he did, though, he took Baronov's cell phone, as well as his money. It was freezing. Within the preternatural afternoon winter darkness came the snow, swirling down in ever-heavier curtains. Bourne knew he had to get out of the area as quickly as possible. He took the SIM card out of his phone, put it in Baronov's, then threw his own cell phone down a storm drain. In his new identity as Fyodor Ilianovich Popov he couldn't afford to be in possession of a cell with an American carrier.

He walked, leaning into the wind and snow. After six blocks, huddled in a doorway, he used Baronov's cell phone to call his friend Boris Karpov. The voice at the end of the line grew cold.

'Colonel Karpov is no longer with FSB.'

Bourne felt a chill go through him. Russia had not changed so much that lightning-swift dismissals on trumped-up charges were a thing of the past.

'I need to contact him,' Bourne said.

'He's now at the Federal Anti-Narcotics Agency.' The voice recited a local number before abruptly hanging up.

That explained the attitude, Bourne thought. The Federal Anti-Narcotics Agency was headed up by Viktor Cherkesov. But many believed he was much more than that, a *silovik* running an organization so powerful that some had taken to calling it FSB-2. Recently an internal war between Cherkesov and Nikolai Patrushev, the head of the FSB, the modern-day successor to the notorious KGB, had sprung up within the government. The *silovik* who won that war would probably be the next president of Russia. If Karpov had gone from the FSB to FSB-2, it must be because Cherkesov had gotten the upper hand.

Bourne called the office of the Federal Anti-Narcotics Agency, but he was told that Karpov was away and could not be reached.

For a moment he contemplated calling the man who had picked up Baronov's Zil in the Crocus City parking lot, but he almost immediately thought better of it. He'd already gotten Baronov killed; he didn't want any more deaths on his conscience.

He walked on until he came to a tram stop. He took the first one that appeared out of the gloom. He'd used the scarf he'd bought at the boutique in Crocus City to cover up the mark the wire had made across his throat. The small seepage of blood had dried up as soon as he'd hit the frigid air.

The tram jounced and rattled along its rails. Crammed inside with a stinking, noisy crowd, he felt thoroughly shaken. Not only had he discovered a Kazanskaya assassin waiting in Tarkanian's apartment, but his contact had been murdered by an NSA assassin sent to kill him. His sense of apartness had never been more extreme. Babies cried, men rustled newspapers, women chatted side by side, an old man, big-knuckled hands curled over the head of his walking stick, clandestinely ogled a young girl engrossed in a manga comic. Here was life, bustling all around him, a burbling stream that parted when it came to him, an immovable rock, only to come together when it passed him, flowing on while he remained behind, still and alone.

He thought of Marie, as he always did at times like this. But Marie was gone, and her memory was of little solace to him. He missed his children, and wondered whether this was the David Webb personality bubbling up. An old, familiar despair swept through him, as it hadn't since Alex Conklin had taken him out of the gutter, formed the Bourne identity for him to slip on like a suit of armor. He felt the crushing weight of life on him, a life lived alone, a sad and lonely life that could only end one way.

And then his thoughts turned to Moira, of how impossibly difficult that last meeting with her had been. If she had been a spy, if she had betrayed Martin and meant to do the same with him, what would he have done? Would he have turned her over to Soraya or Veronica Hart?

But she wasn't a spy. He would never have to face that conundrum.

When it came to Moira, his personal feelings were now bound up in his professional duty, inextricably combined. He knew that she loved him and, now, in the face of his despair, he understood that he loved her, as well. When he was with her he felt whole, but in an entirely new way. She wasn't Marie, and he didn't want her to be Marie. She was Moira, and it was Moira he wanted.

By the time he swung off the tram in Moscow Center, the snow had abated to veils of drifting flakes whirled about by stray gusts of wind across the huge open plazas. The city's lights were on against the long winter evening, but the clearing sky turned the temperature bitter. The streets were clogged with gypsy cabbies in their cheap cars manufactured during the Brezhnev years, trundling slowly in bumper-to-bumper lines so as to not miss a fare. They were known in local slang as *bombily* – those who bomb – because of the bowel-loosening speed with which they bombed around the city's streets as soon as they had a passenger.

He went into a cybercafé, paid for fifteen minutes at a computer terminal, typed in Kitaysky Lyotchik. Kitaysky Lyotchik Zhao-Da, the full name – or The Chinese Pilot in its English translation – turned out to be a throbbing *elitny* club at proyezd Lubyansky 25. The Kitai-Gorod metro stop let Bourne out at the end of the block. On one side was a canal, frozen solid; on the other, a row of mixed-use buildings. The Chinese Pilot was easy enough to spot, what with the BMWs, Mercedeses, and Porsche SUVs, as well as the ubiquitous gaggle of *bombily* Zhigs clustered on the street. The crowd behind a velvet rope was being held in check by fierce-looking face-control bullies, so that waiting partygoers spilled drunkenly off the pavement. Bourne went up to the red Cayenne, rapped on the window. When the driver scrolled the window down, Bourne held out three hundred dollars.

'When I come out that door, this is my car, right?'

The driver eyed the money hungrily. 'Right you are, sir.'

In Moscow, especially, American dollars talked louder than words.

'And if your client comes out in the meantime?'

'He won't,' the driver assured Bourne. 'He's in the champagne room till four at the earliest.'

Another hundred dollars got Bourne past the shouting, unruly mob. Inside, he ate an indifferent meal of an Oriental salad and almond-crusted chicken breast. From his perch along the glowing bar, he watched the Russian *siloviki* come and go with their diamond-studded, mini-skirted, fur-wrapped *dyevochkas* – strictly speaking, young women who had not yet borne a child. This was the new order in Russia. Except Bourne knew that many of the same people were still in power – either ex-KGB *siloviki* or their progeny lined up against the boys from Sokolniki, who came from nothing into sudden wealth. The *siloviki*, derived from the Russian word for 'power,' were men from the so-called power ministries, including the security services and the military, who had risen during the Putin era. They were the new guard, having overthrown the Yeltsin-period oligarchs. No matter. *Siloviki* or mobster, they were criminals, they'd killed, extorted, maimed, blackmailed; they all had blood on their hands, they were all strangers to remorse.

Bourne scanned the tables for Gala Nematova, was surprised to find half a dozen *dyevs* who might have fit the bill, especially in this low light. It was astonishing to observe firsthand this wheat field of tall, willowy young women, each more striking than the next. There was a prevalent theory, a kind of skewed Darwinism – survival of the prettiest – that explained why there were so many startlingly handsome *dyevochkas* in Russia and Ukraine. If you were a man in his twenties in these countries in 1947 it meant that you'd survived one of the greatest male bloodbaths in human history. These men, being in the vast minority, had their pick of women. Who had they chosen to marry and impregnate? The answer was obvious, hence the acres of *dyevs* partying here and in every other nightclub in Russia.

Out on the dance floor, a crush of gyrating bodies made identification of individuals impossible. Spotting a redheaded *dyev* on her own, Bourne walked over to her, gestured if she wanted to dance. The earsplitting house music pumped out of a dozen massive speakers made small talk impossible. She nodded, took his hand, and they shoved, elbowed, and squeezed their way into a cramped space on the dance floor. The next twenty minutes could have substituted for a vigorous workout. The dancing was nonstop, as were the colored flashing lights and the chest-vibrating drumming of the high-octane music spewed out by a local band called Tequilajazz.

Over the top of the redhead Bourne caught a glimpse of yet another blonde *dyev*. Only this one was different. Grabbing the redhead's hand, Bourne eeled deeper into the gyrating pack of dancers. Perfume, cologne, and sour sweat mixed with the raw tang of hot metal and blazing monster amplifiers.

Still dancing, Bourne maneuvered around until he was certain. The blonde *dyev* dancing with the broad-shouldered mobster was, indeed, Gala Nematova.

'It'll never be the same,' Dr. Mitten said.

'What the hell does that mean?' Anthony Prowess, sitting in an uncomfortable chair in the NSA safe house just outside Moscow, barked at the ophthalmologist bent over him.

'Mr. Prowess, I don't think you're in the best shape to hear a full diagnosis. Why not wait until the shock –'

'A, I'm not in shock,' Prowess lied. 'And B, I don't have time to wait.' That was true enough: Having lost Bourne's trail, he needed to get back on it ASAP.

Dr. Mitten sighed. He'd been expecting just such a response; in fact, he would've been surprised at anything else. Still, he had a professional responsibility to his patient even if he was on retainer to the NSA.

'What it means,' he said, 'is that you'll never see out of that eye again. At least, not in any way that'll be useful to you.'

Prowess sat with his head back, his damaged eye numbed with drops so the damn ophthalmologist could poke around. 'Details, please.'

Dr. Mitten was a tall, thin man with narrow shoulders, a wisp of a comb-over, and a neck with a prominent Adam's apple that bobbed comically when he spoke or swallowed. 'I believe you'll be able to discern movement, differentiate light from dark.'

'That's it?'

'On the other hand,' Dr. Mitten said, 'when the swelling goes down you may be completely blind in that eye.'

'Fine, now I know the worst. Just fix me the hell up so I can get out of here.'

'I don't recommend – '

'I don't give a shit what you recommend,' Prowess snapped. 'Do as I tell you or I'll wring your scrawny little chicken neck.'

Dr. Mitten puffed out his cheeks in indignation, but he knew better than to talk back to an agent. They seemed born with hair-trigger responses to everything, which their training further honed.

As the ophthalmologist worked on his eye, Prowess seethed inside. Not only had he failed to terminate Bourne, he'd allowed Bourne to permanently maim him. He was furious at himself for turning tail and running, even though he knew that when a victim gains the upper hand you have to exit the field as quickly as possible.

Still, Prowess would never forgive himself. It wasn't that the pain had been excruciating – he had an extremely high pain threshold. It wasn't even that Bourne had turned the tables on him – he'd redress that situation shortly. It was his eye. Ever since he was a child, he had a morbid fear of being blind. His father had been blinded in an accidental fall getting off a transit bus, when the impact had detached both his retinas. This was in the days before ophthalmologists could staple retinas back in place. At six years old the horror of watching his father deteriorate from an optimistic, robust man into a bitter, withdrawn nub had imprinted itself forever in his mind. That horror had kicked in the moment Jason Bourne had dug his thumb deep into his eye.

As he sat in the chair, brooding amid the chemical smells emitted by Dr. Mitten's ministrations, Prowess was filled with determination. He promised himself he'd find Jason Bourne, and when he did Bourne would pay for the damage he'd inflicted, he'd pay dearly before Prowess killed him.

Professor Specter was chairing a chancellors' meeting at the university when his private cell phone vibrated. He immediately called a fifteen-minute break, left the room, strode down the hall and outside onto the campus.

When he was clear, he opened his cell, and heard Nemetsov's voice buzzing in his ear. Nemetsov was the man Baronov had called to switch cars with at Crocus City.

'Baronov's dead?' Specter said. 'How?'

He listened while Nemetsov described the attack in the car outside Tarkanian's apartment building. 'An NSA assassin,' Nemetsov concluded. 'He was waiting for Bourne, to garrote him as he did Baronov.'

'And Jason?'

'Survived. But the assassin escaped as well.'

Specter felt a wave of relief wash over him. 'Find that NSA man before he finds Jason, and kill him. Is that clear?'

'Perfectly. But shouldn't we also try to make contact with Bourne?'

Specter considered a moment. 'No. He's at his best when working alone. He knows Moscow, speaks Russian fluently, and he has our fake IDs. He'll do what must be done.'

'You've put your faith in this one man?'

'You don't know him, Nemetsov, otherwise you wouldn't make such a stupid statement. I only wish Jason could be with us permanently.'

When, sweaty and entangled, Gala Nematova and her toy boy left the dance floor, so did Bourne. He watched as the couple made their way to a table where they were greeted by two other men. They all began to guzzle champagne as if it were water. Bourne waited until they'd refilled their flutes, then swaggered over in the style of these new-style gangsters.

Leaning over Gala's companion, he shouted in her ear, 'I have an urgent message for you.'

'Hey,' her companion shouted back with no little belligerence, 'who the fuck're you?'

'Wrong question.' Glaring at him, Bourne pushed up the sleeve of his jacket just long enough to give him a glimpse of his fake Anubis tattoo.

The man bit his lip and sat back down as Bourne reached over, pulled Gala Nematova away from the table.

'We're going outside to talk.'

'Are you crazy?' She tried to squirm away from his grip. 'It's freezing out there.'

Bourne continued to steer her by her elbow. 'We'll talk in my limo.'

'Well, that's something.' Gala Nematova bared her teeth, clearly unhappy. Her teeth were very white, as if scrubbed to within an inch of their lives. Her eyes were a remote chestnut, large with uptilted corners that revealed the Asian blood in her ancestry.

A frigid wind swept off the canal, blocked only partially by the gridlock of expensive cars and *bombily*. Bourne rapped on the Porsche's door and the driver, recognizing him, unlocked the doors. Bourne and the *dyev* piled in.

Gala, shivering, hugged her inadequately short fur coat around her. Bourne asked the driver to turn up the heat. He complied, sank down in his fur-collared greatcoat.

'I don't care what message you have for me,' Gala said sullenly. 'Whatever it is, the answer's no.'

'Are you sure?' Bourne wondered where she was going with this.

'Sure I'm sure. I've had it with you guys trying to find out where Leonid Danilovich is.'

*Leonid Danilovich*, Bourne said to himself. *There's a name the professor never mentioned.*

'The reason we keep hounding you is he's sure you know.' Bourne had no idea what he was saying, but he felt if he kept running with her he'd be able to open her up.

'I don't.' Now Gala sounded like a little girl in a snit. 'But even if I did I wouldn't rat him out. You can tell Maslov that.' She fairly spat out the name of the Kazanskaya's leader, Dimitri Maslov.

*Now we're getting somewhere*, Bourne thought. But why was Maslov after Leonid Danilovich, and what did any of this have to do with Pyotr's death? He decided to explore this link.

'Why were you and Leonid Danilovich using Tarkanian's apartment?'

Instantly he knew he'd made a mistake. Gala's expression changed dramatically. Her eyes narrowed and she made a sound deep in her throat. 'What the hell is this? You already know why we were camped out there.'

'Tell me again,' Bourne said, improvising desperately. 'I've only heard it third-hand. Maybe something was left out.'

'What could be left out? Leonid Danilovich and Tarkanian are the best of friends.'

'Is that where you took Pyotr for your late-night trysts?'

'Ah, so that's what this is all about. The Kazanskaya want to know all about Pyotr Zilber, and I know why. Pyotr ordered the murder of Borya Maks, in prison, of all places – High Security Prison Colony 13. Who could do that? Get in there, kill Maks, a Kazanskaya contract killer of great strength and skill, and get out without being seen.'

'That's precisely what Maslov wants to know,' Bourne said, because it was the safe comment to make.

Gala picked at her nail extensions, realized what she was doing, stopped. 'He suspects Leonid Danilovich did it because Leonid is known for such feats. No one else could do that, he's sure.'

Time to press her, Bourne decided. 'He's right on the money.'

Gala shrugged.

'Why are you protecting Leonid?'

'I love him.'

'The way you loved Pyotr?'

'Don't be absurd.' Gala laughed. 'I never loved Pyotr. He was a job Semion Icoupov paid me handsomely for.'

'And Pyotr paid for your treachery with his life.'

Gala seemed to peer at him in a different light. 'Who are you?'

Bourne ignored her question. 'During that time where did you meet Icoupov?'

'I never met him. Leonid served as intermediary.'

Now Bourne's mind raced to put the building blocks Gala had provided into their proper order. 'You know, don't you, that Leonid murdered Pyotr.' He didn't of course know that, but given the circumstances it seemed all too likely.

'No.' Gala blanched. 'That can't be.'

'You can see how it must be what happened. Icoupov didn't kill Pyotr himself, surely that much must be clear to you.' He observed the fear mounting behind her eyes. 'Who else would Icoupov have trusted to do it? Leonid was the only other person to know you were spying on Pyotr for Icoupov.'

The truth of what he said was written on Gala's face like a road sign appearing out of the fog. While she was still in shock, Bourne said, 'Please tell me Leonid's full name.'

'What?'

'Just do as I tell you,' Bourne said. 'It may be the only way to save him from being killed by the Kazanskaya.'

'But *you're* Kazanskaya.'

Pushing up his sleeve, Bourne gave her a close-up look at the false tattoo. 'A Kazanskaya was waiting for Leonid in Tarkanian's apartment this evening.'

'I don't believe you.' Her eyes widened. 'What were you doing there?'

'Tarkanian's dead,' Bourne said. 'Now do you want to help the man you say you love?'

'I *do* love Leonid! I don't care what he did.'

At that moment, the driver cursed mightily, turned in his seat. 'My client's coming.'

'Go on,' Bourne urged Gala. 'Write his name down.'

'Something must've happened in the VIP,' the driver said. 'Shit, he looks pissed. You gotta get outta here now.'

Bourne grabbed Gala, opened the street-side door, nearly burying it in the fender of a hurtling *bombily*. He flagged it down with a fistful of rubles, made the transfer from Western luxury to Eastern poverty in one stride. Gala Nematova broke away from him as he was entering the Zhig. He clutched her by the back of her fur coat, but she shrugged it off, began to run. The cabbie stepped on the gas, the stench of diesel fumes foaming up into the interior, choking them so badly Bourne had to crank open a window. As he did so, he saw two men who'd been at her table come out of the club. They looked right and left. One of them spotted Gala's running figure, gestured to the other one, and they took off after her.

'Follow those men!' Bourne shouted to the cabbie.

The cabbie had a flat face with a distinctly Asian cast. He was fat, greasy, and spoke Russian with an abominable accent. Clearly, Russian wasn't his first language. 'You're joking, yes?'

Bourne thrust more rubles at him. 'I'm joking, no.'

The cabbie shrugged, crashed the Zhig into first gear, depressed the gas pedal.

At that moment the two men caught up with Gala.

# 20

At precisely that moment, Leonid Danilovich Arkadin and Devra were deciding how to get to Haydar without Devra's people knowing about it.

'Best would be to extract him from his environment,' Arkadin said. 'But for that we need to know his habitual movements. I don't have time –'

'I know a way,' Devra said.

The two of them were sitting side by side on a bed on the ground floor of a small inn. The room wasn't much to look at – just a bed, a chair, a broken-down dresser – but it had its own bathroom, a shower with plenty of hot water, which they'd used one after the other. Best of all, it was warm.

'Haydar's a gambler,' she continued. 'Almost every evening he's hunkered down in the back room of a local café. He knows the owner, who lets them play without imposing a fee. In fact, once a week he joins them.' She glanced at her watch. 'He's sure to be there now.'

'What good is that? Your people are sure to protect him there.'

'Right, that's why we aren't going to go near the place.'

An hour later, they were sitting in their rented car on the side of a two-lane road. All their lights were off. They were freezing. Whatever snow had seemed imminent had passed them by. A half-moon rode in the sky, an Old World lantern revealing wisps of clouds and bluish crusty snowbanks.

'This is the route Haydar takes to and from the game.' Devra tilted her watch face so it was illuminated by the moonglow coming off the banked snow. 'He should show any minute now.'

Arkadin was behind the wheel. 'Just point out the car, leave the rest to me.' One hand was on the ignition key, the other on the gearshift. 'We have to be prepared. He might have an escort.'

'If he's got guards they'll be in the same car with him,' Devra said. 'The roads are so bad it will be extremely difficult to keep him in sight from a trailing vehicle.'

'One car,' Arkadin said. 'All the better.'

A moment later the night was momentarily lit by a moving glow below the rise in the road.

'Headlights.' Devra tensed. 'That's the right direction.'

'You'll know his car?'

'I'll know it,' she said. 'There aren't many cars in the area. Mostly old trucks for carting.'

The glow brightened. Then they saw the headlights themselves as the vehicle crested the rise. From the position of the headlights, Arkadin could tell this was a car, not a truck.

'It's him,' she said.

'Get out,' Arkadin ordered. 'Run! Run now!'

'Keep moving,' Bourne told the cabbie, 'in first gear only till I tell you different.'

'I don't think –'

But Bourne had already swung open the curbside door, was sprinting toward the two men. One had Gala, the other was turning, raising his hand, perhaps a signal for one of the waiting cars. Bourne chopped his midsection with his two hands, brought his head down to his raised knee. The man's teeth clacked together and he toppled over.

The second man swung Gala around so that she was between him and Bourne. He scrabbled for his gun, but Bourne was too quick. Reaching around Gala, Bourne went for him. He moved to block Bourne and Gala stamped her heel on his instep. That was all the distraction Bourne needed. With a hand around her waist, he pulled her away, delivered a vicious uppercut to the man's throat. Reflexively, he put two hands up, choking and gagging. Bourne delivered two quick blows to his stomach and he, too, hit the pavement.

'Come on!'

Bourne grabbed Gala by the hand, made for the *bombila*, moving slowly along the street with its door open. Bourne swung her inside, climbed in after her, slammed the door shut.

'Take off!' he shouted at the cabbie. 'Take off now!'

Shivering with the cold, Gala rolled up the window.

'My name is Yakov,' the cabbie said, craning his neck to look at them in the rearview mirror. 'You make much excitement for me tonight. Is there more? Where can I take you?'

'Just drive around,' Bourne said.

Several blocks on he discovered Gala staring at him.

'You weren't lying to me,' she said.

'Neither were you. Clearly, the Kazanskaya think you know where Leonid is.'

'Leonid Danilovich Arkadin.' She was still trying to catch her breath. 'That's his name. It's what you wanted, isn't it?'

'What I want,' Bourne said, 'is a meeting with Dimitri Maslov.'

'The head of the Kazanskaya? You're insane.'

'Leonid has been playing with a very bad crowd,' Bourne said. 'He's put you in harm's way. Unless I can persuade Maslov that you don't know where Arkadin is you'll never be safe.'

Shivering, Gala struggled back into her fur jacket. 'Why did you save me?' She pulled the jacket tight around her slender frame. 'Why are you doing this?'

'Because I can't let Arkadin throw you to the wolves.'

'That's not what he's done,' she protested.

'What would you call it?'

She opened her mouth, closed it again, bit her lip as if she could find an answer in her pain.

They had reached the inner Garden Road. Traffic whizzed by at dizzying speeds. The cabbie was about to earn his *bombily* name.

'Where to?' he said over his shoulder.

There was silence for a moment. Then Gala leaned forward, gave him an address.

'And where the fuck might that be?' the cabbie asked.

That was another oddity about *bombily*. Since almost none of them were Muscovites, they had no idea where anything was. Unfazed, Gala gave him directions and, with a horrific belching of diesel fumes, they lurched into the madly spinning traffic.

'Since we can't go back to the apartment,' Gala said, 'we'll crash at my girl-friend's place. I've done it before. She's cool with it.'

'Do the Kazanskaya know about her?'

Gala frowned. 'I don't think so, no.'

'We can't take the chance.' Bourne gave the cabbie the address of one of the new American-run hotels near Red Square. 'That's the last place they'll think to look for you,' he said as the cabbie changed gears and they hurtled through the spangled Moscow night.

Alone in the car, Arkadin fired the ignition and pulled out. He stamped on the gas pedal, accelerating so quickly his head jerked back. Just before he slammed into the right corner of Haydar's car, he switched on his headlights. He could see Haydar's bodyguards in the rear seat. They were in the process of turning around when Arkadin's car made jarring contact. The rear end of Haydar's car slewed to the left, beginning its spin; Arkadin braked sharply, rammed the right back door, staving it in. Haydar, who had been struggling with the wheel, completely lost control of the car. It spun off the road, its front now facing the way it had come. Its rear struck a tree, the bumper broke in two, the trunk collapsed, and there it sat, a crippled animal. Arkadin drove off the road, put his car in park, got out, stalking toward Haydar. His headlights were shining directly into the wrecked car. He could see Haydar behind the wheel, conscious, clearly in shock. Only one of the men in the backseat was visible. His head was thrown back and to one side. There was blood on his face, black and glistening in the harsh light.

Haydar cringed fearfully as Arkadin made for the bodyguards. Both rear doors were so buckled they could not be opened. Using his elbow, Arkadin smashed the near-side rear window and peered in. One man had been caught in Arkadin's broadside hit. He'd been thrown clear across the car, lay half on the lap of the bodyguard still sitting up. Neither one moved.

As Arkadin moved to haul Haydar out from behind the wheel, Devra came hurtling out of the darkness. Haydar's eyes opened wide as he recognized her. She tackled Arkadin, her momentum knocking him off his feet.

Haydar watched in amazement as they rolled over through the snow, now visible, now not in the headlight beams. Haydar could see her striking him, the much larger man fighting back, gradually gaining the upper hand by dint of his superior bulk and strength. Then Devra reared back. Haydar could see a knife in her hand. She drove it down into darkness, stabbing again and again.

When she rose again into the headlight beams he could see her breathing heavily. Her hand was empty. Haydar figured she must have left the knife buried in her adversary. She staggered for a moment with the aftereffects of her struggle. Then she made her way over to him.

Yanking open the car door, she said, 'Are you okay?'

He nodded, shrinking away from her. 'I was told you'd turned on us, joined the other side.'

She laughed. 'That's just what I wanted that sonovabitch to think. He managed to get to Shumenko and Filya. After that I figured the only way to survive was to play along with him until I got a chance to take him down.'

Haydar nodded. 'This is the final battle. The thought that you'd turned traitor was dispiriting. I know some of us thought your status was earned on your back, in Pyotr's bed. But not me.' The shock was coming out of his eyes. The old canny light was returning.

'Where is the package?' she said. 'Is it safe?'

'I handed it off to Heinrich this evening – at the card game.'

'Has he left for Munich?'

'Why the hell would he stay a minute more than he had to? He hates it here. I assume he was driving to Istanbul for his usual early-evening flight.' His eyes narrowed. 'Why d'you want to know?'

He gave a little yelp as Arkadin loomed out of the night. Looking from Devra to Arkadin and back again, he said, 'What is this? I saw you stab him to death.'

'You saw what we wanted you to see.' Arkadin handed Devra his gun, and she shot Haydar between the eyes.

She turned back to him, handed him the gun butt-first. There was clear defiance in her voice when she said, 'Have I proved myself to you now?'

Bourne checked into the Metropolya Hotel as Fyodor Ilianovich Popov. The night clerk didn't bat an eye at Gala's presence, nor did he ask for her ID. Having Popov's was enough to satisfy hotel policy. The lobby, with its gilt sconces and accents, and glittering crystal chandeliers, looked like something out of the czarist era, the designers thumbing their nose at the architecture of Soviet Brutalism.

They took one of the silk-lined elevators to the seventeenth floor. Bourne opened the door to their room with an electronically coded plastic card. After a thorough visual check, he allowed her to enter. She took off her fur jacket. The act of sitting on the bed rode her mini-skirt farther up her thighs, but she appeared unconcerned.

Leaning forward, elbows on knees, she said, 'Thank you for saving me. But to be honest, I don't know what I'll do now.'

Bourne pulled out the chair that went with the desk, sat facing her. 'The first thing you have to do is tell me whether you know where Arkadin is.'

Gala looked down at the carpet between her feet. She rubbed her arms as if she was still cold, though the temperature in the room was warm enough.

'All right,' Bourne said, 'let's talk about something else. Do you know anything about the Black Legion?'

Her head came up, her brows furrowed. 'Now, that's odd you should mention them.'

'Why is that?'

'Leonid would speak about them.'

'Is Arkadin one of them?'

Gala snorted. 'You must be joking! No, he never actually spoke about them to me. I mean, he mentioned them now and again when he was going to see Ivan.'

'And who is Ivan?'

'Ivan Volkin. He's an old friend of Leonid's. He used to be in the *grupperovka*. Leonid told me that from time to time the leaders ask him for advice, so he knows all the players. He's a kind of de facto underworld historian now. Anyway, he's the one Leonid would go to.'

This interested Bourne. 'Can you take me to him?'

'Why not? He's a night owl. Leonid used to visit him very late.' Gala searched in her handbag for her cell phone. She scrolled through her phone book, dialed Volkin's number.

After speaking to someone for several minutes, she terminated the connection and nodded. 'He'll see us in an hour.'

'Good.'

She frowned, put away her phone. 'If you're thinking that Ivan knows where Leonid is, you're mistaken. Leonid told no one where he was going, not even me.'

'You must love this man a great deal.'

'I do.'

'Does he love you?'

When she turned back to him, her eyes were full of tears. 'Yes, he loves me.'

'Is that why you took money to spy on Pyotr? Is that why you were partying with that man tonight at The Chinese Pilot?'

'Christ, none of that matters.'

Bourne sat forward. 'I don't understand. Why doesn't it matter?'

Gala regarded him for a long time. 'What's the matter with you? Don't you know anything about love?' A tear overflowed, ran down her cheek. 'Whatever I do for money allows me to live. Whatever I do with my body has nothing to do with love. Love is strictly a matter of the heart. My heart belongs to Leonid Danilovich. That's sacred, pure. No one can touch it or defile it.'

'Maybe we have different definitions of love,' Bourne said.

She shook her head. 'You've no right to judge me.'

'Of course you're right,' Bourne said. 'But that wasn't meant as a judgment. I have difficulty understanding love, that's all.'

She cocked her head. 'Why is that?'

Bourne hesitated before continuing. 'I've lost two wives, a daughter, and many friends.'

'Have you lost love, too?'

'I have no idea what that means.'

'My brother died protecting me.' Gala began to shake. 'He was all I had. No one would ever love me the way he did. After our parents were killed we were inseparable. He swore he'd make sure nothing bad happened to me. He went to his grave keeping that promise.' She sat up straight. Her face was defiant. 'Now do you understand?'

Bourne realized that he'd seriously underestimated this *dyev*. Had he done the same with Moira? Despite admitting his feelings for Moira, he'd unconsciously made the decision that no other woman could be as strong, as imperturbable as Marie. In this, he was clearly mistaken. He had this Russian *dyevochka* to thank for the insight.

Gala peered at him now. Her sudden anger seemed to have burned itself out. 'You're like Leonid Danilovich in many ways. You no longer will walk off the cliff, you no longer trust in love. Like him, you were damaged in terrible ways. But now, you see, you've made your present as bleak as your past. Your only salvation is to find someone to love.'

'I did find someone,' Bourne said. 'She's dead now.'

'Is there no one else?'

Bourne nodded. 'Maybe.'

'Then you must embrace her, instead of running away.' She clasped her hands together. 'Embrace love. That's what I would tell Leonid Danilovich if he were here instead of you.'

Three blocks away, parked at the curb, Yakov, the cabbie who had dropped Gala and Bourne off, opened his cell phone, pressed a speed-dial digit on the keypad. When he heard the familiar voice, he said, 'I dropped them off at the Metropolya not ten minutes ago.'

'Keep an eye out for them,' the voice said. 'If they leave the hotel, tell me. Then follow them.'

Yakov gave his assent, drove back around, installed himself opposite the hotel entrance. Then he dialed another number, delivered precisely the same information to another of his clients.

'We just missed the package,' Devra said as they walked away from the wreck. 'We'd better get on the road to Istanbul right away. The next contact, Heinrich, has a good couple of hours' head start.'

They drove through the night, negotiating the twists, turns, and switchbacks. The black mountains with their shimmering stoles of snow were their silent, implacable companions. The road was as pockmarked as if they were in a war zone. Once, hitting a patch of black ice, they spun out, but Arkadin didn't lose his head. He turned into the skid, tamped gently on the brakes several times while he threw the car into neutral, then turned the engine off. They came to a stop in the side of a snowdrift.

'I hope Heinrich had the same difficulty,' Devra said.

Arkadin restarted the car but couldn't build up enough traction to get them moving. He walked around to the rear while Devra took the wheel. He found nothing useful inside the trunk, so he trudged several paces into the trees, snapped off a handful of substantial branches, which he wedged in front of the right rear tire. He slapped the fender twice and Devra stepped on the gas. The car wheezed and groaned. The tires spun, sending up showers of granular snow. Then the treads found the wood, rolled up onto it and over. The car was free.

Devra moved over as Arkadin took the wheel. Clouds had slid across the moon, steeping the road in dense shadow as they made their way through the mountain pass. There was no traffic; the only illumination for many miles was the car's own headlights. Finally, the moon rose from its cloud bed and the hemmed-in world around them was bathed in an eerie bluish light.

'Times like this when I miss my American,' Devra mused, her head against the seat back. 'He came from California. I loved especially his stories about surfing. My

God, what a weird sport. Only in America, huh? But I used to think how great it would be to live in a land of sunshine, ride endless highways in convertibles, and swim whenever you wanted to.'

'The American dream,' Arkadin said sourly.

She sighed. 'I so wanted him to take me with him when he left.'

'My friend Mischa wanted me to take him with me,' Arkadin said, 'but that was a long time ago.'

Devra turned her head toward him. 'Where did you go?'

'To America.' He laughed shortly. 'But not to California. It didn't matter to Mischa; he was crazy about America. That's why I didn't take him. You go to a place to work, you fall in love with it, and now you don't want to work anymore.' He paused for a moment, concentrated on navigating through a hairpin switchback. 'I didn't tell him that, of course,' he continued. 'I could never hurt Mischa like that. We both grew up in slums, you know. Fucking hard life, that is. I was beaten up so many times I stopped counting. Then Mischa stepped in. He was bigger than I was, but that wasn't it. He taught me how to use a knife – not just stab, but how to throw it, as well. Then he took me to a guy he knew, skinny little man, but he had no fat on him at all. In the blink of an eye he had me down on my back in so much pain my eyes watered. Christ, I couldn't even breathe. Mischa asked me if I'd like to be able to do that and I said, 'Shit, where do I sign up?''

The headlights of a truck appeared, coming toward them, a horrific dazzle that momentarily blinded both of them. Arkadin slowed down until the truck lumbered past.

'Mischa's my best friend, my only friend, really,' he said. 'I don't know what I'd do without him.'

'Will I meet him when you take me back to Moscow?'

'He's in America now,' Arkadin said. 'But I'll take you to his apartment, where I've been staying. It's along the Frunzenskaya embankment. His living room overlooks Gorky Park. The view is very beautiful.' He thought fleetingly of Gala, who was still in the apartment. He knew how to get her out; it wouldn't be a problem at all.

'I know I'll love it,' Devra said. It was a relief to hear him talk about himself. Encouraged by his talkative mood, she continued, 'What work did you do in America?'

And just like that his mood flipped. He braked the car to a halt. 'You drive,' he said.

Devra had grown used to his mercurial mood swings, but watched him come around the front of the car. She slid over. He slammed the passenger's-side door shut and she put the car in gear, wondering what tender nerve she'd touched.

They continued along the road, heading down the mountainside.

'We'll hit the highway soon enough,' she said to break the thickening silence. 'I can't wait to crawl into a warm bed.'

Inevitably there came a time when Arkadin took the initiative with Marlene. It happened while she was sleeping. He crept down the hall to her door. It was child's play for him to pick the lock with nothing more than the wire that wrapped the cork in the bottle of champagne Icoupov served at dinner. Of course, being a

Muslim, Icoupov himself had not partaken of the alcohol, but Arkadin and Marlene had no such restrictions. Arkadin had volunteered to open the champagne and when he did he palmed the wire.

The room smelled of her – of lemons and musk, a combination that set off a stirring below his belly. The moon was full, low on the horizon. It looked as if God were squeezing it between his palms.

Arkadin stood still, listening to her deep even breaths, every once in a while catching the hint of a snore. The bedcovers rustled as she turned onto her right side, away from him. He waited until her breathing settled again before moving to the bed. He climbed, knelt over her. Her face and shoulder were in moonlight, her neck in shadow, so that it appeared to him as if he'd already decapitated her. For some reason, this vision disturbed him. He tried to breathe deeply and easily, but the disturbing vision tightened his chest, made him so dizzy that he almost lost his balance.

And then he felt something hard and cold that in a drawn breath brought him back to himself. Marlene was awake, her head turned, staring at him. In her right hand was a Glock 20 10mm.

'I've got a full magazine,' she said.

Which meant she had fourteen more rounds if she missed the kill with her first shot. Not that that was likely. The Glock was one of the most powerful handguns on the market. She wasn't fooling around.

'Back off.'

He rolled off the bed and she sat up. Her bare breasts shone whitely in the moonlight. She appeared totally unconcerned with her semi-nudity.

'You weren't asleep.'

'I haven't slept since I came here,' Marlene said. 'I've been anticipating this moment. I've been waiting for you to steal into my room.'

She set aside the Glock. 'Come to bed. You're safe with me, Leonid Danilovich.'

As if mesmerized, he climbed back onto the bed and, like a little child, rested his head against the warm cushion of her breasts while she rocked him tenderly. She lay curled around him, willing her warmth to seep into his cool, marble flesh. Gradually, she felt his heartbeat cease its manic racing. To the steady sound of her heartbeat, he fell into slumber.

Some time later, she woke him with a whisper in his ear. It wasn't difficult; he wanted to be released from his nightmare. He started, staring at her for a long moment, his body rigid. His mouth felt raw from yelling in his sleep. Returning to the present, he recognized her. He felt her arms around him, the protective curl of her body, and to her astonishment and elation he relaxed.

'Nothing can harm you here, Leonid Danilovich,' she breathed. 'Not even your nightmares.'

He stared at her in an odd, unblinking fashion. Anyone else would have been frightened, but not Marlene.

'What made you cry out?' she said.

'There was blood everywhere . . . on the bed.'

'Your bed? Were you beaten, Leonid?'

He blinked, and the spell was broken. He turned over, faced away from her, waiting for the ashen light of dawn.

# 21

On a fine clear afternoon, with the sun already low in the sky, Tyrone drove Soraya Moore to the NSA safe house nestled within the rolling hills of Virginia. Somewhere, in some anonymous cybercafé in northeast Washington, Kiki was sitting at a public computer terminal, waiting to sow the software virus she'd devised to disable the property's two thousand CCTV surveillance cameras.

'It'll loop the video images back on themselves endlessly,' she'd told them. 'That was the easy part. In order to make the code a hundred percent invisible it'll work for ten minutes, no more. At that point, it will, in essence, self-destruct, deforming into tiny packets of harmless code the system won't pick up as anomalous.'

Everything now depended on timing. Since it was impossible to send an electronic signal from the NSA safe house without it being picked up and tagged as suspicious, they had worked out an external timing scheme, which meant that if anything went wrong – if Tyrone was delayed for any reason – the ten minutes would tick by and the plan would fail. This was the plan's Achilles' heel. Still, it was their only option and they decided to take it.

Besides, Deron had a number of goodies he'd concocted for them after consulting the architectural plans of the building he'd mysteriously conjured up. She had tried to get them herself and struck out; NSA had what she thought was a total lock on the property records.

Just before they stopped at the front gates, Soraya said, 'Are you sure you want to go through with this?'

Tyrone nodded, stony-faced. 'Let's get on wid it.' He was pissed that she'd even thought to ask that question. When he was on the street, if one of his crew dared to question his courage or resolve that would've been the end of him. Tyrone had to keep reminding himself that this wasn't the street. He knew all too well that she'd accepted a huge risk in taking him in off the street – civilizing him, as he sometimes thought of the process when he felt particularly hemmed in by the rules and regulations of white men he knew nothing about.

He glanced at her out of the corner of his eye, wondering if he'd ever have stepped into the white man's world were it not for his love of her. Here was a woman of color – a Muslim, no less – who was working for the Man. Not just the Man, but the Man squared, cubed into infinity, whatever. If she didn't mind doing it, why should he? But his upbringing was about as different from hers as it could get. From what she'd told him her parents had given her everything she needed; he barely had parents, and they either didn't want to give him anything or were incapable of giving it. She had the advantage of a first-class education; he had

Deron who, though he'd taught Tyrone many things, was no substitute for white man's education.

What was ironic was that only months ago, he would have sneered at the kind of education she had. But once he'd met her he began to understand how ignorant he really was. He was street-smart, sure – more than she was. But he was intimidated around people who'd graduated high school and college. The more he observed them maneuvering through their world – how they talked, negotiated, interacted with one another – the more he understood just how stunted his life had been. Street smarts and nothing else was just what the doctor ordered for picking your way through the hood, but there was a whole fucking world beyond the hood. Once he realized that, like Deron, he wanted to explore the world beyond the borders of his neighborhood, he knew he'd have to remake himself from the toes up.

All this was on his mind when he saw the imposing stone-and-slate building within the high iron fence. As he knew from the plans he'd memorized at Deron's it was perfectly symmetrical, with four high chimneys, eight gabled rooms. A spiky fistful of antennas, aerials, and satellite dishes was the only anomalous feature.

'You look very handsome in that suit,' Soraya said.

'It's fuckin' uncomfortable,' he said. 'I feel stiff.'

'Just like every NSA agent.'

He laughed the way a Roman gladiator might as he entered the Colosseum.

'Which is the point,' she added. 'You've got the tag Deron gave you?'

He patted a place over his heart. 'Safe and sound.'

Soraya nodded. 'Okay, here we go.'

He knew there was a chance he'd never come out of that house alive, but he didn't care. Why should he? What had his life amounted to up until now? Shit-all. He'd stood up – just as Deron had – made his choice. That's all a man asks for in this life.

Soraya presented the credentials LaValle had sent her by messenger this morning. Nevertheless, both she and Tyrone were scrutinized by a bookend pair of suits with square jaws and standing orders not to smile. Finally, they passed muster, and were waved through.

As Tyrone drove down the snaking gravel drive Soraya pointed out the terrible gauntlet of surveillance systems an intruder would have to pass in order to infiltrate from beyond the property's borders. This monologue reassured him that they'd already bypassed these risks by being LaValle's guests. Now all they had to do was negotiate the interior of the house. Getting out again was another matter entirely.

He drove up to the portico. Before he could turn off the engine, a valet came to relieve him of the car, yet another square-jawed military type who'd never look right in his civilian suit.

General Kendall, punctual as usual, was at the door to meet them. He gave Soraya's hand a perfunctory shake, then eyeballed Tyrone as she introduced him.

'Your bodyguard, I presume,' Kendall said in a tone someone would use for a rebuke. 'But he doesn't look like standard-issue CI material.'

'This isn't a standard CI rendezvous,' Soraya returned tartly.

Kendall shrugged. Another perfunctory handshake and he turned on his heel, leading them inside the hulking structure. Through the public rooms, gilt-edged, refined, expensive beyond modern-day imagining, along hushed corridors lined with martial paintings, past mullioned windows through which the January sunlight sparked in beams that stretched across the plush blue carpet. Without seeming to, Tyrone took note of every detail, as if he were casing the joint for a high-end robbery, which in fact he was. They passed the door down to the basement levels. It looked precisely as Soraya had drawn it from memory for him and Deron.

They went on another ten yards to the walnut doors leading to the Library. The fireplace contained a roaring blaze, a grouping had been set with four chairs in the same spot where Soraya said she had sat with Kendall and LaValle on her first visit. Willard met them just inside the door.

'Good afternoon, Ms. Moore,' he said with his customary half bow. 'How very nice to see you again so soon. Would you care for your Ceylon tea?'

'That would be wonderful, thank you.'

Tyrone was about to ask for a Coke, but thought better of it. Instead he ordered another Ceylon tea, having not the faintest idea what it tasted like.

'Very good,' Willard said, and left them.

'This way,' Kendall said unnecessarily, leading them to the grouping of chairs where Luther LaValle was already seated, staring out the mullioned windows at the light gathered to an oval over the western hills.

He must have heard the whisper of their approach, because he rose and turned just as they came up. The maneuver seemed to Soraya artfully rehearsed, and therefore as artificial as LaValle's smile. Dutifully, she introduced Tyrone, and they all sat down together.

LaValle steepled his fingers. 'Before we begin, Director, I feel compelled to point out that our own archives department has unearthed some fragmentary history on the Black Legion. Apparently, they did exist during the time of the Third Reich. They were composed of Muslim prisoners of war who were brought back to Germany from the first putsches into the Soviet Union. These Muslims, mainly of Turkish descent from the Caucasus, detested Stalin so much they'd do anything to topple his regime, even becoming Nazis.'

LaValle shook his head like a history professor recounting evil days to a class of wide-eyed students. 'It's a particularly unpleasant footnote in a thoroughly repugnant decade. But as for the Black Legion itself, there's no evidence whatsoever that it survived the regime that spawned it. Besides which, its benefactor Himmler was a master of propaganda, especially when it came to advancing himself in the eyes of Hitler. Anecdotal evidence suggests that the role of the Black Legion on the Eastern Front was minimal, that it was in fact Himmler's fantastic propaganda machine that gave it the feared reputation it enjoyed, not anything its members themselves did.'

He smiled, the sun emerging from behind storm clouds. 'Now, in that light, let me take a look at the Typhon intercepts.'

Soraya tolerated this rather condescending introduction, meant to discredit the origin of the intercepts before she even handed them over. She allowed indignation and humiliation to pass through her so she could remain calm and focused on her mission. Pulling the slim briefcase onto her lap, she unlocked the coded lock, extracted a red file with a thick black stripe across its upper right-hand corner, marking it as DIRECTOR EYES ONLY – material of the highest security clearance.

Staring LaValle in the face, she handed it over.

'Excuse me, Director.' Tyrone held out his hand. 'The electronic tape.'

'Oh, yes, I forgot,' Soraya said. 'Mr. LaValle, would you please hand the file to Mr. Elkins.'

LaValle checked the file more closely, saw a ribbon of shiny metal sealing the file. 'Don't bother. I can peel this back myself.'

'Not if you want to read the intercepts,' Tyrone said. 'Unless the tape is opened with this' – he held up a small plastic implement – 'the file will incinerate within seconds.'

LaValle nodded his approval of the security measures Soraya had taken.

As he gave the file to Tyrone, Soraya said, 'Since our last meeting my people have intercepted more communication from the same entity, which increasingly seems to be the command center.'

LaValle frowned. 'A command center? That's highly unusual for a terrorist network, which is, by definition, made up of independent cadres.'

'That's what makes the intercepts so compelling.'

'It also makes them suspect, in my opinion,' LaValle said. 'Which is why I'm anxious to read them myself.'

By this time, Tyrone had slit the metallic security tape, handed the file back. LaValle's gaze dropped as he opened the file and began to read.

At this point Tyrone said, 'I need to use the bathroom.'

LaValle waved a hand. 'Go ahead,' he said without looking up.

Kendall watched him as he went up to Willard, who was on his way over with the drinks, to ask for directions. Soraya saw this out of the corner of her eye. If all went well, in the next couple of minutes Tyrone would be standing in front of the door down to the basement at the precise moment Kiki sent the virus to the NSA security system.

Ivan Volkin was a hairy bear of a man, salt-and-pepper hair standing straight up like a madman, a full beard white as snow, small but cheerful eyes the color of a rainstorm. He was slightly bandy-legged, as if he'd been riding a horse all his life. His lined and leathery face lent him a certain dignified aspect, as if in his life he'd earned the respect of many.

He greeted them warmly, welcoming them into an apartment that appeared small because of the stacks of books and periodicals that covered every conceivable horizontal surface, including the kitchen stovetop and his bed.

He led them down a narrow, winding aisle from the vestibule to the living room, made room for them on the sofa by moving three teetering stacks of books.

'Now,' he said, standing in front of them, 'how can I be of help?'

'I need to know everything you can tell me about the Black Legion.'

'And why are you interested in such a tiny footnote to history?' Volkin looked at Bourne with a jaundiced eye. 'You don't have the look of a scholar.'

'Neither do you,' Bourne said.

This produced a spraying laugh from the older man. 'No, I suppose not.' Volkin wiped his eyes. 'Spoken like one soldier to another, eh? Yes.' Reaching around behind him, he swung over a ladder-backed chair, straddled it with his arms crossed over the top. 'So. What specifically do you want to know?'

'How did they manage to survive into the twenty-first century?'

Volkin's face immediately shut down. 'Who told you the Black Legion survives?'

Bourne did not want to use Professor Specter's name. 'An unimpeachable source.'

'Is that so? Well, that source is wrong.'

'Why bother to deny it?' Bourne said.

Volkin rose, went into the kitchen. Bourne could hear the refrigerator door open and close, the light clink of glassware. When Volkin returned, he had an iced bottle of vodka in one hand, three water glasses in the other.

Handing them the glasses, he unscrewed the cap, filled their glasses halfway. When he'd poured for himself, he sat down again, the bottle standing between them on the threadbare carpet.

Volkin raised his glass. 'To our health.' He emptied his glass in two great gulps. Smacking his lips, he reached down, refilled it. 'Listen to me closely. If I were to admit that the Black Legion exists today there would be nothing left of my health to toast.'

'How would anyone know?' Bourne said.

'How? I'll tell you how. I tell you what I know, then you go out and act on that information. Where d'you think the shitstorm that ensues is going to land, hmm?' He tapped his barrel chest with his glass, slopping vodka onto his already stained shirt. 'Every action has a reaction, my friend, and let me tell you that when it comes to the Black Legion every reaction is fatal for someone.'

Since he'd already as much as admitted that the Black Legion had, in fact, survived the defeat of Nazi Germany, Bourne brought the subject around to what really concerned him. 'Why would the Kazanskaya be involved?'

'Pardon?'

'In some way I can't yet understand the Kazanskaya are interested in Mikhail Tarkanian. I stumbled across one of their contract killers in his apartment.'

Volkin's expression turned sour. 'What were you doing in his apartment?'

'Tarkanian's dead,' Bourne said.

'What?' Volkin exploded. 'I don't believe you.'

'I was there when it happened.'

'And I tell you it's impossible.'

'On the contrary, it's a fact,' Bourne said. 'His death was a direct result of him being a member of the Black Legion.'

Volkin crossed his arms over his chest. He looked like the silverback in the National Zoo. 'I see what's happening here. How many ways will you try to get me to talk about the Black Legion?'

'Every way I can,' Bourne said. 'The Kazanskaya are in some way in league with the Black Legion, which is an alarming prospect.'

'I may look as if I have all the answers, but I don't.' Volkin stared at him, as if daring Bourne to call him a liar.

Though Bourne was certain that Volkin knew more than he would admit, he also knew it would be a mistake to call him on it. Clearly, this was a man who couldn't be intimidated, so there was no point in trying. Professor Specter had warned him not to get caught up in the *grupperovka* war, but the professor was a long way away from Moscow; his intelligence was only as accurate as his men on the ground here. Instinct told Bourne there was a serious disconnect. So far as he could see there was only one way to get to the truth.

'Tell me how to get a meet with Maslov,' he said.

Volkin shook his head. 'That would be most unwise. With the Kazanskaya in the middle of a power struggle with the Azeri –'

'Popov is only my cover name,' Bourne said. 'Actually, I'm a consultant to Viktor Cherkesov' – the head of the Federal Anti-Narcotics Agency, one of the two or three most powerful *siloviks* in Russia.

Volkin pulled back as if stung by Bourne's words. He shot Gala an accusatory glance, as if Bourne were a scorpion she'd brought into his den. Turning back to Bourne he said, 'Have you any proof of this?'

'Don't be absurd. However, I can tell you the name of the man I report to: Boris Illyich Karpov.'

'Is that so?' Volkin produced a Makarov handgun, placed it on his right knee. 'If you're lying . . .' He picked up a cell phone he scavenged miraculously from out of the clutter, and quickly punched in a number. 'We have no amateurs here.'

After a moment he said into the phone, 'Boris Illyich, I have here with me a man who claims to be working for you. I would like to put him on the line, yes?'

With a deadpan face, Volkin handed over the cell.

'Boris,' Bourne said, 'it's Jason Bourne.'

'Jason, my good friend!' Karpov's voice reverberated down the line. 'I haven't seen you since Reykjavik.'

'It seems like a long time.'

'Too long, I tell you!'

'Where have you been?'

'In Timbuktu.'

'What were you doing in Mali?' Bourne asked.

'Don't ask, don't tell.' Karpov laughed. 'I understand you're now working for me.'

'That's right.'

'My boy, I've longed for this day!' Karpov let go with another booming laugh. 'We must toast this moment with vodka, but not tonight, eh? Put that old goat Volkin back on the line. I assume there's something you want from him.'

'Correct.'

'He hasn't believed a word you've told him. But I'll change that. Please memorize my cell number, then call me when you're alone. Until we speak again, my good friend.'

'He wants to talk to you,' Bourne said.

'That's understandable.' Volkin took the cell from Bourne, put it to his ear. Almost immediately his expression changed. He stared at Bourne, his mouth slightly open. 'Yes, Boris Illyich. Yes, of course. I understand.'

Volkin broke the connection, stared at Bourne for what seemed a long time. At length, he said, 'I'm going to call Dimitri Maslov now. I hope to hell you know what you're doing. Otherwise, this is the last time anyone will see you, either alive or dead.'

# 22

Tyrone went immediately into one of the cubicles in the men's room. Fishing out the plastic tag Deron had made for him, he clipped it on the outside of his suit jacket, a suit that looked like the regulation government suits all the other spooks wore here. The tag identified him as Special Agent Damon Riggs, out of the NSA field office in LA. Damon Riggs was real enough. The tag came straight from the NSA HR database.

Tyrone flushed the toilet, emerged from the cubicle, smiled frostily at an NSA agent bent over one of the sinks washing his hands. The agent glanced at Tyrone's tag, said, 'You're a long way from home.'

'And in the middle of winter, too.' Tyrone's voice was strong and firm. 'Damn, I miss goin' top-down in Santa Monica.'

'I hear you.' The agent dried his hands. 'Good luck,' he said as he left.

Tyrone stared at the closed door for a moment, took a deep breath, let it out slowly. So far, so good. He went out into the hallway, his eyes straight ahead, his stride purposeful. He passed four or five agents. A couple gave his tag a cursory glance, nodded. The others ignored him altogether.

'The trick,' Deron had said, 'is to look like you belong. Don't hesitate, be purposeful. If you look like you know where you're going, you become part of the scene, no one notices you.'

Tyrone reached the door without incident. He went past it as two agents, deep in conversation, passed him. Then, checking both ways, he doubled back. Quickly he took out what seemed to be an ordinary piece of clear tape, laid it on top of the fingerprint reader. Checking his watch, he waited until the second hand touched the 12. Then, holding his breath, he pressed his forefinger onto the tape so that it was flush against the reader. The door opened. He stripped off the tape, slipped inside. The tape contained LaValle's fingerprint, which Tyrone had lifted off the back cover of the file while working the device that slit the security tape. Soraya had engaged LaValle in conversation as a diversion.

At the bottom of the flight of steps, he paused for a moment. No alarm bells were going off, no sound of armed security guards coming his way. Kiki's software program had done its work. Now the rest was up to him.

He moved swiftly and silently down the rough concrete corridor. Buzzing fluorescent strips were the only decoration here, casting a sickly glow. He saw no one, heard nothing beyond the susurrus of machinery.

Snapping on latex gloves he tried each door he came to. Most were locked. The first one that wasn't opened into a small cubicle with a viewing window in one wall. Tyrone had been in enough police precincts to know this was one-way glass. He peered into a room not much larger than the one he was in. He could make out a metal chair bolted to the center of the floor, beneath which was a large drain. Affixed to the right-hand wall was a three-foot-deep trough as long as a man with manacles bolted to each end, above which was coiled a fire hose. Its nozzle looked enormous in the confines of the small room. This, Tyrone knew from photos he'd seen, was a waterboarding tank. He snapped as many photos of it as possible, because there was the proof Soraya needed that the NSA was enacting illegal and inhuman torture.

Tyrone took photos of everything with the ten-megapixel digital mini camera Soraya had given him. Given the huge memory of its smart card, it could record six videos of up to three minutes in duration.

He moved on, knowing he had an extremely limited amount of time. Opening the door an inch at a time, he determined that the corridor was still deserted. He hurried down it, checking all the doors he came to. At length, he found himself in another viewing room. This time, however, he saw a man kneeling beside a table. His arms were drawn back, his bound hands on the table. A black hood had been pulled down over his head. His attitude was of a defeated soldier about to be forced to kiss the feet of his conqueror. Tyrone felt a surge of rage run through him such as he'd never felt before. He couldn't help thinking of the history of his own people, hunted by rival tribes on the east coast of Africa, sold to the white man, brought as slaves back to America. All of this terrible history Deron had made him study, to learn where he came from, to understand what drove the prejudices, the innate hatreds, all the powerful forces inside him.

With an effort he pulled himself together. This is what they'd been hoping for: proof that the NSA was subjecting prisoners to illegal forms of torture. Tyrone took a slew of photos, even a short video before exiting the viewing room.

Once again, he was the only one in the corridor. This concerned him. Surely he would have heard or seen NSA personnel down here. But there was no sign of anyone.

All at once, he felt a prickling at the back of his neck. He turned, retracing his steps at a half run. His heart pounded, his blood rushed in his ears. With every step he took his sense of foreboding increased. Then he broke into a full-out sprint.

Luther LaValle looked up from his reading, said ominously, 'What kind of game are you playing, Director?'

Soraya kept herself from starting. 'I beg your pardon?'

'I've been through these transmission intercepts you claim come from the Black Legion twice now. Nowhere do I find any reference to that name or, for that matter, any name at all.'

Willard appeared, handed General Kendall a folded slip of paper. Kendall read it without any expression. Then he excused himself. Soraya watched him leave the Library with no little trepidation.

To regain her attention, LaValle waved the sheets briefly in the air like a red flag in front of a bull. 'Tell me the truth. For all you know, these conversations could be between two sets of eleven-year-olds playing terrorist games.'

Soraya could feel herself bristling. 'My people assure me they're genuine, Mr.

LaValle, and they're the best in the business. If you don't believe that, I can't imagine why you want a piece of Typhon.'

LaValle conceded her point, but he wasn't finished with her. 'Then how do you know they're from the Black Legion.'

'Collateral intelligence.'

LaValle sat back in his chair. His drink was left untouched on the table. 'Just what the holy hell does *collateral intelligence* mean?'

'Another source, unrelated to the intercepts, has knowledge of an imminent attack on American soil that originates with the Black Legion.'

'Who we have no tangible evidence actually exist.'

Soraya was growing increasingly uncomfortable. The conversation was veering perilously close to an interrogation. 'I brought these intercepts at your behest with the intention of engendering trust between us.'

'That's as may be,' LaValle said. 'But quite frankly these anonymous intercepts, alarming as they seem on the surface, don't do it for me. You're holding something back, Director. I want to know the source of your so-called collateral intel.'

'I'm afraid that's impossible. The source is absolutely sacrosanct.' Soraya could not tell him that her source was Jason Bourne. 'However – ' She reached down to her slim attaché case, pulled out several photos, handed them over.

'It's a corpse,' LaValle said. 'I fail to see the significance –'

'Look at the second photo,' Soraya said. 'It's a close-up of the inside of the victim's elbow. What do you see?'

'A tattoo of three horses' heads attached to – what is this? It looks like the Nazi SS death's head.'

'And so it is.' Soraya handed him another photo. 'This is the uniform patch of the Black Legion under their leader Heinrich Himmler.'

LaValle pursed his lips. Then he put sheets back in the file, returned it to Soraya. He held up the photos. 'If you could find this insignia, anyone could. This could be a group that's simply appropriated the Black Legion's sign, like the skinheads in Germany appropriated the swastika. Besides, this isn't proof that the intercepts came from the Black Legion. And even if they did I have a problem, Director. It's the same as yours, I would think. You've told me – also according to your sacrosanct source – that the Black Legion is being fronted by the Eastern Brotherhood. If the NSA acts on this intel, we'll have every flavor of PR nightmare visited on us. The Eastern Brotherhood, as I'm sure you're aware, is exceedingly powerful, especially with the overseas press. We run with this and we're wrong, it's going to cause the president and this country an enormous amount of humiliation, which we can't afford now. Do I make myself clear?'

'Perfectly, Mr. LaValle. But if we ignore it and America is successfully attacked again, then how do we look?'

LaValle scrubbed his face with one hand. 'So we're between a rock and a hard place.'

'Sir, you know as well as I do that action is better than inaction, especially in a volatile situation like this.'

LaValle was about to capitulate, Soraya knew it, but here came Willard again, gliding up, silent as a ghost. He bent, whispered something in LaValle's ear.

'Thank you, Willard,' Lavalle said, 'that will be all.' Then he returned his attention to Soraya. 'Well, Director, it seems I'm urgently wanted elsewhere.' He stood up and smiled down at her, but spoke with a steely tone. 'Please join me.'

Soraya's heart plummeted. This invitation wasn't a request.

Yakov, the *bombila* driver, who'd been ordered to park across the avenue from the front entrance of the Metropolya Hotel, had been joined forty minutes ago by a man who looked as if he'd been in a fistfight with a meat grinder. Despite efforts to cover it up, his face was swollen, dark as pounded flesh. He wore a silver patch over one eye. He was a surly bastard, Yakov decided, even before the man handed him a fistful of money. He uttered not a word of greeting, but slammed into the backseat, slithered down so even the crown of his head was invisible to anyone glancing casually in.

The atmosphere inside the *bombila* quickly grew so toxic that Yakov was forced to vacate the semi-warmth for the freezing Moscow night. He bought himself some food from a passing Turkish vendor, spent the next half hour eating it, talking to his friend Max, who'd pulled up behind him because Max was a lazy sonovabitch who grasped at any excuse not to work.

Yakov and Max were in the middle of heated speculation that concerned last week's death of a high-level RAB Bank officer, who was discovered tied up, tortured, and asphyxiated in the garage of his own *elitny* dacha. The two of them were wondering why the General Prosecutor's Office and the president's newly formed Investigative Committee were fighting over jurisdiction of the death.

'It's politics, pure and simple,' Yakov said.

'*Dirty* politics,' Max retorted. 'There's nothing pure and simple about *that.*'

It was then that Yakov spotted Jason Bourne and the sexy *dyev* getting out of a *bombila* in front of the hotel. When he struck the side of his cab three times with the flat of his hand, he sensed a stirring in the backseat.

'He's here,' he said as the rear window rolled down.

Bourne was about to drop Gala off at the Metropolya Hotel when he looked out the *bombila* window, saw the taxi that had earlier taken him from The Chinese Pilot to the hotel. Yakov, the driver, was leaning against the fender of his dilapidated junkmobile, eating something greasy while talking to the cabbie parked right behind him.

Bourne saw Yakov glance over as he and Gala exited the *bombila*. When they'd gone through the revolving door, Bourne told her to stay put. To his left was the service door used by porters to take guests' luggage in and out of the hotel. Bourne looked out across the street. Yakov stuck his head in the rear window, huddled with a man who'd been hidden in the backseat.

In the elevator, on the way up to their room, he said, 'Are you hungry? I'm starved.'

Harun Iliev, the man Semion Icoupov sent to find Jason Bourne, had expended hours in contentious negotiations and frustrating dead ends, and finally spent a great deal of money in his pursuit. It wasn't coincidence that had led him at last to the *bombila* named Yakov, for Yakov was an ambitious man who knew he'd never get rich driving around Moscow, fending off other *bombily*, pissing them off by cutting in, snatching their fares from under their noses. What could be more lucrative than spying on other people? Especially when your chief client was the American. Yakov had many clients, but none of them knew how to throw around dollars like the Americans. It was their sincere belief that enough money bought you anything. Mostly, they were right. When they weren't, though, it was still costly for them.

Most of Yakov's other clients laughed at the kind of money the Americans threw around. Chiefly, though, he suspected it was because they were jealous. Laughing at what you didn't have and never would was, he supposed, better than letting it depress you.

Icoupov's people were the only ones who paid as well. But they used him far less than the Americans. On the other hand, they had him on retainer. Yakov knew Harun Iliev well, had dealt with him a number of times before, and both liked and trusted him. Besides, they were both Muslim. Yakov kept his religion a secret in Moscow, especially from the Americans, who, stupidly, would have dropped him like a fake ruble.

Directly after the American attaché contacted him for the job, Yakov had called Harun Iliev. As a consequence, Harun had already inserted himself in the staff of the Metropolya Hotel through a cousin of his, who worked in the kitchen as one of the expediters. He coordinated food orders for the line chefs. The moment he saw the room-service order come down from 1728, Bourne's room, he called Harun.

'We're short-staffed tonight,' he said. 'Get down here in the next five minutes and I'll make sure you're the one to take the order up to him.'

Harun Iliev quickly presented himself to his cousin and was shown to a trolley, neatly covered in starched white linen, laden with covered bowls, platters, plates, silverware, and napkins. Thanking his cousin for this opportunity to get to Jason Bourne, he rolled his trolley to the service elevator. Someone was already there. Harun took him to be one of the hotel managers until, as they entered the elevator, he turned so Harun caught a fleeting glimpse of his pulped face and the silver patch over one eye.

Harun reached out, pressed the button for the seventeenth floor. The man pressed the button for the eighteenth. The elevator stopped at the fourth floor, where a maid got on with her turn-down cart. She exited a floor later.

The elevator had just passed the fifteenth floor when the man reached over, pulled out the large red EMERGENCY STOP button. Harun turned to question the man's action, but the man fired one bullet from an exceptionally quiet 9mm Welrod equipped with a suppressor. The bullet pierced Harun's forehead, tore through his brain. He was dead before he collapsed to the elevator floor.

Anthony Prowess mopped up what little blood there was with a napkin from the room-service cart. Then he quickly stripped the clothes off his victim, donned the uniform of the Metropolya Hotel. He pushed in the EMERGENCY STOP button again and the elevator continued its ascent to the seventeenth floor. After determining that the hallway was clear, Prowess consulted a map of the floor, dragged the corpse into a utility room, then wheeled the cart around the corner to room 1728.

'Why don't you take a shower? A long hot one,' Bourne said.

Gala's expression was mischievous. 'If I stink at least it's not as bad as you.' She began to slip out of her mini skirt. 'Why don't we take one together?'

'Some other time. I have business to attend to.'

Her lower lip comically pouted. 'God, what could be more boring?'

Bourne laughed as she crossed into the bathroom, closed the door behind her. Soon after, the sound of running water came to him, along with tiny curls of steam. He turned on the TV, watched a dreadful show in Russian with the sound turned up.

There was a knock on the door. Bourne rose from his position on the bed, opened the door. A uniformed waiter in a short jacket and a hat with a bill pulled down over his face pushed a trolley full of food into the room. Bourne signed the bill, the waiter turned to leave. Instantly he whirled, a knife in his hand. In one blurred movement, he drew his arm back. But Bourne was ready. As the waiter threw the knife Bourne raised a domed metal top off a chafing dish, used it as a shield to deflect the knife. With a flick of his wrist, he sent it spinning at the waiter, who ducked out of the way. The edge of the domed top caught his hat, spun it off his head, revealing the puffy face of the man who'd strangled Baronov and tried to kill Bourne, as well.

The attacker drew a Welrod and squeezed off two shots before Bourne shoved the cart into his midsection. He staggered back. Bourne threw himself across the cart, grabbed Prowess by the front of the uniform, then wrestled him to the floor.

Bourne managed to kick away the Welrod. The man attacked with hands and feet, moving Bourne so that he could regain possession of the gun. Bourne could see the patch over the NSA agent's eye, could only surmise the damage he'd inflicted.

The agent feinted one way, then caught Bourne flush on the jaw. Bourne staggered and his attacker was on him with another wire, which he whipped around Bourne's neck. Pulling hard on it, he drew Bourne back to his feet. Bourne staggered against the cart. As it skittered away from him, he grabbed the chafing dish, hurled its contents in the agent's face. The scalding soup struck the attacker like a torch, and he shouted but failed to drop the wire, instead pulling it tighter, jerking Bourne against his chest.

Bourne was on his knees, his back arched. His lungs were screaming for oxygen, his muscles were rapidly losing their strength, and it was becoming increasingly difficult to concentrate. Soon, he knew, he'd pass out.

With his remaining strength, he jabbed his elbow into the agent's crotch. The wire slacked off enough for him to get to his feet. He slammed the back of his head into the agent's face, heard the satisfying thunk as the man's head struck the wall. The wire slackened a bit more, enough for Bourne to pull it from his throat, gasping in air, and reverse their positions, wrapping the wire around Prowess's neck. He fought and kicked like a madman, but Bourne held on, working the wire tighter and tighter, until the agent's body went slack. His head toppled to one side. Bourne didn't slacken the wire until he'd assured himself there was no longer a pulse. Then he let the man slide to the floor.

He was bent over, hands on thighs, taking deep, slow breaths when Gala walked out of the bathroom amid a halo of lavender-scented mist.

'Jesus Christ,' she said. Then she turned and vomited all over her bare pink feet.

# 23

'Any way you slice it or dice it,' Luther LaValle said, 'he's a dead man.'

Soraya stared bleakly through the one-way glass at Tyrone, who was standing in a cubicle ominously outfitted with a shallow coffin-like tub that had restraints for wrists and ankles, a fire hose above it. In the center of the room a steel table was bolted down to the bare concrete floor, beneath which was a drain to sluice both water and blood away.

LaValle held up the digital camera. 'General Kendall found this on your compatriot.' He touched a button, and the photos Tyrone had taken scrolled across the camera's screen. 'This smoking gun is enough to convict him of treason.'

Soraya couldn't help wondering how many shots of the torture chambers Tyrone had managed to take before he was caught.

'Off with his head,' Kendall said, baring his teeth.

Soraya could not rid herself of the sick feeling in her stomach. Of course, Tyrone had been in dangerous situations before, but she was directly responsible for putting him in harm's way. If anything happened to him she knew she'd never be able to forgive herself. What was she thinking involving him in such perilous work? The enormity of her miscalculation was all too clear to her now, when it was too late to do anything about it.

'The real pity,' LaValle went on, 'is that with very little difficulty we can make a case against you, as well.'

Soraya was solely focused on Tyrone, whom she had wronged so terribly.

'This was my idea,' she said dully. 'Let Tyrone go.'

'You mean he was only following orders,' General Kendall said. 'This isn't Nuremberg. Frankly, there's no viable defense the two of you can put up. His conviction and execution – as well as yours – are a fait accompli.'

They took her back to the Library, where Willard, seeing her ashen face, fetched her a fresh pot of Ceylon tea. The three of them sat by the window. The fourth chair, conspicuously empty, was an accusation to Soraya. Her grievous mismanagement of this mission was compounded by the knowledge that she had seriously underestimated LaValle. She'd been lulled by his smug, overaggressive nature into thinking he was the sort of man who'd automatically underestimate her. She was dead wrong.

She fought the constriction in her chest, the panic welling up, the sense that she and Tyrone were trapped in an impossible situation. She used the tea ritual to refocus herself. For the first time in her life she added cream and sugar, and drank the tea as if it were medication or a form of penance.

She was trying to get her brain unfrozen from shock, to get it working normally again. In order to help Tyrone, she knew she needed to get herself out of here. If LaValle meant to charge her as he threatened to do with Tyrone, she'd already be in an adjacent cell. The fact that they'd brought her back to the Library allowed a sliver of light into the darkness that had settled around her. She decided for now to allow this scenario to play out on LaValle's and Kendall's terms.

The moment she set her teacup down, LaValle took up his ax. 'As I said before, Director, the real pity is your involvement. I'd hate to lose you as an ally – though, I see now, I never really had you as an ally.'

This little speech sounded canned, as if each word had been chewed over by LaValle.

'Frankly,' he continued, 'in retrospect, I can see that you've lied to me from the first. You never had any intention of switching your allegiance to NSA, did you?' He sighed, as if he were a disciplinary dean addressing a bright but chronically wayward student. 'That's why I can't believe that you concocted this scheme on your own.'

'If I were a betting man,' Kendall said, 'I'd wager your orders came from the top.'

'Veronica Hart is the real problem here.' LaValle spread his hands. 'Perhaps through the lens of what's happened here today you can begin to see things as we do.'

Soraya didn't need a weatherman to see which way the wind was blowing. Keeping her voice deliberately neutral, she said, 'How can I be of service?'

LaValle smiled genially, turned to Kendall, said, 'You see, Richard, the director can be of help to us, despite your reservations.' He quickly turned back to Soraya, his expression sobering. 'The general wants to prosecute you both to the full extent of the law, which I needn't reiterate is very full indeed.'

Their good-cop, bad-cop routine would seem clichéd, Soraya thought bitterly, except this was for real. She knew Kendall hated her guts; he'd made no effort to hide his contempt. He was a military man, after all. The possibility of having to report to a female superior was unthinkable, downright risible. He hadn't thought much of Tyrone, either, which made his capture of the younger man that much harder to stomach.

'I understand my position is untenable,' she said, despising having to kowtow to this despicable human being.

'Excellent, then we'll start from that point.'

LaValle stared up at the ceiling, giving an impersonation of someone trying to decide how to proceed. But she suspected he knew very well what he was doing, every step of the way.

His eyes engaged hers. 'The way I see it we have a two-part problem. One concerns your friend down in the hold. The second involves you.'

'I'm more concerned with him,' Soraya said. 'How do I get him out?'

LaValle shifted in his chair. 'Let's take your situation first. We can build a circumstantial case against you, but without direct testimony from your friend –'

'Tyrone,' Soraya said. 'His name is Tyrone Elkins.'

To hammer home just whose conversation this was, LaValle quite deliberately ignored her. 'Without direct testimony from your friend we won't get far.'

'Direct testimony we will get,' Kendall said, 'as soon as we waterboard him.'

'No,' Soraya said. 'You can't.'

'Why, because it's illegal?' Kendall chuckled.

Soraya turned to LaValle. 'There's another way. You and I both know there is.'

LaValle said nothing for a moment, drawing out the tension. 'You told me that your source for the attribution of the Typhon intercepts was sacrosanct. Does that decision still stand?'

'If I tell you will you let Tyrone go?'

'No,' LaValle said, 'but you'll be free to leave.'

'What about Tyrone?'

LaValle crossed one leg over another. 'Let's take one thing at a time, shall we?'

Soraya nodded. She knew that as long as she was sitting here she had no wiggle room. 'My source was Bourne.'

LaValle looked startled. 'Jason Bourne? Are you kidding me?'

'No, Mr. LaValle. He has knowledge of the Black Legion and that they were being fronted by the Eastern Brotherhood.'

'Where the hell did this knowledge come from?'

'He had no time to tell me, even if he had a mind to,' she said. 'There were too many NSA agents in the vicinity.'

'The incident at the Freer,' Kendall said.

LaValle held up a hand. 'You helped him to escape.'

Soraya shook her head. 'Actually, he thought I'd turned on him.'

'Interesting.' LaValle tapped his lip. 'Does he still think that?'

Soraya determined it was time for a little defiance, a little lie. 'I don't know. Jason has a tendency toward paranoia, so it's possible.'

LaValle looked thoughtful. 'Maybe we can use that to our advantage.'

General Kendall looked disgusted. 'So, in other words, this whole story about the Black Legion could be nothing more than a lunatic fantasy.'

'Or, more likely, deliberate disinformation,' LaValle said.

Soraya shook her head. 'Why would he do that?'

'Who knows why he does anything?' LaValle took a slow sip of his whiskey, diluted now by the melted ice cubes. 'Let's not forget that Bourne was in a rage when he told you about the Black Legion. By your own admission, he thought you'd betrayed him.'

'You have a point.' Soraya knew better than to defend Bourne to these people. The more you argued against them, the more entrenched they became in their position. They'd built a case against Jason out of fear and loathing. Not because, as they claimed, he was unstable, but because he simply didn't care about their rules and regulations. Instead of flouting them, something the directors had knowledge of and knew how to handle, he annihilated them.

'Of course I do.' LaValle set down his glass. 'Let's move on to your friend. The case against him is airtight, open-and-shut, no hope whatsoever of appeal or commutation.'

'Let him eat cake,' Kendall said.

'Marie Antoinette never said that, by the way,' Soraya said.

Kendall glared at her, while LaValle continued, '*Let the punishment fit the crime* would be more apropos. Or, in your case, *Let the expiation fit the crime.*' He waved the approaching Willard away. 'What we're going to need from you, Director, is proof – incontrovertible proof – that your illegal foray into NSA territory was instigated by Veronica Hart.'

She knew what he was asking of her. 'So, basically, we're talking an exchange of prisoners – Hart for Tyrone.'

'You've grasped it entirely,' LaValle said, clearly pleased.

'I'll have to think about it.'

LaValle nodded. 'A reasonable request. I'll have Willard prepare you a meal.' He glanced at his watch. 'Richard and I have a meeting in fifteen minutes. We'll be back in approximately two hours. You can think over your answer until then.'

'No, I need to think this over in another environment,' Soraya said.

'Director Moore, given your history of deception that would be a mistake on our part.'

'You promised I could leave if I told you my source.'

'And so you shall, when you've agreed to my terms.' He rose, and with him Kendall. 'You and your friend came in here together. Now you're joined at the hip.'

Bourne waited until Gala was sufficiently recovered. She dressed, shivering, not once looking at the body of the dead agent.

'I'm sorry you got dragged into this,' Bourne said.

'No you're not. Without me you never would've gotten to Ivan.' Gala angrily jammed her feet into her shoes. 'This is a nightmare,' she said, as if to herself. 'Any minute I'll wake up in my own bed and none of this will have happened.'

Bourne led her toward the door.

Gala shuddered anew as she carefully skirted the body.

'You're hanging out with the wrong crowd.'

'Ha, ha, good one,' she said, as they made their way down the hall. 'That includes you.'

A moment later, he signaled her to stop. Kneeling down, he touched his fingertip to a wet spot on the carpet.

'What is it?'

Bourne examined his fingertip. 'Blood.'

Gala gave a little whimper. 'What's it doing out here?'

'Good question,' Bourne said as he crept along the hallway. He noted a tiny smear in front of a narrow door. Wrenching it open, he switched on the utility room's light.

'Christ,' Gala said.

Inside was a crumpled body with a bullet in its forehead. It was nude, but there was a pile of clothes tossed in a corner, obviously those of the NSA agent. Bourne knelt down, rifled through them, hoping to find some form of ID, to no avail.

'What are you doing?' Gala cried.

Bourne spotted a tiny triangle of dark brown leather sticking out from under the corpse, which was only visible from this low angle. Rolling the corpse on its side, he discovered a wallet. The dead man's ID would prove useful, since Bourne now had none of his own. His assumed identity, which he'd used to check in, was unusable, because the moment the corpse was found in Fyodor Ilianovich Popov's room, there'd be a massive manhunt for him. Bourne reached out, took the wallet.

Then he rose, grabbed Gala's hand, and got them out of there. He insisted they take the service elevator down to the kitchen. From there it was a simple matter to find the rear entrance.

Outside, it had begun to snow again. The wind, slicing in from the square, was icy and bitter. Flagging down a *bombila*, Bourne was about to give the cabbie the address of Gala's friend, then realized that Yakov, the cabbie working for the NSA, knew that address.

'Get in the taxi,' Bourne said quietly to Gala, 'but be prepared to get out quickly and do exactly as I say.'

Soraya didn't need a couple of hours to make up her mind; she didn't even need a couple of minutes.

'All right,' she said. 'I'll do whatever it takes to get Tyrone out of here.'

LaValle turned back to regard her. 'Well, now, that kind of capitulation would do my heart good if I didn't know you to be such a duplicitous little bitch.

'Unfortunately,' he went on, 'in your case, verbal capitulation isn't quite as convincing as it would be in others. That being the case, the general here will make crystal clear to you the consequences of further treachery on your part.'

Soraya rose, along with Kendall.

LaValle stopped her with his voice, 'Oh, and, Director, when you leave here you'll have until ten tomorrow morning to make your decision. I'll expect you back here then. I hope I've made myself clear.'

The general led her out of the Library, down the corridor to the door to the basement. The moment she saw where he was taking her, she said, 'No! Don't do this. Please. There's no need.'

But Kendall, his back ramrod-straight, ignored her. When she hesitated at the security door, he grasped her firmly by the elbow and, as if she were a child, steered her down the stairs.

In due course, she found herself in the same viewing room. Tyrone was on his knees, his arms behind him, bound hands on the tabletop, which was higher than shoulder level. This position was both extremely painful and humiliating. His torso was forced forward, his shoulder blades back.

Soraya's heart was filled with dread. 'Enough,' she said. 'I get it. You've made your point.'

'By no means,' General Kendall said.

Soraya could see two shadowy figures moving about the cell. Tyrone had become aware of them, too. He tried to twist around to see what they were up to. One of the men shoved a black hood over his head.

*My God*, Soraya said to herself. What did the other man have in his hands?

Kendall shoved her hard against the one-way glass. 'Where your friend is concerned we're just warming up.'

Two minutes later, they began to fill the waterboarding tank. Soraya began to scream.

Bourne asked the *bombila* driver to pass by the front of the hotel. Everything seemed calm and normal, which meant that the bodies on the seventeenth floor hadn't been discovered yet. But it wouldn't be long before someone went to look for the missing room-service waiter.

He turned his attention across the street, searching for Yakov. He was still outside his car, talking to a fellow driver. Both of them were swinging their arms to keep their circulation going. He pointed out Yakov to Gala, who recognized him. When they'd passed the square, Bourne had the *bombila* pull over.

He turned to Gala. 'I want you to go back to Yakov and have him take you to Universitetskaya Ploshchad at Vorobyovy Gory.' Bourne was speaking of the top of the only hill in the otherwise flat city, where lovers and university students went to get drunk, make love, and smoke dope while looking out over the city. 'Wait there for me and whatever you do, don't get out of the car. Tell the cabbie you're meeting someone there.'

'But he's the one who's been spying on us,' Gala said.

'Don't worry,' Bourne reassured her. 'I'll be right behind you.'

The view out over Vorobyovy Gory was not so very grand. First, there was the ugly bulk of Luzhniki Stadium in the mid-foreground. Second, there were the spires of the Kremlin, which would hardly inspire even the most ardent lovers. But for all that, at night it was as romantic as Moscow could get.

Bourne, who'd had his *bombila* track the one Gala was in all the way there, was relieved that Yakov had orders only to observe and report back. Anyway, the NSA was interested in Bourne, not a young blond *dyev*.

Arriving at the overlook, Bourne paid the fare he'd agreed to at the beginning of the ride, strode down the sidewalk, and got into the front seat of Yakov's taxi.

'Hey, what's this?' Yakov said. Then he recognized Bourne and made a scramble for the Makarov he kept in a homemade sling under the ratty dash.

Bourne pulled his hand away and held him back against the seat while taking possession of the handgun. He pointed it at Yakov. 'Who do you report to?'

Yakov said in a whiny voice, 'I challenge you to sit in my seat night after night, driving around the Garden Ring, crawling endlessly down Tverskaya, being cut out of fares by kamikaze *bombily* and make enough to live on.'

'I don't care why you pimp yourself out to the NSA,' Bourne told him. 'I want to know who you report to.'

Yakov held up his hand. 'Listen, listen, I'm from Bishkek in Kyrgyzstan. It's not so nice there, who can make a living? So I pack my family and we travel to Russia, the beating heart of the new federation, where the streets are paved with rubles. But when I arrive here I am treated like dirt. People in the street spit on my wife. My children are beaten and called terrible names. And I can't get a job anywhere in this city. 'Moscow for Muscovites,' that is the refrain I hear over and over. So I take to the *bombily* because I have no other choice. But this life, sir, you have no idea how difficult it is. Sometimes after twelve hours I come home with a hundred rubles, sometimes with nothing. I cannot be faulted for taking money the Americans offer.

'Russia is corrupt, but Moscow, it's more than corrupt. There isn't a word for how bad things are here. The government is made up of thugs and criminals. The criminals plunder the natural resources of Russia – oil, natural gas, uranium. Everyone takes, takes, takes so they can have big foreign cars, a different *dyev* for every day of the week, a dacha in Miami Beach. And what's left for us? Potatoes and beets, if we work eighteen hours a day and if we're lucky.'

'I have no animosity toward you,' Bourne said. 'You have a right to earn a living.' He handed Yakov a fistful of dollars.

'I see no one, sir. I swear. Just voices on my cell phone. All moneys come to a post office box in –'

Bourne carefully placed the muzzle of the Makarov in Yakov's ear. The cabbie cringed, turned mournful eyes on Bourne.

'Please, please, sir, what have I done?'

'I saw you outside the Metropolya with the man who tried to kill me.'

Yakov squealed like a skewered rat. 'Kill you? I'm employed merely to watch and report. I have no knowledge about –'

Bourne hit the cabbie. 'Stop lying and tell me what I want to know.'

'All right, all right.' Yakov was shaking with fear. 'The American who pays me, his name is Low. Harris Low.'

Bourne made him give a detailed description of Low, then he took Yakov's cell phone.

'Get out of the car,' he said.

'But sir, I answered all your questions,' Yakov protested. 'You've taken everything of mine. What more do you want?'

Bourne leaned across him, opened the door, then shoved him out. 'This is a popular place. Plenty of *bombily* come and go. You're a rich man now. Use some of the money I gave you to get a ride home.'

Sliding behind the wheel he put the Zhig in gear, drove back into the heart of the city.

Harris Low was a dapper man with a pencil mustache. He had the prematurely white hair and ruddy complexion of many blue-blooded families in the American Northeast. That he had spent the last eleven years in Moscow, working for NSA, was a testament to his father, who had trod the same perilous path. Low had idolized his father, had wanted to be like him for as long as he could remember. Like his father, he had the Stars and Stripes tattooed on his soul. He'd been a running back in college, gone through the rigorous physical training to be an NSA field agent, had tracked down terrorists in Afghanistan and the Horn of Africa. He wasn't afraid to engage in hand-to-hand combat or to kill a target. He did it for God and country.

During his eleven years in the capital of Russia, Low had made many friends, some of whom were the sons of his father's friends. Suffice to say he had developed a network of *apparatchiks* and *siloviks* for whom a quid pro quo was the order of the day. Harris held no illusions. To further his country's cause he would scratch anyone's back – if they, in turn, scratched his.

He heard about the murders at the Metropolya Hotel from a friend of his in the General Prosecutor's Office, who'd caught the police squeal. Harris met this individual at the hotel and was consequently one of the first people on the scene.

He had no interest in the corpse in the utility closet, but he immediately recognized Anthony Prowess. Excusing himself from the crime scene, he went into the stairwell off the seventeenth-floor hallway, punched in an overseas number on his cell. A moment later Luther LaValle answered.

'We have a problem,' Low said. 'Prowess has been rendered inoperative with extreme prejudice.'

'That's very disturbing,' LaValle said. 'We have a rogue operative loose in Moscow who has now murdered one of our own. I think you know what to do.'

Low understood. There was no time to bring in another of NSA's wet-work specialists, which meant terminating Bourne was up to him.

'Now that he's killed an American citizen,' LaValle said, 'I'll bring the Moscow police and the General Prosecutor's Office into the picture. They'll have the same photo of him I'm sending to your cell within the hour.'

Low thought a moment. 'The question is tracking him. Moscow is way behind the curve in closed-circuit TVs.'

'Bourne is going to need money,' LaValle said. 'He couldn't take enough through Customs when he landed, which means he wouldn't try. He'll have set up a local account at a Moscow bank. Get the locals to help with surveillance pronto.'

'Consider it done,' Low said.

'And Harris. Don't make the same mistake with Bourne that Prowess did.'

Bourne took Gala to her friend's apartment, which was lavish even by American standards. Her friend, Lorraine, was an American of Armenian extraction. Her dark eyes and hair, her olive complexion, all served to increase her exoticism. She hugged and kissed Gala, greeted Bourne warmly, and invited him to stay for a drink or tea.

As he took a tour through the rooms, Gala said, 'He's worried about my safety.'

'What's happened?' Lorraine asked. 'Are you all right?'

'She'll be fine,' Bourne said, coming back into the living room. 'This'll all blow over in a couple of days.' Having satisfied himself of the security of the apartment, he left them with the warning not to open the door for anyone they didn't know.

Ivan Volkin had directed Bourne to go to Novoslobodskaya 20, where the meet with Dimitri Maslov would take place. At first Bourne thought it lucky that the *bombila* he flagged down knew how to find the address, but when he was dropped off he understood. Novoslobodskaya 20 was the address of Motorhome, a new club jammed with young partying Muscovites. Gigantic flat-panel screens above the center island bar showed telecasts of American baseball, basketball, football, English rugby, and World Cup soccer. The floor of the main room was dominated by tables for Russian billiards and American pool. Following Volkin's direction, Bourne headed for the back room, which was fitted out as an Arabian Nights hookah room complete with overlapping carpets, jewel-toned cushions, and, of course, gaily colored brass hookahs being smoked by lounging men and women.

Bourne, stopped at the doorway by two overdeveloped members of club security, told them he was here to see Dimitri Maslov. One of them pointed to a man lounging and smoking a hookah in the far left corner.

'Maslov,' Bourne said when he reached the pile of cushions surrounding a low brass table.

'My name is Yevgeny. Maslov isn't here.' The man gestured. 'Sit down, please.'

Bourne hesitated a moment, then sat on a cushion opposite Yevgeny. 'Where is he?'

'Did you think it would be so simple? One call and *poof!* he pops into existence like a genie from a lamp?' Yevgeny shook his head, offered Bourne the pipe. 'Good shit. Try some.'

When Bourne declined, Yevgeny shrugged, took a toke deep into his lungs, held it, then let it out with an audible hiss. 'Why do you want to see Maslov?'

'That's between me and him,' Bourne said.

Yevgeny shrugged again. 'As you like. Maslov is out of the city.'

'Then why was I told to come here?'

'To be judged, to see whether you are a serious individual. To see whether Maslov will make the decision to see you.'

'Maslov trusts people to make decisions for him?'

'He is a busy man. He has other things on his mind.'

'Like how to win the war with the Azeri.'

Yevgeny's eyes narrowed. 'Perhaps you can see Maslov next week.'

'I need to see him now,' Bourne said.

Yevgeny shrugged. 'As I said, he's out of Moscow. But he may be back tomorrow morning.'

'Why don't you ensure it.'

'I could,' Yevgeny said. 'But it will cost you.'

'How much?'

'Ten thousand.'

'Ten thousand dollars to talk to Dimitri Maslov?'

Yevgeny shook his head. 'The American dollar has become too debased. Ten thousand Swiss francs.'

Bourne thought a moment. He didn't have that kind of money on him, and certainly not in Swiss francs. However, he had the information Baronov had given him on the safe-deposit box at the Moskva Bank. The problem was that it was in the name of Fyodor Ilianovich Popov, who was no doubt now wanted for questioning regarding the body of the man in his room at the Metropolya Hotel. There was no help for it, Bourne thought. He'd have to take the chance.

'I'll have the money tomorrow morning,' Bourne said.

'That will be satisfactory.'

'But I'll give it to Maslov and no one else.'

Yevgeny nodded. 'Done.' He wrote something on a slip of paper, showed it to Bourne. 'Please be at this address at noon tomorrow.' Then he struck a match, held it to the corner of the paper, which burned steadily until it crumbled into ash.

Semion Icoupov, in his temporary headquarters in Grindelwald, took the news of Harun Iliev's death very hard. He'd been a witness to death many times, but Harun had been like a brother to him. Closer, even, because the two had no sibling baggage to clutter and distort their relationship. Icoupov had relied on Harun for his wise counsel. His was a sad loss indeed.

His thoughts were interrupted by the orchestrated chaos around him. A score of people were staffing computer consoles hooked up to satellite feeds, surveillance networks, public transportation CCTV from major hubs all over the world. They were coming to the final buildup to the Black Legion's attack; every screen had to be scrutinized and analyzed, the faces of suspicious people picked out and run through a nebula of software that could identify individuals. From this, Icoupov's operatives were building a mosaic of the real-time backdrop against which the attack was scheduled to take place.

Icoupov became aware that three of his aides were clustered around his desk. Apparently, they'd been trying to talk to him.

'What is it?' His voice was testy, the better to cover up his grief and inattention.

Ismail, the most senior of his aides, cleared his throat. 'We wanted to know who you intend to send after Jason Bourne now that Harun . . .' His voice trailed off.

Icoupov had been contemplating the same question. He'd made a mental list that included any number of people he could send, but he kept eliminating most of them, for one reason or another. But on the second and third run through he began to realize that these reasons were in one way or another trivial. Now, as Ismail asked the question again, he knew.

He looked up into his aides' anxious faces and said, 'It's me. I'm going after Bourne myself.'

# 24

It was disturbingly hot in the Alter Botanischer Garten, and as humid as a rain forest. The enormous glass panels were opaque with beads of mist sliding down their faces. Moira, who had already taken off her gloves and long winter coat, now shrugged out of the thick cable-knit sweater that helped protect her from Munich's chill, damp morning, which could penetrate to the bone.

When it came to German cities, she much preferred Berlin to Munich. For one thing, Berlin had for many years been on the cutting edge of popular music. Berlin was where such notable pop icons as David Bowie, Brian Eno, and Lou Reed, among many others, had come to recharge their creative batteries by listening to what musicians far younger than they were creating. For another, it hadn't lost its legacy of the war and its aftermath. Berlin was like a living museum that was reinventing itself with every breath it took.

There was, however, a strictly personal reason why she preferred Berlin. She came for much the same reason Bowie did, to get away from stale habits, to breathe the fresh air of a city unlike those she knew. At an early age Moira became bored with the familiar. Every time she felt compelled to join a group because that was what her friends were doing she sensed she was losing a piece of herself. Gradually, she realized that her friends had ceased to be individuals, devolving into a cliquey 'they' she found repellent. The only way to escape was to flee beyond the borders of the United States.

She could have chosen London or Barcelona, as some other college sophomores did, but she was a freak for Bowie and the Velvet Underground, so Berlin it was.

The botanical garden was built in the mid-1800s as an exhibition hall, but eighty years later, after its garden was destroyed by a fire, it gained new life as a public park. Outside, the awful bulk of the prewar Fountain of Neptune cast a shadow across the space through which she strolled.

The array of gorgeous specimens on display inside this glassed-in space only underscored the fact that Munich itself was without verve or spark. It was a plodding city of *untermenschen*, businessmen as gray as the city, and factories belching smoke into the low, angry sky. It was also a focal point of European Muslim activity, which, in one of those classic action–reaction scenarios, made it a hotbed of skinhead neo-Nazis.

Moira glanced at her watch. It was precisely 9:30 AM, and here came Noah, striding toward her. He was cool and efficient, personally opaque, even withholding, but he wasn't a bad sort. She'd have refused him as a handler if he was; she was senior enough to command that respect. And Noah did respect her, she was certain of that.

In many ways Noah reminded her of Johann, the man who'd recruited her while she was at the university. Actually, Johann hadn't contacted her at college; he was far too canny for that. He asked his girlfriend to make the approach, rightly figuring Moira would be more responsive to a fellow female student. Ultimately, Moira had met with Johann, was intrigued by what he had to offer her, and the rest was history. Well, not exactly. She'd never told anyone, including Martin or Bourne, who she really worked for. To do so would have violated her contract with the firm.

She stopped in front of the pinkly intimate blooms of an orchid, speckled like the bridge of a virgin's nose. Berlin had also been the site of her first passionate love affair, the kind that curled your toes, obliterated your focus on responsibility and the future. The affair almost ruined her, principally because it possessed her like a whirlwind and, in the process, she'd lost any sense of herself. She became a sexual instrument on which her lover played. What he wanted, she wanted, and so dissolution.

In the end, it was Johann who had saved her, but the process of separating pleasure from self was immensely painful. Especially because two months afterward her lover died. For a time, her rage at Johann was boundless; curdling their friendship, jeopardizing the trust they'd placed in each other. It was a lesson she never forgot. It was one reason she hadn't allowed herself to fall for Martin, though part of her yearned for his touch. Jason Bourne was another story entirely, for she had once again been overtaken by the whirlwind. But this time, she wasn't diminished. Partly, that was because she was mature now and knew better. Mainly, though, it was because Bourne asked nothing of her. He sought neither to lead nor to dominate her. Everything with him was clean and open. She moved on to another orchid, this one dark as night, with a tiny lantern of yellow hidden in its center. It was ironic, she thought, that despite his own issues, she had never before met a man so in control of himself. She found his self-assurance a compelling aphrodisiac, as well as a powerful antidote to her own innate melancholy.

That was another irony, she thought. If asked, Bourne would surely say that he was a pessimist, but being one herself, she knew an optimist when she met one. Bourne would take on the most impossible situations and somehow find a solution. Only the greatest of optimists could accomplish that.

Hearing soft footfalls, she turned to see Noah, shoulders hunched within a tweed overcoat. Though born in Israel, he could pass for a German now, perhaps because he'd lived in Berlin for so long. He'd been Johann's protégé; the two had been very close. When Johann was killed, it was Noah who took his place.

'Hello, Moira.' He had a narrow face below dark hair flecked with premature gray. His long nose and serious mouth belied a keen sense of the absurd. 'No Bourne, I see.'

'I did my best to get him on board at NextGen.'

Noah smiled. 'I'm sure you did.'

He gestured and they began to walk together. Few people were around this gloomy morning so there was no chance of being overheard.

'But to be honest, from what you told me, it was a long shot.'

'I'm not disappointed,' Moira said. 'I detested the entire experience.'

'That's because you have feelings for him.'

'What if I do?' Moira said rather more defensively than she expected.

'You tell me.' Noah watched her carefully. 'There is a consensus among the partners that your emotions are interfering with your work.'

'Where the hell is that coming from?' she said.

'I want you to know that I'm on your side.' His voice was that of a psychoanalyst calming an increasingly agitated patient. 'The problem is you should have come here days ago.' They passed a worker tending a swath of African violets. When they were out of her earshot, he continued, 'Then you go and bring Bourne with you.'

'I told you. I was still trying to recruit him.'

'Don't lie to a liar, Moira.' He crossed his arms over his chest. When he spoke again, every word had weight. 'There is a grave concern that your priorities aren't straight. You have a job to do, and a vitally important one. The firm can't afford to have your attention wandering.'

'Are you saying you want to replace me?'

'It's an option that was discussed,' he acknowledged.

'Bullshit. At this late stage there's no one who knows the project as well as I do.'

'But then another option was requested: withdrawal from the project.'

Moira was truly shocked. 'You wouldn't.'

Noah kept his gaze on her. 'The partners have determined that in this instance it would be preferable to withdraw than to fail.'

Moira felt her blood rising. 'You can't withdraw, Noah. I'm not going to fail.'

'I'm afraid that's no longer an option,' he said, 'because the decision's been made. As of oh seven hundred this morning we've officially notified NextGen that we've withdrawn from the project.'

He handed her a packet. 'Here is your new assignment. You're required to leave for Damascus this afternoon.'

Arkadin and Devra reached the Bosporus Bridge and crossed over into Istanbul just as the sun was rising. Since coming down from the cruel, snow-swept mountains along Turkey's spine they had shed layers of clothes, and now the morning was exceptionally clear and mild. Pleasure yachts and huge tankers alike plowed the Bosporus on their way to various destinations. It felt good to roll down the windows. The air, fresh, moist, tangy with salt and minerals, was a distinct relief after the dry hard winter of the hinterlands.

During the night they'd stopped at every gas station, beaten-down motel, or store that was open – though most were not – in an attempt to find Heinrich, the next courier in Pyotr's network.

When it came time for him to spell her, she moved to the passenger's side, put her head against the door, and fell into a deep sleep, from which emerged a dream. She was a whale, swimming in icy black water. No sun pierced the depths where she swam. Below her was an unfathomable abyss. Ahead of her was a shadowy shape. She didn't know why, but it seemed imperative that she follow that shape, catch up with it, identify it. Was it friend or foe? Every so often she filled her head and throat with sound, which she sent out through the darkness. But she received no reply. There were no other whales around, so what was she chasing, what was she so desperate to find? There was no one to help her. She became frightened. The fright grew and grew . . .

It clung to her as she awoke with a start in the car beside Arkadin. The grayish predawn light creeping through the landscape rendered every shape unfamiliar and vaguely threatening.

Twenty-five minutes later they were in the seething, clamorous heart of Istanbul.

'Heinrich likes to spend the time before his flight in Kilyos, the beach community in the northern suburbs,' Devra said. 'Do you know how to get there?'

Arkadin nodded. 'I'm familiar with the area.'

They wove their way through Sultanahmet, the core of Old Istanbul, then took the Galata Bridge, which spanned the Golden Horn, to Karaköy in the north. In the old days, when Istanbul was known as Constantinople, seat of the Byzantine Empire, Karaköy was the powerful Genoese trading colony known as Galata. As they reached the center of the bridge Devra looked west toward Europe, then east across the Bosporus to Üsküdar and Asia.

They passed into Karaköy, with its fortified Genoese walls and, rising from it, the stone Galata tower with its conical top, one of the monuments that, along with the Topkapi Palace and the Blue Mosque, dominated the modern-day city's skyline.

Kilyos lay along the Black Sea coast twenty-two miles north of Istanbul proper. In the summer it was a popular beach resort, packed with people swimming, snacking in the restaurants that lined the beach, shopping for sunglasses and straw hats, sunbathing, or just dreaming. In winter it possessed a sad, vaguely disreputable air, like a dowager sinking into senility. Still, on this sun-splashed morning, under a cloudless cerulean sky, there were figures walking up and down the beach: young couples hand in hand; mothers with young children who ran laughing to the waterline, only to run back, screaming with terror and delight when the surf piled roughly in. An old man sat on a fold-up stool, smoking a crooked hand-rolled cigar that gave off a stench like the smokestack of a tannery.

Arkadin parked the car and got out, stretching his body after the long drive.

'He'll recognize me the moment he sees me,' Devra said, staying put. She described Heinrich in detail. Just before Arkadin headed down to the beach, she added, 'He likes putting his feet in the water, he says it grounds him.'

Down on the beach it was warm enough that some people had taken off their jackets. One middle-aged man had stripped to the waist and sat with knees drawn up, arms locked around them, facing up to the sun like a heliotrope. Kids dug in the sand with yellow plastic Tweety Bird shovels, poured sand into pink plastic Petunia Pig buckets. One pair of lovers had stopped at the shoreline, embracing. They kissed passionately.

Arkadin walked on. Just behind them a man stood in the surf. His trousers were rolled up; his shoes, with socks stuffed into them, had been placed on a high point in the sand not far away. He was staring out at the water, dotted here and there with tankers, tiny as LEGOs, inching along the blue horizon.

Devra's description was not only detailed, it was accurate. The man in the surf was Heinrich.

The Moskva Bank was housed in an enormous, ornate building that would pass for a palace in any other city but was run-of-the-mill by Moscow standards. It occupied a corner of a busy thoroughfare a stone's throw from Red Square. The streets and sidewalks were packed with both Muscovites and tourists.

It was just before 9 AM. Bourne had been walking around the area for the last twenty minutes, checking for surveillance. That he hadn't spotted any didn't mean the bank wasn't being watched. He'd glimpsed a number of police cars cruising the snow-covered streets, more than usual, perhaps.

As he walked along a street close to the bank, he saw another police cruiser, this one with its light flashing. Stepping back into a shop doorway, he watched as it sped by. Halfway down the block it stopped behind a double-parked car. It sat there for a moment, then the two policemen got out of their cruiser, swaggered over to the vehicle.

Bourne took the opportunity to walk down the crowded sidewalk. People were wrapped and bundled, swaddled like children. Breath came out of their mouths and noses in cloud-like bursts as they hurried along with hunched shoulders and bent backs. As Bourne came abreast of the cruiser, he dipped down and glanced in the window. There he saw his face staring up at him from a tear sheet that had obviously been distributed to every cop in Moscow. According to the accompanying text he was wanted for the murder of an American government official.

Bourne walked quickly in the opposite direction, disappearing around a corner before the cops had a chance to return to their car.

He phoned Gala, who was parked in Yakov's battered Zhig three blocks away awaiting his signal. After his call, she pulled out into traffic, made a right, then another. As they had surmised, it was slow going, the morning traffic sluggish.

She checked her watch, saw she needed to give Bourne another ninety seconds. As she approached the intersection near the bank, she used the time to pick a likely target. A shiny Zil limousine, not a speck of snow on its hood or roof, was heading slowly toward the intersection at right angles to her.

At the appointed time she accelerated forward. The *bombila*'s tires, which she and Bourne had checked when they'd returned to Lorraine's, were nearly bald, their treads worn down to a nub. Gala braked much too hard and the Zhig shrieked as the brakes locked, the old tires skidding along the icy street until its grille struck the front fender of the Zil limo.

All traffic came to a screeching halt, horns blared, pedestrians detoured from their appointed rounds, drawn by the spectacle. Within thirty seconds three police cruisers had converged on the site of the accident.

As the chaos mounted, Bourne slipped through the revolving door into the ornate lobby of the Moskva Bank. He immediately crossed the marble floor, passing under one of the three huge gilt chandeliers that hung from the vaulted ceiling high above. The effect of the room was to diminish human size, and the experience was not unlike visiting a dead relative in his marble niche.

There was a low banquette two-thirds of the way across the vast room, behind which sat a row of drones, their heads bent over their work. Before approaching, Bourne checked everyone inside the bank for suspicious behavior. He produced Popov's passport, then wrote down the number of the safe-deposit box on a small pad kept for that specific purpose.

The woman glanced at him, took his passport and the slip of paper, which she ripped off the pad. Locking her drawer, she told Bourne to wait. He watched her walk over to the rank of supervisors and managers, who sat in rows behind identical wooden desks, and present Bourne's documentation. The manager checked the number against his master list of safe-deposit boxes, then he checked the passport. He hesitated, then reached for the phone, but when he noticed Bourne staring at him, he returned the receiver to its cradle. He said something to the woman clerk, then rose and came over to where Bourne stood.

'Mr. Popov.' He handed back the passport. 'Vasily Legev, at your service.' He was an oily Muscovite who continually scrubbed his palms together as if his hands had been somewhere he'd rather not reveal. His smile seemed as genuine as a three-dollar bill.

Opening a door in the banquette, he ushered Bourne through. 'It will be my pleasure to escort you to our vault.'

He led Bourne to the rear of the room. A discreet door opened onto a hushed carpeted corridor with a row of square columns on either side. Bad reproductions of famous landscape paintings hung on the walls. Bourne could hear the muted sounds of phones ringing, computer operators inputting information or writing letters. The vault was directly ahead, its massive door open; to the left a set of marble stairs swept upward.

Vasily Legev showed Bourne through the circular opening and into the vault. The hinges of the door looked to be two feet long and as thick around as Bourne's biceps. Inside was a rectangular room filled floor-to-ceiling with metal boxes, only the fronts of which could be seen.

They went over to Bourne's box number. There were two locks, two keyholes. Vasily Legev inserted his key in the left-hand lock, Bourne inserted his into the right-hand lock. The two men turned their keys at the same time, and the box was free to be pulled out of its niche. Vasily Legev brought the box to one of a number of small viewing rooms. He set it down on a ledge, nodded to Bourne, then left, pulling the privacy curtain behind him.

Bourne didn't bother sitting. Opening the box, he discovered a great deal of money in American dollars, euros, Swiss francs, and a number of other currencies. He pocketed ten thousand Swiss francs, along with some dollars and euros, before he closed the box, pulled aside the curtain, and emerged into the vault proper.

Vasily Legev was nowhere to be seen, but two plainclothes cops had placed themselves between Bourne and the doorway to the vault. One of them aimed a Makarov handgun at him.

The other, smirking, said, 'You will come with us now, *gospadin* Popov.'

Arkadin, hands in his pockets, strolled down the crescent beach, past a happily barking dog whose owner had let it off the leash. A young woman pulled her auburn hair off her face and smiled at him as they passed each other.

When he was fairly near Heinrich, Arkadin kicked off his shoes, peeled off his socks, and, rolling up his trousers, picked his way down to the surf line, where the sand turned dark and crusty. He moved at an angle, so that as he ventured into the surf he was within earshot of the courier.

Sensing someone near him, Heinrich turned and, shading his eyes from the sun, nodded at Arkadin before turning away.

Under the pretext of stumbling as the surf rolled in, Arkadin edged closer. 'I'm surprised that someone besides me likes the winter surf.'

Heinrich seemed not to hear him, continued his contemplation of the horizon.

'I keep wondering what it is that feels so good about the water rushing over my feet and pulling back out.'

After a moment, Heinrich glanced at him. 'If you don't mind, I'm trying to meditate.'

'Meditate on this,' Arkadin said, sticking a knife very carefully in his side.

Heinrich's eyes opened wide. He staggered, but Arkadin was there to catch him. They sat down together in the surf, like old friends communing with nature.

Heinrich's mouth made gasping sounds. They reminded Arkadin of a fish hauled out of the water.

'What . . . what?'

Arkadin cradled him with one hand as he searched beneath his poplin jacket with the other. Just as he thought, Heinrich had the package on him, not trusting it to be out of his sight for an instant. He held it in his palm for a moment. It was in a rolled cardboard cylinder. So small for something with that much power.

'A lot of people have died for this,' Arkadin said.

'Many more will die before it's over,' Heinrich managed to get out. 'Who are you?'

'I'm your death,' Arkadin said. Plunging the knife in again, he turned it between Heinrich's ribs.

'Ah, ah, ah,' Heinrich whispered as his lungs filled with his own blood. His breathing turned shallow, then erratic. Then it ceased altogether.

Arkadin continued to shelter him with a comradely arm. When Heinrich, nothing more than deadweight now, slumped against him, Arkadin held him up as the surf crashed and ebbed around them.

Arkadin stared out at the horizon, as Heinrich had done, certain that beyond the demarcation was nothing save a black abyss, endless and unknowable.

Bourne went willingly with the two plainclothes policemen out of the vault. As they stepped into the corridor, Bourne slammed the edge of his hand down on the cop's wrist, causing the Makarov to drop and slide along the floor. Whirling, Bourne kicked the other cop, who was flung back against the edge of a square column. Bourne grabbed hold of the arm of the first cop. Lifting it, he slammed his elbow into the cop's rib cage, then smashed his hand into the back of his neck. With both cops down, Bourne hurried along the corridor, but another man came sprinting toward him, blocking the way to the front of the bank, a man who fit Yakov's description of Harris Low.

Reversing course, Bourne leapt up the marble staircase, taking the steps three at a time. Racing around the turn, he gained the landing of the second floor. He'd memorized the plans Baronov's friend had procured for him and had planned for an emergency, not trusting to chance that he'd get in and out of the bank without being identified. It was clear Vasily Legev, having recognized *gospadin* Popov, would blow the whistle on him while he was inside the safe-deposit viewing cubicle. As Bourne broke out into the corridor he encountered one of the bank's security men. Grabbing him by the front of his uniform, Bourne jerked him off his feet, swung him around, and hurled him down the stairs at the ascending NSA agent.

Racing down the corridor, he reached the door to the fire stairs, opened it, and went through. Like many buildings of its vintage this one had a staircase that rose around an open central core.

Bourne took off up the stairs. He passed the third floor, then the fourth. Behind him, he could hear the fire door bang open, the sound of hurried footsteps on the stairs behind him. His maneuver with the guard had slowed down the agent, but hadn't stopped him.

He was midway to the fifth and top floor when the agent fired on him. Bourne ducked, hearing the *spang!* of the ricochet. He sprinted upward as another shot went past him. Reaching the door to the roof at last, he opened it, and slammed it shut behind him.

Harris Low was furious. With all the personnel at his disposal Bourne was still at large. *That's what you get*, he thought as he raced up the stairwell, *when you leave the details to the Russians.* They were great at brute force, but when it came to the subtleties of undercover work they were all but useless. Those two plainclothes officers, for instance. Over Low's objections they hadn't waited for him, had gone into the vault after Bourne themselves. Now he was left with mopping up the mess they'd made.

He came to the door to the roof, turned the handle, and banged it open with the flat of his shoe. The tarred rooftop, the low winter sky glowered at him. Walther PPK/S at the ready, he stepped out onto the roof in a semi-crouch. Without warning, the door slammed shut on him, driving him back onto the small landing.

Up on the roof, Bourne pulled open the door and dived through. He struck Low three blows, directed first at the agent's stomach and then at his right wrist, forcing Low to let go of the gun. The Walther flew down the stairwell, landing on a step just above the fourth floor.

Low, enraged, drove his fists into Bourne's kidney twice in succession. Bourne collapsed to his knees, and Low kicked him onto his back then straddled his chest, pinning Bourne's arms. Low gripped Bourne's throat, squeezing as hard as he could.

Bourne struggled to get his arms free, but he had insufficient leverage. He tried to get a breath, but Low's grip on him was so complete that he was unable to get any oxygen into his system. He stopped trying to free his arms and pressed down with the small of his back, providing a fulcrum for his legs, which he drew up, then extended toward his head. He brought his calves together, sandwiching Low's head between them. Low tried to shake them off, violently twisting his shoulders back and forth, but Bourne held on, increasing his grip. Then, with an enormous effort, Bourne spun them both to the left. Low's head hit against the wall, and Bourne's arms were free. Unwinding his legs, he slammed the palms of his hands against Low's ears.

Low shouted in pain, kicked away, and scrambled back down the stairs. Bourne, on his knees, could see that Low was heading for the Walther. Bourne rose. Just as Low reached it, Bourne launched himself down and across the air shaft. He landed on Low, who whipped the Walther's short but thick barrel into Bourne's face. Bourne reared back, and Low bent him over the railing. Four floors of air shaft loomed below, ending in an unforgiving concrete base. As they locked in their struggle, Low slowly, inexorably, brought the muzzle of the Walther to bear on Bourne's face. At the same time, the heel of Bourne's hand was pushing Low's head up.

Low shook loose from Bourne's grip, lunged at him in an effort to pistol-whip him into unconsciousness. Bourne bent his knees. Using Low's own momentum, he slid one arm under the agent's crotch, and lifted him up. Low tried to get a fix on Bourne with the Walther, failed, swung his arm back to deliver another blow with the barrel.

Using all his remaining strength, Bourne hefted him up and over the banister, dumping him down the air shaft. Low plummeted, a tangle of arms and legs, until he hit the bottom.

Bourne turned, went back out onto the roof. As he loped across it, he could hear the familiar rise and fall of police sirens. He wiped blood off his cheek with the back of his hand. Reaching the other side of the roof, he climbed atop the parapet, leapt across the intervening space onto the roof of the adjoining building. He did this twice more until he felt that it was safe for him to return to the street.

# 25

Soraya had never understood the nature of panic, despite the fact that she grew up with an aunt who was prone to panic attacks. When the attacks came on her aunt said she felt as if someone had put a plastic dry-cleaning bag over her head; she felt as if she were being smothered to death. Soraya would watch her huddled in a chair or curled up on her bed and wonder how on earth she could feel such a thing. There weren't even any plastic dry-cleaning bags allowed in the house. How could a person feel as if she were suffocating when there wasn't anything on her face?

Now she knew.

As she drove out of the NSA safe house without Tyrone, as the high reinforced metal gates swung closed behind her, her hands trembled on the wheel, her heart felt as if it was jumping painfully inside her breast. There was a film of sweat on her upper lip, under her arms, and at the nape of her neck. Worst of all, she couldn't catch her breath. Her mind raced like a rat in a cage. She gasped, sucking ragged gulps of air in to her lungs. She felt, in short, as if she were being smothered to death. Then her stomach rebelled.

As quickly as she was able she pulled to the side of the road, got out, and stumbled into the trees. Falling to her hands and knees, she vomited up the sweet, milky Ceylon tea.

Jason, Tyrone, and Veronica Hart were now all in terrible jeopardy because of rash decisions she'd made. She quailed at the thought. It was one thing to be chief of station in Odessa, quite another to be director. Maybe she'd taken on more than she could handle, maybe she didn't have the steel nerve that was required to make tough choices. Where was her vaunted confidence? It was back there in the NSA interrogation cell with Tyrone.

Somehow she made it to Alexandria, where she parked. She sat in the car bent over, her clammy forehead pressed to the steering wheel. She tried to think coherently, but her brain seemed encased in a block of concrete. At last, she wept bitterly.

She had to call Deron, but she was petrified of his reaction when she told him that she had allowed his protégé to be captured and tortured by the NSA. She had fucked up big time. And she had no idea how to rectify the situation. The choice LaValle had given her – Veronica Hart for Tyrone – was unacceptable.

After a time, she calmed down enough to get out of the car. She moved like a sleepwalker through crowds of people oblivious to her agony. It seemed somehow wrong that the world should spin on as it always had, utterly indifferent and uncaring.

She ducked into a little tea shop, and as she rummaged in her handbag for her cell phone she saw the pack of cigarettes. A cigarette would calm her nerves, but standing out in the chilly street while she smoked would make her feel more of a lost soul. She decided to have a smoke on the way back to her car. Placing her cell phone on the table, she stared down at it as if it were alive. She ordered chamomile tea, which calmed her enough for her to pick up her phone. She punched in Deron's number, but when she heard his voice her tongue clove to the roof of her mouth.

Eventually, she was able to get out her name. Before he could ask her how the mission went she asked to speak with Kiki, Deron's girlfriend. Where that came from, she had no idea. She'd met Kiki only twice. But Kiki was a woman and, instinctively, with an atavistic clannishness, Soraya knew it would be easier to confess to her than to Deron.

When Kiki came on the line, Soraya asked if she could come to the little tea shop in Alexandria. When Kiki asked when, Soraya said, 'Now. Please.'

'The first thing you have to do is stop blaming yourself,' Kiki said after Soraya had finished recounting in painful detail what had happened at the NSA safe house. 'It's your guilt that's paralyzing you, and believe me you're going to need every last brain cell if we're going to get Tyrone out of that hole.'

Soraya looked up from her pallid tea.

Kiki smiled, nodding. In her dark red dress, her hair up in a swirl, hammered-gold earrings descending from her earlobes, she looked more regal, more exotic than ever. She towered over everyone in the tea shop by at least six inches.

'I know I have to tell Deron,' Soraya said. 'I just don't know what his reaction is going to be.'

'His reaction won't be as bad as what you fear,' Kiki said. 'And after all, Tyrone is a grown man. He knew the risks as well as anyone. It was his choice, Soraya. He could've said no.'

Soraya shook her head. 'That's just it, I don't think he could, at least not from the way he sees things.' She stirred her tea, more to forestall what she knew she had to say. Then she looked up, licked her lips. 'See, Tyrone's got a thing for me.'

'Doesn't he ever!'

Soraya was taken aback. 'You know?'

'Everyone who knows him knows, honey. You just have to look at him when the two of you are together.'

Soraya felt her cheeks flush. 'I think he would've done anything I asked of him no matter how dangerous, even if he didn't want to.'

'But you know he wanted to.'

It was true, Soraya thought. He'd been excited. Nervous, but definitely excited. She knew that ever since Deron had taken him under his wing he'd chafed at being cooped up in the hood. He was smarter than that, and Deron knew it. But he had neither the interest nor the aptitude for what Deron did. Then she came along. He'd told her he saw her as his ticket out of the ghetto.

Yet she still had a knot in her chest, a sick feeling in the pit of her stomach. She could not get out of her head the image of Tyrone on his knees, hooded, arms held behind him on the tabletop.

'You just turned pale,' Kiki said. 'Are you all right?'

Soraya nodded. She wanted to tell Kiki what she had seen, but she couldn't. She sensed that to talk about it would give it a reality so frightening, so powerful it would throw her back into panic.

'Then we ought to go.'

Soraya's heart tripped over itself. 'No time like the present,' she said.

As they went out the door, she pulled out the pack of cigarettes and threw it in a nearby trash can. She didn't need it anymore.

As planned, Gala picked up Bourne in Yakov's *bombila* and together they returned to Lorraine's apartment. It was just past 10 AM; his meet with Maslov wasn't until noon. He needed a shower, a shave, and some rest.

Lorraine was kind enough to provide the necessities for all three. She gave Bourne a set of towels, a disposable razor, and said if he gave her his clothes she'd wash and dry them for him. In the bathroom Bourne stripped, then opened the door enough to hand the dirty clothes to Lorraine.

'After I put these in the wash, Gala and I are going out to get food. Can we bring you anything?'

Bourne thanked her. 'Whatever you're having will be fine.'

He closed the door, crossed to the shower, turned it on full force. Opening the medicine cabinet, he took out rubbing alcohol, a gauze pad, surgical tape, and antibiotic cream. Then he went back to the toilet, put the seat cover down, and cleaned his abraded heel. It had taken a lot of abuse and was red and raw looking. Squeezing the cream onto the gauze, he placed it over the wound and taped it up.

Then he took his cell phone off the edge of the sink where he'd placed it when undressing, and dialed the number Boris Karpov had given him.

'Would you mind going without me?' Gala said, as Lorraine reached into the hall closet for her fur coat. 'All of a sudden I'm not feeling well.'

Lorraine walked back to her. 'What is it?'

'I don't know.' Gala sank onto the white leather sofa. 'I'm kind of dizzy.'

Lorraine took hold of the back of her head. 'Bend over. Put your head between your knees.'

Gala did as she was told. Lorraine crossed to the sideboard, took out a bottle of vodka, and poured some into a glass. 'Here, take a drink. It'll settle you.'

Gala came up as gingerly as a drunk walks. She took the vodka, threw it down her throat so fast she almost choked. But then the fire hit her stomach and the warmth began to spread through her.

'Okay?' Lorraine asked.

'Better.'

'All right. I'm going to buy you some hot borscht. You need to get some nourishment into you.' She drew on her coat. 'Why don't you lie down?'

Once again Gala did as she was told, but after her friend left, she rose. She'd never found the sofa comfortable. Making sure of her balance, she went down the hall. She needed to crash on a proper bed.

As she was passing the bathroom, she heard a sound like talking, but Bourne was in there by himself. Curious, she moved closer, then put her ear to the door.

She could hear the rushing of the shower more clearly, but also Bourne's voice. He must be on his cell phone.

She heard him say 'Medvedev did what?' He was talking politics to whoever was on the other end of the line. She was about to take her ear away from the door when she heard Bourne say, 'It was bad luck with Tarkanian . . . No, no, I killed him . . . I had to, I had no other choice.'

Gala pulled away as if she'd touched her ear to a hot iron. For some time, she stood staring at the closed door, then she backed away. Bourne had killed Mischa! *My God*, she said to herself. How could he? And then, thinking of Arkadin, Mischa's best friend, *My God*.

# 26

Dimitri Maslov had the eyes of a rattlesnake, the shoulders of a wrestler, and the hands of a bricklayer. He was, however, dressed like a banker when Bourne met him inside a warehouse that could have doubled as an aircraft hangar. He was wearing a chalk-striped three-piece Savile Row suit, an Egyptian cotton shirt, and a conservative tie. His powerful legs ended in curiously dainty feet, as if they'd been grafted on from another, far smaller body.

'Don't bother telling me your name,' he said as he accepted the ten thousand Swiss francs, 'as I always assume they're fake.'

The warehouse was one among many in this soot-laden industrial area on the outskirts of Moscow, and therefore anonymous. Like its neighbors, it had a front area filled with boxes and crates on neat stacks of wooden pallets piled almost to the ceiling. Parked in one corner was a forklift. Next to it was a bulletin board on which had been tacked overlapping layers of flyers, notices, invoices, advertisements, and announcements. Bare lightbulbs at the ends of metal flex burned like miniature suns.

After Bourne had been expertly patted down for weapons and wires, he'd been escorted through a door to a tiled bathroom that stank of urine and stale sweat. It contained a trough with water running sluggishly along its bottom and a line of stalls. He was taken to the last stall. Inside, instead of a toilet, was a door. His escort of two burly Russians took him through to what appeared to be a warren of offices, one of which was raised on a steel platform bolted onto the far wall. They climbed the staircase to the door, at which point his escort had left him, presumably to go stand guard.

Maslov was seated behind an ornate desk. He was flanked on either side by two more men, interchangeable with the pair outside. In one corner sat a man with a scar beneath one eye, who would have been unprepossessing save for the flamboyant Hawaiian print shirt he wore. Bourne was aware of another presence behind him, his back against the open door.

'I understand you wanted to see me.' Maslov's rattlesnake eyes shone yellow in the harsh light. Then he gestured, holding out his left arm, his hand extended, palm-up, as if he were shoveling dirt away from him. 'However, there's someone who insists on seeing you.'

In a blur, the figure behind Bourne hurled himself forward. Bourne turned in a half crouch to see the man who'd attacked him at Tarkanian's apartment. He came at Bourne with a knife extended. Too late to deflect it, Bourne sidestepped the thrust, grabbed the man's right wrist with his left hand, using his own momentum to pull him forward so that his face met Bourne's raised elbow flush-on.

He went down. Bourne stepped on the wrist with his shoe until the man let go of the knife, which Bourne took up in his hand. At once the two burly bodyguards drew down on him, pointing their Glocks. Ignoring them, Bourne held the knife in his right palm so the hilt pointed away from him. He extended his arm across the desk to Maslov.

Maslov stared instead at the man in the Hawaiian print shirt, who rose, took the knife from Bourne's palm.

'I am Dimitri Maslov,' he said to Bourne.

The big man in the banker's suit rose, nodded deferentially to Maslov, who handed him the knife as he sat down behind the desk.

'Take Evsei out and get him a new nose,' Maslov said to no one in particular.

The big man in the banker's suit pulled the dazed Evsei up, dragged him out of the office.

'Close the door,' Maslov said, again to no one in particular.

Nevertheless, one of the burly Russian bodyguards crossed to the door, closed it, turned and put his back against it. He shook out a cigarette, lit it.

'Take a seat,' Maslov said. Sliding open a drawer, he took out a Mauser, laid it on the desk within easy reach. Only then did his eyes slide up to engage Bourne's again. 'My dear friend Vanya tells me that you work for Boris Karpov. He says you claim to have information I can use against certain parties who are trying to muscle in on my territory.' His fingers tapped the grips of the Mauser. 'However, I would be inexcusably naive to believe that you were willing to part with this information without a price, so let's have it. What do you want?'

'I want to know what your connection is with the Black Legion?'

'Mine? I have none.'

'But you've heard of them.'

'Of course I've heard of them.' Maslov frowned. 'Where is this going?'

'You posted your man Evsei in Mikhail Tarkanian's apartment. Tarkanian was a member of the Black Legion.'

Maslov held up a hand. 'Where the hell did you hear that?'

'He was working against people – friends of mine.'

Maslov shrugged. 'That might be so – I have no knowledge of it one way or another. But one thing I can tell you is that Tarkanian wasn't Black Legion.'

'Then why was Evsei there?'

'Ah, now we get to the root of the matter.' Maslov's thumb rubbed against his forefinger and middle finger in the universal gesture. 'Show me the quid pro quo, to co-opt what Jerry Maguire says.' His mouth grinned, but his yellow eyes remained as remote and malevolent as ever. 'Though to tell you the truth I'm doubting very much there's any money at all. I mean to say, why would the Federal Anti-Narcotics Agency want to help me? It's anti-fucking-intuitive.'

Bourne finally pulled over a chair, sat down. His mind was rerunning the long conversation he'd had with Boris at Lorraine's apartment, during which Karpov had briefed him on the current political climate in Moscow.

'This has nothing to do with narcotics and everything to do with politics. The Federal Anti-Narcotics Agency is controlled by Cherkesov, who's in the midst of a parallel war to yours – the *silovik* wars,' Bourne said. 'It seems as if the president has already picked his successor.'

'That pisspot Mogilovich.' Maslov nodded. 'Yeah, so what?'

'Cherkesov doesn't like him, and here's why. Mogilovich used to work for the president in the St. Petersburg city administration way back when. The president put him in charge of the legal department of VM Pulp and Paper. Mogilovich promptly engineered VM's dominance to become Russia's largest and most lucrative pulp and timber company. Now one of America's largest paper companies is buying fifty percent of VM for hundreds of millions of dollars.'

During Bourne's discourse Maslov had taken out a penknife, was busy paring grime from under his manicured nails. He did everything but yawn. 'All this is part of the public record. What's it to me?'

'What isn't known is that Mogilovich cut himself a deal giving him a sizable portion of VM's shares when the company was privatized through RAB Bank. At the time, questions were raised about Mogilovich's involvement with RAB Bank, but they magically went away. Last year VM bought back the twenty-five percent stake that RAB had taken to ensure the privatization would go through without a hitch. The deal was blessed by the Kremlin.'

'Meaning the president.' Maslov sat up straight, put away the penknife.

'Right,' Bourne said. 'Which means that Mogilovich stands to make a king's ransom through the American buy-in, by means the president wouldn't want made public.'

'Who knows what the president's own involvement is in the deal?'

Bourne nodded.

'Wait a minute,' Maslov said. 'Last week a RAB Bank officer was found tied up, tortured, and asphyxiated in his dacha garage. I remember because the General Prosecutor's Office claimed he'd committed suicide. We all got a good laugh out of that one.'

'He just happened to be the head of RAB's loan division to the timber industry.'

'The man with the smoking gun that could ruin Mogilovich and, by extension, the president,' Maslov said.

'My boss tells me this man had access to the smoking gun, but he never actually had it in his possession. His assistant absconded with it days before his assassination, and now can't be found.' Bourne hitched his chair forward. 'When you find him for us and hand over the papers incriminating Mogilovich, my boss is prepared to end the war between you and the Azeri once and for all in your favor.'

'And how the fuck is he going to do that?'

Bourne opened his cell phone, played back the MP3 file Boris had sent to him. It was a conversation between the kingpin of the Azeri and one of his lieutenants ordering the hit on the RAB Bank executive. It was just like the Russian in Boris to hold on to the evidence for leverage, rather than go after the Azeri kingpin right away.

A broad grin broke out across Maslov's face. 'Fuck,' he said, 'now we're talking!'

After a time, Arkadin became aware that Devra was standing over him. Without looking at her, he held up the cylinder he'd taken from Heinrich.

'Come out of the surf,' she said, but when Arkadin didn't make a move, she sat down on a crest of sand behind him.

Heinrich was stretched out on his back as if he were a sunbather who'd fallen asleep. The water had washed away all the blood.

After a time, Arkadin moved back, first onto the dark sand, then up behind the waterline to where Devra sat, her legs drawn up, chin on her knees. That was when she noticed that his left foot was missing three toes.

'My God,' she said, 'what happened to your foot?'

It was the foot that had undone Marlene. The three missing toes on Arkadin's left foot. Marlene made the mistake of asking what had happened.

'An accident,' Arkadin said with a practiced smoothness. 'During my first term in prison. A stamping machine came apart, and the main cylinder fell on my foot. The toes were crushed, nothing more than pulp. They had to be amputated.'

It was a lie, this story, a fanciful tale Arkadin appropriated from a real incident that took place during his first stint in prison. That much, at least, was the truth. A man stole a pack of cigarettes from under Arkadin's bunk. This man worked the stamping machine. Arkadin tampered with the machine so that when the man started it up the next morning the main cylinder dropped on him. The result wasn't pretty; you could hear his screams clear across the compound. In the end, they'd had to take his right leg off at the knee.

From that day forward he was on his guard with Marlene. She was attracted to him, of this he was quite certain. She'd slipped from her objective pedestal, from the job Icoupov had given her. He didn't blame Icoupov. He wanted to tell Icoupov again that he wouldn't harm him, but he knew Icoupov wouldn't believe him. Why should he? He had enough evidence to the contrary to make him suitably nervous. And yet, Arkadin sensed that Icoupov would never turn his back on him. Icoupov would never renege on his pledge to take Arkadin in.

Nevertheless, something had to be done about Marlene. It wasn't simply that she'd seen his left foot; Icoupov had seen it as well. Arkadin knew she suspected the maimed foot was connected with his horrendous nightmares, that it was part of something he couldn't tell her. Even the story Arkadin told her did not fully satisfy her. It might have with someone else, but not Marlene. She hadn't exaggerated when she'd told him that she possessed an uncanny ability to sense what her clients were feeling, and to find a way to help them.

The problem was that she couldn't help Arkadin. No one could. No one was allowed to know what he'd experienced. It was unthinkable.

'Tell me about your mother and father,' Marlene said. 'And don't repeat the pabulum you fed the shrink who was here before me.'

They were out on Lake Lugano. It was a mild summer's day, Marlene was in a two-piece bathing suit, red with large pink polka dots. She wore pink rubber slippers; a visor shaded her face from the sun. Their small motorboat lay to, its anchor dropped. Small swells rocked them now and again as pleasure boats went to and fro across the crystal blue water. The small village of Campione d'Italia rose up the hillside like the frosted tiers of a wedding cake.

Arkadin looked hard at her. It annoyed him that he didn't intimidate her. He intimidated most people; it was how he got along after his parents were gone.

'What, you don't think my mother died badly?'

'I'm interested in your mother before she died,' Marlene said airily. 'What was she like?'

'Actually, she was just like you.'

Marlene gave him a basilisk stare.

'Seriously,' he said. 'My mother was tough as a fistful of nails. She knew how to stand up to my father.'

Marlene seized on this opening. 'Why did she have to do that? Was your father abusive?'

Arkadin shrugged. 'No more than any other father, I suppose. When he was frustrated at work he took it out on her.'

'And you find that normal.'

'I don't know what the word *normal* means.'

'But you're used to abuse, aren't you?'

'Isn't that called leading the witness, Counselor?'

'What did your father do?'

'He was *consigliere* – the counselor – to the Kazanskaya, the family of the Moscow *grupperovka* that controls drug trafficking and the sale of foreign cars in the city and surrounding areas.' He'd been nothing of the sort. Arkadin's father had been an ironworker, dirt-poor, desperate, and drunk as shit twenty hours a day, just like everyone else in Nizhny Tagil.

'So abuse and violence came naturally to him.'

'He wasn't on the streets,' Arkadin said, continuing his lie.

She gave him a thin smile. 'All right, where do *you* think your bouts of violence come from?'

'If I told you I'd have to kill you.'

Marlene laughed. 'Come on, Leonid Danilovich. Don't you want to be of use to Mr. Icoupov?'

'Of course I do. I want him to trust me.'

'Then tell me.'

Arkadin sat for a time. The sun felt good on his forearms. The heat seemed to draw his skin tight over his muscles, making them bulge. He felt the beating of his heart as if it were music. For just a moment, he felt free of his burden, as if it belonged to someone else, a tormented character in a Russian novel, perhaps. Then his past came rushing back like a fist in his gut and he almost vomited.

Very slowly, very deliberately he unlaced his sneakers, took them off. He peeled off his white athletic socks, and there was his left foot with its two toes and three miniature stumps, knotty, as pink as the polka dots on Marlene's bathing suit.

'Here's what happened,' he said. 'When I was fourteen years old, my mother took a frying pan to the back of my father's head. He'd just come home stone drunk, reeking of another woman. He was sprawled facedown on their bed, snoring peacefully, when *whack!*, she took a heavy cast-iron skillet from its peg on the kitchen wall and, without a word, hit him ten times in the same spot. You can imagine what his skull looked like when she was done.'

Marlene sat back. She seemed to have trouble breathing. At length, she said, 'This isn't another one of your bullshit stories, is it?'

'No,' Arkadin said, 'it's not.'

'And where were you?'

'Where d'you think I was? Home. I saw the whole thing.'

Marlene put a hand to her mouth. 'My God.'

Having expelled this ball of poison, Arkadin felt an exhilarating sense of freedom, but he knew what had to come next.

'Then what happened?' she said when she had recovered her equilibrium.

Arkadin let out a long breath. 'I gagged her, tied her hands behind her, and threw her into the closet in my room.'

'And?'

'I walked out of the apartment and never went back.'

'How?' There was a look of genuine horror on her face. 'How could you do such a thing?'

'I disgust you now, don't I?' He said this not with anger, but with a certain resignation. Why wouldn't she be disgusted by him? If only she knew the whole truth.

'Tell me in more detail about the accident in prison.'

Arkadin knew at once that she was trying to find inconsistencies in his story. This was a classic interrogator's technique. She would never know the truth.

'Let's go swimming,' he said abruptly. He shed his shorts and T-shirt.

Marlene shook her head. 'I'm not in the mood. You go if – '

'Oh, come on.'

He pushed her overboard, stood up, dived in after her. He found her under the water, kicking her legs to bring herself to the surface. He wrapped his thighs around her neck, locked his ankles, tightening his grip on her. He rose to the surface, held on to the boat, swung water out of his eyes as she struggled below him. Boats thrummed past. He waved to two young girls, their long hair flying behind them like horses' manes. He wanted to hum a love song, but all he could think of was the theme to *Bridge on the River Kwai*.

After a time, Marlene stopped struggling. He felt her weight below him, swaying gently in the swells. He didn't want to, really he didn't, but unbidden the image of his old apartment resurrected itself in his mind's eye. It was a slum, the filthy crumbling Soviet-era piece of shit building teeming with vermin.

Their poverty didn't stop the older man from banging other women. When one of them became pregnant, she decided to have the baby. He was all for it, he told her. He'd help her in any way he could. But what he really wanted was the child his barren wife could never give him. When Leonid was born, he ripped the baby from the girl's arms, brought Leonid to his wife to raise.

'This is the child I always wanted, but you couldn't give me,' he told her.

She raised Arkadin dutifully, without complaint, because where could a barren woman go in Nizhny Tagil? But when her husband wasn't home, she locked the boy in the closet of his room for hours at a time. A blind rage gripped her and wouldn't let her go. She despised this result of her husband's seed, and she felt compelled to punish Leonid because she couldn't punish his father.

It was during one of these long punishments that Arkadin woke to awful pain in his left foot. He wasn't alone in the closet. Half a dozen rats, large as his father's shoe, scuttled back and forth, squealing, teeth gnashing. He managed to kill them, but not before they finished what they'd started. They ate three of his toes.

# 27

'It all started with Pyotr Zilber,' Maslov said. 'Or rather his younger brother, Aleksei. Aleksei was a wise guy. He tried to muscle in on one of my sources for foreign cars. A lot of people were killed, including some of my men and my source. For that, I had him killed.'

Dimitri Maslov and Bourne were sitting in a glassed-in greenhouse built on the roof of the warehouse where Maslov had his office. They were surrounded by a lush profusion of tropical flowers: speckled orchids, brilliant carmine anthurium, birds-of-paradise, white ginger, heliconia. The air was perfumed with the scents of the pink plumeria and white jasmine. It was so warm and humid, Maslov looked right at home in his bright-hued short-sleeved shirt. Bourne had rolled up his sleeves. There was a table with a bottle of vodka and two glasses. They'd already had their first drink.

'Zilber pulled strings, had my man Borya Maks sent to High Security Prison Colony 13 in Nizhny Tagil. You've heard of it?'

Bourne nodded. Conklin had mentioned the prison several times.

'Then you know it's no picnic in there.' Maslov leaned forward, refilled their glasses, handed one to Bourne, took the other himself. 'Despite that, Zilber wasn't satisfied. He hired someone very, very good to infiltrate the prison and kill Maks.' Drinking vodka, surrounded by a riot of color, he appeared totally at his ease. 'Only one person could accomplish that and get out alive: Leonid Danilovich Arkadin.'

The vodka had done Bourne a world of good, returning both warmth and strength to his overtaxed body. There was still a smear of blood on the point of one cheek, dried now, but Maslov had neither looked at it nor commented on it. 'Tell me about Arkadin.'

Maslov made an animal sound in the back of his throat. 'All you need to know is that the sonovabitch killed Pyotr Zilber. God knows why. Then he disappeared off the face of the earth. I had Evsei stake out Mischa Tarkanian's apartment. I was hoping Arkadin would come back there. Instead, you showed up.'

'What's Zilber's death to you?' Bourne said. 'From what you've told me, there was no love lost between the two of you.'

'Hey, I don't have to like a person to do business with him.'

'If you wanted to do business with Zilber you shouldn't have had his brother murdered.'

'I have my reputation to uphold.' Maslov sipped his vodka. 'Pyotr knew what kinds of shit his brother was into, but did he stop him? Anyway, the hit was strictly business. Pyotr took it far too personally. Turns out he was almost as reckless as his brother.'

There it was again, Bourne thought, the slurs against Pyotr Zilber. What, then, was he doing running a secret network? 'What was your business with him?'

'I coveted Pyotr's network. Because of the war with the Azeri, I've been looking for a new, more secure method to move our drugs. Zilber's network was the perfect solution.'

Bourne put aside his vodka. 'Why would Zilber want anything to do with the Kazanskaya?'

'There you've given away the extent of your ignorance.' Maslov eyed him curiously. 'Zilber would have wanted money to fund his organization.'

'You mean his network.'

'I mean precisely what I say.' Maslov looked hard and long at Bourne. 'Pyotr Zilber was a member of the Black Legion.'

Like a sailor who senses an onrushing storm, Devra stopped herself from asking Arkadin again about his maimed foot. There was about him at this moment the same slight tremor of intent of a bowstring pulled back to its maximum. She transferred her gaze from his left foot to the corpse of Heinrich, taking in sunlight that would no longer do him any good. She felt the danger beside her, and she thought of her dream: her pursuit of the unknown creature, her sense of utter desolation, the building of her fear to an unbearable level.

'You've got the package now,' she said. 'Is it over?'

For a moment, Arkadin said nothing, and she wondered whether she'd left her deflecting question too late, whether he would now turn on her because she had asked about what had happened to that damn foot.

The red rage had gripped Arkadin, shaking him until his teeth rattled in his skull. It would have been so easy to turn to her, smile, and break her neck. So little effort; nothing to it. But something stopped him, something cooled him. It was his own will. He – did – not – want – to – kill – her. Not yet, at least. He liked sitting here on the beach with her, and there were so few things he liked.

'I still have to shut down the rest of the network,' he said, at length. 'Not that I think it actually matters at this point. Christ, it was put together by an out-of-control commander too young to have learned caution, peopled by drug addicts, inveterate gamblers, weaklings, and those of no faith. It's a wonder the network functioned at all. Surely it would have imploded on its own sooner or later.' But what did he know? He was simply a soldier engaged in an invisible war. His was not to reason why.

Pulling out his cell phone, he dialed Icoupov's number.

'Where are you?' his boss said. 'There's a lot of background noise.'

'I'm at the beach,' Arkadin said.

'What? The beach?'

'Kilyos. It's a suburb of Istanbul,' Arkadin said.

'I hope you're having a good time while we're in a semi-panic.'

Arkadin's demeanor changed instantly. 'What happened?'

'The bastard had Harun killed, that's what happened.'

He knew how much Harun Iliev meant to Icoupov. Like Mischa meant to him.

A rock, someone to keep him from drifting into the abyss of his imagination. 'On a happier note,' he said, 'I have the package.'

Icoupov gave a short intake of breath. 'Finally! Open it,' he commanded. 'Tell me if the document is inside.'

Arkadin did as he was told, breaking the wax seal, prying open the plastic disk that capped off the cylinder. Inside, tightly rolled sheets of pale blue architectural paper unfurled like sails. There were four in all. Quickly, he scanned them.

Sweat broke out at his hairline. 'I'm looking at a set of architectural plans.'

'It's the target of the attack.'

'The plans,' Arkadin said, 'are for the Empire State Building in New York City.'

# Book 3

# 28

It took ten minutes for Bourne to get a decent connection to Professor Specter, then another five for his people to rouse him out of bed. It was 5 AM in Washington. Maslov had gone downstairs to see to business, leaving Bourne alone in the greenhouse to make his calls. Bourne used the time to consider what Maslov had told him. If it was true that Pyotr was a member of the Black Legion, two possibilities arose: One was that Pyotr was running his own operation under the professor's nose. That was ominous enough. The second possibility was far worse, namely that the professor was, himself, a member. But then why had he been attacked by the Black Legion? Bourne himself had seen the tattoo on the arm of the gunman who had accosted Specter, beat him, and hustled him off the street.

At that moment Bourne heard Specter's voice in his ear. 'Jason,' he said, clearly out of breath, 'what's happened?'

Bourne brought him up to date, ending with the information that Pyotr was a member of the Black Legion.

For a long moment, there was silence on the line.

'Professor, are you all right?'

Specter cleared his throat. 'I'm fine.'

But he didn't sound fine, and as the silence stretched on Bourne strained to catch a hint of his mentor's emotional state.

'Look, I'm sorry about your man Baronov. The killer wasn't Black Legion; he was an NSA agent sent to murder me.'

'I appreciate your candor,' Specter said. 'And while I grieve for Baronov, he knew the risks. Like you, he went into this war with his eyes open.'

There was another silence, more awkward than the last one.

Finally, Specter said, 'Jason, I'm afraid I've withheld some rather vital information from you. Pyotr Zilber was my son.'

'Your son? But why didn't you tell me that in the first place?'

'Fear,' the professor said. 'I've kept his real identity a secret for so many years it's become habit. I needed to protect Pyotr from his enemies – my enemies – the enemies who were responsible for murdering my wife. I felt the best way to do that was to change his name. So in the summer of his sixth year, Aleksei Specter drowned tragically and Pyotr Zilber came into being. I left him with friends, left everything and came to America, to Washington, to begin my life anew without him. It was the most difficult thing I've ever had to do. But how can a father renounce his son when he can't forget him?'

Bourne knew precisely what he meant. He'd been about to tell the professor what he'd learned about Pyotr and his cast of misfits and fuckups, but this didn't seem the right time to bring up more bad news.

'So you helped him?' Bourne guessed. 'Secretly.'

'Ever so secretly,' Specter said. 'I couldn't afford to have anyone link us together, I couldn't allow anyone to know my son was still alive. It was the least I could do for him. Jason, I hadn't seen him since he was six years old.'

Hearing the naked anguish in Specter's voice, Bourne waited a moment. 'What happened?'

'He did a very stupid thing. He decided to take on the Black Legion himself. He spent years infiltrating the organization. He discovered that the Black Legion was planning a major attack inside America, then he spent months worming his way closer to the project. And finally, he had the key to bringing them down: He stole the plans to their target. Since we had to be careful about direct communication, I suggested he use his network for the purpose of getting me information on the Black Legion's movements. This is how he meant to send me the plans.'

'Why didn't he simply photograph them and send them to you digitally?'

'He tried that, but it didn't work. The paper the plans are printed on is coated with a substance that makes whatever's printed on it impossible to copy by any means. He had to get me the plans themselves.'

'Surely he told you the nature of the plans,' Bourne said.

'He was going to,' the professor said. 'But before he could he was caught, taken to Icoupov's villa, where Arkadin tortured and killed him.'

Bourne considered the implications in light of the new information the professor had given him. 'Do you think he told them he was your son?'

'I've been concerned about that ever since the kidnapping attempt. I'm afraid Icoupov might know our blood connection.'

'You'd better take precautions, Professor.'

'I plan to do just that, Jason. I'll be leaving the DC area in just over an hour. Meanwhile, my people have been hard at work. I've gotten word that Icoupov sent Arkadin to fetch the plans from Pyotr's network. He's leaving a trail of bodies in his wake.'

'Where is he now?' Bourne said.

'Istanbul, but that won't do you any good,' Specter said, 'because by the time you get there he'll surely have gone. It's now more imperative than ever that you find him, though, because we have confirmed that he's taken the plans from the courier he murdered in Istanbul, and time is running out before the attack.'

'This courier came from where?'

'Munich,' the professor said. 'He was the last link in the chain before the plans were to be delivered to me.'

'From what you tell me, it's clear that Arkadin's mission is twofold,' Bourne said. 'First, to get the plans; second, to permanently shut down Pyotr's network by killing its members one by one. Dieter Heinrich, the courier in Munich, is the only one remaining alive.'

'Who was Heinrich supposed to deliver the plans to in Munich?'

'Egon Kirsch. Kirsch is my man,' Specter said. 'I've already alerted him to the danger.'

Bourne thought a moment. 'Does Arkadin know what Kirsch looks like?'

'No, and neither does the young woman with him. Her name is Devra. She was one of Pyotr's people, but now she's helping Arkadin kill her former colleagues.'

'Why would she do that?' Bourne asked.

'I haven't the faintest idea,' the professor said. 'She was something of a cipher in Sevastopol, where she fell in with Arkadin – no friends, no family, an orphan of the state. So far my people haven't turned up anything useful. In any event, I'm going to pull Kirsch out of Munich.'

Bourne's mind was working overtime. 'Don't do that. Get him out of his apartment to a safe place somewhere in the city. I'll take the first flight out to Munich. Before I leave here I want all the information on Kirsch's life you can get me – where he was born, raised, his friends, family, schooling, every detail he can give you. I'll study it on the flight over, then meet with him.'

'Jason, I don't like the way this conversation is headed,' Specter said. 'I suspect I know what you're planning. If I'm right, you're going to take Kirsch's place. I forbid it. I won't let you set yourself up as a target for Arkadin. It's far too dangerous.'

'It's a little late for second thoughts, Professor,' Bourne said. 'It's vital I get these plans, you said so yourself. You do your part and I'll do mine.'

'Fair enough,' Specter said after a moment's hesitation. 'But my part includes activating a friend of mine who operates out of Munich.'

Bourne didn't like the sound of that. 'What do you mean?'

'You've already made it clear that you work alone, Jason, but this man Jens is someone you want at your back. He's intimately familiar with wet work.'

*A professional killer for hire*, Bourne thought. 'Thank you, Professor, but no.'

'This isn't a request, Jason.' Specter's voice held a stern warning not to cross him. 'Jens is my condition for you taking Kirsch's place. I won't allow you to walk into this bear trap on your own. My decision is final.'

Dimitri Maslov and Boris Karpov embraced like old friends while Bourne stood on, silent. When it came to Russian politics nothing should surprise him, but it was nevertheless astonishing to see a high-ranking colonel in the Federal Anti-Narcotics Agency cordially greeting the kingpin of the Kazanskaya, one of the two most notorious narcotics *grupperovka*.

This bizarre reunion took place in Bar-Dak, near the Leninsky Prospekt. The club had opened for Maslov; hardly surprising, since he owned it. *Bar-Dak* meant both 'brothel' and 'chaos' in current Russian slang. Bar-Dak was neither, though it did sport a prominent strippers' stage complete with poles and a rather unusual leather swing that looked like a horse's harness.

An open audition for pole dancers was in full swing. The lineup of eye-poppingly-built young blond women snaked around the four walls of the club, which was painted in glossy black enamel. Massive sound speakers, lines of vodka bottles on mirrored shelves, and vintage mirror balls were the major accoutrements.

After the two men were finished slapping each other on the back, Maslov led them across the cavernous room, through a door, and down a wood-paneled hallway. Mixed in with the scent of the cedar was the unmistakable waft of chlorine. It smelled like a health club, and with good reason. They went through a translucent pebbled glass door into a locker room.

'The sauna's just over there,' Maslov pointed. 'We meet inside in five minutes.'

Before Maslov would continue the conversation with Bourne, he insisted on meeting with Boris Karpov. Bourne had thought such a conference unlikely, but when he called Boris, his friend readily agreed. Maslov had given Bourne the name of Bar-Dak, nothing more. Karpov had said only, 'I know it. I'll be there in ninety minutes.'

Now, stripped down to the buff, white Turkish towels around their loins, the three men reconvened in the steamy confines of the sauna. The small room was lined, like the hallway, in cedar paneling. Slatted wooden benches ran around three walls. In one corner was a heap of heated stones, above which hung a cord.

When Maslov entered, he pulled the cord, showering the rocks with water, which produced clouds of steam that swirled up to the ceiling and down again, engulfing the men as they sat on the benches.

'The colonel has assured me that he will take care of my situation if I take care of his,' Maslov said. 'Perhaps I should say that I will take care of Cherkesov's problem.'

There was a twinkle in his eye as he said this. Stripped of his outsize Hawaiian shirt, he was a small, wiry man with ropy muscles and not an ounce of fat on him. He wore no gold chains around his neck or diamond rings on his fingers. His tattoos were his jewelry; they covered his entire torso. But these were not the crude and often blurred prison tattoos found on so many of his kind. They were among the most elaborate designs Bourne had ever seen: Asian dragons breathing fire, coiling their tails, spreading their wings, grasping with claws outstretched.

'Four years ago I spent six months in Tokyo,' Maslov said. 'It's the only place to get tattoos. But that's just my opinion.'

Boris rocked with laughter. 'So that's where you were, you bastard! I scoured all of Russia for your skinny butt.'

'In the Ginza,' Maslov said, 'I hoisted quite a few saki martinis to you and your law enforcement minions. I knew you'd never find me.' He made a sweeping gesture. 'But that bit of unpleasantness is behind us; the real perpetrator confessed to the murders I was suspected of committing. Now we find ourselves in our own private glasnost.'

'I want to know more about Leonid Danilovich Arkadin,' Bourne said.

Maslov spread his hands. 'Once he was one of us. Then something happened to him, I don't know what. He broke away from the *grupperovka*. People don't do that and survive for long, but Arkadin is in a class by himself. No one dares to touch him. He wraps himself in his reputation for murder and ruthlessness. This is a man – let me tell you – who has no heart. *Yes, Dimitri*, you might say to me, *but isn't that true of most of your kind?* To this I answer, Yes. But Arkadin is also without a soul. This is where he parts company with the others. There is no one else like him, the colonel can back me up on this.'

Boris nodded sagely. 'Even Cherkesov fears him, our president as well. I personally don't know anyone in either FSB-1 or FSB-2 who'd be willing to take him on, let alone survive. He's like a great white shark, the murderer of killers.'

'Aren't you being a bit melodramatic?'

Maslov sat forward, elbows on knees. 'Listen, my friend, whatever the hell your real name is, this man Arkadin was born in Nizhny Tagil. Do you know it? No? Let me tell you. This fucking excuse of a city east of here in the southern Ural Mountains is hell on earth. It's filled with smokestacks belching sulfurous fumes from its ironworks. *Poor* is not even a word you can apply to the residents, who swill homemade vodka that's almost pure alcohol and pass out wherever they happen to land. The police, such as they are, are as brutal and sadistic as the citizens. As a gulag is ringed by guard towers, Nizhny Tagil is surrounded by high-security prisons. Since the prison inmates are released without even train fare they settle in the town. You, an American, cannot imagine the brutality, the callousness of the residents of this human sewer. No one but the worst of the crims – as the criminals are called – dares be on the streets after 10 P.M.'

Maslov wiped the sweat off his cheeks with the back of his hand. 'This is the place where Arkadin was born and raised. It was from this cesspit that he made a name for himself by kicking people out of their apartments in old Soviet-era projects and selling them to criminals with a bit of money stolen from regular citizens.

'But whatever happened to Arkadin in Nizhny Tagil in his youth – and I don't profess to know what that might be – has followed him like a ghoul. Believe me when I tell you that you've never met a man like him. You're better off not.'

'I know where he is,' Bourne said. 'I'm going after him.'

'Christ.' Maslov shook his head. 'You must have a mighty fucking large death wish.'

'You don't know my friend here,' Boris said.

Maslov eyed Bourne. 'I know him as much as I want to, I think.' He stood up. 'The stench of death is already on him.'

# 29

The man who stepped off the plane in Munich airport, who dutifully went through Customs and Immigration with all the other passengers from the many flights arriving at more or less the same time, looked nothing like Semion Icoupov. His name was Franz Richter, his passport proclaimed him as a German national, but underneath all the makeup and prosthetics he was Semion Icoupov just the same.

Nevertheless, Icoupov felt naked, exposed to the prying eyes of his enemies, whom he knew were everywhere. They waited patiently for him, like his own death. Ever since boarding the plane he'd been haunted by a sense of impending doom. He hadn't been able to shake it on the flight, he couldn't shake it now. He felt as if he'd come to Munich to stare his own death in the face.

His driver was waiting for him at baggage claim. The man, heavily armed, took the one piece of luggage Icoupov pointed out to him off the chrome carousel, carried it as he led Icoupov through the crowded concourse and out into the dull Munich evening, gray as morning. It wasn't as cold as it had been in Switzerland, but it was wetter, the chill as penetrating as Icoupov's foreboding.

It wasn't fear he felt so much as sorrow. Sorrow that he might not see this battle finished, that his hated nemesis would win, that old grudges would not be settled, that his father's memory would remain sullied, that his murder would remain unavenged.

To be sure, there had been attrition on both sides, he thought as he settled into the backseat of the dove-gray Mercedes. The endgame had begun and already he sensed the checkmate waiting for him not far off. It was difficult but necessary for him to admit that he had been outmaneuvered at every turn. Perhaps he wasn't up to carrying the vision his father had for the Eastern Brotherhood; perhaps the corruption and inversion of ideals had gone too far. Whatever the case, he had lost a great deal of ground to his enemy, and Icoupov had come to the bleak conclusion that he had only one chance to win. His chance rested with Arkadin, the plans for the Black Legion's attack on New York City's Empire State Building, and Jason Bourne. For he realized now that his nemesis was too strong. Without the American's help, he feared his cause was lost.

He stared out the smoked-glass window at the looming skyline of Munich. It gave him a shiver to be back here, where it all began, where the Eastern Brotherhood was saved from Allied war trials following the collapse of the Third Reich.

At that time his father – Farid Icoupov – and Ibrahim Sever were jointly in charge of what was left of the Eastern Legions. Up until the Nazi surrender,

Farid, the intellectual, ran the intelligence network that infiltrated the Soviet Union, while Ibrahim, the warrior, commanded the legions that fought on the Eastern Front.

Six months before the Reich's capitulation, the two men met outside Berlin. They saw the end, even if the lunatic Nazi hierarchy was oblivious. So they laid plans for how to ensure their people would survive the war's aftermath. The first thing Ibrahim did was to move his soldiers out of harm's way. By that juncture the Nazi bureaucratic infrastructure had been decimated by Allied bombing, so it was not difficult to redeploy his people into Belgium, Denmark, Greece, and Italy, where they were safe from the reflexive violence of the first wave of invading Allies.

Because Farid and Ibrahim despised Stalin, because they were witness to the massive scale of the atrocities ordered by him, they were in a unique position to understand the Allied fear of communism. Farid argued persuasively that soldiers would be of no use to the Allies, but an intelligence network already inside the Soviet Union would be invaluable. He keenly understood how antithetical communism was to capitalism, that the Americans and the Soviets were allies out of necessity. He felt it inevitable that after the war was over these uncomfortable allies would become bitter enemies.

Ibrahim had no recourse but to agree with his friend's thesis, and indeed this was how it turned out. At every step, Farid and Ibrahim brilliantly outmaneuvered the postwar German agencies in keeping control of their people. As a result, the Eastern Legions not only survived but in fact prospered in postwar Germany.

Farid, however, fairly quickly uncovered a pattern of violence that made him suspicious. German officials who disagreed with his eloquent arguments for continued control were replaced by ones who did. That was odd enough, but then he discovered that those original officials no longer existed. To a one, they had dropped out of sight, never to be seen or heard from again.

Farid bypassed the weakling German bureaucracy and went straight to the Americans with his concerns, but he was unprepared for their response, which was one big shrug. No one, it seemed, cared the least bit about disappeared Germans. They were all too busy defending their slice of Berlin to be bothered.

It was about this time that Ibrahim came to him with the idea of moving the Eastern Legion's headquarters to Munich, out of the way of the increasing antagonism between the Americans and the Soviets. Fed up with the Americans' disinterest, Farid readily agreed.

They found postwar Munich a bombed-out wreck, seething with immigrant Muslims. Ibrahim wasted no time in recruiting these people into the organization, which by this time had changed its name to the Eastern Brotherhood. For his part, Farid found the American intelligence community in Munich far more receptive to his arguments. Indeed, they were desperate for him and his network. Emboldened, he told them that if they wanted to make a formal arrangement with the Eastern Brotherhood for intelligence from behind the Iron Curtain, they had to look into the disappearances of the list of former German officials he handed them.

It took three months, but at the end of that time he was asked to appear before a man named Brian Folks, whose official title was American attaché of something-or-other. In fact, he was OSS chief of station in Munich, the man who received the intel Farid's network provided him from inside the Soviet Union.

Folks told him that the unofficial investigation Farid asked him to undertake had now been completed. Without another word, he handed over a slim file, sat without comment as Farid read it. The folder contained the photos of each of the German officials on the list Farid had provided. Following each photo was a sheet detailing the findings. All the men were dead. All had been shot in the back of the head. Farid read through this meager material with an increasing sense of frustration. Then he looked up at Folks and said, 'Is this it? Is this all there is?'

Folks watched Farid from behind steel-rimmed glasses. 'It's all that appears in the report,' he said. 'But those aren't all the findings.' He held out his hand, took the file back. Then he turned, put the sheets one by one through a shredder. When he was finished, he threw the empty folder into the wastebasket, the contents of which were burned every evening at precisely 5 PM.

Following this solemn ritual, he placed his hands on his desk, said to Farid, 'The finding of most interest to you is this: Evidence collected indicates conclusively that the murders of these men were committed by Ibrahim Sever.'

Tyrone shifted on the bare concrete floor. It was so slippery with his own fluids that one knee went out from under him, splaying him so painfully that he cried out. Of course, no one came to help him; he was alone in the interrogation cell in the basement of the NSA safe house deep in the Virginia countryside. He had to quite literally locate himself in his mind, had to trace the route he and Soraya had taken when they'd driven to the safe house. When? Three days ago? Ten hours? What? The rendition he'd been subjected to had erased any sense of time. The hood over his head threatened to erase his sense of place, so that periodically he had to say to himself: 'I'm in an interrogation cell in the basement of the NSA safe house in' – and here he would recite the name of the last town he and Soraya had passed . . . when?

That was the problem, really. His sense of disorientation was so complete, there were periods when he couldn't distinguish up from down. Worse, those periods were becoming both longer and more frequent.

The pain was hardly an issue because he was used to pain, though never this intense or prolonged. It was the disorientation that was worming its way into his brain like a surgeon's drill. It seemed that with each bout he was losing more of himself, as if he were made up of grains of salt or sand trickling away from him. And what would happen when they were all gone? What would he become?

He thought of DJ Tank and the rest of his former crew. He thought of Deron, of Kiki, but none of those tricks worked. They'd slip away like mist and he'd be left to the void into which, he was increasingly sure, he'd disappear. Then he thought of Soraya, conjured her piece by piece, as if he were a sculptor, molding her out of a lump of clay. And he found that as his mind lovingly re-created each minute bit of her, he miraculously stayed intact.

As he struggled back to a position that was tolerably painful, he heard a metallic scrape, and his head came up. Before anything else could transpire, the scents of freshly cooked eggs and bacon came to him, making his mouth water. He'd been fed nothing but plain oatmeal since he was brought here. And at inconsistent times – sometimes one meal right after the other – in order to keep his disorientation absolute.

He heard the scuff of leather soles – two men, his ears told him.

Then General Kendall's voice, saying imperiously, 'Set the food on the table, Willard. Right there, thank you. That will be all.'

One set of shoe soles clacked across the floor, the sound of the door closing. Silence. Then the screech of a chair being hitched across the concrete. Kendall was sitting down, Tyrone surmised.

'What have we here?' Kendall said, clearly to himself. 'Ah, my favorite: eggs over easy, bacon, buttered grits, hot biscuits and gravy.' The sound of cutlery being taken up. 'You like grits, Tyrone? You like biscuits and gravy?'

Tyrone wasn't too far gone to be incensed. 'On'y ting I like betta is watermelon, sah.'

'That's a damn fine imitation of one of your brethren, Tyrone.' He was obviously talking while eating. 'This is damn fine chow. Would you like some?'

Tyrone's stomach growled so loudly he was sure Kendall heard it.

'All you gotta do is tell me everything you and the Moore woman were up to.'

'I don't rat anyone out,' Tyrone said bitterly.

'Um.' The sounds of Kendall swallowing. 'That's what they all say in the beginning.' He chewed some more. 'You do know this is just the beginning, don't you, Tyrone? Sure you do. Just like you know the Moore woman isn't going to save you. She's going to hang you out to dry, sure as I'm sitting here eating the most mouthwatering biscuits I ever had. You know why? Because LaValle gave her a choice: you or Jason Bourne. You know her history with Bourne. She might claim she didn't fuck him but you and I know better.'

'She never slept with him,' Tyrone said before he could stop himself.

'Sure. She told you that.' Munch, munch, munch went Kendall's jaws, shredding the crisp bacon. 'What'd you expect her to say?'

The sonovabitch was playing mind games with him, Tyrone knew that for a fact. Trouble was, he wasn't lying. Tyrone knew how Soraya felt about Bourne – it was written all over her face every time she saw him or his name came up. Though she'd said otherwise, the question Kendall had just raised had gnawed at him like an addict at a candy bar.

It was difficult not to envy Bourne with his freedom, his encyclopedic knowledge, his friendship as equals with Deron. But all these things Tyrone dealt with in his own way. It was Soraya's love for Bourne that was so hard to live with.

He heard the scrape of chair legs and then felt the presence of Kendall as he squatted down beside him. It was astonishing, Tyrone thought, how much heat another human being gave off.

'I have to say, Tyrone, you really have taken a beating,' Kendall said. 'I think you deserve a reward for how well you've held up. Shit, we've had suspects in here who were crying for their mamas after twenty-four hours. Not you, though.' The quick *click-clack* of a metal utensil against a china plate. 'How about some eggs and bacon? Man, this was some big plate of food, I surely can't finish it myself. So come on. Join me.'

As the hood was raised high enough to expose his mouth Tyrone was conflicted. His mind told him to refuse the offer, but his severely shrunken stomach yearned for real food. He could smell the rich flavors of bacon and eggs, felt the food warm as a kiss against his lips.

'Hey, man, what're you waiting for?'

*Fuck it,* Tyrone said to himself. The tastes of the food exploded inside his mouth. He wanted to moan in pleasure. He wolfed down the first few forkfuls fed to him, then forced himself to chew slowly and methodically, extracting every bit of flavor from the hickory-smoked meat and the rich yolk.

'Tastes good,' Kendall said. He must have regained his feet because his voice was above Tyrone when he said, 'Tastes real good, doesn't it?'

Tyrone was about to nod his assent when pain exploded in the pit of his stomach. He grunted when it came again. He'd been kicked before, so he knew what Kendall was doing. The third kick landed. He tried to hold on to his food, but the involuntary reaction had begun. A moment later he vomited up all the delicious food Kendall had fed him.

'The Munich courier is the last one in the network,' Devra said. 'His name is Egon Kirsch, but that's all I know. I never met him; no one I know did. Pyotr made sure that link was completely compartmentalized. So far as I know Kirsch dealt directly with Pyotr and no one else.'

'Who does Kirsch deliver his intel to?' Arkadin said. 'Who's at the other end of the network?'

'I have no idea.'

He believed her. 'Did Heinrich and Kirsch have a particular meeting place?'

She shook her head.

On the Lufthansa flight from Istanbul to Munich he sat shoulder-to-shoulder with her and wondered what the hell he was doing. She'd given him all the information he was going to get from her. He had the plans; he was on the last lap of his mission. All that remained was to deliver the plans to Icoupov, find Kirsch, and persuade him to lead Arkadin back to the end of the network. Child's play.

Which begged the question of what to do with Devra. He'd already made up his mind to kill her, as he'd killed Marlene and so many others. It was a fait accompli, a fixed point detailed in his mind, a diamond that only needed polishing to sparkle into life. Sitting in the jetliner he heard the quick report from the gun, leaves falling over her dead body, covering her like a blanket.

Devra, who was seated on the aisle, got up, made her way back to the lavatories. Arkadin closed his eyes and was back in the sooty stench of Nizhny Tagil, men with filed teeth and blurry tattoos, women old before their time, bent, swigging homemade vodka from plastic soda bottles, girls with sunken eyes, bereft of a future. And then the mass grave . . .

His eyes popped open. He was having difficulty breathing. Heaving himself to his feet, he followed Devra. She was the last of the passengers waiting. The accordion door on the right opened, an older woman bustled out, squeezed by Devra then Arkadin. Devra went into the lavatory, closed the door, and locked it. The OCCUPIED sign came on.

Arkadin walked to the door, stood in front of it for a moment. Then he knocked on it gently.

'Just a minute,' her voice came to him.

Leaning his head against the door, he said, 'Devra, it's me.' And after a short silence, 'Open the door.'

A moment later, the door folded back. She stood in front of him.

'I want to come in,' he said.

Their eyes locked for the space of several heartbeats as each tried to gauge the intent of the other.

Then she backed up against the tiny sink, Arkadin stepped inside, with some difficulty shut the door behind him, and turned the lock.

# 30

'It's state-of-the-art,' Gunter Müller said. 'Guaranteed.'

Both he and Moira were wearing hard hats as they walked through the series of semi-automated workshops of Kaller Steelworks Gesellschaft, where the coupling link that would receive the LNG tankers as they nosed into the NextGen Long Beach terminal had been manufactured.

Müller, the team leader on the NextGen coupling link project, was a senior vice president of Kaller, a smallish man dressed impeccably in a conservatively cut three-piece chalk-striped suit, expensive shoes, and a tie in black and gold, Munich's colors since the time of the Holy Roman Empire. His skin was bright pink, as if he'd just had his face steam-cleaned, and thick brown hair, graying at the sides. He talked slowly and distinctly in good English, though he was rather endearingly weak with modern American idioms.

At each step he explained the manufacturing process with excruciating detail, great pride. Spread out before them were the design drawings, along with the specs, to which Müller referred time and again.

Moira was listening with only one ear. How her situation had changed now that the Firm was out of the picture, now that NextGen was on its own with the security of its terminal operations in Long Beach, now that she had been reassigned.

*But the more things change,* she thought, *the more they stay the same.* The moment Noah had handed her the packet for Damascus she knew she wouldn't disengage herself from the Long Beach terminal project. No matter what Noah or his bosses had determined she couldn't leave NextGen or this project in jeopardy. Müller, like everyone else at Kaller and, for that matter, nearly everyone at NextGen, had no idea she worked for the Firm. Only she knew she should be on a flight to Damascus, not here with him. She had a grace period of mere hours before her contact at NextGen would begin to ask questions as to why she was still on the LNG terminal project. By then, she hoped to convince NextGen's president of the wisdom of her disobeying the Firm's orders.

Finally, they reached the loading bay where the sixteen parts of the coupling link were being packed for shipment by air to Long Beach on the NextGen 747 jet that had brought her and Bourne to Munich.

'As specified in the contract, our team of engineers will be accompanying you on the homeward journey.' Müller rolled up the drawings, snapped a rubber band around them, and handed them to Moira. 'They'll be in charge of putting the coupling link together on site. I have every confidence that all will go smoothly.'

'It had better,' Moira said. 'The LNG tanker is scheduled to dock at the terminal in thirty hours.' She shot Müller an unpleasant look. 'Not much leeway for your engineers.'

'Not to worry, Fräulein Trevor,' he said cheerfully. 'They're more than up to the task.'

'For your company's sake, I sincerely hope so.' She stowed the roll under her left arm, preparatory to leaving. 'Shall we speak frankly, Herr Müller?'

He smiled. 'Always.'

'I wouldn't have had to come here at all had it not been for the string of delays that set your manufacturing process back.'

Müller's smile seemed immovable. 'My dear Fräulein, as I explained to your superiors, the delays were unavoidable – please blame the Chinese for the temporary shortage of steel, and the South Africans for the energy shortage that is forcing the platinum mines to work at half speed.' He spread his hands. 'We've done the best we could, I assure you.' His smile widened. 'And now we are at the end of our journey together. The coupling link will be in Long Beach within eighteen hours, and eight hours later it will be in one piece and ready to receive your tanker of liquid natural gas.' He stuck out his hand. 'All will have a happy ending, yes?'

'Of course it will. Thank you, Herr Müller.'

Müller nearly clicked his heels. 'The pleasure is all mine, Fräulein.'

Moira walked back through the factory with Müller at her side. She said good-bye to him once more at the gates to the factory, walked across the gravel drive to where her chauffeured car sat waiting for her, its precisely engineered German engine purring quietly.

They pulled out of the Kaller Steelworks property, turned left toward the autobahn back to Munich. Five minutes later, her driver said, 'There's a car following us, Fräulein.'

Turning around, Moira peered out the back window. A small Volkswagen, no more than fifty yards behind them, flashed its headlights.

'Pull over.' She pushed aside the hem of her long skirt, took a SIG Sauer out of the holster strapped to her left ankle.

The driver did as he was told, and the car came to a stop on the shoulder of the road. The Volkswagen pulled in behind. Moira sat waiting for something to happen; she was too well trained to get out of the car.

At length, the Volkswagen drove off the shoulder, into the underbrush, where it disappeared from sight. A moment later a man became visible tramping out onto the side of the road. He was tall and narrow, with a pencil mustache and suspenders holding up his trousers. He was in his shirtsleeves, oblivious to the German winter chill. She could see that he had no weapons on him, which, she reasoned, was the point. When he came abreast of her car, she leaned across the backseat, opened the door for him, and he slipped inside.

'My name is Hauser, Fräulein Trevor. Arthur Hauser.' His expression was morose, bitter. 'I apologize for the incivility of this impromptu meeting, but I assure you the melodrama is necessary.' As if to underscore his words, he glanced back down the road toward the factory, his expression fearful. 'I do not have much time so I shall come straight to the point. There is a flaw in the coupling link – not, I hasten to add, in the hardware. That, I assure you, is absolutely sound. But there is a problem with the software. Nothing that will interfere with the operation of the link, no, not at all. It is, rather, a security flaw – a window, if you will. The chances are it might never be discovered, but all the same it's there.'

When Hauser glanced again out the back window a car was coming toward them. He clamped his jaws shut, watched as the vehicle passed by, then visibly relaxed as it drove on down the road.

'Herr Müller was not altogether truthful. The delays were caused by this software flaw, nothing else. I should know, since I was part of the software design team. We tried for a patch, but it's been devilishly difficult, and we ran out of time.'

'Just how serious is this flaw?' Moira said.

'It depends on whether you're an optimist or a pessimist.' Hauser ducked his head, embarrassed. 'As I said, it might never be discovered.'

Moira glanced out the window for a time, thinking that she shouldn't ask the next question because, as Noah told her in no uncertain terms, the Firm was now out of ensuring the security of NextGen's LNG terminal.

And then she heard herself say, 'What if I'm a pessimist?'

Peter Marks found Rodney Feir, chief of field support, in the CI caff, eating a bowl of New England clam chowder. Feir looked up, gestured to Marks to sit. Peter Marks had been elevated to chief of operations after the ill-starred Rob Batt was outed as an NSA rat.

'How's it going?' Feir said.

'How d'you think it's going?' Marks parked himself on the chair opposite Feir. 'I've been vetting every one of Batt's contacts for any sign of NSA taint. It's daunting and frustrating work. You?'

'As exhausted as you, I expect.' Feir sprinkled oyster crackers into the chowder. 'I've been briefing the new DCI on everything from agents in the field to the cleaning firm we've used for the past twenty years.'

'D'you think she'll work out?'

Feir knew he had to be careful here. 'I'll say this for her: She's a stickler for detail. No stone unturned. She's not leaving anything to chance.'

'That's a relief.' Marks twiddled a fork between his thumb and fingers. 'What we don't need is another crisis. I'd be happy with someone who can right this listing ship.'

'My sentiments exactly.'

'The reason I'm here,' Marks said, 'is I'm having a staffing problem. I've lost some people to attrition. Of course, that's inevitable. I thought I'd get some good recruits graduating from the program, but they went to Typhon. I'm in need of a short-term fix.'

Feir chewed on a mouthful of gritty clam bits and soft potato cubes. He'd diverted those graduates to Typhon and had been waiting for Marks to come to him ever since. 'How can I help?'

'I'd like some of Dick Symes's people to be assigned to my directorate.' Dick Symes was the chief of intelligence. 'Just temporarily, you understand, until I can get some raw recruits through training and orientation.'

'Have you talked to Dick?'

'Why bother? He'll just tell me to go to hell. But you can plead my case to Hart.

She's so snowed under that you're the one best suited to get her to listen to me. If she makes the call Dick can yell all he wants, it won't matter.'

Feir wiped his lips. 'What number of personnel are we talking here, Peter?'

'Eighteen, two dozen tops.'

'Not inconsiderable. The DCI is going to want to know what you have in mind.'

'I've got a brief detailing it all ready to go,' Marks said. 'I shoot it to you electronically, you walk it in to her personally.'

Feir nodded. 'I think that can be arranged.'

Relief flooded Marks's face. 'Thanks, Rodney.'

'Don't mention it.' He began to dig into what was left of the chowder. As Marks was about to rise, he said, 'Do you by any chance know where Soraya is? She's not in her office and she's not answering her cell.'

'Unh-unh.' Marks resettled himself. 'Why?'

'No reason.'

Something in Feir's voice gave him pause. 'No reason? Really?'

'Just, you know how office scuttlebutt can be.'

'Meaning?'

'You two are tight, aren't you.'

'Is that what you heard?'

'Well, yeah.' Feir placed his spoon into the empty bowl. 'But if it isn't true – '

'I don't know where she is, Rodney.' Marks's gaze drifted off. 'We never had that kind of thing going.'

'Sorry, I didn't mean to pry.'

Marks waved away his apology. 'Forget it. I have. So what do you want to talk with her about?'

This was what Feir was hoping he'd say. According to the general, he and LaValle required intel on the nuts and bolts of how Typhon worked. 'Budgets. She's got so many agents in the field, the DCI wants an accounting of their expenses – which, frankly, hasn't been done since Martin died.'

'That's understandable, given what's been going on in here lately.'

Feir shrugged deferentially. 'I'd do it myself; Soraya's got more on her plate than she can handle, I imagine. Trouble is, I don't even know where the files are.' He was going to add: *Do you?* but decided that would be overselling it.

Marks thought a minute. 'I might be able to help you there.'

'How badly does your shoulder hurt?' Devra said.

Arkadin, pressed against her body, his powerful arms around her, said, 'I don't know how to answer that. I have an extremely high tolerance for pain.'

The airplane's cramped bathroom allowed him to concentrate exclusively on her. It was like being in a coffin together, like being dead, but in a strange afterlife where only they existed.

She smiled up at him as one of his hands traced its way from the small of her back to her neck. His thumb pressed against her jaw, gently tilted her head up while his fingers tightened on the nape of her neck.

He leaned in, his weight arching her torso backward above the sink. He could see the back of her head in the mirror, his face about to eclipse hers. A flame of emotion flickered to life, illuminating the soulless void inside him.

He kissed her.

'Gently,' she whispered. 'Relax your lips.'

Her moist lips opened beneath his, her tongue searched for his, tentatively at first, then with an unmistakable hunger. His lips trembled. He had never felt anything when kissing a woman. In fact, he'd always done his best to avoid it, not knowing what it was for, or why women sought it so relentlessly. An exchange of fluids, that's all it was to him, like a procedure performed in a doctor's office. The best he could say was that it was painless, that it was over quickly.

The electricity that shot through him when his lips met hers stunned him. The sheer pleasure of it astonished him. It hadn't been like this with Marlene; it hadn't been like this with anyone. He did not know what to make of the tremor in his knees. Her sweet, moaning exhalations entered him like silent cries of ecstasy. He swallowed them whole, and wanted more.

*Wanting* was something Arkadin was unused to. *Need* was the word that had driven his life up to this moment: He needed to revenge himself on his mother, he needed to escape home, he needed to strike out on his own, no matter the course, he needed to bury rivals and enemies, he needed to destroy anyone who got close to his secrets. But *want*? That was another matter entirely. Devra defined *want* for him. And it was only when he was certain he no longer needed her that his desire revealed itself. He wanted her.

When he lifted her skirt, probing underneath, her leg drew up. Her fingers nimbly freed him from his clothing. Then he stopped thinking altogether.

Afterward, when they'd returned to their seats, making their way through the line of glaring passengers queued up to use the lavatory, Devra burst into laughter. Arkadin sat watching her. This was another thing unique about her. Anyone else would have asked, *Was that your first time*? Not her. She wasn't interested in prying his lid open, peering inside to see what made him tick. She had no need to know. Because he was someone who had always needed something, he couldn't tolerate that trait in anyone else.

He was aware of her next to him in a way he was unable to understand. It was as if he could feel her heartbeat, the rush of blood through her body, a body that seemed frail to him, even though he knew how tough she could be, after all she'd suffered. How easily her bones could be broken, how easily a knife slipped through her ribs might pierce her heart, how easily a bullet could shatter her skull. These thoughts sent him into a rage, and he shifted closer to her, as if she were in need of protection – which, when it came to her former allies, she most certainly was. He knew then that he'd do everything in his power to kill anyone who sought to do her harm.

Feeling him edge closer, she turned and smiled. 'You know something, Leonid, for the first time in my life I feel safe. All that prickly shit I give off is something I learned early on to keep people away.'

'You learned to be tough like your mother.'

She shook her head. 'That's the really shitty part. My mother had this tough shell, yeah, but it was skin-deep. Beneath it, she was a mass of fears.'

Devra put her head against the headrest as she continued, 'In fact, the most vivid thing I remember about my mother was her fear. It came off her like a stink.

Even after she'd bathed, I smelled it. Of course, for a long time I didn't know what it was, and maybe I was the only one who smelled it, I don't know.

'Anyway, she used to tell me an old Ukrainian folktale. It was about the Nine Levels of Hell. What was she thinking? Was she trying to frighten me or lessen her own fear by sharing it with me? I don't know. In any case, this is what she told me. There is one heaven, but there are nine levels of hell where, depending on the severity of your sins, you're sent when you die.

'The first, the least bad, is the one familiar to everyone, where you roast in flames. The second is where you're alone on the summit of a mountain. Every night you freeze solid, slowly and horribly, only to thaw out in the morning, when the process begins all over again. The third is a place of blinding light; the fourth of pitch blackness. The fifth is a place of icy winds that cut you, quite literally, like a knife. In the sixth, you're pierced by arrows. In the seventh, you're slowly buried by an army of ants. In the eighth, you're crucified.

'But it was the ninth level that terrified my mother the most. There, you lived among wild beasts that gorged themselves on human hearts.'

The cruelty of telling this to a child wasn't lost on Arkadin. He was absolutely certain that if his mother had been Ukrainian she'd have told him the same folktale.

'I used to laugh at her story – or at least I tried to,' Devra said. 'I struggled against believing such nonsense. But that was before a number of those levels of hell were visited on us.'

Arkadin felt her presence inside him all the more deeply. The sense of wanting to protect her seemed to bounce around inside him, increasing exponentially as his brain tried to come to terms with what the feeling meant. Had he at last stumbled across something big enough, bright enough, strong enough to put his demons to rest?

After Marlene's death, Icoupov had seen the writing on the wall. He'd stopped trying to peer into Arkadin's past. Instead he'd shipped him off to America to be rehabilitated. 'Reprogrammed,' Icoupov had called it. Arkadin had spent eighteen months in the Washington, DC, area going through a unique experimental program devised and run by a friend of Icoupov's. Arkadin had emerged changed in many ways, though his past – his shadows, his demons – remained intact. How he wished the program had erased all memory of it! But that wasn't the nature of the program. Icoupov no longer cared about Arkadin's past, what concerned him was his future, and for that the program was ideal.

He fell asleep thinking about the program, but he dreamed he was back in Nizhny Tagil. He never dreamed about the program; in the program he felt safe. His dreams weren't about safety; they were about being pushed from great heights.

Late at night, a subterranean bar called Crespi was the only option when he wanted to get a drink in Nizhny Tagil. It was a reeking place, filled with tattooed men in tracksuits, gold chains around their necks, short-skirted women so heavily made up they looked like store mannequins. Behind their raccoon eyes were vacant pits where their souls had been.

It was in Crespi where Arkadin at age thirteen was first beaten to a pulp by four burly men with pig eyes and Neanderthal brows. And it was to Crespi that Arkadin, after nursing his wounds, returned three months later and blew the men's brains all over the walls. When another crim tried to snatch his gun away, Arkadin shot him point-blank in the face. That sight stopped anyone else in the bar from approaching him. It also gained him a reputation, which helped him to amass a mini real estate empire.

But in that city of smelted iron and hissing slag success had its own particular consequences. For Arkadin, it was coming to the attention of Stas Kuzin, one of the local crime bosses. Kuzin found Arkadin one night, four years later, having a bare-knuckle brawl with a giant lout whom Arkadin called out on a bet, for the prize of one beer.

Having demolished the giant, Arkadin grabbed his free beer, swigged half of it down, and, turning, confronted Stas Kuzin. Arkadin knew him immediately; everyone in Nizhny Tagil did. He had a thick black pelt of hair that came down in a horizontal slash to within an inch of his eyebrows. His head sat on his shoulders like a marble on a stone wall. His jaw had been broken and reconstructed so badly – probably in prison – that he spoke with a peculiar hissing sound, like a serpent. Sometimes what he said was all but unintelligible.

On either side of Kuzin were two ghoulish-looking men with sunken eyes and crude tattoos of dogs on the backs of their hands, which marked them as forever bound to their master.

'Let's talk,' this monstrosity said to Arkadin, jerking his tiny head toward a table.

The men who'd been occupying the table rose as one when Kuzin approached, fleeing to the other side of the bar. Kuzin hooked his shoe around a chair leg, dragged it around, and sat down. Disconcertingly, he kept his hands in his lap, as if at any moment he'd draw down on Arkadin and shoot him dead.

He began talking, but it took the seventeen-year-old Arkadin some minutes before he could make heads or tails of what Kuzin was saying. It was like listening to a drowning man going under for the third time. At length, he realized that Kuzin was proposing a merger of sorts: half Arkadin's stake in real estate for 10 percent of Kuzin's operation.

And just what was Stas Kuzin's operation? No one would speak about it openly, but there was no lack of rumors on the subject. Everything from running spent nuclear fuel rods for the big boys over in Moscow to white slave trading, drug trafficking, and prostitution was laid at Kuzin's doorstep. For his own part, Arkadin tended to dismiss the more outlandish speculation in favor of what he very well knew would make Kuzin money in Nizhny Tagil, namely, prostitution and drugs. Every man in the city had to get laid, and if they had any money at all, drugs were far preferable to beer and bathtub vodka.

Once again, want never appeared on Arkadin's horizon, only need. He needed to do more than survive in this city of permasoot, violence, and black lung disease. He had come as far as he could on his own. He made enough to sustain himself here, but not enough to break away to Moscow where he needed to go to grab life's richest opportunities. Outside, the rings of hell rose up: brick smokestacks, vigorously belching particle-laden smoke, iron guard towers of the brutal prison *zonas*, bristling with assault rifles, powerful spotlights, and bellowing sirens.

In here he was locked inside his own brutal *zona* with Stas Kuzin. Arkadin gave the only sensible answer. He said yes, and so entered the ninth level of hell.

# 31

While on line for passport control in Munich, Bourne phoned Specter, who assured him everything was in readiness. Moments later he came in range of the first set of the airport's CCTV cameras. Instantly his image was picked up by the software employed at Semion Icoupov's headquarters, and before he'd finished his call to the professor he'd been identified.

At once Icoupov was called, who ordered his people stationed in Munich to move from standby to action, thus alerting both the airport personnel and the Immigration people under Icoupov's control. The man directing the incoming passengers to the different cordoned-off lanes leading to the Immigration booths received a photo of Bourne on his computer screen just in time to indicate Bourne should go to booth 3.

The Immigration officer manning booth 3 listened to the voice coming through the electronic device in his ear. When the man identified to him as Jason Bourne handed over his passport the officer asked him the usual questions – 'How long do you intend to remain in Germany? Is your visit business or pleasure?' – while paging through the passport. He moved it away from the window, passed the photo under a humming purple light. As he did so, he pressed a small metallic disk the thickness of a human nail into the inside back cover of the passport. Then he closed the booklet, smoothed its front and back covers, and handed it back to Bourne.

'Have a pleasant stay in Munich,' he said without a trace of emotion or interest. He was already looking beyond Bourne to the next passenger in line.

As in Sheremetyevo, Bourne had the sense that he was under physical surveillance. He changed taxis twice when he arrived at the seething center of the city. In Marienplatz, a large open square from which the historic Marian column ascended, he walked past medieval cathedrals, through flocks of pigeons, lost himself within the crowds of guided tours, gawping at the sugar-icing architecture and the looming twin domes of the Frauenkirche, cathedral of the archbishop of Munich-Freising, the symbol of the city.

He inserted himself in a tour group gathered around a government building in which was inset the city's official shield, depicting a monk with hands spread wide. The tour leader was telling her charges that the German name, *München*, stemmed from an Old High German word meaning 'monks.' In 1158 or thereabouts, the current duke of Saxony and Bavaria built a bridge over the Isar River, connecting the saltworks, for which the growing city would soon become famous, with a settlement of Benedictine monks. He installed a tollbooth on the bridge, which became a vital link in the Salt Route in and out of the high Bavarian plains on which Munich was built, and a mint in which to house his profits. The modern-day mercantile city was not so far removed from its medieval beginnings.

When Bourne was certain he wasn't being shadowed, he slipped away from the group and boarded a taxi, which dropped him off six blocks from the Wittelsbach Palace.

According to the professor, Kirsch said he'd rather meet Bourne in a public setting. He chose the State Museum for Egyptian Art on Hofgartenstrasse, which was housed within the massive rococo façade of the Wittelsbach Palace. Bourne took a full circuit of the streets around the palace, checking once more for tags, but he couldn't recall being in Munich before. He didn't have that eerie sense of déjà vu that meant he had returned to a place he couldn't remember. Therefore, he knew local tags would have the advantage of terrain. There might be a dozen places to hide around the palace that he didn't know about.

Shrugging, he entered the museum. The metal detector was staffed by a pair of armed security guards, who were also setting aside backpacks and picking through handbags. On either side of the vestibule was a pair of basalt statues of the Egyptian god Horus – a falcon with a disk of the sun on his forehead – and his mother, Isis. Instead of walking directly to the exhibits, Bourne turned, stood behind the statue of Horus, watching for ten minutes as people came and went. He noted everyone between twenty-five and fifty, memorizing their faces. There were seventeen in all.

He then made his way past a female armed guard, into the exhibition halls, where he found Kirsch precisely where he told Specter he'd be, scrutinizing an ancient carving of a lion's head. He recognized Kirsch from the photo Specter had sent him, a snapshot of the two men standing together on the university campus. The professor's courier was a wiry little man with a shiny bald skull and black eyebrows as thick as caterpillars. He had pale blue eyes that darted this way and that as if on gimbals.

Bourne went past him, ostensibly looking at several sarcophagi while using his peripheral vision to check for any of the seventeen people who'd entered the museum after him. When no one presented themselves, he retraced his steps.

Kirsch did not turn as Bourne came up beside him, but said, 'I know it sounds ridiculous, but doesn't this sculpture remind you of something?'

'The Pink Panther,' Bourne said, both because it was the proper code response, and because the sculpture did look astonishingly like the modern-day cartoon icon.

Kirsch nodded. 'Glad you made it without incident.' He handed over the keys to his apartment, the code for the front door, and detailed directions to it from the museum. He looked relieved, as if he were handing over his burdensome life rather than his home.

'There are some features of my apartment I want to talk to you about.'

As Kirsch spoke they moved on to a granite sculpture of the kneeling Senenmut, from the time of the Eighteenth Dynasty.

'The ancient Egyptians knew how to live,' Kirsch observed. 'They weren't afraid of death. To them, it was just another journey, not to be undertaken lightly, but still they knew there was something waiting for them after life.' He put his hand out, as if to touch the statue or perhaps to absorb some of its potency. 'Look at this statue. Life still glows within it, thousands of years later. For centuries the Egyptians had no equal.'

'Until they were conquered by the Romans.'

'And yet,' Kirsch said, 'it was the Romans who were changed by the Egyptians. A century after the Ptolemys and Julius Caesar ruled from Alexandria, it was Isis, the Egyptian goddess of revenge and rebellion, who was worshipped throughout the Roman Empire. In fact, it's all too likely that the early Christian Church founders, unable to do away with her or her followers, transmogrified her, stripped her of her war-like nature, and made from her the perfectly peaceful Virgin Mary.'

'Leonid Arkadin could use a little less Isis and a lot more Virgin Mary,' Bourne mused.

Kirsch raised his eyebrows. 'What do you know of this man?'

'I know a lot of dangerous people are terrified of him.'

'With good reason,' Kirsch said. 'The man's a homicidal maniac. He was born and raised in Nizhny Tagil, a hotbed of homicidal maniacs.'

'So I've heard,' Bourne nodded.

'And there he would have stayed had it not been for Tarkanian.'

Bourne's ears pricked up. He'd assumed that Maslov had put his man in Tarkanian's apartment because that's where Gala was living. 'Wait a minute, what does Tarkanian have to do with Arkadin?'

'Everything. Without Mischa Tarkanian, Arkadin would never have escaped Nizhny Tagil. It was Tarkanian who brought him to Moscow.'

'Are they both members of the Black Legion?'

'So I've been given to understand,' Kirsch said. 'But I'm only an artist; the clandestine life has given me an ulcer. If I didn't need the money – I'm a singularly unsuccessful artist, I'm afraid – I never would have stayed in this long. This was to be my last favor for Specter.' His eyes continued to dart to the left and right. 'Now that Arkadin has murdered Dieter Heinrich, *last favor* has taken on a new and ter-rifying meaning.'

Bourne was now on full alert. Specter had assumed that Tarkanian was Black Legion, and Kirsch just confirmed it. But Maslov had denied Tarkanian's affiliation with the terrorist group. Someone was lying.

Bourne was about to ask Kirsch about the discrepancy when out of the corner of his eye he spotted one of the men who'd come into the museum just after he had. The man had paused for a moment in the vestibule, as if orienting himself, then strode purposefully off into the exhibition hall.

Because the man was close enough to overhear them in the museum's hushed atmosphere, Bourne took Kirsch's arm. 'Come this way,' he said, leading the German contact into another room, which was dominated by a calcite statue of twins from the Eighth Dynasty. It was chipped, time-worn, dating from 2390 BC.

Pushing Kirsch behind the statue, Bourne stood like a sentinel, watching the other man's movements. The man glanced up, saw that Bourne and Kirsch were no longer at the statue of Senenmut, and looked casually around.

'Stay here,' Bourne whispered to Kirsch.

'What is it?' There was a slight quaver in Kirsch's voice, but he looked stalwart enough. 'Is Arkadin here?'

'Whatever happens,' Bourne warned him, 'stay put. You'll be safe until I come get you.'

As Bourne moved around the far side of the Egyptian twins, the man entered the gallery. Bourne walked to the side opening and into the room beyond. The man, sauntering nonchalantly, took a quick look around and, as if seeing nothing of interest, followed Bourne.

This gallery held a number of high display cases but was dominated by a five-thousand-year-old stone statue of a woman with half her head sheared off. The antiquity was staggering, but Bourne had no time to appreciate it. Perhaps because it was toward the rear of the museum, the room was deserted, save for Bourne and the man, who was standing between Bourne and the one way in or out of the gallery.

Bourne placed himself behind a two-sided display case with a board in the center on which were hung small artifacts – sacred blue scarabs and gold jewelry. Because of a center gap in the board, Bourne could see the man, but the man remained unaware of his position.

Standing completely still, Bourne waited until the man began to come around the right side of the display case. Bourne moved quickly to his right, around the opposite side of the case, and rushed the man.

He shoved him against the wall, but the man maintained his balance. As he took up a defensive posture he pulled a ceramic knife from a sheath under his armpit, swung it back and forth to keep Bourne at bay.

Bourne feinted right, moved left in a semi-crouch. As he did so, he swung his right arm against the hand wielding the knife. His left hand grabbed the man by his throat. As the man tried to drive his knee into Bourne's belly, Bourne twisted to partially deflect the blow. In so doing, he lost his block on the knife hand and now the blade swept in toward the side of his neck. Bourne stopped it just before it struck, and there they stood, locked together in a kind of stalemate.

'Bourne,' the man finally got out. 'My name is Jens. I work for Dominic Specter.'

'Prove it,' Bourne said.

'You're here meeting with Egon Kirsch, so you can take his place when Leonid Arkadin comes looking for him.'

Bourne let up on his grip of Jens's neck. 'Put away your knife.'

Jens did as Bourne asked, and Bourne let go of him completely.

'Now where's Kirsch? I need to get him out of here and safely on a plane back to Washington.'

Bourne led him back into the adjoining gallery, to the statue of the twins.

'Kirsch, the gallery's clear. You can come out now.'

When the contact didn't appear, Bourne stepped behind the statue. Kirsch was there all right, crumpled on the floor, a bullet hole in the back of his head.

Semion Icoupov watched the receiver attuned to the electronic bug in Bourne's passport. As they approached the area of the Egyptian museum, he told the driver of his car to slow down. A keen sense of anticipation coursed through him: he'd decided to take Bourne by gunpoint into his car. It seemed the best way now to get him to listen to what Icoupov had to tell him.

At that moment his cell phone sounded with the ringtone he'd assigned to Arkadin's number, and while on the lookout for Bourne he put the phone to his ear.

'I'm in Munich,' Arkadin said in his ear. 'I rented a car, and I'm driving in from the airport.'

'Good. I've got an electronic tag on Jason Bourne, the man Our Friend has sent to retrieve the plans.'

'Where is he? I'll take care of him,' Arkadin said in his typical blunt way.

'No, no, I don't want him killed. I'll take care of Bourne. In the meantime, stay mobile. I'll be in touch shortly.'

Bourne, kneeling down beside Kirsch, examined the dead body.

'There's a metal detector out front,' Jens said. 'How the hell could someone bring a gun in here? Plus, there was no noise.'

Bourne turned Kirsch's head so the back of it caught the light. 'See here.' He pointed to the entry wound. 'And here. There's no exit wound, which there would have been with a shot fired at close range.' He stood up. 'Whoever killed him used a suppressor.' He went out of the gallery with a purposeful stride. 'And whoever killed him works here as a guard; the museum's security personnel are armed.'

'There are three of them,' Jens said, keeping pace behind Bourne.

'Right. Two on the metal detector, one roaming the galleries.'

In the vestibule, the two guards were at their station beside the metal detector. Bourne went up to one of them, said, 'I lost my cell phone somewhere in the museum and the guard in the second gallery said she'd help me locate it, but now I can't find her.'

'Petra,' the guard said. 'Yeah, she just took off for her lunch break.'

Bourne and Jens went through the front door, down the steps onto the sidewalk, where they looked left and right. Bourne saw a uniformed female figure walking fast down the block to their right, and he and Jens took off after her.

She disappeared around a corner, and the two men sprinted after her. As they neared the corner Bourne became aware of a sleek Mercedes sedan as it came abreast of them.

Icoupov was appalled to discover Bourne exiting the museum in the company of Franz Jens. Jens's appearance told him that his enemy wasn't leaving anything to chance. Jens's job was to keep Icoupov's people away from Bourne, so that Bourne had a clear shot at retrieving the attack plans. A certain dread gripped Icoupov. If Bourne was successful all was lost; his enemy would have won. He couldn't allow that to happen.

Leaning forward in the backseat, he drew a Luger.

'Pick up speed,' he told the driver.

Bracing himself against the door frame, he waited until the last instant before depressing the button that slid the window down. He took aim at the running figure of Jens, but Jens sensed him, slowed as he turned. With Bourne now safely three paces ahead, Icoupov squeezed off two shots in succession.

Jens slipped to one knee, skidded off the sidewalk as he went down. Icoupov fired a third shot, just to be sure Jens didn't survive the attack, then he slid the window up.

'Go!' he said to the driver.

The Mercedes shot forward, down the street, screeching away from the bloody body tangled in the gutter.

# 32

Rob Batt sat in his car, a pair of night-vision binoculars to his eyes, chewing over the recent past as if it were a piece of gum that had lost its flavor.

From the time that Batt had been called into Veronica Hart's office and confronted with his treacherous actions against CI, he'd gone numb. At the moment, he'd felt nothing for himself. Rather, his enmity toward Hart had morphed into pity. Or maybe, he had thought, he pitied himself. Like a novice, he'd stepped into a bear trap; he'd trusted people who never should have been trusted. LaValle and Halliday were going to have their way, he had absolutely no doubt of it. Filled with self-disgust, he'd begun his long night of drinking.

It wasn't until the morning after that Batt, waking up with the father of all hangovers, realized that there was something he could do about it. He thought about that for some time, while he swallowed aspirins for his pounding head, chasing them down with a glass of water and angostura bitters to calm his rebellious stomach.

It was then that the plan formed in his mind, unfolding like a flower to the rays of the sun. He was going to get his revenge for the humiliation LaValle and Kendall had caused him, and the real beauty part was this: If his scheme worked, if he brought them down, he'd resuscitate his own career, which was on life support.

Now, sitting behind the wheel of a rented car, he swept the street across from the Pentagon, on the lookout for General Kendall. Batt was canny enough to know better than to go after LaValle, because LaValle was too smart to make a mistake. The same, however, couldn't be said for the general. If Batt had learned one thing from his abortive association with the two it was that Kendall was a weak link. He was too tied to LaValle, too slavish in his attitude. He needed someone to tell him what to do. The desire to please was what made followers vulnerable; they made mistakes their leaders didn't.

He suddenly saw life the way it must appear to Jason Bourne. He knew the work that Bourne had done for Martin Lindros in Reykjavik and knew that Bourne had put himself on the line to find Lindros and bring him home. But like most of his former co-workers, Batt had conveniently dismissed Bourne's actions as collateral happenstance, choosing to stick to the common wisdom that Bourne was an out-of-control paranoid who needed to be stopped before he committed some heinous act that would disgrace CI. And yet, people in CI had had no compunction about using him when all else failed, coercing him into playing as their pawn. But at last he, Batt, was no one's pawn.

He saw General Kendall exit a side door of the building and, huddled in his trench-coat, hurry across the lot to his car. He kept the general in his sights as he put one hand on the keys he'd already inserted in the ignition. At the precise moment Kendall leaned his right shoulder forward to start his engine, Batt flipped his own ignition, so Kendall didn't hear another car start when his did.

As the general pulled out of the lot, Batt set aside the night glasses and put his car in gear. The night seemed quiet and still, but maybe that was simply a reflection of Batt's mood. He was a sentinel of the night, after all. He'd been trained by the Old Man himself; he'd always been proud of that fact. After his downfall, though, he realized that it was this pride that had distorted his thinking and his decision making. It was his pride that made him rebel against Veronica Hart, not because of anything she said or did – he hadn't even given her the chance – but because he'd been passed over. Pride was his weakness, one that LaValle had recognized and exploited. Twenty–twenty hindsight was a bitch, he thought as he followed Kendall toward the Fairfax area, but at least it provided the humility he needed to see how far he'd strayed from his sworn duties at CI.

He kept well back of the general's car, varying his distance and his lane the better to avoid detection. He doubted that Kendall would consider that he might be followed, but it paid to be cautious. Batt was determined to atone for the sin he'd committed against his own organization, against the memory of the Old Man.

Kendall turned in at an anonymous modern-looking building whose entire ground floor was taken up by the In-Tune health club. Batt observed the general park, take out a small gym bag, and enter the club. Nothing useful so far, but Batt had long ago learned to be patient. On stakeouts it seemed nothing came quickly or easily.

And then, because he had nothing better to do until Kendall reappeared, Batt stared at the IN-TUNE sign while he bit hunks off a Snickers bar. Why did that sign seem familiar? He knew he had never been inside, had never, in fact, been in this part of Fairfax. Maybe it was the name: *In-Tune*. Yes, he thought, it sounded maddeningly familiar, but for the life of him he couldn't think of why.

Fifty minutes had passed since Kendall had gone in; time to train his night glasses on the entrance. He watched people of all description and build come in and out. Most were solitary figures; occasionally two women came out talking, once a couple emerged, headed in tandem for their car.

Another fifteen minutes passed and still no Kendall. Batt had taken the glasses away from his eyes to give them a rest when he saw the gym door swing open. Fitting the binoculars back to his eyes he saw Rodney Feir step out into the night. *Are you kidding me?* Batt thought.

Feir ran his hand through his damp hair. And that's when Batt remembered why the name *In-Tune* was so familiar. All CI directors were required to post their whereabouts after hours so if they were needed the duty officer could calculate how long it would take them to get back to headquarters.

Watching Feir walk over and get into his car, Batt bit his lip. Of course it might be sheer coincidence that General Kendall used the same health club as Feir, but Batt knew that in his trade there was no such thing as coincidence.

His suspicion was borne out when Feir did not fire up his car, but sat silent and still behind the wheel. He was waiting for something, but what? Maybe, Batt thought, it was someone.

Ten minutes later, General Kendall emerged from the club. He looked neither to the right nor the left, but went immediately to his car, started it up, and began to back out of his space. Before he'd exited the lot, Feir started his car. Kendall turned right out of the lot and Feir followed.

Excitement flared in Batt's chest. *Game on!* he thought.

After the first two shots struck Jens, Bourne turned back toward him, but the third shot fired into Jens's head made him change his mind. He ran down the street, knowing the other man was dead, there was nothing he could do for him. He had to assume that Arkadin had followed Jens to the museum and had been lying in wait.

Turning the same corner as the museum guard, Bourne saw that she had hesitated, half turned to the sound of the shots. Then, seeing Bourne coming after her, she took off. She darted into an alley. Bourne, following, saw her vault up a corrugated steel fence, beyond which was a cleared building site bristling with heavy machinery. She grabbed hold of the top of the fence, levered herself up and over.

Bourne scaled the fence after her, jumping down onto the packed earth and concrete rubble on the other side. He saw her duck behind the mud-spattered flank of a bulldozer, and ran toward her. She swung up into the cab, slid behind the wheel, and fumbled with the ignition.

Bourne was quite close when the engine rumbled to life. Throwing the bulldozer into reverse, she backed up directly at him. She'd chosen a clumsy vehicle, and he leapt to one side, reached for a handhold, and swung up. The bulldozer lurched, the gears grinding as she struggled to shove it into first, but Bourne was already inside the cab.

She tried to draw her gun, but she was also trying to guide the bulldozer, and Bourne easily slapped the weapon away. It fell to the foot well, where he kicked it away from her. Then he reached over, turned off the engine. The moment he did that, the woman covered her face with her hands and burst into tears.

'This is your mess,' Deron said.

Soraya nodded. 'I know it is.'

'You came to us – Kiki and me.'

'I take full responsibility.'

'I think in this case,' Deron said, 'we have to share the responsibility. We could've said no, but we didn't. Now all of us – not just Tyrone and Jason – are in serious jeopardy.'

They were sitting in the den of Deron's house, a cozy room with a wraparound sofa that faced a stone fireplace and, above it, a large plasma TV. Drinks were set out on a low wooden table, but nobody had touched them. Deron and Soraya sat facing each other. Kiki was curled up in the corner like a cat.

'Tyrone's already totally fucked,' Soraya said. 'I saw what they're doing to him.'

'Hold on.' Deron sat forward. 'There's a difference between perception and reality. Don't let them skullfuck you. They're not going to risk damaging Tyrone; he's their only leverage to coerce you to bring Jason to them.'

Soraya, once again finding fear scattering her thoughts, reached over and poured herself a scotch. Rolling it around in the glass, she inhaled its complex aroma, which called to mind heather and butterscotch. She recalled Jason telling her how sights, scents, idioms, or tones of voice could trigger his hidden memories.

She took a sip of the scotch, felt it ignite a stream of fire down to her stomach. She wanted to be anywhere but here now; she wanted another life; but this was the life she'd chosen, these were the decisions she'd made. There was no help for it – she could not abandon her friends; she had to keep them safe. How to do that was the vexing question.

Deron was right about LaValle and Kendall. Taking her back down to the interrogation room was a psychological ploy. What they'd showed her was minimal, now that she thought about it. They were counting on her to imagine the worst, to let those thoughts prey on her until she gave in, called Jason so they could take him into custody and, like a show dog, present him to the president as proof that, having accomplished what numerous CI initiatives could not, LaValle deserved to take over and run CI.

She took another sip of scotch, aware that Deron and Kiki were silent, patiently waiting for her to work through the mistake she'd made and, coming through the other side, put it behind her. But she had to take the initiative, to formulate a plan of counterattack. That was what Deron meant when he said, *This is your mess.*

'The thing to do,' she said, slowly and carefully, 'is to beat LaValle at his own game.'

'And how do you propose to do that?' Deron said.

Soraya stared down at the dregs of her scotch. That was just it, she had no idea.

The silence stretched out, growing thicker and more deadly by the second. At last, Kiki uncurled herself, stood up, and said, 'I for one have had enough of this gloom and doom. Sitting around feeling angry and frustrated isn't helping Tyrone and it isn't helping us find a solution. I'm going out to have a good time at my friend's club.' She looked from Soraya to Deron and back again. 'So who's going to join me?'

The high–low wail of the police sirens came to Bourne as he sat beside the museum guard in the bulldozer. Up close, she looked younger than he had imagined. Her blond hair, which had been pulled back in a severe bun, had come loose. It flowed down around her pale face. Her eyes were large and liquid – red around the rims now from crying. There was something about them that made him think she'd been born sad.

'Take off your jacket,' he said.

'What?' The guard appeared totally confused.

Without saying anything, Bourne helped her off with her jacket. Pushing up the sleeves of her shirt, he checked the insides of her elbows, but found no Black Legion tattoo. Naked fear had joined the sadness in her eyes.

'What's your name?' he said softly.

'Petra-Alexandra Eichen,' she said in a quavery voice. 'But everyone calls me Petra.' She wiped at her eyes, and gave him a sideways look. 'Are you going to kill me now?'

The police sirens were very loud, and Bourne had a desire to get as far away from them as possible.

'Why would I do that?'

'Because I . . .' Her voice faltered and she choked, it seemed, on her own words, or on an emotion welling up. 'I shot your friend.'

'Why did you do that?'

'For money,' she said. 'I need money.'

Bourne believed her. She didn't act like a professional; she didn't talk like one, either. 'Who paid you?'

Fear distorted her expression, magnified her eyes until they seemed to goggle at him. 'I . . . I can't tell you. He made me promise, he said he'd kill me if I opened my mouth.'

Bourne heard raised voices, using the clipped jargon endemic to police the world over. They'd started their dragnet. He retrieved her gun, a Walther P22, the small caliber being the only option for a silent kill in an enclosed space, even with a suppressor.

'Where's the suppressor?'

'I threw it down a storm drain,' she said, 'as I was instructed to do.'

'Continuing to follow orders isn't going to help. The people who hired you are going to kill you anyway,' he said as he dragged her down from the bulldozer. 'You're in way over your head.'

She gave a little moan and tried to break away from him.

He grabbed her. 'If you want, I'll let you go straight to the cops. They'll be here any minute.'

Her mouth worked, but nothing intelligible came out.

Voices came to him, more distinct now. The police were on the other side of the corrugated wall. He pulled her in the opposite direction. 'Do you know another way out of here?'

Petra nodded, pointing. She and Bourne ran diagonally across the yard, dodging heavy equipment as they picked their way through the rubble and around deep holes in the earth. Without turning around, Bourne could tell that the cops had entered the far side of the yard. He pushed Petra's head down as he himself bent over to keep them both from being spotted. Beyond a crane, a crew chief's trailer was set up on concrete blocks. Temporary electric lines were strung into it from just above the tin roof.

Petra threw herself headlong under the trailer, and Bourne followed. The blocks set the trailer just high enough for them to worm their way on their bellies to the far side, where Bourne saw that a gap had been cut in the chain-link fence.

Crawling through the gap, they found themselves in a quiet alley filled with industrial-size garbage bins and a Dumpster filled with broken tiles, jagged blocks of terrazzo, and pieces of twisted metal, no doubt from whatever buildings had once stood in the now empty space behind them.

'This way,' Petra whispered as she took them out of the alley and down a residential street. Around the corner, she went to a car and opened it with a set of keys.

'Give me the keys,' Bourne said. 'They'll be looking for you.'

He caught them in midair, and they both got in. A block away they passed a cruising police car. The sudden tension caused Petra's hands to tremble in her lap.

'We're going right past them,' Bourne said. 'Don't look at them.'

Nothing further passed between them until Bourne said, 'They've turned around. They're coming after us.'

# 33

'I'm going to drop you off somewhere,' Arkadin said. 'I don't want you in the middle of whatever's going to come.'

Devra, in the passenger's seat of the rented BMW, shot him a skeptical look. 'That doesn't sound like you at all.'

'No? Who does it sound like?'

'We still have to get Egon Kirsch.'

Arkadin turned a corner. They were in the center of the city, a place filled with old cathedrals and palaces. The place looked like something out of Grimm's Fairy Tales.

'There's been a complication,' he said. 'The opposition's king has entered the chess match. His name is Jason Bourne and he's here in Munich.'

'All the more reason why I should stay with you.' Devra checked the action on one of the two Lugers that Arkadin had picked up from one of Icoupov's local agents. 'A crossfire has many benefits.'

Arkadin laughed. 'There's no lack of fire to you.'

That was another thing that drew him to her – she wasn't afraid of the male fire burning in her belly. But he had promised her – and himself – that he would protect her. It had been a very long time since he'd said that to anyone, and even though he'd sworn never to make that promise again, he'd done just that. And strange to say, he felt good about it; in fact, there was a sense now when he was around her that he'd stepped out of the shadows he'd been born into, that had been tattooed into his flesh by so many violent incidents. For the first time in his life he felt as if he could take pleasure in the sun on his face, in the wind lifting Devra's hair behind her like a mane, that he could walk down the street with her and not feel as if he was living in another dimension, that he hadn't just arrived here from another planet.

As they stopped at a red light, he glanced at her. Sunlight was streaming into the interior, turning her face the palest shade of pink. At that precise moment he felt something rush out of him and into her, and she turned as if she felt it, too, and she smiled at him.

The light turned green and he accelerated through the cross street. His cell phone buzzed. A glance down at the number of the incoming call told him that Gala was calling. He didn't answer; he had no wish to talk to her now, or ever, for that matter.

Three minutes later, he received a text message. It read: MISCHA DEAD. KILLED BY JASON BOURNE.

*

Having followed Rodney Feir and General Kendall over the Key Bridge into Washington proper, Rob Batt made sure his long-lens SLR Nikon was fully loaded with fast film. He shot a series of digital photos with a compact camera, but these were only for reference, because they could be Photoshopped in a heartbeat. To forestall any suspicion that the images might be manipulated, he'd present the undeveloped roll of film to . . . well, this was his real problem. For a legitimate reason he was persona non grata at CI. It was astonishing how quickly years-long associations vanished. But now he realized he'd mistaken the camaraderie he'd developed with what had been his fellow directors for friendship. As far as they were concerned he no longer existed, so going to them with any alleged evidence that the NSA had turned yet another CI officer would be either ignored or laughed at. Trying to approach Veronica Hart was similarly out of the question. Assuming he could ever get to her – which he doubted – speaking to her now would be like groveling. Batt had never groveled in his life, and he wasn't going to now.

Then he laughed out loud at how easy it was to become self-deluded. Why should any of his former colleagues want anything to do with him? He'd betrayed them, abandoned them for the enemy. If he were in their shoes – and how he wished he were! – he'd feel the same venomous animosity toward someone who'd sold him out, which was why he'd embarked on this mission to destroy LaValle and Kendall. They'd sold him out – hung him out to dry as soon as it suited their purposes. The moment he came on board, they'd taken control of Typhon away from him.

*Venomous animosity.* That was an excellent phrase, he thought, one that precisely defined his feelings toward LaValle and Kendall. He knew, deep down, that hating them was the same as hating himself. But he couldn't hate himself; that was self-defeating. At this very moment he couldn't believe he'd sunk so low as to defect to the NSA. He'd gone through his line of thinking over and over, and now it seemed to him as if someone else, some stranger, had made that decision. It hadn't been him, it couldn't have been him, ergo, LaValle and Kendall had made him do it. For that they had to pay the ultimate price.

The two men were on the move again, and Batt headed out after them. After a ten-minute drive, the two cars ahead of him pulled into the crowded parking lot of The Glass Slipper. As Batt passed by, Feir and Kendall got out of their respective cars and went inside. Batt drove around the block, parked on a side street. Reaching into the glove compartment, he took out a tiny Leica camera, the kind used by the Old Man in his youthful days of surveillance. It was the old spy standby, as dependable as it was easy to conceal. Batt loaded it with fast film, put it in the breast pocket of his shirt along with the digital camera, and got out of the car.

The night was filled with a gritty wind. Refuse spiraled up from the gutter, only to come to rest in a different place. Jamming his hands in his coat pockets, Batt hurried down the block and into The Glass Slipper. A slide guitarist was up on stage, wailing the blues, warming up for the feature act, a high-powered band with several hit CDs under its belt.

He'd heard about the club by reputation only. He knew, for instance, that it was owned by Drew Davis, primarily because Davis was a larger-than-life character who continually inserted himself into the political and economic affairs of African Americans in the district. Thanks to his influence, homeless shelters had become safer places for their residents, halfway houses had been built; he made it a point to hire ex-cons. He was so cannily public about these hirings that the ex-cons had no choice but to make the most of their second chances.

What Batt didn't know about was the Slipper's back room, so he was puzzled when, after a full circuit of the space, plus an expedition to the men's room, he could find no trace of either Feir or the general.

Fearing that they'd slipped out the back, he returned to the parking lot, only to find their cars where they'd left them. Back in the Slipper, he took another trip through the crowd, figuring he must have missed them somehow. Still, there was no sign, but as he neared the rear of the space he spotted someone talking to a muscled black man the approximate size of a refrigerator. After a small bout of jawing, Mr. Muscle opened a door Batt hadn't noticed before, and the man slipped through. Guessing this was where Feir and Kendall must have gone, Batt edged his way toward Mr. Muscle and the door.

It was then that he saw Soraya walk through the front door.

Bourne almost stripped the car's gears trying to outrun the police car on their tail.

'Take it easy,' Petra said, 'or you'll tear my poor car apart.'

He wished he'd taken a longer look at the map of the city. A street blocked off with wooden sawhorses flashed by on their left. The paving had been torn up, leaving the heavily pitted and cracked underlayer, the worst parts of which were in the process of being excavated.

'Hold on tight,' Bourne said as he reversed, then turned into the street and drove the car through the sawhorses, cracking one and scattering the others. The car hit the underlayer, jounced down the street at what seemed a reckless speed. It felt as if the vehicle were being machine-gunned by a pile driver. Bourne's teeth rattled in his head, and Petra struggled to keep from crying out.

Behind them, the police car was having even more difficulty keeping to a straight path. It jerked back and forth to avoid the deepest of the holes gouged in the roadbed. Putting on another burst of speed, Bourne was able to lengthen the distance between them. But then he glanced ahead. A cement truck was parked crosswise at the other end of the street. If they kept going there was no way to avoid crashing into it.

Bourne kept the speed on as the cement truck loomed larger and larger. The police car was coming up fast behind them.

'What are you doing?' Petra screamed. 'Are you out of your fucking mind?'

At that moment, Bourne threw the car into neutral, stepped on the brake. He immediately changed into reverse, took his foot off the brake, and pressed the gas pedal to the floor. The car shuddered, its engine screaming. Then the transmission locked into place, and the car flew backward. The police car came on, its driver frozen in shock. Bourne swerved around it as the vehicle raced forward into the side of the cement truck.

Bourne wasn't even looking. He was busy steering the car back down the street in reverse. Blasting past the shattered sawhorses, he turned, braked, put the car into first, and drove off.

'What the hell are you doing here?' Noah said. 'You should be on your way to Damascus.'

'I'm due to take off in four hours.' Moira put her hands in her pockets so he wouldn't see that they were curled into fists. 'You haven't answered my question.'

Noah sighed. 'It doesn't make any difference.'

Her laugh had a bitter taste to it. 'Why am I not surprised?'

'Because,' Noah said, 'you've been with Black River long enough to know how we operate.'

They were walking down Kaufingerstrasse in the center of Munich, a heavily trafficked area just off the Marienplatz. Turning in at the sign for the Augustiner Bierkeller, they entered a long, dim cathedral-like space that smelled powerfully of beer and boiled wurst. The hubbub of noise was just right for masking a private conversation. Crossing the red flagstone floor, they chose a table in one of the rooms, sat on wooden benches. The person closest to them was an old man sucking on a pipe while he leisurely read the paper.

Moira and Noah both ordered a Hefeweizen, a wheat beer still clouded with unfiltered yeast, from a waitress dressed in the regional Dirndlkleid, a long, wide skirt and low-cut blouse. She had an apron around her waist, along with a decorative purse.

'Noah,' Moira said when the beers had been served, 'I don't hold any illusions about why we do what we do, but how do you expect me to ignore this intel I got right from the source?'

Noah took a long draw of his Hefeweizen, fastidiously wiped his lips before answering. Then he began to tick off points on his fingers. 'First, this man Hauser told you that the flaw in the software is virtually undetectable. Second, what he told you isn't verifiable. He might simply be a disgruntled employee trying to get revenge on Kaller Steelworks. Have you considered that possibility?'

'We could run our own tests on the software.'

'No time. There's less than two days before the LNG tanker is scheduled to dock at the terminal.' He continued ticking off points. 'Third, we couldn't do anything without alerting NextGen, who would then turn around and confront Kaller Steelworks, which would put us in the middle of a nasty situation. And, fourth and finally, what part of the sentence *We've officially notified NextGen that we've withdrawn from the project* do you not understand?'

Moira sat back for a moment and took a deep breath. 'This is solid intel, Noah. It could lead to the situation we were most worried about: a terrorist attack. How can you —'

'You've already taken several steps over the line, Moira,' Noah said sharply. 'Get your tail on that plane and your head into your new assignment, or you're through at Black River.'

'It's better for the moment that we don't meet,' Icoupov said.

Arkadin was seething, barely holding down his rage, and only then because Devra, canny witch that she was, dug her fingernails into the palm of his hand. She understood him; no questions, no probing, no trying to pick over his past like a vulture.

'What about the plans?' He and Devra were sitting in a miserable, smoke-filled bar, in a run-down part of the city.

'I'll pick them up from you now.' Icoupov's voice sounded thin and far away over the cell phone, even though there could be only a mile or two separating them. 'I'm following Bourne. I'm going after him myself.'

Arkadin didn't want to hear it. 'I thought that was my job.'

'Your job is essentially over. You have the plans and you've terminated Pyotr's network.'

'All except Egon Kirsch.'

'Kirsch has already been disposed of,' Icoupov said.

'I'm the one who terminates the targets. I'll give you the plans and then take care of Bourne.'

'I told you, Leonid Danilovich, I don't want Bourne terminated.'

Arkadin made an anguished animal sound under his breath. *But Bourne has to be terminated,* he thought. Devra dug her claws deeper into his flesh, so that he could smell the sweet, coppery scent of his own blood. *And I have to do it. He murdered Mischa.*

'Are you listening to me?' Icoupov said sharply.

Arkadin stirred within his web of rage. 'Yes, sir, always. However, I must insist that you tell me where you'll be when you accost Bourne. This is security, for your own safety. I won't stand helplessly by while something unforeseen happens to you.'

'Agreed,' Icoupov said after a moment's hesitation. 'At the moment, he's on the move, so I have time to get the plans from you.' He gave Arkadin an address. 'I'll be there in fifteen minutes.'

'It'll take me a bit longer,' Arkadin said.

'Within the half hour then. The moment I know where I'll be intercepting Bourne, you'll know. Does that satisfy you, Leonid Danilovich?'

'Completely.'

Arkadin folded away his phone, disentangled himself from Devra, and went up to the bar. 'A double Oban on rocks.'

The bartender, a huge man with tattooed arms, squinted at him. 'What's an Oban?'

'It's a single-malt scotch, you moron.'

The bartender, polishing an old-fashioned glass, grunted. 'What does this look like, the prince's palace? We don't have single-malt anything.'

Arkadin reached over, snatched the glass out of the bartender's hands, and smashed it bottom-first into his nose. Then, as blood started to gush, he hauled the dazed man over the bar top and proceeded to beat him to a pulp.

'I can't go back to Munich,' Petra said. 'Not for a while, anyway. That's what he told me.'

'Why would you jeopardize your job to kill someone?' Bourne said.

'Please!' She glanced at him. 'A hamster couldn't live on what they paid me in that shithole.'

She was behind the wheel, driving on the autobahn. They had already passed the outskirts of the city. Bourne didn't mind; he needed to stay out of Munich himself until the furor over Egon Kirsch's death died down. The authorities would find someone else's ID on Kirsch, and though Bourne had no doubt they'd eventually find out his real identity, he hoped by that time to have retrieved the plans from

Arkadin and be flying back to Washington. In the meantime the police would be searching for him as a witness to the murders of both Kirsch and Jens.

'Sooner or later,' Bourne said, 'you're going to have to tell me who hired you.'

Petra said nothing, but her hands trembled on the wheel, an aftermath of their harrowing chase.

'Where are we going?' Bourne said. He wanted to keep her engaged in conversation. He felt that she needed to connect with him on some personal level in order to open up. He had to get her to tell him who had ordered her to kill Egon Kirsch. That might answer the question of whether he was connected to the man who'd gunned down Jens.

'Home,' she said. 'A place I never wanted to go back to.'

'Why is that?'

'I was born in Munich because my mother traveled there to give birth to me, but I'm from Dachau.' She meant the town, of course, after which the adjacent Nazi concentration camp had been named. 'No parent wants *Dachau* to appear on their child's birth certificate, so when their time comes the women check into a Munich hospital.' Hardly surprising: Almost two hundred thousand people were exterminated during the camp's life, the longest-standing of the war, since it was the first built, becoming the prototype for all the other KZ camps.

The town itself, situated along the Amper River, lay some twelve miles northwest of Munich. It was unexpectedly bucolic, with its narrow cobbled streets, old-fashioned street lamps, and quiet tree-lined lanes.

When Bourne observed that most of the people they passed looked contented enough, Petra laughed unpleasantly. 'They go around in a permanent fog, hating that their little town has such a murderous burden to carry.'

She drove through the center of Dachau, then turned north until they reached what once had been the village of Etzenhausen. There, on a desolate hill known as the Leitenberg, was a graveyard, lonely and utterly deserted. They got out of the car, walked past the stone stela with the sculpted Star of David. The stone was scarred, furry with blue lichen; the overhanging firs and hemlocks blocked out the sky even on such a bright midwinter afternoon.

As they walked slowly among the gravestones, she said, 'This is the KZ-Friedhof, the concentration camp cemetery. Through most of Dachau's life, the corpses of the Jews were piled up and burned in ovens, but toward the end when the camp ran out of coal, the Nazis had to do something with the corpses, so they brought them up here.' She spread her arms wide. 'This is all the memorial the Jewish victims got.'

Bourne had been in many cemeteries before, and had found them peculiarly peaceful. Not KZ-Friedhof, where a sensation of constant movement, ceaseless murmuring made his skin crawl. The place was alive, howling in its restless silence. He paused, squatted down, and ran his fingertips over the words engraved on a headstone. They were so eroded it was impossible to read them.

'Did you ever think that the man you shot today might have been a Jew?' he said.

She turned on him sharply. 'I told you I needed the money. I did it out of necessity.'

Bourne looked around them. 'That's what the Nazis said when they buried their last victims here.'

A flash of anger momentarily burned away the sadness in her eyes. 'I hate you.'

'Not nearly as much as you hate yourself.' He rose, handed her back her gun. 'Here, why don't you shoot yourself and end it all?'

She took the gun, aimed it at him. 'Why don't I just shoot you?'

'Killing me will only make matters worse for you. Besides . . .' Bourne opened up one palm to show her the bullets he'd taken out of her weapon.

With a disgusted sound, Petra holstered her gun. Her face and hands looked greenish in what light filtered through the evergreens.

'You can make amends for what you did today,' Bourne said. 'Tell me who hired you.'

Petra eyed him skeptically. 'I won't give you the money, if that's what you're angling for.'

'I have no interest in your money,' Bourne said. 'But I think the man you shot was going to tell me something I needed to know. I suspect that's why you were hired to kill him.'

Some of the skepticism leached out of her face. 'Really?'

Bourne nodded.

'I didn't *want* to kill him,' she said. 'You understand that.'

'You walked up to him, put the gun to his head, and pulled the trigger.'

Petra looked away, at nothing in particular. 'I don't want to think about it.'

'Then you're no better than anyone else in Dachau.'

Tears spilled over, she covered her face with her hands, and her shoulders shook. The sounds she made were like those Bourne had heard on Leitenberg.

At length, Petra's crying jag was spent. Wiping her reddened eyes with the backs of her hands, she said, 'I wanted to be a poet, you know? I always equated being a poet with being a revolutionary. I, a German, wanted to change the world or, at least, do something to change the way the world saw us, to do something to scoop that core of guilt out of us.'

'You should have become an exorcist.'

It was a joke, but such was her mood that she found nothing funny in it. 'That would be perfect, wouldn't it?' She looked at him with eyes still filled with tears. 'Is it so naive to want to change the world?'

'*Impractical* might be a better word.'

She cocked her head. 'You're a cynic, aren't you?' When he didn't answer, she went on. 'I don't think it's naive to believe that words – that what you write – can change things.'

'Why aren't you writing then,' he said, 'instead of shooting people for money? That's no way to earn a living.'

She was silent for so long, he wondered whether she'd heard him.

At last, she said, 'Fuck it, I was hired by a man named Spangler Wald – he's just past being a boy, really, no more than twenty-one or -two. I'd seen him around the pubs; we had coffee together once or twice. He said he was attending the university, majoring in entropic economics, whatever that is.'

'I don't think anyone can major in entropic economics,' Bourne said.

'Figures.' Petra was still sniffling. 'I have to get my bullshit meter recalibrated.' She shrugged. 'I never was good with people; I'm better off communing with the dead.'

Bourne said, 'You can't take on the grief and rage of so many people without being buried alive.'

She looked off at the rows of crumbling headstones. 'What else can I do? They're forgotten now. Here's where the truth lies. If you omit the truth, isn't that worse than a lie?'

When he didn't answer, she gave a quick twitch of her shoulders and turned around. 'Now that you've been here, I want to show you what the tourists see.'

She led him back to her car, drove down the deserted hill to the official Dachau memorial.

There was a pall over what was left of the camp buildings, as if the noxious emissions of the coal-fired incinerators still rose and fell on the thermals, like carrion birds still searching for the dead. An ironwork sculpture, a harrowing interpretation of skeletal prisoners made to resemble the barbed wire that had imprisoned them, greeted them as they drove in. Inside what had once been the main administrative building was a mock-up of the cells, display cases of shoes and other inexpressibly sad items, all that was left of the inmates.

'These signs,' Petra said. 'Do you see any mention of how many Jews were tortured and lost their lives there? 'One hundred and ninety-three thousand *people* lost their lives here,' the signs say. There's no expiation in this. We're still hiding from ourselves; we're still a land of Jew-haters, no matter how often we try to stifle the impulse with righteous anger, as if we have a right to be the aggrieved ones.'

Bourne might have told her that nothing in life is as simple as that, except he deemed it better to let her fury burn itself out. Clearly, she couldn't vent these views to anyone else.

She took him on a tour of the ovens, which seemed sinister even so many years after their use. They seemed alive, appeared to shimmer, to be part of an alternate universe overflowing with unspeakable horror. At length, they passed out of the crematorium and arrived at a long room, the walls of which were covered with letters, some written by prisoners, others by families desperate for news of their loved ones, as well as other notes, drawings, and more formal letters of inquiry. All were in German; none had been translated into other languages.

Bourne read them all. The aftermath of despair, atrocities, and death hung in these rooms, unable to escape. There was a different kind of silence here than the one on the Leitenberg. He was aware of the soft scuff of shoe soles, the whisper of sneakers as tourists dragged themselves from one exhibit to another. It was as if the accumulated inhumanity stifled the ability to speak, or perhaps it was that words – any words – were both inadequate and superfluous.

They moved slowly down the room. He could see Petra's lips move as she read letter after letter. Near the end of the wall, one caught his eye, quickened his pulse. A sheet of paper, obviously stationery, contained a handwritten text complaining that the author had developed what he claimed was a gas far more effective than Zyklon-B, but that no one at Dachau administration had seen fit to answer him. Possibly that was because the gas was never used at Dachau. However, what interested Bourne far more was that the stationery was imprinted with the wheel of three horses' heads joined in the center by the SS death's head.

Petra came up beside him, now her brows knitted together in a frown. 'That's damn familiar.'

He turned to her. 'What do you mean?'

'There was someone I used to know – Old Pelz. He said he lived in town, but I think he was homeless. He'd come down to the Dachau air raid shelter to sleep, especially in winter.' She pushed a stray lock of hair behind one ear. 'He used to babble all the time, you know how crazy people do, as if he was talking to someone else. I remember him showing me a patch with that same insignia. He was talking about something called the Black Legion.'

Bourne's pulse began to pound. 'What did he say?'

She shrugged.

'You hate the Nazis so much,' he said, 'I wonder if you know that some things they gave birth to still exist.'

'Yeah, sure, like the skinheads.'

He pointed at the insignia. 'The Black Legion still exists, it's still a danger, even more so than when Old Pelz knew it.'

Petra shook her head. 'He talked on and on. I never knew whether he was speaking to me or to himself.'

'Can you take me to him?'

'Sure, but who knows whether he's still alive. He drank like a fish.'

Ten minutes later Petra drove down Augsburgerstrasse, heading for the foot of a hill known as Karlsburg. 'Fucking ironic,' she said bitterly, 'that the one place I despise the most is now the safest place for me.'

She pulled into the lot outside the St. Jakob parish church. Its octagonal baroque tower could be seen throughout the town. Next door was Hörhammer's department store. 'You see there at the side of Hörhammer's,' she said as they clambered out of the car, 'those steps lead down to the huge air raid bunker built into the hill, but you can't get in that way.'

Leading him up the steps into St. Jakob, she led him across the Renaissance interior, past the choir. Adjacent to the sacristy was an unobtrusive dark wooden door, behind which lay a flight of stone stairs curving down to the crypt, which was surprisingly small, considering the size of the church above it.

But as Petra quickly showed him, there was a reason for the size: Beyond it lay a labyrinth of rooms and corridors.

'The bunker,' she said, flicking on a string of bare lightbulbs affixed to the stone wall on their right. 'Here is where my grandparents fled when your country bombed the shit out of the unofficial capital of the Third Reich.' She was speaking of Munich, but Dachau was close enough to feel the brunt of the American air force raids.

'If you hate your country so much,' Bourne said, 'why don't you leave?'

'Because,' Petra said, 'I also love it. It's the mystery of being German – proud but self-hating.' She shrugged. 'What can you do? You play the hand fate deals you.'

Bourne knew how that felt. He looked around. 'You're familiar with this place?'

She sighed heavily, as if her fury had left her spent. 'When I was a child my parents took me to Sunday Mass every week. They're God-fearing people. What a joke! Didn't God turn his face away from this place years ago?

'Anyway, one Sunday I was so bored I snuck away. In those days, I was obsessed with death. Can you blame me? I grew up with the stench of it in my nostrils.' She looked up at him. 'Can you believe that I'm the only one I know who ever visited the memorial? Do you think my parents ever did? My brothers, my aunts and uncles, my classmates? Please! They don't even want to admit it exists.'

Seemingly weary again. 'So I came down here to commune with the dead, but I didn't see enough of them, so I pushed on and what did I find? Dachau's bunker.'

She put her hand on the wall, moved it along the rough-cut stone as caressingly as if it were a lover's flank. 'This became my place, my own private world. I was only happy underground, in the company of the one hundred and ninety-three thousand dead. I felt them. I believed that the soul of each and every one of them was trapped here. It was so unfair, I thought. I spent my time trying to figure out how to free them.'

'I think the only way to do that,' Bourne said, 'is to free yourself.'

She gestured. 'Old Pelz's crash pad is this way.'

As they picked their way along a tunnel, she said, 'It's not too far. He liked to be near the crypt. He thought a couple of those old folks were his friends. He'd sit and talk to them for hours, drinking away, just as if they were alive and he could see them. Who knows? Maybe he could. Stranger things have happened.'

After a short time, the tunnel opened out into a series of rooms. The odors of whiskey and stale sweat came to them.

'It's the third room on the left,' Petra said.

But before they reached it, the doorway was filled with a hulking body topped by a head like a bowling ball with hair standing up like the quills of a porcupine. Old Pelz's mad eyes looked them over.

'Who goes there?' His voice was as thick a fog.

'It's me, Herr Pelz. Petra Eichen.'

But Old Pelz was looking in horror at the gun on her hip. 'The fuck it is!' Hefting a shotgun, he yelled, 'Nazi sympathizers!' and fired.

# 34

Soraya entered The Glass Slipper behind Kiki and ahead of Deron. Kiki had called ahead, and no sooner were they all inside than the owner, Drew Davis, came waddling over like Scrooge McDuck. He was a grizzled old man with white hair that stood on end as if it were shocked to see he was still alive. He had an animated face with mischievous eyes, a nose like a wad of chewed-up gum, and a broad smile honed to perfection on TV ops and stumping for local politicos, as well as his good works throughout the poorer neighborhoods of the district. But he possessed a warmth that was genuine. He had a way of looking at you when you spoke with him that made you feel he was listening to you alone.

He embraced Kiki while she kissed him on both cheeks and called him 'Papa.' Later, after the introductions, when they were seated at a prime table that Drew Davis had reserved for them, after the champagne and goodies had been served, Kiki explained her relationship with him.

'When I was a little girl, our tribe was swept by a drought so severe that many of the elderly and newborn grew sick and died. After a time, a small group of white people arrived to help us. They told us they were from an organization that would send us money each month, after they'd set up their program in our village. They had brought water, but of course there wasn't enough.

'After they left, thinking of broken promises, we fell into despair, but true to their word water came, then the rains came until we didn't need their water anymore, but they never left. Their money went for medicines and schooling. Every month I, along with all the other children, got letters from our sponsor – the person sending the money.

'When I was old enough, I started writing back to Drew and we struck up a correspondence. Years later, when I wanted to go on to higher learning, he arranged for me to travel to Cape Town to go to school, then he sponsored me for real, bringing me to the States for college and university. He never asked for anything in return, except that I do well in school. He's like my second father.'

They drank champagne and watched the pole dancing – which, much to Soraya's surprise, seemed more artful, less crass than she had imagined. But there were more surgically enhanced body parts in that one room than she'd ever seen. For the life of her she couldn't figure out why a woman would want breasts that looked and acted like balloons.

She continued to drink her champagne, all too aware that she was taking tiny, overly dainty sips. She'd like nothing better than to take Kiki's advice, forget about her problems for a couple of hours, kick back, get drunk, let herself go. The only trouble was, she knew it would never happen. She was too controlled, too closed in. *What I ought to do*, she thought morosely as she watched a redhead with gravity-defying breasts and hips that seemed unattached to the rest of her, *is get smashed, pull off my top, and do some pole dancing myself.* Then she laughed at the absurdity of the notion. She'd never been that kind of person, even when it might have been age-appropriate. She had always been the good girl – cool, calculating to the point of overanalysis. She glanced over at Kiki, whose magnificent face was lit up not only by the colored strobe lights but also by a fiercely experienced joy. Wasn't the good girl's life drained of color, of flavor? Soraya asked herself.

This thought depressed her even more, but it was just the prelude, because a moment later she looked up to see Rob Batt. *What the what?* she thought. He'd seen her, all right, and was making a beeline right at her.

Soraya excused herself, rose, and walked in the other direction, toward the ladies' room. Somehow Batt managed to snake his way to a position in front of her. She turned on her heel, threaded her way around the tables. Batt, running up the waiters' aisle from the kitchen, caught up with her.

'Soraya, I need to talk to you.'

She shook him off, kept going, out the front door. In the parking lot she heard him running after her. A light sleet was falling, but the wind had failed entirely, the precipitation coming straight down, melting on her shoulders and bare head.

She didn't know why she'd come out here; Kiki had driven them from Deron's house, so she had no car to get into. Maybe she'd been disgusted by the sight of a man she'd liked and trusted, a man who'd betrayed that trust, who'd defected to the dark side, as she privately called LaValle's NSA because she could no longer bear to utter the words *National Security Agency* without feeling sick to her stomach. The NSA had come to stand for everything that had gone wrong in America over the last number of years – the power grabs, the sense felt by some inside the Beltway that they were entitled to do anything and everything, laws of democracy be damned. It all boiled down to contempt, she thought. These people were so sure they were right, they felt nothing but contempt and perhaps even pity for those who tried to oppose them.

'Soraya, wait! Hold on!'

Batt had caught up with her.

'Get out of here,' she said, continuing to walk away.

'But I've got to talk to you.'

'The hell you do. We have nothing to talk about.'

'It's a matter of national security.'

Soraya, shaking her head in disbelief, laughed bitterly and kept on walking.

'Listen, you're my only hope. You're the only one open enough to listen to me.'

Rolling her eyes, she turned to face him. 'You've got some fucking nerve, Rob. Go back and lick your new master's boots.'

'LaValle sold me out, Soraya, you know that.' His eyes were pleading. 'Listen, I made a terrible mistake. I thought what I was doing would save CI.'

Soraya was so incredulous she almost laughed in his face. 'What? You don't expect me to believe that.'

'I'm a product of the Old Man. I had no faith in Hart. I –'

'Don't use the Old Man routine with me. If you really were his product you'd never have sold us out. You'd have hung in there, become part of the solution, rather than making the problem worse.'

'You didn't hear Secretary Halliday, the guy's like a goddamn force of nature. I got sucked into his orbit. I made a mistake, okay? I admit it.'

'There's no excuse for your loss of faith.'

Batt held up his hands, palms-outward. 'You're absolutely right, but, for God's sake, look at me now. I'm being thoroughly punished, aren't I?'

'I don't know, Rob, you tell me.'

'I have no job, no prospect of getting one, either. My friends won't answer my calls, and when I run into them on the street or a restaurant, they act like you did, they turn away. My wife's moved out and taken the kids with her.' He ran his hand through his wet hair. 'Hell, I've been living out of my car since it happened. I'm a mess, Soraya. What could be a worse punishment?'

Was it a flaw in her character that her heart went out to him? Soraya wondered. But she showed no trace of sympathy, simply stood, silent, waiting for him to continue.

'Listen to me,' he pleaded. 'Listen —'

'I don't want to listen.'

As she began to turn away again, he shoved a digital camera into her hand. 'At least take a look at these photos.'

Soraya was about to hand it back, then she figured she had nothing to lose. Batt's camera was on, and she pressed the REVIEW button. What she saw was a series of surveillance photos of General Kendall.

'What the hell?' she said.

'That's what I've been doing since I got canned,' Batt said. 'I've been trying to find a way to bring down LaValle. I figured right away that he might be too tough a nut to crack quickly, but Kendall, well, he's another story.'

She looked up into his face, which shone with an inner fervor she'd never seen before. 'How d'you figure that?'

'Kendall's restless and bitter, chafing under LaValle's yoke. He wants a bigger piece of the action than either Halliday or LaValle is willing to give him. That desire makes him stupid and vulnerable.'

Despite herself, she was intrigued. 'What have you found out?'

'More than I could've hoped for.' Batt nodded at her. 'Keep going.'

As Soraya continued to scroll through the photos her heart started to hammer in her chest. She peered closer. 'Is that . . . Good God, it's Rodney Feir!'

Batt nodded. 'He and Kendall met up at Feir's health club, then they went to dinner, and now they're here.'

She looked up at him. 'The two of them are here at The Glass Slipper?'

'Those are their cars.' Batt pointed. 'There's a back room. I don't know what goes on in there, but you don't have to be a rocket scientist to figure it out. General Kendall is a God-fearing family man, goes to church with his family and LaValle's every Sunday like clockwork. He's very active in the church, very visible there.'

Soraya saw the light at the end of her own personal tunnel. Here was a way to get both her and Tyrone off the hook. 'Two birds with one photo shoot,' she said.

'Yeah, only trouble is how to get back there to snap 'em. It's invitation only, I checked.'

A slow smile spread across Soraya's face. 'Leave that to me.'

For what seemed a long time after Kendall had kicked him until he vomited, nothing happened. But then, Tyrone had already taken note that time seemed to have slowed down to an agonizing crawl. A minute was made up of a thousand seconds, an hour consisted of ten thousand minutes, and a day – well, there were simply too many hours in a day to count.

During one of the periods when his hood was taken off, he walked back and forth the narrow width of the room, not wanting to go near the far end with its ominous waterboarding tub.

Somewhere inside him he knew he'd lost track of time, that this slippage was part of the process to wear him down, open him up, and turn him inside out. Moment by moment he felt himself sliding down a slope so slick, so steep that whatever he did to try to hold on to it failed. He was falling into darkness, into a void filled only with himself.

This, too, was calculated. He could imagine one of Kendall's underlings coming up with a mathematical formula for how far a subject should break down each hour of each day he was subject to incarceration.

Ever since he had suggested to Soraya that he might be useful to her he'd been reading up on how to handle himself in the worst situations. There was a trick he'd come across that was useful to him now – he needed to find a place in his mind where he could withdraw when the going got really rough, a place that was inviolable, where he knew he'd be safe no matter what was done to him.

He had that place now, he'd been there several times when the pain of kneeling with his arms locked high behind him became too much even for him. But there was one thing that frightened him: that damn trough on the other side of the room. If they decided to waterboard him he was done. For as far back as he could remember he'd been terrified of drowning. He couldn't swim, couldn't even float. Every time he'd tried to do either he'd choked, had to be hauled from the water like a three-year-old. He'd soon given up, figuring it didn't matter. When was he going to go sailing or even lie on a beach? Never.

But now the water had come to him. That damn trough was waiting, grinning like a whale about to swallow him whole. He was no Jonah, he knew that. That fucking thing wasn't going to spit him out alive.

He looked down, saw that the hand he held out in front of him was trembling. Turning away, he pressed it against the wall, as if the cinder block could absorb his unreasoning terror.

He started as the sound of the door being unlocked ricocheted around the small space. In came one of the NSA zombies, with dead eyes and dead breath. He put down the tray of food and left without even glancing at Tyrone, all part of the second phase of the plan to break him down: make him think he didn't exist.

He went over to the tray. As usual, his food consisted of cold oatmeal. It didn't matter; he was hungry. Taking up the plastic spoon, he took a bite of the cereal. It was gummy, had no taste whatsoever. He almost gagged on the second bite because he was chewing on something other than oatmeal. Aware that his every move was monitored, he bent over, spit out the mouthful. Then he used the fork to paw open a folded piece of paper. There was something written on it. He bent over further to make out the letters.

DON'T GIVE UP, it read.

At first, Tyrone couldn't believe his eyes. Then he read it again. After reading it a third time, he scooped the message up with another bite of oatmeal, chewed it all slowly and methodically, and swallowed.

Then he went over to the stainless-steel toilet, sat down on the edge, and wondered who had written that note and how he could communicate with him. It wasn't until some time later that he realized this one brief message from outside his tiny cell had managed to restore the balance he'd lost. Inside his head, time resolved itself into normal seconds and minutes, and the blood began once again to circulate through his veins.

Arkadin allowed Devra to drag him out of the bar before he could demolish it completely. Not that he cared about the thuggish patrons who sat in stupefied silence, watching the mayhem he wreaked as if it were a TV show, but he was mindful of the cops who had a significant presence in this trashy neighborhood. During the time they'd been in the bar he'd noticed three police cruisers pass slowly by on the street.

They drove through the sunshine down littered streets. He heard dogs barking, voices shouting. He was grateful for the heat of her hip and shoulder against him. Her presence grounded him, wrestled his rage back down to a manageable level. He hugged her more tightly to him, his mind returning with feverish intensity to his past.

For Arkadin, the ninth level of hell began innocently enough with Stas Kuzin's confirmation that his business came from prostitution and drugs. Easy money, Arkadin thought, immediately lulled into a false sense of security.

At first, his role was as simple as it was clearly defined: He'd provide the space in his buildings to expand Kuzin's brothel empire. This Arkadin did with his usual efficiency. Nothing could have been simpler, and for several months as the rubles rolled in he congratulated himself on making a lucrative business deal. Plus, his association with Kuzin brought him a boatload of perks, from free drinks at the local pubs to free sessions with Kuzin's ever-expanding ring of teenage girls.

But it was this very thing – the young prostitutes – that became Arkadin's slippery slope into hell's lowest level. When he stayed away from the brothels, or made his cursory weekly checkups to ensure the apartments weren't being trashed, it was easy to turn a blind eye on what was really going on. He was mostly too busy counting his money. However, on those occasions when he availed himself of a freebie or two, it was impossible not to notice how young the girls were, how afraid they were, how bruised their thin arms were, how hollow their eyes, and, all too often, how drugged up most of them were. It was like Zombie Nation in there.

All of this might have passed Arkadin by with a minimum of speculation had he not developed a liking for one of them. Yelena was a girl with wide lips, skin as pale as snow, and eyes that burned like a coal fire. She had a quick smile and, unlike some of the other girls, she wasn't prone to bursting into tears for no apparent reason. She laughed at his jokes, she lay with him afterward, her face buried in his chest. He liked the feel of her in his arms. Her warmth seeped into him like fine vodka, and he grew used to how she found just the right position so that the curves of her body meshed perfectly with his. He could fall asleep in her arms, which for him was something of a miracle. He couldn't remember when he'd last slept through the night.

About this time, Kuzin called him into a meeting, told him he was doing so well he wanted to increase his partnership stake with Arkadin.

'Of course, I'll need you to play a more active role,' Kuzin said in his semi-intelligible voice. 'Business is so good that what I need most now is more girls. That's where you come in.'

Kuzin made Arkadin the head of a crew whose sole purpose was to solicit teenage girls from the populace of Nizhny Tagil. This Arkadin did with his usual frightening efficiency. His visits to Yelena's bed were as plentiful but not as idyllic. She had grown afraid, she told him, of the disappearances of some of the girls. One day she saw them; the next they had vanished as if they'd never existed. No one spoke of them, no one answered her questions when she asked where they'd gone. In the main, Arkadin dismissed her fears – after all, the girls were young, weren't they leaving all the time? But Yelena was certain the girls' disappearances had nothing to do with them and everything to do with Stas Kuzin. No matter what he said, her fears did not subside until he promised to protect her, to make sure nothing happened to her.

After six months Kuzin took him aside.

'You're doing a great job.' A mixture of vodka and cocaine slurred Kuzin's voice even further. 'But I need more.'

They were in one of the brothels, which to Arkadin's practiced eye looked oddly underpopulated. 'Where are all the girls?' he asked.

Kuzin waved an arm. 'Gone, run away, who the fuck knows where? These bitches get a bit of money in their pocket, they're off like rabbits.'

Ever the pragmatist, Arkadin said, 'I'll take my crew and go find them.'

'A waste of time.' Kuzin's little head bobbled on his shoulders. 'Just find me more.'

'It's getting difficult,' Arkadin pointed out. 'Some of the girls are scared; they don't want to come with us.'

'Take them anyway.'

Arkadin frowned. 'I don't follow you.'

'Okay, moron, I'll lay it out for you. Take your fucking crew in the fucking van and snatch the bitches off the street.'

'You're talking about kidnapping.'

Kuzin laughed. 'Fuck me, he gets it!'

'What about the cops?'

Kuzin laughed even harder. 'The cops are in my pocket. And even if they weren't, d'you think they get paid to work? They don't give a rat's ass.'

For the next three weeks Arkadin and his crew worked the night shift, delivering girls to the brothel, whether or not they wanted to come. These girls were sullen, often belligerent, until Kuzin took them into a back room, where none of them ever wanted to go a second time. Kuzin didn't mess with their faces, as that would be bad for business; only their arms and legs were bruised.

Arkadin watched this controlled violence as if through the wrong end of a telescope. He knew it was happening, but he pretended it had nothing to do with him. He continued to count his money, which was now piling up at a more rapid clip. It was his money and Yelena that kept him warm at night. Each time he was with her, he checked her arms and legs for bruises. When he made her promise not to take drugs, she laughed, 'Leonid Danilovich, who has money for drugs?'

He smiled at this, knowing what she meant. In fact, she had more money than all the other girls in the brothel combined. He knew this because he was the one who gave it to her.

'Get yourself a new dress, a new pair of shoes,' he'd tell her, but frugal girl that she was, she'd merely smile and kiss him on the cheek with great affection. She was right, he realized, not to do anything to call attention to herself.

One night, not long after, Kuzin accosted him as he was leaving Yelena's room.

'I have an urgent problem and I need your help,' the freak said.

Arkadin went with him out of the apartment building. A large van was waiting on the street, its engine running. Kuzin climbed into the back, and Arkadin followed. Two of the brothel girls were being guarded by Kuzin's pair of personal ghouls.

'They tried to escape,' Kuzin said. 'We just caught them.'

'They need to be taught a lesson,' Arkadin said, because he assumed that was what his partner wanted him to say.

'Too fucking late for that.' Kuzin signaled to the driver, and the van took off.

Arkadin settled back on the seat, wondering where they were going. He kept his mouth shut, knowing that if he asked questions now he'd look like a fool. Thirty minutes later the van slowed, turned off onto an unpaved road. For the next several minutes they jounced along a rutted track that must have been very narrow because branches kept scraping against the sides of the van.

At length, they stopped, the doors opened, and everyone clambered out. The night was very dark, illuminated only by the headlights of the van, but in the distance the fire of the smelters was like blood in the sky or, rather, on the undersides of the belching miasma churned out by hundreds of smokestacks. No one saw the sky in Nizhny Tagil, and when it snowed the flakes turned gray or even sometimes black as they passed through the industrial murk.

Arkadin followed along with Kuzin as the two ghouls pushed the girls through the thick, weedy underbrush. The resiny scent of pine perfumed the air so strongly, it almost masked the appalling stench of decomposition.

A hundred yards in the ghouls pulled back on the collars of the girls' coats, reining them in. Kuzin took out his gun and shot one of the girls in the back of the head. She pitched forward into a bed of dead leaves. The other girl screamed, squirming within the ghoul's grasp, desperate to run.

Then Kuzin turned to Arkadin, placed the gun in his hand. 'When you pull the trigger,' he said, 'we become equal partners.'

There was something in Kuzin's eyes that at this close range gave Arkadin the shivers. It seemed to him that Kuzin's eyes were smiling in the way the devil smiled, without warmth, without humanity, because the pleasure that animated the smile was of an evil and perverted nature. It was at this precise moment that Arkadin thought of the prisons ringing Nizhny Tagil, because he now knew beyond a shadow of a doubt that he was locked within his own private prison, with no idea if there was a key, let alone how to use it.

The gun – an old Luger with the Nazi swastika imprinted on it – was greasy with Kuzin's excitement. Arkadin raised it to the height of the girl's head. She was whimpering and crying. Arkadin had done many things in his young life, some of them unforgivable, but he'd never shot a girl in cold blood. And yet now, in order to prosper, in order to survive the prison of Nizhny Tagil, this was what he had to do.

He was aware of Kuzin's avid eyes boring into him, red as the fire of Nizhny Tagil's foundries themselves, and then he felt the muzzle of a gun at the nape of his neck and knew that the driver was standing behind him, no doubt on Kuzin's orders.

'Do it,' Kuzin said softly, 'because one way or another in the next ten seconds someone's going to fire his gun.'

Arkadin aimed the Luger. The shout of the report echoed on and on through the deep and forbidding forest, and the girl slid along the leaves, into the pit with her friend.

# 35

The sound of the bolt being thrown on the 8mm Mauser K98 rifle echoed through the Dachau air raid bunker. That was the end of it, however.

'Damn!' Old Pelz groaned. 'I forgot to load the thing!'

Petra took out her handgun, pointed it in the air, and squeezed the trigger. Because the result was the same as what had happened to him, Old Pelz threw down the K98.

'*Scheisse*!' he said, clearly disgusted.

She approached him then. 'Herr Pelz,' she said gently, 'as I said, my name is Petra. Do you remember me?'

The old man stopped muttering, peered at her carefully. 'You do look an awful lot like a Petra-Alexandra I once knew.'

'Petra-Alexandra.' She laughed and kissed him on the cheek. 'Yes, yes, that's me!'

He recoiled a little, put a hand on his cheek where she'd planted her lips. Then, skeptical to the end, he looked past her at Bourne. 'Who's this Nazi bastard? Did he force you to come here?' His hands curled into fists. 'I'll box his ears for him!'

'No, Herr Pelz, this is a friend of mine. He's Russian.' She used the name Bourne had given her, which was on the passport Boris Karpov had provided.

'Russians're no better than Nazis in my book,' the old man said sourly.

'Actually, I'm an American traveling under a Russian passport.' Bourne said this first in English and then in German.

'You speak English very well, for a Russian,' Old Pelz said in excellent English. Then he laughed, showing teeth yellowed by time and tobacco. At the sight of an American, he seemed to perk up, as if coming out of a decades-long drowse. This was the way he was, a rabbit being drawn out of a hat, only to withdraw again into the shadows. He wasn't mad, just living both in the drab present and in the vivid past. 'I embraced the Americans when they liberated us from tyranny,' he continued proudly. 'In my time I helped them root out the Nazis and the Nazi sympathizers pretending to be good Germans.' He spat out the last words, as if he couldn't stand to have them in his mouth.

'Then what are you doing here?' Bourne said. 'Don't you have a home to go to?'

'Sure I do.' Old Pelz smacked his lips, as if he could taste the life of his younger self. 'In fact, I have a very nice house in Dachau. It's blue and white, with flowers all around a picket fence. A cherry tree stands in back, spreading its wings in summer. The house is rented out to a fine young couple with two strapping children, who send their rent check like clockwork to my nephew in Leipzig. He's a big-shot lawyer, you know.'

'Herr Pelz, I don't understand,' Petra said. 'Why not stay in your own home? This is no place to live.'

'The bunker is my health insurance.' The old man cocked a canny eye her way. 'Do you have any idea what would happen to me if I went back to my house? They'd spirit me away in the night, and that's the last anyone would ever see of me.'

'Who would do that to you?' Bourne said.

Pelz seemed to consider his answer, as if he needed to remember the text of a book he'd read in high school. 'I told you I was a Nazi hunter, a damn fine one, too. In those days I lived like a king – or, if I'm honest, a duke. Anyway, that's before I got cocky and made my mistake. I decided to go after the Black Legion, and that one intemperate decision was my downfall. Because of them I lost everything, even the trust of the Americans, who at that time needed those damn people more than they needed me.

'The Black Legion kicked me into the gutter like a piece of garbage or a mangy dog. From there it was only a short crawl down here into the bowels of the earth.'

'It's the Black Legion I came here to talk to you about,' Bourne said. 'I'm a hunter, too. The Black Legion isn't a Nazi organization anymore. They've turned into a Muslim terrorist network.'

Old Pelz rubbed his grizzled jaw. 'I'd say I'm surprised, but I'm not. Those bastards knew how to play all the cards in all the hands – the Germans, the Brits, and, most importantly, the Americans. They toyed with all of 'em after the war. Every Western intelligence service was throwing money at them. The thought of having built-in spies behind the Iron Curtain had them all salivating.

'It didn't take the bastards long to figure out it was the Americans who had the upper hand. Why? 'Cause they had all the money and, unlike the Brits, weren't being tight-fisted with it.' He cackled. 'But that's the American way, isn't it?'

Not waiting for an answer to a question that was self-evident, he plowed on. 'So the Black Legion took up with the American intelligence machine. First off, it wasn't difficult to convince the Yanks that they'd never been Nazis, that their only goal was to fight Stalin. And that was true, as far as it went, but after the war they had other goals in mind. They're Muslims, after all; they never felt comfortable in Western society. They wanted to build for the future, and like a lot of other insurgents they created their power base with American dollars.'

He squinted up at Bourne. 'You're American, poor bastard. None of these modern-day terrorist networks would've existed without your country's backing. Fucking ironic, that is.'

For a time he lapsed into muttering, broke into a song whose lyrics were so melancholy tears welled up in his rheumy eyes.

'Herr Pelz,' Bourne said, trying to get the old man to focus. 'You were talking about the Black Legion.'

'Call me Virgil,' Pelz said, nodding as he came out of his fugue state. 'That's right, my Christian name is Virgil, and for you, American, I will hold my lamp high enough to throw light on those bastards who ruined my life. Why not? I'm at a stage in my life when I should tell someone, and it might as well be you.'

'They're in the back,' Bev said to Drew Davis. 'Both of them.' A woman in her mid-fifties with a thick frame and a quick wit, she was The Glass Slipper's girl wrangler, as she wryly called herself – part disciplinarian, part den mother.

'The main interest is in the general,' Davis said, 'isn't that right, Kiki?'

Kiki nodded. She was closely flanked by Soraya and Deron, and all of them were clustered in Davis's cramped office up a short flight of stairs from the main room. The pounding of the bass and drums thumped against the walls like the fists of angry giants. The room had the appearance of an attic or a garret, windowless, its walls like a time machine, plastered with photos of Drew Davis with Martin Luther King, Nelson Mandela, four different American presidents, a host of Hollywood stars, and various UN dignitaries and ambassadors from virtually every country in Africa. There was also a series of informal snapshots of him with his arm around a younger Kiki in the Masai Mara, totally unselfconscious, looking like a queen-in-training.

After her talk with Rob Batt in the parking lot, Soraya had returned to her table inside and filled in Kiki and Deron on her plan. The noise from the band on stage made eavesdropping impossible, even by anyone at the next table. Because of her longtime friendship with Drew Davis, it had been up to Kiki to create the spark that would light the fuse. This she did, resulting in this impromptu meeting in Davis's office.

'For me to even contemplate what you're asking, you have to guarantee blanket immunity,' Drew Davis said to Soraya. 'Plus, leave our names out of it, unless you want to piss me off – which you don't – as well as pissing off half the elected officials in the district.'

'You have my word,' Soraya said. 'We want these two people, that's the beginning and the end of it.'

Drew Davis glanced at Kiki, who responded with an almost imperceptible nod.

Now Davis turned to Bev.

'Here's what you can do and what you can't do,' Bev said, reacting to her boss's cue. 'I won't allow anyone on my ranch who's not there for legitimate purposes – that is, either a patron or a working girl. So forget just barging in there. I do that and tomorrow we have no business left.'

She wasn't even looking at Drew Davis, but Soraya saw him nod in assent, and her heart fell. Everything depended on their gaining access to the general while he was in the midst of his frolics. Then she had a thought.

'I'll go in as a working girl,' she said.

'No, you won't,' Deron said. 'You're known to both the general and Feir. One look at you and they'll be spooked.'

'They don't know me.'

Everyone turned their heads to stare at Kiki.

'Absolutely not,' Deron said.

'Ease up there,' Kiki said with a laugh. 'I'm not going through with anything. I just need access.' She mimed taking photos. Then she turned to Bev. 'How do I get into the general's private room?'

'You can't. For obvious reasons the private rooms are sacrosanct. Another rule of the house. And both the general and Feir have chosen their partners for the evening.' She drummed her fingers against Davis's desktop. 'But in the case of the general there *is* one way.'

*

Virgil Pelz took Bourne and Petra farther into the bunker's main tunnel, to a rough-hewn space that opened out into a circle. There were benches here, a small gas stove, a refrigerator.

'Lucky someone forgot to turn off the electricity,' Petra said.

'Lucky my ass.' Pelz settled himself on a bench. 'My nephew pays a town official under the table to keep the lights on.' He offered them whiskey or wine, which they refused. He poured himself a shot of liquor, downed it perhaps to fortify himself or to keep himself from sinking back into the shadows. It was obvious he liked having company, that the stimulation of other humans was bringing him out of himself.

'Most of what I've already told you about the Black Legion is basic history, if you know where to look, but the key to understanding their success in negotiating the dangerous postwar landscape lies in two men: Farid Icoupov and Ibrahim Sever.'

'I assume this Icoupov you speak of is Semion Icoupov's father,' Bourne said.

Pelz nodded. 'Just so.'

'And did Ibrahim Sever have a son?'

'He had two,' Pelz replied, 'but I'm getting ahead of myself.' He smacked his lips, glanced at the bottle of whiskey, then decided against another shot.

'Farid and Ibrahim were the best of friends. They grew up together, each the only sons in large families. Possibly, this is what bonded them as children. The bond was strong; it lasted for most of their lives, but Ibrahim Sever was a warrior at heart, Farid Icoupov an intellectual, and the seeds of discontent and mistrust must have been sown early. During the war their shared leadership worked out just fine. Ibrahim was in charge of the Black Legion soldiers on the Eastern Front; Farid put in place and directed the intelligence-gathering network in the Soviet Union.

'It was after the war when the problems began. Stripped of his duties as commandant of the military end, Ibrahim began to fret that his power was eroding.' Pelz clucked his tongue against the roof of his mouth. 'Listen, American, if you're a student of history you know how the two longtime allies and friends Gaius Julius Caesar and Pompey Magnus became enemies infected by the ambitions, fears, deceptions, and power struggles of those under their respective commands. So it was with these two. In time, Ibrahim convinced himself – no doubt abetted by some of his more militant advisors – that his longtime friend was planning a power grab. Unlike Caesar, who was off in Gaul when Pompey declared war on him, Farid lived in the next house. Ibrahim Sever and his men came in the night and assassinated Farid Icoupov. Three days later Farid's son, Semion, shot Ibrahim to death as he was driving to work. In retaliation, Ibrahim's son, Asher, went after Semion in a Munich nightclub. Asher managed to escape, but in the ensuing hail of gunfire Asher's younger brother was killed.'

Pelz scrubbed his face with his hand. 'You see how it goes, American? Like an ancient Roman vendetta, an orgy of blood of biblical proportions.'

'I knew about Semion Icoupov, but not about Sever,' Bourne said. 'Where's Asher Sever now?'

The old man shrugged his thin shoulders. 'Who knows? If Icoupov did, Sever would surely be dead by now.'

For a time, Bourne sat silent, thinking about the Black Legion's attack on the professor, thinking about all the little anomalies that had been piling up in his mind: the oddity of Pyotr's network of decadents and incompetents, the professor saying it was his idea to have the stolen plans delivered to him via the network, and the question of whether Mischa Tarkanian – and Arkadin himself – was Black Legion. At last, he said, 'Virgil, I need to ask you several questions.'

'Yes, American.' Pelz's eyes looked as bright and eager as a robin's.

Still, Bourne hesitated. Revealing anything of his mission or its background to a stranger violated every instinct, every lesson he'd been taught, and yet he could see no other alternative. 'I came to Munich because a friend of mine – a mentor, really – asked me to go after the Black Legion, first because they're planning an attack against my country, and second because their leader, Semion Icoupov, ordered his son, Pyotr, killed.'

Pelz looked up, a curious expression on his face. 'Asher Sever gathered his power base, which he'd inherited from his father – a powerful intelligence-gathering network strewn across Asia and Europe – and ousted Semion. Icoupov hasn't been running the Black Legion for decades. If he had, I doubt whether I'd still be down here. Unlike Asher Sever, Icoupov was a man you could reason with.'

'Are you saying that you've met both Semion Icoupov and Asher Sever?' Bourne said.

'That's right,' Pelz said, nodding. 'Why?'

Bourne had gone cold as he contemplated the unthinkable. Could the professor have been lying to him all the time? But if so – if he was in fact a member of the Black Legion – why in the world would he entrust the delivery of the attack plans to Pyotr's shaky network? Surely he would have known how unreliable its members were. Nothing seemed to make sense.

Knowing he had to solve this problem one step at a time, he took out his cell phone, scrolled through the photos, brought up the one the professor had sent of Egon Kirsch. He looked at the two men in the photo, then handed the phone to Pelz.

'Virgil, do you recognize either of these men?'

Pelz squinted, then stood and walked nearer to one of the bare lightbulbs. 'No.' He shook his head, then, after a moment's further scrutiny, his forefinger jabbed at the photo. 'I don't know, because he looks so different . . .' He returned to where Bourne sat, turned the phone so they could both see the photo, and tapped the figure of Professor Specter. '. . . but, damn, I'd swear this one is Asher Sever.'

# 36

Peter Marks, chief of operations, was with Veronica Hart in her office, poring over reams of personnel data sheets, when they came for her. Luther LaValle, accompanied by a pair of federal marshals, had swept through CI security, armed with their warrant. Hart had only the briefest of warnings – a phone call from the first set of security guards downstairs – that her professional world was imploding. No time to get out of the way of the falling debris.

She barely had time to tell Marks, then stand up to face her accusers before the three men entered her office and presented her with the federal warrant.

'Veronica Rose Hart,' the senior of the stone-faced federal marshals intoned, 'you are hereby placed under arrest for conspiring with one Jason Bourne, a rogue agent, for purposes that violate the regulations of Central Intelligence.'

'On what evidence?' Hart said.

'NSA surveillance photos of you in the courtyard of the Freer handing a packet to Jason Bourne,' the marshal said in the same zombie voice.

Marks, who was also on his feet, said, 'This is insane. You can't really believe – '

'Shut it, Mr. Marks,' Luther LaValle said with no fear of contradiction. 'One more word out of you and I'll have you put under formal investigation.'

Marks was about to reply when a sharp look from the DCI forced him to bite back his words. His jaws clamped shut, but the fury in his eyes was unmistakable.

Hart came around the desk, and the junior marshal cuffed her hands behind her back.

'Is that really necessary?' Marks said.

LaValle pointed at him wordlessly. As they marched Hart from her office, she said, 'Take over, Peter. You're acting DCI now.'

LaValle grinned. 'Not for long, if I have anything to say about it.'

After they'd gone, Marks collapsed into his chair. Finding that his hands were trembling, he clasped them together, as if in prayer. His heart was pounding so hard he found it difficult to think. He jumped up, walked over to the window behind the DCI's desk, stood staring out at the Washington night. All the monuments were lit up, all the streets and avenues were filled with traffic. Everything was as it should be, and yet nothing looked familiar. He felt as if he'd entered an alternate universe. He couldn't have been witness to what just happened, NSA couldn't be about to absorb CI into its gigantic corpus. But then he turned around to find the office empty and the full horror of seeing the DCI frog-marched out in handcuffs swept over him, made his legs weak, so that he sought out the big chair behind the desk and sat in it.

Then the implications of where he sat, and why, sank in. He picked up the phone and dialed Stu Gold, CI's lead counsel.

'Sit tight. I'll be right over,' Gold told him in his usual no-nonsense voice. Did nothing faze him?

Then Marks began to make a series of calls. It was going to be a long and harrowing night.

Rodney Feir was having the time of his life. As he accompanied Afrique into one of the rooms in the back of The Glass Slipper, he felt as if he were on top of the world. In fact, popping a Viagra, he decided to ask her to do a number of things he'd never tried before. *Why the hell not?* he asked himself.

While he was undressing he thought of the information on Typhon's field agents Peter Marks had sent him via interoffice mail. Feir had deliberately told Marks he didn't want it sent electronically because it was too insecure. The info was folded into the inside pocket of his coat, ready to give to General Kendall before they left The Glass Slipper tonight. He could have handed it over while they were at dinner, but he'd felt, all things considered, that a champagne toast after all their treats had been consumed was the proper way to cap off the night.

Afrique was already on the bed, spread languidly, her large eyes half closed, but she got right down to business as soon as Feir joined her. He tried to keep his mind on the proceedings, but seeing as how his body was totally in it, there wasn't much point. He preferred dwelling on the things that made him truly happy, like getting the better of Peter Marks. When he was growing up it was people like Marks – and, for that matter, Batt – who'd had it all over him, brainiacs with brawn, in other words, who'd made his life miserable. They were the ones who had the cool circle of friends, who got all the great-looking girls, who rode in cars while he was still tooling around on a scooter. He was the nerd, the chubby – fat, really – kid who was made the butt of all their jokes, who was pushed around and ostracized, who, despite his high IQ, was so tongue-tied he could never stick up for himself.

He'd joined CI as a glorified pencil pusher, and, yes, he'd worked his way up the professional ladder, but not into fieldwork or counterintelligence. No, he was chief of field support, which meant that he was in charge of gathering and distributing the paperwork generated by the very CI personnel he longed to be like. His office was the central hub of supply and demand, and there were days when he could convince himself that it was the nerve center of CI. But most of the time he saw himself for what he really was – someone who kept pushing electronic lists, data entry forms, directorate requests, allocation tables, budget spreadsheets, personnel assignment profiles, matériel lading bills, a veritable landslide of paperwork whizzing through the CI intranet. A monitor of information, in other words, a master of nothing.

He was enveloped in pleasure, a warm, viscous friction spreading outward from his groin into his torso and limbs. He closed his eyes and sighed.

At first, being an anonymous cog in the CI machine suited him, but as the years passed, as he rose in the hierarchy, only the Old Man understood his worth, for it was the Old Man who promoted him, time after time. But no one else – certainly none of the other directors – said a word to him until they needed something. Then a request came flying through CI cyberspace as quick as you could say, *I need it yesterday.* If he got them what they wanted yesterday, he heard nothing, not even a nod of thanks in the hallway, but should there be any delay at all, no matter the reason, they'd land on him like woodpeckers on a tree full of insects. He'd never hear the end of their pestering until they got what they wanted, and then silence again. It seemed sadly ironic to him that even in an insider's paradise like CI he was on the outside.

It was humiliating to be one of those stereotypical Americans who time and again got sand kicked in his face. How he hated himself for being a living, breathing cliché. It was these evenings spent with General Kendall that gave his life color and meaning, the clandestine meetings in the health club sauna, the dinners at local barbecue joints in SE, and then the delicious chocolate nightcaps at The Glass Slipper, where he was for once the insider instead of having his nose pressed to someone else's window. Knowing that he couldn't be transformed he had to settle for losing himself in Afrique's bed at The Glass Slipper.

General Kendall, smoking a cigar in the corral, the colloquial name for the parlor room where the girls were paraded for the benefit of the patrons, was enjoying himself immensely. If he was thinking of his boss at all, it was of the heart attack this scene he was enacting would cause LaValle. As for his family, they were the farthest thing from his mind. Unlike Feir, who always went for the same girl, Kendall was a man of diverse tastes when it came to the women of The Glass Slipper, and why not? He had virtually no choice in any other areas of his life. If not here, where?

He sat on the purple velvet sofa, one arm thrown along the back, watching through slitted eyes the slow parade of flesh. He had already made his choice; the girl was in her room, undressing, but when Bev had come to him, suggesting that he might want something a bit more special – another girl to create a threesome – he hadn't hesitated. He'd been just about to make his choice when he saw someone. She was impossibly tall, with skin like the darkest cocoa, and was so regal in her beauty that he broke out into a sweat.

He caught Bev's eye and she came over. Bev was attuned to his desires. 'I want her,' he said to Bev, pointing at the regal beauty.

'I'm afraid Kiki's not available,' she said.

This answer made Kendall want her all the more. Venal witch; she knew him too well. He produced five hundred-dollar bills. 'How about now?' he said.

Bev, true to form, pocketed the money. 'Leave it to me,' she said.

The general watched her pick her way through the girls to where Kiki was standing, somewhat apart from the others. While he observed the conversation his heart began to beat in his chest like a war drum. He was sweating so much he was obliged to wipe his palms on the purple velvet of the sofa arm. If she said no, what would he do? But she wasn't saying no, she was looking across the corral at him, with a smile that raised his temperature a couple of degrees. Jesus, he wanted her!

As if in a trance, he saw her coming across the room toward him, her hips swaying, that maddening half smile on her face. He stood up, with some difficulty, he noted. He felt like a seventeen-year-old virgin. Kiki held out her hand and he took it, terrified that she'd be repulsed if it was damp, but nothing interfered with that half smile.

There was something intensely pleasurable about allowing her to lead him past all the other girls, enjoying the looks of envy on their faces.

'Which room are you in?' Kiki murmured in a voice like honey.

Kendall, inhaling her spicy, musky scent, could not find his voice. He pointed, and again she led him as if he were on a leash until they were standing in front of the door.

'Are you sure you want two girls tonight?' She brushed her hip against his. 'I'm more than enough for any man I've been with.'

The general felt a delicious shiver travel down the length of his spine, lodge itself like a heated arrow between his thighs. Reaching out, he opened the door. Lena writhed on the bed, naked. He heard the door close behind him. Without thinking, he undressed himself, then he stepped out of the puddle of his clothes, took Kiki's hand, padded over to the bed. He knelt on it, she let go of his hand, and he fell on Lena.

He felt Kiki's hands on his shoulders, and, groaning, he lost himself within Lena's lush body. The pleasure built along with the anticipation of Kiki's long, lithe body pressed against his glistening back.

It took him some time to become aware that the quick flashes of light weren't a result of the quickened firing of nerve endings behind his eyes. Drugged with sex and desire, he was slow to turn his head directly into another battery of flashes. Even then, negative images dancing behind his retinas, his fogged brain couldn't quite piece together what was happening, and his body continued to move rhythmically against Lena's pliant flesh.

Then the camera flashed again, he belatedly raised his hand to shield his eyes, and there was stark reality staring him in the face. Kiki, still dressed, continued to take shots of him and Lena.

'Smile, General,' she said in that sensual, honeyed voice. 'There's nothing else you can do.'

'I've got too much anger inside me,' Petra said. 'It's like one of those flesh-eating diseases you read about.'

'Dachau is toxic for you, so is Munich now,' Bourne said. 'You've got to go away.'

She moved to the left-hand lane of the autobahn, put on some real speed. They were on their way back to Munich in the car Pelz's nephew had bought for him under the nephew's name. The police might still be looking for both of them, but their only lead was Petra's Munich apartment, and neither of them had any intention of going anywhere near it. As long as she didn't get out of the car, Bourne felt it was relatively safe for her to drive him back into the city.

'Where would I go?' she said.

'Leave Germany altogether.'

She laughed, but it wasn't a pleasant sound. 'Turn tail and run, you mean.'

'Why would you see it that way?'

'Because I'm German; because I belong here.'

'The Munich police are looking for you,' he said.

'And if they find me, then I'll do my time for killing your friend.' She flashed her headlights so a slower car could get out of her way. 'Meanwhile I have money. I can live.'

'But what will you do?'

She gave him a lopsided smile. 'I'm going to take care of Virgil. He needs drying out; he needs a friend.' Nearing the city, she changed lanes so she could exit when she needed to. 'The cops won't find me,' she said with an odd kind of certainty, 'because I'm taking him far away from here. Virgil and me, we'll be two outlaws learning a whole new way of life.'

Egon Kirsch lived in the northern district of Schwabing, known as the young intellectual quarter because of the mass of university students that flooded its streets, cafés, and bars.

As they came abreast of Schwabing's main plaza, Petra pulled over. 'When I was younger I used to hang out here with my friends. We were all militants, then, agitating for change, and we felt connected to this place because it was from here that the Freiheitsaktion Bayern, one of the most famed resistance groups, commandeered Radio Munich near the end of the war. They broadcast messages to the populace to seize and arrest all local Nazi leaders, and to signal their rejection of the regime by waving white sheets out of their windows – an action that was punishable by death, by the way. And they managed to save a large number of civilian lives as the American army swept in.'

'At last we find something in Munich that even you can be proud of,' Bourne said.

'I suppose so.' Petra laughed, almost sadly. 'But I among all of my friends was the only one who stayed a revolutionary. The others are corporate functionaries or Hausfraus now. They lead sad, gray lives. I see them sometimes, trudging to and from work. I walk by them; they don't even look up. In the end, they all disappointed me.'

Kirsch's apartment was on the top floor of a beautiful house of stone-colored stucco, arched windows, and a terracotta tile roof. Between two of his windows was a niche holding a stone statue of the Virgin Mary cradling the baby Jesus.

Petra pulled into the curb in front of the building. 'I wish you well, American,' she said, deliberately using Virgil Pelz's phrasing. 'Thank you . . . for everything.'

'You may not believe it, but we helped each other,' Bourne said as he got out of the car. 'Good luck, Petra.'

When she'd driven off, he turned, went up the steps to the building, and used the code Kirsch had given him to open the front door. The interior was neat and spotlessly clean. The wood-paneled hallway gleamed with a recent waxing. Bourne climbed the carved wooden staircase to the top floor. Using Kirsch's key, he let himself in. Though the apartment itself was light and airy, with many windows overlooking the street, it was steeped in a deep silence, as if it existed on the bottom of the sea. There was no TV, no computer. Bookcases lined one entire wall of the living room, holding volumes by Nietzsche, Kant, Descartes, Heidegger, Leibniz, and Machiavelli. There were also books by many of the great mathematicians, biographers, fiction writers, and economists. The other walls were covered with Kirsch's framed and matted line drawings, so detailed and intricate that at first glance they seemed to be architectural plans, but then suddenly they came into focus and Bourne realized the drawings were abstracts. Like all good art, they seemed to move back and forth from reality to an imagined dream world where anything was possible.

After taking a brief tour of all the rooms, he settled down in a chair behind Kirsch's desk. He thought long and hard about the professor. Was he Dominic Specter, the nemesis of the Black Legion, as he claimed to be, or was he, in fact, Asher Sever, the leader of the Black Legion? If he was Sever, he'd staged the attack on himself – an elaborate scheme that had cost a number of lives. Could the professor be guilty of such an irrational act? If he was the leader of the Black Legion, certainly. The second question Bourne had been asking himself was why the professor would entrust the stolen plans to Pyotr's thoroughly undependable network. But there was another enigma: If the professor was Sever, why was he so anxious to get those plans? Wouldn't he already have them? These two questions went around and around in Bourne's head without producing a satisfactory solution. Nothing about the situation he found himself in appeared to make sense, which meant that a vital part of the picture was missing. And yet he had the nagging suspicion that, like Egon Kirsch's drawings, he was being shown two separate realities – if only he could decipher which was real and which one was false.

At length, he turned his mind to something that had been bothering him ever since the incident at the Egyptian Museum. He knew that Franz Jens had been the only one to follow him into the museum, so how on earth did Arkadin know where he was? Arkadin had to have been the one to kill Jens. He also must have given the order to kill Egon Kirsch, but, again, how did he know where Kirsch was?

The answers to both questions were firmly rooted in time and place. He hadn't been tailed to the museum, then . . . As a chill spread through him, Bourne went very still. With no physical tail, there had to be an electronic tail somewhere on his person. But how had it been put there? Someone could have brushed up against him in the airport. He rose, slowly undressed. As he did so, he went through every item of clothing, looking for an electronic tag. Finding nothing, he dressed, sat again in the chair, deep in thought.

With his eidetic memory, he went through every step of his journey from Moscow to Munich. When he recalled the German Immigration officer, he realized that his passport had been out of his possession for close to half a minute. Taking it out of his breast pocket, he began to leaf through it, checking each page both by sight and by touch. On the inside of the back cover, stuck in the fold of the binding, he found the tiny transmitter.

# 37

'How wonderful it is to breathe the good night air,' Veronica Hart said as she stood on the pavement just outside the Pentagon.

'Diesel fumes and all,' Stu Gold said.

'I knew LaValle's charges wouldn't stick,' she said as they crossed to his car. 'They're patently trumped up.'

'I wouldn't begin celebrating just yet,' the attorney said. 'LaValle's put me on notice that he's going to take those surveillance photos of you and Bourne to the president tomorrow for an executive order to have you removed.'

'Come on, Stu, those were private conversations between Martin Lindros and a civilian, Moira Trevor. There's nothing in them. LaValle's banking on hot air.'

'He's got the secretary of defense,' Gold said. 'Under the circumstances that alone is enough to make trouble for you.'

The wind was whipping up and Hart caught her hair, pushed it off her face. 'Coming into CI and marching me out in cuffs . . . LaValle made a big mistake grandstanding like that.' She turned, looked back at the headquarters of the NSA in which she'd been incarcerated for three hours until the moment Gold showed up with his order from a federal judge for her temporary release. 'He'll pay for humiliating me.'

'Veronica, don't do anything rash.' Gold opened the car door, ushered her inside. 'Knowing LaValle as I do it's more than likely that he wants you to go off half-cocked. That's how fatal mistakes are made.'

He went around the front of the car, got behind the wheel, and they drove off.

'We can't let him get away with this, Stu. Unless we stop him he's going to hijack CI right out from under us.' She watched the Virginia night turn into the district night as they crossed the Arlington Memorial Bridge. The Lincoln Memorial rose up before them. 'I made a pledge when I signed on.'

'Like all DCIs.'

'No, I'm talking about a personal pledge.' She very much wanted to see Lincoln sitting on his chair, contemplating all the unknowns that lay before every human being. She asked Gold to make a stop there. 'I never told anyone this, Stu, but the day I officially became DCI I went to the Old Man's grave. Have you ever been to the Arlington National Cemetery? It's a sobering place, but in its own way a joyous place as well. So many heroes, so much courage, the bedrock of our freedom, Stu, every one of us.'

They'd come to the memorial. They both got out, walked up to the majestic floodlit granite statue, stood gazing up into Lincoln's stern, wise face. Someone had left a bouquet of flowers at his feet, withered heads nodding in the wind.

'I stayed at the Old Man's grave for a long time,' Hart continued in a faraway voice. 'I swear I could feel him, I swear I felt something stir against me, then inside me.' Her gaze swung around to fix on the attorney. 'There's a long, exemplary legacy at CI, Stu. I swore then, and I'm swearing now, that I won't let anything or anyone damage that legacy.' She took a breath. 'So whatever it takes.'

Gold returned her stare without flinching. 'Do you know what you're asking?'

'Yes, I believe I do.'

At last, he said, 'All right, Veronica, it's your call. Whatever it takes.'

Feeling invigorated and invulnerable after his workout, Rodney Feir met General Kendall in the champagne room, reserved for those VIPs who had consummated the evening's pleasures and wanted to linger, with or without their girls. Of course time spent in there was far more expensive with the girls than without.

The champagne room was decorated like a Middle Eastern pasha's den. The two men lazed on voluminous pillows while being served the bubbly of their choice. This was where Feir planned to hand over the intel on Typhon's field agents. But first he wanted to luxuriate in the pure pleasure provided in the back rooms of The Glass Slipper. After all, the moment he set foot outside, the real world would come crashing in on him with all its annoyances, petty humiliations, drudgery, and the piquancy of fear that preceded every move he made to advance LaValle's position vis-à-vis CI.

Kendall, his cell phone at his right hand, sat rather stiffly, as befitted a military man. Feir thought he must be slightly uncomfortable in such lush surroundings. The men chatted for a time, sipping their champagne, exchanging theories about steroids and baseball, about the chances of the Redskins making the play-offs next year, the gyrations of the stock market, anything but politics.

After a time, when the bottle of champagne was nearly exhausted, Kendall looked at his watch. 'What d'you have for me?'

This was the moment Feir had been keenly anticipating. He couldn't wait to see the look on the general's face when he caught a glimpse of the intel. Reaching into the pocket in the lining of his coat, he brought out the packet. A low-tech hard copy was the safest way to smuggle data out of the CI building, since security systems were in place to monitor the comings and goings of any device with a hard drive large enough to hold substantial data files.

A smile broke out across Feir's face. 'The whole enchilada. Every last detail on the Typhon agents across the globe.' He held up the packet. 'Now let's talk about what I get in return.'

'What do you want?' Kendall said without much enthusiasm. 'A higher grade? More control?'

'I want respect,' Feir said. 'I want LaValle to respect me the way you do.'

A curious smile curled the general's lips. 'I can't speak for Luther, but I'll see what I can do.'

As he leaned forward to take the intel, Feir was wondering why he was so solemn – no, worse than solemn, he was downright glum. Feir was on the point of asking him about it when a tall, elegant black woman began snapping a series of photos.

'What the hell?' he said, through the blinding string of flashes.

When his vision cleared, he saw Soraya Moore standing beside them. She had the packet of intel in her hand.

'This isn't a good night for you, Rodney.' She picked up the general's cell phone, thumbed it on, and there was the conversation between the general and Feir recorded and regurgitated so everyone could hear his treachery for themselves. 'No, I would have to say that all things considered it's the end of the line.'

'I'm not afraid to die,' Devra said, 'if that's what you're worried about.'

'I'm not worried,' Arkadin said. 'What makes you think I'm worried?'

She bit into the chocolate ice cream he'd bought her. 'You've got that deep vertical indentation between your eyes.'

She wanted ice cream even though it was the middle of winter. Maybe it was the chocolate she wanted, he thought. Not that it mattered; pleasing her in little ways was strangely satisfying – as if in pleasing her he was also pleasing himself, although that seemed like an impossibility to him.

'I'm not worried,' he said. 'I'm thoroughly pissed off.'

'Because your boss told you to stay away from Bourne.'

'I'm not going to stay away from Bourne.'

'You'll piss off your boss.'

'There comes a time,' Arkadin said, walking faster.

They were in the center of Munich; he wanted to be in a central location when Icoupov told him where he was meeting Bourne in order to get there as quickly as possible.

'I'm not afraid to die,' Devra repeated, 'the only thing is, though, what do you do when you no longer have memories?'

Arkadin shot her a look. 'What?'

'When you look at a dead person what do you see?' She took another bite of ice cream between her teeth, leaving little indentations in what was left of the scoop. 'Nothing, right? Not a damn thing. Life has flown the coop, and with it all the memories that have been built up over the years.' She looked at him. 'At that moment, you cease to be human, so what are you?'

'Who gives a shit?' Arkadin said. 'It'll be a fucking relief to be without memories.'

Soraya presented herself at the NSA safe house just before 10 AM, so that by the time she cleared the various levels of security, she was being ushered into the Library precisely on time.

'Breakfast, madam?' Willard asked as he escorted her across the plush carpet.

'I believe I will, today,' she said. 'A fines herbes omelet would be nice. Do you have a baguette?'

'We do, indeed, madam.'

'Fine.' She shifted the evidence damning General Kendall from one hand to the other. 'And a pot of Ceylon tea, Willard. Thank you.'

She walked the rest of the way to where Luther LaValle sat, drinking his morning cup of coffee. He stared out the window, casting a jaundiced eye on the early spring. It was so warm the fireplace held only cold, white ash.

He did not turn when she sat down. She placed the evidence file on her lap, then said without preamble, 'I've come to take Tyrone home.'

LaValle ignored her. 'There's nothing on your Black Legion; there's no unusual terrorist activities inside the US. We've come up blank.'

'Did you hear what I said? I've come for Tyrone.'

'That's not going to happen,' LaValle said.

Soraya brought out Kendall's cell phone, played back the conversation he'd had with Rodney Feir in the champagne room of The Glass Slipper.

'*Every last detail on the Typhon agents across the globe,*' came Feir's voice. '*Now let's talk about what I get in return.*'

General Kendall: '*What do you want? A higher grade? More control?*'

Feir: '*I want respect. I want LaValle to respect me the way you do.*'

'Who cares?' LaValle's head swung around. His eyes were dark and glassy. 'That's Feir's problem, not mine.'

'Maybe so.' Soraya slid the file across the table toward him. 'However, this is very much your problem.'

LaValle stared at her for a moment. His eyes were now full of venom. Without lowering his gaze, he reached out, flipped open the file. There he saw photo after photo of General Kendall, naked as sin, caught in the midst of having intercourse with a young black woman.

'How is that going to look for the career officer and devout Christian family man when the story comes out?'

Willard arrived with her breakfast, snapping down a starched white tablecloth, setting the china and silverware in a precise pattern in front of her. When he was finished, he turned to LaValle. 'Anything for you, sir?'

LaValle shooed him away with a curt flick of his hand. For a time, he did nothing more than leaf through the photos again. Then he took out a cell phone, placed it on the table, and pushed it toward her.

'Call Bourne,' he said.

Soraya froze with a forkful of omelet halfway to her mouth. 'I beg your pardon?'

'I know he's in Munich, our substation there picked him up on their CCTV monitoring of the airport. I have men in place to take him into custody. All that's needed now is for you to set the trap.'

She laughed as she set down her fork. 'You're dreaming, LaValle. I have you, not the other way around. If these photos become public, your right-hand man will be ruined both professionally and personally. You and I both know you're not going to allow that to happen.'

LaValle gathered up the photos, slid them back into the envelope. Then he took out a pen, wrote a name and address on the front of the envelope. When Willard glided over at his beckoning, LaValle said, 'Please have these scanned and sent electronically to *The Drudge Report*. Then have a courier deliver them to *The Washington Post* as soon as possible.'

'Very good, sir.' Willard tucked the envelope under his arm, vanished into another part of the Library.

Then LaValle took out his cell phone, dialed a local number. 'Gus, this is Luther LaValle. Fine, fine. How's Ginnie? Good, give her my love. The kids, as well . . . Listen, Gus, I have a situation here. Evidence has come to light regarding General Kendall, that's right, he's been the target of an internal investigation for some months now. Effective immediately, he's been terminated from my command, from the NSA in toto. Well, you'll see, I'm having the photos messengered over to you even as we speak. Of course it's an exclusive, Gus. Frankly, I'm shocked, truly shocked. You will be, too, when you see these photos . . . I'll have an official statement over to you within forty minutes. Yes, of course. No need to thank me, Gus, I always think of you first.'

Soraya watched this performance with a sick feeling in the pit of her stomach that grew from an icy ball into an iceberg of disbelief.

'How could you?' she said when LaValle finished his call. 'Kendall's your second in command, your friend. You and he go to church together with your families every Sunday.'

'I have no permanent friends or allies; I only have permanent interests,' LaValle said flatly. 'You'll be a damn sight better director when you learn that.'

She then drew out another set of photos, this one showing Feir handing a packet to General Kendall. 'That packet,' she said, 'details the number and locations of Typhon field personnel.'

LaValle's disdainful expression didn't change. 'What's that to me?'

For the second time, Soraya struggled to hide her astonishment. 'That's your second in command taking possession of classified CI intel.'

'On that score you should see to your own people.'

'Are you denying that you gave General Kendall orders to cultivate Rodney Feir as a mole?'

'Yes, I am.'

Soraya was almost breathless. 'I don't believe you.'

LaValle produced an icy smile. 'It doesn't matter what you believe, Director. Only the facts matter.' He flicked the photo away with his fingernail. 'Whatever General Kendall did, he did on his own. I have no knowledge of it.'

Soraya was wondering how everything could have gone so wrong, when, once again, LaValle pushed the phone across the table.

'Now call Bourne.'

She felt as if there were a steel band around her chest; the blood was singing in her ears. *Now what?* she said to herself. *Dear God, what can I do?*

She heard someone with her voice say, 'What should I tell him?'

LaValle produced a slip of paper with a time and an address on it. 'He needs to go here, at this time. Tell him that you're in Munich, that you have information vital to the Black Legion's attack, that he has to see it for himself.'

Soraya's hand was so slick with sweat, she wiped it on her napkin. 'He'll be suspicious if I don't call him on my own phone. In fact, he might not answer if I don't, because he won't know it's me.'

LaValle nodded, but when she produced her phone, he said, 'I'm going to listen to every word you say. If you try to warn him I promise your friend Tyrone will never leave this building alive. Clear?'

She nodded, but did nothing.

Observing her like a frog split open on a dissecting table, LaValle said, 'I know you don't want to do this, Director. I know how *badly* you don't want to do this. But you *will* call Bourne and you *will* set the trap for me, because I'm stronger than you are. By that I mean my will. I get what I want, Director, at any cost, but not you

– you *care* too much to have a long career in intelligence work. You're doomed and you know it.'

Soraya had stopped listening to him after the first few words. Acutely aware that she had vowed to take control of the situation, to somehow turn disaster into victory, she was furiously marshaling her forces. *One step at a time,* she told herself now. *I have to clear my mind of Tyrone, of the failed ploy with Kendall, of my own guilt. I have to think of this call now; how am I going to make the call and keep Jason from being captured?*

It seemed an impossible task, but that kind of thinking was defeatist, totally unhelpful. Still – what was she to do?

'After your call,' LaValle said, 'you'll stay here, under constant surveillance, until after Bourne is taken into custody.'

Uncomfortably aware of his avid eyes on her, she flipped open her phone, and called Jason.

When she heard his voice, she said, 'Hi, it's me, Soraya.'

Bourne was standing in Egon Kirsch's apartment, staring down at the street when his cell phone rang. He saw Soraya's number come up on the screen, answered the call, and heard her say, 'Hi, it's me, Soraya.'

'Where are you?'

'Actually, I'm in Munich.'

He perched on the arm of an upholstered chair. 'Actually? In Munich?'

'That's what I said.'

He frowned, hearing echoes in his head from far away. 'I'm surprised.'

'Not as much as I am. You came up on the CI surveillance grid at the airport.'

'There was no help for it.'

'I'm sure not. Anyway, I'm not over here on official CI business. We've been continuing to monitor the Black Legion communications, and at last we got a breakthrough.'

He stood up. 'What is it?'

'The phone's too insecure,' she said. 'We should meet.' She told him the place and the time.

Glancing at his watch, he said, 'That's a little over an hour from now.'

'Right as rain. I can make it. Can you?'

'I think I can manage,' he said. 'See you.'

He disconnected, went over to the window, leaned on the sash, replaying the conversation word by word in his mind.

He felt the jolt of a dislocation, as if he had moved outside his body, experiencing something that had happened to someone else. His mind, recording a seismic shift in its neurons, was struggling with a memory. Bourne knew he'd had this conversation before, but for the life of him he couldn't remember where or when, or what significance it might have for him now.

He would have continued on with his fruitless search had not the downstairs bell rang. Turning from the window, he went across the living room, pressed the button that released the outer door's lock. The time had finally come when he and Arkadin would meet face-to-face – the assassin of legend, who specialized in killing killers, who had slipped in and out of a Russian high-security prison without anyone being the wiser, who had managed to eliminate Pyotr and his entire network.

There was a knock on the door. He kept away from the spy hole, kept away from the door itself, unlatching it from the side. There was no gunshot, no splintering of the wood and metal. Instead the door opened inward and a dapper man with dark skin and a spade-shaped beard stepped into the apartment.

Bourne said, 'Turn around slowly.'

The man, hands where Bourne could see them, turned to face him. It was Semion Icoupov.

'Bourne,' he said.

Bourne produced his passport, opened it to the inside cover.

Icoupov nodded. 'I see. Is this where you kill me at the behest of Dominic Specter?'

'You mean Asher Sever.'

'Oh, dear,' Icoupov said, 'there goes my surprise.' He smiled. 'I confess I'm shocked. Nevertheless, I congratulate you, Mr. Bourne. You've come by knowledge no one else has. By what means is a complete mystery.'

'Let's keep it that way,' Bourne said.

'No matter. What's important is that I don't have to waste time trying to convince you that Sever has played you. Since you've already uncovered his lies, we can move on to the next stage.'

'What makes you think I'm going to listen to anything you have to say?'

'If you've discovered Sever's lies, then you know the recent history of the Black Legion, you know we were once like brothers, you know how deep the enmity between us runs. We are enemies, Sever and I. There can be only one outcome to our war, you understand me?'

Bourne said nothing.

'I want to help you stop his people from attacking your country, is that clear enough?' He shrugged. 'Yes, of course you're right to be skeptical, I would be if I was in your place.' He moved his left hand very slowly to the edge of his overcoat, pulled it back to reveal the lining. There was something sticking out of the slit pocket. 'Perhaps before anything untoward happens, you should take a look at what I have here.'

Bourne leaned in, took the SIG Sauer Icoupov had holstered at his belt. Then he pulled the packet free.

As he was opening it up, Icoupov said, 'I went to a great deal of trouble to steal those from my nemesis.'

Bourne found himself looking over the architectural plans for the Empire State Building. When he glanced up, he found Icoupov watching him intently. 'This is what the Black Legion means to attack. Do you know when?'

'Indeed, I do.' Icoupov glanced at his watch. 'Precisely thirty-three hours, twenty-six minutes from now.'

# 38

Veronica Hart was looking at *The Drudge Report* when Stu Gold escorted General Kendall into her office. She was sitting in front of her desk, the monitor turned toward the door so Kendall could get a clear view of the photos of him and the woman from The Glass Slipper.

'That's just one site,' she said, waving them to three chairs that had been arranged opposite her. 'There are so many others.' When her guests were seated, she addressed Kendall. 'Whatever is your family going to say, General? Your minister, and the congregation?' Her expression remained neutral; she was careful to keep the gloat out of her voice. 'I understand that a goodly number of them aren't fond of African Americans, even as maids and nannies. They prefer the Eastern Europeans – young blond Polish and Russian women. Isn't that right?'

Kendall said nothing, sat with his back ramrod-straight, his hands clasped primly between his knees, as if he were at a court-martial.

Hart wished Soraya were here, but she hadn't returned from the NSA safe house, which was worrying enough; she wasn't answering her cell, either.

'I've suggested that the best thing he can do now is to help us tie LaValle in to the plot to steal CI secrets,' Gold said.

Now Hart smiled rather sweetly at Kendall. 'And what do you think of that suggestion, General?'

'Recruiting Rodney Feir was entirely my idea,' Kendall said woodenly.

Hart sat forward. 'You want us to believe you'd embark on such a risky course without informing your superior?'

'After the fiasco with Batt, I had to do something to prove my worth. I felt I had the best chance romancing Feir.'

'This is getting us nowhere,' Hart said.

Gold stood up. 'I agree. The general has made up his mind to fall on his sword for the man who sold him down the river.' He moved to the door. 'I'm not sure how that computes, but it takes all kinds.'

'Is that it?' Kendall looked straight ahead. 'Are you done with me?'

'We are,' Hart said, 'but Rob Batt isn't.'

Batt's name got a reaction out of the general. 'Batt? What does he have to do with anything? He's out of the picture.'

'I don't think so.' Hart got up, stood behind his chair. 'Batt's had you under surveillance from the moment you ruined his life. Those photos of you and Feir going in and out of the health club, the barbecue joint, and The Glass Slipper were taken by him.'

'But that's not all he has.' Gold lifted his briefcase meaningfully.

'So,' Hart said, 'I'm afraid your stay at CI will continue awhile longer.'

'How much longer?'

'What do you care?' Hart said. 'You no longer have a life to go back to.'

While Kendall remained with two armed agents, Hart and Gold went next door, where Rodney Feir was sitting, guarded by another pair of agents.

'Is the general having fun yet?' Feir said as they took seats facing him. 'This is a black day for him.' He chuckled at his own joke, but no one else did.

'Do you have any idea how serious your situation is?' Gold said.

Feir smiled. 'I do believe I have a handle on the situation.'

Gold and Hart exchanged a glance; neither could understand Feir's light-hearted attitude.

Gold said, 'You're going to jail for a very long time, Mr. Feir.'

Feir crossed one leg over the other. 'I think not.'

'You think wrong,' Gold said.

'Rodney, we have you stealing Typhon secrets and handing them over to a ranking member of a rival intelligence organization.'

'Please!' Feir said. 'I'm fully aware of what I did and that you caught me at it. What I'm saying is none of that matters.' He continued to look like the Cheshire Cat, as if he held a royal flush to their four aces.

'Explain yourself,' Gold said curtly.

'I fucked up,' Feir said. 'But I'm not sorry for what I did, only that I got caught.'

'That attitude will certainly help your case,' Hart said caustically. She was done being manhandled by Luther LaValle and his cohorts.

'I'm not, by nature, prone to being contrite, Director. But like your evidence, my attitude is of no import. I mean to say, if I *were* contrite like Rob Batt, would it make any difference to you?' He shook his head. 'So let's not bullshit each other. What I did, how I feel about it is in the past. Let's talk about the future.'

'You have no future,' Hart said tartly.

'That remains to be seen.' Feir kept his maddening smile trained on her. 'What I'm proposing is a barter.'

Gold was incredulous. 'You want to make a deal?'

'Let's call it a fair exchange,' Feir said. 'You drop all charges against me, give me a generous severance package and a letter of recommendation I can take into the private sector.'

'Anything else?' Hart said. 'How about a summer house on the Chesapeake and a yacht to go with it?'

'A generous offer,' Feir said with a perfectly straight face, 'but I'm not a pig, Director.'

Gold rose. 'This is intolerable behavior.'

Feir eyed him. 'Don't get your knickers in a twist, counselor. You haven't heard my side of the exchange.'

'Not interested.' Gold signaled the two agents. 'Take him back down to the holding cell.'

'I wouldn't do that if I were you.' Feir didn't struggle as the agents grabbed hold of either arm and hauled him to his feet. He turned to Hart. 'Director, did you ever wonder why Luther LaValle didn't try a run at CI while the Old Man was alive?'

'I didn't have to; I know. The Old Man was too powerful, too well connected.'

'True enough, but there's another, more specific reason.' Feir looked from one agent to the other.

Hart wanted to wring his neck. 'Let him go,' she said.

Gold stepped forward. 'Director, I strongly recommend –'

'No harm in hearing the man out, Stu.' Hart nodded. 'Go ahead, Rodney. You have one minute.'

'The fact is LaValle tried several times to make a run at CI while the Old Man was in charge. He failed every time, and do you know why?' Feir looked from one to the other, the Cheshire Cat grin back on his face. 'Because for years the Old Man has had a deep-cover mole inside the NSA.'

Hart goggled at him. 'What?'

'This is bullshit,' Gold said. 'He's blowing smoke up our ass.'

'Good guess, counselor, but wrong. I know the identity of the mole.'

'How on earth would you know that, Rodney?'

Feir laughed. 'Sometimes – not very often, I admit – it pays to be CI's chief file clerk.'

'That's hardly what you –'

'That's precisely what I am, Director.' A storm cloud of deep-seated anger momentarily shook him. 'No fancy title can obscure the fact.' He waved a hand, his flash of rage quickly banked to embers. 'But no matter, the point is I see things in CI no one else does. The Old Man had contingencies in place should he be killed, but you know this better than I do, counselor, don't you?'

Gold turned to Hart. 'The Old Man left a number of sealed envelopes addressed to different directors in the event of his sudden demise.'

'One of those envelopes,' Feir said, 'the one with the identity of the mole inside NSA, was sent to Rob Batt, which made sense at the time, since Batt was chief of operations. But it never got to Batt, I saw to that.'

'You –' Hart was so enraged that she could barely speak.

'I could say that I'd already begun to suspect that Batt was working for the NSA,' Feir said, 'but that would be a lie.'

'So you held on to it, even after I was appointed.'

'Leverage, Director. I figured that sooner or later I'd need my Get Out of Jail Free card.'

There was the smile that made Hart want to bury her fist in his face. With an effort, she restrained herself. 'And meanwhile, you let LaValle trample all over us. Because of you I was led out of my office in handcuffs, because of you the Old Man's legacy is a hair's breadth from being buried.'

'Yeah, well, these things happen. What can you do?'

'I'll tell you what I can do,' Hart said, signaling the agents, who grabbed Feir again. 'I can tell you to go to hell. I can tell you that you'll spend the rest of your life in jail.'

Even then, Feir appeared unfazed. 'I said I knew who the mole is, Director. Furthermore – and I believe this will be of especial interest to you – I know where he's stationed.'

Hart was too enraged to care. 'Get him out of my sight.'

As he was being led to the door, Feir said, 'He's inside the NSA safe house.'

The DCI felt her heart thumping hard in her chest. Feir's goddamn smile was not only understandable now, it was warranted.

*Thirty-three hours, twenty-six minutes from now.* Icoupov's ominous words were still ringing in Bourne's ears when he saw a flicker of movement. He and Icoupov were standing in the foyer, the front door was still open, and a shadow had for a moment stained the opposite wall of the hallway. Someone was out there, shielded by the half-open door.

Bourne, continuing to talk to Icoupov, took the other man by his elbow and moved him back into the living room, across the rug, toward the hallway to the bedrooms and bath. As they passed one of the windows, it exploded inward with the force of a man swinging through. Bourne whirled, the SIG Sauer he'd taken from Icoupov coming to bear on the intruder.

'Put the SIG down,' a female voice said from behind him. He turned his head to see that the figure in the hallway – a young pale woman – was aiming a Luger at his head.

'Leonid, what are you doing here?' Icoupov seemed apoplectic. 'I gave you express orders –'

'It's Bourne.' Arkadin advanced through the welter of glass littering the floor. 'It was Bourne who killed Mischa.'

'Is this true?' Icoupov turned on Bourne. 'You killed Mikhail Tarkanian?'

'He left me no choice,' Bourne said.

Devra, her Luger aimed squarely at Bourne's head, said, 'Drop the SIG. I won't say it again.'

Icoupov reached out toward Bourne. 'I'll take it.'

'Stay where you are,' Arkadin ordered. His own Luger was aimed at Icoupov.

'Leonid, what are you doing?'

Arkadin ignored him. 'Do as the lady says, Bourne. Drop the SIG.'

Bourne did as he was told. The moment he let go of the gun, Arkadin tossed his Luger aside and leapt at Bourne. Bourne raised a forearm in time to block Arkadin's knee, but he felt the jolt all the way up into his shoulder. They traded punishing blows, clever feints, and defensive blocks. For each move he employed, Arkadin had the perfect counter, and vice versa. When he stared into the Russian's eyes he saw his darkest deeds reflected back at him, all the death and destruction that lay in his wake. In those implacable eyes there was a void blacker than a starless night.

They moved across the living room as Bourne gave way, until they passed under the archway separating the living room from the rest of the apartment. In the kitchen Arkadin grabbed a cleaver, swung it at Bourne. Dodging away from the executioner's lethal arc, Bourne reached for a wooden block that held several carving knives. Arkadin brought the cleaver down on the countertop, missing Bourne's fingers by less than an inch. Now he blocked the way to the knives, swinging the cleaver back and forth like a scythe reaping wheat.

Bourne was near the sink. Snatching a plate out of the dish rack, he hurled it like a Frisbee, forcing Arkadin to duck out of the way. As the plate shattered against the wall behind Arkadin, Bourne withdrew a carving knife like a sword out of its scabbard. Steel clashed against steel, until Bourne used the knife to stab directly at Arkadin's stomach. Arkadin brought the cleaver down precisely at the place where Bourne was gripping the knife, and he had to let go. The knife rang as it hit the floor, then Arkadin rushed Bourne, and the two closed together.

Bourne managed to keep the cleaver away, and at such close quarters it was impossible to swing it back and forth. Realizing it had become a liability, Arkadin dropped it.

For three long minutes they were locked together in a kind of double death grip. Bloody and bruised, neither managed to gain the upper hand. Bourne had never encountered someone of Arkadin's physical and mental skill, someone who was so much like him. Fighting Arkadin was like fighting a mirror image of himself, one he didn't care for. He felt as if he stood on the precipice of something terrible, a chasm filled with endless dread, where no life could survive. He felt Arkadin had reached out to pull him into this abyss, as if to show him the desolation that lurked behind his own eyes, the grisly image of his forgotten past reflected back at him.

With a supreme effort Bourne broke Arkadin's hold, slammed his fist against the Russian's ear. Arkadin recoiled back against a column, and Bourne sprinted out of the kitchen, down the hall. As he did so, he heard the unmistakable sound of someone racking the slide, and he flung himself headlong into the main bedroom. A shot splintered the wooden door frame just over his head.

Scrambling up, he headed straight for Kirsch's closet, even as he heard Arkadin shout to the pale woman to hold her fire. Pushing aside a rack of clothes on hangers, Bourne scrabbled at the plywood panel in the rear wall of the closet, searching for the clips Kirsch had described to him at the museum. Just as he heard Arkadin rush into the bedroom, he turned the clips, removed the panel, and, crouching almost double, stepped through into a world filled to overflowing with shadow.

When Devra turned around after her attempt to wound Bourne, she found herself looking at the muzzle of the SIG Sauer that Icoupov had retrieved from the floor.

'You fool,' Icoupov said, 'you and your boyfriend are going to fuck everything up.'

'What Leonid is doing is his own business,' she said.

'That's the nature of the mistake,' Icoupov said. 'Leonid has no business of his own. Everything he is he owes to me.'

She stepped out of the shadows of the hallway into the living room. The Luger at her hip was pointed at Icoupov. 'He's quits with you,' she said. 'His servitude is done.'

Icoupov laughed. 'Is that what he told you?'

'It's what I told him.'

'Then you're a bigger fool than I thought.'

They circled each other, wary of the slightest move. Even so, Devra managed an icy smile. 'He's changed since he left Moscow. He's a different person.'

Icoupov made a dismissive sound in the back of his throat. 'The first thing you need to get through your head is that Leonid is incapable of change. I know this better than anyone because I spent so many years trying to make him a better person. I failed. Everyone who tried failed, and do you know why? Because Leonid isn't whole. Somewhere in the days and nights of Nizhny Tagil he was fractured. All the czar's horses and all the czar's men can't put him back together again; the pieces no longer fit.' He gestured with the SIG Sauer's barrel. 'Get out now, get out while you can, otherwise, I promise you he'll kill you like he killed all the others who tried to get close to him.'

'How deluded you are!' Devra spat. 'You're like all your kind, corrupted by power. You've spent so many years removed from life on the streets you've created your own reality, one that moves only to the wave of your own hand.' She took a step toward him, which prompted a tense response from him. 'Think you can kill me before I kill you? I wouldn't count on it.' She tossed her head. 'Anyway, you have more to lose than I do. I was already half dead when Leonid found me.'

'Ah, I see it now,' Icoupov nodded, 'he's saved you from yourself, he's saved you from the streets, is that it?'

'Leonid is my protector.'

'God in heaven, talk about deluded!'

Devra's icy smile widened. 'One of us is fatally mistaken. It remains to be seen which one.'

'The room is filled with mannequins,' Egon Kirsch had said when he'd described his studio to Bourne. 'I keep the light out with blackout shades because these mannequins are my creation. I built them from the ground up, so to speak. They're my companions, you might say, as well as my creations. In that sense, they can see or, if you like, I *believe* that they have the gift of sight, and what creature can look upon his creator without going mad or blind, or both?'

With the map of the room in his mind, Bourne crept through the studio, avoiding the mannequins so as not to make noise or, as Kirsch might have said, so as not to disturb the process of their birth.

'You think I'm insane,' he'd said to Bourne in the museum. 'Not that it matters. To all artists – successful or not! – their creations are alive. I'm no different. It's simply that after struggling for years to bring abstractions to life, I've given my work human form.'

Hearing a sound, Bourne froze for a moment, then peered around a mannequin's thigh. His eyes had adjusted to the extreme gloom, and he could see movement: Arkadin had found the panel and had come through into the studio after him.

Bourne liked his chances here far better than in Kirsch's apartment. He knew the layout, the darkness would help him, and if he struck quickly, he'd have the advantage of being able to see where Arkadin couldn't.

With that strategy in mind, he moved out from behind the mannequin, picked his way toward the Russian. The studio was like a minefield. There were three mannequins between him and Arkadin, all set at different angles and poses: One was sitting, holding a small painting as if reading a book; another was standing spread-legged, in a classic shooter's pose; the third was running, leaning forward, as if stretching to cross the finish line.

Bourne moved around the runner. Arkadin was crouched down on his hams, wisely staying in one place until his eyes adjusted. It was precisely what Bourne had done when he'd entered the studio moments before.

Once again Bourne was struck by the eerie mirror image that Arkadin represented. There was no pleasure and a great deal of anxiety at the most primi-tive level in watching him do his best to find you and kill you.

Picking up his pace, Bourne negotiated the space to where the mannequin sat, reading his painting. Keenly aware that he was running out of time, Bourne moved stealthily abreast of the shooter. Just as he was about to lunge at Arkadin, his cell phone buzzed, the screen lighting up with Moira's number.

With a silent curse, Bourne sprang. Arkadin, alert for even the tiniest anomaly, turned defensively toward the sound, and Bourne was met with a solid wall of muscle, behind which was a murderous will of fiery intensity. Arkadin swung; Bourne slid backward, between the legs of the shooter mannequin. As Arkadin came after him he ran right into the mannequin's hips. Recoiling with a curse, he swung at the man-nequin. The blade struck the acrylic skin and lodged in the sheet metal underneath. Bourne kicked out while Arkadin was trying to pull the blade free, and made contact with the left side of his chest. Arkadin tried to roll away. Bourne jammed his shoulder against the back of the shooter. It was extremely heavy, he put all of his strength into it, and the mannequin tipped over, trapping Arkadin underneath.

'Your friend gave me no choice,' Bourne said. 'He would've killed me if I hadn't stopped him. He was too far away; I had to throw the knife.'

A sound like the crackle of a fire came from Arkadin. It took a moment for Bourne to realize it was laughter. 'I'll make you a bet, Bourne. Before he died, I bet Mischa said you were a dead man.'

Bourne was about to answer him when he saw the dim glint of a SIG Sauer Mosquito in Arkadin's hand. He ducked just before the .22 bullet whizzed over his head.

'He was right.'

Bourne twisted away, dodging around the other mannequins, using them as cover even as Arkadin squeezed off three more rounds. Plaster, wood, and acrylic shattered near Bourne's left shoulder and ear before he dived behind Kirsch's worktable. Behind him, he could hear Arkadin's grunts combined with the screech of metal as he worked to free himself from the fallen shooter.

Bourne knew from Kirsch's description that the front door was to the left. Scrambling up, he dashed around the corner as Arkadin fired another shot. A chunk of plaster and lath disintegrated where the .22 impacted the corner. Reaching the door, Bourne unlocked it, pulled it open, and sprinted out into the hallway. The open door to Kirsch's apartment loomed to his left.

'No good can come of us training guns on each other,' Icoupov said. 'Let's try to reason through this situation rationally.'

'That's your problem,' Devra said. 'Life isn't rational; it's fucked-up chaos. It's part of the delusion; power makes you think you can control everything. But you can't, no one can.'

'You and Leonid think you know what you're doing, but you're wrong. No one operates in a vacuum. If you kill Bourne it will have terrible repercussions.'

'Repercussions for you, not for us. This is what power does: You think in short-cuts. Expediency, political opportunities, corruption without end.'

It was at that moment they both heard the gunshots, but only Devra knew they came from Arkadin's Mosquito. She could sense Icoupov's finger tighten around the SIG's trigger, and she went into a semi-crouch because she knew if Bourne appeared rather than Arkadin she would shoot him dead.

The situation had reached boiling point, and Icoupov was clearly worried. 'Devra, I beg you to reconsider. Leonid doesn't know the whole picture. I need Bourne alive. What he did to Mischa was despicable, but personal feelings have no place in this equation. So much planning, so much spilled blood will come to nothing if Leonid kills Bourne. You must let me stop it; I'll give you anything – anything you want.'

'Do you think you can buy me? Money means nothing to me. What I want is Leonid,' Devra said just as Bourne appeared through the front doorway.

Devra and Icoupov both turned. Devra screamed because she knew, or she thought she knew, that Arkadin was dead, and so she redirected the Luger from Icoupov to Bourne.

Bourne ducked back into the hallway and she fired shot after shot at him as she walked toward the door. Because her focus was entirely concentrated on Bourne, she took her eyes off Icoupov and so missed the crucial movement as he swung the SIG in her direction.

'I warned you,' he said as he shot her in the chest.

She fell onto her back.

'Why didn't you listen?' Icoupov said as he shot her again.

Devra made a little sound as her body arched up. Icoupov stood over her.

'How could you let yourself be seduced by such a monster?' he said.

Devra stared up at him with red-rimmed eyes. Blood pumped out of her with every labored beat of her heart. 'That's exactly what I asked him about you.' Each ragged breath filled her with indescribable pain. 'He's not a monster, but if he were you'd be so much worse.'

Her hand twitched. Icoupov, caught up in her words, paid no attention until the bullet she fired from her Luger struck his right shoulder. He spun back against the wall. The pain caused him to drop the SIG. Seeing her struggling to fire again, he turned and ran out of the apartment, fleeing down the stairwell and out onto the street.

# 39

Willard, relaxing in the steward's lounge adjacent to the Library of the NSA safe house, was enjoying his sweet and milky midmorning cup of coffee while reading *The Washington Post* when his cell phone buzzed. He checked it, saw that it was from his son, Oren. Of course it wasn't actually from Oren, but Willard was the only one who knew that.

He put down the paper, watched as the photo appeared on the phone's screen. It was of two people standing in front of a rural church, its steeple rising up into the top margin of the photo. He had no idea who the people were or where they were, but these things were irrelevant. There were six ciphers in his head; this photo told him which one to use. The two figures plus the steeple meant he was to use cipher three. If, for instance, the two people were in front of an arch, he'd subtract one from two, instead of adding to it. There were other visual cues. A brick building meant divide the number of figures by two; a bridge, multiply by two; and so on.

Willard deleted the photo from his phone, then picked up the third section of the *Post* and began to read the first story on page three. Starting with the third word, he began to decipher the message that was his call to action. As he moved through the article, substituting certain letters for others as the protocol dictated, he felt a profound stirring inside him. He had been the Old Man's eyes and ears inside the NSA for three decades, and the Old Man's sudden death last year had saddened him deeply. Then he had witnessed Luther LaValle's latest run at CI and had waited for his phone to ring, but for months his desire to see another photo fill his screen had been inexplicably unfulfilled. He simply couldn't understand why the new DCI wasn't making use of him. Had he fallen between the cracks; did Veronica Hart not know he existed? It certainly seemed that way, especially after LaValle had trapped Soraya Moore and her compatriot, who was still incarcerated belowdecks, as Willard privately called the rendition cells in the basement. He'd done what he could for the young man named Tyrone, though God knows it was little enough. Yet he knew that even the smallest sign of hope – the knowledge that you weren't alone – was enough to reinvigorate a stalwart heart, and if he was any judge of character, Tyrone had a stalwart heart.

Willard had always wanted to be an actor – for many years Olivier had been his god – but in his wildest dreams he'd never imagined his acting career would be in the political arena. He'd gotten into it by accident, playing a role in his college company, Henry V, to be exact, one of Shakespeare's great tragic politicians. As the Old Man said to him when he'd come backstage to congratulate Willard, Henry's betrayal of Falstaff is political, rather than personal, and ends in success. 'How would you like to do that in real life?' the Old Man had asked him. He'd come to Willard's college to recruit for CI; he said he often found his people in the most unlikely places.

Finished with the deciphering, Willard had his immediate instructions, and he thanked the powers that be that he hadn't been tossed aside with the Old Man's trash. He felt like his old friend Henry V, though more than thirty years had passed since he'd trod a theater stage. Once again he was being called on to play his greatest role, one that he wore as effortlessly as a second skin.

He folded the paper away under one arm, took up his cell phone, and went out of the lounge. He still had twenty minutes left on his break, more than enough time to do what was required of him. What he had been ordered to do was find the digital camera Tyrone had on him when he'd been captured. Poking his head into the Library, he satisfied himself that LaValle was still sitting in his accustomed spot, opposite Soraya Moore, then he went down the hall.

Though the Old Man had recruited him, it was Alex Conklin who had trained him. Conklin, the Old Man had told him, was the best at what he did, namely preparing agents to be put into the field. It didn't take him long to learn that though Conklin was renowned inside CI for training wet-work agents, he was also adept at coaching sleeper agents. Willard spent almost a year with Conklin, though never at CI headquarters; he was part of Treadstone, Conklin's project that was so secret even most CI personnel was unaware of its existence. It was of paramount importance that he have no overt association with CI. Because the role the Old Man had planned for him was inside the NSA, his background check had to be able to withstand the most vigorous scrutiny.

All this flashed through Willard's mind as he walked the sacrosanct hallways and corridors of the NSA's safe house. He passed agent after agent and knew that he'd done his job to perfection. He was the indispensable nobody, the person who was always present, whom no one noticed.

He knew where Tyrone's camera was because he'd been there when Kendall and LaValle had spoken about its disposition, but even if he hadn't, he'd have suspected where LaValle had hidden it. He knew, for instance, that it wouldn't have been allowed to leave the safe house, even on LaValle's person, unless the damaging images Tyrone had taken of the rendition cells and the waterboarding tanks had been transferred to the in-house computer server or deleted off the camera's drive. In fact, there was a chance that the images had been deleted, but he doubted it. In the short amount of time the camera had been in the NSA's possession, Kendall was no longer in residence and LaValle had become obsessed with coercing Soraya Moore into giving him Jason Bourne.

He knew all about Bourne; he'd read the Treadstone files, even the ones that no longer existed, having been shredded and then burned when the information they held became too dangerous for Conklin, as well as for CI. He knew there had been far more to Treadstone than even the Old Man knew. That was Conklin's doing; he'd been a man for whom the word *secrecy* was the holy grail. What his ultimate plan for Treadstone had been was anyone's guess.

Inserting his passkey into the lock on LaValle's office door, he punched in the proper electronic code. Willard knew everyone's code – what use would he be as a sleeper agent otherwise? The door opened inward, and he slipped inside, shutting and locking it behind him.

Crossing to LaValle's desk, he opened the drawers one by one, checking for false backs or bottoms. Finding none, he moved on to the bookcase, the sideboard with its hanging files and liquor bottles side by side. He lifted the prints off the walls, searching behind them for a hidden cache, but there was nothing.

He sat on a corner of the desk, contemplated the room, unconsciously swinging his leg back and forth while he tried to work out where LaValle had hidden the camera. All at once he heard the sound the heel of his shoe made against the skirt of the desk. Hopping off, he went around, crawled into the kneehole, and rapped on the skirt until he replicated the sound his heel had made. Yes, he was certain now: This part of the skirt was hollow.

Feeling around with his fingertips, he discovered the tiny latch, pushed it aside, and swung open the door. There was Tyrone's camera. He was reaching for it when he heard the scratch of metal on metal.

LaValle was at the door.

'Tell me you love me, Leonid Danilovich.' Devra smiled up at him as he knelt over her.

'What happened, Devra? What happened?' was all he could say.

He'd extricated himself at last from the sculpture, and would have gone after Bourne – but he'd heard the shots coming from Kirsch's apartment, then the sound of running feet. The living room was spattered with blood. He saw her lying on the floor, the Luger still in her hand. Her shirt was dyed red.

'Leonid Danilovich.' She'd called his name when he appeared in her limited field of vision. 'I waited for you.'

She started to tell him what had happened, but blood bubbles formed at the corners of her mouth and she started to gurgle horribly. Arkadin lifted her head off the floor, cradled it on his thighs. He pushed matted hair off her forehead and cheeks, leaving red streaks like war paint.

She tried to continue, stopped. Her eyes went out of focus and he thought he'd lost her. Then they cleared, her smile returned, and she said, 'Do you love me, Leonid?'

He bent down and whispered in her ear. Was it *I love you*? There was so much static in his head, he couldn't hear himself. Did he love her, and, if he did, what would it mean? Did it even matter? He'd promised to protect her and failed. He stared down into her eyes, into her smile, but all he saw was his own past rising up to engulf him once again.

'I need more money,' Yelena said one night as she lay entangled with him.

'What for? I give you enough as it is.'

'I hate it here, it's like a prison, girls are crying all the time, they're beaten, and then they disappear. I used to make friends just to pass the time, to have something to do during the day, but now I don't bother. What's the point? They're gone within a week.'

Arkadin had become aware of Kuzin's seemingly insatiable need for more girls. 'I don't see how any of this has to do with you needing more money.'

'If I can't have friends,' Yelena said, 'I want drugs.'

'I told you, no drugs,' Arkadin said as he rolled away from her and sat up.

'If you love me, you'll get me out of here.'

'Love?' He turned to stare at her. 'Who said anything about love?'

She started to cry. 'I want to live with you, Leonid. I want to be with you always.'

Feeling something unknown close around his throat, Arkadin stood up, backed away. 'Jesus,' he said, gathering up his clothes, 'where do you get such ideas?'

Leaving her to her pitiful weeping, he went out to procure more girls. Before he reached the front door of the brothel Stas Kuzin intercepted him.

'Yelena's wailing is disturbing the other girls,' he said in his hissing way. 'It's bad for business.'

'She wants to live with me,' Arkadin said. 'Can you imagine?'

Kuzin laughed, the sound like nails screeching against a blackboard. 'I'm wondering what would be worse, the nagging wife wanting to know where you were all night or the caterwauling brats making it impossible to sleep.'

They both laughed at the comment, and Arkadin thought nothing more about it. For the next three days he worked steadily, methodically combing Nizhny Tagil for more girls to restock the brothel. At the end of that time he slept for twenty hours, then went straight to Yelena's room. He found another girl, one he'd recently hijacked off the streets, sleeping in Yelena's bed.

'Where's Yelena?' he said, throwing off the covers.

She looked up at him, blinking like a bat in sunlight. 'Who's Yelena?' she said in a voice husky with sleep.

Arkadin strode out of the room and into Stas Kuzin's office. The big man sat behind a gray metal desk, talking on the phone, but he beckoned Arkadin to take a seat while he finished his call. Arkadin, preferring to stand, gripped the back of a wooden chair, leaning forward over its ladder back.

At length, Kuzin put down the receiver, said, 'What can I do for you, my friend?'

'Where's Yelena?'

'Who?' Kuzin's frown knit his brows together, making him look something like a cyclops. 'Oh, yes, the wailer.' He smiled. 'There's no chance of her bothering you again.'

'What does that mean?'

'Why ask a question to which you already know the answer?' Kuzin's phone rang and he answered it. 'Hold the fuck on,' he said into it. Then he looked up at his partner. 'Tonight we'll go to dinner to celebrate your freedom, Leonid Danilovich. We'll make a real night of it, eh?'

Then he returned to his call.

Arkadin felt frozen in time, as if he was now doomed to relive this moment for the rest of his life. Mute, he walked like an automaton out of the office, out of the brothel, out of the building he owned with Kuzin. Without even thinking, he got into his car, drove north into the forest of dripping firs and weeping hemlocks. There was no sun in the sky, the horizon was rimmed with smokestacks. The air was hazed with carbon and sulfur particles, tinged a lurid orange-red, as if everything were on fire.

Arkadin pulled off the road and walked down the rutted track, following the route the van had taken previously. Somewhere along the line he found that he was running as fast as he could through the evergreens, the stench of decay and decomposition billowing up, as if eager to meet him.

He brought himself up abruptly at the edge of the pit. In places, sacks of quicklime had been shaken out in order to aid the decomposition; nevertheless it was impossible to mistake the content. His eyes roved over the bodies until he found her. Yelena was lying in a tangle where she'd landed after being kicked over the side. Several very large rats were picking their way toward her.

Arkadin, staring into the mouth of hell, gave a little cry, the sound a puppy might make if you mistakenly stepped on its paw. Scrambling down the side, he ignored the appalling stench and, through watering eyes, dragged her up the slope, laid her out on the forest floor, the bed of brown needles, soft as her own. Then he trudged back to the car, opened the trunk, and took out a shovel.

He buried her half a mile away from the pit, in a small clearing that was private and peaceful. He carried her over his shoulder the whole way, and by the time he was finished he smelled like death. At that moment, crouched on his hamstrings, his face streaked with sweat and dirt, he doubted whether he'd ever be able to scrub off the stench. If he knew a prayer, he would have said it then, but he knew only obscenities, which he uttered with the fervor of the righteous. But he wasn't righteous; he was damned.

For a businessman there was a decision to be made. Arkadin was no businessman, though, so from that day forward his fate was sealed. He returned to Nizhny Tagil with his two Stechkin handguns fully loaded and extra rounds of ammunition in his breast pockets. Entering the brothel, he shot the two ghouls dead as they stood at guard. Neither had a chance to draw his weapon.

Stas Kuzin appeared in the doorway, gripping a Korovin TK pistol. 'Leonid, what the fuck?'

Arkadin shot him once in each knee. Kuzin went down, screaming. As he tried to raise the Korovin, Arkadin trod heavily on his wrist. Kuzin grunted heavily. When he wouldn't let go of the pistol, Arkadin kicked him in the knee. The resulting bellow brought the last of the girls from their respective rooms.

'Get out of here.' Arkadin addressed the girls, though his gaze was fixed on Kuzin's monstrous face. 'Take whatever money you can find and go back to your families. Tell them about the lime pit north of town.'

He heard them scrambling, babbling to one another, then it was quiet.

'Fucking sonovabitch,' Kuzin said, staring up at Arkadin.

Arkadin laughed and shot him in the right shoulder. Then, jamming the Stechkins in their holsters, he dragged Kuzin across the floor. He had to push one of the dead ghouls out of the way, but at last he made it down the stairs and out the front door with the moaning Kuzin in tow. In the street one of Kuzin's vans screeched to a halt. Arkadin drew his guns, emptied them into the interior. The car rocked on its shocks, glass shattered, its horn blared as the dead driver fell over onto it. No one got out.

Arkadin dragged Kuzin to his car and dumped him in the backseat. Then he drove out of town to the forest, turning off at the rutted dirt track. At the end of it, he stopped, hauled Kuzin to the edge of the pit.

'Fuck you, Arkadin!' Kuzin shouted. 'Fuck –'

Arkadin shot him point-blank in the left shoulder, shattering it and sending Kuzin down into the quicklime pit. He peered over. There was the monster, lying on the corpses.

Kuzin's mouth drooled blood. 'Kill me!' he shouted. 'D'you think I'm afraid of death? Go on, do it now!'

'It's not for me to kill you, Stas.'

'Kill me, I said. For fuck's sake, finish it now!'

Arkadin gestured at the corpses. 'You'll die in your victims' arms, hearing their curses echoing in your ears.'

'What about all *your* victims?' Kuzin shouted when Arkadin disappeared from view. 'You'll die choking on your own blood!'

Arkadin paid him no mind. He was already behind the wheel of his car, backing out of the forest. It had begun to rain, gunmetal-colored drops that fell like bullets out of a colorless sky. A slow booming coming from the smelters starting up sounded like the thunder of cannons signaling the beginning of a war that would surely destroy him unless he found a way out of Nizhny Tagil that wasn't in a body bag.

# 40

'Where are you, Jason?' Moira said. 'I've been trying to reach you.'

'I'm in Munich,' he said.

'How wonderful! Thank God you're close by. I need to see you.' She seemed slightly out of breath. 'Tell me where you are and I'll meet you there.'

Bourne switched his cell phone from one ear to the other, the better to check his immediate surroundings. 'I'm on my way to the Englischer Garten.'

'What are you doing in Schwabing?'

'It's a long story; I'll tell you about it when I see you.' Bourne checked his watch. 'But I'm due to meet up with Soraya at the Chinese pagoda in ten minutes. She says she has new intel on the Black Legion attack.'

'That's odd,' Moira said. 'So do I.'

Bourne crossed the street, hurrying, but still alert for tags.

'I'll meet you,' Moira said. 'I'm in a car; I can be there in fifteen minutes.'

'Not a good idea.' He didn't want her involved in a professional rendezvous. 'I'll call you as soon as I'm through and we can – ' All of a sudden, he realized he was talking to dead air. He dialed Moira's number, but got her voice mail. Damn her, he thought.

He reached the outskirts of the garden, which was twice the size of New York's Central Park. Divided by the Isar River, it was filled with jogging and bicycle paths, meadows, forests, and even hills. Near the crown of one of these was the Chinese pagoda, which was actually a beer garden.

He was naturally thinking of Soraya as he approached the area. It was odd that both she and Moira had intel on the Black Legion. Now he thought back over his phone conversation with her. Something about it had been bothering him, something just out of reach. Every time he strained for it, it seemed to move farther away from him.

His pace was slowed by the hordes of tourists, American diplomats, children with balloons or kites riding the wind. In addition, a rally of teenagers protesting new rulings on curriculum at the university had begun to gather at the pagoda.

He pushed his way forward, past a mother and child, then a large family in Nikes and hideous tracksuits. The child glanced at him and, instinctively, Bourne smiled. Then he turned away, wiped the blood off his face, though it continued to seep through the cuts opened during his fight with Arkadin.

'No, you can't have sausages,' the mother said to her son in a strong British accent. 'You were sick all night.'

'But Mummy,' he replied, 'I feel right as rain.'

*Right as rain.* Bourne stopped in his tracks, rubbed the heel of his hand against his temple. *Right as rain;* the phrase rattled around in his head like a steel ball in a pachinko machine.

Soraya.

*Hi, it's me, Soraya.* That's how she'd started off the call.

Then she'd said: *Actually, I'm in Munich.*

And just before she'd hung up: *Right as rain. I can make it. Can you?*

Bourne, buffeted by the quickening throngs, felt as if his head were on fire. Something about those phrases. He knew them, and he didn't, how could that be? He shook his head as if to clear it; memories were appearing like knife slashes through a piece of fabric. Light was glimmering . . .

And then he saw Moira. She was hurrying toward the Chinese pagoda from the opposite direction, her expression intent, grim, even. What had happened? What information did she have for him?

He craned his neck, trying to find Soraya in the swirl of the demonstration. That was when he remembered.

*Right as rain.*

He and Soraya had had this conversation before – where? In Odessa? *Hi, it's me* coming before her name meant that she was under duress. *Actually* coming before a place where she was supposed to be meant that she wasn't there.

*Right as rain* meant it's a trap.

He looked up and his heart sank. Moira was heading right into it.

When the door opened, Willard froze. He was on his hands and knees hidden from the doorway by the desk's skirt. He heard voices, one of them LaValle's, and held his breath.

'There's nothing to it,' LaValle said. 'E-mail me the figures and after I'm done with the Moore woman I'll check them.'

'Good deal,' Patrick, one of LaValle's aides, said, 'but you'd better get back to the Library, the Moore woman is kicking up a fuss.'

LaValle cursed. Willard heard him cross to the desk, shuffle some papers. Perhaps he was looking for a file. LaValle grunted in satisfaction, walked back across the office, and closed the door after him. It was only when Willard heard the grate of the key in the lock that he exhaled.

He fired up the camera, praying that the images hadn't been deleted, and there they were, one after another, evidence that would damn Luther LaValle and his entire NSA administration. Using both the camera and his cell phone, he linked them through the wireless Bluetooth protocol, then transferred the images to his cell. Once that was completed, he navigated to his son's phone number – which wasn't his son's number, though if anyone called it a young man who had standing instructions to pass as his son would answer – and sent the photos in one long burst. Sending them one by one via separate calls would surely cause a red flag on the security server.

At last, Willard sat back and took a deep breath. It was done; the photos were now in the hands of CI, where they'd do the most good, or – if you were Luther LaValle – the most damage. Checking his watch, he pocketed the camera, relatched the door to the hidden compartment, and scrambled out from under the desk.

Four minutes later, his hair freshly combed, his uniform brushed down, and looking very smart indeed, he placed a Ceylon tea in front of Soraya Moore and a single-malt scotch in front of Luther LaValle. Ms. Moore thanked him; LaValle, staring at her, ignored him as usual.

Moira hadn't seen him, and Bourne couldn't call out to her because in this maelstrom of people his voice wouldn't carry. Blocked in his forward motion, he edged his way back to the periphery, moving to his left in order to circle around to her. He tried her cell again, but she either couldn't hear it or wasn't answering.

It was as he was disengaging the line that he saw the NSA agents. They were moving in concert toward the center of the crowd, and he could only assume that there were others in a tightening circle within which they meant to trap him. They hadn't spotted him yet, but Moira was close to one of the pair in Bourne's view. There was no way to get to her without them spotting him. Nevertheless, he continued to circle through the fringes of the crowd, which had grown so large that many of the young people were shoving one another as they shouted their slogans.

Bourne pushed on, although it seemed to him at a slower and slower pace, as if he were in a dream where the laws of physics were nonexistent. He needed to get to Moira without the agents seeing him; it was dangerous for her to be looking for him with NSA infiltrating the crowd. Far better for him to get to her first so he could control both their movements.

Finally, as he neared the NSA agents, he could see the reason for the sudden rancor of the crowd. The shoving was being precipitated by a large group of skinheads, some wielding brass knuckles or baseball bats. They had swastikas tattooed on their bulging arms, and when they began to swing at the chanting university students, Bourne made a run for Moira. But as he lunged for her, one of the agents elbowed a skinhead aside and, as he did so, caught a glimpse of Bourne. He whirled, his lips moving as he spoke urgently into the earpiece with which he was wirelessly connected with the other members of what Bourne assumed was an execution team.

He grabbed Moira, but the agent had hold of him, and he began to jerk Bourne back toward him, as if to detain him long enough for the other members of the team to reach them. Bourne struck him flush on the chin with the heel of his hand. The agent's head snapped back, and he collapsed into a group of skinheads, who thought he was attacking them and started beating him.

'Jason, what the hell happened to you?' Moira said as she and Bourne turned, making their way through the throng. 'Where's Soraya?'

'She was never here,' Bourne said. 'This is another NSA trap.'

It would have been best to keep to where the garden was most crowded, but that would put them in the center of the trap. Bourne led them around the crowd, hoping to emerge in a place where the agents wouldn't spot them, but now he saw three more outside the mass of the demonstration and knew retreat was impossible. Instead he reversed course, drawing Moira farther into the surging mass of demonstrators.

'What are you doing?' Moira said. 'Aren't we headed straight into the trap?'

'Trust me.' Instinctively he headed toward one of the flashpoints where the skinheads were clashing with the university students.

They reached the edge of the escalating fight between the two groups of teens. Out of the corner of his eye Bourne saw an NSA agent struggling through the same mass of people. Bourne tried to alter their course, but their way was blocked, and a resurgent wave of students pushed them like flotsam at the tide line. Feeling the new influx of people, the agent turned to fight against it and ran right into Moira.

He barked Bourne's name into the microphone in his earpiece, and Bourne slammed a shoe into the side of his knee. The agent faltered, but managed to counter the chop Bourne directed at his shoulder blade. The agent drew a handgun, and Bourne snatched a baseball bat from a skinhead's grip, struck the agent so hard on the back of his hands that he dropped the handgun.

Then, from behind him, Bourne heard Moira say. 'Jason, they're coming!'

The trap was about to snap shut on both of them.

# 41

Luther LaValle waited on tenterhooks for the call from his extraction team leader in Munich. He sat in his customary chair facing the window that looked out over the rolling lawns to the left of the wide gravel drive, which wound through the elms and oaks lining it like sentinels. Having verbally put her in her place after returning from his office, he contrived to ignore Soraya Moore and Willard who, after the second time, had given up asking him if he wanted his single-malt scotch refreshed. He didn't want his single-malt scotch refreshed and he didn't want to hear another word from the Moore woman. What he wanted was his cell phone to ring, for his team leader to tell him that Jason Bourne was in custody. That's all he required of this day; he didn't think it was too much to ask.

Nevertheless, it was true that his nerves were pulled tighter than a drawn bow-string. He found himself wanting to scream, to punch someone; he'd almost launched himself like a missile at Willard when the steward had approached him the last time – he was so damn servile. Beside him, the Moore woman sat, one leg crossed over her knee, sipping her damnable Ceylon tea. How could she be so calm!

He reached over, slapped the cup and saucer out of her hands. They bounced on the thick carpet, along with what was left of the tea, but they didn't break. He jumped up, stomped the china beneath his heel until it cracked and cracked again. Aware of Soraya staring up at him, he snapped, 'What? What are you looking at?'

His cell phone buzzed and he snatched it off the table. His heart lifted, a smile of triumph wreathed his face. But it was a guard at the front gate, not the leader of his extraction team.

'Sir, I'm sorry to bother you,' the guard said, 'but the director of Central Intelligence is here.'

'What?' LaValle fairly shouted his response. He was flooded with bitter disappointment. 'Keep her the fuck out!'

'I'm afraid that's not possible, sir.'

'Of course it's possible.' He moved to the window. 'I'm giving you a direct order!'

'She's with a contingent of federal marshals,' the guard said. 'They're already on their way to the main house.'

It was true, LaValle could see the convoy making its way up the drive. He stood, speechless with confusion and fury. How dare the DCI invade his private sanctuary! He'd have her in prison for this outrage!

He started, feeling someone standing next to him. It was Soraya Moore. Her wide lips were curled in an enigmatic smile.

Then she turned to him and said, 'I do believe it's the end of days.'

\*

The maelstrom closed around Bourne and Moira. What had once been a simple demonstration was now a full-blown melee. He heard screams and shouts, hurled invective, and then, under it all, the familiar high-low wail of police sirens approaching from several different directions. Bourne was quite certain the NSA hit squad had no desire to run afoul of the Munich police; it was therefore running out of time. The agent near Bourne heard the sirens, too, and with his hands clearly still half numb from the bat grabbed Moira around the throat.

'Drop the bat and come with me, Bourne,' he said against the rising tide of screams and shouts, 'or so help me I'll break her neck like a twig.'

Bourne dropped the bat but, as he did so, Moira bit into the agent's hand. Bourne drove his fist into the soft spot just below his sternum then, taking hold of his wrist, he turned over the arm at an awkward angle, and with a sharp blow broke the agent's elbow. The agent groaned, went to his knees.

Bourne dug out his passport and earbud, threw the passport to Moira as he fitted the electronic bud into his ear canal.

'Name,' he said.

Moira already had the wallet open. 'William K. Saunders.'

'This is Saunders,' Bourne said, addressing the wireless network. 'Bourne and the girl are getting away. They're heading north by northwest past the pagoda.'

Then he took her hand. 'Biting his hand,' he said as they stepped over the fallen agent. 'That was quite a professional move.'

She laughed. 'It did the trick, didn't it?'

They made their way through the mob, heading southeast. Behind them, the NSA agents were shoving their way toward the opposite side of the mass of people. Ahead, a corps of uniformed policemen outfitted in riot gear were trotting along the path, semiautomatics at the ready. They passed Bourne and Moira without a second look.

Moira glanced at her watch. 'Let's get to my car as quickly as possible. We have a plane to catch.'

*Don't give up.* Those three words Tyrone had found in his oatmeal were enough to sustain him. Kendall never came back, nor did any other interrogator. In fact, his meals came at regular intervals, the trays filled with real food, which was a blessing because he didn't think he could ever get oatmeal down again.

The periods when the black hood was taken off seemed to him longer and longer in duration, but his sense of time had been shot, so he didn't really know whether or not that was true. In any case, he'd used those periods to walk, do sit-ups, push-ups, and squats, anything to relieve the terrible, bone-deep aching of his arms, shoulders, and neck.

*Don't give up.* That message might just as well have read *You're not alone* or *Have faith,* so rich were those words, like a millionaire's cache. When he read them he knew both that Soraya hadn't abandoned him and that something inside the building, someone who had access to the basement, was on his side. And that was the moment when the revelation struck him, as if, if he remembered his Bible correctly, he were Paul on the road to Damascus, converted by God's light.

*Someone is on my side* – not the side of the old Tyrone, who roamed his hood with perfect wrath and retribution, not the Tyrone who'd been saved from life in the gutter by Deron, not even the Tyrone who'd been awed by Soraya. No, once he spontaneously thought *Someone is on my side,* he realized that *my side* meant CI. He had not only moved out of the hood forever, but also stepped out from under Soraya's beautiful shadow. He was his own man now; he'd found his own calling, not as Deron's protector, or his disciple, not as Soraya's adoring assistant. CI was where he wanted to be, in the service of making a difference. His world was no longer defined by himself on one side and the Man on the other. He was no longer fighting what he was becoming.

He looked up. Now to get out of here. But how? His best choice was to try to find a way to communicate with whoever had sent the note. He considered a moment. The note had been hidden in his food, so the logical answer would be to write a note of his own and somehow hide it in his leftovers. Of course, there was no way to be sure that person would find the note, or even know it was there, but it was his only shot and he was determined to take it.

He was looking around for something to use to write when the clanging of the door brought him up short. He turned to face it as it opened. Had Kendall returned for more sadistic playtime? Had the real torturer arrived? He took a fearful glance over his shoulder at the waterboarding tank and his blood turned cold. Then he turned back and saw Soraya standing in the doorway. She was grinning from ear to ear.

'God,' she said, 'it's good to see you!'

'How nice to see you again,' Veronica Hart said, 'especially under these circumstances.'

Luther LaValle had come away from the window; he was standing when the DCI, flanked by federal marshals and a contingent of CI agents, entered the Library. Everyone else in the Library at the time goggled, then at the behest of the marshals beat a hasty retreat. Now he sat ramrod-straight in his chair, facing Hart.

'How dare you,' LaValle said now. 'This intolerable behavior won't go unpunished. As soon as I inform Secretary of Defense Halliday of your criminal breach of protocol – '

Hart fanned out the photos of the rendition cells in the basement. 'You're right, Mr. LaValle, this intolerable behavior won't go unpunished, but I believe it will be Secretary of Defense Halliday who'll be leading the charge to punish you for your criminal protocols.'

'I do what I do in the defense of my country,' LaValle said stiffly. 'When a country is at war extraordinary actions must be undertaken in order to safeguard its borders. It's you and people like you, with your weak-willed leftist leanings, that are to blame, not me.' He was livid, his cheeks aflame. 'I'm the patriot here. You – you're just an obstructionist. This country will crack and fall if people like you are left to run it. I'm America's only salvation.'

'Sit down,' Hart said quietly but firmly, 'before one of my 'leftist' people knocks you down.'

LaValle glared at her for a moment, then slowly sank into the chair.

'Nice to be living in your own private world where you make the rules and you don't give a shit about reality.'

'I'm not sorry for what I did. If you're expecting remorse, you're sorely mistaken.'

'Frankly,' Hart said, 'I'm not expecting anything out of you until after you're waterboarded.' She waited until all the blood had drained from his face, before she added, 'That would be one solution – *your* solution – but it isn't mine.' She shuffled the photos back into their envelope.

'Who's seen those?' LaValle asked.

The DCI saw him wince when she said, 'Everyone who needs to see them.'

'Well, then.' He was unbowed, unrepentant. 'It's over.'

Hart looked past him to the front of the Library. 'Not quite yet.' She nodded. 'Here come Soraya and Tyrone.'

Semion Icoupov sat on the stoop of a building not far from where the shooting had taken place. His greatcoat hid the blood that had pooled inside it, so he didn't draw a crowd, just a curious glance or two from pedestrians hurrying by. He felt dizzy and nauseated, no doubt from shock and loss of blood, which meant he wasn't thinking clearly. He looked around with bloodshot eyes. Where was the car that had brought him here? He needed to get out of here before Arkadin emerged from the building and spotted him. He'd taken a tiger from the wild and had tried to domesticate him, a historic mistake by any measure. How many times had it been attempted before with always the same result? Tigers weren't meant to be domesticated; neither was Arkadin. He was what he was, and would never be anything else: a killing machine of almost preternatural abilities. Icoupov had recognized the talent and, greedily, had tried to harness it to his own needs. Now the tiger had turned on him; he'd had a premonition that he would die in Munich, now he knew why, now he knew how.

Looking back toward Egon Kirsch's apartment building, he felt a sudden rush of fear, as if at any moment death would emerge from it, stalking him down the street. He tried to pull himself together, tried to rise to his feet, but a horrific pain shot through him, his knees buckled, and he collapsed back onto the cold stone.

More people passed, now ignoring him altogether. Cars rolled by. The sky came down, the day darkened as if covered with a shroud. A sudden gust of wind brought the onset of rain, hard as sleet. He ducked his head between his shoulders, shivered mightily.

And then he heard his name shouted and, turning his head, saw the nightmare figure of Leonid Danilovich Arkadin coming down the steps of Kirsch's building. Now more highly motivated, Icoupov once again tried to get up. He groaned as he gained his feet, but tottered there uncertainly as Arkadin began to run toward him.

At that moment, a black Mercedes sedan pulled up to the sidewalk. The driver hurried out and, taking hold of Icoupov, half carried him across the pavement. Icoupov struggled, but to no avail; he was weak with lost blood, and growing weaker by the moment. The driver opened the rear door, bundled him into the backseat. He pulled an HK 1911 .45 and with it warned Arkadin away, then he hustled back around the front of the Mercedes, slid behind the wheel, and took off.

Icoupov, slumped in the near corner of the backseat, made rhythmic grunts of pain like puffs of smoke from a steam locomotive. He was aware of the soft rocking of the shocks as the car sped through the Munich streets. More slowly came the realization that he wasn't alone in the backseat. He blinked heavily, trying to clear his vision.

'Hello, Semion,' a familiar voice said.

And then Icoupov's vision cleared. 'You!'

'It's been a long time since we've seen each other, hasn't it?' Dominic Specter said.

'The Empire State Building,' Moira said as she studied the plans Bourne had managed to scoop up in Kirsch's apartment. 'I can't believe I was wrong.'

They were parked in a rest stop by the side of the autobahn on the way to the airport.

'What do you mean, wrong?' Bourne said.

She told him what Arthur Hauser, the engineer hired by Kaller Steelworks, had confessed about the flaw in LNG terminal's software.

Bourne thought a moment. 'If a terrorist used that flaw to gain control of the software, what could he do?'

'The tanker is so huge and the terminal is so complex that the docking is handled electronically.'

'Through the software program.'

Moira nodded.

'So he could cause the tanker to crash into the terminal.' He turned to her. 'Would that set off the tanks of liquid gas?'

'Quite possibly, yes.'

Bourne was thinking furiously. 'Still, the terrorist would have to know about the flaw, how to exploit it, and how to reconfigure the software.'

'It sounds simpler than trying to blow up a major building in Manhattan.'

She was right, of course; and because of the questions he'd been pondering he grasped implications of that immediately.

Moira glanced at her watch. 'Jason, the NextGen plane with the coupling link is scheduled to take off in thirty minutes.' She put the car in gear, nosed out onto the autobahn. 'We have to make up our minds before we get to the airport. Do we go to New York or to Long Beach?'

Bourne said, 'I've been trying to figure out why both Specter and Icoupov were so hell-bent on retrieving these plans.' He stared down at the blueprints as if willing them to speak to him. 'The problem,' he said slowly and thoughtfully, 'is that they were entrusted to Specter's son, Pyotr, who was more interested in girls, drugs, and the Moscow nightlife than he was in his work. As a consequence, his network was peopled by misfits, junkies, and weaklings.'

'Why in the world would Specter entrust so important a document to a network like that?'

'That's just the point,' Bourne said. 'He wouldn't.'

Moira glanced at him. 'What does that mean? Is the network bogus?'

'Not as far as Pyotr was concerned,' Bourne said, 'but so far as Specter saw it, yes, everyone who was a part of it was expendable.'

'Then the plans are bogus, too.'

'No, I think they're real, and that's what Specter was counting on,' Bourne said. 'But when you consider the situation logically and coolly, which no one does when it comes to the threat of an imminent terrorist attack, the probability of a cell managing to get what it needs into the Empire State Building is very low.' He rolled up the plans. 'No, I think this was all an elaborate disinformation scheme – leaking communications to Typhon, recruiting me because of my loyalty to Specter. It was all meant to mobilize American security forces on the wrong coast.'

'So you think the Black Legion's real target is the LNG terminal in Long Beach.'

'Yes,' Bourne said, 'I do.'

Tyrone stood looking down at LaValle. A terrible silence had descended over the Library when he and Soraya had entered. He watched Soraya scoop up LaValle's cell phone from the table.

'Good,' she said with an audible sigh of relief. 'No one's called. Jason must be safe.' She tried him on her cell, but he wasn't answering.

Hart, who had stood up when they'd come over, said, 'You look a little the worse for wear, Tyrone.'

'Nothing a stint at the CI training school wouldn't cure,' he said.

Hart glanced at Soraya before saying, 'I think you've earned that right.' She smiled. 'In your case, I'll forgo the usual warning about how rigorous the training program is, how many recruits drop out in the first two weeks. I know we won't have to be concerned about you dropping out.'

'No, ma'am.'

'Just call me Director, Tyrone. You've earned that as well.'

He nodded, but he couldn't keep his eyes off LaValle.

His interest did not go unnoticed. The DCI said, 'Mr. LaValle, I think it only just that Tyrone decide your fate.'

'You're out of your mind.' LaValle looked apoplectic. 'You can't –'

'On the contrary,' Hart said, 'I can.' She turned to Tyrone. 'It's entirely up to you, Tyrone. Let the punishment fit the crime.'

Tyrone, impaling LaValle in his glare, saw there what he always saw in the eyes of white people who confronted him: a toxic mixture of contempt, aversion, and fear. Once, that would have sent him into a frenzy of rage, but that was because of his own ignorance. Perhaps what he had seen in them was a reflection of what had been on his own face. Not today, not ever again, because during his incarceration he'd finally come to understand what Deron had tried to teach him: that his own ignorance was his worst enemy. Knowledge allowed him to work at changing other people's expectations of him, rather than confronting them with a switchblade or a handgun.

He looked around, saw the look of expectation on Soraya's face. Turning back to LaValle, he said: 'I think something public would be in order, something embarrassing enough to work its way up to Secretary of Defense Halliday.'

Veronica Hart couldn't help laughing, she laughed until tears came to her eyes, and she heard the Gilbert and Sullivan lines run through her head: *His object all sublime, he will achieve in time – let the punishment fit the crime!*

# 42

'I seem to have you at quite a disadvantage, dear Semion.' Dominic Specter watched Icoupov as he dealt with the pain of sitting up straight.

'I need to see a doctor.' Icoupov was panting like an underpowered engine struggling up a steep grade.

'What you need, dear Semion, is a surgeon,' Specter said. 'Unfortunately, there's no time for one. I need to get to Long Beach and I can't afford to leave you behind.'

'This was my idea, Asher.' As he had braced his back against the seat, some small amount of color was returning to Icoupov's cheeks.

'So was using Pyotr. What did you call my son? Oh, yes, a useless wart on fate's ass, that was it, wasn't it?'

'He *was* useless, Asher. All he cared about was getting laid and getting high. Did he have a commitment to the cause, did he even know what the word meant? I doubt it, and so do you.'

'You killed him, Semion.'

'And you had Iliev murdered.'

'I thought you'd changed your mind,' Sever said. 'I assumed you'd sent him after Bourne to expose me, to gain the upper hand by telling him about the Long Beach target. Don't look at me like that. Is it so strange? After all, we've been enemies longer than we've been allies.'

'You've become paranoid,' Icoupov said, though at the time he had sent his second in command to expose Sever. He'd temporarily lost faith in Sever's plan, had finally felt the risks to all of them were too great. From the beginning, he'd argued with Sever against bringing Bourne into the picture, but had acquiesced to Sever's argument that CI would bring Bourne into play sooner or later. 'Far better for us to preempt them, to put Bourne in play ourselves,' Sever had said, capping his argument, and that had been the end of it, until now.

'We've both become paranoid.'

'A sad fact,' Icoupov said with a gasp of pain. It was true: Their great strength in working together without anyone in either camp knowing about it was also a weakness. Because their regimes ostensibly opposed each other, because the Black Legion's nemesis was in reality its closest ally, all other potential rivals shied away, leaving the Black Legion to operate without interference. However, the actions both men were sometimes obliged to take for the sake of appearance caused a subconscious erosion of trust between them.

Icoupov could feel that their level of distrust had achieved its highest point yet, and he sought to defuse it. 'Pyotr killed himself – and, in fact, I was only defending myself. Did you know he hired Arkadin to kill me? What would you have had me do?'

'There were other options,' Sever said, 'but your sense of justice is an eye for an eye. For a Muslim you have a great deal of the Jewish Old Testament in you. And now it appears that that very justice is about to be turned on you. Arkadin will kill you, if he can get his hands on you.' Sever laughed. 'I'm the only one who can save you now. Ironic, isn't it? You kill my son and now I have the power of life and death over you.'

'We always had the power of life and death over each other.' Icoupov still struggled to gain equality in the conversation. 'There were casualties on both sides – regrettable but necessary. The more things change the more they stay the same. Except for Long Beach.'

'There's the problem precisely,' Sever said. 'I've just come from interrogating Arthur Hauser, our man on the inside. As such, he was monitored by my people. Earlier today, he got cold feet; he met with a member of Black River. It took me some time to convince him to talk, but eventually he did. He told this woman – Moira Trevor – about the software flaw.'

'So Black River knows.'

'If they do,' Sever said, 'they aren't doing anything about it. Hauser also told me that they withdrew from NextGen; Black River isn't handling their security anymore.'

'Who is?'

'It doesn't matter,' Sever said. 'The point is the tanker is less than a day away from the California coastline. My software engineer is aboard and in place. The question now is whether this Black River operative is going to act on her own.'

Icoupov frowned. 'Why should she? You know Black River as well as I do, they act as a team.'

'True enough, but the Trevor woman should have been on to her next assignment by now; my people tell me that she's still in Munich.'

'Maybe she's taking some downtime.'

'And maybe,' Sever said, 'she's going to act on the information Hauser gave her.'

They were nearing the airport, and with some difficulty Icoupov pointed. 'The only way to find out is to check to see whether she's on the NextGen plane that's transshipping the coupling link to the terminal.' He smiled thinly. 'You seem surprised that I know so much. I have my spies as well, many of whom you know nothing about.' He gasped in pain as he searched beneath his greatcoat. 'It was texted to me, but I can't seem to find my cell.' He looked around. 'It must have fallen out of my pocket when your driver manhandled me into the car.'

Sever waved a hand, ignoring the implied rebuke. 'Never mind. Hauser gave me all the details, if we can get through security.'

'I have people in Immigration you don't know about.'

Sever's smile held a measure of the cruelty that was common to both of them. 'My dear Semion, you have a use after all.'

Arkadin found Icoupov's cell phone in the gutter where it had fallen as Icoupov had been bundled into the Mercedes. Controlling the urge to stomp it into splinters, he opened it to see whom Icoupov had called last, and noticed that the last incoming message was a text. Accessing it, he read the information on a NextGen jet due to take off in twenty minutes. He wondered why that would be important to Icoupov. Part of him wanted to go back to Devra, the same part that had balked at leaving her to go after Icoupov. But Kirsch's building was swarming with cops; the entire block was in the process of being cordoned off, so he didn't look back, tried not to think of her lying twisted on the floor, her blank eyes staring up at him even after she stopped breathing.

*Do you love me, Leonid?*

How had he answered her? Even now he couldn't remember. Her death was like a dream, something vivid that made no sense. Maybe it was a symbol, but of what he couldn't say.

*Do you love me, Leonid?*

It didn't matter, but he knew to her it did. He had lied then, surely he'd lied to ease the moments before her death, but the thought that he'd lied to her sent a knife through whatever passed for his heart.

He looked down at the text message and knew this was where he'd find Icoupov. Turning around, he walked back toward the cordoned-off area. Posing as a crime reporter from the *Abendzeitung* newspaper, he boldly accosted one of the junior uniformed police, asking him pointed questions about the shooting, stories of gunfire he'd gleaned from residents of the neighboring buildings. As he suspected, the cop was on guard duty and knew next to nothing. But that wasn't the point; he'd now gotten inside the cordon, leaning against one of the police cars as he conducted his phony and fruitless interview.

At length, the cop was called away, and he dismissed Arkadin, saying the commissioner would be holding a press conference at 16:00, at which time he would be free to ask all the questions he wanted. This left Arkadin alone, leaning against the fender. It didn't take him long to walk around the front of the vehicle, and when the medical examiner's van arrived – creating a perfect diversion – he opened the driver's-side door, ducked in behind the wheel. The keys were already in the ignition. He started the car and drove off. When he reached the autobahn, he put on the siren and drove at top speed toward the airport.

'I won't have a problem getting you on board,' Moira said as she turned off onto the four-lane approach to the freight terminal. She showed her NextGen ID at the guard booth, then drove on toward the parking lot outside the terminal. During the drive to the airport she'd thought long and hard about whether to tell Jason about whom she really worked for. Revealing that she was with Black River was a direct violation of her contract, and right now she prayed there'd be no reason to tell him.

After passing through security, Customs, and Immigration, they arrived on the tarmac and approached the 747. A set of mobile stairs rose up to the high passenger door, which stood open. On the far side of the plane, the truck from Kaller Steelworks Gesellschaft was parked, along with an airport hoist, which was lifting crated parts of the LNG coupling link into the jet's cargo area. The truck was obviously late, and the loading process was necessarily slow and tedious. Neither Kaller nor NextGen could afford an accident at this late stage.

Moira showed her NextGen ID to one of the crew members standing at the bottom of the stairs. He smiled and nodded, welcoming them aboard. Moira breathed a sigh of relief. Now all that stood between them and the Black Legion attack was the ten-hour flight to Long Beach.

But as they neared the top of the stairs, a figure appeared from the plane's interior. He stood in the doorway, staring down at her.

'Moira,' Noah said, 'what are you doing here? Why aren't you on your way to Damascus?'

Manfred Holger, Icoupov's man in Immigration, met them at the checkpoint to the freight terminals, got in the car with them, and they lurched forward. Icoupov had called him using Sever's cell phone. He'd been about to go off duty, but luckily for them had not yet changed out of his uniform.

'There's no problem.' Holger spoke in the officious manner that had been drummed into him by his superiors. 'All I have to do is check the recent immigration records to see if she's come through the system.'

'Not good enough,' Icoupov said. 'She may be traveling under a pseudonym.'

'All right then, I'll go on board and check everyone's passports.' Holger was sitting in the front seat. Now he swiveled around to look at Icoupov. 'If I find that this woman, Moira Trevor, is on board, what would you have me do?'

'Take her off the plane,' Sever said at once.

Holger looked inquiringly at Icoupov, who nodded. Icoupov's face was gray again, and he was having more difficulty keeping the pain at bay.

'Bring her here to us,' Sever said.

Holger had taken their diplomatic passports, passed them quickly through security. Now the Mercedes was sitting just off the tarmac. The 747 with the NextGen logo emblazoned on its sides and tail was at rest, still being loaded from the Kaller Steelworks truck. The driver had pulled up so that the truck shielded them from being seen by anyone boarding the plane or already inside it.

Holger nodded, got out of the Mercedes, and walked across the tarmac to the rolling stairs.

'*Kriminalpolizei,*' Arkadin said as he stopped the police car at the freight terminal checkpoint. 'We have reason to believe a man who killed two people this afternoon has fled here.'

The guards waved him past Customs and Immigration without asking for ID; the car itself was proof enough for them. As Arkadin rolled past the parking lot and onto the tarmac, he saw the jet, crates from the NextGen truck being hoisted into the cargo bay, and the black Mercedes idling some distance away from both. Recognizing the car at once, he nosed the police cruiser to a spot directly behind the Mercedes. For a moment, he sat behind the wheel, staring at the Mercedes as if the car itself were his enemy.

He could see the silhouettes of two male figures in the backseat; it wasn't a stretch for him to figure that one of them was Semion Icoupov. He wondered which of the handguns he had with him he should use to kill his former mentor: the SIG Sauer 9mm, the Luger, or the .22 SIG Mosquito. It all depended on what kind of damage he wanted to inflict and to what part of the body. He'd shot Stas Kuzin in the knees, the better to watch him suffer, but this was another time and, especially, another place. The airport was public space; the adjacent passenger terminal was crawling with security personnel. Just because he had been able to get this far as a member of the *kriminalpolizei*, he knew better than to overstep his luck. No, this kill needed to be quick and clean. All he desired was to look into Icoupov's eyes when he died, for him to know who'd ended his life and why.

Unlike with the moment of Kuzin's demise, Arkadin was fully aware of this moment, keyed in to the importance of the son overtaking the father, of revenging himself for the psychological and physical advantages an adult takes with a child. That he hadn't, in fact, been a child when Mischa had sent Semion Icoupov to resurrect him never occurred to him. From the moment the two had met, he had always seen Icoupov as a father figure. He'd obeyed him as he would a father, had accepted his judgments, had swallowed whole his worldview, had been faithful to him. And now, for the sins Icoupov had visited on him, he was going to kill him.

'When you didn't show for your scheduled flight, I had a hunch you'd show up here.' Noah stared at her, completely ignoring Bourne. 'I won't allow you on the plane, Moira. You're no longer a part of this.'

'She still works for NextGen, doesn't she?' Bourne said.

'Who is this?' Noah said, keeping his eyes on her.

'My name is Jason Bourne.'

A slow smile crept over Noah's face. 'Moira, you didn't introduce us.' He turned to Bourne, stuck out his hand. 'Noah Petersen.'

Bourne shook his hand. 'Jason Bourne.'

Keeping the same sly smile on his face, Noah said, 'Do you know she lied to you, that she tried to recruit you to NextGen under false pretenses?'

His eyes flicked toward Moira, but he was disappointed to see neither shock nor outrage on her face.

'Why would she do that?' Bourne said.

'Because,' Moira said, 'like Noah here, I work for Black River, the private security firm. We were hired by NextGen to oversee security on the LNG terminal.'

It was Noah who registered shock. 'Moira, that's enough. You're in violation of your contract.'

'It doesn't matter, Noah. I quit Black River half an hour ago. I've been made chief of security at NextGen, so in point of fact it's you who isn't welcome aboard this flight.'

Noah stood rigid as stone, until Bourne took a step toward him. Then he backed away, descending the flight of rolling stairs. Halfway down, he turned to her. 'Pity, Moira. I once had faith in you.'

She shook her head. 'The pity is that Black River has no conscience.'

Noah looked at her for a moment then turned, clattered down the rest of the stairs, and stalked off across the tarmac without seeing the Mercedes or the police car behind it.

Because it would make the least noise, Arkadin decided on the Mosquito. Hand curled around the grips, he got out of the police car, stalked to the driver's side of the Mercedes. It was the driver – who doubtless doubled as a bodyguard – he had to dispense with first. Keeping his Mosquito out of sight, he rapped on the driver's window with a bare knuckle.

When the driver slid the glass down, Arkadin shoved the Mosquito in his face and pulled the trigger. The driver's head snapped back so hard the cervical vertebrae cracked. Pulling open the door, Arkadin shoved the corpse aside and knelt on the seat, facing the two men in the backseat. He recognized Sever from an old photograph when Icoupov had showed him the face of his enemy. He said, 'Wrong time, wrong place,' and shot Sever in the chest.

As he slumped over, Arkadin turned his attention to Icoupov. 'You didn't think you could escape me, Father, did you?'

Icoupov – who, between the sudden attack and the unendurable pain in his shoulder, was going into delayed shock – said, 'Why do you call me father? Your father died a long time ago, Leonid Danilovich.'

'No,' Arkadin said, 'he sits here before me like a wounded bird.'

'A wounded bird, yes.' With great effort, Icoupov opened his greatcoat, the lining of which was sopping wet with his blood. 'Your paramour shot me before I shot her in self-defense.'

'This is not a court of law. What matters is that she's dead.' Arkadin shoved the muzzle of the Mosquito under Icoupov's chin, and tilted upward. 'And you, Father, are still alive.'

'I don't understand you.' Icoupov swallowed hard. 'I never did.'

'What was I ever to you, except a means to an end? I killed when you ordered me to. Why? Why did I do that, can you tell me?'

Icoupov said nothing, not knowing what he could say to save himself from judgment day.

'I did it because I was trained to do it,' Arkadin said. 'That's why you sent me to America, to Washington, not to cure me of my homicidal rages, as you said, but to harness them for your use.'

'What of it?' Icoupov finally found his voice. 'Of what other use were you? When I found you, you were close to taking your own life. I saved you, you ungrateful shit.'

'You saved me so you could condemn me to this life, which, if I am any judge, is no life at all. I see I never really escaped Nizhny Tagil. I never will.'

Icoupov smiled, believing he'd gotten the measure of his protégé. 'You don't want to kill me, Leonid Danilovich. I'm your only friend. Without me you're nothing.'

'Nothing is what I always was,' Arkadin said as he pulled the trigger. 'Now you're nothing, too.'

Then he got out of the Mercedes, walked out on the tarmac to where the NextGen personnel were almost finished off-loading the crates. Without being seen, he climbed onto the hoist. There he hunkered down just beneath the operator's cab, and after the last crate had been stowed aboard, when the NextGen loaders were exiting the cargo hold via the interior stairwell, he leapt aboard the plane, scrambled behind a stack of crates, and sat down, patient as death, while the doors closed, locking him in.

Bourne saw the German official coming and suspected there was something wrong: An Immigration officer had no business interrogating them now. Then he recognized the man's face. He told Moira to get back inside the plane, then stood barring the door as the official mounted the stairs.

'I need to see everyone's passport,' the officer said as he approached Bourne.

'Passport checks have already been made, *mein Herr*.'

'Nevertheless, another security scan must be made now.' The officer held out his hand. 'Your passport, please. And then I will check the identity of everyone else aboard.'

'You don't recognize me, *mein Herr*?'

'Please.' The officer put his hand on the butt of his holstered Luger. 'You are obstructing official government business. Believe me, I will take you into custody unless you show me your passport and then move aside.'

'Here's my passport, *mein Herr*.' Bourne opened it to the last page, pointed to a spot on the inside cover. 'And here is where you placed an electronic tracking device.'

'What accusation is this? You have no proof –'

Bourne produced the broken bug. 'I don't believe you're here on official business. I think whoever instructed you to plant this on me is paying you to check these passports.' Bourne gripped the officer's elbow. 'Let's stroll over to the commandant of Immigration and ask them if they sent you here.'

The officer drew himself up stiffly. 'I'm not going anywhere with you. I have a job to do.'

'So do I.'

As Bourne dragged him down the rolling stairs, the officer went for his gun.

Bourne dug his fingers into the nerve bundle just above the man's elbow. 'Draw it if you must,' Bourne said, 'but be prepared for the consequences.'

The official's frosty aloofness finally cracked, revealing the fear beneath. His round face was pallid and sweating.

'What do you want of me?' he said as they walked along the tarmac.

'Take me to your real employer.'

The officer had one last blast of bravado in him. 'You don't really think he's here, do you?'

'As a matter of fact I wasn't sure until you said that. Now I know he is.' Bourne shook the official. 'Now take me to him.'

Defeated, the officer nodded bleakly. No doubt, he was contemplating his immediate future. At a quickened pace, he led Bourne around behind the 747. At that moment, the NextGen truck rumbled to life, heading away from the plane, back the way it had come. That was when Bourne saw the black Mercedes and a police car directly behind it.

'Where did that police car come from?' The officer tore himself away from Bourne and broke into a run toward the parked cars.

Bourne, who saw the driver's-side doors on both vehicles standing open, was at the officer's heels. It was clear as they approached that no one was in the police car, but looking through the Mercedes's door, they saw the driver, slumped over. It looked as if he'd been kicked to the passenger's side of the seat.

Bourne pulled open the rear door, saw Icoupov with the top of his head blown off. Another man had fallen forward against the front seat rests. When Bourne pulled him gently backward, he saw that it was Dominic Specter – or Asher Sever – and everything became clear to him. Beneath the public enmity, the two men were secret allies. This answered many questions, not the least of which was why everyone Bourne had spoken to about the Black Legion had a different opinion about who was a member and who wasn't.

Sever looked small and frail, old beyond his years. He'd been shot in the chest with a .22. Bourne took his pulse, listened to his breathing. He was still alive.

'I'll call for an ambulance,' the officer said.

'Do what you have to do,' Bourne said as he scooped Sever up. 'I'm taking this one with me.'

He left the Immigration officer to deal with the mess, crossing the tarmac and mounting the rolling stairs.

'Let's get out of here,' he said as he laid Sever down across three seats.

'What happened to him?' Moira said with a gasp. 'Is he alive or dead?'

Bourne knelt beside his old mentor. 'He's still breathing.' As he began to rip off the professor's shirt, he said to Moira. 'Get us moving, okay? We need to get out of here now.'

Moira nodded. As she went up the aisle, she spoke to one of the flight attendants, who ran for the first-aid kit. The door to the cockpit was still open, and she gave the order for takeoff to the captain and the co-pilot.

Within five minutes the rolling stairs had been removed and the 747 was taxiing to the head of the runway. A moment later the control tower cleared it for takeoff. The brakes were let out, the engines revved up, and, with increasing velocity, the jet hurtled down the runway. Then it lifted off, its wheels retracted, flaps were adjusted, and it soared into a sky filled with the crimson and gold of the setting sun.

# 43

'Is he dead?' Sever stared up at Bourne, who was cleaning his chest wound.

'You mean Semion?'

'Yes. Semion. Is he dead?'

'Icoupov and the driver, both.'

Bourne held Sever down while the alcohol burned off everything that could cause the wound to suppurate. No organs had been struck, but the injury must be extremely painful.

Bourne applied an antiseptic cream from a tube in the first-aid kit. 'Who shot you?'

'Arkadin.' Tears of pain rolled down Sever's cheeks. 'For some reason, he's gone completely insane. Maybe he was always insane. I thought so anyway. Allah, that hurts!' He took several shallow breaths before he went on. 'He came out of nowhere. The driver said, 'A police car has pulled up behind us.' The next thing I know he's rolling down the window and a gun is fired point-blank in his face. Neither Semion nor I had time to think. There was Arkadin inside the car. He shot me, but I'm certain it was Semion he'd come for.'

Intuiting what must have happened in Kirsch's apartment, Bourne said, 'Icoupov killed his woman, Devra.'

Sever squeezed his eyes shut. He was having trouble breathing normally. 'So what? Arkadin never cared what happened to his women.'

'He cared about this one,' Bourne said, applying a bandage.

Sever stared up at Bourne with an expression of disbelief. 'The odd thing was, I think I heard him call Semion 'Father.' Semion didn't understand.'

'And now he never will.'

'Stop your fussing; let me die, dammit!' Sever said crossly. 'It doesn't matter now whether I live or die.'

Bourne finished up.

'What's done is done. Fate has been sealed; there's nothing you or anyone else can do to change it.'

Bourne sat on a seat opposite Sever. He was aware of Moira standing to one side, watching and listening. The professor's betrayal only went to prove that you were never safe when you let personal feelings into your life.

'Jason.' Sever's voice was weaker. 'I never meant to deceive you.'

'Yes, you did, Professor, that's all you know how to do.'

'I came to look upon you as a son.'

'Like Icoupov looked upon Arkadin.'

With an effort, Sever shook his head. 'Arkadin is insane. Perhaps they both were, perhaps their shared insanity is what drew them together.'

Bourne sat forward, 'Let me ask you a question, Professor. Do you think you're sane?'

'Of course I'm sane.'

Sever's eyes held steady on Bourne's, a challenge still, at this late stage.

For a moment, Bourne did nothing, then he rose and, together with Moira, walked forward toward the cockpit.

'It's a long flight,' she said softly, 'and you need your rest.'

'We both do.'

They sat next to each other, silent for a long time. Occasionally, they heard Sever utter a soft moan. Otherwise, the drone of the engines conspired to lull them to sleep.

It was freezing in the baggage hold, but Arkadin didn't mind. The Nizhny Tagil winters had been brutal. It was during one of those winters that Mischa Tarkanian had found him, hiding out from the remnants of Stas Kuzin's regime. Mischa, hard as a knife blade, had the heart of a poet. He told stories that were beautiful enough to be poems. Arkadin had been enchanted, if such a word could be ascribed to him. Mischa's talent for storytelling had the power to take Arkadin far away from Nizhny Tagil, and when Mischa smuggled him out past the inner ring of smoke-stacks, past the outer ring of high-security prisons, his stories took Arkadin to places beyond Moscow, to lands beyond Russia. The stories gave Arkadin his first inkling of the world at large.

As he sat now, his back against a crate, knees drawn up to his chest in order to conserve warmth, he had good cause to think of Mischa. Icoupov had paid for killing Devra, now Bourne must pay for killing Mischa. But not just yet, Arkadin brooded, though his blood called out for revenge. If he killed Bourne now, Icoupov's plan would succeed, and he couldn't allow that, otherwise his revenge against him would be incomplete.

Arkadin put his head back against the edge of the crate and closed his eyes. Revenge had become like one of Mischa's poems, its meaning flowering open to surround him with a kind of ethereal beauty, the only form of beauty that regis-tered on him, the only beauty that lasted. It was the glimpse of that promised beauty, the very prospect of it, that allowed him to sit patiently, curled between crates, waiting for his moment of revenge, his moment of inestimable beauty.

Bourne dreamed of the hell known as Nizhny Tagil as if he'd been born there, and when he awoke he knew Arkadin was near. Opening his eyes, he saw Moira staring at him.

'What do you feel about the professor?' she said, by which he suspected she meant, *What do you feel about me?*

'I think the years of obsession have driven him insane. I don't think he knows good from evil, right from wrong.'

'Is that why you didn't ask him why he embarked on this path to destruction?'

'In a way,' Bourne said. 'Whatever his answer would have been it wouldn't have made sense to us.'

'Fanatics never make sense,' she said. 'That's why they're so difficult to counteract. A rational response, which is always our choice, is rarely effective.' She cocked her head. 'He betrayed you, Jason. He nurtured your belief in him, and played on it.'

'If you climb on a scorpion's back you've got to expect to get stung.'

'Don't you have a desire for revenge?'

'Maybe I should smother him in his sleep, or shoot him to death as Arkadin did to Semion Icoupov. Do you really expect that to make me feel better? I'll exact my revenge by stopping the Black Legion's attack.'

'You sound so rational.'

'I don't feel rational, Moira.'

She took his meaning, and blood rushed to her cheeks. 'I may have lied to you, Jason, but I didn't betray you. I could never do that.' She engaged his eyes. 'There were so many times in the last week when I ached to tell you, but I had a duty to Black River.'

'Duty is something I understand, Moira.'

'Understanding is one thing, but will you forgive me?'

He put out his hand. 'You aren't a scorpion,' he said. 'It's not in your nature.'

She took his hand in hers, brought it up to her mouth, and pressed it to her cheek.

At that moment they heard Sever cry out, and they rose, went down the aisle to where he lay curled on his side like a small child afraid of the dark. Bourne knelt down, drew Sever gently onto his back to keep pressure off the wound.

The professor stared at Bourne, then, as Moira spoke to him, at her.

'Why did you do it?' Moira said. 'Why attack the country you'd adopted as your own?'

Sever could not catch his breath. He swallowed convulsively. 'You'd never understand.'

'Why don't you try me?'

Sever closed his eyes, as if to better visualize each word as it emerged from his mouth. 'The Muslim sect I belong to, that Semion belonged to, is very old – ancient even. It had its beginnings in North Africa.' He paused already out of breath. 'Our sect is very strict, we believe in a fundamentalism so devout it cannot be conveyed to infidels by any means. But I can tell you this: We cannot live in the modern world because the modern world violates every one of our laws. Therefore, it must be destroyed.

'Nevertheless . . .' He licked his lips, and Bourne poured out some water, lifted his head, and allowed him to drink his fill. When he was finished, he continued. 'I should never have tried to use you, Jason. Over the years there have been many disagreements between Semion and myself – this was the latest, the one that broke the proverbial camel's back. He said you'd be trouble, and he was right. I thought I could manufacture a reality, that I could use you to convince the American security agencies we were going to attack New York City.' He emitted a dry, little laugh. 'I lost sight of the central tenet of life, that reality can't be controlled, it's too random, too chaotic. So you see it was I who was on a fool's errand, Jason, not you.'

'Professor, it's all over,' Moira said. 'We won't let the tanker dock until we have the software patched.'

Sever smiled. 'A good idea, but it will avail you nothing. Do you know the damage that much liquid natural gas will do? Five square miles of devastation, thousands killed, America's corrupt, greedy way of life delivered the hammer blow Semion and I have been dreaming of for decades. It's my one great calling in this life. The loss of human life and physical destruction is icing on the cake.'

He paused to catch his breath, which was shallower and more ragged than ever. 'When the nation's largest port is incinerated, America's economy will go with it. Almost half your imports will dry up. There'll be widespread shortages of goods and food, companies will collapse, the stock exchanges will plummet, wholesale panic will ensue.'

'How many of your men are on board?' Bourne said.

Sever smiled weakly. 'I love you like a son, Jason.'

'You let your own son be killed,' Bourne said.

'Sacrificed, Jason. There's a difference.'

'Not to him.' Bourne returned to his agenda. 'How many men, Professor?'

'One, only one.'

'One man can't take over the tanker,' Moira said.

The smile played around his lips, even as his eyes closed, his consciousness fading. 'If man hadn't made machines to do his work . . .'

Moira turned to Bourne. 'What does that mean?'

Bourne shook the old man's shoulder, but he'd slipped into deep unconsciousness.

Moira checked his eyes, his forehead, his carotid artery. 'Without intravenous antibiotics I doubt he'll make it.' She looked at Bourne. 'We're near enough New York City now. We could touch down there, have an ambulance waiting –'

'There's no time,' Bourne said.

'I know there's no time.' Moira took his arm. 'But I want to give you the choice.'

Bourne stared down at his mentor's face, lined and seamed, far older in sleep, as if it had imploded. 'He'll make it on his own, or he won't.'

He turned away, Moira at his side, and he said, 'Call NextGen. This is what I need.'

# 44

The tanker *Moon of Hormuz* plowed through the Pacific no more than an hour out of Long Beach harbor. The captain, a veteran named Sultan, had gotten word that the LNG terminal was online and ready to receive its inaugural shipment of liquid natural gas. With the current state of the world's economies, the LNG had become even more precious; from the time the *Moon of Hormuz* had left Algeria its cargo had increased in value by over 30 percent.

The tanker, twelve stories high and as large as a village, held thirty-three million gallons of LNG cooled to a temperature of –260 degrees. That translated into the energy equivalent of twenty billion gallons of natural gas. The ship required five miles to come to a stop, and because of the shape of its hull and the containers on deck Sultan's view ahead was blocked for three-quarters of a mile. The tanker had been steaming at twenty knots, but three hours ago he'd ordered the engines into reverse. Well within five miles of the terminal, the ship was down to six knots of speed and still decelerating.

Within the five-mile radius to shore his nerves became a jittery flame, the nightmare of Armageddon always with him, because a disaster aboard the *Moon of Hormuz* would be just that. If the tanks spilled into the water, the resulting fire would be five miles in diameter. For another five miles beyond that thermal radiation would burn any human to a crisp.

But those scenarios were just that: nightmares. In ten years there'd never been even a minor incident aboard his ship, and there never would be, if he had anything to say about it. He was just thinking about how fine the weather was, and how much he was going to enjoy his ten days on the beach with a friend in Malibu, when the radio officer handed him a message from NextGen. He was to expect a helicopter in fifteen minutes; he was to give its passengers – Moira Trevor and Jason Bourne – any and all help they requested. That was surprising enough, but he bristled at the last sentence: He was to take orders from them until the *Moon of Hormuz* was safely docked at the terminal.

When the doors to the cargo bay were opened, Arkadin was ready, crouched behind one of the containers. As the airport maintenance team clambered aboard, he edged out, then called from the shadows for one of them to help him. When the man complied, Arkadin broke his neck, dragged him into the deepest shadows of the cargo bay, away from the NextGen containers. He stripped and donned the man's maintenance uniform. Then he stepped over to the work area, keeping the ID tag clipped to it out of full view so that no one could see that his face didn't match that on the tag. Not that it mattered: These people were here to get the cargo off-loaded and onto the waiting NextGen trucks as quickly as possible. It never occurred to any of them that there might be an impostor among them.

In this way, Arkadin worked his way to the open bay doors, onto the loading lifts with the container. He hopped onto the tarmac as the cargo was being loaded onto the truck, then ducked away beneath the wing. Finding himself alone on the opposite side of the aircraft, he walked away at a brisk, business-like clip. No one challenged him, no one even gave him a second look, because he moved with the authority of someone who belonged there. That was the secret of assuming a different identity, even temporarily – people's eyes either ignored or accepted what looked correct to them.

As he went, he breathed deeply of the clear, salt air, the freshening breeze whipping his pants against his legs. He felt free of all the leashes that had bound him to the earth: Stas Kuzin, Marlene, Gala, Icoupov, they were all gone now. The sea beckoned him and he was coming.

NextGen had its own small terminal on the freight side of the Long Beach airport. Moira had radioed ahead to NextGen headquarters, giving them a heads-up and asking for a helicopter to be ready to take her and Bourne to the tanker.

Arkadin beat Bourne to the NextGen terminal. Hurrying now, he used the badge to open the door to the restricted areas. Out on the tarmac he saw the helicopter right away. The pilot was talking to a maintenance man. The moment they both squatted down, examining one of the runners, Arkadin pulled his cap low on his forehead, walked briskly around to the far side of the helicopter, and made himself busy there.

He saw Bourne and Moira emerge from the NextGen terminal. They paused for a moment and he could hear their argument about whether or not she should come, but they must have had it before, because the fight was hammered out in brief, staccato bursts, like shorthand.

'Face facts, Jason. I work for NextGen; without me you won't get on that copter.'

Bourne turned away, and for an instant Arkadin felt a foreboding, as if Bourne had seen him. Then Bourne turned back to Moira, and together they hurried across the tarmac.

Bourne climbed in on the pilot's side, while Moira headed to Arkadin's side of the copter. With a professional smile, he held out a hand, helping her up into the cockpit. He saw the maintenance man about to come across, but waved him off. Looking up at Moira through the curved Perspex door he thought of Devra and felt a lurch in his chest, as if her bleeding head had fallen against him. He waved at Moira, and she lifted her hand in return.

The rotors began to swirl, the maintenance man signaled for Arkadin to come away; Arkadin gave him the thumbs-up sign. Faster and faster the rotors spun, and the copter's frame began to shudder. Just before it lifted off, Arkadin climbed onto the runner and curled himself into a ball as they swung out over the Pacific, buffeted by a stiff onshore wind.

The tanker loomed large in the passengers' vision as the copter sped toward it at top speed. Only one other boat could be seen, a commercial fishing vessel several miles away beyond the security limits imposed by the Coast Guard and Homeland Security. Bourne, who was sitting directly behind the pilot, saw that he was working to keep the copter's pitch at the correct angle.

'Is everything okay?' he shouted over the roar of the rotors.

The pilot pointed to one of the gauges. 'There's a small anomaly in the pitch; probably the wind, it's gusting up quite a bit.'

But Bourne wasn't so sure. The anomaly was constant, whereas the wind wasn't. He had an intuition what – or, more accurately, who – was causing the problem.

'I think we have a stowaway,' Bourne said to the pilot. 'Take it in low when you get to the tanker. Skim the tops of the containers.'

'What?' The pilot shook his head. 'Too dangerous.'

'Then I'll take a look myself.' Unstrapping himself, Bourne crept toward the door.

'Okay, okay!' the pilot shouted. 'Just get back in your seat!'

They were almost at the bow of the tanker now. It was unbelievably big, a city lumbering through the Pacific swells.

'Hang on!' the pilot shouted as he took them down far more quickly than normal. They could see members of the crew racing across the deck, and someone – no doubt the captain – emerged from the wheelhouse near the stern. Someone was shouting to pull up; the tops of the containers were coming at them with frightening speed. Just before they skimmed the top of the nearest container, the copter rocked slightly.

'The anomaly's gone,' the pilot said.

'Stay here,' Bourne shouted to Moira. 'Whatever happens stay on board.' Then he gripped the weapon lying astride his knees, opened the door and, as she screamed his name, jumped out of the copter.

He landed after Arkadin, who had already leapt down onto the deck and was scuttling between containers. Crew members rushed toward them both; Bourne had no idea whether one of them was Sever's software engineer, but he raised a hunting crossbow and they stopped in their tracks. Knowing that firing a gun would be tantamount to suicide on a tanker full of liquid natural gas, he'd had Moira ask NextGen to have two crossbows in the copter. How they procured them so quickly was anyone's guess, but a corporation of NextGen's size could get just about anything at a moment's notice.

Behind him, the chopper set down on the part of the foredeck that had been cleared, and cut the engines. Doubled over to avoid the rotors, he opened the copter door and looked up at Moira. 'Arkadin is here somewhere. Please stay out of the way.'

'I need to report to the captain. I can take care of myself.' She, too, was cradling a crossbow. 'What does Arkadin want?'

'Me. I killed his friend. It doesn't matter to him that it was in self-defense.'

'I can help, Jason. If we work together, two are better than one.'

He shook his head. 'Not in this case. Besides, you see how slowly the tanker is moving; its screws are in reverse. It's within the five-mile limit. For every foot we travel forward, the danger to thousands of lives and the port of Long Beach itself grows exponentially.'

She nodded stiffly, stepped down, and hurried along the deck to where the captain stood, awaiting her orders.

Bourne turned, moving cautiously among the containers, in the direction he'd glimpsed Arkadin heading. Moving along the aisles was like walking down the canyons of Manhattan. Wind howled as it cut across corners, magnified, racing down the aisles as if they were tunnels.

Just before he reached the end of the first set of containers, he heard Arkadin's voice, speaking to him in Russian.

'There isn't much time.'

Bourne stood still, trying to determine where the voice was coming from. 'What d'you know about it, Arkadin?'

'Why d'you think I'm here?'

'I killed Mischa Tarkanian, now you kill me. Isn't that how you defined it back in Egon Kirsch's apartment?'

'Listen to me, Bourne, if that's what I wanted I could have killed you anytime while you and the woman slept aboard the NextGen 747.'

Bourne's blood ran cold. 'Why didn't you?'

'Listen to me, Bourne. Semion Icoupov, who saved me, whom I trusted, shot my woman to death.'

'Yes, that's why you killed him.'

'Do you begrudge me my revenge?'

Bourne said nothing, thinking of what he would do to Arkadin if he hurt Moira.

'You don't have to say anything, Bourne, I already know the answer.'

Bourne turned. The voice appeared to have shifted. Where the hell was he hiding?

'But as I said we have little time to find Icoupov's man on board.'

'It's Sever's man, actually,' Bourne said.

Arkadin laughed. 'Do you think that matters? They were in bed together. All the time they posed as bitter enemies they were plotting this disaster. I want to stop it – I *have* to stop it, or my revenge on Icoupov will be incomplete.'

'I don't believe you.'

'Listen, Bourne, you know we haven't much time. I've avenged myself on the father, but this plan is his child. He and Sever gave birth to it, fed it, nurtured it through its infancy, through its adolescent growing pains. Now each moment brings this floating supernova closer to the moment of destruction those two madmen envisioned.'

The voice moved again. 'Is that what you want, Bourne? Of course not. Then let's join together to find Sever's man.'

Bourne hesitated. He didn't trust Arkadin, and yet he had to trust him. He examined the situation from all sides and concluded that the only way to play it was to move forward. 'He's a software engineer,' he said.

Arkadin appeared, climbing down from the top of one of the containers. For a moment, the two men stood facing each other, and once again Bourne felt the dislocating sensation of looking in a mirror. When he stared into Arkadin's eyes, he didn't see the madness the professor spoke of; he saw himself, a heart of darkness and pain beyond understanding.

'Sever told me there was only one man, but he also said we wouldn't find him, and even if we did it wouldn't matter.'

Arkadin frowned, giving him the canny, feral appearance of a wolf. 'What did he mean?'

'I'm not sure.' He turned, walking down the deck toward the crew members who had cleared the space for the copter to land. 'What we're looking for,' he said as Arkadin fell into step beside him, 'is a tattoo specific to the Black Legion.'

'The wheel of horses with the death's head center.' Arkadin nodded. 'I've seen it.'

'It's on the inside of the elbow.'

'We could kill them all.' Arkadin laughed. 'But I guess that would offend something inside you.'

One by one, the two men examined the arms of the eight crewmen on deck, but found no tattoo. By the time they reached the wheelhouse, the tanker was within two miles of the terminal. It was barely moving. Four tugboats had hove to and were waiting at the one-mile limit to tow the tanker the rest of the way in.

The captain was a swarthy individual with a face that looked like it had been deeply etched by acid rather than the wind and the sun. 'As I was telling Ms. Trevor, there are seven more crewmen, mostly involved in engine-room duties. Then there's my first mate here, the communications officer, and the ship's doctor, he's in sick bay, tending to a crewman who fell ill two days out of Algeria. Oh, yes, and the cook.'

Bourne and Arkadin glanced at each other. The radioman seemed the logical choice, but when the captain summoned him he, too, was without the Black Legion tattoo. So were the captain and his first mate.

'The engine room,' Bourne said.

At his captain's orders, the first mate led them out onto the deck, then down the starboard companionway into the bowels of the ship, reaching the enormous engine room at last. Five men were hard at work, their faces and arms filthy with a coating of grease and grime. As the first mate instructed them, they held out their arms, but as Bourne reached the third in line, the fourth man looked at them beneath half-closed lids before he bolted.

Bourne went after him while Arkadin circled, snaking through the oily city of grinding machinery. He eluded Bourne once but then, rounding a corner, Bourne spotted him near the line of gigantic Hyundai diesel engines, specifically designed to power the world's fleet of LNG tankers. He was trying to furtively shove a small box between the structural struts of the engine, but Arkadin, coming up behind him, grabbed for his wrist. The crewman jerked away, brought the box back toward him, and was about to thumb a button on it when Bourne kicked it out of his hand. The box went flying, and Arkadin dived after it.

'Careful,' the crewman said as Bourne grabbed hold of him. He ignored Bourne, was staring at the box Arkadin brought back to them. 'You hold the whole world in your hand.'

Meanwhile Bourne pushed up his shirtsleeve. The man's arm was smeared with grease, deliberately so, it seemed, because when Bourne took a rag and wiped it off, the Black Legion tattoo appeared on the inside of his left elbow.

The man seemed totally unconcerned. His entire being was focused on the box that Arkadin was holding. 'That will blow up everything,' he said, and made a lunge toward it. Bourne jerked him back with a stranglehold.

'Let's get him back up to the captain,' Bourne said to the first mate. That's when he saw the box up close. He took it out of Arkadin's hand.

'Careful!' the crewman cried. 'One slight jar and you'll set it off.'

But Bourne wasn't so sure. The crewman was being too vocal with his warnings. Wouldn't he want the ship to blow now that it had been boarded by Sever's enemies? When he turned the box over, he saw that the seam between the bottom and the side was ragged.

'What are you doing? Are you crazy?' The crewman was so agitated that Arkadin slapped him on the side of the head in order to silence him.

Inserting his fingernail into the seam, Bourne pried the box apart. There was nothing inside. It was a dummy.

Moira found it impossible to stay in one place. Her nerves were stretched to the breaking point. The tanker was on the verge of meeting up with the tugboats; they were only a mile from shore. If the tanks went, the devastation to both human life and the country's economy would be catastrophic. She felt useless, a third wheel hanging around while the two men did their hunting.

Exiting the wheelhouse, she went belowdecks, looking for the engine room. Smelling food, she poked her head into the galley. A large Algerian was sitting at the stainless-steel mess table, reading a two-week-old Arabic newspaper.

He looked up, gesturing at the paper. 'It gets old the fifteenth time through, but when you're at sea what can you do?'

His burly arms were bare to the shoulders. They bore tattoos of a star, a crescent, and a cross, but not the Black Legion's insignia. Following the directions he gave her, she found the infirmary three decks below. Inside, a slim Muslim was sitting at a small desk built into one of the bulkheads. In the opposite bulkhead were two berths, one of them filled with the patient who had fallen ill. The doctor murmured a traditional Muslim greeting as he turned away from his laptop computer to face her. He frowned deeply when he saw the crossbow in her hands.

'Is that really necessary,' he said, 'or even wise?'

'I'd like to speak with your patient,' Moira said, ignoring him.

'I'm afraid that's impossible.' The doctor smiled that smile only doctors can. 'He's been sedated.'

'What's wrong with him?'

The doctor gestured at the laptop. 'I'm still trying to find out. He's been subject to seizures, but so far I can't find the pathology.'

'We're near Long Beach, you'll get help then,' she said. 'I just need to see the insides of his elbows.'

The doctor's eyebrows rose. 'I beg your pardon?'

'I need to see whether he's got a tattoo.'

'They all have tattoos, these sailors.' The doctor shrugged. 'But go ahead. You won't disturb him.'

Moira approached the lower berth, bending over to pull the thin blanket back from the patient's arm. As she did so, the doctor stepped forward and struck her a blow on the back of her head. She fell forward and cracked her jaw on the metal frame of the bunk. The pain pulled her rudely back from a precipice of blackness, and, groaning, she managed to roll over. The copper-sweet taste of blood was in her mouth and she fought against wave after wave of dizziness. Dimly she saw the doctor bent over his laptop, his fingers racing over the keys, and she felt a ball of ice form in her belly.

*He's going to kill us all.* With this thought reverberating in her head, she grabbed the crossbow off the floor where she'd dropped it. She barely had time to aim, but she was close enough not to have to be accurate. She breathed a prayer as she let fly.

The doctor arched up as the bolt pierced his spine. He staggered backward, toward where Moira sat, braced against the berth frame. His arms extended, his fingers clawing for the keyboard, and Moira rose, swung the crossbow into the back of his head. His blood spattered like rain over her face and hands, the desk, and the laptop's keyboard.

Bourne found her on the floor of the infirmary, cradling the computer in her lap. When he came in, she looked up at him and said, 'I don't know what he did. I'm afraid to shut it off.'

'Are you all right?'

She nodded. 'The ship's doctor was Sever's man.'

'So I see,' he said as he stepped over the corpse. 'I didn't believe him when he told me he had only one man on board. It would be like him to have a backup.'

He knelt down, examined the back of her head. 'It's superficial. Did you black out?'

'I don't think so, no.'

He took a large gauze pad from the supply cabinet, doused it with alcohol. 'Ready?' He placed it against the back of her head, where her hair was plastered down with blood. She moaned a little through gritted teeth.

'Can you hold it in place for a minute?'

She nodded, and gently Bourne lifted the laptop into his arms. There was a software program running, that much was clear. Two radio buttons on the screen were blinking, one yellow, the other red. On the other side of the screen was a green radio button, which wasn't blinking.

Bourne breathed a sigh of relief. 'He brought up the program, but you got to him before he could activate it.'

'Thank God,' she said. 'Where's Arkadin?'

'I don't know. When the captain told me you'd gone below I took off after you.'

'Jason, you don't think . . .'

Putting the computer aside, he helped her to her feet. 'Let's get you back up to the captain so you can give him the good news.'

There was a fearful look on his face. 'And you?'

He handed her the laptop. 'Go to the wheelhouse and stay there. And Moira, this time I really mean it.'

With the crossbow in one hand, he stepped into the passageway, looked right and left. 'All right. Go. Go!'

Arkadin had returned to Nizhny Tagil. Down in the engine room, surrounded by steel and iron, he realized that no matter what had happened to him, no matter where he'd gone, he'd never been able to escape the prison of his youth. Part of him was still in the brothel he and Stas Kuzin had owned, part of him still stalked the night-time streets, abducting young girls, their pale, fearful faces turned toward him as deer turn toward headlights. But what they'd needed from him he couldn't – or wouldn't – give them. Instead, he'd sent them to their deaths in the quicklime pit Kuzin's regime had dug amid the firs and the weeping hemlocks. Many snows had passed since he'd dragged Yelena from the rats and the quicklime, but the pit remained in his memory, vivid as a blaze of fire. If only he could have his memory wiped clean.

He started at the sound of Stas Kuzin screaming at him. *What about all* your *victims?*

But it was Bourne, descending the steel companionway to the engine room. 'It's over, Arkadin. The disaster has been averted.'

Arkadin nodded, but inside he knew better: The disaster had already occurred, and it was too late to stop its consequences. As he walked toward Bourne he tried to fix him in his mind, but he seemed to morph, like an image seen through a prism.

When he was within arm's length of him, he said, 'Is it true what Sever told Icoupov, that you have no memory beyond a certain point in time?'

Bourne nodded. 'It's true. I can't remember most of my life.'

Arkadin felt a terrible pain, as if the very fabric of his soul was being torn apart. With an inchoate cry, he flicked open his switchblade, lunged forward, aiming for Bourne's belly.

Turning sideways, Bourne grabbed his wrist, began to turn it in an attempt to get Arkadin to drop the weapon. Arkadin struck out with his other hand, but Bourne blocked it with his forearm. In doing so, the crossbow clattered to the deck. Arkadin kicked it into the shadows.

'It doesn't have to be this way,' Bourne said. 'There's no reason for us to be enemies.'

'There's every reason.' Arkadin broke away, tried another attack, which Bourne countered. 'Don't you see it? We're the same, you and me. The two of us can't exist in the same world. One of us will kill the other.'

Bourne stared into Arkadin's eyes, and even though his words were those of a madman Bourne saw no madness in them. Only a despair beyond description, and an unyielding will for revenge. In a way, Arkadin was right. Revenge was all he had now, all he lived for. With Tarkanian and Devra gone, the only meaning life had for him lay in avenging their deaths. There was nothing Bourne could say to sway him; that was a rational response to an irrational impulse. It was true, the two of them couldn't exist in the same world.

At that moment Arkadin feinted right with his knife, drove left with his fist, rocking Bourne back onto his heels. At once he stabbed out with the switchblade, burying it in the meat of Bourne's left thigh. Bourne grunted, fought the buckling of his knee, and Arkadin jammed his boot into Bourne's wounded thigh. Blood spurted, and Bourne fell. Arkadin jumped on him, using his fist to pummel Bourne's face when Bourne blocked his knife stabs.

Bourne knew he couldn't take much more of this. Arkadin's desire for revenge had filled him with an inhuman strength. Bourne, fighting for his very life, managed to counterpunch long enough to roll out from under Arkadin. Then he was up and running in an ungainly limp to the companionway.

Arkadin reached up for him as he was half a dozen rungs off the engine room deck. Bourne kicked out with his bad leg, surprising Arkadin, catching him under the chin. As he fell back, Bourne scrambled up the rungs as fast as he could. His left leg was on fire, and he was trailing blood as the wounded muscle was forced to work overtime.

Gaining the next deck, he continued up the companionway, up and up, until he came to the first level belowdecks, which according to Moira was where the galley was. Finding it, he raced in, grabbed two knives and a glass saltshaker. Stuffing the shaker into his pocket, he wielded the knives as Arkadin loomed in the doorway.

They fought with their knives, but Bourne's unwieldy carving knives were no match for Arkadin's slender-bladed switchblade, and Bourne was cut again, this time in the chest. He kicked Arkadin in the face, dropped his knives in order to wrest the switchblade out of Arkadin's hand, to no avail. Arkadin stabbed at him again and Bourne nearly suffered a punctured liver. He backed away, then ran out the doorway, up the last companionway to the open deck.

The tanker was at a near stop. The captain was busy coordinating the hookups with the tugboats that would bring it the final distance to the LNG terminal. Bourne couldn't see Moira, which was a blessing. He didn't want her anywhere near Arkadin.

Bourne, heading for the sanctuary of the container city, was bowled over as Arkadin leapt on him. Locked together, they rolled over and over until they fetched up against the port railing. The sea was far below them, churning against the tanker's hull. One of the tugs signaled with its horn as it came alongside, and Arkadin stiffened. To him it was the siren sounding an escape from one of Nizhny Tagil's prisons. He saw the black skies, tasted the sulfur smoke in his lungs. He saw Stas Kuzin's monstrous face, felt Marlene's head between his ankles beneath the water, heard the terrible reports when Semion Icoupov shot Devra.

He screamed like a tiger, pulling Bourne to his feet, pummeling him over and over until he was bent back over the railing. In that moment, Bourne knew that he was going to die as he had been born, falling over the side of a ship, lost in the depth of the sea, and only by the grace of God being brought in to a fishing boat with their catch. His face was bloody and swollen, his arms felt like lead weights, he was going over.

Then, at the last instant, he pulled the shaker from his pocket, broke it against the rail, and threw the salt in Arkadin's eyes. Arkadin bellowed in shock and pain, his hand flew up reflexively, and Bourne snatched the switchblade from him. Blinded, Arkadin still fought on, and he grasped the blade. With a superhuman effort, not caring that the edges cut into his fingers, he wrested the switchblade away from Bourne. Bourne heaved him backward. But Arkadin had control of the knife now, he had partial vision back through his tearing eyes, and he ran at Bourne with his head tucked into his shoulders, all his weight and determination behind the charge.

Bourne had one chance. Stepping into the charge, he ignored the knife, grabbed Arkadin by his uniform jacket and, using his own momentum against him, pivoted from the hip as he swung him around and up. Arkadin's thighs struck the railing, his upper body continuing its flight, so that he toppled head-over-heels over the side.

Falling, falling, falling . . . the equivalent of twelve stories, before plunging beneath the waves.

# 45

'I need a vacation,' Moira said. 'I'm thinking Bali would do me quite well.'

She and Bourne were in the NextGen clinic in one of the campus buildings that overlooked the Pacific. The *Moon of Hormuz* had successfully docked at the LNG terminal and the cargo of the highly compressed liquid was being piped from the tanker to onshore containers where it would be slowly warmed, expanding to six hundred times its present volume so it could be used by individual consumers and utility and business power plants. The laptop had been turned over to the NextGen IT department, so the software could be parsed and permanently shut down. The grateful CEO of NextGen had just left the clinic, after promoting Moira to president of the security division and offering Bourne a highly lucrative consulting position with the firm. Bourne had phoned Soraya, each of them bringing the other up to date. He'd given her the address of Sever's house, detailing the clandestine operation it housed.

'I wish I knew what a vacation felt like,' Bourne said when he'd finished the call.

'Well . . .' Moira smiled at him. 'You've only to ask.'

Bourne considered for a long time. Vacations were something he'd never contemplated, but if ever there was a time to take one, he thought, this was it. He looked back at her and nodded.

Her smile broadened. 'I'll have NextGen make all the arrangements. How long do you want to go for?'

'How long?' Bourne said. 'Right now, I'll take forever.'

On his way to the airport, Bourne stopped at the Long Beach Memorial Medical Center, where Professor Sever had been admitted. Moira, who had declined to come up with him, was waiting for him in the chauffeured car NextGen had hired for them. They'd put Sever in a private room on the fifth floor. The room was deathly still, except for the respirator. The professor had sunk deeper into a coma and was now unable to breathe on his own. A thick tube emerged from his throat, snaking to the respirator that wheezed like an asthmatic. Other, smaller tubes were needled into Sever's arms. A catheter attached to a plastic bladder hooked to the side of the bed caught his urine. His bluish eyelids were so thin Bourne thought he could see his pupils beneath them.

Standing beside his former mentor he found that he had nothing to say. He wondered why he'd felt compelled to come here. Maybe it was simply to look once more on the face of evil. Arkadin was a killer, pure and simple, but this man had made himself brick by brick into a liar and a deceiver. And yet he looked so frail, so helpless now, it was difficult to believe he was the mastermind of the monstrous plan to incinerate much of Long Beach. Because, as he'd said, his sect couldn't live in the modern world, it was bound to destroy it. Was that the real reason, or had Sever once again lied to him? He'd never know now.

He was abruptly nauseated by being in Sever's presence, but as he turned away a small dapper man came in, allowing the door to close at his back.

'Jason Bourne?' When Bourne nodded, the man said, 'My name is Frederick Willard.'

'Soraya told me about you,' Bourne said. 'Well done, Willard.'

'Thank you, sir.'

'Please don't call me sir.'

Willard gave a small, deprecating smile. 'Pardon me, my training is so ingrained in me that's all I am now.' He glanced over at Sever. 'Do you think he'll live?'

'He's alive now,' Bourne said, 'but I wouldn't call it living.'

Willard nodded, though he seemed not at all interested in the disposition of the figure lying in the bed.

'I have a car waiting downstairs,' Bourne said.

'As it happens, so do I.' Willard smiled, but there was something sad about it. 'I know that you worked for Treadstone.'

'Not Treadstone,' Bourne said, 'Alex Conklin.'

'I worked for Conklin, too, many years ago. It's one and the same, Mr. Bourne.'

Bourne felt impatience now. He was eager to join Moira, to see the sherbet skies of Bali.

'You see, I know all of Treadstone's secrets – all of them. This is something only you and I know, Mr. Bourne.'

A nurse came in on her silent white shoes, checked all of Sever's feeds, scribbled on his chart, then left them alone again.

'Mr. Bourne, I thought long and hard about whether I should come here, to tell you . . .' He cleared his throat. 'You see, the man you fought on the tanker, the Russian who went overboard.'

'Arkadin.'

'Leonid Danilovich Arkadin, yes.' Willard's eyes met Bourne's, and something inside him winced away. 'He was Treadstone.'

'What?' Bourne couldn't believe what he was hearing. 'Arkadin was Treadstone?'

Willard nodded. 'Before you – in fact, he was Conklin's pupil just before you.'

'But what happened to him? How did he wind up working for Semion Icoupov?'

'It was Icoupov who sent him to Conklin. They were friends, once upon a time,' Willard said. 'Conklin was intrigued when Icoupov told him about Arkadin. Treadstone was moving into a new phase by then; Conklin believed Arkadin was perfect for what he had in mind. But Arkadin rebelled. He went rogue, almost killed Conklin before he escaped to Russia.'

Bourne was desperately trying to process all this information. At last, he said, 'Willard, do you know what Alex had in mind when he created Treadstone?'

'Oh, yes. I told you I know all of Treadstone's secrets. Your mentor, Alex Conklin, was attempting to build the perfect beast.'

'The perfect beast? What do you mean?' But Bourne already knew, because he'd seen it when he'd looked into Arkadin's eyes, when he understood that what he was seeing reflected there was himself.

'The ultimate warrior.' Willard, one hand on the door handle, smiled now. 'That's what you are, Mr. Bourne. That's what Leonid Danilovich Arkadin was – until, that is, he came up against you.' He scrutinized Bourne's face, as if searching for a trace of the man who'd trained him to be a consummate covert operative. 'In the end, Conklin succeeded, didn't he?'

Bourne felt a chill go through him. 'What do you mean?'

'You against Arkadin, it was always meant to be that way.' Willard opened the door. 'The pity of it is Conklin never lived to see who won. But it's you, Mr. Bourne. It's you.'

## ABOUT THE AUTHORS

Eric Van Lustbader was born and raised in Greenwich Village. He is the author of over twenty bestselling novels, and his work has been translated into more than twenty languages.

After a successful career in the theatre, Robert Ludlum launched his career as a bestselling writer with *The Scarlatti Inheritance* in 1971, the first of twenty-two consecutive international bestsellers.